BEYOND THE CITADEL
The Complete Trilogy

by
Simon Marinker

TRAFFORD

Canadian Cataloguing in Publication Data

Marinker, Simon, 1913-
   Beyond the citadel

   ISBN 1-55212-238-7

   I. Title.
PS8576.A663B49 1999   C813'.54   C99-910281-8
PR9199.3.M355B49 1999

ISBN 1-55212-238-7

TRAFFORD

This book was published 'on-demand' in cooperation with Trafford Publishing.
On-demand publishing is a unique process and service of making a book available for retail sale to the public taking advantage of on-demand manufacturing and Internet web marketing. **On-demand publishing** includes promotions, retail sales, manufacturing, order fulfilment, accounting and collecting royalties on behalf of the author.

Suite 2, 3050 Nanaimo St., Victoria, B.C. V8T 4Z1, CANADA

Phone	250-383-6864	Toll-free	1-888-232-4444 (Canada & US)
Fax	250-383-6804	E-mail	sales@trafford.com
Web site	www.trafford.com	TRAFFORD PUBLISHING IS A DIVISION OF TRAFFORD HOLDINGS LTD.

Order this book online at: www.trafford.com/robots/99-0007.html

10   9   8   7   6   5   4

Introduction

'BEYOND THE CITADEL' is a trilogy consisting of three books in continuity.
Book One: 'Crossing The Moat'
Book Two: 'Castle Gardens'
Book Three: 'Assault On The Ramparts'

* * *

Publication of 'Beyond The Citadel' is dedicated to the loving memory of MAUREEN, for her abiding courage, beauty and elegance.

* * *

The author acknowledges the unfailing encouragement of his family and friends. Special thanks also go to Guy Barton for being the original satirist of 'The Ants And The Bees' in Book Three of the trilogy, and to Jonathan Lomas for research material in his book, 'First And Foremost In Community Health Centres' (University of Toronto Press). The author also wishes to thank his son Peter for first suggesting the title of this trilogy.

* * *

This is the biography of a Canadian surgeon, his life and times. It is based on a series of conversations between the narrator and Dr. Philip Bosnar over a five-year period between 1985 and 1990, during which the tape recorder was allowed to run freely. The protagonist of this book was encouraged to speak openly about his hopes and dreams, his successes and failures. He was also asked to include, as far as possible, the people and events that influenced his personal life and chosen career.

The title of this biography, which has been written as a trilogy, is derived from the classic novel by A.J. Cronin entitled 'The Citadel,' which had a profound influence on Philip Bosnar when he was a young doctor on the threshold of his professional future. It is the story of the central character's journey through the trials and temptations of medical practice to his eventual confrontation with the medical establishment.

Since there was no chronological order to the recorded reminiscences, the narrator has elected to use his own alternating time sequences that seemed appropriate to a study of the surgeon's growth and development from youth to maturity. These time sequences interrelate his earliest development with the ultimate direction of his life as an ethical leader and attempted reformer of his chosen profession.

* * *

Is this a fictionalized autobiography? That is a question asked of most writers of narrative novels, and the author of this trilogy is no exception. The answer is that all the character are based to a varying degree on people the author has known, but are mostly composites.

Several locations are fictionalized, but only the names of famous (as well as infamous) national and international individuals are clearly stated.

Finally, historical and other events of the twentieth century are presented as seen through the eyes of the central character, Philip Bosnar.

Book One

Crossing the Moat

Chapter 1

1939

It was 7.30 on a fine July morning and the new arrivals found it hard to believe that this smoke-belching behemoth had been thundering across such a vast continent, speeding from one province to another during the night while they lay in their intimate little sleeping compartment. The Canadian Pacific Railway train, surely a mile long, must represent the heart and soul of this huge country. It somehow typified the pioneer energy that could consolidate so enormous an expanse of the Earth's surface into one single nation.

Their faithful porter or steward (or whatever his official status might be) awakened them at 8 o'clock with a loud knocking at the door and a welcome pot of tea. Unlike his counterpart in the Hollywood version of train travel, he wasn't a kind and helpful Negro with a toothy grin and a voice like that of Paul Robeson. He was a dour and scrawny Scotsman whose heart of gold – if any – was kept carefully concealed, and he departed without a single word or change of expression.

As Philip watched the perfection of her slender body with unstinting admiration, Patricia's adorable oval face with its crowning glory of thick coppery hair was turned toward him with the hint of a smile. She awoke reluctantly with a prolonged stretching of her beautiful naked limbs, and pulled up the window blind to view the outer world in all its moving splendor. It seemed to be racing by in an ever-changing panorama: from the present to the past and on into the future, or so it seemed. Yesterday, it had been a continuation of the endless dark forests and countless lakes and rivers. Today, it was great fields of grain stretching to the limitless horizon.

Philip was no expert on trees, but it was obvious that the majority of them were an assortment of evergreens. They were different types of pine, fir, spruce and others whose names must still be learned. Here and there, a large gathering of maple trees took their theater bows to the passing travelers, and sometimes a coven of oak trees displayed the gnarled contours of their limbs in a dance of defiance. Occasionally, an isolated column of poplars strode by like a platoon of fresh recruits marching in perfect step, but looking lost in an unknown land. As for the lakes, they seemed huge by English standards. (*Later on, they would think of those in the 'Old Country' as mere ponds. Whenever they flew over this part of Canada – without the matchless imagery of train travel – they would see these same great stretches of water as tiny puddles glinting in the sun, as if left by the glaciers that retreated northward not so very long ago.*)

This morning, they were entering prairie country. There were seas of waving wheat, perhaps rye or barley, swaying restlessly to the constant rhythm of the wind and seeming to reflect both the bright warm sunlight and a scattering of clouds in an endless sky. What a wonderful way to meet a new and strange country, thought Patricia. She smiled with the realization that while they were expending so much energy and enthusiasm making love during the night, this mighty clanging, clattering, fire-breathing monster was carrying them closer with seven league boots, mile by rapid mile, to a new and unknown life.

After the view of picturesque Quebec City from the deck of the *S.S. Montclare*, and a brief glimpse of cosmopolitan Montreal before boarding their train, the short bus tour of Toronto had been a bit of a disappointment. The Royal York Hotel was imposing enough, with its strange geometric structure and sloping green roofs. But Bay Street, the financial center of Canada so extolled by their shipboard companions, seemed sterile and dull. It was so different from the exciting and historic City district of London, a veritable rabbit warren of international commerce and mercantile wealth.

The residential areas they saw in outlying communities beyond the suburbs of Toronto, were not the stately homes of the affluent but the ordinary homes of average families. They looked, for the most part, rather dilapidated: flimsy structures of peeling white-painted clapboard, with sagging front porches. Philip and Patricia found their appearance depressing. Where were the permanent houses, no matter how humble, made of bricks and mortar? Perhaps Canadians had to use up as much wood as possible or the towns and villages, even the cities, would be engulfed by expanding forests – the way equatorial jungles sometimes threatened to swallow up the native dwellings in their midst.

The side trip to Niagara Falls was much more worthwhile. Besides, it was thrown in free of charge by the travel agency in Wolverhampton. The world-famous waterfalls lived up to their advance billing, and were spectacular and awe-inspiring in the brilliant morning sunshine. Lunch, however, at what looked like a better than average restaurant, proved a decided letdown. Patty (the nickname Philip used most of the time for his beloved Patricia, both in thought and spoken word) ordered a plain omelet, which was hard to find in a welter of lettuce and potato crisps. Philip felt bold and ordered what was vaunted as a popular Canadian dish, namely 'Chicken a la King'. Not the King of Great Britain and Empire, one hoped, but presumably Mackenzie King, Prime Minister of the Dominion. As soon as he laid eyes on the soggy gray mess, Philip began to have doubts about the worthy gentleman who gave his name to the dish. By the time he'd explored the contents of his plate he developed a decided antipathy toward Mr. King and summoned the waiter.

"I can see the a la King quite plainly," he complained, "but where in blazes is the chicken?" The waiter looked stricken at this affront to the national dish, but agreed to bring him a cold chicken sandwich instead, this time with real chicken.

After lunch, their biggest thrill came when they were standing at the guard rail, staring at the mighty roaring cascade and churning torrent below. Patty suddenly looked at Philip in horror and screamed, "There's a hideous great insect on your collar!" It was their first encounter with the ubiquitous Canadian grasshopper or, more accurately, the North American locust. Unlike its innocent little green namesake in Britain, this was a monstrous brown creature with hungry jaws, one that flew off with an angry clatter when Philip swatted it away in disgust.

"Don't see many o' them 'round these parts," a helpful bystander informed them. "Them's prairie pests.

The hot tea was delicious, and they both took their time getting ready for breakfast in the dining car. They began to reminisce about their trip across the Atlantic. They recalled embarking from grimy old Liverpool, then gliding along the west coast of Scotland past Greenock under forbidding skies, and finally plunging into the open heaving ocean. The first morning was a rough one for poor Patty, suffering her first and last attack of sea sickness. She wasn't helped by the sounds of pandemonium coming from the next cabin through the thin intervening wall, with a foreign-sounding baritone voice imploring, "Please, Marianne, please try not to throw up!" followed by desperate sounds of retching and wailing.

The seasickness pills weren't helping Patty, so – at her persistent request – Philip left her alone to her private misery that he prayed would soon pass. After contacting their steward and asking him to check from time to time and see if his wife was all right, he went up on deck. The morning was crisp and bracing, the dull clouds of yesterday had almost cleared, and after a few fast turns around the almost deserted upper deck, he ventured down to the magnificent dining room. It, too, was almost deserted, and he was glad his own slight queasiness had been blown away by the sea air. The dining steward showed him to his table, where he was the lone occupant so far. He felt a terrible guilt as he devoured his bacon and eggs, mushrooms and fried tomatoes. Like an unfeeling and gluttonous pig, he thought, and he cursed his huge appetite as he thought of his beautiful bride suffering in her bed of sorrow, alone and abandoned by her loved one. By the time he got back to their cabin, she was feeling better and had even summoned the courage to try a few sips of tea, brought to the cabin by their considerate steward. Next door, the death scene of poor Marianne continued unabated, despite the heart-rending entreaties of her grieving husband.

On the speeding train, that last day but one before arriving at Moosejaw, the journey had eaten up not only the fleeting miles but most of their precious dollars as well. Delicious meals in the dining car, with gleaming silver and sparkling white linen, would now remain only a mouth-watering memory. As they took their seats in the main passenger car, they looked with newfound favor on the ancient native Indian, dressed like everyone else in casual North American attire, droning his irritating chant, "Chocolates, peanuts, Coca-Cola!" Irritating? Heavens, no! thought Patty. It was a song from Heaven, and for the next two days she and Phil discovered the delights of salted roast peanuts and tangy Coca-Cola, not to mention the economic benefits to their shrinking resources. (*Strangely enough, in years to come, it would be these last two days, the long lean days of peanuts and 'coke' that they'd remember more than any other of their cross-Canada journey, as a timeless signpost in their new life in a new country.*)

The following day, their morning tea was accompanied by two of the largest, most mouthwatering doughnuts Patty had ever seen or tasted. Dear considerate Scotty, she thought, he doesn't miss a thing, and she was glad Phil had set aside a generous tip from their shrinking funds for their unsmiling but all-knowing porter. Fortunately, there should still be enough for a night at the hotel in Moosejaw and a small dinner. Perhaps they could even have another sumptuous banquet of tea and doughnuts for breakfast the following morning. Both she and Philip were coming to appreciate, at firsthand, the value of a Canadian dollar and its limitations. "Good Lord, we mustn't become tightwads!" she scolded herself with a shudder.

When they arrived at the city that served as a railway hub for Saskatchewan, they were dismayed at its small size and low outdated buildings. Even by Toronto standards, Moosejaw was more like a nineteenth century small town than a city. "Surely," said Philip, as he felt his heart sink in unison with Patty's, "Vanwey can't be much smaller than this."

The cheerful bellboy who helped them with their luggage and showed them to their hotel room, was very talkative and proud of his city. In reply to Patty's apprehensive enquiry, he assured her that, although Vanwey of course wasn't that big, it was a busy and progressive town, with friendly people, and it was beginning to emerge from the "hard times." (***This new and ominous expression would become an integral part of their lives in the early years of their prairie experience.***)

After getting cleaned up and changed, they went down for dinner. The regular dining room was being used for the weekly Rotary Club meeting, so they were shown instead into a relatively bare room with half a dozen tables set up for the evening meal. Only one of these was occupied, by a couple of salesmen from Winnipeg. Their loud conversation concealed few business secrets and even fewer personal ones. The meal was a pleasant surprise. It consisted of steaming vegetable soup and a delicious 'Western Sandwich' of toast, scrambled eggs, fried onions and bits of ham, with a pot of excellent tea. The chairs were comfortable and the service was good. Even the loud sounds of singing, speechmaking and conversational roar coming from the club meeting next door, failed to dampen the young couple's feeling of contentment. That night, they slept little, making love and wondering aloud what lay ahead.

The following day, after a hastily swallowed breakfast of tea and doughnuts (never again could they be as scrumptious as those in their own little 'sleeperette'), they paid the bill, tipped the bellboy and took the rickety bus back to the railway station. Their new train looked much smaller than the one which had brought them this far, but it was fairly comfortable and far from crowded. As they watched the passing parade of still more fields of grain, not as opulent as those of the previous day, the farm buildings began to take on a more dilapidated appearance and the agricultural machinery looked rusted and abandoned. Even the brilliant sunshine failed to cheer up the forlorn scene. It only made everything appear very hot and very dusty. The cattle of yesterday seemed more scarce in this parched land, and there were even fewer horses. On their way across Manitoba, the travelers had enjoyed seeing the occasional herd of Holsteins, the big rumpy farm horses, even a few thoroughbreds prancing over to the railroad tracks and displaying their glossy splendor to admiring onlookers. The contrast was somewhat discouraging.

From time to time, the unhurried train passed tall white 'grain elevators' – the Bosnars were learning new names of the unfamiliar from their obliging fellow travelers – with small clusters of huts around them, and the names of towns and villages on railway signs. These clusters, they were informed, were the actual towns and villages, but Phil and Patty refused to be dismayed. Finally, the engine slowed down and squealed to a halt by a small platform, and they decided this must be the rail junction before reaching Vanwey. But at that moment the conductor called out, "Vanwey, Vanwey. Anyone for Vanwey?" and they thought they'd be reaching their final destination in a short while. There was to be no short while, however, and this was no junction. Dear God in heaven, thought Patty, suddenly seized with an illogical urge to laugh, welcome to grand and glorious Vanwey, Dr. and Mrs. Bosnar, as the conductor began to give them a hand with their luggage.

The figure that came to greet them to this dusty prairie oasis was straight out of Hollywood westerns. He was short and stocky, with a broad and ruggedly handsome face, and a shock of untidy white hair; yet according to their advance information he was only in his fifties. The wide-brimmed light gray Stetson hat which he removed to swat away a mosquito, complemented a suit of navy-blue serge, flared jacket, waistcoat with watch-chain; and a large unconcealed gun in holster resting in familiar comfort at his right hip.

Here was the legendary Doc' of all the Roy Rogers, Gene Autry and Hopalong Cassidy western film classics. Everything about this man looked vigorous, almost aggressive, yet the pallor of his complexion seemed entirely uncharacteristic in these surroundings, where even the air itself seemed scorched.

"Well, here they are, Dr. Tom, safe and sound," boasted the conductor, as if he'd personally conveyed the new arrivals through the perils of the Atlantic and across a vast continental wilderness to this destination.

"Sure good to see you Bosnar, and you too, missus," announced Dr. Blaikie with unconscious male chauvinism.

"Won't hurt to have a good-looking gal like you around the place," he added with clumsy gallantry.

As Philip loaded the luggage into the trunk of Dr. Blaikie's large yellow Buick four-door sedan, Patty was suddenly asked, "How did you like the train trip? Pretty long and tiring I guess."

"Oh no," she insisted, "we thought it was wonderful, such marvelous...." but her voice trailed off as Blaikie stopped listening to her answer and hurried across the platform to exchange a private joke with the conductor. The sound of their bellowing laughter was soon drowned out by metallic stirrings of the train as it began to pull out of the lonely station.

(Tom Blaikie was a man of instant – almost impatient – decisions. He knew right away that he was attracted to this gorgeous copper-haired Irish lass with the shy smile. He admired the perfect long oval of her face, the Grecian nose and the sexy mouth. A bit like that young actress, Loretta Young, he thought. He had already noted with appreciation that her body was tall, erect, slender and lithe, but with all the correct curves in the right places. Hell, he grumbled to himself, if circumstances were different I could sure go for a knockout like this one. Who knows, thought the demon in the black recesses of his mind – the one that was always challenging his self-control – this young fella with the veddy veddy English accent doesn't seem like much of a threat. Sure doesn't look very strong, he told himself as he sized up his new surgeon.

He observed that Philip Bosnar was rather thin, about five foot ten in height and weighing a scant one hundred and forty-five to one hundred and fifty pounds. He had thick dark brown hair, almost black, and worn English style; a bit too full for Canadian custom, with lots of fussing around the forehead and sideburns. His eyes were dark brown below thick black bat-wing eyebrows and his thin, almost bony face was dominated by a large nose. Like an Armenian merchant, Blaikie chuckled to himself, yet somehow the overall impression was that of a reasonably handsome young Englishman: a true 'toff' who might add social prestige as well as surgical skills to the practice, especially with the paying patients from North Dakota.)

At the same time that he was taking an initial inventory of his youthful passengers, Blaikie announced the layout of the streets they were traversing at slow speed. His voice was loud, twangy and high-pitched.

"We're going west now down Fifth Street and then we'll take a left at 4th Avenue."

After the turn he said, "That's the Station Hotel on the right and the Queen's Hotel on the left. That's Stu Raimey's law office on the left, with Mark Standwick's next door, and that corner brick building is my hospital, with Jake the Greek's restaurant on the ground floor. Over on the right that's another doctor's office, between Sam Grigsby's billiard parlor and Doc Swenson's café on the corner. Pete Forsyth ain't got much of a practice, I'm afraid. Should've never left me, the stubborn bugger. Excuse the language, missus."

As the car lurched into a wide turn, he continued,

"Now we're heading back east on Fourth Street, that's our Main Street. On the corner there, that big yellow building is the business headquarters of South Saskatchewan Light and Power. Over on the right, that's the Bank of Montreal and next door those are the town council offices. Those two stores on the left are Schneider's furniture and Berman's Fashions for men, women and kids. Pretty good clothes and quite cheap."

They came to the end of the block at the corner of Third Avenue, where a large modern-looking office building stood in solitary splendor.

"This is our establishment. It's called the Blaikie Building by most folks in Vanwey," their guide announced with considerable pride and satisfaction. "We'll park in back and I'll take you up to your suite."

They drove down a small alleyway separating the medical building from the adjoining firehall, and into a wide parking area. As they got out of the car, it seemed as though the brown surface of dusty baked ground rose up like an outer layer of the earth's crust, with the clickety-clackety sound of dry beating wings as thousands of ugly grasshoppers rose in unison. They flew away in a deadly dark cloud to find another resting place, perhaps preparing to ravage some nearby doomed wheat field.

Blaikie entered through the back door, and took the young couple up the back stairs to his living quarters. These were very spacious and furnished in a combination of comfort and good taste. Sprawled in a large soft armchair was a young man about the same age as Philip. He ignored their entrance with studious disrespect and addressed their host without preamble.

"Bill Simmons was here just now, Dr. Tom. He said he'd sell you a couple of fine Black Angus cows if you're interested."

Blaikie threw his Stetson onto one of the coffee tables.

"Want you to meet Phil Bosnar, our new surgeon. And this is his lovely bride."

The figure in the chair still didn't rise.

"Want you to meet Sam Walters, my assistant, and this," as he brought forward a large, but not obese, woman of about forty, "this here is Marcie, who runs the whole show. Even tries to run me sometimes."

"Thought we were having some chicken sandwiches and coffee, Marcie," Walters complained, looking impatiently at his wristwatch. The message came through to Phil and Patty at the same moment, loud and clear, as though shouted out by this cocky fellow, still sprawled in his chair and relaxed in open blue shirt and red galluses. `This is my territory. I've staked it out and no newcomer is going to push me aside. Besides, right now I'm too busy to bother with a lot of social mumbo-jumbo'.

"Take no notice of his bad manners," Marcie admonished, defusing the tense moment, "Sam always likes to show off."

Blaikie showed his agreement with a noisy cackle, and Walters acknowledged temporary defeat with a shrug and guilty grin.

He stood up, shook hands with the Bosnars and said, I'll show you where the bathrooms are, so you can clean up after your long trip." He sounded almost cordial.

After a tasty lunch, they were given a tour of the ground floor by Dr. Tom – as he insisted they call him and they obliged with some discomfort.

"I designed the whole layout myself," he told them proudly, "and it's worked out pretty good." In fact, so it had.

A large and comfortable waiting room led off through a wide passageway to three consulting rooms, one much larger than the other two, but all three furnished in fashionable modern style. Alternating with these were two well-equipped and thoroughly up-to-date examining rooms. To the left of the main front entrance was a receptionist's enclosure, with a wide front shelf holding a card-file system at one end and a swing-up section at the other. Behind this was a typing desk, some file cabinets and a black wall-phone, There was also a large green Chubb's floor safe that looked as if it weighed a ton.

At the western end of the building was the X-ray room, fully lead-shielded, with equipment by General Electric. It consisted of a tilting table, mobile overhead X-ray tube enclosure and a good fluoroscopy unit. Next to this area was a large room designated for minor surgery, but with obvious deficiencies. The sterilizer was oldfashioned and unsafe and the operating light was poor. Overall, however, the standards were fairly high for a small town medical practice, and Philip joined his bride in complimenting their beaming host on the high quality of his facilities.

The waiting room was empty except for two young women waiting to see Dr. Walters. A few loose papers rustled on Marcie's desk, and a million particles of prairie dust danced in the shafts of sunlight finding their way into the drowsy interior of Dr. Tom's domain. But the slight breeze didn't come from the dead stillness outside that presaged a storm. It came from the electric fans that whirred without pause in almost every room of the building.

The remainder of that first day in Vanwey went by in a blur of activity for the young newly-weds. First they were conducted to the Bank of Montreal at the request of Philip, who admitted being low in cash. With no spontaneous offer forthcoming from Blaikie, there was no alternative. They were introduced to the manager, who was very accommodating and gave Dr. Tom's new surgeon a loan of two hundred dollars. One hundred dollars was made available in crisp new bills and the rest went into the Bosnar account with a small deduction for interest.

Next, they were driven back to the Blaikie hospital on Fourth Avenue. They walked up a flight of stairs to the right of the restaurant, and arrived at the second floor. To the left of the corridor was the hospital section, with all the familiar sights and smells of institutionalized sickness. To the right were the individual residential suites. Number six, the one reserved for the Bosnars, was immediately opposite the wide double doors leading into the hospital.

Dr. Tom showed them through his realm with unconcealed pride. There were two eight-bed wards, one for males and one for females, two private rooms and a four-bed children's ward with two cribs. The operating room seemed reasonably well-equipped but too small, with adjoining scrub sinks but no changing room. It also doubled as a delivery room for obstetrical cases. The premises as a whole were rather cramped and dingy, the overall ventilation was poor, and the numerous table fans fought a losing battle against the assault of bedpans and two colostomy cases in the male ward. (A colostomy is an artificial opening made in the large bowel by the surgeon, often temporary but sometimes permanent, and in the late '30s odor problems were difficult to manage. Today, such management is straightforward and easy to teach the patient, with excellent appliances available from several surgical supply firms.)

After introductions to three members of the nursing staff who were in obvious awe of their revered Dr. Tom, the visitors were shown into their apartment, and Patty prayed the hospital wouldn't insinuate its objectionable aura beyond its double doors, into the corridors and perhaps even further.

The 'Suite' consisted of a large bed-sitting room, with a Murphy pull-down bed on the left. It could be kept concealed when company was present. Beyond this was a small three-piece bathroom, and to the right there was a small alcove equipped as a kitchen-dinette, with a large primitive sink, an electric range and a roasting oven. To the right of the doorway, food refrigeration was provided by a massive ice-box. On the opposite wall, there was a wide settee covered in flowered chintz that could seat four people, and three unmatched armchairs completed the seating arrangement. A small glass and metal table and two tube-metal chairs were kept in the kitchen.

The windows opposite the Murphy bed looked out on Fourth Avenue below, and were fitted with Venetian blinds and beaded side curtains. In addition to overhead light fixtures in the main room, kitchen and bathroom, there were two table lamps on small side tables and one tall floor lamp between the settee – called a 'davenport' – and the window. The furniture was augmented by a large and noisy floor-model electric fan. Not quite what I had in mind, thought Patty as she surveyed her new abode, but it was rent-free so one could hardly complain. The agreement reached with young Ted Blaikie, their London intermediary, was that the initial salary would be one hundred and fifty dollars monthly, with a comfortable suite and the use of a car owned by the practice, both without charge.

The luggage was brought upstairs by Philip, and after handing over two keys to the suite, Dr. Tom went down with his new colleague to the light green two-door Ford. It was parked by the curb and placed at the disposal of the newcomers. While Patty stayed to check out the contents of the apartment and unpack, Philip was taken on a test drive by his employer. He found it much easier than he'd imagined, despite the fact that the steering wheel, gearshifts and foot-controls were all on the left side instead of the right, and driving was on the right side of the street instead of the left. Dr. Blaikie introduced him to a strange local custom. When making a left turn on a busy street it was customary for the driver to swing the left-hand door open wide, then close it again when the turn was complete.

They stopped at the police headquarters on Fifth Street East. A large, well-built man with a ruddy good-humored face greeted them at the head of the stone steps.

"Been another scorcher today, Dr. Tom, eh?" he said, wiping his sweating face with a large blue handkerchief.

"You bet," Blaikie concurred, but Philip noticed he never seemed to perspire. "Want you to meet our new surgeon from England. Name's Phil Bosnar, and this here's Jock McDougal, our popular Chief of Police, a good man to have on your side."

The main purpose of the meeting turned out to be the provision of a driver's license for his junior associate, without the customary formalities. It was becoming apparent that doing Blaikie a favor ultimately meant doing yourself a favor.

By the time they returned, it was arranged for Philip to start practice at 8 a.m. on the following Monday, when he'd meet Blaikie at the hospital. The older man drove off without further ado, and when Philip got back to the apartment he found Patty looking fresh and pink following a shower and change. She was wearing a short white cotton tennis dress and looked like a million in the floor-fan's cooling breeze. Philip was delighted to see that she'd almost completed unpacking for both of them. She was starting to hang up their clothes on the rack to the right of the Murphy doors and placing their smaller items in the drawers on the left. Philip gave her a great bear hug and a long and fervent kiss. It seemed so long since they were alone and could express their deep love and passion in the privacy of their own abode.

After a quick shower and change into light gray slacks and blue summer shirt, he began to feel human again. Before completing the unpacking with Patty, he decided he'd better check the contents of the violin case. He wasn't really worried. The leather case was an excellent one, with top-grade velvet padding guarding the silky-toned violin and his favorite bow. At no time during the long journey, had he permitted anyone else to handle the case. He kept it in his own protective grasp, just as Patty hung onto her precious handbag at all times. He wasn't surprised when he found his violin intact. In fact, it was in almost perfect tune, even though he'd never played it since the ship's concert.

The next item of business was to check out the Murphy bed. It came down smoothly, and was of more than adequate size, but they were thankful they were slender and not too tall. Patty found the kitchen contents somewhat skimpy, with a shortage of knives, forks and spoons, even dishcloths. But the oven and stove were adequate, the ancient toaster worked and the wash-up sink was fully functional.

"I've got some shopping I must take care of tomorrow morning," she declared, "and get some kitchenware, as well as some food."
She gave a slight shudder, knowing full well that so far in her life she and cooking had been total strangers.

"We're getting a bit low on cigarettes, too," Philip noted, "and I must pick up something to drink. The old boy suggested I go to the liquor store on 5th Avenue and get a bottle of scotch and a bottle of rye."

"Good! Then we'll be able to celebrate our arrival."

By now, they were starting to feel much better, and were shaking off most of the earlier doubts that had clouded their day. Outside, there was the sound of distant thunder and the occasional flash of lightning on the horizon, but so far not a drop of rain despite the rapidly darkening sky. They were getting hungry and agreed it was high time they had a good supper, so they went downstairs to the restaurant of 'Jake the Greek'. It was a name almost impossible to resist, with its strong flavor of the pioneer west.

When they entered, they were greeted by a tall and dignified gentleman dressed in a smart three-piece lightweight business suit and wearing goldrimmed glasses. He introduced himself in cultured English as Stavros Jakopoulos, but was quite content with being called Jake the Greek.

"I saw you both arrive earlier today with Dr. Tom, and I hope you and Mrs. Bosnar will be very happy here."

After a few more pleasantries, he showed them to a cozy booth where they enjoyed an excellent meal, well served and entirely unhurried. The restaurant was a welcome surprise. It was clean and well furnished, and must have had a good interior decorator. Although almost full, there was no noisy or disorderly behavior at any time during their stay. Patty decided that this place could prove a life saver for her poor husband, until such time as she could learn to make something more elaborate than banana sandwiches, for this represented the limit of her culinary powers at the moment. That night, they both slept like the dead, the accumulating fatigue of travel and the steady tension of adjustment to new places, new faces and new values, catching up with them at last.

The next day was hot, dry and dusty once again, with a film of what felt like fine sand covering everything they touched. The newcomers soon found that brushing off the dusty coating accomplished nothing. It returned at once in the same
thickness as before. After breakfast, and wearing their lightest summer clothes, they went their separate ways for some shopping, hoping to pick up whatever stray pieces of local information they could. Philip purchased scotch and rye at the liquor store, then went another two blocks to Eckstrom's Groceries and picked up cigarettes and soft drinks. He was astonished to find out how much could be learned by simply listening to the casual conversation and not-so-casual gossip of other shoppers, as well as asking the occasional question. The nature of his enquiries and obvious British accent – totally unamericanized – identified him at once as the new surgeon Dr. Tom was said to be bringing out from England.

He learned that the wheat crop was once again disappointing, but perhaps better than last year, the grasshoppers were still a major problem and nearby Midale had been hit late yesterday afternoon with a nasty hailstorm. Most important of all, however, was the statement that there was still no sign of rain, "and the Lord knows we need it," like a combined complaint and prayer. It sounded reminiscent of Christ's anguished words, "My God, my God, why hast thou forsaken me?" Here, thought Philip, nothing is more important than the weather, and here, drought becomes an overwhelming disaster, like fire, flood, earthquake and epidemic.

Walking back to the corner of Fifth Street and Fourth Avenue, he peered through the steamy windows of Swenson's Cafe. It looked like a hangout for the more raucous elements, and even the loudest conversation must have found it hard to compete with the deafening 'bonga-bonga' rubbish emanating from a jukebox in the far corner. Nearer at hand, Sam Walters was in plain view, holding forth at the crowded front counter, with an appreciative audience guffawing at his humor. He was clearly at home with this loutish group and accepted as one of the `good old boys'. Philip crossed the street and went back to the apartment.

After putting his purchases away in the kitchen he turned on the radio, (he and Patty must be careful not to call it a 'wireless' over here), and was just in time for the 11 o'clock news. There were some items of local interest, mainly agricultural topics and some references to the production figures at the nearby strip mines. Then, there were some comments about Premier Duplessis of Quebec and his complaints about the unfair way Ottawa was dealing with French Canada. There followed a few perfunctory reports from Europe hinting that Hitler was becoming more ravenous with each swallowed mouthful of territory. The reports also made it clear to Philip that Neville Chamberlain and Eduard Daladier saw exactly what was happening but were urging their people to bury their heads in the sands of official reassurance.

He tried not to let these thoughts depress him too much and concentrated on happier things. Most of all, there was his good fortune at falling so deeply in love with his adorable Patricia, and the miracle of having that love reciprocated beyond his wildest dreams. How very different was this love affair from his earlier youthful passions. There was a reality to this present bond between them, a feeling of permanence and depth. While it was every bit as romantic and passion-ate as his very first love, it was the real stuff of mature emotion, adult perception and total consum-mation.

Patty arrived just before noon, loaded with sundry household supplies and groceries, a genuine cornucopia.

"Darling, you've every right to look proud." he exclaimed. "You've managed marvels in so short a time and I bet you're exhausted" He took the parcels from her and put them away in the kitchen, then returned for a prolonged embrace.

"For lunch," Patty announced breathlessly, "we're having cucumber sandwiches and tea, and for dinner we're having ham and salad. How about that!" she added, with a note of justifiable triumph. After lunch, they drove around town in leisurely fashion. The afternoon was a drowsy one and suited their own dreamy state, and they experienced a comfortable euphoria. They drove down to the western end of Mainstreet, past the business section and as far as the handsome new Colle-giate. On the way, they noticed that aside from two main central blocks occupied by offices and stores (few locals called them `shops'), the sidewalks were unpaved boardwalks and the buildings had the false fronts of the pioneer west. To the east, there was a gravel highway that led past the Jeremy coal mines to the town of Bonchance, twelve miles away.

They decided not to take that route today, turning off instead and driving south. This took them through the residential areas of Third, Second and First street, and brought them to a wonderful panoramic view of the broad valley that fell away from the town into the distance. Philip parked on the south side of the street and they stayed awhile to enjoy the tranquil view. The win-dows were kept closed to shut out marauding insects, and they checked the radiator before pro-ceeding further. It was protected, as were all car radiators in Vanwey, by a broad screen mesh that was anchored with wire loops. According to the town map, the valley road would lead through Squirrel River Park and Resort (owned by Jake the Greek), across the bridge spanning the river, past Sundstrom's Market Gardens and on to the air field, five miles away. They would save that drive for another day.

Driving back to Mainstreet, they began to realize that this tiny spot of dusty prairie on the vast face of Canada was beginning to grow before their very eyes into a real town, with its own individual characteristics and flavor. When they returned to the apartment with their loot, it was time for Patty to get ready for her well-planned banquet. Phil cooperated by dashing out to get some assorted flavors of ice-cream from the restaurant below. It was a dessert fit for royalty, in keeping with their regal dinner.

Later that evening, they relaxed by the open window and enjoyed the first cooling breeze of the past two days as they listened to the Saturday night revelries of a small prairie town. It was a microcosm of western Canada, just emerging from its pioneer past. The beer parlors at the hotels were doing a great business, and the strollers on the sidewalks could be heard in an endless Babel of foreign lan-guages: German, Ukrainian, French, Swedish, Polish, Russian and Chinese. English was heard from time to time, sometimes with a Scottish accent, sometimes Irish or Welsh, sometimes American and sometimes that strange mixture known as Canadian, in which "Out and about," became "Oat and aboat."

Phil and Patty looked at each other, and all of a sudden the dam of disappointment broke for both of them. They laughed until their sides ached, and continued until tears rolled down their cheeks and they collapsed in exhaustion. After a while, Phil got up without a word and fixed them both a drink: a mild rye and ginger ale for Patty and a stiff scotch and soda for himself. Going over to the ice box, he chipped off a few pieces of ice with the resident ice pick, and after cleaning off the occasional grasshopper wing, he dropped the ice into both drinks. Then, turning serious, they raised their glasses in a toast, "To our new home and our new country, Canada!"

They resolved that henceforth there would be no disparaging comparisons with anything English, or indeed anything European. They were the new immigrants, the new Canadians, and this was where their loyalties would lie.

CHAPTER 2

1929

At fifteen, Philip (named Philippe at birth) Bosnar was short and skinny for his age but strong for his size. Although he wasn't very good at Gym classes he was surprisingly skilled with his fists, a fact the bullies among his fellow pupils soon discovered to their cost. He was never aggressive and it upset him, more than he'd ever admit, whenever he was drawn into a fight and gave his surprised opponent a bloody nose. His energies lay in other directions: the gathering of knowledge, dreams and ambitions yet to be realized, worlds to be conquered. This, after all, was his glorious England, mother of a vast global family and fully recovered from the awful losses of the Kaiser's war. These were the twilight days of a golden Edwardian era, a time when even the son of Jewish immigrant parents could aspire to a knighthood and possibly a peerage.

"Study hard, Phileep, and you will make it to the top," his mother would urge him. (All his family members and closest friends pronounced his name Phileep, in the French style.)

He was a good student but never a 'swot' – that derisive term for a bookworm. As a matter of fact, he enjoyed considerable popularity with his classmates at Brewers School despite his high marks. Perhaps it was because he was always ready to help anyone in difficulty with his studies, or because he was an incorrigible practical joker: always up to some mischief or other and the frequent recipient of punishing cane strokes across his bottom. He endured these with a smile, and soon acquired the nickname of 'Smiley' among both his fellow pupils and teachers. They hardly ever called him Philip or Bosnar, and whenever his Mum and Dad visited the school for special events, they found themselves labeled as the parents of 'Smiley Bosnar even by members of the teaching staff from the Headmaster down.

It was a fine secondary school, situated in the heart of London's East End, and Philip was proud to say he attended Brewers, just as others might brag about Eton or Harrow. It was basically a boys' school, with a small section for girls in a much less impressive building two blocks away. The girls' section was all but hidden out of sight, as if to proclaim that Brewers was a house of learning where men could be men and women could be pursued but always kept out of the masculine dominion.

So far, Philip hadn't encountered any girls who aroused his romantic yearnings. The daughters of his parents' Jewish friends, even the most attractive ones, seemed more like cousins, and the thought of a love affair with any of them seemed almost incestuous. As for the Gentile friends of his 17-year-old sister, Pauline, they seemed much too old to interest him. In any event, his first order of business was getting through the matriculation exams at the end of the school term, preferably with Honors. To pass with Honors required very high marks – called Distinctions – in at least five of the eight subjects, a tough proposition even for the élite few in each matriculating class. What made it more difficult in Philip's case, was the fact that he'd skipped a class level because of his high performance in recent term exams, and he felt a strange sense of inadequacy as he listened to the torrent of knowledge coming from his new classmates. Some of them suggested that he try catching up with his studies and homework in the reading room department of the Trevor Road Public Library. He prayed this would work out well, since he'd always done his homework at home. Above all, he hoped the change of lifestyle wouldn't hurt his chances in the 'Matrics'.

There were three important considerations.

First, passing with honors would earn him a scholarship for free studies up to university entrance, provided he then passed the 6th form exams for Intermediate B.A. or B.Sc.

Second, helping his father, a warm-hearted and gentle man whose strength of character and unflagging optimism had so far been rewarded with one financial disaster after another. This courageous person, the only true Christian he'd ever met in terms of the Nazarene's moral code, was still reeling in the throes of the current economic depression. He deserved to be rewarded with success, if only through the accomplishments of his son.

Third, he was beginning to question the choice of Law as his chosen career and was now looking more toward Medicine as his life's vocation. This new decision had been strongly influenced by the three fascinating volumes of 'The Science of Life' by H.G.Wells and Thomas Huxley. They were a birthday present from his father's business partner, and he read them with the intensity of a starving man offered a feast of the world's most tempting foods.

Even if he achieved total success in his matrics, he would still offer to go out and get a job – any job at all – just to help out with the family's finances. He had a fair idea of how fierce the family opposition to such an idea would be. It would come from his Dad more than anyone, and he knew how remote were his chances in the hostile environment of massive nationwide unemployment.

His mother was the real disciplinarian of the Bosnar clan, but she tried to conceal that fact from friends and relatives, pretending her husband was the final arbiter of behavior in the Bosnar household. Her standards and expectations were very high, and her husband appeared to back her to the hilt while making generous concessions to his children behind her back. She knew what was going on and secretly approved, even as she vehemently condemned his duplicity. In truth, this small bundle of energy, five feet high and weighing all of seven stone (ninety-eight pounds), loved her children more than life itself but couldn't conceal her burning ambition for their success, especially that of her Phileep. Her determination that he would not fail was the driving force behind her every thought and action concerning his progress, and he was glad he hadn't let her down so far.

The true irony lay in the fact that he was determined to overcome any obstacle to his own objectives, and required no additional persuasion. If it meant becoming a leading student, then that must be his contribution to a brighter future for his family; but most of all for the father he admired so much. He hoped he would retain his mother's drive in the process and never lose his father's moral values.

His first few nights at the library were a pleasant surprise. There were four broad tables, placed along most of the length of the study area, with lots of room for each student to spread out books and writing materials. Reference volumes were readily available from the supervising librarian, a middle-aged man with goldrimmed pince-nez and prissy manner, who pursed his lips in disapproval whenever he had to shush a noisy student into guilty silence. His trousers were far too short and he walked with mincing steps that were the object of much amusement and ribald whispers. Although fully aware of his young charges' unkind comments, he kept the place running in a decent and orderly fashion and made it a conducive environment for study.

The students were mostly boys of Philip's own age: a couple of his classmates from Brewers and some from the rival Standish secondary school that was located in teeming Whitechapel. It was celebrated for the highest scholastic standing in London, and perhaps in the whole of England. He'd met the renowned 'Quickshot' Martin from that institution, who was reputed to have a clear run at top marks in the forthcoming matrics. Martin seemed a likable chap, with a ready sense of humor and little vanity about his accomplishments, and Philip decided he was a most worthy rival. There were some boys from Traynor secondary school in lower Stepney, and a few girls from the female sections of Brewers, Standish, and Traynor (Pauline's house of learning). A few university students were present from nearby Queen Mary's College, and Philip recognized at least two of these as substitute teachers who taught classes at Brewers. Needless to say, there was a certain amount of clandestine flirtation going on, with surreptitious gestures and meaningful glances. There were even whispered invitations and assignations from the boldest among them.

By the fourth night, he'd entered fully into the spirit of doing his homework at the library and using the reference facilities to full advantage. Suddenly, his concentration was interrupted by the regal entrance of a beautiful, golden-haired girl. She was petite in stature but beautifully proportioned, and she commanded the unconcealed adulation of the two university students who were her escorts. They were just completing a lively exchange, which dropped quickly to a smiling silence as the doors swung open and the intimate trio came through. The girl's dazzling smile struck Philip with an impact no other smile had ever done before, and he felt an urgent need to know all about this young lady with the smile of angels. He waited until the librarian had gone across to the main library for a few minutes and asked his closest companion, "WHO is that smasher?"

"Oh, that's Dora Henderson, darling of the student world. She's head of the senior students, champion swimmer and diver, and she's admired by all the chaps at Traynor and all the gals as well."

Philip noticed that she'd put on some horn-rimmed glasses, but these only seemed to augment her delicate good looks, especially her eyes. They had a most unusual color and he believed they must be violet. At five minutes before the 10 o'clock closing time, one of her escorts, a darkly handsome brute in his early twenties, with a dashing air of self-confidence, came over and put his hand on her unprotesting shoulder. She rose from her chair, put on her mackintosh, and they both went out together in happy familiarity.

The weeks passed by, and Philip continued to study well at the library and began to catch up on all the subjects he'd missed by skipping a class. But he was always restless and uneasy until the 'golden girl' came laughing through the swing doors with her admiring escorts. When she'd taken her seat at the desk parallel to his, and almost immediately across from him, he waited for her to put on those attractive glasses of hers before he was able to settle down. Once in a while, he looked up from his books and their eyes would meet in cordial recognition as fellow-students, but nothing more.

By the last week in March, with his sixteenth birthday fast approaching, this nightly library ritual of non-courtship was shattered by an accusation delivered by his sister, Pauline. It came as a veritable bolt from the blue.

"I was talking to Dora Henderson today. She's our top student, you know, and a wonderful girl. She said she was worried that you weren't concentrating on your matric studies and were gaping at her instead." Philip blew up.

"That's a bloody patronizing remark for her to make and a bloody conceited one as well. She's the guilty party, always looking around and turning on that enticing smile of hers at anyone who happens to glance her way."

He felt ashamed at his fury.

"We'll just see if I'm not concentrating enough to pass my matrics."

From that time forth, he added something new to the library ritual. Each night, as soon as Dora Henderson left the library with her husky escort, Philip would leave, too. He would follow some twenty paces behind them, until the couple parted company at the junction of Mile End Road and Congrave Street. She and her beau would exchange a few words, but there were no embraces or gestures of affection, which seemed strange. Just goodbye until next time. She would walk down Congrave and Mister Queen Mary's College would continue along the Mile End Road. As for Philip, he would cross the road and proceed toward his home in Grantham Square.

One night, shortly after his sixteenth birthday, she was walking home alone, and he was keeping pace in his faithful rearguard position when she lost patience and decided to confront him. She stopped abruptly in her tracks, turned to face him and waited until he was close.

"Is this a bet or a trial of patience?" she asked coolly.

She was accurate on both counts, he thought in amazement. Some of his pals who shared his confidences were already betting he'd succeed, against all odds, in establishing a romantic relationship with her.

"It's neither one," he lied "but I must confess I'd much sooner walk WITH YOU than behind you."

She laughed merrily, and he knew the ice was broken. Forever, he felt quite sure. He walked along with her for the rest of the way, exchanging a few aimless pleasantries, then accompanied her to the end of Congrave and her house at 27 Birnham Place. Step One, thought Philip, as he walked home with elation in his stride and joy in his heart.

During the next few months, they got to know each other much better, and from time to time he accompanied her home from the library, gradually taking over from her college escort. On the way, they would discuss many things: her ambition to become a good teacher and perhaps do some writing, his to become a skillful surgeon and perhaps make some new discoveries in medicine. They talked about British politics in general and Oswald Moseley in particular, a dangerous demagogue whose Fascist thugs roamed London's Eastend in search of racial and political victims. Philip loved the sound of Dora's voice. It was soft and cultured in tone, and her perfect use of the English language won his admiration. It seemed an odd coincidence when she now confided to Pauline how much she loved listening to her brother express his views on a wide range of topics.

It was obvious that Philip and Dora were enjoying each other's company more and more as the weeks passed into late spring, and both looked forward eagerly to each new meeting. He was changing from a callow fifteen-year-old boy to a young man of sixteen, and growing taller almost from one day to the next. His voice had found a good low level, his acne was clearing and he was shaving each morning. His thoughts, too, were more adult, more practical, more responsible. He wanted to take her in his arms, to protect her and give her all his love. She, in turn, seemed to experience a different kind of feeling toward him, but still not a truly adult male-female bond of love. Perhaps, after matriculation and the summer vacations, their relationship would burst into full blossom. In the meantime, their closeness and intimate friendship gave him a happiness that let him fly through his studies at top speed.

English was his best subject, French and German came next, then Chemistry and Physics, Algebra, Geometry and Trigonometry, and finally History and Geography. He found these last two subjects difficult, mainly because of the boring way his schoolmasters presented their material in these areas. He began to concentrate on them, doing his own research and accumulating not just facts, but logic and patterns of thought as well. His friends and boosters at Brewers noticed his rapid progress at classes, and some even expressed the belief that their Smiley might surpass Standish's Quickshot in matric results. They were all eagerly following Smiley's romantic progress as well, and were shortening the odds against failure. It was a strange feeling for him to know that he had a widening group of supporters pulling for his success in both enterprises, and he appreciated the warmth of their good wishes.

As the time for exams came closer, his former tensions of self-doubt continued to disappear, until he felt fully relaxed in the confident belief that he'd perform well. At the same time, there was the sad realization that he'd soon be parted from his beloved Dorie during the summer holidays, while she in turn told him how much she'd miss him while they were apart.

"But don't you worry, Phil," she assured him, "I promise not to forget you and I'll be back from Cornwall with my aunt and uncle by the end of July."
He knew she'd lived with them since she was three years old. Her parents had perished in a terrible gas explosion that destroyed their home, the result of a faulty stove. Mercifully, she was playing outside at the time and was spared, thank God!

The matric examinations came and went, and he was off to school camp for two weeks in the coastal region of South Kent, with its pleasant beaches and wide playing fields. This would be followed by a further two weeks on the Isle of Wight, after results of the matric exams were announced: an annual custom. He'd enjoyed the summer camp's activities for the past two years, and this year was better than ever. His progressive headmaster, Dr. Ellsmere, had arranged – through his European educational contacts – for a contingent of students to come to the Kent camping grounds from the University of Tübingen in Bavaria, from the École spéciale de Paris in France, and the Vienna College for Young Ladies in Austria. This new and unexpected development opened up new horizons for Philip, giving him an opportunity to polish up his linguistic skills in French and German, both of which he could already speak almost like a native.

He found the Austrian girls, in their late teens, quite delightful. They were pretty, charming and vivacious, proficient at a wide variety of sports and speaking excellent English. Their leader, and by far the most popular with the Brewers' 6th-formers, was a tall and striking brunette called Mimi. The French lads, by contrast, were withdrawn and surly, played nothing but soccer, and only with their French classmates. The Germans, around seventeen and eighteen, were fine-looking, strapping lads. Their handsome leader, whom they called Count Rudi, was a blue-eyed blond giant: a true Nordic God of Teutonic Aryan mythology. When it was discovered how well Philip could speak their language they soon adopted him as "Unser englischer Freund, Smiley."

From that time forth he became their constant companion, and they began inviting him over to their quarters to share their beer and sausage and teach him the strange German speech of Bavaria, as well as songs in that dialect. He learned to join them in lusty renditions of *"Als die Römer Fresch geworden"* (When the Romans got cheeky), and the nostalgic *"Mussiden, mussiden vom Städtel hinaus, Städtel hinaus und Du mei Schatz bleibst hier"* (Must I leave this little town, while you, my dearest, stay here.) He was even persuaded to sing a *Hochdeutsch* solo, the famous and beloved ballad: "Ich weiss nicht was soll est bedeuten das ich so traurig bin" (I know not how to explain it, how to account for my sadness.) They began taking him on their marches across the surrounding fields and ditches at the magic hour of dusk, and he joined them in roaring their vigorous marching songs, beating out the heavy rhythm with their tramping boots.

The first hint of anything unwholesome came on the fifth day: rumors and innuendoes from his German friends, suggesting it was wise to stay away from Mimi because she was A JEW. It was the first time in his life that he'd ever been directly involved in any situation of open antisemitism, and he was stunned to see that the obscene stain of Adolph Hitler's paranoid racism could contaminate people as fine as Count Rudi. He decided not to over-react, but to deal with each situation as it developed.

The second event occurred three days later. During the night, a group of German students entered the French hut, tied one of the students to his mobile bunk, and stifled his cries with a gag. They carried him down to the waters edge and left him there. By the grace of God, the tide was going out, but the unfortunate victim of this 'prank' was in pretty bad shape when he was discovered by a local resident who was taking his dog for an early morning run. It was fortunate that the victim recovered with no obvious after-effects. Although there was a very tense atmosphere in the camp compound with feverish activity behind the scenes, the matter was hushed up. After all, the local police had no wish to become involved in any messy diplomatic commotion.

The third incident took place one week later. The avuncular professor in charge of the Tübingen group delivered an interesting lecture that day on the origin, significance and impact of national anthems. Philip loved to hear Dr. Schemmler deliver his views in flawless Hochdeutsch accents, and attended the outdoor classes of this gentle and cultured man whenever he could. The professor had an unblemished background as a democratic moderate, having served in the Weimar republic during its dying days. Oddly enough, his students didn't seem to hold him in very high regard. His most interesting comments on that day concerned the opening lines of the German national anthem.

'*Deutschland, Deutschland über Alles'* he explained, did not mean `Germany above all nations. What it really meant was `*Ich liebe Deutschland über Alles'*(I love Germany more than any other country). This information was followed by a slow departure of the class, until all but Philip had left.

He didn't see the venerable teacher for several days, and was shocked when he finally observed him limping along to the German dining area, with both eyes blackened and swollen, and a nasty cut across his upper lip.

"You must forgive the appearance of a clumsy, absent-minded old professor, Herr Smiley," he apologized, "I should never have gone stumbling around in the dark. My pleasant nightly walk ended up instead in a most unpleasant fall."

That night, for the first time, Philip had difficulty sleeping, and during the following week he felt something of real value had changed between him and his German friends. They still treated him with respect and affection and tried to make him feel like one of their own, but he found it difficult to reciprocate.

One day Count Rudi took him aside.

"Smiley, my good friend, let us go for a walk," he said. It was quite a long walk and when they were finally out of all earshot they sat down on the soft green wildgrass.

"You are intelligent, Smiley, so you must be aware of what is going on behind the scenes in our New Germany." He accentuated the word "NEW" as if it were part of an emerging national title.

"After the war we were betrayed by the politicians, by the damn Communists and most of all by the Jews."

Philip waited with seething anger before dropping his bombshell; he could afford to wait. The time was near.

"All our students at the university will be in the forefront of the New Order, in the birth of the Third Reich. We will be ready to take up the banner of such heroes as my uncle, the Baron Klaus von Eisenwald, one of Bavaria's most honored judges. Even now he is shaping our new laws, starting with those against undesirable political elements and inferior races."

He paused for effect and studied Philip's face intently.

"We are going to need special friends in many countries, but especially in England. France we really detest. Italy we despise. The Slavs we will eventually destroy."

It was quite a speech, but Philip still held his tongue.

"So you see, Smiley, why you could be so useful to us over the coming years."

Rudi paused with a satisfied sigh, obviously pleased with the sense of a difficult job well done.

"You Goddamn fool, Rudi!" Philip exploded, "Don't you know I'm a Jew, and even if I weren't, crazy bigotry like yours would make me vomit. I hate Stalin's Communism just as much as you, but I don't want to beat up, imprison or kill anyone who thinks that way. As for France, that's where I was born. As for the Slavs, my forbears came from Poland and some may have intermarried. And as for your madman, Adolph Schickelgruber, the man's an insult to the human race."

To Philip's absolute amazement, Rudi laughed.

"Don't be so naive, Smiley. Don't you know that we Nazis of aristocratic background make our own decisions and our own exceptions. You would not be the first. As for that vulgar little Austrian pervert, we will take care of him once he's done the initial dirty work for us." He caught his breath, then continued.

"We thought, just thought mind you, that you might be a Jew, but we all agreed that it would not make the slightest difference. You're really like one of us you know, Smiley, and we need you."

"No, Rudi, I could never be one of you, and I could never be your undercover agent, or help your New Order in any way, if that was your real purpose."

"That is not true," protested Rudi, "It was your friendship first and foremost that we wanted. You must believe me."

"I'm sorry," said Philip quietly but firmly, "but you and your Nazi pals have finally destroyed that."

There was nothing more to say and they walked back in sad silence. The twilight was beautiful, and overhead the seagulls were leaving sea and shore for their inland sanctuaries.

The next day was one of rising excitement in the English boys' camp. The news had filtered down from the Headmaster and masters to the 6th-formers, and from them to the 5th-formers, that the matriculation results were due to be announced later that day. Somehow, the air of expectation seemed more than just that. Whenever they passed by his group in the sports field, the masters seemed to glance at him so often that he wondered if his imagination was playing tricks. They seemed to be talking in a conspiratorial fashion, with lowered voices and whispers, and he had the feeling that something very special was brewing. He was hardly in the mood for any unpleasant surprises after the emotional turmoil of yesterday, and he was glad when the dinner bell rang and the Brewers campers were greeted with the sight of a veritable banquet laid out on the food tables.

There was a festive air and a lot of laughter and happy commotion at the head table. Dr. Ellsmere held up his hand for silence, and the students all settled quietly into their appointed places.

"Boys of Brewers School, this is a proud day for us as your teachers, and for you as our pupils. The overall matriculation results this year have been the best for decades, and they will be posted in the information area following this special dinner." He took a sip of water and went on, "Before I give you my special news I would like to introduce our honored guest for this occasion." He motioned for the person on his right to stand, and for a moment Philip couldn't believe his eyes. The beaming gentleman who rose was his own beloved father, and he thought he must be dreaming.

The Headmaster continued, "This is the father of Philip Bosnar, better known to most of you as Smiley."

There was a lot of clapping as well as obvious bewilderment.

"We have invited him to share our joyful news that his son not only gained distinction in every subject, but received the highest marks in England."

What followed was total pandemonium, with Philip almost in a state of speechless shock while waves of cheering and congratulation broke over him. Half dazed, he moved like a sleepwalker to the head table and threw his arms around his Dad as they both fought back their tears. After dinner, he thanked all the masters for their wonderful gesture to his father and indeed to his family, and Ellsmere said that he would seek the schoolboard's permission to declare an annual school holiday in celebration of the event. Philip went outside with his Dad and spent a private half hour with him, until it was time to catch the evening train back to London. Rafael Bosnar gripped his son's right hand in both of his and said in a very quiet voice,

"Phileep, you have made me the happiest man in the world."

If anyone had asked him to relate what happened during the next two weeks, he would have been unable to answer. Time passed by on the beautiful Isle of Wight in a sort of pleasant delirium. He knew his current success didn't make him any cleverer or more important. He must put all the acclamation behind him and get on with his life, with his obligations and his future. Now that he'd brought joy to his family, and proved to himself that he could build solid accomplishment on determination and effort, he could face the future with confidence. It was time to get back to

London, to see his family and friends, to join his beautiful Dorie once again and lay firm claim to her love. But first of all, he must confront his father with the proposition that he take time off his school schedule and earn some money for at least a year or two, if at all possible.

He always felt guilty thinking how hard his Dad worked, through the most difficult times, to maintain a comfortable standard of living for his family. Despite his deepening debts, a facade of middle-class lifestyle was always maintained, although his creditors knew that Rafael Bosnar's word was his ironclad bond. Philip looked forward to the day when he could, at last, lift the heavy burden of debt from those weary shoulders. Regardless of developments, he was re-solved to pursue his dream of becoming a surgeon, but realized how disappointed the old Head-master would be.

Dr. Ellsmere had set his heart on helping young Bosnar to become a barrister-at-law. He used to come into the classroom from time to time, presiding as judge during one of the mock-courtroom trials, and always seemed to enjoy listening to Smiley Bosnar hold forth as counsel for the defense. Strings were being pulled by the old man and vital contacts made through the old boys' network. All these efforts would now be wasted and there would be the inevitable sense of betrayal and hurt.

Holidays finally came to an end, and he was home again. It was fun to join his friends kicking a football around in the street or practicing their cricket skills, and to watch the older boys playing tennis in the park. Both courts were occupied most of the time, and he was anxious to arrange a few games for himself before the summer was over. It was one of his favorite sports and he always felt relaxed after a good game of singles. On the first Sunday evening after getting back, he broached the subject of leaving school and getting a job, and was promptly shot down in flames by his appalled family.

"If you do this," his irate father warned him, "you would destroy all our hopes and every-thing I have worked for."
His mother and sister joined the assault with a vengeance, and he knew he'd lost.

After dinner, which tasted heavenly (he'd almost forgotten his Mum's genius in the kitchen), Pauline took him aside.

"I bumped into Dora Henderson this afternoon," she confided with a knowing smile. "She asked me to let you know she'll be at the library tomorrow evening. Don't let Mum know," she added, "you know how she is. She'd either have hysterics or put on one of her dramatic scenes of motherhood betrayed."

"Not to mention my affront to the entire Jewish race."
Even as he laughed, he knew that he'd have to face the maternal wrath sooner or later and establish his independence in such personal matters.

The following Monday evening, he entered the reference library shortly after 8 o'clock. The regular custodian was on his summer vacation and his place was taken by a younger and easy-going East Indian. All the usual gang were there and it was almost like a social club. They gathered around Philip excitedly, and exhibited a hero-worship that he found embarrassing. At 9 o'clock, the buzz of conversation died down suddenly as Dora entered, and they all waited in hushed expecta-tion as she came over to Philip. He rose at once and walked out with a possessive arm around her slim waist, all eyes watching in approval and admiration.

At first, Philip reflected, he'd been the Don Quixote in hopeless pursuit of his Dulcinea,

but now he'd conquered the windmills and she belonged to him. She'd never looked more beautiful, and seemed vibrant and aglow. They went for a long walk, and wanted to know all about each
other. She told him that she had high marks in her Intermediate B.A. exams, and that all the local
schools knew about his matriculation triumph. Philip congratulated her in turn, and told her how
proud he was of her excellent exam results. He gave a brief account of his camping holidays, but
didn't mention the unpleasantness with the German group. This was no time for politics; it was a
time for loving reunion, and they couldn't show how much they'd missed each other until they
were quite alone.

It was curious how the residents of Congrave Street and Birnham Place behaved as
the young couple passed by. This was a very rough neighborhood, mostly tough Cockneys and the
dregs of Anglo-Jewish misfits. It was an enclave where summer nights were filled with loud coarse
language and raucous laughter, as the locals gathered along the pavement to enjoy the cooling
night-breezes of summer. As Dora and Philip passed by, the swearing and guffaws seemed to subside and the loungers stepped aside to let them pass. It was almost as though they were co-conspira-
tors in this unlikely romance and wished it well.

At last, they arrived at her door and Dora invited him in. She showed Philip into the
front parlor and turned on a small table lamp. She looked at him for a long silent moment. He
seemed so much taller, so much older and more mature than the callow youth she first knew. This
was her man and to him and him alone she would give her love.

Time stood still; then with a tiny cry escaping from her throat, she rushed across the
room. Now, as if they had been lovers all their lives, she melted into his arms while her lips eagerly
sought his.

CHAPTER 3

1939 cont'd

During their first two months in Vanwey, Phil and Patty learned many new things and made many new friends. The first of these was discovered by Patty when she went around the corridor one morning, hoping to borrow some sugar from an available and accommodating neighbor. She soon found one and was invited to stay for coffee, which the helpful neighbor confessed was always percolating in her apartment from morning to night. This new (*and ultimately life-long*) friend of Patricia Bosnar was Ruth Steffanson, a part-time schoolteacher who possessed a quick mind, a warm and caring nature and a bubbling sense of humor.

Three years earlier, this splendid young Canadian lass of solid pioneer stock, with distant origins in the Scottish highlands, had married Olaf Steffanson, now known as Alf. He was an experienced accountant of Swedish origin, but hadn't been too successful so far. Nevertheless, he was a conscientious and sensitive individual who believed passionately in the philosophy of free enterprise and open competition. Despite his disappointments, he retained untarnished dreams of a bright future in this new land. He and Philip soon became good friends and shared a keen and common interest in politics, international affairs, chess, bridge and poker.

Theodore Sundstrom was a bluff and hearty American expatriate in his early sixties. He was named for Theodore ('Teddy') Roosevelt, the president who became his lifelong hero and the model on whom he patterned himself. Sundstrom tackled his business ventures the way the legendary Teddy had once charged the heights of San Juan. He feared only one person, his beloved wife, the svelte and socially ambitious Helen. She was his former secretary, a lady of impeccable diction and a melodious laugh that could steal center stage of any conversation. They were both warm and generous people, and Helen Sundstrom guided Patty unerringly through the complex thickets of Vanwey's 'high society'.

Theodore would often encourage Phil with an avuncular arm around the shoulder and a forceful "Bully, young fella!" He had the snort and thumb-to-nose flick of the experienced boxer, as well as the telltale movements of his thick shoulders. As a former intervarsity middleweight champion, he could still put on a formidable display with any young challenger. Philip liked him a lot and would value his support in difficult times to come.

Another good friend and future champion of lost causes for the Bosnars was the lawyer Herb Adams, a delightful elf of a man with a ruddy smooth complexion and expressive hands that were used to full advantage in lively discussion. His wife Hilda, elegant doyenne of Vanwey's senior smart set, was well cast as a social leader: white-haired, coiffed to perfection and utterly charming. She adored her husband and admired him despite his meager and unprofitable law practice.

Within a short time, Phil and Patty came to share that admiration. They knew he was

President of both the Saskatchewan Law Society and the Vanwey District Conservative Association. He was also a devout but progressive Roman Catholic, and organist at the Holy Cross Cathedral. His reputation for honesty, fair play and decency, was in sharp contrast to that of Mark
Standwick, his professional competitor. Standwick was head of the local Orange Lodge, a shrewd
and successful scoundrel and the great and good friend of Dr. Tom Blaikie, for whom he acted as
legal advisor.

        The most fascinating couple of all were the Freikopfs. George Freikopf was owner of
South Prairie Light and Power and the employer of Alf Steffanson, who managed the firm's books
and acted as financial adviser. An allround athlete, George was still an excellent badminton player
and above average golfer at the age of forty. He owned and managed a small string of racehorses
and was a fine rider in the bargain. His Swiss ancestors had come to the New World almost a
century before. They settled in North Dakota and became successful farmers, growing flax, barley
and wheat and eventually adding a fine Guernsey dairy herd.

        He had been one of the youngest senators in the U.S. government and represented his
home state in an effective manner. While in office, he improved the lot of its depressed farming
communities and expanded its tenuous industrial base. After leaving politics, his business interests
took him northwards to Saskatchewan where he met Dorothy Parsons, a bright and attractive schoolteacher. He soon married her and settled in Vanwey on a full-time basis.

        They lived in a large and pleasant home on First Street, overlooking the valley, and
entertained quite often. But although George was active in the town's civic affairs he never became
a Canadian citizen. Dorothy joined him in many of his activities and enjoyed a well-deserved
reputation as a charming hostess, despite her job of raising three small children.

        Through these first few friendships, the Bosnars met many new friends and acquaint-
ances, some of whom would play a pivotal part in their future lives. The evening parties kept
proliferating and so did the casual gossip. It was said that Blaikie was still living in sin with Marcie
Crofts, but would never marry her despite her high hopes for such a union when she first came to
work for him in 1934. Ten years earlier he'd been involved in a messy extramarital affair with
Marcie's predecessor in that department. Mrs. Blaikie, a devout Catholic, announced her adamant
refusal to divorce him and took their son Edward to live with her in Winnipeg. That was where the
rest of her family dwelt, and that was where she could pick up the pieces of her life after her
disastrous marriage. At least her husband paid for the boy's education and saw him through medical school. He even brought him out to Vanwey from time to time as a locum G.P.

        In most ways Edward detested his father's brutal attitude toward life, women, Catho-
lics, Jews and 'furriners'. In other ways he respected him for the boldness and strength of will
which, to his great regret, he'd never inherited. He even believed the legend of his father's
preeminence as a country surgeon, and it was this false concept which he'd conveyed to the Bosnars
– in all innocence – when they met at the Strand Palace Hotel in London in April of 1938; a
thousand years ago, it now seemed.

        Blaikie's pathological bigotry was shared by a small circle that included lawyer
Standwick and several of the town's leading merchants. Some of these had been members of the
Ku Klux Klan when it flourished in the prairie border towns during the depressed early 30s. The
malignant influence of this central core of racism permeated many areas of an otherwise decent
community, and there were even murmurs of discontent about accepting Mort Schneider as the

solitary Jewish member of the Rotary Club. It was a turn of events that made it easy for Philip Bosnar to reach his final and irrevocable decision. Since he'd never been asked and the subject had never been raised, he would henceforth be known as a non-practicing Catholic, thus facilitating his new role as a fighter against the plague of antisemitism.

The perverse bigotry directed against Jews had already swept across Europe and was threatening to destroy the values of Christian civilization itself. Philip Bosnar's final answer to Count Rudi and his Nazi sympathies could now be clearly defined: Undercover, yes, but against what you stand for and never on the side of racial and religious intolerance." (Declarations and arguments against antisemitism would come far more convincingly from a non-Jew).

Phil and Patty had already freely discussed the problems of religious intermarriage: in particular, the raising of their children. The first decision reached was that both parents should live the forgivable fiction of belonging to the same faith, and the second was that they should be known as non-practicing Catholics. That wasn't too difficult, since Philip had usually been considered by most who met him as Gentile. Besides, by virtue of an amusing mix-up at the Hôpitale de Sainte Therese in the Montmartre, he'd been baptized a Catholic by an overzealous hospital priest, and was registered as such in the hospital archives. It was hoped this deception would protect their offspring from the major cross-prejudices of life at school, but it was the firm intention of both parents to reveal the simple truth to the children when they were old enough.

(In years to come Philip and Patricia would sometimes question the wisdom of the deception, but always came up with the same answer: it was worth it. Even their two children, when they were grown up and differed on many political viewpoints, would affirm their agreement on this subject and respect their parents' motives. So far as the truth eventually emerging or interim suspicions being voiced, there was no great problem. Those to whom the real truth seemed so important weren't the ones who mattered very much to Phil and Patty, and those who did matter to them would hardly care one way or the other. Aside from these future considerations, it would be interesting to see Blaikie's reaction if he found out such a 'frightful' truth about his new associate.)

Patty was happy to observe that Phil's reputation as a surgeon was starting to spread, and even as a general physician he was respected and well-liked. Unfortunately, his relations with Dr. Tom were deteriorating with each passing week, while Sam Walters stayed shrewdly out of sight. It was obvious the young G.P. wasn't helping the situation. He knew on which side his bread was buttered and echoed all the old man's hatreds and prejudices.

They still imposed a rigid boycott of the new sixty-bed Sisters' hospital, located at the far west end of First Street. Philip was forbidden to admit any patients there and was warned against having anything to do with the Black Witches. That was what Blaikie liked to call the nursing nuns of the Sisters of St. Cecilia, even though they wore gleaming white habits during the summer months.

Philip soon discovered that his renowned boss was a poor diagnostician and a clumsy operator. His postoperative management consisted of coarse humor and cackling laughter during morning ward rounds, ordering his patients to stop feeling sorry for themselves. Marcie gave the general anesthetics; she was, after all, a graduate nurse. Although she did her best, it was difficult to get adequate and safe muscular relaxation with her outdated 'Open Ether' technique, using a mask and drip-bottle rather than a gas-flow machine. That was why Philip came to depend more and more on spinal anesthesia to provide safe and reliable pain relief and relaxation for abdominal surgery, especially when the patient was very large or distended.

He soon became adept at giving 'spinals' with minimal fuss or difficulty and hardly any discomfort to the patient. By combining this method with adequate preoperative medication, excellent results were obtained. Of course the patient had to be placed in the correct position, thus avoiding too high a level of spinal blockade that could impair breathing. It was essential for a nurse to stay with the patient throughout the procedure, to check for a safe upper level of sensory loss and watch the respiration and blood pressure.

By taking these precautions it was possible to avoid unpleasant side effects or difficulties; and by using the finest possible spinal needle and keeping the patient flat for twenty-four hours, it was possible to avoid the dreaded 'post-spinal headache'. During this first day of full recumbency the patient was turned frequently, leg movements were encouraged and assisted, and the patient was made to take deep breaths and cough effectively. Only in this way could one avoid the formation of clots in the leg veins or the collapse of one or both lungs.

Philip learned to enjoy all aspects of medical practice and could count his professional blessings:-

He was good with children and they in turn were often his best patients, whether medical or surgical.

He learned all the Canadian proprietary drug preparations, a far cry from the British multi-drug formulae that one had to concoct according to traditional apothecary methods.

He enjoyed handling his obstetrical cases and made sure there was always adequate relief from undue pain.

He became skilled at forceps deliveries, with minimum damage to the stretched soft tissues, careful repair of any damage, or the deliberate incision known as 'episiotomy'(which was done to prevent extensive tearing, using supplementary local anesthetic).

He was highly selective in choosing those mothers who needed Cesarean Section, and his results were rewarding to mother, child and surgeon.

He learned how to become adept at reading cardiograms, as well as performing thorough fluoroscopic examinations in the X-ray room in order to increase his accuracy in radiological diagnosis.

He became proficient at skin-testing for allergic disorders, and treating certain cases by progressive desensitization to the offending substance when clearly identified. The commonest offender proved to be ragweed, and a special oily solution of the extract seemed to benefit a majority of the patients.

As for those female disorders requiring surgical correction, what he saw in his practice made him very sad. So many of these long-suffering souls had been misdiagnosed as ovarian cysts, backwardly tipped wombs or both. Their real problem often remained overlooked, namely *'Cystocele and Rectocele'*. In this condition the muscular supports around the pelvic organs become stretched and damaged – usually during delivery of the baby – and fail to provide the necessary support to the bladder, vagina and rectum. The weakness may progress until the womb descends through the stretched vagina and down between the thighs. After a while the unfortunate woman loses control of her urinary bladder and her rectum, and she cannot strain, cough or sneeze without increasing her incontinence and discomfort.

Many of these sufferers had undergone a so-called *'Triple Procedure'*. This operation consisted of removing small and mostly inoffensive cysts of the ovary, sometimes the needless removal of the ovaries themselves, fixing the womb in a forward-tilted position and removing the appendix if still present. Although the operation itself was a simple one, any temporary psychological relief was usually followed by a disappointing return of unpleasant symptoms. These were then diagnosed as 'adhesions' and could lead to one or more additional and unnecessary operations. In many cases, what the patient really required was an appropriate vaginal repair and nothing more. A number of these women had been fitted with messy, uncomfortable and often ineffective internal supports known as 'pessaries'. This was the equivalent of prescribing a truss for the control rather than the cure of a hernia.

Dr. Philip Bosnar began to give serious consideration to the idea of abandoning general surgery and specializing in obstetrics and gynecology. In the end, however, he decided against it for three reasons, which he discussed in depth with Patty. The first was having to leave the challenge, scope and infinite variety of general surgery. The second was facing the irregular hours of obstetrics, with urgent calls to the hospital at any hour of the day and night and inevitable disruption of family life. An alternative was to yield to temptation and employ frequent artificial induction of labor or Cesarean section, thus tailoring ones practice to a more orderly time-table. The third reason was that although helping women in distress could be a glorious example of modern chivalry, the idea of never examining or treating a male patient seemed unnatural and somehow abhorrent. Philip enjoyed the give and take of discussing weather and crops with his male patients, as well as sports events and even current politics. He would have missed these far too much.

By a strange twist of fate, it was in this very specialty, obstetrics and gynecology, that the fuse was lit, leading to the eventual explosion between Philip and the formidable, even dangerous, Dr. Tom. The patient was a woman from a small town in North Dakota, some twenty miles away, and she was scheduled for surgery the next morning. The diagnosis was a massive and steadily enlarging ovarian cyst, possibly malignant, and Philip was asked to examine the patient prior to surgery. She was a very obese forty-year-old female with a benign past history, family history and functional enquiry. Although married for fifteen years she'd never been pregnant; in fact she now wondered whether she was entering a premature 'change of life'. Her menstrual periods had become erratic and finally stopped at the beginning of the current year; and although the large swelling in her belly gave her some indigestion she felt quite well in all other respects.

Her general physical examination revealed no significant abnormalities, but her abdominal examination produced a real surprise. What had been diagnosed as a giant ovarian cyst was the size and shape of a full term pregnancy. At first, Philip thought he detected some abnormal muscle spasms. Then he wondered if these might be the fetal movements of an unborn offspring. A stethoscope applied near the patient's navel removed any lingering doubt; the baby's heart was beating lustily! Telling the patient not to get dressed and to remain on the examining table, Philip excused himself and said he would talk with Dr. Blaikie. He hated having to do this, but at least it would save the old man from putting the finishing touches to a catastrophic error.

"I don't believe you," the older man screamed when he received the unwelcome news, his face suffused with rage, "you're wrong, wrong, wrong!"

He dashed out violently, almost knocking Philip down, and didn't return for almost half an hour. When he came back, his face was pale and covered in sweat. It was the first time Philip had ever seen him perspire.

"Fucking smart aleck," was all Blaikie said, almost in a whisper, but the glare of hatred was one it would be difficult to forget. The surgery was cancelled but the patient never came back to Dr. Tom.

(*Such are the capricious twists of fate that, many years later, she would become a devoted patient of Dr. Bosnar.*)

Meanwhile, the news from Europe grew worse, and Philip's direst predictions were becoming day by day, inexorable realities. Neville Chamberlain's appeasement policies had left a stench of betrayal in the Nazi conclaves at Berchtesgarten, Godesberg and Munich, and effectively laid the groundwork for the rape of Austria and Czechoslovakia. They would no doubt lead to the invasion of Poland by brutal force of arms and the use of *'Schrecklichkeit'*, (terror against civilians).

Surely, thought Philip, the public must see the actions of this British scarecrow in their true light. They were NOT the misguided attempts of a man of peace, but a contrived collaboration with the evil forces of Nazism and Fascism to take over Europe. Was all this in preparation for eventual war against the Soviet Union? No sacrifice of other nations or peoples seemed too great to accomplish this purpose; not even the sadistic plans to torture and murder millions of humans whose sole crime was being Jews. All who opposed this policy in occupied Europe would suffer the same fate, while men like Chamberlain, Daladier and their cronies would avert their gaze as freedom and democracy were trampled underfoot.

There was one small spark of hope. The British people were starting to rally to those in parliament who clamored for Churchill to take over as Prime Minister, just as Philip Bosnar had been doing with mounting frustration for the past year. If this were resisted and Britain failed to come to Poland's assistance, a popular revolution was not an impossibility, even in staid old Britain. The decent common man in this home of democracy and freedom could stomach just so much national hypocrisy and betrayal before rising up in righteous anger and throwing out the corrupt rulers.

From time to time, the Bosnars took a weekend drive across the border to North Dakota. Their favorite city was Minot, and their favorite spot was the Leland-Parker Hotel, which they found opulent but inexpensive. Shopping was all that could be wished and there were some excellent stores and boutiques attached to the hotel. On one occasion in late August, they decided to take advantage of the reasonable American prices and go on a shopping trip. Patty had one hundred Canadian dollars with which to splurge to her heart's desire and returned after three hours, exhausted but proud, having purchased Melmac Pearl tableware sufficient for a dozen settings, with table napkins and cutlery for the same number. To complete the bonanza, two bridge-tables and eight folding chairs were delivered to their hotel room from the store, and the visiting new Canadians celebrated their bounty that evening with dinner, drinks, and a night of ardent love.

The next day, they completed their hedonistic weekend by attending a special afternoon Premiere performance of 'Gone With The Wind'. The film was magnificent and the theater was the ultimate in splendor. It was a memorable event and they drove back to Vanwey in blissful contentment, with their green Ford groaning under its packed load. Their relief was great when they were passed through customs without any fuss.

With the drums of approaching war in Europe beating ever more loudly on the radio and in the daily press, a new concern was distracting Philip. Since he didn't yet possess a permanent license to practice in Canada it was necessary for him to take the basic qualifying exams: namely the L.M.C.C. (Licentiate of the Medical Council of Canada). That meant returning to such subjects as basic sciences, pathology, clinical medicine and the didactic aspects of obstetrics, gynecology and public health.

From an examination point of view, these were the kind of theoretical studies he'd left behind with his English Fellowship in the specialty of Surgery, and he began to feel very rusty. It was only a few months before exams, and with only fifteen other holders of the English F.R.C.S. diploma across Canada, he thought what a terrible disgrace it would be if he failed his forthcoming exams. He must try to get down to studies, although this was becoming difficult because of his worsening relations with Blaikie, whom he found increasingly incompetent and vindictive.

The Bosnars were also starting to pick up disquieting bits of additional information about the older man that made their association with him even more distasteful. First, Philip suspected that the revered Dr. Tom was engaged in the unethical splitting of fees with those doctors who referred cases to him from the surrounding countryside. This had recently been confirmed by an indiscreet Marcie, after consuming one refreshing double gin-and-tonic too many. Second, it was common knowledge that – following Marcie's arrival on the scene – her predecessor had raised embarrassing difficulties about severing her relationship with her employer, once torrid but now cooling.

When all other threats failed her, she threatened suicide. Her reluctant lover apparently remained undismayed. It was even whispered that she obtained the pills for ending her life from her beloved and helpful Dr. Tom, and she died at the ripe old age of forty-one. The whole affair was hushed up and neither the police nor anyone else raised a noticeable fuss, but the horrible rumors persisted. In due course Marcie moved in to fill the void, God was in His Heaven and all was right with the world.

Finally, there was the story of the strike. In the mid-30s, the local economy was a shambles, unemployment was up, wages were down, and matters boiled over into violent strikes. A force of two hundred angry strikers marched on Vanwey from the neighboring coal mines of Bonchance, closed for nearly four months. It was a threatening situation and both the Mounties and army troops were called in to assist the local police.

As the hours passed, matters turned irreversibly ugly, shots were fired, and men lay bleeding in the streets. Three of the wounded strikers managed to crawl to the stairway leading up to the Blaikie Hospital, which they knew well. With gun drawn and loaded, the redoubtable Dr. Tom denied them access, and refused to give medical aid to the dying men.

"Let the Commie bastards die," he roared, "they get no help from me."
These were the stories circulating below the tranquil surface of life in Vanwey, and they were about the community's own revered folk-hero.

One day, Philip made up his mind to look through the Catholic Sisters' hospital, Blaikie or no Blaikie, and he drove out there at 11 o'clock on a Monday morning and parked his car in the visitor's area. As he was about to enter, a tall well-built man came out through the front entrance, looked at him carefully and asked, "Aren't you Philip Bosnar, the new surgeon from England?" and Philip nodded.

The individual facing him had conservatively cut fair hair, a healthy outdoors complexion, a pleasant and quite handsome face in spite of his professorial spectacles, and a cultured voice. He was smartly dressed in a lightweight gray suit, white shirt and striped blue tie, neatly knotted. Philip was favorably impressed.

"I'm Peter Forsyth," the stranger announced, scarcely waiting for a reply, "and I'd like to show you through the hospital if I may."

"I'd certainly appreciate that," Philip replied, "if you can spare the time."
So this was the man who left Blaikie before the arrival of Sam Walters, he thought. What a complete contrast from his former associate. Here was someone who looks and sounds like a modern doctor and not like a character out of the penny westerns.

Philip's gracious guide introduced him to the Sisters, who proved both friendly and charming, and it was obvious that they knew all about his entry into the Blaikie practice. The hospital boycott was also well-known to them, along with the fact that the mighty Dr. Tom had arranged a special Orange Lodge parade against the nuns' Hospital just a year ago.

The visiting surgeon was most impressed with Sister Mary Sybil, the Mother Superior, a woman of regal bearing and easy good humor. She looked far too young for her status in the hospital hierarchy; and bloody goodlooking, too, thought Philip irreverently.

"If you ever decide to admit your patients here, Dr. Bosnar," she said, her eyes twinkling with mischief, "I promise we won't kill them off." They all laughed out loud and the ice was broken. She was certainly his kind of nursing sister, Philip had to admit, and for a brief and absurd moment he compared her dignified good looks with those of poor old Marcie, that patient soul whose only hope lay in the eventual demise of her Dr. Tom and acquisition of her promised inheritance.

Dr. Bosnar, welcome newcomer from the Blaikie practice, was impressed with the hospital. The wards were bright, airy and roomy, without the unwholesome crowding of Dr. Tom's Hospital. The main operating room was superb and the minor O.R. was more than adequate. The obstetrical department was first class and it was obvious that Forsyth had been a major force in aiming at the highest modern standards. On this point the nuns left no doubt; he'd been a loyal friend and a progressive influence.

Finally, after inspecting the new and impressive X-ray department, Dr. Bosnar complimented Forsyth and the nuns and expressed his gratitude before taking his leave and promising to return.

"The next time you must bring Mrs. Bosnar," the Mother Superior told him, and he promised he would, although he wondered if she might pressure poor Patty into joining them in the chapel. Of course if it came to that, he might come under the identical pressure, but that was in the future and he would deal with this type of problem as each situation arose.

As he drove away from the fine modern structure, with its attractive facade of Roman Tile bricks, he began to think seriously, for the first time, of leaving the dangerous and incompetent character whose practice he'd joined with stupid optimism and sight unseen. First, however, there was the L.M.C.C. exam, and then he'd confront Blaikie and try to reach a new understanding, both professional and financial. It must also include his use of the first class hospital run by the Sisters of St. Cecilia. If it came to an impasse, he would resign and consult the provincial College before taking any definitive action.

Despite the looming shadows of continuing conflicts within the practice and of the forthcoming exam, life in general was very good. Phil and Patty were surrounded by a growing circle of interesting and amusing friends. Social life was an endless round of afternoon luncheons or teas for the ladies, with either Mah Jong or Contract Bridge, late night poker sessions for the men, or mixed evening dinner parties followed by bridge, usually four to six tables. The Bosnars began to entertain more often and with increasing success, and Philip took pride in the knowledge that his lovely wife had become such an excellent hostess and sought-after guest.

Notwithstanding a growing food and liquor bill, they were managing their finances without scrimping, and were paying off their bank loan without too much difficulty. For exercise, they played tennis on a cement hardcourt they discovered behind Smither's Dyeing and Cleaning on 5th Street, and sometimes they ventured a round of imperfect golf on the hilly nine-hole course one mile north of the railroad tracks.

With shared problems, their love became deeper and more intense. Both realized how completely right their choice had been, and how wrong it would have been to accept defeat because of presumed 'impossibly different' backgrounds. Both were changing. In Phil, she was seeing a strength, resilience and determination that surpassed even her own expectations. In Patty, he was witnessing a rich and versatile intelligence that complemented her stunning red-haired beauty. No wonder she was so popular with the men, he thought. She even took his occasional merciless teasing and turned it into positive accomplishment.

"Patty, why not try something new and revolutionary?" he'd approached her one day during their first month in Vanwey,

"Instead of banana sandwiches how about trying MEAT!"
She knew he'd been sneaking off to Jake the Greek's for the odd steak, so she made him literally eat his words by becoming a good cook, and it was obvious that one day her culinary art would be beyond reproach.

What made every day a bright new experience, was their shared interest in so many areas. The daily news, local, national and international; politics, religion and movies. You name it, they discussed it, and there was always the daily 'scuttlebutt'. All these gave them a growing intellectual bond that strengthened rather than challenged their physical love and gave each day a rich diversity.

Eventually, with foot-dragging reluctance, Mackenzie King's government declared war on Germany, one whole week after the mother country's declaration. By this time, of course, Poland was dying; its brave army unable to survive its gaping wounds, and its civilians in agony on the rack of terror and enslavement. Meanwhile, Mackenzie King refused to institute conscription despite the eagerness of most Canadians to crush Hitler and all he stood for.

This Prime Minister was known as one who was always counting votes, and he knew what would happen to the millions of Quebec votes if the anglophobes of French Canada were drafted into the armed forces fighting for the cause of 'Les Maudits Anglais'. He need make no more than token gestures toward support of the Allies opposing the Nazis. But he reckoned without the innate decency of most of his countrymen, especially those who were anglophile at heart and who detested Hitler and his Nazi scum.

As for the Bosnars, their attitude was clear and unwavering. Whoever was prepared to fight against Hitler was on the side of the righteous. Whoever was prepared to look the other way had no real quarrel with Nazi atrocities. On September the 4th, Philip wrote the British Medical Association, offering his services to the British Armed Forces as a surgical specialist with special experience in trauma. He explained his position as a recent arrival in Canada, and stated that his wife was available for parallel service as an expert surgical nurse. The reply arrived one month later, coldly formal and negative.

'Since you now reside in Canada, and since the British armed forces have more than enough doctors and nurses in all categories, you should apply to the Canadian authorities'. No 'Thank you', and no 'So sorry'. Just don't bother us. After all there's a war on!

As exam time approached, Philip put aside the war for the present and applied himself to the books. When it was time to leave for Winnipeg, where the exams were being held, he and Patty found the parting much more wrenching than they'd anticipated. After all, he consoled himself, they had decided – in keeping with their progressive views – that if a marriage was really sound and not just a matter of appearances, there should be no hesitation in taking separate trips. In his own reasoning, the argument went even further. A marriage that couldn't survive such separations lacked the mutual trust that was the essence of the bond. Fidelity shouldn't hinge on constant proximity, but rather on the ability of two people to maintain and strengthen their love through all situations, whether together or apart. On this particular occasion, both felt it would be easier for Philip to 'cram' if Patty wasn't with him.

Winnipeg proved to be a far more modern city than he'd imagined, but it was cold and blustery and the reputation of the Portage and Main corner for freezing winds was no exaggeration. His hotel room, however, was warm and comfortable, and he had an early dinner followed by two hours of deep sleep, from which he awoke fully refreshed.

Before getting down to his studies, he phoned Dr. Alan Simpson to let him know he was in town and ready for the LMCC exams that were starting the next morning. Simpson was a great chap whom he'd recently met at Blaikie's office. His father was a respected country doctor in Crampton, some thirty miles west of Vanwey, and he sent the occasional surgical patient to Blaikie, although he preferred Regina for the more serious operations.

Alan was his father's pride and joy, and in 1935 had been appointed as head of the Surgical Department at the prestigious St. Augustine Hospital, where he soon became an authority on tumors and their characteristics. He and Philip hit it off right away, and when they got around to discussing their views on a wide variety of surgical topics, they found a remarkable confluence of opinion and background knowledge. Before parting company, Philip promised to contact his new friend as soon as he got to Winnipeg.

By a stroke of luck on this occasion, Alan answered as soon as Philip phoned him, and he said he was eager to arrange a 'bash' for the successful candidate as soon as the exams were over. But now it was time to draw the drapes, spread out all his books on the bed, most of them lightweight but intensely detailed synopses, and settle down to a high-pressure absorption ritual that was so successful in past exams and scholarships. With each passing moment his speed increased; first the words, then the sentences and soon the pages, flying from the open books into the avid depths of his mind, ready to be disgorged the next morning.

It was amazing how his previous knowledge of these subjects came flooding back from his memory to reinforce the present osmosis, and by 4 a.m. he felt ready for any challenge in tomorrow's subjects. The rest could wait; he cleared the books off the bed and in fifteen minutes was fast asleep.

The next few days went by like a dream. He awoke each morning in response to a six-thirty call placed with the hotel operator, showered and shaved, had a light breakfast, and read the Winnipeg Free Press on his bus trip to the General Hospital, where the L.M.C.C. exams were being held. The written papers were in the morning and the orals after lunch, and it soon became obvious from the examiners' comments that his English Fellowship degree was widely known. Philip even wondered if Simpson might have 'spilled the beans', to use a popular gangster-film expression. In any event, he found the examiners pleasant and they treated him with respect. He found the written exam questions straightforward and the orals a romp, with a fair amount of good-humored exchange between candidate and examiner.

So it was with a song in his heart that he walked back to the hotel and phoned his darling Patty.

"I've missed you so much already," he declared, and she said she felt the same way, even though it had only been a few days.

"How were the exams?"

"Oh they were a breeze, much better than I ever dreamed."

"See, I told you not to worry, the way you do with all your exams."

"I'll phone you as soon as I know when I'm coming home."

HOME, he thought; how incredible that, already, he could think of their little apartment in a dusty prairie town as home.

Almost as soon as he hung up, the phone rang again and it was Alan Simpson, sounding very excited.

"Phil, you sly bastard, you got some pretty fantastic marks in your exams. All the guys at the Med. Arts Club are talking about it. I'll pick you up for dinner in two hours, and afterward we'll celebrate by getting roaring drunk. I've asked John Kinsley to join us. He was one of your inquisitors in the surgery orals."

Vera Simpson proved to be an elegant hostess, and her dinner of roast venison, with sweet potatoes and corn on the cob, was a cordon bleu tribute to her husband's hunting prowess. The food was preceded by dry martinis, then accompanied by a rich Burgundy and followed by Hennessy Five Star Brandy. The hostess drank only a small quantity of gin and ginger-ale, while the men filled their glasses with no thought of tomorrow.

After dinner, the threesome got steadily more drunk until Mrs. Simpson excused herself and said she was off to bed. By the grace of God and a happy capacity for alcohol, Philip was able to stand up with a semblance of decorum, and he complimented his hostess on the excellence of the meal and the sparkling dinner conversation – most of it relating to the changing medical scene in Canada.

John Kinsley was a fascinating fellow. He had an unending store of risqué jokes, and when it came to the subject of surgery, he was a superb talker, especially when it involved his special interest, the history of surgery. It appeared that he was known throughout Manitoba as a topflight general surgeon as well as a lecturer of renown, but he was the unfortunate victim of severe recurrent bronchitis. It had plagued him ever since a life- threatening bout of pneumonia at the age of seven.

Alan was finding it difficult to keep awake, and was using straight scotch to fend off slumber. John was treating his bronchitis by chain-smoking Sweet Caporals and drinking straight rye, while Philip stayed with the Hennessy. By 2.30 a.m, all three were out cold just where they lay, sprawled out on the comfortable davenports.

It was 10 o'clock on a bright Saturday morning when they began to show signs of life, but each brilliant shaft of sunlight that found its way through the partly drawn curtains was an agonizing reproach to the three sinners. Vera was busying herself in the kitchen and announced that breakfast sausages and coffee would be ready in half an hour, to allow for their slow recovery to normal health. The recipe for this recovery, to which the reluctant visitor was now introduced, was an abomination known as a Prairie Oyster, consisting of a raw egg in a glass of tomato juice, with the addition of Worcestershire sauce for character and Tabasco for inspiration. It was down the hatch without fuss or delay, and a round of well-deserved applause from his fellow-sufferers. As for Philip, he had serious misgivings about his chances of survival from this repulsive shock to his system. To his great surprise, he soon began to feel better and even his rebellious stomach began settling to a peaceful submission.

Alan ushered him into the largest of three bathrooms and gave him shaving cream, brush and razor with a fresh blade. He soon emerged, after a prolonged and restorative shower and shave, looking and feeling like a human being once more.

"Thank God you're a man who can handle his liquor," Alan commented with open approval, and Kinsley added, "You're pretty good at handling a hangover, too."

"I told John you're our kind of Englishman," said Alan, but Phil corrected him.

"That's because I was born in France I guess."

"Is that right?" asked Kinsley, with a broad grin, "then where's your Frog accent?"

"That's only for my Frog patients," countered Phil and they all chuckled at his riposte.

"Where the hell's the breakfast you promised us, Vera?" yelled Alan, "we're bloodywell starving!"

After breakfast, Alan led Philip into his small study at the back of the house, closed the door and asked his guest to sit down. Then, taking the opposite chair he asked: "Phil, what are your plans?"

"Well, I suppose I'll go back to Vanwey and continue with my practice."

"Now come on, who are you kidding? You know you can't stay with that crazy sonofabitch and his stooge. What about the armed forces?"

Philip brought Alan up to date on the matter of his efforts, first to London and then to Ottawa. His host listened attentively and thought for a few moments before speaking.

"Look, I'm due to go overseas next month as I.C. surgery with a base hospital unit that'll be operating out of the Bournemouth area in England, and I have to find a suitable replacement as chief of surgery at San Augies when I leave. How about taking the job?"

"Christ Almighty! I couldn't do that. It wouldn't be fair to the guys expecting to step into your shoes when the time comes."

"That's no argument. We're trying to get away from the old school tie system inherited from the British and select the right man for the right job."

"No, Alan, I couldn't have that on my conscience."

"I believe you're wrong Phil. You have a fine academic base, you're a good speaker and I know you've already acquired a reputation as a classy surgeon. In any case, most of the guys up for my job will enlist in the next few months so they wouldn't be hostile, especially when they hear how your own enlistment efforts have failed." There was another long pause before Philip replied.

"Now listen Alan, I'm grateful for this and in fact for everything you've done already, but my first duty is to my own patients in Vanwey. I intend to have things out with the old boy and I know that the moment our break-up takes place Peter Forsyth will offer me a place in his growing practice and I'll accept. If the situation changes in any unexpected fashion I can let you know right away. In the meantime I intend to keep on trying to enlist as that was my intention from the outset." Alan nodded his understanding and they left the study to join the others. It was obvious that Kinsley and the hostess knew what had been discussed, as Simpson shook his head almost imperceptibly from side to side when they joined the others in the living room.

Kinsley drove Philip back to his hotel but refused his invitation to join him for the proverbial 'hair of the dog' and perhaps some lunch later. He had to get over to the hospital for ward rounds before the weekend visitors started flooding in and disrupting the orderly conduct of hospital procedure. He did, however, insist that Philip come over to his house for a cocktail party that evening, "any time after eight." All the examiners would be there and he was sure Philip would receive many similar invitations before leaving the city. John gave him a card with his home address and phone number and left.

As it turned out, there were invitations and parties indeed for the next few days, and Philip had to postpone his departure. He made many new influential friendships and learned many new aspects of the University medical environment, some of them interesting, some disturbing and some that would no doubt affect his future life.

CHAPTER 4

1929-31

August was a month of mixed emotions for Philip Bosnar. On the international front, he was appalled at what was taking place in continental Europe. He wondered how a fundamentally decent society like the British could ignore the rape of basic human values and liberty in Germany, with the clear threat of engulfing all of Europe in the same evil. There were rumors of pogroms against chosen victims of Nazi racial doctrines, carried out by gangs of brownshirted thugs.

Defenseless people were beaten and brutalized and there were plans to have their property confiscated or destroyed. Next would come public degradation and loss of position for Jewish schoolteachers, university professors, scientists and even heads of industry. Children with the wrong parents would be barred from schools and students from universities. As a hideous accompaniment to the hellish game of hunting down genetic undesirables, the doomed quarry was pilloried without respite in a campaign of vicious articles and caricatures. These appeared in 'Der Stürmer', a trashy newspaper run by the infamous Julius Streicher, known criminal pervert and antisemite.

Much of the news about the vile Nazi excesses and plans for the next phase was either omitted from most British newspapers or relegated to obscure corners and abbreviated columns at the foot of the pages. No one inch headlines for these stories! We don't want to upset the public or stir up bad feelings against the poor Germans. Look how badly they were treated in the Treaty of Versailles; how they suffered in the terrible collapse of their currency! Somebody else has to suffer for these sins; let's just see who's available. Only the pro-Communist Daily Worker carried the stories with any degree of prominence. But these were with clear political bias for the most part, as though antisemitism didn't exist in Russia; as though Nazi brutality was primarily directed against lily-white socialists fighting for liberty and enlightenment.

What distressed Philip wasn't only the gutless policies of the recent Baldwin government and the general apathy of the public. It was the dangerous and misguided reaction of those who reacted to their loathing of Nazism and Fascism by embracing Communism. Little did they seem to realize that Josef Stalin was far from the great emancipator his international propaganda sought to present to those with left-leaning idealism. Although Philip refused to be seduced by such deception, he had to give the Soviet Union credit for its open opposition to Hitler, Mussolini, and Franco. Much as one might detest Stalin, he could prove a valuable ally if Britain ever had to fight Germany again.

It was in the midst of this turmoil of the spirit, and with Count Rudi's revelations still fresh in his memory, that Philip one day received a package by special delivery. It measured about ten by twelve inches, bore German stamps and was postmarked Tübingen. He carried it into the kitchen, where his mother was preparing some sandwiches for lunch, and opened it up. Inside was a thick gilt-edged card embossed with the Tübingen University coat of arms. On both sides of this impressive card were dozens of short handwritten messages, all signed and mostly in English.

'Dear Smiley, we have not met but please come to our Schwartzwald next summer'

'Please be our guest next year, I look forward to our meeting'

'I hear you are like one of us, Smiley, let us show you the real Germany'

'Next year we must meet in beautiful Bavaria'

There were many more and he thought, so much *Gemütlichkeit*, concealing so much *Schrecklichkeit*.

Suddenly his pent-up anger, disgust and frustration, broke the bounds of sane and civilized behavior, and he found himself ripping the invitation to shreds as his mother watched in horror. At that moment, in the clear imagery of his fevered imagination, he envisioned an old Hasidic Jew (so totally different from his own father) beaten and kicked as he was forced to scrub a dog-befouled pavement under the curses and jeers of Stormtrooper bullies, somewhere on the back streets of beautiful Tübingen.

That evening, he explained the background of such bizarre conduct to his stunned parents and sister, recounting his experiences at summer camp. They understood, and their somber silence was sufficient response as he conveyed his thoughts, holding nothing back. It was after midnight before they finally went to bed.

On the romantic front, he'd now taken Step Two and it was irrevocable. His relationship with Dora was exhilarating but strange. Prior to his matric exams, she had been – in many intangible ways – the dominant figure in their romance. She was an unattainable Dulcinea to his Don Quixote, while his companeros cheered him onward in his bold quest for the fair maiden's hand. Now, instead, he had become the admired victor and she, his faithful and adoring sweetheart.

Their life together, for whatever hours they could steal from each day's separate requirements, was complete as far as it went, in both the emotional and intellectual sense. They would meet at the library during most weekdays, arriving one hour earlier than in the past and leaving together before nine. They would take the familiar walk to her house and go into the quiet privacy of the front parlor. Her aunt and uncle rarely came back before 11 o'clock, and if they arrived sooner than expected they always retired discreetly to the back of the house. As soon as the young couple were alone they hugged each other in long and passionate embrace and exchanged ardent endearments. Afterward, when they separated in order to catch their breath, they would discuss their futures: his as a surgeon and hers as a teacher.

They disagreed on few items of morality, philosophy or political viewpoint, but there were two points of dispute which resulted in a temporary truce rather than capitulation on Philip's part. The first was Dora's insistence that she would never "go to bed" with him until their future marriage was a certainty. The second was her conviction, almost a premonition, that he would eventually marry a suitable Jewish bride and thus make his parents happy. When he assured her that this could never happen, she replied with an enigmatic smile that should his marriage fail she'd be happy to become his mistress. Her convoluted logic disturbed him, but to this warm and passionate girl the two ideas weren't contradictory, and her resolve couldn't be shaken. In any event, he was determined never to force Step Three of their relationship without her prior consent.

On weekends, Saturday was their main evening out. They used to meet at her place at

8 o'clock in the evening, then take the Stepney Green underground train to Blackfriars Station. This led them to the Thames embankment and what became their favorite walk. Strolling along the promenade, they chatted about the day's events, their individual activities, current news items of interest, and always the future. From time to time, they stopped and descended the steps leading down to the water's edge. There they could kiss and fondle to their heart's content, away from prying eyes and in a magic peaceful world of their own. Only the sound of the Thames lapping below their feet and the glow of reflected lights from the South Bank served as a backdrop to the fervor of their embraces and their secret thoughts.

Approaching Westminster bridge, they next turned north toward the brilliant confusion of Trafalgar Square on a Saturday night. They worked their way to Admiralty Arch and then along the Mall, walking along slowly under the row of trees running parallel to St. James Park on their left. There was a beautiful tranquility to the deserted park and leaf-strewn pavement that seemed to shut out the rest of London with its bustling humanity. Continuing on toward Buckingham Palace and passing small clusters of daytime tourists lingering in the palace square, they turned left and proceeded along the high-walled Palace grounds that protected the royal abode with a cloak of silence and darkness.

Eventually, they arrived at their destination: Hyde Park, a quiet and gentle place at night, where lovers could be seen sitting together on the benches or strolling with their arms around each other. Conversation was hushed and even laughter was subdued. It was a haven for romance, where couples seemed to obey a hidden pact respecting each other's right to privacy. An occasional pair could be discerned embracing or mating on the grass, in secluded areas well away from the lights, and any inadvertent intruder would back away in apologetic haste.

Philip usually selected an empty bench in a shadowed area, rather than a grassy patch, and he had to be on constant guard not to let the ardor of their embraces go beyond the containment of his passions. Both learned how to draw back before the moment of no return, winding down their desires to a safer level of self-control and continence.

The warmth and brightness of summer cooled to the chilling drizzles of autumn, and his meetings with Dora were no longer a well-kept secret from Philip's parents. Whenever he came home after 11 p.m. on weekdays or midnight on Saturdays, his mother would "go off the deep end," to use the family expression. She warned him against the dangers of becoming involved with a seductive "Shiksa," a modern Delilah who could sap his strength of purpose and pursuit of greatness. He tried to reassure her that this was a normal and natural romance with a decent girl; that outmoded religious taboos were out of place in a progressive world. On most such occasions he tried to divert her wrath with reason and humor, but once in a while she would drive him too far and he'd reply in anger.

"Be careful," he cautioned on more than one occasion, "Don't let your attitude become like that of the Nazis."

When this caused her to run off to bed in tears, he felt like the lowest of criminals. If his beloved mother was trying to make him feel guilty she was certainly succeeding, but not on the basis of her arguments. His Dad, as always, was the great conciliator, most often after his Mum had left the room. Once, after a stormy scene, he advised, "Remember, Phileep, always treat your mother with kindness and understanding even when you are quite sure she is wrong." Lest Philip feel vindicated he added, "Remember as well, my son, there are many times when she would have been right. We live, and hope that we learn".

His sister was usually asleep by the time these arguments occurred, but if she happened to be present she was careful not to commit herself, lest her mother's anger be diverted in her direction. It so happened that Pauline was going through a very difficult time with a hopeless affair that was draining her emotionally. The object of her wild and desperate love was a man in his early sixties. Dr. Sidney Berentson was a charismatic lecturer at Queen Mary's College, where he gave a special extracurricular evening course in social and political philosophy. Although Philip had met and admired him for his brilliance, and Berentson always insisted that nothing could ever come of the affair, he and Pauline were still meeting from time to time, away from their classes. By a strange twist of logic, it was her Mum who showed the greater tolerance in this matter while her Dad seemed to fear a tragic outcome.

One evening, his Dad broached him on the subject of his romantic involvement with Dora. It was evident that he didn't take it lightly.

"Do you intend to marry her some day?" he asked.

"Yes, after I'm fully qualified and can earn my own living."

"Do you realize how long that will be?"

"Yes, Dad, between ten and twelve years."

"What about your physical relations. Is there any chance you will get foolish and she will become pregnant?"

"We've discussed that openly and honestly, and we've agreed not to go all the way before marriage. If our agreement ever changed and we did in fact go to bed together then I'd take the necessary precautions."

"Remember, Phileep, even though I know how mature you have become, nothing is certain. Man proposes, God disposes."

That ended the discussion. Thank heaven it was open and honest, and he felt he had an understanding friend on whom he could rely throughout this romance-filled period of his life. Not only did this prove to be true, but from time to time his Dad slipped a few pound notes onto his study table. When he protested, his Dad would say, "You can't take your lady out and never spend money."

He could hardly dispute this ultimate wisdom and accepted with deep gratitude.

The first few weeks back at school constituted a period of readjustment. Many of his friends had failed their exams and didn't follow Philip into the 6th form. Others went into the Arts division, namely literature and languages with a strong element of history, geography and philosophy. On the Science side, most of the students took Higher Maths, Chemistry, both inorganic and organic, and advanced Physics. A few, like Philip, took Botany, which bored him to tears, and Zoology, which he loved.

The zoology master was a real character. His shiny blue serge suit was hopelessly short in the sleeves but was pressed to within an inch of its precarious life, while his shapeless trousers terminated a jaunty six inches above his ankles. He was a great naturalist, a keen observer of wildlife, a natural pantomimist and comedian. His portrayal of an amoeba, with its spreading and engulfing pseudopods, was a thrilling classic. His transformation into a young salamander venturing for the first time onto perilous dry land was a riotous masterpiece, and his metamorphosis into a prehistoric saber-toothed tiger was the stuff of nightmares. He also managed to overcome his student's inborn squeamishness (and this was absolutely vital for Philip), to the extent that he could now dissect a frog, a dogfish, and even a rabbit, without flinching. (He would never lose his deep aversion to the smell of formalin, however, and rabbit in any form whatever would become his least favorite meat dish.)

Dr. Ellsmere could never forgive Philip for what he considered a personal betrayal. The interview in the headmaster's study was painful and memorable.

"Sit down Smiley." Philip sat, looking and feeling guilty.

"You know of course that I have made all the arrangements and spoken to the right contacts so that your entry into the wonderful world of English law will be a smooth and successful one?"

"Yes, Sir, and I want you to know how grateful I am."

"Dammit young man, I'm not interested in your gratitude but in your commonsense. We both know you have the gift of effective speech and convincing logic. We both know how persuasive you can be in our monthly mock trials."

"That's probably because you acted as the judge for these sessions, thought Philip, but he said, "I hope you'll understand and forgive me, sir. For the past few months I've grown determined to become a surgeon. I don't believe it's a passing fancy. It's nothing I planned, but it has a lot to do with the stuff I've been reading on the subject."

The headmaster seemed to become more ancient as he grew angrier.

"I heard all that nonsense yesterday from your father when I asked him to use his influence with you. I told him that H.G. Wells and his confounded Science of Life shouldn't take priority over our carefully laid plans."

Philip could see with dismal clarity that the interview was getting nowhere, and even Ellsmere finally gave up and dismissed him. Things would never be the same between them. Something precious was gone; and when the old man died of a stroke in January of 1930, Philip Bosnar felt somehow responsible.

Over the next two years Philip made many new friends, but only two of these turned out to be really close. The first was Bob Vermier, two years his senior and returning to Brewers after a year's absence. He was stocky, a good wrestler and a strong swimmer. On the scholastic side, he was a fine practical scientist whose favorite subject was physics, with maths and chemistry not far behind. His parents had come to England from Holland at the turn of the century, and they were the proud owners of a successful shoe retail business about a mile east of Brewers School. Unfortunately, during the past year there had been an increasing number of break-ins and burglaries, with considerable losses and soaring insurance rates.

Bob Vermier decided to leave school for one year and put his known talents to work in helping the family business. First, he rearranged the entire display system, both in the front windows and inside the store, then he devised and installed a superb burglar alarm system with triple-lock safety devices, front and back. He set up multiple trip mechanisms all over the premises. These were activated at closing time and turned off the next morning. Last but not least, he improved the night lighting system and changed the front protective grill. Within six months, the break-ins stopped and the insurance company agreed to lower the premium rates.

At school, Vermier was known as a hard worker, and would have headed his class except for difficulty with some of the Arts subjects. "History, geography and languages put me to sleep," he complained to Philip, who reminded him that this would no longer be a problem in the Science 6th form. The two often compared notes as their courses proceeded in different directions, and both enjoyed discussions on a variety of subjects.

(Their futures would run parallel for many years but would eventually diverge widely. As Philip's father was so fond of saying, "Man proposes, God disposes.")

The second of Philip's new friends was Arty Jones, who lived only two streets away from the Bosnars and attended Standish School. Arty, who was the same age as Philip, was the son of sturdy Welsh parents, and hoped to become a qualified electrician. A keen cross-country walker, he belonged to a hiking club with about thirty members of both genders. Once in a while, he invited Philip to join the group for a Sunday hike, and this was an exhilarating experience. It was wonderful to learn the joys of striding through England's glorious and everchanging countryside, and to discover that he was able to continue for hours on end without a vestige of fatigue. He and Arty also enjoyed soccer and cricket, but most of all they were devoted to tennis and played whenever both were free.

Morrie Kahn had been Philip's closest friend for many years. He was a cheerful fellow, the irreligious son of devout orthodox Jews, a year older than Philip and a 5th form pupil at Traynor School. A born comedian and mimic, he had a face like Charlie Chaplin minus the mustache. He was also the only person who could drop in at the Bosnar home at any time without invitation or advance notice, yet always welcome. His quick wit and clever impersonations kept Mrs. Bosnar in stitches, while his knowledge and love of music were refreshing to Philip, who shared both with growing enthusiasm.

It had been Morrie who dragged him off between the ages of thirteen and fifteen to Sunday concerts at the Albert Hall, where they stood in line for hours in all weathers, waiting for the cheap seats in the 'Gods'. Once inside the vast auditorium, the sorcery of a Heifetz would transport them to paradise with his flawless Zigeunerweiser; a Casals, with his haunting Swan of Tuonela; a Backhaus, with his breathtaking Appassionata. Philip was initiated into the secret rites of slipping into the Artist's Room during the encores, so they'd be ready to obtain – if they were lucky – those treasured autographs that were beyond all dreams of wealth.

Both played the violin and had studied music for years. Kahn took his lessons at home from a mediocre musician who played with a cinema orchestra in London's West End. Philip had met him a few times at his friend's house, and contrary to Morrie's adulation, remained unimpressed. The instructor's playing was uninspired, and he taught his pupil snatches of popular classics instead of regular exercises and standard compositions. These were absolutely necessary for the hard climb to proficiency in this most demanding of instruments. Two items stuck in Philip's memory for many years. The first was the instructor's doleful and horsefaced features and the second was his vociferous obsession with Communism. It seemed that Morrie was learning more about far left political philosophy than the art of the violin.

As for Philip's own musical education, he was fortunate in having been placed in the rigorous musical program at the Guildhall School of Music at age eleven, and was slowly and steadily developing his skills, both as an orchestral player and soloist. For a few years, he seemed destined for a musical career, with successes in music festivals and trial concerts. By the age of fourteen, however, he knew this could never be. He could never settle for a berth in a cinema orchestra, and he knew the virtuosity of the world's foremost violin soloists was light years out of reach.

By 1930, Bob Vermier had become his closest friend at school and Arty Jones his best friend out of school. Morrie Kahn was gradually drifting away and becoming far too involved with the Communist cause and the daughter of his persuasive music instructor. She was a young lady who shared her father's political views and his equine features. What Morrie had gained in dialectical polemics he appeared to be losing in his sense of humor. He was becoming a bore, and Philip was saddened. His Mum was puzzled and distressed; she could no longer look forward to the unexpected and hilarious incursions by her favorite comedian, often with spur-of-the-moment meals she gladly prepared on the spot.

Of course, all three friendships took a distant second place to Philip's continuing and undiminished romance with Dora. The lending library on Trevor Road featured less and less in their lives and he knew he was spending too much time away from his studies, but felt that every stolen hour together was worth the occasional twinge of conscience about his neglected work. Nevertheless, he wasn't wholly irresponsible. He was determined to get high marks that would be enough to pass the Intermediate B.Sc. exams in 1931. Perhaps he could even win a Gordon Leaving Scholarship in the Science section. He might as well forget about a scholarship to Cambridge. In the first place, he'd need to work twice as hard and in the second place, going to Cambridge would mean seeing much less of his family and his beloved Dorie.

Philip's marks in the Intermediate B.Sc. were much better than expected, considering how little time he'd spent with his books. But they weren't quite good enough for a Cambridge scholarship, and a part of him (the pride factor) felt a bit upset, while Dora and his parents never showed the slightest evidence of disappointment. It was clear that Cambridge wasn't an important item in their hopes for his future, and he felt relieved.

During his final month at Brewers, he was pleased to learn that Bob Vermier had won the Science prize, mainly for his work in physics, which was of the highest caliber. But he was surprised when he, Phil Bosnar, was awarded the Arts prize for proficiency in French, German, and English Literature. He'd continued with these subjects despite his enrollment in the Science section of the 6th form, in order to substitute for advanced maths and physics.

Philip had learned his pre-matriculation French from Monsieur Barak, an English Jew whose parents came from Lebanon. He was a very strict teacher, and his credo was that the only pathway to language was through pronunciation. His set piece came from the street rebellion scene in Victor Hugo's Les Miserables: 'Courfeyrac tout-à-coup aperçu quelq'un au bas de la barricade, dehors dans la rue sous les balles. Gavroche avait sortit par la coupure et était paisiblement occupé à vider dans sont panier des gibernes pleine de cartouches'.
Philip practiced this excerpt so often in his early years that he would remember it for the rest of his life.

As for German, his instructor was a kindly Viennese gentleman who spoke about ten languages fluently and was a first class teacher. In his 3rd form, Smiley used to be known for his pranks and his mimicry of Herr Neimann's Teutonic mannerisms. Whenever he was caught, his punishment was 'detention', which meant staying after school to memorize designated lines from his studies. The first was a dozen lines of Goethe's works in German, the second was twenty. Within a month it had reached a hundred, but he'd mastered the art of rapid memorization and soon began to appear in the German masters' study with his penalty successfully completed in very short order.

One day, when he entered, the master greeted him with a cordial, "Sit down Smiley," which was a good sign. It had always been "Bosnar" up to now.

"Let's not waste time on your lines. We both know you can memorize them as fast as I can fill my pipe and that you enjoy showing off to me. Frankly I enjoy these sessions because I think you have a flair for languages and I wonder what plans you have for your future."

"That's awfully kind of you, Sir. Quite honestly I have no special plans except that I like studying language and literature. My Dad can read and write French, German, Russian, Polish, Hebrew and Yiddish. I'm certain I could never match that."

"I'm so glad we had this little chat, Smiley. Now let us have some tea together and we'll have more chats from time to time."

Philip didn't think it was much of a chat, but replied, "I'm afraid I've given you a lot of trouble in class, Sir. That won't happen again I promise you."

From that time forth, this portly pink-faced Austrian, his shiny head as bald as the proverbial billiard ball and rolls of flesh adorning the back of his neck, became Philip's all-time paragon of schoolmasters. (*When the day came, three years later, for him to receive his Arts award at the annual prize-giving ceremony, he almost burst out laughing as he examined the expensively bound set of six volumes. It was a collection of Goethe's works in German and he knew he would always treasure them.*)

As far as English Literature was concerned, he received his 6th form lessons from a teacher who was dull and uninspiring. Mr. Snavely couldn't even put a semblance of human feeling into the immortal works of the mighty John Milton. Philip, however, must have drawn some unconscious inspiration from these studies when he wrote a three-page poem, commencing with the lines:

> **'O harp, I cannot hear your whispered trill,**
> **Nor violin your mellow strains so plaintive,**
> **O flute, your rippling trickle like the spheres**
> **Of crystal that in heav'n fore'er do tinkle,**
> **Nor list to throbbing tune of mystic orient,**
> **Nor feel the solemn bass of organ grand,**
> **But I must ever meditate and ponder**
> **My greatest joy and grief since I was born.**
> **Still do I hear her silv'ry voice so soft,**
> **Melodious and appealing in its charm.**
> **I see her wondrous hair of burnished gold,**
> **Her eyes entreat me as in days before.'**

It was a disturbing opus and gave him a feeling of unwelcome prophecy, so he put the poem away and forgot about it.

As far as the Gordon Leaving Scholarship was concerned, a most unusual decision was reached. Smiley Bosnar was summoned to the headmaster's office for an interview. Dr. Braithwaite was a handsome and impressive man, with brown hair turning to gleaming silver. He'd been a cricket and rowing 'Blue' at Oxford, and he filled his predecessor's shoes with a reputation for firmness but fairness. He was widely respected by both students and teaching staff and Philip held him in high regard.

"How does it feel, Smiley, now that you'll soon be leaving for your first year in Medicine?"

"A bit excited I suppose, Sir."

"I asked you here to discuss this year's Gordon Scholarship. It appears we have a bit of a problem."

Philip waited for him to continue.

"Both you and Vermier really deserve it, and as you know, we generally alternate between the arts and science sections. This year it was supposed to be the science section."

"As far as science is concerned, Sir, it should certainly go to Vermier."

He wasn't just being noble, he really believed it.

"Glad to hear you say so. I know you're both awfully good friends."

The headmaster smiled mysteriously and slowly loaded his pipe.

"You might be interested to know that Vermier thought you should have it, since you took more subjects."

He now grinned broadly and revealed his closely kept secret.

"Well, young man, I've discussed the matter with the Old Boys' Association, and they've agreed to split the award between the two of you. Never been done before," he added with unconcealed satisfaction.

Philip was relieved when he won an entrance scholarship to the prestigious St. Clements College Hospital. It would certainly make his situation much more comfortable financially, and the medical school was renowned for its fine teachers. Although he wasn't able to see Dora quite as often, they still had their Saturdays and sometimes Sundays as well if they were both free. She told him all about her courses at teachers' college: at the present time, she was doing the full B.A. course at Queen Mary's College and studying ancient Anglosaxon Literature. He, in turn, told her all about the wonderful world of the microscope and explained the mysteries of histology. He glossed over some of the messier features of anatomical dissection, with its reek of formalin and the brown wizened corpses that were scarcely recognizable as human beings. It seemed impossible that he was now one of the least squeamish in the gruesome dissection hall, when he'd been so sure the reverse would be true.

What really upset him, however, were the cats used in the experimental department of the physiology laboratory. Even though they were well looked after by the lab's considerate animal-keeper, Philip could never accept the idea of subjecting these poor creatures to any form of suffering, no matter how laudable the objective.

The actual physiology lectures were brilliantly delivered by the renowned 'Tommy' Wrongwell, whose textbook on the subject was an international classic. His classes were as lucid as his textbook was abstruse, and each new chapter became crystal clear after listening to his logical explanations. On the other hand, Wrongwell had no patience at all with inattentive students, and he thought that surgeons were "totally ignorant of anything but cutting up people." Both categories were treated with withering sarcasm.

Old man Fleetwood, who taught anatomy, seemed about a hundred years old. He'd lectured on the subject since the mid-1890s, and was also a brilliant archaeologist and expert on Egyptian hieroglyphics. His collection of bones and cadavers took the place of friends and lovers, and his trusted assistant looked after both. During anatomy lectures, Professor Fleetwood might suddenly call out in his squeaky nasal twang, "William, bring me the left temporal bone of a mongoose, and don't take all day," and sure enough the little ogre soon came trotting back with the appropriate scrap of bone which the old man accepted without comment, then used it to illustrate a point in comparative morphology. As for William's appearance, Philip felt he could have passed as an associate of Burke and Hare, the Edinburgh body-snatchers.

The professor was reputed to have had himself lowered into the abdominal cavity of an elephant's carcass at the London Zoo, and dissected his way from the inside out. He claimed it was the only way one could really understand anatomy. Although – unlike William and the Portuguese 'Anatomy Demonstrator' – the professor never took his lunch in the dissecting hall, he wasn't above presenting a set of filthy quotations that provided the mnemonics for specific sets of names in anatomy: memory aids for the exams. Everyone used these and blessed old Fleetwood for his help.

Life with Dora was now far less concealed. It was accepted as an open secret with the Bosnars' friends and acquaintances, but never discussed. Despite a continuing archaic fear of religious intermarriage, with its reputation for disaster (especially for the children of such a union), there was enough confidence in their esteemed Phileep to believe he was one person who could make it work. If he failed, there could be little hope for the triumph of reason over prejudice and bigotry, despite the world's advances in other areas of human progress.

Meanwhile, Philip found it very difficult at times to contain his passions, most of all when he and Dora indulged in torrid 'necking', their youthful bodies pressed close together and their eager hands caressing each other. On such occasions, after he got home and went to sleep, he obtained vicarious consummation in realistic wet dreams, and wondered if she obtained similar relief. On the subject of taking the final step, she remained firm and he, faithful to his pledge.

One evening, they were sitting together in her front room, laughing at amusing reminiscences and speculating about their future, with the sounds of a winter rainstorm rattling the windows of their cozy retreat. Suddenly she turned serious.

"Do you have a secret life away from me, Phil, of which I know nothing?"

"If you mean do I have another sweetheart, you know the answer is No, Dorie. I'm not capable of cheating." He paused a moment, then continued, "I'm just as sure you have no other sweetheart aside from me, but I realize you have your own friends just as I have mine. You enjoy your swimming and other sports, just as I enjoy my tennis, the odd game of cricket or soccer, and occasional hiking."

She threw her arms around his neck and kissed him ardently, a hint of moisture visible below her glistening violet eyes. All at once her mood changed, and she gave him a happy smile as she announced,"Now I've got a secret to show you. I just have to get something from the hall closet and won't be long."

While he waited for the surprise, he reflected that she never revealed much of her life away from him, but he felt no resentment. He knew she was entering a world of teachers and education, just as he was entering a world of doctors and medicine. When she returned, she was carrying a large leather-bound book bearing the title DIARY in embossed gold letters. She sat down beside him and leafed through the pages until she found the entry she was looking for.

"I want you to look at this page, but nothing else," she requested. He gave his promise and read the selected page, written in her neat lettering.

'February 6, 1929.

Oh, something terribly funny happened tonight. Pauline Bosnar's little brother who gazes at me soulfully in the Trevor Road library has been following me part way home every night when I leave. Tonight I decided to confront him and asked Is this a bet or a trial of patience?" He turned out to be quite witty and charming and I hated to discourage him. After all `Faint heart ne'er won fair lady' so there's hope for him yet, the poor young lad'.

He wanted to read more but she took the diary away from him and said, "Perhaps some other time".

After he left, she wondered why she hadn't shown him the entry dated February 6, 1930, which commenced with the words, **'He came, he saw, he conquered'**.

At the same moment, a reflective Philip Bosnar, walking home through the subsiding drizzle, speculated that life was full of funny little tricks. God had a unique sense of humor.

CHAPTER 5

1939-40

It was a pleasant fall day (that was what they called autumn in Canada and the Bosnars were rapidly becoming assimilated), when Philip arrived back in Vanwey. Patty was there to meet him at the station, and she looked radiant and gorgeous. He wanted to take her to bed without delay, and stay there until the following morning. Instead, he had to settle for ardent hugs and kisses, embarrassing his lovely wife and delighting the approving onlookers.

When they got home, with Patty driving expertly and opening the left door, prairie-style, at the appropriate turns, he found that she'd prepared a sumptuous lunch. He showered and changed, then joined her at the kitchen dinette. Indoctrinated since childhood in the Irish tradition that real men don't share in women's housework, Patty refused any offers of help from her husband. That was her job, she reminded him, and surgery was his. He realized this would never change, and proved to be prophetic.

The lunch was delicious, and over steaming hot tea and mouthwatering apple pie she asked him all about Winnipeg and his new friends. He filled her in with as many details as possible and made her very happy.

"There was only one sour note," he admitted reluctantly, "and that was at one or two of the cocktail parties, when bigotry reared its ugly head."
He described the incidents but cleaned up the language, as he was well aware that she found obscenities offensive.

The first episode was at John Kinsley's home. Everyone was getting a bit high, mostly on rye whisky, and a small group of his recent examiners were conversing noisily. As soon as they spotted him, they beckoned him to join them. One of their group, a heavyset man with deep red complexion, was holding forth in an aggressive manner.

"What I do," he was saying, "is mark 'em all down by twenty percent, otherwise the fucking Jewboys will swamp our goddam profession."

"Oh stuff it, Vance," protested one of his colleagues, "you're full of shit. How the hell do you know which candidates are Jews?"

"I'm not alone," came the smug reply, "a bunch of us go over the list of candidates before each exam, and once we figure out who the kikes are we cut their marks."
Philip's mouth remained open in shock and amazement, but he managed to splutter, "You must be crazy!" He drew a deep breath and continued, "Jesus Christ! That would be breaking every rule..." but he was interrupted by the red-faced speaker, who stared at him with a strange expression for a moment or two then shook his head and growled, "It's you bloody do-good liberals who'd let any alien bastard into medicine, Kike, Nigger or Chink."
He grinned at the newcomer's obvious disgust, and Philip decided to let the matter drop, but not

without a feeling of guilt. Now that he knew the score, he told himself, there'd be better opportunities to tackle this problem in future; by effective flanking attacks rather than self-defeating direct confrontation. So, for the moment, although it was against every fiber of his being, he held his tongue and the conversation drifted into pleasanter topics. At some of the ensuing parties, he heard similar racist remarks by other guests and realized that the problem was a fairly general one.

Patty listened to his account in sober silence. At times like this she found herself feeling more Jewish than her husband, and was outraged rather than offended.

"How about your new friends in Winnipeg?" she asked, "Are they infected with the same virus?"

"I doubt whether either Alan Simpson or John Kinsley are prejudiced, but one never knows." He paused thoughtfully, then added, "I was tempted to drop my facade in spite of our pledge. In any event, if and when the truth comes out we'll find that real friends remain true friends."

By the end of November, a reply finally arrived from Ottawa, politely informing Dr. Philip Bosnar that he should apply to the U.K. authorities for entry into the British armed forces, and he perceived that he was just another pawn in a futile game between two rigid bureaucracies. He'd have to find another way.

As for the Blaikie practice, relations with 'good old Dr. Tom' came to a head shortly before the new year, and they had a real blow-up. It was all about hostile attitudes; financial arrangements; different approaches to medicine, surgery and obstetrics; and acceptable standards of performance. Everything came out into the open, even the unethical splitting of fees and the older man's unwelcome attentions to Patty.

"I'd like to leave this practice as soon as convenient," he concluded.

"That's Okay with me," came the reply, "let's say the end of March. That'll give me time to get another surgeon." Then he added, as if by afterthought, "If you go back to England we'll forget what you owe me."

"Owe you! I don't owe you a damn cent as far as I know." Blaikie scowled and his face darkened.

"We'll see about that," he warned grimly, and Philip felt there was nothing more to say.

Later that day, he phoned Joe McShane, Registrar of the Saskatchewan College of Physicians and Surgeons, and discussed the entire situation. He'd met this decent official once before. A short time after his arrival in Vanwey, the Registrar had hastened his temporary licensure to practice and invited him to present a paper at the summer meeting of the College membership. It was held at Little Sparrow Lake, and he and Patty had a wonderful time there. His paper, 'Recent Advances in Gastric Surgery', was well received and McShane was the perfect host. Before saying goodbye to the young couple he surprised them by remarking, without preamble, "If that old bugger Tom Blaikie gives you any trouble just give me a shout." Thus, it wasn't entirely unexpected that the present phone-call proved so productive. The registrar sounded like a true friend, and informed him that if he wished to stay and practice in Vanwey it wouldn't be unethical in any way. He also added a somewhat cryptic comment, "If any financial arguments arise be sure to let me know."

A short time later, Peter Forsyth phoned Philip and came up to the Bosnar apartment.

"This is where I started when I first joined the Blaikie practice," he commented as he looked

around. He revealed his knowledge of the blow-up and added, "Good old Dr. Tom has been spreading his own version of the affair with allusions to thirty pieces of silver."
Philip guessed that Forsyth would be making him an offer and wasn't surprised when it came.

"Would you be willing to join me and replace Tim Grady? He enlisted a month ago and will be leaving very soon. Your monthly salary would start at $250, with car expenses and incidentals, plus one annual medical meeting in Canada or the U.S."
Philip accepted cheerfully and they had a couple of stiff drinks of Canadian Club to celebrate the occasion. They liked each other, and what was just as important, Patty had met Forsyth only once and was favorably impressed. As always, her judgment was impeccable.

As for her beloved husband, he soon discovered that his new colleague was a competent surgeon, despite having no special surgical qualifications. He was also an excellent all-round G.P. and chose his office staff well. Valerie Cruickshank, his office nurse-receptionist, was capable and pleasant, well-trained and experienced, and she did a lot for the practice. The office building was modern, spacious and well equipped. The only item lacking was an X-ray facility, but this was no problem, as patients requiring radiological service were simply referred to Saint Cecilia Hospital. The nuns had the latest equipment with all the necessary protective shielding, and enjoyed the expertise of a first class X-ray technician. It would be a bonus for Philip, since he knew he hadn't taken suitable precautions to protect himself during the many X-ray examinations he'd performed at the Blaikie building.

On New Year's Eve, the Bosnars threw a party and invited a group of their closest friends, including the Forsyths. Kitty Forsyth was a plump and boisterous individual with an earthy sense of humor that enlivened any party she attended. Patty made sure there was enough coffee, and Phil took care of the alcoholic refreshments with a generous supply of Seagrams V.O. and Cutty Sark, an assortment of mixes and lots of chipped ice. Extra chairs were provided by the Steffansons, and the glowing hostess had outdone herself with a delicious assortment of sandwiches and cakes.

The evening was a resounding success, and after a hearty rendition of Auld Lang Syne and an inebriated round- robin exchange of kisses, the party continued into the early hours of 1940. Nobody seemed to notice the prolonged embrace and lingering kiss bestowed on her husband by an aroused Patty. When the happy guests departed, at long last and with reluctance, it was 2 o'clock and the young couple were ready for bed, but not for sleep. Patty was more than a devoted wife. She was a passionate lover.

On the last day of March, the Bosnars were happy to move out of their apartment and into their new home. It was a furnished bungalow on Fourth Street East and more than adequate. The owner was Peter Forsyth's brother-in-law, a goodhumored Scot who managed his family's bakery business. As for the rent, it was most reasonable by local standards and Patty couldn't be happier with the furniture and accessories.

Although the house was sheer luxury compared with their recent abode, she and Phil would often find themselves coming up with amusing reminiscences of their apartment days that produced a chuckle or two; nostalgia so soon? First, there was the constant battle against the pervasive odors from Dr. Tom's hospital. Then, there was the ancient iceman barging into their apartment unannounced, depositing a fresh load of ice – complete with frozen grasshoppers – into the icebox at 6 o'clock on their first Tuesday morning, and taking away the remains of the old. And who could forget the rattlesnake scare on the first night of August? Since their arrival in Vanwey they often heard rumors about snakes, rattlers as well as the harmless garden variety, and the new Canadians listened to tales about these nasty slithering creatures with some apprehension. They wondered if they'd ever encounter a poisonous serpent, perhaps even one that could wander into people's living quarters.

The day had been unbearably hot and they went to bed early with bedclothes off and windows wide open, hoping for a night breeze. At 3 a.m. Philip awoke with a feeling of dread, all senses alert. The room was in pitch-black darkness and the sound he heard chilled him to the bone. It was a RATTLE, SLITHER, pause...rattle, slither, pause. He carefully edged himself over the side of the Murphy bed and realized to his horror that he was barefoot, almost naked and without weapon. The nearest light switch was in the bathroom. In a split second he leaped across the space between bed and bathroom and turned on the light, casting a subdued illumination over the entire suite. Fortunately, the rattle and slither sounds remained at the open windows.

As his eyes began to adjust to the half-light, the only weapons he could think of were his shoes. He hated to turn on the overhead light since this would awaken Patty, who was sleeping like a baby. With a shoe in each hand, he advanced inch by inch toward the deadly sounds. The fear was passing and he felt poised for instant combat. Then he saw his enemy for the first time, just as the ominous rattle sounded once more. The night breeze was moving the beaded side curtains, producing the rattle. The shifting beads caught the side of the table lamp before sliding down to produce the ominous slithering sound. He inhaled deeply, closed the window and returned to bed feeling sheepish but relieved. His beauteous wife slumbered on, unaware of what might have been the life and death struggle of her darling.

Then there was the unexpected visit of 'Big Red' Haynes on a Saturday afternoon in mid-December. The fierce prairie winter had really set in. There were deep snow drifts all over town and blizzards were forecast for Monday. Every driver had chains on his wheels, a load of sand in the trunk, and a large shovel. Philip hated to drive to the hospital or make housecalls in this weather. Although the apartment temperature was a pleasant sixty-five degrees Fahrenheit, the outside temperature was twenty below zero and it wasn't a day for expecting visitors. There was a loud knock at the door and – lo and behold – who should appear on their doorstep but Big Red Haynes from their Atlantic crossing!

Like most shipboard promises to visit one another after completing the voyage, Red's vow hadn't been taken seriously, yet here he was, larger than life. He was given an enthusiastic greeting and welcomed inside. The unexpected guest was anxious to know how they were getting along, and how they were acclimatizing to life on the Canadian prairies. Philip poured a large scotch and soda for Haynes, one for himself and a mild rye and ginger-ale for Patty, then brought him up-to-date on most of the important details, but omitted anything unpleasant. Big Red declared he was astounded at their successful adjustment to Canadian life and asked his hostess, with a sudden unabashed directness, "Are you pregnant yet, Patricia?"

"Not yet," she replied, blushing slightly, "but we have lots of time before starting a family," and departed into the kitchen to prepare tea and sandwiches.

"By the way, I hope you like tea," she called out.

"Tea's just fine. You know, Patricia, I'd forgotten how beautiful you are. You're a lucky dog, Bosnar." More typical Haynes, thought Philip, direct but charming.

The visitor now informed them that he'd recently been promoted to vice-president of Canadian Schemmler Tableware, with headquarters in Toronto, and was doing a tour of western outlets. He was on his way from Winnipeg to Calgary, driving some three hundred miles a day, and decided to drop in on his Vanwey friends. Always the keen salesman, he made them promise to change to Schemmler's Extra Fine Tableware before the year was out. After two pleasant hours together, he thanked them for their hospitality and said he had to leave. He gave the Bosnars his card, put on his outdoor clothes and galoshes, shook hands with Phil and gave Patty an enthusiastic kiss on the lips before saying goodbye. His visit had been just as entertaining as it was surprising.

The more they reminisced, the more incidents from their recent apartment life they seemed to recall. But now was the time to look forward once again to the future and see what life had to offer in the '40s.

The next two months were happy ones. The Bosnars and Forsyths got along well, and from a professional point of view things could hardly be better. Pete and Phil were not only compatible in all phases of their practice but had become close friends in a short space of time. McShane was enthusiastic about the new association, and so were their mutual friends and acquaintances. The state of internecine warfare in Dr. Tom's 'ménage a trois' prior to Dr. Bosnar's departure had by now become an open secret, although Phil and Patty had been scrupulous in avoiding any discussion of the matter with anyone in Vanwey.

The two associates in the Forsyth practice went about their office duties with quiet efficiency, never hesitating to talk to each other about their cases, or to seek formal consultation on difficult areas of diagnosis, therapy, or complex surgery. It was the same in the hospital. For average operations they assisted each other, mostly using spinal or local anesthesia. For lesser operations requiring the specific use of general anesthesia, or when the patient refused spinal or local, each would do the 'gassing' for the other. For more advanced surgery, which was always done by Philip, they called in Dr. Sharp to give the anesthetic.

Clifford Sharp was a mild-mannered and obliging G.P. who ran a mine contract practice in nearby Bonchance. In addition to referring his surgical cases to the Forsyth practice, he gladly agreed to gas for their cases when needed. He was capable and congenial, and they both liked and trusted him. It was a very satisfactory arrangement and they considered themselves lucky. As for Patty, she thought the new turn of events was almost too good to be true and admitted that she was delighted.

Into this idyllic setting, the vindictive Dr. Tom Blaikie dropped his bombshell with unabashed glee. He announced that he was suing Philip Bosnar for 'moneys advanced', for transportation and associated expenses of bringing the couple to the Vanwey practice. Patty was stunned and Philip, remembering Blaikie's dark warning ("We'll see about that") was outraged. The writ served by lawyer Standwick contained the word 'advanced' rather than 'forwarded' or 'sent', and it seemed that in Canada 'advanced' implied a loan. Philip could hardly have the old rogue's son brought back from Africa to testify against his own father.

The Bosnars had clear recollections of the interview with young Ted Blaikie in London, before he left for the colonial medical service in Kenya, and there was no room for genuine misunderstanding. The moneys in question were being SENT and not loaned, to defray all travel expenses, since it was Blaikie senior who commissioned Bosnar to fill a specific need in the Vanwey practice. Unfortunately, this had all seemed so perfectly logical and proper that he'd failed to get this particular transaction in writing. 'Like a stupid idiot', he told himself.

He discussed the problem in excruciating detail with his worried wife, and that proved therapeutic. It was decided he should first phone McShane at the College and then consult Herb Adams. In addition, both agreed that Peter Forsyth must be brought into the distressing situation without delay. Peter didn't mince words,

"That's just typical of the old crook," he exclaimed.

"He brought the two of you all the way from England because he wanted a Fellowship surgeon and he undertook to pay all expenses. His son Ted acted as the old man's agent and arranged the transfer of funds to cover travel and related costs for both of you. In my opinion you owe him nothing. He made your stay with him impossible, just as he did with me and others before me."

"That's what I was hoping you'd say. I'm grateful, and Patty will be so relieved when I tell her. This has been one hell of a worry to her and your reaction will mean a whole lot."

The College Registrar's response was just as positive when Philip phoned and told him what had happened.

"You and I, Phil, know each other well enough for you to call me Joe, and to tell me all the details no matter how embarrassing you find them."
He listened in silence while Philip filled him in with all the sorry details, starting with Ted Blaikie and the London interview, going on to professional disagreements in the Vanwey practice and the final blow-up and resignation, followed by the impending lawsuit.

"The old devil is either bluffing or he's trying to scare you out of town. Now that you've joined forces with Forsyth, a move I strongly endorse, you represent a real threat to his practice. What's worse, you threaten his pocket book."

"What do you think I ought to do?"

"You should fight the case and win. Get yourself a good lawyer and tell him everything you've told me, leaving nothing out."

"Thanks a lot, Joe, I can't tell you how much I appreciate your interest and I'll be sure to follow your advice."

"Don't let it get you down, Phil. This time pistol-packing Tom has bitten off more than he can chew. Remember me to that gorgeous Irish redhead of yours." They were on the phone almost half an hour, and Philip felt as if a great load had been lifted off his shoulders. With a light heart he phoned Herb Adams for an office appointment.

At 10 o'clock the following morning, he was shown into the small and unpretentious Adams office by the elderly office secretary. It was well known that she'd remained with her boss through the very worst of times, and had retrieved all the I.O.Us he invariably threw out.

"So far as the claim is concerned Blaikie doesn't have a leg to stand on," the lawyer declared after hearing his client out without interruption, "but you have to realize it won't be that simple. If you don't defend the case he can tell everyone that he nailed you trying to swindle him. If you fight the case and win you'll be fully vindicated. If you lose you'll be out of pocket but your honor will be intact and the town's sympathy will be with you, and not with him. They'll simply conclude that the old devil has pulled another fast one."

"In that case let's go ahead, Mr. Adams, (Mrs. Adams was the only one who ever addressed him as `Herb') and see if we can't win the battle in the courtroom."

The lawyer rotated his wrists to free his shirt- cuffs from the sleeves of his navy blue gabardine jacket. It was a familiar gesture, signifying either the planning of a play at bridge or the elaboration of an opinion.

"Perhaps I'm being overly cautious, Philip, but I want you to know that Mark Standwick is one of the shrewdest fellows around, some would say `shifty', and he's respected for his ability but not his ethics. On top of hat, the case will come up before old Judge Tompkins, who's not only pixilated but was once Standwick's senior partner in their law practice."

"Will that work against us, do you think?"

"It might, and that's why I don't want to take any chances."

"What do you have in mind?"

"I'm sure you've heard of M.A. McPherson in Regina. He's one of the best barristers in Canada, and was nominated more than once for leadership of the federal Conservative party. Only young Diefenbaker from Prince Albert is his rival in the West. I want you to come with me to Regina to meet this man. I know he'll be favorably impressed by you and will agree to take this case in a consultant capacity."

"I don't know what to say. Of course I'll be glad to come with you, but I have every confidence in you handling my defense."

"Don't worry. I'll remain on the case."

"What about his fees, won't they be awfully high?"

"I'm sure he'll waive his customary fee in a case like this if he believes a fine new Canadian is being victimized by an unscrupulous opponent like Blaikie."

They shook hands and Philip went home to tell Patty all about the interview. By this time she'd lost most of her anxiety and was feeling much more confident about the entire affair.

"Don't you worry darling, we'll show them," she declared with proud defiance, and they drank a toast to Blaikie's defeat.

McPherson proved to be a most impressive individual and Philip liked him right away. He was waiting for them when they arrived at his sumptuous suite of offices, some two blocks from the Saskatchewan Hotel – where they'd checked in after driving up from Vanwey. When Philip looked at the famed lawyer, he saw a quiet gray person in his middle forties, with a clean-shaven and strongly-lined face that was full of humor and intelligence. His diction was cultured and his accent carried a hint of Edinburgh in his background. When he put on his gold-rimmed glasses he looked like a kindly professor, but it would be a mistake to underestimate his strength. This was a man accustomed to power and knew how to use it.

After introduction and formalities, he seated his two visitors in handsome mahogany armchairs, upholstered in brown Moroccan leather and facing him across a huge mahogany desk, its leather top matching the chairs. There were some eighteenth century steeplechase prints on the walls and the entire atmosphere was intimate and comfortable.

"First of all, Dr. Bosnar, I want you to tell me everything you've already told my colleague Mr. Adams. Don't leave out any details and if there are any additional points you may have omitted please let's have them now."

Once again Philip heard himself going over all the details of his familiar tale of woe. It was like an actor going through the performance of a play: one which has become so familiar that the memorized lines begin to lose their meaning. McPherson pondered for quite a while, then turned to Adams and asked,

"Can you think of a single reason why we shouldn't win this case? Because I can't."
Herb Adams agreed emphatically with this defiant optimism and it was obvious he was pleased. Then it was Philip's turn once again.

"I must be direct with you, doctor. Do you have any money or property?"

"Not much money I'm afraid. I get $250 a month and we live in a rented bungalow. Enough to live on but no savings so far."

"What about debts?"

"We've managed to pay off our initial bank loan."

"Nothing else owing?"

"Well, there is one other obligation," Philip conceded reluctantly. "Before coming to Canada I took over my father's business debts and still send $50 to England every month. He was hit pretty hard during the depression years, and it's the least I can do."
The man opposite said nothing but looked at him long and hard, as if searching for the real person under the composed exterior. Finally he stood up and shook his client's hand warmly.

"You just leave everything to me, doctor. Adams and I will look after you and you musn't worry about the fee. We'll talk about that after we win the case."

When Philip got back from Regina, he learned that Blaikie was over in England. Rumor had it that he was trying to get commissioned as a surgeon in the Canadian Army. It seemed that he'd functioned as such in France during the First World War, but it seemed a bit far-fetched at this stage of his life. Perhaps he'd arranged a meeting overseas with his son, who might be on special leave at this time. In any event, it was all very strange; but Dr. Tom was a strange character who made weird decisions.

In the meantime, the daily routine of the Bosnars remained relatively unchanged. Patty was enjoying a rich social life, with many new friends and activities. She was on the hospital auxiliary and had been made a member of the IODE. They both roared with laughter at this latest honor. She, the daughter of flaming IRA zealots, now defending British imperialism! It seemed only yesterday that she was able, for the first time in years, to rise for the British National Anthem without feeling intense guilt and the necessity of at least a hundred Mea Culpas.

Philip was getting along well in his practice and was handling some challenging surgical cases with gratifying results. Perhaps he was drinking a bit more than he should, but he was never inebriated and did most of his imbibing during social evenings. It wasn't very long before he was dragooned into the Rotary Club and this became an avenue to many interesting new friendships.

April the ninth was the Bosnars' combined birthday and the occasion for a small party at their home. Although Patty was a year younger than her husband, both had the identical birth date and felt that this established some kind of special bond ordained by the celestial guardian of their destiny. It was also the day that Hitler sent his armed hordes into peaceful Denmark and Norway, two small nations with a joint population of less than ten million and pledged to neutrality.

The radio was full of analytical commentaries by Matthew Halton and Ross Munro, with dire pronouncements of impending disaster by the Canadian Broadcasting Company's resonant bass-baritone, Lorne Green, the 'Voice of Doom'.

To Philip, the news appeared as the obscene development of his predicted program for the subjugation of Europe, commencing with the domination by Germany's naval forces of its lifelines in the Baltic. Next would come the Low Countries of Belgium, Holland and tiny Luxembourg, followed by France. Unless Chamberlain could be thrown out and replaced by Churchill or even Anthony Eden (Philip's own paragon of honest fearless statesmanship), Britain itself must fall to the triumphant bestiality of the Nazis.

Although the impending trial hung heavily over their heads, the Bosnars wouldn't allow its shadow to darken their daily lives. They began to improve their contract bridge game and enjoyed it more with each session. In truth, however, Philip preferred his poker games, preferably for high stakes. There was a regular group, and they played at each other's homes about twice a month. Alf Steffanson played scientifically while George Freikopf relied on his luck and was a good card-holder – just as he was in bridge. Big Jim Qualen, who ran the King Edward Hotel, was a good sport and a bluff, kindhearted fellow. Jock McTeague, the town mayor, was the proverbial canny Scot, who loved the game but appeared to hate parting with a single penny at the table. The new chief of police enjoyed the game but enjoyed the company more. Rounding out the group was the local chief of C.P.R. operations, a man who liked people, loved parties and was a pretty fair player. As for Philip, he was rapidly becoming an enthusiastic and better than average poker player.

Patty soon found that Mah Jong was her favorite game, but mainly as a backdrop to her lunches or teas with 'The Girls'. Her husband was starting to spend more time practicing on his violin, but avoided tedious exercises that might dull his renewed interest. By a stroke of luck he was contacted by a young piano teacher who was keen on developing a violin and piano duo. Mayor McTeague approached him at about the same time, and invited him to perform at the annual concert that promoted local talent. It was usually held at the beginning of May and took place in the Princess movie theater.

The soloist and his accompanist decided on Beethoven's Spring Sonata for Violin and Piano. It was a piece that sounded impressive but was, in fact, quite straightforward. Depending on the amount of applause, he might play Brahms' Hungarian Dance No 5 or Drdl's Souvenir as an encore. It certainly felt good to get back to the musical instrument of his boyhood.

CHAPTER 6

1933

By his second year at medical school Philip had passed his exams in anatomy, physiology, histology and organic chemistry and commenced his first contact with real live patients on the wards. This was an enormous thrill, and for the first time he began to feel like a doctor. The famed Dr. Hugo Sapian, M.D. (Doctor of Medicine), F.R.C.S,F.R.C.P. (Fellow of the Royal Colleges of Surgery and Medicine), was the instructor in clinical medicine. After his London Fellowship in surgery, this gifted man had run into two severe obstacles: first, he was only 5 feet 2 in height, and second, he was afflicted with stubborn pustular facial acne. This meant that he not only had to stand on a special platform to operate and that proved hard on his back, but his patients fell victim to a high incidence of wound infection. After a while he felt compelled to give up his surgical career and he became a celebrated medical specialist instead.

Along with rest of the 'clinical clerks', as they were known, Philip Bosnar learned to take the patient's medical history, starting with the age, occupation and family history: any illness or untimely death and any obvious or probable familial or inherited diseases. Next came the patient's history of past illness or accident, pregnancy or surgery, as the case might be.

The patient's symptoms came next; first the patient's version, then the search for exact details. This was followed by the functional enquiry: a careful review of every bodily function, any abnormality or alteration of these functions. In a way it was straight detective work, requiring patience, tact and persistence.

The physical examination came next with a planned approach. First, grant the patient privacy by drawing the curtains and conversing in a quiet and sympathetic voice, then asking the patient to disrobe completely and cover up any area not being examined in order to preserve dignity. Commence with the general appearance: good color or definite pallor, fat or thin, tall or short, clear skin or eruptions, muscular or wasted, surgical scars or deformities. The list kept growing as observation improved. After this came the check-out of each area, starting with the head and neck, and ending not with the feet but with the rectum!

"If you don't put your finger in it you may put your foot in it," was the charming way Dr. Sapian impressed this warning upon them.

One day, the great man approached Philip and looked at his notes on the patient he had just examined.

"Details, Bosnar," he admonished, "details. Is this man Caucasian, East Indian, African, Mongolian, Eskimo? Has he recently visited any country where he may have picked up a particular endemic infection or parasite. Details!"

"I'm sorry, Sir, those are points I missed," Philip apologized

"Of course you did," came the cheerful reply. "I see you've noted the patient's extreme

pallor. That's good, but what about his expression? Is it tranquil or does it reveal discomfort, pain, or agony? Is his mind clear or does it appear to be dulled?"
Philip looked crushed.

"Cheer up, Bosnar, this is a good report, but never forget, details! He never forgot.

On another occasion, they were all given a demonstration of the importance of observation. Dr. Sapian asked the students if they had tested the patient's urine. Was it clear or murky, of abnormal odor, fragrant or foul. Was it obviously bloody; if the patient was female, was she menstruating? Had they tested for sugar, acetone, ketone, bile elements, protein? What about the microscope, had they seen pus cells, red cells, crystals, clear casts, granular casts, parasites, other abnormal items or clues? Any urine tests? Yes, cultures for bacterial growth. Anything else?

"No, gentlemen? You astound me? Have you forgotten the taste test?"
He picked up the bedside specimen, dipped his finger in and tasted it. To their horror they were all instructed to follow. Fighting nausea, they all complied and found the taste less objectionable than they feared.

"And now gentlemen, we come to the importance of careful observation," their mentor declared, his face beaming.

"Had you watched more closely you would have observed that I dipped my right MIDDLE finger in the urine but I put my right INDEX finger in my mouth."
There was some doubtful laughter at this revelation, but they promised to honor his request never to reveal his secret to the next group of clinical clerks.

Philip Bosnar and his fellow students were learning how to examine the eyes, ear, nose and throat; becoming adept at using the ophthalmoscope, the nasal speculum, and the auriscope for examining the ears. They became proficient with the stethoscope and sphygmomanometer (for blood-pressures) and became familiar with X-rays. They learned the elements of neurological investigation, employing the cottonwool stick for light touch, the pin for superficial pain, the hot and cold water flask for temperature sensation, and the tendon pinch for deep pain. Then there was the 'knee hammer' for tendon reflexes and the large tuning fork for vibratory sense. There was the finger to nose test, the Romberg test for balance, and the joint-motion test to determine positional sense. It seemed there were no limits to the number of procedures and special tests, but meantime they were becoming experts in their restricted professional duties.

It was now becoming decision time for Philip, and the issue at hand was Primary Fellowship. The London, or more correctly the English F.R.C.S, was held in two parts. The Primary was in the subjects of advanced anatomy and physiology, and had a terrifying reputation for difficulty – with a formidable failure rate. Unfortunately, it was one hurdle that had to be cleared before one could sit for the F.R.C.S. Finals in surgery, pathology and bacteriology, and its failure rate was still high. That was why many candidates opted for the Edinburgh one-phase exam, although its prestige was not as great.

Most of the British candidates for Primary were doctors who were completing or had completed their surgical training. Most of the Commonwealth candidates were established surgeons who had put aside funds to take the special courses in designated schools such as St. Clement's and then remain for the exams. They came from Australia and New Zealand, from Canada and South Africa, from India and Nigeria.

The current failure rate was about 80 percent in the Primary and about 70 percent in the Final. It was felt that this was the best opportunity to take the Primary, as at this time the subjects were still fresh in memory and one simply had to polish up the fine details to absolute perfection. The only snag in this plan was that it meant completing the special course studies concurrently with those involved in a successful dressership, and that was a back-breaking load.

Philip decided he'd give it one try, all or none. His new pals at the hospital told him he was crazy; candidates required at least three attempts before getting through. At home, his parents worried that he might taking on too heavy a load but didn't discourage him, while Dora was confident he could do it and volunteered to help him with his memory tests. These were of the utmost importance, and anatomy in particular was largely a matter of the straightforward memory of a thousand detailed facts; every bone, joint, ligament, capsule, muscle, tendon, nerve, artery, vein, lymphatic and lymph node. Every organ and gland, duct and tube, names in both English and Latin, new terminology and old. What were their spatial relationships to each other, by which foramina did they enter and leave? They would allow for no error in this examination, nor faulty memory.

He found himself relearning physiology with a depth of understanding and a fundamental admiration for the ingenious way each structure in the body, large or small, was intrinsically related to a specific function. It was all part of an incredible grand design, and he felt eager to glimpse its inner workings and decipher the complex blueprint of this design. He read his books with a new insight, and experienced the thrill of a new understanding.

In anatomy, simply building up his memory was not enough; it was necessary to visualize the structure and texture of each part. On rare occasions he would find a segment of Gray's Anatomy that didn't quite make sense. He would then fall back on that amazing little condensed text, 'Jamieson's Companion to Anatomical Studies'. A fraction of the size of Gray's, without a single illustration, its description of spacial relationships were superb. He even felt himself impelled to construct models with colored plasticine, in order to obtain clarification of a particular problem. What were the folds and recesses of the `*Peritoneum*' (the inner lining membrane of the abdomen)? What was the exact relationship of the brain's interior structure to the overlying cerebral convolutions? These two questions alone took two weekends of patient modelling, and there were others. Often it was necessary to begin with a single bone and build up layer by layer, cord by cord, until suddenly the whole picture became crystal-clear and the text acquired the intimacy of a friend.

Eventually he felt himself ready for battle, but his fellow clinical clerks would taunt him with such remarks as, "Do you think you stand a chance?", "Wait till Lazenby gets you," or worse still, "Get rid of the rope on your bathrobe!"

It wasn't that they were heartless, it was simply their way of handling the impact of a recent tragedy.

Trevor Copeland was a serious young man of thirty-one years, the son of a well-known gynecologist on staff at the Middlesex Hospital. He was a conscientious student and worked hard at his studies, yet he'd failed his Primary on four successive attempts, mainly the result of Lazenby's actions in the physiology Orals. Sir Edward Lazenby was renowned for his pioneer work on vitamins and their role in such diseases as rickets and scurvy. As an examiner he was notorious for his unfair methods, almost to the point of sadism. It was said that he enjoyed nothing more than failing any candidate from Wrongwell's course.

Two weeks before the Primaries, a deeply depressed Copeland came to a decision. He couldn't face another Primary failure and the disgrace this would bring, especially to his father. He took a large helping of scotch whisky then removed the rope from his bathrobe and hanged himself. This was to be his ultimate test, and he passed it on the first try. After the initial shock and grief, the medical students covered the vulnerability of their emotions with comments in appallingly bad taste. There was an expression of outrage in the London Times, in an Editorial entitled '**Examination or Murder?**'

The examination was held in the traditional Queen's Square Hall off Kingsway. Philip found the papers almost too straightforward. This was a written examination with only a few fortunates getting any chance, so it seemed logical to give ones answers a novel approach. He gave his answers in anatomy almost as if he were modelling in plasticine, and went even further into detail. Each paper contained two questions, to be answered in detailed essay form. The first question in physiology had to do with the neurological connections in certain types of muscle reflex and gave an example.

Philip took his life in his hands and started his essay by pointing out that this was a particularly bad choice, since it contained important exceptions to the rule. It was true hubris, what the Jews called chutzpah, and he knew he was 'going for broke'. Aside from this one act of bravado he followed his routine of commencing his essay with a carefully categorized skeleton-table of the subject, giving him a working modus operandi and sending a message to the examiner that the candidate possessed a clear and orderly mind.

The anatomy Orals were reasonably difficult but not unfair, and revolved mainly around the identification of points on the floor of the cranium, where each tiny foramen was the conduit for a particular nerve or blood vessel. Everything had to be clearly and correctly identified. There was also a session on the origins and insertions of the muscles of the hand and forearm.

Finally there was the physiology Oral, with the hated Lazenby. Sir Edward was a large and pompous fellow, with an expression of combined smugness and faint boredom. He gave Philip a somewhat scornful look and asked him to examine the slide under the microscope?

"What's that?" he asked.

"It's a cross-section of the spinal cord, Sir."

"Yes, yes, but what level?"

"The midthoracic level, if it's from an adult human."

"What's it stained with?"

"Cajal stain. He gave it the Spanish pronunciation, Kahal.

"What's that and who's he?"

"It's a special brown stain invented by Ramon y Cajal, the great Spanish neurohistologist."

"What if I told you that we don't have a single Cajal stain in this entire collection? He deliberately pronounced the `j' as J for John, not the Spanish H. and Philip felt his hackles rising.

"Then its an excellent imitation."

"Haven't you ever heard of the Weigert-Pal stain?"

"Yes, it's a different nerve stain that has a blue color."

"Is that so. What's the easiest way to take your life?

"Sticking your head in the gas oven."

Now it was raw anger that made Philip give a slight emphasis to the word "your". A tiny smile flickered across the inquisitor's face and he asked, "So if I stick MY head in the gas oven would my asphyxia be accompanied by convulsions? No, you say? But if I were to squeeze YOUR windpipe and asphyxiate you, would you have convulsions?"

"Yes, I certainly would."

"Why the difference? And give me exact details, no generalities. Explain the ventilation processes and blood-gas chemistry involved, as well as the cardiovascular mechanisms that might come into play."

He listened to Philip's highly technical reply with an air of waning interest. Then he interrupted him with what appeared to be a suppressed yawn and said, as if at random, "Oh well. Tell me all you know about the Thalamus and Hypothalamus."

As his candidate described each detail, the examiner would hound him with, "Anything else?" until the subject could be pursued no further.

After the exam, in order to wind down his rage and get Lazenby out of his system, Philip went straight to the Stoll Theater, ordered a tray of Devonshire splits and a pot of tea, and sat through four hours of movies. (***He would never remember a single moment of what he was watching.***)

Out of twenty-one candidates who 'sat' the examination from St. Clement's, only three passed. He was one of the fortunate ones and was convinced it was mainly luck, as each of the other candidates knew the subjects backward, forward and inside out. Old Professor Fleetwood congratulated the successful candidates with the reassuring comment, "It's a test of yer ignorance, gentlemen, not yer knowledge!"

One day Tommy Wrongwell took Philip aside and told him, "You'll be interested to know what Professor Lazenby told me after he quizzed you. He said, 'I tried my best to trip that young whippersnapper of yours, Wrongwell, but he wouldn't weaken.' By the way, Bosnar, you'll be glad to know there were several Cajal stains in that collection. I used them myself while examining my own candidates."

It was great to get back to the clinical work on the medical wards. He wasn't interested in his new-found fame and popularity, but was happy for his loved ones whose faith was rewarded. He soon left the recent lofty heights of surgical ambitions and came down to earth with the mundane issues of the color, consistency and odor of human sputum and feces.

After completing his year on the medical wards, he was more than ready for his clinical dressership on the surgical wards and in the operating theaters. The routine on the surgical floor was similar to that of the medical floors, with one difference. Surgical dressers had to take care of major dressings on request, and were also responsible for preparing the patient for surgery. What was meant by 'prepping' was the washing, shaving, and application of an antiseptic solution to the area destined for the surgeons knife.

Before commencing these duties, however, the clinical dressers were introduced to the operating suite, and would have to witness their first operation. Their mentor, the handsome and aristocratic Cedric Mantel, was going to operate on a middle-aged man for what had been diagnosed as a bowel tumor. They watched the great man as he removed his jacket, collar and tie as well as his shoes. He put on a pair of large white rubber boots and a white waterproof apron, then a cap and mask from special containers in the 'Scrub-room'. He rolled up his shirt-sleeves and proceeded to scrub his hands and forearms from fingertips to elbow, using a sterilized nail brush and liquid soap.

The 'Theater Sister', (the name used for the head nurse in the operating rooms), was queen of this realm, and she instructed the nervous students to remove their jackets and leave them in the changing room. They were then ushered into the scrub-room to observe the surgeon's routine and don caps and masks that were handed out to them. Next came clean – but not sterilized – gowns of white linen, which they tied on to cover their clothes.

They followed their Chief into the operating room, where two nurses, already scrubbed, capped, masked and gowned, were laying out the instruments and sutures. One of them handed the surgeon a sterile towel with which he dried his hands and forearms, and a sterile gown, held wide open. He drove his arms into the sleeves and a junior nurse fastened the ties at the back; sterile talcum powder was then shaken on his hands. At last came the gloves, into which the hands were thrust with a masculine flourish of deep entry that almost carried sexual overtones, especially as the performance took place under the adoring eyes of his female helpers. Mantel's assistant had gone through the same routine a little earlier, according to protocol. He was the registrar, and he received his adulation at a more subdued level.

The patient, already put to sleep in the adjoining room, was lying on the operating table. His belly was completely uncovered by removing the overlying sterile towels, and the skin was repainted with iodine solution over the traditional levels of nipples to upper thighs. More sterile towels were then applied to isolate the operative area, and finally a large 'Lap' drape was opened up to cover the entire abdomen, (*'Lap' was short for laparotomy, which meant cutting open the belly*). At the upper end the sterile sheet with a large central aperture was thrown across a metal bridge, called an 'Ether Screen', isolating the wound area from the anesthetic region.

The surgeon was handed a scalpel with an expert snap of the handle and he promptly made a vertical deep gash, eight inches long, down the mid-portion of the exposed belly. Just as promptly, two of the students dropped as if poleaxed to the hard and polished tile floor. Fortunately they both missed the operating table; less fortunately, a third had fallen forward and broken his nose. Mantel was duly sympathetic but knew he always enjoyed this, year in and year out.

Philip's first 'preop. prep.' was a 16 Stone (224 lb) man, aged fifty-three, who worked as a bricklayer. He had been hoarding his large scrotal hernia for many years, concealing it from the intrusive gaze of doctors until it was too large to endure and resisted all attempts to accomplish its previous 'reduction', namely the return of its contents to the proper body cavity, his ample belly.

Armed with the equipment handed to him, Philip descended upon the apprehensive but cooperative patient. The patient's gaze was focussed on the shaving-cup and cylinder of soap, the large shaving-brush and a 'cut-throat' straight razor. The upper portion of the razor's voyage was smooth sailing, so to speak, but both skipper and passenger were conscious of dangerous shoals ahead. As Philip approached the sweating victim's family jewels, the watching eyes grew progressively wider. At long last, some forty minutes later, the ordeal was over for both of them, each covered with sweat, but no sutures were required and blood transfusion wouldn't be necessary.

The following morning, when the great surgeon surveyed his field of potential conquest, he gave a slight quiver and turned to his waiting students.

"I don't know who is responsible for this," he remarked, "but I must certainly thank him for commencing the operation."
Philip made a desperate attempt to become the Invisible Man of H.G. Wells, but with total lack of success.

The four months spent on 'C.M.'s service were valuable, and Philip picked up the art of detecting the symptoms, signs and pathology of surgical diseases. He learned about the value of special tests, especially blood tests and X-rays, and of careful patient-evaluation to help with a decision in doubtful cases. He acquired the techniques of skillful dressings and trauma-free surgical preps. Above all, he learned the tricks of the trade in basic operative procedure.

When the group was transferred to the service of Simons-Barstow, a new dimension was added; this eminent specialist was nearing the end of his career but was still world-famous for his pioneer work on cancer of the breast. His monograph on the subject, published in a well-illustrated book, contained his original dye injection studies on lymphatic spread of the malignant tumor, and was regarded as an international classic.

Philip picked up the fine details of radical breast surgery and found joy in his chief's excellent results, both technically and in the improved survival rates – compared with figures published by other surgeons. The implantation of radon needles into the intercostal spaces, in order to destroy cancer cells between the front ribs and prevent their spread to the interior of the chest, seemed highly original as well as logical.

One of the cases turned over to Philip was a daunting challenge, both to his ingenuity and to his senses. The patient was a 65-year-old man who'd been operated upon three weeks previously for a large central abdominal hernia. He had developed a feared complication known as *'Symbiotic gangrene'*. (This was a unique type of wound infection in which two separate types of bacteria, each moderately infective, combined to produce a most virulent combined infection, which literally caused the death and putrefaction of the involved tissues, extending from skin to underlying soft structures). The sickening stench was appalling, and since it was midsummer, the patient could mercifully be moved out onto the balcony.

A search of the hospital chart and a discussion with the nurse in charge revealed the fact that every possible kind of treatment had been tried, but nothing managed to halt the inexorable march of the destructive process. Those involved had tried Dakin's chlorinated solution in water and in paraffin, acriflavine in glycerine and in paraffin, iodoform gauze, even scarlet red ointment, but all to no avail. As a final desperate try the patient had been suspended for a whole week in a tub of constantly flowing and changing warm saline, but it proved quite useless.

Philip first checked the patient's diabetic status and satisfied himself that the management was not at fault and that the sugar level stayed under tight control. Next he considered the type of organisms they were dealing with, and it seemed that these were *'anaerobic'*, that they thrived best in an environment deprived of oxygen. He covered the entire wound area with wet dressings of hydrogen peroxide, changed every three hours. Next, he obtained some rubber catheters and cut out a series of tiny holes in the terminal eight inches. He went to the surgical stores and obtained a glass connector with six outlets, previously used for irrigations with Dakin's fluid. The catheters were connected to the glass connector and this in turn was inserted tightly into a single hose which was connected to the outlet valve of an oxygen cylinder. The sister thought the young medical student was crazy, but was intrigued and gave him every encouragement.

The stench remained in Philip's system for days. Whatever he ate or drank smelled and tasted of the death and decay of human flesh. Even his cigarettes stank and nauseated him. By the fourth day he had lost all sense of smell, and the dreadful aroma no longer bothered him. At the same time, the steady trickle of oxygen, bubbling at slow speed into the patient's wound night and day, began to take effect, and a week later there was diminished infection and signs of healing. Another two weeks, and healing was just about complete; it would even be unnecessary to perform any grafting. The patient was ecstatic, and both Philip and his Chief were gratified by the remarkable result. As for the nurses and other patients, they were happy to breathe clean air once more.

The last four months in the tour of surgical wards were under the aegis of the great Sir Grant Grant-Sutton. This fine and cultured Scottish gentleman, with refined and gentle manners, his soft Edinburgh accent and amazing memory for names and faces, was said to be the world's greatest surgeon. Philip marvelled at his superb operative skills and the courage with which he faced even the most fearsome surgical challenges at the operating table. His surgical assistant was the house-surgeon Arnold Chadwick, and whoever watched them working together was convinced that the assistant's adroit movements, dovetailing artistically with those of his chief, could cut the operating time by as much as 50 percent. It would be a sad loss for the great man when his house-man moved on to other fields.

The weeks passed by at unbelievable speed, and Philip enjoyed every aspect of his work on this service. One, 'Sir G-squared-S' as he was affectionately known, was conducting his student group on regular afternoon ward rounds, accompanied by the sister and house-surgeon. After an exhaustive review of the first five patients he came to the bed of a young woman in her early twenties; she seemed to be rather agitated and watched the parade anxiously.

"Can any of you speak French?" he enquired of the group.

"Bosnar can," came several voices.

"Sufficient to converse with this patient, Mr. Bosnar? She is visiting here from France and speaks hardly any English."

"I think I can manage, Sir."

"In that case I would appreciate it if you would kindly take over the history and physical of this patient. We already have her urinalysis which is normal, and her blood count which shows a mild '*neutrophil leukocytosis*' (increase in white blood cells). She probably has acute appendicitis but I would like your own evaluation."

Philip's feet were ten feet off the ground and his head was in the clouds. The language presented no problem and the rest was easy. Diagnosis: early acute appendicitis.
Several of his pals now suggested that he ask the Chief if he might do the appendicectomy himself under guidance.

"Good God!" he protested, he'd be furious."

"Don't you believe it. The old man gave one of his dressers a haemorrhoidectomy two years ago."

Philip gave the great man the details of his history and examination and concluded with his diagnosis: early acute appendicitis.

"And what do you think we should do, Mr. Bosnar?"

"Take out her appendix without delay, Sir, and may I request the privilege of doing the procedure under guidance?"

Philip couldn't believe it was his own voice delivering such a request.

"Of course you shall, young man. You've certainly earned it."

He turned to his houseman with a smile.

"You'll give him a hand won't you, Chadwick? Why don't you set the case up for 2.30?"

The prospective surgeon was still in a dreamlike state when he made his three inch incision in the lower right abdominal quadrant. There was very little bleeding, and the young lady was nice and slender, so he soon reached the peritoneum without difficulty.

"Let me place these retractors for you," offered his assistant.

"You'll notice there's no sign of peritonitis and here's the cecum sitting up nicely. Now if you put your finger under the cecum and flip it upward and outward the appendix should pop out," and by God so it did! "I can leave you now. Sister Lomax can look after you for the rest."

This must be a wonderful dream. Soon Dora would enter, naked, and they would make violent love without restraint.

"Let me adjust these retractors so they stay in place."

It was the same Sister Lomax who'd been made Dame of the Order of the British Empire only two years ago.

Philip remembered the ceremony in the front courtyard, when King George the Fifth, accompanied by Queen Mary and with a host of important officials standing by, made the presentation before a crowd of applauding students: "For courage above and beyond the call of duty." There had been an explosion in the operating room and fire had broken out just next to the oxygen cylinder and the ether. Sister Lomax immediately wheeled the patient on the operating table out of the theatre, ordered everyone out, then returned and put out the blaze single-handed. This was the heroic woman now helping him to finish up his operation.

The appendix was quite inflamed but came out easily. Drainage wasn't required and wound closure was straightforward. Like the facile Chadwick, his substitute assistant made everything simple and he was humbly grateful to her.

At six o'clock, as promised, he went to meet Dora at Victoria Station, where her train would be arriving from Croydon in about ten minutes. He remembered how excited she was when she first landed the job as part-time English instructor at an excellent grammar school located in that sleepy town in Surrey, some eight months ago. She took classes from Tuesday to Friday, and then came home for long weekends.

She loved her new job, and was very proud that she was fully accepted by the teaching staff and her pupils. Not only that, but she was now drawing a small wage that gave her a newfound feeling of true worth and even independence. The headmaster, a semi-invalid who might have to give up his job because of recurrent illness, had been most helpful and thought she could be recommended for a fulltime staff appointment.

When Philip saw her coming through the gate, he caught his breath at how vibrant and radiant she appeared. The new position was, without a doubt, helping her to blossom into full womanhood and he was happy for her. They embraced each other and walked a short distance to a cozy little restaurant, one that had become a Friday evening favourite for them. As was the new custom, she insisted on paying for the meal and he put up no argument. She brought him up-to-date on the week's happenings at her school, and discussed the perfection of Shaw's *Saint Joan*, the current subject in her class. As they were finishing their icecream desserts Philip could hardly contain his precious secret.

"I've got some exciting news to tell you, but I'll save it for our walk."

They took an underground train to Blackfriars and walked along the embankment arm in arm, while he carried her valise with his free hand. The evening was beautiful and the late summer twilight seemed to carry a special magic. Dora listened happily to his description of the events leading up to his first surgical operation and then to the details of the actual appendicectomy. But at times she seemed a thousand miles away, and then she would apologize and ask him to repeat some point of his thrilling narrative. There was something different about her tonight; perhaps they were both excited about all the new events that seemed to be closing in on them with each passing week.

As they reached Trafalgar Square she suddenly said,

"Let's not walk any further. Let's go home instead."

Perhaps, thought Philip, this was the night when she'd say Yes and he would – at long last – reach Step Three. When they arrived at her home and entered the front parlour she whispered, "I'd like to leave the lights off, Phil," and he felt uneasy. On the way home she'd hardly said a single word, and even now he found it impossible to gauge her mood. They sat together on the sofa in silence, but he didn't feel her body softening into his, the way it always did. There was a silence between them, but not the warm, sweet silence of lovers. Strangers then? What was happening?

His body grew cold and his heart felt encased in lead. He couldn't believe the words that escaped from his mouth. Surely they were being uttered by some malicious stranger.

"It's over, Dorie, isn't it?"

"Yes, Phil," came the quiet reply, "it's over."

"Is it something I've done or failed to do?" he asked.

"It's nothing like that. It was bound to end sooner or later and now it has."

Philip's brain refused to function any further and there seemed nothing more that he could say; his vocal cords seemed frozen.

After a long and deadly pause they kissed as friends, not lovers, and parted with shattering politeness. He staggered home in a state of shock and went straight to bed.

That night he endured bad dreams. Perhaps the worst was the one in which a sneering Mr. Snavely, his 6th Form English master, read from his pupil's poem in a nasty, scornful manner,

'But I must ever meditate and ponder

My greatest joy and grief since I was born.'

The whole class hooted in derisive laughter as the schoolmaster set fire to the poem with a lighted match, while Philip shouted "Why? Why?"

He was still trying to shout the question when he awoke in a cold sweat and then, after a restless eternity, sank back into a fitful sleep.

CHAPTER 7

1940

The courtroom was almost full. It was on the second floor of the new courthouse, built in 1937 and situated on the south side of Fourth Street, two blocks east of the Blaikie building. Philip was seated at the left-hand lawyers' table, between Adams and McPherson. Just behind them, sitting nervously in the front row, was his darling Patricia, and at her own request none of her friends were there to give her comfort. It was tacitly agreed between them that they should not be present as observers, in case there was anything that might come up to embarrass the young couple. It was better that way, and Patty drew courage from the obvious confidence of Phil and his counsel. In any event, the trial, which was scheduled for 2 p.m. on the afternoon of Monday, the second of May, didn't get under way until 2.30.

Judge Tompkins, now about seventy-five years old, quite senile and absentminded, had difficulty controlling the court proceedings. There he sat on his thronelike chair, his apple-cheeks glowing with satisfaction, his great bulk impressive in its robes, and his expression benign but vacant. To the right of the defense table sat a resplendent Dr. Tom, sporting a new gray silk suit and looking more like Savile Row than OK Corral. He fidgeted with nervous anticipation at the prosecutor's table, and whispered with obvious agitation into the ear of his suave lawyer Mark Standwick.

After the lengthy preliminaries, which seemed to take forever, the trial got under way. The plaintiff was sworn in and questioned about his credentials, but Standwick was interrupted by the judge who declared, "I'm sure the defense will concede the doctor's long career and excellent reputation."

McPherson rose angrily to his feet and replied, "We are prepared to concede only that he is a qualified medical doctor of many years."

Standwick looked like a cat that had just swallowed the cream.

"Tell us, doctor, did you send a five hundred dollar money order to Dr. Philip Bosnar?"

"I sure did."

"When was that, and to which address did you send the money?"

"I sent it on March the fifth, 1939, and addressed it to Dr. P.Bosnar, care of Dr. F.G.Stroud, thirty-five Victoria Terrace, Stafford, Staffordshire, England."

"What was the money for?"

"Objection, your Honor. No money order has been produced as evidence in this court."

"Overruled. I hardly think the money order needs to be produced," said the judge with a cordial smile, and McPherson sat down, seething.

"Would you like me to repeat the question?"

"That won't be necessary. It was an advance to cover the cost of Dr. Bosnar coming to

Vanwey with his wife."

"By `advance' I take it you mean loan."

"Objection!" McPherson was on his feet again. "The term `advance' does not always signify a loan. In England it could simply signify paying for something ahead of time."

"Overruled. The witness may state his intention."

"Sure I meant a loan. I don't hand out money for honeymoon trips."

"Objection again, your Honor, I really must protest."

"Overruled. Learned counsel will have his opportunity to cross-examine."

Things weren't going well, thought Patty, as she noted the growing frustration of Philip's lawyers and Standwick's smug expression.

"Did you at any time, either by spoken or written word, promise to turn over this money with no expectation of repayment?"

"You mean an outright gift? Not a chance!"

"Did Dr. Bosnar at any time, either by spoken or written word, indicate that he considered this payment an outright gift?"

"Never. I'd have laughed in his face."

"In fact you expected that a qualified doctor would never Welch on a debt like this."

Patty's heart sank like a stone. McPherson was on his feet at once, his face flushed with anger.

"Your Honor, I must protest this whole line of leading questions and defamatory comments, based on nothing but assumptions and plaintiff's interpretations. It is beyond the bounds of propriety."

The drowsy judge roused himself and remarked in gentle reproach,

"Mr. Standwick, you really should avoid any defamatory comments by you or your client against the defendant."

"We apologize, your Honor, but my client is deeply hurt and disappointed by the conduct of his former associate."

He turned back to Blaikie.

"Did you fire Dr. Bosnar or did he quit?"

"I tried real hard to make it work, but he was always acting hoity-toity, telling me where I was wrong. Me! With all my years of practical experience. I sure felt like firing him, and more than once."

"I must protest again, your Honor, in the strongest terms."

"Oh very well. You really must control your client, Mr. Standwick. Please proceed."

And so it dragged on, with question, answer, objection, over-rule and apology. The proceedings seemed to be moving in frustrating circles of legal indecision. As for the old Judge, he was yawning and nodding off when Standwick announced he was finished with his direct examination of the witness.

"In that case, Mr. Standwick," said the judge in a sleepy voice, "you may cross-examine the defendant."

All three lawyers looked nonplussed, and an uneasy murmur ran through the courtroom. It was Adams who broke the tension and saved the court further embarrassment by rising to say he was ready to cross-examine the plaintiff.

After a few moments of confusion the judge roused himself and said grumpily, "Of course, of course, let's get on with it."

"Now, doctor, tell me, did you or did you not seek to obtain the services of a qualified surgeon early in 1939?"

"Yes I did, that's right."

"And you were especially eager to get one with the English Fellowship of the Royal College of Surgeons?"

"Sure. I was hoping to get a first-class man."

"And so you did. There are only sixteen surgeons with this degree in the whole of Canada, isn't that so?"

"About that many, I guess."

"Or that few, to put it in perspective. So it could be said that you sought Dr. Bosnar and not the other way around. In fact it was an advantage for your practice."

"Well I sure wanted the right man."

"And that's why you were prepared to pay for the Bosnars to come to Vanwey, isn't that so?"

"Not their expenses. I never promised that."

"But you sent a money order for five hundred dollars."

"Yes, but it was an advance, a loan."

"Is that what you told Dr. Bosnar or was there a written contract?"

"No. I just took it for granted."

"Whatever you took for granted could hardly be an obligation on Dr. Bosnar to repay you, could it?"

"Objection, your Honor. The question is argumentative and prejudicial."

"I withdraw the question, your Honor."

But the point had been made with the judge and with the people of Vanwey.

"You didn't get along very well with Dr. Bosnar, did you?"

"No, he was hard to get along with, always disagreeing with anything I said or did."

"But surely in surgical matters he was the expert and not you?"

"Objection, your Honor. Irrelevant and immaterial."

"Sustained."

"Exception! This matter was raised by my learned friend himself, in direct examination of this witness."

"Maybe so, but I want you to get off this line of questioning."

He was too late. The rugged face of Dr. Tom, self-styled hero of the wild west, was contorted with rage and he snarled,

"But you don't know what I found out when I went over...." It was obvious he was out of control and Herb Adams astutely cut him short.

"We are not interested in your discoveries. No more questions."

Judge Tompkins, barely awake, consulted his large gold pocket-watch and announced, "This would be a good time to adjourn. The court will reconvene at 10 o'clock tomorrow morning."

There was a brief conference in one of the counsel chambers between the Bosnars and their two lawyers, and McPherson seemed surprisingly upbeat.

"Things aren't going too well, are they?" asked Patty.

"Oh, I believe we scored some excellent points in cross- examination," McPherson countered, "don't you all agree?"

They did, but Philip felt compelled to add, "I've never known a judge to be so blatantly prejudiced in favor of the plaintiff."

"That will probably work in our favor," Adams reassured him, "as the judgment will balance things out by rendering a verdict for the defense."

Before they parted for the day McPherson asked Philip, "What was all that nonsense about what Blaikie thought he found out? Anything we have to worry about?"

"Nothing at all," came Philip's reply, but he knew it had been a close call. Thank God, a wise Herb Adams had shut the old man's mouth up before he could do any harm.

The Bosnars went straight home, and before going out for dinner at Jake the Greek's they held a brief council of war.

"Let's see now," Philip commenced, "on the basis of questions and answers so far I would put McPherson and Adams well ahead of Standwick."

"I know," Patty conceded, "but you must admit the judge ruled heavily in favor of the other side."

"Maybe so, but McPherson's point about balancing things up with a verdict in our favor makes good sense. Besides, I thought Blaikie came completely apart under cross-examination."

"What about that little item just before the close when Blaikie suggested he had something on you?" She sounded a bit worried.

"You know what that was, Patty. He must have found out when he was in England that the Bosnars are a Jewish family and hoped to toss it into the trial as bait for Vanwey's antisemites, maybe even pressure us to leave town."

"That's what I thought," she agreed, and he continued.

"They must have laughed him out of Canadian headquarters in England when he offered his services as a veteran army surgeon. I bet it was just another grandstand act on his part."

"Do you think he met his son in London?" she asked.

"If he did it's obvious he was unable to get Ted to support his version of the five hundred dollars in a signed affidavit."

"I wonder, when he was unsuccessful along those lines, if he ferreted around for anything he could use against you."

"There was absolutely nothing to use other than my origins and if I'm asked the direct question in court I'll give them the direct reply," and his voice hardened, "if not, they can go to hell and hint as much as they like."

The next morning, the trial resumed shortly after 10 and Philip was sworn in. McPherson confirmed his client's degrees and surgical experience in three senior resident hospital appointments. This testimony went unchallenged.

"Tell the court how you came to learn that Dr. Tom Blaikie was looking for a qualified surgeon."

"I first heard about it in Stafford, England, where I was working as assistant in a surgical practice. At the Stafford General Hospital I met a Dr. Medford from Saskatchewan who knew Dr.

Tom Blaikie very well and told me he was looking for a surgeon, preferably with his English F.R.C.S."

"When was this?"

"The first week of March, 1939."

"Please continue, Doctor."

"I discussed the matter with my fiancee, and we agreed to a meeting with Dr. Edward Blaikie, as arranged by Dr. Medford. We met the following week at the Strand Palace Hotel in London."

"And what was discussed at that meeting?"

"We talked about the nature of Dr. Tom Blaikie's practice and requirements, and the fact that I would be an important addition to the practice and the scope of surgery that could be handled."

"What about financial arrangements?"

"I was to start at one hundred and fifty dollars a month plus the rent-free use of a flat, what was called a `suite' by my interviewer."

"Not a very princely remuneration, was it?"

"Objection, your Honor!" Standwick roared indignantly.

"I withdraw the question. Now what about travel expenses?"

"I explained that moving to Canada and all the way to Saskatchewan with my wife, after our marriage in early July, would involve a considerable expenditure on my part and this would have to be covered by Dr. Blaikie senior."

"Was an amount agreed upon?"

"I said that five hundred dollars should cover all my expenses."

"And this was the amount agreed upon?"

Standwick leapt to his feet.

"Your Honor, I really must object to this in the strongest terms. Dr. Blaikie's son is not here to confirm the alleged interview."

"If my learned friend wishes to refute our version of the agreement then surely it is up to him to produce the witness. We contend that the burden of proof is on the plaintiff."

"I'm afraid I must allow the question to stand, Mr. Standwick."

"Thank you, your Honor. Shall I repeat the question?"

"That won't be necessary. It was the amount agreed upon."

"Was there anything in your conversation with Dr. Edward Blaikie to indicate that you would be expected to repay that five hundred dollars to Dr. Tom Blaikie or anyone else at any time in the future?"

"Absolutely not."

"And no written letter or contract committing you to return that amount of money to Dr. Tom Blaikie or anyone else at any time?"

"Absolutely not, Sir."

"Thank you for your forthright answers, Dr. Bosnar. I have no further questions."

"Well I sure have a couple," Standwick remarked in a threatening tone of voice. He walked slowly across to the witness stand and looked Philip over with distaste. After a while he pointed his finger at him and asked, "You thought you were too good for our Dr. Tom, didn't you?"

Philip waited for the objection, but none came. It seemed strange.

"No, Sir, I wouldn't say that."

"So Dr. Tom is the baddie and you're the goodie-goodie. Just how good are you? Do you go to church on Sundays?"

Still no objection! The defendant looked at the old judge who seemed quite content, at his lawyers who looked perplexed, and at Patty who looked disgusted rather than dejected.

"No I don't."

"Why don't you?" Herb Adams rose to his feet, looking annoyed, and spoke up.

"Objection! This line of questioning is uncalled for and is quite irrelevant to the matters under consideration."

"Do you have a point to make, Mr. Standwick?"

"I do have a point, your Honor."

"Then I will allow it."

"I don't go to church because, although I believe in God, I have no affiliation with any one denomination."

"Indeed! And what do you call your religion?"

"I call it `Nondenominational Monotheism', Sir."

"How interesting."

The point was never made and therefore never challenged. Perhaps, thought Patty, Philip's lawyers weren't so stupid after all; but her peace of mind was soon shattered.

"In addition to paying for your trip to Vanwey with your brand-new wife what else was Dr. Tom supposed to pay for?"

"I'm sure I don't know what you mean."

"I'll just bet you don't. How about your wife's underwear? Was he supposed to pay for that as well?"

Standwick's face was a study in malicious triumph and his smirk was an affront.

"Objection, your Honor! This is really too much."

"Withdrawn. I'm finished with this witness. Quite finished."

Thus, in an atmosphere of anticlimax, the trial drew to a close at ten minutes before noon on Tuesday, the seventh of March. Judge Tompkins announced he would review the testimony and deliver his verdict later that month. It would be in written form to counsel for both sides.

Adams and McPherson were confident that because the judge had displayed such open bias in the plaintiff's favor he would have to rule for the defendant, otherwise it would look like a rigged trial. Philip and Patricia were not quite so sure but kept their peace.

"Mark Standwick sure didn't help his case with all that church nonsense," McPherson observed, and the Bosnars both agreed.

In the week prior to the trial, the German war machine smashed through the brave but feeble resistance of peaceful, neutral Norway. This was almost Déjà Vue to those who, like the Bosnars, had watched the inexorable march of the Nazi forces across the face of Europe. In early April it had been Denmark. Despite its inability to offer any resistance, that little country would not submit to a brutal takeover without mounting a series of labor strikes and acts of sabotage against the invaders. History would record, to its undying glory, the courage with which Denmark defied the new campaign of terror against the mere six thousand Jews in the entire country. It took the shining example set by the Danish monarch, so aptly named 'Christian', in wearing the Star of

David himself when the Jews were ordered to do so, for thousands of his countrymen to do likewise.

One week after the Vanwey trial, at dawn on May the 10th, the Germans smashed into Holland, Belgium and tiny Luxembourg. From the skies and across the flaming cities and countryside, the myth of the Phony War was finally blown to shreds, and the hideous results of Chamberlain's sycophantic policies shocked the British public out of its slumbers. Now, they could understand that 'Appeasement' meant capitulation. Shouts for his resignation echoed across the land and reached into the hallowed halls of parliament. By the grace of God and to the enormous relief of the Bosnars, Winston Churchill could now rise, phoenix-like, from the ashes of British politics. He could take his place as Prime Minister and become the hope of the free world. No matter his youthful exploits of derring-do, his erratic swings of political direction, his early obsession with the 'Communist Plot'. This was the man for the hour, and from him would flow a surging national resolve to destroy the Nazi beast.

There was one aspect of these developments that disturbed Phil and Patty: the extraordinary apathy of the average Canadian on the street. Despite the stirring news reports of a Lorne Green in Canada or a Matthew Halton in England, most people in Canada's prairie environment were more concerned with the weather and the crops. Even the trial, which was supposed to re-establish Dr. Tom as the righteous 'White Hat' of the West, failed to divert much attention from these central issues of daily concern. The shocking news about the methodical obliteration of Rotterdam from the skies by a merciless Luftwaffe, and the machine-gunning of fleeing civilians on the crowded highways and byways of the Low Countries, barely succeeded in arousing much indignation.

It seemed that *Schrecklichkeit* had not yet outraged the average citizen in serene Vanwey. As for such minor technicalities as Stars of David and concentration camps, they seemed to go unnoticed. Was this some new form of voluntary amblyopia, a visual suppression that comes from indifference?

"There are none so blind as those who will not see," quoted Patty bitterly.

The concert was a success. It was very well received by the mixed audience who packed the theater. The local women's choir was unexpectedly professional, and the solo soprano had the looks and voice to produce the warmest response. When Mayor McTeague, Master of Ceremonies, came to introduce Philip, he indulged in a little rib-poking. "If Dr. Bosnar, who's brought his violin ALL THE WAY from England, can wield his bow anything like he uses his scalpel then we're in for a treat. Otherwise we may have to ask Miss Connally to play the piano as soloist instead of accompanist." The crowd roared with laughter and applauded.

"At least," he added with a wicked grin, "I hope he plays in tune. Can't stand an out-of-tune fiddle myself."

That brought the house down. It also completely relaxed the performers and resulted in a commendable effort by both of them, including two encores, all received with enthusiastic applause. As a serendipitous bonus, the Bosnars made many new friends that evening, and it might serve to remove some of the unpleasant taste left by the recent court-case.

On May the sixteenth, the Wehrmacht crossed the Meuse and penetrated the northern hinge of the 'impenetrable' Maginot Line. The Bosnars found black humor in comparing this to the former attitude of their contemporaries, just before they left the Old Country. That overconfidence, too, had been breached by the implacable march of events. History rarely forgave blunders of judgment.

By the last week of May, the remaining troops of the British Expeditionary Forces were huddled on the beaches of Dunkirk, with the Luftwaffe trying desperately to annihilate them from the skies. Miracles, however, still seemed to happen, and three hundred thousand troops were brought back to the shores of England by a dogged British Navy, supplemented by a gallant mini-armada of private boats and pleasure craft.

No such miracle greeted Phil and Patty in Judge Tompkin's lengthy and convoluted verdict that arrived at this time. Every single argument for Blaikie was rationalized and supported. Every single argument for Philip was minimized and discarded. The verdict was for the Plaintiff without costs. If this was Canadian justice then it deserved nothing but contempt.

Herb Adams wasted no time in arranging another trip to Regina, to confer with M.A.McPherson on June the first.

"Believe me, Philip," the great man said when they were seated in his office, "I am just as shocked as you and Adams. This is a grave miscarriage of justice and I couldn't imagine that Judge Tompkins would let his former association with Standwick govern his decisions to such an extent." Philip felt he must speak up right away.

"My colleague, Dr. Forsyth, thinks I should appeal. So does the registrar of the provincial college of physicians and surgeons."

"How about your wife?"

"Although she thinks I could win such an appeal she isn't keen on dredging up this whole mess once again in front of a gaping audience".

"She's one smart Irish colleen. We should win the appeal plus costs, but it wouldn't be worth it. You might even get a hostile write-up in the papers."

"We certainly wouldn't want to risk that," Adams commented thoughtfully.

"Besides," added McPherson, "we want you coming out of it looking like the victim and not the aggressor. You'd be surprised how that can affect your practice."

"How about the legal fees? I'd like to pay these right away."

"Don't you worry about them. They won't be too heavy."

Indeed they weren't. The combined fee was a mere one hundred and fifty dollars and it was obvious that the eminent Regina barrister had foregone his customary fee. Phil and Patty would never forget this act of generosity and wrote him the warmest letter of appreciation.

"I'm really glad he decided against an appeal," Patty remarked, "and he's probably right about the effect on your practice."

Despite the necessity of another bank-loan, they both felt as if a great weight had been lifted from their shoulders.

Two weeks later, the triumphant columns of the Wehrmacht goose-stepped through the Arc de Triomphe, and a gloating Führer strutted, pranced and hopscotched obscenely on the Champs Elysee, while sobbing Parisians who watched from the sidewalks shed bitter tears of shame and sorrow. The city of lights was about to descend into the foul darkness of brutal occupation. All too soon, its cherished freedoms and artistic culture would fall victim to Nazi savagery. The trains would be filled with Frenchmen destined for slave labor in Germany's arms factories; except for the Jews. These were destined for other trains that headed for the death camps of occupied Europe.

Despite the grim news from overseas and the threat of widening German conquest, there was still no thought of conscription in the Mackenzie King government. He was accused by his opponents of catering to the francophone anglophobes of Quebec. These elements had no taste for risking life and limb on behalf of Les maudits Anglais. What puzzled the Bosnars most was that the stalwarts of La Belle Provence showed only scant concern for the fate of France, home of their ancestors. Philip wrote a forceful letter on the moral necessity for conscription, and took it around to the new editor of the Vanwey Gazette.

Doug Conway was the son of the former editor, Stephen Conway, a brilliant journalist revered by the local population. The senior Conway's recent funeral was one of the largest ever held in this part of the province. The flag at the Town Hall flew at halfmast and all places of business were closed for the day. The Bosnar letter was duly published, despite young Conway's staunch affiliation – like that of his late father – to the Liberal party and this conscription matter was, in a strange way, the start of a strong and lasting friendship.

Conway junior was very keen on a campaign for the compulsory pasteurization of milk and asked Phil for his help. Not only would this process reduce the incidence of various milk-borne diseases but, in particular, would all but eliminate the scourge of Bovine Tuberculosis. Unlike Pulmonary TB, which affected the lungs and was also known as Human TB, the bovine organism affected the bones, joints, kidneys, intestines and other viscera as well as the lymph nodes of the neck and other areas. Bovine TB could strike any child exposed to raw milk, especially native Indians, who had none of the white man's inborn immunity.

All these facts were published in a front page appeal, which was followed by a short daily column on various aspects of the subject. Conway's attempt to get support from the Blaikie practice got him nowhere. He was simply told to go to hell. The dentists and drugstore owners remained silent, but there were numerous complaints from the public about pasteurization: how it spoiled the taste of the milk, and how it destroyed its natural health-giving qualities. Needless to say, Peter Forsyth strongly supported the campaign, but was far from optimistic about the outcome.

"The people aren't really against progress," he explained, "it's just that they don't want it to come too fast."

He was absolutely right; a write-in referendum was conducted, and of the thirteen hundred and twenty-seven replies, five hundred and forty-three were in favor of pasteurization and seven hundred and eighty four against. The most telling blow was an eleventh hour door-to-door distribution of vicious propaganda leaflets. These attacked the campaign and its promoters, and were circulated by a local printer whose business was in direct competition with the Gazette's printing department, and who was an active former member of the now defunct Ku Klux Klan.

The summer of 1940 saw Philip's practice growing at a fast rate. He was getting far more surgical cases, and many of these would formerly have gone to Regina, Winnipeg or the Mayo Clinic. Not only were many of his new patients converts from the Blaikie practice, but they were coming from towns and villages that were further away from Vanwey, and in increasing numbers from North Dakota border towns. Sam Walters left for Winnipeg, where he planned to specialize in ophthalmology, and his place was taken by a Dr. Brent Slocum, who had his specialist certification in Obstetrics and Gynecology and also did some general surgery. Slocum was a big easygoing fellow with a sweet-natured wife, and Philip found him a pleasant change from his sour and uncouth predecessor. Perhaps Walters needed to get married to the right kind of wife.

Dr. Tom was starting to use the Sisters' hospital once in a while, and Slocum was using it for most of his admitted patients. The old Blaikie hospital was obviously destined for early conversion into apartments, but it wasn't likely that the owner would starve. In addition to his practice, even though it was falling off, he had widespread investments in real estate all over town. Beside these, he was the proud owner of a fair-sized herd of cattle, most of which were prize Hereford Whitefaces. The farm was situated right on the U.S.A. border, and the Bosnars vividly remembered their first visit to the property about a week after their arrival in Vanwey.

Blaikie drove his aging Buick, with Sam Walters in front and Marcie in the back, where she shared her space with a large buffalo-hide car warmer and sundry hospital dressing tables needing repairs or a fresh coat of enamel. Phil and Patty followed behind and found it difficult to keep up with the lead car. It was being driven as if by a madman, raising great clouds of dust from the gravel and dirt roads. Visibility became minimal, and following the first car was treacherous.

When they arrived, they found that the farm wasn't very impressive and the buildings looked a bit neglected. The place was handled by a Meti family who were among the poorest of Blaikie's patients. The Hereford cows lacked the charm of Jerseys and Guernseys, the grace of Holsteins and the sturdiness of Black Angus stock, and their undercarriage was far less impressive than the more familiar dairy cattle Phil and Patty had previously known. They found it peculiar that there was nothing to indicate where the international border ran and felt it would be easy to cross into either country without challenge, especially at night.

Some of Blaikie's enemies claimed that the farm's strategic location made it an ideal location for the smuggling of Canadian booze into a thirsty U.S.A. during the bleak and arid years of Prohibition. It was even hinted that it was during these perilous times Dr. Tom first carried a gun, along with one or two hard-eyed characters who 'took care' of any threats to the farm's safety. Others believed the good doctor made his fortune, like many of that era, by selling prescriptions of which the main ingredient was ethyl alcohol. The guns were used to fend off mayhem by any disgruntled bootleggers who registered displeasure at such unethical competition.

There was no clear proof of these allegations, just conjecture and rumor, but there was always the cautionary remark that 'dead men tell no tales'. Perhaps it was a constant reminder of what happened to the key witness in a notorious 'rum-running' trial a few years previously. He'd been shot dead while being driven to the Vanwey courthouse with his Royal Canadian Mounted Police escort. Silence became more than golden after that particular incident, and people were wary of imparting any knowledge of details. Above all, they were careful not to mention names.

By August of 1940, the CBC was broadcasting news of the Battle of Britain, describing the waves of Luftwaffe bombers sweeping over southern English seaports. It was good to learn that R.A.F. bombers were starting to attack enemy bases in occupied western Europe, but the satisfaction was short-lived. In September came the shocking news of the fire-bombing of London by fleets of German planes. This was the infamous doctrine of *Schrecklichkeit*, so dear to the hearts of the Nazi High Command. First, destroy cities and their civilian populations. Next, destroy the will to resist and finally, the will to survive. Civilian targets had now become more important than military ones. It was to be the standard pattern for Nazi warfare.

Peter Forsyth, whose name had been on the list of army reservists, was now called up to join a Canadian base hospital that was being set up in the south of England. He was happy with the call-up, in sharp contrast to his wife and three small children who dreaded his departure. As for his practice, he left it confidently in the hands of Philip Bosnar. This was now the third week of September, when the threat of impending snowfall was already evident in the chilling winds and freezing rains sweeping across the prairie plains, and Peter would soon be off to the training camps of southern Ontario and the unknown hazards of wartorn Britain.

Patty commented that he looked very young and jaunty in his dress uniform, with his shining Sam Browne belt and smart swagger-stick. Phil knew he'd miss him in more ways than one. At the same time, he envied him more than he could admit and cursed the stubborn inertia of the British and Canadian bureaucrats who kept him in civvies. Meanwhile, the news from his family was disturbing. His Dad had sent his wife and ten-year-old son to the safety of Bath, that serene city of grace and history, while he remained behind in London to safeguard the continuity of his business. At night, he carried out his rooftop fire-watcher duties, in keeping with his responsibilities as district fire warden.

Philip felt like a shirker in the peace and safety of southern Saskatchewan, light years away from the European War. Patty reminded him that he couldn't do much about it, and that perhaps an opportunity might still arise. She understood how he must be feeling, and despite her desperate wish for him to stay, she almost hoped he'd be able to fulfill his ambition and get over to England as an army surgeon.

There was one incident that marred the pleasant atmosphere of Forsyth's departure. One of the drugstore owners threw a Bon Voyage party for him and made the tactless error of including Dr. Tom Blaikie's name on the guest list. The Forsyths and Bosnars managed to avoid him during most of the evening, and everybody seemed to be having a good time, chatting, eating, drinking, and wishing Peter all the best. It appeared, however, that Blaikie wished to do his well-wishing in private. He took his former associate by the arm and dragged him off into the coat-room. When they emerged some ten minutes later, the older man had a self-satisfied smirk but Peter looked somewhat shaken and pale.

After the Bosnars got home from the party, Phil said, with some bitterness, "I guess the bastard just had to get it off his chest," and Patty replied, "True, but I didn't think the Peter Forsyth we know so well would go into shock at the news that you're Jewish."

"Don't worry, Patty," he consoled her with a smile, "As it has been written, `This too shall pass', and I'm sure no harm has really been done." **(He was right as it turned out, but in the strangest of ways, and Peter Forsyth would treasure his friendship with Philip to the day he died.)**

According to news reports of the war in Europe, the nightly agony of London continued unabated, but German pilots were paying heavily for their brutal war on women and children, the sick and the elderly. St. Paul's proud and battered dome symbolized the determination of Londoners to defy the hateful enemy; to survive the nightly shower of fire, destruction and death, without being forced to their knees. It was from these steadfast and resilient citizens, that the defiant Winston Churchill seemed to draw inspiration for his most stirring oratory, and the free world applauded.

CHAPTER 8

1934-35

Rafael Bosnar knocked on his son's door and was invited to come in. The room was a large combination bedroom and study on the third floor, with a bookcase containing various medical volumes pertinent to his current studies. It was decorated on the top shelf with an impressive array of large multicolored crystals. These were made by Philip during his matriculation year and they masqueraded as giant emeralds, rubies, amethysts and sapphires.

During the daytime, he could look out on the Square below, and the park and tennis courts just across the street. At night, however, he kept the curtains drawn so that no distraction would interfere with his concentration. It was rare for anyone to interrupt him during his studies, except to call him for a meal – if they hadn't, he probably wouldn't eat at all – and when his Dad entered, Philip knew at once he'd come to talk.

He was seated at a wide oak desk covered with books and papers, notebooks and journals, and the quilted eiderdown on his brass bedstead was covered with a similar array of study material. As usual when he was working, he'd been prowling the room, stopping once in a while to check a reference, and he only sat down to write a note elucidating some tricky point in the text. The calendar on the wall behind him was turned to the month of May, 1934.

"Come and sit down, Dad. Here, take this chair, you'll find it more comfortable." His father sat down and looked concerned.

"I'm worried about you. Something's wrong. Are you ill?"

"No Dad, I'm not ill, just off my food a bit, that's all."

"You can tell that to anyone else but not to your father. He knows you much too well. If you're not ill it must be either your work at the hospital or something to do with your ladyfriend."

"It's nothing you have to worry about Dad, honestly."

"Well, we can forget about your hospital work, as I'm sure you would have told me. That leaves Dora Henderson. You didn't get her pregnant, did you?"

"No Dad I didn't. Perhaps it would have been better if I had."

"You've broken up. That's it, isn't it? Of course, I should have known right away. Your whole timetable has been off for the past week, and you seem somewhere else when we're talking to you."

He came around to where his son now sat half-slumped in his chair, and put a comforting arm around his shoulder. Silence.

"All right, if you won't tell me then I must ask you directly. Have you two broken up? Is it just a quarrel or for good?"

Philip exploded out of the stifling intensity of self-doubt he'd endured for the thousands of dragging moments since he asked the fatal question, "It's over isn't it?" He went over the essentials of his grand passion, and was gratified to find his father didn't dismiss it as no more than a boyish crush. When he described that final day with all of its bizarre improbability, he was able to convey the strange fatalism that seemed to hold the final scene in its inexorable grasp. He related how he found himself unable to insist that she tell him why it must end now, just when the future looked so bright.

"It may be over, Phileep, and perhaps it's just as well it happened now rather than later, but don't you intend to find out why?"

"I'm afraid I know why, but I've always avoided admitting the truth to myself. It's because I never insisted on going to bed with her no matter how strongly she seemed to protest." He knew this snide comment was unworthy but he was too bitter for restraint.

"That's nonsense. You know it would be against everything you were taught about how to treat the opposite sex."

"Maybe, Dad, but in future I won't make stupid promises like that ever again. I'm afraid I'm headed for a life of love 'em and leave 'em from now on."

"No, my son. When you meet your real life partner and fall deeply in love, you will change your mind. But first you must know the truth from your Dora."

Philip felt so much better after this meeting that he began to plan for his next and perhaps final meeting with Dora. First the letter: forceful, dominant, irrefutable in its powerful logic. Then the meeting, with a reawakening of the romantic forces that had led to such a lasting attraction, or the final death knell of a love affair gone hopelessly astray.

'My darling Dorie,

Whatever the malevolent Genie or Demon that forced its way between us and voiced my destructive question, I stand guilty of permitting it to ruin not only what might have been a glorious evening but the happiness of two young lives.

You, my love, were no less guilty by closing a shutter, with your cold reply, against any hope of rekindling the fires of our emotions against the chilling sorcery of senseless resignation.

I repeat, 'Senseless' because no matter how I try to analyze our final scene, it still emerges as a tasteless Theater of Stupidity, lacking rhyme or reason.

Were we each becoming too obsessed with our own career triumphs? I really don't believe so. We were far too careful to plunge into that familiar pitfall. Even if it had been true we surely possess the intellectual courage to tackle such a problem with open honesty.

Was it the fact that I never had sexual intercourse with you, despite your stubborn protestations and my foolish pledge? I confess my own sins of omission and am prepared, nay eager, to make abundant amends? In fact I can think of no better way to erase the dark blot of our insane farewell.

You have no idea how many times in past encounters I had to clench my teeth and restrain my surging passions when we shared our mounting intimacies, or have you?

If our romance is to be resurrected, our future must be more in keeping

with the divine laws of nature and the ways of a man and his beloved.

As you quoted in your diary, 'Faint heart ne'er won fair lady' and by God I am no faint heart. I ask you to meet me next Monday at the Brenthaven station, when I arrive on the 6 p.m. train.

We must meet. We must talk. After that? Perhaps a love rekindled, perhaps a love laid to rest, but in the name of Heaven not a love needlessly squandered.

Philip.'

He studied hard over the weekend and kept his mind off the forthcoming meeting. As usual, during his free moments, he read every newspaper on which he could lay his hands: from the *Daily Express* to the *Star* and from the *Times* to the *Daily Worker*. It seemed that the evil virus of Fascism was spreading across Europe, yet the counterforce of Communism believed no less in the doctrine of letting the end justify the means. Just as Hitler and his malignant entourage had refined Fascism into the ultimate evil of Nazi terror, Stalin had twisted and deformed Russian Communism into the intimidation and enslavement of personal freedoms. Democracy, frail, uncertain and inefficient, still seemed the only hope for the survival of civilization, and now was the time for free nations to unite and present a strong and effective front against the forces of repression and tyranny. Now, while there was still time. Soon, it would be too late. For many of the oppressed in Europe it was already too late.

The train arrived on time and Dora was there to meet him. He'd never seen her looking more ravishing. Her face was flushed and she turned her brilliant smile into an incandescent greeting as she approached him.

"I'm glad you decided on this meeting," she said, "the last one was rather dismal, wasn't it."

Philip felt as if he'd been kicked in the stomach. She was talking in such a bright and offhanded manner, almost as if she were chatting about recent poor weather. It was as though her real thoughts were elsewhere, and he noticed she was carrying a small bouquet of wildflowers.

"I'm here to find out what the hell went wrong, Dora," he said roughly, "and polite chatter be damned." She gave his arm an intimate squeeze.

"You have every right to be angry, Phil darling. Come and walk along with me. I'm going to visit one of our teachers in hospital. The doctors have diagnosed advanced colitis, and have started blood transfusions to combat the bleeding."

Was this the reason for her preoccupation? Was her radiance associated with a new role of ministering angel to the sick and suffering: to a less self-centered attitude toward life?

"I'm sorry if I sound unsympathetic," he conceded as they slowly walked together, her arm linked with his, "but I find your attitude hard to understand. Visiting a sick friend is all very commendable but I doubt if her fate hangs on your bringing her flowers this very evening."

"I promised," she replied brightly, and Philip found his anger hard to control.

"For the love of God, don't you realize what this meeting is all about? We're here to decide the future of two healthy young people who've been in love with each other for five years. Now I want to know if it's really over. Or were you just the victim of a strange black mood that engulfed us both for no valid reason."

They had reached the end of the quiet street, and the hospital was just across the road. Dusk was falling and the hospital lights were beginning to come on, one by one, giving the scene a storybook quality. Suddenly, Philip had a sense of displacement in time as well as space, and Dora's voice seemed to be coming from some remote region where he was a foreigner.

"Listen," said the quiet voice, "It really is over. In a way I've always known it had to end some time. I'm amazed it lasted this long. I'll always love you, but I know I could never bring you true happiness as your wife."
He stood silent as she continued.

"You may have thought you loved me, but in truth it was a long-lasting romantic infatuation on your part and quite different from the love I feel for you. I was the challenge and you were the successful suitor, just like the mediaeval romances. But now it's time for real life to take over from fantasy."

"I'm certainly grateful you've got it all worked out," he gritted, "now I won't need a psychiatrist to tell me what went wrong. I don't intend to stand here like a bloody fool and debate your analysis with you. It's quite obvious you don't need mine."

"Please forgive me, my darling," she begged him, "but it was a bet after all and never a trial of patience. Only the bet was really with yourself and you won that long ago."

"I hope you haven't thrown happiness away with your bizarre logic."

"Perhaps, but I'm sure that when you meet the right woman you'll understand the meaning of genuine love. When that happens I hope you'll think more kindly of me."
There was nothing more to say. A quick hug, a quick kiss and she was gone. He walked rapidly to the station without looking back.

He kept himself very busy during the following year and soon forgot the deep feeling of betrayal and resentment at his breakup with Dora. His family noticed he was studying with more focused concentration and was engaging in many more activities. The medical school orchestra he'd started a year ago was now up to twenty-four members, and it was becoming recognized as a bonafide university orchestra. It had begun with five medical students like himself and one of the pathology instructors, who not only taught himself how to play the cello but actually constructed the instrument on which he played. The entire venture had taken him twelve months and was a true labor of love. It was this kind of dedication that injected itself into the project and made it so successful.

Rehearsals took place every Wednesday after the day's regular work period, and were held in the Students' Common Room. At first, there was heated and even physical opposition to the weekly cacophony that now intruded into the tranquil peace and quiet of the premises. As the weeks passed into months and the musicians learned to play in tune and tempo, objections turned to approval and even support. Philip was a strict conductor and insisted his baton be followed at all times, especially by the tympanist, and anyone playing out of tune was told in no uncertain terms that such deficiencies wouldn't be tolerated.

By early 1935, the orchestra was almost reaching professional levels and the rehearsals were attracting a growing audience of students. They crowded into the common room, and when there was no available space inside they gathered outside, listening to the rehearsals in silence but applauding an especially fine performance. A repertoire of standard classical works was gradually built up in both numbers and length, and in increasing complexity and difficulty with each succeeding month.

As the group of instrumentalist grew in size and variety, it was possible to build up potential concert programs consisting of overtures and symphonic works. The latter were performed as individual movements and were later supplemented with concertos for solo instrument and orchestra. The members decided that Philip should be soloist at the first concert, so he chose the opening movement of the Mozart Fourth Violin Concerto as a reasonable choice, while the orchestra pursued its role of accompaniment with true professionalism.

To top off the entire enterprise, Philip made a remarkable discovery of hidden talent, quite by chance. From time to time, while he was enjoying his lunch-time game of chess in the Common Room, he'd listen to one of the senior students playing hot jazz or popular favorites with an easy touch and adroit sense of rhythm, and envied him his effortless talent. One Friday evening in the winter of 1934, Philip had wandered into the Common Room looking for one of his chess-playing friends who'd promised him a late game. The lights were off and the room looked deserted, but it seemed that somebody had a record playing on the gramophone, just behind the grand piano. Chopin's Ballade in G minor, one of his longtime favorites, was being performed with an exquisite touch and he guessed the artist was probably Alfred Cortot, the French virtuoso.

When it was finished, Philip turned on the lights and crossed the floor to remove the record. To his astonishment it wasn't a record. It was the live dilettante of jazz and popular music revealing his true genius, but doing so privately and not for public display.

"Sorry for busting in on you like this, Meredith," he apologized, "but that was sensational. Where on earth did you learn to play like that?"

It was an interesting story and Meredith told it with modesty. His father had been a career diplomat and was posted to Vienna for a period of ten years following the World War, and that was where he grew up. His mother was a concert pianist, and she saw to it that her son received a first class training at the Wiener Conservatorium, where he showed considerable promise at the piano. Her tragic death came like a bolt out of the blue when she was thrown from her horse during a morning canter, and it changed her son's life completely. He gave up all ideas of becoming a professional musician and went into Medicine instead. Philip made him promise to perform at their first concert and arranged for him to attend some special rehearsals.

Then there was Sidney Carstairs – ah, Carstairs! He was a short bundle of energetic self-importance and was always trying to promote his own advancement despite mediocre talents. He came from Sheffield and hadn't lost the accent. In fact many claimed he exaggerated it. He always sported a large meerschaum pipe which he puffed vigorously but rarely filled, and he never walked, he bustled. One day he bustled up to Philip and commenced with typical hubris.

"Bosnar, old chap, Ah've bin chattin' with a bunch of the fellas and they all think you're givin' me student choir a raw deal."

"I've no idea what the devil you're talking about," Philip replied with some annoyance.

"You had no right to bar us from your concert plans."

"Actually, it was to be a concert of the orchestra with a few soloists."

"As leader of the choir Ah resent our bein' excluded."

"Look here Carstairs, you may resent what you like, but all you had to do was ask me and I would have said yes, as long as the rest of the orchestra agreed. You didn't have to chat with a bunch of the fellas, as you put it so quaintly, before asking me."

"Sorry if Ah've offended you, Bosnar, and thanks for agreein' to include us. Mebbe we could discuss the program sometime."

It was typical of the bumptious fellow, thought Philip. First do a little preliminary lobbying, then attack and finally apologize.

The concert was a huge success. The students' restaurant was easily converted into a concert hall and was filled to overflowing. Philip's parents and sister were in the front row and had a most enjoyable evening, although Pauline tried to chew her fingernails to the elbows with nervousness, especially during the violin concerto. The highlight of the evening was Meredith's superb rendition of Chopin's Ballade in G minor, and it received a well-deserved and deafening round of applause. After the concert, Philip took his family across to the Crown and Thistle pub, a favorite drinking retreat for the medical students. He introduced his family to as many of his friends as he could, and their pleasure was complete.

There was one little incident that would be remembered by the orchestra players for a long time. They all wore dark business suits for the concert, as did the choir members. Philip and Meredith wore black tie and dinner jackets, but Carstairs – ah, Carstairs! – upstaged them all, with resplendent white tie and tails. Afterward, he heard someone say that he looked like a pompous penguin and that produced an outburst.

"One day," he promised darkly, "Ah'll thumb me nose at you snobbish bastards. Ah know you look down on us chaps from what you call `the grubby midlands'. You'll see. Once Ah've chosen me specialty Ah'll make it to the top o' me profession."

(They all laughed, never dreaming that one day he would.)

It was an interesting year. Pathology and bacteriology were fascinating subjects and Philip was lost in wonder as he began to understand how the various diseases were caused. First there were the congenital diseases, including anatomical birth defects and those which interfered with normal physiology.

Then the acquired diseases, that could be divided into traumatic, infective, neoplastic and degenerative. Trauma included physical injury such as fractures, burns or frostbite, poisons and toxins such as snakebite and insect stings, acid and alkali destruction of tissues.

Infective diseases included acute infections, such as those due to streptococcal and staphylococcal bacteria, pneumonia, meningitis and gonorrhea. Chronic infections were such conditions as tuberculosis and syphilis. Viral diseases included such conditions as influenza and infantile paralysis ('Polio' in America, and 'Heine-Medin disease' in continental Europe). There were also parasitic diseases such as malaria and intestinal worms, as well as various fungal and yeast-like infestations.

Neoplastic diseases included benign tumors such as fibroid tumors of the uterus, and malignant tumors that included a whole spectrum of disordered and uncontrollable cell growth, threatening limb and life.

Finally, the degenerative disorders, which increased with advancing years but may well have started in youth. These were cardiovascular conditions such as arteriosclerosis, chronic osteoarthritis, and senile osteoporosis.

There were divisions and subdivisions, variations and cross-classifications that reminded Philip of his chess manuals. The panorama was dazzling, and gradually a clearer understanding of the immense science of medicine was emerging.

Philip's personal life was becoming fuller and more balanced. His circle of friends, both from the university students of London's Eastend and his own medical school, was constantly expanding. He was becoming more interested in hiking trips with Arty Jones and his cross-country group whenever the weather was suitable, and was renewing his love affair with music in general and his violin in particular.

Caught in the mainstream of London's seething youth, he found himself involved with amateur dramatic groups, young writers and painters, and even – despite his revulsion against what he considered 'music hall stuff'- members of the Stepney Gilbert and Sullivan Society. In truth, despite his musical snobbery, he had to admit that G & S music and lyrics were starting to sound more and more like the light operas of the great Rossini.

Among these new spheres of friendship there were quite a few attractive young women, but Philip wasn't ready for even the most transient personal relationships with the opposite sex. They'd have to wait until he passed his final examinations. The effect on these young ladies was just the reverse, and he couldn't understand why they seemed to find him attractive and tended to pursue him. His face, especially his nose, was showing some of the battering he'd been getting lately in the boxing ring. Against the advice of the boxing coach, he'd been engaging in some unauthorized sparring sessions with much heavier opponents, and his facial features suffered the consequences. Although he eventually gave up this sport, he never lost his interest in watching a well-matched fight.

Jack Dempsey had been one of his boyhood idols, but Philip long ago accepted the sad truth that Gene Tunney was by far the better boxer, just as he'd been forced to face the fact, in his early teens, that Jascha Heifetz was a greater violinist than his idol, Fritz Kreisler. He remembered his fury at the so-called 'Long Count' which, he was sure, had robbed the 'Manassa Mauler' of regaining the heavyweight championship from Tunney in their second fight. Much later, he conceded with great reluctance that the faster Gene represented a new era in boxing, skill versus raw power.

His current idols were some of his medical instructors, and of these, Mike Soames – who taught morbid anatomy and histology – was his favorite. He spoke like an 'Orstrihlean' but was actually from Sussex. His lectures were gems of sheer brilliance and his freehand drawings in colored chalk were masterly. Then there was Sir Leonard Wappel, who limped on an artificial limb (some said he'd lost a leg in the war), and who was personal Physician to the Royal Family. He taught his students the secrets of the hidden microscopic world. These were the arcane mysteries of bacteriology and microbiology, first revealed by such giants as Louis Pasteur and Robert Koch.

Last but not least there was Dr. Courtland, that quiet and civilized gentleman who was Philip's first cellist as well as his instructor in general 'morbid anatomy' (the non-microscopic study of pathological specimens).

The new theoretical and practical sessions in cardiology, under the tough auspices of Dr. Ian Blanding, were detailed and instructive, and Philip got a great thrill out of learning the interpretation of electrocardiograms, sometimes known by the elitist continental abbreviation, EKGs. Blanding was acquiring wide recognition for his original work on progressive EKG changes in acute coronary occlusion.

The course in Obstetrics and Gynecology was rather humdrum, but watching the mighty Walter Blaney operate was a revelation. He was totally ambidextrous, cutting and sewing with either hand and with equal facility. It often seemed as if each hand took turns acting as surgeon and assistant to the other. He was even considered by many to be superior to the great Professor Wertheim of Germany, the surgeon who introduced his radical operation for the treatment of cancer in the lower portion of the womb. An oft-repeated colloquialism was that, even in this operation, Blainey could always out-Wertheim Wertheim!

Eric Ransford, soon to be knighted, was head of the new department of urology and taught his students all about kidney stones, prostate disorders, infections and strictures of the genitourinary tract. Philip soon picked up the tricks of the trade in everything from circumcisions to cystoscopies and catheterizations, and above all, the art of prostatectomy.

During his final year in Internal Medicine, Philip learned all about infectious diseases such as whooping cough, measles, scarlet fever and diphtheria. The latter was particularly rampant in the London area and accounted for a high annual death rate among children. He learned all about the newest theories of immunity, and about active immunization by vaccines and passive immunization by injections of specific serum. He learned their applications to the field of public health, but found the rest of that subject boring in the extreme.

The weekly outing to the Northeastern Hospital for Infectious Diseases proved interesting beyond all expectation. Here, he was able to see for himself the full range of complications that could follow what often seemed simple childhood infections: obstruction of the larynx in diphtheria, nephritis in scarlatina, and pneumonia in whooping cough. Then there were the occasional exotic and deadly infections in sailors who came off ships from far-off ports of call: smallpox, typhoid, typhus, even bubonic plague. Most of these latter cases ended up quietly, even surreptitiously, in the Hospital for Tropical Diseases.

By the late summer of 1935, Philip Bosnar entered the two-phase practical training program in obstetrics. The first part consisted of night duty as an undergraduate houseman in residence at St. Clement's College Hospital. Here, he was able to handle a fair number of standard deliveries under close supervision and fine anesthetic facilities on hand when needed, particularly for 'Primips' (the first-timers).

He learned when and how to perform a neat 'episiotomy' under local anesthesia – that merciful cut to enlarge the vaginal outlet and prevent a massive tear – and how to sew it up expertly following delivery. He learned when and how to perform forceps extractions at different levels with specific types of instruments, and he watched the occasional performance of Cesarean Section by the experts. He acquired the art of detecting fetal distress in time, and how to resuscitate the distressed infant following complicated labor.

After the first phase of his training in obstetrics, he journeyed to Stratford in East London, where he lived in 'digs' (a boarding house) for the next few weeks, and did his obstetrics at the Queen Charlotte Hospital, a 'lying-in' hospital (one devoted to obstetrics). Most of the day, he carried out prenatal examinations in the outpatient department. He learned to detect the earliest signs of the dreaded toxemia of pregnancy and take the appropriate measures, and to make an early diagnosis of twins or breech presentations. He handled a number of routine and forceps deliveries, assisted at Cesarean Sections and performed internal and external version to correct malposition of the infant.

His chief, built like a professional wrestler, was aptly named Mr. Brewes. Of course, anyone possessing the degree of F.R.C.O.G. (Fellow of the Royal College of Obstetrics and

Gynecology) was entitled to be called Mister instead of Doctor. An F.R.C.S. degree entitled one to the same esteemed title, and Philip dreamed of the day he would be called MISTER Bosnar with that unique inflection. Watching Mr. Brewes filled him with admiration, most of all at his gentleness and delicate technique, and it was only much later that he learned his muscular chief was President of the Royal College of Obstetrics and Gynecology.

Philip was well aware that all his wealthier chums had gone across to Dublin to get their Ob.Gyn. training at the prestigious Rotunda Hospital, but he felt in no way short-changed and was sure he was receiving the best possible training in this field. He loved helping his patients through various phases of their distress during the time of impending and actual birth. One of the most thrilling elements of this training period was what they called "going out on the district." This meant home deliveries, usually very difficult ones and most often at the request of the attending midwife who'd run into trouble.

One thing was soon abundantly clear to Philip: these midwives were no amateurs. The women were well-trained, dedicated and efficient workers in their field, and in most cases handled their responsibilities with efficiency and dispatch. He felt they could teach him a lot, just as he'd been taught so much by most of the experienced nurses with whom he worked, especially in the departments of surgery and Ob.Gyn, albeit in an extracurricular fashion. As he progressed, he was conscious of owing them a great and permanent debt of gratitude despite the fact that many of these senior nurses, called 'Sisters', were referred to as 'Dragon Ladies', especially the older and more experienced ones.

Philip learned a great deal about people, too. The boarding house at which he stayed was run by a husky Maltese in his middle forties and his older English wife. Salvatore Mazzini was possessed of striking good looks, a strong artistic inclination, and a deep love of Italian opera, especially those of Puccini and Verdi. He would often hum snatches of his favorite arias until his wife screamed for him to stop. Lottie Mazzini was a devotee of raucous music hall favorites and had no time for what she called, "hysterical Wop nonsense." Salvatore did most of the housework, including the superb cooking, while his faded blonde spouse, parading in housecoat and curlers at all hours, seemed to do most of the complaining. Nevertheless, Philip was happy and comfortable in their house, enjoyed his meals, and in particular looked forward to his musical discussions with Salvatore.

There were three other boarders. One was a skinny piano-tuner who sometimes played popular tunes on the upright piano in the parlor, those he knew were Mrs. Mazzini's favorites. At such times, her husband found urgent duties requiring his attention in the basement. The other two boarders were retired schoolteachers. The small slender one, Miss Collins, was an excellent pianist, but she only played when the mistress of the house was out on a shopping trip. The large heavyset one, Miss Jenner, was reputed to have been a fine singer in earlier and better times.

One day, Miss Jenner told Philip she'd been well on her way to an operatic career, and even accepted for entry into the Covent Garden company, when disaster struck. She was singing a Donizetti coloratura excerpt in rehearsals when her voice disappeared without warning and she was not even able to speak. The management called in their throat specialist and he diagnosed the problem as a case of 'chronic granular laryngitis', despite the fact that she never smoked and had no known allergies. She had just suffered her first acute attack of vocal failure and there would be others. The specialist warned her against singing, shouting, or even excessive talking, as these might exacerbate the condition. She remained faithful to these instructions most of the time, but slipped once or twice and paid the penalty.

What Philip failed to notice, was a careful conspiracy already taking place between his fellow boarders and Mr. Mazzini. On the Monday of Philip's last week at the boarding house, Salvatore announced that he had two tickets to the London Palladium for a new musical revue, said to be the hottest show in town. They were dress circle seats for Thursday night's performance and he wondered if the piano-tuner would like to go with Mrs. Mazzini. Both were delighted at this thoughtful gesture and Salvatore soon found himself smothered in the grateful embraces of his bosomy wife, and embarrassed by the piano-tuner's profuse thanks.

On the Thursday evening, following a sumptuous dinner and Mrs. Mazzini's departure with her ecstatic escort, Philip was asked to sit in the large armchair on the far side of the parlor. Miss Collins sat at the piano while Miss Jenner and Salvatore stood on either side. What followed, sent shivers down Philip's spine, as he found himself overwhelmed by a whole evening of Tosca and La Boheme. Miss Jenner sang with an amazing clarity of tone and subtle inflections of the deepest emotional understanding. The statuesque Maltese brought a dramatic intensity to the roles of Mario and Rodolfo, with a rich tenor voice that blended magnificently with the soprano of his tragic heroines. Miss Collins' accompaniment on the piano was nothing short of inspired.

The entire performance was a tour de force, and the audience of one responded, time and again, with wild applause and loud bravos. As the last duet drew to a close, tears were streaming unashamedly down the cheeks of all three performers. Philip became aware of a large lump in his throat that made it difficult to speak. He had to blow his nose loudly before telling them how marvellous they'd been and how much he appreciated what they'd given him. It was a gift of beauty and a gift of love – the shared love of music – and one he could never forget. He left on the Saturday morning, and the Tosca and Mimi of Thursday night could only bid him goodbye in a hoarse whisper.

At home, the routine was much the same except for slight changes in his time table. Except for Wednesday evenings and the continuing orchestra rehearsals, Philip usually arrived to meet his family at about 6 o'clock in the early evening, when the winter darkness had already fallen. Supper was served at 7 and he was expected to tell his family all about his day's activities, or at least those parts that would be most interesting to them. He tried his best to have them share, with vicarious avidity, his day-by-day experiences and new areas of knowledge. In the eyes of Klara Bosnar, her Phileep was already England's greatest doctor and would soon be its foremost surgeon. The residents of Grantham Square treated him as if they believed her claims, and just as his father was always called "Rafael The Gentleman," Philip was now known as "Phileep The Doctor."

During their conversations around the dinner table, his family never made the slightest reference to his breakup with Dora, and concealed both their relief and deep sympathy. After dinner, he always went upstairs to study but stopped off to visit his little brother Clayton in his parents' bedroom on the second floor. He adored little Clayton as if he were his own child rather than a brother who was seventeen years younger than him.

When Klara Bosnar made the extraordinary discovery that she was pregnant, after so long a gap, the secret was kept as long as possible from her children. Perhaps she prayed for a miscarriage, but most of all she blamed her husband for being careless. In truth, Rafael Bosnar was both shocked and delighted, since he'd assumed they'd both reached that safe plateau of married life when precautions were of doubtful necessity. It was Pauline who first made the discovery, and soon she and her brother were making witty remarks intended to reduce their mother's embarrassment. But, as soon as they were informed these were in poor taste, they stopped.

The choice of name was an interesting one. Klara Bosnar had one real weakness, that of becoming romantic about every attractive man who entered her life. It might be Eric Freedman, the Polish scientist who'd been a welcome guest in their home since his early student days. It might be their family doctor or dentist, and it most certainly was Clive Brook, that most suave and handsome of all English film-stars. Her last magnificent obsession had been Mr. Clayton, the charismatic young surgeon who operated on her in the spring of 1930 for 'chronic' appendicitis, at the Charing Cross Hospital. She'd worshipped him for months and seemed to identify him with the Swedish actor Nils Asthor, who starred in that heartbreaking film 'Sorrel and Son'. It was the story of a brilliant young surgeon who was called upon to operate on his own dying father, a tragic figure who sacrificed everything in his life for the success of his son.

In any event, 'Clayton' was the name chosen for the new infant and he was adored by every member of the family, and by none with more intensity than Philip, who behaved like a doting new father, even now that the little chap had reached the wonderful age of five. The minute he finished his supper, Clayton was permitted to play until bedtime. In the summer, it was on the pavement in front of the house, but when the days grew short, it was in the second floor front room serving as both a bedroom for his parents and a playroom for the youngster. The little lad was given one special responsibility before going to bed each evening, and that was to clean up his toys from the floor and stow them away neatly. Philip loved to spend at least half an hour playing with his beloved brother before retiring to his own room and getting down to the books.

His finals in January of 1936 were called the 'Conjoints', otherwise known as the M.R.C.S,L.R.C.P. (Member of the Royal College of Surgeons and Licentiate of the Royal College of Physicians), that Philip thought sounded far too important. However, when a medical student made it safely to shore after braving the pounding seas of so many arcane subjects, as well as the dangerous shoals of practical Medicine, perhaps he'd earned the honored titles, if only for sheer endurance.

Philip had to admit the written papers were straightforward and the orals eminently fair. He encountered no difficulty in passing, and was happy to do so while still only twenty-two. What now faced him was far more important as far as his future might be concerned. The most sought after awards in the medical school were the two Broughton scholarships in a wide range of clinical medicine and pathology, and the Larkin Gold Medal in a wide range of general surgery, including the special field of surgical pathology. These exams took place after the finals, while the subject matter was still fresh in the minds of the contestants.

He knew the competition would be tough, as his closest rival was the unpleasant and unpopular Felix Ainslie, a man who possessed great powers of concentration and a near-photographic memory. Sadly, he was also a staunch and vocal supporter of Oswald Moseley's black-shirted Fascists. Where Philip might have an edge, was in the pressing knowledge that winning one of these awards was essential if he wished to get Grant-Sutton's house job next Autumn.

The Broughton exams seemed fairly standard, but Philip concentrated on revealing – as far as possible – the small practical applications of each discipline that he'd picked up during his clerkships and dresserships. As for the Larkin paper, it was a dream: 'Discuss surgical drainage'. Out of the time allotted for each essay, he spent the first forty-five precious minutes cataloguing and categorizing the different divisions and subdivisions of this vast subject into a full-page chart, with carefully numbered compartments and segments. Working from this base, he was able to formulate a cogent presentation which he hoped would strike a chord with his examiner, Eric Ransford, the topflight general surgeon turned topflight urologist.

He made a point of stressing the urological aspects, such as drainage of a blocked kidney, blocked ureter, blocked bladder or blocked urethra, and didn't fail to include drainage of a perinephric abscess (pus around the kidney), as well as surgical drainage of the Space of Retzius (located in front of the bladder) in prostate removal. Nevertheless, he tried not to stint on the other subdivisions, and went for details, always details. As for the orals, these were a pleasant scientific chat with his eminent examiner on a wide range of subjects, and he felt at ease.

When the results came out, he was stunned. Getting the gold medal was a real gift from Heaven, while winning the second Broughton (the first was won by Ainslie) completed a veritable cornucopia beyond his wildest dreams, and he knew this would consolidate his chances of landing a job with Sir Grant Grant-Sutton.

His family was overjoyed: his mother's bosom burst with pride at her Phileep, his sister shed tears of joy, his father seemed to glow with an inner happiness and even little Clayton seemed to understand that something wonderful had happened to his big "bruvva." Philip was aware of an immense gratitude to his Creator, but recognized with the wisdom of experience that today's triumphs did not preclude tomorrow's disappointments.

Now it was time to get a good houseman job, especially one that paid a decent stipend. He couldn't afford the luxury of an unpaid house physician job at St. Clement's. Besides, he wanted to get as much surgical training and practical experience as he could before taking his final F.R.C.S. exam at the earliest opportunity. This wouldn't be until 1938, when he reached the mandatory minimum age of 25.

He perused the advertisements in the medical journals with great care, and finally applied to the Royal Gwent Hospital in Newport, located on the Welsh border not far from Cardiff. There was an opening for Senior Casualty officer, and a good salary was offered. When his application was accepted, he felt his primary Fellowship must have given him a distinct advantage.

(It was here, in his very first job, that he would get a solid grounding in emergency surgery, in premarital sex, and in getting to know Canadians. These interesting 'Colonials' would prove to be the first ingredient in Dr. Philip Bosnar's decision, years later, to seek fame and fortune across the Atlantic.)

CHAPTER 9

1940-41

In July of 1940, the Baltic states of Lithuania, Latvia, and Estonia were repossessed by the Soviet Union. This coldblooded act appeared to Philip Bosnar as another page in Stalin's diary of perfidy. First, the partition of Poland in the autumn of 1939, with the Soviets grabbing the eastern half, then the invasion of brave little Finland by Stalin's army in November. As for France, Philip's birthplace and home to his father's surviving relatives, this once proud nation was now a vassal state of its Nazi overlords; with a Fascist-oriented and doddering Marshal as puppet president and a corrupt prime minister readily doing their bidding. Soon, the trains would be hauling their victims eastward in crowded cattle cars, some to slave labor in the war factories, others to concentration camps.

In Britain, the bombardment of London's civilians, especially in the teeming Eastend, continued to destroy historic buildings and humble homes alike, to cripple and murder innocent men, women, children, the sick and the elderly, in a nightly ordeal of fire and explosion. Philip thanked God that this Schrecklichkeit was forging the steel of London's resilience in the flames of its tormentors. He thought of his uncomplaining father spending night after sleepless night in the chill and damp of the London autumn, fire-watching for the fellow-citizens of his adopted country. Even the loneliness that followed the dispatch of his beloved wife and child to the safety of historic Bath, failed to distract him from the urgent sense of duty that energized his nightly vigil.

Looking out at the starry night sky above Vanwey, Philip wondered if at this very moment his father's thoughts were with his son, in merciful safety across the seas. It was at such moments that he felt he must, by hook or by crook, get into uniform and over to wartorn Britain. He would at least have the opportunity to share his family's dangers, and feel a sense of genuine involvement in the most righteous war of human history.

Peter Forsyth was now in Sussex, helping to set up a base hospital that one day might find its way to continental Europe, when the great day of Allied invasion finally came to pass. In the meantime, he would be studying the surgery of warfare, attending special seminars and watching the leading contemporary surgeons at work in London's operating theaters. How Philip envied him! But he tried to shut out all thoughts of the wrenching separation from Patty, the price he must pay. He was well aware that Pete's separation from his wife was far less wrenching, as it was in the hearts of so many Canadians who flocked to the colors. To such men, going to war almost constituted an escape from marriage, although it must be distressing to leave ones children and other loved ones.

Meanwhile, in the safety of Saskatchewan's prairie environment, there were the pressures of the Bosnar practice, which by December was growing by leaps and bounds. Patients were coming from a hundred mile radius, and whenever he referred a particular type of case to the appropriate specialists in Regina or Winnipeg, they were beginning to banter about referring some of their tough cases back to him in Vanwey. In nearby North Dakota, the doctors arranged for a professional border pass which permitted him to be called for emergency operations in critical surgical situations. One way or another, his reputation appeared to be growing and the former trickle of American patients was reaching flood proportions. It was nice – for a change – to be paid with real money rather than chickens, loads of grain, eggs by the dozen, or just promises.

In the Sisters' hospital, he shared available bed space with the Blaikie practice, but was keenly aware that a disproportionate number of Slocum's patients were being admitted when they could just as easily be treated as outpatients. Many seemed slated for major surgery on the flimsiest of clinical indications, and there were rumors via the nurses' grapevine about the removal of normal gallbladders for flatulent indigestion and normal uteri for excessive menstrual bleeding. Slocum refused to submit his operative specimens for the customary pathology examination (at the university laboratories in Saskatoon), and this was a great worry to all concerned, especially the Sisters. Warnings were given and ignored, but no other action was taken. As far as Dr. Bosnar was concerned, the situation was a disappointment. He'd hoped that the popular and personable new man in Blaikie's practice would be someone with whom he could work and organize a plan of reciprocity for emergency coverage.

Dr. Tom died suddenly in late September under obscure circumstances, and although there were dark hints of foul play, the issue was never pursued by the police. It was reported that he'd fallen down the stairs in the early hours of the morning while Marcie was away visiting her sister in Regina. There was a private funeral, but Sam Walters, who arrived from Calgary on hearing the news, was barred attendance. Whatever his reaction, he telephoned Philip and arranged to meet him the following morning in the lobby of St. Cecilia's.

Philip came down from the O.R. with a white lab coat covering his operating greens, and Walters rushed over to the elevator and greeted his former adversary with surprising warmth and friendliness.

"Nice to see you looking so well, doctor," he said cheerfully, "Hope you've forgiven me for being such a rotten prick, the way I treated you."

"That didn't bother me too much at the time. I just couldn't figure out why. As a matter of fact I even wondered if you might be a bit crazy."

Walters laughed and replied, "I'm surprised you didn't guess. I had the old fart eating out of my hand before you arrived and was scared everything would change unless I eased you out."

"Well, you sneaky bastard, you sure managed that, but I really should thank you instead of condemning you. Things couldn't have turned out better for me."

"Listen Philip, is there somewhere we can talk in private?"

He'd lowered his voice conspiratorially and Philip led the way to the radiography office which he knew would be empty at this time. He was about to learn the real reason for Sam Walters' trip to Vanwey.

"I must tell you that those of us close to Dr. Tom realized he had quite a lot of money stashed away. Marcie was just waiting for him to die, since she was bound to inherit a good chunk of his loot, with the rest going to young Ted. The old man hated his first wife, actually his only wife 'cos he never got a divorce, and he had no use for his brother in Winnipeg. They fell out when Sandy sided with Mrs. Blaikie against brother Tom."

Walters took out a pack of Sweet Caps and offered one, but Philip refused and lit one of his own.

"Get to the point, Sam," he said, looking at his wristwatch.

"OK, OK, I'm getting there. After you left I tried hard to improve my position with the old bugger but it didn't work out so I left. I knew he always kept a heap of cash in that big Chubb safe downstairs, but after he kicked the bucket they opened the safe and it was empty. At first they thought it might be Marcie, but she was mad as a wet hen and she sure is no actress. Anyway, she shouldn't beef. I wouldn't be surprised if he kept his latest will there, leaving a chunk to me. Now we'll never know. Slocum has gotten very buddy-buddy with lawyer Standwick and God knows what they've cooked up between them."

"Do you have any proof or is this all conjecture?" Philip asked impatiently.

"Hang on a minute," Walters insisted, "I know there's no proof, but I'll bet Slocum got to the safe first, the sly bugger. Just ask the guys who knew him when he was interning at the Winnipeg General. He's the kind of sneak who can knife you in the back while shaking hands and giving you a friendly laugh. At least when I knife you it's with no pretense at being friendly."

"Granted all you say is true, Sam, what's the real purpose of this meeting?" asked Philip.

"Just thought I'd warn you. Owed you at least that much. Just watch him and never turn your back."

They walked to the big exit door leading to the parking lot and Walters turned on an afterthought.

"Rotten shame about the trial. Pure spite. The old fart won the trial but lost the town. May even have cost him his life." With that he was gone, and Philip found it impossible to wish him good luck.

It was difficult not to like Brent Slocum. He was lanky, athletic and good-humored, and there was little doubt about his popularity. He was a good pianist, especially when it came to jazz, and he was a bit of a ladies' man, which certainly didn't hurt his practice. Both the Bosnars were fond of his pretty little wife Debbie, and Philip found it hard to believe the reports that his competitor was becoming increasingly abusive to the hospital Sisters and nursing staff. According to Dr. Sharpe of Bonchance, the Blaikie fee-splitting act with referring doctors was still flourishing under present auspices, with Marcie well aware of all that went on, although she wouldn't be remaining long in Vanwey. With increased surgery it would have been nice for Philip to have a reciprocal arrangement with Slocum for anesthesia, but he wasn't interested. He had his own nurse for the job; she was supposed to be specially trained but Philip had watched her performance and didn't consider her too reliable.

At this point in time, Patty showed what she was really made of. She volunteered to go to Winnipeg and get training as a nurse-anesthetist, and was very persuasive. Philip gave in without much argument, since he remembered her superb past performance in any duties pertaining to the OR. In early October, he wrote Dr. Aikenhead, professor and chief of anesthesia at the Winnipeg General Hospital, and explained all his particular circumstances. He remembered being introduced to him at one of the post-exam parties, and how impressed he was with him as a scholar and a gentleman, someone of real depth and well-deserved reputation.

True to form, Aikenhead phoned back a few days later and said he'd be delighted to take Patricia under his wing and make her into a really competent anesthetist. She stayed with him for just over one month, living in the nurses' quarters and coming home for weekends to break the separation and loneliness. At the end of the training period, her mentor assured Philip that she could handle any assignment given her, and it was soon evident he hadn't exaggerated.

Philip wrote him a long letter of appreciation and asked him to send his bill for the excellent tuition he'd given to Patty. In reply, Aikenhead declared what a pleasure it had been and insisted that he wouldn't dream of charging a fee. It was evident that he was impressed with his student, and in return she arranged to have a set of volumes about antique furniture sent to his home, as she'd learned that this was one of his major interests. At the same time, Philip phoned John Kinsley, to thank him for the hospitality he'd shown Patty while she was in Winnipeg, and to bring him up to date on the situation in Vanwey. Kinsley, in turn, promised to come out and spend some time with the Bosnars, and Philip planned to book some special major surgical cases for the chosen dates.

For the next two months, everything worked to perfection as Patty took on her new duties with enthusiasm. She got along very well with the Sisters and nursing staff, and whenever Philip needed her, she rose to the occasion without a qualm. She hadn't the slightest difficulty with the new Boyle gas-machine, and handled her intravenous procedures smoothly and efficiently.

Now that everything seemed to be working out so well, Phil drove up to Regina and went straight to the Army Medical headquarters, where he had an hour-long interview with Lieutenant-Colonel Hughes, the D.M.O. (District Medical Officer). This was the man who ran the medical show for MD12, (Military District number 12). During their conversation, it became clear that it would take a lot of effort to get through all the red tape and bureaucratic inertia of the Canadian Army before he had any hope of joining up, let alone getting back to Britain and bringing Patty with him as an army surgical nurse. The D.M.O. was sympathetic and said he'd see what he could do and would get back to him, but it was obvious that nothing more could be done, at least for the present.

That evening, when he got back to Vanwey, Philip heard the news on the radio: Neville Chamberlain, Hitler's perennial appeaser, had died at his home in Hampshire, unmourned and unrevered. At least he was spared the guilt, some five days later, of witnessing the barbaric destruction of beautiful historic Coventry by the Luftwaffe.

One morning in early December, Dr. Bosnar was halfway through his morning operating list and was finishing up a ventral hernia repair, when there was a sudden commotion at the head of the table. Patty had just fainted. All that was left to do was the final wound closure, and Philip left that to Cliff Sharpe, his assistant, then hurried to his wife's side. The fainting spell was very brief and Patricia insisted on completing the anesthetic. She certainly looked fine and her pulse and blood pressure were quite normal.

After the surgical patient was wheeled out to the recovery area, the O.R. Sister took Patty into a small anteroom and laid her down on the couch. It was there, at Philip's request, that Sharpe examined her and found no evidence of any grave cause for her unusual spell. Was it due to an overlooked leakage of anesthetic gas, Philip wondered? No, the G.P. reassured him, and delivered the laconic verdict: it was simply a case of overlooked early pregnancy.

When the prospective father recovered from the shock, he joined his radiant wife in unrestrained happiness, and there were congratulations all round from the O.R. nurses and ecstatic Mother Superior – who'd been sent for as soon as the fainting spell occurred. That day, the brilliant new career of young Mrs. Bosnar came to an abrupt end, and she would never again resume the nursing career of which her husband had been so proud.

During the past few months, a strong friendship had developed between the Mother Superior and Dr. Philip Bosnar. She consulted him frequently on medical matters and ways to improve hospital standards. He, in turn, sought her help with problems in the nursing department, and was glad to receive her shrewd suggestions for improving ward rounds and instruction of nurses in general. She was very worried about Dr. Slocum and his abusive manner toward the nursing staff, his improper utilization of beds and his refusal to send his surgical specimens to Saskatoon for the usual pathology examination. Philip could only advise her to talk to the culprit directly, and if this failed, to put her complaints in a formal letter and request a written reply. He made it clear that it was inappropriate for him to get into the situation directly, unless Slocum was willing to accept him in the capacity of advisor or arbiter. So it was left at that, but Philip had a nasty premonition that this problem would, sooner or later, reach crisis proportions.

There was only one subject on which he and the Superior had regular arguments. It was about the Vatican's official position on Nazism, and in particular that of Pius the XIIth. His failure to condemn the appalling atrocities of the Nazi regime in the strongest possible terms, and to place the Catholic church unequivocally against Hitler's satanic policies, was a betrayal of Christianity and civilized mankind. Hitler's persecution of the Catholics, his frenzy against the Jews, his oppression of political opponents, his slave labor and death camps: none of these seemed to excite more than mild reproof from His Holiness. If Jesus Christ could condemn the ungodly policies of the Sanhedrin, then surely – as current inheritor of the forthright Nazarene's mantle of responsibility – the Pope should have the courage to thunder his outrage at the evildoers of his day.

Sister Mary Sybil took the view that His Holiness was working frantically behind the scenes, rather than placing the Vatican openly on the side of the Allies and thereby enraging a demented Führer into even worse acts of vengeance. With each passing week, he felt her defense weakening and sensed her inner concern that his accusations might prove to be true (may the Good Lord forbid!). He didn't press his advantage. Time and history would be the merciless judge.

On the same subject, Patty felt even more strongly (if that were possible) than her husband. She felt morally betrayed by the world leader of the Catholic Credo in which she was raised, and she despised him for besmirching the world's Catholics with his cowardly bleatings against "acts of violence." (No specifics, PLEASE!) In a strange fashion, she always seemed to arrive at positions identical to those of her beloved husband on matters of politics and morality. It wasn't simply a matter of conversational osmosis or even telepathy, for she was always fiercely independent in her judgment and conclusions. Instead, it was as though their reasoning mechanisms had entered into synchrony. Yet this didn't stop them from having many lively discussions in which each was prepared to act as devil's advocate, so as to ensure total objectivity in reaching their decisions.

On the subject of religion there were no differences, yet he harbored a secret admiration and gratitude for her resilience. Not once had she made the slightest move to attend a church service since coming to Canada, despite strong pressures – real or implicit – from Monsignor

Kelly, the hospital Sisters and Catholic friends like the Adams. She and Philip were simply accepted as non-practicing Catholics and that was that. Any other interpretations were kept strictly private and never openly discussed.

The news from the war fronts seemed nothing more than a series of advances and retreats, alternating attack and defense, triumph and defeat. At times it seemed that nothing could stop the Nazis from winning the war, not even their preoccupation with maintaining extermination camps right across Europe, an obsession that must have diverted massive resources in military manpower and transportation from their primary war effort.

In Britain, there were extraordinary attempts in the highest circles to conceal the truth behind a bizarre solo flight: that of a deranged Rudolph Hess to Scotland on May 12, 1941. It was reported that his parachute landing was made in order to meet with the Duke of Hamilton for private talks. Nobody in authority seemed to offer a believable explanation. What was published instead, was the feeble excuse that the noble Duke was unavailable because he was on flying duties with the R.A.F. For twenty-four hours a day?

What an extraordinary coincidence, that this scion of British aristocracy happened to be one of the leading figures in an Anglo-German friendship society: one that flourished even during the worst days of prewar Nazi aggression and terror. Appeasement was evidently still alive and well, even with its prophet safely in the ground. How about a nice declaration of peace between the United Kingdom and the Third Reich? Then, on to Moscow with banners proudly flying, the Union Jack and the Swastika side by side. Poor demented Rudolph; too bad he'd jumped the gun. Forty days after they locked him away, his beloved Führer declared war on Russia and ordered his generals to attack along a two thousand mile front.

That summer, the Bosnars became increasingly immersed in the Canadian way of life and the unique culture of the prairies. Their accents became tinged with a North American twang and they shared the common concern about the weather, the crops, provincial and federal politics, the affluent East versus the depressed West, the sinister machinations of Bay Street and the heroic performance of the Canadian armed forces.

At this exact time, the powerful influence of the Mother Country was destined to make itself felt throughout the life of Vanwey. A Commonwealth pilot-training base was being established five miles south of town, with most of the officers British, but a few Americans as well. The trainees were equally divided between British and Canadians.

Early in July, Philip drove out to the base and sought out the Medical Officer, Graham Hobart, a pleasant and friendly G.P. from Nova Scotia who was delighted to learn that Dr. Bosnar was a full-fledged surgical specialist. This was the start of a strong affiliation between the Bosnars and the R.A.F, one that would last for the next two years.

Hobart and his wife Ethel became good friends of Phil and Patty and often came to their home for a visit. Patty expected her baby in mid-July and found Ethel most helpful. Meanwhile, Philip met the top brass at the pilot-training station and arrangements were made for him to act as civilian surgical consultant to airforce personnel and their families, in full liaison with Squadron Leader Hobart.

Patty was beginning to get very large, and Cliff Sharpe was checking her closely for water retention and possible early toxemia of pregnancy. Fortunately, this complication didn't develop and she remained mobile and active throughout her pregnancy, although she hated to be seen looking "so enormous," as she called it. Meanwhile, Philip was making more frequent trips to the airfield and going up with one of the top instructors for low-flying maneuvers, skimming the telephone wires (or so it seemed to Philip), and filling him with a new hunger, that of flying. He even did well in his tryout on the flight-simulator which duplicated a standard cockpit, with a pilot's view of takeoff, flight and landing.

He was surprised he hadn't flunked this apparatus, known as a Link Trainer, since he had only monocular vision, with right-sided Suppression Amblyopia. This condition, a veritable loss of effective vision in the affected eye, never bothered him in daily life, not in reading and not in operating. He simply used a parallax technique with imperceptible head movements for depth perception. It was doubtful, however, whether he could ever pass the strict standards necessary for a pilot's license. In any event, the matter was permanently settled when Patty learned of her "crazy" husband's unauthorized flying escapades, and made him give his solemn pledge to cease and desist for now and evermore. He kept his pledge, albeit with extreme reluctance, but he was developing a strong bond with the R.A.F. officers and trainees, out of which many new friendships developed. He'd never lose his love of everything associated with flying, and would always feel the closest empathy with these winged warriors who soared into the wide open skies.

Patty was due to have her delivery on the twenty- first of July, but the next three days passed serenely without the slightest sign of labor. She was now very large and weighed an astonishing one hundred and seventy pounds. Other than this most unwelcome expansion, she remained cheerful and healthy, with a normal blood pressure and normal urinalysis. By the 28th, Philip felt impelled to take some action, and after dinner he took her for a drive to the airbase and back. The trip was always rather bumpy and this one was no exception. His overdue wife, of course, knew exactly what was going on and was more than willing to cooperate.

Labor started shortly after midnight. Phil phoned Dr. Sharpe, who admitted his patient to the obstetrical unit on the third floor of St. Cecilia's. As soon as he arrived, he checked her carefully and found a normal 'occipito-anterior lie', with the baby's head descending nicely into the true pelvis. The fetal pulse remained strong and steady, and although this was going to be a large baby, there was no evidence of disproportion. Dr. Sharpe doubted whether he'd need to employ forceps, except possibly in the very last moments of delivery.

Once Patty was reassured, she asked Phil to leave her alone and go off somewhere where he could be called when the baby was born. He phoned his favorite drinking buddy, Doug Conway, who was delighted to join him at Bert Shank's Dominion Hotel. Bertie set aside a large room for their use, complete with chesterfield, table, chairs and telephone. He also was thoughtful enough to provide two bottles, one of Seagrams VO rye whisky and one of Cutty Sark scotch, a large club soda, a pitcher of iced water, some tumblers and a minibucket of ice. He joined his guests for one quick drink then wandered off to bed, leaving them to their celebrations.

Doug Conway needed no special reason to party. He was a brilliant editor, probably even better than his famous father, and a lightning wit, and he was blessed (or cursed) with an enormous capacity for alcohol. Philip valued his friendship and found it most stimulating, because of the vigorous intellect and devastating humor of the man. But there was a price to pay, namely his own increasing consumption of alcohol, mostly in the evenings. By force of habit, he timed his drinks carefully and always managed to stay on the right side of inebriation. Doug drank twice as much, yet remained only mildly drunk and fully functional, except on those occasions when the black mood overtook him and he went on a prolonged and solitary binge.

Most of the time, Conway liked company when he was attacking the bottle, and Philip was his favorite companion, especially at the newspaper office. That was where they reviewed the next day's editorial page together and stayed to discuss sundry news topics – laughing uproariously at the occasional hilarious incident or situation. On this particular occasion, there were two reasons for celebration. One was the awaited arrival of the Bosnars' firstborn. The other was the safe arrival of the Conways' third child a week earlier, a fine baby boy.

Philip had seen the petite Jenny Conway (born Genevieve Duval in Trois Rivieres, Quebec) safely through her last pregnancy until the final week, at which time her life and that of the baby were suddenly threatened by the dreaded complication of Placenta Previa. (This is a condition in which the placenta is situated in the region of the uterine outlet, producing massive hemorrhage in severe cases and initiating fetal distress). Jenny's had been the most severe type, requiring blood transfusion and emergency Cesarean section. Mother and child had come through the ordeal safely, and were back at home, healthy and happy. Doug was so overjoyed that he went on the wagon for forty-eight hours. Gratitude to his close friend required no eloquent words. It was almost tangible and could never fade.

Philip kept his drinks carefully paced and remained fully sober, phoning the hospital every hour to make sure all was going well in the labor room. At long last, about 2 o'clock, he drifted off to sleep. Doug was already snoring loudly, his glass still half full and his ashtray heaped with butts. At 6.45, the phone rang loudly and cleared every cobweb from Philip's brain. The news was marvelous, and it was announced over the phone by a triumphant Clifford Sharpe. At exactly 6.30, Patty had given birth without fuss or complication, to a fine bouncing baby boy weighing nine and a half pounds. She required very little anesthetic and only the slightest assistance with low forceps. A small episiotomy was needed to prevent tearing and this had been nicely repaired, so there should be no further trouble. The boy was big and strong, with perfect appendages and a lusty pair of lungs. By the grace of God he had his mother's good looks.

Doug was finishing his drink and lighting another cigarette as he slowly came up to the surface, and he insisted that Philip repeat the phone message word for word. They had a hasty trip to the bathroom, freshened up, got themselves looking half decent, then went out to the Bosnars' new Chrysler car and sped off to the hospital.

Patty was still sleepy, but looked radiant and serenely happy. The nurse brought in the baby and Dr. Bosnar became just another overwhelmed new father, completely captivated by the sight of this gorgeously proportioned little fellow, with finely shaped head and perfect features. The infant's hair was silky and very blonde, his body and limbs were strong and presented a full complement in all departments, and he greeted the befuddled grinning stranger with ear-shattering howls of disapproval. Philip was ecstatic as he kissed his beautiful wife, mother of his perfect firstborn man-child, and promised to return later that day. Doug remained discreetly in the background, but came forward before leaving to admire the baby and give Patty a congratulatory kiss. He and the proud father then drove back to the hotel, and Cliff Sharpe agreed to meet them there for breakfast.

By 10 o'clock they'd finished their bacon and eggs, ordered up by the ever-considerate Bertie, and all three felt more human, even if they didn't look it. Doug Conway thought it was now time for some serious drinking and Philip concurred, but not before informing the hospital switchboard that he was signed out for the rest of the day to Dr. Slocum. This sort of situation was the one and only unwritten agreement between their two practices that was honored without question.

Heavy persuasion was required to convince the abstinent Dr. Sharpe that this was a special occasion. He could therefore make an exception by accepting one small and well-diluted glass of scotch. After gallantly agreeing, he was out cold in fifteen minutes. They awakened him for lunch at 1 o'clock, and he felt fully recovered and refreshed. Doug was well on his way to the happy state, while Phil had gone through a fair quantity of scotch but was still compos mentis and steady on his feet.

A short time later, they all went down to the dining room where Bertie joined them for a light lunch. It was, he announced, "on the house," in honor of the two doctors who were reciprocal actors in the joyful event, of Patty, and above all, the newest member of the Bosnar lineage. Phil thanked his companions, settled up with Bertie, made sure Cliff was well enough to drive back to Bonchance, left Doug to continue his party at the newspaper office and drove home. After a shower and shave, a change of clothes and phone calls to the hospital and to Patty's closest friends, he was ready to go back and bask in the glory of a happy new mother and wonderful child.

Two weeks later, they moved into their new house on Third Street West, just a couple of blocks from the hospital. Their new abode was a rambling, one-storey, red brick bungalow, with a good garden space at the back that would be suitable for a children's play area, a vegetable plot and some flowering areas. It was comfortable, reasonably priced and theirs.

The house-warming was a rousing success. All their closest friends came, including the Hobarts from the air base. Baby James Spencer Bosnar was the center of attraction, and he refrained, with admirable self-control, from crying and screaming even when his proud father approached. Philip felt this augured extremely well for their future father-son relationship, and he was delighted with the name he and Patty had agreed on. He felt sure their son would like it, too. As for Patty, she looked resplendent in a new white summer dress, her weight mercifully back to a fashionable one hundred and fifteen pounds.

The Hallidays were most helpful during the party, and the buxom and motherly Mrs. H. was a blessing to Patty at an important time in her life. This middle-aged couple, who lived in a humble cottage a couple of blocks away, had offered their services during Patty's second trimester of pregnancy. Mr. H. was willing to do odd jobs as handyman, and his wife would be a combination nanny and baby-sitter for the new child. In this joint capacity she was worth every cent of her wages. It was, the new parents hoped, the beginning of a long and warm relationship.

Philip was making frequent trips to the air base, but sticking to his pledge of refraining from flying. He was getting to know an ever-widening group of pilots and in turn was widely recognized and accepted as one of their kind. He was even accorded honorary membership in the officer's mess, a privilege that included Patty in the frequent social functions at the station. She and Philip, in their turn, began to entertain the airmen and their wives with increasing frequency, and introduced them to their Vanwey friends.

By the end of summer, a powerful new social force had entered the fabric of daily life in Vanwey, and – in an almost imperceptible fashion – the town seemed to become more caught up and involved in the fate of Britain and the war in Europe. On the professional side, the airforce brass officially designated Philip Bosnar as civilian physician to the airmens' families, a duty he was happy to assume in addition to serving as surgical consultant to the base. Those requiring major surgery were transferred to St. Cecilia's, and there was no problem with service red tape.

Easing of the rules was not only due to the efforts of Squadron Leader Hobart, but to the overall base commander, Group Captain Cummings. This dignified R.A.F. veteran was in his early fifties, tall and gray-haired, and he reminded Philip of Percy Marmont, that well-known British film star of the early thirties, and one of his longtime personal favorites. Cummings was the quintessential English aristocrat, a man who could adapt to any location and culture in the true tradition of last century's colonial leaders. He fitted smoothly into Vanwey's alien environment and was soon popular with the locals, even those who ordinarily laughed at the veddy English types (such as the expatriate remittance men scattered across the rough prairies, with their absurd airs and graces).

One late summer evening, at an outdoor barbecue party thrown by the Sundstroms in their valley home, Phil and Patty watched the Group Captain's superlative performance and were filled with admiration. He was served corn on the cob, known in Britain as 'maize' and considered only fit for livestock consumption. With perfect aplomb, he soldiered bravely through the messy ordeal without the slightest break in his impeccable table manners, and paid his hosts a glowing compliment on the excellent taste of the novel food, to which he was a total stranger but an enthusiastic learner.

The dances at the base were first class, and the dance band under the baton of Flight Lieutenant Richard Mallory was of top professional standard. The food was delicious and the drinks were plentiful. Mrs. H was always delighted to babysit little Jamie on all such occasions, and the lively fellow never gave her the slightest trouble.

The Bosnars did their best to reciprocate the generous airforce hospitality, but it was difficult to maintain adequate liquor stocks in their home because of wartime rationing. The boss of the local liquor board outlet was a patient of Philip's and did his best to slip him an extra bottle from time to time, but it still became necessary to take an occasional trip across the border into North Dakota and smuggle some extra supplies into Canada. Meanwhile, it was good to see that more officers' wives were arriving week by week. This meant that airforce families were moving into rented homes around town, thus leading to a desirable mixing of civilian and service society, with an easy breakdown of earlier barriers.

During their occasional forays into the U.S.A, Phil and Patty became aware of a welcome drift away from anti-British isolationism and a growing desire by the average American to join in the Allied crusade against the Third Reich and its supporting nations. The great Franklin Delano Roosevelt, idolized by the Bosnars, seemed to be winning out against the pro-axis policies of Senators Gerald Nye, Hamilton Fish and their fellow propagandists, especially Henry Ford and Charles Lindbergh.

Philip felt sure that, at any moment, the Americans would openly enter the war on the side of the Allies. With each passing week, there were more U.S. flyers arriving at the Commonwealth base in the valley and they confirmed these impressions, although they believed it would take Japan's entry into the war to mobilize Americans into an all out war against the Axis forces. In support of these hopes, it was noteworthy that Churchill had met with Roosevelt on the high seas for a consultation on military policy that was published as the Atlantic Charter. The date was August 12, 1941.

Kinsley came out from Winnipeg toward the end of August, and stayed with the Bosnars for three days. Philip arranged for the visiting surgeon to assist him in a few heavier OR cases specially booked for that time. The first was a difficult *Abdomino-Perineal Resection* (removal of the rectum and adjoining colon for cancer of the lower rectum). Customarily, this operation was done first through the abdomen, with establishment of a permanent colostomy, then completed from below with the patient's legs up in stirrups. A newer technique had been introduced by Lloyd-Davies of St. Mark's Hospital in London, England. Bosnar and Kinsley used it on this occasion with great success.

It was a synchronous operation, with one surgeon and assistant working above and the other surgeon and assistant below. The trick was to get the patient's legs up and out of the way, to make room for the lower team without crowding the upper team. In this morning's case, the large stirrups worked very well with the aid of some ingenuity in placing the scrub nurses, drapes, separate instrument tables and trays. The table tilt and height had to be just right, as well as the lighting. The two surgeons felt like pioneers, and although it might be some time before this method became accepted as standard, they felt that at least they had given the new technique a major boost.

That evening, Philip and John discussed the main advantages of the synchronous approach. It saved time and it saved blood, but it would be decades before it became commonplace. Later that evening, after dinner, John slipped into the kitchen and told Patty, "Your husband's a crackerjack surgeon. He shouldn't be working in a small place like this."

"I don't believe he'll move before he gets into the war," she informed him, "but perhaps later on."

Kinsley never pursued the subject.

By September of '41, the German mechanized spearhead advanced to within twenty miles of Leningrad, and to the south they captured Kiev, capital of the Ukraine. The long-suffering people of Greater Russia forgot about the tyranny of Stalin's communism and knew only the cruel atrocities and indiscriminate carnage inflicted by the Nazi invaders. Perhaps, Philip conjectured, this was what the Russian population needed to shake them out of defeatist hopelessness and strengthen their resolve to snatch victory from the jaws of defeat. It wouldn't be Josef Stalin and his bemedalled generals, but the suffering common man of the USSR, who could accomplish this by sheer human sacrifice. This brave people – not its strutting leaders – deserved Britain's friendship and alliance in common cause. The great Churchill, longtime foe of Soviet Russia, clearly recognized these truths and acted accordingly, for which Philip once again felt a deep sense of gratitude.

It amazed Patty that her husband managed to maintain what seemed like an elaborate balancing act. His practice was growing by leaps and bounds, his surgery was increasing daily, he was heavily involved with the airforce, he was obsessed with the progress of the war, he was involved with the Sisters and their trouble with Slocum, he was drinking rather heavily with Conway, yet he managed to remain on an even keel and was always sober when on duty.

Occasionally, he might cut loose at a party, as he did on the night of the big R.A.F. dance early in October, celebrating the 30th anniversary of Group Captain Cummings' service with the airforce. Liquor flowed freely and Philip Bosnar felt his affection growing steadily for this wonderful group of people who swarmed around his gorgeous Patricia. The dance band seemed to be working so hard and so willingly, and none more vigorously than the sweating double-bass player. It was obvious the poor fellow needed a rest, and Philip nobly mounted the bandstand where – without argument – he took over the massive instrument for the next hour, plucking away enthusiastically although he'd never played a double-bass in his life. By sheer good luck, his performance didn't disrupt the proceedings, and Patty assured him later that he hadn't done too badly at all. Cummings, always the diplomat, graciously complimented him for his friendly assistance, and Philip's R.A.F. cronies got an enormous kick out of the occasion. They treated him as if he belonged to their outfit and was no mere stuffed-shirt civilian.

Little Jamie was the Bosnars' pride and joy and he filled Patty's void when Philip was at his busiest and away from the house most of the day. During the night she was instantly awake at the slightest sound of disturbance from the baby's crib. Philip, on the other hand, could sleep soundly through the greatest commotion, and even the baby's lustiest howls wouldn't disturb his peaceful slumbers. Let the phone ring just once, however, and he was on instant alert – 'All Systems Go!' Within seconds he could phone the border staff at the customs station, telling them he'd be coming through at top speed in answer to an emergency call from the US that required his urgent surgical intervention. He could also transmit a detailed set of orders to the hospital without the slightest hesitation or difficulty. Other than these professional interruptions, he could sleep through an earthquake.

It hadn't always been thus, and in earlier days he found it very difficult to reach the surface when awakened from a deep sleep. One early morning, a few months after coming to Canada, he'd been roused by the insistent ringing on his side table. He reached out sleepily and Patty heard his angry voice shouting, "For Heaven's sake, whoever you are, speak up. I can't hear a damn thing you're saying."

"Darling, you're talking to the alarm clock," she said.

From that time forth, he was a changed person and no nocturnal or early morning phone-call would ever again catch him at a disadvantage.

CHAPTER 10

1936-37

The Royal Gwent Hospital was everything Philip could have hoped for, and when he arrived there in March to take up his duties, he found that it a well built hospital, modern, spacious and well equipped. The wards were large and airy, and they appeared well run by the supervising nursing Sisters, who were efficient and experienced. The 'honoraries' (attending consultant staff) were pleasant and helpful and of generally high standard. It was a busy hospital and the nearby steelworks provided a steady stream of industrial accidents, most of which were of the minor variety and ended up in the Casualty department. Only the major ones went to the operating theaters. These were of high quality and the level of surgery wasn't all that different from the London teaching hospitals such as St. Clement's.

The Casualty department, which would be Philip's sphere of activity, was an efficient one. According to the hospital grapevine, its fine record rested to a large extent on the no-nonsense shoulders of Nurse Gwynneth Evans. She was a sturdy young nurse in her late twenties, short and brown- haired, and she came from the Rhonda valley. What she lacked in prettiness she made up in brisk expertise, an attractive personality and a sympathetic attitude toward her patients. Philip soon found he could learn something from this diminutive bundle of energy almost every day, and she in turn spared no effort to be as helpful as possible.

Beside Philip, the house staff consisted of three Canadians, one Afrikaner from Johannesburg and an Irish Jew from Dublin. Gil Turner was the senior resident, and he was a veritable tower of strength. A big easy-going fellow with blond good looks, he had come over to England in the summer of 1934 to get his F.R.C.S., and after he'd accomplished that, he spent six months with the world-famous Professor Lorenz Böhler at the *Unfallkrankenhaus* in Vienna. Here, he learned in practical terms what Dr. Bohler had written in his superb textbook on traumatic orthopedics, a work that was handsomely illustrated and published in at least a dozen languages. It was one of the classical texts that Philip devoured from cover to cover.

Gil's father was head of the famous Turner Clinic in Edmonton, Alberta, and he was grooming his son to take over the growing group practice. As part of the training period, Gil had taken on this job at the Royal Gwent, confident that it would provide excellent practical experience. He was given his own surgical lists, and it didn't take Philip long to perceive that Turner was the best surgeon in the hospital, both in technique and academic knowledge.

Bart Farley was tough and thickset, with a wrestler's powerful build. As a matter of fact, he'd been intercollegiate wrestling champion in his weight division while at university in Toronto, Ontario. When sober, he was a pleasant and likeable chap with a great sense of humor. When drunk – and this didn't happen very often – he was apt to go on the rampage, and on those occasions it took about four strong men to handle him. On Philip's first night, when his new colleagues threw a party for the incoming Senior Casualty Officer, Farley ran wild. Philip had sore muscles for days as a reward for being part of the search-and-subdue party.

The third Canadian, Lou Dalgleish from Fredericton, New Brunswick, was quiet and studious, and he planned to take his English Fellowship in 1937, as did Farley. Meanwhile, he was marking time as house physician, and at the end of his six month tour of duty hoped to take over a senior surgical residency. Both he and Farley were doing as much studying as possible, but while Dalgleish spent more time at the books, Farley seemed able to absorb more essential practical knowledge, with a better chance of making the grade when the fateful examinations came due.

Mickey Lavin, an Irish Jew from Dublin, was an ugly but charming rascal who suggested that Philip should contact Nurse Beatty as soon as possible, as she was very amiable to new housemen and wasn't standoffish like the untouchable Evans in Casualty. It soon transpired that her name wasn't Beatty but Walton, and she was affectionately known as BT, short for Big Tits, in honor of her superstructure. She proved most congenial and was the first of his many sexual conquests at this pleasant institution, but never without the protection so reliably provided by Rameses Medical and Surgical Supplies.

Dick Vanderveldt came from Boer stock. His grandfather had been a general in Oom Paul's guerilla war against the British. He was very tall, slender and athletic, and was both charming and good-humored, but with one notable exception. Whenever the subject of the 'Kaffirs' (blacks) came up, usually after the evening meal when the conversation wandered away from medical matters, Dickie's pro-Apartheid fanaticism transformed him into a raving bigoted monster who regarded all blacks as subhuman creatures. They were either to be kept in total submission or wiped out if they threatened the white man's supremacy.

By the end of the first month, Philip had learned many new things in the field of practical surgery. He became speedier in cutting and sewing, but at the same time more attentive to detail, so that speed was never at the cost of carelessness. With the help of Nurse Evans, he became slick at plaster cast technique and even enjoyed his application of almost two hundred casts each month, part of his duties as resident in charge of the Fracture Clinic. He also became adroit at injecting varicose veins in the Wednesday outpatient Vein Clinic, and was happy to observe the good results, although he soon recognized that most were on a rather short-term basis and some patients even seemed to get worse.

Assisting Gil Turner was a special joy. The Canadian was smooth and capable, and he made his operations look so effortless. Their discussions during these sessions, whether clinical, theoretical or operative, were on an enjoyable one-to-one basis that Philip deeply appreciated. They didn't always agree and, in fact, during evening professional discussions they sometimes got into some pretty strong debates, but Philip was gratified to find he could hold his own on many such occasions. The senior resident might call him a "stubborn Limey bastard," yet he secretly enjoyed these active exchanges and they became good friends, with a high level of mutual respect.

Gil showed him how to put on body casts for spinal fractures and plaster appliances for certain types of fractured jaw. He instructed him in the exact finger movements to accomplish a clean and efficient prostatectomy, a procedure that was done through the lower abdomen and via the opened bladder. Turner's girl friend, who'd joined him from Edmonton, stayed in a small flat close to the hospital. Sometimes in the evening, when she was with her beloved Gil, she begged Philip to play his violin for them. The lights would be turned down, and with the mood set by the flickering glow from the fireplace in the houseman parlor, he would take out his violin and ask them what they wanted to hear.

"Something romantic, Phil. You know what I mean." Chopin's Nocturne in E flat major, transcribed for violin from the original piano version, was a great favorite, as was the slow movement from Mendelssohn's Violin Concerto.

"Give us lots of the old vibrato," Gil demanded, "and some of that schmaltzy double-stopping stuff."

Philip was happy to oblige and delighted that they enjoyed his unaccompanied playing. This was usually tough on the uninitiated listener, so he had to keep his bowing and tone as smooth and silky as possible. He varied his tempo in harmony with the romantic mood but kept a meticulous accuracy of pitch, since the slightest imperfection would be revealed by the absence of piano or other instrumental accompaniment.

The months seemed to pass by more rapidly than seemed possible, yet hardly a moment appeared to be wasted. From a professional standpoint, his growth was steady in both the theory and practice of surgery, and he already looked forward to 1938, when he'd become eligible for the final Fellowship exams at the age of 25. He kept in touch with his family by writing them twice a month, and his father's replies were always a pleasure to read, so full of affection, optimism and detailed news.

Socially, his life was full and happy. He was never without a ladyfriend, but his only steady friendship was with Nurse Evans. Perhaps it was a strange exception, but their relationship remained strictly platonic. In fact, they hadn't even exchanged so much as a kiss, and that never changed. From time to time, they took a trip together into nearby Cardiff for a bit of shopping and a leisurely afternoon tea, with watercress or cucumber sandwiches and scrumptious Devonshire Splits. If the day was very sunny, they would take a train into the countryside and bask in the beauties of nature along the serene valleys of southern Wales.

On one such outing, she showed him the sanatorium by the edge of the Usk River where she'd spent two years as a child with Tuberculosis of the lungs. She'd been completely clear since the age of 14, but still submitted annually to a stringent series of tests and X-rays to confirm her cure, and so far there were no residual after-effects from her childhood disease. Like most families in this part of the country, hers had its fair share of TB victims and her father had died of the deadly infection at an early age. Naturally, the coal miners were the worst, and it seemed that the coal and rock dust made the lungs a fertile field for Koch's Tubercle Bacillus, as if anthracosis and silicosis weren't enough.

It was such a rotten shame, thought Philip, that in the midst of such tranquil beauty there should be such pestilence, not to mention dire poverty. He had come to love these simple people who endured so much and complained so little. In the Casualty department, they were so appreciative that he felt rewarded beyond any monetary recompense, and he wanted to thank them for the experience they gave him instead of the other way around.

During the lunch breaks, when there was sufficient time, Vanderveldt and Bosnar enjoyed a fast set of tennis on the grass courts behind the hospital. They seemed well matched, and when Van suggested that the loser should buy the Guinness they both enjoyed with their meal at the Legion restaurant near the hospital, Philip agreed. At first, they shared the honors, but it soon became evident that Van, once he got used to the asphalt court surface, was going to win every single time, if only by a slender margin.

"You're too good for me Van," Philip conceded one day, "I'm afraid the Guinness bets are off, unless of course you're prepared to spot me one game per set."

Van got quite furious.

"Not on your life!" he declared, "If the bets are off so are the games."

Philip decided he wouldn't challenge this ultimatum – after all, he enjoyed the games too much – but he felt that Van needed a lesson and went to work accordingly. For the next few tennis sessions, he would order a Guinness for himself but not for Van. These first three times, Van would venture a gentle, "You owe me a Guinness," but when the number got to four the expression on Philip's face warned him not to pursue the matter. Van was quite sure the debt would be paid, but just how and when remained a puzzle.

Some time later, they'd just completed a closely fought set and sat down for a quick lunch. When the waiter came over and asked his customary, "What is your pleasure today, Gentlemen?" they both ordered ham sandwiches and Philip ordered the Guiness.

"I'd like the usual and please bring nine for my friend. I want them served now," he told the astonished waiter, "and not left till later. My friend has won these Guinesses `fair and square' on a tennis bet and I want him to enjoy his winnings here and now."

The waiter grinned and brought up a side-table on which he served up the ten glasses of thick black stout with their creamy heads of rich foam. Van looked stunned but uttered no protest. The word soon got around to the other occupants of the dining room and they were enjoying the scene immensely. Moreover, Van found himself in the embarrassing position of being unable to refuse the fruits of his many victories: the appended bets on which he insisted.

An unrepentant Philip Bosnar left the place with the satisfaction of a debt well paid, in the certain knowledge that his conqueror – on a point of arrogant pride – would drink himself into oblivion unless his outraged stomach rebelled first. Philip lost no time in reporting to the medical floor that Dr. Vanderveldt was unwell and that he, Dr. Bosnar, would be happy to cover for his colleague until he recovered. The tennis was continued for the rest of their stay at the Gwent, but the bets were irrevocably cancelled from that day forth.

About the middle of his term of residency, Philip received an unexpected letter from 'Skinny' Thompson, a fellow student of his year at St. Clement's. Skinny was built like a tank and weighed a beefy sixteen stone (224 lbs). He was a valuable member of the medical school rugby team, a jolly chap who was extremely popular at all levels of student and staff. As a student, he was below average and found his surgical studies the hardest of all. It was small wonder that he was deliriously happy when he passed his finals in that troublesome subject. He considered Philip one of his closest friends at medical school and that was his stated reason for this particular letter. He wrote that he was doing a six month junior house physician job on Sapian's 'firm', and planned to go for the Grant-Sutton job in the autumn.

The real purpose of the letter was to warn his friend that he, Thompson, had the job locked up for a number of reasons. Not the least of these was the eminent surgeon's promise to Skinny's father that his son would get the position whenever he applied. This promise was given last February, when Thompson senior was admitted to the private wing of St. Clement's for removal of a bowel tumor by Grant-Sutton. Of course, Skinny's popularity on and off the rugby field would hardly be a deterrent.

Philip took great care with his reply. First, he had to wait for his anger, disappointment and resentment to subside, and only then would he put pen to paper.

'I realize,' he wrote, **'that the Grant-Sutton job is the most prestigious of the lot, but I always thought you weren't keen on surgery. For myself, surgery is my life's ambition, and no power on earth could dissuade me from applying for this particular H.S. appointment.'**

At the risk of sounding conceited he added, **'It seems to me that my Primary Fellowship and Larkin Gold Medal should make me front runner and – if that isn't enough – I intend to get my MB,BS as soon as I finish this stint, and needless to say I shall go flat out for Honors in Surgery.'**

Philip thought it unnecessary to remind his friend that the coveted appointment was only awarded after a preliminary written exam given by the great man. He did, however, conclude: **'May the best man win (and it may even be a dark horse) and we shall remain the best of friends.'**

When the Canadians learned about Skinny Thompson's letter, they showed some dismay but no particular surprise.

"Typical of the Old Boys Network," Turner observed sardonically, "and just what I'd expect in Merrie England."

"Why the hell didn't you go to Eton's and Oxford like rahlly decent cheps?" asked Dalgleish, in an uppity English accent.

"Then you'd never have this kind of horseshit to deal with for the rest of your life," Farley chipped in. "If you have any sense you'll cut your losses and think about going to Canada."

"Perhaps I'll give it some thought after I've got my Fellowship finals in '38, but thanks anyway for the suggestion."

The idea struck him as most amusing. Born in Paris to parents who were eloping runaways from Warsaw, raised, educated and trained in London, Philip Bosnar found it hard to think of himself as another expatriate to colonial Canada, and learning to speak with an American twang. He knew so little about this vast subcontinent. Let's see, he thought, there was Toronto and Montreal, there were prairies with oodles of wheat, there were Great Lakes and a place called Saint Pierre Dulac. He appreciated the suggestion with thanks, then soon put it out of his mind.

The news items he was able to glean from their places of concealment in the newspapers and wireless broadcasts were becoming ominous. The Austrian government, under its right-of-center Chancellor Schuschnigg, was being forced to submit to Hitler's growing demands, while Austrian Nazi Stormtroopers were growing in strength day by day. They were parading openly and terrorizing political 'undesirables' and, of course, the Jews. Vicious philosophies of the Third Reich, conceived by Hitler, popularized by Goebbels, systematized by Goering, pogromized by Streicher and refined to the most exquisite cruelty by Himmler, would now be duplicated inside a hapless Austria.

Where would be next? Who would be next? Where were the counterforces and where the resistance? Certainly not in Britain or France. The League of Nations? What a joke! That illustrious institution had become a hollow showcase for aspiring public speakers, their florid expanses of oratory concealing narrow national self-interest and a refusal to take concerted action against the marauding despots of Europe.

In such an international atmosphere of moral default, it became all too easy for Hitler to repudiate the Locarno treaty and occupy the demilitarized zone of the Rhineland on March the 8th. That the triumphant troops of the Reichswehr were entirely unopposed came as no surprise to Philip. It was now easy for General Franco to mount his civil war – with blatant help from Italy and Germany – against the legitimate left-of-center Spanish government.

Philip remembered his outraged sense of betrayal when the League of Nations stood idly by as it watched the rape of Abyssinia. On October 3rd, without any declaration of war, the armed forces of Italy crossed into this primitive African country, steeped in biblical history: General Graziani from Somalia and General De Bono from Eritrea. It was a pathetic case of modern guns, tanks, planes and poison gas against the loyal but defenseless subjects of Emperor Haile Selassie, while the League dithered and debated.

The infamous Hoare-Laval treaty, proposed on December 13, sickened even the strongest stomachs in England and France, so slanted was it in favor of the aggressive Italians. Mercifully, it was repudiated at the insistence of Anthony Eden, the steadfast British diplomat who replaced Samuel Hoare as Foreign Minister. It was unfortunate that Eden's efforts at spurring united pressure from the Mediterranean nations – France, Yugoslavia, Greece and Turkey – were doomed to failure. There was a great deal of cluck-clucking at Mussolini's brutal invasion, but only ineffectual sanctions that could be circumvented at will and the behest of self-interested regimes.

Shortly after graduation in his Finals, Philip had reached a decision. According to what he could read and hear on the wireless, Abyssinia was not only undermanned, outgunned and isolated, but even lacked the adequate medical personnel needed to provide proper care of the wounded. He wrote forthwith to the Ethiopian Legation, offering his services as a surgeon in that wartorn country. The reply was almost immediate: he was advised to contact the British Red Cross, and he telephoned their headquarters right away. The official who replied told him they might be able to use him in the Southern Red Cross unit in Ethiopia. However, since they would prefer someone with military experience, they'd have to let him know later. Later came soon enough, when newspapers and broadcasts screamed the headlines that the Southern Red Cross Hospital unit had been wiped out by an Italian bombing raid. It was only fitting, thought Philip, that the crimson cross on the hospital roof provided such a perfect target for General Graziani's bombers.

That was the end, at least for the time being, of Dr. Philip Bosnar's career as a military surgeon. Now the months had passed, and when the victorious Italian forces entered Addis Ababa on May 5, the world seemed to look the other way. Hailie Selassie escaped to Palestine, where he rested awhile before travelling to the safety of England. On June 13, he electrified the civilized world with a ringing and heartrending presentation on behalf of his stricken nation. But the oratory and not the cause was the focus of the League's attention, and a broken ruler retired to the tranquil beauty and grace of historic Bath in the heart of England's countryside.

Philip was sorry when the time came for him to leave the happy medical and social environment of the Royal Gwent. It had been a fine experience, and he felt his scope had been expanded in all directions, especially in clinical and practical surgery. He had developed the keenest interest in the surgery of trauma, and if – God forbid! – Hitler ever plunged Europe into a second world war, Dr. Bosnar would be well equipped to take on the responsibilities of advanced military surgery, preferably in a base hospital, but if necessary, in a front line casualty unit.

He gave his fond farewells to his fellow residents, to his erstwhile 'lady-loves', and most of all to his sad-eyed Gwynneth Evans, who finally threw caution to the winds and gave him a long and passionate kiss. He was glad he hadn't stayed long enough for her to develop a non-platonic interest in him, as he could never bring himself to hurt her in any way. But now it was off to London, away from the musical Welsh language and lilting Celtic accents in this gentle oasis between two countries and two cultures. It was back to teeming London and to his home and family; back to the books and onward to his M.B,B.S. exams. With any luck, it might even be the coveted Honors mark in Surgery.

The whole family came to meet him at the station. His Dad, bless his heart!, hired a chauffeur-driven limousine for the occasion so that his beloved son could be brought back home in style. His Mum and Dad looked so young, Pauline so beautiful and Clayton grown-up beyond belief, and they all gave Philip an ecstatic welcome, although at first the little fellow wasn't quite sure who this new arrival might be. The first bear-hug and kiss soon rectified that uncertainty.

When Philip got back to the friendly privacy of his room he felt ready for a determined attack on his books. Before embarking on the major assault, he contacted his neighborhood friends and let them know he was back in circulation. He told them that although he'd be studying hard he'd still be available for the occasional tennis game or an evening stroll along the Mile End Road. In this way his life would retain some balance.

The focal centers of his day would be Bailey and Love's Textbook of Surgery and Letheby Tidy's Synopsis of Medicine, but there would be time for mealtime talks with his family on a variety of subjects, games with his adorable little brother, and a detailed analysis of the day's news from the daily newspapers and BBC broadcasts. At midnight he would search out the broadcasts from Radio Stuttgart and glean a few kernels of truth from the huge coating of Nazi propaganda. He would listen to some of Hitler's ranting speeches in his vulgar German accent, and get a clear blueprint for present tyranny and future conquest.

On the occasional evening he joined his pals and their girl-friends for a pleasant evening stroll, exchanging gossip, setting up assignations, or arguing about the pros and cons of Communism and Gilbert and Sullivan. The debates never got too heavy, the laughter was unrestrained and the romance totally non-binding. Along with occasional daytime tennis sessions, they served as pleasant diversionary interludes to his hours of single-minded and concentrated study, when he effectively shut out the rest of the world. Time was short, so there were no concerts and no cinemas, but there was still the odd moment when he felt constrained to take out his violin and play some old favorites or improvise some new ones.

Before settling down to a genuine high-pressure preparation for his exams, there was the small matter of an 'Annual Awards' ceremony held by the medical school of St. Clement's College Hospital in London's ornate Queen's Hall. This event was always well attended by the students and their families, as well as every one of the honoraries, registrars and housemen who weren't on duty at the time. Philip's Mum and Dad could hardly contain their excitement.

Pauline agreed to stay home with Clayton and her new fiancé, a stocky American from Cleveland who worked at the Dagenham Ford car factory in the East Thames area. He had come over some two years ago as floor supervisor in the auto finishing department, and decided to stay. He and Pauline first met at one of Dr. Berentson's night classes, and the lecturer decided to act as matchmaker for his favorite pupil. Such was the tortuous course of true love, Philip thought whimsically.

When the Bosnars arrived at Queen's Hall it was already filling up, and after Philip got his parents safely seated in the first balcony, he went below to join the other prize winners seated in the front rows. The opening address was the customary high-sounding stuff one expected from the Dean. Philip wondered with an inward smile if the stubborn Dr. Harold Blevins would relent in his uncompromising opposition to the Common Room Orchestra, now that its founder was high on the awards list. Maybe with the passage of time there would be a change of heart.

The prizes were awarded in ascending order, commencing with first year students and up the line until it reached the senior winners of scholarships and prizes. When his rival's name was called as winner of the first Broughton Scholarship, there was polite but perfunctory applause as he mounted the platform. It should have been more, thought Philip. Perhaps it was because the poor fellow wasn't very popular, but the importance of the award deserved better recognition. When his own name was announced as winner of the second Broughton and the Larkin medal, he found the applause embarrassing by contrast.

He knew it was partly because of the outrageous racket created by students of his final year, and partly because many in the audience remembered his name in connection with the students' orchestra and concert. To his enraptured mother, however, the heavenly noise could only mean acknowledgement of her boy's brilliance and universal popularity, while Philip – rather ashamed for himself – was overjoyed for them.

Once the glorious summer months had passed, with their tempting distractions, Philip found it much easier to settle down to a more uninterrupted industry. He still made weekly trips to the Lewis lending library on Gower Street and scanned the latest medical journals and books. He also dropped in on St. Clement's, nearby, and tried to pick up gossip about forthcoming house jobs, but was unable to shake his fear that Grant-Sutton's might go to Thompson.

When the M.B,B.S. exams came at last, it almost seemed an anticlimax, and Philip poured forth his knowledge in effortless abundance. He would have been a hypocrite to feign surprise at his good results and Honors in Surgery, but the big test would come when he competed for the treasured house surgeon job to the Great One.

It was a bleak winter day in early January of 1937, the kind of day that found Londoners scurrying through the streets, with heads and bodies bent low against the chilling rain and umbrellas turning hopelessly inside out in the mean winds gusting around every corner. Everyone seemed to make a mad rush for the nearest bus or underground station and Philip had been among the fastest, running all the way from his house to the Stepney Green station.

But now it was late afternoon, and the rain was turning to sleet. It could be heard rattling threateningly against the windows of Sir Grant's private office in his surgical wing, cancelling with its frigid sound the warmth coming from a large electric heater on the opposite side of the tastefully furnished room.

"Your marks and scholastic achievements are well ahead of the other candidates, Bosnar, and that is beyond question." Sir Grant's voice, with its soft Scottish inflections, was warm and kindly. Nevertheless, Philip found himself shivering slightly as the eminent surgeon continued, "I believe your friend, Skinny Thompson, has informed you of my promise to give him the job at this time."

"He wrote me the information, Sir, but not the precise justification."

"Some actions, my idealistic young friend, become necessary rather than justifiable."
Philip fought back his bile.

"At any other time there would have been no question." Sir Grant was still trying to rationalize, thought the stricken Philip, as his fallen idol continued with inexorable gentleness.

"The appointment will certainly be yours the next time around, and you must be sure to apply."

"Thank you, Sir," and he struggled to keep his voice firm and steady, "but no thanks."
The subject was closed, the interview was over, Man had proposed, God had disposed.

Dr. Philip Bosnar put his disappointment squarely behind him and set about looking for an alternative position as good as or even better than the one snatched from his expectant grasp. Ironically, it was Skinny who phoned him and told him about the upcoming vacancy at the Athlone Hospital in Walthamstow. Was it friendship, or simply expiation? Philip wouldn't permit disillusion to deteriorate into cynicism, and he chose friendship. The job was one of the best in London, outside of the major medical schools. It was a registrarship (senior residency), and the honoraries included such topnotch specialists as Richard Vaughan in Surgery and Hawksley in Medicine. In fact, the major medical schools provided most of the staff appointments at this ancient hospital as a secondary position. What a triumph the registrar's job would be, Philip fantasized, and what an antidote to the sour taste of defeat. So he sat down and wrote his application.

When he was called for interview one week later, he found the candidates for registrar had been narrowed down to two by the selection committee, on the basis of credentials, past performance and testimonials. The other candidate was a solid-looking man from Leeds, considerably taller and beefier than Philip, and five years older. He'd served in several house jobs over the past two years, had a good record, and he too had his Primary Fellowship. In addition, he held a B.Sc. in Physiology.

Philip considered himself clearly outgunned after their face-to-face interviews with the selection committee, and even more so when he heard his rival recounting his practical experiences at the housemen's dinner table. It was a genuine shock to Philip, therefore, when he learned later that evening that he – and not the man from Leeds – had received the final nod. Needless to say, his rival was bitterly disappointed and he had every right to feel that way, but each passing year and new experience taught Philip the inevitable lesson that for each winner there had to be a loser.

The following morning, before turning over his duties to his happy successor, the outgoing registrar took him on a comprehensive tour of the hospital and spelled out his duties in a broad but undetailed manner.

"Now there's one thing I must warn you about," he impressed on Philip, "Colonel Hardisty, our gynecologist, is a stickler on form. First, he likes being met by the registrar on his operating mornings. He arrives in a chauffeur-driven Rolls Royce, is met by you, then you hold the door open for him and help him off with his coat."
Philip stared at him in disbelief, but his instructor was serious.

"Don't hang up his coat unless he asks you to or he can get quite cross."

"As far as I'm concerned he can go and fuck himself," was Philip's irreverent reply. "I'll give him the best professional service I can but that's all."
Then, when he noticed his colleague's worried look, he added, "No disrespect, needless to say!" and they both guffawed.

"There's just one more item, Bosnar. He doesn't want any one but the registrar to assist him at surgery, and I'll leave you to learn for yourself just how tough he is to assist."

With the exception of the imperious Colonel, every honorary he met during the next two weeks seemed pleasant and helpful. He knew Vaughan from St. Clement's, where he was renowned for his superb thyroid surgery, for his all-round technical skill in the operating theater, and for his black- haired, dark-eyed attractiveness to the opposite sex. He was married to a ravishing society beauty, renowned for her artistic professional photography. The couple were frequently shown in the smarter magazines, arriving at the opera, the theater, the ballet or wherever: he, resplendent in his scarlet lined cloak, she, in her gowns and furs. What a dashing, smashing pair, like a pair of film stars! That was how all his student and resident admirers thought about them, and Philip endorsed their adulation.

Hawksley was a good-humored and brilliant young physician, and old Dr. Rubin, head of anesthesia, was a kindly orthodox Jew who made friends easily and had few enemies. The two exceptions at this institution, he learned via the hospital rumor mill, were Hardisty and "that old pisspot Maxwell," who was away in Australia but would be back the following month. Philip also learned that Hardisty, after leaving the army medical corps at the end of the war with the rank of Captain, had remained in the reserves and now held the rank of Lieutenant Colonel. He insisted on being called `Colonel' rather than the customary surgical title of Mister, especially by his subordinates. He was handsome in a florid military manner, with a guardsman's ramrod back and the bristling mustache of a senior regimental officer.

His new registrar was an immediate disappointment to him. The trouble started when the honorary was met by Philip, not at the door, but well back in the corridor. Philip introduced himself politely but only received a disinterested grunt in return. The next hurdle was the operating list. The first case was a vaginal repair for '***Cystocele and Rectocele***', 'dropped bladder and rectum' in the patient's vernacular. The anesthetized patient, a female in her forties, with eight children to her credit and a history of difficult deliveries, was put up in stirrups, prepped and draped. Hardisty seated himself on a padded stool at the foot of the table, which was then raised until the operative area was at his eye level. As was his experience with many such procedures, Philip edged himself carefully to the left side of the surgeon, in order to stand inside the patient's right thigh.

"No, no, not there!" came a loud stage whisper from the theater sister.

She was big and fat, with a noisy asthmatic wheeze and long past her prime. The mutual antipathy with Philip was instantaneous and almost molecular. It appeared that the Colonel required his assistant to stand on the outside of the patient's right thigh and assist by Braille. This would have been bad enough with ordinary technique, but Hardisty prided himself on his mastery with the Bonney-Reverdin technique.

In this method, a special needle is used. It is a very large needle that takes large tissue bites and has a slotted opening for the suture material. The surgeon makes his needle-bite, opens up the slot, and the assistant places a length of suture in the slot, which is then closed and the threaded needle drawn back and out, after which the suture is tied. The aperture's opening and closing is accomplished by pressing and releasing a spring device at the base of the fixed needle-holder. The assistant must work in synchrony with the surgeon, taking a prepared length of suture from the scrub-nurse and feeding it into the needle with an artery forceps.

Philip had always prided himself on being facile with this technique, and was more accustomed to the operator's praise than the obvious displeasure of his present chief. On the second occasion, a week later, he tried standing on a platform so that he could reach down in a diving motion to make the essential moves. He felt and probably looked like a praying mantis, and although his visibility was somewhat improved, his back ached for days. After the third weekly session, he'd reached the limit of his patience. With the malevolent cooperation of the nursing supervisor, the Colonel had been a real bastard and the showdown must no longer be delayed. The other theater nurses could almost feel it coming.

"Mr. Hardisty," Philip commenced his counterattack, "I would appreciate it if you would give me a few minutes of your time before leaving."

"Is it anything important, Bosnar?"

"Definitely, Sir."

"Can't it wait? I'm in a bit of a hurry."

"Definitely not, Sir."

"Very well then, if you insist"

When they were changed into regular attire, Philip led Hardisty into the small private office across from the theater suite and pulled out a chair for the honorary while he remained standing.

"Thank you for giving me this time. We've got off to a bad start and I feel the situation must be rectified as soon as possible."

"And just who do you think is to blame?"

"Perhaps both of us. In the first place I'm hopelessly inefficient as a butler or a valet, but I've been told that I'm a damn good surgical assistant and resident."

"Then why the devil don't you prove it?"

"Only if I can see what you're doing. For me, Sir, light still travels in straight lines and doesn't penetrate a female thigh or bend around it just to let me see."

"All right then. We'll try it your way, but don't crowd me, Bosnar."

The gynecologist had turned from crimson to purple at Philip's last remark, and his final warning showed marvellous self-control. It was the start of a wonderful new professional relationship, but on a personal level the Colonel never went beyond icy politeness.

Working with Richard Vaughan was a joy. This superb surgeon, who was Philip's real chief, was undemanding and invariably cordial, and he displayed an open appreciation of his resident's performance. He inspired Philip to use the scalpel's sharp edge whenever possible in preference to blunt dissection. He would graciously hand over a large operating list, usually on Fridays, with an apologetic, "Bosnar, I'm feeling rather tired after this morning's heavy cases. Would you mind finishing up the rest of the list today," then, as Philip choked back his ecstatic thanks, "I may pop in from time to time but if you need me just ask the nurses to give me a shout." Of such stuff is hero worship born and sustained.

Stuart Davies, the junior surgeon, was reasonably proficient, and although inordinately vain he was quite good to work for and gave Philip all his cystoscopic work.

"You've done quite a few of these, haven't you?" he asked casually one morning, "How about taking them off my hands? It shouldn't take you too long to catch on, I'm sure." He was right as it turned out, and Philip started to become quite expert at passing the scope, usually under low spinal, viewing the interior of the bladder in detail after a thorough irrigation with saline, and identifying the ureteric openings and prostate. (The ureters are the tubes conducting the kidney's urine to the bladder for expulsion).

He became adept at passing fine catheters up these tubes for the purpose of injecting dye and taking X-ray pictures of the kidneys, ureters and bladder. He found himself able to identify pathology of the urinary tract in the very earliest stages. Not only did he find himself enjoying these 'Cysto lists' more and more, but Davies even started to turn over his prostatectomies in increasing quantities, followed by other cases. Dr. Bosnar's cup was full!

It took the return of the voyaging Maxwell to pollute the contents of that cup. Hubert St. John Maxwell was a very important man. He was about 60 years old but looked, moved and spoke like a man in his nineties. He was chief of staff and senior surgeon, and he was also incompetent and obtuse, with the stubborn incorrectability of premature senescence. Unfortunately, he possessed heavy political power in this venerable institution and was backed up by the Sister in charge of the main surgical ward and by the gross dragon-lady who ruled over the operating theater suite.

It seemed that he was the longest serving honorary in the institution, and in his day had squired both of these women. They still loathed each other, but would unite without hesitation to defend his shabby performance against any new challenge. Everyone else in the hospital knew the truth but appeared powerless to do anything about it.

Whenever Philip assisted Maxwell, in order to spare one of his terrified house surgeons, he had to keep on constant alert in order to make sure the old surgeon wasn't going astray. For the heavier cases, Sister Wheezy would 'scrub in' herself and she, too, would be on surreptitious guard. The difficulty came with emergency evening cases. Customary procedure was for the registrar to phone the honorary surgeon on call, and he in turn would usually tell him to go ahead, with a houseman assisting. The honorary only came along if specifically requested, or if the registrar was off call that evening. Maxwell always came to the hospital when on call, and got thoroughly in the way when he stayed to assist. Philip found the only way to keep his unwelcome assistant's hands out of the open abdomen was to hand him three retractors rather than the customary two, and politely ask him to pull them in three directions at once.

During the next few months, Dr. Bosnar and his house staff enjoyed a happy and convivial life. On the professional side, they were intensely loyal to him and carried out his directions without question. On a personal level, they enjoyed a good time, playing cards and drinking beer in the evenings. They were men of his year who'd graduated with him from St. Clement's, and he gradually became aware – through their infallible grapevine – that it was his fallen idol, Grant-Sutton, who'd engineered his selection over the candidate from Leeds. This was no doubt in order to make amends, but gave Philip scant comfort.

Free beer was provided through the benevolence of the hospital board chairman, owner of a local brewery. The resident staffmen never allowed themselves to get drunk, but all agreed that the quality of the brew was excellent. Excellence was totally absent, however, from the piano recital given each evening by their self-styled keyboard virtuoso. His lugubrious rendition of 'Ain't

She Sweet', played Andante Sostenuto, brought pangs to Philip's tortured eardrums, but he kept his mouth (not to mention his violin case) judiciously shut.

Lunch was quite pleasant. It was a joint meal in the medical staff dining room, with both honoraries and house staff attending and chatting together without formality. Beer was available with meals and the privilege was never abused. Some of the housemen found the lunches uncomfortable and felt they were unable to relax in the presence of their chiefs, but Philip found this was true only when Hardisty or Maxwell were there to chill the atmosphere. Dr. Rubin attended as often as possible and was always served special meals that didn't transgress his strict Kosher rules. He was always a welcome addition to the group and usually had a ready joke available for his colleagues, but never in questionable taste.

Dr. Bosnar's salary as registrar was barely enough to cover cigarettes, an occasional trip to the local cinema and the odd meal at a decent restaurant. Fortunately he was good at card games, especially pontoon, otherwise known as twenty-one, vingt-et-un or blackjack. The houseman sitting room was often visited by residents from other hospitals who knew all about the beer facilities. They were always welcome, as long as they came after supper.

The 'colonials', especially South Africans, loved to gamble, and their favorite game was pontoon. It seemed they were never short of cash and were willing to challenge Philip head to head, with the Athlone house staff staking their registrar to whatever was needed to finance an all-night game. This was held from time to time on a Friday evening, as the Saturday mornings had very light duty requirements.

Philip's housemen had their confidence justified and rewarded with fairly regular winnings, while Philip, even at moderate stakes, was able to double his monthly income. There was even the occasional morning when, after giving the visitor a handsome breakfast, they would pay his cab fare back to his own hospital base.

By the fourth month, however, a series of incidents, mostly involving Maxwell and his two supportive Sisters, was building up to a crisis, and it took the needless death of a 3-year-old child to explode the crisis into concerted action: one that shook the hospital from top to bottom and would reverberate in the hospitals of the entire metropolis.

CHAPTER 11

1941-42

Valerie Cruickshank was dying. This vigorous young woman, so full of robust vitality, such an asset to the Forsyth-Bosnar practice both as receptionist and nurse, so respected by patients and employers alike, was fading away to a brown misery. It had started last spring, but she told no one. She was never one to fuss about minor incapacities. First, there was the gradual loss of appetite, which she actually welcomed as she thought she was overweight, although with her height and big-boned frame this wasn't too noticeable. Then there was the progressive nausea followed by early jaundice, with her eyes showing the first yellow tint, while at the same time her urine became darker and her stools paler. There was no pain whatever, and when Forsyth asked Philip to see her in consultation, the surgeon could find no evidence of local tenderness or abdominal mass.

The *serum bilirubin* studies (the levels and types of bile pigments in the blood) revealed a true obstructive jaundice, and although special gallbladder X-rays showed a non-functioning organ, the barium studies showed an ominous indentation of the duodenum (the first loop of small intestine) which confirmed Philip's suspicion that the probable diagnosis was cancer of the pancreas. (When a malignant tumor invades the right side of the organ, known as the 'sweetbread' in common parlance, it compresses the lumen of the bile duct, backing up the bile and causing jaundice as well as other progressive symptoms so typical of this fatal condition. Vomiting follows nausea, visible wasting follows diminished intake of food, and intractable generalized itching follows the deepening yellow-to-brown discoloration of the skin.)

Nurse Cruickshank was no fool and no coward. On the contrary, she was a straightforward realist who insisted on being kept fully informed of Dr. Bosnar's opinions and suspicions. When she was given the facts she didn't break down. Instead, she requested that he go ahead as soon as possible with exploratory laparotomy (opening the belly and checking the organs by direct vision and palpation). This, she decided, would be the only way he could rule out his grim suspicions or, alternatively, do whatever was possible to cure or alleviate the condition.

With Forsyth present, Philip put forth his position without concealment.

"Valerie, you must understand that everything points to a carcinoma of the pancreatic head. It may well be inoperable."

"I understand that, but what if it's operable?"

"In that case it would mean a radical Whipple procedure."

"Refresh my memory, if you wouldn't mind."

"Of course. It's a procedure in which the tumor and adjoining pancreas is removed along with part of the stomach and the entire duodenal loop. Things are then joined up and the bile duct and pancreatic duct are reimplanted."

"How dangerous is an operation of that size?"

"It carries quite a high risk and a low cure rate, and even in successful cases there may be permanent digestive upsets or diabetic problems following the surgery."

"What would make it inoperable?"

"If the tumor involves the main underlying blood-vessel called the Portal Vein."

"What then?"

"There is still the possibility of a palliative bypass to sidetrack the bile duct, and if necessary, do a gastric bypass at the same time."

"I'd like you to go ahead and I'd like Dr. Forsyth to assist."

"No, Valerie. If it were almost any other abdominal condition I would willingly go ahead, but there are too many on-the-spot decisions that might require a pathologist in attendance to read tissue samples, and other details."

He paused for a few moments to let his words overcome her resistance.

"It would be hard to justify going ahead here. I'd prefer to arrange for your immediate transfer to Dr. Thorlakson's service in the Winnipeg General Hospital. He has excellent facilities and the largest experience of such cases in the midwest if not in the whole of Canada."

With characteristic strength of character she accepted Dr. Bosnar's decision with reluctance but without fuss, and he was grateful for Peter's support at this difficult time.

Three days later, she was explored by the Winnipeg surgeon and found to have an inoperable cancer of the head and body of the pancreas. A palliative double bypass was performed and, as soon as she was well enough to travel, she was transferred to the Sisters hospital in Vanwey. Philip had looked after her faithfully, ever since.

By November of 1940 she was in the terminal stage of her malignant syndrome. Her face and body were greenish brown and shrunken, an indwelling gastric tube was attached to intermittent suction in order to minimize vomiting, and she was receiving fluids and essential chemicals intravenously to reduce thirst and weakness. She was permitted to sip clear fluids of her own choice and at her own will. Now, her abdomen was becoming distended with fluid due to obstruction of the venous outflow, and she was suffering more from pain than from itching.

The nurses were instructed to pay close attention and never to forget her behind the closed door of her private room. Above all, they were not to withhold her palliative injections of narcotic and sedative drugs even as the dosage needed to be increased week by week.

One day, she asked to see him without her nurse present. Her face revealed her suffering, her voice revealed her weakness, and her words revealed her courage.

"I know I won't live much longer, Dr. Bosnar, and I feel I can allow myself to be completely candid. I've admired you from the very first, just as I've always loved Peter from the time I became his office nurse."

Her words were interrupted by a severe fit of coughing.

"Now I need you to promise me something."

"Whatever I can possibly do for you, Valerie."

"I realize things are going to get pretty rough for me from now on but, unlike most people in my condition, I want to live every minute of every day that's left to me. Please do nothing that will shorten my life even if it prolongs my discomfort."

"I promise."

She gave him a wonderful smile and squeezed his hand in gratitude. As he fought back his tears he noted that she used the word "discomfort," not "agony," not even "pain."

Two weeks later she died, mercifully, in her sleep.

A few days after the funeral, her father came to see Philip, and he was old and bent from years of toil and hardship on the dusty sunbaked earth of southern prairie farmland. Despite his bowed back and twisted joints, his rugged weathered face still showed strength and courage. Philip brought a jaw-jutting look of pride to the old man's face when he recounted his daughter's last request.

"That's one thing me and my missus taught our Val. Good old-fashioned religion and a respect for the life the Good Lord gave us."

He left with his head as high as he could force it, and carried his walking-cane as if it were the staff of Saint John the Baptist.

Although Philip and his patients missed his late office-nurse with a deep sense of loss, her place was soon filled by an excellent replacement. Susan O'Reilly was an attractive and skilled office nurse who stepped into the breach at the specific request of her good friend and former classmate, Valerie Cruickshank. The replacement was arranged when Valerie first recognized the seriousness of her condition, and whenever Philip watched the high standard of O'Reilly's performance and her happy disposition, he felt a debt of gratitude to Valerie for her selfless foresight.

Patty became very fond of the new nurse during the ensuing months and, when James Spencer Bosnar was born, it was Susan O'Reilly who became his devoted admirer and slave. She even became his proud Godmother. The new baby and nurse seemed to take to each other right away, and Patty felt that if it ever became necessary, she wouldn't hesitate to leave the baby in Susan's safe hands at any time, although the nurse might have to fight the redoubtable Mrs. H. for the privilege.

As for Philip's practice, in the absence of Forsyth he was becoming almost too busy, and he decided that sooner or later he must take on an associate to lighten the load. He was determined, however, to be very careful when the time came to make his selection.

Meanwhile, winter was approaching, and he knew that between Christmas and the New Year there would be one party after another, both at home and with friends, as well as the splendid dinner dances at the airforce officers' mess. He must lay down an adequate stock of rye and scotch, with lesser quantities of gin, rum and sherry. Anything less than a total of one hundred bottles might prove dangerously low.

In the first week of January, the fabled beauty queen arrived from England. Flight Lieutenant Tom Jeffries had bragged to his fellow officers about his gorgeous bride almost from the time he first arrived on the base, and everyone was dying to see last year's reputed winner of a beauty contest at Bournemouth. Jeffries, a dashing rogue blessed with striking good looks of his own, confided to Philip that his wife was worried about some varicose veins marring the flawless splendor of legs, and he wanted her to have a thorough examination.

"But please remember, Phil old chap, she's a very shy person."

When she eventually appeared at the office to keep her appointment, Susan O'Reilly announced her arrival with a wry grin.

"There's a voluptuous English dish waiting for you to give her a complete examination."

The word "complete" was spoken with roguish emphasis.

"She already has all the men drooling in the waiting room."

As Loretta Jeffries was shown into his consulting room, Philip had to admit she was indeed quite a good-looking 'dish', but without the depth of true beauty like that of his own lovely Patricia. For one thing, the patient's curvaceous body – although eye-catching and seductive – could benefit from a weight-reducing program.

Philip took the usual detailed history, then said he'd be back shortly to examine her. He asked O'Reilly to get her gowned and he'd let her know when to come back for the patient's physical examination. When he re-entered his office he was stopped in his tracks. The luscious Loretta, Flight Lieutenant Jeffries' "very shy" wife, was seated in nonchalant total nudity, facing the door expectantly and smoking a casual cigarette. He rushed out in desperate haste and ordered his nurse, whose mirth was now almost hysterical, to gown the brazen creature immediately and stay for the entire examination.

By the grace of God there were no further embarrassments, and he was happy to inform the patient that she was entirely healthy, and that she had a few tiny and harmless superficial venous clusters which required no special treatment at the present time. He made no return appointment.

In the evenings, after a hard day's work, Philip still liked to drop into the Gazette offices up the street and hoist a few glasses of scotch and soda with Doug Conway, discuss current events of interest and go over the next day's editorial in critical detail. Regardless of how serious the conversation, Doug's lightning wit always managed to spot some amusing aspect of the news, Phil would pick up the mood and repartee, and they'd soon have each other in stitches. How wonderful it felt when they finally fell back exhausted with laughter and alcohol, the tears literally streaming down their cheeks!

Once in a while, after leaving the Gazette offices just before 11, they'd catch Jake the Greek as he was closing up his restaurant for the night. Doug would plant a large and very determined foot in the closing door and announce, "Jake, we're very hungry."

The scenario would then continue as follows, with only minor variations.

"Sorry, Gentlemen, but I'm closed."

"Not quite," Phil chimes in.

"Think how hard we've been working," Doug insists, "especially the Doctor."

"I'm not only exhausted, I'm starving," Phil adds, and Jake capitulates.

"Very well, Gentlemen, but only a small snack."

With unrelenting pressure Jake is forced into retreat. The small snacks grow into sumptuous steaks, the steaks acquire the companionship of fried onions and potatoes, and further persuasion produces pie a la mode and coffee.

The meal is embellished by political debates, and is followed by a 'coup de grace': they shoot craps for the bill, double or quits. Jake invariably loses, and Phil worries about the duodenal ulcer for which he's been treating the restaurant owner for the past six months and which stubbornly fails to improve.

From time to time, Philip Bosnar and Alf Steffanson got together for a game of chess or a discussion of the world geopolitical scene and the current state of the war. The news from the Russian front was grim indeed. By September of 1941 the German forces had captured the Ukrainian capital Kiev, and in the north they penetrated to within twenty miles of Leningrad. One month later, they took Odessa on the Black Sea as well as the industrial city of Kharkov to the northeast, while Moscow was under siege. The two friends shared an intense dislike for the brutal Soviet dictator, the pipe-puffing Stalin with his heavy mustachios and crafty smile. Both, however, felt a profound sympathy for the brave, embattled citizens of the Soviet Union.

By November, Japan was making threatening moves in the far Pacific, and mounting complaints of 'encirclement' bore an ominous similarity to those of Hitler just before he plunged Europe into war. Phil and Alf had long hoped that the U.S.A. would be forced into a war with Japan, and might then be dragged, kicking and screaming, into war against Hitler and his Fascist partners.

This would be a cup of hemlock to such Fascist-lovers as Senators Nye and Hamilton Fish in politics, Ford and Lindbergh in industry, Father Coughlin in religion, and the vicious KKK and Bund members who now operated undercover. President Roosevelt had made it clear that he wished his country to enter the war on Britain's side, but so far had been thwarted by the powerful isolationist lobby, the far right Nazi-lovers and the Anglophobes. Perhaps Japan's Premier Tojo and his fellow warlords could accomplish for F.D.R. what his supporters could not. At least, that was the devout hope shared by Alf and Philip.

The attacking planes of the Rising Sun, swooping low over sleepy Pearl Harbor in the early morning light of December 7, blasted the U.S. Pacific Fleet to smithereens without benefit of a declaration of war. They exploded the myth of U.S. isolationist neutrality and gave the hard-pressed Allies much needed help in their time of need.

The main roads of southern Saskatchewan were of gravel, a rough surface that sent its stones bouncing a flamenco rhythm against the underside of the car's chassis and creating a steady clatter of castanets, taking considerable adjustment for drivers accustomed to smooth-paved surfaces. Side roads were somewhat more even. They were dirt-surfaced, dusty in dry weather and slippery when the rains changed dirt to mud.

But when the blizzards of winter came, driving on either surface could be life-threatening, and on the night of December 12 the Bosnars came face to face with that awesome fact for the first time in their lives. It had been a pleasant late afternoon when they set out, in a convoy of half a dozen cars, for the city of Burnest some fifty miles away. The occasion was a concert and dinner-dance in honor of the South Saskatchewan Regiment. Invited guests included the Mayor of Vanwey and his wife, the Chief of Police and his wife, the Freikopfs, Conways, Bosnars, Group Captain Cummings and a few senior army officers and their wives.

The evening was a huge success and everyone had an enjoyable time. Philip wore his white tie and tails, and was relieved to find at least a dozen other men wearing the same formal attire, with some displaying an impressive array of medals. Patricia Bosnar was the undisputed Belle of the Ball, at least as far as her proud husband was concerned. She looked stunning in her simple strapless black evening gown, and the dark velvet was a perfect complement to her fair complexion and copper-colored hair. Philip's chest swelled with unabashed pride, and he didn't even complain when the dashing George Freikopf asked her for a few too many dances.

When they started back, however, he started to worry.

The night was pitch black, with no visible moon. It was after 1 a.m. and few lights were showing. Phil had been careful with his drinks and was cold sober, but he knew the others had been far less temperate and were now feeling no pain. The plan was for Phil and Patty to be fourth in line, with three cars ahead and two behind, and it sounded like a sensible arrangement.

As they left Burnest, all lights disappeared, the snowfall got heavier and in another ten minutes the blizzard struck, full force! Instead of slowing down, the convoy leaders increased their speed to over sixty miles an hour, in the carefree conviction that the sooner they got home the safer they'd be. Now, the feeling of worry deepened to a clear sense of danger and, as the rear lights of the car ahead faded to a hazy pink, they knew they were in deep trouble.

Driving snow beat angrily against the windshield in a remorseless onslaught of converging white projectiles, and howling icy gusts tried to push the car off the road, first to one side and then the other. The slick road surface made them all too aware of the deep ditches (called 'sloughs' by prairie dwellers) on either side, and their struggling heater, bravely protecting them against numbing hypothermia, couldn't stop the windshield and windows from fogging up.

Phil and Patty never understood how they were able to complete this nightmare journey through winter's deadly gauntlet, and when they reached the warm safety of their home they thanked God for postponing their day of final reckoning, and hoped this would be far off into the distant future.

The festive season went by in a dazzling whirl of social activities, and even their generous stock of alcoholic supplies was dwindling to a few forlorn bottles as the young couple settled down to the icy blasts and snow drifts of winter. Philip was becoming a veteran in the use of tire chains, sand-gravel mixtures and snow shovels, to help him through the frequent obstacles of travel during this difficult season. He also became expert at helping others when they got stuck in the snow and needed assistance.

Phil and Patty learned to live with the fact that often, after a heavy snowfall, they were almost house-bound. The town came to a halt and most of the offices and stores stayed closed. Philip didn't attempt to use his car on these occasions and left it in the garage. The streets were blanketed with thick impassable snow and wouldn't be negotiable until snow-plows could be brought in.

He limited himself to trudging to the hospital in the morning, knee-deep in the soft white stuff and clad in a heavy duffel coat, with the hood drawn over his head and hands protected by fur-lined gloves. Although his calf-high winter boots kept out most of the snow, he remained keenly aware of the dangers of frostbite. At the end of the morning, after surgery and ward rounds, he struggled back home, always with the threat of unpredictable winds suddenly whipping up and reducing all visibility and progress to near-zero.

The most intrepid traveller at this time, and a Good Samaritan to those on the Bosnars' street block, was the fearless Angus Jackson. This fine fellow, married to Peter Forsyth's sister and erstwhile landlord to Phil and Patty, volunteered to do the shopping for his neighbors, if only for the barest essentials. He was dressed as warmly as possible and exhibited a special ingenuity at protecting himself against the elements.

On his head, he carried the additional protection of a cardboard box, with a cut-out in front into which he'd glued a transparent plastic rectangle that assured visibility. He wore mukluk boots, with hide thongs that could be tightened to keep out the snow. As for provisions, these were loaded onto a light sled that he dragged along behind him.

He made several such trips a day and all the beneficiaries felt indebted to his selfless endeavors. Had he accepted their grateful offers of a chill-defying libation at each home, he would have been beyond any form of travel except one into happy oblivion.

With the spring came warmer air, the renewal of exuberance, the planting, the thaws, and then – to temper optimism – the floods. The great valley became a lake, and each tiny village downstream to the swollen Burnley River became a puddle of miserable discomfort. In some areas, this was not without compensation, and the Bosnars remembered the visit to Grimby during their first Canadian summer.

Blaikie must have had a big laugh over that episode. He'd sent Philip out on an urgent visit, to see a woman with severe abdominal pains and bloody bowel movements, and she was "too sick to be moved." The patient was a farmer's widow who lived alone in the village of Grimby. Instructions of how to get there were somewhat vague, but Philip was assured that once he arrived he'd be directed to the patient's home by local villagers.

Patty decided she wanted to accompany her husband and they set off, first eastward then swinging south onto a narrow dirt road. As they came over the crest of a small hill they were greeted by an incredible sight. The maps showed this area as farmland. Instead, as far as the eye could see, there were miles and miles of sand dunes stretching toward the international border. Here was a mini-Sahara desert where there should have been grain-bearing prairie earth, and the new Canadians felt reality slip away as they surveyed the dismal arid scene. So this was what a decade of drought and grasshoppers could do to a fertile country!

After passing a lonesome elevator back and forth several times, in search of the elusive village, they discovered that this forlorn structure with its few surrounding huts was, indeed, the village of Grimby. A woman with American-Indian features came forward from one of the dwellings and escorted Philip to his patient.

The elderly woman lying in bed insisted she was feeling much better after several doses of wild strawberry and wouldn't dream of going into hospital. Her medical history revealed similar attacks of lesser intensity for several years, especially when she ate meat that wasn't fresh, and the examination supported a diagnosis of ordinary Gastroenteritis, commonly known as 'Summer Flu'. Nevertheless, Philip took a small stool sample in the sterile container he'd brought along, for bacteriological examination.

"I've got a bottle of medicine and some sulfa pills I want you to take," he said, "but if you're not feeling better by tomorrow we'll have to bring you into hospital for special tests. In the meantime stay in bed and drink lots of clear liquids. No alcohol, of course."
The patient was grateful and apologetic.

"I wouldn't have brought you all the way out here but Dr. Tom insisted."

Her neighbor undertook to keep an eye on her, and Philip felt quite sure she would. These farm people seemed tied together in a bond of mutual hardship and he respected them for it.

As they drove away from that forlorn place, Phil and Patty expressed the devout hope that one day this terrible desert scene would be transformed into acre upon billowing acre of wheat, rye, corn, alfalfa and whatever other bounty nature could restore, abundant and endless as far as the eye could see. As for the Blaikies of this world, they could enjoy their little jests, but could they ever attain true empathy with their less fortunate but stalwart compatriots?

At long last, summer burst upon the southern prairies in all its glowing splendor, and a decade of drought, grasshoppers and despair, even the recent floods that inundated the valley, seemed to fade into a distancing past. New cars were appearing and new farm machines displayed their shining splendor, while fields of growing crops filled the landscape and prosperity appeared close at hand for Vanwey and its surrounding farmlands.

Philip's thoughts often strayed at this happy time to a game of tennis, a round of golf or a dip in the river down at the Sandstrum's place. Only rust, sundry pests, hungry birds, too much rain, too little rain, hail, low prices for grain and those damn financiers in Bay Street, could spoil the prospect of better times. What if the Japanese were winning the war in the Pacific and news reports shuddered with tales of atrocity against Canadian prisoners in Hongkong and American prisoners in the Philippines?

As for the rest of the war news, who was this guy Rommel who was beating the hell out of British forces in North Africa? Those who, like the Bosnars, kept abreast of world news, knew who this 'newcomer' was. He was the fabled Desert Fox, yesterday's Nazi zealot, today's respected military genius and a leader who now threatened to drive the British out of Africa. This was no time, however, for darker thoughts. Everyone knew Canada was beginning to flourish and the western allies were bound to win the war in the long run, while cautious words of warning were boring at best and seditious at worst.

In late June, Philip received a severe blow. He would soon be losing his closest friend and drinking buddy, Doug Conway.

"I've been asked to take over as the editor of a paper in Northern Ontario," Conway confided to his devastated friend, "it's a great opportunity, and the pay is a lot better than I'm making here, and they're prepared to give me a fine house, free and clear, as an added inducement."
Philip tried not to look as stricken as he felt. There would be no more liquor-inspired bull sessions, no more assaults on Jake the Greek's establishment, no more late night games of blackjack or poker.

"Waddya think I ought to do, old sport? Who the hell's gonna to keep you sober, who's gonna make sure you get to the midnight mass with your bloody fiddle, who's gonna keep you from joining up with Slocum?"

Conway's eyes glinted devilishly, but couldn't conceal the pain.

"You rotten bastard, you know bloody well you have to go, so why the blazes ask me!" Phil retorted in kind, but Doug wasn't fooled for a moment.

"I'll miss you just as much, you stubborn Limey bugger," he said, and his voice was gruff with emotion.

By the end of July the Conways were gone, but not before they were wined, dined and honored at a round of parties given by their many friends, all of whom would miss them dearly. The Gazette would continue under new management, but for the Bosnars it would never be the same.

During the past year there had been several occasions on which Dr. Bosnar was called upon to attend airforce officers' pregnant wives at delivery time, and he was happy to take on this assignment and bring greater joy to the airbase, as well as the unfamiliar sound of bawling infants. Daphne Leigh-Jones was a very special case. She was the glamorous wife of Squadron-Leader Ronnie Leigh-Jones, and both were great favorites with Phil and Patty. He was the pleasant 'Algy' type widely popularized in the works of the inimitable P.G.Wodehouse, but the foppish facade concealed a sharp mind and strong character.

Daphne was the typical blonde and blue-eyed English Rose, and in addition to her prewar career as barrister-at-law, was known as a glamorous stage actress best suited to such light roles as Noel Coward's Blithe Spirit. After several previous miscarriages it was gratifying to bring her through to term on this occasion, and the Leigh-Jones were overjoyed when Philip also brought her through a smooth labor to the delivery of a fine-looking baby girl.

On the second day following delivery, Daphne started to bleed. All her clotting factors came back normal and there was no evidence of retained membranes or concealed infection. When the bleeding got severe enough to require a blood transfusion, Dr. Bosnar decided to wait no longer before performing a curettage under general anesthesia. This had to be done with extreme gentleness because of the delicate and friable nature of the uterus so soon after delivery. There was no evidence of retained membranes or placental fragments, and he was puzzled. There was no sign of concealed uterine or vaginal tears and the response to uterus-contracting drugs remained negative. He even tried intravenous calcium; it had worked empirically for him in the past for a few cases of bleeding of unknown origin, but to no avail at this time.

In despair, after an intense search of the medical literature failed to help, he phoned Dr. McQueen in Winnipeg, the professor of Ob.Gyn. who'd been his L.M.C.C. examiner.

"When you did the curettage did you pack her?"

"Just a vaginal pack."

"If she doesn't stop bleeding in 48 hours, repeat the D and C and pack the uterus."

"I planned to do that if you approved, but my main worry is whether I can avoid hysterectomy and how long I can postpone the decision."

The professor remained silent for a long while, then, "Let's see what happens first. There's still time to decide."

Three days later Philip was on the phone again.

"I'm afraid nothing has worked. The second curettage came up empty, and the tightest uterine packing has failed. I'd be most grateful if you could come here for direct consultation and final decision."

The professor was flown out of Winnipeg on a special RCAF plane provided at Bosnar's urgent request. He spent a long time with the patient, going over her medical and family history point by point. His physical examination was as detailed as possible and he went over her hospital chart with the proverbial fine-toothed comb, then sat down with the husband to give his summation.

Before he could start, Ronnie Leigh-Jones spoke up with typical British candor.

"Professor McQueen, I want you to know how much we appreciate your help, but it's only fair to tell you that we have every confidence in Dr. Bosnar and it was he alone, and neither my wife nor I, who requested another opinion."

"I quite understand," McQueen replied pleasantly, "and I must tell you that Dr. Bosnar has done everything I would have done in his place."
He paused a few moments before continuing.

"In my opinion we don't have to make any drastic decisions for the present, but if there is no improvement over the next two days then we are both agreed that hysterectomy may have to be considered."

"I earnestly hope not," said Daphne "but if it should become necessary then we both would want our good friend Dr. Bosnar to perform the surgery."

"You couldn't be in better hands," McQueen assured them as he stood up and shook hands all round.

As he was leaving the hospital to enter the R.C.A.F. staff car, he turned and said quietly to Philip, "Keep your fingers crossed."

The next day Philip crossed not only his fingers, but toes as well, as he carefully removed the uterine pack. Twelve hours later the hemorrhage stopped and never returned.

The annual summer fair took place in a large field just west of Vanwey. Phil thought it only fitting that he and Patty should attend this fun-filled event at least once this year, and be seen by his patients as relaxed and informal young Canadians rather than stiff English expatriates. Patty hated the carnival rides her husband enjoyed so much, and she was quite content to watch him take the Rollacoaster, the Octopus and other crazy rides, defying all the laws of gravity and common safety. With each successive foray into sublime vertigo his boyish excitement seemed to carry him back to the slim young enthusiast who'd first captured her heart. Watching him now, with his thick black hair all dishevelled and his clothes awry, she knew she loved the youngster in him that would never die. Where she sought stability he sought challenge, yet each had the resilience to complement the other.

After a while it started to get dark, the fairgrounds became a fairyland of lights, calliope music, cheerful shrieks and joyous laughter. It seemed to Patty that every second person they bumped into was a patient of Phil's, and that gave her a warm and wonderful feeling of belonging. Phil was still looking for the ultimate thrill-ride and was delighted when he found it in a devilish contraption called a 'Moon Swing'. This was a double swing for two occupants who were strapped into special seats before being put into motion by the operator. Once started, the swings were projected into a giant arc of 180 degrees, one after the other. The passengers were suspended upside down for a few moments before being swung down again, and the whole process was repeated over and over with increasing speed and gravitational force. Philip couldn't conceal his eagerness, but nobody in the small cluster of watchers seemed very keen to share a ride with him.

Suddenly he spotted a familiar face. It was Tom Thurston, a G.P. practicing in the small neighboring town of Fennert. Thurston was a quiet and gentle man in his thirties and a rather timid soul, or so it seemed to Philip. He recoiled in horror at Philip's suggestion that he share the ride with him, but Philip bought the two tickets anyway and kept up his persuasion and reassurance until his quarry weakened. The ride was marvellous and Philip came back to ground totally exhilarated. Thurston, sad to say, came down looking green and fighting nausea.

Dr. Philip Bosnar, surgical specialist and prominent Vanwey citizen, felt like a miserable worm as he watched this gentle person and valued colleague slink away into the darkness beyond the giant tent, heaving up his guts. But after a while, the enticing aroma of hot dogs reminded the young couple that they were ravenous. They consumed their steaming savory snacks with gusto and washed them down with ginger ale. Patty was ready to leave, while her stubborn husband insisted, "One more ride, just for the road." That was a big mistake.

The human inner ear is a marvellous organ of balance, with its three semicircular canals of spacial recognition, its *Vestibule* (the communicating chamber) and its *Cilia* (myriad tiny fibrils) all combining their actions to maintain balance. This mechanism was now challenged by 'Bosnar's Last Ride'. It was only a simple inoffensive roundabout kind of ride, but it was horizontal and it came too soon after the vertical Moon Swing and hot dogs.

Philip realized two things as the speed began to pick up and his head began to swim. First, he was going to be very, very sick. Second, the roundabout seemed surrounded by the smiling faces of his patients. The fates relented as their mortified doctor found a large pocket handkerchief into which he was able to vomit unobtrusively whenever his vehicle swung around inward, away from the gaze of his audience. Then, when the ordeal reached its conclusion, he carried the loaded handkerchief like a handbag to the nearest trash can and got rid of it.

A few months later he learned that Captain Tim Thurston, Medical Officer in his regiment, had distinguished himself during the Dieppe raid with great gallantry and heroism, 'Above and Beyond'. The Bosnars swelled with admiration for this quiet and self-effacing hero. It was some time before they learned all the details. It was obvious that the Dieppe raid was a colossal military blunder, and when Thurston found himself trapped on the landing beach, he not only took care of the wounded but paused from time to time to fire his gun. He was aiming at the invisible enemy pouring down a withering hail of bullets from the high ground. According to witnesses who returned from that terrible debacle, their M.O. (Medical Officer) had to be dragged back to a waiting offshore craft, "with his chest shot full of holes," and he kept wanting to return to his wounded men.

When he received the George Medal (and it should have been the Victoria Cross!), Phil and Patty sent him a wire telling him how proud of him they were, and how overjoyed to learn that he'd made a good recovery from his honorable wounds. In Thurston's letter of reply, there was the usual gentle modesty, but one sentence really tickled the Bosnars: **'Believe me, Philip, compared to that awful Moon Swing it was a breeze'**.

Later that year Philip asked Patty if she'd like to accompany him to a meeting of the Canadian Medical Association in Toronto. She was overjoyed at the suggestion and started to make the necessary preparations right away. By this time, Jamie was a strong and beautiful boy who was easy to look after, and between Mrs. H. and Susan O'Reilly there'd be no problem whatever. Meanwhile, Philip made the usual arrangements with Slocum and there were no objections.

When the Bosnars boarded the train, there were several other doctors and their wives already in their carriage, travelling from the western provinces. They all looked so important and so prosperous, thought Patty, and worse still they all seemed to know each other so well; exchanging easy conversation from which she and Philip seemed excluded. He was confident the situation would change before journey's end, and the opportunity arose when the steward announced dinner call. Phil and Patty were halfway down the waiting line when he became aware of a commotion up front. It seemed that the wife of one of western medicine's leading lights had got a speck of coal grit into her eye from one of the partly opened windows, and no one could get it out.

The moment, thought Philip with elation, was heaven sent. How many times had he removed such painful tiny brutes from suffering patients at the Royal Gwent! First, you told the patient to open the opposite eye and keep it open, no matter what. Next, you gently took hold of the upper eyelid on the offending side, starting with the lashes and then the rim of the lid itself. Next, with slight counterpressure on the lid from above, you flipped it inside out.

Philip remembered how he used to practice the trick on himself, and how he exploited the special art when giving his shameless imitation of the Hunchback of Notre Dame at parties. He was no Charles Laughton, but with his upper lid flipped inside out and his eye rolled up; with his tongue forcing the opposite cheek outward and his right shoulder thrown upward and forward; and with the lights turned off and a flashlight shining upward, he could still be scary enough.

Now, however, was the moment of truth. With Patty clinging to his waist, he worked his way toward the dining car.

"Excuse me, please." – "I must get forward." – "I'm here to help." – "I'm experienced at this sort of thing."

When he reached the poor woman at last, he saw that she was well into eye spasm. Using all his memorized skill he soon had the patient calmed, the lid flipped up and her eye looking obediently downward. He produced a clean handkerchief, gently lifted out the offending black granule and presented it to the smiling lady as if it were a rare jewel.

From that moment onward and to the end of the trip he OWNED the train, and there was no conversation that failed to include both Bosnars at its center. The others wanted to know everything about the young couple and Patty was ecstatic. She and Phil even got into some friendly bridge games and that made the trip seem much shorter.

Toronto seemed to have grown since they last saw it, but no doubt this must be by comparison with Vanwey rather than with the major cities of England. They found the Royal York Hotel gracious and impressive, and their room on the twelfth floor was large and comfortable, with a good view of the city below. After dinner in the stylish coffee shop, Philip attended an evening meeting concerning medical office management while Patty wandered around the enticing boutiques inside the hotel.

The following morning, they decided that since it was such a gorgeous day they'd stroll over to Bloor Street for breakfast. Too bad they hadn't reckoned with the vagaries of abbreviated hotel maps. The one next to the phone on a side table showed Bloor Street as two blocks up from the hotel, first College and then Bloor. But it failed to show the many additional streets running parallel to these, and the two travellers from the prairies discovered every one of these on their safari into the high country of an interminable Yonge Street.

By the time they got to Bloor Street and found a decent restaurant, they were more than ready for a glorious lunch of ham omelettes, toast and jam, with cup after cup of hot tea. Replete and rested, they took a taxi back to the hotel so Phil could get to his afternoon meetings on time and Patty could go shopping. The meetings proved worthwhile, and most of the presentations were of high quality, well-delivered and informative, with good slides and case presentations.

On the second day, Philip ran into someone he thought he might never see again. It was none other than his first resident 'boss' at the Royal Gwent, Gil Turner. Neither of them could believe his eyes and both were delighted. The world was becoming a very small place, indeed, and their professional travel was hastening its contraction. Gil asked about every detail of Phil's progress since the happy days of Newport, and about his decision to come to Vanwey. The Albertan, in turn, described his decision to leave England in 1937 and take over the reins of the Turner Clinic in Edmonton from his ailing father. The old man died shortly after his son's return, Gil married his sweetheart and they now had two little girls.

That night, the Bosnars threw a party for the Turners in their hotel room. There were introductions all round, and these included Dr. Max Fremont, a pediatrician who was Mrs. Turner's favorite brother and who came along, too. Phil had a bottle of Johnny Walker Red Label and one of Seagrams V.O. ready for the event, and he had room service send up some assorted sandwiches, ice and extra glasses.

Everybody loved everybody, everybody drank too much, each reminiscence was greeted with peals of happy laughter, and Fremont proved to be the popular comedian of the group. As the supplies dwindled Gil picked up the phone and called room service. Then, in his best oriental accent, he shouted, "Doctaw Bossinaw secletally speakin', need maw stuff, loom tweref ereven. Then Fremont seized the phone and asked, "Is that Womb Service? You must give me Womb Service!"

After the pandemonium subsided and the group stopped screaming with laughter, it became possible for the poor restaurant staff at the other end of the line to take an intelligible order for fresh supplies of food, drink and ice. It was a memorable night, and when the party came to an end at 2 a.m. they all went to bed in happy exhaustion.

(This would be the last meeting between these two surgeons. After Turner's return to Edmonton he was afflicted by a series of heart attacks, each more severe than the one before, but he refused to modify his work pattern and was actually finishing a difficult operation when he had his final attack. The patient made a wonderful recovery but his surgeon died two days later. His premature death was a great loss to his profession and to his country. He was a brilliant, bold and innovative surgeon, who always preferred to lead rather than follow.)

CHAPTER 12

1937

Wednesday evening was Dr. Bosnar's night off. For the first three months at the Athlone he usually stayed in and was available for any surgical emergency case. As the house staff became more proficient and trustworthy with each passing week, and as his house surgeon, Willie Seale, developed his skills in the operating theater, he began to enjoy the occasional evening out. On this particular evening he'd arranged to take in a Westend film with Scottie McEwen, a pretty little X-ray technician. She was rather sweet, good company and not too demanding, so their friendship remained on a light and uncommitted level.

Just as he was ready to depart for the evening he was called to see a patient in the emergency department, an adorable little 3-year-old boy who'd been diagnosed by Seale as a possible intestinal *Intussusception*. (This is a condition, most prevalent at this age, in which a segment of contracting small intestine telescopes itself into the neighboring bowel, causing an acute obstruction. The affected loop is often the one closest to the right colon, and as the protrusion progresses around the colon the advancing intrusive segment can progress as far as the anal outlet.)

Philip confirmed the diagnosis and congratulated the beaming houseman on his astuteness. The preliminary clinical notes were excellent. The symptoms, which had commenced that morning, were characteristic: first the colicky pains that became steadily more violent, then the persistent vomiting, and finally the passage of blood-stained mucus from the rectum. There was no fever and the blood count was within normal limits, but the brave little chap was very dehydrated and an IV was set up at once with glucose in saline. The abdomen was only slightly distended and there was still the occasional tinkling metallic sound of obstructive peristalsis. There was a tender area in the left upper quadrant and the impression of a sausage-shaped mass in the left lower quadrant. X-rays of the abdomen were also most suggestive, with an absence of gas where the right colon should be showing.

Philip was chagrined to find that Maxwell was the honorary on call, and he phoned him without delay, albeit with considerable reluctance. After giving him all the details, he said, "If you don't mind, Sir, I'd like to set up for a laparotomy right away and get this intussusception reduced before it becomes fixed."

"But I do mind, Bosnar. You know very well that you're off duty this evening, and there's absolutely no reason at all for you to stay. I've already arranged to go ahead at nine o'clock and the house surgeon on call can assist me, so you're really not needed."

Maxwell's tone was as deliberately offensive as his words and Philip was too furious to reply. He slammed down the phone angrily and analyzed what he'd just heard.

First of all, it was obvious that the old bastard had been surreptitiously informed about the case by his private network: probably one or both of his two dragon ladies. Second, as a result he'd made it pointedly clear he wanted the case for himself and had no intention of letting the registrar get his hands on such a surgical prize.

During the film, which Scotty enjoyed from beginning to end, Philip remained distracted and almost unaware of what was happening on the big screen. He was unable to fight off his mood of depression, and even when his lively companion tried to cheer him up once or twice with an unashamedly full kiss on the lips, he was only aware that she always managed to bite him every time with those sharp little incisors of hers. As he licked away the salty drop of blood on his lower lip, he wondered if that old tosspot, Maxwell, was at this very moment botching a perfectly straight-forward operative procedure.

After the show, they found a cozy little night spot off Tottenham Court Road where they could enjoy a small snack and some drinks. Scotty had a glass of port and Philip belted down a double John Jameson with some soda water. Despite a slight easing of gloom, he couldn't go to bed without dropping in to see the little patient, and was partially reassured when he saw him sleeping peacefully like a pale Botticelli angel, with cherub's lips and golden curls.

The following morning, as the housemen all joined him at the breakfast table, they broke the bad news and he felt shattered. The little lad had expired shortly before 6 a.m. Philip pushed his breakfast tray away from him and fought back waves of dizziness and grief.

"That isn't the worst of it, Phil," Willie Seale's voice rose above the buzz of conversation around him. "Old Maxwell simply made a small incision, put in his hand and announced that there was no sign of intussusception, just tuberculous mesenteric nodes. Then he closed up."

"Did you believe the old fake?" asked Philip, his eyes bulging.

"I guess not, but I couldn't be sure," Willie replied quietly, looking downcast.

"Then why the fucking hell didn't you call me when I came back?" He felt himself slipping out of control and suddenly stopped. Standing up, he reached across, put an apologetic hand on Seale's shoulder and said, "It wasn't your fault, Willie. Let's set up a postmortem right away and we'll see what happened."

An hour later Philip stood appalled beside the little body on the autopsy table, the viscera fully exposed. There for all to see and weep, was a massive intussusception now black with gangrene, the blood-choked intestine floating in putrid peritoneal fluid. No tuberculous mesenteric nodes.

NO TUBERCULOUS NODES!

Get Mr. Maxwell over here right away," he ordered his assistant through clenched teeth, "and tell him it's a matter of the utmost urgency."

When the Athlone's senior honorary surgeon arrived on the scene, he was red-faced, annoyed and out of breath.

"What's all the big fuss about?" he enquired petulantly. Philip simply pointed to the black mess in the center of the table and answered with icy control.

"That, Mr. Maxwell, is what all the fuss is about. Will you tell the parents the truth or shall I?"

The old man seemed on the verge of a stroke, as his unwilling eyes absorbed the dreadful scene, and he staggered out of the room looking haggard.

That night, the house staff held a council of war.

"Something's got to be done," Philip declared, after giving the rest of them the gruesome details of the autopsy and Maxwell's reaction. Everyone agreed and it was young Finch-Roberts who spoke up at this point. The son of Britain's foremost expert on infectious diseases, he was doing a month's locum in the outpatient department and all the residents liked him.

"My Dad told me about a situation like this one, where they couldn't get rid of a rotten apple in the barrel, the hospital board wouldn't act, and the staff was helpless because of the culprit's political friends. They had to threaten a mass walkout of the resident staff before any changes were made."

"Did it work?" he was asked.

"Yes," he replied "but only just."

"Then I guess it's a gamble," Philip conceded. "Are we ready to vote on it?"

They all voted "Yea," without reservation and Finch-Roberts spoke up again.

"First, we ought to draft a set of concrete complaints, the really obvious ones that can't be refuted. Then we should demand that these complaints be dealt with and that all necessary corrective action should be undertaken without further delay."

Everyone endorsed his suggestion, and it was proposed that he and the registrar get together and draft the requisite memorandum. Their present term of duty was until the end of July, 1937, and their resignation, in the event the memorandum was rejected, would be as of June 30. Philip decided to discuss the matter with Mr. Vaughan and Dr. Rubin. They both gave him their full support, and agreed that the only way to get the dangerous Maxwell off staff and introduce much needed reforms was by submitting a set of demands and threatening to resign in support of their conditions. This would avoid the stigma of a strike and re-enforce their moral position beyond question.

The presentation, dated May 21, 1937, was sent to the Board of Management and to the Medical Committee. It read well, polite but firm. Both copies were signed by each and every member of the resident staff. Many of the honoraries felt sure the resignations could never be accepted. The allegations were true from start to finish. Maxwell should have been booted out long ago along with his pet Sisters and even the Matron, who consistently failed to stop the rot. Their optimism proved unjustified.

The resignations were accepted by the board without comment, and a pall of desperation hung over the hospital for days. Finally, Philip Bosnar called another meeting of his house staff.

"Listen, chaps, we've only got a little over a month to go. Let's not lower our standards and leave like a pack of dogs with our tails between our legs. Let's go out in a blaze of glory instead and give the performance of our lives. We'll give them a demonstration of just how good we are and make sure they'll never forget what a great bunch of residents they've lost, just because they were too stupid and too stubborn to change their rotten ways. Maybe we're the ones who had to clean up a mess that should have been taken care of by our predecessors, but if that's the case we should be bloody proud and not dejected."

He sat down, somewhat embarrassed by his oratory, and mumbled,

"Sorry about the long speech," but his apology was drowned out in a burst of enthusiastic handclapping and shouts of "Well done, Phil old boy!"

The remainder of their time turned out to be remarkably pleasant, and the honoraries were friendlier than ever, except for the icy Hardisty. Maxwell was hardly ever to be seen, thank God! The two dragon-Sisters and Matron were almost objectionably sweet and cooperative, and the tempo of the hospital settled into a steady and efficient rhythm. Philip was proud of his house-men and admired the proficiency they now displayed. He even felt entitled to some of the credit. As for his own standards, he felt that despite all the problems and difficulties, he'd learned a lot and improved a lot. Above all, he was learning to be a leader and take difficult decisions.

Dr. Rubin now insisted that Dr. Bosnar come to his home every Friday evening for the Shabbas meal. The Rubins were Orthodox Jews and they conducted a beautiful ceremony, with the ritual lighting of candles in their woven silver Minora and the blessings delivered in ancient bibli-cal Hebrew. The motherly Mrs. Rubin, her plump face agleam with religious ardor and apprecia-tion of her husband's melodious chant, made Philip feel like one of the family as she fussed over her 'honored guest' and made sure he was well looked after. Although he accepted the Yarmulka she handed him, he made no attempt to join in the ceremony – that would be hypocritical for such a disbeliever – but he felt a strange nostalgia tugging him back to his childhood and his early Hasidic zeal.

During the delicious repast, with its shining 'chalah' (a plaited loaf of bread), chopped liver and 'gefilte' fish (chopped fish with special herbs and popular vegetables), 'knaydle' soup (dumplings in chicken broth) and 'salt beef' (kosher corned beef), the two Rubin children, boys of nine and eleven, chattered away happily but otherwise behaved like perfect little gentlemen.

The other guest was a charming Jewish girl of about nineteen or twenty, obviously quite Orthodox, and it soon became evident that the main object of the occasion was that of serious matchmaking. Dr. Rubin, as fine a host as he was an anesthetist, kept telling his wife what a won-derful person Dr. Bosnar was, far beyond any point of embarrassment, and his wife in turn extolled the many superlative virtues of the blushing young lady. This was their way of quickening the romantic interest of the young pair, but Philip was sure it had just the reverse effect.

In any event, these warm and friendly Friday evenings went on for a whole month before the Rubins – bless their kind hearts – decided their 'Shatchan' (matchmaker) efforts had failed to produce the desired march to the 'Chupa' (the ceremonial wedding canopy) and the smashed wineglass of marital good fortune. Nevertheless, thought Philip, the interlude had served to remind him that a lot could still be said for the old-time Jewish religion of his ancestors.

The most pleasant turn of events came when it was time to leave the Athlone. Philip asked all the honoraries with whom he'd worked, excepting Maxwell, for the customary testimo-nial letters. The ones he'd obtained from the Royal Gwent were very flattering, and he was sure these wouldn't be as good. To his great joy they turned out even better, and the most surprising of all was the one from Hardisty. The unbending Colonel not only praised his work in glowing terms but paid tribute to **'Dr. Bosnar's firmness of resolve and leadership qualities'**. As in the past, Philip marveled at the Good Lord's sense of humor.

He began to wonder what to do next, and he certainly needed to get the bad taste of the Athlone residency out of his system before applying for the next one. A more important considera-tion was his shortage of cash, and he'd need to pick up some well-paid locum jobs as soon as possible. They'd have to be general practice, preferably far away from his present location in Walthamstow. First, however, his batteries needed recharging and he was sure he'd feel much better after a fortnight's holiday, but where?

The problem was soon solved by his favorite X-ray technician, when he met her for afternoon tea on the Saturday after leaving the Athlone for the last time. He arrived a bit late at the small tea room near the Charing Cross Hospital, a favorite relaxing spot with the hospital's resident staff. A big rugged-looking chap was with her, his face displaying the same goodlooking features as those of the petite Scotty but in bolder version, and it was no surprise when she introduced him as her brother.

"This is my little brother Hamish." she said with a laugh. "He has his real estate office close by and keeps a bachelor flat on the second floor. I knew you wouldn't mind if I asked him to join us."

Hamish seemed a likable fellow, and soon proved himself a good conversationalist. His sister had obviously told him all about the residents' manifesto and walk-out at the Athlone, and he made it clear that he admired Philip for his stand.

"That took guts," he remarked succinctly.

"Well, all my resident staff were in this together, and they deserve full credit."

"Too bad the previous bunch of residents didn't have the gumption to act before things got that bad."

Philip didn't feel like pursuing the matter.

"Let's change the subject," he suggested, "and talk about something pleasant, like holidays."

Tea arrived, with lots of scrumptious Devonshire Splits, and between creamy mouthfuls Scotty and her brother came up with a great idea.

"Hamish and I are going up to Stornoway on Monday. Mummy lives there, all alone. We've both tried to get her to move to London after Daddy died but she refuses to budge."

"We've been a mite worried lately about her health." said Hamish. "She never complains, but we get regular reports on her condition from a cousin who lives close by."

"Tell me about Stornoway. I'm not too familiar with the place."

"It's in the outer Hebrides, on the Island of Lewis and Harris, and that's where Hamish and I were born. The place is right away from civilization. That's why Jeannie and I have always had a bit of a wild streak."

"I've never noticed your sister's wild streak so far."

"That's probably because she's spent too much time in London."

"Speak for yourself, Hamish. You're the one who's become the polished English type, complete with a fancy London flat."

"Listen, Dr. Bosnar, why don't you come up to the Island next week and join us. We can get you comfortably put up at a top-flight boarding house. You'll find the food simple but delicious."

"You know, Hamish, that sounds like a hell of a good idea. I'll start making arrangements right away, but first I must spend a week at home with my family."

Thus it was arranged that Philip would join the McEwens in far-off Stornoway: land of the Gaelic tongue, magical mists, wild scenery, untamed sheep, native crofters and Harris Tweed. He should be able to time his arrival one week from next Tuesday, and they all shook hands on it.

The train journey was a memorable one. Philip reserved a lower sleeper and slept like a top, as the Flying Scotsman puffed its way northward to the magnificent wilds of Scotland and its Atlantic Islands. The following morning, he rose refreshed and ready for an early breakfast. After a shave and general toilet in the men's washroom, he dressed and entered the dining area as hungry as a wolf. This was true luxury at its finest. He was seated alone at a table facing the engine. The table linen was gleaming white, the cutlery sparkling and of ornate high quality, and the glassware of graciously designed cut crystal. Outside, the early morning was glorious and the view magnificent.

As he worked his enthusiastic way through a fruit cocktail, a small platter of delicious tiny grilled fish and the main dish of aromatic bacon and eggs with mushrooms and fried tomatoes, he revelled not only in the superb quality of such a royal feast but in the glorious scenery through which they were speeding. By the time he'd finished his third cup of tea and polished off the toast and jam, he was sure he'd never be able to eat again but didn't regret a single hedonistic moment of his matchless breakfast.

At Edinburgh, he changed trains for Inverness, and the surrounding scenery became even more breathtaking. On enquiry from his fellow-travelers he was informed that these were the legendary Trossachs. How fascinating, he thought: this was the romantic locale of Sir Walter Scott's 'Lady of the Lake' and 'Rob Roy,' and he revelled in the picturesque wild countryside to the limits of his imagination and the reading memories of his childhood. As they passed into the untamed northeastern highland country, he felt a desperate urge to get outside and paint or photograph the glory that Mother Nature now spread before them in careless abundance. There it was, heaped slope on craggy slope, forest on mountain meadow, up and up into the mists of legend.

At Inverness, he changed trains once again, this time bound for the western shores and the Kyle of Lochalsh. The final train journey traversed the starker northern highlands: land of heroic vistas and the aura of myth and mystery. Scotland was truly a land of abiding splendor, and he could understand the Scots' fierce pride for their unique homeland, where the skirl of pipes calls out to the wild winds of the North in a dialogue of timeless history.

The McBraine steamer that ferried him across the choppy waters of the Minch was surprisingly small, and carried only about two dozen passengers. As they journeyed northward, the seas got rougher and the ferry boat's chugging engine seemed to labor. Once, it actually stopped and Philip wondered if the exhausted pistons had finally given up. Far from it; it took more than angry seas to stop these intrepid seamen and their flimsy craft. Looking out over the port side rail, he could barely make out the lone oarsman heaving his small rowboat against the snarling seas and approaching the McBraine steamboat at his peril. The boat had come from one of the tiny islands dotting the Minch. When it got dangerously close and in imminent hazard of being dashed against the larger vessel, the lone mariner lowered his oars and transferred a package into the long-handled net lowered from above. It must be some mail in a waterproof wrapping. Then, in return, mail for his lonely speck of sea-encircled land was lowered carefully by the same means. The notorious Captain Bligh could have done no better!

Philip found the rising excitement of the trip winning hunger's fight against the threat of seasickness, and when they were well under way once more, he opened up the coverings of his giant Cadbury chocolate bar, broke off a piece and took a generous bite. He also offered his chocolate in unthinking generosity to several of his fellow passengers on deck, but they fled as though offered a dose of poison.

At last they came in sight of the Isle of Lewis and Harris, then the port of Stornoway itself. The smell of dead herring assaulted him like a massive blow, and for a few moments he found himself unable to breathe. Despite the choking miasma, it appeared that the town's entire population had come to greet the steamer's arrival and welcome the passengers ashore. On enquiry, he was told by a crewman that this was standard procedure. After all, this was their lifeline to the outside world, and it reduced their sense of isolation and abandonment.

He soon spotted the McEwens waving madly at the back of the crowd and they helped him into their borrowed car, an ancient Austin Minor. Scotty gave him a great big welcoming kiss and he tasted his blood in the Hebrides for the first time. It tasted of dead herring, as would everything else for the first few days. Hamish laughed his head off when Philip mentioned the problem.

"It's destroyed even my celebrated appetite. I doubt if I'll be able to eat anything while I'm here."

"You'll get used to it, Phil," Scotty assured him, "and then you'll be eating our good plain food with a healthy appetite and enjoyment."

"Without its herring trade, you must remember, poor Stornoway would probably just fade away." Hamish informed him, and Philip remarked, "I suppose the dreadful odor of dead fish must be like an expensive perfume to the local population."

Mrs. Grant's boarding house was all he could have wanted. She was a buxom widow in her sixties, full of good humor and anxious to take good care of her young guest, the "important London surgeon." Philip assured her that he was only of hospital resident status and begged to be addressed at all times as "Phil." She, in turn, never called him anything other than "Dr. Bosnar." The bedroom assigned to him was spacious, and the old iron bed with its huge mattress most comfortable. The bathroom was close by and there was no shortage of hot water. After a great night's sleep, he awoke early, obtained unchallenged access to the bathroom, and came down to breakfast with a hunger that was only partially neutralized by the all-pervasive smell that lingered in every corner. It took two more days before he became cheerfully immune to the fishy miasma, and his morning oatmeal porridge, bacon and eggs, no longer tasted of expired *Clupia harengus*.

Once his appetite returned full force, he was afraid that all of Mrs. Grant's magnificent food would make him gain too much weight, so he filled his days with long walks and occasional tennis games on a nearby hard-court that had seen better days. Sometimes these activities were shared with the vivacious Scotty, sometimes with her athletic brother, and sometimes all three joined forces.

On the fourth day, he was introduced to their charming mother, a thin little gray-haired lady looking old far beyond her years. Her tiny waterfront house was spotless, and all its humble contents were neat and tidy, down to the last carefully preserved knickknack. The old lady wore the conventional Stornoway black attire, and her traditional black shawl was hanging on a peg in the corner. She thanked Philip in English – with a heavy Scottish accent – for his small bouquet of local wildflowers, but seemed far more at home with her native Gaelic, into which she lapsed when addressing her devoted children. They all shared a large pot of tea with her, then left for a tour of Lever Castle, more a historical art museum than a castle.

Lord Leverhulme's gift to the islanders was a beautiful edifice, built in tasteful architectural style and located by the edge of a quiet stretch of water. The furnishings, paintings and artifacts were all of high quality and Philip was impressed. This was a gift in the grand manner and the people of Lewis were proud and grateful.

One morning, Hamish invited him to go "handline fishing." He warned Philip it might be very cold, and that warning turned out to be accurate in the extreme. Despite extra layers of clothing and a heavy mackintosh covering, his teeth were soon chattering with the penetrating chill; as the sea breezes found their way through every weave and seam of his protective attire. Even the brilliant sunshine seemed unable to combat the frigid air. Hamish had set his stage carefully.

"Sorry, Phil," he said apologetically, "if I sound oldfashioned, but I have to ask you the direct question."

"Fire away," Phil replied, keeping his voice cheerful, as he knew full well what was coming.

"What are your intentions toward my sister? In spite of her spunkiness, she's easily hurt and I know she's much keener on you than she shows."

"Let me put it this way, Hamish. I find her a good friend and an enjoyable companion. Any romantic overtones are quite non-binding, and I've never shown the slightest intention of entering into a serious affair with Jeannie, much less any suggestion of marriage."

That seemed to satisfy his sturdy oarsman and the subject was never raised again.

Once in a while, on an afternoon stroll together, Phil and Scotty would pause and sit down on a grassy hummock to enjoy the tranquil scene. The only disturbances to their peaceful serenity were the screaming wild seagulls and an occasional threatening ram. The gulls were reputed to be unusually fierce, while the rams looked huge to Phil's untutored eyes, and were armed with great menacing horns. The atmosphere was otherwise idyllic and Philip was careful not to encourage the growing amorous tendencies of his lively companion. On one such occasion, Scotty broke through his reserve.

"I'm quite aware you've no intention of marrying me, Philip, but that doesn't mean we can't make love, does it?"

To emphasize her point she kissed him hard on the mouth and he found himself once more tasting his own blood with the distinctive flavor of dead herring. Perhaps, he thought, this was an ancient Hebridean love potion, recaptured from the mists of time. In any event, they both shed their clothing impediments on the spot and made love to the point of exhaustion, while the magical landscape smiled on their pleasure.

As the days passed by, Philip began to spend an increasing amount of time on his own, and that was quite agreeable to the young McEwens, as they had many business items to take care of in connection with the family finances, and would be driving into the center of town quite often. On one such day he took the vaunted bus trip to the southern end of the island and the hills of Harris.

The journey proved a spectacular foray into travel sickness and dire peril. As the rickety vehicle careened recklessly over the narrow potholed winding highway, Philip stole an occasional glance through the window and kept himself pressed against it so that he could maintain his stability on the lurching turns. He caught his breath when, at what felt like dizzying heights, great chunks on the side of the road appeared to have dropped away, and one could gaze straight down at an unimpeded panorama of the valley far below.

As if that weren't enough to give his passengers a thrill, the intrepid driver engaged in a lively Gaelic conversation with an old fellow behind him, often turning to face his chatty passenger, with the bus rattling ahead unerringly as though it remembered the way. Showing a keen understanding of the inexorable laws of nature, the driver stopped his bus once in a while, so that the distressed travelers could heave up their insides by the roadside to their hearts' content, while others obtained alternative visceral relief on the opposite side of the vehicle.

Harris was a bit of a disappointment. Philip had expected to see a host of busy crofters weaving their sturdy tweeds of worldwide fame. He even wore his impressive rust-brown suit of 'Genuine Harris Tweed' for the special occasion. Sad to say, the native crofters were few, forlorn and far between, and he learned that most of this precious fabric was now produced in the mechanized looms of Manchester. Only the wool came from this area, but the ancient skilled craft was disappearing and the romance would soon be gone forever.

Exciting as this hair-raising and memorable trip proved to be, an even greater thrill was to follow. One warm morning, around 10 o'clock, he took his swimsuit and towel with him and walked along to the nine hole golf course. Then he wandered down to the beach, known locally by a Gaelic name which sounded to his ear like 'The Cocheleb'. He'd always been a poor swimmer with no buoyancy whatever in fresh water. The sea was something else entirely, a watery paradise of pounding waves and heaving swells, carrying him up and down to its own restless rhythm, refreshing his body and renewing his vitality with its primordial solution of metallic salts and dissolved oxygen. It was a miraculous liquid that so closely matched his own blood plasma and internal body fluids.

When he entered the seductive blue-gray billows that surged toward him, he gasped at the incredible chill of these northern seas. Despite his most intense efforts at adjusting to the freezing embrace numbing him to the bone, he soon had to withdraw in abject defeat, his skin matching the color of the waves. Running back to his pile of towel and clothing he rubbed himself dry and continued toweling vigorously until he felt his circulation restored, then began dressing and felt warm again. It was at this moment of tingling exhilaration that Philip Bosnar made his big mistake.

The deserted wide sandy beach was covered with every conceivable variety of seashell in untouched and unspoiled splendor, and he bent down eagerly to pick up some choice specimens. In an instant they were upon him, wave upon screeching wave of attacking seagulls, fierce beyond any dreams, bent upon pecking him to shreds, but aiming mostly for his eyes. These fearsome predators were much closer to their dinosaur ancestors than the friendly scavengers of his childhood experiences around the Thames and southern seasides. He covered his head with his towel, picked up his clothes and ran blindly away from the shore and in the direction of the golf links. Only when he was safe from renewed attack did he remove his cover. He found himself stared at curiously by a foursome of golfers on the adjoining fairway, and he didn't feel like offering any explanation.

That afternoon, he visited the small Stornoway hospital as a matter of interest, and found the resident in charge an informative fellow from Aberdeen. He had his Edinburgh F.R.C.S. and was capable of a wide range of general and traumatic surgery. When he heard about Philip's experience on the beach the resident told him he'd been pretty lucky.

"Last year," he related, "a visiting golfer wasn't so lucky. He hooked his ball onto the `Cocheleb' and as he picked it up the gulls attacked him and he lost an eye."
When his listener looked horrified, he explained.

"You see, that stretch of sandy beach is the main nesting ground of the local seabird population, and if they believe you're threatening one of the many eggs buried just below the surface, they attack in force. They go mostly for the eyes and what you did to protect yourself was exactly right."

Despite the extreme comfort of his bed at the boarding house, Philip found it very difficult – after the first dreamless night – to fall asleep. Outside at this late hour, it was still as bright as midday. The sun shone in insistent brightness through his drawn blinds and curtains, beckoning him outside. Once or twice he surrendered to temptation, got dressed and walked the half mile down to the main jetty. He strolled among the fishermen fixing up their small boats and endless nets for the following morning's trawling and marveled at their patience.

Lately, he'd become engrossed in a recently purchased book, and fell asleep still reading it, night after night. The name of the new work by A.J.Cronin was **'The Citadel'**, and Philip lost himself in its fascinating depths. Here was a man who could write with deep understanding of his subject, involving his readers in the central character's conflicts of conscience and ambition, of service to his fellow mortals versus the dizzying climb to power and affluence.

The story was obviously a fictional autobiography. It carried its protagonist, an idealistic young Scottish physician, through the stifling penny-pinching back country of mine-contract practice in South Wales, and up into the venal heights of 'high society' private practice in the fashionable West End of London. Philip was familiar with the locales described in the South Wales segment of the novel, and he wondered how much things had changed since the early 20s, the period described by Dr.. Cronin, as seen through the eyes of his imperfect hero, Dr. Manson. As for the lucrative type of so called 'fashionable practice,' Philip had seen for himself the endless array of brass plates on the front of those imposing Victorian residences in such places as Harley Street and Wimpole Street, where great specialists had their offices. He also knew that most of these plates represented pretenders: vulgar types who paid exorbitant prices for the borrowed eminence of an impressive address but occupied the premises for as little as one hour a week.

The Citadel was a brand new work by this physician-turned-author, like so many doctors before him, and Philip understood why the critics were so effusive in their praise. By the time he'd finished the book he knew what he must do when he returned to London. He would search the advertisements in the Lancet and B.M.J. (British Medical Journal); first, for a locum in the mining country of South Wales; then, in the elegant medical salons of fashionable practice in London. In this way, he could duplicate the earlier experiences of the fictional Dr. Manson and reach his own conclusions. It seemed an excellent way of shaping his future path in the exciting profession he'd chosen.

On the journey back to London he reflected on the message of moral maturation he'd received from Cronin's inspired pen. Such development and growth could only come from a rich diversity of medical practice in various environments, not just the ivory tower of a major teaching hospital in London. He found himself wondering how he'd behave if, like the leading figure in this tale of ideals, temptations and strife, he might ultimately find himself confronting the forces of organized medicine in a conflict of principles.

CHAPTER 13

1943

The date was December 7, and it seemed a thousand years since Pearl Harbor. Philip was in one of his despondent moods about the war's progress. He'd hoped, on this anniversary of Japan's sneak attack, that the armed might of the U.S.A. would have registered a long series of resounding victories against the Axis forces. Patty tried to cheer him up.

"You worry too much, darling. Look at El Alamein. Military experts are saying it might well be the turning point of the war."

"Maybe. They're saying the same thing about the Russian break-through at Stalingrad. They could be right, as long as Montgomery doesn't let up on the chase, and the Russians likewise."

"Then why the long face?"

Philip tried to convey his gnawing doubts without sounding like a Jeremiah. He pointed out that both of these victories had been snatched from the jaws of defeat. They came at the end of long retreats and a string of enemy victories. Thank God the Germans had stretched their supply lines hopelessly in both cases!

He went on to deplore the terrible beating taken by Allied forces in the Pacific, the Death March of American P.O.Ws in the Philippines and the brutal treatment of Canadians by the Japanese in Hongkong. The Sons of Nippon had learned their lessons well from their Nazi friends.

"But that," he concluded, "doesn't justify the rotten treatment of second generation Japanese-Canadians by the Mackenzie King government."

There was another aspect of the war that he found deeply disturbing. How the devil could they put a man like Eisenhower in charge of the allied forces in North Africa? He'd always been a desk officer, a military bureaucrat whose experience was acquired to a large extent while serving as a subordinate in McArthur's office, never in battle.

"A lot of overseas authorities are saying it should have been Alexander, or even Montgomery, and I think they're right. If nothing else, a man of integrity like Alexander would never associate himself with a miserable turncoat like Admiral Darlan."

Patty asked him to explain his revulsion and he obliged with a detailed analysis. Darlan, he pointed out, was the man who first jockeyed with the senile Petain and sleazy Laval for top position in the Vichy puppet government. He was a notorious admirer of the Hitler regime and a confirmed hater of the British. Most of all, he still seemed to carry the stench of the old French military establishment that sent an innocent Dreyfus to rot in the cages of Devil's Island.

As soon as Darlan thought Britain and the Americans might be winning the war, he sneaked across to Algiers, where he was taken prisoner – a most convenient event. The next news about him was his appointment as High Commissioner for French Colonial Africa, with the full approval of General Eisenhower. The excuse given was that he was the only high official who could get the French troops in Africa to join the Allies. What about De Gaulle? He should have been the logical choice, but instead, the Allies had made a lasting enemy of this future leader of France. Then, when it was much too late, the turncoat admiral ordered the French Fleet to North Africa, with the foregone conclusion that the great Armada would be scuttled instead. Once Philip got all these misgivings off his chest, he felt much better and gladly accepted Patty's offer of something to wet his whistle. She knew how to handle her husband when he got all wound up.

Christmas Eve Midnight Mass was rapidly approaching and Philip started to get his violin into trim for the occasion. For three years he'd been called upon to perform during the services, with Herb Adams at the organ. Adams was the church organist at the Catholic cathedral and an excellent accompanist, and between them they worked out a suitable program each year. This year they chose the Meditation from Thais, music from Samuel Barber's Adagio for Strings and the Negro spiritual, Goin' Home.

On each of the previous occasions the cathedral had been crowded to overflowing, with many people standing at the back of the building. This time, the rehearsals had gone smoothly and the somber Monsignor thought the selected program expressed profound religious feelings. Philip had been working hard on perfecting a special viola-like sound for this type of music: what he called his "Celestial Tone."

He had to smile when he remembered last Christmas Eve. He and Doug Conway were on a bit of a bender after dinner, when his friend asked him to play some of the music he'd prepared for the Midnight Mass.

"Not on your life, old boy. You know you hate serious music, and violin most of all."

"Go ahead anyhow. Maybe I'll get religion. I might even become a Catholic."

"Never! Think of all those confessions."

"Go ahead and play. Do it just for me."

"Oh very well, but remember, it won't sound very good without accompaniment."

He brought his violin case inside from the back seat of his car, took out the instrument and tuned it while Doug winced, then adjusted the bow's tension.

They were alone in the rear office of the Gazette and there were no extraneous sounds to disturb them. He began to play the popular Schubert's Ave Maria. To his astonishment, the acoustics were perfect and the notes sang with haunting beauty. As he played, he noticed a strange transformation on Doug's face. The lines of mirth were replaced by a strange fixed intensity, and when the double-stopping passage filled the air with its simple harmonies, Doug could no longer hide his appreciation. As the last notes faded away into absolute silence, Doug blew his nose noisily and said, "Phil, you old bugger, I never knew you could make a fiddle sound like that."

The Mass was first-class, and Philip was gratified that the musical program was well received. He was seated in the choir area and the choir leader almost spoiled his complimentary remarks by whispering, "The Goddam place is swarming with unbelievers."

On second thoughts, Philip decided the comment was hilarious in the circumstances.

The festive season was now upon them, and crisis was at hand. The customary annual supply of liquor had failed to materialize and the manager of the local liquor board was apologetic.

"Sorry, Dr. Bosnar, but there was such a rush of orders I couldn't put aside the usual supply for you. Rationing was much tighter this Christmas for some reason."

The Bosnars counted their stocks. Forty-seven bottles and that was all! They'd invited their airforce friends to an open house party on Boxing Day, and they dreaded the moment when supplies petered out. Perhaps, before they got below a certain point, the odd bottle could be scrounged from their closest friends. Besides, they wouldn't have to contend with the gargantuan thirst of the absent Doug Conway. If necessary, Philip was even prepared to go teetotal himself.

At 3 o'clock on the afternoon of the party, the airforce guests started to arrive in large numbers, and the hosts felt their hearts sinking. Then, wonder of wonders, each officer produced a bottle of liquor and it was possible to breathe freely once again. It was a great party, and Phil wondered how their airforce friends found out about their last minute shortage. Patty was convinced that R.A.F. intelligence must be the finest in the world, and Phil agreed.

It wasn't long after the holiday season that the Bosnars read and listened, enthralled, to the extraordinary news about Darlan. He'd been killed by a young Frenchman on Christmas Eve. The assassin had entered the High Commissioner's office without difficulty or challenge, and emptied his handgun into the unsuspecting victim. Darlan fell mortally wounded, and as soon as the gunman turned away, he was seized and imprisoned; then executed by a firing squad not long after his arrest.

Several important details were missing from the news reports, and apart from the information that the killer was twenty years old, all particulars were withheld. Who was this young Frenchman? Where did he come from? Who were his parents? What were his motives: political, personal, right wing, left wing? Was he a hired killer for the Free French, for the British, for a dissident element in the Eisenhower command, the Laval group, or maybe even the Germans? How did he enter these heavily guarded headquarters with such ease, and why the hasty execution with no published report of an investigation or trial?

The whole affair smelled of a set-up and doublecross. Philip envisaged a young patriot who might have lost a member of his family, and blamed Darlan for complicity in the pro-Nazi atrocities taking place in occupied France. Perhaps the assassin had been promised amnesty or a contrived escape and disappearance. Two items received only the scantiest attention in the press. The first was the political convenience of the assassination. It eliminated a grave embarrassment to Eisenhower and his cohorts, and it made the way clear for General Giraud (and perhaps even DeGaulle) to join the Allied campaign in North Africa. The second was the obvious astonishment of the assassin on facing a firing squad, as described by those present at his execution.

Ultimately, however, it would be a simple decision that dead men tell no tales. The world would never know, but the enquiring Bosnars of this world would always speculate. Once the U.S. high command in North Africa was prepared to be contaminated by such corruption, the stench could never again be entirely dispelled. Out of such expediency and compromise would come an overriding political philosophy: that the end always justified the means.

The unexpected arrival of Dr. Alvin Masters in late January was a pleasant surprise. He applied for a position in the practice, having heard from his friends in Vanwey that Dr. Bosnar was looking for a G.P. to join him. Philip checked his credentials and found them more than adequate. All of Masters' former teachers and department heads in Toronto mentioned his quick mind and pleasant personality, and during his one month's trial in Vanwey he proved the accuracy of both comments. An additional recommendation was the fact that Masters was certified unfit for military service by virtue of an active duodenal ulcer. This would satisfy the stringent requirements of the Procurement and Assignment Board, should Philip now enlist. Masters' commencing salary was agreed at $350 a month, increasing later on if all worked out well.

The new arrival was Jewish and had changed his name from Meissner. He was a good-looking young man in his late twenties, with dark curly hair, and he was married to a pretty little Jewish girl. It was obvious they were deeply in love and Philip assured them that they'd find Vanwey a happy and friendly place. It was a sad disappointment, therefore, when Masters' entry into the Rotary Club ran into unexpected difficulties. It appeared there were still a few members in the club who felt that adding a second Jew to the membership would be going too far. Mort Schneider was more than enough, they insisted. Philip's solution was simple. He discussed the matter with a group of Vanwey's leading Rotarians: Adams, Sundstrom, McTeague and the young United Church Minister, Norman Evans. They all responded by threatening to resign and Masters was soon accepted as a new member.

Group Captain Leacox had taken over from the patrician Cummings as senior officer at the base, and the Bosnars found him an affable replacement. One Saturday afternoon in mid-April, he paid them a surprise visit. He was full of boyish enthusiasm and told them he was the bearer of glad tidings. "Why don't we have a drink first?" he suggested, his cheeks glowing with excitement, and Philip did the honors.

"How would you like to come into the R.A.F. with the acting rank of Wing Commander?" the visitor asked without preamble.

"My God, that would be terrific!"

"I'm pretty sure I can swing it. I've contacted the top brass in London and told them all about you."

"That's awfully decent of you."

"I told them how hard you've tried to enlist both over there and over here. I've also told them about your fine work as civilian surgeon to our base."

"Do you mind telling me where you got all the details?"

"From several sources, but mainly from Squadron Leader Graham Hobart, our chief M.O. He even gave me all your degrees. Very impressive I must say,"

"As you can see, my wife is pregnant and well along. She's carrying our second child and I wouldn't want to leave before the baby's born next month."

"Of course not, but I think you should go ahead and get yourself measured for a uniform."

After he left, the Bosnars found it difficult to absorb what their jovial guest had just told them. Patty felt a genuine sense of elation for her husband, even though she dreaded his impending departure, now that her second baby was on the way. Perhaps it was just as well. With each passing month, his thoughts seemed to dwell more and more on the war, and if he didn't get overseas pretty soon, he'd be very difficult to live with.

He tried to keep his enthusiasm in perspective. He would just love to get overseas, and a Wing Commander's rank in the R.A.F. would be icing on the cake. But the thought of leaving his adorable Patty behind, along with their beloved little lad and a new baby, filled him with a sense of separation and betrayal that he couldn't suppress. Meanwhile, his new associate was working out well, and there was no doubt he'd take good care of the practice if and when his superior had to leave.

On the following Saturday, the jovial Group Captain returned, but not so jovial this time. He was glum and apologetic, and hoped he hadn't raised Bosnar's expectations too high during his previous visit. Philip assured him no R.A.F. uniform had been ordered as yet, and asked what had gone wrong. It was the old familiar bureaucratic game that could be so damnably frustrating, and Philip could almost sense what was coming next.

Apparently, some minor fuss-pot in the London H.Q. had taken it upon himself to enquire about Bosnar's call-up status in Canada. Ottawa's reply, for reasons that made no sense whatever, was that the Canadian armed forces held first claim to his specialist services. It went on to state that he was eligible for call-up as soon as he had a satisfactory replacement, one who was medically unfit for military service. This was pure garbage, Philip fumed. He'd already informed the D.M.O. of MD12 about Masters and his special status, as far back as early February, and hadn't received so much as an acknowledgement.

The Bosnars and their visitor decided to fill their glasses at this point and drink to the abolition of red tape and its abominable functionaries. Philip also expressed his appreciation to the Group Captain for his efforts and insisted he had no reason to feel apologetic.

That night, he phoned John Kinsley in Winnipeg and was overjoyed to reach him without delay. He poured out his entire story about the Wing Commander fiasco, and felt better right away when Kinsley shared his anger.

"One of the reasons I thought I'd better phone you is to try and pull some strings. I believe J.L.Anderson is now an army Colonel and has a fair amount of clout on matters of army medical recruiting."
Anderson had been professor and head of Internal Medicine at the Winnipeg General, and was one of his L.M.C.C. examiners.

"He's a bloody good man and a close friend of mine," Kinsley replied with enthusiasm. "I'll get onto him right away and things should start moving in a couple of months, allowing for the usual delays and office snafus."
Philip slept well that night and Patricia was happy to observe that he smiled in his sleep. It was clear the phone call had cheered him up more than he'd admit.

Their second child, Florian, arrived on May 24, 1943. It was a nice easy delivery and they were blessed with a beautiful little blonde-haired daughter, weighing 6 lbs 8 oz. She was tiny but perfect, like a Caravaggio miniature, and she would be Jimmy's little sister and playmate in the years to come. The baby had a wonderful pixie expression and never cried. Three weeks passed and she never cried at all. She almost never seemed to sleep, either, and didn't seem the least bit interested in her bottle. Patty never attempted to breast-feed her, after her difficulties the last time, and Philip began to worry. Florian seemed to remain perfectly happy, serene and content, and there was no weight loss; but neither was there any weight gain.

He searched his books and journals to no avail. Next, he phoned the professor of pediatrics at the Winnipeg General and the infancy department at Toronto's Sick Children's Hospital, but came up with few good answers. The most he could hope to accomplish by transferring their adored little baby, would be to convert her into a pin-cushion of tests and ever more tests with little promise of resolving the problem.

There was only one place where he found the faintest suggestion of how to proceed. It was in a three volume German classic, 'Kinderkrankheiten' (diseases of children), about twenty years old. It hinted that in some similar cases – where the temperature, blood count and urinalysis were normal – it might be a case of concealed mineral or vitamin deficiency. After a long and difficult discussion with Patty, she swallowed her reluctance and bravely agreed to let him place the baby in hospital for a two week trial program of management.

He contacted Mrs. Charters, a veteran who'd taken care of Patty in 1941 when she developed her breast infection, and who now did special nursing. He set up a continuous intravenous drip of glucose in saline, with a small daily dose of Vitamin B complex and Vitamin C. Every four hours around the clock, a bottle of formula would be offered to the little tot, varying the brand of milk, the mixture and the taste, with added flavors of fruit or chocolate until the magic formula could be found.

For the first week nothing happened, but they persisted. By the start of the second week, the infant began to sleep. She also began to cry and show an interest in the bottle. On the twelfth day they found the magic formula, a simple Carnation Brand mixture with a slight orange flavor. Little Florian began to finish her bottles with evident delight, and from that moment on she never looked back. On the fourteenth day she was back home, showing every sign of flourishing, and they all breathed more easily.

It wasn't until the end of May that he received his official call to report to the Regina H.Q. at 0900 hours on June 1. He phoned Kinsley the same evening to thank him for his efforts, and asked him to convey his thanks to Anderson. A series of meetings followed, first with Mayor Jock McTeague, who was his accountant and also Pete Forsyth's, then with Alvin Masters and Kitty Forsyth.

McTeague had always chided Philip for being far too generous in his income sharing arrangements with Forsyth when he left to enter the army. It worked out as 65 percent to Bosnar and 35 percent to Forsyth, and Philip thought that was fair. The new arrangement would be 50 percent to Masters, 30 percent to Bosnar and 20 percent to Forsyth. All parties agreed to this arrangement, and it was calculated – by including certain tax advantages worked out by McTeague – that Philip's 30 percent from the practice along with his army pay, would be pretty close to his current income.

A letter was sent to all his patients that he was turning them over, if they were agreeable, to his new partner Dr. Masters. At the same time, an appropriate notice was inserted in the Vanwey Gazette. It was hard beyond words saying goodbye to his beloved Patty, to his husky 2-year-old son and his sweet little daughter, now thriving, but he gave his solemn promise to get back home as often as possible. He also left her a consoling memento: a lovable black and white cocker spaniel, 2 years old. Patty took one look, was quite overwhelmed and named him 'Whiskers' without hesitation.

Acting Captain Philip Bosnar, surgical specialist to MD12, soon found out what a small cog he was in the vast creaking machinery of the Canadian Army. He was assigned to the outpatient department of Regina Military Hospital, and his duties were to examine new recruits of the South Saskatchewan Regiment and check them for such defects as hernias, varicose veins, hemorrhoids, bunions, or any other problems that needed surgical correction before enlistment was accepted. He was assigned no duties whatever in the hospital wards and was automatically excluded from any operative surgery. Any cases requiring surgery were still being transferred out to the civilian surgeon in the D.P.N.H. (Department of Pensions and National Health), just as they were prior to Philip's arrival.

His boarding arrangements, on the other hand, were more than acceptable. Since the medical officers' regular quarters were full, he was put up at the Saskatchewan Hotel, with breakfast and dinner in the hotel dining room. This was a pleasant luxury, at the taxpayer's expense of course. He was flattered by his smart dress uniform, with shining Sam Browne belt and flashy swagger stick; and as he walked to the hospital in the morning and returned in the late afternoon, he enjoyed the ritual of being saluted by passing privates and N.C.Os and snapping back a smart salute in return. He was careful to stride rather than stroll, to keep his head high and his shoulders back, as befitted an officer in His Majesty's Armed Forces. None of those sloppy U.S. army customs!

As new surgical specialist to Regina Military Hospital, Captain Bosnar decided to approach the O.C. in charge of hospital activities, Major Pines, a man he knew fairly well. He remembered him as an unpleasant individual who'd been one of Blaikie's chums from up the line, a substandard G.P. who used to send all his surgery to that worthy gentleman, often with little to justify any operation at all.

"Don't expect to change everything here just because you think you're a bigshot surgeon," was the O.C's helpful response when Philip asked what his operative duties would be, and it was clear that there'd be no relief in that direction.

He asked to see Lt-Col. Ackland, the D.M.O. he'd met once or twice in the officers' mess and who seemed quite likeable. Ackland was a short, fat, jolly fellow in his early fifties, with a bull neck and purple complexion that suggested he might be strangling inside his collar and tie. He had a good reputation as a decent commanding officer, and Philip looked forward to having an honest discussion with him. The first two occasions that he tried, however, he didn't get past the Colonel's deputy, Major Ratch, a confirmed cynic known for his sarcasm and obstructive attitude.

"Just waddya wanna to see the Colonel about?" he asked nastily. Philip told him, but avoided details.

"I'm not gonna to let you bother the old man with petty problems like that. He'd have my ass for breakfast and yours, too."
So this was the infamous military red tape in full entangling action, Philip thought, wielded expertly by a power-hungry bureaucrat.

On the third attempt, after making sure that Ratch wasn't around and with the help of the orderly room sergeant, he managed to see the D.M.O. and was given a courteous and sympathetic hearing.

"Be patient a little while longer, Bosnar, and we'll see if we can't get things changed. Can't waste your specialist talents, you know."
But he sounded unconvincing and Philip knew he had a struggle on his hands. He also knew there

was no chance of getting overseas until he'd completed his basic training at Camp Borden in Ontario, and there was scant hope of doing any operating before that time.

He managed to get back to Vanwey every two weeks, in full military regalia, and Patty glowed with pride. Thin as he was, he looked vigorous, sinewy and fit in his perfectly tailored uniform, and she was happy to note that his color was improved as well. She shared his frustrations as he recounted them in detail, and listened with amusement as he repeated the caution given by Lieutenant Harold Blevin, whose older brother ran the Princess Movie Palace in Vanwey.

"Take my advice, Phil," he'd admonished, "I know your beef is absolutely right, but stop beating your brains out."
He paused to fill his pipe and Philip felt his hackles rising, since he never liked waiting while some self-satisfied sonovabitch carried on foreplay with his bloody pipe.

"You're up against the army establishment now. It's you against the system and you can't win."

"Well the crappy system's wrong and I'm going to give it my best shot trying to beat the odds."
Blevin walked away sadly, giving his fellow officer a look of pitying wisdom. The perfect under-ling, thought Philip. He should go far in the system, any system in fact that required blind and unquestioning acquiescence.

"Only the remarkable Captain O'Dowd tried to encourage me," Phil told Patty. "He alone urged me to keep trying, no matter who told me otherwise."

"What makes him so remarkable?' she enquired?

"Let me tell you. Here's a big, tough-looking chap with the scarred and battered features of a prize fighter, but with a quiet manner and gentle cultured voice. Some ten years ago he was a successful country doctor, happily married to a lovely wife, and with three small children."

"So far, so good."

"It was a comfortable family with only one problem: his chronic problem, alcohol. Nothing his wife could say or do, nothing his friends could say or do, nothing his minister or partner in practice could say or do, made the slightest bit of difference."

The narrator stopped to sip his scotch and soda and clear his throat.

"One night he was driving his family home from a school play. He'd made several trips to the washroom during the evening and had almost emptied the liquor in his hip flask."

Patty folded her arms and huddled her shoulders in chilled premonition.

"He'd fortified himself before, during and after dinner, and when it came time to return home, his wife pleaded with him to give her the keys and let her drive the car, but all in vain. It was a rotten night, wet and very dark, and he went off the highway and overturned the car as he swerved to avoid an oncoming truck."

"Oh my God! How awful."

"He was the only survivor. The others were killed instantly, and he underwent extensive plastic surgery, but his face was marked for life. He spent the next three years in a psychiatric unit until he was considered both rational and safe for discharge."

"What happened then?"

"He chose to stay on at the institute for five more years, doing postgraduate study and be-coming a qualified psychiatrist himself."

"What an incredible story, and how terribly, terribly sad." Patty had tears in her eyes.

"Since the accident," Philip concluded, "he's never taken a single drop of alcohol, and never driven a car."

Summer passed in the slow tedium of dull duties, and Philip fought hard not to become contaminated with the cynicism so widespread in the army and so well exemplified by Major Ratch. He found a fellow medical officer in his early twenties who was a keen tennis player, and they played once or twice a week. Whenever he could, he kept abreast of all the current medical journals and read all the latest literature on military surgery – its organization, operative techniques and innovations. Every lunch hour, he played chess with O'Dowd or table tennis with other M.Os in his group. Most of all, however, he spent his spare time studying the latest war news in searching detail.

Even though they were strongly slanted toward American military predominance and triumphs, the articles in Life Magazine always thrilled him, with its panoramic battle scenes drawn in such impressive detail by Leydenfrosst. It seemed extraordinary that few of the other officers, medical or otherwise, seemed to know or care very much about what was happening overseas. The total rout of Rommel's forces in North Africa, the invasion of Sicily and assault on Italy appeared to go unnoticed. Even Mussolini's resignation and the transfer of his government to Marshall Badoglio was a surprise to the others when Philip mentioned it. Didn't they even listen to the radio newscasts?

As for the Pacific War, it might as well be taking place on another planet. Didn't they know about the brutal island-by-island war of attrition fought by the Americans: the dreadful naval engagements, with every ship a floating time bomb for its crew? For these sailors, death by explosion, burning or drowning, played a one-sided game of odds with each successive battle.

Eventually, it was time for Camp Borden and a train journey eastward with his fellow medical officers. There were about two dozen of them, and several were strangers to Philip, but they soon got to know each other after the first few hours and the first few drinks. After a while, they separated into small groups, playing poker or bridge for the rest of the long trip. From time to time, he looked out of the window at the same scenery that so fired his imagination that first time, four long years ago. Good Lord, he thought, was it only four years? Time now passed quickly on the train, and he began to feel a wonderful sense of cameradie, the feeling of true army spirit. These, he thought, were the kind of men he'd like to have with him when he went overseas and faced the common dangers.

Camp Borden, no doubt named for the former Prime Minister of Canada, Sir Robert Borden, and located near the charming city of Barrie, was a typical army camp of rolling plains and scattered bush. Philip had read up on Barrie and discovered it was situated on Lake Simcoe, a point in its favor. He remembered that it was Borden who introduced conscription in World War 1, and he reflected with chagrin that now in 1943 there was still no conscription.

The newly arrived M.O. trainees were assigned to one of the endless long flat huts that were set row on monotonous row. They were directed to a nine of small rooms, each with comfortable double bunks, and there was a large shower-and- toilet common facility. Despite the late

September chill, with a temperature in the low 50s Fahrenheit, the hut was unheated and hot water had not yet been turned on.

As soon as the men had selected their fellow occupants, tossed coins for upper or lower bunks and got unpacked, Staff Sergeant Stockley took roll-call and issued tabs to cover their pips of rank.

"Your unit is known as A.22," he informed them with a pleasant smile, "and while you're here you're nothing but a bunch of miserable privates, and you'll answer to me." He sucked his teeth thoughtfully and added, "Or else!"

Once again he paused as he sized up the men facing him.

"Anyone caught with liquor in this hut will have me to deal with, understood?"

His new charges shuffled and nodded their heads.

"UNDERSTOOD?" he roared. "YES SIR!" they all answered smartly, and he left them with, "I'm sure glad we understand each other."

A runner arrived with two messages. The first was that medical inspection would take place at 1600 hours in the Sick Bay, located five huts to the south, and the second was for trainee Bosnar to report at once to Colonel Oakes. Philip made sure his battledress was tidy, and after asking a few directions on the way, soon found himself in the awesome presence of his commanding officer, a man to be respected and feared by all ranks under his command.

"Have a seat, Bosnar," he said in a cordial tone of voice and Philip felt relieved. Here was no military automaton, he thought, and was grateful for the pleasant discovery.

"You've got the highest medical credentials in your outfit and you're the oldest among your fellow trainees. Our physical training course can be pretty strenuous at times so if there are any parts you'd rather avoid you have my permission to do so."

"I wouldn't dream of missing any part of the training, Sir, with all due respect and thanks." The C.O. waited for him to continue.

"For one thing I believe I can match the younger chaps in fitness, and for another I wouldn't want to go through my training here as a guy enjoying special advantages."

"Good man!" said Oakes approvingly and shook his hand. "Hope you have a good time here."

When Philip got back to his hut his companions were curious about his interview, but he told them it was nothing important.

At the sick parade, they were shocked to discover they were going to receive some inoculations.

"But we've already had our shots a week ago," they protested.

"Too bad," drawled the Camp M.O. with total lack of interest, "your documents haven't arrived yet, so as far as I'm concerned you haven't had your shots."

There were more protests, and the French Canadians in their outfit, numbering about a dozen, shouted their anger at this stupid and stubborn "Maudit Anglais. Sale cochon!"

"Get those sleeves up and no more nonsense," said the M.O. and they got their repeat inoculations despite all protests.

That evening in the giant mess hall, Philip was annoyed to find that the 'Frenchies' (or 'Frogs' as some of the less congenial Anglos called them) were clustered well away from the rest, at the far end of the long table, and spoke nothing but a French dialect. This must be the 'Jouale' he'd heard about and which he had difficulty understanding. Toward the end of the meal he went over to the group.

"Listen, you crazy bunch of dung-eaters," he said in his best French, "why the hell do you have to sit by yourselves? We're all in the same damn war whether we like it or not."

They stared at him as he continued, "I thought we were all Canadians, no matter which province we came from."

Then he finished up in English, "For God's sake, smarten up, you stupid bastards!"
Later on, he noticed a definite decline in the segregation between the two groups as they enjoyed their drinks at the bar, and he felt encouraged.

The following morning after breakfast, the new recruits were taken for their first route march, with Major Fieldgate in the lead. It seemed to Philip that the major was deliberately setting a tough pace for his green marchers. Just behind him he could hear Solly Berman, whose father ran the Klassy Klothing store in Vanwey, grumbling at the top of his voice as he clomped along, hopelessly out of step. He was six foot four inches of total incoordination and he bellowed, "For Christ's sake tell that stupid fanatic up front to slow down!"
If the major heard, he showed no sign and kept up the pace.

After a while, Philip felt himself becoming hot and faint, and he felt that he'd lost all sensation in the soles of his feet. He knew it couldn't be the march, as he was a damn good walker, and it couldn't be his army boots, as they fitted well and felt comfortable. It must be those bloody repeat shots, he told himself, and he noticed several others starting to wilt. One in particular was looking very groggy and seemed about to fall. He was the tall Quebecker whom Philip had nicknamed 'Mon General' since he looked so much like de Gaulle.

"Excuse me, Sir," he shouted at the top of his voice, as he broke ranks and rushed forward, "this man is sick and I'd like to take him back to his bunk."
Another marcher broke ranks at the same time, and thus was born a close army comradeship. Philip had first noticed this impressive fellow-officer at the Regina railway station. He looked very much the military type, with his erect bearing and clipped regimental mustache, and at first Philip was sure he must be at least a lieutenant-colonel. He turned out to be a fellow captain instead: Bill Kramer, a budding surgeon from Regina.

With the major's permission they helped Mon General back to their hut, half-carrying the stricken fellow part of the way. They managed to get him back to his bunk and covered him with blankets until he stopped shivering. Then they got hold of the camp M.O. and almost dragged him to see the patient. By this time, the Quebecker had warmed up under the blankets and was starting to sweat profusely. Even so, he still registered a fever of 103.5 degrees Fahrenheit, and a scared-looking M.O. diagnosed pneumonia and ordered the patient transferred to the camp hospital. He was warned by Bosnar and Kramer that if their friend failed to make a rapid recovery they'd submit a full report to the C.O. Although this proved unnecessary, the M.O. was a chastened man from that time forward. Mon General returned to duty two days later, as good as new, and the French Canadians no longer sat apart at mealtimes (or any other times, in fact) as the grapevine ran its customary path through the whole of A.22.

This wasn't the only piece of information to work its way to the trainees. It seemed that the substance of Philip's interview with Colonel Oakes had also filtered down, and he'd unwittingly acquired the title of 'Happy Pappy'. This proved a wonderful way of taking up sides and breaking the boredom of their daily classes. Thus, there soon developed two subgroups who transcended the previous ones of Anglo-Canadians and Franco-Canadians. They were the Happy-Pappys over twenty-five and Anti-Pappys under twenty-five, infantile but impassioned. At the end of each session in the lecture room, after the lecturer had departed, all hell broke loose as the two cliques went for each other with great bravado but few casualties, apart from the odd black eye or bruised rib. It was a perfect outlet, and Philip was sure Staff Stockley knew all about it and secretly approved.

The morning shave with cold water wasn't the most desirable way of starting each new day and the cold shower was worse. After the first few mornings, Philip found himself with few companions in the showers, and a bond of endurance was formed between these hardy (some said "foolhardy") types who emerged each day, blue and shivering, from the chilly cascade. The days passed by in morning parades on the vast parade square, drill routines, obstacle courses, stretcher-bearing up and down steep slopes, and gas drill with chemical nauseants and eye irritants. There were lectures on military law and the logistics of army corps, divisions, regiments, battalions and companies; armored troops, infantry, artillery, support troops, engineers and heaven knows what else. In addition, there were all the details of frontline MO duties and field surgical units, their logistics and functional organization.

So much of this information appeared useless to Philip that he often used the lectures to catch up on his sleep, especially after lunch. He soon learned to get himself wedged between two obliging companions, and slept with his head tilted forward in a position of concentration and his pencil held in note-taking position. As for the periodic exams, he was thankful that these were of the multiple choice type. They enabled him to place his confidence in the law of averages and the pin-choice method. It was maddening for a dedicated and hard-studying fellow like Arthur Fitzgerald to get marks that weren't all that far ahead of Philip Bosnar's random selection, but they were good pals and eventually shared many a laugh about the stupidity of the whole thing.

Far and away the most enjoyable duty was their compulsory attendance at the camp movie theater for a series of Frank Capra films entitled 'Why we fight'. Written, directed and produced for U.S. troops, they were, nonetheless, an effective set of propaganda presentations for Canadians as well. As far as the facts went, they seemed pretty accurate, and the motivational impact was strong. The historical background was essentially sound, the photography superb, and the musical score stirring. Too bad, thought Philip, that so many infamous details about the three Axis partners were now being revealed for the first time.

The films recounted the rise of Mussolini and Fascism in Italy and the rise of Hitler and Nazism in Germany.

They recalled the assault by the Japanese militarists on China, the Spanish Civil War, and the appeasement policies of the West.

They detailed the prewar growth of atrocities based on racial and political grounds, the rape of Ethiopia, Czechoslovakia, Austria and Albania.

They described the brutal attack on Poland that launched the second World War, then the violation of Denmark and Norway, the Low Countries and France.

They replayed the agony of Pearl Harbor and the rape of the Philippines, Malaya, Singapore and Hongkong.

They focused on the treachery of Germany's onslaught against Russia and pinpointed the threat to Africa, India and Australia. All in all a magnificent revue, thought Philip as he applauded its message as well as its history.

After the first two weeks, when the hot water and radiators were turned on in the hut, when civilization returned to A.22 and everybody knew everybody else, Philip and his good buddy Bill Kramer began to make plans. Bill was of Ukrainian-German stock, a not too strict Roman Catholic and a fierce hater of dictatorships in general and Nazism in particular. Although serious and studious, he had a humorous side to his nature that appealed to Philip. They discussed many topics, including the stringency of certain rulings handed down by Colonel Oakes.

Because of an appalling lack of performance and discipline shown by the last A.22 contingent, all privileges had been and still were suspended. These included all alcoholic beverages in the huts and all leaves of absence during the current term of training. Kramer and Bosnar both agreed that something should be done to rectify this unhappy situation. They finally settled on the one method that might work. It was daring, it was simple, and it even had an outside chance. The campaign would make use of one of the training camp's most formidable weapons:

RUMOR!

So it came to pass that two scheming brains combined forces to construct a Machiavellian plan which would lead to the triumphant emancipation of A.22.

CHAPTER 14

1937 cont'd.

It was a wonderful wedding and everyone agreed that the bride looked radiant. Philip had to concede he'd never seen Pauline look lovelier, yet in a way his heart ached for her. He knew only too well that her true love, crazy and illogical as it might seem, belonged to a broken down old savant, powerful in intellect but frail in physique. Yet he consoled himself that this slow, plodding, broad-framed American would be a good, if totally unexciting, husband for her and an attentive father for her children.

No miracle could ever make Irving Kline look attractive, "not even the coming of the Messiah," as the bride's mother observed succinctly. His body, like his mind, moved to a slow and steady cadence; but if one had the patience, it would be perceived that he always accomplished his objective, no matter how long it took. There seemed little doubt that he was in love with Pauline, as much as he could be in romantic love with any woman, and Philip was confident he'd be a faithful husband. Irving wasn't the type to explore the tempting pastures of infidelity.

The synagogue service was impressive and Cantor Solomon was in fine voice. Philip felt like an impostor, with the yarmulka perched on the back of his head and his memory struggling to recapture those flowing phrases of biblical Hebrew he'd once mastered. They were, after all, the ones in which he'd placed such sincere faith as a child. The *Chupa* ceremony (a mock tent above the bridal pair) was duly enacted with profound religious fervor, and the crushed wine glass evoked a magnificent chorus of "*Mazel Tov*," with loud weeping from the overjoyed female celebrants.

In his heart, Philip knew he could never be a bridegroom in this type of wedding, nor would he ever be married in a synagogue, cathedral, chapel, mosque or oriental temple. No, it would be a simple civil affair, with the pledge of eternal love to his chosen life-partner carrying an import beyond the confines of any one religion. He was certain of one thing. When he found the one he adored above all else, if he were ever that fortunate, no sectarian ritual would be required to sanctify his marriage vows.

It wasn't that he'd abandoned all religion, but rather that he wanted to embrace all faiths in a universal moral code while preserving the time-honored pageantry of diverse religious customs. Perhaps it was mainly for their historic value or pure ethnic nostalgia. In truth, he enjoyed not only the spectacle of the different services, but the music as well, be it Gregorian chant, Russian Orthodox choir, Cathedral organ or Cantor's melodic invocation.

One month after his sister's wedding, in the late summer of 1937, he was on his way to Aberglavairy in the Black Mountain district of South Wales. By a stroke of luck, he'd seen the advertisement in the BMJ shortly after his return from the Hebrides and applied without delay. A locum tenens was required for two weeks, to look after a busy general practice in this coal-mining town of eight thousand, and he was delighted to seize the opportunity.

Now he'd see for himself what the fictional Dr. Manson had experienced in days gone by, and make his own comparisons with the locations and people so eloquently described by A.J. Cronin in The Citadel. He would talk with, examine and treat these simple hardworking folk in their own depressing environment. It would be a far cry from the cloistered atmosphere of a London teaching hospital, with its disciplined wards and gleaming operating theaters. Here, he could visit his patients in their own humble homes, and practice the social as well as the scientific aspects of medicine.

Much to his surprise, his first impression of Aberglavairy was far from depressing. When he got off the train, the sun was shining brightly, the air was clear and refreshing and there was a pleasant breeze blowing toward the distant hills enshrouded in summer clouds. A pretty young woman, blonde, slender and probably in her early twenties, came to greet him and help with his luggage.

"I'm Gwen Morgan, Dr. Evans' dispenser and assistant," she announced brightly as they shook hands.

"And I'm Dr. Bosnar. Very pleased to meet you."
She looked amused at his awkward stiffness and led him to an ancient Morris two-seater parked alongside the charming little railway station.

"Dr. Evans asked me to look after you and make sure you have everything you want while you're with us."
As she drove toward the far-off hills, she maintained her merry chatter.

"The doctor's gone up to London for the England-Wales rugby game and I sure hope he has a good time. He's such a hard worker and hardly takes any time off. Other than his work, rugby's his only outside interest. He trains the local team and helps the schoolboys get started early into the game. He's got a great knack with the young lads and shows 'em how to avoid getting hurt."

"You're obviously very proud of Dr. Evans, and I'll do my best to fill his shoes while he's away."

When they got closer to the hills, the grimy little town came into view, and what had looked like low-lying clouds became a smoky fog of gritty coal dust that made his eyes smart, his throat raw and his breathing difficult. As he went into a spasm of coughing and spluttering his driver smiled and observed, "I see you've had your first taste of fresh Black Mountain air. Don't worry, it's not as bad as it seems and you'll soon get used to it."
Philip took out his handkerchief, coughed and blew his nose, and the white linen turned black.

They were now driving past the colliery pits, with their ancient machinery and ubiquitous layer upon layer of coal dust. It lay on the ground, the buildings and machines; but most of all on the coalminers themselves. Their faces were almost invisible under thick black layers of grime, and their working clothes looked filthy. Yet, as far as Philip could tell, they seemed quite cheerful, walking about briskly, talking to each other with evident animation, whistling, even singing.

"You must remember, Dr. Bosnar, that music is almost as important as breathing to our people in these valleys," she commented. "It seems as if they're always practicing for the Eisteddfod, and sometimes I think if they ever stop singing they'll die."

All at once, Philip was seized with an immense admiration, even affection, for these brave Welsh workmen who could look hardship and adversity in the eye, not with a complaint but with a song. Their countryside was devoid of trees and grass. All vegetation, it seemed, was destined for inevitable extermination. There were only monstrous slag heaps on all sides: huge latter-day pyramids that were monuments to the mindless despoliation of God's green Earth, shutting out what little sunlight might find its way into this blighted landscape.

Was this, Philip asked himself, the price of progress at the tail end of the industrial revolution? Was it all really worthwhile? What happened when there was no more coal; no more coal gas; no more coal-derived chemicals; no more non-renewable fuels to wrench from the long-suffering ground? What would the face of Mother Earth look like when that day finally arrived?

The house in which the doctor's office was located was large and well-built, with an attractive exterior. It was situated in a busy street on the outskirts of the main town, and proudly displayed a struggling garden with a large moth-eaten lawn and a number of sad-looking trees. The 'surgery' facilities were more than adequate for standard general practice, and the spacious living quarters located on the first and second floors had comfortable old-fashioned furniture.

Mrs. Evans hadn't accompanied her husband to London. She was a plump and friendly matron in her middle fifties and did her best to make Dr. Bosnar feel thoroughly at home. It didn't take him long to get into the daily routine. Breakfast was served in the upstairs dining room at 8 a.m, and after reading the morning papers, Philip was ready for morning surgery, which started at 9 sharp.

Most of the patients were interested in repeats of their prescribed medicines, and Philip soon got used to such requests as "Please may I have another bottle of me brown `Bronical' medicine, doctor?" or "I need more of me `Gasteric' medicine. It does me so much good." Even more important was the request for a disability certificate, so vital for the truly sick, so convenient a camouflage for the leadswinger, and so precious to the hypochondriac. As far as the prescriptions were concerned there was no real difficulty. The formulae were standard and clearly marked on the patient's case record. The medicines were prepared by the attractive dispenser with expert skill and speed, and the white paper wrapping and red wax seal were impeccable.

Unfortunately, there were far more problems related to the disability certificate, since Dr.Bosnar insisted on examining his patient before donating his magic signature.

"How are you feeling, Mr. Jones? Is the pain in your left side getting any better? Are you coughing up any blood?"

The genuine patient didn't mind answering such questions, while the hypochondriac was only too delighted and hard to divert from an endless array of symptoms for which there was no known disease. The medical impostor, on the other hand, was trouble from the start, and Philip was thankful that this type of pseudopatient was comparatively rare. First, there was the resentment at any questioning whatever, an attitude of "Are you hinting that I'm lying?"

As for physical examination, this was an unpleasant confrontation.

"Doc Evans wouldn't put me through all this nonsense, he'd take my word for it."

With groaning reluctance, a few square inches of skin would be exposed for Dr. Bosnar's inquisitive fingers and stethoscope, but it was a losing proposition. Even the genuine patients were difficult enough to examine, finding it hard to remove sufficient layers of clothing for a proper diagnostic examination.

Gwen Morgan was very helpful and seemed to retain her good humor at all times. She knew most of the patients and their ailments in remarkable detail, and she passed on her knowledge to Philip to the best of her ability. Another gem of information came his way when she showed him the secret rites of mixing medicinal ingredients in correct and careful proportions, and how to wrap the bottle and apply the sealing wax with neatness and efficiency. This part of the procedure, she emphasized, was of great importance to the patient in assessing the quality of medical care. Last but not least, she even gave him valuable guidance on how to handle the identifiable hypochondri-acs and fakers, and his gratitude knew no bounds.

At 11.30 a.m. the door to the surgery was routinely locked and it was time for the morning home visits. Several bottles of medicine were made up in advance, as well as sundry boxes of pills and jars of ointment. All these items had been carefully annotated by the dispenser. She kept accurate records that included a list of those patients requiring visits. Taking his brand-new black leather doctor's bag with him, he accompanied Miss Morgan to the antiquated Morris, and she drove him around to various addresses on her list of Panel patients, with an up-to-date summary of each case. (Panel patients were those on the National Health Scheme). Before leaving the car, he was handed the specific bottle, pillbox or jar to place in his bag, ready for each particular home visit. It was easy to understand how this kind of detail would impress patients and build essential confidence.

He admired these bedridden unfortunates, many of them women with complications following childbirth. A majority, however, were coal-miners with acute bronchitis or assorted oc-cupational injuries not severe enough to warrant hospitalization. The remainder were children with influenza, septic sore throat or childhood fevers. Family members were willing and helpful, and they functioned as effective amateur nurses. Their appreciative trust was heartwarming and made the visiting doctor's task much easier.

Although the houses were inadequate, cramped and scantily furnished, they were models of cleanliness for the most part, and the sick-rooms were kept tidy and sanitary. It saddened Philip to observe that many of the occupants of these humble homes had chronic coughs, and some appeared to be afflicted with emphysema as well. He felt sure investigation would reveal a high incidence of anthracosis and silicosis.

One pleasant custom appeared to be observed as a matter of course, and was both charming and hazardous. At the end of each visit, after all the questions had been answered and all the instructions given, he was offered a small glass of straight whisky, already poured and beckon-ing on the kitchen table and awaiting his departure. He was careful to take only a token sip. To refuse might appear churlish, and to take the entire drink would lead to impaired sobriety by the fourth or fifth visit. Eventually, he might be able to build up his tolerance so he could respond to the hospitable glass in more convincing fashion.

The visits were usually over before 1 o'clock and then it was time for lunch. After lunch, he had almost an hour to himself during which he could read some of the books and journals in Dr. Evans' library. At 2 o'clock it was time for visits to patients 'on the Hill'. These were the private non-Panel patients who resided in fine spacious houses on the hilltops, well above and beyond the smoke and grime which the prevailing winds kindly blew across the Monmouthshire border. The occupants were mine owners, managers, senior engineers, wealthy shopkeepers and their families, and their residential area seemed a world apart from the pervasive coal dust and choking fog below.

House calls to these people were made in Dr. Evans' gleaming black Daimler, driven by a chauffeur in smart livery; he was also the Evans' gardener and odd job man. The homes were sumptuously furnished, the accents of the dwellers were English rather than Welsh, and there was often a special nurse in attendance for the sick member of the family. To add a touch of irony when he was about to leave, Philip was offered a cup of tea or, at most, a tiny glass of sherry rather than a healthy shot of whisky.

Sometimes in the late evening, after the evening surgery and following dinner, he would wander over to the pub on the corner of the street and settle down with a pint of bitters to observe the locals in their relaxed habitat. The atmosphere was convivial without becoming rowdy and there was much lively conversation, most of it in sing-song Welsh. At any time and the prover-bial drop of a hat, someone would start a popular native melody on the concertina and soon every-one was singing lustily with joyful abandon.

It was in this pub, The Red Unicorn, that he got to know a few G.P.s practicing in the area. They were a decent bunch of fellows and they informed him about local customs and folklore. After the 10 o'clock official closing time, they joined the proprietor in the saloon bar and played 'Fingers Up' for drinks. Then they got into discussions on a wide range of subjects, everything from sports to politics, from medicine to music, but always returning to the unhappy theme of local unemployment and economic depression. They also expressed concern about the laxity of safety regulations in the mine shafts and the high rate of accidents.

Compensation for such accidents was grossly inadequate, and too many complaints by the miners could result in extensive lay-offs or even firing on some convenient pretext. Al-though his newfound companions spoke without restraint in this safe assembly, they warned Philip not to air such views in less trustworthy surroundings or he'd soon be stigmatized as a 'Bolshie'.

At the end of two weeks, Philip began to feel like a bona fide Black Mountain native and wished he could have stayed longer. He felt that the patients had accepted him well, he was able to discuss current events in Aberglavairy with the locals, and he even managed the odd phrase in Welsh, much to the delight of the townsfolk with whom he conversed whenever possible.

The day before he was due to leave, he got his wish. Mrs. Evans approached him with a request that he continue as a locum for another two weeks. She'd been in touch with her husband, and in view of the excellent report on Dr. Bosnar's performance, she was authorized to double his salary if he agreed to stay on for the extra fortnight. Philip was delighted, and in his heart he knew the charming and vivacious Gwen must have played a large part in this eleventh hour decision.

Thus was born a torrid physical relationship between the two co-workers, and from that time until his ultimate departure they held clandestine trysts – in her bedroom on the second floor and his on the first. He suspected Mrs. Evans knew what was going on but decided to turn a blind eye; perhaps she even approved. As for Gwen and Philip, despite the passion of their affair, they both realized it was only a transient involvement of two intense young individuals whom fate had brought together for a brief gleam of joy in this gloomy corner of the universe.

By the third week of his locum, his patients were starting to learn the fine art of undressing for the doctor's physical examination, without affront or embarrassment. There were few spurious requests for disability certificates and a deep sense of total acceptance by his patients and the town. People on the streets recognized him and tipped hand to forehead in respectful greeting. He even got to know some of the local gypsies who were camped in their wagons on the northern outskirts of Aberglavairy.

On his first visit to see a sick little gypsy boy with a severe type of scarlet fever, Philip was amazed at the mother's extraordinary sanitary precautions. She had taken a few sheets and soaked them in a solution of Lysol. After wringing them out, she hung them from ceiling hooks in a series of baffles, separating the caravan into compartments. In each compartment there was a bowl of water and a scrap of carbolic soap.

When the mother took Dr. Bosnar into the patient's quarters, she covered her mouth and nose with a piece of cloth tied behind her head. When he asked where she'd picked up such essentials of hygiene, she said she was just doing what other members of the gypsy family always did in similar cases. He congratulated her, left some medications and instructions and promised to call daily. Within a week, the little lad was much improved and Philip was treated to some gypsy dancing and singing in his honor. What was lacking in artistic quality was more than compensated by the wild abandon of the performers.

One late night in the Red Unicorn's saloon bar, the world was made much smaller. In company with the proprietor and G.P. regulars, he listened over the short wave wireless to a championship heavyweight fight between Joe Louis and Tommy Farr. For a while it appeared as if the popular Welsh heavyweight champion might take the fight from the implacable Negro by his clever boxing, but in the end it was the sheer power of Louis' punches that gave him the victory. It was very late when Philip got back to his quarters, but Gwen was still waiting for him.

Thus it would be until the time came for him to leave the practice, the town and people of Aberglavairy and the Black Mountain country of South Wales. There were no tearful farewells and no promised letters or future meetings. For Mrs. Evans, there was a large bouquet of carnations and profuse thanks for her excellent care and the sumptuous meals she'd prepared for him. For Gwen, there was a single red rose, a simple goodbye, a final kiss at the railway station and no regrets or sadness on either side. It had been a joyful interlude for both, and their memories would soon fade as life's journeys took them into separate paths.

No matter how hard he tried, Dr. Bosnar found it impossible to obtain a locum tenens appointment – even for the shortest time – in the hallowed precincts of Harley Street or Wimpole Street. These and other fashionable addresses were the ones that led the fictional Dr. Manson into the alluring temptations of London's high society practice; into its corruption, venality, betrayal of medical ethics and debasement of moral values. It was a milieu where some doctors of limited competence could indulge their desperate reach for social and professional 'advancement'.

Just as he was about to give up, Philip found what he was looking for. It was a fashionable general practice in the Epping Forest area, equally divided between Panel patients and a large segment of private patients who enjoyed the privilege of Dr. Gable's 'Rooms' in Harley Street. Prior to commencing his two week locum appointment, he asked Dr. Gable if he'd mind letting him spend a week watching his employer conduct his daily practice. Using this pretext as a basis for his research, and applying his conversations with the private patients he saw from time to time, he was able to build up a clear picture of what really went on under the respectable surface of the practice.

Every Thursday morning, for exactly one hour, Dr. Gable had purchased the right to use the hallowed premises from one of London's most eminent physicians. The exorbitant price also covered the services of an impressive butler, who offered sherry to the exalted few in the waiting room. There were at least a dozen mediocre doctors who paid through the nose for a similar privilege at this one address, but they all found it worthwhile, not only for their image but for financial reward.

In the case of Dr. Gable, he reaped his main benefit from surgical patients. Suppose, for example, one of his patients required a hysterectomy. He would arrange her admission to his favorite private 'Clinic' where, from what Philip saw for himself, the facilities were hopelessly inadequate, even by minimum standards. It was clear that Gable had a special arrangement with the Matron of this pretentious establishment, and another that he maintained each year with the surgical registrar and junior anesthetist from one of the teaching hospitals in the city's Westend.

The actual operation was performed by the registrar, but it was Dr. Gable who was the surgeon of record and accepted the surgeon's fee, at a rate depending on the patient's financial status. The patient then paid the assistant's fee and the anesthetist's fee separately, and this handsome extracurricular source of income was deeply appreciated by the junior participants in the 'ghost surgery' conspiracy. The patient would no doubt boast to her society friends about the great surgical accomplishments of Dr. Gable, with rooms in Harley Street and offices in Epping Forest. As for the worthy Dr. Gable, large, fleshy, prosperous-looking and dressed in the impeccable best that Savile Row had to offer, the Matron and nurses treated him like royalty.

The practice itself, once Philip assumed his duties, wasn't all that different from his recent locum in South Wales, except that the environment was superior in every way. The patients were much cleaner and the air purer, but trivial complaints were more frequent, especially from the more affluent. Two weeks passed uneventfully, and he felt he was still basically on track with the professional if not the personal voyage of the fictional Dr. Manson.

There was one event during this locum that was mildly disturbing. He'd sent a card to Scotty McLeod informing her of his current address and she phoned him repeatedly to arrange a meeting. When he saw her, for the first time since Stornoway, he noticed a subtle change. She seemed far more possessive and wanted to know everything about his experiences in South Wales, but although he did his best she still seemed dissatisfied. She chided him with keeping her in the dark about his activities and was anxious to know just what were his plans for the future.

By the second meeting he felt something had changed in their friendship, and she was seeking a more permanent relationship. He decided the time had come to tell her, once and for all, that he had no plans for a lasting affair, much less marriage. Yet despite his candor and careful words she made him feel like a cad. Shortly thereafter, she phoned him with the exciting news that she'd just become engaged to a handsome young lawyer from Aberdeen, and he wished her all the luck and happiness in the world.

The third locum was in the district of Tottenham and it was enjoyable in all respects. Philip was aware that he'd become, willy-nilly, a competent general practitioner. He knew how to handle his patients and get their confidence, and he was expert in dispensing medicines: wrapping and waxing the bottles in a manner that left nothing to be desired. His visits to bedridden patients – for which he drove the gleaming Vauxhall car provided by the practice – were pleasant outings, and he enjoyed his employer's spacious house with its impressive rooms and offices. There was also a first-class tennis hardcourt at the back of the residence, and he thought that spoke well of his employer.

He'd met Dr. Marcus briefly just before taking over his GP practice, and was intrigued. Marcus was a widower in his mid-forties, barely five foot six inches in height and blessed with the comfortable belly of a sedentary individual. But to Philip's surprise he turned out to be a talented golfer, and his cabinets and mantelpieces were replete with a multitude of trophies and cups won in tournaments all across England, Wales, Scotland and Ireland. On this particular occasion he was headed for a tournament in Devon and obviously felt quite confident of winning.

It was evident from the excellent quality of his patients' records that Marcus ran a high-grade general practice and this was gratifying to Philip, as it made his locum work simpler and more rewarding. Mrs. Emma Sondheim, the large and impassive Swedish house keeper, ran the household well and was a great cook in the bargain. She was in her late fifties, had been with the Marcus menage for a dozen years, looked after her employer with great devotion and had never been known to lose an argument. Philip thought she was great.

Sunday was his favorite day. There was no morning or evening office, almost no house calls, and the house was quiet and peaceful. On the third Sunday of his current locum, however, he was beset by a strange feeling of restlessness and uncertainty. The long walk following breakfast failed to dispel his mood, and even in the waning light of late afternoon he still had that feeling of disquiet, almost premonition.

Perhaps it was the muffled sound of distant churchbells, cascading their incessant descending major scales and reminding him nostalgically of his boyhood reaction to such sounds. Or was it the haunting melodies of Schumann's Piano Concerto, to which he'd been listening on the phonograph and still echoed in his mind? It could be the delayed shock reaction when he learned about the Japanese bombing of Shanghai just a few days ago.

The daily papers gave all the gruesome details of this outrageous attack on a defenseless open city and its thousands upon thousands of dead and wounded civilians. There was a desperate shortage of doctors and more raids were expected, and it was almost instinctive for him to write the Chinese Embassy and offer his services right away.

The setting sun had long since dropped behind the rooftops that were still visible through the windows of the darkened room, and he was about to turn on the lights when a sudden loud ringing of the telephone startled him. In that very instant he knew! For a few moments he let the phone ring while he collected his thoughts. Then he lifted the receiver, and without waiting for the voice at the other end of the line, he said quietly, "It's you Dora, isn't it?"

"Yes, Philip, it's me. I hope I haven't disturbed you, but I was anxious to get in touch with you. Your mother was kind enough to give me your number when I phoned your home."

"It's been a long time, Dora, and I imagine it must be something pretty important or you wouldn't have called."

"It's important to me, at least, and perhaps you may find it's important to you as well." Philip's mind was racing, but his thoughts were controlled, coldly calculating and without a shred of warm sentiment.

"Why don't we have supper together tomorrow evening, if you can make it?" he suggested. "I can book a table at Chez Vassily's, just off Leicester Square. Would 8 o'clock be suitable?"

"Yes, Philip, that would be lovely. I look forward to seeing you again."

That was all, no earthquakes or volcanoes, but despite the plan forming in his mind he resented the way she'd opened a door he'd closed so tightly, years ago. Despite the soft invitation in her voice, he thought with some satisfaction, she was headed for a very unpleasant surprise. This time it was his turn, not hers, to terminate the romance, but not until he felt his charade had reached the peak of deception. He determined not to weaken, no matter how great the temptation to let bygones be bygones.

He met her the following evening, just in front of the restaurant, and he had to admit she looked as attractive as ever, yet older and not quite so vibrant. All this changed, however, when she saw him and flashed that dazzling smile of hers, which no doubt was meant to captivate him. She spoke first, almost as if to set the mood of their first meeting since the bitter farewell in Brenthaven.

"For a moment," she said brightly, "I didn't recognize the handsome stranger as Philip Bosnar, the man I once knew."

"Thanks for the compliment, Dora. I must say you're looking as beautiful as ever."
He was glad she was dressing in stylish good taste, as he admired the simple two-piece light brown costume she was wearing, with a multicolored silk scarf at her throat.

Vassily was an elderly White Russian, one of those secondary aristocratic émigrés who flocked first to Paris after the Bolshevik revolution, then later on to London. He ran a simple and inexpensive restaurant, specializing in choice Russian and French dishes as well as discreet intimacy.

He led the couple to a quiet corner where they could converse in relative privacy, and they settled on the Chicken Kiev to simplify matters and allow them to concentrate on discussion.

"Tell me what you've been doing, Philip, since I last saw you."

"Nothing too exciting I'm afraid. I qualified in January last year and have gone through two residencies and three locums."

"What about your FRCS finals?"

"Well, as you know, those exams can't be attempted before the age of twenty-five, so I hope to be ready in about a year."

"Any new lady friends?"

"A few here and there. Nothing serious and certainly nothing permanent."

"So you still haven't found your one and only?"

She paused briefly, then asked, "By the way, how did you know that I was the one on the phone yesterday?"

"Oh, the old Bosnar intuition, I imagine. But tell me about yourself. What have you been doing? Have you found your own true love?"

"You sound sardonic and I don't blame you. I wasn't entirely honest with you at our last dreadful meeting in Brenthaven. Nor for some time previously, in fact."

Dishes came and went. Drinks came and went. Eating and drinking became entirely incidental to the growing intensity of their conversation.

"Do you remember when you met me at the station after that glorious letter you sent me?" she asked.

"How could I forget?"

"I was going to visit one of the teachers who was ill in hospital."

"Yes, you were carrying flowers and were totally preoccupied with your sick friend."

"That sick friend was our headmaster and my lover."

"I see. Do go on."

"I don't blame you for sounding so bitter. I should never have tried to conceal the truth from you. Jim Stevens had become a chronic invalid by the time I first met him. He was suffering from a particularly dreadful form of colitis and from time to time there were severe hemorrhages requiring blood transfusion. Medications became ineffective and surgery was tried without success."

There was a long silence and the waiter poured more coffee for them.

"At first it was just pity and compassion on my part. Here was a fine, brave man, a person of intellect and courage, and he was being destroyed by his disease and by his bitch of a wife."

"I presume she didn't show him your pity and compassion."

"What she showed him was a selfish heartlessness. She convinced him that he'd lost his manhood and would never again be able to perform in bed."

"I imagine that type of accusation could become self- fulfilling."

"Absolutely. The thought of irreversible impotence was an additional burden and it was too much for him to bear. He'd always been strong and virile until his colitis laid him low."

"When did you become his mistress?"

"As his wife grew more hostile and more distant he began to feel isolated and inadequate. Meanwhile I began to fill the emptiness in his life by the warmth of our new friendship. I knew he was falling in love with me and did nothing to discourage him."

"How old a man is he?"

"He was in his middle fifties."

"WAS?"

"Yes. He died a month ago."

"I'm sorry. Please go on."

"The truth is that I always knew his days were numbered and he might have a fatal hemorrhage at any time. Anyhow, after a while, and especially when his wife finally left him, I found myself actually falling in love with this afflicted lonely man."

There was another long silence before she was able to continue.

"After a while the intimacies began to increase. The kisses grew more ardent, the caresses more passionate, and it was inevitable that he invite me to sleep with him, if only to reaffirm his manhood."

"And were you successful?"

"Strangely enough I was able to remove his self-doubt and dispel the impotence to which his wife had condemned him. But the more I was able to restore his manhood the more I realized that I was actually playing at being in love. It was still you, Phil, with whom I was genuinely in love, and all the sympathy and compassion in the world couldn't conceal that fact."

It was all beginning to sound as though she were reading from a book.

"And now he's dead," he said, without expression.

"Yes, now he's dead and doesn't have to suffer any more. As for me, I have no regrets. Only the satisfaction of knowing I was able to bring some happiness into the remainder of his lonely life, some warm affection where there'd been only cold rejection."

"You gave him more than that. You gave him your desirable body, the one you denied to me."

"Oh, Phil, you can't imagine how often I've mentally chastised myself for being so thoughtless and so heartless. It must have been sheer hell for you to honor the unnatural pledge I forced on you. Blame it on a misguided innocence or just naive prudishness, but in the end it was still cruel and unforgivable."

"I survived."

"So I see, but I doubt if you've ever really forgiven me. You know I deceived you, but you weren't the only one. As time went by and I went to bed with my lover, it was you, Phil, I was making love to, not him. It wasn't his ailing body I was holding in my arms but your young and healthy body. Does that make it even ? Please tell me."

"In the long run, Dorie, we follow our own individual compulsions. Sometimes in order to be generous to one person we find ourselves hurting another. Sometimes the priorities seem beyond our control."

He tried not to sound sententious but knew he'd been entirely unsuccessful.

Dinner was long over, and the last of the coffee was as cold as a lost love. They walked together for the next hour, along quiet and darkened streets; each lost in wordless reminiscent meditation, before parting for the night. She said she was staying in town for the next few days with some friends, and he arranged to meet her daily until she went back to Brenthaven.

Over the next few days, he carefully built up the new romance and her amorous expectations. They took long walks in Regents Park, had lunches in outdoor cafes, teas in out-of-the-way little restaurants, always off the beaten track: places where they could exchange a kiss, a caress or even a hug with no one to raise an eyebrow. They strolled through New Bond Street arm in arm or around each other's waists, looking in shop windows and chatting as though they had only the present and no past. He felt her anticipation quickening and her optimism rising beyond the wildest expectations. Now, at last, was the time for the complete and unexpected let-down.

He chose a charming little spot just off Piccadilly circus, where they could sit and talk over a pot of tea and some buttered crumpets.

"I can't tell you how much I've enjoyed the last few days, Philip," she said breathlessly, "How about you?"

"For me, my dear, it's been a rare experience."

She looked at him, catching something chilling in his tone.

"There were so many questions I needed answered, and now you've given me those answers. I had to know why you found it necessary to smash our beautiful romance so ruthlessly and senselessly? No, Dora, please don't interrupt me. I had to know why it was necessary for me to ask, `It's over, isn't it?'

Why couldn't you have been the one to tell me first that it was all over and give me the real reason we had to part?"

As his voice grew harsher Dora turned pale.

"You placed me in a male chastity belt then betrayed me. The rest, my fair lady, is simply your conscience balm."

She was fighting back tears but he was not yet through.

"I can never forgive you for your dishonesty. When you casually turned your back on so many precious years between us I could have killed you. This moment, however, is a far better conclusion. Goodbye, my one-time sweetheart!"

Without looking at her he threw some money on the table, rose sharply and strode away at full speed. To his horror, he saw her out of the corner of his eye, running wildly to follow him. He'd left the side street and was crossing Piccadilly Circus on the green traffic light when he heard the blaring horns and turned around. Dora was running across the busy Circus, oblivious to lights and traffic, in blind pursuit.

He thanked God she arrived by his side unhurt. "You can't leave this way." she gasped. His anger was gone and he felt drained.

"It's over, Dora, believe me. It's been over since our last meeting in Brenthaven." She stared at him for a few long moments, her face ashen, then turned and slowly walked away. Philip felt guilty beyond words, painfully aware that the completion of his masterly charade had brought him no joy.

He was restless all night and slept poorly. When the telephone at his bedside rang at 5 a.m. he was already half awake, but he was shocked when he heard Dora's distraught voice, calling him from Brenthaven.

"Tell me the truth, Philip, have you poisoned me?"

"Get hold of yourself, Dora, and don't talk nonsense."

"Well, you did say you wanted to kill me, didn't you?"

"All that's in the past, for heaven's sake!"

"Maybe so, but I've had terrible stomach cramps and attacks of vomiting all night long. I feel as if I'm going to die."

She sounded somewhat hysterical.

"Have you called your doctor?"

There was a long pause and he could hear her rapid breathing.

"No, I thought I'd better call you first."

"Now listen carefully. I'm going to take the first morning train to Brenthaven, but if you feel any worse before I get there, be sure to call your doctor. Now give me your address and I'll write it down."

He dressed quickly, told Mrs. Sondheim to postpone the morning office until 2 p.m, gulped a quick glass of milk and departed.

The train arrived at Brenthaven promptly at 9 and he took a taxi to Dora's address. It was an attractive old- fashioned cottage, genuinely Tudor, and she was waiting at the front gate to greet him. She had a large Alsatian dog with her and looked very fragile in her dressing gown.

"Thank you for coming, Philip. I'm feeling a lot better now, but a bit foolish for panicking." They went inside, with the dog licking his hand.

"He likes you, Philip, and as a rule he's not very friendly with strangers."

They sat down together on the couch in her small front parlor and talked quietly in a spirit of gentle nostalgia.

"You don't really hate me, do you?" she asked.

"Of course I don't. And I shouldn't have treated you so roughly. It was a cruel and empty vengeance."

"But I deserved it."

"I tried hating you, Dorie, but it didn't work. I tried revenge but that didn't work either. They were both ways to conceal my pain and anger."

There was a moment of silence and she drew closer.

"Please hold me tight, Phil, I want you to leave me with happy memories this time."

He felt the familiar contours of her body pressing against him and noticed that she was trembling, while her violet eyes seemed brighter than he'd ever seen them before. This must be another of God's jokes, he thought. He knew she was aroused and Step Three was finally his for the taking. Yet he couldn't take it, now that the offer was so unmistakable. The passion would be there and what remained of affection, but it would be an act of contrition after all.

"I must go now, Dorie," he said at last, disengaging himself gently. She had stopped trembling and seemed at peace.

"Take care of yourself," he continued, "because now that I've got some heavy things off my chest I honestly wish you nothing but happiness."

She kissed him goodbye and he walked back to the station with a great sense of truths revealed and doubts resolved.

CHAPTER 15

1943

Kramer and Bosnar started their rumor insidiously. They would each select a likely subject and ask him, in a conspiratorial semi-whisper, "Have you heard the latest? Maybe it's only the contrast with the last group but it's rumored we're considered the best A.22 ever."

"Where in hell did you get that load of bullshit?"

"It's not bullshit. The word's out all over the camp. As far as I can tell, the information came down from the C.O. himself."

"Well, maybe you're right, I'll ask around."

That was the start, and the reliable army grapevine was set into smooth motion.

"Don't spread it around yet, but I've been hearing the same thing," said Staff Sergeant Stockley when asked. "It's certainly the best since I came here in '42. I'll check it out."

The upward diffusion was now well under way and Phase Two was started a few days later. By this time, the Captain was proud to confirm the Staff Sergeant's information, the Major confessed he'd known for some time, and the good Colonel couldn't be bothered to refute a fait accomplit that seemed to keep his entire outfit in such high morale and motivation.

"They say we're going to get a forty-eight hour leave," went the scuttlebutt.

"Keep it to yourself. If word gets out too soon it may fuck things up."

"Don't worry. I won't tell a soul."

Needless to say, it might as well have been put on the P.A. system, and the forty-eight hour leave was duly announced for the following weekend. Kramer and Bosnar surveyed the results of their scheme with a sense of worthwhile accomplishment, but they decided to postpone Phase Three until after the weekend leave.

Philip was invited to join two of his newfound army pals for the weekend. 'Slick' Murdock and Archie Wright would be good fun, and the proposed trip to Detroit sounded most promising. The three of them left camp at 5 p.m. on Friday afternoon, resplendent in dress uniform and Sam Browne belt, with their rank's insignia uncovered. They caught a ride into Toronto then took a bus to Detroit. From the bus terminal, a taxicab took them to the Brook-Cadillac Hotel, where they registered without difficulty. A coin flip decided room occupancy and Philip won. He'd have a single room to himself and his companions would share a double.

After getting settled and unpacked, they went down to the main bar and had their first American bourbon highball. All three agreed that it was delicious and deserved a repeat. Next, it was decided to sample some of the hotel's food. As soon as the head waiter spotted their Canadian uniforms, he shepherded them to a well-placed table with a great show of respect and cordiality. Several diners came over to shake hands and tell them what wonderful allies Canadians were to the good old USA. Philip found it all very embarrassing but accepted their effusiveness in good grace.

Following a superb and very expensive dinner a council of war was held as to what they should do next. They settled without dispute on a pub crawl, and it was decided that each would go his separate way and they'd all meet the following morning to exchange their experiences at breakfast. It seemed that almost every second door along the teeming streets led into a cocktail bar or tavern. Philip elected to avoid the taverns and stick to the better-looking establishments, of which there were quite a few. He decided to restrict himself to just one drink at each bar, and sip it slowly while enjoying the company and watching the passing parade. If and when he reached the point of becoming tipsy, he intended to slow right down, and if matters threatened to get out of control he'd get a cab back to the hotel before falling flat on his face.

For the first few bars, he thoroughly enjoyed his night on the town. Everyone wanted to talk to him, to buy him a drink. Some of the ladies came over to admire his smart Canadian dress uniform. One or two wanted to see his medals, but he told them he kept them in a drawer under lock and key, every single one. He was able to decline sundry invitations to "join the party" without sounding too standoffish, until he hit bar number five. As soon as he got there, he was adopted by half a dozen officers of the United States Marine Corps.

These were not the stiffnecked trained killers and overdisciplined military robots of screen and fiction. They were decent warmhearted guys, who wanted his company and were determined he should not go dry as long as they had anything to do with it. When he tried to return their generous hospitality, he was told in the friendliest fashion to keep his hand away from his pocket or they'd cut it off.

Each time he left to visit the next bar, they went along with him, and after a while he felt himself drifting into a pleasant dreamlike state, in which he was surrounded by the warmest friendship, conversation, laughter and music. As he began to lose touch with his bearings, he was vaguely aware that their party had been joined by a couple of very jolly young ladies. He guessed he must have reached somewhere close to his twentieth bar, and now there was a muffled discussion about taking a quick trip to Windsor.

His last waking recollection was that of a happy ride in the back of a crowded car with a perfumed lovely on his lap. His bladder felt rather full and he doubted if he could hold on much longer. He was vaguely aware that they were driving through some kind of underground tunnel, but as he lapsed into unconsciousness he really didn't care.

It was 11 o'clock in the morning when he awoke in his hotel room, and he became aware of several disturbing facts in rapid sequence. The first was that he had the daddy of all hangovers. The second was that he was lying fully dressed on top of the bed, and when he tried to move he was punished with a blinding headache. The third was that the room and bed were fully made up, and the fourth was that his uniform looked freshly pressed and spotless. He put his hands in his pockets and found he had almost as much money as when he'd started.

Although he tried hard to recall the events of last night, all he could come up with after the tunnel ride was a blur of music, drinks, laughter, and a voice that kept saying, "It looks like the poor guy's passed out again." He felt as if he'd been comatose for an eternity, and – just to complete his mystification – when he looked in the bathroom mirror he found himself freshly shaved.

After a while, he phoned room service for a large pot of coffee and a Bromoseltzer, then called the front desk.

"This is Captain Bosnar in Room 517. Would you mind telling me if you saw me come into the hotel this morning?"

"Yes, indeed, Sir. A couple of Marine Officers helped you in. You were very sick and they took you up to your room. Are you feeling better now, Sir? Is there anything we can do for you?"

"No, thank you very much."

A sudden terrible thought assailed him.

"Would you mind telling me what day this is?" he asked very calmly.

"Why, Sir, it's a beautiful Sunday morning."

And that, thought a chastened Captain Philip Bosnar RCAMC, must have been one hell of a lost weekend!

After a few more phone calls, the three weekenders met downstairs for brunch and Philip was quizzed without mercy about his Saturday disappearance.

"We were worried as hell when you didn't show up yesterday and we didn't hear from you."

"You sly bastard, I bet you had yourself one whale of a time in some babe's boudoir."

"No way. I'd have been bloody useless anyhow, as I was totally out of it most of the time."

"Don't you remember anything at all?"

"Only what I've already told you."

"No perfume or blonde hairs on your uniform?"

"Sorry to disappoint you but there was no sign of anything resembling debauchery. Just a hangover and the vague memory of an awful lot of drinking."

"Well, you just go ahead and stick to your story. We'll draw our own conclusions. By the way, you owe us some money. We stocked up on a supply of liquor that we have to pack carefully in our suitcases before we go back. We'll split the supplies and the bill three ways. Okay?"

The customs officers at the border showed no interest whatever, and the threesome could have smuggled the Statue of Liberty into Canada without challenge for all the attention they got. It was a delighted bunch of trainees who greeted them when they got back to camp and revealed their precious loot, and everyone coughed up his share of the bill.

There was one more essential piece of business, however, that needed immediate attention before embarking on a program of discreet drinking parties. Philip sought out Staff Sergeant Stockley, poured him a long and heavy scotch and soda and a milder one for himself.

"Here's to you, Staff, for all your efforts to make us the best of the A.22s. By the way, is there any truth to the stories we've been hearing about a special banquet Colonel Oakes is giving in our honor?"

"As far as I know, it's definitely been planned. Not too many know about it yet."

The banquet, two weeks later, was a roaring success: lots of great food, no shortage of liquor, and endless toasts. When the C.O. finished his tribute to the fine trainees of A.22 there was hardly a dry eye in the place. The final March Past, with Colonel Oakes taking the salute, was icing on the cake. The marchers looked and sounded a bit sloppy, and the sound of Solly Berman's clomping boots, totally out of step with every other member of the formation, could surely be heard as far as Barrie.

Afterwards, the two conspirators quietly congratulated each other on a successful experiment conducted with smooth precision and careful attention to detail, and Kramer promised to keep in touch after they left Camp Borden. Philip had never felt so completely fit in all his life, but his weight had dropped from 145 to 135 pounds. Of course he knew why: late nights, too much drinking after hours, then awakening in the obscenely early mornings to the sounds of the bugler's Reveille and the marching band's merciless rendition of The Lincolnshire Poacher.

Now, there was only one more item of importance before they all left camp and were replaced by a new training class for aspiring M.Os: the list of overseas assignments. These were duly read out by the Major with appropriate pomp and ceremony, and his announcements were met with whoops of joy or groans of disappointment, depending on individual hopes and inclinations. The name of Bosnar was NOT among those slated for overseas duty and Philip felt crushed and in dire need of consolation.

It was just as well he'd found out, only the day before, that his former colleague and resident wrestler at the Royal Gwent, Bart Farley, was here in Camp Borden, serving as temporary drill instructor. Philip sought him out with desperate speed and found him in a nearby officers' mess, sipping beer with some fellow stalwarts. Farley was surprised and delighted to see him once again and gave him a hearty welcome. After they'd settled down at a quiet table with their beers, and brought each other up to date on the intervening years since Newport, Philip told his companion about his shattering disappointment. Farley was sympathetic.

"If you want my opinion, Phil, someone back in Regina may have had something to do with this."

"I suppose it could be Major Crane, my hospital O.C.; on the other hand our D.M.O's 2 I.C. would really get his kicks out of seeing me stuck in Regina. I'd simply have to go on examining recruits for surgical conditions I wouldn't get to fix. I'm starting to sound paranoid, for Christ's sake!"

"No, I don't think so. If you want my advice, ask to see Colonel Oakes and put the matter up to him fair and square."

The next morning, he got his interview with the C.O. but it was no use. Oakes explained that because the Captain's documents were specifically marked, the posting was irrevocable. Philip stared at his documents with a feeling of despair. The message stamped on the front was only too clear: ESSENTIAL HOME WAR ESTABLISHMENT SPECIALIST PERSONNEL. It seemed he was trapped.

By the time he got back to Vanwey, he was starting to feel less pessimistic. Rejoining his adorable Patty seemed to give him newfound strength and resolve. After he told her about the duty assignments, she didn't bother with expressions of sympathy.

"You'll find a way, I'm sure of that," she insisted.

"You know something, Patty, you're absolutely right. I'm not going to let this thing get me down."

They put their arms around each other and kissed long and hard. They'd been apart too long, and now they were together again they were aware how deeply they'd missed each other. Each felt incomplete without the other, as though some special ingredient was missing from a miraculous elixir.

The children looked great. Jamie was glowing with healthy vigor and was a dynamo of energy. It took him a little while to remember who the uniformed stranger was, then gave him all his affection. As a matter of fact it wasn't long before he'd worn his father out completely.

"My God, Patty, Borden was never as exhausting as this," Philip laughed breathlessly. As for Florian, she was like an adorable little fairy, and his heart swelled with pride and joy to see how she was flourishing. He felt he could kiss and cuddle her forever, and she seemed to return his adoration, cooing and gurgling with delight. Once or twice he was sure she was trying to speak the very words themselves.

Before driving back to Regina, he checked in with Alvin Masters at the office. The practice was going well and Susan O'Reilly confirmed Philip's impression that his colleague was doing an excellent job. He'd certainly proven himself a lucky find for the practice.

When Captain Bosnar returned to his former duties at the Regina Military Hospital, he found that life in the city was much the same. He got his old room back at the Saskatchewan hotel, as well as his old assignment: surgical assessments of recruits. Harold Blevin was still on hand to assure him that nothing decided by the army brass could ever be changed, but this only served to harden his resolve.

Evening meals at the hotel were becoming a problem. Despite an excellent and varied menu, everything began to taste the same and he found himself remembering the last delicious meal served by Patty. It was just a simple beef roast with all the trimmings, but what a glorious aroma and taste! He decided that henceforth he'd ask the Czech headwaiter to select his meals, and that seemed to work out well.

His new dining companion proved to be an interesting person, one who'd seen for himself the shocking results of Fascism's spread through central Europe, even before World War 2. Philip soon found himself enriched by their after-dinner conversations, and the Czech seemed to enjoy the Canadian officer's viewpoints on a wide variety of subjects, from political philosophy to opera. As for the meals, they seemed to become more palatable day by day.

One of the toughest enemies Philip had to fight was boredom. There was just so much one could read, whether medical, fictional, national or world affairs. There were just so many movies worth seeing and just so many games of bridge, cribbage or poker one could play in the officers' mess before the bar closed. There was the occasional dance, but Philip wasn't interested in getting involved with any of the nurses or female medical officers. It was great news, therefore, to learn that there was a first class poker establishment downtown, and from time to time he tried his luck at that well-run establishment, with mostly favorable results.

Colonel Frederick Crawford was a man for whom Philip had great admiration. As Dr. Crawford, senior surgical specialist at the Winnipeg Medical Center, he was renowned as an outstanding thoracic surgeon. He was short in stature but strikingly handsome, with fine strong features crowned by an abundance of the whitest possible hair. Despite his small build, Crawford was an imposing figure, and once a month Philip spotted him for a few moments during one of his lightning visits to the Regina Military Hospital. On these occasions, the eminent visitor spent most of his time with Colonel Ackland and much less with Major Pines. He'd browse through the hospital wards before briefly inspecting the outpatient department; then it was out to his staff car and off to the next assignment.

During one of these visits Philip seized opportunity, not only by the forelock but by

the short hairs as well. The Colonel poked his head around the corner of Philip's office and enquired pleasantly, "Everything all right here, Bosnar?"
Crawford prided himself on his sterling memory for names and faces. Philip drew a deep breath for maximum resonance and replied, "NO, SIR," very slowly and deliberately. The great man looked at his wristwatch and said, "Mustn't keep my driver waiting or he'll start sulking. Will this take very long?"

"If you'd be kind enough to come into my office, Sir, I'll try to be as brief as possible."
Colonel Crawford sat down and made himself comfortable, while Philip closed the door with the feeling that his fellow M.Os had their ears pressed against the thin walls of the adjoining offices.

He began with a rapid survey of his training, qualifications and experience, and continued with his attempts to get into the army, first in the U.K. and then in Canada. He described the offer of a high commission with the R.A.F. and how that was shot down in flames by the bureaucracy in Ottawa. Next, he told about the stultifying non-operating duties assigned to him in Regina, while the real surgery went outside to an ancient civilian surgeon in the DPNH and an army assistant from this very medical unit. All these shenanigans took place with the full knowledge and consent of Majors Pines and Ratch. Finally, he described his crushing disappointment at being designated Essential Home War Establishment Specialist Personnel.

By now, he knew he'd shot his bolt, but he was still poised on a surging hubris and couldn't retreat.

"I know," he concluded, "that what I've just said could land me in a court-marshal, Sir, but I simply have to see this through to the end, no matter what the consequences are."
Crawford looked at him searchingly, and it was difficult to tell what he was thinking.

"Let me see what I can do, Bosnar," he said, "and I'll get back to you in a week or so."
After he left, the room rapidly filled with his colleagues, full of praise, congratulations and good wishes. The walls had provided very fine hearing for the ears pressed against them.

One day, Philip ran into the orderly room sergeant from the D.M.O's headquarters.

"D'you mind me asking you something, Captain Bosnar?" he asked without preamble.

"Of course I don't mind. What did you want to ask?"

"Has Major Ratch been making things difficult for you, Sir?"

"You know that's something I can't discuss with you, Sergeant, but thanks for your interest anyway."

"With your permission, I just wanted you to know I'm aware of what's going on and might be able to put a word in the right ear."

"I'm sure you'll do whatever you think is right."

A week later, Philip was having lunch at the officers' mess in the hospital when he heard an excited exchange across the table.

"Did you hear what's happened to Major Ratch?"

"Yes, the old man got wind of some of the shenanigans his 2 IC was up to."

"Somebody finally blew the whistle."

"I hear he's been posted to the boondocks."

"Right. I believe it's good old Goose Bay, Labrador."

"Can't think of a better place, can you?"
The Vanwey surgeon left the dining table in deep thought. He was beginning to appreciate the fact

that officers might lead the parades and take the salutes, but it was N.C.Os who made the Army machinery run.

Shortly thereafter, Colonel Crawford reappeared as promised and sought Philip in his office.

"Tell me, Major Bosnar, how would you like to take over as I.C. Surgery at Thornton Military Hospital? Yes, you've just been promoted to acting Major."

Thornton military camp, situated an easy ride from the pleasant city of Saskatoon, was a veritable prairie wilderness, except for a collection of low buildings set in groups of eight to twelve, mostly in parallel. Connecting these buildings was a network of narrow roadways and lines of car tracks in the grassy stretches. Some of the buildings were of more substantial structure and one of these served as the regimental Headquarters of Colonel Roger Ashton, D.S.O,M.C, the famed 'Tiger of Thornton'.

A much larger and imposing building was the hospital, built like a genuine civilian hospital and not at all like a military structure. Surrounding the hospital was a cluster of army huts, of which the largest contained the M.O. bar and sleeping quarters, and across the main roadway, the nurses' bar and sleeping quarters. Then there was the dining area and main officers' mess for the use of both nurses and medical officers.

After Philip had settled down and unpacked in the room assigned to him, with a clear view of the adjoining tennis hardcourts, he went across to the dining area in time for dinner. The matron, Captain McGillicuddy, a hard-bitten hard-drinking and hard-smoking veteran of army duty, introduced him to the nurses, and the O.C. Hospital, Lieutenant Colonel Robert Maitland, introduced him to the other medical officers and the Quartermaster.

The O.C. seemed a refined and friendly type, and the following morning he took Major Bosnar on a tour of the hospital. He showed him its spacious wards and operating rooms; its isolation areas, emergency and outpatient areas; and its laboratory facilities, record rooms and central supply area.

It was far better in every way than Philip could possibly have dreamed, and he was overjoyed.

Everyone seemed cordial and cooperative, with good morale in all ranks, and he knew he was going to be very happy here. This was a top-grade modern hospital, and the department of surgery was his domain. It wasn't the overseas posting on which he'd set his hopes, but at least it was the next best thing and he'd be doing real surgery. It wouldn't be just the standard operations of civilian practice, but challenging reconstructive surgery on the evacuated wounded from the battlefields of Europe.

Within the next few days, he had the surgical lists running smoothly and was able to integrate a harmonious surgical team. Hector Tremblay was a capable O.R. assistant, Bill James gave competent anesthesia, Francis Doyle was a good urologist who was studying for his specialty exams, and the O.R. nurses were efficient and friendly, but strictly no- nonsense. Aside from these members of his surgical team, there was Captain Jack Hanson, permanent army Quartermaster and a great help in matters of military procedure and protocol; Dick Levinson, a crackerjack internist; and Pat Drake, a budding young GP who hoped to pick up some experience in general surgery, his chosen field.

Last but not least there was Bob Maitland, the O.C. whom Philip liked and respected from the moment he first met him. It was strange how soon these two built up a level of cordiality and cooperative effort that was reflected at every level of the hospital's operation and through all ranks. Philip soon realized that this older and experienced senior officer, one who exemplified all the finer aspects of army service, would be his closest friend at Thornton, and he felt flattered by the regard in which his superior held him.

A month after the arrival of Major Bosnar, there was an election for president of the Officers' Mess, and he was duly railroaded into the job by the familiar technique of "Move..." : "Second...": Bang, bang! He had mixed feelings about these new duties. But at least he'd have an opportunity to keep the lid on excessive high jinks between M.Os and nurses – that could wreck the orderly function of any such army establishment. On the other hand, it would do little to curtail his own drinking habits, and the temptations of alcohol were notorious in the armed forces.

Day by day, he settled into his new routine and found it both pleasant and comfortable. At 7.30 each morning he was awakened by Corporal Tom Kennedy, who doubled as batman and bar steward, with a welcome cup of hot tea and his boots freshly shined. At 8 a.m. he had a light breakfast, then did his morning ward rounds with the head nurse. Next came the scheduled operating list, and that brought him to lunch break some time between noon and 1 o'clock. In the afternoon there was the routine work on the wards, charts to be completed and the occasional emergency or urgent operation; and if time and weather permitted, a fast game of tennis singles with one of his fellow officers.

After dinner, which was served between 6 and 7, he retired to the bar area. This was the main social meeting- ground for conversation, listening to records or radio, or playing interminable games of cribbage. During the entire evening until the bar steward gave him his routine enquiry, "Permission to close the bar, Sir?" there was a constant round of drinks, each member of the group taking his turn at buying the round. Once in a while, some officers from other outfits would wander over and spend some time in the M.O's mess, and occasionally a few nurses would be invited in for a drink.

Everything seemed to be running smoothly, but Philip had been warned that his first run-in with 'Tiger' Ashton, the terror of Camp Thornton and implacable enemy of every medical officer in the Canadian Army, was just a matter of time. The first specific bone of contention was the manner in which Philip conducted his surgical consultations on both officers and other ranks in the entire camp.

His predecessor had foolishly consented to hold these examinations on a sick parade basis, with prospective examinees lined up outside the examining office. Philip, on the other hand, felt he was a surgical specialist first and a soldier second, and in order to put his expertise to its best use he must consider his patients in the same way: as patients first and soldiers second. That was why he gave these individuals separate appointments, with half an hour allotted to each.

As predicted and now confirmed by his colleagues, "the shit really hit the fan," and the Camp Commandant reacted with purple fury. He fumed over the phone that he'd never permit such sheer rubbish in his camp. It was a calculated risk, but with Maitland's secret approval Philip took it anyway and refused to budge from his position.

The army grapevine came to his rescue a few days later. It was about 8.30 in the evening when Colonel Ashton strode into the medical officers' mess accompanied by two captains from his HQ. Everyone present stood up smartly as the Camp Commandant took off his cap – as did his two juniors – and said, quite cordially, "Sit down, Gentlemen. I'm just here to make a social call on the Major."

He shook Philip's hand with a crushing grip, and was introduced to all present.

"May I get you a drink, Sir?" asked Philip, "and perhaps your adjutants would care for one as well?"

When drinks had been served and he and Ashton were settled in a quiet corner, deep in the soft and comfortable leather armchairs, the Camp Commandant spoke first.

"You're a stubborn bastard, Major, and I kind of admire that, but I must warn you. Don't push your luck."

"Certainly not if I can help it, Sir."

"You realize, of course, that separate appointments really bugger up the system in this establishment?"

"Yes, and I owe you an apology on that score, but the sick parade system can never afford the time and environment for a really thorough surgical consultation. They tell me you're quite a stickler for thoroughness yourself, if you'll permit me to say so."

"You've got quite a way with words, you cheeky devil. I think I'd better have another drink." When the second drink was served, Ashton changed course.

"I hear you're quite a chess player and not too bad at bridge either. Perhaps you'd care to join me some free evening and we'll see just how good you really are."

It didn't take a genius to diagnose that here was an avid fan of both games and one who was happy to find a fellow enthusiast.

During the next few weeks Philip got to know Ashton very well. He looked like a slimmed down version of that great soldier, Viscount Alexander of Tunis, and he came from similar austere Northern Irish Protestant stock. He was ramrod straight, and his stiff stride almost concealed a slight limp due to a shattered right leg, a legacy of World War 1. It was said that there was enough metal in that leg to render any nearby compass useless, and any change of weather carved lines of pain on his proud and handsome face.

Ashton was permanent army, and between wars had taken time out to win his air force Wings. These were worn proudly along with the many ribbon decorations on his battle dress tunic. Tough as nails but scrupulously fair, he ran a tightly disciplined camp. Nevertheless he wasn't immovable, and he appreciated initiative as much as he admired strength of purpose. Despite the wide differences in background and attitude, especially on politics and religion, this 55-year-old career officer and 30-year-old army surgeon were soon becoming close friends, but Philip at no time showed any hint of familiarity that might upset the balance of their different ranks and responsibilities.

Of all his qualities, perhaps this was the one that impressed the hard-bitten Colonel Ashton the most, and he decided that the young surgeon could always count on him for any reasonable favor. In the meantime, Philip enjoyed the occasional game of bridge or tight chess battle with the Camp Commandant, whenever he was invited over to the Headquarters Mess. The fact that he was better at these games than his superior officer seemed to cause no resentment, and he was relieved.

A new medical officer arrived at the hospital to bring the medical staff up to full strength, and Major Bosnar was delighted to have him on his surgical team as an extra anesthetist and general assistant. The new arrival, Karl Tomchuk, was a rugged weather-beaten Manitoban of solid Ukrainian peasant stock. His family farmed about fifty miles due west of Winnipeg and he was no stranger to the hard life of a prairie farmer. He looked to be at least in his late forties, had trouble with his back and showed some evidence of generalized arthritis, and it was hard to figure out how he ever got into the Army. More to the point, however, although they soon became good friends the new man never divulged the reason for enlisting at his age, which he must have falsified on his documents. They read: '37'.

Tomchuk was a keen bridge player and was soon busy arranging bridge games in the closely knit medical community. Such games became increasingly popular during the icy blasts of winter in Thornton, and all agreed that even the North Pole couldn't be any worse so far as winter weather was concerned. Cribbage was still the number one evening game, and since each game was played on a double-or-nothing financial basis, some of the card debts were climbing to serious proportions. But as they soared by geometric progression it became doubtful if they could ever be collected in reality.

Once in a while, Philip caught a ride in one of the camp vehicles going into Saskatoon. He became very fond of the little city, with its serene university atmosphere and the downtown stores where he could to pick up some suitable Christmas presents for Patty and the children. He found the Bessborough Hotel gracious and charming, and had the occasional meal there with one or two fellow officers. Above all, he enjoyed the fine view of the South Saskatchewan River as it swept its magnificent watery expanse past the hotel on its way to the northeast.

With the North African rout of the German army complete and Rommel's troops chased out of Tunisia back to the Italian boot, the invasion – first Sicily then the murderously unyielding Italian peninsula itself – was filling an increasing number of the beds with wounded Canadian soldiers returning from the fighting fronts. Now, even General McNaughton would have been satisfied with the honorable blooding of his countrymen on the field of battle. These new patients were not sullen or bitter but cheerful and optimistic, almost eager for the surgery that would restore them to normal; at least, in some cases, to an acceptable level of normality.

This was the kind of work Major Bosnar had been waiting for, and he poured all his skill and experience unstintingly into the best reconstructive work he'd ever done in his life. He worked in concert with other members of his surgical team, and the operating rooms were filled with a feverish atmosphere of accomplishment experienced by all who worked there. The standard of performance began to reach new heights, and Maitland was overcome with pride at the work done in his hospital. In fact, it reflected as much on the intelligent and diplomatic handling of his staff as on those engaged in the actual treatment of the patients. With typical honesty, he expressed his deep gratitude to the chief of surgery for the revitalization of the surgical department.

Philip got back to Vanwey for Christmas and Boxing day, and the family had a wonderful time together. The war in general seemed very far away, and Thornton was only another transient interlude in their lives. Now that he seemed so happy and fulfilled in his new appointment and there was little likelihood he'd be sent overseas, Patty felt content and secure. As for her beloved husband, he appeared free from the stress that plagued him in Regina and it was obvious that he had, at last, become comfortable in the army. Above all, she felt his love more strongly than ever, and she knew that when he returned from the army it would be with a sense of having performed a useful wartime service. She was confident he'd be the same Phil as before, and not changed in the way so many servicemen were when they returned to their families and civilian life. She thanked God that his frustrations had been overcome, and gave her beloved full credit for his fighting spirit and stubborn determination.

The Christmas tree looked magnificent and the decorations were outstanding. Philip felt exhilarated as he took movie shots of little Jamie and his baby sister under the tree, enjoying their toys and bubbling with excitement, their mother glowing with pride and deep affection. He tried to capture for the indefinite future the sheer charm and joy of the precious moment. The fleeting thought that his associate had been celebrating the feast of **Hanukah** not so long ago, added a sense of the mysterious machinations of Fate to the occasion. He was sure Alvin's boyhood in the smothering maternal arms of Judaism hadn't been so very different in most aspects from his own. Yet here he was, completely at home and at ease with the Christmas celebration and all its trappings.

The icy grip of winter in the white and windswept expanse that was Camp Thornton softened to a soggy and untidy spring, and life at the hospital settled into the steady rhythm of the proverbial well-oiled machine. Beside this, there was a new-found cameradie on the wards between patient and medical officer: one that was a constant reward to both sides and was amply complemented by open flirtation between patient and nurse. Morale was tremendous, and it was quite a sight to watch a delighted young soldier carrying his bedpan for all to see, its proudly displayed contents testifying to the successful termination of his colostomy life. At another time it might be a compound fracture case, with the patient bravely trying out his metal-strutted and bone-grafted femur, and bearing weight for the first time since he was targeted in the sights of a German 88 cannon.

By and large, the war news was slowly but surely veering in favor of the Allies. The Italian government and population were allying themselves with the Allied forces against the common enemy, Nazi Germany. Mussolini and his Fascist cronies were rejected by those who once stood by the thousands to cheer hysterically as he postured and ranted from his balcony. Now, this barrel-chested exhibitionist was deflated, reviled and ridiculed, and Italy was no longer his. Only the Germans could be depended upon to defend his former empire against the advancing forces of the Allied Command, and his grandiose visions were turning to ashes in his mouth.

Fascism had released man's most despicable qualities, whether in triumph or defeat, and Nazism's foul stain on the banner of human progress could never be washed clean, even after the last Nazi had been destroyed. At least for the present, it was satisfying to see the Italian people liberated, no matter how painfully, from the brutal embrace of modern barbarism. Perhaps, after all, there was hope for the forces of freedom and enlightenment.

CHAPTER 16

1938

By the end of autumn, Philip Bosnar still found himself short of funds and decided on one last G.P. locum before seeking his next hospital residency. There was a two week locum in Limehouse and the stipend was most attractive, but the location made him wonder. His boyhood memories of Sax Rohmer's thrillers came to mind in a flash, with their opium dens, crime and vice beyond belief, and the sinister figure of Dr. Fu Manchu – that oriental archdemon – slinking through the fog-enshrouded back alleys of Limehouse.

Even at this time, the district was notorious for its soaring crime rate, gambling dens and opium parlors. The robbing of innocent victims who ventured into the streets after dark, was usually conducted by throwing a loaded sandbag aimed at the head, then searching the unconscious body for loot. Pockets were rifled, watches and rings stripped from wrists and fingers, and even boots and clothing removed if the quality made it worthwhile.

It was said that criminals in this region of East London were rarely caught by the police. For one thing, the waterfront area was a veritable warren of crowded flimsy dwellings and narrow reeking alleys through which it was difficult to run, let alone drive. For another, it was reported that there were miles of connecting underground tunnels, and one of the main entries to this system was also its most popular pub, the Orange Dragon. It was frequented by white, yellow and black, Aussie sailor and East Indian lascar, American and Oriental tourist, respectable businessman and notorious criminal alike. Only one kind felt himself imperilled in the pub's seething environment, and that was any policeman who entered to search the premises for his quarry. As long as he was there for a friendly beer and nothing more, he was as safe as in a cathedral.

Philip decided he'd give it a try. After all, surely a local doctor or his locum tending to the medical needs of his district would be off limits to the criminal element. At least it should be an interesting experience and one for which he'd be well paid. At worst he might get sandbagged, but only if he was careless. As it happened, the locum position justified his optimistic approach in the main, and he was glad he'd gone ahead. His principal was a grizzled old Irishman, whose advanced alcoholic state was revealed by a bulbous red nose, dilated cheek-venules, and a pervasive aroma of gin – for which strong peppermints failed to provide adequate camouflage. Aside from this chronic affliction, his careful clinical notes and the attitude of his patients, some of them the dregs of society, indicated a well-conducted and well-motivated general practice.

It was evident that Dr. Sean O'Flynn, a veteran of dockside general practice, was determined to give them a better deal than life had dealt him, or perhaps he'd dealt himself. At least he was better off than one or two colleagues who dropped in now and then after evening office hours, scrounging for available drugs and stinking of chloral hydrate. They often slept off the vile stuff in the waiting room, and on such occasions Philip instructed his nursing assistant, an ancient and formidable Negress, to keep lots of hot coffee available for the time of awakening.

On some evenings, after a supper of sorts concocted by the same all-purpose assistant, he felt himself smothering for lack of fresh air and compelled to escape into the darkened streets outside for a brisk walk. On the third such unwise foray into the menacing unknown, he received the beating he so richly deserved. He'd reached his fourth street and turned left, away from the docks, in order to complete a rectangular route: eight streets east, four north, eight west, four south and so back to the surgery. Unfortunately, he didn't get that far. Half a dozen youthful thugs who couldn't have been more than 16 or 17 appeared out of nowhere and attacked him with their fists. He was on the ground and thoroughly searched in a matter of minutes. When they found he carried very little money and only an inexpensive wristwatch, they expressed their disappointment with a few well-aimed kicks that left his ribs sore for days.

His dark-skinned 'Girl Friday' gave him little sympathy but delivered a valuable lesson in local survival.

"If you goin' walkabout these parts all toffed up you goin' get yoh head bashed in sometime, Doctah," she scolded him. "You gotta dress rough and make sure you dirty yoh face good."

Her instructions were delivered in a catchy singsong accent. It didn't sound like the ordinary Caribbean lilt one might associate with Jamaica or the Bahamas. Perhaps she was Haitian, even a voodoo priestess, though he wasn't keen on asking even if she did fit the part.

From that time forth, he wore the roughest clothes he could find in a nearby secondhand clothing store, complete with ratty scarf and shabby cloth cap, before going out for his nocturnal walks. There were other important details. The first was to rub dirt on his face and the second was to find a different route. In any event, the stratagem seemed to work and he strode the dangerous pavements like the most confident of local toughs. At the end of two weeks, even his dusky mentor accepted him as though he were a bonafide Limehouse GP, and he in turn came to appreciate the warm heart and basic intelligence hiding behind that voodoo exterior.

After this strong taste of London's subculture, the very antithesis of high society practice, Philip felt more than ready for his next hospital appointment. The most attractive advertisement was for a surgical registrar at the Norfolk and Norwich hospital. He sent in his application, replete with testimonials from his former chiefs at St. Clement's and subsequent residencies. His reply arrived sooner than expected, informing him that he was one of two final candidates selected for interview, and he was given an early September appointment with the selection committee.

Although he arrived for his meeting with a fair degree of optimism, he realized the final decision might hinge on more factors than his record. He wasn't worried about the Royal Athlone affair, as the final verdict on that episode seemed to have come down hard on the side of the resident staff and against the hospital management. It was now widely known that there had been a total shake-up from top to bottom. Most of the honorary staff had supported the residents' complaints and forced a few resignations, the board of governors was replaced and the Matron and a few of the older Sisters were pensioned off. It had been an important warning to other hospitals to clean up their act.

The members of the house staff at the 'N and N' were very congenial, and after questioning Philip at length they decided that he should get the job "without a doubt." The other candidate, arriving almost an hour later, was a fresh-faced Australian, about the same age as Philip and with equivalent credentials. He seemed a likeable chap, and a lot more sophisticated and well-mannered than most doctors that he'd met so far from 'down under'.

The Bosnar interview consisted of introductions to the members of the selection committee, a casual review of his education and practical experience, and a friendly chat about his plans, ambitions, interests and outlook. He emerged with the impression that he'd scored well. Then it was the other candidate's turn, and it seemed that his interview took quite a bit longer than his own.

After about fifteen suspense-filled minutes he was recalled to the committee room. The chief surgeon was the spokesman and he was the one who addressed him now.

"We want you to know, Dr. Bosnar, that you impressed us very favorably. On the other hand so did Dr. Johnson, who is a visitor to this country and hopes to sit for his Final Fellowship at the end of this residency if chosen, after which he will return to Melbourne and take over his father's surgical practice. We feel that this fact weighs rather heavily in his favor and that you, on the other hand, can have another opportunity to take this appointment the next time around."

He paused to fill his pipe and Philip felt his gorge rising. Always the special circumstances, he thought, always the special reason. Would it never end?

"We would like to know what you think we ought to do."

There was a very long pause before he replied in a quiet and controlled voice.

"I'm sure you gentlemen will consider all the facts at your disposal and make your decision in the fairest possible manner." Someone spoke up from the other end of the table, rather injudiciously it would seem.

"Of course, doctor, your appointment next time would be guaranteed."

Of course! echoed Philip's mind, and what about the other aspiring candidates at that time?

His disappointment was somewhat tempered by that of the residents who'd been waiting in the commonroom, hoping to hear that the St. Clement's candidate was the one selected. Johnson was sitting quietly on his own, reading a magazine and looking embarrassed. Philip went over and congratulated him. After all, to be a good loser was still an integral aspect of the British ethic, even though it was sometimes bloody difficult.

Back in London, he found himself in what seemed like an unreal and fractionated world. He felt as if his hopes and dreams were passing him by. Perhaps the chaps at Newport had been right after all, and he belonged in Canada or even the United States rather than here in England. In any event, he'd look for a well-paying senior residency, no matter where, and no matter the size or prestige of the hospital. From now until the Final F.R.C.S. he'd be marking time as it were, reading, studying, and getting in as much practical operating experience as he could, and perhaps some relaxation as well.

The hospital appointment he decided to explore was the one in Dover, Kent. This historic area was not all that far from the summer camping grounds of his boyhood memories, and he thought it worth looking at. At least a trip to the famed Cliffs of Dover and picturesque Dover Castle would be worthwhile.

His application was accepted so rapidly that he wondered if he was overqualified for the job. Once again he said goodbye to his Mum and Dad, who never failed to get very emotional on these occasions, and to Clayton, his cherished young brother who was getting to be quite a big boy but still hated to see Philip go, no matter where or when. Even though the youngster was now seven years old and had started elementary school, there was still more of a father-son relationship between them than a filial one. Before leaving, Philip assured Clayton that he'd be right back if he decided not to stay for the job.

He enjoyed the train journey down to Dover. It was late October, but the weather was fine, the sun was shining and the countryside looked lush and fertile. On arrival, he took a taxi to the Alexandra Infirmary, situated next to the central police station. Nearby, he noticed a well-kept public tennis court, and that was a plus.

As soon as he got to the hospital, he sought out the superintendent and introduced himself. He was then introduced to Sister Tregarth, the Matron. She was a stern-looking woman in her forties who seemed pleasant enough and sounded very Welsh. He was also introduced to Dr. Driscoll, the outgoing senior resident, a jovial Canadian who was going back home to Nova Scotia the very next day. He told Philip he'd enjoyed his stay in Dover, found the job interesting and felt sure the visitor would, too.

"You'll find it different from the larger hospitals, especially those in London," he commented, "but in many ways you'll have more authority and independence."

A tour of the hospital with Driscoll came next. The wards all looked roomy and bright, the operating theaters were modern and the obstetric and pediatric departments were well up to standard. Driscoll introduced Dr. Bosnar to all the Sisters en route and to his houseman, a black-haired Irishman with an infectious grin and John Gilbert mustache. His name was Terence Fogarty and he looked like a fun-loving sort of chap. Yet, in spite of all these encouraging first impressions, the cordial and even welcoming atmosphere, Philip had just about decided not to take the job. It was far too small a place, and he doubted if the honorary staff would be up to much or whether he could learn anything at all in so unimpressive an institution.

The last port of call was the busy Casualty.

"We certainly can't miss that," Driscoll remarked with a laugh as they entered, "or Nurse Clancy would never forgive us. After all, this is the best run joint in the whole place, and the most popular."

Philip thought his host was being a trifle heavy-handed but he paused to take in the scene. The department appeared more than adequate in equipment and space. Its main operating table and overhead light were of excellent quality and the entire place seemed well run. He was struck by the quiet efficiency of the young nurse who was gently cleansing the wounds of a patient lying on the table, an elderly man who'd been involved in a car collision. An orderly brought in a tray with some flasks and she swiftly set up an intravenous drip with a minimum of fuss. Her cheeks were flushed, perhaps as much from Driscoll's comments as her efforts for the injured man.

She had a gorgeous figure and a regal bearing. Her hair, just showing under her white nurse's cap, was a coppery red, and her eyes were an unusual bluish-green, but perhaps it was just the light. The smart blue and white uniform appeared tailored for her small-waisted figure and seemed to complement her natural colors. No wonder this is the most popular place in the hospital, thought Philip. The object of his scrutiny showed only a momentary interest in the visitor and smiled briefly when introduced at a distance.

"I believe you've persuaded me to stay," Philip told his grinning guide. "You Canadians are pretty good salesmen."

"And you British have a pretty good eye for the better things in life."

After unpacking in his quarters and changing into hospital clothes, he joined the others for supper and the departing resident proposed a toast to his successor, even though it was only with lemonade. He wished him luck and a happy stay. Then, almost as an afterthought, he added, "I'm willing to bet you'll marry that girl."

"Which girl is that?"

"Don't be coy, Bosnar, you know I mean Nurse Clancy. I saw the way you looked at her just before you decided to stay."

"You've got a great imagination, old chap. Our damp English climate must have affected your brain."

Just as Driscoll anticipated, Philip found his residency enjoyable. Each of the honoraries was interesting, some almost to the point of strangeness. Mr. Pawley, an eccentric Ulsterman from Belfast, was the senior surgeon. He was explosive in everything he did, and hardly ever seemed at rest. When he spoke, he concealed a slight stutter with loud staccato speech, scattering a wide spray of saliva at his listeners. His goldrimmed pince-nez gleamed with restless enthusiasm, and he was always coming up with new gadgets for the management of patients, some of them quite good but many hopelessly impractical. In the operating theater he was fast but clumsy, yet he'd been kissed by the unseen arbiter of every surgeon's destiny. No matter how badly he handled a case and how completely he ignored the limitations of surgical anatomy, his patients always did well postoperatively.

Whenever he started an operation, his standard request, was, "Come on, dearie, let's have a knife, a fork and a piece of string and we'll get this job over and done with."
No matter that he almost invariably managed to puncture the femoral vein during his hernia repairs, or that he closed a perforated duodenal ulcer by taking a bite of the common bile duct to cover the hole; his patients thrived without complication. If Philip occasionally drew his attention to these technical hazards, Pawley would comfort him with a brusque, "Don't worry, my dear fellow, everything's fine," and damn it all, he was always right, the lucky bugger!

Claudius Sifton was the very opposite of 'Uncle Willie' Pawley. He was diminutive and neat where the older man was big and sloppy. His dress was tidy and dignified, his manner quiet and disciplined. In the operating theater he was fastidious to a fault, taking infinite care with each step of the operation. He even had his own selected instruments down to the exact specification of needles and suture material. Quiet and congenial as a rule when operating, he could blow up in a frenzy of rage if his scrub-nurse showed any clumsiness or inattention during an important stage of the procedure. His postoperative care was well ahead of its time and his surgical knowledge superb.

Yet, despite all these factors in his patients' favor, his complication rate was inordinately high and his death rate excessive. It seemed that regardless of how punctilious was his performance, his luck and that of his patients was as bad as that of Pawley was breathtakingly good. Everyone in the hospital knew this, but nobody had so far come up with any explanation. As for Dr. Bosnar, he prayed the Good Lord would grant him luck as well as skill in his chosen profession. He and his patients would need both.

The Proberts were an amusing young couple. Margaret ('Maggie') was the gynecologist and an incurable flirt whom the residents kept at arm's length. Her husband Stephen, who was by far the better looking of the two yet never strayed, gave the anesthetics for her cases, and the two got along well most of the time. Once in a while, however, they'd get into a quarrel during surgery, and matters would reach a point of no return when Maggie threw her husband one insult too many. At such times he simply left, and Philip had to step into the breach and try to coax him back to his patient, while one of the nurses carried on with the anesthesia pending his return.

On other occasions, such as a difficult hysterectomy, after applying so many artery forceps that the entire pelvis was converted into a fixed mass of gleaming metal, she would plead, "Do something, please, Bosnar!" in her most plaintive voice, and he would take over.

"Why don't you have a cup of tea and take a short rest," he'd suggest respectfully, and as soon as she withdrew he would remove the forceps one by one. Most were unnecessary anyhow, and only about four required the insertion of suture- ligatures.

"You might as well finish up, Bosnar," she'd say when she came back, and he was happy to oblige.

Cunningham was a tall fine-looking gray-haired man in his early fifties, with a neatly clipped military mustache and a distinguished bearing. He was the anesthetist for Pawley's cases and was inclined to doze during operations, but fortunately neither he nor the patient ever ran into trouble. He and Probert alternated on anesthesia for Sifton's cases and prayed for his success, but to no avail. Cunningham's favorite place for whiling away the occasional free half-hour was the Casualty department, where he would enjoy a quiet cup of tea in the chart area, lounging next to the gas heater. Philip got the impression that it was Nurse Clancy who was the main attraction, and tea was as good an excuse as any to socialize.

Starbuck was a great bear of man, a lot like the well known character actor, James Robertson Justice. He was the senior physician, and was always ready with a rough joke and a mighty laugh. He was also the accredited police surgeon, a position that really suited his style.

McLeary, the eye surgeon, was built like Charles Laughton and had soft delicate hands that shook badly until his instrument was about one inch from the patient's eye, at which point his threatening 'intention tremor' would magically cease.

Burford, the E.N.T. surgeon, was a veteran of the old school who'd never fully come to grips with modern antisepsis. He could scrub, gown and glove with assiduous care, then scratch his itchy nose. Alternatively, he might need a certain type of curette and take one (unsterilized!) from the instrument cupboard, then use it with nary a qualm. His infection rate was far below average for his line of work.

From all these wonderful, imperfect chiefs, Philip Bosnar learned an incredible amount of valuable practical knowledge, and discovering how not to do something was no less instructive than the best and simplest way of doing something. These were the secret 'gimmicks' the little items that were never found in textbooks, but were more precious than gold.

The first professional encounter between Dr. Philip Bosnar and Nurse Patricia Clancy was far from promising. A young worker had sustained a deep and extensive gash on the back of his right thigh, the result of an accident at the Clathorpe machine shop near the harbor, where major marine engine repairs were carried out and there was the occasional mishap. Such injuries were usually the result of worker carelessness, lack of equipment safeguards, or both, as was readily admitted by the patient on the table.

"Nurse, I'd like a fresh bottle of one percent procaine, half a dozen small Spencer Wells, toothed and non-toothed thumb forceps, and..." but that was as far as Philip got. With green eyes blazing and cheeks flushed with anger, she informed him icily, "Really, Doctor Bosnar, I believe I'm fully capable of setting up for a straightforward case like this without special instructions." She looked absolutely gorgeous, and he watched her with unconcealed admiration as she got everything ready in a matter seconds, without a wasted move.

Nurse Clancy, in turn, liked the way this conceited and much-too-thin but attractive young man handled such a nasty wound with skill and gentleness. She liked the reassuring way he had with the anxious patient and how he was able to complete his repair with minimal discomfort to the injured man. The resident's black hair and deep brown eyes, in combination with a large and rather irregular nose, suggested a certain foreign quality: Italian? Greek? Perhaps Jewish? She felt herself softening toward him and was impressed when, after completing the dressing and injecting the patient against tetanus, he turned to her and said,

"Nurse Clancy, I want you to know how sorry I am if I've offended you. Detailing the instruments I need for any job has been a longtime habit and was no reflection on your obvious capabilities."

His remorse seemed so genuine that she felt herself drawn to this disturbing newcomer. Taking advantage of her changing mood, Philip asked, "May I make amends by taking you out some evening?"

Three days later, they had their first rendezvous. They arranged to meet outside the Barclay's Bank building at 7 p.m, and he asked her to suggest a quiet restaurant. She directed him to the Crypt, an underground cave-like dining place with individual alcoves, like monastic cells, carved out of the bare rock, giving the diners a feeling of intimate and softly illuminated privacy. The food was inexpensive and simple, but extremely tasty, and they both enjoyed it.

Afterwards, they walked along the cliff's edge toward the Castle, and were glad they were wearing their heavy coats against the chill night breezes. They continued their stroll, descending the cliff steps down to the seafront and proceeding toward the lights of the harbor.

Before going back through town to the hospital, they stood for quite a while at a guardrail on the seashore and kissed, while the twinkling lights of a far-off steamer adding to their sense of intimacy in the dark. At that moment, Philip knew that he loved this beautiful Irish girl, proud but shy, independent but warmhearted, as he had never loved anyone before. He wanted her both in body and mind, not just for an affair – no matter how passionate – but for a lifetime: marriage, children, the whole thing.

How totally different, he thought, from the uninvolved attitude he'd built up against the opposite gender for the past few years. It wasn't just her beauty; it was her soft sweet voice with its lilting Irish brogue; her attitude, demeanor and humor; her sense of values that she so openly revealed as they conversed during their meal. He would avoid committing himself to any declaration until they'd met on several more occasions and he could consolidate his early impressions.

On their fourth outing, he took her to see the Barrymores in an exciting film, *Moby*

Dick. To tide them over until the show ended, Philip gave Patricia a box of assorted chocolates, and during the first whale-hunt scene he managed to dislodge a large filling from an upper molar. She'd just offered him a chocolate and he'd bitten into a hard toffee center with more vigor than caution. Within minutes, he was sweating with agony and hoping he could last the evening.

Afterwards, they walked to the Grand Hotel and he ordered a sherry for her and a scotch and soda for himself, to be followed by a small supper. Patricia noticed that he looked drawn and pale and insisted on knowing what was wrong. Only when he found himself unable to eat his meal did he admit to what was wrong, and she chided him for not having told her sooner.

"To be perfectly honest, Patricia," he confessed, "I hoped the whisky might do the trick and ease the pain, but I was wrong."

On their way back to the Royal Alexandra, she stopped him and they stood together in one of the darkened doorways along the quiet street. As they put their arms tightly around each other and kissed fervently, she knew she was deeply in love with this intruder into her peaceful life: this fierce but gentle; aloof but compassionate; stubborn yet ultimately reasonable stranger; for whom she felt something far beyond mere passion and who was changing her life.

The next morning, the staff dentist replaced the filling and said, "You must have spent a very rough night." He was quite right, to be sure, but – during the sleepless hours – Philip was diverted from his screaming cavity by the sure thought that Patricia was his and he could soon declare himself and obtain her declaration in return.

A fortnight later, on a glorious and unusually warm moonlit evening, they declared their love in the deep shadows behind the Castle walls, away from the rest of the world. They placed their coats on the ground and held each other close while they spoke of their feelings for each other. Then they made love, without restraint or feelings of guilt. This was a physical union that, despite all its passion and intensity, went far beyond mere self-gratification, and Philip knew he could never give her up, no matter the difficulties, religious or otherwise.

During the next few weeks, whenever they dined together at the Crypt, the Grand Hotel, or Enrico's new Italian restaurant, they discussed the future and the problems to be overcome.

"How could we possibly get married, Philip, with me a Catholic and you Jewish. Even though you're not a practicing Jew, I'm a practicing Catholic who goes to confession and attends Mass. The church would never let me marry outside the faith. Then there's your family and mine."

"You don't have to worry about my family, Patricia. They're conditioned to the idea of my marrying a Gentile."

"That may be, but I have two sisters who are nuns and one younger brother who's going to become a priest."

"I don't pretend it will be easy, especially for you, my darling, but I believe our future happiness makes any effort worthwhile, no matter what the odds. If people like us can't go against those odds and beat the doom-sayers then there'll never be any progress. Millions of people will be separated from their loved ones by outdated prejudices of the past."

"I agree with everything you say, Philip, and I know how strong your determination is, but there are certain difficulties even you can't overcome."

"Time will tell, but you mustn't underestimate your own strength. I believe in the power of your love and that makes me hopeful."

Patricia wanted to believe him, but in her heart she wasn't optimistic, despite the eloquence and honesty of their discussions.

Meanwhile, Terry Fogarty was trying out one nurse after another and Philip listened to his inflated tales of conquest with distaste and boredom. The fellow was such an oaf: he ate sloppily and drank noisily, and he had an endless fund of jokes, sometimes quite funny and always quite filthy. Every Saturday evening he took off with one of the local chiropractors, a shifty-looking blond dandy, and they went looking for prostitutes. Sooner or later, Philip felt sure his junior houseman would come back with a large dose of venereal disease, and he hoped he could personally administer the unpleasant therapeutic measures. Meanwhile, the thought of this libertine spreading his infection around the nursing staff disturbed him deeply and he told him so in no uncertain language.

In spite of these issues, they both got along quite well and even did a fair amount of drinking together, especially on the occasional late evening when all was quiet in the hospital. Terry Fogarty often got drunk, while Philip found it hard to get even mildly tipsy, even though they matched drink for drink. One subject was sacrosanct between them. On no account was Fogarty permitted to make the remotest off-color reference to Patricia. It was a quiet understanding that any infraction of this rule would lead to violence, and therefore the occasion never arose. Terry was a lover, not a fighter!

As each day passed, Philip enjoyed his stay at the 'Alex' more and more. His relations with the honorary staff were excellent and he was getting a great deal of work. This included a large percentage of the prostatectomies, some gallbadders and gastrointestinal cases, some hernias and colorectal surgery, some eye cases including cataracts and assorted muscle corrections for squint, mastoidectomies for advanced middle ear infections, and routine nasal procedures. There were some vaginal repairs, hysterectomies and classical Cesarean sections, and always the daily circumcisions, tonsils, adenoids, and skin grafts. In addition, most of the good emergency cases were left to him, without interference but with guidance when he requested it.

His duties on the surgical wing were rewarding, even though Sister Prudence Claridge, a character straight out of Emily Bronte, kept telling him how Dr. Driscoll always did things when he was senior resident. Philip didn't mind, as it was a familiar hospital phenomenon. Besides, dear old 'Pru' was soon loyal to Driscoll's replacement and cooperative to a fault. Unfortunately, she disapproved of Nurse Clancy, and was heard to complain that the Irish hussy was too pretty for her own good and was liable to turn men's heads. Philip hated to tell her that her warning came too late, and made up his mind he would eventually break the prejudice.

Christmas was approaching and after that the New Year, and he realized this would be his first yuletide season, be it Hanukah or Christmas, that he hadn't been at home with his parents. Perhaps it was an omen, a sign that the tightly knit Bosnar family was at last separating into its components, and perhaps one day it would be seas and continents that separated them, just as it was in the case of his mother when she came to England and her relatives went to America.

The yuletide holiday at the Alex was quiet, peaceful and enjoyable, culminating in a glorious festive dinner, with roast goose, chestnut dressing, and lots of plum pudding. There were bottles of wine and whisky from the honorary staff, but nobody drank to excess. Boxing Day was another matter entirely. After the customary exchange of small gifts between doctors and nurses, the day progressed into a veritable bacchanale, with the honoraries and even Matron getting somewhat tiddly and exchanging a good deal of affection. Everyone was kissing and hugging everybody else, Fogarty passed out cold and Philip rescued Patty (the new and accepted nickname for his adored Patricia) from the amorous advances of a convivial Dr. Cunningham.

Philip took her to his quarters and locked the bedroom door. Then, far from the 'madding crowd' below, they made wonderful unhurried love. When they finally emerged to join the others, they ran into Sister Tregarth on the stairs. The young lovers were convinced she not only knew exactly what was going on but strongly approved.

Early in the new year, several of the nurses came down with a severe type of influenza, and some of the more senior nurses had to pitch in and do double duty. One of these was Nurse Clancy, and Sister 'Pru' bristled when the red-haired beauty arrived in her domain to a chorus of appreciative whistles from the occupants of the men's surgical ward. Within a matter of days, however, the older woman was completely won over as she watched the new arrival going about her new duties without difficulty, confusion or complaint. Not only was she popular with the patients but with the other nurses as well, and her time off was always secondary to the unfinished duties at hand, a detail that wasn't lost on the Sister in charge.

About a week later, Philip was approached by Pru Claridge in strictest confidence.

"I understand, if you'll forgive me for mentioning it, that you and Nurse Clancy are going out together."

Philip was about to say it was none of her business when she continued, "I think you've made a wonderful choice, Dr. Bosnar. She's a very fine person and extremely competent."

"Thank you, Sister. I'm so glad you like her. She means an awful lot to me."

"I shouldn't wonder! Good luck to both of you."

From that time onward, the previously dour Sister became a devoted friend to both of them, and they sometimes invited her to join them for a trip to the beach or an afternoon tea. The old spinster seemed to blossom with a newfound youth in the joy of their companionship.

Professionally, this was an exciting year in medical history. The new drug Prontosil, related to the aniline dyes, was a beacon to the future conquest of microbial infections, and might well prove the forerunner of even more powerful and safer antibacterial drugs in the future. Philip found that his patients with postoperative soft tissue infection, pneumonia or urinary infection responded extremely well, and he felt eternally grateful to Dr. Domagk and his parent chemical firm – I.G. Farben Industries – where Prontosil had been developed. This was truly an example of science in the service of humanity, even at the purely commercial level. The thought didn't occur to him at the time, but it was just such firms that produced the obscene poison gas used in the 1914-18 World War.

On another medical front, he was greatly disturbed in the matter of major thermal burns and new trends in their management. The present gold standard of therapy was the tannic acid treatment. Based on extensive clinical studies in Detroit and commencing in the mid-twenties, Dr. Davidson of Detroit's Henry Ford Hospital had introduced his special tannic acid techniques and was touted as the next winner of the Nobel Prize in Medicine.

The pathological basis seemed sound. Victims of major burns were subject to a state of dangerous shock, brought about by severe loss of fluid volume due to seepage from the smallest blood vessels. This loss centered on the burned area, where there was an enormous loss of serum into the surrounding tissues and into the dressings, and such a large fluid deficit required massive intravenous replacement. A dilute solution of tannic acid applied to the surface of the cleansed and debrided burn, served to minimize fluid loss by forming an impermeable protective crust, thus reducing seepage.

The most serious complication in the past had always been invasion of the burned area by bacteria, causing serious infection and even fatal septicemia. This infection could be minimized by application of the coagulative tannic acid solution, and now that Prontosil was at hand, the microbial invasion could be stopped in its tracks.

That was the theory. In practice, however, Dr. Bosnar was having some secret and very disturbing doubts. To start with, it seemed to him that pain was a major feature in the production of burn-shock, and had to be minimized by medication – or even carefully administered anesthesia – before the open area could be adequately cleansed and loose dead material removed. He refused to 'scrub the wound clean' (as advocated in the texts) and used gentle washing, instead, with soft gauze soaked in warm saline. He hated to apply the tannic acid solution, which he knew would destroy living cells so essential to the healing process in the burn. After all, didn't it work by coagulating and thereby destroying vital proteins? Some of these troubling thoughts were beginning to appear in the medical literature, but mainly the subject of purulent infection gathering under a tannicized crust that prevented its escape. It was suggested that part of the crust's edge be excised, pus released and silver nitrate applied to the exposed area.

Then there was the matter of reported deaths from liver failure. These burn patients were found to have died from '*Progressive necrosis of the hepatic central lobules*' (Toxic death of liver cells throughout this vital organ).

The fatal complication was regarded as an unfortunate side effect of that wonder drug Prontosil, and was even considered an acceptable risk when one looked at the overall figures. That conclusion was all very well unless it turned out that it was the toxicity of tannic acid and not Prontosil that was at fault.

With the advent of summer, Philip and Patricia took long walks along the cliffs, toward Folkestone in the west or St. Margaret's Bay in the east. There were afternoons on the beaches, sometimes with Pru Claridge joining them and disporting herself in the latest swim costume of the 20s. There were tennis games and feasts of strawberries with Devonshire cream, sometimes to the bursting point. With the approach of July, the annual Summer Ball in aid of the Royal Alexandra Infirmary drew near. It was held each year on the second Saturday evening of July, with Sir Henry and Lady Clathorpe as official hosts. Not only did the Clathorpe shadow loom large over most of the major commercial enterprises in Dover, but Sir Henry was also ex-mayor of the city and perennial chairman of the Hospital board.

When the fateful night arrived, Bosnar and Fogarty held a council of war. They both agreed that this was one of the high points of the Dover's social scene – black tie at the very least – and it was guaranteed to be a most orderly affair and a devastating bore. The Matron, Sisters and nurses were traditionally among the early guests, then the board members, the honoraries, residents and junior administrative staff. The two residents agreed that their salvation lay in getting a bit drunk before submitting to the endless tedium of the evening's deadly formalities. There was only one small problem.

"You know how I am with alcohol, Terry, I never seem to get drunk. Maybe it's metabolic."

"It's nothing of the kind, boyo. It's just that you always sip your drinks slowly instead of knocking them down."

"That's not the reason, I'm sure."

"Well we can easily find out. I'll pour you two glasses of neat Jameson and you can just drink one after the other before we leave for the Grand Hotel."

Philip went ahead steadily, and finished both glasses without unnecessary slowness. He felt marvellous, and on the way over in the taxi, which he shared with a giggling Fogarty, he felt engulfed by a great aura of friendliness and goodwill toward the entire human race. He saw everything through a miraculous fog of happiness, but when he entered the Grand Ballroom he found it hard to spot his adored Patricia.

Where could she be hiding from him? In actual fact, he found it hard to distinguish any one individual out of the hazy mass of people swaying from side to side and up and down, even though the music wasn't even playing. It was enough to make one feel nauseated. Aha! he thought triumphantly, at least he'd identified his hostess, the large and formidable Lady Clathorpe, resplendent in a backless pink satin evening gown.

He staggered to the center of the floor, and before the apoplectic glare of her husband, slapped her resoundingly across the bare expanse of her back, burbled a jovial "How are you, old horse?" and passed out cold.

CHAPTER 17

1944-45

Any attempt to face the outside elements during the vicious winter season was fraught with the danger of severe frostbite, a condition all too common in this inhospitable part of Saskatchewan. The unpleasant affliction could strike at the nose, fingers, earlobes or toes, and aside from an immediate possibility of losing any of these appendages during the acute phase, there were permanent effects of altered sensation and marked sensitivity to future cold exposure.

Major Bosnar felt humiliated by the thought that a winter freeze-up could keep him locked indoors until the spring thaw. He put on a standard pair of cotton pajamas, two pairs of socks, battle dress buttoned up to the very top, and his heavy army boots. In addition, he put on a heavy scarf, his overcoat and forage cap – with the side-flaps turned down over his ears. Next, he used a sheet of heavy transparent X-ray film cut to shape as a visor, with the upper edge fixed under his cap and the lower edge jammed against his scarf. With this simple equipment, he could face the most daunting winter storms, and deliberately plow himself through any snowdrift in his path for the sheer joy and exhilaration of the experience. At such times, he felt a great kinship with those hardy natives who were the real pioneers and inheritors of this awesome land, and most of all with the incredible Inuits, to whom arctic ice and snow were both hunting ground and playground.

At long last (and it seemed forever), it was spring, with the seasonal thaw cascading floodwaters all over the camp. The ground was turning into a thick glue-like mud, the kind that sucked remorselessly at wheel and boot alike. The stark, bare trees were starting to reveal their earliest buds and, along with the occasional songbird, signalled new birth and new life in this bleak and cheerless landscape. The patients on the surgical wards were all doing well, and new ones kept arriving from the Italian front, presenting ever new challenges to the surgical team.

Lieutenant-Colonel Maitland and Major Bosnar had everything going smoothly, creating a dedicated partnership in which respect for those of lesser rank and authority was never sacrificed for greater efficiency. Needless to say, they weren't unaware of the popularity they enjoyed as a result of this attitude, and they noted the high morale of patients and hospital staff alike. Witnessing this extraordinary change in what had once been a disjointed and sloppy department of surgery, Tiger Ashton was heard to extoll the change and even take some of the credit.

"Always knew the blasted M.Os could be made to work decently if you kicked 'em in the rear from time to time," he declared, leaving the clear impression it was he who did the kicking. It wasn't worth disputing, since everyone in the camp already knew the truth and were still chortling about the surgical sick parade impasse and its peaceful solution. In many ways, Ashton was entitled to some of the credit, as he was fully cooperative in following up on any request or suggestion coming from Philip and his O.C.

June 6, 1944, D.Day! It just didn't seem possible after so long a period of setbacks, frustrations and disappointments. First, the 'phony war' and then Dunkirk, the fall of France and the German onslaughts in Russia, the dreadful Allied losses to the U-boats, and the Dieppe disaster, most disappointing of all. Was it possible that the high brass had actually learned something about modern sea-borne invasion from the debacle of Dieppe? Philip's head reeled as he thought of the vast D.Day armada heading for the Normandy coast, the mighty Anglo-American airforce filling the skies and huge armies coming ashore; all committed to the invasion of continental Europe and destruction of the Third Reich. Perhaps the Dieppe raid was nothing more than a sacrificial gambit and prelude to a much larger and deadlier game.

Japan could wait. For the present, all the power and purpose of the Allied forces must bear down inexorably on vaunted Fortress Europa, penetrate its fortifications and devastate Germany city by city, until the enemy begged for mercy and was ready to sign an unconditional surrender.

Peter Forsyth would soon be shipping out to France and then to wherever it was decided to set up his base hospital, the lucky devil! Philip could only wish he were there during this remarkable period of retribution and restitution. Now the hunter would become the hunted, and the infamy of a demonized state would be revealed for the whole world to see: Dachau; Bergen-Belsen; Auschwitz; Ravensbruck; Buchenwald; Mauthausen; Sachsenhausen; and only his Satanic Majesty knew how many more.

During the summer months, there was a periodic visit to the hospital by Colonels Crawford and Anderson. They always stopped for an hour or two with Major Bosnar, and after the first few visits were all on a first name basis. He always enjoyed these pleasant occasions and the interesting chats they afforded, and he made it clear that he owed them both a great debt of gratitude. They, in turn, congratulated him on fitting so well into his new post, but he always gave Maitland full credit for his fine hospital management and unstinting support of the surgical staff.

Another senior officer who made periodic visits to the hospital was Brigadier General Lasalle, G.C.O. (General Commanding Officer) of MD12. This regular army officer was widely feared for his draconian methods, and like so many others at his level of command, held a deep-seated dislike for doctors in uniform. It was rumored that he'd once studied for a medical career but was unable to complete his course because of his poor performance in the exams.

When it came to relations with Major Bosnar, there had been no hint of friction so far, and perhaps that was because of Bosnar's secret weapon: never making any request that Lasalle could refuse. Even when the surgeon was in a position to ask for special favors, he resisted the temptation and built up his position of strength for a more appropriate time. The Brigadier had to admit to a grudging liking for this self-composed Maudit Anglais with his Oxford English accent and correct deportment.

This might be just the place for his daughter (and the light of his life) Lisette, to commence her career in physiotherapy career under the watchful and responsible eyes of Bosnar and Maitland. Destiny also decreed that Madame Lasalle should have been referred to Bosnar for a breast lump, which proved entirely benign on excision and biopsy, and that a strange bond should grow between these two totally different men following the event.

When she arrived in due course at Thornton Military Hospital, Lisette proved to be a

delightful surprise. She was tall and slender where her parents were short and beefy, and she revealed a contagious sense of humor where her parents seemed to have none. As for the vaunted
problems of bilingualism, she could speak both English and French without the trace of an accent.
Lisette was an excellent worker, and every one of her patients soon adored their charming and
unaffected 20-year-old angel of mercy, with her shy manner and silky fair hair.

Major Bosnar was careful to deal with her in the most correct manner, since it would
be all too easy to grant her special latitude because of her charm and the power wielded by her
father. In return, she accelerated the rehabilitation of his patients to such an impressive degree that
it was duly noted by the entire staff.

After a glorious summer, with lots of tennis to fill the free hours, and with the glowing
news from Europe that the Germans were being driven out of France, the fall months seemed to
pass quickly into a dark and dismal winter. Now the news wasn't quite so good: the V.1 flying
bombs that showered London with death and destruction were being replaced by V.2 rockets. These
were even deadlier, and were heard only after they landed and exploded their huge payload. Some
of the new rockets were being used against key allied targets, the Port of Antwerp in particular.
Since this was where Forsyth was now stationed, Philip hoped he would be spared.

The Battle of the Bulge that threatened to split the Allied forces might have succeeded
had Bastogne fallen. According to the latest reports, it was US General McAuliffe's succinct reply
of "NUTS!" to German surrender demands that stopped the counter-offensive in its tracks and sent
the enemy scurrying back, with Field Marshall Von Rundstedt in disgrace. As for the plot to assas-
sinate Hitler, it had been a dismal failure, despite reports that his right arm was useless and his
speech impaired. He was still healthy enough to send the conspirators and their supporters to a
miserable death: hanging by a wire noose around the neck and suspended from meat hooks. Their
wives and children were sent off to perish wretchedly in concentration camps.

In early February, two new officers were assigned to Thornton Military Hospital. They'd
been on active duty with the European invasion forces, and although both were Lieut.-Colonels
they were placed under Major Bosnar's authority in the surgical department. The first of these was
an orthopedic surgeon named Philip Austin, with the military bearing of a Roman centurion. The
second – and Philip could hardly believe his eyes – was none other than his friend and partner Peter
Forsyth, looking a bit older and heavier, but otherwise much the same as when he left the Vanwey
practice.

The reunion party between these two friends started at 5.30 p.m. and went on until
closing time at 10, and they exchanged a great deal of news and information about events on the
war front and the home front. It was obvious that Forsyth was drinking far more heavily than
before and there was no way Philip could keep up with him. Perhaps it was because the V.2 attacks
on Antwerp had caused such havoc, and made working in the O.R. quarters so hazardous and
emotionally exhausting. That was why hospital personnel in that area were being rotated for home
service duty after such a short stay at the war front.

The extent to which Forsyth had been affected overseas wasn't entirely apparent until
a week later in the officers' mess. He was sitting at ease in the depths of an armchair when the bar
steward made his customary request to Major Bosnar.

"Permission to close the bar, Sir?"

"No, Goddamit," growled Forsyth, "leave the bloody place open."

"Go ahead Corporal and close up," said Philip, quietly.

"Thank you, Sir. Any last orders?"

"Let's have a bottle of Cutty Sark and put it on my tab," barked Forsyth, and his stubborn expression cooled any thought of contradiction. The other M.Os drifted away, one by one, and went off to their sleeping quarters, since it looked as if a nasty situation might be building up. As it happened, Peter gradually settled into an alcoholic euphoria and embarrassed Philip with the profusion of his gratitude.

"Nobody else could've kept our practice going the way you did, Phil. I could never repay you for the way you fought the odds and doubled our practice."

Only by the slightest slurring of his speech could one tell he was well on his way to a drunken stupor. For the last few rounds he'd been spiking both drinks with a small capful of "my secret ingredient from Antwerp," a clear fluid that he carried in a flat silver flask.

"This stuff is guaranteed to bring out the flavor of any drink," he boasted to Philip, who had no difficulty diagnosing the colorless liquid as pure ethyl alcohol. By the time they'd worked their way through scores of reminiscences and were having difficulty seeing each other clearly, they called it a night and staggered off to sleep.

The following morning, the batman found it impossible to rouse Forsyth and was worried about his faint pulse. He reported at once to Major Bosnar, who was facing his own purgatory. The numerous aches in his body were reaching their zenith in a blinding headache, and his stomach rejected the taste and aroma of any food at all with wave after wave of nausea, retching and diarrhea.

After satisfying himself that his good friend would live, Philip retired once more to the toilet, where – in the depths of his misery – he took a solemn vow to swear off alcohol for the duration of his army service and probably beyond. He kept his pledge, and thereafter, whenever he was involved in the customary rounds of drinks in the officers' mess, he restricted himself to ginger ale or coca-cola.

Peter finally surfaced at 1400 hours and became functional by 1500 hours, never dreaming he was destined for chronic alcoholism; while Philip felt he might have been snatched from a similar fate, just in time.

Aside from his alcoholic problem, Forsyth was a good medical officer and had developed a genuine proficiency in trauma-related surgery. Austin, on the other hand, was a capable but slow orthopedic surgeon who wasn't keen on Forsyth tackling any cases that could be considered as orthopedic, and they fought each other all the time.

Poor Maitland found them impossible to control and begged Philip to take over the problem. As I.C. Surgery, the latter invited them into his office, and told them the rot had to stop "right here and right now." He informed them that this was an order he expected them to obey even though they both outranked him, and they accepted his decision without argument. Furthermore, he assured them that if they failed to get along they'd probably find themselves posted to a much less attractive location. Even Goose Bay, Labrador, couldn't be ruled out.

"It's team effort here, chaps," he reminded them, "and there's no room for primadonnas." After that, they got along surprisingly well, even though Philip knew they still detested each other.

He managed to divide up the surgical cases so they each had enough to do, and Maitland was grateful beyond words.

It was a strange feeling for Philip to find himself so effective in the role of peace-maker, and he felt he was acquiring the qualities of leadership without even trying. The recent turn of events seemed providential, since Maitland was now posted back to a higher desk job in Ottawa and asked Bosnar to take over as O.C. Hospital for the time being, while continuing as IC Surgery. Philip made it clear that he sought no promotion in rank, as this might lead to a desk job and divorce him from any more active surgery.

He still managed to get back to Vanwey every second weekend and this served to unite the family, so that the little ones got used to the sight of their Daddy dressed up like a soldier, and Patty was happy he didn't have to carry a gun. She had to admit she loved seeing him in his resplendent dress uniform, although she thought he still looked too thin.

On one or two occasions, his breakfast companion on the train journey to Vanwey was an impressive individual who was a fine conversationalist. His bright yellow hair looked as if it had been marcelled and his heavy brows beetled into a thoughtful frown whenever he drove home a point in discussion. His smile was toothy, his voice resonant and his deportment impressive, and he could converse on a wide variety of subjects. Philip always enjoyed his company, and it was only after their fourth meeting that he discovered his companion was not only a celebrated lawyer but the rising star of Canadian Conservatism, John Diefenbaker.

As far as his trips home were concerned, Philip came dangerously close to losing them when questioned by Brigadier Lasalle. The top brass was on one of his periodic visits to Camp Thornton and, above all, to see his daughter, although his official excuse was to find out how Major Bosnar was coping with his joint assignment.

"I'm managing just fine, thank you Sir."

"Good. I've had some nice reports about you, especially the way you've kept two Lieutenant-Colonels from coming to blows. That takes diplomacy. By the way, Major, how's my daughter getting along?"

"She's doing very well, Sir. She's a good worker and everyone likes her."

"And do you manage to see your family from time to time?"

"Yes, thank you. I get back to Vanwey every second weekend."

The Brigadier looked puzzled and Philip knew he'd said too much.

"But that would mean a forty-eight hour leave twice a month instead of once a month, wouldn't it?"

"That's right, Sir."

"But surely that must cause some complaints from your fellow officers in the hospital?"

"No it doesn't. You see, I give them all the same forty-eight twice a month. With our two extra surgeons it makes the arrangement quite comfortable and no loss of efficiency, Sir."

Lasalle choked a little on his cigar, and changed direction with the hint of a smile.

"I'm told you still hope to go overseas."

"That's true, Sir, and why I decided to wear this volunteer badge for service in the Pacific. But I'd much prefer Europe."

"Of course you would, and good luck to you."

The weekend leave arrangement continued unchanged and Philip conceded he'd had a close shave. Henceforth, he would always remember to apply the golden rule of army life and carry it into the civilian milieu: 'You no try, you no get!'

Once in a while, he found the ritualistic element of army life so absurd that he took some risks which might easily have backfired. One such occasion occurred when there was an unexpected visit to the camp by General Crerar, and Philip received a phone-call at 0730 hours from his adjutant.

"Major Bosnar, you will kindly parade your officers and other ranks in front of the hospital at 0900 hours for inspection by the General, to be followed by a tour of the entire hospital facility."

"I'm afraid that's quite out of the question. We have a complete list of operations scheduled to commence at 0800 hours and wouldn't be available for a hospital tour before 1100 hours at the earliest. Then we can take a thirty minute break, but definitely no parade."

The voice at the other end sounded somewhat hysterical.

"You don't seem to understand. This is the adjutant to General Crerar speaking...." but Philip cut him short.

"I understand perfectly, but I'm running a hospital with real live patients and there's no way we can stop at a moment's notice for inspection parades. Please inform the General we'll be honored to accommodate him at 1100 hours and have him inspect the entire hospital, with the exception of the isolation ward."

The inspection went off perfectly, and Philip was impressed with Crerar's interest and knowledge of hospital matters. He asked some searching questions, was very good with the patients and displayed a courtly charm to the nursing staff. Matron McGillicuddy was in seventh heaven. At 1130 hours the inspection was over, and the General left with a few kind remarks. An hour later, his adjutant phoned Philip once more, his voice full of respect. He asked if the Major was free to join the General for lunch at 1300 hours at Colonel Ashton's quarters. Philip replied he'd be happy to accept the kind invitation, and was pleased to learn that battle dress would be just fine. The meal turned out to be quite informal and General Crerar was a charming and gracious visitor. Colonel Ashton, the Tiger of Thornton, was glowing with pleasure, and after lunch he kept the guests in fits with a repertoire of jokes, mostly ribald but never vulgar.

Some time later Philip found out that Crerar had given Thornton Military Hospital high marks in every category. Needless to say, this was one more feather in Ashton's cap, while Philip almost felt sorry for the unfortunate adjutant, whose concepts of military protocol and priority must have been rudely shattered.

The spring and summer of 1945 passed by in a glorious series of military victories for the Allies, and Philip felt exhilarated with the news that each day brought the Anglo-American forces closer to the heart of the Third Reich, while the Russians continued their inexorable advance from the East. So much was happening so quickly, as if this was a special kind of wine that had to be swallowed in fast gulps, again and again, in order for the full flavor to be appreciated.

Paris was liberated and De Gaulle marched down the Champs Elysee in lofty splendor, his tall figure held in erect defiance of residual enemy snipers lurking on the rooftops. The French troops could now join in wild enthusiasm with the British, Commonwealth, American, Polish and other allied troops in chasing the enemy to his lair.

Italy now belonged to the antifascist forces and was the newest ally in the fight against the Germans. The hated Mussolini had been caught by the partisans when he tried to cross the northern border in company with his mistress. He was disguised as a German soldier trying to join the retreat to Innsbruck when both were recognized. They were shot and their corpses hung up by the heels like carcasses of meat. Philip was sickened by the gruesome details, and by the thought that yesterday's strutting dictator had finally descended from his balcony of triumph to a disgusting death, his body defiled; possibly by some of the same Italians who'd cheered themselves hoarse in earlier times!

There was little satisfaction in such events, and later, when Hitler committed suicide in his bunker with Eva Braun (his new wife and former mistress) and their bodies were burned, it was a hollow anticlimax. It seemed obscene that such a human fiend could expiate his sins with a quick bullet in the head, while the ruins of Berlin were still being pounded to rubble. For him, there would be no inviting sign displaying the hopeful message, *'Arbeit macht frei'* (Work will make you free). At least not in this world.

The Yalta conference on the fate of the post-war world now saw a dying President Roosevelt striving for an effective and revitalized League of Nations, to be called the United Nations. It would be up to the Big Three, the U.S.A., Great Britain and the U.S.S.R., to make sure there would never be another war. These were the visions of a great statesman, while visibly losing his fight against a terminal illness.

Although the Germans surrendered in May and every vestige of the Nazi legacy was being systematically destroyed, Philip remained unconvinced. So many German citizens and their fellow-travellers in the Ukraine, Poland, Rumania, Hungary, Austria, Latvia, Lithuania and Estonia, had shown themselves ready to accept or even participate in the Holocaust of stricken Europe, that it might take generations for the scourge to be wiped out beyond reincarnation. Until then, every rock should be turned over lest it conceal the deadly Nazi pestilence.

For the immediate present, however, all eyes were on the Pacific, where a deadly war of attrition dragged on, island by island and bunker by bunker; where deaths on both sides were in fearsome numbers and few prisoners were taken. Iwo Jima had fallen to the American flag and even the impregnable fortress of Okinawa had been taken by gallant US forces after a long and costly assault.

It wasn't long after that event when Philip met Major-General Fenwick, head of all Canadian army medical services, on tour of Thornton's facilities and personnel.

"You'll be happy to know, Bosnar, I've selected you to head up a Field Surgical Unit in Okinawa if you're still gung-ho about getting overseas."

"That would be just great, Sir, especially now I've missed the European posting."

"Jolly good! I'd like you to get started right away choosing a team from your M.O. volunteers, and we can start the Pacific training program right away."

"I'd appreciate it if you could let me have a detailed list of my requirements in personnel and equipment, and any pertinent instructions."

"No problem. To start with you'll all have to take a trip to a special training area in Georgia, preferably two at a time and in alphabetical order."

Philip wasn't as elated as he thought he might be, and was uncertain as to how he'd break the news to his darling Patty. In the meantime, he held an informal meeting with those members of his medical staff who were Pacific volunteers and told them what had transpired. They were all excited and looked forward to their Georgia trip, although they understood this would include some tough jungle training and a series of unpleasant inoculations. On the other hand, there was a clear possibility of promotions for each of them, and in any event, they were all bound to find it an exciting adventure and a wonderful professional experience. The plans were well under way, and the first two selected M.Os were already getting ready for their trip south when news of the atomic bomb dropped on Hiroshima swept through the camp.

There could be little doubt now that the war against Japan was over to all intents and purposes and the little Emperor would have to surrender. But in the name of human decency, at what a hideous price! Yet, if it was true that this would shorten the war and thus save countless lives, then some could argue that it was worth it. Nevertheless, it meant that the Allies, too, had crossed that terrible moral chasm beyond which innocent civilians, women and children, the old and the sick, were in the very forefront of the agony, death and destruction of modern warfare.

Was this what all the proud banners, resplendent parades and historic tales of derring-do, had come to? Was this, henceforth, to be a legitimate field of combat for brave warriors? These were disturbing questions, yet out of the conflicting emotions facing Philip Bosnar during these cataclysmic days, his overall sense was one of relief that the horrible carnage and suffering would now be over and families would be reunited once again.

Despite the fact that all unit O.Cs in Camp Thornton, as elsewhere across the country, had received strict orders to close the bars on VJ Day, Major Bosnar decided this was one celebration he hadn't the heart to suppress, even though he'd be restricting himself to soft drinks. On September 2, the news of V.J. Day was flashed around the world and he sent for his Quartermaster. He showed him a large official-looking letter from Ottawa, addressed to Lt-Col. R.L.Maitland, O.C. Hospital.

"I want you to note this letter is being redirected to Colonel Maitland without being opened," he said. "After all, if the bumf-boys in Ottawa can't keep track of officers' reassignments that's not our affair, wouldn't you agree?"

"Absolutely, Sir!"

"Fine. In that case see if you can get this letter out to its correct address as soon as possible."

Thus it came to pass that on the evening of September 2, 1945, the bar at the Medical Officers Mess was the only one in Camp Thornton to remain open, and probably one of the very few in all of Canada's military establishments. The celebrations remained quiet and orderly, and by good fortune Forsyth and Austin were both on leave, so that took care of one tricky problem. Slowly and steadily, some officers from other units started drifting in, as did the matron and some of the nurses.

The infallible army grapevine was working at full capacity and it was no surprise when the Tiger himself, in full dress uniform and considerably under the weather, strode in with his customary escort of two captains and shouted, "Bosnar, you rotten swine, why didn't you invite me to your goddam party?" Philip breathed a sigh of relief. It was obvious he'd got away with his deception without repercussion, and he asked Corporal Kennedy to serve drinks to the new arrivals. He also told him to pour a good stiff drink for himself, which the steward accepted with thanks. Then, lifting his own glass of coca-cola diluted with club soda, Major Bosnar proposed a toast.

"Colonel Ashton, with your kind permission, I ask you all to raise your glasses and drink to our final victory over Japan and the release of our brave comrades from the prison camps. To Victory, and to Peace!"

The bar closed down at midnight, but it was 2 a.m. before the two faithful watchdogs succeeded in getting their stumbling Camp Commandant to his feet and on his way back to his quarters.

The next morning, the Q.M. fulfilled his duty by announcing there might be some delay in locating Colonel Maitland's present address and perhaps the Major might consider opening the letter in case it was something urgent. It was opened ceremoniously in the orderly room, and the Q.M. read the contents aloud: All mess-bars were to remain closed for twenty-four hours following the announcement of V.J. Day, by order of General Crerar.

The following month was mainly concerned with a winding down process. To Philip's great relief, the two warring Lieut.-Colonels received transfer orders to Regina prior to their discharge. As a matter of fact it had been possible, with careful handling, to derive the best effort from both of them, and by the time they left, they were getting along fairly well. Philip was more than satisfied with their chief contribution: bringing the latest surgical advances from the battle front to his surgical department.

One Friday evening after dinner, Brigadier Lasalle called him up from Regina, and he wondered what was afoot. It turned out that Lisette had decided on the spur of the moment to visit her parents for the weekend but found herself short of funds.

"Do you think you could lend her some money, Bosnar? She'll pay you back for sure on Monday morning."

"No problem, Sir. I'll see to it right away."

His fellow officers, picking up the gist of the phone conversation, were chuckling their heads off.

"You sure have the old boy eating out of your hand."

"Why don't you escort the gorgeous Lisette to Regina, yourself, you old smoothie."

"Boy, I wish I had your chance, Phil. I'd sure take the longest, slowest route."

Philip simply smiled at them.

"It's a lucky thing I don't have a dirty mind like yours," he laughed, and was greeted with mock protestations of injured innocence. They were a great bunch of fellows, he had to admit, and he was proud of the way they'd kept their romantic aspirations under wraps and never did anything to cause him undue embarrassment.

Late in September, Ashton had him over for dinner and after the meal he wanted to know what Philip's plans were following discharge.

"First, I have to get back to Vanwey and bring the practice up to peak performance. Then, after we've arrived at a suitable financial settlement between the three partners, we'll decide who stays and who leaves. Personally, I'm keen on practicing in Vancouver or at least some major center on the West Coast, but that won't be for a few years yet."

"How about coming to my city, Edmonton? I can give you all the right connections and could guarantee you a top-drawer practice in no time at all. I'm not without influence, you know, and Edmonton is going to be the boomtown of the next twenty years, mark my words."

Philip expressed his gratitude, and noted his host's disappointment when he showed no enthusiasm for the offer. Then Ashton had another idea.

"Why don't you let me fix you up with a base hospital command in Germany? You could take your time making up your mind while enjoying the perks of a full colonel's rank, with your family living in a fine home nearby. Of course it would be a desk job but you'd be in charge of all the work done in the hospital."

"I'm afraid I'd go batty behind a desk, and I'm not fussy about living in Germany until some of the stink has gone."

"Don't be a chump, Bosnar. The Krauts will probably be our allies in the next war with the Bolshies."

The discussion petered out after that, and Philip felt he'd somehow offended his benefactor.

The following month, the new O.C. Hospital arrived, much to Philip's relief, and took over the unpleasant duty of closing down the wartime footing of the institution. There was only the simplest routine surgery to handle, and all the remaining serious cases would be shipped out to various veteran's hospitals such as Deer Lodge in Winnipeg and Sunnybrook in Toronto.

At the beginning of November, his discharge papers were complete and he took his final leave of the hospital. The sadness of the occasion was somewhat diminished by the army's final surprise for him. Brigadier Lasalle, terror of all medical officers and lord of Military District 12, sent his staff car and driver to pick up Major Bosnar. He would drive him to Regina in time to get him back to Vanwey the same day.

When Philip compared this day with his initial experiences in the Canadian army, he couldn't help smiling. Somehow, nothing in the past two years seemed to make the slightest sense, yet he knew he was a stronger man and a far better surgeon. He also knew he should be thankful to God that the crazy contradictions of military bureaucracy had somehow spared him to return, safe and sound, to his loved ones.

It was wonderful being back in civilian life; in his own home, in civvie clothes, with his beloved wife and adorable children. To play rough and tough with his robust son and so very gently with his little fairy princess, was a joy beyond all expectation. It was exciting to see them developing individual traits of character, some of Patty's and some of his, yet ever-changing into unique qualities of individual personality and the development of separate identity. It was such a joy to eat the wonderful food his darling wife served him every day. What a fantastic talent she had developed in the kitchen, with every meal so tasty and enjoyable!

Above all, it was glorious to have the warm and beautiful body of his adorable Patricia next to him in bed, night after night. She was his to hold and to love, with every one of her soft curves finding its reciprocal contour in the eager embrace of his firm body. Theirs was a passionate love that could survive any separation and would last for a lifetime, come what may. That was what they both felt, as they realized how lucky they were to share such a divine gift.

The practice was doing quite well but there were a few problems. Susan O'Reilly had left to look after her ailing parents in Guelph, and she was replaced by an older nurse-assistant, a doctor's widow who wasn't as good as her predecessor and who found the work a bit too much for her. Upstairs, above the offices, Alvin Masters had done wonders, converting the old cramped storage rooms to an up-to-date pharmacy and dispensary – where patients could obtain their pre-scriptions at cost, with a minimum dispensing fee.

"Some of the local druggists have been really ripping off our patients," he explained to Philip, "even with stock brand-name pharmaceuticals, and our system saves them at least thirty percent on their drugs."

Philip approved heartily but added a note of warning, "Don't be too shocked if the local druggists complain to the College of Physicians and Surgeons. After all, we're on their territory."

Sure enough, a letter arrived in due course from the new College registrar, Dr. Fraywell, demanding that their dispensary be shut down or charges of unethical conduct might be raised. It was a vague and unsatisfactory letter, and both Philip and Alvin felt like telling Fraywell to back up his charge or get lost, but it hardly seemed worth fighting about or making new enemies. They closed down the upstairs venture and converted it into a laboratory for standard blood and urine testing. Philip was sorry to learn his good friend, Joe McShane, had died a few months ago from a massive heart attack, and knew he'd miss him dearly. He was a fine man and the right person for the job of College registrar. It would be hard to fill his shoes.

During some of his weekend army leaves to Vanwey, Masters had acquainted Philip with a few of the problems he'd been encountering at the hospital, but now that his partner was back in full practice he gave him all the details, and they were really bad.

"Al, you should have told me about some of these difficulties before now."

"I thought it better to wait until you were in a position to do something about them."

First, there was the matter of hospital beds: a progressive cramming process by which Brent Slocum had been monopolizing the admissions. The moment a patient was discharged, Slocum had an "emergency case" requiring instant admission, be it an "acute bunion," a suspected "acute abdomen" that included almost any belly ache, or even cases of infected skin eruptions that were bound to increase the dangers of hospital inpatient cross-infection.

When Philip started to investigate the situation, he found there was no real attempt to justify these spurious emergency admissions. Moreover, there were numerous bed-patients in the corridors due to overcrowding of the wards. These corridor cases were used mainly for Slocum's overnight admissions, so he could obtain first access to empty beds on the wards the very next day. Even Philip had to marvel at the sheer simplicity of the fraudulent system. What made all this possible, was the fact that the inimitable Sister Mary Sybil had been replaced by a dear old doddery nun, Sister Margaret Anthony. She was hopelessly unaware of what was going on, and thus, twice as dangerous.

On the other hand, one who was by no means unaware was Sister Elizabeth in the O.R. She had taken over shortly after Philip left, and had fallen under Slocum's influence ever since, although it was hard to figure out why this was so. Alvin thought it was because she disliked him for being a Jew.

"Once or twice I was tempted to tell her I had nothing whatever to do with killing Jesus, but she wouldn't have taken my word for it anyway."

Like most of life's little annoyances, Alvin could always find a refreshing point of humor in the situation, and Philip found it easy to laugh with him, but not to the point of ignoring the problem.

Slocum's predominance in O.R. schedules and assignment of nursing help could be tolerated no longer, and Philip discussed his entire plan of action with Herb Adams, who was chairman of the hospital board. Adams's summation was straight to the point. Dr. Slocum, the lawyer declared, was a ruthless opportunist; Sister Margaret Anthony was a senile incompetent; and Sister Elizabeth could well be an incurable antisemite.

"What's your plan, Philip?" he asked.

"I'm going to write to the Reverend Mother Superior of the Order of Saint Cecilia in Gresham, Ontario, outlining the entire situation. I shall recommend that Sister Margaret Anthony should be transferred to supervisory duties at the convalescent wing in the valley, and Sister Claudia take over as Superior in her place. She's a fine sturdy person with a strong character and an excellent background in nursing and hospital administration. I know she'd love the job and would do it well."

He went on to say he'd have a little chat with "our fat and sneaky O.R. Sister," and set her straight in no uncertain terms. Then he'd call a meeting of all three doctors and set up a formal medical staff with clear-cut rules and privileges, and with strict regulations covering such items as admissions and discharges.

"I'm afraid this won't include Pete Forsyth as he isn't rejoining our practice."

"I know. He's going to join a small medical group in Calgary and we're all going to miss him."

"I'll miss him very much. He's asked me to come out and join him there but I believe my place is here, at least until the present hospital mess is cleared up, and if I decide to move to a larger center at some later date it would probably be to the West Coast."

"What happens if you get no satisfactory response from the Mother House in Gresham?"

"Then I won't hesitate to involve the Archbishop and the Provincial Minister of Health."

"Good for you, Philip. Go for it!"

Chapter 18

1938 cont'd.

It was the first time in his life he'd ever been drunk, and it made up for all his previous sobriety. This time it was sheer alcoholic coma. Philip awoke at 2.30 a.m. and found himself in his own room at the hospital, reclining in his bed in Fowler's position (45 degrees above horizontal), so familiar for surgical patients. A gastric tube that came out of the left side of his mouth was attached to a suction and irrigation setup. There was also an oxygen tank next to the bed, with facial mask and tubing affixed, but these were lying on the bedcovers with the valves shut off. In addition, he observed that an intravenous had been set up in his left arm, and he realized he was being treated for acute alcoholism.

Much to his surprise, he felt reasonably well aside from a slight general weakness, and at this point of his recovery he was pleased to see his bluff and hearty savior, Dr. Starbuck.

"Glad to see you finally awake. Let's see how groggy you are. What's the date?"

June the 8th or 9th, I think."

"What year?"

"1938, I'm pretty sure."

"You really tied one on, my young friend. Fogarty told me how you belted those drinks down, one after the other without any mix. You must have thought you had some special immunity, you stupid blighter."

"What can I say? I guess it was an experiment that went sour."

"More like a bet or a challenge you just couldn't resist, I'd say."

"It looks as if you saved my life, Sir, and I'm very grateful."

"As a matter of fact, when I got you back here you didn't have much of a pulse or blood pressure, and I guessed your blood alcohol had flipped over the top. Your vitals have come back to normal in the past hour, and except for looking a pale shade of green you're pretty well back to your usual self."

He paused, grinned broadly and asked, "By the way, who the hell is this `Patty' you've been yelling for since you started coming round?"

The matron had just crept quietly into the room and supplied the answer.

"Oh that's his own true love, Nurse Clancy. Right now she's furious with him but I've got her waiting outside and I'll make sure she sees him before she goes back to bed."

"With two terrific people like you on my side how can I lose?" Philip said with feeling.

His two visitors left and a few minutes later Patty came in.

As soon as she saw him, her anger gave way to concern, but she made him promise he'd never again take thoughtless chances like that with his safety.

"Remember," she admonished him, "part of you belongs to me now, and I don't want you to take any crazy risks."

It was a close shave, and the superintendent told him in confidence that it was fortunate he enjoyed such a good reputation throughout the hospital. It was decided, at the top administration levels, to dismiss the entire incident as an innocent youthful prank that went astray, and nothing more. Philip knew how earnestly good old Starbuck and Tregarth must have gone to bat for him and he loved them for it.

For the rest of his stay at the Alex he made every effort to expiate the sinful lapse, and his chiefs in turn kept allocating more and more important operative cases to his exclusive care. The harder he worked, the more carefully he arranged his spare time, so he could share it whenever possible with his beloved Patty. Their tacit engagement was now recognized by the entire hospital staff at all levels and that made concealment unnecessary, but both stuck to the rules and there was no overt display of affection in front of patients or staff.

As if divine Providence was ready to send them a sign of approval, Nurse Patricia Clancy was now appointed to take charge of the number 2 Operating theater, where Philip did most of his cases. It was soon obvious to all concerned, and especially to Philip, that she was an absolute 'natural' in the theater, whether in her supervisory duties, as scrub- nurse or surgical assistant. It was in her latter capacity that the two young lovers found their most natural and satisfying professional partnership, and it was no exaggeration to claim that she cut his operating time by as much as fifty percent.

They would never forget the puny two week-old infant with a *Strangulated inguinal hernia'* a hernia in the groin with obstructed blood-flow to the contents), where speed was the absolute essence of success. From incision to final suture took less than fifteen minutes. Not a single move was wasted by either one and the baby did fine. It was almost as though some form of telepathy existed between them in the theater and no requests or instructions were necessary. Philip was reminded of Grant-Sutton working with Chadwick, and how he'd marveled at the almost catalytic effect of the assistant in that fabled team.

Dear old erratic Uncle Willie was especially kind to his senior resident and turned over most of the operations on non-private patients, and after a while the other honoraries began to follow suit. Philip became aware of a constant widening of his scope, as well as a growing independence of decision and action with the patients on his wards.

It was strange, sometimes, to observe that the greatest reward could come from the least spectacular cases. For example, poor Mr. Tarpole, an 86-year-old scarecrow of a man, was dying of laryngeal cancer. He was quite beyond curative radiation or surgery, and was being kept as comfortable as possible with regular doses of morphine and tube-feedings. Nothing more was to be considered, especially anything of a surgical nature.

One afternoon, Philip caught sight of him struggling to breathe – to force some air into his lungs through the strictured barrier of his vocal cords – and he knew what he must do, orders or no orders. He helped the old gentleman into a wheelchair, took him down to theater number 2 and said,

"Mr. Tarpole, I'm going to make a hole in your windpipe to let you breathe. I'll be using injections of local anesthetic and finish up with a special tube in your lower neck. Is that agreeable to you?" The patient nodded his head vigorously, and half an hour later was back in his bed breathing easily and writing profuse expressions of gratitude on his writing pad. Everyone associated with the case was deeply touched, and even though death within a matter of weeks was inevitable, the patient had been given a measure of comfort for which morphine was no longer needed as often as before.

As a final measure of the extent to which he'd been accepted into the fabric of Dover's social life, Dr. Philip Bosnar received an invitation to play lead violin in a performance of J.S.Bach's St. Matthew's Passion. After a dozen intensive rehearsals, the concert was held at The Church of Christ the Redeemer, with Sir Henry and Lady Clathorpe glowing their approval from the front pew.

A week later, Philip left for London and was ready and eager to commence the Final Fellowship course for which he'd registered at the London Hospital on Mile End Road. At about the same time, Patty succeeded in finding a job at the Hampstead General Hospital, where she'd be working with a surgical group headed by the nationally acclaimed surgeon, Sir Heneague Ogilvie.

Despite all the variety of professional and emotional elements occupying his daily life and never far from his mind, Philip was forever conscious of what was taking place in Europe – especially Great Britain. When the troops of the Third Reich marched into Austria on May 10, he found it difficult to get the bad taste of betrayal out of his mouth. Where in God's name were Britain and France, let alone the League of Nations? Why was the Anschluss such a foregone conclusion, with Austrian troops welcoming the invaders instead of resisting them?

This type of debacle could hardly occur in a vacuum, but rather as the final scene in a carefully organized drama of deception and intrigue. First the formation of an Austrian Nazi movement, then its infiltration into political seats of power and subversion of the defense forces themselves. Didn't the leaders of Britain and France comprehend – in excruciating detail – Germany's organization and financing of the Austrian Nazi network, and the series of escalating demands to Austria's government, to a point of no return?

Philip was painfully aware that the cancer eating away at the peace of Europe, and possibly the world, had shown its first diagnostic symptoms and signs much earlier. As far back as October 1935, Hitler had withdrawn Germany from the League of Nations and disavowed the Geneva Disarmament Conference. Mussolini, who contrasted the Führer's brutal daring with the obsequious retreat of the Anglo-French partnership, wasn't the kind to look a gift horse in the mouth and soon invaded Abyssinia with impunity while the League cluck-clucked.

Now, however, it was the last of summer and no time for such grim reflections. Instead, Philip decided to take Patty for a glorious carefree weekend in Ostend, the coastal playground of Belgium. The Channel crossing was remarkably smooth and pleasant and they were even unable to resist the offer of "Teabreadabutter," bawled out to the passengers by a white-coated steward as he ran around the decks every half hour. One presumed the first class passengers enjoyed more elegant fare.

After debarkation and the perfunctory customs and immigration routines, they took a taxi downtown and checked in at a charming little hotel, Le Maison Palomar, which had a good rating with the Cooks' travel people, even if the young lovers had to climb two steep flights of stairs to their room. The bed-sitting room, bedecked with an abundance of chintz, was nonetheless charming, and it looked out on a busy, noisy street, filled with the sights, sounds and smells of mixed Gallic and Flemish cultures.

It was time for a late lunch, so Phil and Patty wandered along the crowded streets and inspected the sidewalk cafe's until they both selected the same small corner establishment, one with the special romantic aura they were seeking. The lone waiter found them a nicely placed table and Philip ordered Deux Dubonnets avec soda. The assorted paté sandwiches they had for lunch were delicious and were washed down with hot and very sweet café au lait. Then they were off to see the sights.

Rather than waste time and money going to the Kursaal and watching the gamblers stake their bets, they decided instead to go exploring on a Bicycle a deux that they rented for a few hours. This was a side-by-side tandem capable of surprisingly good speed once they got into rhythm. Aside from provoking choice curses from annoyed tram drivers whenever the tandem's wheels got stuck in the recessed tracks, Phil and Patty had a wonderful time on their novel vehicle. They found they could make great progress along the seafront promenade, cruising along with the ease of veterans.

They went north to the famed war zone of Zeebrugge, with its imposing memorial and museum in remembrance of the sacrifices made by its citizens and armed forces during the Great War of 1914. They toured around merrily like two school children on a country outing, and got back to Ostend tired and hungry, as the sun was setting over the rooftops.

After a bath and change of clothes, they sought out their chosen sidewalk cafe and enjoyed a sensational meal, served by Henri, the same waiter who was now their friend and adviser. Following assorted hors d'oeuvres that Phil wolfed with abandon and Patty approached with more caution, there was some great vichyssoise, served cold, then a culinary masterpiece of coq au vin avec haricots verts et pommes de terre Guillaume'. The latter were tiny baked potato cakes that tasted like the golden latkes (highly flavored potato cakes) his mother cooked at home, and they were mouthwatering. During this classic repast, they drank a simple vin ordinaire (their waiter informed them it was a beaujolais), and although sharp and unsweetened to their taste, they found it most refreshing. Patty had some petits gatteaux for dessert while Phil had a glace Chartreuse. Finally some espresso café and cigarettes to finish off the memorable meal. Le billet was reasonable, and the pourboire left for their exemplary host was generous.

By midnight, they were ready to flop into the large and creaky brass bed and melt into each other's arms, but when sleep came at last, it wasn't for very long. At 5 a.m, the street vendors came down the street in a noisy gallop, bringing their fruit and vegetables, their fresh fish, French loaves and assorted meats, and singing off-tune as they ran – a sort of universal alarm clock for the neighborhood. A chorus of barking dogs followed the running vendors and acclaimed the new day with noisy enthusiasm. By 7 a.m, the young lovers were more than ready for breakfast, and Philip phoned downstairs to have it sent up. The buttered croissants, still hot, with iced petits suisses (cream cheese patties) tasted heavenly, and the café au lait was just right.

After breakfast, it was a tour of Bruges with its historic Cathedral, a monument of Gothic splendor, and a walk around the old city, where its incredibly ancient ladies could be seen crafting their inimitable lace. Their artistry and energy were awe-inspiring, and Philip found himself comparing their speedy movements and intricate needlework with those of the most gifted surgeons he'd worked with. He had to admit the surgeons came in a distant second.

The rest of their stay in Ostend was a joyful unwinding, with Fellowship finals, the dark international scene, family religious obstacles and all other worries cast completely aside. So buoyed were they and so full of optimism and even bravado, that despite the heaving surging seas on their return trip across the channel they remained out on deck for the entire crossing. Only one lone figure remained with them: a young Belgian who'd boarded with them and now sat rigidly in his deck chair, his face a muddy green and covered with large beads of sweat from hairline to chin.

"Avez vous besoin d'assistance, Monsieur." Philip asked him, but the poor fellow remained motionless and only managed to mutter a faint "Non, merci."

The channel lived up to its vile reputation until they actually landed, and when the young couple set foot on England's reassuring shore they were ready to face anything.
Philip's money was running low and he even entertained a brief thought about returning to Ostend on his own and risking his remaining capital at the Kursaal's tables. A reassessment of his finances, however, reassured him that he could pay for the F.R.C.S. course and still manage to subsist, especially as he'd be living at home. Anyhow, once he'd passed his exams, if indeed he were that fortunate, he'd be in a position to earn some real money and plan his future with Patty.

It was strange, but despite what seemed like insurmountable obstacles with her devout Catholic family in Ireland, he never doubted her strength and determination to stay firm against all odds, or that the two of them would forge a successful and enduring marriage. Together or apart, they seemed integral parts of one complete entity, and the thought of living apart seemed to contravene the very laws of nature.

There were twenty-five members of the Fellowship class at the London Hospital and these included Australians, South Africans, Canadians, Egyptians and East Indians, of whom one was a diminutive Maharani. She was resplendent in a gilded sari and wore a precious jewel in her nose. They were nearly all practicing surgeons and the average age was between thirty-five and forty. The man in charge of the course was the very antithesis of everything Philip Bosnar expected. He'd visualized a patrician savant, a man of culture and refinement over and above his reputation as a distinguished surgeon. Instead, Mr. Trevor Russell was a large untidy individual with a loud and raucous Cockney accent, and his language to the members of his course was vulgar and insulting. His dress, as well as his overall demeanor, could only be described as slovenly, as if challenging the stereotype.

Within forty-eight hours, this boorish individual commanded Philip's deepest respect, and he recognized him for the great teacher he really was. The unpleasant facade was no more than that, and if one could survive his acid tongue one could learn a great deal. A South African was the first casualty.

"Now tell us, Fletcher, whaddya fink's the trouble wiv this poor old bloke?"

"In my opinion, Sir, the patient has an acute attack of diverticulitis in the pelvic colon."

"And whaddya mean by vat?"

"I mean that he has an acute inflammation of..." but he got no further. At that very moment, Russell let out a triumphant yell: "OH, GOODIE. INFLUMMITION! Now vat's somethin' we'd all wanna hear abaht!"

Gone, was the erudition with which the hapless Fletcher was poised to expound on the pathology of the patient's condition, and gone, the outpouring of pertinent clinical and surgical facts in support of his opinions. Instead, he was trapped in a subject more appropriate to a first year medical course, and on which he would now be grilled and humiliated for the next half-hour.

"What a waste of time and what uncouth rudeness," was the common verdict on their unmannerly tutor's spot inquisitions. But a moment's reflection should make the candidates aware that they'd learned more about this subject than they could ever get from their reading. Moreover, Trevor Russell could take any other so-called 'simple subject' like gallstones, and by the time he'd ferreted out the last desperate reply from his unlucky victim, he'd instilled into his class the ability to think a piece of knowledge through to its ultimate possibilities. The whole world of surgical and pathological theory became a wonderful integrated tapestry of information.

There were six other lecturers and demonstrators, covering abdominal surgery, neurosurgery, urology, gynecology, orthopedics, head and neck surgery, chest surgery, vascular surgery and surgical applied anatomy. They were all excellent and behaved like polished gentleman, showing every courtesy to their hard-studying candidates. But not one had the dynamic impact of Trevor Russell, at least as far as Philip was concerned. He took everything the dreaded Cockney instructor chose to throw at him and tried to give as good as he got. The others either feared their tormentor or simply detested him. This was no Lazenby – of Primary Fellowship memories – trying to confuse and mislead, but a determined teacher digging out the truth from his charges, no matter how it hurt. He was organizing their thoughts so they could absorb their book knowledge more effectively.

Philip did most of his reading from a superb three-volume work on surgery by Rodney Maingot, which he set out to absorb from cover to cover. This required a special technique of reading, the one he'd used for his M.B., B.S. exams, as there were several other books which had to be studied, plus notes and medical journals. The formula was 20 pages the first day, 30 the second, 45 the third, 60 the fourth, 80 the fifth and 100 the sixth day. Once he was able to cope with 500 pages a day, he speeded up no further but kept a large reading capacity in reserve for special occasions.

Each day brought new intensive detail to the specialized information he was storing in his mind, but he still found time to scan the daily newspapers and listen to the BBC broadcasts and what he considered even more important, the radio broadcasts from Germany.

It seemed incredible to Philip that the public at large and even his fellow students seemed blithely oblivious of the terrible tragedy that was shaping up, first for Czechoslovakia and then for the whole of Europe. The malign forces that could unilaterally reject Versailles, Locarno and Geneva, that could remilitarize the Rhineland, march into Austria and threaten Czechoslovakia, wouldn't stop at the Sudetenland but would gobble up the entire country. If that happened, after a quick gulp of Danzig it would be Poland's turn. All these dark considerations raised the same awful question. At what point would Chamberlain and Daladier show some semblance of backbone and declare, "Cross this line and we fight?"

More amused than depressed, Philip began to observe that his friends and companions regarded him as a hopeless obsessive at best and a determined warmonger at worst. No one, least of all the western statesmen, seemed prepared to deal harshly with criminal perverts to whom beatings, torture and killings were acceptable modes of political conduct. Would these vile practices become precedents for a universal norm by the end of the century? So far, there were few public voices raised in concern about such matters. In England, there was Anthony Eden and the redoubtable warhorse, Winston Churchill. In France, there was that modern Joan of Arc, Madame Tabouis, political columnist to the *Paris Oeuvre*. This remarkable little lady, a chronic invalid who was born into a family of wealth and fascist sympathies, had the courage to defy her milieu and speak out boldly against submission to Hitler.

Every Saturday at 3 p.m, Patty went to meet Phil at Hampstead Heath underground station. They embraced with unconcealed fervor, oblivious of passers-by, then walked arm-in-arm for the next hour, exchanging as much news as possible about his Fellowship course and her work at the hospital. During the rest of the day, they tried to compensate for all the time they'd been forced apart by the pressures of separate duties and commitments. Both felt the keenest interest in every aspect of each other's experiences. Two things were clear about Patty's present state of mind. First, she was determined that nothing be permitted to interfere with Phil's intense concentration on his present studies, and would make no demands to see him more often. Second, and far more exhilarating, was her total commitment to marrying her beloved, no matter what the rest of her family might feel. He had an idea that she'd gradually broken down the barriers of religious parochialism, in her own quiet and determined way, until marrying out of the true faith was no longer equated with making a pact with the devil.

He had to laugh at her single deception. Since no other member of her family had ever known anyone as exotic as a Jew, she decided to soften the cultural shock by labeling Phil a Protestant and suggesting that conversion was in the offing. He was amused by the thought that her family might even accept a Jew into its devout Catholic midst, rather than an alien follower of the demonic Martin Luther and apologist for the murderous Oliver Cromwell, tyrant and regicide.

Phil and Patty loved to climb the Heath and stroll over to Spaniard's Walk for afternoon drinks and sandwiches of cucumber and watercress. After dark, they would wander down to a small restaurant, Le Petit Fontainbleu, and enjoy a light and tasty supper. Then it was back to the dark privacy of the Heath, where they took their place near – yet totally isolated from – all the other loving couples enjoying the crisp evening air, the moon, the stars and each other. All too soon, it was time to walk back to the underground station and say goodbye for another whole week, with Patty returning to her quarters at the hospital and Phil to his studies.

During the week, Patty never failed to put in a phonecall to her beloved at exactly 9 each night, and this had the effect of breaking their sense of separation; just a few words of deep affection and that was all one needed. Once in a while, Philip let himself go on geopolitical affairs, whenever the newspapers or radio got him really worked up. At such times, her sympathetic understanding and emotional support always made him feel much better. They both seemed on the same wavelength, and it was remarkable that this daughter of the Irish Republican Army and this staunch English Conservative Jew could reach such convergent views.

By September of 1938, Philip felt he was fighting a campaign on many fronts.

First and foremost, it was imperative that he study to his absolute limit in order to pass his final F.R.C.S. without the dread necessity of a retry.

Second, he felt compelled to stay abreast of British and world affairs, as he was convinced that this next month represented the crossroads of history, perhaps for generations to come.

Third, he must keep his family ties intact and never lose sight of his financial obligations and an early opportunity to take over the family debts.

Fourth, he must prepare for 1939 with a clear plan of action: directed either at an eventual honorary staff appointment at St. Clement's or a private surgical practice. Such a practice would have to be at a less exalted level, either in Britain or as far away as Canada. As for his beloved Patty, one way or another he was determined to marry her not later than the summer of 1939.

He consolidated his studies and operative cadaver dissections to such a degree that, by the middle of September, he was able to concentrate at night on the machinations of the Appeasement Gang. This infamous group included Neville Chamberlain and his personal adviser, Horace Wilson; Ambassador to the Third Reich, Nevile Henderson; and Foreign Secretary, Lord Halifax. There were others, but these four were actively seeking friendly relations with the Nazi leaders and their hirelings.

From Philip's perspective, Chamberlain and his intimate surrogates were not the well-intentioned peace-loving dupes as characterized by the media and their public apologists. Instead, they were true admirers of the Nazi regime, even though they recognized Hitler as a vulgar demented megalomaniac. Their obsessive hatred of the Soviet Union blinded them to the monstrous evil of the Third Reich. Hadn't they studied the Nuremberg Laws or the rantings of 'Mein Kampf' or did they simply choose to ignore them? Meanwhile, a nervous public, busy digging trenches and testing gasmasks, applauded as their leaders went through the charades of Berchtesgarten, Godesberg and Munich, debating the order of the menu and type of condiments while Hitler prepared to devour the entire territory of Czechoslovakia and a good deal more.

The final straw that broke the camel's back, so to speak, was a speech delivered over the BBC by a tremulous Prime Minister to his quaking public on September 27, the eve of the Munich four-power meeting. It sounded like the death knell of all the moral values Philip Bosnar had always embraced so proudly. These had always been emblematic of Britain's legendary sense of fair play and support for the underdog – and to hell with the risks! He was so stunned that only the occasional phrase stuck in his mind: "this faraway country," and "these people of whom we know nothing." Translation: "Forget the principles of collective security. Tear up mutual defense agreements! Abandon the victim and genuflect to the insatiable marauder!"

Philip thanked God the Conservative Party could still produce men of courage and principle, men like Eden and Churchill, and now – like a bolt from the blue – a reborn Duff Cooper, who exposed the shallow mockery of Munich by resigning as Lord of the Admiralty. The delays and vacillation over mobilization of the Northern Fleet had proved to this staunch blueblood what he'd long suspected. These appeasers never had the slightest intention of stopping the Nazis in their piecemeal conquest of Europe, so long as it was made to look all very diplomatic and respectable: meetings, memoranda and treaties, with only the prospective victim denied a voice in defense of its fate.

The examinations came at last, and Philip found the papers very fair. The candidates were required to discuss renal tumors in essay form. This meant a description of the pathology, clinical features, investigations, treatment, operative details, complications, results and prognosis. Above all, were there any original ideas one could inject into the discussion, indicating a desire to look to the future for further advances? Another paper was even more challenging: 'A 56-year-old workman has fallen 20 ft. off a scaffolding and sustained a severe compression fracture of the 3rd thoracic vertebral body. Discuss your approach, including examination, treatment and complications'. His answers seemed to write themselves, especially after setting up the usual preliminary skeleton outlines, and the allotted time seemed adequate for including all important details, as long as one avoided longwinded prose to conceal ignorance or uncertainty.

The Orals were a different matter entirely, and this was where one stood or fell. There was an acute consciousness of ones surroundings, for this was the fabled Royal College of Surgeons in the historic confines of Lincoln-in-Fields, and the results would be announced in this building as soon as the last of the Orals were over. There would be a resplendent Beadle in traditional regalia, directing each candidate by pointing his ornate mace up the stairs for success or downward for failure.

At first, everything seemed to be going smoothly. He was taken to a huge table covered with every conceivable kind of surgical instrument, and asked to name each one handed to him by one of the two examiners. This was perfect for Philip, as he could name, describe and expand on just about every surgical instrument in the huge Downs Catalogue.

The operative session came next, with each candidate assigned an area on one of the preserved cadavers. He was required to reset the upper third of the left fibula for a large benign tumor. Of course, the real trap was in avoiding injury to the common peroneal nerve without compromising the resection. Before touching the bone, Philip carefully identified the attenuated nerve and separated it from the tumor in order to place an identifying tape around the endangered structure. Only then did he proceed with dissection around the fibula, separating the bone from all vital structures below the knee joint before completing the resection.

The very last Orals, held at 10 a.m, were a pleasant surprise. He recognized his examiner as Sir Charles Pannett, President of the Royal College of Surgeons and a man with a reputation for fairness and decency toward his candidates. The second man, who took notes and helped with the actual marking, was a friendly chap with an obvious sense of humor.

Philip felt almost certain that he'd be quizzed on the subject of *Actinomycosis*, a disease usually affecting farmers and causing *granulomas* (inflammatory tumors) of the jaws and intestine in most instances. A week earlier, he'd learned that a new surgical book had just arrived at Lewis's reference library. It was the latest monograph on Actinomycosis and was written by that eminent authority, Zachary Cope. He had so speeded up his daily reading schedule that he was able to take the underground train to Warren Street Station, dash to the library on Gower Street and race through the new book, cover to cover, absorbing only the high points. He was back home and resuming his regular reading in the space of three hours.

"Let's see," said Pannett cordially, shall we talk about Actinomycosis this morning or shall we find out what you know about Duodenal Ulcer?"
Without waiting for a reply, the examiner continued, "I'm pretty sure you've seen far more D.Us than Actino, and perhaps you've just read Cope's new work, so we'll go for D.U."
Ah well, thought the disappointed Philip, such is fate, but I certainly came close.

The questions were searching but essentially fair, and he was careful to seize any opportunity to score an extra point whenever one presented itself. Thus, when he was asked what operation he would select for the treatment of a 45-year-old male bus driver with a proven duodenal ulcer, his answer was unequivocal.

"I wouldn't operate on this patient, Sir, but rather advise a course of comprehensive medical treatment."

The associate examiner smiled faintly, "Would you care to amplify your reply?"

"My point is that surgery should be reserved for specific complications such as acute perforation, massive hemorrhage which cannot be medically controlled, or severe pyloric obstruction."

"Anything else?"

"Persistent failure to respond to carefully supervised medical treatment, advanced posterior penetrating ulcer, or a case labeled as intractable by the physician in charge."

"Anything else?"

"If the X-rays reveal advanced distortion of the pyloro- duodenal region and there is the possibility of a pyloric malignancy."

The examiners seemed unoffended by his approach, but they proceeded to bombard him with questions on the pathology and investigation of Duodenal Ulcer, and what he would consider adequate medical treatment before contemplating surgery. He was also questioned about exact surgical techniques, and even the history of these operations and the pioneers who developed them. So far, thought Philip, so good, and he still felt composed.

Then Sir Charles seemed to zero in on him, and for the first time the cool candidate felt as though the heat had been turned up to tropical level.

"Tell me what you know about hemangiomas of the face?"

"They are mostly congenital and many disappear spontaneously within a few years."

He went on to give a detailed classification of these blood vessel tumors and went, step by step, through the various forms of treatment, both operative and non-operative; especially those he'd used to treat such conditions successfully in those failing to resolve by themselves.

"Yes, I quite agree, but what about those giant cavernous hemangiomas of the face, those formidable diffuse tumors that can bleed copiously if one is not careful?"

The floor under Philip's feet felt almost imperceptibly softer as he answered, "An attempt should be made to locate the main feeding vessels and ligate them if possible."

"Anything else?"

"One could attempt a combination of selective compression combined with sclerotherapy using dilute sodium morrhuate, or one might even try X-ray therapy which sometimes helps to ablate these swellings."

Now the floor was becoming even softer and he felt compelled to add, "I should mention that I've never actually dealt with one of these giant hemangiomas but I'd feel obliged to proceed very cautiously."

The associate examiner's smile was now quite unconcealed.

"What about the injection of boiling water into these tumors?"

"I would never use such a method"

"Why not?"

"I understand it has been abandoned as too dangerous and can cause massive sloughing and dangerous bleeding."

Both examiners were smiling pleasantly and Philip now stood ankle-deep in soft manure.

"Which surgical journals do you prefer for your regular reading?"

"I prefer the British Journal of Surgery, S.G. and O. (Surgery, Gynecology and Obstetrics) and Annals of Surgery."

"What about The Medical Press and Circular?"

"Once in a while it carries some good articles but it isn't as authoritative as the ones I mentioned."

"Well, my young friend, it's nice to meet a discriminating reader," Sir Charles remarked cheerfully, as Philip felt the manure reaching up to his sweating armpits, and he wished his two examiners were less friendly and would simply blast him for stepping into the danger zone.

As soon as the Orals were over, Philip dashed downstairs to the library and sought out the latest issue of The Medical Press and Circular. As though trapped in some bizarre film thriller on a theme of Déja Vue, he looked in horrified fascination at the leading article. It was a beautifully written and illustrated monograph on 'The Boiling Water Treatment of Massive Facial hemangiomas', and the author was none other than Sir Charles Pannett.

Although he joined a group for lunch at a nearby pub, he was unable to swallow so much as a mouthful of food, and no amount of beer could eliminate the terrible dryness in his mouth. At 2 p.m, the arcane ritual began, as the Beadle called out each candidate's name from the front door of the John Hunter Room. Then, once the cringing individual was out of sight of his or her nerve-wracked companions, the ornate mace was pointed to heaven or to hell, or at least that's how it seemed.

Philip Bosnar knew, when his name was called, that this was a mere painful formality, and he was halfway down the stairs when he heard a voice shouting, "No Sir. It's upstairs. UP-STAIRS!" and he saw the Beadle – or was it an archangel? – pointing the lance of fate upward to F.R.C.S. and glory.

The initiation ceremonies were short and sweet. All the main examiners were there and Sir Charles gave a short speech, welcoming the successful candidates as Fellows, almost as surgical kinfolk. Henceforth, instead of being addressed as Doctor, they would be called Mister, in a manner sounding like a title of esteem. Yet this new title still carried an echo of humbler origins, going back to the days of the lowly barber-surgeon.

Each new Fellow passed down the receiving line and was greeted with a handshake and a warm, "Welcome to the Fellowship."
Pannett had a few extra words for Philip.

"You know, Mr. Bosnar, the boiling water method is really well worth trying," he said, "and the Medical Press and Circular is a much better journal than most surgeons think. Congratulations and good luck!"
Philip was so overcome with gratitude he was speechless.

CHAPTER 19

1946-47

It was April and he was thirty-three years old. More importantly, it was over ten years since graduation and first internship and time to take stock of his life. The Army had been a strange interlude. Despite the disappointment of not getting overseas the pluses far outweighed the minuses, and overall he'd been treated well and came out of it a better and stronger person. He was certainly a better surgeon than when he'd entered the armed forces. He'd also learned that the Canadian army wasn't run by its generals and colonels but by its noncommissioned officers. Philip Bosnar was fortunate to have the sergeants and corporals on his side, almost from the time he put on his uniform, and their loyalty and support had been valuable throughout his brief but eventful army career. As for Patty and the children, although it would be impossible to love them more intensely than before his army stint, he seemed to appreciate them more than ever and to understand how fortunate he was to have them.

Across the Atlantic, his parents, sister and young brother had emerged from the war safe and sound, as had his brother-in-law and close friends, and he was grateful. Some of his continental relatives had been less fortunate. His father's sister, one of Warsaw's leading actresses, and her husband, a brilliant architect, had been exterminated along with their 15-year-old son and two daughters, aged 10 and 12, in the gas-chambers of Auschwitz. Two of his cousins, sons of Rafael Bosnar's older sister, had been caught as members of the French Resistance, 'interrogated' until near death, then sent to an extermination camp in one of the oh-so-busy cattle trains made readily available by a cooperative Vichy regime.

In Vanwey, Estelle and Alvin Masters had become their close friends, as had the Jacksons, especially Gladys Jackson, Peter Forsyth's sister. Just as her husband Angus was very factual and prosaic, she was a jolly person of high intellect and unfailing good humor, with a special affection for Patty and Phil. The McTeagues had become much closer, too, along with their three attractive daughters. The relationship even survived the hurdle of Jock McTeague's optimistic but erroneous calculation of taxation exemptions, which cost the Bosnars a bundle. It had become obvious that he was a much better mayor than accountant.

On the hospital front, the Mother General flew out from Gresham, and after frank discussions with Dr. Bosnar and Sister Claudia, decided to follow his recommendations to the letter. Sister Margaret Anthony was dispatched to the convalescent hospital in the valley, making her divinely happy, and she was replaced by Sister Claudia as new Mother Superior.

Slocum and his new associate Dr. Spurling, a prissy little self-important fellow, attended a special meeting with Bosnar and Masters, at which Philip was elected Chief of Staff, without opposition. He was given authority and responsibility for rules of Admission and Discharge, Records, and (what would now be essential) Privileges based on credentials. Any of these rulings could be changed by a vote of three to one, or by appeal to the College of Physicians and Surgeons.

For a while there was a vast improvement in the hospital situation, and even Sister Elizabeth seemed able to contain her prejudices. But the first challenge to the new system came from the pushy Spurling who, without so much as a "by your leave," began to book a series of major orthopedic cases in the O.R. Philip took him aside and informed him that if he wished to perform these operations he should take his Certification in Surgery or, better still, his Canadian F.R.C.S. Both Slocum and Masters had their certification in surgery and Bosnar had his English and Canadian F.R.C.S. degrees).

The deeply offended Spurling soon decided he'd leave Vanwey and seek his professional fortune elsewhere, perhaps where they didn't have such restrictions.

The bed situation had improved considerably and so had the O.R. inequities, which meant that Philip and Al now had their fair share of operating time and an adequate allocation of O.R. nurses. Sister Elizabeth was becoming more cooperative, while she was becoming embarrassed by the high proportion of apparently normal organs removed by Brent Slocum and never sent for routine pathological examination. A further problem, and one that troubled Sister Claudia a great deal, was the lack of information on Slocum's charts, especially the absence of many operative records over a three year period. She confided in Philip that whenever she raised the subject with the offender he would tell her he'd take care of it in due course. At other times he became abusive and insisted it was nobody else's business.

Had the previous College Registrar Joe McShane (whom Philip knew so well and trusted so much) been alive, the solution would have been much simpler. A discreet phone call would have produced an appropriate and effective warning from the College. Sad to say, Herb Fraywell was a different kind of individual in almost every way, and his intrusion into the situation might simply add fuel to a smoldering fire.

There were two fortuitous developments at this time that Philip couldn't have predicted. Dr. Harry Medford, brother of Philip's best man at his wedding in 1939, started sending him patients and – after assisting him once or twice – referred all his operative cases to the Bosnar practice. The same thing happened with Bill Govern, the new G.P. in Bonchance. Philip had the honor of attending Viola Govern during her pregnancy and delivering a fine baby girl, and the Bosnars were delighted to know that she was named Patricia.

It soon transpired that Medford and Govern had both become somewhat disenchanted with Slocum, fee-splitting or no fee-splitting. They knew Philip never split fees and respected him for it. As his practice grew, there was considerable pressure on Philip to purchase the brand new Thurston House on 2nd Street. The pressure came especially from the Freikopfs, Sundstroms and McTeagues. The latter would become next-door neighbors if the deal went through. Jack Thurston had built this home for his daughter and her family, but her husband had been posted to New Brunswick, so the house had never been occupied and remained unfurnished.

It was a gracious Dutch Colonial two-storey building with a large basement, a sturdy covered garage and a spacious yard in the back, with a few trees, swings, seesaws and sandlot, where the children could play with their friends. The house was built of light beige bricks, the kind usually called Roman Tile. 'Old man Thurston', who'd retired in 1945 as manager of Vanwey's

Saskatchewan Clay Products, was willing to sell the property to Philip for $12,000, and Patty felt this was a very reasonable price for a home and surroundings with which she'd fallen in love at first sight.

They moved into their new abode (the finest in Vanwey) in the summer of 1946, and found it a great place to live and to entertain, a task at which Patty excelled. The children were thrilled with their upstairs quarters and the large back-lot playground they could share with their neighborhood friends.

By the end of summer, with the practice going smoothly, Philip flew back to London to see his family after a separation of seven years. The trip in the TransCanada Airlines' converted Lancaster bomber was hot and bumpy. They put down at Gander in Newfoundland, Keflavik in Iceland and Shannon in Ireland, before cruising over the familiar countryside of southwest England en route to London.

Philip's father met him at the airport and they embraced each other with unashamed emotion before loading the luggage aboard the shiny new Bosnar car. It was an impressive Morris Saloon, all gleaming black except for bright metal sidestrips and white sidewall tires, and the drive to the new Bosnar home in Hendon was smooth and comfortable. The house was a charming three-storey brown brick building with a charming little rose garden in front, and crowding the entrance area was the entire London contingent of Philip's family.

There was little change in his parents except that they looked a bit older. Pauline hadn't changed much except that she moved more like a middle-aged housewife, while Irving Kline seemed broader and slower than ever. They had their two little daughters with them, both looking more like their father than their mother. Young Clayton was the big surprise: no longer an adorable little boy but a fine-looking fellow of 16, and the new relationship would take a lot of adjustment.

The greetings, hugs and kisses must have lasted a full half-hour before entering the house, and as soon as Philip set foot in the living room there was wine and macaroons for all, so typical of his dear thoughtful and energetic Mum. It was the beginning of a wonderful two weeks and Philip was treated like royalty. They tried to catch up on seven years of news, but even by staying up late and talking into the small hours of the morning, it was an impossible task. His Dad, by custom, was sent off to bed early, as he still left for work each morning at 8 and didn't get home until 6.30.

Philip spent as much time as possible with Clayton, and by the time he was ready to leave they could truly accept each other as brothers. It was nice to know that Clayton was doing well at school although, unfortunately, he was no longer writing his excellent poems. When he was staying in Bath with his mother, his English master had always encouraged his poetic efforts, and whenever Phil and Patty received copies of these works – written by the youngster from the age of ten – they were thrilled to read them and felt proud of their gifted little relative. They remembered how exciting it was to see one of Clayton's poems published in the London Times, along with a letter of praise from the Poet Laureate. It may have been a coincidence, but the poems became more scarce following the spite raid on tranquil historic Bath by an unopposed squadron of the Luftwaffe.

Rafael Bosnar no longer admired Josef Stalin and was turning back to religion, albeit the modern 'Reform Synagogue' that was strongly British in character. He was one of so many left-wing intellectuals who became disillusioned with Russia's communist regime. First, it was the arrogant behavior of the Soviet commissars in Spain during the Civil War, distorting the moderate liberal aims of the Republican government into Stalinist propaganda. Then there was the signing of the Ribbentrop-Molotov pact; the spurious political trials and execution of so many dedicated Communists; and the Russian incursions into Poland, the Baltic states, Rumania, Bulgaria, Hungary, Czechoslovakia and East Germany.

Philip was careful to avoid any reference to the many political arguments he used to have with his beloved Dad, in which he always categorized Stalin as a black-hearted dictator with few genuine ideals. For this diplomatic avoidance, his Dad was deeply grateful, and the subject was never raised.

When Philip learned that his boyhood friend Morrie Kahn was perennially involved in street demonstrations on behalf of the British Communist Party, he decided not to bother contacting him. He tried on several occasions to phone his former hiking companion, Arty Jones, but there was never anyone to answer the call and he finally gave up. He was more successful in getting through to Bob Vermier and was rewarded with an immediate invitation to come over for dinner that very evening.

Vermier had a fascinating story to tell. After gaining his doctorate in physics, with original work on a new electron diffraction camera, he became a research scientist at the Siemen's radio tube division. When he discovered he was being paid less than the boys who cleaned his equipment, and when he complained but obtained no satisfaction, he made up his mind. He quit his job and joined his wife in her little millinery shop on Oxford Street, borrowing some money to add a men's hat department to the premises. The bigendered store became steadily more prosperous and the Vermiers were busy and happy.

After the arrival of their first child, World War 2 broke out and Vermier was ordered to report to the Research Department of the R.A.F, for special work on the possible use of certain types of radiation for military purposes. When peace was declared, he was discharged with a special commendation, but went back to his hat shop and had stayed there ever since.

By the time Philip had to say goodbye to his Mum and Dad, to his brother and sister and her husband, it was as though he'd never left them, but the family made him promise to send Patty and the children over as soon as possible.

When he got back to Vanwey, he and Patty decided it would be a nice gift for his parents to bring them over for a visit, acquaint them with life on the Canadian prairie, and have them see their grandchildren. Unfortunately, his Dad couldn't leave his business at this time because of a recent rush of orders from Harrods and Selfridges, and it was difficult to get additional good workers. His Mum, however, said she'd be delighted to come out for two weeks. The trip was arranged for June 1947 and the plane tickets were purchased and sent over to London.

Philip's mother had a smooth flight, and that was followed by a wonderful time in Vanwey. She was astounded at Patricia's superb cooking and the efficient way she ran the household, and they developed a deepened bond of affection. As for the children, their grandma adored them madly and her affection was returned with interest. She was introduced to Phil and Patty's many close friends and they, in turn, found her charming and witty and treated her like a visiting member of British Royalty. Of course, the family in London had long ago accepted the fact that Klara Bosnar behaved as if she were a member of feudal nobility, and nicknamed her 'The Duchess' behind her back.

The weather stayed warm, bright and sunny, and Philip's mother had a delightful time, but the highlight of her visit was quite unexpected, at least as far as Philip was concerned. Patty introduced her to all the Sisters of St. Cecilia, and they toured the hospital and had tea together. She got on well with the nuns, especially Mother Superior, and this led to a small conspiracy.

One morning, as the first case of a busy operating schedule, Dr. Bosnar had booked a left-sided colectomy for cancer of the descending colon, with Dr. Masters assisting and Dr. Govern 'gassing'. He was about two thirds of the way through the procedure, when two new figures quietly entered the operating room, suitably gowned and masked. One was large and broad, the other tiny and slim. He realized at once that Sister Claudia had transgressed a few O.R. rules in order to satisfy his mother's eternal dream of watching her son perform an actual surgical operation.

When Philip delivered the large operative specimen from the patient's open abdomen, tears of pride and joy spilled down her mask and she left the theater with her head high. Philip said nothing, but to his surprise it was Sister Elizabeth who remarked, "I'm glad your mother was able to see that."

The incident was never discussed further, but he could well imagine how its description would be embellished by the time it reached the house in Hendon.

There was one more happy memory his Mum could take back with her, namely her new relationship with Patty. Her daughter-in-law, an Irish Shiksa, had now become a true and treasured daughter and genuinely kith and kin.

Toward the end of summer, a fierce correspondence occurred between official circles in Regina and Saskatoon on the one side and Vanwey on the other. Slocum had recently refused, point blank, to do anything about his unwritten operative records, and whoever objected could go to hell: that included Sister Claudia and Dr. Bosnar. Since Slocum had recently been joined by Dr. Trelawny, a young Canadian surgeon who had just obtained his English F.R.C.S, this was an ideal moment for the Sisters to suspend Slocum from the hospital staff, pending completion of his blank operative charts, and to transfer his hospital patients to the new associate.

Trelawny told Sister Claudia in confidence that he was quite willing to cooperate with this arrangement until the matter was cleared up, but Slocum reacted violently. He delivered petitions to the College, the Ministry of Health and the Archbishop in Regina, signed by many of his patients and supporters. This was accompanied by wild accusations against the Sisters of St. Cecilia, and against Bosnar in his capacity as chief of staff. He threw out dire warnings of his widespread influence and political connections.

The Sister Superior now became involved in a painful correspondence with representatives of the Saskatchewan Hospital Commission, the Archbishop's office in Regina and the provincial College of Physicians and Surgeons. All three, it was now revealed, had been subjected to intense political pressure by Slocum's supporters, and had transferred that pressure to Sister Claudia, but true to character, she hadn't flinched.

The onslaught began with a phone call from a representative of the provincial Hospital Commission, requesting an immediate explanation of her suspension of Slocum's hospital privileges. Sister Claudia gave him a brief summary and followed it up with a detailed written report of all the events leading up to the suspension.

She related Dr. Slocum's longstanding antagonism to the nursing staff, his abusive behavior and persistent refusal to abide by the most elementary rules of professional conduct. Although she had approached the Commission on several previous occasions about the problem, no help was forthcoming. Furthermore, she had been advised that it was in the hospital patients' best interest that she, and she alone, had the right to suspend the offending doctor. This sole authority had also been recently confirmed at a meeting of Canadian Hospital Superintendents which she attended.

Sister Claudia had dealt with the matter in accordance with the highest ethical standards of her position as Mother Superior and Hospital Superintendent. She even waited until Dr. Slocum took on an associate who was fully qualified to handle his hospital patients, and she stressed this point in her correspondence. Her letters were sent not only to the Hospital Commission, but to the monsignor representing the Archbishop, and to a violently hostile Dr. Fraywell. This unpleasant individual not only overstepped his authority as College Registrar but failed to do his duty regarding Slocum's unprofessional behavior.

Herb Adams, as Chairman of the Hospital Board, delivered his opinion in no uncertain terms, one that coincided with that of Sister Claudia, while Dr. Bosnar pulled no punches in his letter of censure to Fraywell. He pointed out where his own duties lay. These were protection of the patients' best interests and the smooth and efficient operation of St. Cecilia's Hospital, with maintenance of the highest possible standards of medical and nursing care.

In conclusion, he reminded the Registrar that he should be guided by the same principles. Instead of adopting a belligerent stance toward the Mother Superior and issuing threats against the chief of staff, he should discipline the offending staff member in accordance with the provisions and obligations of the College.

On September the 6th, Sister Claudia wrote Dr. Slocum, informing him that since Dr. Trelawny had now decided to leave Vanwey and practice elsewhere, she was lifting Slocum's suspension from the medical staff in fairness to his patients. There was only one proviso: that he sign and abide by a set of rules that would cover each member of the medical staff. They included appropriate behavior toward the Sisters and nurses, maintenance of basic clinical and operative records, and compliance with hospital policy regarding the correct allocation of hospital beds.

Slocum held out for a month before signing this declaration. Then, with his tail between his legs, he tried hard to comply with its requirements. With all his contacts and political pull, all he'd accomplished was to lose an excellent associate who refused to become embroiled in such a nasty situation. Strangely enough, after this crisis Slocum showed much greater cordiality toward Philip Bosnar, and this attitude was reciprocated as far as possible.

As for Fraywell, having been caught in flagrante delicto, so to speak, as an unconcealed lobbyist for a delinquent college member, he faded quietly from the picture, but his enmity toward Philip Bosnar did not fade.

Monsignor Hughes was rather more depressed than usual. He was always morose, but the thought of going into hospital and having surgery troubled him very much. It wasn't the operation itself; after all it was only a hernia and lots of men had that. Besides, he had the greatest confidence in Dr. Bosnar, who was his friend as well as his surgeon. What distressed him was the dreaded revelation, to all who saw him undressed in the hospital, that he'd neglected his hernia to the point where it dwarfed his genitals and exposed his celibacy as a shameful physical defect.

Philip examined the 53-year-old priest with great care in sparing him the slightest embarrassment. He promised that when he was under the anesthetic the same care would be exercised, avoiding the slightest unnecessary exposure. That promise helped the patient to a degree, but his spirits still required considerable boosting, and Philip felt bold measures were necessary. He wrapped up a dozen copies of 'Esquire' magazine and delivered them to the Monsignor's hospital room with an attached note that read, **'I believe these will be good for you'**.

After all, this racy journal was essentially harmless and brought innocent joy to many a man without turning him into a raving salivating sex maniac. The shapely, elegant and lightly-clad young ladies so tastefully portrayed with brush and pen by the renowned Vargas, were never vulgar or objectionable, and surveying them with an appreciative but unoffended eye might well restore the Monsignor's lost sense of manhood and dispel his gloom.

The operation went smoothly and the recovery was splendid, with the devout patient obeying all postoperative orders with good cheer and without complaint. One week after his discharge from hospital he had the magazines returned to his surgeon's office, along with a huge volume on Catholic theology. The appended note read: **'I believe for my part that this book will be good for you'**.

It took Philip six weeks of 'blood, sweat and tears' to get through the massive tome. He found it replete with arcane discussions on comparative theology, obscure biblical interpretations by ancient savants (both revered and heretical), and long quotations in Latin and Greek. He sought assistance from his Italian and Greek patients, but even they were stumped by the esoteric nature of the book's contents.

Eventually, he finished reading it to the best of his ability, and returned it in person to the Monsignor, after first phoning him at the rectory.

"Come in, doctor, come and sit down over here next to me. It was nice of you to bring that heavy book over by yourself. I could have had it picked up at your office with no trouble at all."

"You're looking extremely well Monsignor. How are you feeling?"

"I'm feeling just fine, thank you. No pain and walking well, thanks to you. Will you join me in a dry sherry? It's a Portuguese Amontillado and has a very pleasant bouquet."

"Thank you, that would be delightful, and give me an opportunity to drink to your continued good health."

"By the way, Doctor, how did you like the book?"

"It was certainly interesting and profound, but I must confess that some of it was a bit over my head."

"In that case I sincerely envy you. Most of it was way over my head and I just couldn't get through it at all."

On the way home, Philip couldn't help chuckling at the dry humor of this austere priest. He'd exacted his perfect revenge for the racy magazines sent by his surgeon, albeit with impudent humor but benign intentions.

One of Philip's most interesting cases toward the end of 1947 was a young woman with grossly deformed hands, the result of 'burned out' rheumatoid arthritis of the most severe kind. Her fingers were distorted and the knuckle joints appeared completely dislocated. He was surprised to learn that she'd been working as personal secretary to 'Tommy' Douglas, the new Saskatchewan Premier and Minister of Health. She was recently forced to give up her position because she found it impossible to continue typing, and she'd heard that Dr. Bosnar had a special interest in patients with severe, crippling arthritis.

This interest was entirely fortuitous, and started back in September of 1939 when he was treating a middle-aged lady for grossly arthritic knees. She lived above a grocery store on Main Street and her husband had to carry her up and down the stairs. Her knee-joints were bent almost to a right angle with contracted ligaments and tendons. She'd been through numerous ineffectual treatments, including massive vitamin injections and bee-venom. In addition, she and her devoted husband had spent most of their money on various quack treatments at so-called 'Arthritis Clinics', where they believed it was less important to give than to receive.

When Philip upbraided them for such folly they, not without justification, challenged him to do better. He took up the challenge and admitted the patient to hospital. After a series of hinged plaster casts with adjustable screw controls, a series of special exercises, injections of gold in oil and large doses of aspirin (along with antacids to protect the stomach lining), followed by graduated ambulation on crutches, he was able to remove her casts. Three weeks later, after intensive mobilization exercises in warm water baths, she was discharged and walked up the stairs to her rooms for the first time in seven years.

It was little wonder that Philip never lost interest in this affliction in all its dreadful forms, and that he should now be confronted with one more formidable challenge. Since the new patient was right-handed, he decided to attack the left hand first. She fully understood that this was an experimental approach, but was more than willing to go ahead.

The plan was to expose the affected joints at operation, with tourniquet control to keep the area free of blood. He would remove the heads of the metacarpals (the soft knuckle bones), reposition and repair the tendons and ligaments as far as possible. Following surgery, he would suspend the fingers individually on a special overhead frame and encourage very early finger exercises.

To the amazement of everyone, and despite no attempt to reshape the cut ends of the metacarpals, the new joints appeared to work well, and the patient returned from Regina in three months to have the other side done.

During the long and severe winter months, a new dimension was added to his practice after he returned to civilian life. The establishment of a private flying club at the site of the old airforce base south of town now made it possible to fly out of town for surgical emergencies in outlying hospitals. This proved most helpful when the roads were blocked and even snow machines couldn't get through.

He would first question the referring physician in detail over the phone, then relay an itemized set of preoperative instructions as well as the precise layout of operative instruments he'd require. If any were lacking he'd bring them himself in a sterilized bundle. He would then phone the flying club and they'd dispatch a light four-seater plane with pilot and co-pilot. He'd meet them by car in a suitable landing strip on the outskirts of town, and they'd take off smoothly on ski floats.

On arrival at a field located near his destination, they were picked up by the local doctor and driven to the hospital. After a cup of coffee and a cigarette, Philip would examine the patient carefully and issue last minute instructions before operating. Following the appropriate surgery and further detailed instructions, Philip had more coffee and cigarettes before returning to the plane. It was usually necessary to thaw out the frozen engine with a portable blowtorch before they could take off for their return flight. Each such flight was an exciting departure from the normal routine, and Dr. Philip Bosnar looked forward to each such occasion.

In early February 1948, St. Cecilia's Hospital was faced with a strike by its non-nursing workers, including orderlies and technicians. Such an unpleasant event had never happened in the past, and it was a new and terrifying experience for the Sisters.

Six months earlier the hospital had hired a new X- ray technician, a very strong-minded individual with a good record in his chosen field. What wasn't known at the time of hiring (an unfortunate omission) was his even more impressive record as a union organizer and labor agitator. The evenings were soon taken up with bargaining sessions, with the union representative, a Mr. Shackley from Yorkton arguing the hospital workers' case, and Dr. Bosnar delegated to argue the Sisters' case.

Every attempt was made to convince Shackley and his committee of hospital employees that the hospital management had no objection whatever to granting the increased salaries demanded by the union. All that was required was an increase from the Ministry of Health in the already restricted hospital budget. This fell on deaf ears, with Shackley ranting and raving about "bloodsucking hospital capitalists growing fat on the backs of impoverished and exploited workers."

There was even a veiled suggestion that the hospital authorities were probably reactionary warmongers as well. Shackley was a perfect throwback to the worst days of the Industrial Revolution, when fiery Marxists were the only defense against rapacious factory owners, with their oppression of workers and vicious strike-breaking methods.

Meeting after meeting seemed to bog down in the same impasse, except that Shackley now contended the strike position was supported by the C.C.F. government and the Health Ministry of Tommy Douglas.

"That just proves he knows the management of this hospital has the money to pay a fair wage but wants to grind down its underpaid workers." Then more polemics, a few gratuitous lessons in Lenin's economic theories for good measure, and nothing accomplished.

At the end of the second week Philip had taken all he could stomach from the fervent Comrade Shackley and phoned Premier Douglas in Regina. After introducing himself and being told, "I know who you are, Dr. Bosnar," he apologized for disturbing so busy a political leader and explained in summary the labor impasse at St. Cecilia's.

"May I discuss this matter with you and any committee you feel appropriate, as soon as possible. I can drive up to Regina any time you say."

"How about next Monday at 2 p.m. Dr. Bosnar?"

"That's most considerate of you, Mr. Premier. I shall be there."

Philip found himself looking forward to meeting this little battler who was so renowned as a consummate politician of the Socialist left. Unlike his own father, Philip had always been what could be termed a moderate Conservative, and had always remained suspicious of the possible infiltration and subversion of Socialism by Communism, Moscow style.

On the other hand, he'd seen the Baldwin-Chamberlain drift toward a marriage with the Fascists and Nazis of Europe during the 30s, and had lost faith in this style of 'Conservatism without a heart'. As for the Liberalism of politicians like Mackenzie King, its duplicity and hypocrisy sickened him. At least Tommy Douglas believed in his principles, yet he never lost his Scottish sense of humor.

Here was a man whose character and ambition were forged in the unpleasant experiences of his youth. As a young boy, he suffered from *'Chronic Osteomyelitis'* of the leg (a persistent bone infection), following a fall in his native Scotland. This affliction led to many operations, both before and after his family's move to Winnipeg, just before World War 1. He was cared for by both incompetent and skilled doctors, and decided that one day he'd make it possible for every patient to have good medical care regardless of ability to pay.

Languishing in the draughty waiting rooms of hospital outpatient departments, and experiencing the different levels of hospital treatment, he became determined that one day there would be universal hospitalization unrelated to a patient's means.

Puny of build and handicapped by his infirmity, he determined to remedy that situation as well, and eventually took the lightweight boxing championship of Manitoba for two years running. Shy as a young boy and not very much of a talker, he grew up to become not just a political speaker but a true orator of dynamic impact and lightning wit, especially when dealing with hecklers.

Philip looked forward to meeting this courageous leader who, although revered by the working class, was feared by businessmen, free enterprisers (doctors most of all!), and the middle class in general. He wondered how well he would fare when up against so formidable an opponent.

CHAPTER 20

1938-39

Now that he had his Fellowship and could be called 'Mister,' he realized that what he had was a successful professional past but not necessarily a successful future. In fact, what loomed ahead of his F.R.C.S. in the closing days of 1938 was an enormous gulf of uncertainty. To help bridge this chasm he'd need a great deal of help, advice and sheer good luck. So far as help was concerned, he'd first have to see what the medical advertisements had to offer in the 'Lancet' or 'B.M.J.' (British Medical Journal).

Perhaps he should have been encouraged by the small card which arrived one day at 12 Grantham Square, addressed to Philip Bosnar, M.B,F.R.C.S. It was enclosed in an envelope bearing a faint aura of perfume, and he recognized both the perfume and the handwriting. The postmark was Croydon and the message was short.
'Congratulations on your wonderful success with the Fellowship. I'm immensely proud of you.' and it was signed,'From D.H. with love.' and it left him vaguely disturbed, but happy nonetheless. He knew she would always remain a part of his earliest manhood, but that fact could never diminish the greater love he felt for Patricia, one that he would cherish forever.

Once in a while, he wandered up to St. Clement's to find out what was in the wind, but there was nothing promising. He decided to write the one man whose advice would be honest and forthright, and who would refuse to bend the truth just to ease his anxiety. He wrote Mr. Vaughan and asked him what it would take to obtain a junior Honorary staff appointment: preferably at St. Clement's, but if not, then at a comparable hospital.

In reply, Vaughan congratulated him on getting his Fellowship finals at the first attempt, and offered several items of advice to help him get the appointment he sought. First, go after the very best registrar jobs – the ones paying the least – and sit for the London M.S. (Master of Surgery), which required a thesis on original work done by the candidate. Next, and most importantly, concentrate on one particular facet of surgery, whether it was the parotid gland, the venous system, or colorectal surgery. Every general surgeon, it would appear, needed a special 'gimmick' that would provide him with specific identification, enabling him to start publishing a series of papers for the journals.

As soon as Philip got this reply, he decided this projection was not for him. It would entail up to ten years of hard slogging at minimum pay, and that was something requiring a self-centered attitude beyond mere dedication.

The Stafford advertisement brought him back to the real world. It was for a well-paid job as assistant to a general surgeon, and the only proviso, aside from suitable qualifications and credentials, was the candidate's possession of a car for house calls and hospital visits.

Philip found a nice little Morgan two-seater just off Portland Place, and the salesman soon asked pointedly how he intended to pay for this attractive vehicle. He asked to see the manager, a smooth and charming individual with impeccable attire and hard eyes. 'Nothing ventured,' Philip showed him the Lancet advertisement.

"If I get this car," he suggested, "I'll test-drive it up to Stafford, and I'm certain I'll land the job following my interview."

"You've got one hell of a bloody nerve, that's for sure, but I'm half inclined to believe you."

"Well, here's my record at school, hospitals and locums which you can check if you wish, but I need to have the car by Thursday and I can give you a five pound deposit."

The manager choked slightly but seemed to be making up his mind.

"Come on over here," he said, "and we'll make out the papers. My wife always said I've got a balmy streak and I guess she's right."

On Thursday morning, Philip Bosnar drove his shiny new car, its unusual bluish color looking quite attractive, up to Stafford, where he had his interview with a congenial Dr. Stroud, F.R.C.S.(Edin.) and his vivacious wife. The interview was successful, and the high point was reached with chuckles of appreciation when Philip confessed how he'd purchased the car. He used his rising hubris to ask if he could have his first month's salary ahead of time, so that he could honor his commitment to the car dealers with an appropriate down-payment, and Stroud gave him a cheque for which Philip signed a receipt and locum contract.

When he got back to London and paid the manager a substantial first instalment on the Morgan, there was great joy on both sides of the transaction.

"I guess I'm a pretty good judge of character. Have to be in this job," boasted the manager, swelling with pride and a certain degree of relief, all the more so when his enterprising customer paid him in cash.

There was one more essential detail: getting Patty fixed up with a suitable job at the Stafford Royal Infirmary. With her splendid nursing background, there was no trouble having her accepted as a senior nurse in the Department of Surgery. It was in this hospital that Phil and Patty first ran into Chuck Medford, the Senior Surgical Resident who was over from Canada in search of his English F.R.C.S. He was a cheerful, heavy-set, brown-haired fellow, with the build and moves of a heavyweight boxer. He proved to be a gentle and soft-spoken chap, his voice only rising whenever he showed his appreciation of a funny remark with an earsplitting guffaw.

Medford declared that in his opinion Philip would be crazy to remain in 'Merrie Olde England', dragging out ten years of his life in pursuit of a holy grail that might turn out dross rather than gold. He just happened to know the very place for Philip and Patricia. There was a very busy practice in Vanwey, Saskatchewan, with a great deal of major surgery, and it was becoming too much for the head of the practice, Dr. Thomas Blaikie: famed far and wide as 'Doctor Tom, the Prairie Surgeon'. His son, Ted Blaikie, who would shortly be on his way to Kenya as medical officer in the British Colonial Service, was now in London and authorized to search for a new surgeon to join his father, preferably someone with his English Fellowship in surgery.

"If all goes well," Chuck Medford declared, I plan to return to Canada after getting my English Fellowship, and between the two of us we could try to set up a South Saskatchewan Clinic, just the way the Mayo clinic was started in a small Minnesota farm community called Rochester." It all sounded very exciting and very promising, and both Phil and Patty were enthusiastic.

Shortly after this fateful conversation they took a trip to London and met Ted Blaikie at the Strand Palace Hotel, a meeting set up for them by Chuck Medford. The younger Blaikie was a genial individual, slender and darkhaired, with an engaging manner and cultured speech. If his father was anything like this, the young couple thought, it would certainly be great, and they warmed still further to the prospect.

"You're exactly what my father has been looking for," said their interviewer after he perused Philip's credentials, "and I don't think you'll be disappointed with the surgical scope of the practice."

"As you may well imagine," Philip confessed, "after all this studying, courses and exams, I'm pretty well broke. Would your father be prepared to pay travel expenses for the two of us? We plan to get married before leaving the country, and our expenses would have to be covered or we couldn't dream of traveling to Canada right now."

"Well I know my Dad wants someone as soon as possible and I'm sure he'll take care of all travel expenses for both of you."

"In that case Patricia and I will say yes to your proposition, providing the salary and financial arrangements are satisfactory."

"I'm authorized to tell you the commencing salary will be $200 a month, rising by increments 'til you reach full partnership in two years. There'll also be a rent-free suite in the hospital building owned by my father."

By British standards this sounded decidedly opulent and would make it much easier to assume the family debts, a plan to which Patty, true to her fine character, gave her unstinting and generous approval. It seemed a far better deal than the occasional surgical practice in the provinces that came up for sale from time to time and required a large capital outlay – quite aside from the uncertainties of what, in truth, would be the purchase of a 'pig in a poke'.

The Stafford practice was a bit disappointing. It was mainly general practice, with little opportunity for major surgery, but Dr. Stroud was convivial and his wife proved intelligent and well-informed, especially on the subject of politics. She'd been private secretary to the infamous Prime Minister Ramsay McDonald, and – since she was an ardent socialist in her bias – she engaged Philip in some fierce political arguments, in which her husband acted as wise arbiter and philosopher.

On weekends, there were tennis foursomes arranged by Dr. Stroud and played on the cement hardcourt behind the surgery. On Sunday afternoons, whenever possible, Philip took Patty out into the countryside, and the outings included driving lessons, which she enjoyed and absorbed with enthusiasm. Sometimes, after supper with the Strouds, they amused Philip with anecdotes about the hidden political tableau: intrigues and power struggles behind the scenes, mostly concealed from the public at large. It became all too easy to develop a certain cynicism about political leaders and prominent statesmen, those whose outward idealism was so tainted with prejudice and amour propre.

There was one additional matter requiring attention without further delay: taking over the Bosnar family debts once and for all. Philip approached the manager of Barclay's Bank in Stafford, requested and obtained a large loan sufficient to cover all the debts, but there was one proviso. In the absence of any tangible collateral, it was necessary for someone of financial substance to countersign the bank loan for the full amount, and Philip decided to approach Stroud, although he felt uncomfortable about asking him to back so large an amount.

"It's something I've never done in my life," was Stroud's reply, "but my wife agrees that we should make a special exception in your case, because we trust you fully."

"I'm grateful to you both and you may be sure I'll send the bank fifty dollars each month until the debt is fully discharged."

The Strouds were told all about the practice in Canada and expressed their confidence that he was making the right choice, especially as he was planning to get married before leaving England. There was also the growing uncertainty of developments in the U.K, with Europe under increasing threat of war. As a matter of fact, Philip doubted whether there'd be war in the foreseeable future. It wouldn't be necessary, as long as Hitler saw all his territorial demands granted by the appeasement gang controlling British foreign policy. If, by some unforeseen occurrence, war did break out after all, Philip would offer his specialist services at once to either the British or Canadian army.

He planned to sail for Canada some time in July, and as soon as Dr. Blaikie's cheque arrived in the amount of $500, he booked passage on the *S.S. Montclare* and managed to obtain a well-placed outside cabin close to the main stairway. One special feature that seemed a civilized departure from the general rule was having First and Second class combined into one 'Deluxe' class and the Third class designated as Tourist. Since this voyage would be their actual honeymoon, Phil and Patty had no hesitation in choosing the Deluxe accommodation. A brochure illustrating the ship's facilities revealed a palatial dining room and a magnificent central stairwell that was artistically ornamental but not unduly 'glitzy'. The various interiors revealed excellent taste combined with maximum comfort and quiet luxury.

The travel tickets were picked up at the Cook's travel agency in the neighboring city of Wolverhampton, and this thriving center – a bustling metropolis by comparison with Stafford – soon became one of their weekend meccas. It was an excellent place for a good meal at one of several fine restaurants, and for the occasional worthwhile film.

When the weather was hot, they chose a pleasant drive to Cannock Chase, its hilly contours perfectly suited to both picnickers and lovers. Close by and only a short distance from Stafford, was the government-planned forest, its young trees arranged in straight avenues that crisscrossed the entire area with right-angled geometric precision. It was an ideal place for Patty to polish her driving skills, and a peaceful retreat where few cars were ever encountered except on national holidays.

There was now the important matter of the wedding, and this posed a few problems. Both Phil and Patty agreed it should be a completely non-religious ceremony at a Registry Office, and Chuck Medford consented to act as best man, with his own fiancee as Patty's bridesmaid. All four had become close friends during the preceding few months, and they discussed their plans without reservation. It was decided that in early July they'd all meet in Liverpool, the Montclare's embarkation port for the newlyweds' transatlantic voyage.

By a stroke of luck, Philip was able to land a fortnight's locum in Liverpool at just the right time, and he arranged for his parents to meet Patty in that city three weeks before the wedding, so they could at least get to know and like each other before the parting. He planned to drive down to London later, to say a fond farewell to his beloved family and his closest friends. Pauline would no doubt take the parting very hard and little Clayton even harder, and he acknowledged once again that one person's rising fortunes so often spelled sorrow for others.

Meanwhile, he left the Stroud practice with warm feelings and best wishes all round, and with a flattering letter of commendation. He drove up to Liverpool and arranged accommodation for Patty and his parents at a small but comfortable hotel close to the Richards surgery, where he'd be doing his final locum. The rooms were booked for the following week.

On arrival at the Richards home, a roomy old house with the surgery located at the front of the ground floor, he was greeted by Stella Richards, an attractive young lady whom he took to be Dr. Richards's daughter. She showed him through the patients' waiting area, the consulting room, examination room and the rest of the house, with admirable quiet efficiency.

His bags were put away in a comfortable upstairs bedroom, after which they sat down in the cozy downstairs parlor. There was an inviting brick fireplace for cold spells that could come at any time, but the most prominent feature was a huge radio-gramophone combination of which Stella Richards seemed very proud, and she demonstrated its excellence by playing her newest and favorite record, Deep Purple: a romantic melody that appeared to send her into raptures.

The first shock came at lunch, when she said,

"Tomorrow I'll take you to meet my husband. He's in a nearby nursing home with one of his frequent gastric ulcer attacks. He's already had two operations but still gets bad hemorrhages from time to time."

Philip couldn't get himself to believe that this petite and vivacious individual, still more child than woman, was the doctor's wife.

"How old is your husband?" he asked and quickly amended his gaffe with, "How long has he had this illness?"

"He's fifty-six and he's had this trouble for over twenty years."

She looked at him boldly, and he felt uncomfortable at the unconcealed invitation in those flashing dark brown eyes, the aura of her musky perfume and the gloss of her shiny black hair – cut short in girlish fashion.

Here was no child, he thought. No indeed! This was a dangerous, flirtatious woman, accustomed to testing the vulnerability of any man she desired. Perhaps it was all quite innocent and his snap interpretation did her an injustice, but whatever the truth he would tread warily and give her not the slightest encouragement.

Following the afternoon surgery, he took a quick shower and went into the parlor, where Mrs. Richards introduced him to two of her closest friends, Lester Pollock and his wife, Emily. They made a lively threesome and invited him to join them in a dry sherry. He learned that they'd booked a supper-table at the Grand Hotel for that evening, and requested that Philip join them. Black tie, of course. He also learned that the Richards children were staying in the country with their aunt for the long weekend. It was now Friday, and they'd left early that morning.

When the festive foursome arrived at the hotel in Pollock's handsome Daimler (as befitted a self-styled 'high society dentist'), the ladies looked dazzling in their evening gowns, and the men quite dashing in their dinner jackets. It all seemed a bit excessive to Philip, until he discovered that this was their regular Friday night supper-dance, courtesy of the convivial Pollocks. He got through a difficult evening, treading a fine line between getting too close to his prearranged dancing partner and staying too unsociably distant.

After the first two hours it became obvious that the oh-so-friendly Emily was doing everything possible to ignite a romantic affair between her intimate friend and the new young locum. Philip wondered how often this had happened to previous locums and decided to cool the situation without further delay.

"I'd like you to join me," he declared in a loud voice, "in a toast to my absent fiancee, Patricia Clancy, to whom I shall be getting married later this month."

The toast was joined by all, but in an atmosphere that was perceptibly chilly.

"Well," grumbled Emily, somewhat tipsy, "you're not married yet, so don't act like an old spoilsport!"

This admonition seemed to cheer up Philip's dancing partner and restore a glow to her youthful cheeks. The new locum had now been served unmistakable notice by this strange Pollock woman, that she took personal responsibility for the extramarital romances of her alluring protégé. He decided he'd have to watch his step with great care if he intended to elude Emily's byzantine maneuvers.

On Sunday, he drove down to London and had a wonderful reunion with his Mum and Dad, his beloved little brother, his grieving sister and her husband. They discussed his unobtrusive wedding plans and the forthcoming Canadian adventure. They also debated his plea that they, too, should plan to move to Canada if at all possible, but they persuaded him that such a move would be totally out of the question. It was obvious they were convinced that he and his darling Patty would eventually return to England, sooner rather than later.

To keep their hopes alive, Philip told them that if the Vanwey practice turned out to be a dud he'd spend some time at either the Mayo Clinic or Johns Hopkins, before coming back and seeking his professional fortunes closer to home. It was quite clear that he'd inherited his father's indomitable optimism.

He talked at length about Patricia, a paean of praise they'd heard many times before and which they now accepted. Since the wedding wouldn't take place in a church or synagogue, and since none of Patricia's relatives would be in attendance, it was only right and proper that none of the Bosnar clan should be present. Philip felt this was a correct decision, although he understood how painful it must be for the parents.

Monday's surgeries were straightforward and there were no untoward incidents. There was a delightful meeting with the beautiful Richards children, who were full of happy mischief but basically well-behaved, warm and friendly. Philip knew they'd captivate him completely before he finished his locum, and when they invited him to join in their games he was happy to accept. As a matter of fact, it was soon apparent that they'd adopted him as a special playmate.

In the background there was the constant sound of their mother's favorite records: Deep Purple, Red Sails In The Sunset, Underneath The Arches, and Jealousy. Stella Richards was still as flirtatious as ever, but it seemed a matter of habit rather than conscious effort. As a matter of fact Philip found her scant attire (no matter how fashionable) and her heavy perfume (no matter how seductive) most embarrassing. He wondered how long he could keep his distance before arousing her hostility.

On Tuesday, soon after the morning surgery, she took him to meet her husband. He was lying in bed in a private room, looking pale and wan, and in his eighties rather than his fifties. He had a blood transfusion dripping slowly into his left arm and his speech was impaired by a tube traversing his mouth and entering his beleaguered stomach. His morose expression brightened for a moment at the sight of his smiling young wife, then hardened into suspicious hostility when he eyed the latest pretender to his domain. Or at least, thought Philip, that could be how Dr. Richards might view the situation from his position of helplessness.

Emily Pollock was a frequent visitor to the Richards home and she was constantly trying, in her devious way, to get something started between Stella and Philip, despite his forthcoming marriage. It was evident – in her strange book of morality – that this was no impediment to a torrid affair between these two, which the perverse Emily could experience vicariously. To counter these plans, Philip remained on guard and trod cautiously during his hours away from the practice.

On Wednesday evening there was a small after-dinner party upstairs, and Emily Pollock managed to get Philip and Stella locked into a small study at the back of the house, in the course of one of the many parlor games. It was all so contrived, that Philip wasn't surprised when Stella began making bold physical advances, and he was compelled to rebuff her firmly before the situation got out of hand. When the room was finally unlocked, Stella was furious and a vicious Emily asked why he couldn't act like a real man to this poor love-starved beauty.

"Get someone else for your hired gigolo," was Philip's reply through clenched teeth. The other guests continued with their fun but the party broke up shortly thereafter.

By a strange coincidence, Philip received an unexpected phone call the next morning. It was a man's voice,

"Has she been after you yet?"

"Who is this?"

"Why, I'm your predecessor, old chap. First she seduced me, aided and abetted by the helpful Emily. Then she threatened me when I cooled off. I thought I'd better warn you as one locum to another. Just watch your step before you get in too deep."

"Thanks for your warning. I'll be very careful."

"Remember Potifar's wife in the bible, old chap. Your modern version has a very dangerous sponsor."

That was all, but now Philip was fully alert to the perils of the situation.

He was glad when Saturday came around. He'd survived the dangers of Friday evening by simulating an influenzal attack, not caring whether his coughing and sniffling were believed. The important thing was that he was spared a command performance at the weekly supper-dance.

In the afternoon, he met his parents at the railway station and drove them over to their hotel. He got them comfortably settled, then ordered afternoon tea to the room. They had a leisurely meeting, with a conversation that was full of hopes for the future. They were going to miss each other dreadfully but didn't let this fact intrude on their happy projections.

On Sunday, Patty arrived and within the hour she and Philip's parents were hobnobbing like old friends. It was clear that this new and unexpected intimacy was breaking down Patty's long-held fears and shy reserve. A deep relationship of the warmest kind had taken hold between his parents and his bride-to-be, and his Mum drew him aside to confess quietly,

"Phileep, if you have to marry a Shiksa thank God you've chosen this one. We love her like a daughter."

His parents returned to London while Patty stayed on in Liverpool and did some shopping.

The final showdown with Stella came soon enough. It had been a pleasant day, in which Philip had managed to spend a happy hour with Patty. When he returned to the Richards abode after supper, he found Stella Richards in an excited mood: her cheeks flushed, her eyes shining much too brightly and a certain breathlessness in her speech. As soon as he came into the house, the Victrola was turned on and the haunting voice of Hutch singing Jealousy echoed through all the rooms.

She sat as if transfixed, listening intently to each word of the familiar song, with the lights down low, and she remained motionless as though in a trance. When she spoke at last, it was to complain that she'd been very frightened, "left all alone in this big house with nobody to protect me."

She moved over on the davenport to press against him, and she was clad in a short silken nightgown with matching negligee. Both were almost transparent.

"Now listen, Stella," he started, (he knew that calling her Mrs. Richards would just enrage the little lady), "you're a very attractive young woman, but even if you weren't married I'd find the present situation unacceptable."

He felt her body stiffen.

"You just can't get it into your head that I'm soon going to marry the woman I love."

Her eyes stared straight ahead as he continued, "I could never betray her by going to bed with you, no matter how bloody attractive you are."

She stood up in a fury, her eyes blazing and her voice suddenly harsh.

"What if I told the police you've been trying to take advantage of me in my husband's absence. Emily thinks they'd believe me and I could make it stick."

"I think you're both crazy. All I have to do is to get hold of a few previous locums and your lies would be exposed to everyone."

She rushed out of the room, and her last audible words were muffled by her sobs.

"Damn you to hell, you self-righteous bastard!"

That was their last real encounter. After that, she stayed away from him most of the time and remained cold and aloof, much to his relief. As for the children, they still showed they loved him and he returned their affection in full.

Philip was now convinced that Europe was becoming a lost cause, and Great Britain seemed destined to reduce itself to defeatist helplessness. Austria had been handed over to the marauding forces of the Third Reich by its treacherous Nazi underground and sympathizers in the armed forces. Czechoslovakia had been dismembered and then devoured. Poland would be next – after disposing of Danzig in one gulp.

The only possibility of stopping this process of conquest by threat and common extortion, was by accepting Russia's approaches. This meant signing a clearcut pact of mutual military assistance in the face of any German threat against the smaller nations of Europe. Despite the fact that the Soviets had been completely excluded from the Munich negotiations, their chief diplomatic contact and a committed friend of the British, Maxim Litvinov, had been persistently rebuffed by the appeasement gangs in Britain and France.

It seemed inevitable that the Soviets would give up in desperation and turn to their hated enemies, to sign a non-aggression pact and stave off a Nazi attack. It was also clear that if it were left to Vyacheslav Molotov ('Old Ironpants'), Litvinoff's head would roll and the treaty between the Soviet Union and Germany would be signed, sealed and delivered.

As far as the international media were concerned, it appeared that only the American broadcaster, William Schirer, and Madame Tabouis of the *Paris Oeuvre*, expressed a clear understanding and analysis of the situation. This brave little French lady, a semi-invalid whose aristocratic family were Fascist sympathizers, had the courage to write the truth. Her book, 'Blackmail or War', dispelled all the lies and apologias for the Nazi ravages and Hitler's plans for military conquest. Meanwhile, Schirer kept the western world informed about what was really happening in the Third Reich, from his vantage point in Berlin, but few listened.

By the end of June, the locum was finished and the joint menace of Stella and Emily was mercifully lifted from Philip's shoulders. He drove down to London for the last time and to Grantham Square for final farewells to his family. It was painful enough saying goodbye to his beloved parents, who were unbearably brave for the occasion. Dear affectionate Pauline broke down completely, sobbing that he'd always been her anchor whenever events seemed about to cast her adrift.

The most heartbreaking parting of all was with 9-year-old Clayton. He stood forlornly on the stairway, his beautiful face ashen and his expression uncomprehending. So great was his shock and so desperate his sense of loss that there was no room for tears. 'Until we meet again, my dear young brother' resounded in Philip's brain, but words would not come.
He found his voice at last with his father, "Keep the car, Dad, It's paid up in full and the papers are all in order."
Was this his inspiring speech of farewell to those he loved so deeply? Only in literature did the divine poetic phrases fall with sublime artistry from the protagonist's lips.

On the train back to Liverpool, he began to picture what Patty's last meeting with her family in Ireland must have been like: the pain, the uncertainty. What kind of a husband would this alien, smoothtalking stranger be to their beloved Patricia, and in a far-off land, besides? What religious battles did the future hold for the newlyweds, and even more so for their children? How could a marriage ceremony not blessed by the Church survive the perils of so diverse a background?

At last, July came to England with the world still holding its breath, month after frustrating month, and here they were; Patty looking stunningly beautiful in her pale beige dress of Shantung silk; Philip looking distinguished in his smart St. Clement's Hospital blazer; and the time-honored questions floating on the still air of the registry office.

"Do you Philip Bosnar take this woman Patricia Clancy...?"

It was the third day out from Liverpool, the sun was bright and warm, the Atlantic swell was at its friendliest, and with the possible exception of the perpetually stricken Mimi in the next cabin, seasickness was disappearing from the list of travel inconveniences. The decks were alive with happy promenaders, with deck chair loungers awaiting their cup of hot Bovril, playing children livening up the peaceful scene and sports enthusiasts displaying their deck-tennis skills.

At mealtimes, the dining-room was filled with passengers enjoying the sumptuous meals, the magnificent spaciousness of the vast hall, the gleaming mahogany furniture and superb chandeliers. The ship's orchestra was in fine fettle and played a nicely balanced selection of classics and popular music. From time to time the newlyweds tried their hand at the pingpong table, and in fact Patty persuaded Phil to enter the shipboard knockout tournament. He thought he might do pretty well, as it used to be one of his favorite games at medical school.

They soon made new friends on the crossing. There was the Winnipeg representative of Ingram and Bell (a Canadian medical supply company), and she promised to let her Saskatchewan agent know about the new Canadians.

A middle-aged couple from Prince Albert almost adopted them. They ran a chain of hardware stores and were able to instruct the Bosnars about points of interest pertaining to Saskatchewan, its history and its politics.

Then, there was The Wild Bunch at the next table to theirs in the dining-room. It included Big Red Haynes, senior executive in a tableware firm with branches right across Canada. There was Tiny Eaton, a tall and slender athlete who was one of the heirs to the Eaton millions. He and Big Red, along with their hearty young companions, were returning from a rowing Regatta in England where they'd represented Canada with a fair degree of success. They were always up to high jinks of one sort or another, and they showed a great deal of warm friendliness toward Phil and Patty. Needless to say, there were the usual promises to come and visit after the voyage was over, but the Bosnars took them with a large grain of salt.

The table tennis tournament ended according to form, although Philip was pleasantly surprised when he beat Big Red in the semifinals, and decided his opponent must have been battling a hangover at the time. Eaton was a different cup of tea entirely, and when he whispered just before the finals, "Let's make this look good, shall we?" Philip was nonplused and somewhat affronted. As soon as the preliminary knock-up started, however, Philip knew he'd be lucky if he took a single point in the match. His lanky opponent simply stood back about eight feet from the table and clobbered whatever ball Philip delivered. The final scores of 21-16 and 21-18 were entirely due to the champion's sporting largess.

"Thanks for the lesson," Philip told Eaton.

"Don't sell yourself short, doctor," came the reply, "You play a damn good game."

The ship's concert was an absolute disaster. Philip was third on the list and played a couple of Kreisler favorites and the traditional Brahms Hungarian Dance No 5. The Wild Bunch, sitting together and poised for mischief, maintained a complete silence during his performance, then applauded politely. They were waiting like beasts of prey for the unfortunate little soprano who was next on the program.

Under ordinary circumstances, the lady could probably sing quite well, but the saboteurs had prepared a nasty accompaniment. Whenever her voice rose in volume they tore strips from newspapers concealed under their table and the result was disastrous. It sounded as if she had an appalling rasp in her voice, and her performance concluded with a grating crescendo. As soon as she finished, her saboteurs yelled boisterously for the longest time.

The rest of the concert was a debacle, and when it came to a merciful end, the tray was passed around for a collection to be split among the cabin boys. There was mostly silver and a few dollar bills on the tray until it was passed to the Wild Bunch. But when it was moved to the next group all the silver was gone. A great deal of tut-tutting and angry murmurs from the audience followed this outrage until the collection appeared to be over, at which point the pranksters piled the tray high with five and ten dollar bills. Everyone roared with laughter and The Wild Bunch became instant favorites with all the passengers, especially after they apologized to the soprano and she forgave them for their youthful high jinks.

On the last day of their journey, at the end of their smooth passage down the magnificent Gulf of St. Lawrence, the *S.S. Montclare* dropped anchor at the port of Montreal. There was excitement on board, and a great deal of anxiety about the French-Canadian immigration officers who would soon be swarming over the decks. It was a strange interlude for Phil and Patty. They'd thought of Canada as an essentially British country like Australia and New Zealand, but at the moment it seemed more like a part of France and they realized they must reassess their perspective.

"Have you got your employment papers?" someone asked them.

"I don't have a single paper about employment. I'm joining a medical practice."

"These goddamn Frogs won't give a hoot. They've got a new act of parliament called the Mining and Immigration Act or something of the sort, and if you don't have your papers they can ship you back to the U.K. They might even make you pay for the return."

Patty showed some concern, especially when the immigration officers appeared on deck, speaking a strange French dialect and browbeating the passengers. When Philip was approached by one of these officials he decided to speak up first.

"Je suis un chirurgeon, et je suis né à Paris."

This information brought a friendly smile from the Quebecker.

"Bienvenue à Quebec, Monsieur, Madame."

With that, the official drew some large chalk crosses on their luggage and left.

The newlyweds were puzzled until they left the ship. On the arrival platform at dockside, they were almost embarrassed as they watched their shipmates having their luggage clumsily opened and the contents unceremoniously dumped out by customs officers, while their own luggage went untouched and was waved ahead to the waiting porter.

WELCOME TO CANADA! Or at least to French Canada.

CHAPTER 21

1948-49

Philip was ushered into a large chamber by a uniformed attendant. It was beautifully furnished in oak-wood and old leather and the broad windows facing west provided more than ample illumination. He thought this was probably the cabinet room but failed to recognize the half dozen men gathered around the table, with the exception of the Premier, who came over briskly to shake his hand and then introduced him to the others. They were cabinet ministers and senior civil servants who were most closely involved in the new government's health plan. The feisty little leader opened up the proceedings briskly and without preamble.

"We understand you're having trouble in your negotiations with your hospital workers other than qualified nurses."

"Yes, Mr. Premier, and this includes technicians and secretarial staff who richly deserve a raise."

"That's a bit of a surprise, doctor," one of the others commented, "we thought you opposed such a raise."

"Far from it. I've repeatedly informed Mr. Shackley, the union representative, that we aren't against an increase, but the amount of increase would depend on the level of government funding to our hospital. On each occasion he would proceed to harangue the meeting with references to a penny-pinching reactionary hospital board, only interested in grinding its long-suffering workers deeper and deeper into poverty."

"Are you saying that Mr. Shackley is the main impediment to a settlement."

"With respect, Sir, I'm afraid I am. It seems this individual is determined to use outdated polemics that drive a wedge between the union members on the one hand and the Sisters on the other."

"What you're saying" came a voice from the end of the table "is that you think he's just spouting outmoded Marxist philosophy instead of looking for a settlement."

"I think the doctor has already made that quite clear. Is there anything else? Any questions or comments?"

There were endless questions and various opinions, but at the end of an hour none of these really added anything beyond what had already been said. Eventually, after the lengthy discussion had subsided to a low murmur, the Premier rose.

"Dr. Bosnar, I would like to thank you for coming here and helping us to clarify the situation. This meeting is adjourned, but I'd like you to stay for a few moments, doctor, if you can spare the time."

"It would be my pleasure, Mr. Premier."

"Great! Let's loosen our ties, take off our shoes, and I'll order up a pot of tea. As far as the union demands are concerned I'll see to it that the difficulty is resolved."

After tea had been served, along with some chocolate biscuits which Douglas confessed were his weakness, the conversation was resumed.

"First of all I should tell you how pleased we all are with the great work you did for my former secretary. Her hands are so much better and she's praising you far and wide."

"Thank you, Sir, I'm flattered."

"It's come to my attention that you've had a longstanding special interest in arthritis."

"That's quite true, especially the crippling variety known as Rheumatoid Arthritis."

"How would you like me to set up a government-sponsored Arthritic Center in Vanwey, with you in charge?"

"I'm afraid I'd have to decline with thanks. In the first place, I'm a general surgeon and this center would need an internist with a special interest in rheumatology as well as an orthopedic surgeon. Secondly, such a center would be more logically placed in Regina or Saskatoon where such specialists can be found."

"Well thanks anyway for being so honest with me, although I must say I'm a bit disappointed."

"For my part, Mr. Premier, I want to thank you both for this meeting and for your offer of a special center. I'm indebted and hope to meet you again, perhaps less formally."
The meeting was over but would not be forgotten.

The next round of negotiations with the union committee took place a few days later. This time, the obdurate Shackley wasn't present to poison the proceedings with his tedious propaganda. Instead, there was a cordial Scot from Edinburgh by the name of Ian Stuart, with a soft accent and a reasonable manner to match. The union settled for a raise of one third less than the original demand, and both sides received a guarantee that the Ministry of Health would provide the necessary funds to cover the shortfall. So that was the end of that.

This appeared to be an appropriate time for the Bosnar family to take a two week vacation. It was decided that they'd take the car, a reliable maroon-colored Chrysler, and drive to Vancouver. The trip would give the children an opportunity to see the spectacular Rocky Mountains and the scenic Pacific coast as well.

The drive was superb, and all four had a great time. The children were in a state of joyous excitement throughout. Crossing the border into North Dakota, they journeyed across Montana and through the mountains to Idaho. The views were sensational and ever-changing, and the immense beauty of the North American continent was driven home to the enthralled travelers. Philip made sure they stopped at the most photogenic panoramas and took both still pictures and movies. They drove through Billings, Butte and Anaconda, marveling at the immensity of the copper mines, great man-made spiral craters in the red-brown earth. Then, it was through Missoula into Idaho, past Coeur D'Alene and on to Spokane.

On their way through the Rockies, they caught their breath at the grandeur of the snowclad mountains and great wooded valleys far below. It was an inspiring experience, and the glory and constant variety of their surroundings restored a sense of balance to ones human experiences and problems, which somehow seemed picayune by comparison.

They stayed in Spokane overnight, and after a generous breakfast, serviced the car for the drive north into Canada. The border was crossed at Blaine and the immigration and custom officials on both sides were friendly and helpful. After entering Vancouver from the south, they drove into Stanley Park and across the grandiose Lion's Gate bridge before settling on a small but comfortable motel. They took a double unit that would give them lots of room for relaxation.

This would be an excellent opportunity for Philip to scout the possibility of setting up or joining a surgical practice in Vancouver, and Patty agreed. He phoned Dr. Karl Sefton, one of the city's leading surgeons, and got an appointment for the following morning, a Saturday, at 10 o'clock. The meeting was at the surgeon's residence in Shaughnessy Heights, and after introducing himself, he was taken for a stroll in the sumptuous gardens behind the old three-storey house.

"What can I do for you, Dr. Bosnar?"

"I was hoping you could advise me on the feasibility of practicing surgery in this city. I've had nine years in Saskatchewan, including a couple of years in the army, and here is my resumé."

They sat down on an ornamental bench while Dr. Sefton studied the credentials carefully. He handed the documents back to Philip and rose.

"There's no question that you're good enough to practice in this city, but right now you'd starve."

"Why is that?"

"Since World War 2 there's been a huge influx of doctors into Vancouver, especially general surgeons, and many have had to leave after almost hitting the poverty line. You might have a slight chance of survival as a thoracic surgeon, a urologist, a gynecologist or an orthopedic surgeon. This is the day of the sub-specialist."

He paused for a while to watch his listener's reaction.

"The days of the general surgeon are numbered, especially in an overcrowded center like Vancouver. As for getting on a hospital staff you'd be at the end of a long line. I'm sorry to pour cold water on your plans but I think you came to me for the truth and that's what I'm giving you." Philip left his host with thanks for the candor of his advice, but felt crushed as he drove back across Lion's Gate bridge, oblivious to the inspiring panorama below.

For the next few days, the family had a great time, exploring Capilano Canyon and crossing the swaying Capilano Bridge with intrepid abandon. They drove to West Vancouver and out to Horseshoe Bay, then returned to meander through Stanley Park, taking long walks through its many trails. They also enjoyed the bustling port area, where ships of all nations were assembled at the docks and made them feel that the whole world was assembling at this very place.

Finally, it was time to go back, this time by way of Rogers pass and the Canadian mountain ranges. They stopped off briefly to visit the renowned Banff Springs hotel, with the foaming Bow river below and the beautifully layered Rocky Mountains close by, all artistically mirrored in each of the many small lakes. Then, on to the 'wild west' city of Calgary, home of the Forsyths and the Calgary Stampede. The Bosnars and Forsyths had a warm reunion and dined together in the pleasant and spacious Forsyth home, and the children played together as if they'd never parted. The next day, Phil and Patty took all the children to the Calgary Stampede and found the afternoon thrilling beyond their wildest expectations, especially the hair-raising Chuckwagon races.

All too soon, it was time to bid their hosts goodbye. The Bosnars were glad Peter was doing well in his new group practice, although they couldn't help noticing that he and Kitty were drinking far too heavily. Philip consoled himself with the thought that his friend was too fine a person and far too good a doctor to let himself go down the drain.

8-year-old Beth Forsyth, a rather difficult child, said she was going to visit her aunt Gladys and uncle Angus in Vanwey, and could Philip drive her there? The Bosnars said they were quite prepared to take her along for the trip, and she rode happily in the back of the car with her former prairie pals. The return journey detoured through Glacier National Park, a scenic gem of spectacular mountains and gleaming mirror lakes; then on through Montana until they reached the North Dakota border and headed toward Vanwey.

Perhaps Philip should have predicted that something might go wrong on this, the last morning of their continental drive, and less than thirty miles from Vanwey. It had rained heavily during the night after long weeks of dry weather and parched ground, and the dirt road was as slick as if coated with oil. Traction was becoming increasingly difficult and a slight crown in the center of the road made it difficult to avoid a progressive sideslip, no matter how Philip tried to keep his speed under control. In a matter of minutes he realized that a roll-over into the deep right culvert was inevitable.

"Hold on everybody and keep calm," he warned, "we're going to roll over slowly to the right."

He maintained his grip on the steering wheel with his left hand and reached over tightly against Patty's body to grasp the right hand door handle. A moment later, they rolled an unbelievably gentle three hundred and sixty degrees into the culvert, landing right side up. Patty, Jamie and Florian were remarkably calm and even seemed to be enjoying the excitement of the experience, but Philip's relief was soon shattered by Beth Forsyth's sudden attack of screaming hysteria. Patty leaned over to the back seat, and once she'd assured herself that none of the children was hurt in any way, she slapped the hysterical girl firmly across the face. By the grace of God that aborted the screaming attack before it could spread to the others.

The North Dakota Highway Patrol arrived shortly thereafter with their tow truck, and hauled the Chrysler back onto the highway and further, to a point where the road wasn't as slippery.

"Believe me, Sir, this would have happened no matter who was driving," said the officer in charge, after taking note of the particulars. "You see, there's an alkaline lake just to the left of that stretch of road. After a heavy rainfall the alkali seeps into the road surface and makes it soapy. You folks should have no trouble the rest of the way. Good luck to you."

"We can't thank you enough for everything. If you're ever up in Vanwey please look us up. Here's my card."

They drove on to Vanwey with the car showing no marks of the close encounter, and stopped at the Jacksons to deliver their unblemished guest into the outstretched arms of Gladys.

"Oh Auntie, Dr. Bosnar turned his car over in a ditch!"

"Let's get the blazes out of here," came the fierce whisper from Patty, her face crimson with anger. There would be an opportunity to give Gladys and Angus the true details at another time, but Patty felt badly hurt by their ungrateful young passenger's casual distortion of what really happened. If it hadn't been for the cool way their driver had handled such a dangerous situation, she insisted, none of them might have come out of he accident unscathed.

Al Masters came over to see Philip that evening.

"You'll be interested to know that Slocum contacted me yesterday and wants to meet with us as soon as possible with a special proposal. He wouldn't say what it was."

"I wonder what he's got up his sleeve."

"Perhaps he's going to leave town, though I don't see why he should. He's certainly behaving much better in the hospital and he's got a pretty good practice in spite of all his crazy behavior."

"Let's set up the meeting for next Monday evening in our office and see what he has to say."

The three met in Philip's consulting room at 8 o'clock in the evening and got right down to business. Brent Slocum had a plan, quite a grandiose one in fact. He had put a down payment on the large office building at the corner of Main Street and Sixth Avenue. The former occupants, Vanwey Trust and Loan Company, had moved to larger premises on Third Avenue and put their present building up for sale. Slocum made an offer that was accepted, and intended to finance the deal himself, with the help of his friendly bank manager. His idea was to set up a clinic in which all three would practice together and gradually expand if the partnership turned out well. He thought Dr. Bosnar should be the professional head of the clinic.

Philip thanked him politely for his offer and agreed to think about it for a while. Masters suggested another meeting for the following Monday, but Slocum said he'd prefer it sooner than that and they settled on Thursday, same time, same place. They parted cordially, with Slocum obviously excited and Masters somewhat inscrutable. Bosnar could hardly believe the turn of events. It seemed so illogical, so totally out of character for Slocum, yet in a convoluted sort of way it was just the unexpected change of direction one saw from time to time in so erratic a character. Like a chameleon, he could change his image as circumstances required, and right now he required Philip to head his new clinic while he, Slocum, faded into the background. That was now, but the future could quickly see the colors change if Slocum found it necessary to resume the offensive.

Alvin sprang his surprise at the next meeting. He expressed gratification at Brent Slocum's change of attitude toward the colleagues he'd tried to cheat and harass in the past. He was pleased that the suggestion to make Philip professional head of the new clinic came first from Slocum. He was also in entire agreement that Slocum should confine his practice to Ob.Gyn. in which he held his Certification, and all other major general surgery would go to Philip except as otherwise delegated by him.

There was only one remaining question: would Slocum agree that Philip should have, at all times, the final say in any ethical decisions pertaining to the practice? Since this would include such vital matters as unnecessary surgery, fee-splitting and exorbitant billing, it was the key question and the answer – unfortunately for Vanwey's medical future – was a categorical No!

That was the end of it. The lines had been clearly drawn and Philip knew that as long as Brent had influential figures like Fraywell in his corner he'd probably thrive and grow wealthy. Philip also realized to his sorrow that, once he and his family left Vanwey, Slocum would eventually drive Masters out of town.

The clinic proposal had come at a strange time. It was now 1948, and the Bosnar-Masters practice was doing very well, yet the day was fast approaching when Philip felt he should move on with Patty and the children to a more challenging future: one with larger professional scope for him and better educational facilities for the youngsters. The place to go, and this was Patty's strong desire, was somewhere on the west coast.

The most attractive prospect without a doubt was the Kaiser-Permanente Foundation in California, a giant group practice system with its own hospitals and a remuneration system based on qualifications, experience, performance and seniority. It was not in any way associated with the accepted system of fee-for-service, and beyond hoping to be accepted he even allowed himself to dream of a posting in the San Francisco area.

The initial correspondence with the Foundation's authorities was encouraging and they found Philip's resume most acceptable. In fact, Philip was prompted to apply for a working visa in the U.S.A, one that he received without delay. San Francisco, from all he'd heard, read, and seen in magazines and movies, was just about the most civilized city in the whole of North America. It was a place where they could bring up the children in an environment of civic pride ('the Naples of the Pacific Coast!') and great opportunity for the future.

The children were now five and seven, with Jaimie at elementary school only a few blocks from their home, and Florian not yet at school age. They played together vigorously, and in the absence of a Kindergarten or good educational facilities at school, Phil and Patty made sure they were constantly exposed to good music and intelligent discussions in the home, on a wide variety of subjects. What the children missed in education, they made up in strenuous games with a large group of pals from their neighborhood.

The ample back yard, with its swings and sand lots, proved a blessing to the children and their friends. Jaimie was especially fond of the large elm tree behind the garage, where he could practice his climbing skills both summer and winter. He and his sister usually got along extremely well and loved to race on their tricycles, with Jaimie permitting Florian to take short cuts as a sort of legitimate equalizer.

Aside from the poor level of teaching at their school, it soon became evident that their joy was clouded by a bully who lived across the street. He was a large good-looking kid with a broad red face, and he was a year older than Jaimie. When the bully was with his doting parents he was the model of decorum, but at school he was an unholy terror.

Philip decided it was time to pass on a few basic lessons in self-defense, both for the young lad and the protection of his sister. He purchased some boxing gloves that were just the right size for the little chap and started with simple techniques.

First, good footwork, watching the opponent, especially his eyes, and ducking at the right moment. After a while this might make him swing wildly and the advantage is yours.

Next lesson, in front of the mirror, jab, jab and jab again with your left fist, with your right hand protecting your head. Keep your head tucked into your shoulder. Learn to take a punch, but hang on in a clinch if you have to. If he misses with a blow, bring your right fist across, straight and hard.

Final lesson, learn to counterpunch, vary your attack with blows to the body or uppercuts. Don't worry about fancy combinations at this stage of the game. Never start a fight but keep your boxing skills mainly for bullies, that's the only way they'll ever learn.

Patty stood by quietly but watched apprehensively. A few weeks later Jamie brought home a note from his teacher. '**If the purpose of your son's boxing lessons is for self-defense it has gone far beyond its objective.**'

The disappointment arrived near the end of the year. Philip was informed by the California State Medical Board that although they were prepared to recognize his degrees, they couldn't grant reciprocity to his postgraduate surgical training in the U.K. This was at least partially understandable, since the postwar training programs were much more stringent, lasted much longer, and all had to take place in top-flight university teaching hospitals. As if that were not enough, however, they even questioned his basic British medical qualifications, even though he had his Canadian L.M.C.C.

Canadian degrees were mostly recognized in reciprocity, but what Philip had to contemplate was going back to passing exams in basic sciences, and losing (at best) about five years of his life in studies and exams. During this time there would be no surgery and no income. That was the end of the great American dream, and Patty offered the consoling thought that perhaps in years to come they'd be thankful they'd remained in Canada.

By mutual consent, they decided to look for other promising opportunities, and even take another look at the west coast. They flew out to Edwardia in celebration of their birthdays, leaving the children in the capable hands of Mrs. Halliday, their ever-faithful housekeeper, who was now called 'Auntie Mildred' by the children. Changing planes at Vancouver, where it was drizzling, they took the small twelve-seater to Edwardia, Garden City of Vancouver Island, where the sun was shining and the air was pure.

After riding into town by airport bus and enjoying the delightful parkland scenery on the way, they entered a city that was much larger than they'd imagined and were impressed by the cleanliness of its orderly streets. Edwardia appeared to be dozing peacefully in the afternoon sun and most of the passers-by looked welldressed and unhurried.

They took a taxi to the famed Prince Albert Hotel, with its ivy-covered facade, green-painted rooftops and cupolas. It was situated across from the impressive Royal Harbor with its dozens of sailboats lying at anchor, as if waiting in readiness for the next race. Next, they went over to the registration desk, with a helpful porter bringing their luggage along. There was quite a crowd collecting at the registration area, and when the porter asked if they had reservations and Philip told him they hadn't, he quizzically wished them luck.

It was at this moment that the capricious fates intervened. A hefty slap landed on his shoulder and a familiar voice rebuked him.

"For Christ's sake, Phil, surely you don't expect to get in here without an advance booking." It was none other than John Kinsley, Philip's good friend from Winnipeg. He said he'd moved out to Edwardia a couple of years ago, to get his failing lungs out of Winnipeg's freezing winters and cut down on his busy operative schedule. Since his arrival, he'd been getting steadily busier but still maintained a safety backup by functioning as `resident doctor' to this prestigious C.P.R. hotel.

"You don't really deserve it," he told Philip, "but let me see what I can do."

Within the hour he arranged for Phil and Patty to move into a comfortable bed-sitting room on the second floor, although they had no idea how he managed it.

"Get yourselves settled, have some dinner and then I'll join you about 9 o'clock with Jane Crocket, my wild Irish secretary, and we'll all get smashed. She's nothing to look at but a barrel of laughs at a party."

"Why don't you join us for dinner here, in the hotel dining room?" Patty asked.

"Sorry, I can't. Got a dinner meeting at the Chelmsford Hospital but I'll skip out early."

The party started shortly after 9 and the serious drinking about an hour later. As Kinsley had accurately informed them, his secretary was no beauty queen and Mrs. Kinsley had nothing to worry about, but the newcomer delivered a barrage of jokes from the moment she entered, and her screams of laughter could be heard on the decks of the sailboats moored below. Patty stayed with mild drinks of gin and ginger ale, while the others attacked a bottle of Ne Plus Ultra whisky with a vengeance. It was a great reunion and a wild night, and the party finally broke up at about 3 in the morning, but not before Kinsley had made a clear offer to Philip.

"I need a good man to join me in my practice and you're just the right guy for the job. I'll find Patricia a house she'll like and make sure you get on staff at our hospitals without delay." The offer was loud and firm, even though John was having increasing trouble with his diction, and Philip couldn't be sure his friend was really serious.

Phil and Patty were awakened without mercy at 7.30 the following morning, and the ringing phone sounded like the shrieking of an enraged banshee. It was Kinsley, God bless his unfeeling heart.

"I'll pick you up about 9 o'clock, Phil, and take you up to the hospitals to meet some of the guys." The reluctant risers tried to moisten their parched throats with generous draughts of cold water, but these only seemed to reach the palate before absorbing into desiccated mucous membranes. Altogether, it took about four or five large tumblers of water before the divine liquid reached their stomachs. They phoned down for orange juice, toast and tea, and Phil got himself ready for his trip to the hospitals.

By the time Kinsley phoned their room from the front foyer, Philip looked and felt like a human being again. As for Kinsley, he looked remarkably fresh and there was even some healthy color in his cheeks. His breathing seemed less labored, too. The drive to the Chelmsford Hospital was about two miles, and the hospital proved to be a fully modern institution with up-to-date facilities in all departments. They went up to the operating room suite on the top floor and Kinsley introduced Philip to the O.R. nurses.

"Dr. Bosnar will be joining me fairly soon," he announced confidently, "and I want you to be really nice to him."

That was typical of John Kinsley, thought Philip, although he was still taken aback. It wasn't just the verification of his drunken offer from the night before, but the easy manner in which he'd taken Philip's acceptance for granted. He decided to humor his sponsor even if the offer proved no more than a temporary enthusiasm resulting from their unexpected meeting after so many years. He was ushered into the doctors lounge, where he was served a cup of coffee and introduced to half a dozen staff doctors. There were further introductions on the wards, the emergency and outpatient departments, the X-ray department and laboratory.

Next, they drove to St. Peter's hospital, run by a nursing order of Roman Catholic nuns.

"I don't do much work in this place," Kinsley remarked. "Too rundown, too much interference by the Sisters, and too much hospital politics." The hospital didn't measure up to the Chelmsford but was a perfectly satisfactory institution in which the patients could receive a high standard of medical care. Philip thought how happy he'd be to have such a facility at his disposal for operative cases.

After another round of introductions in all major departments they left and returned to the Prince Albert Hotel. Patty joined them for lunch in the coffee shop, and following an enjoyable meal – the hangover fading fast – they said goodbye to Kinsley and thanked him for getting them accommodation, for the party, the trip to the hospitals and the introductions. The offer to join Kinsley's practice was carefully not mentioned.

"You'll be hearing from me." were Kinsley's parting words.

That afternoon, they took a walk around the picturesque harbor and mingled with the tourists. They admired the hanging flower baskets adorning the lamp-posts, and took one of the horse and buggy tours of the city.

"What a marvelous place to live and for you to practice," Patty enthused. "I'm sure the children would just love it."

"Mustn't get your hopes up, Patty. Besides, the kids might miss all that lovely prairie snow."

The next move was up to Kinsley, and if his offer remained firm they'd be hearing from him in due course. Patty's eyes were shining and turning from green to blue, a sure sign she was happy and excited. Philip took care not to reveal he'd already fallen in love with this charming city and hoped the offer would turn out to be a true bill. Working with Kinsley would be a real thrill, and working in those two hospitals would be a privilege.

They decided not to return to Vancouver by air, and took the ferryboat instead. It was a memorable trip, gliding past the steep wooded shores of the Gulf Islands, and through the seething waters of Active Pass; then across the Straits of Georgia to the mainland. Vancouver's weather had changed for the better, and their plane to the east took off in warm sunshine and a cloudless sky.

When they got home, the children greeted them with wild enthusiasm, and if Mrs. H's report could be believed, they'd behaved like angels during their parents' absence. By this time, they'd adopted their surrogate aunt completely and saved their best behavior for her. The news that the family might be moving to the west coast was the cause of much excitement, especially when Patty described the beauties of Edwardia.

Of course, Alvin Masters had to be brought into the picture right away.

"I'll certainly be lost without you, Phil, but I felt you must be getting restless and looking for a practice in some major center with more scope."

"It's not just that, Al. It's the better educational opportunities for the kids and a better life for Patty."

"Well I sure hope it works out for you and I wish you luck. You must be getting fed up with local medical politics."

"There's always the chance of running into a different brand of medical politics, even in an ideal place like Edwardia."

The call from Kinsley came two weeks later.

"Well, you lucky S.O.B, I've got just the house for you. It's not completed yet, but it's well built, it's in a super location on the scenic bus tour and has a knockout view. I've jewed 'em down to seventeen five, and the mortgage is damn reasonable. Patricia will love it. How soon can you get here?"

"Thanks for your efforts on the house, John. I'm sure we'll love it. I'll send Patty out to see for herself and then I'll head down to the Mayo Clinic and Owen Wangensteen's unit in Minneapolis and brush up on the latest surgical techniques. I should be able to join you by the beginning of July."

Two days later, after a quick flight, Patty was back in Edwardia and phoned Phil.

"It's a wonderful house, darling, tudor style and roomy. The upstairs needs finishing and so does the basement. The garden will need quite a bit of landscaping, but when it's all finished it should be perfect for us. Just wait till you see the view."

"That's just great, Patty. Go ahead and confirm the purchase, and come back home as soon as you're satisfied the preliminaries are OK."

She returned to Vanwey by the end of the week and was still bubbling with enthusiasm.

"I can convert the front into a terrific rock garden, and perhaps we can put in a small lawn next to the garage at the back of the house."

The sale of their home on Third Street was somewhat disappointing. Once the word was out that they'd soon be leaving, it became a buyer's market, and they had to sell for the same price they'd paid four years earlier, namely $12,500. Philip had already established a firm reputation as one who never got the best of a financial deal, and he accepted the unpalatable fact philosophically. Patty, willing and reliable as ever, stayed behind to make all the final arrangements. She would look after the orderly transfer of household goods to British Columbia and a thousand other details that invariably crop up at the last moment in such a major move.

Philip, on the other hand, fixed his sights on his forthcoming visit to the fountains of surgical knowledge in Minnesota. He drove first to Rochester, home of the world famous Mayo Clinic, and checked in at a comfortable hotel that was reasonably priced and located close to the Clinic's hospital complex. The town itself had an unfortunate moribund quality, unrelieved by the countless churches and chapels, and still less by the many funeral parlors. These seemed to be competing, in the true spirit of free enterprise, for a smoother entry of their clients into the Kingdom of Heaven. Patients paraded the sidewalks in wheelchairs, on artificial limbs or just crutches and canes, with the light of faith in their Mayo doctors shining in their eyes. It wasn't quite the passionate fervor of a Lourdes but a religious intensity nonetheless, with the aroma of disinfectant replacing the holy aura of incense.

The hospital areas had a magic of their own for such as Dr. Philip Bosnar, as he marveled at the steady stream of physicians and surgeons who came from all over the world to watch the Mayo staff doctors at their work. They came to listen to their presentations and observe their skilled surgical technique. It took him very little time to realize that the best man to watch was the celebrated Dr. Clagett. Although primarily a thoracic surgeon, he was also an excellent general surgeon and a cogent communicator. Philip decided to spend most of his time with this paragon, and did his best to 'steal his brains' from a well-chosen vantage point in the O.R. observer gallery. Clagett soon learned to recognize his Canadian visitor and they began to discuss various aspects of the surgical cases in a valuable person-to-person fashion.

To Philip's surprise, just as this one surgeon was outstanding, several of the others were disappointing, and he was learning how to avoid their imperfections as well as how to emulate the best methods. Every evening, after dinner at the hotel, he settled down with his notebook and took down copious notes and commentaries on the day's proceedings, with illustrations as necessary to clarify the words.

After a most enlightening five days he drove to Minneapolis and checked in at the Radisson Hotel. Following a light snack at the coffee shop he felt unable to pursue his studies, as it was simply too hot and sticky. He showered and changed, then went down to a spacious bar that carried the exotic name, 'Turquoise Lounge', and was decorated accordingly. Above all, it was cool and inviting, with a relaxing ambiance that took his mind off the intense search for knowledge that filled his recent days. The icy Tom Collins was just what he needed as he sat at the bar and looked at the few people seated at the tables.

He noticed a nearby group, consisting of several prosperous-looking young men and a smartly dressed young woman. They seemed to be having a lively time, punctuated with laughter and animated conversation, and one of the men waved him a hello and came over to the bar with typical American friendliness and hospitality.

"Say. Why don't you come over and join us?" he asked.

"Forgive me, but I'd rather not if you don't mind. I'm feeling a bit bushed and am off to an early night's sleep."

"That's OK, but at least let me buy you a drink. You're a Limey, aren't you? Same again for my friend, bartender."

"Thanks a lot. Actually I'm a Canadian, but lived most of my life in England."

This information appeared to initiate an introduction.

"By the way, my name's Sam Birdwell. I'm field representative for Kodak."

He was a big chap, about six feet tall, built like a football player and endowed with the characteristic curiosity of his countrymen. It wasn't long before he learned that Dr. Philip Bosnar was down here from Canada to visit the famed surgical unit of Dr. Owen Wangensteen; that he was married to an Irish girl who wasn't with him on this professional trip, and he'd be returning to southern Saskatchewan in a week.

After refurbishing his new acquaintance's glass and switching to plain ginger ale for himself, Philip soon found himself joining the others at their table and being introduced all around. They were a convivial group, and when he finally excused himself, he wondered if his evenings would remain as free for study as he'd hoped. As if reading his thoughts the jovial Birdwell called out, "We'll be meeting again for drinks, Doctor, before you go back to Canada." The others registered their approval, and Philip felt a bit worried.

Dr. Wangensteen was everything he was reputed to be, an exceptional surgeon and a lucid teacher. He showed the visiting Canadian every courtesy and withheld nothing from his probing curiosity. There wasn't a single facet of his surgical skill and knowledge that Philip missed or failed to store for future application. The other surgeons in the unit were also impressive, but none as much as Dr. Robert Varcoe, a jolly fellow whose huge bulk concealed an artistic delicacy of operative technique.

At the end of a long and crowded day, Philip stopped off at a small restaurant for his evening meal, then returned to his hotel room to complete his notes of the day's operations and discussions. At 9 o'clock the phone rang,

"Come on down, doctor, and join us for a drink. You must be due for a little relaxation."

"No thanks, old chap. I've got some writing to do and then I'm off to bed."

But Sam Birdwell and his friends, with the best of intentions, were not to be denied ('Hands across the border' and all that sort of international goodwill), and the other members of the group added their persuasions over the phone. After a while, Philip gave up and joined them for one drink, then excused himself and went back upstairs.

Day after day, this routine was repeated and it became more and more difficult to get away from the group, which had now expanded to six men and four women. They were all in their thirties and forties and all quite charming, well-mannered and amusing. It became more difficult to rebuff them, but by the fourth evening he asked the switchboard to keep his phone clear. The operator informed him that he'd have to keep his phone off the hook. He hoped Birdwell and his companions wouldn't regard this as Limey snobbery and take offense. At least they didn't take the step of banging on his door, so it was likely they respected his need to study. In any event his evenings remained uninterrupted until the morning before his departure. There was a message for him at the desk from Birdwell. 'We'd like you to be our guest for a farewell dinner this evening. If you can make it, meet us in the bar about 7 o'clock.' Philip was deeply moved.

The dinner was a great success. The entire group foregathered in the Turquoise Lounge for a couple of drinks, then moved to the main dining room for an excellent meal. With a pleasing background of music played by a small string ensemble, the conversation centered on Philip's visit and what he thought of the medical facilities he'd seen, in Minnesota generally and Minneapolis in particular.

"First let me say that you Americans are the most friendly and hospitable people I've ever met in my life. I felt awful not being able to join you for the past few evenings but I simply had to study. Hope you weren't offended. The Mayo Clinic was great but the Minneapolis unit under Dr. Owen Wangensteen was even better."

The conversation continued, back and forth, and Philip was once again impressed with the genuine warmth of these people. Could Canadians ever show a similar level of hospitality in similar circumstances? The answer, he knew, was No, even at the level of major hospital centers (except when the visitor had a special relationship with one or more members of the medical staff).

Shortly before midnight the enjoyable evening drew to a close and the bandleader announced, "We shall now play 'When Irish eyes are smiling' in honor of Dr. Boston's wife who is back in Canada." Everyone applauded and Philip was quite touched, even if they couldn't get his name right.

CHAPTER 22

1949 cont'd–Retrospective

The last few days in Vanwey were associated with a surprising level of nostalgia. There were so many goodbyes to so many friends, so many farewell parties and so many gifts. The Sisters of Ste. Cecilia were devastated by the news of their imminent departure.

"How can we ever get on without you, Dr. Bosnar?" Sister Claudia protested with tears running down her broad cheeks.

"But Sister, it isn't as if you haven't known for weeks that we'd be leaving."

"I only knew that you MIGHT leave, and that gave me room to hope and pray you might stay after all."

"Time marches on for all of us, Sister, and nobody is indispensable. You'll get along just fine after I've gone."

"We'll never forget you, Dr. Bosnar, and all you've done for our hospital."

"You'd be surprised. If I come back for a visit to this hospital in a few years, they may ask who I am and how I spell my name."

"That's impossible. We'll always remember you and your lovely wife, and we'll certainly miss those beautiful children of yours."

Philip and Patricia found themselves reminiscing every evening, after the children had gone to bed. First, there were the memorable incidents, both amusing and sad.

***

There was the time when Philip was called out to make a housecall on Jim Quayle, who phoned to say he thought he was having a heart attack. It was a few days before Christmas and the weather had been dreadful. The snow was falling steadily and the wind was rising toward blizzard conditions.

Philip liked Big Jim except for his one failing: he was a confirmed hypochondriac and was always phoning his favorite doctor to make unnecessary housecalls. Up to the time Mrs. Quayle died following a stroke, it was she who was the one who phoned for housecalls, only one of which proved to be necessary – the final one. When the situation started getting out of hand, Philip informed his recalcitrant patient that henceforth his fee for housecalls would be doubled. On each such occasion the culprit would show his remorse.

"You're absolutely right, Doc," he'd confess, "you've never charged me enough anyway," by way of a mea culpa.

"Why don't you get yourself another doctor, Jim?"

"I couldn't do that, Doc, and you can charge me as much as you like."

"That's not the point, my friend. I simply can't keep on making these unnecessary housecalls."

Nothing had worked, however, no matter how much he charged. The Quayles were well off and money was no problem. Driving to the large Quayle home on this miserable night was no easy matter and Dr. Bosnar wasn't in a good mood when he arrived.

"Come on in, Doc. The door isn't locked."

The patient's voice was loud and lusty, and his appearance, sitting comfortably by the fire in his bright red dressing gown, was one of exuberant good health. When Philip questioned and then examined his patient, it was obvious that his symptoms, if any, were due to overindulgence at the dinner table. Philip proceeded to take him to task in the strongest possible terms, and pulled no punches.

"This is positively the last time. Make no mistake."

He was seething as he got ready to leave.

"Oh, by the way," Big Jim's hearty voice sang out as Philip was about to open the front door, "there's something for you by the coat rack. Be sure to take it with you."

It was a case of Ne Plus Ultra Scotch Whisky and Philip felt about two inches tall. He read the card: **'A Merry Christmas to my favorite doctor and friend. Sorry for all the trouble I've been.'** The sound of a soft chuckle from the incorrigible Jim Quayle did nothing to make him feel any better.

***

Then, there was the classic example of Judge Tompkins' notorious absentmindedness. He was driving to Regina in late January on some legal business and agreed to drive three of Vanwey's finest ladies to a church committee meeting in the Capital City. He was halfway there when, in a moment of distraction, he skidded his car into some heavy snow on the side of the road. His three passengers put their backs into the task confronting them and soon had the good judge free to continue his journey.

The rest of the trip was uneventful, as was the return journey two days later. It was only then that His Honor was reminded he'd left these three good women stranded on the highway in their Sunday finest, madder than wet hens. By the grace of God, they were picked up an hour later by a good Samaritan and driven on to their destination.

***

Jock and Doris McTeague were blessed with three good-looking and very marriageable daughters. The youngest, Sylvia, was a flashing-eyed raven-haired beauty, innocently flirtatious and adored by all who knew her. She was always full of laughter and a joy to her parents and friends. When she reached the age of twenty, she was wooed and won by a handsome navy lieutenant.

Charlie Prentice first came to Vanwey as part of a team of young oil geologists surveying the area for some of the largest oil companies in North America. The young scientists became good friends of Phil and Patty and were often entertained at their home, along with their wives or lady-friends. There were lunches and informal dinners, and the Bosnars were soon receiving confidential advice to put whatever spare cash they had into purchasing local farmland areas:

those designated as most promising for oil exploration. Unfortunately, Phil and Patty hadn't the money for such a speculation at that time and were unwilling to borrow from the bank.

Everyone was delighted when Sylvia McTeague and Charlie Prentice were wed, and the reception at her parents' home was a great occasion. The bride's bubbling good humor was a perfect counterpoint to the groom's serious, scientific nature and the Bosnars thought this might be a perfect union.

The couple were divinely happy for the first year, until one day Sylvia complained of a headache and weakness in her right arm. Within twenty-four hours she was dead, and the diagnosis was 'Fulminating Polio'. Vanwey was shocked into total disbelief and Philip felt a special rage, since he knew that research teams were on the verge of a breakthrough in the war against this dread destroyer of human limb and life.

Prentice joined the Canadian navy and went on to make his own discoveries in the saving of human lives, by his researches into radar and the degaussing of enemy magnetic mines. He even got Philip to join him in thermocouple experiments aimed at diagnosing hidden malignancy, by readings of temperature abnormalities deep inside body tissues.

***

1946-48 had seen a remarkable exodus of their friends from Vanwey. With the arrival of a socialist C.C.F. government in the province, George Freikopf turned his company over to the socialists as he had no intention of trying to run his business their way. He would be a free enterprise capitalist to the very end and moved to Edmonton, where he set up a natural gas company with the aid of American friends who helped put up the money. It was typical of George that he'd already started to plan for the transition since the end of the war, and by 1949 the company was already a growing success story.

Following the Vanwey power company's dissolution, the Steffansons moved to Saskatoon, where Alf started an upholstery business. But this was unsuccessful so they moved once again, this time to Edwardia, where Alf resumed his true profession of accountancy. The Steffanson's latest move would be a boon for the Bosnars, who sorely missed their close friends and were looking forward to a reunion with great anticipation.

Angus and Gladys Jackson had also moved to Edwardia, where they set up a small hardware store in one of the new suburbs, and they'd help to make Phil and Patty feel at home.

Another family that had moved out to Edwardia was the Torwalds. He was Danish in origin and she was a Scottish 'blueblood' related to the famed General Mackintosh of the Burma campaign. Henry Torwald was a civil engineer with headquarters in Vanwey and when his firm was nationalized by the C.C.Fs he decided it was time to make his move. There were a few more Vanwey families who decided to move to Edwardia at this time and it was obvious that the Bosnars weren't destined to die of loneliness in their new abode.

Prior to the departure of the Freikopfs to Edmonton, George bequeathed the care and use of his favorite thoroughbred filly to Patty, of whom he was extremely fond. Patty was a superb rider and had almost grown up on horseback as a child in semirural Ireland; in addition, she looked stunning in her Jodhpurs. Phil, on the other hand, was a complete novice when it came to surviving on the back of a horse – a fact of which the animal was invariably aware.

The first time the two of them went riding together, he was able to put on a brave front, and finished his ride at an impromptu gallop to the barn, from which he appeared to arrive unscathed. What he concealed was the painful fact that both his ankles were skinned by stirrups which were far too large. It took a couple of weeks before he was able to ride again with only moderate pain, but this time he wore the right stirrups and conducted himself like a veteran horseman, or at least he thought so.

***

On several occasions, he and Patty were accompanied by a third rider who was even more of a novice than Philip. He was Hugo Peyton, midwestern representative of Ingram and Bell. He was a hale and hearty young man, always full of fun and blessed with an infectious uproarious laugh. The Bosnars always looked forward to his monthly arrival from Winnipeg, and usually entertained him at their home. The children loved him and he seemed to fill the house with happy laughter.

Phil and Patty were overjoyed when he told them he'd met the girl of his dreams and planned to get married in late summer. They begged him to bring her along the next time around. But there was no next time around. The shocking news reached them a short time later that Hughie had killed himself: no details, no reason given. The Bosnar family was shocked and grief-stricken and their agonized question of "Why?" was never answered. Had his beloved cooled toward him? Had he made a shattering discovery about her or about himself? Had there been religious or family incompatibilities? These and other scenarios were endlessly conjectured without resolution, and only time would soften the nagging and unanswered questions.

***

The most recent incident was the 'Great Fire'. Ten days prior to their projected departure from Vanwey, Philip was seeing a few patients in his afternoon office and was gratified there weren't too many for him to examine. His equanimity was shattered by the sudden wail of a passing fire engine, soon followed by the Firechief's red Buick limousine. Someone outside called out, "Where's the fire?" and someone else replied, "It's the Bosnar house." Philip controlled his panic, excused himself to the waiting patients and drove straight home. He had to park nearly a block from his house because of the crowds. It seemed that most of Vanwey's population had come to see the fire, and if possible, explore the interior of the Bosnar household. They were soon dispersed by the Firechief, one of Philip's most loyal patients, who told them to go home as it was only a false alarm.

Patty had gone over to have lunch with Ruth Steffanson, leaving a roast in the oven on low heat. Some of the beef juice must have splashed onto the wall of the oven, producing a cloud of thick smoke that soon filled the kitchen. As soon as the children noticed this, Jamie had the presence of mind to call the Fire Department before rushing his little sister out of the house. At the same time, Patty heard the sirens and phoned the central exchange to find out where the fire was. When she was told, she rushed over to her home but couldn't get through because of the curious mob. She and Philip managed to fight their way to the front door at just about the same time, and were greatly relieved that things weren't worse. They felt extremely proud of their children, especially their enterprising son.

A few days later, at the weekly Rotary luncheon, there was a special farewell ceremony, with good luck wishes from Philip's fellow members and he was gratified to find Premier Tommy Douglas at his table. He was there as guest speaker and was kind enough to add a few complimentary remarks of his own about the departing member. As the piece de resistance of the meeting and to the appreciative laughter of the audience, the Firechief made his own special presentation to Dr. Bosnar, "to remind you of your narrow escape from such a disastrous conflagration." It was a miniature firetruck, and a grinning Philip accepted it with profuse thanks on behalf of his quick-thinking young son.

As far as Patty was concerned, she was glad there was no damage to the stove or kitchen, but her beautiful roast was a total loss after its losing encounter with the fire extinguisher.

***

Another favorite subject for reminiscences was in the realm of spectacular and unusual cases which Philip had encountered during the past ten years. Patty often asked why he didn't publish these cases.

"I could never rush into print with isolated cases," he explained. "You see, as far as I am concerned, unless one is prepared to present and analyze a large series of similar cases it simply becomes an interesting anecdote at best and an ego trip at worst. It's too bad that a great deal of what's published in the medical journals is based on inadequate numbers, backed up with a hodge-podge of assorted graphs, and colored by the prejudices of the author. Only in a major university hospital setting is it possible to have the concentrated volume on which to base reliable statistics and conclusions."

Nevertheless, Philip liked discussing some of his more interesting cases with his medical friends.

One of the most fascinating was a young woman, Mrs. D, weighing 90 lbs, married for six years, childless, and increasingly ill for the past two years. The diagnosis was a right-sided *Pyonephrosis* (a blocked kidney filled with pus). X-ray investigations proved that she had an obstruction to the outflow of urine, producing a gross dilatation of the kidney. Secondary infection had converted this distended organ into a veritable abscess.

The symptoms were severe: backache, progressive loss of weight, weakness, night sweats and intermittent attacks of fever and chills. She had a history of tuberculosis in childhood with kidney and gland involvement, but there had been no sign of active TB for many years. There was no evidence of any kidney function on the right side but the left kidney was entirely normal, so that surgery to remove the infected kidney was a feasible method of dealing with the problem.

The operation, which was conducted through the customary loin incision, was a difficult one but went fairly smoothly. There was only one slight hitch: it was necessary to excise a small adherent area of *Peritoneum* (the lining of the abdominal cavity and the intestinal coating), with the possibility of infective contamination producing a dangerous peritonitis.

As soon as the operation was over, Philip contacted R.C.A.F. medical headquarters in

Ottawa. Penicillin, a new antibiotic which wasn't yet generally available, had been used on the war fronts to control and combat infection in grossly contaminated wounds, with excellent results.

Two days later, the magical antibacterial agent arrived in Vanwey by R.C.A.F. plane, but not before the patient was having the first severe chills and fever. Fortunately she made a smooth recovery thereafter and suffered no toxic side effects (such as those reported in many cases with this new agent). After twelve months, she was strong and healthy, weighed a staggering 130 lbs and gave birth to her first child, a bouncing baby girl. Her husband was ecstatic and they named the girl Philippa.

***

Then there was the case of Mr. T, a heavyset man in his forties who worked for the city council. He could be seen regularly, struggling along Mainstreet as he swung his heavy, useless right leg in an arc with each painful step. He'd broken his right thigh just below the hip joint during a football game, at the age of eighteen. The fracture failed to heal and he was sent to Regina, where they operated and put in a metal device. Ordinarily, this might have worked well, but the wound became infected and he developed Osteomyelitis (a severe infection and destruction of bone). Several more operations followed: in Regina, Winnipeg and finally in the Mayo Clinic, but all to no avail. He now came to Dr. Bosnar to see if anything more could be done.

The entire right lower limb had become quite useless and there were severe contractures of the muscles around the hip, knee and ankle. The knee was almost fixed in flexion and was a source of increasing pain. The patient had begged to have his leg removed and replaced with an artificial limb but was consistently advised against it. There was the danger of infection flaring up once again, he was told, and fitting a suitable prosthesis would be difficult and probably unsuccessful.

Philip couldn't agree with this negative assessment. First of all, infection was not all that likely and could be handled by the new miracle antibiotics. Second, the affected limb was totally useless and more of a painful burden to its owner with each passing year. Third, with the advances in prosthetic engineering there was no reason why a new 'tilting table' type of artificial limb shouldn't work. Even at its worst, it would be better than the patient's present unfortunate state.

Since this was the type of surgery best performed from both the front and the back, the fully anesthetized patient was placed on his side and the right lower limb was suspended at an angle of thirty degrees from the vertical axis. Amputation was carried out just below the actual hip joint, through healthy bone, and a large flap of muscle, soft tissues, fat and skin, was carried forward to provide a good thick cover for the bone and enable the patient to sit comfortably into the top of the tilting table prosthesis.

Mr. T. was made of pretty stern stuff and enjoyed an excellent recovery with minimal complaint. Instead of the usual post-amputation depression he was positively upbeat. Within six months he was managing with crutches and within a year he was walking remarkably well with just a cane. As for pain, it became a distant memory, much to the delight of patient and surgeon alike.

***

Philip's recollection of his most memorable cases seemed to expand with each description, and he began to realize that ten years in a small prairie town hadn't been a waste of time but a rich learning and creative experience. Even at a less elite level there had been cases he would always remember as stepping stones in his professional growth. There was the time he acquired a deep interest in the painful and incapacitating condition known as Sciatica. He found several articles that suggested the use of 'Caudal Blocks' in the management of such cases. The caudal canal could be entered through a notch just above the tailbone, and it led to the spinal space outside the *'Dura'*, (a thick layer that protects the spinal fluid compartment). An injection into this canal, of dilute Novocain in a quantity of saline, often resulted in partial or complete relief of the pain. As a rule, a total of three injections were necessary to obtain longlasting relief.

Practice made perfect and Philip soon learned to be proficient in this art. More importantly, he enjoyed the triumph of seeing Mr. W, a salesman for surgical supplies, play eighteen holes of golf, a game he'd been unable to play for the past five years because of his affliction. Thus, when Hingson and Hastings in the U.S.A. reported their technique of 'Transcaudal Anesthesia' for obstetrical delivery, Dr. Bosnar was ready, willing and able. The only snag was that he'd been steadily turning over his obstetrics to Alvin Masters. He decided to restrict his obstetrics to transcaudals, on special request from the patient, and most came from closest friends, doctors' wives and nurses.

It was very time-consuming but highly rewarding. The mothers enjoyed a high degree of comfort and were spared all of the worst pains of delivery. But Philip had to stay close by at all times, to make sure that the local anesthesia didn't spill over into the spinal fluid canal. The babies, too, seemed to enter the outside world in a more vigorous state: pink and alert, and with immediate lusty cries of protest at being ejected from the comfort of a warm fluid environment.

***

Things were likely to be quite different in Edwardia. There would be no more obstetrics of any kind, and perhaps (God forbid!) even gynecology, at which he was particularly experienced and adept. With the alarming growth of each new subspecialty – urology, orthopedics, proctology, plastic surgery and more – perhaps general surgery was ultimately destined to become confined to surgical conditions of the navel. It seemed that the old aphorism, about those who got to know more and more about less and less, might become a fact at some future time, and Philip shuddered at the thought.

He had developed virtually every facet of 'General' surgery since his first internship, and felt at home from the cranium above to the toes below. Was all this to be wasted? He devoutly hoped not. At least, he would do everything in his power to prevent it, but not to block the development of subspecialties per se. In his professional philosophy, the two need not be mutually exclusive, any more than the theory of evolution and belief in a Creator. The secret was to find a plane of ideas that were coexistent rather than conflicting.

Another possibility to be considered was that of moving into new and challenging branches of operative surgery, such as the advancing field of cardiovascular surgery, in which he'd become increasingly interested in recent years. One thing was certain and that was how much he looked forward to working with John Kinsley. Not only was John a capable and innovative surgeon but he was a brilliant authority on medical history, particularly as it pertained to advances in surgery. Philip knew he'd enjoy the weekly 'Ward Rounds', in which there would be a discussion of interesting cases and topics by members of the staff, with the housemen in attendance. There would be cut and thrust debates, in which ones knowledge or ignorance were soon exposed and to stringent peer review. As John had carefully pointed out to him the last time they met, "Here's where they separate the men from the boys."

***

Much had changed in southern Saskatchewan since their arrival in the summer of 1939. The days of the awful droughts of the 'Hungry Thirties' were gone. Decrepit farm buildings with unpainted exteriors were being renovated and freshly painted. Rusting farm machinery and broken down cars were being replaced by shiny new combines and bright new Cadillacs. Instead of getting paid in eggs, chickens and loads of grain, he was now paid cash from thick rolls of bills which newly prosperous farmers took from their pockets. It was no longer necessary to depend on American patients for the only reliable source of income.

As for the landscape, instead of large areas of grassland converted to parched, cracked earth or sand-dune, there were recurrent floods in the great valley south of the town – a result of heavy rainfalls. It seemed the Bosnars were leaving Vanwey just as prosperity was coming around the corner. The second decade of their Canadian experience was now upon them. A new life and new worlds to conquer.

Patty and the children were fully ready to meet the challenge ahead, BUT WAS HE?

Book Two

Castle Gardens

CHAPTER 23

1916

Philip Bosnar's recollections of this time and its thrilling danger were sketchy at best and – like so many of his memories – were rounded out by matters revealed long after the facts. It is only in this fashion that memories become a coherent narrative and make sense of events which, at the time of occurrence, may seem senseless or bewildering. Yet, for all that, it is remarkable how much the constantly aging brain permits one to snatch fragments of memory from the hazy amnesic past, like torches of light in a dense fog.

Eventually, as such lights are added, the entire scene becomes illuminated and the individual pictures assemble themselves into one continuous happening. Three to four years old from an adult perspective seems barely out of infancy. To the developing mind of a little child it is a wonderland of new discoveries, and it provides the brilliant pieces of a later and inevitable mature mosaic. What were some of these earliest remembered discoveries in the life of Philip Bosnar?

There was shouting in the streets, people were running, women were crying and his parents tried to keep him and his sister calm. He really couldn't understand what all the excitement was about but could hear snatches of talk about 'zeppelins' and air-raids. From the way everyone was pointing up to the sky it became apparent that the large, silvery gray, elongated and balloon-like contraption above them, droning along in leisurely fashion, was the object of all this excitement.

The occasional booming sound followed by rising plumes of smoke must be the air raid, and in answer to his persistent questions, his know-it-all older sister informed him that they were being bombed by the Kaiser's airships. The family's descent from the top floor of number 13 Grantham Square was fast but orderly, from the moment the warning siren started its up and down incessant wailing. With the same orderly speed, but without the slightest panic, they all made their way to the underground platform of Stepney Green subway station.

They stayed there, with the crowds milling around them, until the steady sound of the 'All Clear' came faintly down to their level and he was sorry to learn the excitement was all over. After all, this was as close as small children like him could get to the thrills and dangers of the Great War. How he envied the dashing soldiers with their khaki uniforms and shining guns: smiling heroes who'd have all the fun of beating the enemy and winning the war for the Bosnar family, for England and Empire!

They got back home about an hour later and his bladder contents were rescued from accidental release by the speed with which he rushed out to the W.C. facilities behind the back of the house. He was quite happy to be living in the family's crowded quarters on the top two floors of the house, but detested having to run the gauntlet of the Kelmans sitting around the kitchen table as he made his way to the outdoor lavatory, cold and draughty in the winter, hot and abuzz with insect life in the summer.

He always had the impression that the Kelmans were timing him, and this thought never helped very much when he was faced with occasional digestive upsets of either rapid or sluggish bowel activity. He felt that good manners ought to be observed by the Kelmans by moving from the kitchen to another room at such times, rather than remaining as the focus of his embarrassment. At least he had to give them credit of not talking to him on his way to and from his essential transits. Despite the fact that such an arrangement must have been a constant source of irritation to his parents, he never heard a single word of complaint, not even from Pauline, who insisted that they'd soon be moving. As it happened, she was right, but not quite in the way she thought.

It was that cigar-shaped zeppelin which convinced his Dad the only safety for his family was to get them out of London. That was why, in early 1917, he found himself transplanted to a place called Manchester, where people talked in a funny way. Mum and Pauline came with him, but Dad stayed behind where he had his work to look after.

(Rafael Bosnar had completed a course of studies at the prestigious Timpson School of Cutting and Designing and was starting to instruct his own pupils privately. Lately, the number of pupils was growing week by week, and although this kept him increasingly away from home, it was proving a definite blessing to the restricted family coffers.)

The place where Philip stayed in Manchester, along with Pauline and his Mum, was a pleasant roomy three-storey house in a quiet residential area, away from the city center. The family with whom they stayed, the Danzigs, were jolly and friendly and made them feel welcome. Most important, their 7-year-old son, Harry, was a perfect playmate for him and never treated him like a baby. Harry's sister was nine years old and she and Pauline got along famously. More to the point, they left the two boys alone to their own devices.

Mr. Danzig was in the window-blind business, and there were always dozens of imperfect Venetian blinds kept in a storage room on the top floor. That was where Philip and his new friend played out their imaginary tales of derring-do. Harry had an inexhaustible imagination and was able to construct scenarios of castles, dragons and armored knights, with hair-raising conflicts and courageous rescues. His only equipment for these mighty epics was the pile of slatted window-blinds which he could fashion, or so it seemed, into a thousand shapes of fantasy, with a running narrative derived from stories he'd heard and loved. Little did Philip Bosnar realize at the time that these graphic scenes were the true precursor of his later infatuation with motion pictures and the twentieth century era of vicarious experience and adventure.

It has generally been assumed that romantic love can only invade the heart and senses when we are old enough to be ready for consummation, but that is a great untruth. In the first place, it depends on an accurate understanding and definition of the range of consummation. In Philip Bosnar's case it was simply a total enslavement to the beautiful creature who was his kindergarten teacher during these wondrous days.

This fair lady, with her nut-brown hair that felt like silk and eyes the color of the deepest sea, seemed to return the deep affection he felt for her, and when she conveyed him around the streets of Manchester, pointing out each place of interest, he experienced a sense of safety and delight akin to that which he'd only felt in his mother's embrace. The sensation of her arms around him and the spontaneous way she cuddled him up against her was total consummation for him, and this heavenly bliss represented his very first affair of the heart.

(The memory of those golden days would stay with him forever, and it was only much later that he realized his feeling for this divine maiden was reciprocated by her own love for a funny little boy: one so responsive to her emotional need for the love of children.)

The days passed rapidly and were filled with happiness. He marveled at the versatile mind and body of his friend Harry, who could twist himself into any shape, jump like a circus acrobat and climb like a monkey. The war seemed far away and the only real excitement came from the increasingly complex games originating in the inventive mind of his friend: using the old window blinds as if they were the walls and roofs of buildings, the girders of bridges or the bodies of warships and planes.

Into their world of make-belief came the sudden cold reality of crime. It was a series of burglaries in their area that – according to the gossip of the grown-ups – was keeping the police baffled and the residents very nervous. There were even front page headlines in the local newspapers, which Mr. Danzig read out to them daily: 'Cat Burglar Puzzles Police For Third Week'. The full story described the cat burglar as having a poor taste in jewelry, often leaving expensive items and picking up worthless gaudy baubles instead.

One dark and dismal day there was considerable turmoil and confusion in the Danzig household. A great deal of whispering was going on between the grown-ups and everyone seemed upset. The situation reached its climax with the arrival of the police and pretty soon the whole truth came out. Mrs. Danzig had become more and more suspicious over the past few days. She knew how fond her little boy was of anything that looked pretty, like brooches, rings, watches, and bracelets, and how he loved to play with his mother's collection of inexpensive jewelry, the flashier the better. When she added this fact to his acrobatic agility, she decided to search his 'treasure box,' always considered off limits to anyone else. What she found made her call her husband, who came home immediately and called the police. Harry owned up right away and said the whole thing was a lark, but once he started it was too exciting to stop.

In a way, it was a good thing for him to be caught by his own mother, at least that's what Philip's Mum said, since who knows what might have happened if he'd been caught by anyone else. Fortunately, because of Harry's age, the police settled for "a darned good spanking" by Mr. Danzig and a promise by both parents that they'd keep him under stricter control. For the next fortnight, Harry's sister and Pauline were deeply shocked and treated him like a murderer, and then the whole affair blew over.

Philip had to admit that this episode, so traumatic to the others, in no way affected his own friendship with the young criminal, and sad to say, even made him admire his chum all the more. (*He often wondered, long after that fateful day, whether Harry Danzig eventually became an international jewel thief, so glamorized in the movies by such as Donald Niven and Cary Grant. Or did he, instead, become a giant of industry, which seemed to require similar inborn talents, and become a national figure with a changed name: perhaps Lord Danes of Manchester.*)

There was one other incident in this period of his life that remained indelibly in his memory, and he never failed to marvel at the strange coincidence. From all that was being said around the house, at kindergarten and in the streets, the war was coming to an end and the soldiers were coming home. In a large field behind the Danzig house there was now considerable activity: the entire grassy area was occupied by American soldiers. They looked so much more relaxed and so untidy by comparison with the British soldiers. Most of the time, they were engaged in lining up to be counted, doing simple drills or just marching to the tune of their brass band. Once in a while, there was a game of something that looked like the English game of rounders, but wasn't. There was even an occasional boxing match that he enjoyed very much, but serious fights sometimes broke out, in which they nearly all seemed to join. Everyone would strike out in all directions and some would be badly hurt, until loud whistles blew and they all stopped.

One morning after breakfast, his Mum was looking out of the kitchen window when she suddenly got very excited and shouted, "That's my brother Jack, I'd know him anywhere!"

"But it must be ages since you last saw him, Klara."

"That's true but I had photos of him a couple of months ago, showing him in uniform, and I'm sure it's him."

Nothing could stop her now, and she went straight over to the tent area at the far end of the field, where she was allowed to see the officer in charge. According to her later account, the officer confirmed that there was indeed a Sergeant Jack Stransky in his outfit, and what followed was a wild and happy reunion, with lots of disbelief, laughter and tears.

As for Philip, it was marvelous to have a real live uncle, and in the American army no less: an uncle who now spoiled him with presents and took him everywhere, whenever he had some free time. Philip's favorite place was the fairground, and in addition to the rides, he loved the balloons and what his uncle called "cotton candy." His esteemed American relative wasn't invariably rewarded for his marvelous generosity and patience while acceding to his nephew's every new request. This was completely contrary to Philip's upbringing in London, but for his part, Sergeant Stransky was enjoying his new role as the fabulous uncle from across the sea.

Occasionally, when the excitement of the rides, food and drinks were too much, and when his uncle had the misfortune to be carrying him, the little boy's full bladder failed its trained continence. Sometimes, (dare he confess?) the disaster was even greater and his unfortunate benefactor was forced to cope with the ungodly mess. Philip knew he'd carry his guilt for a long long time!

By the time his poorly rewarded American hero left, the endless war was over; and after the wild city celebrations, the cheering in the streets and parties in the homes, it was time for him to return to London and home, along with his Mum and sister Pauline. His Dad, who'd only seen them once a month when he came up to Manchester by train, greeted them at the railway station and helped them with their luggage. They took the underground back to Stepney Green and got a taxi to Grantham Square, not to number 13 but to number 12, where his Dad had rented the entire house for the four of them! He was in great form and seemed overjoyed to have them all back together again, with no more zeppelins trying to drop bombs on them.

Philip was glad to learn that Great Britain had not only beaten the wicked old Kaiser, but forced him to go to a place in Holland called Exile, probably a special prison for starting the war. When he learned what Exile meant, and that it wasn't a prison, he marveled at the amazing kindness and forgiveness of the British monarch and began to collect pictures of George the Fifth and Queen Mary to pin on the wall above his bunk. No wonder they had so great an Empire, with such decent and kind-hearted rulers on the royal throne!

CHAPTER 24

1949-50

The trip to the west coast was along the same route they'd taken two years earlier, and proved even more enjoyable on this occasion. It wasn't only that they knew what to seek and where to linger for full immersion in the artistry of nature all around them. It was that Jamie and Florian now shared their appreciation and behaved like seasoned travellers. As though emulating their example, their black and white cocker spaniel, Whiskers, never gave them a moment's trouble. He showed canine maturity by curbing his natural functions until the mandatory gas-station stops. As for the children, they were so excited throughout the trip that they were ready for bed as soon as they pulled up at their motel each evening, after ten hours on the road.

Breakfast time was 7.30 each morning, a tasty and substantial meal that would get them off to a good start for the day. A light lunch was timed for about noon, coinciding with a gasoline fill-up, and dinner was eaten at leisure about an hour before checking in at the motel of their choice. Whiskers' appetite was never overlooked. In addition to his regular dog food and water, there was always a treat from the doggie bag, specially saved for him after every meal.

As before, they stopped overnight at Spokane before their final run into British Columbia. Then they took their time to absorb the matchless grandeur and awesome heights of Steven's Pass, as they turned northwards into the Cascade Range before emerging onto the coastal plain.

It was at this stage of the journey that little Florian blossomed forth with the unmistakable blistered eruption of chicken-pox, and the family held a serious council of war. It was just possible the immigration officials at Blaine might insist on a quarantine period before permitting their reentry into Canada, although neither parent was sure about this tricky point.

After wrestling with his conscience, Philip decided to bend the truth if questioned and call it an allergic rash. He covered the telltale vesicles with calamine lotion from their first aid kit, both to alleviate the itching and support the deception. As it happened, when they got to the border, the busy officials on the Canadian side paid no attention to the little girl's camouflaged rash and they all breathed more easily.

The ferry ride to Edwardia was a wonderful thrill for the children, and they "oohed" and "aahed" at each passing ship and the ever-changing shore lines of the Middle Gulf Islands. It was as though their youthful imaginations were fired by this thrilling maritime experience, so different from that of their prairie birthplace and its arid plains.

For the moment, it was difficult to feel nostalgic about summer's grainfields stretching to distant horizons, or winter's snowy vastness when Mother Nature converted the dusty land to a winter playground for the youngsters and their cavorting canine companion. Poor Whiskers! He had to remain in the car below deck, and from time to time either Phil or Patty went below, to make sure he was all right and comfort him so he wouldn't get too panicky at all the strange goings-on.

After debarkation, the drive into Edwardia was as picturesque as ever and the city just as photogenic as they remembered it. The children were delighted with their new home on Imperial Drive and Philip had to admit he loved it at first sight, even though quite a bit of work might be necessary before final completion.

The Tudor-styled house faced a scenic highway, where tourist buses drove by at regular intervals and individual tourist cars in a continuous stream, and the first rule was laid down right away. The front of the house was off limits to the children as a play area, and this was accepted without protest. There was ample play room behind the house, at the upper end of a sloping driveway to the garage. When they were a little more agile, they could climb the rocks with Whiskers, up to the rail-protected lookout. From that vantage point, they could enjoy a wide panorama of the city below and the Olympic mountains across the blue waters separating Canada and the United States.

A handsome wrought iron stairway led to a large oaken front door adorned with matching wrought iron fittings. It opened into a small entrance hall with a large living room on the right and a stairway to the upper level on the left. The living room had large picture windows through which sea and mountains were clearly visible, and led to an ample dining room off to the left, with a view of Mount Baker to the southeast. This magnificent cone could be seen to greatest advantage in the late afternoon, when the declining sun painted a pink glow on its snowy crown.

The kitchen led off the dining room to the back door, and the kitchen windows looked out at the garage and a large house at the far end of the winding driveway. The master bedroom was almost as large as the living room and looked out on the same view through its own picture window. Beyond this room, there was a superb den adjoining the driveway, with bushes concealing the house next door and ensuring ones own privacy. This, thought Philip, would make a perfect study, where he could turn to his books and journals with minimum interruption.

Upstairs, there were two bedrooms and a much larger room with a great view of the bay and seafront that stretched below and to the west, and beyond that, the city – all clean and gleaming. It looked like a duplicate Cote d'Azure, designed by and for Englishmen, just as they had created places like Eastbourne and Torquay on the Old Country's southern coast.

This large upstairs room would be the children's very own indoor play area. Later on, it would have a ballet practice-bar for Florian and a toy train set for Jamie (and his father). Until that time there would be dolls, a doll's house and a doll's wardrobe for the growing girl, and endless Meccano sets of increasing complexity for the growing boy (and his father, of course).

There were two bathrooms, one for the children's bedroom and one for the master bedroom. The basement was still unfinished but would make an excellent ping-pong room in due course. Surprisingly, because the house was built on a rocky incline, the basement windows gave a clear view of the roadway below and the sea and mountains beyond. Patty had ambitions to create a colorful rock garden extending from the front of the house around to the side: providing a flowering western perimeter to the driveway.

The whole family revelled in plans for the future of their precious new home. They were captivated by this wondrous city of inviting seashores, entrancing mountain views, British accents and British atmosphere. To complete the magic aura there were the famed hanging baskets through most of the city, filled with bouquets of fresh blossoms.

John Kinsley's office was located downtown, with good parking nearby. It was a four-storey office building, with a large drugstore on the ground floor, and it was located on Colonial Street, a main thoroughfare. An oldfashioned elevator with ornamental brass fittings took Philip to the third floor, and a short distance along the wide corridor he found number 304, with its frosted glass door bearing a newly painted sign announcing that these offices were occupied by John Kinsley F.R.C.S.C. and Philip Bosnar F.R.C.S.(C. & Eng.), Surgical Specialists.

The office nurse and general manager, Miss Eva Gregory, was a brusque veteran with gold-rimmed glasses and a loud nasal twang that Philip would find a bit annoying, although her efficiency and loyalty would prove beyond question. Miss Elsie Crocket, who remembered Dr. Bosnar from the rousing party at the Prince Albert Hotel, greeted him warmly and enquired about Patricia. She was responsible for looking after the books and the phoned-in appointments, and her breezy good humor were a perfect antidote to Nurse Gregory's astringent manner.

Philip soon fell into a daily routine that depended largely on the times of surgical bookings, most of which were at the Chelmsford hospital and started at 8 a.m. He enjoyed assisting his senior associate and learned a lot from his operative technique. It was obvious that Kinsley was highly regarded by the nurses and the local medical profession, and Philip was proud to be associated with him.

As soon as the first case was finished, the operative report written up and the postoperative orders given, Kinsley would settle down by the phone in the surgeon's lounge with a cup of coffee, and discuss the day's stock market situation with his broker. This routine was followed after almost every case and it was soon obvious that the financial market was a major part of his daily life.

After the morning list was over, they both donned their long white hospital coats and did their ward rounds together, usually accompanied by a head nurse. Kinsley discussed each case with Bosnar so that his patients and methods soon became familiar. From time to time, they went across town to St. Peters Hospital, whenever John had a postoperative case there or a patient to see in Emergency. At this smaller hospital, the atmosphere was polite and correct but not too cordial. It was obvious the Kinsley practice wasn't regarded as friendly to the Catholic institution, and Philip made up his mind to treat the two hospitals in a more evenhanded manner as time passed. This could only happen after he developed his own clientele, with his patients encouraged to make their own choice wherever possible. Of course, a lot would depend on the Sisters' ability to match their rival institution in providing the necessary facilities for his basic requirements.

As soon as the morning's hospital work was completed, the two surgeons would drive back to their office, and pick up any messages. They listened to Nurse Gregory's twanging recital of current information about patients to be seen that afternoon – in remarkably pertinent detail – and settled down to a lunch of sandwiches and coffee. After another priority session with his brokerage house, Kinsley would enter into a lively discussion with his colleague, who felt flattered by the respect shown for his knowledge and viewpoints. It was clear he was going to be treated as a professional equal, albeit a junior associate in the practice. The two men had a great deal in common, with similar professional attitudes in many ways, despite vast differences in their backgrounds of training and experience; and their opinions on Canadian politics, the Quebec question and world affairs in general, seemed remarkably parallel.

Despite a warm and happy family, with two little girls, a little boy and a loving wife, it seemed that in many ways John Kinsley was a lonely man, with few close friends. He enjoyed a wide range of acquaintances, especially among the social elite. His gracious Georgian home on fashionable Hargrave Terrace received frequent mention and photographic coverage in the social columns of the 'Edwardia Gazette', often with pictures of Margaret Kinsley and her delightful children. But it was evident that Mrs. Kinsley, although a matchless chatelaine, failed to provide her husband's restless intellect with the conversational challenges it craved, and Philip soon found himself invited by phone, two or three times a week, to "come over and have a drink."

These invitations always came around 9 o'clock in the evening and meant a series of intense discussions on a wide range of current affairs, of the Canadian medical profession in general and the Edwardia medical profession in particular. By the end of the first liberal scotch and soda, Mrs. Kinsley would put down her knitting, her crocheting or petit-point, excuse herself and go off to bed. Only then did Kinsley relax completely, refilling their glasses ("Just a very small one for me, John") and exploring his favorite subject – the history of surgery since ancient times.

The first few weeks were busy ones, especially for Patty. It seemed that all the energy and conscientious effort she'd formerly put into her career as a surgical nurse were now transferred into the even more difficult duties of wife and mother, in a new environment – albeit a delightful one. She chose the new furniture: essentially modern but not too severe, with an attractive white mahogany dining room set as the piece de resistance. As usual, her tastes coincided with Philip's, and he watched in admiration as their new house became a most attractive home. A large amount of good rich soil was ordered, along with a number of shrubs and rose bushes that would complement the developing rock garden and camouflage the oil-tank just below the basement windows.

The international news these days was far from encouraging. As Phil and Patty discussed the daily papers, radio broadcasts and magazine articles, they began to wonder who had really won the war. England was a political and economic shambles, and her worldwide empire was coming apart at the seams. Japan and West Germany were destined for a miraculous recovery, mainly due to the largesse of the U.S.A. and their own incredible industrious efforts.

Josef Stalin had succeeded in surrounding his vast nation with a buffer of 'friendly' satellite countries, all with Communist governments and all Moscow-dominated. Thus, the world was once again dangerously polarized and the West's new enemy would be Soviet Russia and its growing empire, while its new allies would be West Germany and Japan.

Canada was distancing itself from Great Britain, if not its monarchy, and seemed to be coming under the military and industrial dominance of the U.S.A.

Antisemitism was still alive and well, not only in the neofascist and neonazi pockets of western Europe and South America but in the U.S.S.R. and its subservient satellites as well.

There was one small gleam of hope. The General Assembly of The United Nations had at last got off its collective rear-end, and voted to recognize the new state of Israel, even if only by a close margin. It was only a year ago that Ben Gurion's government had proclaimed the birth of a new State of Israel and placed its infant life on the line.

The pro-Arab British Military Government of its Palestinian mandate had systematically disarmed the Jewish settlers prior to evacuating the troubled area. No self- respecting Arab country on Israel's borders could resist such a mouth-watering opportunity, and they all closed in for the kill.

The whole world knew that Jews are not fighters, but God decided that on this occasion the joke was on their enemies, and the attacking Arab forces were successfully repelled. Against such fierce determination, born within the decade on the blood-soaked streets of the Warsaw Ghetto, not even the crack Jordanian troops of Glubb Pasha could prevail.

Now, the new state of Israel had its latter-day prophets: Prime Minister Ben Gurion, a refugee from Poland, and President Chaim Weitzman, a Professor of Chemistry from England. Now, the new nation had its modern Maccabee, Moshe Dayan, an intrepid young military hero whose black eye-shade concealed his missing eye but not his smiling good looks. Now, the words of the Holocaust Remembrance, engraved in the hearts of its survivors, sprang to life on the embattled borders of the new State of Israel. NEVER AGAIN!

Philip Bosnar's surgical practice was continuing to grow, often by transfer from Kinsley, especially certain types of surgery Kinsley preferred to turn over to his new associate. These included thyroid surgery, prostatectomies and ventral hernias, and they would form a good initial base from which to build up a word-of-mouth surgical practice. Some of his patients wanted to "try the new surgeon in the Kinsley practice," even more so after a recommendation by the senior partner. There were also a few referrals from general practitioners, internists and pediatricians whom Philip had met: those who liked his manner and approach to surgical problems, and were willing to "give the new boy on the block an early break."

Within three months, the combined surgical practice had grown to the point where Kinsley and Bosnar assisted each other only on the most important operations, using the intern staff as assistants in the other cases. This afforded Philip an opportunity to instruct his young assistants in surgical anatomy, pathology and operative technique, as well as preoperative and postoperative management.

With expert anesthesia now available, and by virtue of technological advances in anesthetic machines and equipment, the scope of his surgery and associated safety factors was greatly augmented. At the same time, the O.R. nursing staff was becoming more accustomed to Dr. Bosnar's methods and preferences, and treated him less as a junior to the formidable Kinsley than an independent and experienced surgeon in his own right. The same was true on the wards, and Philip began to conduct more and more of his ward rounds on his own. It was simply a matter of the available time.

Even lunches were becoming less of an office ritual, and Philip found it unproductive to wait while his colleague conducted extensive financial transactions with his brokers over the phone. He found it simpler to drive home for his lunches. The hugs and kisses revitalized him and the meals were certainly tastier. Patty was happy to spend the time with her beloved and he was still able to get back for the afternoon office in good time. He was able to see John and have a quick chat before seeing their first patients.

Neither one hesitated to call in the other when there was an interesting clinical problem to discuss or an unusual feature to present. The evening invitations continued, but Philip was no longer reticent about voicing a polite refusal when it interfered with his own plans for that particular evening. He had no objection to accepting the majority of emergency calls for the practice, as these often provided the most interesting surgical cases. There were certain shibboleths and sacred cows, however, which he unhesitatingly kicked aside, not only in dealing with emergencies but also in handling routine cases on the wards.

The one that offended him most was that any kind of pain-relieving drugs should never be administered to a patient until a clearcut provisional diagnosis had been established. This inhumane rule was based on the hypothesis that such medication would mask the clinical features and obscure the diagnosis. His own experience was exactly the reverse. A patient thrashing around in pain, moaning and groaning or retching and vomiting, was hardly in an ideal state for accurate questioning and even less for careful and painstaking examination. On the contrary, once that patient was settled down by an appropriate analgesic or narcotic, perhaps an antinauseant or antiemetic, then he or she became much more amenable to providing a worthwhile history and submitting to a careful physical examination.

The procedural code he'd established for himself, and which he taught his nurses and interns, was in the form of two triads:-

First, treat the severe and painful symptoms.

Second, treat the condition (the underlying pathology).

Third. treat the individual, since patients differ in gender, age, occupation, pain tolerance and attitude, quite aside from underlying conditions such as diabetes, obesity, cardiovascular, pulmonary and renal deficits.

In treating the patient's surgical condition in hospital, there was a second triad:-

First, the total therapy by the surgeon in charge, including preoperative, operative, and postoperative.

Second, the management: such as consultation with other specialists and further investigations as indicated.

Third, the disposition: back to work, rehabilitation, referral to a special center, office or outpatient follow-up.

Despite the congenial atmosphere between the two surgeons, their growing friendship and increasing mutual respect, there was one disappointing issue that was becoming a point of growing contention between Kinsley and Bosnar. It was the continued G.P. nature of the practice. When Kinsley had first moved out to B.C. for his health, he found Edwardia a closed shop as far as getting surgical referrals. He was compelled to engage in general practice and rely mainly on that type of practice as a source of operative surgery. An additional bonus was landing the position of resident physician to the prestigious Prince Albert Hotel. This, in turn, led to the doubtful blessing of acquiring a foothold in high society circles, and with it, a 'carriage trade' general practice. These patients were unquestionably well-paying individuals with good connections, but often quite demanding, and Philip felt it humiliating for them to insist on housecalls from Kinsley at any time of the day or night, all too often on flimsy pretexts.

The nadir, from Philip's point of view, was reached one miserable, cold wet night in late November. John had finished a tough surgical case just an hour earlier and wasn't feeling too well. He begged Philip, who'd assisted him in the operation, to drive him to Killmarnock Castle, home of the legendary Duggan family and immortalized in the best-seller 'From Iron-mine to Peerage'. The reason for the nocturnal emergency visit was that the new 2-week-old baby grandson had failed to move his bowels on cue, and might need an enema. No sooner had one of Edwardia's finest surgical teams arrived than the infant heir to the Duggan legacy produced a monumental offering, bringing happy smiles of relief to the doting family and a refusal by the doctors – with the most insincere thanks – to stay for tea and cookies.

Philip had made repeated attempts to get John to turn over his general practice to genuine G.Ps. What might be lost in direct surgical cases would be more than compensated by an increase in referrals, once their 'firm' was recognized as a genuine specialist practice, by referral only. Appropriate cards of announcement could be sent out to the medical profession at large.

Following the case of the Duggan baby, Philip tried to press his advantage but to no avail, and the subject remained a closed issue thereafter. There was no doubt that some of the other surgeons in town were far busier, each with their own regular referral base, and John Kinsley hinted darkly that most of these fixed referral patterns were based on financial considerations.

"Do you mean fee-splitting?" Philip asked, directly.

"Yes, in one form or another," was John's cryptic reply but didn't elaborate further.

In due course Philip learned, largely as a result of scuttlebutt and some imprudent remarks in the surgeon's lounges, that sometimes the inducements might not be the crude splitting of surgical fees but special club memberships or specific patterns of social entertainment. Even the setting up of new doctors in practice, by financing office rentals or furnishings, in exchange for congenial professional arrangements, wasn't excluded. Philip took a twofold vow. First, he would never indulge in such tactics, no matter the professional cost. Second, if he were ever in a position of adequate authority he would do his utmost to abolish these unethical methods, at least in British Columbia.

By the summer of 1950, Philip's practice was well established and he was fairly busy with his surgical cases, hospital ward rounds – often repeated in the evening if there was a patient requiring critical care – and surgical meetings that were held once a week. These hospital meetings gave him an opportunity to sharpen his mind when matching knowledge, experience, logic and judgement with those of his professional peers.

By tacit agreement and good fortune, he was spared the necessity of handling general practice except in some emergency situations. He and John Kinsley were getting along well and worked together harmoniously, most noticeably in the O.R. Their surgical viewpoints were closely aligned, as were their opinions about what was right and what was wrong with the medical profession, especially in the field of general surgery.

As for family life, Phil and Patty were enjoying a widening circle of friends. Of these, the closest were still those they'd known in Vanwey, prairie dwellers who'd finally decided to come out to Edwardia and live the good life, not so much for themselves as for their children. Among their most recent friends from Vanwey were the Torwalds. Henry and Matilda Torwald, known to their friends as Hank and Mattie, had put all their savings into a small property on the northbound highway, across from the Oaklands golf course. Hank, who came from solid Danish stock, was a man of high intelligence but wasn't afraid of hard manual labor. He was building a small six-unit motel from the ground up and this meant that he, Mattie and their two small children were living in very rough bohemian style. Although they enjoyed few amenities of comfort, all four Torwalds exuded a happy optimism. Fortunately, Mattie – who was descended from a warrior family in the Scottish highlands – had a shrewd eye for commercial possibilities and a natural bent for figures and balance sheets.

Phil and Patty were confident the Torwalds would succeed, and to this end, the Bosnars were among their earliest paying customers. During their first week in Edwardia, while the contractors were putting finishing touches to the upper floor of their house and before all the furniture arrived, the Bosnar family stayed in one of the Torwalds' newly completed motel units, where the two families hobnobbed together and had lots of fun. They had come to know each other well during the last few years in Vanwey, where Hank, a well-trained civil engineer, worked successfully on various provincial projects. Despite strong socialist leanings, he'd found the new CCF government too stifling for his free-style methods and decided to leave for a new career on the west coast. Phil and Patty held the Torwalds in high esteem and never stopped admiring their industry and pioneer spirit.

The Steffanson family, too, had decided to come out to Vanwey. They purchased a charming bungalow along the Spurling inlet, with an excellent waterfront access to a recreational area located some four miles out of town. Alf was going to continue his accountancy on a freelance basis and Ruth intended to do part-time teaching some time in the future, whenever the necessity and opportunity arose.

As for the Jacksons, they opened up a bakery in the Truscott Bay suburban area and purchased a fine home in that district, about five miles east of the Bosnar domicile. It was an area in which the family could enjoy the new lifestyle of coastal British Columbia. Angus Jackson was a veritable fountain of knowledge about all pragmatic matters, or more precisely those gleaned from such academic journals as Popular Mechanics and Household Improvements. Gladys, on the other hand, took a personal interest in the individuals she met and knew, and she left no doubt about those she liked and those she didn't. She was very fond of both Phil and Patty and her affectionate regard was warmly reciprocated.

Dick Southerby was an Englishman through and through. This former Scotland yard detective had met his future wife Moira in Vanwey about six years ago. He was a Flight Lieutenant at the Commonwealth air base at the time, and she was the daughter of a senior officer in the R.C.M.P. They were good company and lively conversationalists who shared many interests with Phil and Patty, especially classical opera. It was the Southerbys, in fact, who first introduced them to the glorious voice of the Swedish tenor, Jussi Bjoerling, on English recordings. It was also Dick who suggested that Philip might get started on his proposed basement project and said he'd be happy to help in any way.

Another offer of such help came from Glen Parsons, a G.P. who sometimes sent surgical cases to the Kinsley-Bosnar practice, and he and his exuberant wife soon became close friends of the Bosnars. Their basement project commenced with a strategy meeting, over inaugural drinks with Parsons and Southerby, during which careful plans were laid, measurements taken and blueprints prepared. Philip was careful to conceal the fact that he was a hopelessly amateur carpenter, and was relying on the pride of his two helpers to provide much of the basic workmanship over the next few weeks.

He set up a couple of saw-horses and cut a number of measured pieces of knotty pine plywood with a sharpened handsaw, the others pitching in whenever he got a bit tired and decided it was time to replenish the drinks. The oil-burning furnace was covered with sheets of asbestos insulation and outer panels of plywood, and a hinged doorway provided access to the furnace for servicing and repairs. The plastered walls were covered with laminated panels of knotty pine, and these were nailed into place to the musical accompaniment of periodic hammer blows on sensitive thumbs. Philip's vocal lead in this chorale remained unchallenged.

He also set up the small room next to the main basement space as a workshop, where all the carpentry and sundry additional tools, paints, stains, varnishes and brushes were kept. Once in a while he would require an additional piece of two-by-four that was usually made available by Glen Parsons from his own elaborate workshop. On the first such occasion Glen told Philip to help himself.

"Molly and I will be out this evening so we'll leave the doors unlocked. I'll leave the lights on so you can go down the stairs and help yourself."

What he failed to tell Phil was that there would be unexpected company, When he entered the Parsons' basement there was a quiet patter of little feet, and looking up at him in steely alertness was the most perfect Doberman Pinscher he'd ever seen. There was menace in every line of this finely tuned instrument of destruction, and the intruder decided against any sudden moves or hasty retreat. Walking slowly and steadily across the floor, he murmured, "Good dog," "There's a good boy," and other inanities in a voice that remained steady enough to quell any canine suspicions.

He found the appropriate piece of lumber left for him and walked back with studied nonchalance. The dog followed him at a distance of no more than six inches, poised – or so it seemed to Phil's taut senses – for instant destruction at the slightest wrong move. It was only when he got back into his car that he was able to draw his first deep breath and restore his failing oxygen supply.

Even with the generous help of his two friends, it took three weeks to finish the project. He did all the staining and varnishing himself and Patty was very happy with the results. The rough ceiling with its pipes were concealed by textured white panels which brightened up the basement considerably. They were easy to put up and most of this was done by his two expert friends.

Next, he bought some inexpensive ivory and brown 6 by 6 inch floor tiles and some special floor cement. He drew up a simple pattern, with panels of alternating color, and started the final stages of the enterprise with Patty's enthusiastic approval. The unevenness of the rock-blasted floor, however, made the tile sealing process too difficult, and they were forced to yield this phase to professionals.

To complete the playroom, Phil and Patty went downtown to Eaton's sports department and purchased 'top-of- the-line' table tennis equipment. Within the first week after setting these up, they were playing some vigorous games and even the children were becoming interested in the indoor sport.

The heating system was a good one, even though the furnace seemed to have an insatiable thirst for oil, and there was a cosy feeling in the new playroom as the winds of winter pounded against the front of the house. At times, these winds – from the frigid white peaks across the waters – seemed intent on forcing their blasts through the sturdy windows of their basement haven.

As for the children, something seemed missing and they were beset by a strange restlessness, one that would only disappear with the passage of time. It was that strange absence, in their first British Columbia December, the absence of glorious, white, fluffy snow!

CHAPTER 25

1950-51

It was amazing how suddenly winter passed into an exquisite west coast spring. Philip's mentor in photography was Jason Shelby, a cardiologist who was also a superb photographer and taught him many tricks of the art. The second-hand Kodak Reflex 2 he sold Philip turned out to be a fine instrument and produced first-class transparencies. Shelby showed him how to compose his photographs so they were more than mere snapshots. He taught him to use back light effectively, and how to judge the skies for different effects of clouds, sunshine and shadow.

Ansco color film was the popular choice at the time, and Shelby initiated his willing pupil in the secrets of film processing without benefit of a darkroom. It was simply a matter of using a light-trap tank, going through the fourteen stages outlined in the printed instructions and making sure the water was kept in the right temperature range. By the time his thirty-seventh birthday came around, Philip had produced some good landscapes and seascapes, as well as memorable studies of Patty and the children relaxing in the front garden, with Whiskers trying to steal the show.

The practice was going well and Philip was gratified to find himself gaining recognition in both hospitals as an experienced and skilled surgeon in his own right; and no longer in the shadow of his senior partner. It was an ideal relationship in many ways, and the head nurse of the Chelmsford O.R. suite commented in her usual salty manner, "You two ornery devils make a goddamn good team." For most cases, however, it was more appropriate and less time-consuming to utilize the surgical interns as assistants, and Philip enjoyed the opportunity of training these eager young men in the art as well as the science of surgery.

He taught them to operate in a clean and bloodless field by appropriate attention to specific details: avoiding rough technique, controlling capillary ooze with firm pressure and applying fine arterial forceps to specific points of bleeding. He demonstrated the trick of one-handed knots and encouraged them to practice in their own quarters, using ordinary cotton and a pencil, until they became quite proficient. In addition, he instructed them in preoperative assessment of the surgical patient and early recognition of impending postoperative complications.

As far as the overall Kinsley-Bosnar practice was concerned, there was only one small fly in the ointment and it refused to stop buzzing. Nearly all the surgeons in the city had dropped their general practice and were seeing only referred patients. Several of Philip's growing number of friends in the profession asked him, point blank, why the hell he didn't do the same. Loyalty prevented him from revealing that his senior partner remained adamant in refusing to go along with the idea. Only Glen Parsons knew the truth and offered his prediction.

"I hate to say this, Phil, but I'm afraid you and John are bound to part company, maybe by next year. It's a bloody shame, because you're both good men and should be enjoying a much larger share of this town's surgery."

The idea of leaving John Kinsley was so abhorrent that Philip put the thought as far out of mind as he could, but it was always there to disturb him. Sooner or later, John was bound to come to grips with the situation and it could be his suggestion, and not Philip's, that they dissolve their partnership. If that ever happened, it must be on the most cordial possible terms and in no way detrimental to their mutual friendship and respect.

The summer of 1950 was a splendid one and the Bosnar family were having a marvelous time, especially the children. They loved to climb up the rocks above the back driveway with Whiskers; to the Sanchez lookout or the memorial for Sir Anthony Chelmsford. Sir Anthony was the founder of Edwardia Lumber Products (a dominant factor in the city's early prosperity) and a benefactor without parallel in all charitable enterprises. His grandson, Hector, was current president of the company and Chairman of the Board at the hospital bearing his proud family name.

As the weather got progressively warmer, Jamie and Florian loved to go down to the beach and play for hours in the sand and surf, but they were only permitted to go into the sea when accompanied by one or both parents. In any event, the water was usually much too cold, even in midsummer, for them to stay in for more than a few minutes. At other times, the whole family would go for long drives, either following the corrugated coastline to the southeast or northward over the spectacular Strongway Mountain highway as far as the little valley town of Groverdale.

As a rule, they stopped over at the Skyview Lodge and had a leisurely snack while watching the restaurant's proud new attraction: a large television set boasting a twelve inch screen. There, they could enjoy their 'Chicken in a Basket', with coca-cola for the children and hot tea for their parents, and watch Charlie Ruggles dispensing his whimsical philosophy from behind the counter of his country general store.

From time to time they spent a few days in Vancouver, a city that rivaled Hong Kong in its stunning panoramas, with the gleaming mountains of the Coastal Range as a backdrop beyond compare. They enjoyed its hotels, theaters and downtown shopping area, and thrilled to its vital tempo but had no wish to share it.

Another place they liked to visit was Seattle, a short and bumpy plane-trip away. It was not yet a beautiful city, but the people were warm and friendly and there was an exciting feeling of bustling prosperity. The restaurants were of the highest standard, both in food and interior decor, and the shopping was good and reasonably priced. As for the children, whenever they were left behind in Edwardia, they stayed with friends: either the Steffansons or the Torwalds. At both homes, they felt really welcome and could socialize with children of their own age group.

Patty felt her horizons expanding in the new and exciting environment, and her days were filled with getting the children off to school in the mornings, taking care of a rock garden that increased in splendor week by week, and reveling in the fine views from almost every window of the house. She looked forward to Philip's brief lunches at home and even more to the evening meals, when the family gathered together. At other times, she never felt alone as long as Whiskers was around, and there was always that magic link with her many friends: the telephone.

One of Philip's newest friends was Cliff Robins, a fine young fellow who'd been one of his favorite interns, always ready to assist in the O.R. and always displaying a sharp wit that added to his charm. He was an excellent athlete and tennis was his favorite game. Every Sunday morning, the two would meet at the Harvey Street public courts for an hour or two of singles, then join Patty and the children for a late breakfast. Cliff was always welcome in their home, and his unfailing good humor and sense of fun made him one of their favorite young men.

They really missed him when he embarked on a postgraduate course in pathology at the Vancouver General Hospital. In August, they learned of his forthcoming marriage to a young student-nurse in the pediatric department at the Vancouver General. Since Cliff was a Catholic, albeit non- practicing, and she was a Lutheran (also non-practicing), the young couple wisely decided on a quiet civil ceremony, thus avoiding family squabbles. Phil and Patty sent them a Spode place setting in their favorite pattern, after consulting Cliff's older sister on the choice. She lived with her widowed mother in Edwardia, and both approved of the gift but not the marriage.

It wasn't until the Christmas holidays that the Bosnars met the new bride. Melanie Robins was a jolly warmhearted girl of nineteen, a raven-haired brunette with flashing, dark brown 'come-hither' eyes. She was someone who could turn into quite a beauty once she got rid of her remaining baby fat. Even so, she already looked dangerously sexy in the eyes of other doctors' wives. Patty was no exception, even though she found herself becoming very fond of the new arrival, and Philip, for his part, required no warning to avoid showing too much attention to this potential seductress.

A few days prior to Christmas, Glen Parsons came up with a brainwave, and Philip Bosnar fell for it.

"Why not chop down your own Christmas tree, Phil, instead of buying one of the mangy specimens being sold around town at rip-off prices."
He drove Phil and Patty about fifty miles north into a densely wooded area. On arrival, he parked his station wagon in a small clearing before leading them through the underbrush for about a quarter of a mile. It was a place where the fir trees stood tall and proud, and where all sounds of human activity seemed a thousand miles away.

"It seems such a dreadful pity to cut down one of these gorgeous trees," Patty protested, and Phil added with his customary pragmatism, "Are you quite sure it's legal, Glen?"

"Don't you worry about a thing. Everybody does it and nobody gets excited as long as you don't chop down too large a tree, too many trees, or start a fire. Here's one that's just the right size."

It looked awfully big, but Philip wasn't about to challenge Glen on such matters since he wasn't well enough versed in forestry. The axe he brought with him looked like a children's toy alongside the sturdy trunk to be severed, and both Bosnars were fast losing their enthusiasm for this great pioneering venture. Nevertheless, Philip rolled up the sleeves of his heavy mackinaw shirt and attacked the tall timber with bold abandon. As his axe recoiled with a clanging quiver of protest, he realized he was in for a hard day's work.

It was just as well that Glen spelled him off for increasing periods, and after the second hour there was some evidence of early progress. After about four hours of unremitting toil and with their backs complaining bitterly, the great Douglas fir was finally toppled. And as the tree's crown crashed down through the underbrush they could have sworn it made a sound like the sigh of a mortally wounded animal. It was only when Glen said, "Now we'll just chop off the top seven feet and it should be just right for your living room," that Patty and Phil were overcome by a deep sense of guilt at the dreadful waste. Sensing their dismay, Glen reassured them cheerfully,

"Don't worry about the rest of the tree. Some Indians from the nearby reserve will be quite happy to chop it up for firewood, and the forest will be none the worse for the loss of one small fir tree."

Philip was especially fond of the transition from late winter to earliest spring in Edwardia. Although the air was chill and the skies were gray, with only an occasional fitful gleam of sunlight cutting a brassy path through the overcast, the spindly trees in Hillcrest Park were displayed in a sort of naked innocence. Their intricately patterned branches and twigs revealed the earliest buds, shy harbingers of nature's rich fabric of foliage and blossom that would soon adorn their freezing limbs.

Warm greenery would soon drive away winter's cold with the energy blazing down on this blessed planet from its nearest star, and the trees would once again lift their verdant leaves in homage to their cosmic benefactor. It was a wondrous time to walk through the park's hushed pathways, where there were few visitors at this time of year and the stillness was only broken by the sound of an occasional thrush singing its delighted appreciation of the changing season, or the amusing quack of a quarrelsome duck. This was the best time of year to take along a camera, to try and capture the wonderful solitude of the moment. Gliding serenely through this tranquil and un-hurried fairyland were those graceful ballet dancers of the ornamental ponds, the magnificent white swans, performing their smooth pas de deux, pirouettes and arabesques. It was that magical mo-ment of time when the sleeping beauty of winter awaited the solar prince's reawakening kiss.

Springtime eventually burst upon Edwardia in a riot of yellow: crocuses, daffodils, and masses of golden broom adorning 'waste' patches of earth and the very rocks themselves. As for Patty's garden, it had become a fantasy of color, where every photograph of the family seemed better than the last, set against house and rock garden or the backdrop of the Sanchez Straits and white-crested mountains beyond.

John Kinsley was off to San Francisco for two weeks, partly as a vacation break and partly to attend a surgical meeting at which he was presenting a paper on 'Massive Gastric Hemorrhage'. During his absence there were three events that played a great part in deciding Philip's future course.

The first involved one of Kinsley's wealthy patients, a plump and pleasant woman in her early sixties who'd undergone a combined abdominoperineal resection for rectal cancer, one week earlier, at St. Peters. Kinsley performed the abdominal procedure from above and Philip performed the perineal procedure from below. The operation went smoothly and the prognosis was considered favorable, since no secondary deposits of malignancy were found.

Her initial postoperative recovery was entirely satisfactory, but on the sixth night after surgery she developed pain and tenderness in the lower right abdomen and a high fever. Since she'd had a previous appendectomy and her urine was clear, as was the chest X-ray, Philip was forced to consider an unsettling possibility, namely a retained gauze pack: the surgeon's night-mare! He contacted Fred Ivanov, the radiologist, and arranged for a portable X-ray of the abdomen to be performed with the utmost discretion. Ivanov was reliably circumspect and soon phoned Philip to confirm his worst fear.

He put through a call to Kinsley, giving the long distance operator a number at which he could be located. It took about twenty minutes before he reached his associate and gave him the bad news.

"For God's sake, Phil, don't tell her it's a pack that's been left inside. It would be all over the newspapers in no time at all."

"I have to tell the patient and her daughter something, John, especially as I plan to operate this afternoon."

"You'll think of something, I'm sure of that, but definitely no mention of a retained pack. Is that quite understood?"

"If you say so, John."

"OK then, and I'm sure everything will go fine."

Philip went back to see the patient and her daughter, who were handling their anxieties well.

"I'm afraid I'm going to have to perform a small secondary operation this afternoon, Mrs. McPhee. It shouldn't take long but it will mean another general anesthetic, although a short one, and I expect you to make a rapid recovery."

"What exactly is the trouble, Dr. Bosnar?" asked the daughter. "Mother seemed to be doing so very well."

"The fever, pain and tenderness in the lower right area of the belly all point to the same thing. An abscess is developing in that location and could be caused by foreign material. We need to look inside, drain the abscess if necessary and remove the cause."

"We have every confidence in your judgement, doctor, and know you'll do what's best."

Dr. Bosnar left the room and let out a great sigh of relief but still felt like a charlatan. He'd skirted the demon phrase, "retained gauze sponge," and used the euphemistic terms, "abscess" and "foreign material" instead. Was he being really honest? Would it have helped the patient in any way to know the precise truth? Was it worth it to inflict a damaging blow to the reputation of a valued colleague? After all, there had been the usual mandatory double count of sponges, packs and instruments by the O.R. nursing staff before commencing the abdominal closure, and Kinsley had received the magic words, "All counts correct, doctor." There had been no reason to suspect that the doubly confirmed count might be wrong, and it was all too easy for a pack to hide undetected in the abdominal cavity of an obese patient at the end of the operation.

The secondary procedure was fast and simple. As soon as the patient was asleep he made a small incision in the lower right side and removed the pack, which was surrounded by inflamed *'omentum'*. (The omentum is a fatty apron that covers the intestines and has great protective and healing qualities. It surrounds any inflamed or injured area, thus localizing abscess formation and preventing general peritonitis.) Luckily, a true abscess had not yet formed in this case, so drainage was unnecessary. Despite the discretion and confidentiality with which the whole affair had been handled, the operating room was crowded with nursing staff, the Medical Director, the Mother Superior, and the O.R. supervisor, as well as Fred Ivanov. It was the latter who summed up the tricky situation with a cheerful remark, "Well done, Philip! Problem neatly solved."

The O.R. supervisor, spoke up next.

"This should never have happened, Dr. Bosnar, if my nurses had done their count properly. It's their responsibility to double-check the count, especially in this kind of case. Please convey our deepest apologies to Dr. Kinsley, and we thank you for dealing with the complication so promptly." The Mother Superior also had something to say.

"You've saved the hospital a great deal of embarrassment, doctor, and we're all very grateful."

Philip felt much better, and was relieved that the patient and her family didn't press him further about his findings at surgery. Best of all, Mrs. McPhee did very well and was discharged one week later.

The second case was a bizarre experience. Philip had taken Patty and the children out to dinner at their favorite informal dining spot: the restaurant at the Empire Hotel on Bedford Road. The children always enjoyed the food and comfortable booths of this place, so it had become a popular outing for all of them – at least once a week – and a well-deserved break for Patty. As usual, Philip left the restaurant's phone number with the answering service, and was glad the meal was almost finished when he got his emergency call. It was one of Kinsley's elderly patients and sounded like a possible heart attack. Philip wasted no time getting to the patient's home, especially when the old gentleman refused to go to hospital by ambulance, the first and logical choice.

When he arrived at the designated address, a comfortable bungalow on the northern side of the city, it was the patient himself who let him in. He was a husky Yorkshireman in his middle seventies, who said he'd been gardening when he was seized with severe chest pains and had to stop and rest.

"I'm much better now, doctor, and my Mum ought never to've called you."

His Mum! Good God, there she was, sitting quietly in a corner like an ancient duplicate of Whistler's Mother and knitting away furiously to cover her deep concern for her son. She must be well on her way to a hundred, Philip thought, as he turned his attention to the patient.

"I often get these attacks, doc, whenever I do too much shovelling. It's just strained muscles but my Mum's sure it's me old ticker."

"Do you ever get short of breath?"

"Not so's I'd notice, doc. Always been strong as an ox."

I can believe it, Philip thought. Here was a typical Yeoman of Olde England. Yet even this type wasn't immune to a heart condition.

"Tell me, Mr. Tacklebury, have you ever had your heart checked by a doctor? Have you had any cardiograms or X-rays?"

"Never needed 'em. Always led the good clean life, no liquor, no smoking and never married. Just look after me dear old mum."

"I just want to examine your heart and blood pressure so I'd like you to take your clothes off down to the waist"

This was going to be a major endeavor, as the old Yorkshireman believed in many layers of clothing. To pass the time during the lengthy undressing process, Philip questioned him about his past history and even about Yorkshire. It was an area about which he knew little but the patient was happy to describe, and he even start reminiscing. When the last garment was peeled down to the belt, Philip applied his stethoscope. Mr. Tacklebury was eager to keep talking about his boyhood near the historic city of York, and had to be shushed while the doctor listened to a heartbeat that was strong, regular and free of murmurs. 'Kerblonk, went the heartbeat, kerblonk, kerblonk...' and then silence: a ghastly terminal silence, as the old gentleman slowly and gently slid off his chair onto the floor, quite dead.

When Philip had confirmed that his patient was beyond all hope of resuscitation, he turned and addressed the old lady, who'd stopped knitting and sat rigidly in her chair.

"I'm terribly sorry, ma'am, but I'm afraid your son is dead. It must have been a massive heart attack."

"Knew for sure 'e wouldn't make it this time. Stubborn as a mule 'e were, but a wunnerful son to me. I'll be follerin' me son to the grave very soon now."

"I'll phone the coroner right away, ma'am, and if there's anyone I can call for you, friends, neighbors or family, I'll be glad to do so."

"No need, doc, I can manage."

She resumed her knitting and was quietly accepting one more tragedy in her long life.

"I'll cover up your son's body with a sheet if you'll show me where I can get one."

"No, you're a busy man, I'll tend to all that. This is the last of my eight children that I'll see buried and I don't need no help. You'll send me your bill, doc?"

"There'll be no charge. I'm just sorry I couldn't save him. Perhaps if he could have been diagnosed sooner there might have been a chance."

"I guess it were God's will, doctor."

Philip stayed awake that night thinking about the old Yorkshireman. The Edwardia Medical Society must get behind an urgent campaign to educate the public. Anyone with a history of chest pains, particularly with exertion, must seek medical advice without delay. In the case of an acute attack, an ambulance should be dispatched at once in order to give emergency care on the spot, such as oxygen inhalation or artificial respiration, and take the patient straight to the emergency department of the nearest hospital. In addition, the ambulance men should undergo a special course of training, so they could become experts at administering supportive care between the patient's residence and the hospital.

As expected, he had difficulty with the coroner, a pigheaded and difficult gentleman.

"No need for an autopsy on this old chappie, Dr. Bosnar. It's an open and shut case of myocardial infarction."

"That may be so but we have no medical documentation of any coronary disease, and no substantiating cardiograms. Only an autopsy can establish the exact cause of death."

"Rubbish. Go ahead and fill out the death certificate."

"If you're going to be that stupid about it, Sir, it's up to you to write the death certificate, and it'll be on your conscience."

By now he was fuming. No wonder, he thought, it was often rumored that (with this ignorant bastard as coroner) Edwardia would be the easiest place in Canada to get away with murder. He planned to discuss every aspect of the case at the next medical society meeting, even if it meant making waves.

Case number three came only a couple of days prior to Kinsley's return. It was 2.30 in the morning when the phone rang at Philip's bedside. It had been a particularly heavy day at both the hospitals and the office, and when he heard the arrogant and obviously drunken voice coming at him over the phone he was not amused.

"I want you to come over to the Empire Suite at the Prince Albert Hotel right away. My name is Malcolm deWitt Frazier and I'm a good friend and patient of John Kinsley. There's been a nasty fight with my ladyfriend. We're both cut quite badly and have to be stitched up."

"In that case you should both go down to the emergency department at the hospital of your choice. Do you need an ambulance?"

"Jesus Christ, man, no fucking ambulance and no fucking hospital. I don't want the police crawling all over the place and my name in the papers. I'm an important man and don't need that kind of shit. So get your goddam clothes on and come over right now."

Controlling his rage, Philip assembled his emergency suturing kit with a supply of local anesthetic and dressings, plus a few vials of tetanus toxoid if needed. In twenty minutes, he was shown into the hotel suite on the top floor by a rapidly sobering Mr. Godalmighty Frazier.

He recognized the handsome florid face at once; he'd seen it often enough in the newspapers. 'Premier Bennett's Shadow Man' was how they described him, a political wheeler-dealer who was also the owner of a prosperous real estate company, and one whose family appeared in the social columns of the local press even more often than the Kinsleys. He was badly cut around the face and shoulders but none of the wounds were deep and there was very little bleeding.

The young lady was still very drunk and the whole place smelled like a booze joint. She'd been savagely beaten up and displayed bruises and swellings around the face and breasts. Her lower lip was split and her front teeth loosened. There was also a severe gash on the top of her head where it was obvious she'd been struck with a heavy object, but no suggestion of concussion or other intracranial injury. She was holding a towel pressed against the gash to stop the bleeding.

Philip gathered that they'd got into a violent argument after partying for several hours.

"This rotten sonofabitch pretended he was going to divorce his wife and marry me," she informed the doctor in a loud and drunken voice, glaring murderous hatred at her treacherous lover.

"I told him I'd had enough of that crap and it was time to put up or shut up. As for more excuses he could shove 'em up his ass."

She began to sob, and that made it even more difficult for Philip to make out what she was saying.

"I guess I got really mad," Frazier interjected, "and with all that scotch inside me I went wild and slapped her around a bit."

"Yeah, with a fucking bottle," added his unnamed paramour, "so I smashed the bottle against the wall and let him have a bit of his own medicine."

It was 4 o'clock by the time Philip finally got through sewing them up, and the female of the species looked far more presentable. She was sober by now and checked her appearance in the mirror.

"Thanks a lot, doctor. I appreciate what you've done."

His Highness added his own grudging thanks but Philip brushed him aside and told him his stitches should come out in a week, except for those on his face: these should come out in four days. The same orders applied to the woman, and he instructed her that if there was any problem with her head injury she should report to one of the emergency departments without delay. He got back to bed at 4.30 and managed a couple of hours sleep before rising to get ready for his morning list at the Chelmsford.

That afternoon at the office, it gave him the greatest pleasure to send Mr. Malcolm deWitt Frazier the largest medical bill he could possibly justify, about four times what he'd have charged him in an emergency department. He chuckled at the thought of this frustrated adulterer, staggered by the size of the bill, but not ready to jeopardize his shaky marriage with an official protest that would let the cat out of the bag for the whole world to see.

The gun barrels of the terrible second World War had scarcely cooled when two new expressions found their way into western lexicon and the political thinking of the western peoples. The first was "Cold War," attributed to the American financier and presidential adviser, Bernard Baruch, and the second was "Iron Curtain," one of Winston Churchill's graphic expressions – spelling out the dangers of Soviet Russia's steady expansion and ever-present threat to the western democracies.

All western eyes, it seemed, were exclusively focused on Europe, from the Baltic in the north to the Mediterranean in the south, and Asia seemed too far away to constitute a danger. It was a time when the Berlin blockade forced the U.S.A. to risk armed conflict in order to relieve the besieged West Berliners with a courageous Airlift; a time when the U.S.S.R. forbade its satellite states to accept the beneficence of the Marshall plan; a time when Czechoslovakia fell to its Communist minority takeover; and a time when little attention was paid to Mao tse-Tung's takeover of China. The shocking end-result of all these east-west tensions was the invasion of South Korea by the Communist North. Poised at the Yalu River, the massed forces of China waited for the moment when it would be most opportune to enter the expanding conflict.

The international news was now most alarming, and it filled the newspapers, magazines and radio broadcasts as though each item had only just occurred in some sort of historic vacuum. The Chinese Communists of Mao tse-Tung, the westerners were now informed, had routed the forces of Chiang Kai-Shek and driven the Kuomintang government into political exile on the island of Formosa, now called Taiwan. It was hardly surprising, therefore, when the armed forces of the U.S.A. aided by the UN-sponsored forces of Europe and the British Commonwealth, were locked in a war of attrition with North Korea. Worse still, the North Koreans were backed up by formidable Chinese forces, perhaps as many as half a million (in spite of official denials by the Chinese authorities). This was a new kind of war, one in which the terrible power of the atomic bomb could not be used lest it unleash a frightful third World War.

Philip reached a fearful and terminal conclusion. Never again would any war be won: there could only be losers. This meant that Capitalism and Socialism must learn to live together on this fragile planet or there would be no survival for either political system, for their peoples or, perhaps, even the planet itself!

CHAPTER 26

1951-52

Mickey Bosworth was a pleasant young chap in his late twenties. He recently returned from two years in Britain, where he'd been doing a number of surgical house jobs overseas and tried both his English and Edinburgh F.R.C.S. exams without success. It was clear that John Kinsley was Bosworth's idol, and the young doctor followed his mentor around with religious constancy, both on ward rounds and as assistant in the O.R. He always waited patiently in the doctors' lounge while Kinsley finished up his financial discussions with his broker.

It was becoming obvious to Philip that Bosworth had gone across to the U.K. in the secret hope that there'd be an opportunity to join his paragon in practice, just as soon as he could write the magic letters F.R.C.S. after his name. His failure to accomplish this ambition must have been a double blow to his professional hopes and Philip felt sorry for him.

For his part, John Kinsley was kind and supportive toward his youthful admirer and encouraged him to apply for Canadian Certification in General Surgery. It wasn't surprising, therefore, that the subject of Bosworth's future came up one day in late October of 1951, when John and Philip were having coffee at the office during a break between patients.

"Tell me, Phil, what do you think of the idea of young Mickey joining our practice as a junior assistant and later as junior partner?"

"Do you really think our practice is big enough to justify taking on a third man? He's a nice enough chap and thinks the world of you, but he wouldn't get any major surgical privileges at either hospital even if there were enough surgery for the three of us."

"I agree, but he'd be a useful man for me to have around and could build up quite a good general practice."

"That would only reduce our referrals from G.Ps even further, and besides, I was hoping we could eventually get out of general practice and become strictly referral surgeons."

"Oh for God's sake, Phil, haven't you got rid of that bee in your bonnet yet? That stuff you want to eliminate from our practice is still our bread and butter, and don't you forget it."

"I'm afraid we'll have to agree to differ on that point, John."

"No, I'm sure you're wrong and too stubborn to change your mind."

"In that case perhaps Mickey Bosworth would be a better partner for you than I am, but not because I like and admire you any the less."

"To be honest with you I've been thinking along the same lines. I think you'd do just fine on your own, and I hope you find your referred work growing steadily after you leave here."

"I wouldn't set up in separate practice in this city unless I was sure you and I could remain good friends and part with no ill feelings on either side."

"Of course not, you crazy French Limey. You know how much I think of you and how much

I've enjoyed our friendship. Go ahead with your plans and best of luck."

It was all so simple and so final. Philip knew, with a sinking feeling in his gut, that life in Edwardia could never be quite the same and his close relationship with John Kinsley, the man to whom he owed so much and whom he admired so much, would never be quite the same. In the cut-throat competition for referred surgery, he and John would now be friendly rivals but no longer partners, and he felt oppressed with a great sense of loss.

When he repeated the conversation and final decision to Patty, she was saddened and disappointed, yet it was no surprise to her. She understood the depth of friendship between Kinsley and Philip, as well as the differences that separated them; and she endorsed his decision (but not without a fair measure of regret). Both realized how much he owed this fine person and they would never forget.

In due course, Philip found a suitable office some two blocks from John Kinsley's premises, with a pleasant waiting room and enclosure for his nurse-receptionist, a comfortable consulting room and a large examining room that could double as a minor operating room for simple procedures requiring only local anesthesia. The rent wasn't exorbitant and there was a large pharmacy on the corner of the block. He was able to work out a satisfactory deal with one of the surgical equipment companies for office furniture, instruments and the dozens of accessories, such as sterilizer, mobile operating light and suction apparatus. The monthly payments were reasonable and flexible, depending on his level of income.

The most valuable acquisition, however, was his new nurse-receptionist, an attractive and dynamic little brunette. She was newly married, good-humored, warm and friendly to the patients and an excellent worker. Philip considered himself most fortunate and Patty, who came to see for herself, agreed enthusiastically. There was no doubt that she and Grace Thornbury would get to like each other more and more with each meeting, and this was in sharp contrast to the way she felt about his previous nurse at the Kinsley office.

"I'm pretty sure she's going to be really good for your practice, darling. Especially the way she handles patients and people in general. She has the magic touch."

Needless to say, a growing number of doctors approached Philip to offer their congratulations and good wishes, but he was careful to make it clear that the parting was on cordial terms; that he continued to admire Kinsley as a surgeon and value him as a friend. In any event, the referrals of surgical cases increased very slowly over the next few months and didn't quite match the enthusiasm with which his act of independence had initially been greeted. His ever-cheerful office nurse assured him it was still much too early to tell how things would go, and urged him not to be too impatient or discouraged.

By the summer of 1952, the picture had brightened considerably and the Bosnar practice reached the stage of solvency, with a reasonable monthly balance after paying office expenses, his nurse's salary and sundry incidentals. It was enough for the family budget to emerge out of red ink, although well below the levels of income enjoyed by most of his surgical colleagues. Nevertheless, there were several developments that he found reassuring. The anesthetists at both hospitals were most cooperative and liked his work in the operating room. He had a pleasant relationship with the internes, who said they enjoyed his tutorials, and he was starting to become involved in the administrative aspects of his specialty.

His rigid stand against dichotomy (the splitting of professional fees as a quid pro quo reward for referrals) had earned him the nickname of 'Mr. Clean' but failed to accelerate the referrals to his practice by those who applauded his ethical stand. There were encouraging exceptions to the rule and his nurse pointed out that these were becoming more frequent. Thus, one of the leading specialists in Internal Medicine began sending him a few interesting cases, then a second internist and eventually a third and fourth, each with the occasional referred patient.

Two of the most prominent surgeons in the city became admiring supporters of Philip's ethical positions on various controversial situations – specifically those pertaining to the several surgical specialties. One of these supporters was Erskine Ridgeway, an imposing individual who resembled Viscount Alexander of Tunis, and like that distinguished soldier, was an Ulsterman. He had the bearing of a British guardsman and a clipped English accent to match, without a trace of northern Irish brogue. He was the leading general surgeon in Edwardia, a keen skier and mountain climber, and he had a reputation for the highest moral standards in all facets of his life; and an aversion to drinking, smoking, fee-splitting and Catholicism.

His wife was an attractive English lady, prominent in social work and a strong advocate for the legalization of addictive drugs. She argued convincingly that classifying drug-possession as a criminal offense paralleled the failure of Prohibition to diminish the use and sale of alcoholic beverages during the American 'Roaring Twenties'. Only the crooks grew wealthy, she pointed out, while the addicts became pitiful pariahs in society and all too often died from contaminants added by those whose greed for profit left no room for human compassion. In Margaret Ridgeway's philosophy, drug-addiction and alcoholism were metabolic disorders to be treated medically and not punitively.

Philip's second supporter, Ellery Farnsworth, Edwardia's leading gynecologist, was a fiery bantam of a man with a formidable will and a temper to match, and he detested fee-splitting as much as other less obvious incentives for referrals. He was highly regarded across the province and was current president of the Canadian Pacific Surgical Association (C.P.S.A.). As a speaker at ward rounds and hospital meetings, he was an orator of renown and was nicknamed 'The Silver Tongue'.

Farnsworth was a man to be either feared or admired, and he made few friendships. One of these was with Philip Bosnar, a comparative newcomer, and they got along well right from the start. His extracurricular passions were his high-speed motorboat and four-seater seaplane, and from time to time he took Philip along for an enjoyable run in each of these. It was too bad that his extremely goodlooking wife was an incurable alcoholic.

The third boost to Philip's advancement in the medical profession, not only of Edwardia but of British Columbia as a whole, was his newfound friendship with Virgil Stanford. This gentleman was the very personification of a successful surgeon, from his aristocratic bearing to the carnation in the buttonhole of his beautifully tailored coat. He projected, at first sight, an overbearing and pompous manner both in speech and style, while his posture suggested a cleverly concealed corset.

Stanford was a successful urologist, but more in social than professional terms. His family represented the 'old money' of Edwardia, and with it a wide access to the city's carriage trade. He was prominent in the political side of surgery, was club doctor to the local hockey team, Commodore of the Royal Edwardia Yacht Club and a senior member of the Empire Union Club as well as a district director of the Rotary club. In his capacity as treasurer of the C.P.S.A, he had valuable connections with fellow surgeons in Vancouver, New Westminster and other centers in the rest of the province.

What first promoted a strong friendship between these two men of vastly different backgrounds and life styles, it would be hard to say. Perhaps it was initiated by Stanford when he introduced himself to Philip and commented with cordial candor.

"I'm glad you decided to leave John Kinsley and strike out on your own. He's a damn good man, but he needs someone who'll always follow him around rather than an equal, or what would be worse, a partner who might surpass him in caliber and reputation."

Mrs. Farnsworth was independently wealthy and a gracious hostess, although she was inclined to be imperious with those outside her social circle. She was extremely fond of Patty, from the moment they first met at one of her celebrated cocktail parties.

Although these three dominant figures seemed determined to stand firmly behind Philip in his aims and ambitions, they were unable to increase his referrals. They never hesitated, however, to call him into difficult cases as a second consultant, and asked him to assist in any operation requiring a second surgeon. These opportunities helped to solidify his growing reputation among the nurses, the public and the medical fraternity, and he was grateful.

In addition to referrals from specialists in Internal Medicine there was an increasing number of referrals from family doctors, who began to use him for their surgical patients. First among the internists was Hector Brand, a man whose manner identified him as the most English of Englishmen, with rumpled tweedy apparel, well-worn pipe and accent to match. Philip found him a delightful fellow, with a sharp brain, a fine knowledge of literature and a wonderful sense of humor. His wife, the daughter of an English country vicar, was equally engaging, and both Phil and Patty got to enjoy exchanging visits with them from time to time and admiring their lively children, all as English as could be.

The cream of the jest turned out to be the eventual revelation that Brand was an American, born and raised in Virginia and of solid American forbears. One of his ancestors had actually fought with Washington against the British Colonial forces and lost his life in the cause. As present heir to the proud family escutcheon, Hector Brand had originally set out to be a writer and spent ten years in England, five of them perfecting his writing skills at Oxford University. When he discovered that many of the leading authors whom he studied had been either practicing or retired physicians, he succumbed to the temptation of becoming a physician himself and never looked back. His written consultations were gems of sparkling literary style and Philip always enjoyed reading them. The two doctors took to each other from the very first meeting, and their friendship and professional bond was based on mutual admiration and respect.

A second internist who sent him cases was Willie Morton. He was a blond young giant with a quiet voice and manner that concealed a devilish passion for practical jokes. Some of these came dangerously close to the boundaries of propriety. The worst example was one occasion when he asked Philip to examine a private room patient, an elderly spinster who had emphysema and diabetes, complicated by recurrent phlebitis of the veins in her legs. Midway through the examination Morton rushed into the room in simulated panic, and pointing to the surgeon's long white lab coat, asked him excitedly, "Are you sure you're not one of the painters working on this section today." They all laughed off the incident but it was the kind of close call that left Philip wondering what, when and where the next prank might be. But in spite of this one failing, the redoubtable Willie was a competent physician and congenial friend.

A third internist was Jimmie Brock, a close friend of John Kinsley since their days together at the Winnipeg General Hospital. He'd always sent his surgical patients to Kinsley but now made a point of calling on Philip's services whenever his former partner was away or unavailable. As time went by, it seemed these occasions gradually grew more frequent. In any event, Brock proved to be a man of character, great charm and a large measure of basic clinical wisdom.

One advantage of being less than fully occupied with elective cases in Philip's practice was that he was more available for emergency cases, and some of these were extremely interesting. Aside from those covered by Workman's Compensation, many emergency patients proved to be transients to whom payment of the surgeon's fee was a low priority, no matter how grateful they might be, but he felt that he was still the winner on balance.

Another advantage of free time was the opportunity to attend various medical meetings and weekly ward rounds. It was where he could cross debating swords with his surgical colleagues, in the presentation and discussion of unusual and controversial cases. A further advantage was the time available to spend with those internes who displayed a special interest in surgery. One might even hope – if and when they decided to settle in the city following their term of duty – that they'd be inclined to send their referrals to the staff surgeons whose work they most admired. *(That this hope was quixotic would only become evident with the passage of time.)*

Herb Rogers was the youngest of the internists and the most brilliant. He gave one the impression of being both discriminating and idealistic, yet he appeared to have a strange preference for Jerry McDougall as his surgeon. This apparent paradox was hard to understand at first, since McDougall, although likable and amusing, was known as a 'clock watcher': one who tries to complete an operation as rapidly as possible, often at the expense of careful technique and gentle handling of tissues. To be fair, on the other side of the surgical equation there was the 'putterer': the tediously slow surgeon who takes twice as long as most of his colleagues for even the simplest operation.

Philip knew only too well that the best technique was one which was neither too fast nor too slow, but had the flexibility to speed up in critical situations or slow down for a condition requiring meticulous dissection. All the finest surgeons he'd ever observed followed this intermediate course and he prided himself on adhering to that approach as a working rule.

It appeared that there was a tacit arrangement in which several doctors worked as an unofficial group. In this particular context, Rogers and McDougall got most of their respective referrals from three family physicians who worked in loose association with them. There were several such unofficial medical groups and most of these were under contract to companies such as the Canadian Pacific Railway or organizations such as the Fraternal Order of the Falcon. From time to time, Rogers would send Philip a surgical referral when McDougall was unavailable or the patient expressed a firm personal choice of Dr. Bosnar. In either event he was happy to see these patients since he always enjoyed working with this internist.

On the home front, the Bosnars were enjoying the new life in Edwardia to the full. Patty had done wonders with the rock garden and was proud of its splendid roses in a profusion of different varieties and colors. The shrubs were coming along splendidly and the ultimate compliment for her efforts was the increasing frequency with which tourists slowed their cars along the Terrace to photograph her garden.

For the past year both children had been transferred to private schools, since they offered a much wider curriculum and higher standards for their pupils, both in studies and sports. Jamie was enrolled in the Handleigh School for Boys and Florian in the Dorset school for Girls, two years later. Handleigh was an excellent establishment, run on similar lines to such English schools as Eton and Harrow, but without mandatory boarding. The headmaster was English, as were most of the masters, and the sports facilities were first rate, with the accent on cricket, rugby and soccer. There was also a well-trained army cadet corps, and young James Bosnar (just about the smallest member of the outfit) had the proud honor of serving as one of its buglers.

On special historic occasions and in celebration of various national and local events, the cadets assembled on the lawn in front of City Hall, a rococo structure of early Victorian design. Then, they would march off in proud formation along the waterfront esplanade, resplendent in their smart khaki battle-dress and carrying the school colors. After marching through the central business district, the cadets returned to the City Hall where they were reviewed with full military dignity by the commanding officer of the local Armories. Philip swallowed hard as he beheld his son and heir making his early mark on Her Majesty's Canadian Armed Forces. Striding along with proud chest forward and shoulders back, their diminutive bugler marched and blew with the confidence of a veteran while his moist-eyed mother glowed with joy and pride.

Jamie seemed to be growing much more slowly than his sister, and this was a source of vexation similar to that felt by his father during the early 20s (when he was much smaller than his sister until reaching his sixteenth birthday). He had a wide circle of friends and none closer than Freddy Steffanson, oldest child of Ruth and Alf Steffanson. Of all his subjects at school, Jamie soon found that his favorite by far was English Literature, and the reason went beyond his enthusiasm for the subject itself.

His English master, Desmond Gates, an Englishman from Somerset, was his idol. Although tough and demanding with his pupils, he knew how to teach, how to inspire, and for the chosen few, how to become a life model. Young James, as Gates invariably called him, never Jamie, now determined that he'd follow the shining path of English letters for his chosen career, either as teacher or writer. He would steer clear of the siren call of his father's vocation, notwithstanding the glamour of surgery.

Florian loved her new school and its severe headmistress, a widow from Cornwall – from whose craggy landscape she seemed to have derived her permanent looks and manner. She was Florian's idol, and a person for whom she would do anything. Florian wasn't as good a student as her brother, but that was mainly because she had too little interest in studying rather than any lack of intelligence. Dorset School for Girls was strongly oriented toward its track and field program. The annual Sports Day was one of the most important events of the year, religiously attended by the parents, most of all by doting mothers. It was a source of disappointment for Phil and Patty that their lithe and agile daughter, so promising in her ballet classes at the Sottini studios, should show such a lack of interest in school sports, with the possible exception of field hockey.

One day, Patricia Bosnar received a phone call from the headmistress, inviting her to take afternoon tea with her at the school, but failing to indicate the purpose of what must be more than a mere social invitation. The next day, when tea had been poured and buttered scones served, the headmistress came right to the point.

"First, I must tell you that I am quite fond of your daughter and believe she has great possibilities. The only trouble is her lack of desire in certain areas and this should be rectified or she will not reach her potential. With her natural intellect she simply needs to study a bit harder and I have few worries on that point."

Patty felt she'd better say something.

"Just what is it about Florian that you find disturbing?"

"It's simply that she has shown no interest whatever in our sports program and I fear that this may handicap her physical development at an important phase of her growth. Our sports counselor informs me that sports activities are the surest safeguard against postural defects that may become progressive."

When her guest showed concern but remained silent the headmistress became bluntly specific.

"I believe you and your husband should do all you can to persuade Florian to enter our sports program, especially track and field, without further delay."

No mention of this conversation was ever made to their daughter, but both Phil and Patty began a campaign of gentle and persistent persuasion. They pointed out that by participating in track and field events she would improve her aptitude for more advanced ballet routines and thus increase her strength, stability and stamina, as well as her posture and physical attractiveness. The campaign seemed to work, and two weeks before Annual Sports Day, Florian began to put in one hour daily at the school track, after classes.

When the great day arrived, Patty accompanied her daughter to the games, and both parents assured her they wouldn't be disappointed as long as she did her best, and trying was more important than winning. Secretly, they hoped their darling girl wouldn't be humiliated at the games.

Philip arrived home after a long day at the office and found Patty looking bright-eyed and elated. He discovered that Florian had returned in triumph, laden with cups and ribbons from track and field events, in most of which she'd come either first or second. They both congratulated the proud victor and realized that here was an individual who, at so tender an age, revealed a special capacity for rising to any challenge, no matter how unforeseen. All that was required was a suitable incentive. They would apply this idea to Florian's performance at the annual music conservatory exams, where she'd be competing in the under-10 piano event.

Jamie's fellow bugler in the army cadets was Billie Arngrim, the son of Harry Arngrim, whom the Bosnars had known in Vanwey as a pilot at the Commonwealth training base. Billie was only a couple of inches taller than Jamie, and for their diminutive size they could create quite a thunderous cacophony as they practiced their art, often forcing Phil and Patty to cover their ears in self-protection. In due course, however, the two young musicians began to conquer their gleaming instruments and produce the sweeter sounds so stubbornly denied to the uninitiated.

As the fearsome squeals and squawks of the bugles gave way to mellower tones, the Bosnars were able to tolerate the practice sessions without their former apprehension, and even looked forward to the performance of various bugle calls, from Reveille to the Last Post (or Taps as it was often called in North America). Personally, Philip had mixed nostalgic memories of these calls from his training days at Camp Borden, and to Patty they brought back memories of loneliness when her beloved husband was away from her in the army.

The second-hand piano the Bosnars had acquired from the Torvalds in 1950, at a bargain price, was a beautiful Baldwin baby grand. It was of dark mahogany with a port wine underglow and an unblemished surface. The harp strings required a certain amount of refurbishing and tuning, but after the work was completed (and it was worth every cent of the high price they paid the experts), the instrument sounded like a Steinway. An excellent teacher was found for the children and they both showed an encouraging facility for the instrument. But whereas Jamie showed keenness and practiced regularly, his sister showed far less enthusiasm, as piano practice held a low priority in her youthful interests.

Armed with the experience gained from the Sports Day incident, both parents now applied psychological pressure. They suggested to Florian that when the time came for her first performance at the forthcoming Conservatory Festival she might shame the family by a poor showing, especially when she had such potential. Perhaps it was this added touch that did the trick, as three weeks later Florian scored very high marks in the under 10 group.

Jamie got the expected high marks in his age division, and continued to show an interest in improving his musical skills, whereas Florian devoted all her energies to ballet and was bound and determined to become a professional ballerina. Now that she'd proven her ability to perform well at both sports and piano, on demand so to speak, she felt it was time to devote all her energies to her chosen vocation. So her parents gave up on this decision and put up a ballet bar on the back wall of the upstairs playroom, where Florian could practice to her heart's content.

On weekends, whenever he wasn't on emergency call and the weather was good, Philip would drive the family into the countryside to enjoy the rugged splendors of the Pacific coastline or the wonderful feeling of remoteness in the deep forests, where only the song of birds or rustle of little animals in the underbrush broke the stillness. Whenever the weather grew stormy and the winds started to blow, mighty waves would crash against the rocks in wild abandon, sending great fountains of spray into the air. The forests became symphonies of tumultuous sound as rampaging blasts of air rushed through the thrashing leaves, with each tree an individual performer in nature's orchestra. The children found pleasure in sharing these experiences and observations with their parents and it helped them appreciate anew the wonders of this vast land into which they had been born.

When the weather was at its worst there was always the radio, and the whole family enjoyed the Jack Benny show and Lux Theater most of all. Most of the CBC programs were disappointing but there were two notable exceptions: the 'Prairie Schooner' with its superb country music orchestra, and the plays produced by Andrew Allen. These plays were performed by such first class Canadian actors as John Drainie, Mavor Moore and Tommy Tweed, and written by topflight Canadian authors. As for television, the programs seemed geared to the lowest possible denominator of public taste and the Bosnars decided it was not for them.

The news from Vanwey was exciting. The whole area surrounding the town was enjoying an oil boom. Unproductive farmlands were converting to profitable oil properties, causing a genuine wave of prosperity to roll across all segments of the community. Alvin Masters was collecting outstanding fees that he'd written off as uncollectible, and he enclosed a sizable and welcome cheque in his letter, as Philip's share of the bonanza.

The most deserving of all the beneficiaries during this oil boom, at least as Phil and Patty were concerned, was Herb Adams. This most ethical of lawyers, a man of infinite patience and generosity who always translated his Catholicism into personal charitability rather than narrow dogma, was now catapulted into instant wealth. His wife and daughters were delighted, while he was simply bewildered. All those slips of paper with IOUs for unpaid legal fees suddenly translated into deeds for small plots of land that included substantial oil finds.

The Bosnars were happy for this deserving and long-suffering paragon of the legal profession, but they couldn't help remembering those eager young oil geologists and seismologists who were so confident that Southern Saskatchewan would become a significant oil field. They'd been so enthusiastic when they urged Philip to invest his money in promising land sites at a time when he had no money to invest.

As for Alvin Masters, his practice was doing well but he was becoming frustrated with the unfair competitive methods used by Brent Slocum. Al was contemplating a move back to Toronto, where his wife's family lived, and he was studying hard for his Fellowship in surgery. Philip wished him all the luck in the world. He certainly deserved it.

On the national scene, it seemed there would never be any lasting accommodation between English-speaking Canada and its French-speaking population, especially in Quebec. It seemed idiotic that the media still referred to Quebec's provincial parliament as the 'National Assembly'. Another idiocy was that in order to practice medicine in that province one had to take a special examination other than the L.M.C.C. (Licentiate of the Medical Council of Canada). It appeared that all the francophone political leaders, no matter what their party, were determined to preserve some sort of lopsided special status for Quebec in the nation, far beyond the rest of the provinces, and that seemed to presage a move toward a separatist state at some time in the not-too-distant future.

It was also worrying to Phil and Patty that the federal leaders were consistent in catering to Quebec's francophone population in exchange for votes at election time. As far as Phil and Patty were concerned, this seemed at the expense of consolidating a true nationhood free of historic prejudices and obsessions. Sad to say, Louis St. Laurent, the new Prime Minister, wasn't much of an improvement on his predecessor, Mackenzie King, except for a certain amount of oldfashioned charm, a more pleasant appearance and a less unpleasant speaking voice. His policies were just as devoid of vision and merely entrenched the status quo. Canada cried out for a bold leader: for a man of decision.

On the international scene, it appeared that the ever-present dangers of postwar antagonisms, with East and West glaring at each other across the checkpoints of Berlin, were obliterating memories of the fearful holocaust that still left its stench over continental Europe. There were disturbing reports of neonazi and neofascist groups springing up all over the western world and of the escape of some of the worst war criminals to South America; even to Canada and the U.S.A. It seemed all that was needed was a proof of anticommunism and these criminals against humanity could count on a helping hand from the military and immigration authorities. It was this type of attitude, Philip insisted, that made communists out of moderates. In any case, the new witch hunts in America were now finding communist subversives in every closet and under every bed.

"I suppose," Phil observed sardonically to Patty, "it keeps the F.B.I. ferrets busy and the

House Unamerican Activities Committee happy, so I guess it serves some purpose," and she agreed with a shudder.

Strange to note, the North American paranoia about communist spies had started in Canada with the defection of Igor Gouzenko, an official of the Russian Embassy in Ottawa who was almost frustrated in his attempts to obtain sanctuary. It was this man's revelations that led the intelligence authorities of Canada and the U.K. to apprehend two highly placed British atomic scientists who were conveying atomic secrets to Russia. There followed an epidemic of guilt by association or innuendo.

The great American atomic physicist, Robert Oppenheimer, was treated as a disloyal security risk by U.S. intelligence authorities, without a shred of evidence. Not that there was a total absence of genuine cases. Professor Pontecorvo, a Canadian atomic scientist who defected to Russia, was one of several bona fide examples. On the other hand, the indictment of Alger Hiss on a trumped-up charge of spying for Russia and camouflaged as a charge of perjury, was based on the bizarre testimony of Whittaker Chambers, a magazine editor who'd undergone some sort of moral reawakening but was obviously deranged.

In the long run, this sort of national paranoia was bound to lead to the worst kind of political persecution: one closely akin to the police-state methods of the hated postwar enemy, Godless Communist Russia. Much more to the point, and despite all the frenzied activities of the intelligence agencies, the atomic genie was out of the bottle not only for the West but for the East as well. Neither side dared use its deadly new weapons for fear of awful reprisal – a stalemate of terror. Now the whole world must realize that henceforth wars could never again be won, only lost. The United States had already received its first lesson about the new realities of war in the dismal stalemate of the Korean War, with both sides back at the 38th parallel and so many huge losses but no gains.

Here, in this glorious haven of peace, natural beauty and tranquillity, in this matchless gem of a city on Canada's western shores, all such dangers (both imagined and real) seemed impossibly remote. If there was any place on earth where man had devoted himself to the glorification of nature's beauties and turned his back on ugliness, it was Edwardia. It was home to the magnificent oaks and smoothly-sculptured bronze arbutus; to the flowering cherry trees with their heavy profusion of pink blossoms; to the flaming rhododendrons and glowing azaleas; to the voluptuous tulips and glistening heather; and to the fragrant multicolored roses and gleaming dogwood. These and so many more were augmented by a stunning array of birds of every description. As if that were not sufficient to entrance the senses, Mother Nature had also blessed Edwardia with an abundance of wildflowers and flowering shrubs that rivaled the spectacular public and residential gardens.

It was difficult to live in such a paradise and resist the temptation to turn ones back on the world's never-ending strife. No wonder they called this place 'Lotus Land'. That was its beauty and that was its danger.

CHAPTER 27

1919-20

Peacetime London was a wonderful place. No more air raids, no more nasty zeppelins dropping their bombs on houses and people. At the age of six, Philip was beginning to appreciate the fact that people suffered in war and some lost their lives, even when they weren't fighting at the front. The summer was long past, and these were the wondrous and mysterious gray days, when the skies seemed to come down toward the ground, bringing their great cloud cover with them, almost within touching distance; when sturdy trees in the park and in front of houses shed their leaves onto the ground. From time to time, the winds would whip up these fallen victims of approaching winter into a mad frenzy of dancing. Round and round went the leaves and up and up, swirling and flying before falling down once again in sheer exhaustion.

Soon, it would be time for the school plays, and for the first elementary class his teacher had chosen a scene from the French historic romance, Aucassin and Nicolette. Much to his surprise Philip was asked to play the nobleman, Aucassin. His Mum was thrilled to bits but he wasn't too happy despite the great honor. It seemed a bit sissy to him, and he wasn't looking forward to coming out on stage in front of all those cockney ruffians, with their great big boots and filthy swear-words. He'd been chosen for the part less by his teacher, an old battle axe, than by the gorgeous Rosemary Highness, who was selected (who else!) for the part of Nicolette. Her glowing coppery curls and round dimpled face were just right for the part, and she seemed to like him very much, which was just fine as far as he was concerned. Of course, he could never feel the way he did in Manchester, where he'd lost his heart to the divine kindergarten teacher.

The worst thing about the play was that it included singing, something he always hated to do. There were those who could sing and those who couldn't and he belonged in the second category. It was hard to explain, since he was the only one in his family who didn't have a good singing voice. The story of Aucassin and Nicolette was all about two young people who loved each other, were parted from each other, then came together again and everything ended up just fine. Not much of a plot, he thought, for all the talking and singing; but since it was supposed to be an ancient and very famous story from France, he supposed one shouldn't complain. Anyhow, it all seemed to go off pretty well and all the parents applauded, especially his Mum and Dad. They didn't even seem bored.

When school closed for the Christmas Holidays, his family would be enjoying all the delicious Hanukah foods, with almonds and raisins for him and Pauline. But they didn't celebrate the Jewish festival the way all their neighbors did, nor did they join the crowds going to Shul (synagogue) at the far corner of the Square. He supposed his Mum and Dad weren't religious in that way.

His biggest thrill came on Christmas morning, when his Dad awakened him with a great big gift-stocking made of white netted material and containing a magic assortment of miniature toys. There were little horses and carts, ships and planes, even some buses and trams; there were picture cards, postage stamps from different countries, tiny shovels and pails, toy soldiers and even a little cannon. It seemed as if the profusion of treasures pouring from these magic stockings would never end, and in later years, whenever Philip Bosnar thought back to those days, he knew there was never the most expensive gift given to him that was as precious as those magic stockings packed with a small child's wonder and joy.

Wintertime in London often brought with it the heavy fog that blotted out everything, no matter how close. The only way one knew if someone was nearby was by listening closely for footsteps, coughing, nose-blowing, talking, laughing, whistling and many other people sounds that one might hardly notice at other times. There were disembodied shouts from who knows what direction, the blare of motor horns and clippety-clop of horses.

On the Mile End Road, one could hear rather than see the traffic groping its slow way through the thick gloom. Day turned into night and Philip was sure that all the robbers, murderers and spies must be having the time of their lives. In fact, he found himself feeling sorry for the brave policemen who would be facing unseen foes. He wondered why it wasn't possible to have a special kind of illumination, one that could penetrate the fog and light up the darkened streets of this great city – now reduced from a speedy hustle and bustle to a wary, frightened crawl.

In general, school days were fun. The lessons weren't too hard and the games were exciting and challenging. It was always a mark of esteem to be chosen early on someone's team, whether for cricket or football, but in the latter it was wise to avoid the murderous boots of the cockney opposition, and his shins bore testimony to the times he was careless.

As far as illness was concerned, he considered himself pretty lucky. The worst time was when he had his tonsils out. He hated the rotten taste in his mouth, the aching in his throat when he tried to swallow anything and the bloody fluid he seemed to be spitting for days on end. Perhaps, he thought, it would all be worthwhile if it stopped his frequent bouts of what his doctor called 'Septic Throat'. That would make all the misery of the operation worthwhile.

There was one illness that brought him unexpected happiness shortly after his seventh birthday. It was diagnosed as a severe attack of Scarlet Fever and was a great worry to his family, although his sore throat didn't compare with having his tonsils out. Apart from a rash and very high fever, he seemed to be doing well. However, after a few days at home, where he was looked after in quarantine, the doctor became worried about complications and he was transferred to a special hospital out in the country.

As the first week passed, he felt much better, and whenever the weather was good, he was allowed to go outside in the spacious hospital grounds. It was just perfect in every way; the air was so pure and the countryside so beautiful! Since the hospital was situated at the top of a rise, it was possible to see for miles. He could see fields of grain; cows and horses; sheep and goats. There were woodlands and little ponds, and in the further distance, one could even see and hear a passing train.

Although he never quite lost the guilt of that happy time, he had to admit he didn't miss his family nearly as much as he should have done. Yet, on the two occasions when they were permitted to visit him during the next few weeks, he was delighted to see them, and it wasn't just for the baskets of oranges, apples, pears, bananas and grapes that they brought him, nor the chocolates and fruit jellies.

One of his favorite ways of whiling away the time, whenever he was back in bed during these long quiet days at the hospital, was drawing pictures on whatever paper was available. He'd picked up this form of amusement from his former good friend and expert burglar, Harry Danzig, whose many skills included a great talent with paper and pencil. Philip used to admire his exciting drawings of battles, trains and great liners at sea, and Harry took the time to show him the right way of using a pencil to greatest advantage.

Philip never lost his liking for this art form. In his present hospital confinement, however, the available paper was far less than the subjects he wished to draw, and it took the nurses a long time to find out who was responsible for the disappearance of toilet paper from the lavatories. They even indulged his venture into crime by admiring his sketches. Eventually he was found out by the head nurse, and she gave him the very dickens and made him promise never to repeat his guilty act.

Despite this lapse, he would always remember the happiness of his days in that convalescent fever hospital, where he was blissfully unaware of the serious complications for which he was admitted and from which he recovered completely. When he got back home, he realized how much he'd missed his family and familiar surroundings at number twelve Grantham Square, not to mention his Dad's stories and his Mum's delicious meals. He even appreciated Pauline's sterling qualities, usually unnoticed, and found out how much he loved her.

It was good to walk through the park and watch the tennis players, and to see the familiar faces of his friends and their parents; but at night he dreamed of pastures and woodlands, of hills, lakes, and distant trains puffing away on the horizon.

CHAPTER 28

1953

Life in Edwardia had settled into a pleasant routine and Philip Bosnar's comfortable and unhurried professional routine left time for a rich social life, both with old friends and new, old interests and new. It seemed hardly possible, but he was now in his fortieth year and that should represent some sort of watershed, yet he didn't feel that much different from his thirtieth birthday. Was he settling into some kind of comfortable rut in this land of lotus eaters? He decided that he must continue to move forward and go on developing whatever potential the good Lord had given him; to make whatever waves were necessary in order to project the essential professional and social reforms he considered necessary.

The children were growing up nicely and had not yet reached the dreaded revolutionary phase, becoming so prevalent among the younger generation of the middle classes. James and Florian were happy, healthy and not ashamed to appear, among their peer group, reasonably well dressed, clean and tidy. Fortunately they enjoyed a wide circle of friends, their bicycles, their games and their hobbies.

One of the newest friends of Phil and Patty was their son's English master, Desmond Gates, a popular fellow in company, vigorous, flamboyant and witty. He was an excellent conversationalist and a formidable debater, and they liked to have him at their parties. His wife, Priscilla, whom Philip loved to tease by calling her 'Prillie', was a sweet little English lass, very shy, very blond and very pretty, and kidding her seemed to be the best antidote for her natural reserve. It wasn't long before this couple began to show up at all the parties attended by the Bosnars.

The Robins, who were now back in Edwardia, were nearly always invited to the Bosnar parties. Cliff was working in the Pathology department at St. Peter's Hospital and Philip was glad to have him back and to resume their weekend tennis sessions, but Patty offered the roguish suggestion that he was even more glad to have Cliff's wife, Melanie, back in town. She had matured into a most attractive young lady and wasn't ashamed to flirt with those men she liked. Privately, Philip was flattered more by Patty's latent jealousy than by any attention he might receive from the opposite gender. After all, philandering was no longer his avocation, since he first met Patricia Clancy in Dover and fell deeply in love. He'd become an incorrigible 'one-woman man', but it was nice to know this wasn't taken for granted. As for his beloved wife, with her redheaded good looks, she was a great favorite with the men, but had eyes for none but her husband, and he was thankful.

Virgil Stanford and his charming wife were outside the Bosnars' social circle. They were older and had different interests from theirs, yet they seemed determined to enrich the Bosnars' Edwardia experience both socially and professionally. During the past few months they had put their intentions into practice. There were cocktail parties and dinners at their gracious home and they were at great pains to introduce them to a new circle of friends, some of them quite prominent in the life of the city. Virgil put up Philip's name for membership in the prestigious Empire club, which he accepted, and the Rotary club, which he declined with thanks. He also put them both up for membership in the Royal Edwardia Yacht Club, but they decided to wait until next year. More importantly, he nominated Philip for membership in the Canadian Pacific Surgical Association and encouraged him to take an active part in its activities, both professional and social.

One development saddened Philip deeply, and Patty no less. He and John Kinsley seemed to be drifting apart, and as a matter of fact, John seemed to be withdrawing from his professional friends to a rather alarming degree. It was said that his right wing political views were becoming more extreme all the time, and he was scared that communists were taking over the country. As for his professional association with the amiable Mickey Horsford, it wasn't the greatest success.

The young man wasn't Kinsley's intellectual equal, and at best could only function as a glorified house surgeon to his senior associate. On the few occasions that Philip saw Kinsley he seemed to be not as well, and he worried about his former associate's persistent cough and occasional shortness of breath. He was glad Kinsley had taken over the position of Chief of Surgery at the Chelmsford, and felt that this would – at the very least – give them an opportunity of seeing each other at the weekly surgical ward rounds on Saturday mornings.

Surgical Ward Rounds at the Chelmsford were first class and John was a good chairman, but he began to arrive later and later and leave earlier and earlier, delegating one of the other surgeons to take over with increasing frequency. There appeared to be no particular antipathy on Kinsley's part, but the warmth in their relationship had almost gone even if the respect was still there. Phil and Patty tried to invite the Kinsleys to their home from time to time but eventually gave up when there was no positive response. Patty knew how hurt her husband was but he assured her that he could never forget what this fine individual had done for him ever since they first met in Winnipeg so long ago.

Glen Parsons decided it was high time Philip joined the ranks of B.C. sports fishermen and at least try his hand at early morning trolling for coho salmon. When he finally agreed, he had no idea what was in store for him, but Glen assured him that all he needed was a good rod and spinning gear, suitable line, weights, lures, and hooks, and gave him the necessary detailed instruction.

"Be sure to dress warmly," he cautioned, "and be ready at 4 a.m. because that's when I'll be picking you up."

Patty thought this was typical masculine lunacy and Philip was inclined to agree with her. At 4a.m. he was ready at the foot of the front steps as Glen drove up. The novice fisherman was clad in heavy Mackinaw and thick woolen sweater, rough heavy trousers and boots over ordinary cotton pajamas – his favorite insulating protection. For additional measure against the morning chill, even though this was early May, he had his silver hipflask filled with neat Irish whisky.

They drove through the pitch-black darkness for forty minutes until they reached Bluewater Bay, and Glen parked his car by the marina's general store and restaurant. He led the way to the dock, untied a small dinghy equipped with a tiny outboard motor, and after paying the old native Indian in charge, they were off like Captain Ahab and his crew in pursuit of the great white whale.

They weren't alone on this broad and well-sheltered bay, safe from the white caps of the outer seas. It was obviously a popular location for the primitive art of trolling, with many boats, large and small, rowboat, inboard and outboard; and while Philip steered with the tiller Glen checked for the best place to slow down and cast their lines. He put his line out first and fixed his rod in one of the side holders, then checked Philip's gear and did the same. It wasn't very long before the chill began to penetrate their very substantial clothing and Philip offered his friend a swig from his flask. Glen took one short sip, choked and then declined a second swallow with strangled thanks. It was almost apologetically that Philip took a hefty draft of the fiery elixir and felt it coursing through his body and restoring his circulation.

They trolled patiently until daylight, and Philip couldn't understand why they hadn't been luckier. On all sides great shimmering coho salmon were leaping out of the water, almost as if they were trying to jump into the boats and save the fishermen the trouble. By 7 o'clock the two doctors had actually landed a couple of fine specimens, at least sixteen inches long, and Philip was halfway through his whisky. He was glad they'd each caught a fish, and that Glen was so adroit with his gillhook and had the decency to whack the fish over the head with the butt end of the hook, "to save them from drowning in air."

As a surgeon, Philip supposed he should have volunteered to clean the fish, but his companion was happy to exhibit his prowess and did a neat and tidy job before packing them in ice. By this time they were both famished and devoured a huge breakfast at the marina restaurant. The meal was rough and ready but the bacon and scrambled eggs, toast, jam and great mugs of tea were fit for the gods, and by agreement Philip footed the bill.

When they got back, Patty was less than enthralled with her darling's smelly presentation, wrapped in old newspaper. But later on, after baking the coho in the oven, and with a hot sauce concocted by Philip – with ketchup, malt vinegar and Worcestershire sauce – she had to agree that it made a delicious lunch.

From that time forth Glen Parsons and Philip repeated their fishing outings at least once a month, and although Glen always refused the raw liquor, they had many a long discussion while putt-putting along, waiting for the line to scream and the rod to arch, and praying they hadn't snagged bottom. As they became more blasé', the conversation became more important than the fishing and they talked about many things.

"How's the practice going, Phil?" Glen asked on one such occasion.

"Pretty well, I guess, but I seem to have reached a plateau and wouldn't mind an increase of about thirty percent over my present volume. It's an increase I could manage quite easily, but I don't seem able to crack certain entrenched arrangements and concealed groupings."

"You realize, old boy, that some of the big companies like the C.P.R. and organizations like the Fraternal Order of the Falcon have their own medical contracts with certain doctors, and that cuts into your field of referrals quite a bit. Then of course you don't split fees or sponsor new G.Ps; that cuts another chunk of work out of your reach. All things considered, I think you've done bloody well, and what's more you've retained your self respect."

"I'm not sure you're making me feel much better, Glen, and certainly no wealthier. Perhaps one day one of the new medical groups will make me an offer to be their surgeon. If the terms are right I might even accept."

Glen thought for a moment before confessing to his friend, "The day will come, Phil, when I may be facing the same decisions. I hope to get my surgical fellowship or certification one day. But as low man on the totem pole I'll probably have to get my surgical work from my own general practice."

Virgil Stanford's twin-masted schooner was his pride and joy, and the object of admiration and envy throughout the membership of the Royal Edwardia Yacht Club. Its hardy solid teak hull and polished gleaming mahogany decks were superb; with its white canvas aloft at full rigging she was a sleek and elegant craft, a combination of speed and stability. The first time the Bosnars were invited aboard for a day's cruise, Patty was far from enthusiastic but Philip assured her that this was the safest possible sailing craft and that its powerful diesel engines were a secure backup in bad weather and heavy seas.

They came aboard at 11 o'clock by Philip rowing the dinghy clumsily to where the schooner 'Palomena' lay at anchor, halfway between dockside and outer breakwater. Philip wasn't used to the wide open rowlocks and his oars kept slipping out as a result, much to Patty's increasing sense of unease. Once they were aboard, however, and had hoisted a couple of drinks with their hosts and other guests, she felt fine and her nervousness disappeared. The day was glorious, the seas were calm, and after pulling up anchor and clearing the breakwater under low power, the sheets were hoisted aloft and the engines turned off.

Virgil looked most impressive in his Commodore's blazer, yachting cap and white slacks. His wife Jessie was a gracious hostess, and her relaxed good humor combined with her friendly attention to Patty made it an enjoyable trip for both Bosnars. For Philip's part, he was happy to pitch in from time to time with the lines, under the expert guidance of the skipper.

They headed for Plymouth Island and arrived there at 2.30 after a glorious sail. After dropping anchor on the lee side of the island, lunch was served, consisting of a fine assortment of sandwiches, cakes, and more drinks, but Patty was starting to get worried. The tall and generous Tom Collins drinks were starting to catch up with her, and she was much too shy to use the very public 'Head', situated forward of the main cabin, with only a draw curtain separating the two. Finally, by 3.30 she could hold out no longer, and defying the crowded occupancy of the cabin, was compelled to answer nature's urgent call. She would always insist that a malicious fate conspired to silence the assembled guests just as the sounds of a miniature waterfall emerged from her side of the curtain. Luckily the guests were used to the sound effects of a ship's head, of which this was far less embarrassing than most, and she emerged quite relieved in more ways than one. The return voyage was smooth and uneventful and a good time was had by all, but Philip's beloved wife vowed that she'd never become a sailor and had no ambition to own a boat.

They had both, for some time, noticed that boat ownership was almost a sine qua non in the medical, dental and legal professions. Yet closer scrutiny revealed the strange fact that for every hour spent out at sea about twelve hours were spent scraping, painting, caulking and routine repairing, and all-in-all it hardly seemed worthwhile. Only Gordie Sharpe, one of the anesthetists at St. Peter's, and the internist Hector Brand, used their boats sufficiently. Both owned simple and unimpressive sloops.

Philip enjoyed going out with either one of these excellent yachtsmen and helping with the rigging and other duties, but Patty had no ambitions to join them. The truth was that, while he enjoyed going out on his friends' boats and pitching in as necessary, he hadn't the slightest desire to own a boat. One of the main symptoms of the boat-ownership syndrome was a constant desire to exchange ones own boat for a larger one at least every couple of years, and that was a condition Philip didn't envy.

Apart from his professional and social activities, there were three other activities that occupied his spare time. The first was music, and both he and Patty shared an enthusiastic love of music, especially the classics. His own tastes veered in the direction of symphonies, violin and piano concertos, solo instrumentalists and chamber ensembles, with a strong affinity for music of the baroque. Patty enjoyed all these musical forms but was developing a very strong taste for Italian opera, and Puccini was her clear-cut favorite, even ahead of the mighty Verdi. Listening to the heart-throbbing melodies of La Boheme, Madama Butterfly and Tosca, sent her into raptures, and the heavenly voices of Jussi Bjoerling and Licia Albanese could keep her enthralled by the hour.

They both enjoyed good popular music except for some of the recent rubbish that was developing from the latest rowdy but popular cultists: performers who parlayed bad music and worse lyrics into an international frenzy, mostly by virtue of their deafening bonga-bonga drum beat, their crazy hairstyles and weird dress. Perhaps by the time they'd earned their millions from an undiscerning and bemused public, they might acquire enough talent to sing some decent songs with worthwhile lyrics, but their music could never aspire to the melodious heights of a Glen Miller, a Benny Goodman, or a Duke Ellington.

Phil and Patty both loved good dance music, whether Big Band or small sophisticated Combos, and they loved dancing on rare occasions such as the annual Medical Society dance and the Artillery Ball. It was nice to dress up in resplendent evening gown for Patty and formal white tie and tails for Philip. They both enjoyed the slow foxtrot, the Latin rhythms of the rumba and samba – and most of all – the exotic tango. They also shared a marked distaste for the waltz and the polka. Holding his beautiful darling close to him and dancing cheek to cheek, they were once again the romantic young lovers of 1938 and traveled back in time and space to the gleaming white Cliffs of Dover.

Philip was playing his violin less often, and that was mainly due to the fact that he no longer had a regular piano accompanist. Nevertheless he still enjoyed playing, and developed a set of solo anthologies: those that were favorites of Patty, those that the children enjoyed, and his own favorites, including improvisations, transcriptions and original compositions. The latter were based on memories of his mother's songs from her native Poland which she used to hum while working in the kitchen.

The weekly concerts given in Townsend Hall by Klaus Hausemann and the city symphony orchestra were more of a social than a musical event, and the suave young Austrian conductor was far more notable as a darling of the dowagers than as an orchestral conductor. His speaking voice, with its perfect English diction and faint Viennese flavor captivated his audience but failed, in Philip's opinion, to compensate for his musical shortcomings. The symphony performances lacked any emotional quality and Hausemann conducted as though he was a human metronome, without what his fellow continentals would call 'Verstandt', that inner appreciation of the musical message. After attending these concerts faithfully for two seasons the Bosnars finally gave up, and now satisfied themselves with records and radio.

From time to time they and the Steffansons would enjoy a friendly game of bridge either at the one home or the other, and Patty was developing into quite a keen player. There were also periodic poker games, strictly stag, with a small group of doctors, including Bud Sawyer from the Army base out at Greenpoint, in the western section of Edwardia. Sawyer occasionally filled in as anesthetist at one or other of the hospitals in town whenever there was a temporary shortage. Another player was Alf Steffanson, who never lost his keenness for the game and was always a welcome addition.

After a while the games moved out to the Army Officers' Mess on a regular monthly basis, starting at 8 o'clock in the evening and ending at 2 a.m. Two additional players joined their group and proved to be an excellent choice: they were both professional gamblers and were scrupulously honest and most pleasant companions. The stakes were high and the game was played seriously, with a minimum of drinking. No money changed hands until the end of the game, and all players started off with equal stacks of chips, but could cash out at any time or buy further chips if they were running low.

The steward, a middle-aged corporal, looked after their refreshments, and at midnight the game was recessed for fifteen minutes while steak sandwiches were served. These were in fact choice tenderloins between thin slices of toast, and they were devoured with deep appreciation. Two dollars were removed by the steward from each 'pot' and this paid for the food, beverages, and a substantial gratuity for their attentive corporal. Most of the time Philip came out ahead, and when he got home and slipped quietly to bed he made a point of stacking his winnings on Patty's side table.

On the international front this had been a strange year. Josef Stalin, the tyrant of Communist Russia, was finally dead, to the relief of his oppressed subjects. It was easy to speculate that his death from "natural causes" may have been expedited by a bullet or a dose of poison. Of even greater importance to some was the execution of the archfiend, Lavrenti Beria, lord of the Soviet secret police, the man responsible for countless executions of political foes, real or imagined, and for the appalling prison camps of the frozen north. The so-called Doctors' Plot had proven a vile fabrication. A group of Jewish doctors were blamed by Stalin for the death of Andrei Zhdanov, the popular political leader from Leningrad. If, indeed, this man had been murdered, then it was most likely by Beria's men on the orders of Stalin, in order to eliminate yet another rival to the communist throne. One couldn't help wondering if the death of the dictator might have prevented an antisemitic bloodbath.

What about his successors? The pale, moonfaced Georgy Malenkov was now Chairman of the Council of Ministers, but it was Nikita Khrushchev, First Secretary of the communist party, who seemed to have the real power. This short stocky bald-headed Ukrainian peasant, with his earthy sense of humor and blunt direct manner, seemed just the right kind of leader to rescue Soviet Russia from the doctrinaire despotism of Stalin. Perhaps it might now be possible for the U.A. to ease up on its paranoid witch-hunt for communists; but it would take both sides of the Iron Curtain to ease the deepening Cold War.

Of course the madness in America had started with the disclosures of Igor Gouzenko in Canada, and these proved genuine. Then came the Alger Hiss case, a doubtful one at best, but at least giving a political boost to Richard Nixon, his shifty prosecutor. Yet another opportunist was the junior senator from Wisconsin, Joseph McCarthy. This unpleasant individual had begun in 1950 by accusing the Truman administration of "coddling communists" in the State Department. What followed was a mounting witch-hunt that wrecked the careers of many distinguished writers and film-makers. At the same time, the House Unamerican Activities Committee, under the chairmanship of John Parnell Thomas, was an organization he was able to dominate and put to his own use.

In the U.K. the two atomic spies, Alan Nunn May and Klaus Fuchs had simply been imprisoned without much muss or fuss. In the U.S.A., on the other hand, the Rosenbergs, a pair of rather naive and misguided dupes, were executed, and the Eisenhower administration as well as the entire country was immersed in guilt and shame at the heartlessness of such a decision. There wasn't even any clear proof that the secrets they passed on to the Russians were of any great value. Surely, in any event, it must have been obvious that any military secret possessed by one nation must sooner or later be discovered or stolen by its enemy.

The government of Harry Truman had been a surprisingly strong and effective one, considering the fact that he had to follow the awesome F.D.R. It was a no-win stalemate in the dismal Korean War and the recall of General Douglas MacArthur that led to Truman's decision not to run again. The American nation, in its sense of humiliation, was ready for the proverbial 'Man on the White Horse' and Dwight Eisenhower, recent Commander-in-Chief of the NATO forces in Europe, was an obvious choice. He wasn't a great leader and had little capacity for firm decisions, and when he actually managed to make one, such as the Darlan fiasco in World War 2 and the recent sacrifice of the Rosenbergs to the lunatic right, it was almost invariably the wrong one.

In Korea, the game of war-truce-war-truce had finally run itself down at the cost of one million dead and countless wounded or rendered homeless. Conditions for the prisoners of war had been frightful – with their high deathrate from starvation, disease and physical abuse.

A new element in this conflict was the technique known as 'brain-washing' employed by the North Korean captors and – without a doubt – their Red Chinese allies. It consisted of intensive and repeated psychological indoctrination of the prisoner, combined with physical torture until he did the enemy's bidding. Surely, it seemed to Patty, it was imperative, from now on, that all combatants be given advanced permission to confess to anything the enemy desired, but with advance and subsequent repudiation. Otherwise, the alternative was the routine issuance of cyanide pills, and the order to fight to the death in any situation: a sort of Western Kamikaze mentality. Philip concurred wholeheartedly.

When all was said and done, however, although he admired the firmness and honesty of Harry Truman and applauded his decision to recall MacArthur, he still had ambivalent thoughts about the flamboyant general with the corncob pipe. As a person, his arrogance and towering vanity offended him. As a political thinker his ultra-right extremism scared him. But as a soldier, he had to concede that he was a military genius, and probably even greater than the vaunted Rommel. More than once he'd observed to Patty that he didn't think the popular hero 'Ike' was fit to shine MacArthur's boots.

McArthur's military exploits in the war against Japan were master strokes of strategy and he knew how to snatch victory from the jaws of defeat. In the Korean war he'd held back the attacking communist forces before they could take Pusan, and his landing at Inchon would remain as one of the great engagements of military history. Had it not been for the intervention of Mao tse-Tung's hordes pouring across the Yalu River there was little doubt that North Korea would have fallen to the U.N. forces.

MacArthur's ultimate plan to bomb the Chinese bases in their Manchurian sanctuary may well have proven strategically successful, and it was doubtful that the U.S.S.R. would actively have intervened, but he pushed his plan too far. He forgot that while he was Commander of the U.N. forces his President was also his Commander-in-Chief and had the final word. The General of World War 2 had to defer to the Captain of World War 1 and found it impossible. Listening to his stirring farewell address to the joint Congress, one could understand why.

"Old soldiers never die," he quoted nostalgically from the well-known army song, "they simply fade away," and many a tear was shed by his millions of listeners.

For the past few weeks Philip had started to spend one or two nights a week at the Edwardia Chess Club. At Brewers' School, one dark winter's lunch hour in 1928, he'd wandered into the Chess Room and then, by watching the players and reading some of the available books on the subject, he steadily began to improve to the point where he was able to join the school team at the lowest board. Their club was in the third division, but over the next two years they worked their way up to the first division. Philip improved to the level of playing at third board and after a while he took over as team captain. Their first board Larry Frome was an excellent player who nearly always won his interschool games, but the one exception was the formidable Wilson's School, London's perennial champions.

Wilson's first board was a strange chap by the name of Harry Golombek; he was tall and gawky, with a taut bony face and an ungainly manner. It was said that his parents had come to Canada from Eastern Europe at the turn of the century, and although he grew up in London, he was inclined to be withdrawn and uncommunicative. It was unnerving to watch him play; he hardly ever looked at the board, and gazed instead at the ceiling as if he were playing 'Blindfold Chess'. He beat Frome quite handily and Philip lost his game in the same manner. The final score was 7 to 0 for the Wilson team, a genuine drubbing, and Philip made up his mind to follow the chess fortunes of their unusual top player.

(Over the years Harry Golombek was destined to become Great Britain's strongest player, a polished and charming English gentleman, the popular founder and adjudicator of the International Chess Federation and a respected ambassador of goodwill for his adopted country. He became a writer of chess manuals and – eventually – a knight of the realm. Philip marveled at the extaordinary metamorphosis and was lost admiration of this unique person. Nietsche himself would have marveled at this triumph of the will.)

During the intervening years, Philip played many friendly but serious games with his favorite opponent, Alf Steffanson, and they had some great games. In the army, he was able to polish up his game and could now give a fairly good account of himself except against a real Chess Master. In 1950, while discussing some financial matters with his bank manager Cy Hastings, he was asked if he ever played chess. It turned out that the manager was the city champion and had held that honor for some considerable time.

"Why don't you come up to the chess club tonight at eight o'clock sharp?" he asked, "I'm playing a simultaneous match and I'll save one of the boards for you."
After further persuasion Philip agreed.

"I'm sure I'm not in your class," he said, "but I'll come along anyway."

It wasn't very far into the game when he knew just how right he was. Hastings was destroying him and he was fighting for his life on the checkered board. He knew two chess tricks in these situations. The first was to hold on and give ground grudgingly; the second was to follow his well-worn adage: "You no try, you no get." After a while his opponent became just a trifle impatient and went for the artistic kill, but blundered instead with an attempt at overkill. The position suddenly gave Philip a winning combination, totally unplanned and an absolute fluke.

His victory was more embarrassment than triumph, but since his was the only winning game for the challengers, he realized he'd better do some real studying of the game and get in lots of practice, or the accident of his win would be obvious to the entire club. The result of this experience was a much improved standard of play and a steady climb in the ranking.

By early 1951, Cy Hastings was posted to Winnipeg and Philip decided to go after the city championship, and he estimated this would take about seven or eight years of hard but thoroughly enjoyable effort.

Patty, too, was starting to show some renewed interests, and first and foremost among these was the formation of a new Art Gallery for the city. An exploratory committee had been formed and she was asked to serve as one of its members. Philip was delighted when she accepted and was confident she would do a fine job, as with everything she attempted. During the past year he'd witnessed, with unabashed admiration, her remarkable dress-making abilities when she completed a set of beautiful ballet costumes for their dancing daughter. These were so splendid and artistic that – with Florian modeling expertly – he took a complete roll of color transparencies, to be treasured by the entire family in the distant future. These were their golden days and Philip was determined to keep his cameras busy, both his old 8mm movie camera and his ever-reliable Reflex 2.

Now, if only his practice would continue to grow, their lives would be complete. Both his wife and his office nurse told him he was being too impatient and expressed complete confidence in the future. Philip hoped their optimism would be justified. To bolster his own optimism, he decided to take the family on a long motoring trip as soon as the children were out of school for the summer holidays.

They all drove down to Oregon, and once the prevailing off-shore fog had cleared, the coastline with its marvelous wide beaches and great rocks jutting out of the surf were a unique visual experience and a perfect opportunity for Philip's photographic efforts. He drove the Chrysler right down onto the beach and they enjoyed the view and invigorating sea air; it was great to see the children having such a good time. Portland, the 'City of Roses', was well worth visiting and they stayed there for twenty-four hours before proceeding on their way to San Francisco. From time to

time the scenery along the coastal road was so magnificent that they simply had to stop and im-
merse themselves in the breathtaking spectacle, while he took some shots with his Reflex 2.

San Francisco, 'The American Naples', was all they'd heard and dreamed of, and
more. The weather remained perfect and they took advantage of the brilliant sunshine to explore
the glistening city from one end to the other. Philip learned to drive the hilly streets and kept his
hand close to the handbrake to avoid rolling back whenever they stopped on an uphill slope. They
visited Fisherman's Wharf and sampled its superb seafood, and they drove out to see the Golden
Gate Bridge at sunset. They also decided to take the children with them to the Top of the Mark, the
famed penthouse cocktail lounge of the Mark Hopkins Hotel.

The headwaiter was extremely helpful, and when they told him they were from Canada
and this was a special treat for the children, he promptly got them an excellent corner table with a
superb view of the city. The grown-ups settled for some excellent 'Bay Specials', a super gin fizz,
and the children were brought exotic non-alcoholic colored drinks in tall glasses, with whipped
cream and Maraschino cherries on top. They were absolutely overjoyed and felt like regular customers rather than small fry.

The next day they took in Chinatown and the bell-clanging cablecars that careened
downhill to Market Street. They looked across the Bay at the prison fortress on Alcatraz Island,
drove out to Pebble Beach and watched the sea lions frolicking offshore. They observed the huge
flow of traffic across the Bay Bridge to Oakland and Berkeley across the water, then drove to the
fairgrounds where the children took a delirious series of rides, almost to the point of exhaustion.
The whole family agreed it was a pity they couldn't have taken Whiskers along, but it would have
been a bit too much. In any event, when the Southerbys volunteered to look after him during their
friends' absence, the Bosnars gratefully accepted. They knew how much they liked dogs, and Whiskers was one of their favorites.

The following day the travelers took a city tour to the old Spanish missions, to Tel-
egraph Hill, the Nob Hill area, special buildings of architectural elegance, and the city parks. Philip
tried to capture some of the sights with his camera, but there was a special atmosphere about these
scenes that no photograph could ever capture.

On the third day they took a leisurely drive around the Monterey Peninsula, watched
the artists at work, and were exhilarated by the wild waves crashing against the craggy rocks
below. They watched as the incoming tide sent great plumes of spray upward against the impressive homes poised in perilous overhang on the cliffs above. The twisted shapes of the Monterey
pines stood out boldly, like rugged guardians of the windswept shores, and Philip found it hard not
to purchase easel and paint there and then, and join the inspired throng of artists reveling in Nature's breathtaking display. Meanwhile, his cameras would have to suffice.

Whenever and wherever possible, he tried to include one or more members of the
family in unposed positions but in chosen colors of apparel to complement each scene. Then, as the
sun started to set, they drove out to the Giant Redwood Park, where only the giant wooden voice of
Nelson Eddy, singing 'Trees' on a recording that came from concealed loudspeakers, interfered
with the grandeur of these ancient living monuments.

The following day they bade a sad farewell to glorious San Francisco, America's
picture city, and drove down toward Los Angeles. On the journey southward they were impressed
with the garden-like beauty of Santa Barbara and the beflowered elegance of a large motel; where

some of the occupants were soaking up the mid-day sun around a large swimming pool and others were enjoying outdoor drinks or lunch.

Taking a chance, Philip parked the car close by and went into the office of the motel, where he tried his prepared gambit. After telling the desk clerks they were from Canada and how impressed they were with their fair city and this motel, he asked if they could stay for an outdoor lunch. They replied that they'd be delighted to have the Canadian visitors stay as long as they wished, and perhaps at some other time they might stay for a few days or weeks. As a matter of fact, especially after availing themselves of the excellent washroom facilities and enjoying a superb outdoor lunch, the Bosnar family was sorely tempted to remain for a few days, but decided they'd better press on.

They didn't go all the way into Los Angeles but stopped instead at a convenient motel in Malibu Beach, situated just across the road from the seashore. After a clean-up and change of clothes they drove to a Beachcomber Restaurant nearby, where they enjoyed a Polynesian-style dinner and some delicious drinks in hollowed-out fresh pineapple. The ones for James and Florian were well diluted and they thought they were absolutely "the greatest".

After breakfast at the motel the following morning, Philip couldn't resist a quick swim in the ocean: the rolling breakers were just too inviting. He hadn't reckoned with the strong undertow, one that was a new and disturbing experience for him, but doubtless quite commonplace for Californians.

They drove into Los Angeles, thick with smog and humanity, with dense motor traffic and fast food emporia, with ugly billboards and America's most unattractive buildings. The fabled Sunset Strip was a severe disappointment, so they decided they should at least take a tour of the 'Homes of the Stars' and Universal Studios. The sumptuous houses were impressive, but like the studios that followed, appeared almost devoid of human habitation. Perhaps the entire film community went into hiding at the approach of the bus tours.

Taking a wrong turn, after driving away from the tour terminus, they suddenly found ourselves in the thick of multiple columns of cars, each vehicle driven by suicidal and homicidal pilots trying to break the sound barrier. It was their first experience of the celebrated Freeway system and for a few moments they thought it might be their last.

About three miles further along they were able to edge the car to an exit, find their way out of town and head for the famed Knott's Berry Farm. This proved to be an ideal playground for the children, with reconstructed streets and scenes from the old Wild West, and a re-enacted shootout at the O.K.Corral, with Wyatt Earp and Doc Halliday taking on the bad guys in the black hats. There were saloons, gamblers and the dance girls, bank hold-ups and posses chasing robbers. The children enjoyed their ride on a miniature steam-train of the last century, complete with cow catcher in front.

There was even a paddle-boat steamer on a miniature Mississippi River, miners panning for gold, and a marshal guarding his gaol against an attempted rescue by the prisoner's dastardly pals. Last but not least, their was a stirring native Indian war dance, with the Chief in full feathered regalia coming straight for Philip's movie camera with his tomahawk. It was an entrancing experience for both children, and by the time they got to the motel in San Bernadino they were both more than ready for bed.

The next day they would embark on their journey across the notorious Mojave Desert, then on to the mighty Grand Canyon.

CHAPTER 29

1953-54

By the time they got to Barstow, it was getting really hot, and they stopped at a gas station to have the engine checked out. They put a fresh supply of cold water in the radiator and installed a dry ice cooler for the trip across the Mojave Desert. As they approached the scorched town of Needles, they were delighted to see a large motel complete with swimming pool and a sign advertising 'The Desert's Coolest Refrigerated Units'. They checked in for the day and decided not to resume their journey until nightfall.

The unit was spacious, with two king size beds and a heavenly air-conditioning system that sent a gentle current of cold air over their toasted bodies. Patty was the sensible one, and after showering, lay down between the cool sheets for a siesta.

Florian and James thought they ought to put on their swimsuits and enjoy the pool, and their carefree father joined them happily. Of course it turned out to be sheer lunacy in that heat, and crossing the pathway to the pool was like running over hot coals. So, after a brief romp in the warm water, with the sun beating down on their heads, they decided to follow Patty's example. At noon, the outside temperature on the giant outside thermometer registered 110 degrees Fahrenheit, and they stayed inside.

By 1.30, they were feeling a bit peckish and got a quick snack at the local restaurant, then returned to their refrigerated room to sleep for the rest of the afternoon, in blissful relief from the cruel heat. When it got dark enough, they resumed their journey eastward and were delighted when, after a few vivid lightning flashes, the rains came down in a torrential cloudburst, relieving the lingering heat of the day.

When they got to the town of Flagstaff, they were ready to freshen up and have a decent meal, and they found a reasonably modern restaurant. Everyone in the crowded interior wore large cowboy Stetson hats and riding boots to match, and the washrooms bore the signs 'Steers' and 'Heifers'. The atmosphere of the noisy dining room was rough and ready, but the meal was first rate and the service beyond reproach.

They arrived at Sunset Lodge on the South Rim of the Grand Canyon in the early hours of the morning and parked the car. The children remained sound asleep in the back. As Phil and Patty stood by the guard rail bordering the canyon, in pitch-black darkness, they heard a frightening sound coming up to them from far below, like a monster breathing deeply. It was the distant roar of the raging Colorado River, but to the uninitiated visitors it sounded as though the canyon was a great prehistoric beast trying to inhale them into its depths.

For the next few days, they stayed at this enthralling place and never tired of watching the canyon's everchanging colors and patterns, and the capricious versatility of its moods. The sheer dimensions of its depth and width, and the realization that a river's ceaseless flow could carve such a great chasm into the multilayered rock, awakened a sense of wonder and perspective in all of them.

On the third morning, they drove out to Bryce Canyon in southern Utah. By the time they got there, it was raining hard and there didn't seem much worth waiting for. Other tourists parked nearby appeared to reach the same conclusion, and the cars left one by one; but Philip was suddenly seized with the stubborn determination of a frustrated photographer. He decided to wait out the shower and prayed for the sun to come out and illuminate the scene.

Thirty minutes later, the rain stopped and they all held their breath as brilliant shafts of sunshine converted the carved shapes lining the rocky slopes into a vast amphitheater of gleaming statues. They seemed fashioned in gold and were arrayed in magnificent crescents, row upon endless row, on a vast terraced floor of white marble. It was an unforgettable sight, and Philip knew the photographs he took would more than match those he'd already taken of the Grand Canyon.

The next morning, they set out for Zion National Park, where they stayed for three enjoyable days. They explored the exquisite architecture of a multihued wonderland, like a storybook city built of Nature's finest stone, in colors of red, yellow and orange. It was adorned by great rocky towers and cathedrals, as though planned to house giant supermen rather than mere mortals. The weather remained perfect, the facilities and service couldn't be bettered, and Philip kept his cameras busy. The children had a fine time in the swimming pool and glowed with health and happiness, while Patty felt totally relaxed and even humored Phil's demands that she pose time after time.

It was hard for the Bosnars to tear themselves away from this fairyland of magical hues and contours, but on the third day they were off again, this time heading northward across the Nevada desert. The highway was crowded with the corpses of countless jack-rabbits, victims of the modern combustion engine and uncaring mankind. Misnamed Homo Sapiens, this strange species responded only to the clatter of slot machines that resounded in every gas station, restaurant and store of this primitive locale.

The twenty-four hours they spent in Reno produced an amusing incident. All four family members went into Harrah's, one of the largest casinos, and were dismayed to find that there were no facilities for children. So far, there hadn't been a single place where they hadn't taken them along, and Philip was sufficiently annoyed to ask for the manager. A pleasant individual came forward and asked what he could do for them. He was so damnably polite that it was hard to proceed.

"We're down here from Canada on a grand tour of the Western States and this is the first place we've been where there aren't any facilities for children."

"I'm happy to say you're quite mistaken, Sir. Upstairs on the second floor we have a special movie theater for children, and playrooms as well. These are all supervised by trained nursing personnel, and the children are checked in and out by name and by time."

"In that case I owe you my humblest apologies and I'll be sure to spread the word to my friends when I get back."

Phil and Patty checked in the youngsters upstairs, where they had the time of their lives for the next three hours. Meanwhile, their father played the blackjack tables, with Patty at his side to bring him luck.

Then it was northward to Crater Lake, where they all had to put on extra clothing against the high elevation's brisk atmosphere. The children played to their heart's content with a family of cute chipmunks, while Patty served as movie director and Philip as cinematographer. After a night's stay at the lodge, they were off to Mount Hood, where they took the chair lifts and watched the skiers winding their way down the glistening mountainside.

Some more photography, then they were on their way back to their own matchless British Columbia, with a thousand images in their memories and a host of still photos and 8 mm. movies. Most of these turned out surprisingly well, but none better than those of Bryce Canyon, taken on that unpromising rainy morning.

The fish weren't biting, the fog was closing in and it was a time for chewing the fat. The two fishermen kept the putt-putt motor running at minimum speed, so other boats heading in their direction would be aware of their presence. As for finding their way back, Glen Parsons had his faithful compass with him and they were both confident of a safe return.

"What do you think, Glen. Should I go ahead or do you think it's just a pipe dream?"
For the past year, Philip had become fascinated by the remarkable advances in cardiovascular surgery. As he read about the pioneer efforts of men like Carrel in France, Matas and Blalock in the U.S.A. and, more recently, Crafoord in Sweden, he felt a surge of excitement and a mounting desire to be part of this brave exploration of new surgical frontiers. From time to time he had discussed this latest dream with Patty, and she encouraged him to go ahead with his enquiries.

That was the matter he now broached with his good friend and fishing partner, and the reply took him by surprise.

"Pipe dream or not, Phil, I think you should go right ahead and talk it over with some of the senior guys in the surgical specialties. I'm sure they'll give you all the encouragement and help they can. Don't forget you've made a pretty good reputation for yourself in this city, and in only a few short years."

"Hold on there, I think you're bullshitting me."

"No I'm not, Phil. It's just guys like you who'd be expected to try breaking new ground. You've obviously had your fill of stomachs, gallbladders, spleens and guts, breasts and thyroids. Not to mention varicose veins, piles and all the humdrum stuff of general surgery. It's no wonder you're showing signs of middle life crisis. At least you haven't gone bonkers over another woman."

"Holy shit, Glen! That was quite a piece of oratory, and you haven't even shared any of my rotgut. But thanks anyway for your opinion and optimism. I guess I'll go ahead. After all I'm the one who's always repeating, `You no try you no get', so I'd better practice what I preach."

The entire family enjoyed radio, and in addition to the excellent newscasts, topflight plays, comedy programs and sports events, there was little doubt that the general standard of programs was far superior to much of the drivel being peddled on television. There was magic in the power of the mind to visualize the action through the airborne waves of radio broadcasts, whether Canadian, American or even the BBC. It was somehow akin to the blind man who 'sees' to such a remarkable degree with his hearing and other intact senses.

Phil and Patty were always amazed at how one could picture the action during broadcast sports events, especially as the annual championships approached: hockey's Stanley Cup, football's Grey Cup, and most of all, baseball's World Series. By listening carefully to the sportscasters it was even possible to acquire an expert knowledge of the games' finer points. Now, with startling suddenness, all that changed.

The circumstance was quite an ordinary one. Whenever Philip walked to his office from the parking lot, he'd glance at the windows of the newly rebuilt Hudson's Bay Store. On this particular occasion, he found himself riveted by what he saw taking place on the 14 inch screen of an Electrohome television set that was on display, with the sound track carried to passing pedestrians by outside loudspeakers. What he saw and heard was living, breathing history, and he knew he must buy a television set without delay.

The program showed the Army-McCarthy hearings, with the unctuous junior Senator from Wisconsin bullying witnesses who were called before the Senate Investigating Committee. He was aided and abetted by an unwholesome lawyer, Roy Cohn, as well as other members of this infamous committee. Against all these forces of reaction and anti-red hysteria, only one resolute champion of democratic freedoms faced up to the challenge. He was a man who symbolized courageous justice versus cowardly innuendo. All the oily McCarthy interruptions of, "Mr. Chairman, Mr. Chairman, Point of order," couldn't deflect the dignified Judge Joseph Welch from his determined stand on behalf of the American Constitution against the forces of a modern witch-hunt.

For the next few days and until the end of the hearings, Phil and Patty watched their new TV set in fascination as Judge Welch, with humor and wisdom, stripped the cloak of official respectability from the sinister inquisitor, and left him in naked dishonor and disgrace. A single outraged comment was the only one spoken in anger by this gentle jurist, as he stood facing the snickering McCarthy, "In the name of God, Sir, have you no sense of decency?"

That was the beginning of the end for Joe McCarthy and for the infamous political persecutions that – during the earlier House Unamerican Activities Committee – had cost the 'Hollywood Ten' their freedom and career. The infamous chairman of that committee, John Parnell Thomas, had subsequently gone to jail for the red-blooded patriotic crimes of income tax evasion and embezzlement of congressional funds.

Perhaps the real guilt for this entire red-baiting spectacle lay with Dwight. D. Eisenhower, the irresolute president of his nation. His predecessor, Harry Truman, firm and unwavering as a national leader, had the guts to recall and demote the popular American hero, General MacArthur; while that great desk warrior, 'Ike', couldn't even stifle a dangerous demagogue in his own political party.

1954 was a year of international ferment, and the news, both home and abroad, now took on a new dimension on their 14 inch screen. The Cold War seemed to be reaching its climax in the rubble of post-war Berlin. What amounted to the siege of West Berlin by the Soviet Kommandatura seemed a challenge to the West that was just short of war. One could only gasp at the audacity of the American airlift, risking its brave air crews as they flew through fog and peril to feed the beleaguered West Berliners.

The western world applauded a compassion that defied the threat of war to carry out its mission of mercy. Without a doubt, this was America's finest hour of recent times, and it showed that Cold War paranoia hadn't fatally dulled the national conscience. By the grace of God, this was not to be another Korean-type war, with massive loss of life followed by a return to the status pro quo. What was now revealed was the more human face of a schizoid national mentality, and Philip was glad to sing its praises. Perhaps one day, when there were no more racial or political hatreds, a truly United States of America could achieve its genuine rather than its aggressive 'Manifest' destiny.

It was hard for Phil and Patty to accept the latest moral and political paradox in the United States. The president had been so firm in refusing to accede to world-wide pleas for clemency toward the Rosenbergs. But now, he was showing flabby indecision in suppressing racial disorders and lawless oppression against the American Negro in the southern states. His election platform, that he would be the peacemaker in war-ravaged Korea, was an affront to all who had fought and died in that divided country, and to all who followed the no-peace-no-war stalemate of the past few years. Sadly, it appeared that the majority of Americans were not keen students of twentieth century history.

With India and Pakistan now independent countries, and the members of the British Commonwealth of nations seeking increasing autonomy from the mother country, it seemed to Philip that Canada was drawing away from Britain at an accelerating pace. It was becoming more and more oriented toward its giant neighbor to the south. As this change became increasingly apparent, the demands of Quebec seemed to become more stridently proclaimed. The concept of a bilingual nation was a progressive one, but only if matched by a willingness by francophone Canadians to accept the idea of a united Canada; with Quebec as just another province, albeit one of great importance. The French language must retain its essential role in current Canadian life as well as its place in history, but ethnic pride must not explode into wild separationist excesses.

Phil often discussed these matters with Patty in considerable depth, and she saw many parallels with the sad history of her beloved Ireland during the first half of the twentieth century. It would be tragic, she thought, if religious differences were ever added to the already explosive ethnic and linguistic mix in Canada. She'd witnessed both antisemitism and anticatholicism during her Vanwey years, and knew about the violent antiprotestant demonstrations in Quebec. As far as she and Phil were concerned, the sooner the Orange Lodge and Knights of Columbus disappeared from multi-ethnic Canada, the better. As for hate organizations like the Ku Klux Klan, the last vestiges of this odious philosophy still existed in rural Alberta and even rural Saskatchewan.

They noticed that both children were showing an increasing interest in daily news, especially the discussions of current national and international affairs between their parents, and they were beginning to ask pertinent questions. Not only were they exhibiting a social awareness on a broadening scale, but – aside from childish mischief – were each exhibiting a development of character and outlook that was most encouraging.

Both thought they'd been baptized as infants, and considered themselves the Christian offspring of Roman Catholic but non-practicing parents. They knew their parents attended no particular church service but had no aversion to any form or denomination of worship, and they felt free to join their friends in whatever church activities they chose to pursue. Aside from these family details, they also recognized the fact that their parents opposed all forms of religious or racial intolerance. Both youngsters had chosen to enter the Scout and Girl Guide movements and thoroughly enjoyed their annual camping holidays in the countryside, and they took part in whatever prayers were held in the course of their activities.

Phil and Patty found no fault with the basic tenets of the Scout credo, basically that of self-reliance, love and respect for parents, and good deeds as well as good intentions toward others. They were happy the children could belong to such an organization without sectarian religious restraints. By next summer, they would both be ready learn about their origin and their heritage: their 'roots', so to speak. Privately, Philip was already toying with the idea of sending Patty and the children over to England and Ireland next year, so they could get to know both of their families in more intimate and interesting detail. It would also enable their grandparents to get to know them and enjoy their company on a daily basis, and for a period of months.

Armed with a superb set of testimonials from the leading surgeons of the city, Dr. Philip Bosnar wrote to Professor Clarence Crafoord at the Carolinska Institute and Hospital in Stockholm, Sweden. Perhaps he should have asked Kinsley for one of those testimonials, but they seemed to have drifted too far apart and he felt it would be a presumption on his part. The big surprise was the letter of recommendation from Dr. Leslie Foster, whose illustrious surgical career had ended shortly after Philip's arrival in Edwardia.

In earlier days, when well-trained and well-qualified surgeons were few and far between on the West Coast, this bantam-sized bundle of energy was renowned from Anchorage in Alaska to San Diego in California. His reputation brought him patients from cities and towns between these two places and made him one of the busiest surgeons in Canada. He lived fairly modestly, was a generous patron of the arts and other good causes, and indulged his one and only extravagance, namely his own private planetarium, to which Philip had been invited from time to time, along with a few other fortunate visitors. Other than that, Philip saw the retired surgeon a few times at the weekly ward rounds, where his comments were always witty and wise.

Dr. Foster believed in the old-fashioned and honorable way of billing: if the patient was wealthy the bill was high, if in straitened circumstances the bill was torn up. It was socially desirable, ethically without fault, and in keeping with Philip's own sentiment in such matters. To charge less than the minimum fee schedule (other than complete cancellation of the bill) was considered unethical and an unfair method of competing for patients.

Patty thought the eminent surgeon's support would be invaluable to her husband's plans, since he actually knew Dr. Crafoord and had spent some time with him, both in Stockholm and at a meeting in Leyden, Holland. Foster suggested that Bosnar would be well advised to spend a year in Sweden, then six months with Gunnar Bauer in Leyden and another six months with Lord Brock in London, England.

The reply from Stockholm came much sooner than expected, and was partly good news and partly bad. Professor Crafoord would be pleased to have Philip Bosnar join him in the capacity of observer for as long as he wished to stay, but felt he could demonstrate all the Canadian surgeon needed to know in less than twelve months. Although Dr. Bosnar might have an opportunity to 'scrub in' with him, he was unable to offer his visitor any sort of salaried position, and Philip must be prepared to finance his own residence and meals.

This was now an entirely different situation and Philip's course was quite clear. If he could arrange the financing of such a project he'd go, taking Patty and the children with him. But he'd require the ironclad guarantee of an appointment as cardiovascular surgeon in the new unit that was being planned for Vancouver.

He discussed the matter fully with the family before broaching the matter with Dr. Nelson Richfield. He saw him two weeks later, at an executive committee meeting of the C.P.S.A. of which they were both members. Richfield was the highly respected Professor of Surgery at the

U.B.C. medical faculty in Vancouver and a man whom Bosnar really admired. He was quite straight-forward in his advice.

"To be perfectly honest with you, Phil, we now have an excellent young chap being groomed for our new department of cardiovascular surgery and it would probably be many years before we could take on a second man in that field. I'd be only too glad to recommend you for a similar opening anywhere else across the country."

"I'm afraid that won't do me much good, but thanks, anyway. You see, the only way I could possibly raise the necessary bank loan to cover all my considerable costs for this project, would be a guaranteed appointment when I get back."

"Well, I guess you know best. I'm sure you'd make a damn good cardiovascular surgeon but I can't help wondering why you'd want to drop all your general surgery."

"I believe general surgery is gradually becoming dismembered. Before I came to B.C. a lot of my best work was in gynecology. Now this work goes to our several Ob.Gyn. fellows. The same sort of thing applies to other fields of work such as urology and orthopedics. Each new subspecialty cuts down some of the scope of general surgery and Edwardia is getting more subspecialists each year."

"There's a lot of truth in what you say, but if you have to give up your plans to do cardiovascular work how about special fields of interest?"

"You may have something there, I must admit. In the past two years I've had several cases of parotid tumor, major diaphramatic hernias with reflux esophagitis, deep vein incompetence and plastic surgery problems. Perhaps I'll apply myself more and more to specific expertise in these conditions."

"I'm pretty sure you'll find it satisfying, and I don't think you'll be disappointed in the long run."

When Philip recounted this conversation to his beloved wife she was more irritated than disappointed and couldn't help observing, "There's always someone else, isn't there? Just like merry old England. I think Canada's caught the disease, don't you?"

"Maybe. Like good old-fashioned nepotism, the old boy's network is alive and well in this country. Strangely enough, I don't feel particularly bad about the whole affair and I think I'll take Richfield's advice about special interests."

"You've always said that what makes a good chess player is the ability to convert a losing position into an unexpected win by using the right tactics."

"Let's hope I prove right in this particular instance. At least we don't have to worry about lean times for the family over the next few years."

"Tell me more about these special interests of yours."

"You know it's a funny thing but these are almost the same as those of Sterling Thomas, Assistant Professor of Surgery at U.B.C. They include parotid tumors, major diaphragmatic hernias, venous problems of the lower limbs and certain plastic procedures."

"Give me some details."

"First of all, there's the correct surgery for benign parotid tumor, a carefully performed removal of either the superficial lobe or the entire gland, depending on the location of the lump. This operation entails accurate dissection and preservation of the facial nerve and all its branches. The entire dissection has to be scrupulously photographed as a permanent record."

"Why do you do that?"

"To reassure the patient in case there's a temporary facial weakness. The weakness disappears in a matter of weeks as a rule."

"What about hernias of the diaphragm?"

"The commonest variety is the one called a sliding hiatus hernia. These cases require no surgery unless they're accompanied by severe esophageal reflux not responding to medical treatment. The others that I see are the result of injury, and are repaired through the chest. Lately, I've had a couple of really spectacular examples of massive hernias due to crushing auto accidents."

"You'll have to draw some of your diagrams for me when you have more time"

"As for deep vein problems of the legs, I'll go into that subject at some other time, as well, and with some more diagrams."

"And the plastic surgery?"

"That involves various types of pedicle grafts, rotation grafts, correction of advanced Jug Ears, and surgery for Dupuytren's contracture of the hand, among other types of related surgery."

"It sounds to me as if you have more than enough to keep you interested beyond your standard operations, don't you agree, darling?"

"I guess so, Patty. The variety is certainly there, but the volume needs to be considerably increased if I'm going to feel really successful in this very conservative city."

"As far as I'm concerned, you're that already."

It was at times like this, that Philip realized what a lucky S.O.B. he was in having a wife like his adorable Patricia. Always loyal and understanding, there wasn't a single aspect of his daily life that he couldn't discuss with her in detail, and she was always deeply interested in his work. At heart she'd never stopped being a surgical nurse, and he had no hesitation talking over his surgical ideas with her.

August brought a beautiful combination of brilliant sunshine and warm clear air. It also brought the popular Prince Philip on a visit to their fair city. The crowds came out to see him, with tourists outnumbering local citizens. All were all dazzled by the royal motorcade, with the smiling Prince spreading his well-known charm. He waved enthusiastically to the cheering crowd from the back seat of a special touring car, made available for the occasion. It was a pale salmon-colored Monarch convertible, with its ivory- white top folded down for the fine weather, a perfect choice for the occasion.

The following Saturday, Philip was driving down Thurston Avenue when he spotted the beautiful vehicle, now on display in the center isle of Brownlow Motors' showroom. At that moment, Philip Bosnar knew he must own that very car, for it was love at first sight. After a few minutes with the manager, whom he knew well as a patient, agreeable terms were arrived at, including the trade-in of Philip's Chrysler. The price was reasonable, and one hour later he proudly drove the new car home. The family was overjoyed and the new convertible became the latest wonder in the life of the Bosnars.

In days to come, this magnificent automobile would become a popular Bosnar trademark, and many of their friends were eager to be driven around in the 'Prince Philip Car', always with the top down, no matter what the outside temperature. Philip was too dazzled by the sheer beauty of his new car to recognize that this was just the psychological lift he needed to compensate for his recently shattered dream of cardiovascular surgery, and it helped to propel him wholeheartedly into his work, putting his set-back behind him.

After all, he told himself, it would have been quite a wrench to leave all his gastrointestinal surgery aside, quite aside from his other special interests in general surgery. Perhaps his regrets might have proven greater than his excitement over the new subspecialty, no matter how glamorous or lucrative.

He was now becoming more heavily involved in the activities of the C.P.S.A. and those of the Section of General Surgery in the B.C. Medical Association. He was asked to serve as program chairman for the following year in the one organization and to take an active role in the decisions of the other. His main efforts were directed at preserving General Surgery from becoming fractionated into a plethora of subdivisions, and eliminating the widespread custom of splitting the surgical fee with the referring doctor. These activities now brought him into contact with some of Vancouver's finest surgeons, some of whom became good friends.

It wasn't only friends who were being acquired by these new activities, however, but enemies as well – in Vancouver, Edwardia and across the province. Most of these were general practitioners, a fair number were surgeons, but the most implacable was his old nemesis Herb Fraywell, former Registrar of the Saskatchewan College of Physicians and Surgeons. He was now Executive Secretary of the B.C.M.A. and in a position to complicate Philip's program, mainly behind the scenes and for purely vindictive motives.

Philip kept quiet about this aspect of the situation, except to Patty, but he felt sorry for some of his colleagues. They were already feeling the pinch because of their attempts to improve the climate of surgical practice. It was obvious they were in for a long hard struggle, but in the end it would be worth it. He felt sure of that, and so did his loyal wife.

The Bosnars' social life was very satisfying and their circle of friends was constantly expanding. Philip's chess activities were increasing and he was developing into a strong challenger for the top ten in the city's ranks, but not quite ready for the championship. Their friends, Hank and Mattie Torwald, sold their small motel for a good profit and bought a property closer to the city center: one they were busy improving and converting into a larger motel with some two dozen units. It seemed they were on the march, and Phil and Patty were happy to see them moving into better times.

Florian was working hard on her ballet endeavors but was running into some problems with her ankles, and her parents wondered if she might have to give up her precious dancing ambitions. James was now an accomplished bugler and deeply involved in the cadets as well as the scouts. Patty was very busy as new president of the Edwardia Arts Society and enjoying it greatly, and Philip was starting to get interested in a new activity. It was tape-recording, more than a hobby and almost a new obsession, to which he'd been introduced by Dr. Stanovitsky.

Emil Stanovitsky was an interesting and versatile family doctor, with a large practice that included many families of European origin. He'd come to Canada from England shortly after World War 2, and married a gregarious and amusing Englishwoman shortly after his arrival in Edwardia. They were both interested in the arts, especially music, with a special enthusiasm for Broadway musicals. Anita Stanovitsky was a tireless hostess and her parties were famous for their excellence and the quality of her guests. She chose them mostly for their ability to participate in sophisticated conversation. She usually dominated these conversations herself, and had the talent of breaking into anybody's train of delivery by brilliant timing, while few ever tried to interrupt her. She was simply too adroit and much too practiced.

Emil was a quiet man and had an old-world charm and graciousness. His speech was cultured, and he could speak both French and German with a fair degree of fluency. He had many hobbies, including astronomy and photography, and had recently taken up tape-recording. These were mostly of interesting conversations, poetic readings and live instrumental recordings.

Phil and Patty became very fond of this unusual couple and found themselves invited to their soirees with increasing frequency. One apparent paradox puzzled them. Anita never seemed to eat anything at all, and according to Emil she never ate a decent meal or indulged in snacks, yet she remained extremely rotund and weighed close to two hundred pounds. She carried off her size with a flair and always dressed in appropriate style, with a penchant for bright colors to offset her rosy complexion.

Neither Emil nor Anita had the slightest interest in bridge or chess and carefully re-frained from expressing any political views, but they loved to reminisce about their experiences in prewar continental Europe. Emil was a non- practicing Jew of Czechoslovakian birth and Anita was a faithful British Anglican from Oxfordshire. Most of the Stanovitsky's regular guests were highly entertaining, and none more so than Colonel and Mrs. Bradford. He was a widely traveled adventurer with countless anecdotes of his colorful life, and she was a painter of wild life.

They'd met while on a photographic safari in the foothills of Mount Killimanjaro and found they had a great deal in common. Their marriage was hardly an affair of the heart, since he was a typically stiff and unromantic colonial while she was plain, dowdy, and rather mannish. Nevertheless, they got along well and seemed to enjoy each other's commentaries on a wide vari-ety of subjects. Bradford was in his early eighties but bright as a dollar, and his wife was some ten years younger and as chirpy as a sparrow. They both took a strong liking to the Bosnars and the feeling was entirely mutual.

The colonel's story was a fascinating one. The son of a vicar in Oxfordshire, he'd been a competent steeplechase rider in his youth and won several cups. He enlisted in the British army at the outbreak of the Boer War and soon rose to the rank of captain. After the war he started to study medicine, but changed his mind and became a mining engineer instead. His travels took him to Mexico, where he made his early fortune before having his first dangerous brush with vicious rebels and banditos who began to infiltrate the area. Some of the mine workers were simply shot in cold blood, but he managed to escape and hide in the dense brush below the silver mine.

"Now, doctor," he said, with a wry smile, "I'd like your opinion of this surgical job." Without further ado, he pulled up his left sleeve and showed Philip the stump of his left forearm, expertly amputated above the wrist.

"A perfect job. Was it a war-wound, Colonel?"

"Not at all. In my hurry to get away from the marauders I took a bad fall. It resulted in a nasty compound fracture of the left forearm. It rapidly became infected, and within forty-eight hours was showing signs of gangrene. I'd fled without rations, and aside from the machete that never left my side, my backpack only held a primitive first aid kit and a few artery forceps."

The narrator renewed their drinks before continuing.

"My delirium dulled the pain and I was able to do an open amputation just above the compound fracture. I was able to control most of the major bleeding, and several days later, more dead than alive, managed to crawl back to the mine where my faithful staff, all that remained, nursed me back to health."

"What an amazing story! The stump has certainly healed beautifully."

"Not only that, but I could hammer a nail into wood with that stump when I was younger." He promised to tell Philip the rest of his story at a later date, on condition that they arrange to play some games of chess together, since he was a devotee of the royal game and knew Philip was, too.

Another of the Stanovitsky's friends and frequent guests was Archbishop Slater, a convivial Englishman who was fond of lively company and had an appreciative palate for good Scotch whisky and French cognac. Patty found him most delightful.

The Mayfairs were the least attractive couple of this group, and hardly the type one would imagine having much in common with the Stanovitskys. Dr. Mayfair was a pompous, pretentious and self-centered G.P. and his wife Cynthia always behaved in an embarrassing theatrical manner. It seemed that she'd first met Anita in prewar Vienna, and they'd remained close friends ever since.

Anita Mowbray, later Stanovitsky, was recuperating at that time from an unpleasant divorce, leaving an embittered first husband and alienated daughter behind. She was enjoying the cosmopolitan cafe' society, with its smartly uniformed Austrian officers, all punctiliously well-mannered and displaying great charm. They were the heel-clicking, hand- kissing variety, with a touch of Viennese *Gemutlichkeit*. As for Cynthia Killop, later Mayfair, she was a small-time stage actress who found herself stranded in Vienna when her traveling theater group ran out of money.

Phil and Patty never found out how these two had survived in a strange country for two years without financial support or employment, but would never dream of trying to find out. The Mayfairs never became their friends and Philip could never have guessed that Anthony (**"Please DO NOT call me Tony!"**) would visit his home, years later, to make him a strange offer and reveal some well-guarded secrets of the medical profession in Edwardia.

In national affairs, 'Uncle Louis' St. Laurent was still running a lack-luster government in the true tradition of Mackenzie King and the nation cried out for a new type of leadership. In international affairs, the debacle of Korea seemed destined to be repeated in Indochina. The colonial French had finally been soundly defeated by the little yellow men of Vietnam, and the fall of the French fortress at Dienbienphu signaled the end of the white man's influence in this part of the world. Not all the saber-rattling threats of John Foster Dulles, Eisenhower's opinionated Secretary of State, failed to arrest the march of history; even when he threatened to use the atom bomb if the Vietnamese didn't stop their onslaught.

What crackpots like Dulles failed to realize, was that atom bombs were useless in fighting jungle warfare and guerilla tactics. Moreover, spying or not, the enemy – sooner or later – was always bound to get the same weapons as those of their opposite number and vice versa. Unless either side was willing to use its deadly weapons without warning (and that would lead to world catastrophe), threats of this kind were really absurd. Thus, the Vietnam they now witnessed was divided, like Korea, into a Communist North and a supposedly Democratic South, with a demilitarized zone at the 17th instead of the 38th parallel.

Anyone reading the scant news about this latest hot spot in the Far East was bound to conclude that the Eisenhower regime seemed determined to repeat the debacle of Korea at some time in the future. The heavy hand of Mao tse-Tung was replacing that of the late Josef Stalin, and one could only draw cold comfort from the increasing antagonism between Peiping and Moscow. This time, there would be no intervention by the United Nations. The Americans would have to go it alone, and Phil and Patty felt sorry for the poor devils who'd be sent to their deaths in the reeking jungles of Vietnam.

One day in the distant future, some great Western leader would finally realize that left alone, every Communist regime contained the seeds of its own reform and eventual path to democratization. It might be a slow process, but the possibility of global annihilation was simply unacceptable as an alternative.

The news from London was mainly upbeat. Clayton was doing well at his brother's old medical school and was now editor of the St. Clement's Journal. It was nice to know that his writing talents weren't going to waste. Their Dad was still working as hard as ever, but his health was fairly good and he was still the eternal optimist. Their Mum missed being surrounded by her children and found the telephone or letters a poor substitute. Lately, she'd been taking treatment for spells of depression, with favorable results.

Pauline was working in a Westend ladies' fashion shop and augmenting the family coffers. Irving was still at the same job but was getting a bit impatient at the slowness of long overdue promotion. Their older daughter was studying to be a teacher while her younger sister had no time for continuing her education, and thought only of boys and the city's bright lights. Her ambitions ran more in the direction of becoming a movie star at best or a beautician at worst. She seemed destined to pursue her wild ways and bring grief to her devoted mother. It was an era of juvenile emancipation, with its attendant delinquency, and it was extolled by the popular young singing idols. English youth seemed to be taking a bad turn.

Clayton's enrollment in the medical school at St. Clement's Hospital was a strange one. After matriculating successfully from the prestigious Smithson High School in Hendon, he served his two year stint in the British Army before applying to St. Clement's. His application was turned down right away, with the suggestion that he apply to one of the provincial medical schools, since it was doubtful if they could accept any new applications for at least three years. Two weeks later, Clayton's disappointment turned to joy when he received an invitation to meet with Sir Harold Plummer for interview.

By virtue of the strange rotational system at St. Clement's, Dr. Plummer, Philip's old foe from the early days of the Medical School Orchestra, was now Dean once more. He wanted to know if Clayton was related to Philip Bosnar, and on learning that they were brothers, he proceeded to relate Philip's entire student career at the medical school and hospital, in nauseating detail and with special hyperbole about his work with the orchestra.

Plummer was now the official patron of the orchestra (God's unique sense of humor, once again!), and the seasonal concerts were called The Common Room Rehearsals, in honor of their early beginnings. Each year since Philip's departure, the orchestra engaged the services of a rising young professional conductor, paid for by the medical school and with Plummer's blessings.

As for the astounded Clayton, he was told to report for the First M.B. course the following Monday, and Philip was delighted at the news. Perhaps Clayton was destined to be the one member of the Bosnar family who would benefit from the old boy's network system, and what a delicious irony that would be.

CHAPTER 30

1923

Pauline and Philip had a good childhood and loved their parents dearly; they appreciated the depth of affection and devotion lavished upon them by their parents and felt themselves privileged. It was not a laissez-faire household by any stretch of the imagination, and both of them were given a code of behavior, a strong sense of right and wrong, and an ambition to do their best in life. Being a child meant games and toys, sweets and chocolates, holidays and birthday parties. It also meant duties, responsibilities and broad planning for the future. Above all it meant education and the painstaking build-up of knowledge, judgement and a diversity of skills and activities.

Philip was ten years old and memories of the Great War were already fading into the past, and not just for children. Once a year, however, the historic event was brought back forcibly, not in its true horror, but as a joyful celebration. All day long, on November the 11th, breaking only for the two minutes of reverential silence at the 11 a.m. sound of the cannon, there were foot races, jumping events, and to keep the spirits high, egg-and-spoon events and three-legged contests.

After the awarding of prizes in each age division, tables and chairs were brought out from the houses into the streets and arranged in rows for the evening festivities. By nightfall, Grantham Square became a fairyland of lights and decorations. There were hanging signs of colored paper bunting stretching from the houses to the park-railings across the street, paying tribute to 'Victory in 1918', to 'The Royal Family' and to 'Our Brave Soldiers, Sailors and Airmen'.

It was a wonderful, magical time, when the food never tasted better – with a myriad new dishes – and if any room was left following the main courses, there was icecream, apples and oranges, bananas and pears, dates and grapes, figs and nuts. All the adults pitched in nobly and many a proud household displayed helmets and bayonets mounted on its walls, complementing the many Union Jacks and other banners flying on all sides.

To top it all off there was an evening amateur concert at which many a brave instrumentalist or vocalist performed before an appreciative audience, and budding comedians were received with loud laughter and applause. Philip's Dad mystified all of them with his amazing feats of magic, and the glorious night came to a close with an impassioned singing of the National Anthem. It seemed that Armistice Day was always blessed with beautiful weather, and the next day the clouds that gathered overnight shed their tears in memory of the fallen warriors. Grantham Square returned to normal, a quiet oasis of Jewry in the heart of the Gentile world of London's Cockneys.

It never occurred to Philip to question the fact that all the dwellers of this sequestered enclave were exclusively Jewish. It was almost a ghetto in reverse, with the families of yesterday's impoverished immigrants enjoying a standard of living and aspiring to heights of advancement far beyond the levels of the neighboring Cockneys of Stepney Green. In the northwestern corner was a fine old synagogue, seldom full except for the high holidays of Rosh Hashonah (The New Year of the Old Testament) and Yom Kippur (The Day of Atonement).

Of the entire Bosnar household, Philip was the only one who was devoutly religious in the true Orthodox fashion.

There were several factors contributing to this premature piety. In the first place he'd fallen under the powerful influence of the Reverend J.K.Goldbloom, the charismatic headmaster of the 'Talmud Torah' Cheder (Hebrew School) attended by Philip every Tuesday and Thursday evening. He'd started at the age of nine, mainly at the suggestion of two close friends at the Tredegar School, both with fathers who were Cantors at nearby synagogues.

When he first asked his parents if he could enroll, they were somewhat dismayed but went along with the idea without argument. For a long time he'd known that his Dad was almost free of most Orthodox restraints, and his Mum fashioned her behavior not to conflict with her husband's beliefs and non-beliefs. Aside from the avoidance of non-Kosher foods and observance of the Leviticus injunction against the mixing of meat and milk products on the same plate, and aside from some minor concessions to the religion of their ancestors, theirs was not an Orthodox home.

J.K.Goldbloom was a striking individual, with the face and beard of an Old Testament Prophet. He was a learned rabbi, an excellent teacher of standard biblical Hebrew, Talmudic Aramaic and modern Palestinian Hebrew and – above all – an ardent and dedicated Zionist. His magnetic personality influenced Philip's thoughts profoundly, and the ancient religion with its arcane traditions crashed into his childish imagination with the impact of a divine revelation. He became an ardent student of the language and religion of his 'People', and often got up at the crack of dawn so that he could accompany one of the elders to early morning service.

Philip's favorite was a wise old man who had recently been brought out from the Ukraine to live with his son's family in Grantham Square. They could only converse in Hebrew or Yiddish, and in their early morning walk along the Mile End Road toward the old gentleman's favorite temple of worship he learned the meaning behind various customs and traditions of Jewish religious practice. This was also the beginning of a growing conviction that Zionism was the true beacon beckoning the Children of Israel back to the Promised Land from which they had been driven so long ago, back from their long exile in the squalid ghettos of Europe.

His youthful zeal and enthusiasm left no room for the vexing questions that would trouble him in only a few more years. Belief had its own worldly rewards, and he would never lose his appetite for all the delicious savory dishes that were the bounty of Jewish cuisine, nor for that delightful humor born of ghetto life and its oppressions: to read the works of Shalom Aleichem was to rock with laughter at the glorious wit of this 'Yiddish Mark Twain'.

Learning about the life of Theodore Herzl, bon vivant and high society dandy of 19th century Vienna, was a revelation: that such a man could actually be the father of modern Zionism sent his mind racing with new perspectives. Herzl had been no strict observer of orthodoxy; he was more concerned with the issue of specific and recognized nationhood rather than the true faith of his people.

Philip loved the joys of Passover, its rituals and the way his parents catered to his fervent belief and his recital of the age-old question: ***"Mah Nishtanah Halayla hazed Halayla echod?"*** (why is this night so unique?), followed by his father's brave account – also in Hebrew –

of the exodus from ancient Egypt. He loved the Matzos and all the special foods of this great celebration. It seemed that each religious holiday had its own special food items and delicacies. *Purim*, with its cooked kidney beans and chick peas, *Sukas*, with its figs and dates, *Hanukah*, with its ***Rojinkas un Mandlen*** (raisins and almonds) for the children.

Only Yom Kippur – the day of atonement – was a time for long hours of solemn prayer, as well as a day and night of strict fasting. Aside from Rosh Hashonah this was the one time that Rafael Bosnar allowed himself to be coerced by his little Phileep to accompany him to the synagogue services and join him in the rigorous avoidance of any food for the duration of the official fasting period. His closest friends were quite religious, while the Bosnar home was considered suspect where orthodox practice was concerned. This didn't bother his friends but only their parents, who feared that their precious son's faith might become subverted.

The elementary school he attended was a very tough one, which was hardly surprising, since the majority of the pupils were rough, tough Cockneys, the ultimate representatives of an aggressive gentile world. (In later years he would come to admire the true worth of this courageous and resilient breed who could look adversity in the eye with a cheeky joke and a raunchy song). At this time in his life they represented danger. His mother liked his hair cut in pageboy style (as against the close brush cut of the Goyim) and occasionally liked to dress him in Russian tunics (*Robashkis*) with embroidered shoulders; she would then send him off to school with the customary command, "Don't get into any fights."

"But what if they start the fight and hit me first?"

"Never mind. Just stay away from the ruffians."

He had to be satisfied with this strange reasoning but privately prepared himself for battle. He knew full well that once he was spotted in such an unmanly garb it would be open season for his assailants. Necessity became his temporary mother of protection and taught him to go for the quick knock-down, or at least return home with no visible marks of battle on his face. Of one thing he was sure: at least in the interest of self-preservation and because – unlike the Russians and Poles – he didn't think the Robushki was a particularly masculine attire, this would be the last year he'd ever wear such attire. Come next birthday, that was to be his first birthday wish.

The next few years were, to a large extent, preparations for his Barmitzvah at the age of thirteen. In the meantime his life was a joyful one. His schoolwork wasn't too hard and his report cards seemed to make his parents happy. He enjoyed his games, both in school and in the Square, but above all he loved his shiny red scooter almost obsessively, and made it a vehicle that could match the speed of all those bicycles ridden by older boys and adults. He could outmaneuver them without difficulty and often propelled and guided his magic conveyance without touching the handlebars. ("Look, no hands!").

He had spent three weeks of the last two summers in Reigate, Surrey. His parents left him there in the care of a fine reliable family, the Inskips, and he formed a very warm friendship with their youngest son, George. The Inskips were Scottish Presbyterians and most dependable people; they liked Philip's parents and appeared to be rather fond of him. He and George often went blackberry-picking together. As they went about filling their baskets, they guiltily popped the most succulent black berries into their mouths. Divine retribution often faced them the following day if their gluttony went too far, or if their appetites tempted them into eating the less ripened red berries. Then, between bouts of colicky diarrhea, they'd swear off blackberries entirely, but only until the next berry-picking foray.

On a clear day, Philip loved to sit alongside the small group of artists gathered atop the hilly slopes above the town. He'd take along his drawing book and sketch the landscape, sometimes by the hour. (***These drawings would be treasured over the years by his parents, along with his later water colors and pottery designs***). His greatest thrill, however, came from his daredevil scooter rides. He would start in the roadway at the very top of the hill, and after one or two firm strokes of the right foot, he was off and coasting. With hands off the handlebars and body pressed forward against the steering column, he felt the surging acceleration in every fibber of his being as the glory of gravity took charge and the wind in his ears sang a song of joy. Down, down, down he careened in an ecstasy of speed, until finally decelerating onto the broad level ground of the town square. Then three times around the square, still coasting, and he was ready for a climb back up the hill.

This summer, his pride of accomplishment with this wondrous vehicle, which he likened to Sinbad's flying carpet, resulted in humiliating disaster. His parents had arrived on the early train to take him home and he was eager to show them the extent of his progress on the scooter. He was eager to have them watch his "death-defying" downhill ride from a vantage point halfway down the slope. The customary silky-smooth rotation of the front wheel was suddenly arrested by an errant stone in its path, some twenty feet from where his apprehensive parents were watching from a grassy area beside the roadside.

At any other time, the stone would have been seen and easily avoided, but on this occasion his mind and eyes were fixed on his Mum and Dad, in anticipation of their breathless adulation. Unfortunately, instead of such praise he found himself flying through the air, landing ignominiously on the edge of the road. Both knees were scraped and bleeding, but nothing was seriously damaged other than his pride. A friendly motorist came by and gave all three a lift to the doctor's office in the town square, where Philip's wounds were cleansed and the dirt and gravel carefully and skillfully removed. After the dressings were applied, he felt as good as new, except for the humiliation.

Perhaps the game that captured his imagination the most was the 'Diablo'. While his schoolchums played on the pavements with their spinning-tops, he honed his skills with this remarkable flying object. It was shaped like a double cone with its waist at the center, and was made of inexpensive light-colored wood. The propelling apparatus was a length of strong twine tied at each end to a firm wooden stick. The operator of the device placed the Diablo on the ground with the string resting on the undersurface of the spinning reel at its waist. Starting gradually, the wooden sidesticks were raised in alternating motion, creating a rotational motion that increased in power as the sticks were moved with increasing force and velocity. Finally, when the Diablo was humming audibly on the string, the sticks would be thrust apart, pulling the string taut and projecting the double cone upward.

Philip had reached the plateau of expertise when he could propel his diablo beyond the rooftops with that final and essential flick of the wrists, until it was almost out of sight; then he would keep it in visual focus until he caught it back on the string and repeated the action. Once in a while, as he watched his spinning projectile soaring up to the skies, he fantasized about the day when it would keep ascending, freeing itself at last from the earth's imprisoning gravity and flying onward into space; perhaps to land eventually onto the outstretched string of another boy just like himself, on some far-off world.

CHAPTER 31

1955

The patient was a 75-year-old man who was admitted to the emergency department of the Chelmsford Hospital after shooting himself in the left side of the chest with his revolver. When Philip Bosnar saw him, after being called downstairs on the P.A. system, the patient was still fully conscious and quite lucid. He'd pumped no less than three bullets into what he thought was his "bad heart," and couldn't understand why he was still alive. He had an intravenous of Ringer's solution running in his left arm and the first unit of matched blood running in his right arm. His blood pressure and other vital signs were better than one would have expected and his cardiogram showed only minimal abnormalities.

"Why did you try to kill yourself, Mr. Jenkins?"

"What d'you doctors care, anyway?"

"I care very much and I'm going to try and save your life."

"Think you can, Doc?"

"I'll give it my best shot but you have to promise you won't try again. Otherwise it's all wasted."

"Okay, you've got my word on it."

"I must tell you that the safest way to operate on you would be under a local anesthetic. I'll make sure you get enough oxygen and try to keep you as comfortable as possible."

"Go right ahead, Doc. I promise not to kick up a fuss."

By the time they got him up to the O.R. he was stable and tranquil, and they ran a dilute Demerol drip to start with, before putting in the Novocaine block. Bosnar took out a major portion of the left 5th rib and got excellent exposure of the damage. There was a laceration of the lower left lung, a hole in the `pericardium' (the smooth fibrous envelope around the heart), and a shallow three inch tangential gouge in the left ventricle. There was also a four inch rent in the left diaphragm, but no evidence of injury to the underlying spleen or stomach. There was only about half a pint of blood in the left chest and hardly any in the abdomen. Some of the damage was caused by rib fragments driven inward by the impact of the bullets. Two of the bullets were recovered from the chest and the third was found in the patient's clothing.

The rib fragments were removed, the diaphragm was repaired, the damaged portion of lung was removed, and finally a few silk sutures were placed to close the gouged wound on the heart's surface. The chest cavity was washed clean with warm saline, the pericardium was left unsutured (to prevent a postoperative build-up of pressure due to blood seepage from the ventricular wound), and a large suction tube was sutured into the left chest. Then some more Novocaine was injected into the tissues around the incision and the chest closed. The patient made an excellent recovery and everyone was delighted.

"Good morning, Mr. Jenkins. How are you feeling today?"

"Just great, Doc, thanks to you."

"Well, you helped by being such a cooperative patient. I'm glad to see you've had a good breakfast."

"Did you get a good look at my heart? Did it look fairly healthy?"

"Aside from the injury it didn't look too bad, but the arteries of the heart weren't all that good. I'm getting a heart specialist to see you today and arrange for further investigation and medication. Now I want you to tell me why you did such a crazy thing. They tell me you were sitting in your neighborhood park at the time."

It all came out in a torrent of angry words. The patient was a veteran of World War 1 and had been severely gassed, apparently with mustard gas. His health had never been the same since he came back home and he was sure his heart had been affected. He got short of breath on the least exertion and often got pains down his left arm. He'd made frequent trips to the doctors of the D.V.A. (Department of Veterans' Affairs) and had always been reassured that there was nothing organically wrong with his heart.

After a while he felt they believed he was faking it in order to get an increased veteran's disability pension, and he got so frustrated that his war efforts weren't being appreciated by his country, that he decided to kill himself. Although Philip felt considerable sympathy for the old fellow, he got the distinct impression that he was still disoriented, so he left instructions that the nurses were never to leave him unattended for any length of time, night and day, and arranged for a psychiatric evaluation.

Eight days later, after what seemed like a smooth and uneventful recovery, the patient died suddenly in the middle of the night and couldn't be revived. An autopsy revealed coronary artery disease and acute coronary thrombosis. This had occurred despite the continuous intravenous heparin (a clotting inhibitor) ordered by the cardiologist. A second finding was the presence of a degenerative cavity in the right frontal lobe of the brain, probably the result of a previous stroke. Philip's profound disappointment as Mr. Jenkins' surgeon was mixed with deep sympathy for the patient, a desperate man whose self-diagnosis was ignored by the DVA physicians; and he felt a sense of dark irony about the entire situation.

He phoned the coroner without delay and gave him all the facts. The coroner wanted to label it death by suicide, but Philip disagreed strongly.

"This man tried, but failed, to commit suicide. He actually died as the result of a heart condition he himself had diagnosed, but one the D.V.A. doctors repeatedly denied."

This argument fell on deaf ears, and on the day of Jenkins' interment, a saddened surgeon offered his silent apology on behalf of his professional brethren. Perhaps their own hearts had been found somewhat wanting in this tragic affair.

It wasn't the first case in which he was involved where the operation was successful but the patient died. It was a well-recognized feature in the practice of surgery, and experience showed that – over the years and after many operations – there were also cases where the patient was expected to die but made a remarkable recovery. Without that balancing factor, most surgeons might give up their perilous profession.

There were examples of this precarious balance. For instance, Tom Pettigrew was a capable and conscientious neurosurgeon who faced an appalling mortality rate with such cases as brain tumor or vascular malformation. His colleagues concealed their sympathy for his unhappiness by greeting him with the cheery enquiry, "Had any survivals lately, Tom?" and Pettigrew would smile sadly and murmur, "Not too many."

Sometimes the burden was too much for a surgeon to bear. Stirling MacDowell had joined Edwardia's medical fraternity two years ago, a well-trained, highly qualified and very competent orthopedic surgeon. He was pleasant, likable, and came from one of the leading families in the community. Since his arrival in the city, he'd encountered nothing but good luck in his work until his most recent case: a 43-year-old construction worker with a severe lumbar disk protrusion. Despite the surgeon's customary unhurried and careful procedure, an inadvertent rent opened up in the back of the aorta (the main arterial trunk of the abdomen) and the patient rapidly expired on the table.

MacDowell went into an acute depression and found himself unable to resume his regular practice. A month later, despite the support and advice of his colleagues and his family, he left town and headed for California. Since then, Philip was happy to learn that the disheartened orthopod had finally accepted a professor's job in that sunny state, and would be teaching and performing orthopedic surgery. All his colleagues wished him the best of luck, and they knew that – apart from skill – luck would always be an important factor in operative surgery. It was the redoubtable Erskine Ridgeway who, when a well-executed piece of surgery on one of his patients was followed by a disaster, made the bitter judgement, "Surgery isn't a science. It's a sport!"

All postoperative deaths and complications were discussed in full at special 'Ward Rounds'. These were neither on the wards, nor were they conducted as rounds, but rather as clinical-pathological conferences, at which the doctors involved were given an opportunity to present their version of each particular case prior to full discussion. There was a mounting apprehension in the medical profession, particularly among the surgeons, that the U.S.A. pattern of medicolegal litigation, with increasing awards and expanding media publicity, threatened to spread its baleful influence to Canada. Nobody could object to appropriate legal action and sufficient awards in cases of genuine and proven malpractice. But where misapplied, the results could be harmful to a doctor's career even when found innocent of all charges.

In the course of time, such a trend could lead to the over-investigation of patients, a tendency to avoid bold but necessary decisions, and an overall attitude of 'defensive medicine/. In the long run, this would slow down medical progress and react to the disadvantage of the patient. All medical and surgical management carried risks, and these required the judgement and experience of the attending doctor in making final decisions and discussing those decisions with the patient.

The reason for hospital rounds, meetings and committees, was to maintain the highest possible standard of medical care and to conduct a continuing overview of medical staff privileges in the hospital. In serious cases of questioned competence or aberrant conduct, it was sometimes necessary to involve the College of Physicians and Surgeons. This was in order that appropriate action be taken regarding possible suspension of the license to practice medicine.

Most direct litigation seemed designed to bypass this stringent self-policing mechanism and was based on the myth that doctors always cover up for each other in such situations. In most areas of keen professional competition, the reverse was often the case, and many a lawyer's writ was based on one or more overcritical remarks made to the patient or family by a second doctor.

Philip felt it behooved all doctors to learn more about the entire issue of medico-legal actions and courtroom procedure. As a medical student, he had the good fortune to have his instruction in Forensic Medicine and Medical Law by an eminent authority on those arcane subjects. Later, when Philip was doing his surgical residencies, he was frequently called as a medical witness in cases involving damages for industrial injuries, and he learned a great deal about court procedure and how a sharp lawyer could twist the truth.

Two cases always stuck in his memory, and he had pleasant recollections of the impressive courtrooms of the King's Bench Division, located in the Inner Temple Law Courts off the Strand. The first of these two court case concerned a 56-year-old workman in a large construction company. He had sustained a nasty fracture of the right wrist when he fell from a faulty platform, a distance of about ten feet. Although the fracture had healed in good position and he was making a progressive functional recovery, he still complained of pain and weakness in the affected joint. The patient's lawyer was suing for increased compensation and called Dr. Bosnar as the medical witness.

Philip had quite an easy time describing his treatment of the case and outlining some of the possible complications. Counsel for the employer's insurance company gave him a hard time regarding these complications, especially the possibility of 'long-term post-traumatic arthritis'. Both lawyers were K.C. (King's Counsel) barristers, the presiding judge was impressive in his lordly robes and the courtroom was crowded with law students. The medical witness for the defense was a veteran insurance doctor who, although he looked as if he was no stranger to alcohol, gave his evidence in a calm and professional manner. The defense lawyer then tried to make him refute Philip's earlier testimony. Again and again he badgered his witness to disagree with Philip until the old gentleman decided he'd had enough.

"If you're asking me to say my colleague gave an incorrect opinion you're wasting your time, as he is absolutely right."

That was essentially the end of the case, and as the insurance physician stomped out of the witness box, his face red with anger, he came over to his young colleague and loudly invited him to lunch. The lunch was most enjoyable, the workman won his award, and Philip had a feeling of pride, both for his own resolute testimony and the dignified performance of an aging insurance doctor, who proceeded to celebrate his act of courage by taking most of his lunch in liquid form.

The second memorable case was held in a different courtroom but in the same location and in very similar circumstances. It was a 38-year-old workman employed by the London Passenger Transport organization, who suffered persistent disability following prolonged use of a pneumatic drill. Philip was aware in general terms of the various disorders that could result from such a vibrating tool, but he decided to check on the latest literature just to be sure. He knew that topflight barristers made it their business to be fully versed in up-to-date and relevant medical information.

The day before the trial, he paid a hasty visit to Lewis's Lending Library on Gower Street, and was pleased to find that the latest issue of Proceedings of the Mayo Clinic contained a detailed article on the subject at hand. It subdivided the complications and sequelae of pneumatic drill injuries into four main categories, but further subdivided the fourth into subgroups A and B. It seemed to Philip that these subgroups should have been listed as separate groups, making five in all. He obtained a copy of the article and studied it repeatedly until bedtime.

The following morning, the defense lawyer approached him pleasantly as he sat in the witness box, and enquired with a friendly smile, "You know of course, doctor, that there are four types of damage in such cases?" Philip knew the scenario all too well. He was supposed to say "Yes," the barrister would pounce on him with a roar of "WHAT ARE THEY?" and he would collapse in a mumble of ignorance. The smart devil had done his reading but this witness was ready for him.

"Five, Sir," he corrected his inquisitor just as pleasantly, and the barrister went into a frantic search of his documents but failed to pursue the issue effectively. Instead he tried a different tack.

"How long since you got your medical degree, doctor? I see, and what is your special training in this field? I see, and now suppose I tell you that our medical witness is Dr. Russell Brain, and his opinion is quite different from yours. What would you say, then?"
Philip summoned all his eloquence before replying.

"I would yield to no one, Sir, in my high regard for Dr. Russell Brain as the world's foremost expert on Neurology. But in this particular case I enjoy one special advantage. I looked after this patient."
His inquisitor turned purple and started to bluster, but his Lordship cut him short.

"I believe the learned young doctor has fully answered your question."
It was nice to know that the workman won his full award for damages.

Two weeks later, in addition to the customary stipend of ten guineas for his court appearance, Philip received an extra ten guineas from the workman's lawyer with a letter of thanks for his 'decisive testimony'. The lesson he learned then – and he wished it would be learned by the entire medical profession – was that doctors should never genuflect before the legal establishment simply as a matter of custom.

James was still a bit smaller than his sister, but both he and Florian were now old enough to be told the truth about their parents and their origins.

"Tell me, children, do you remember much about your last trip to England and Ireland with your mother?"

"Just a little, Dad. I know we all had a good time."

"You were only four and six years old at the time."

"We thought you should have come with us."

"This time I'm going to send you over with your mother for a much longer stay. I want you to spend a lot of time with your Jewish grandparents in England and your Roman Catholic grandmother in Ireland. Your Irish grandfather died in an accident when your mother was just a young girl."

"Does that make us Jewish, too, or are we Catholic?"

"Nothing has changed, and you can still be whatever you want to be. The choice will always be yours."

"Why didn't you tell us before," they asked, almost in unison, but for the most part they seemed to be taking turns. This time they were answered by their mother.

"We just thought it would be easier for you, and easier for your Dad and me, too. Sometimes in a mixed marriage like ours it's easier not to dwell too soon on religious differences."

"Not only that," Philip added, "but unlike Edwardia, a lot of people in Vanwey weren't too fond of Jews when we first came there. Some didn't even like Catholics, so we felt it better to wait until you were ready and to tell you before we told anyone else."

"That's fine, Dad. We think you did the right thing."

It had been so much easier than they had imagined, but the real test would come when the children spent more time with the two families and their cultural backgrounds, each with its own history of persecution and suppression.

Philip booked passage for his three loved ones on a P&O ship, the *S.S. Orsova*, with a large outside cabin. It was arranged that when they got to London his Dad would meet them and drive them to Hendon. Philip would have loved to go with them, but that was out of the question at this time. He was comforted by the thought that if Patty was able to survive her earlier trip to England when the kids were very small, it would be a cinch this time, when they seemed so grown up.

They'd be traveling via the Panama Canal and taking a side trip to the island of Trinidad, and that should be an interesting diversion before their long transatlantic voyage. Following their stay in England and Ireland, he'd arranged for them to get a tour of France, Belgium and Holland before returning to Edwardia by air.

A month prior to the departure date, Whiskers expired peacefully, saddening the entire family, but none more than poor Patty. Their beloved black and white cocker spaniel had been her constant companion, and there were few places she'd go without taking him along. He was wonderful with the children, and always made sure Philip wouldn't feel left out by greeting him with boisterous affection when he came home from hospital, office or poker game; never barking if the hour was very late. Patty would miss her long jaunts with Whiskers along the breezy seafront, his careful balancing act whenever she was tending the rock garden, and her hillside sprints up to the lookout with the dog leading the way.

When the time came for the children and their mother to depart, Philip could comfort himself with the thought that the trip was not only a suitable birthday present for his beloved wife, but surely a therapeutic interlude after the demise of the irreplaceable Whiskers. This forthcoming trip would be far different from the last time they went overseas – when they were still living in Vanwey. The comparison was a strange one. On that occasion, the trip only lasted a couple of weeks, whereas this time, it would be for months.

For their earlier trip they'd taken the train to Montreal, and then down to New York, where they embarked on that dowager of Cunard liners, the sumptuous Queen Elizabeth. This time they would be leaving Edwardia by sea and proceeding through the Panama Canal.

He remembered 1947, the year of his family's last trip to England. It was the first time he'd ever tried the bachelor domestic life and it was a strange experience, even if only for such a short time. He remembered how Patty filled the fridge's freezer compartment with lots of steaks and other choice goodies before she left, so he wouldn't starve to death in her absence.

One day, after a heavy day at the hospital and the office, he'd returned home as hungry as the proverbial bear. He fried some onions and cut up some potatoes to make french fries, then got ready to put a large T-bone steak into the electric fry-pan when, to his horror, the power went off. Of course, he should have known at once what happened and why. During the card game at George Freikopf's house the previous evening, he'd warned that there might be a temporary 'power-out' the next day, lasting about an hour, for transformer repairs. He assured Philip that in the event of a dire emergency at the hospital, they could switch it back on at the main power station.

With a feeling of guilty desperation, Philip phoned the station's chief engineer and said, in a voice of controlled panic, "Please turn the power back on for thirty minutes. Yes indeed, it's an emergency." The power was turned back on, the steak was magnificent, his ravenous hunger was assuaged and fortunately nobody was any the worse or the wiser for the event, but Philip's conscience took a severe beating.

Back then, with Patty and the children overseas, he sometimes had to lunch between operations when there was a long surgical list, and the Sisters would prepare a sumptuous meal for him in the Bishop's Room. The table would be covered with spotless Irish linen, and there would be a matching table napkin in its engraved solid silver ring, a silver tea service and even a bottle of fine Bordeaux. Those times, he now realized with nostalgia, were gone forever. He and his fellow staff doctors were simply cogs in an expanding hospital machinery and got no special treatment whatsoever.

This time, he was learning to fend for himself and having less trouble looking after his nutritional needs with each passing week. There was only one problem, an insidious one: for the first time in his life he was starting to get fat. The cause wasn't obvious at first: it was just a question of supply and demand. No matter how much he'd eaten, he refused to waste any food, so he left nothing to be thrown out. Even when he was too tired to be bothered cooking his own meal, he'd send out for Chinese food, invariably more than he could manage. Whatever was left at the end of the meal was placed in a chafing dish and left to simmer until he was ready for a midnight snack, when he'd finish the remaining hot food without a worry in the world.

While his family was overseas, he tried to keep himself in shape with frequent games of tennis at the Chestnut Road hardcourts. His favorite opponent was his young friend and former house surgeon, Cliff Robins, a strong player who beat him regularly. On Sunday mornings, they were joined from time to time by Cliff's wife Melanie, now a raven-haired and flashing-eyed femme fatale. They played a threesome, and whenever Cliff faced the two of them, Philip enlivened the game by shamelessly cheating on every close call. Cliff's loyal spouse would have objected but was too busy laughing hysterically at this blatant unfairness. Philip insisted it was an essential handicap when playing against such a superb player as her athletic husband.

After the Sunday games, he always invited his friends up to the house for breakfast, on one condition: they had to wash up after the meal. The first time this happened, Melanie discovered that his orange-squeezer was developing green mold, but he covered his embarrassment by insisting he was growing a rare type of pure penicillin. To complete his delinquency, he wasn't above leaving a pile of accumulated dirty dishes in the kitchen sink to be washed and dried by his guests! It was his temporary bachelor privilege.

One Saturday afternoon, the Parsons came up to the Bosnar house. They spotted Philip at the picture window, looking out across the Straits through his binoculars, and decided to make him a generous and unexpected offer.

"Sorry to learn about poor old Whiskers," Glen remarked, by way of introducing the reason for the unexpected visit.

"Yes, it's been specially tough on Patty."

"How about another dog, as soon as she gets back?"

"I'm not sure she'll be ready for one for quite a while."

"You know Glen and I raise pedigreed standard French poodles," said his wife.

"Yes, Molly, I've seen some of them. They're really magnificent."

"Well, how about a pup from a forthcoming litter? No charge of course."

"That's a most generous offer, but I'm afraid my darling can't stand poodles. She just hates that funny haircut they have for the dog shows, the one that makes them look rather naked around the butt."

"Perhaps she'd like the Dutch cut. Actually, that's the one Molly and I prefer. Anyhow, give it some thought, and when the time comes she may change her mind."

Somehow, Philip doubted that she ever would, unless she lost her heart to a poodle pup placed right in her arms. Who could tell?

On the international front, Philip noted that the Cold War was getting no less paranoid, but it was comforting to know that Senator Joseph McCarthy had been totally discredited and was reported to be drinking himself to death. The U.S.A. had taken a very strange turn since the frustration and humiliation of the Korean War and the French debacle in Vietnam. These had occurred despite the rattling of the atomic saber by John Foster Dulles in both cases. It had reached the point where showing sympathy for the underprivileged was subversive. Moreover, speaking out against the use of the atom bomb and opposing war between the East and West military giants, were regarded as communist sympathies.

To consider the Syngman Rhee government of South Korea a fascist dictatorship, and not a democracy by the widest stretch of the imagination, was to be labeled a left- wing extremist. To have fought for the Spanish Loyalists against Franco and his German-Italian alliance was evidence of communist subversion. To be a former Nazi, it now seemed, was the one clear political protection against any accusation of being a communist or 'fellow traveller'.

One could hardly lay the entire blame for such insanity on such political opportunists as John Parnell Thomas, Richard Nixon and Joseph McCarthy. The sinister figures who made these witch-hunts possible were reactionary extremists like the Dulles brothers and J.Edgar Hoover. All these contemporary inquisitors were men who'd never caught a single communist spy in their lives. Their failure was a glaring one, when it was obvious that the real spies had been roaming far and wide across the continent (both before and after the revelations of Igor Gouzenko, Soviet defector to Canada).

Instead, innocent men and women faced vicious interrogation committees; where innuendo and perjury pilloried them as disloyal; where they were judged guilty until proven innocent; and where – under psychological rather than physical torture – they were asked to name accomplices, (an exact parallel to Hitler's Gestapo and Stalin's OGPU). Even the total discredit of Parnell Thomas and McCarthy, and the growing evidence that Julius and Ethel Rosenberg were pitiful left-wing dupes without access to major atomic secrets, failed to halt their country's march toward Fascism.

Was it no longer possible for a middle-of-the-road conservative to look at both sides of a political issue, national or international, on its own merits? Was it necessary to prove ones patriotism by extolling armed intervention and searching for home-grown Commies under every bed? What had happened to religious morality, when a Cardinal Spellman could eulogize people like Joe McCarthy from the pulpit of his cathedral; where Southern Baptist ministers could support lynchings in Dixieland and the suppression of basic constitutional rights in its black communities? When it finally came, as come it must, the backlash to all this insane suppression of democratic freedoms would inevitably divide the entire nation and result in revolution or war. As long as Canadians kept their national identity and democratic freedoms strong, they might be spared the same fate in their precious nation, so vast and yet so fragile!

The news from England was mostly good, marred only by the report of Florian's middle-ear infection with which she'd been afflicted on arrival in Hendon. She had to be admitted to the local hospital where she not only made a fine recovery but, as a doubtful bonus, picked up a solid Lancashire accent from the patient in the next bed. After her recovery, she was enrolled on a temporary basis in the Edith Cavell day school for girls while James entered Smithson's day school for boys, Clayton's old stamping ground. They were both getting an excellent education but finding the standards extremely high.

Patty and the children were getting to know the Bosnar family in London more intimately and the experience was reciprocal, so that what Philip had hoped for seemed to be taking place. They'd met Clayton's wife Martha, whom he married last winter, and found her a pleasant, well-educated Jewish girl who was as non-orthodox as her husband. After Clayton's wild romances with several Gentile girls, his Mum hoped Martha would be a steadying influence and help him to settle down to his studies. She and Clayton were living in a small house quite a distance from Hendon, but tried to visit his parents every weekend if at all possible.

During the school holidays, Patty and the children went across to Ireland and restored old family ties in a heart-warming reunion. Later, they visited her young brother Francis in Southampton and her older sister Bridget in London. Before the final phase of their stay in Europe, Patty planned to visit some of their R.A.F. friends from Vanwey, and Philip looked forward to hearing about them and seeing some of the snapshots and home movies she promised to bring back with her. In the meantime, he sent her a monthly cheque to cover the costs of her overseas stay and hoped she'd let him know at once if she ran short of funds. Knowing how much he missed his beloved wife and children, he realized how much she must be missing him, as would the children whenever their youthful adventures permitted them to project their thoughts back across the vast Atlantic Ocean.

The 'separation phenomenon' in children wasn't unknown to anyone taking care of patients in the pediatric wards of a hospital. Parents invariably missed their children far more than the other way round. Homesickness only seemed to affect these young patients soon after parental visits, and in almost direct proportion to those visits. For most parents this was a hard truth to swallow, but Philip recognized it as perfectly natural, and in no way trivialized the children's love for their parents. It was simply a matter of greater adaptability at a tender age.

The great day came at last, and Philip watched his three loved ones walk down the portable metal stairway onto solid British Columbia ground. Their eyes searched the waiting throng and they walked right past him without a trace of recognition! The solution to this startling occurrence wasn't hard to find, and they all had a hearty guffaw about it whenever the subject came up in days to come. As a result of Philip's unregulated home cooking, he'd blossomed from a respectable 160 lbs to an unpardonable 185 lbs, with an expanded waistline and cheeks like those of a well-fed chipmunk. Patty and the children gave him all the details of their thrilling adventure, and for the next week or two they pored over the snapshots and home movies of their trip. They were viewed and analyzed with joyful interest, and Patty provided a running commentary throughout.

True to his promise, Glen Parsons drove up to their house a fortnight later and deposited a chocolate-brown bundle of canine delight into Patty's arms, and she was instantly captivated by the adorable puppy. It was one of a litter of five tiny standard French poodles, the liveliest and most mischievous of the group, and went by the elegant name of Gigi d'Antibes. It was the most delightful and thoughtful gift Patty could have hoped for, and it came at an ideal time. There was little doubt that Gigi would fill the great void left by the demise of their treasured Whiskers, not only for Patty but for the entire family, and it was a kindness they could never repay.

But tragedy still hadn't exacted its full payment, and it wasn't long after this event that the ever-cheerful and convivial Molly Parsons, forever on the lookout for people and projects she could help, was unable to help herself. It was in her fight against the overwhelming attack of acute leukemia that terminated her young life in the late November of 1955.

Patty was glad to see that the rock garden hadn't gone to rack and ruin in her absence. Philip had watered the rose bushes faithfully, and their Chinese gardener came once a week to do whatever else was necessary to keep the garden in peak condition. The children now spoke with English accents, but after the strict discipline and special uniforms of the London schools, they both wanted to leave their private schools and attend Maple Bay public school, a coeducational secondary school in their district. There, they could select there own attire and hairstyle and enjoy considerable freedom from discipline. As Phil confessed to Patty, he wasn't too overjoyed by this change of school but, after all, this was the middle 50s and things were changing fast, especially where the basic rights of teenagers were concerned. These rights were being espoused by the current crop of doctrinaire child psychologists and counselors, and it was disturbing to note that little was said about the basic responsibilities of the present day's teenager in the 'New Society'.

Philip's surgical practice was humming along steadily, although not quite at the rate he'd hoped for. He was still getting patients coming out to Edwardia once in a while, both from the Vanwey area and North Dakota, and it was touching to see such loyalty from his former patients. If they required extensive hospitalization, he urged them to return home so they could be close to their families. Otherwise, he went ahead with the necessary surgery, realizing that this long trek from the prairies would eventually come to an end in the course of time.

One such patient who came out to consult him was Preston Macready, Ruth Steffanson's brother, an entertaining individual with a great sense of humor and an inexhaustible fund of stories. He was afflicted by a large gastric ulcer, with intractable pain and occasional bleeding, but was incapable of sticking to any special diet or medication, and even more so of avoiding cigarettes and alcohol. Macready was an obvious candidate for partial gastrectomy and Philip persuaded him to go back home and get a good surgeon closer to his farm in Saskatchewan. With considerable reluctance, both he and his wife accepted Philip's advice and it was good to learn that the patient had undergone the requisite surgery shortly thereafter, in the city of Saskatoon.

Unfortunately, the patient did very badly during the following months and returned to Edwardia suffering from abdominal pain, weight-loss and severe regurgitation. This time, he insisted on having Philip look after him and was admitted to the Chelmsford Hospital as a private-room patient. Investigation proved that he had a considerable obstruction at the outlet of his gastric remnant as well as marked Reflux Esophagitis with Sliding Hiatus Hernia (regurgitation of gastric contents into the delicate interior of the lower gullet, associated with a gross widening of the aperture in the diaphragm).

The operation went well, and the obstruction proved to be due to a heavy band of adhesions across the gastric outlet. The reflux and associated hernia were easy to correct and there was no sign of recurrent ulcer or any malignancy. After this second operation, Macready made a splendid recovery and was able to return home two weeks later. He was also able to return to his former diet and resume his smoking and drinking habits despite being advised against both. His farm prospered, however, and he raised a fine family. (***Thereafter, he spent every winter in Edwardia, where he and his wife, whom the Bosnars had known in Vanwey as the oldest daughter of the Adams, became their longtime friends.***)

Toward the closing months of the year, a small event occurred which set a pattern for Phil and Patty which would affect the rest of their lives, and the blame was his, and his alone. Steve Arngrim, whom they knew fairly well from their Vanwey days and whose son Billy was Jamie's school chum and fellow bugler, came over to see Philip with what he called a "sure fire" proposition. If he had about $20,000 to spare, the surgeon could make a very large profit by investing in the early shares of Crestwell Mines, an outfit in the B.C. interior that had struck a rich deposit of copper and silver. Philip told him the most he could spare at the time was about $5,000 and Arngrim said that was better than nothing. Since he was one of the first investors and had purchased a large number of `vendor' shares, he had enough inside information to assure Philip the mine had a guaranteed future.

Sure enough, for the next few months the share value kept going up, starting at $2 and going up steadily until it reached $9, and the Bosnars were delighted. Then the shares started to slide, at first slowly and then more rapidly. When they fell to $3, Philip had an urgent phone call from Arngrim.

"Listen, Phil, I have some good news for you. I've got inside information that the shares may reach an all time high in the next week."

"What makes you say that, Steve?"

"They've just struck some major new deposits and when the news leaks out, the shares will take off."

"Well, that's certainly encouraging news. Frankly I was considering getting rid of my Crestwell stock."

"Don't even think of doing that. Just sit tight and watch your shares climb. I'll keep in touch."

Over the next week, the share value dropped to $1.25 and then the stock disappeared entirely from the market listings. As for Steve, Philip never heard from him again, although he was happy to note that James and Billy remained good friends. After all, as Patty observed, it wasn't

Billy's fault that his father had cost the Bosnars five thousand hard- earned dollars. Philip agreed, but could hardly consider himself blameless in the matter.

One of the phenomena Philip was observing more often each year and which he found disheartening, was the annual metamorphosis of the Chelmsford Hospital interns. All year round he enjoyed working with these eager young men, teaching them as much as he could, both at bedside and in the operating room, as well as in the emergency department whenever the occasion arose. They seemed to enjoy their sessions and were eager to assist at his operations, almost to the point of favoritism over his fellow-surgeons. Thus, it was not unnatural to expect that he might be the recipient of some of their surgical referrals when they went out into private family practice in the city, especially those cases involving his special interests and acknowledged expertise. When this failed to occur, he began to take a closer interest in their new pattern of referral. Not only was this referral to surgeons they'd never assisted, but many of these same surgeons did all of their cases at St Peter's. To make matters worse, some were at the lower end of the totem pole where professional reputation was concerned.

When he discussed these observations with Farnsworth, Ridgeway, and Stanford, they told him of their similar experiences over the years, and stated that a wooing process took place as soon as a house surgeon was ready to move downtown, and the work usually went to the highest or earliest bidder. After that revelation, whenever Philip felt tempted to stop spending so much time instructing his interns, he combated the temptation by remembering that those who stopped teaching usually stopped learning as well.

Mark Symes was a jovial gynecologist who'd come to Edwardia about the same time as Philip, and was about five years his senior. He phoned one evening and asked Phil and Patty to come over for "some drinks and a chat." The Bosnars were fond of both Mark and his wife Betty, and they gladly accepted the invitation, but not without a certain degree of curiosity. When they got to the Symes home and all four had their inaugural drinks, they settled down to conversation. Both the Symes looked upset, and it was obvious that their host was a bit inebriated, but he spoke up without too much trouble.

"You know me well, Phil, right?"

"Right, old chap."

"Then you know that I feel the same way you do about things, right?"

"What things?"

"Don't be so goddamn coy. You know bloodywell what I'm talking about. All those low down, rotten tricks of the trade that come under the polite name of `soliciting'. It's people like you who've had the guts to fight this dirty stuff openly, and what the hell's it got you?"

"The same as it's got you, Mark, self-respect."

"I've had enough of that crap. It doesn't put food on the table or buy shoes for the kids, right?"

"No, I guess it doesn't."

"You're goddamn right it doesn't. Well I can't afford all that high-minded stuff any more and I wanted to tell you to your face, with both our wives present. Now you can spit in my eye or we can have another drink. Waddyasay, old sport?"

"I say let's have another drink. Believe me when I tell you I know just what you've gone through, all these lean years. Your decision is yours alone and nobody has the right to judge you. This won't make the slightest difference to our friendship."

(But it did. From that time onward Mark Symes always tried to avoid Philip, and the Symes couple became strangers, to the deep regret of the Bosnars. Nevertheless, they were happy for Mark and Betty when they moved into a fine new home, two years later.)

CHAPTER 32

1956

For the past few years, there had been an influx of three new orthopedic surgeons to the city and they were all quite busy, right from the start. The reasons weren't hard to find. In the first place, a good deal of the more advanced work in this specialty had been going to Vancouver and there had even been a monthly visit to the Edwardia hospitals by one of Vancouver's leading 'orthopods', with a two-day session of outpatient clinics. One was held at the Chelmsford and one at St. Peters, with the full cooperation of the medical staffs. This would now be a thing of the past, which was just as well if Edwardia intended to grow as a Medical Center.

A second consequence of the presence of these newcomers, was a considerable reduction of work in this field by every well-trained general surgeon. It also meant that most emergency accident cases were seen first by the orthopods; so one more avenue was closed to the general surgeon.

There was one aspect of the matter for which these new specialists were given full credit, namely the absence of resentment toward those few surgeons who continued handling straightforward orthopedic procedures in which they were experienced. The new orthopods were even prepared to be helpful, in sharp contrast to Vancouver, New Westminster and other centers across the province. In their own city, perhaps the handwriting was already on the wall.

Tony Blaze was a big, bluff, rough and ready sort of fellow, good at his orthopedic work but not outstanding. Marcel Bonin, on the other hand, was a short stocky French Canadian, cheerful and outspoken but never controversial, and he did his job efficiently. The real 'Whiz Kid' was Sid Brophy, tall and athletic, happy-go-lucky and a first-class man in his chosen field. Within twelve months of his arrival he was the busiest orthopedic surgeon in the province. The fact that he was an incurable workaholic enabled him to cope and so did his life style as a confirmed bachelor.

When time permitted, he loved the ladies and loved to party, and despite the best efforts of his friends he began to show an increasing affinity for alcohol, an affinity that by the summer of 1956 was becoming a dependency. He started to show up late for his cases, often unsteady and unkempt, his behavior was becoming erratic and confused, and his skillful hands developed increasing shakiness. His practice started to fall off, he began to leave town for long periods of time and then disappeared completely from the city.

Brophy's friends and colleagues all agreed that, for some incredible reason, this man of great natural talent, youth, looks and popularity, with everything to live for, had become a tragedy waiting to happen. Perhaps there was a lesson for all of his colleagues: not to be too impatient, not to look for everything too soon. Such blessings did not come unmixed.

By October of that year, a shocking piece of news filtered back to Edwardia from across the border. Sid Brophy, the Whiz Kid, had been found in a cheap motel in Tacoma, dead from an overdose of sleeping pills and surrounded by empty liquor bottles. Everyone was deeply shocked, not only the doctors but the nurses and Sisters who'd all adored him at both hospitals and the hundreds of patients who had so much reason to thank him, for their limbs, their health, even their lives.

Andy Plantage, the orthopod who replaced him, never drank, smoked or swore. He was a competent surgeon but a self-righteous prig and a colossal bore, and he could never match the skill (or charm!) of his predecessor. The Whiz Kid had been a comet that flashed across the skies of Edwardia's medical world into the great void, and the brilliance of his memory would not soon fade.

Another interesting individual who arrived in their midst at the beginning of the year was Reginald Asquith, an internist who came out from the U.K. with excellent credentials. He had his English M.D. and F.R.C.P. (Doctor of Medicine and Fellow of the Royal College of Physicians, both English specialist degrees in Internal Medicine) and now had his Canadian Fellowship as well. He was highly intelligent, an excellent speaker and a sworn foe of the British National Health Insurance Plan. As such, it followed quite logically that he should become the popular standard bearer of the war against State Medicine, or what was the more pejorative term: 'Socialized Medicine'.

Here was a first-rate specialist who claimed to have experienced the evils of so dictatorial a plan in person, and one whose God-given eloquence could serve as the inspiration for a counterattack. This would commence at the level of the local Medical Society, then the provincial body and ultimately that august national body, the Canadian Medical Association. His fiery orations at medical meetings summoned up images of street barricades and noble resistance – "Contra nous de la tyrannie!" It also made those few who took the longer, wider and more objective look at the issues, seem like traitors to his great cause.

Philip Bosnar was one of those few, one of those traitors. It wasn't that he had such an enthusiasm or high regard for government-run enterprises. It was a distaste for the dog-eat-dog business atmosphere that seemed the pervasive force in current medical practice, instead of professional ethics and morals. He felt one could learn a great deal from even the mistakes made under the British system. After all, since some form of National Health Insurance was now inevitable, it was better for organized medicine to utilize its energies in drawing up a blueprint for the government to follow.

Bosnar discussed these dangerous thoughts with some of his closest and most trusted colleagues. They appreciated that he was far from being a socialist, and that he was a great believer in free enterprise and honest competition. But where, he asked, was the free enterprise in their own profession, when so many referrals – especially in surgery – had less to do with ability and results than other less appropriate standards of comparison? What about the contracts between doctors and various insurance organizations? What about restrictions under the Workman's Compensation Act, sinecure appointments in D.V.A. hospitals and wasteful moment-to-moment 'free choice' of doctor.

There was the Armed Services system of medical care. Philip's own experiences at Thornton tended to endorse the practicability of such a system, whereas the D.V.A. set-up seemed to embody the worst features of bureaucratic waste, inefficiency and political patronage. In truth, he still felt that non-governmental private practice was a pretty good system, but it was the doctors' own abuses that were turning all three political parties toward the alternative, and the public would happily go along with them. While the Reginald Asquiths could trumpet appeals for doctors to be prepared for extreme action if necessary, others like Philip Bosnar were taking a long hard look at the strong and weak points of each system.

His friend Joe Purdy, a local G.P. who was chairman of the Economics Committee, confided that he thought the best way to calm Asquith down was to put him on his committee, where he could be kept from issuing inflammatory statements and making too much fuss. Philip's reply was firm.

"You're wrong, Joe. I think that will simply give him a springboard from which to launch an ambitious political career."

"You have to admit he's a brilliant guy."

"No argument, especially his ability to arouse strong feelings among his fellow M.Ds. What we really need is a group of quiet workers capable of reasoning from positions of pragmatic wisdom and who'll stay away from polarizing the two sides."

"That's quite a mouthful, Phil. You're another of those goddamn British orators. What are you getting at?"

"I'm saying we don't need demagogic approaches to a problem that's going to face all of us in the next decade. Let's clean up our own act first and then see what's wrong with the plans and proposals of the Federal Government."

"Well, I guess time will tell, but frankly I think your idealism may be just as dangerous in the long run as some of the hot-headed extremists. What's more, Philip, it's your kind who usually take the knocks, so don't expect any thanks for your views."

Colonel Bradford was as good as his word, and he resumed the stories of his adventurous past as soon as he and Philip had played a few chess games. He was a pretty fair player and it was obvious that in his younger days he'd been well above average. Now, however, although he sailed through the standard openings without difficulty, he tended to slip up in the middle game and hated to get involved in the geometrics of the end game. He felt about the end games the way Phil and Patty felt about compulsory figures in international skating contests, and he simply couldn't be bothered. Nevertheless, he could still come up with the odd flash of brilliance that made the games interesting. At heart, this very correct and stiff upper lip British prototype was really a buccaneer, a Mississippi riverboat gambler. But it was hard for Philip to visualize him facing his earlier perils with a devil-may-care attitude.

The colonel resumed his interrupted story.

"After the first bandito raid there were others, but I'd set up an early warning system above the mines that worked perfectly until the lookout passed out one day, on an overgenerous intake of tequila."

He paused to refill their glasses.

"This time I didn't get away, and the leader recognized me and told his men not to bother with the others but set up a hanging party for me. He was quite polite, even apologetic, and explained that in these revolutionary times it was important to make an example of gringos like me."

"Why like you?"

"Because, like the Federales, I was taking wealth from this poor country while the peasants starved."

"How were the banditos different."

"Ah! They only stole from the rich so they could help the poor. I knew differently but didn't argue. They set up a special kind of hanging party. It would provide some much-needed entertainment for his men."

"That sounds pretty nasty."

"They tied my hands behind my back and fixed a noose around my neck. The end of the rope was thrown over one of the high girders on the ore-loading platform. It was explained to me that one of the men would pull down on the rope and if I was still alive a second man would help the first. If I was still alive after the third one joined the hanging party then they'd let me go."

"Did you believe that last promise?"

"Of course not. I could only pray for a miracle, and by God it came. There was the sudden sound of a gunshot and a loud shout of `Alto, companeros!' The leader of the hanging party and his men all stood to attention as a short fat Mexican got off his horse, loaded with guns and bandoleros of ammunition. It was my old drinking pal and former numero uno muleteer, Pancho Villa, now the feared Commandante of a spreading revolution."

"Did he recognize you?"

"Right away, even with the noose around my neck and dirt on my face. He reprimanded his troops for mishandling a gringo friend of the revolution, and after freeing me, rode off with his men, all firing their guns as a farewell salute. Before leaving, he whispered to me, `These are dangerous times, my friend, to remain in this troubled country', and I took his advice."

The narrator took a long draught from his glass before embarking on the next episode of his story.

When he got back to the United States, Bradford was just about broke. He'd made his first million and then lost it when he had to flee Mexico. Villa had saved his life, but his revolution cost the Englishman his mine and his fortune. Against his better judgement he was forced to sell the large tract of orchard country he owned in Southern California. He got good money for the sale, but lived to see that land become the eastern suburb of a new city, the city of angels, Los Angeles!

That was the way Bradford had lived his roller-coaster life, making and losing fortunes, and finishing up here in British Columbia in comfortable but far from wealthy circumstances. He and his wife were always good company as guests, and excellent hosts in their house, which was set in the woodlands beyond the northern perimeter of Edwardia. Philip enjoyed Bradford's stories and the colonel enjoyed their chess games.

James and Florian were growing up, and the influence of their new school was obviously much greater than that of their recent English schools. These were the days of teen-age rebellion, as exemplified by the fine young actor and 'Rebel Without Cause', James Dean. It was a time when all the boys tried to dress like him, wear their hair like him and behave like him (What Philip referred to indelicately as the 'permanent slouch'). The girls on the other hand were boy-crazy bobby-soxers, and it was as though every middle class family endured its own James Dean and Natalie Wood teenagers.

Every father worried about his rebellious offspring and every understanding mother sprang to their defense. It seemed incredible that these misguided young people could grow up into the finest of adults, after such negative influences at a crucial time of their lives.

There were other dangerous forces at work as well. Both Jamie and Florian reported to their parents, with considerable concern, what their school counselor had advised them. They were instructed to believe that they really owed their parents nothing, since they hadn't asked to be born in the first place. Conversely, their parents owed them everything since they had the responsibility of giving them a good home and basic material comforts.

"Is that the way you see things?"

"Of course not, Mum, of course not, Dad. We owe you both a great deal and we believe the counselor was wrong."

Nonetheless, Phil and Patty couldn't help wondering how many children believed this new heresy and kept it from their parents. It was important to give this rebel generation correct guidance, yet one must be careful not to stifle growth and individuality with excessive discipline and disapproval. At least, they weren't raising a couple of conformist zombies and for that they were more than grateful. Most of the friends their children brought home were the kind Phil and Patty were happy to accept as 'suitable', but there must have been those they didn't meet, and those of whom they might not approve. Meanwhile, Florian had to give up her ballet because of ankle problems, and James was showing less interest in music and more in political theory.

The Totem theater group headed by Sam Payne gave some first-class performances at the Thunderbird Theater, and Phil and Patty tried to see as many of their plays as possible. After a while, they began to invite the group up to the house for informal drinks and a bite of food. They also started taking James and Florian to the theater from time to time and the children thoroughly enjoyed it, especially when they were invited backstage between acts. They got to know the members of the cast and others behind the scenes, and this would make a lasting impression on them at their vulnerable age. Just how vulnerable and just how deep an impression, their parents would discover in the course of time.

With the advent of the winter season, Patty was becoming a real hockey fan, and there was little question that television had a great deal to do with this. She and Philip started to go to the occasional live game and both enjoyed the fast action. They were even toying with the idea of getting season tickets for the 1957 season. Now that the children were growing up and developing their own social interests, this might be a great idea for the two adults. They were already becoming keen fans of the annual World Series of baseball, and Philip enjoyed the build-up for the Canadian football Grey Cup, though he doubted if Patty could ever become a football fan.

This was, for Patty and Philip at least, the glorious time of Anthony Eden's emergence from the political shadows. After the war years and Winston Churchill's inspired leadership, the British electorate had shown its appreciation of their leader by casting him out in favor of the deadly dull Clement Attlee. It was evident the Socialist programs had failed to produce the expected millenium and an aging Churchill, bloodied but unbowed, was once more called to don the heavy mantle of leadership.

Last year, he'd finally been forced to retire in ill-health, and Eden became the new Prime Minister of Great Britain. It had been a year in which the tenuous peace – or more correctly the ceasefire – of the Middle East was threatened by the increasingly hostile boasts of Egypt's dictator, the aggressive Gamel Abdel Nasser, that he would "throw the Zionists into the sea." When this was followed by warlike preparations, buttressed by Soviet arms supplies, and the mobilization of Egyptian troops in the Sinai, Israeli forces struck first.

Nasser's recent unilateral nationalization of the Suez Canal, repudiating Egypt's treaty with Britain and France and closing that international waterway to Israeli shipping, was threat enough. When the Gulf of Aqaba was then closed to Israel, the result was a foregone conclusion. Israeli forces attacked, demolished the Egyptian resistance and took vast numbers of prisoners, before advancing toward the Suez Canal. At the same time, Britain and France attacked positions on the western side of the Canal zone.

It was precisely at this crucial moment in that explosive area, when the influence of the Egyptian firebrand dictator could have been crushed once and for all, that John Foster Dulles got into the act with the blessing of his President. One might have thought this devout hater of godless Soviet Russia, and anything beneficial to the Communist cause, would applaud such a joint action by America's democratic allies. Instead, he joined the U.S.S.R. and its Communist bloc in putting unbearable pressure on Anthony Eden.

Eden was forced to withdraw from the Suez area along with his French counterpart, and leave Nasser as rampant victor by default. With this one act of betrayal, Eden was isolated and Britain with him, while Israel was guaranteed an implacable enemy on its western approaches. Why, Philip asked himself, would the U.S.A. permit Dulles to abandon its Cold War allies and play into the hands of the Soviets and the forces of Islamic extremism? One reason was the well known deep antipathy between Dulles and Eden, which neither tried to hide, and another was associated with the incredible blunder of the Americans in the Aswan Dam fiasco.

When Nasser first turned to the U.S.A. for financial assistance in constructing the massive power dam on the Nile, he was initially promised the necessary funds by Dulles. Later, he was turned down on the pretext that too much Russian influence in Egyptian affairs was being accepted by Egypt. This proved to be an absurd charge, but it enabled a delighted Soviet Union to take over the role of benefactor in completing the Aswan project.

Now, by this latest act of about-face and betrayal of America's allies, Dulles was once more trying to gain an influence for America in the Middle East, replacing the traditional influence of Britain and France. As a political gambit, it was a dismal failure; furthermore, it made Nasser the unchallenged leader of all the Arab States aligned against Israel.

When America's betrayal was soon followed by Lester Pearson's craven action in the United Nations (acting on behalf of Canada but in concert with the U.S.A. against his mother country), it was ironic that he should be awarded the Nobel Peace Prize, a modern equivalent to the biblical thirty pieces of silver. The third, and perhaps the most reprehensible of all the reasons for the actions of John Foster Dulles and his President at this particular time, would be revealed to Philip personally at a later date, and he was appalled at what he learned. In any event, the betrayals changed the course of history in this troubled part of the world and sealed the political fate of Anthony Eden, one of the noblest statesmen of his day.

An incredible addendum to the Suez debacle was the abject behavior of the pious Dulles in response to Hungary's invasion by Soviet troops and tanks at about the same time, to suppress a national uprising against the country's Moscow- controlled leaders. After all the anticommunist rhetoric of his entourage, where was the courageous American response to this brutal act of aggression by the Cold War enemy, the type of response he found so easy to apply against Cold War allies in the Suez crisis?

On the national front, Philip watched with dismay as Canada's Nobel hero paraded his outmoded bow tie into the halls of the U.N. and perhaps, eventually, into the Prime Minister's office. Canada was becoming a sycophantic nation that seemed to be losing its way and its heritage. Meanwhile, the more Canada distanced itself from Mother England, the more Quebec seemed to clamor for special recognition and special rights. The francophile extremists grew in power as the anglophiles became progressively more obsequious. Soon the national anthem would be changed, and even the nation's precious Union Jack.

On December the 11th Patty reminded Philip that this was an important anniversary, and he realized he should have remembered.

"Exactly twenty years ago I was sobbing my heart out in Folkestone, along with the other nurses, listening to King Edward explain to the people why he must give up his throne so he could marry the woman he loved."

"In my opinion the whole affair was a put-up job engineered by Stanley Baldwin."

"Did he really hate Edward that much?"

"Politically, he regarded the young King Edward the 8th as a threat. As Prime Minister, Baldwin had made a mess of the unemployment situation and ignored the plight of the coal miners in a sagging industry. It was Edward, first as Prince of Wales and then as King, who showed real concern."

"You're right. I remember the newsreels showing Edward promising those poor people that something would be done."

"That promise cost him the throne. The hounds of Fleet Street were let loose and Mrs. Simpson became the Scarlet Woman. All that archaic rubbish about marrying a divorcee was simply to line up the Archbishop of Canterbury in Baldwin's corner, and with him the Church of England."

"Didn't you feel sorry for his poor brother?"

"Most people did. He was painfully shy and had a horrendous stutter."

"You have to admire his sheer courage in overcoming both."

"No question about that."

"I sure hope the Windsors found the happiness they deserve, especially the Duke, and I don't believe she just wanted the throne. The way she stuck by him through all those indignities makes me believe she really loved him."

"I'll drink to that."

Whether by choice or political necessity, the Sisters at St. Peters brought in a new hospital administrator to take over those duties from the Mother Superior in the winter of 1954. Dr. Edwin Fourget was a pompous young fellow, handsome and suave but lacking in humor and handicapped by a sense of personal infallibility. He began to justify his new appointment by making a series of changes in areas requiring no such changes. It was a typical example of the old adage: "If it ain't broke don't fix it." When he began to intervene in operating room procedure without benefit of discussion with the surgeons, Philip felt – along with others – that he'd gone too far.

The straw that broke the camel's back was a memorandum to the medical staff that henceforth only a new type of antiseptic solution was to be used in the O.R. It was a known fact that each surgeon tended to favor those specific materials in the conduct of his or her field of practice which consistently produced the best results. In Dr. Bosnar's case, for example, he hadn't the slightest doubt that iodine preparations were the best sterilizing solutions for painting a patient's skin prior to an operation. However, some surgeons found these solutions irritating, and in Bosnar's case any kind of iodine preparation caused his eyes to water and brought on coughing spells. Moreover, some patients developed a severe rash following their application. That was the reason he and several of his surgical colleagues remained faithful to their use of merthiolate solutions. They were highly antiseptic and non-irritating, and they spread in an even and visible fashion.

In replying to the memorandum, Philip indicated it would be unwise to dictate such matters and bring in 'Novoprep', an untried product; especially without consulting the medical staff and where there was no significant cost-saving. What followed, was a series of unpleasant letters from Fourget, suggesting that Dr. Bosnar was an enemy of the Sisters' hospital, and might consider taking all his work to the Chelmsford.

In a way, that was the opening Philip needed, and after discussing the matter with all his colleagues in the department of surgery, he wrote his final letter on the matter.

> **'Dear Dr. Fourget:**
>
> **First, let me say I found the tone of your letters increasingly offensive, and following consultation with my surgical colleagues I have decided to acquaint you with the following facts.**
>
> **Since my arrival in this fair city I have endeavored to remain scrupulously unbiased in my hospital practice. If you can tear yourself away from issuing offensive memoranda long enough to make the enquiry, you will find I have always admitted about the same number of patients to each hospital, that my reputation for cooperation is the same at both hospitals and has never before been questioned.**
>
> **The path upon which you have embarked is a dangerous one, and unless you are challenged at this point by one or more senior surgeons, you might be encouraged to dictate the type of scalpels we should be using or the type of suture material, and so on ad infinitum. Surgery is an art as well as a science, and one does not dictate to artists what paints or brushes they must use.**
>
> **I expect a prompt apology from you and the issuance of a new memorandum cancelling your previous 'orders'. Otherwise I shall take appropriate action in concert with my colleagues to see that you are disciplined or replaced.**
>
> **Yours truly,**
> **Philip Bosnar'**

Copies were sent to the chief of medical staff, chief of surgery and Mother Superior. Although it would take three more months before final resolution, Dr. Fourget eventually submitted his resignation to the Sisters. His resignation was accepted and the search was on for a suitable replacement.

Both hospitals had recently been through the periodic accreditation review, and although both received a favorable rating, Dr. Giscard O'Dwyer, chief of the Accreditation Committee, was extremely tough and outspoken in his critical comments and made strong recommendations for the improvement of hospital management and procedure. A devout Catholic, born and raised in Montreal, O'Dwyer was an uncompromising critic who made all the previous accreditors seem like pussycats by comparison. His most favorable impression during his short visit, was that of the city itself and the sheer beauty of this part of British Columbia.

Everyone was surprised when Mother Superior took a gamble and asked him if he'd consider taking on the position of hospital administrator, thus putting his own recommendations into practice. To the delight of all concerned, he accepted. Difficult as he was, and to some degree a bit ruthless, he was a likeable individual who worked with the medical staff rather than against them. In due course, he and Philip became good friends, with many similar viewpoints as well as a few deep divisions of opinion. He was always completely open with Philip, even when he disagreed most fiercely with him.

The first such disagreement was his action in the Department of Radiology, the second was in relation to a G.P's privileges, and the third was in an offer that he personally made to Philip. The first two resulted in tragedy, the third was simply an education in hospital politics.

Gavin Mackenzie was a first-rate ophthalmologist, and he and his vivacious wife Ellen were valued friends of the Bosnars. Philip first met him in Winnipeg after the LMCC exams, as a close friend of John Kinsley. Since coming to B.C., he and Mackenzie found that they and their wives got along famously. The eye specialist was a quiet introverted type with a gentle dry wit. On the other hand, his wife was boisterous and possessed a hilarious sense of humor. Both were victims of severe arthritis and came to B.C. for their health and Gavin's semi-retirement. Instead of cutting his practice to a minimum, however, he'd become one of the busiest eye specialists in all of B.C. and his skills were known far and wide.

When he found out that Philip was a victim of right-sided *Suppression Amblyopia* he asked him if he'd like to regain normal binocular vision. (Suppression Amblyopia is a condition where, as a result of an uncorrected visual defect in one eye, the vision on that side is progressively suppressed until it is almost never used at all.) Philip said he'd be delighted if it were possible, but doubted it very much.

"What makes you say that, Phil?"

"Well, when I was a medical student and consulted Maurice Whiting, one of London's finest ophthalmologists, he said not to bother. He was confident it wouldn't interfere with my ambition to become a surgeon but I must simply compensate with good well-positioned lighting, and learn to utilize parallax for depth perception."

"He was right up to a point but I still think we have a good chance of improving things for you."

"Do you really think it's worthwhile at my advanced age?"

"For Christ's sake, man, you're not even forty-five yet. Sure it's worthwhile."

"What do I have to do? Or perhaps I should ask what do you have to do?"

"First I'll check you for a combination of astigmatism and myopia that's the likeliest combination in such cases, then you'll have to wear glasses all the time until you get used to them, and I'll give you some eye exercises to do in your spare time."

He gave Philip the full examination, checking for glaucoma and any retinal changes, then arranged for him to have two pairs of glasses, one for regular reading and later for operating, and one without correction to get him used to wearing spectacles. Philip was deeply grateful for his kind concern and later, as his binocular vision returned, his gratitude knew no bounds.

There was one amusing item concerning Gavin, and if Phil and Patty were given a thousand chances at guessing Gavin's favorite interest outside his profession they'd never have succeeded. The Mackenzies were not the least bit reticent about telling them, even though Ellen whooped with laughter at their friends' reaction. It was the grunt-and- groan pseudo-sport of professional wrestling!

Since it was the twentieth year since his graduation, the Larkin Medal, the Broughton Scholarship and loss of the Grant-Sutton job to Skinny Thompson, Philip felt this might be an appropriate time for him to take a trip to England. By a happy coincidence, he'd recently received a letter from the Dean's secretary at St. Clements Medical School, announcing a reunion meeting of alumni at London's Savoy Hotel, to be held in mid-September. Philip replied that he'd be pleased to attend, and if his old friend Skinny Thompson was available, he'd like him to come as his guest. Thompson accepted the invitation without delay and with profuse thanks.

After Philip's arrival in London, when he went to pick up the reunion tickets at the Dean's office in his old Medical School, he learned a bit more about Thompson's career. After the prestigious house-surgeon's job with Grant-Sutton, he decided he wasn't 'cut out' to be a surgeon and set his sights on becoming a radiotherapist. He then adroitly managed to get a position as house physician to the eminent Dr. Max Hindermayer. Following this, he concluded that his real field lay in diagnostic radiology, and after a series of strategic residencies, he obtained a professorship in Birmingham.

When they shook hands in the large antechamber to the dining room, Philip noticed how much his friend had aged. He looked like a prosperous and overfed banker, and the white tie and tails – standard attire for such an occasion – revealed overly comfortable proportions that were in sharp contrast to Philip's more youthful contours. They strolled over together to pay their respects to the guest of honor, none other than Surgeon-Admiral Sir Grant Grant-Sutton, and were greeted warmly.

"So nice to see you again, Bosnar. I hear you've been making quite a name for yourself in Canada."

"I wouldn't go that far, Sir, but I must say I've found my surgical career in Canada an interesting challenge."

"You're being much too modest if I've been correctly informed, and it was nice of you to come to this affair and invite your old friend, Skinny Thompson, to come as your guest."

There was something delightfully ironic about the occasion, and somewhere deep inside, Philip felt that an old wound was being healed. Not only that, but he soon found himself surrounded by many of his own vintage. They congratulated him on having the foresight to come to Canada, long before so many others thought of doing the same thing. He hadn't the heart to disillusion them. It seemed the grapevine must have resulted in a considerable magnification of his professional and other accomplishments in the New World across the sea.

At his family's home in Hendon, he found his parents in good health and fine form, so that they never stopped exchanging information and viewpoints. They had greatly enjoyed the long visit of Patricia and the children, and as far as they were concerned she was a true daughter rather than an in-law. His Dad had at last given up smoking completely, but unfortunately put on far too much weight, and that didn't help the breathlessness arising from his chronic emphysema and bronchitis.

On the political front, he'd suffered a devastating disillusionment with the Soviet Union. The revelations of Stalin's monstrous transgressions, so fearlessly exposed by Nikita Khrushchev, demolished the raison d'être for his earlier political convictions. He was compensating for his former infatuation with atheistic communism by a return to the religion of his forefathers, albeit the modern Reform Synagogue with its English-style services.

Pauline was healthy and happy, although her husband seemed destined to remain in his present job forever, while Clayton was doing well in his medical studies and seemed oriented toward psychiatry, although he was well aware of Philip's long held anti-Freudian views.

Shortly before his departure from London, his Mum asked him if he ever communicated with Dora Henderson. He confessed that the thought had never crossed his mind, and in any event, he had no idea what had happened to her.

"Oh, she's still at the same school. Why don't you give her a call. I'm sure she'd like to hear from you."

He saw her crossing the small cobbled courtyard leading to the restaurant, and his first reaction wasn't the shock of instant recognition after so many years, but an inner chuckle he found hard to suppress. She looked the typical middle-aged English headmistress, hardly surprising since that was precisely what she was. The determined small firm steps were still there and the funny clenching of those baby-sized fists.

She was wearing a light blue raincoat and a rather severe cloche hat of matching color, hardly flattering but eminently respectable and appropriate to her profession. It was as though she'd made up her mind before meeting him, that this was to be the new Dora and there was to be no emotional nonsense, much less any romantic attempts at recapturing the distant past. (Another world, another time!)

As he watched her from the doorway of Alfredo's, a pleasant and unpretentious family-run establishment of quiet good style and excellent food, she looked up, and after a moment of indecision, suddenly recognized him despite his changed appearance. At that moment, her face became radiant with the dazzling smile of old, and it seemed as if the sun broke through the gloomy clouds in a glorious blaze of light. Perhaps the blaze was simply in his mind, a sudden remembrance of that first incandescent smile that so captivated him when he was a runty 15-year-old and she was an acknowledged school goddess of 18, worshipped by her contemporaries of both sexes and idealized by his own sister.

Jorge, the proprietor, a jolly fat Mexican who chose the name Alfredo's because he thought it sounded more elegant, welcomed them into the dining room with a cordial flourish. He helped Dora off with her coat and even persuaded her to part with her hat before seating them at a pleasant and discreetly placed corner table.

During the meal, as she let her fierce independence lapse for the occasion by letting him order the food and wine, each was engaged in a surreptitious sizing up of the other. Oddly enough, apart from the smile, there wasn't much left of her former vibrant good looks. There was a good deal of gray in the natural gold of her hair that he remembered so well. It had always been her crowning glory, ever since she was a bright and sparkling little girl behind the counter of the crowded fish-and-chip shop run by her uncle and aunt. Her eyes, with their strange violet color, still dominated her elfin face with its tiny features.

"You're heftier than I remembered you," she observed, "but not fat or paunchy for your age. You certainly look successful and self-possessed, almost smug."
He kept quiet and still, as she continued and tried to make awkward amends.

"No, that's unfair. Perhaps I just feel resentful that men so often look more handsome at this age, while few women have the same good fortune. Especially career spinsters like me."

"I'm afraid I can't agree with your assessments."

The excellent food was a scarcely noticed counterpoint to their questions and answers. Was she still teaching at the Brentcloisters in Surrey? Had she ever married? When had he gone to Canada and why? What about his wife? What was her religion? He knew this wasn't just idle and impertinent curiosity on her part, as they recalled how their own different religious backgrounds hadn't made the slightest difference in their relationship.

By the time the superb meal had been consumed and appreciated, they were both aware that her questions far outnumbered his, and for some reason it made him feel guilty, almost self-centered.

"I'm still teaching, and was promoted to headmistress after the war, when it became a girl's school and changed its name to Brentcloisters, although it professes no particular religious affiliation. How about your move to Canada?"

"In a way, Dora, I made up my mind to go to Canada after the so-called Munich Accord. I saw it as a craven betrayal by the Chamberlain gang and it made me wonder about the future of freedom and democracy in continental Europe, if not in Britain itself."

"And your wife?"

"She's a wonderful Irish colleen from County Wicklow. It was love at first sight and we still love each other deeply. We have two children, a 15-year-old boy and a 13-year-old girl."

He couldn't help noticing how stilted he sounded.
As they lingered over their wine, they scarcely noticed its excellence as they probed each other for answers that might magically peel away the years of separation.

Suddenly, an unpleasant thought struck him and the wine turned bitter in his mouth. He knew why he felt so guilty. She was far more interested in his answers than he in hers, and there was far more for him to tell her than she could possibly tell him. He began to regret taking the suggestion (or was it the advice?) of his mother – dear God, his mother of all people! – to see her once more, perhaps for the last time.

"No, Philip, I've never married. From time to time I've had affairs of varying length but little depth and no permanence. I know now there could never be another like Philip Bosnar for me."

She continued to talk rapidly, almost as if she relished his embarrassment, and he knew it was the wine that was talking.

"Even though you and I never consummated our love, my affairs with various lovers never carried the same intensity of true passion I felt for you."

He decided to take charge of the conversation before it got out of hand. He told her how he'd met Patricia at the start of a surgical residency in Dover, and how much he'd admired her for her beauty, her character, her intelligence and her outstanding professional ability as a surgical nurse. The fact that she was born in the south of Ireland and raised as a devout Catholic failed to sway his determination to marry her, as he was convinced he'd met the one person with whom he wished to share the rest of his life.

Time seemed to have passed very quickly in the cosy little dining room, yet there was still so much to ask and so much to say about many things, past and present. It was high time they vacated the table and imposed no further on the patience of their understanding host. Philip took care of the bill, left an appreciative tip and complimented the beaming Jorge on the perfection of the meal.

Outside, the air was fresh and for London almost fragrant, following the brief shower that cleared the sky while they were dining. September of 1956 had been a pleasant month so far, and they both enjoyed the short walk to the taxicab rank behind the new pathology wing of his old medical school. He'd accompany her to Victoria station and see that she caught the last train to Brenthaven. Most of all, he hoped the goodbye wouldn't become maudlin.

CHAPTER 33

1926

Rafael Bosnar placed his hands on his son's shoulders and looked earnestly into his eyes. His voice was quiet and serious.

"You know, Phileep, that your parents are not Orthodox Jews, especially your father."

"Yes, Dad, I know that."

"But your Barmitzvah is very important to us. It means that at your thirteenth year of life you become more of a man and less of a child."

"I understand, and I think I'm ready."

"To you it is still the religious side that is important, but to me it is the way you deal with your life, your family, and all those you meet."

"Both sides are important to me, Dad."

"God has given us love, but too many people find it easier to hate. Try not to hate people but only the bad things that they do. You have a duty to make this a better world, and that means being brave. Not brave with a sword, a gun, or your fists, but brave in speaking out for the good and against the bad that is in all of us."

"I'll try to make you and Mum proud of me, Dad."

The Barmitzvah was a great success. First, there was the synagogue service, with his reading from the Torah's scroll in poetic biblical Hebrew, wearing his new Tallis (a white prayer shawl with black striping and tasselled ends, worn like a scarf) and a new Yarmulka on the back of his head, both gifts from a distant uncle. Then the banquet at Griswold Hall, where such receptions were commonplace, the food delectable and the small orchestra very lively and very professional. There were over a hundred guests, mostly friends, neighbors, close and distant relatives. Most of the gifts brought by these fine people, even the handful of Gentiles among them, consisted of one or two bright golden sovereigns. These were intended to go toward his future education.

The guest of honor was none other than his idol, the peerless J.K.Goldbloom, rabbi, teacher and Zionist protagonist. It was he who proposed the official toast to Philip, seated to his right at the head table. The great man expounded to his entranced audience on the historic significance of the Barmitzvah celebration, then went on to talk about the renowned Theodore Hertzl, Viennese man of letters and bon vivant, the illogical founder and inspirational proponent of modern Zionism.

Philip Bosnar, he declared in ringing tones, showed promise of becoming just such a leader in the coming Zionist struggle for a national Jewish homeland. Although born in France, the speaker continued as he placed his hand on the boy's head, he was a typical young Englishman just as Hertzl had been a typical young Austrian, and his aptitude in the difficult Hebrew language as well as his religious fervor, made him ideally suited for such a destiny. Mr. and Mrs. Bosnar glowed with pride, the guests applauded wildly, and Philip was torn between happy gratitude and gnawing self-doubts.

This year seemed to be a major turning point in his life, quite apart from the ritual Jewish celebration of Barmitzvah. He kept feeling more and more British and less and less Jewish. Now that he was entering Brewers secondary school he began to read more extensively and brought home several books from the library on Trevor Road, each and every week.

First among his new interests was a study of other religions: Roman Catholicism, Greek and Russian Orthodox Catholicism, the diverse Protestant religions, Hinduism, Buddhism, Islam, Confucianism, Taoism, Zen and Zoroaster. One was forced to concede that the members of each faith believed just as fervently – as he once did – in the sanctified truth of their own beliefs and the fallacy of others. In all cases, believers felt they'd inherited God's chosen religion, and it was important to find out why. He began to read that most forbidden of all texts, the New Testament (surely the pathway to Hell!), yet he found it mostly inoffensive. in fact, he wondered why Judaism had so resolutely turned its back on Jesus Christ.

There was no denying that Jesus was a Jew, even though he became a reformer and nonconformist. That was why he had to die, because he threatened the Roman occupation authorities just as much as he threatened the corrupt high priests of the Sanhedrin. Those whose position he threatened had no difficulty in assembling an organized gang of hooligans to demand this troublemaker's execution by the Roman authorities.

The various chapters of the New Testament seemed to contain many contradictions as far as Philip was concerned, and many questions were left unanswered. In the first place, Christ wasn't a Hebrew name but may have referred to the Latin (Roman) word Christus, a translations of the Hebrew Moshiah, meaning Messiah or Anointed One. So what was his real name? It was far more likely to have been the Hebrew Yeshua ben Yusef (Jesus the son of Joseph), and to his followers and disciples, Yeshua Hamoshiah. On the other hand, perhaps the word Krystos – or one closely similar – might have an alternate arcane meaning in ancient Greek, namely The Crucified One!

The story of the virgin birth was almost identical to those he'd learned in his studies of Greek mythology and the Hellenic faith, but made little sense in modern terms. What about the faithful plodding Joseph, the honest carpenter who taught the growing boy Jesus his craft, and who gave his wife his love and devotion even though the child wasn't his? Didn't he deserve at least as much religious adulation as 'Holy Mary', mother of Jesus?

Paradoxically, Christianity seemed to reject the fact that Jesus or Yeshua was born, raised and died a Jew. To Philip's developing sense of logic and rapidly expanding intellectual curiosity, it seemed that accepting the truth of Christ's Judaism should lead to the death of antisemitism.

(But he would learn in time that bigotry trod a dark and sinister path far removed from the enlightened path of logic.)

Prejudice came in many guises. He always winced when he listened to the words of that comical Yiddish folk song, born in the ghettoes of Eastern Europe: 'Oy, Oy, Schicker iss ah Goy!' (Oho, Oho, The Gentile is a drunkard). In this and similar songs the Jew was always the devout talmudic scholar, the Gentile always the drunk. It was a crude antidote to the memory of those terrible pogroms in which drunken ruffians were let loose on a defenseless Jewish population.

He found a modicum of remedy for his troubled soul in a wonderful short story by Israel Zangwill. It was about a little Jewish boy who accidentally wanders into a Cathedral. His eyes and imagination open wide as he sees the magnificent vaulted interior and stained glass windows, with oblique shafts of celestial light coming through to illuminate the worshippers. How his spirits soar with the glorious music rising from the mighty organ, and how entranced he is by the rich vestments of the clergy and the angelic harmonies of the choir, almost giving the congregation a glimpse of heaven. In a state of childish rapture he returns home and tries to convey this new experience to his kind and understanding parents.

Philip felt guilty about his neglect of serious reading, especially when compared with his sister's appetite for the books of her favorite authors: Thomas Hardy, Ethel Mannin, John Galsworthy and D.H.Lawrence. Even some of his own schoolmates humbled him with their knowledge of good literature, while he wasted his reading time with the more lurid 'penny dreadfuls', the mysteries of Edgar Wallace and Conan Doyle and the adventures of Jules Verne.

The sad truth was that his only serious reading up to now had been the 'Jewish Encyclopedia' and 'World-wide Theology'. It was high time he read some worthwhile books, and for the next year he would devour the works of George Bernard Shaw, the plays of John Galsworthy, the novels of Charles Dickens and Joseph Conrad, and the poems of Keats and Shelley.

Recently, he'd become fascinated by the wonders so well described and illustrated in the two volumes of 'The Outlines of Science', a present from his father. It was edited by H.G.Wells and opened up the whole universe to the reader, from the infinitely small atoms and their structure to the infinitely vast reaches of space and its galaxies. Never again could he take the night sky for granted, or think of the sun and moon in quite the same way. He plunged into Charles Darwin's theory of evolution, and even found himself – in some primitive way – understanding the basics of Albert Einstein's theories of relativity, gravity, space-time and new dimensions beyond those ordinarily perceived by humans. He tried hard to visualize the Hypercube, a four-dimensional figure bounded on each side by a cube just as the ordinary cube is bounded on each side by a square.

Much of this growing scientific curiosity came from his Dad. From time to time, Philip used to come down with an attack of acute septic throat. These attacks came on quite often before he had his tonsils out, and at their worst made breathing very difficult. Nowadays, they only came on about twice a year, but never with the same severity as those before his tonsils came out.

In some ways he almost enjoyed these sessions, although he still hated having his throat swabbed by the doctor, every day until cured, with an iodine preparation. He much preferred his Mum's treatment with semolina in hot chicken broth. The taste and texture were divine, and his throat always seemed to derive great comfort from the thick liquid's healing qualities. It seemed to have the properties of an internal poultice.

At these bedridden times, his father would come up to his room and take his mind off his misery with wondrous magic tricks. There were those involving a top hat, from which a whole series of eggs dropped out and disappeared into his hand one by one; and the pound note wrapped in a piece of paper that was ignited with a match and burned to ashes, from which the intact pound note emerged afresh. Then, there was the endless series of silk handkerchiefs that emerged from his father's sleeve and changed with a flick of the wrist into a bouquet of flowers; and finally a whole series of mystifying card tricks.

Following this display of magic, his Dad would talk about the works of Professor Flammarion and Jules Verne, both masters of scientific fiction and literary voyagers into a limitless future. He talked about the universe and Man's future journeys into outer space. He outlined his theories about antimatter and antigravity and postulated that these would be the engines of journeys to the stars, perhaps in the lifetime of Pauline and Philip. At such times, Philip's imagination would soar to incredible heights, and his space vehicle always took the shape of a giant spinning Diablo, stabilized in its flight like a mighty gyroscope. Of course all these flights of fancy were before his Barmitzvah and therefore before the age of reason.

(Rafael Bosnar had ignited a fire of scientific curiosity in his son that would never be extinguished, and set in motion an imagination that would open up the wonders of the cosmos for him throughout the rest of his life.)

In many ways, Philip's life was taking a distinctly new turn, and in some ways less than desirable. Two of his closest friends were Sidney Klinefeld and Dave Brackman. Sidney was a pleasant and brainy lad who was the finest student of biblical language he'd ever met. In fact, his grasp of advanced Hebrew and talmudic Aramaic showed a true genius Philip knew he could never match. He and Sidney often exchanged visits at each other's home and sometimes they were invited to stay for a meal.

One Friday afternoon, they were strolling through the park at Grantham Square. The air was clear, the sun was shining, the birds were singing and the 'poing' of a well-hit tennis ball were all combined into a reassuring sign that God was in his Heaven and all was well with the world. Sidney revealed his ambition to enter Yeshiva (a Jewish seminary college) when he was a bit older, and study to become a rabbi. Since he was a great favorite of Mrs. Bosnar, Philip invited him home and suggested that perhaps he might stay and have some tea and cakes. Sidney's reply shattered Philip's safe and civilized world.

"I don't think I can ever come to your house again, Phil. Your parents don't keep a frum (strictly orthodox) home."

Shocked and outraged, Philip grated out his reply.

"If that's the way you feel, Sid, you can go your own way and I'll go mine. That's the finish for us, I'm sorry to say."

When his Mum asked why he was so glum and why he didn't want his usual tea and cakes, not even his favorite watercress sandwiches, he told her the truth and she wept inwardly for him. But later, when she reflected on the incident, she felt exhilarated by her son's strength of character.

As for his friendship with Dave Brackman, this also suffered an inevitable erosion as Dave showed an increasing submission to the strictures of his parents' orthodoxy. The change occurred at precisely the time when Philip was questioning that same orthodoxy and breaking away. Eventually they spent less time together and the relationship faded.

His friends at the new school were mostly Gentiles. Some were Church of England, some Presbyterian and some Catholics. Although over a quarter of the pupils at Brewers were Jewish, only a few of these were close friends of Philip, and he found his social horizons shifting.

Where his new teachers were concerned, he liked them all with one possible exception. That was Dr. Paul Frampton, who taught basic mathematics and general science.

Although he was a capable instructor, he had a cold and sarcastic manner. He taught his pupils all about evolution of the species by natural selection and periodic mutation. When asked by some of the students how these ideas could be reconciled with the Old Testament, he suggested they make up their own minds on the basis of available scientific evidence. He said he'd like to see some essays on the subject from those pupils who had the nerve to write them, and had the same suggestion for those pupils in his class who felt they understood the new physics and mathematics of the universe at large.

Philip was not only ready, but eager to take up the challenge on both subjects, and started his first essay with the bible's account of the creation of Man. At some stage in the development of the higher primates, he argued, there came a level of brain power, two-legged agility of locomotion and the adroit use of tools by skillful hands, which differentiated early Man from his antecedents. At that moment in history, he postulated, it could be said that God created the earliest creature who could be classified as Man, and The Almighty's experimental technique included what they now knew as Natural Evolution.

'It is likely', he wrote, **'that beside survival of the fittest and the intervention of favorable mutations, adaptation to environment was passed down the hereditary chain in some subtle fashion'**. As for the biblical `Days' of creation, in terms of infinite time and in the divine pattern, each Day – no doubt – was measured in millennia or even eons. Great allowance had to be made for poetic license, and for the translations and re-translations from ancient Hebrew manuscripts into Greek, Latin and English. Some passages needed to be seen as folklore or symbolic representation, and the story of the creation of the first woman from Adam's rib must surely refer to some primordial rite held by early human tribes following mating and reproduction.

The first man and woman soon had human company, as higher primates were evolving into humans with increasing frequency, and as Adam and Eve produced their own offspring. The essay concluded with the hope that science and religion might draw closer together in interpreting the manifold wonders of the world around them.

When he submitted his composition to Dr. Frampton (neatly typed by his sister Pauline on his Dad's office typewriter machine), he was hurt and disappointed by the derisive attitude of his teacher, who deliberately read out disconnected segments to the class out of context, thus concealing the essay's true meaning and flow of logic.

To his surprise, however, several of his new school chums asked for a copy of the complete essay to show their parents. Even more unexpected was the news that their parents were excited by the views and arguments expressed in his essay, and even thought them constructive. In fact, this favorable reaction encouraged him to go ahead with his second presentation, regarding gravity, the fourth spacial dimension and Einstein's theory of relativity.

'Space', he wrote, 'should be thought of as inter-reacting fields of force like sheets of elastic'. When a physical body entered such a force field it warped the elastic sheet in proportion to its weight, or more accurately, its mass. Thus, it produced a localized impetus so that a second mass would be propelled toward it, or more accurately, the space warp. This was the force of gravity. The further apart these objects, the less the degree of propulsion and thus the less the force of gravity.

All individual motion and even individual time itself was relative to external motion and time, and the only absolute limit to motion was the speed of light, 186,000 miles a second. The closer the velocity of an object approached the speed of light the heavier it became, and the slower its time would become relative to its initial mass and time measurement.

As for the fourth dimension in space, which Man was unable to experience or comprehend (and there might be other dimensions!), there was an obvious reason. The Good Lord had endowed Man with only three semicircular canals in the balancing system of his inner ear. So, when the inevitable question was asked, "OK smartie, where's the fourth dimension?" the answer would be, "Why, you stupid oaf, it's where the fourth semicircular canal would be if we had one."

Strangely enough, Dr. Frampton treated this second venture with genuine respect, and was responsible for Philip skipping a class at the beginning of his second year. He was finding it easy to make new friends, and there was no longer that sharp division between Jew and Cockney that existed at Tredegar school. Here at Brewers, not all Gentiles were Cockney, – and he found it increasingly difficult to think of them as Gentiles – and several of the Jewish boys seemed more Cockney than the real article. He began to resent thinking about his school chums in these terms, and he disliked making the differentiation.

He discovered he was a good student with a special aptitude for exams, but he retained a sense of mischief that often got him into trouble for his pranks. Thus, he was no stranger to punitive caning, usually well-deserved. On some occasions, he was punished when he didn't deserve it, but that only made up for the times when he should have been chastised but wasn't.

Now that he was no longer taking Hebrew lessons (and he was thankful he'd made it to the top class before leaving the Cheder) he devoted his linguistic energies to the study of French and German. Pupils were allowed to choose between the classical languages of Latin and ancient Greek and the modern languages, which he felt would be far more useful in the future.

One day, he was surprised and dismayed when Monsieur Barak, their French master, held a special meeting for the Jewish boys and discussed the problem of antisemitism and how to deal with it. Philip knew it existed, and had studied the grotesque history of this perverted aberration in the Jewish Encyclopedia, as well as other sources. But he'd never really encountered it in person, except for some harmless name-calling at elementary school. In a way, most of his nonJewish friends seemed to regard him as one of their own, without any hint of difference between them.

Surely, Philip suggested after Monsieur Barak had finished and left the classroom, the best way to counter antisemitism in England was to be more English than ones antagonists; more athletic, more courageous, better spoken and more correctly behaved. The same technique was applicable in other countries. In actual fact, with the advent of the late Edwardian era, it was no longer impossible for a Jew to acquire a knighthood or even a peerage. That made the Zionist movement seem unnecessary as far as Philip was concerned. Somehow the concept of a separate Jewish State carried a divisive quality that was out of touch with the modern spirit of religious and racial tolerance in the civilized world.

How different had his attitude been so recently, when – on the eve of his thirteenth birthday – his father's close friends arranged for Philip to meet the Chief Rabbi of Great Britain at his home in the Finsbury Park area. They had actually conversed in the three languages, English, Yiddish and ancient Hebrew, and as they strolled around the great man's magnificent gardens, he talked about the world scene in general and Zionism in particular, as well as the perils of religious intermarriage.

As an illustration of these dangers, the Chief Rabbi pointed to the tragic mistake made by that fine writer of English prose, Israel Zangwill. The son of immigrants who fled the Russian pogroms, Zangwill had been raised in London's teeming East End enclave of Whitechapel, where he grew up to become a distinguished man of letters in his adopted language. He fell in love with a young Christian lady and married her, ignoring the dire warnings of family and friends. Despite his confidence that he could overcome all difficulties, the marriage inevitably blew apart, and this should serve as a warning to others who had the same inclination.

Two things puzzled Philip after he thanked the Chief Rabbi for his hospitality and kindness in giving him so much valuable time and advice.

First, why warn a boy not yet fourteen about the dire and dreadful dangers of religious intermarriage? Did the rabbi detect something in his enthusiastic young guest, something that was hidden from the boy? The idea seemed too ridiculous to pursue.

Second, why on earth would the spiritual leader of British Jewry have Grecian-style statues all over his spacious garden when they were forbidden by rabbinical law? Could it be that each such law had its exceptions, or was the Chief Rabbi setting new breakaway trends and preparing to free his flock from the strict confines of narrow and outdated orthodoxy?

The two questions were too complex, even paradoxical, for Philip's logical mind.

CHAPTER 34

1958

When the credentials of Heiko Noguchi were first shown to him, Philip Bosnar was awestruck and insisted both hospitals should accept his application without delay. Born in Vancouver and educated in Winnipeg, Noguchi had trained in the most prestigious neurosurgical centers of Boston, Baltimore, Edinburgh and London, where he served his residencies with distinction. All his chiefs spoke of him in superlatives and Bosnar felt they were lucky to get a man of his caliber in Edwardia's medical milieu. The new neurosurgeon and Tom Pettigrew could cover each other when one was away, share an emergency call system and assist each other in special procedures. They could also discuss interesting cases in both practices.

Philip was surprised to see how young Noguchi looked when he arrived in town, more like a teenager than a man in his early thirties. He seemed shy and reserved, short in stature and frugal in conversation, but otherwise pleasant and unassuming. All members of the hospital staffs tried to make him feel at home, with one notable exception.

Ian Grosvenor was a tall, cadaverous, patrician Scotsman, whose soft accent came unmistakably from Edinburgh, that civilized city of scholars. After completing his surgical training and obtaining his F.R.C.S.(Edin.) degree, he joined his brother's group practice in Hong Kong. Then came the war and years of horror as a prisoner of the Japanese. He emerged from the POW camp a living skeleton, more dead than alive. Since those terrible days, this otherwise charming and gracious gentleman could never be confronted by a "son of Nippon," as he put it, without going through a fear-hate reaction that left him pale and sweating, with hands trembling and voice shaking.

When Noguchi became aware of the Grosvenor problem, he became even more withdrawn and Philip made up his mind that something must be done to remedy the situation. At first, he tried talking to Grosvenor, but it was like being up against the proverbial brick wall. Next, he tried to break through Noguchi's protective shell by asking if he might watch him work in the O.R, and after a while the neurosurgeon started to discuss his cases and operations with him. Before long, Philip discovered that Noguchi's outside interests were car-racing, tennis and music. They began to play tennis singles once a week, alternating between Bosnar's hard court club and Noguchi's grass court club. Since they were well matched, there was a good deal of banter and laughter during the games and they rapidly became friends.

Once or twice, Philip had him up to the house for drinks and Patricia took an instant liking to him. In return, Philip was invited up to Heiko's bachelor pad, where he proudly showed off his set of drums, his conductor's baton and his key to a *Playboy Bunny Club* in New York. He accompanied his jazz records on the drums with considerable skill, and conducted his classical records with more enthusiasm than expertise, but always with a vigorous baton and childlike enjoyment.

Philip learned that Heiko was a third generation Canadian, and that his family had a prosperous grocery business in Vancouver prior to World War 2. Then came internment, loss of property, home, self-respect and national identity. Heiko was deeply hurt but not bitter. Beyond everything, he detested anyone associating him with the atrocities of the Japanese armed forces during the dreadful '40s. As for his plans, he looked forward to taking his Canadian F.R.C.S. exam in neurosurgery later that year, so as to complement his American Boards diploma in that specialty.

The Murrays were an elderly couple who loved good music and intellectual conversation, yet they could hardly be considered elitist snobs. It was that – in their opinion – a world losing its basic standards of excellence must have its havens of refuge from the vulgarities of modern pop music and the obscenities of modern literature and art. Dr. Murray was retiring chief of radiology at the Chelmsford and his energetic wife was widely known for her prize-winning roses. Once a month, they held a 'musicale' at their gracious home, built like a Victorian English vicarage. The old gentleman loved to show off his huge sound system and collection of classical records, and his regular guests included the Blounts and Ridgeways. Emily Blount was a G.P. with a special interest in pediatrics and her husband Eric was a popular junior high school teacher.

After at least one complete symphony and a concerto or piece of chamber music, tea and cakes were served, and discussions on various topics in the fields of science, art and philosophy completed the evening. At first, the Bosnars thought they might be bored to tears, but in actual fact they found themselves enjoying these sessions more and more, as they got to know each other better and formality gave way to relaxed and open debate.

Emily Blount was not only a good physician, but a fine equestrienne besides. It came as a great shock, therefore, to learn she'd been thrown from her favorite horse and sustained serious and irreversible brain damage. Every effort was made by both of Edwardia's neurosurgeons to improve her situation, but to no avail. She was (and would remain) a human vegetable, sustained by tubes, intravenous fluids, medications and a mechanical respirator. The effect on her husband was devastating. He walked around in a state of emotional shock, like a zombie, and for some time was unable to come to grips with the truth of what had happened. Patty tried hard to improve the situation by inviting him for the occasional quiet informal dinner, and he gradually seemed to return to normalcy and an objective grasp of the tragedy. As for the Murrays' musicales, after a while the participants grew further apart and eventually the get-togethers stopped completely.

The James Dean era of youthful hero worship had now been compounded by the singing Pop Idol, Elvis Presley. It wasn't that his songs were all bad, in fact some were quite good, and he had a fine baritone voice when he wasn't croaking out his more raucous stuff; it was the pelvic gyrations and the projected sexual image that were so disgusting. Schoolboys were sporting pompadour haircuts and black leather jackets, and their kyphotic slouch was accompanied by a lecherous sneer. Meanwhile, shrieking schoolgirls worshipped at the shrine of the newest star in the musical firmament, while their brains drowned in a raging sea of hormones.

Would James and Florian ever emerge from these dark days of unsavory role models and distorted peer pressure, and would their innate sense of values and core of solid character come through to shape their adult personalities? Phil and Patty devoutly hoped so, and beyond indicating they didn't share their offsprings' adulation of the current wonder-boy, they didn't compound the problem by laying down stringent rules doomed to failure.

Jason Shelby had done a great deal for Philip's photography and the results were testimony to his influence. As a person, Shelby revealed two entirely separate characters. He was sophisticated and suave, an intellectual aesthete with a sharp mind and biting wit, fastidious and almost obsessive about cleanliness. Socially, he was intolerant almost to the point of snobbishness, yet he had a certain undeniable charm. Among the attributes he valued most were those exemplified by the lady he'd chosen to be his life's partner. Sylvia Shelby was an attractive and intelligent young lady who complemented her husband's social graces. He was very proud of her and they appeared to be the perfect couple, yet to those few friends like Philip Bosnar, who knew Jason really well, there was a darker side to this complex man. He became, on certain unpredictable occasions, an unkempt neurotic and self-centered hypochondriac, with an uncontrollable dependence on narcotic prescriptions and a paranoid suspicion of his wife.

Beside teaching Philip the techniques of good photography and the art of composition, he introduced him to the great outdoors. Whenever he was in the mood, he asked Philip to accompany him on camera trips to such places as the Elwha River and Olympic Mountains, to Shuksan Glacier and Mount Rainier, and to the Forbidden Plateau on Vancouver Island. Each trip lasted one or two days, and Philip kept his trusty Kodak Reflex 2 busy with a score of 'shots', in the hope that at least half of them would turn out well. Above all, he found himself intoxicated by the pure air and glorious scenery, and he acquired a genuine affection for the unspoiled wilderness and its isolation from urban hustle and bustle.

As for Shelby, he would take out his huge old-fashioned Graflex, mount a large plate into the slot and take one picture, no more and no less. Of course, the sky had to be just right, the clouds and the shadows just perfect and then, Presto, the one shot would be a prizewinner every time. Although Philip could never match his mentor's expertise, he was more than happy with his transparencies, and his friends complimented him on his results. He no longer did his own color processing, as the firm of Munshaw in Vancouver now did excellent work at reasonable prices.

One consequence of all this interest in scenic photography was a growing desire to put some of his scenic pictures on canvas, and Philip enrolled in a small art class run by Joseph Fraser, an ancient gnome-like Scotsman from Aberdeen, who taught him the use of oils and the selection of brushes; how to paint landscapes, seascapes and still life. Most important of all, he taught him that there was no such thing as true individual color. It was never to be considered an absolute but only a matter of color contrast. Thus, for example, walking along a country road and looking at the dull brownish gray of the wild-grass on the sides, it was necessary to look more abstractedly at the colors through narrowed lids. This created the magic of color contrast, so that the wild-grass took on a striking purplish hue as seen against the contrasting greens and yellows of the neighboring shrubs and trees. For the rest of his life, Philip Bosnar would feel a debt of gratitude to this fine art instructor for showing him how to look at nature, and he could only hope that somewhere in the vast and spectacular universe the old chap was still painting away happily in his own special fashion.

As program chairman for the C.P.S.A, Philip Bosnar was delighted when Henry Harkens of Seattle consented to be guest speaker at their next scientific meeting, to be held at Harrison Hot Springs. This distinguished professor, formerly president of the American College of Surgeons, was also co- editor of one of the best current textbooks of surgery. He was an excellent surgeon and fine lecturer, and Bosnar had got to know him well at various professional meetings, but most of all through his membership in the local Surgical Travel Club. This club was a small group of Edwardia surgeons who travelled to such neighboring centers as Seattle, Portland, Vancouver, and Edmonton. The leading surgeons in these places were only too happy to show the visitors their surgical techniques, their animal experiments and research projects, and to discuss their ideas, cases and theories with them.

Seattle had some topnotch surgeons, men such as Joel Baker and Alvin Merendino. In Portland, there was Professor Livingstone, an expert on the physiology of pain mechanisms and prevention of postoperative complications, and Allen Boyden, an authority on surgery of the biliary tract. Boyden wasn't as flamboyant as Waltman Walters of the Mayo, but in Bosnar's opinion, his operating technique was far superior. In Vancouver, there was the talented Rocke Robertson, and Walter Mackenzie still reigned supreme in Edmonton.

These surgical leaders were generous with there exchange of information, and Philip enjoyed his discussions with them on a one-to-one basis. In talking to Harkens, he was amazed to learn that the professor was under great stress with the pressures of his teaching schedule, his crowded operative lists and the necessity of turning one paper after another. Then there were his frequent speaking engagements, not only across the U.S.A. but in far off places. He told Bosnar that he envied his life style and, by contrast, feared that he'd soon crack under the strain of his seventy hour work week.

(Neither of them knew at that time that Harkens' life was already drawing to its close long before the allotted three score and ten, although he may well have had his premonitions. Many a time since then, Philip would reflect on the fact that there is a down-side to ambition, to advancement and recognition; and how, so often, the price is much too high.)

Once in a while, Philip took a photographic trip with a volunteer member of the family. Last October, young James accompanied him on a drive up the Fraser Canyon Highway. The road was in terrible shape, with great pot-holes and large chunks of roadway torn off, mostly at a bend in the highway and on the canyon side, where the fall-away was precipitous. But the weather was glorious and so were the fall colors of pale crimson, burnt umber and pastel yellow, with the river an endlessly winding silvery serpent, far below. They stopped only once, and that was to watch the churning waters racing through the narrows of Hell's Gate. When they arrived at Kamloops, Philip tried to order the famous Kamloops steaks but found that this was impossible. These choice foods, they were informed, were "for export only" and not available locally. They also learned that a car had gone over the side near Hell's Gate, about two hours after Philip and James went through that location, and no survivors had been found.

The return trip was uneventful. The light was perfect for photography, and Philip took many pictures during half a dozen stops, with James wearing his brightest and most photogenic red shirt. They detoured to Keremeos, and the stunning scenery made it worthwhile. The car was parked by the side of the road and they sat down in the tall grass, with father photographing son looking out at the wonderful view. James's cheerful cooperation proved he had the true soul of an artist, but neither of them had the slightest inkling that they were in the heart of rattlesnake country!

From time to time, Patty accompanied her husband on a trip to the Okanagan Valley, to catch the spectacular Apple Blossom season. They were getting used to comforting remarks from the locals such as, "Too bad you weren't here last week," or, "one more week and it'll be perfect." This year, however, they'd cheated the odds and arrived at the ideal time. The orchards were in full bloom and Philip's camera was kept busy, but there was a price to pay for success.

They were going back by way of the Hope-Princeton Highway, but they gassed up the car first, and had the young lad at the pumps check oil, water and tires. As they climbed steadily upward, the scenery unfolded around them until they leveled out, with the river far below on the right side and B.C's unspoiled beauty as far as the eye could see. Cruising along at a steady 60 m.p.h, there was a sudden loud bang and all vision ceased. Without the slightest sign of panic, Patty asked, "Do you think we hit a deer or a horse?" and Philip replied mechanically, "I'm not sure, darling," but his brain was racing.

The human mind is an extraordinary mechanism, and its ability to compress judgement and calculation into fractions of a second has saved countless lives. Philip knew two things at once. First, the hood had slipped its catch and flown up against the windshield. Second, he must remember the highway at the very moment before it was blotted from view. They were on a marked curve of the road to the left, and coming toward them on the other side of the road was a large yellow bus. He took his foot off the throttle, gently snubbed the brakes again and again, at the same time trying to steer the car along the remembered trajectory around the bend and avoid dropping into the river below, or plowing into the bus just ahead. When the car came to a merciful stop and he got out, the bus had already stopped on the other side and a white-faced driver was running toward him, shouting, "You folks sure had a lucky escape. Looked like you could see through that hood the way you kept to the bend."

An inspection of the hood made it clear that the young gas attendant at their last stop hadn't fastened the hood down properly, and they were lucky the windshield hadn't shattered under the impact when the hood flew up. The bus driver got some wire from his tool kit and fastened the hood down to the catch, as a stop-gap until they got home. Philip thanked the good Samaritan with all his heart, and remembered to thank the Good Lord for His mercies in their time of peril. From that time forth, he would always check the hood-catch whenever it had been opened, especially by someone else.

The annual scientific meeting of the C.P.S.A. was a great success and Patty had a marvellous time. The social program was first-rate and there were special events and tours arranged for the ladies. One of the reasons the Bosnars enjoyed these surgical meetings so much was the warm friendship they encountered from the Vancouver surgeons and their wives. In some ways, the Vancouver entourage provided the atmosphere of a home away from home, both professionally and socially.

Harrison Lake was breathtaking in its jewel-like splendor and matchless serenity, and the hotel accommodation was beyond reproach. There was only one moment of near panic, and that was the day before the meeting. The first paper was to be presented by none other than Dr. Crawford, Philip's noble mentor from his army days; but instead of the usual 35mm. slides he had an old fashioned set of large slides for which they had no suitable projector. Taking advantage of his friendship with the managers of Edwardia's photographic stores, Philip got their help in hunting down the right kind of projector and all was well.

Crawford had moved from Winnipeg to Vancouver and was still quite an active surgeon despite his advanced years. His paper was on the subject of Parathyroid Tumors, and there were few Canadian surgeons who could challenge his experience in this field. On the first night of the meeting, at the official opening banquet, the renowned surgeon came over to the Bosnars' table, a short but striking figure with his shock of gleaming white hair and firm stride of authority. After formal introductions, he sat down next to Patty and told her, with a remarkable memory for details, about the first encounter at the Regina Military Hospital. He recounted how Philip, a mere captain, had challenged him, a full colonel, to clear up the corruption and mismanagement in the surgical division of MD12.

"I knew right then I liked this guy for his gumption and honesty," he declared, "and I got him his promotion and the Thornton posting."

He glowed with pride, and Patty told him how grateful they both were for his efforts. He departed with some gallant compliments to Patty, and after he left she had to admit she found him quite fascinating. This came as no great surprise, since Crawford was not only a leader in his profession but an attractive and charismatic personality.

When they got back from their glorious week at Harrison, Phil and Patty were saddened by the news that the Shelbys had divorced. Jason closed his office and disappeared from the city, and it was rumored he'd gone south to practice in the United States. Philip wondered if he went to the southwest desert country of Arizona. He'd always claimed that the arid place was God's country, where the splendid colors of earth, sky and desert wildflowers were beyond compare, and a photographer could find his own special Paradise. Philip remembered the countless times Jason had shown him pictures of that region from his collection of photography magazines, and how incredibly vivid they were. Of course, having experienced the wonders of the Grand Canyon, Bryce Canyon, the Painted Desert and Zion National Park, he could understand Jason's emotional ties to those hot dry vistas of everchanging hues.

As for Sylvia, she moved to Vancouver, where she managed a small and fashionable boutique of women's clothing. Phil and Patty felt extremely sorry for her, but knowing how difficult Jason must have become before their final breakup, perhaps she'd be better off this way. Shortly before leaving Edwardia she confided to Philip that she'd always remain in love with that half of Jason's personality she admired so much; but she could never forget how painful it was to try and accommodate herself to that other darker side, the one hidden from most others.

The meeting of the Edwardia Medical Society was engaged in extolling the virtues of M.S.A, the physician-managed medical insurance scheme in British Columbia, and Dr. Bosnar felt the time had come to speak out.

"With your permission, Mr. Chairman, I wish to draw attention to some of the defects of this system and hope we haven't set a dangerous precedent for our federal government to follow. In the first place I believe it's wrong to accept a discounted fee schedule, with a percentage deduction to compensate for collection expenses. Surely it would be preferable for us to lower our own fee schedule by the appropriate amount, otherwise the ten percent may become twenty or thirty percent in the course of time as the bureaucracy grows. In the second place it would seem that our minimum fee schedule, which was instituted to prevent cut-rate fees as a method of soliciting patients, has suddenly been changed to a maximum schedule. Just when did this happen, and with whose approval?"

What followed was sheer confusion, and it was obvious to several of those present that once again doctors in general, and their economics committees in particular, were digging their own graves. Later on, when the politicians were doing to the doctors what they seemed so eager to do to themselves, there would be loud outcries against Socialized Medicine.

As a member of the special committee on medical services to old age pensioners, Bosnar felt the time had come to face some painful facts with a little more courage and honesty.

"For one thing," he declared, "it's unseemly for doctors to approach the B.C. government each year, hat in hand, asking for an increase in O.A.P. payments that are so far below the regular fee schedule. I propose that if the government continues to take credit for this fee reduction our alternative suggestion should be the complete abolition of all payment for the care of these most seriously afflicted patients."

There were murmurs of approval and a few hand-claps.

"In any event," he continued, "the media should be kept fully informed and the doctors' position clearly laid out for the public. After all, the large discount we've accepted so far is the best kept secret by our news media, while the politicians have been getting all the credit for any cost savings."

The proposal was placed in the form of appropriate motions and passed without dissent. It got no further than the Economics Committee of the B.C. Medical Association, but at least a blow had been struck against the idea of double standards in the matter of O.A.P. medical fees. The mere concept of charging nothing, rather than accepting a huge unilateral discount from the government, caused bad dreams for too many leaders of the medical profession. They seemed to forget that the prerogative of tearing up bills for the indigent had always been treasured by their noble profession. This latest proposal would have forced the 'Wacky Bennett' government to fish or cut bait, and would have provided a solid basis for future negotiations in a much broader context.

A viable alternative that might be considered at some future time, to deal with the problems of O.A.P. medical coverage, would be a per capita annual payment to doctors, but such a 'capitation' system would no doubt be considered the ultimate sacrilege by organized medicine, along with such blasphemies as salaried physicians.

As Philip got to know Erskine Ridgeway better, he discovered hidden facets of the man's personality and background that steadily increased his admiration. During World War 2, while serving as senior surgical consultant with the Eighth Army, Ridgeway became friendly with several Jewish officers who told him all about the history of the Zionist dream, and of serious plans to make the State of Israel a reality after the defeat of Germany and her allies.

He was fascinated with that entire area of the Middle East known as Palestine, and was eager to learn more about the communal farms set up by those Jewish pioneer men and women who were determined to convert sunbaked desert into a modern 'land of milk and honey'. That was why, once he was out of the army, this austere Protestant son of Ulster joined a kibbutz in the Galilee, learned to speak some modern Hebrew, worked on the land and took his place alongside the others, with loaded rifle in hand, whenever marauding Arabs attacked the compound in the dead of night. He also set up an emergency surgical unit and performed several operations during his stay.

When he left after six months, he was confident that the State of Israel would become a reality and the native Arabs would be the beneficiaries, unless persuaded by their leaders – the pashas and mullahs – to fight against the Jews. A special feast was held to honor Ridgeway as a 'Gentile friend of Israel,' and he was given the title and special medal of 'Honorary Kibbutznik'.

From time to time, he and Philip would meet for bull sessions on world affairs. Each would take turn in presenting a specific topic for discussion, and brought along a set of notes outlining information obtained from the newspapers and magazines. This year, for example, Philip offered to present the world's unluckiest statesman.

"My choice is Anthony Eden, a man for whom I have the highest admiration," Philip commenced. "In my opinion, this fine statesman, with his impeccable record of moral decisions and strategic judgement, was scuttled by men and nations who should have been his allies. That, beyond all else, was the real instrument of his bad luck."

"Why do you think he was right at the time of the Suez Canal crisis and all the others were wrong?"

"Well, let's suppose that in July of this year the President of Panama announced he was unilaterally nationalizing the Panama Canal. There would have been cries of outrage by Dulles and his cronies, invasion by U.S. forces, and support rather than opposition from Britain and Canada."

After a short break, Ridgeway presented the case of Nikita Krushchev as the world's luckiest statesman. He did so with admirable brevity.

"He's popular at home, has had the courage to denounce Stalin, and has developed into a true world leader. He may even succeed in reforming communism into a more moderate form of socialism." Philip, none too sure about the fortunes of this ebullient Soviet leader, countered, "You've certainly made a strong case for Khrushchev's good luck but I've got a feeling that sooner or later he'll stumble and the Russian wolves will be waiting for him."

The news about Heiko Noguchi was greeted by all who knew him with shock and disbelief. He'd failed his Canadian Fellowship! When his colleagues first questioned him about it, he drew back into his shell, but later on gave them a few significant details. The written exam was perfectly straightforward and gave him no trouble at all, but the orals examiner was hostile right from the start. His questions were peculiar and the answers seemed to dissatisfy him, no matter what they were. On one occasion he asked Noguchi, "Is that the way they do things in Japan?"

There seemed little doubt that this was a case of naked racial intolerance and Philip was determined it should not go entirely unchallenged. Accordingly, a meeting was arranged with the department chiefs in both hospitals, and a small delegation was chosen to enquire into the reasons for Heiko's unexpected failure. When the details were finally unearthed, a month later, they were hard to believe. The question that resulted in failure was extraordinary and certainly not one to ask in an exam of this caliber.

"You are called to see a patient who has been admitted to Emergency in a small hospital some twenty miles away. He has sustained a severe head injury in a car accident and cannot be moved. When you get there and decide to explore for a probable epidural hemorrhage you discover that there are no neurosurgical instruments. How would you proceed?"

Noguchi's answer was perfectly logical.

"Before leaving my city for the outlying hospital I would have made sure they had the equipment I require for an exploration. Then, if necessary, I could bring a sterile bundle of the requisite instruments with me."

The correct answer, according to the official record, was that a carpenter's brace-and-bit should be obtained from the hospital's stores and this could be used for burr-holes instead of the usual Hudson drill. It was the expressed opinion of the delegation that the question was a stupid one and the candidate's reply entirely sensible, but the examination result wasn't changed and Noguchi refused to have the matter pursued any further.

One year later, he passed the Canadian F.R.C.S. in neurosurgery with one of the highest marks ever recorded. He thereupon left Canada, this time for good, and accepted an appointment in Wisconsin as Professor of Neurosurgery; then proceeded to write a concise book on the subject that would be useful for exam candidates. At the time of his departure, he carried with him the best wishes of his colleagues and Philip Bosnar's personal friendship. His honor had been satisfied, while Canada lost a distinguished native son to the dark undercurrent of racial bigotry.

CHAPTER 35

1958-59

This was obviously going to be an extremely busy year. First of all, Philip Bosnar was deeply involved in the affairs of the regional surgical society and the provincial section of general surgery, and there was still a lot to be done with their plans for outlawing fee-splitting. They were working on a standard pledge to be signed by all surgeons across the province, and which would be backed by permission to have their books audited in a specific search for evidence of any irregularities along these lines. Members of the special committee would be the first to undergo such an audit in order to avoid any 'holier-than-thou' appearance. Needless to say, Bosnar and his fellow members were hardly the most popular surgeons in B.C. and the Vancouver committee members were already feeling the pinch, with a clear-cut reduction of referrals and a marked chill in the doctors lounges at the hospitals.

Bosnar felt genuinely sorry for these men and applauded their courage, especially since he observed no such effects in Edwardia. The reason was that whatever could happen had already happened and those who didn't approve of his stand weren't sending him cases, anyway, and were hardly among his most cordial friends.

Over and above these responsibilities, he was informed that he'd shortly be nominated as next Chief of Surgery at Chelmsford Hospital, and it was in this context that Vincent O'Dwyer approached him with a proposition. O'Dwyer, the new administrator at St. Peter's, was born in Montreal, the son of an Irish father from Cork and a Quebec Francophone mother from Trois Rivières. His father was a police captain and had met his mother when she was working as court stenographer. Like his parents, he'd been brought up to be fully bilingual.

He was basically fairminded but believed in acting on impulse, since he considered himself a good judge of people and was rarely proven wrong. On those few occasions when his impulse was wrong, however, the results could be tragic and they spoiled an otherwise good administrative record. One of his less admirable qualities was a tendency to apply pressure politics in order to get his own way, and Philip knew he'd be the recipient of such pressure, sooner or later.

Over the years, listening first to radio broadcasts and then watching TV, Patty had become – like her husband – a rabid hockey fan, and they'd held season tickets for the past year, rarely missing a home game of the Edwardia Lions. They even become team sponsors during the past season and had tickets to all home games. By pure chance, O'Dwyer had a season's seat next to theirs, immediately behind the penalty box, and he and Philip got to discuss the merits and shortcomings of the players, as well as the officials – who often seemed blind as bats.

O'Dwyer was a fanatical fan of the Montreal Canadians, but still enjoyed the local games as an experienced and well-informed hockey afficionado. He and Philip tended to get more than a bit excited during the games but rarely argued about technical points. Occasionally, the administrator had the surgeon over to his house to watch a football game between the Montreal Alouettes and their hottest rivals, especially the Edmonton Eskimos. Philip always bet against Montreal and that made the game more enjoyable, the arguments more energetic, and the consumption of beer more liberal. On one such occasion O'Dwyer suddenly tackled Philip about his persistent loyalty to the Chelmsford when it came to active staff membership.

"I don't understand why you stick with that bunch of Orangemen, Phil. You know how they hate us and besides, what the hell have they ever done for you?"

"In the first place, Vince, I honestly don't believe we should place religious barriers between the two hospitals, and although competition is a good thing it should be constructive rather than destructive."

"You haven't answered my question."

"The Chelmsford has given me and my patients good service and that's all I expect. St. Peter's gives no less, and I let my patients decide where they wish to be admitted, except in certain emergency situations."

"You could get a lot more from St. Peter's if you switched. I guarantee you'd see your practice double in the next two years, starting with emergencies. Why d'you think an internist like Reg Asquith has built up such a big practice in just a few years?"

"Well, in the first place he's a darn good internist, and in the second place he's politically popular."

"It's more than that, my friend. He knows that most of the G.Ps feel more comfortable at St. Peter's and they send their work to specialists like Asquith who promote our hospital and give it all their support."

"Maybe so, but there are also those who may benefit from a strong preference for the Chelmsford. Personally I don't believe those are the kind of factors that should affect one's volume of work."

"Merde, mon ami! Why don't you open your eyes and take a good look at the real world and the way it runs? How do you Anglos say it? You scratch my back and I'll scratch yours."

They agreed to disagree and Philip never gave the slightest consideration to changing his active staff membership from one hospital to the other. Perhaps there was another reason for his determination not to be a turncoat: two incidents for which he could never forgive Vince O'Dwyer, and the administrator knew it. The first was that involving a G.P. and the second concerned a radiologist.

Emil Stanovitsky was a good family doctor, and he had an excellent practice, including a high percentage of continental Europeans who'd settled in their fair city. His privilege list at the Sisters' hospital included a fair number of surgical procedures that he'd performed competently for a good many years. It included the removal of certain small benign tumors and cysts, and vein stripping for varicose veins. There were several established G.Ps who enjoyed such privileges and most of the surgeons – Philip, for one – had no objection. It wasn't uncommon for certain procedures to lie in what might be called: "gray areas", and although no new privileges were being granted along such lines, none were removed without compelling reason.

Even in the broad specialty of general surgery, although many procedures in urology, gynecology, and orthopedics were still on Philip Bosnar's list at both hospitals, he gradually withdrew from certain surgical operations as new subspecialists came into the city. Some of the general surgeons, especially Harry Grote, Chief of Surgery at St Peter's, bitterly opposed any surgical procedures being done by G.Ps – especially Stanovitsky. But Philip had watched Emil in the O.R. once or twice, and in addition, the G.P. had assisted him in several major procedures on his patients and proved he was surgically quite adept and a careful technician.

Unfortunately one of his patients died of acute pulmonary embolism (a sudden blood clot in the lung circulation) three days after surgery, a standard vein stripping. Although there was nothing in the autopsy to indicate any lack of competence on Emil's part or any failure to anticipate such a disastrous outcome, he had all his surgical privileges removed without so much as a hearing in his presence.

Philip spoke at considerable length to Grote, to O'Dwyer and many others on the staff of St. Peter's but to no avail. It seemed there was a lot of envy and a certain amount of prejudice involved in this decision, and he advised Stanovitsky to get himself a good lawyer. But Emil wouldn't even consider such an action, since "it might hurt the nuns", whom he liked so much and to whom he had always been loyal. When the chips were down, Philip thought bitterly, it was not only where you give your loyalty, but who you are and what friends do you have.

From that time forth, happy, kindly, gregarious Emil was a broken man, frequently sick and often seriously depressed. Even his bubbly, irrepressible wife, who could have cheered up Job in his time, was unable to work her magic with her husband. His opponents, both seen and unseen, had smashed his confidence and injured his self-respect, perhaps irreversibly.

Freddy (Feodor) Ivanov was an Englishman to the core in both deportment and diction, and a thoroughly civilized sort of chap except for his political views, which were well to the right of Ghengiz Khan. He came by these naturally, having been born into a family of aristocratic White Russians who fled to England when Lenin and his Bolsheviks took over the destiny of Mother Russia, "like a plague of locusts on our helpless motherland." For the past ten years this patrician gentleman had presided over the radiology department at St. Peter's with regal panache, as if he were current representative of the Romanovs' Imperial Crown. He didn't simply read his X-rays in ones presence; he had tea served ceremoniously while he expounded on the films mounted on his viewing box, and on world politics in general.

What Ivanov exemplified was an oldworld charm and grace rather than the latest advances in his specialty, but those of the medical staff who knew him well and understood his strengths as well as his weaknesses, could see the handwriting on the wall. It would be hard for Freddy to step down from his throne when the time came, and the secret fears that haunted him in this regard were evident only to those who knew him best. He'd never really recovered from the death of his wife two years previously and was having difficulty raising his 12-year-old boy on his own. Luckily, his unmarried older sister was staying at his house and his son adored her.

One day, a Dr. George Selkirk arrived from Winnipeg without any advance notice, to take over as the new head of St. Peter's Department of Diagnostic Radiology, with Ivanov demoted to second in command. This was an action decided upon by Vincent O'Dwyer and the Executive Committee without any discussion whatsoever with Ivanov.

For the next few days the fallen radiologist showed the new arrival every single item of the department in a spirit of helpful cordiality. He told Philip and some of his other friends that he liked the newcomer for his attitude and his obvious expertise, and he certainly revealed no resentment. On Friday, he went home shortly after 4 o'clock. He told his sister and son that he was taking a long trip, and said his goodbyes. Then he went out into his garage and hanged himself.

For the next few weeks a great pall hung over the hospital and the staff all realized that St. Peter's Hospital had lost one of its key personalities – one who simply couldn't be replaced. (**Sister Mary Patrick, the nun in charge of the X-ray technician staff and a devoted friend of her chief, not only departed from the hospital but left her holy order entirely and went down to California, where she became a senior hospital radiographer.**)

Gigi had grown up to be a most beautiful dog. In her smart Dutch cut, with her deep chocolate-brown coat and her bejeweled collar, she looked like a prizewinner, but was far too independent-minded for the Bosnars to consider entering her in any dog show. She was born to mischief, and when she was enrolled in dog-training class she managed in four short lessons to disrupt the class completely. Even the most obedient dogs became delinquent under her guidance, and the lady in charge of the classes was quite willing to pay Patty, in order to keep Gigi as far away as possible from her other pupils.

All the Bosnar family members were extremely fond of their gorgeous poodle and proud of her aristocratic appearance and bearing; none more than Patty, who had once been so prejudiced against any kind of poodle, large or small. Now she was hooked for life. Florian was only too happy to pose for pictures with Gigi, who was a natural show-off, and they made an eye-catching photogenic pair. It was strange how Gigi learned, like Whiskers before her, to keep off the flowers in the rock garden, and she was like a mountain goat when it came to scampering up to the Lookout with her mistress. When the weather was fine the two of them went down to the seafront, where the poodle had her frenzied runs on the broad stretches of grass above the rocky bays, while Patty had long walks at full speed that kept her as fit as a fiddle.

Phil and Patty were surprised and delighted when Jim Leigh-Jones came to visit them in Edwardia. He was on a business trip to Seattle but made a special point of stopping off to pay them a visit; he looked extremely well and had gained a bit of weight since they saw him last. His wife Daphne and three daughters – who remained home – were all well, and his electrical business was flourishing. The Bosnars had known for some time that Jim was one of the first of Britain's postwar business millionaires, and on each of their trips to England they'd visited his huge mansion in Buckinghamshire, with over thirty rooms and large grounds adjoining a golf and country club.

Leigh-Jones was a very shrewd businessman, despite his carefully cultivated pose as an effete aristocratic fop, and his central secret of success was to treat all his employees as if they were members of his family. Once a year, without fail, he closed down his huge London plant and offices and took all his employees and their families on a long weekend to the coast of France, in the Paris Plage area, with all expenses paid. It was the stuff of commitment and loyalty, and his workers resolutely refused to join any union; they always gave an honest day's work for an honest day's pay. Their employer was a confirmed nonconformist and claimed that this attitude was born when he returned to Britain after the war and visited his neighborhood 'Off License' liquor store to replenish his meager stocks.

"I'm sorry, chum, but I don't seem to have your name on our customer list," he was told.

"Of course you don't, I've only just got back to England."

"Where have you been since we opened a few years ago?"

"I've been overseas with the Air force."

"Well, there you are! You can't expect to get any supplies here if you're not on our list. Try us in a couple of months and leave your name."

After that and similar experiences, Jim invariably looked for 'No Parking' areas to park his car, and wherever the advertisements extolled the virtues of a particular brand of product over 'Brand B', he invariably sought out Brand B for his own purchases. In fact, he almost started a national trend along those lines in England and was very proud of it. Phil and Patty sent Daphne and her family all their love, and asked Jim to say how pleased they were that she never had a repetition of the dangerous complication she'd experienced after her delivery in far-off Vanwey.

There was no doubt about it, Philip's friend Emil Stanovitsky was dying. After a number of heart attacks, labelled as 'Coronary Occlusions', he became increasingly feeble, and for the past month he'd been a private room patient on the medical floor of Chelmsford Hospital. Despite the best of care under a team of excellent internists and cardiologists, he lapsed into a chronic state of increasing cardiac failure. He was getting intensive medication and careful monitoring, yet he was failing day by day, and it was apparent to Philip that he'd lost the will to live some time ago.

The day before he died, Emil Stanovitsky asked his wife and nurses to leave him alone with his friend for a few minutes, then spoke quite lucidly, slowly and calmly.

"I've really been very fortunate, Phil, with more good friends than most and a wonderful marriage, although I would have loved to have some children. Please make sure a good man takes over my practice when I'm gone and Elsie gets an adequate deal on the takeover. She may be a bit strapped even with the insurance and our savings. I'm a bit disappointed at my colleagues in St. Peter's and feel a bit let down by the nuns. I know you did all you could to change things around and I'm grateful, but I'll die still wondering who wanted to ruin me and hurt my practice."

"All I can say, Emil, is that you're a damn fine doctor and your patients love you. The same, of course, goes for your loyal office nurse, Fran Michaels, who literally worships you. As for your opponents, they have to live with what they've done and I doubt if they've derived any benefit. You have my word that I'll try to get the right man to take over your practice, and I'll make sure Elsie gets a fair deal on the transaction."

Emil closed his eyes and drifted off into sleep with a happy smile on his face. That would be the way Philip would always remember this gentle soul, a doctor who was kind and thoughtful and should have had no enemies, except for reasons of envy or intolerance. This man of many interests and old world courtliness was also the man who had introduced him to the expanding world of tape-recording, and for that Philip Bosnar would always be grateful.

As President of the C.P.S.A, Dr. Bosnar was glad a first-class program had been arranged and their guest speaker would be the internationally famous Richard Cattell of the Lahey Clinic; his main topic would be advances in biliary and pancreatic surgery. It was agreed unanimously that members of the Society should be careful not to embarrass their guest by asking him anything at all about his experiences as Anthony Eden's surgeon. The entire meeting, held at the Prince Albert Hotel, went like a dream. The accommodations and facilities were beyond reproach, and the papers were of the highest standard, as were the discussions and commentaries. Cattell was in fine form and his presentations exceeded their highest expectations. Bosnar was sorry to detect just a trace of tremor in the hands and the fixed facial expression that were the early signs of Parkinsonism, but so far, the guest speaker seemed at the top of his form.

On the Saturday evening after the end of the meeting, the two were sitting in the main bar of the hotel, chatting over their glasses of Cutty Sark and soda when Dr. Cattell suddenly astounded Bosnar by asking, "Would you like me to tell you about my involvement in the Anthony Eden case?" Bosnar could feel the sudden silence as several of his colleagues drew close to catch a conversation that was so unexpected.

"I'd love to hear it, but before your arrival we decided it would be wrong to ask you."

"Well, as you probably know, he had his gallbladder out in 1953 and following surgery he developed a persistent drainage of bile and slight jaundice. He was opened up again and they found that his common bile duct had been damaged to the extent that the surgeon was unable to effect a repair."

"What was done then?"

"They simply put in a drainage tube as a temporary measure before a commitment was made as to the next step. It so happened that I was over in Britain at the time as guest lecturer when I was contacted by Winston Churchill."

He paused as they slowly finished their drinks and then continued while the bar attendant took a repeat order.

"I was informed the Queen wished to see me, and Churchill had his chauffeur pick me up at my hotel and drive me to Buckingham Palace in the company of the great man himself. He introduced me to the Queen, who was most charming but nevertheless quite direct. 'Mr. Cattell,' she said, using the British surgical Mister rather than Doctor, 'we would like you to take over the care of our Mr. Eden. He is very dear to us and we are very worried about him'. I tried to explain that I would find it awkward to operate away from my home ground at the Lahey Clinic, and that I was quite sure that the excellent British surgeons would handle the case expertly."

"How did she react to that?"

"Quite calmly and firmly. 'Of course, Mr. Cattell,' she said, 'we would expect you to perform the necessary surgery at the Lahey Clinic and we can arrange the immediate transportation of Mr. Eden to America'."

He went on to tell about the operation and two unpleasant side issues. At exploration, the common duct was hopelessly fibrosed right up to the liver, with no visible stump. He therefore used a vitallium Y-tube to insert into the right and left hepatic ducts and implanted the single end into a loop of upper intestine. The operation was difficult but successful, although it wasn't made any easier by old Dr. Lahey, head of the clinic, who was long past his prime but insisted on 'helping' at the surgery. Throughout the operation he kept trying to interfere, with such remarks as, "Let me do it, Dick, I can get at it better from this side."

Philip couldn't resist telling his narrator about the trick he'd used at the Athlone Hospital, handing his troublesome assistant three retractors instead of the customary two. Cattell roared with laughter and thought he should have patented the procedure.

The other awkward business concerned Mrs. Eden, who was supercilious toward everyone at the hospital and a constant embarrassment to her husband. One of her most frequent and gratuitous comments that hardly endeared her to all concerned was, "I really can't see why this operation couldn't have been done in London." As for Eden, he was an ideal and uncomplaining patient, and the nurses all loved him.

When they finished their second drinks Cattell decided to complete his story. Before discharging his distinguished patient he warned him that it might become necessary at some future time to change the vitallium tube if it ever became clogged with what is known as Biliary Mud. That warning, by sheer misfortune, proved prophetic at the worst possible time in world history. It was at the time of the Suez Crisis that Prime Minister Eden reached the stage of chills and high fever, and faced the possibility of having to return to the Lahey for replacement of the Y-tube. Unhappily, therefore, it was a desperately ill man whom John Foster Dulles (in concert with the Soviets and Canada!) was able to bully into abandoning a course which might have prevented continued strife in the Middle East. It was a course that would also ensure an international waterway which couldn't be closed to any nation on the decision of a dictator like Gamal Abdel Nasser.

"Do you think Dulles knew how desperately ill Eden was at that particular time." Philip felt he simply had to ask the question, and Cattell looked at him long and hard before answering.

"You bet he knew," he replied quietly, "and so did President Eisenhower."

Dick and Millie Southerby were two of the Bosnars' favorite people. They were both now working in the provincial civil service and enjoyed gardening and opera. Their comfortable bungalow was located near the woodlands on the eastern edge of the city and they had everything they wanted in life with one enormous exception. The Southerbys had no children, and after extensive medical investigation they were told they could never have a child of their own. For the past five years they'd been trying to adopt a child, and for the past five years the adoption agency officials had been putting them through one cruel frustration after another. It simply made no sense.

"Here's a couple who love children intensely," Philip protested angrily, after the Southerbys left the Bosnar abode one evening, having related their latest disappointment to them, "and they can't get to first base. They have a good home and would make devoted foster parents."

"I agree. The whole system seems grossly unfair."

"A couple of school kids can do it in the back of a car and have a baby they don't want, and couldn't look after, anyway. Then again, a couple of drunks or junkies can produce babies at any time, to be born into a world of squalor and child neglect, while society looks the other way."

"What bothers me is the number of cases of child abuse being uncovered throughout the fifties, right across the country."

"You're absolutely right, Patty. Sometimes I think the less qualified you are for parenthood the less concerned the authorities seem to be. On the other hand, if you're like Millie and Dick, and have all the qualifications to give a baby affection, a good home, and a safe and happy future, you're almost regarded with suspicion by the adoption agencies. They seem to be looking for new reasons to block the desperate search by people like our friends. It's just so bloody unfair and so lacking in logic it drives me up the wall."

"When I watch the Southerbys with our children, year by year, it makes me feel like weeping for all their disappointments."

The Bosnars were delighted to see how well the Torwalds were doing. Their motel was always full and they were thinking of selling and then buying a larger motel in the area of the Royal Harbor adjoining the large complex of civil service buildings. Quite close to their present property was the popular Swiss Alpine Restaurant and through the Torwalds Phil and Patty got to know the family that ran it. Despite the fact that the restaurant was a fair distance out of town its reputation for good food at reasonable prices had spread far and wide and the restaurant was always full. Heinrich and Elsa Mittendorf were not Swiss, they were German, and had come to Canada after World War 2, but not directly. First, they went to Argentina, but after staying there for three years decided to come up to a cooler climate.

Elsa's mother, Madam Kaiserling, had come with them; she was a cello teacher and had taught some of the leading concert artists on both sides of the Atlantic. The old lady was truly charming, with a never-ending series of anecdotes about her most famous pupils and a deep concern about the future of Germany. She was convinced that until that divided nation was reunited it could never find its lost soul.

Heinrich was very quiet and had to be drawn out in conversation; he had a furtive look about him and seemed to be dominated by his vigorous wife. He'd been a prominent and highly respected industrial chemist before leaving Germany but was afraid the communists were after him, as they were in so many similar cases, because of the strong anti-red sentiments he was known to have held as a young man.

Elsa was a typical full-bosomed Aryan blonde, a true Walkurie of Nordic folklore. She'd been a physical fitness instructress for women and still exercised religiously each day. Although she deplored the excesses of the Nazis during the Third Reich, she thought the Führer had done a great deal for the common people during his earlier political career. He'd brought the nation out of the terrible post-war depression, restored national pride, and eliminated the communist forces and other undesirable elements.

As the Bosnars got to know these interesting people better there was no denying that they were very likeable, and in spite of Elsa's brashness, essentially Gemütlich. Thus, when Philip let his suspicious mind fashion a scenario of dark fantasy he felt a bit guilty. In this fantasy he saw Heinrich busily helping to produce Zyklon B for his company – I.G.Farben – and in fear for his life as a hunted war criminal after the defeat of the Third Reich. He could see Elsa leading her troop of big-bosomed blonde Brunhildas, smiling their ecstatic adoration at the beloved Führer as they showered him with flowers. As for Madam Keiserling, she was the traditional German matriarch who could enjoy her family and its rising fortunes while remaining blandly oblivious of the horrors around her.

Patty thought Philip was being unfair and even somewhat paranoid: harboring such unworthy thoughts about a family of likeable people who were only trying to become good Canadians. Philip countered with a few comments of his own.

"You must realize, Patty, that when Eichmann is finally picked up by the Mossad his neighbors will probably say they found him very charming and likeable, and I've no doubt the same will be said about Mengele. It's not that I have any concrete reason to suspect the Mittendorfs, but I'm certain that right across North America there must be hundreds of war criminals and their families who are living out their lives as respectable citizens without a breath of suspicion about their dark past. As for South America, that's a veritable haven for such fugitives from world justice."

"Even if you're right, we musn't abandon our sense of democratic justice. This tells us that people are innocent until proven guilty. Millions were tortured and killed by the Nazis because they were judged guilty from birth. We must have a different concept of justice."

"You're absolutely right and your ethical judgement is perfect, darling, but at the same time we must never forget the old saying that the price of liberty is eternal vigilance."
(Decades later they would remember this conversation when it was revealed that Canada, no less than the United States, had so many war criminals living in its midst, enjoying the good life and above suspicion for all those years.)

Mrs. Betty Thurston was a very sick old lady, living with her husband in retirement about 50 miles north of the city. She was sent to see Bosnar by her physician, Dr. Percy Brooks, and was soon diagnosed as having a large cancer of the stomach, the kind that is called a 'fungating' tumor. In Bosnar's experience this type of stomach malignancy often carried a better outlook following surgery than the smaller ulcerating type. Despite her age, seventy-six, and her anemia, Bosnar was able to get her into good condition for surgery and the operation went well, despite its magnitude. It was necessary to remove nearly all of the stomach along with part of the pancreas (what is known more commonly as the sweetbread), and a large segment of bowel. Following surgery she did remarkably well and her two sons, who had travelled up from Detroit, expressed their gratitude. They were senior executives at G.M. Motors and had arranged for their mother to have a private room and special nurses. Their father was a man of few words and sour disposition, but he did manage to mumble: "Thank you, Doc." The sons insisted that Bosnar send the bill to them and left their address; they also insisted he use the Michigan fee schedule as a guide, which would be in excess of a thousand dollars, rather than the B.C. fee which was considerably less.

Bosnar finally decided a fair bill would be $750 in Canadian dollars, most reasonable by American standards, and when his patient was discharged, doing remarkably well, he sent his bill to Detroit. The months passed without any reply and he decided to send the bill directly to the patient. This time the reply came fairly promptly: it included the patient's O.A.P. (old age pension) number and a request that the surgeon submit an itemized account.

When his blood pressure had settled down, Dr. Bosnar wrote his reply. He started by saying that his O.A.P. payment could be sent to charity, since it would be an insult to the degree of difficulty, the expertise, and the experience required to perform such surgery.

'As for the itemized account,' he continued, 'it is quite simple:
To saving a human life by advanced surgery ————$750.00
For an education in lack of appreciation ——deduct $750.00
Account due ————$000.00'

After that he felt much better, but he reminisced that such ingratitude was rare in those days when each bill was within the control and judgement of the attending doctor rather than a third party agency. It would appear there was something to be said for the time-honored system, –

akin to Noblesse Oblige – but only if his own profession didn't abuse it. It would be a sad day for Canadian Medicine if it ever became converted to a business rather than an honorable calling.

From time to time Peter Forsyth came out to Edwardia to visit his sister Gladys and her family. Phil and Patty used to see him on these occasions both at the Jacksons and at their own home. Besides these joint visits, which included dinner and light social conversation, Pete and Philip used to have a quiet lunch together in one of the more secluded restaurants. As soon as they were assured of privacy, Pete revealed the terrible losing fight he'd been waging with his deadly enemy – Alcohol. His appearance showed it, but not as clearly as one might have thought, and although it hadn't yet affected his practice significantly, his family life was breaking apart. Philip liked his onetime partner and friend very much and respected his abilities, but he knew, with great sadness, that he was heading down a deadly path which could have only one end.

The orbiting of Sputnik last year meant the race for space was on and the Russians were the leaders in orbiting vehicles; more importantly they were in the lead for missiles that could carry nuclear warheads. Almost a decade ago, Philip had been sufficiently intrigued by the subject to buy a copy of Willy Ley's book The Conquest of Space, with color illustrations by Chesley Bonestell. The book dealt with the logistics, in terms of mathematics and physics, required for space travel; first, around the earth and then to the moon and beyond; first unmanned and then manned. It discussed the possibility of a moon orbit and landing, as well as space stations and the future exploration of deep space. It revealed the secrets of the elliptical trajectory – not parabolic – and the importance of 'Mass Ratio', namely the proportion of rocket weight plus payload and fuel to that of the fuel itself, and of the velocity at what was called *'Brennschluss'*, the moment all fuel was consumed. Reading this amazing work again at this time made him marvel at the incredible accuracy of its predictions and its deadly implications in this era of the H-bomb and worldwide tensions between the superpowers.

By the end of 1957 the U.S, Russia and the U.K. had each independently and success-fully exploded a thermonuclear bomb whose destructive force was measured in units called mega-tons, each of which was the equivalent of one million tons of T.N.T. These newer devices could devastate huge areas by the release of overwhelming blast forces, by ultra-thermal incineration, and by the massive release and spread of radioactivity. Now, the circling of their imperilled globe by a little shining sphere launched successfully by Soviet scientists, made them all conscious of new and deadly possibilities. Now, giant missiles could be projected into extraterrestrial pathways and silently deliver their lethal payloads on unsuspecting cities. Then would come the great bang, the immense fireball, and for the lucky ones, instant oblivion.

The time had come for both sides to get the monstrous genie back into the bottle and foreswear, for all time, the use of such advancing technology to destroy civilization, if not the beautiful planet itself.

CHAPTER 36

1927

It hardly seemed possible that only one year ago he was devoutly immersed in the surviving rituals, some religious and some superstitious, of his ancient faith. He prayed in *Tallis* (the prayer shawl) and sometimes even in *Tefilim*, also known as Phylacteries, (small leather boxes containing selected passages from the five books of Moses, one bound to the forehead with leather thongs and one to the left arm with a long and narrow strap wound seven times around the left forearm and hand). The prayers were always in biblical Hebrew, and the head was covered with a cap or *Yarmulka*. All other faiths were false and all other customs out of step with the dictates of the one true God.

Now he knew this was all illusory: that theirs was just one of many religions, the inheritor and partial imitator of other more primitive religions, and the forerunner of two of the most widely accepted faiths in the world, Christianity and Islam. Even the synagogue services had their close parallel in form, apparel, music, and posture, to many other services in church and mosque.

Racially, too, he was not unique, but a mixture of Middle East Semite, European Slav, and quite possibly Aryan and Negroid as well. Ancient historic exile in far off lands, with conquest, enslavement, rape and even intermarriage, had produced a racial chameleon in which specific categorization was no longer possible, and in fact no longer desirable, if racial prejudice was to be eliminated. As for religion, all faiths should be respected, but similarities rather than differences should be sought.

On the issue of Zionism, he was inclined to be against the idea, since the 1920s seemed to be an age of racial and religious tolerance to a degree the world had never seen before. The dying days of antisemitism, it would seem, were those of the Dreyfus Affair, a miscarriage of justice in Fin de Siecle France, an event about which he'd heard in many discussions between his parents and their friends. Although he knew the broad outlines of that national scandal, and who had not read about – and applauded – the stirring 'J'accuse!' in which the great Emile Zola attacked the blatant intolerance and injustice of his beloved France in the national press?

When Philip's father offered to take him to the premiere performance of 'Dreyfus' in the Westend he jumped at the idea, and when warned that he might find the film rather harrowing, he replied he was old enough to handle it and was believed. It proved to be an excellent foreign work, well directed and well acted, with the leading actor handling the title role with a quietly dignified performance.

The film showed Captain Alfred Dreyfus as a rather stiff and formal French officer, the only Jewish officer in the French Ministry of War. He was a reserved and non-gregarious type and the very antithesis of a popular fellow like Major Esterhazy, another officer in his department, one who was a gambler, womanizer, and bon vivant. At home with his family, Dreyfus was shown to be a warm and loving husband and father, adored by his wife and children.

In 1894, on the flimsiest of evidence, he was tried by a military tribunal on a charge of spying for the Germans. One of the documents for the prosecution was declared by the most questionable witnesses to be in the handwriting of the accused; this evidence was hotly contested by the most eminent handwriting experts but feverishly pursued by a Major Henry. Aided and abetted by a virulent and antisemitic press, as well as an aroused public that clamored for his conviction, Dreyfus was found guilty and sent to rot in the tropical hell of the Devil's Island penal colony: a living death where he would be subjected to special brutality by the guards.

As if that were not quite enough to quench the mob's thirst for vengeance, there was a public ceremony of degradation before sending the victim out of its sight. The buttons and insignia were ripped from his tunic and his sword was broken in two. This delectable spectacle was followed by wild anti-Jewish riots all over the country and a further outpouring of racial and political hatred by the extreme right wing, military and ecclesiastic organs of the press.

Next came the backlash, as men of decency and conscience began to challenge this gross miscarriage of justice. Within the War Ministry itself there was a Lt.Col. Picquart, who proved that the traitor had to be Major Esterhazy, and that the evidence against Dreyfus was a pack of forgeries and lies. Picquart was soon transferred to another assignment where he could no longer be effective in his fight against this perversion of justice. Even the General who headed the War Ministry reached such a level of doubt that he resigned; but it was clear that France's military machine wasn't going to be swayed from its distortion of the legal system. As for Esterhazy, he went through a mockery of a trial and was acquitted.

At this point in the film, the great writer Emile Zola, who'd been vainly trying to mobilize the forces of decency against prejudice and hatred, was shown sending his scathing denunciation of the government and the military establishment to the press, under the famous headline 'J'Accuse!' For his pains, he was brought to trial and sentenced to one year in prison and a fine of 20,000 francs. Nothing, however, could now halt the inexorable march of truth.

In exile, disgrace and penury, now living in Britain, Esterhazy tried to make some money by selling his true story to the press, and the world learned how he betrayed the French military secrets to the German Embassy in Paris for money, to cover his mounting gambling losses. Back in France, Major Henry committed suicide when his duplicity was revealed, and the laborious process of investigation, reinvestigation, trial and retrial dragged on endlessly. while the greatest intellectuals of France fumed against official intransigence. Finally, a haggard but indomitable Dreyfus was brought back from Devil's Island, broken in body but not in spirit, and still supported by a loyal wife and brother who never stopped their efforts to obtain his release.

In the closing portion of the film, the audience was shown the reinstatement of the unjustly punished officer, his decoration with the Legion of Honor, and the cheering crowds – no longer an antisemitic mob – enjoying the ceremony. The theater orchestra struck up the stirring opening bars of the Marseillaise, and the Parisian populace was shown singing the words, which were displayed on the screen. As if on cue, the entire audience stood up and joined in the singing of the anthem, whether or not they knew the words. There was hardly a dry eye in the theater, and Philip only got as far as 'Le jour de gloire est arrivé' before he felt his eyes fill with tears.

On the way home he asked his Dad if the day of glory really did arrive for France on that fateful day of vindication, and whether the fearsome specter of racial and religious hatred might ever again return to the land of his birth. His dad replied that this could only happen if the fanatical right wing of the militia, government and church had its way, and that was why the socialists and communists were so important. Privately, Philip wasn't quite so sure about his reasoning, but he knew what an idealist his father was and respected him for it.

London's streets were changing. Horses and carts were being replaced by lorries, and the acrid smell of horse manure was now replaced by the choking fumes of petrol. Only the great wagons of London's breweries, with their magnificent Clydesdale horses, still resisted change. How Philip loved the gleaming, clinking, brass fittings, the painstakingly plaited tails and feathered hooves of the magnificent beasts! As for the draymen, these mighty fellows revealed a capacity for hoisting fully loaded beer barrels onto and off the wagons, matched only by that of their stomachs for the foaming brew itself. It would be a pity if these wonderful reminders of a bygone era were to disappear forever.

Sometimes, when he took a bus ride through London's streets, he sat in the open top section – weather permitting – and from that vantage point he could survey the exciting and never-ending panorama of the traffic and passing parade: people of all ages, sizes, and color, residential houses, shops, and office buildings. It was thrilling to watch the dray wagons refuse to be pressured so much as an inch off course by the buses. The huge iron-shod cartwheels were more than a match for the bus-tires they challenged. The city of Dickens had not yet disappeared completely.

There was another aspect of London he was coming to appreciate more and more, mostly in the company of his father. This was the wide array of museums: the Tate Gallery, National Gallery, Natural History Museum and the great London Museum. Last but not least there was the daunting Madame Tussaud's Wax Museum. There was so much to see, so much to absorb: a veritable unending feast to satisfy an endless intellectual hunger. How, he wondered, was it possible to store even a tiny fraction of all this information in ones mind, even in the space of an entire lifetime?

The important thing, his Dad reminded him, was never to be satisfied with ones knowledge but always seek for more. Never looking to the future without knowing about the past. Never being content with ones own point of view but understanding that of others.

It was a time for learning something about his origins, and he absorbed each new item of information with growing interest. His mother was born into a strictly Hasidic family, the Stranskys, in which her rigidly orthodox father studied the Talmud and prayed morning, noon and night, and her pious mother always wore the traditional wig known as the Sheitle. There were two closely guarded secrets in the Stransky family. The first was that the two sons were socialist revolutionaries and were involved in acts of sabotage against the Tsar's regime, and the second was that the 17-year-old daughter was being courted by a 'Freethinker'. To a Hasid, a freethinker wasn't much better than a Gentile, and a Gentile was someone who beat up or killed Jews when he was drunk.

Philip's father was born into a definitely nonreligious family; his mother had died when he was quite young and he'd been brought up by a father who served at one time as an officer in the Tsar's Polish army. Rafael Bosnar studied in a 'Gymnazium', a military academy where fencing, especially with sabers, was the most important subject. After completing his education, including many languages – of which English and French were paramount – he decided to become an artist and philosopher like his brother.

When Rafael Bosnar and Klara Stransky first met at the wedding of mutual friends, it was love at first sight, and the young lovers knew they must leave the country as soon as possible. In the first place, her father would flatly forbid such a union. In the second place, with the possibility of Russia soon becoming involved in a major European War, to stay in Warsaw might be a fatal error. The senior Bosnar, Paul Philip, had been one of the only Jews with officer's rank in the Tsar's forces and he knew from unguarded chatter in the officers' mess that any non-Christian soldier sent to the fighting front was unlikely ever to return alive. In truth this fact was no secret to the Jewish community.

Paul Philip arranged for Rafael and Klara to get out of the country, and they eloped with his blessings and a sizeable gift of cash to tide them over the next few months. They made it as far as Paris, where Rafael had some relatives, and the young couple moved into a small flat, actually a converted garret, in the Montmartre district, and started married life. For Rafael the hardest challenge was that of making a living, and for Klara it was cooking a meal or doing any housework at all, if it came to that. She'd never been called upon to perform such duties at home. They were always done by the Polish servants, while the family ran its grocery store and the paterfamilias communed with God.

When Pauline was born in 1911 and Philip was born two years later, necessity became the mother of adaptation, and Klara became a proficient housewife and devoted mother, while Rafael became a designer in a 'coutourier' establishment on the Left Bank, and an adoring father. By the winter of 1914, with Paris under wartime restrictions, a shortage of milk combined with an absence of heat in the humble abode to threaten the infant Philip's life with a combination of rickets and double pneumonia, and a kindly old doctor's instructions were simple: "Get the little fellow over to England at once or he will be dead very soon." Fortunately, Pauline hadn't succumbed to these deprivations and remained healthy.

England proved a warm haven for the family and Philip Bosnar would always feel a debt of gratitude to his adopted country. France, too, was a special place. It was the romantic city to which his parents had eloped, his own birthplace, and the home of several of his father's relatives. Philip had been over to visit these relatives once or twice with his parents, and he got to know the sights and sounds of that unique metropolis, especially the left bank and the district of Montmartre.

Unlike Warsaw, Jews weren't persecuted here, and it seemed to Philip that this added to its special position in world esteem, although he also knew it hadn't always been thus. The shocking Dreyfus Case had taken place only a few decades ago, and the echoes of the affair still hadn't died down completely. The film he'd seen so recently must have brought back bitter memories to the older generations.

Now that he was fourteen, he found his interest in the various school subjects undergoing a gradual change. The new progression from arithmetic to algebra and geometry revealed a logic of almost artistic dimensions, whereas trigonometry seemed dry and of no foreseeable application. Chemistry and physics were fascinating, and unlocked some of the secrets of the inanimate world as well as the inner workings of industrial processes – such as the production of steel and aniline dyes. He enjoyed some of the practical experiments, and tasted the excitement that people in research or creative invention experienced as they labored to solve the hidden mysteries of nature.

History seemed extremely dull, involving an endless series of wars and a useless procession of dates to memorize. At least when he was in elementary school, Mr. Rogers used to fire his pupils' imagination with panoramic scenes of historic events, scenes that he drew in chalk right across the wide blackboard: drawings which remained planted in ones imagination.

Geography was even worse, and Philip found it difficult to get thrilled by the physical contours and figures of industrial production and exports of various countries across the world. One day, he promised himself, he'd find a way to make history and geography meaningful and stimulating in a way that was far removed from his present studies.

Languages were a different matter. He loved English with its rich variety, its subtlety and its intricate grammar; and French and German seemed to be coming almost naturally – the spoken aspect most of all.

He began to wonder what he'd be in future: certainly not a doctor, as he still got very squeamish at the mere sight of blood. Perhaps he might grow up to be a trial lawyer, a barrister. He was always fascinated by films about courtroom battles, and loved to witness the magnificent pageantry of the lawcourts. There, high up on the judge's bench, sat his Lordship, above mere mortal men, and below – like actors before an admiring audience – were the opposing barristers, their knowledge and ingenuity, their eloquence and personalities deciding the fate (even life or death) of the prisoner in the dock. What challenge, what power, and what immense responsibility were the daily commonplace of such a noble career!

Surely the historic curled periwig, the black gown and white cravat, were no less impressive than a surgeon's cap and mask, gown and gloves. Well, perhaps not quite as dramatic, never stained with blood; although the skillful prosecutor might have blood on his soul, (perhaps a prisoner wrongfully hanged for a murder he did not commit). It was going to be a difficult decision, and perhaps it would be better to wait until matriculation before making up his mind.

On warm and sunlit days he was always glad to get into a game of cricket or soccer, or even go for a long run around the park when no games were available. His Dad had bought him a tennis racket and press, along with half a dozen used but serviceable tennis balls, and he intended to make full use of these. Mr. Granach, who'd recently become Mr. Grant, was an all-round sportsman in his mid-thirties, and he lived just a few doors away from the Bosnars. He was very good with children and had long been a favorite of Philip's.

Mr. Grant's parents and grandparents had all been born in England and he spoke and behaved like a genuine Anglosaxon. As for his appearance, his blue eyes and light brown hair were more in keeping with the name Grant than Granach. He was a steady rather than a brilliant tennis player and he taught Philip the basics of the game, always being careful to aim the ball toward his pupil rather than away from him. He didn't bother showing him how to serve, hit forehand, backhand, volley or smash, but let him develop his own style by correcting his own mistakes and by watching his instructor.

In this way, Philip was able to practice and enjoy the game at the same time. As some of the boys in the district became available for tennis, he began to arrange games with them, and less with the patient and helpful Mr. Grant, which made him feel guilty. To his relief, his mentor didn't seem to mind at all, and would no doubt be looking for another tennis pupil. (It was from individuals like this that ones youthful development gained almost as much as from ones parents and teachers, and society owed them a great debt).

When the weather was bad and the mood wasn't compatible with reading, he would take out his violin, tune it carefully, check the position of the bridge, adjust the bow's tension, apply the resin and play his favorite short pieces. Only then was he ready to attack the scales, arpeggios and exercises so essential to the growth of ones playing ability. After forty-five minutes of practice, he was ready to play his selections from the classics, and then either improvise or play some music from the last film he'd seen.

God's magic kiss, which He bestowed on the fortunate virtuoso, had passed him by, but he was happy to perform well enough to enjoy the violin and give enjoyment to those who heard him. Luckily, most of these were unable to recognize the absence of the true virtuoso's matchless touch. It was like the art of painting. The museums and Stately English Homes were full of fine landscapes and portraits, but only few of these had the magic stroke of a Rubens, a Turner, a Rembrandt or a Gainsborough.

Philip's love of good music had its origins in the Sunday Promenade Concerts to which his father had started taking Pauline and him since he was seven. It was wonderful to watch the renowned Sir Henry J. Wood conducting the London Symphony Orchestra, using his baton and body movements to blend all those assorted instruments into a harmonious unity: one that conveyed the tempo, volume, and emotional message of the music from Maestro to performers to audience. As time passed, he found himself differentiating between various interpretations of the same piece by different conductors and orchestras and choosing the ones he liked best.

At home, there was the H.M.V. gramophone with operatic recordings of Caruso, Martinelli, Gallicurci, and Melba. They were Mum's favorites as well as his; and whenever Mr. Robinson (formerly Rabinovitch) came to visit the Bosnars, they always encouraged him to sing some arias from Italian Opera in his rich baritone voice. After he'd partaken of a little too much Concord wine he would launch into the Russian songs of his youth and Philip's Dad would join him, both in the songs' mellifluous original language.

(During these early years Philip Bosnar realized that music had entered his soul, and long after the time when he would finally lay aside his violin, his love for this most wonderful of all art forms would never leave him.)

CHAPTER 37

1960

Philip Bosnar's duties as Chief of Surgery at the Chelmsford were by no means onerous and he found most of them enjoyable. As far as the interns were concerned, these duties consisted of a joint tour of surgical floors at regular intervals, in order to examine and discuss interesting cases. The interns would select the cases and then outline the patients' full history, past, present, family and functional. Each intern would examine a patient and describe his or her findings, after which the others could check the significant items known as Physical Signs, or add some examination of their own.

Any available laboratory findings were presented, and additional tests that might be added were suggested. Next, any available X-rays were placed on the view box and discussed in detail; suggestions for additional X-rays were also considered. Finally, each intern was asked to give a provisional diagnosis and present a recommended line of treatment. Rather than adopt the customary didactic approach of listing all the possible diagnoses in some sort of priority order, which he called 'Method A', Dr. Bosnar preferred the provisional diagnosis method, which he called 'Method B'.

He made a point of voicing his diagnostic opinion – or at least his leading suspicion – immediately, pending later completion of the investigation. Not only did this Method B appeal to him as being more honest and less evasive, but a clinician's batting average over the long run was a pretty fair indicator of diagnostic acumen.

It seemed to Philip that the day would come when Norbert Wiener's theories of Cybernetics would produce the technology to use Method A to maximum advantage. If the day ever came when such machines could outplay humans at Chess, then doctors could simply feed the necessary information into the machine and out would come something like the following:

X. Additional information required. ....
Y. Additional investigation required. ....
Z. Diagnosis 1. 75% ....
Diagnosis 2. 12% ....
Diagnosis 3. 7% ....
Other Dxs, each less than 6%

....
....
....
....

Perhaps treatment would be handled the same way during this millennium, but if that day ever came, something precious might be lost to the traditional profession: namely the ART of medical practice.

Dr. Bosnar would next ask the interns to tell him how they would treat the patient while awaiting completion of the investigation. Next came the recommended line of treatment on the basis of each diagnosis that had so far been suggested: operative details, type of anesthesia, which complications had to be guarded against in this particular patient and what special precautions had to be taken to prevent these complications. What would be the earliest indications of such complications, and if there were no complication what was the recommended postoperative management?

On Saturday mornings at 9 a.m. the medical staff had what were erroneously called 'Surgical Ward Rounds'. As a rule each case presentation was made by the intern looking after that patient, and additional information was provided as required by the attending staff doctor. The lab findings were given by the pathologist and the X-rays were discussed by the radiologist. The operative details were given by the surgeon and additional items of treatment were outlined by the surgeon and other attending specialists who were involved. The operative specimen was displayed and the microscopic sections were projected on the screen, once again by the pathologist. In many respects he was the key man. The success or failure to date was described, and then as chairman – after questions were asked – Dr. Bosnar led off the discussion that followed. Happily, there was an excellent attendance at these meetings, and this made all the effort worthwhile.

From time to time there were 'Death Rounds', an unpleasant but essential review. Each surgeon presented his own fatal case or cases, and in addition to the usual routine the pathologist presented the results of the autopsy findings. Other rounds were devoted to post-operative complications and these were most instructive. One of Dr. Bosnar's duties, as he saw them, was to make sure that deaths and complications were discussed in an objective rather than a prosecutorial manner. Any breaches of professional standard and any evidence of negligence or incompetence were dealt with by the Tissue and Audit committee, of which he'd been a member for several years. If the findings indicated any of the above defects, the matter was turned over to the Chief of Staff and the Medical Administrator for appropriate action, but only after giving the individual staff-member an opportunity to defend his or her conduct of the case.

Another duty of the Chief of Surgery was a review of hospital charts in the department of surgery. In order to avoid the slightest hint of a 'holier than thou' attitude, he divided each month's charts between the various staff members in his department so that they passed judgement, as it were, on each other, and he was no more immune to criticism than the others; thus their comments were recorded in an objective manner and no one felt unfairly dealt with.

There were three other committees of which he was a member. The most important was the Executive Committee, consisting of Chief of Staff, Medical Administrator, and chiefs of medical departments. Their business had to do with broad hospital policies, the review of departmental reports and recommendations for the improvement of patient care. They were also involved in hearings associated with restrictive and disciplinary measures.

Integrating with such measures was the Credentials Committee, whose main concern was the annual review of privileges. Most meetings of this committee dealt with applications for increased privileges, and these had to be accompanied by evidence of expertise in the particular area and by a recommendation from the chief of the department. Others concerned removal of existing privileges, based on facts that could be substantiated and not on mere opinions. It was also considered essential in such cases that the doctor concerned be given a full hearing before the Executive Committee.

In serious cases of diminished competence or negligence the facts were communicated to the B.C. College of Physicians with the recommendation, where indicated, that a further period of training be undertaken by the culprit before considering reapplication for staff privileges. In this manner, and by the structure of interlocking committees, a detailed check was kept at all times on the standards of performance by the staff doctors; thus protecting the patients on the one hand and instituting a powerful and effective self-policing mechanism on the other, to a degree not found in any other profession.

Although no such system was foolproof, the current one seemed most effective but still required two criteria to make it work. The first was that it must be free from politics or prejudice, and the second was avoidance of a holier-than-thou attitude.

The importance of the first criterion was exemplified without the slightest doubt by the tragic case of Emil Stanovitsky, and the second by the dictum enunciated by one of Edwardia's most successful surgeons, Dr. Grote. After performing a certain type of operation twenty times he declared that no surgeon should be given privileges in this operation unless he had previously done at least twenty such procedures!

Then, of course, there was the occasional subspecialist who recommended that general surgeons should be prohibited from performing surgery in what he considered as his own private domain. Since some of the general surgeons could perform such operations at least as well as the subspecialist, the argument lacked validity.

The most productive committee of which the Chief of Surgery was automatically chairman and which included senior O.R. nurses, was the Operating Room Committee. This was concerned with keeping all O.R. equipment and nursing personnel up to standard and instituting improvements where necessary; in this respect the opinions and recommendations of the anesthetist on the committee were most important. Safety precautions were scrutinized in such areas as gas lines, oxygen equipment, dangers of explosion or fire, electrical safety, sterile environment, and the prevention of infection.

At one of the first of these meetings, Dr. Bosnar recommended that the hospital Purchasing Committee should have adequate representation by members of the medical staff, in order to avoid the danger of unilateral decisions in the purchase of materiel and equipment. Such decisions without medical staff input had – unfortunately – been the rule rather than the exception at both hospitals, and promoted fears of pressure tactics by suppliers as well as involvement of purchasing agents in preferential deals. It was hoped that the new arrangement would remove such fears.

James had chosen English Literature as his main subject at Edwardia University, which he was now attending. In some ways, his parents were sorry he'd never shown the slightest interest in the profession of Medicine or any of its many subdivisions. Philip was equally disappointed by his son's lack of interest in any other scientific field, and in a way he blamed himself. After all, James knew only that his father's work involved a lot of hard effort, long hours and a great deal of continued study; that it was preceded by long years of training, and followed by earning a great deal of money. How Philip wished that were true!

Since he never discussed any of his cases with his son, the lad was unable to gauge the immense reward of saving a human life, improving a human existence, or reducing the suffering of a doomed patient. Unlike his own father, Philip somehow lacked the gift of imparting to his own son the wonders of the universe and the unbelievable scope and excitement of science; not just medical science.

The boy seemed to like the theater, and Sam Payne's repertory group had obviously left its mark, so when he was given a part in the College Drama Society's production of O'Neill's 'Ah Wilderness!' he was thrilled. As a matter of fact, his parents thought he did pretty well, and wondered whether his future might lie in Drama, either as writer or actor; but it was too early to say.

As for Florian, she had grown into a beautiful young lady, and was interested in becoming a model. The gorgeous Melanie Robins had been a successful model for several years, and was highly thought of by the heads of Eaton's, Hudson's Bay and several other stores and boutiques that employed her for their fashion displays. Needless to say, she served as a persuasive role-model for Florian, although, to be fair, there was never a hint of direct encouragement.

As soon as she'd passed her Grade 12 exams, Florian was determined to enroll in a modelling school, then move to Vancouver where the opportunities were so much better. It was too bad, Phil and Patty thought, that the fates had conspired to give their daughter weak ankles and thwart what might have been an illustrious ballet career. She still looked and moved like a true ballerina, all flowing motion and artistic natural poses, with a face and expression to match.

Cliff Robins had recently stepped up the ladder of success in the laboratory department of St. Peter's Hospital, and in a way Philip could claim some responsibility. He was sitting in the records room of the Sisters' hospital, dictating some notes, when he was approached by Sister Ethel Margaret. She was a likeable elderly nun who was head of the records department and very good at her job. Philip was very fond of her and always enjoyed talking to her and exchanging light banter.

"Why don't you like our new dictating machines, Doctor Bosnar? You're usually so progressive."

"I could pretend that I like to have the secretary read back my dictation and modify or delete any passages that don't sound right, but we both know that isn't the real reason. I like to dictate my notes to someone who can smile and even sit on my lap if need be."

The Sister didn't bother to conceal her amusement but quickly returned to serious questioning.

"What do you think of our new case review forms?"

"I think they have considerable potential, and should provide a useful self-assessment mechanism for each staff doctor."

They went through each column of the form, starting with the admitting diagnosis, the investigation, treatment, operation, length of stay, complications, death and final diagnosis.

"Of course, doctor, the last column is the most important one."

"Why do you say that, Sister?"

"Because that's the pathology report and tells us if the diagnosis was confirmed."

A small devil now made him take up the challenge.

"In that case we need one more column: the one that tells us if the pathology report is correct."

The Sister's smile faded.

"I believe you should take that up with the path. lab, Dr. Bosnar."

"You're absolutely right, Sister. I'll do that right now."

For some considerable time there had been a growing dissatisfaction with the accuracy of Dr. Malcolm Seaton's reports, and with a certain bias when it came to declaring some tissue specimens normal and others showing positive pathology. This was at its worst in such cases as milder degrees of acute appendicitis and borderline malignancy.

Philip phoned his office and told his nurse he might be a bit late, then went straight to Seaton's inner sanctum, where he told him exactly what he'd said to Sister Ethel Margaret. His demeanor discouraged any thought Seaton might have of trying to put him off, and he requested fifty random slides from his own major surgical cases and fifty from those of Seaton's bosom pal, Harry Grote. It soon became apparent that slides with almost identical appearance were being reported differently with a frequency that indicated patent dishonesty.

When the slide examination was over, Philip asked Seaton if he'd care to have a review of the slides for the past five years by the Professor of Pathology at U.B.C. and he turned quite pale. He admitted he may have been in error in some of his reports, but Philip pointed out that there was a pattern to these 'errors' that made them indefensible. Seaton was unable to reply, and one month later offered his resignation. Cliff Robins was named the new Chief of Pathology and his appointment was confirmed by the Executive Committee and the Board. From that time forward, the surgeons at St. Peter's no longer complained of incorrect or biased reports from that department.

Although his many official duties kept him busy, the fact remained that during the past year Philip's G.P. referral base had suffered considerably. This had little to do with the political situation or his professional reputation – since this was at its highest level since his arrival in Edwardia.

In the first place, Emil Stanovitsky's illness and death meant that Philip no longer had as many referrals from his practice except for those from his successor, Fred Jurgens. As for Stanovitsky's office nurse, who'd remained with the practice out of a deep sense of loyalty, she did her best to encourage referrals to Philip, and he was grateful.

In the second place Clark Grayson, a busy and capable fine young G.P. who'd been sending him an increasing amount of surgical work over the past three years, approached him one day with a problem. Grayson looked more like a schoolboy than a physician, and his manner was so engaging that it was easy to understand his popularity.

"I've got a decision to make, Philip, and since you're a good friend and have a lot of experience I thought I'd better ask your opinion. As you know, my practice has grown pretty large and I've been run off my feet. Brenda thinks I'm working too hard and hardly ever see my family, and she's quite right. I've been thinking of quitting general practice and going into Ear, Nose and Throat surgery; do you think that would be the right decision? After all, I'm thirty-five years old with three kids and a large mortgage so it isn't going to be easy."

"I hate to say this, Clark, especially since I've been getting a lot of my best cases from you, but your family comes first and also your lifestyle, so I'd have to say you should go ahead, but do so reluctantly."

Philip hated to see him go, not only for his referred work, but because he and his wife were two of the Bosnars' favorite people. (*Such are the fortunes of war that years later, after returning to Edwardia, Grayson built up such a huge E.N.T. practice that he was twice as busy as he'd been as a G.P.*)

Mrs. Cranbourne, who replaced Grace Thornbury when she left to raise a family of three small children, was the widow of a doctor who was killed in a car collision a year ago. She seemed pleasant enough but lacked the drive and sparkling personality of her predecessor. At first she did nothing whatever to give Philip any cause for complaint, and then matters took a very bad turn. A growing number of patients began to complain about receiving bills for his services long after they had paid.

With the help of his accountant, who went through his books in meticulous detail, Philip discovered that his worthy new office nurse had been writing off the uncollected fees as paid in full and dunning those who had fully settled their accounts. The worst, however, was yet to come. Some of his colleagues with whom he'd enjoyed the warmest of relations and who usually sent him some surgical referrals, began telling him of Mrs. Cranbourne's rudeness over the phone. Not only that, but she wasn't above refusing to give their patients an early appointment, stating that her boss was much too busy to see them at this time.

Philip's blood ran cold as he picked up more and more of these enlightening stories, and he made up his mind that his errant widow was probably deranged and must be fired before she could do any more harm to his practice. Nature preempted him, however, and instead of being a source of anxiety to Philip she became instead one of his most fascinating surgical patients. She began to complain increasingly of severe attacks of abdominal pain, sometimes upper, sometimes lower, sometimes right-sided and sometimes left-sided. Examination of her belly revealed a large mobile lump that appeared to be located in the first part of the colon, in the lower right quadrant. The next time he examined her, however, the lump was in the left upper quadrant, and thereafter the lump changed its position from time to time.

Investigation proved that she had an ***Intussuscepting Neoplasm*** of the Cecum (a telescoping tumor of the pouch at the commencement of the colon). In addition, there was marked anemia but no sign of secondary growths elsewhere. The operation consisted of removal of the right half of the colon with its contained tumor plus a short segment of small intestine. The pathological sections revealed a rare form of malignancy known as an ***Angiosarcoma*** (a cancer of the blood vessels), and following a smooth recovery she was referred to the Cancer Clinic for further evaluation. She was also advised to quit her job for the time being and take it easy for a month, with full pay.

It was now that Philip began to give serious thought to joining one of the medical clinics which seemed to be springing up all the time. He made up his mind that he wouldn't put out any feelers in this direction but would keep his eyes and ears open for any new opportunity; it would be preferable if he were approached first by one of these groups before making a decision.

One advantage of such a clinic was that each had its own medical building with provisions for expansion. Another was the presence of a fixed referral base, with capacity for steady increase. The main advantage, however, was the team approach to medical practice, and he felt sure that expanding clinics were the wave of the future, when unfettered individualism would become increasingly outdated. The ideal proportion would be five physicians to one surgeon, but even as few as three to one might be enough to start with, as long as outside referrals continued.

A good antidote to all these thoughts, problems and considerations was the city chess club, and Philip was now approaching the point where he would soon be ready to challenge the top players for the championship. From time to time he played in various intercity matches, usually at second or third board, and by watching some of the best players he was able to pick up a good deal of knowledge about the game that wasn't in the textbooks on chess, both in tactics and strategy. Above all, he learned that demeanor played a great part in winning or losing. The player who is convinced he has a losing position must behave as if he's winning. Since the player who thinks he's winning is apt to get a bit impatient and try for the quick, artistic kill, it is better to keep him waiting with slow, thoughtful moves, but played with full confidence. Many a losing game has been converted into an unexpected win by such psychological tactics; or at least into a satisfying draw.

One of the most frequent players at the club was old Mr. De Havilland, well into his eighties, physically frail but with a mind that remained very bright, and a notable tendency to arrogance. He was the father of those two well-known film stars, Olivia De Havilland and Joan Fontaine, and from time to time they came up from California to visit the old gentleman.

Despite his age and infirmity he could still give a pretty fair account of himself across the chess board, and one could always be sure of an enjoyable game with him. After a while he became increasingly cordial toward Philip, who began to know the older man better and learn something about his fascinating background.

It was common knowledge that De Havilland had spent some time in Japan, and that his second wife was Japanese. Of his two daughters, Joan had never accepted her father's oriental wife and hadn't kept her father's name, while Olivia was more forgiving and did keep the De Havilland name. At first, only Olivia came to visit her father, but later on Joan softened and began to visit him, too. This also helped to heal the rift between the two sisters that had lasted so long. Philip was impressed by De Havilland's considerable prowess and came to realize that his apparent arrogance was simply a protective mechanism against brash youth. ¨
(Chess today is essentially a young player's game and requires physical stamina as much as mental resilience.)
De Havilland told him many interesting yarns about his experiences in earlier days, when he followed the great Alekhine all over the globe at a time when the Russian expatriate was world champion; it wasn't long before he became accepted as an unofficial member of the champion's large entourage. He not only followed all the champion's games, but also all of the post-game analyses by Alekhine's team of experts, and there was a time when De Havilland actually had all of these historic games memorized. Having lived in Japan for so long, he had steeped himself in the Samurai folklore and the cult of Bushido; he also learned the Japanese war game of 'Go', played with pieces on a board and based on military maneuvers. In De Havilland's opinion Go was the only game that was more complex and mentally demanding than chess.

After a while, with the ice entirely broken, the old man invited Philip to his home for a game. This was something he'd never done before with any of the other club members, Philip was told, and he felt flattered. When he arrived, at eight o'clock sharp, the room into which he was led seemed very dark, but a special overhead light illuminated the exquisite ivory chess set and beautifully inlaid chess table that rightfully belonged – along with the pieces – in a museum.

Through the comparative gloom Philip could see that the place was decorated and furnished in authentic oriental style. His host was dressed in a Japanese kimono and was in stockinged feet. Philip asked if he'd prefer him to take off his shoes and was told that it wasn't really necessary, but he took them off anyway. At that moment a wraithlike figure dressed in traditional female Japanese style shuffled into the room, bowed and took his shoes. There was no attempt by his host to introduce them, so Philip took the initiative and said, "Thank you, Mrs. De Havilland," with a return bow.

During the game, a closely fought Sicilian Defense with his host playing the white pieces, the silent little lady brought in tiny cups of oriental tea, and rice cakes that proved to be delicious. The old man still said not a word, so this time and with a feeling of resentment at his behavior, Philip rose from the chess table, bowed and said, "Arrigato, Mrs. De Havilland. My name is Philip Bosnar and I appreciate your hospitality." She bowed in return and smiled with delight. Now he knew why this feudal British aristocrat had married her, and he found it hard to accept his dominant male attitude, even though his wife found it perfectly natural and quite compatible with so very durable a marriage.

When the first pledges were sent out last year the number of signed returns was less than 20 percent of the provinces surgeons. The rest were unwilling (or unable?) to commit themselves to a pledge against splitting fees and agreeing to have their books audited. Since Philip was the first in Edwardia to have such an audit, he got a worried phone call from the firm of Wilson, Bates, and Wilson, who handled legal and accountancy services for his practice. They had just been visited by a Vancouver accountant asking to see Dr. Philip Bosnar's books for the past five years, and weren't quite clear what it was all about. When Philip explained how it originated, and that he himself had been involved in initiating this unusual audit, they were most relieved and promised to provide their full cooperation.

For some reason Philip felt reasonably confident that within the next year or two the number of positive pledges from B.C's surgeons would rise to over 80 percent; in the meantime there was the strongest support from some of the leading surgeons in Vancouver, considerable opposition from most of the other areas, and lukewarm support in Edwardia. It was a measure not likely to win a popularity award but one worth pursuing before it was too late.

One day, Philip had an unexpected caller. Dr. Anthony Mayfair ("Do NOT call me Tony!") phoned him on a Saturday afternoon and asked if he could come up to the house. The youngsters were out for the afternoon and Patty took the dog out for a walk so that Philip could be alone with his visitor. Mayfair was unusually cordial, and acted as though he were Philip's lifelong friend.

"You know, Phil old chap, you could've had the biggest surgical practice in the city if only you'd played ball with the G.P.s. You see, everyone knows how good your work is but that's not enough."

"Now come on, you know where I stand on such matters, and I'm not going to change now."

"That's not why I'm here. You see, I'm leaving town to train as a urologist in Boston and I'd like you to take over my practice. All I'd want in return is 20 percent of your net take from the practice for the next four years, and once you've seen my books you'd be sure you're getting a bargain. My practice includes two contracts with large city firms, and a staff appointment at the D.V.A. hospital. Over the years a lot of my surgical cases have gone to local surgeons, and I'm sure you'd be getting all of these in future."

"Well it's kind of you to say all those nice things and I didn't want to interrupt you. I must confess I found several of your points extremely interesting. Why don't we have a beer before we continue?"

After they'd settled down with their beers, Philip resumed.

"You must understand that the reason I left the Kinsley practice was in order to confine myself to referred surgery and leave general practice to the G.Ps. To combine the two tends to make a surgeon keep looking for possible operative surgery in his medical patients and I think that tends to produce a distorted approach. As for the built-in D.V.A. appointment that goes with your practice I wouldn't touch it with a ten foot barge pole."

"I haven't heard that good old English expression for ages, but I'd like to know why you said it."

"When I first came to Edwardia I enquired at the Director's office in the Massey Veteran's Hospital if I could serve in the surgical department. I pointed out that I was in the R.C.A.M.C. during the war as I.C. Surgery at the Thornton Military Hospital, with the rank of major. They told me there was no room for me on their staff: they already had a surgeon in charge and a second surgeon wasn't needed. Frankly, I've come to the conclusion that the whole D.V.A. medical setup is a fucking racket and I'd see them in hell before joining their staff as anything less than a surgical consultant with operating privileges."

"I guess you're not interested in my proposition."

"In some ways I found your proposition bloody interesting, in more ways than you can imagine, but my answer is No."

"Well, that means you're too interested in staying pure to give a shit about making a good income for yourself and your family. No wonder the guys call you `Mr. Clean'. I hope you find it's worth it."

On the international front, Harold MacMillan had taken over as British Prime Minister following the resignation of Eden. He could never fill his predecessor's shoes, but at least he'd been the strongest supporter of Eden's policies during the Suez crisis and that would always be to his credit. He'd visited Khrushchev in Moscow and was in close consultation with Adenauer in Bonn and de Gaulle in Paris. These were not easy men to deal with. Adenauer was too stiff-necked and seemed to take the generosity of Germany's former enemies for granted. If there was any remorse for his nation's guilt during the Hitler era he managed to keep it low key. As for de Gaulle, this man was still consumed by injured pride and political vanity, and there was little reason for Britain and the U.S.A. to trust him.

President Eisenhower, ever since the death of his baleful guru John Foster Dulles, seemed to have become a changed man and was even showing glimpses of moral leadership. One could only hope he'd eventually become a man of decision, and the right decisions at that. There was no doubt that the dynamic little peasant Khrushchev was the man firmly in charge of the Soviet political superstructure, and his unabashed desanctification of Stalin plus his friendly attitude toward the West were encouraging. Now, if only he could keep the reactionary forces of the KGB in check and start a genuine disarmament program, there might be some real hope for world peace.

As far as Germany was concerned, Philip hoped it would remain disunited. Memories of the infamous Third Reich were still too fresh and the temptations of a renewed militarism were too great to accept the clear dangers of reunification.

CHAPTER 38

1961

Walter Langley was a big handsome fellow, with an engaging manner and a successful general practice. Three years earlier, he'd started the foundation of a small clinic by building a first-class set of offices and examining rooms, along with a basic laboratory and small operating room. He was joined by two other G.Ps, and between them they built up a thriving group practice. Their first surgeon left a few months ago, apparently dissatisfied with the financial arrangements, and they were looking for a new surgeon.

There was no doubt that Langley was well known across the city, and his former prowess as an amateur hockey player was widely recognized. Even the Seattle sports pages carried glowing reports of 'the great big smiling Canadian, the finest hockey defenseman outside the NHL'. He'd put on a bit of weight since those days but still looked like a good man to have on your side in a free-for-all.

Despite his general popularity in town and a wide circle of friends and acquaintances, especially in athletic circles, he seemed to have a lot of enemies within the medical profession itself. There were dark hints of unprofessional behavior, and warnings not to be seduced by his smooth tongue; yet Philip had always found him polite, respectful and well liked by his patients. He was a man's man and a lady's man; entirely at home with the roughest and toughest of his male patients and enjoying the adulation and loyalty of his female patients.

The city doctors seemed to know – before Philip had any inkling – that Langley would be approaching him on behalf of small group, and as a result, Philip received many a dire and gratuitous warning. His reply was always the same: that he never decided on the basis of rumor but preferred his own assessment. During the next few months Philip saw nothing about Langley that could verify the adverse rumors. He was said to have a problem with alcohol, but although Philip saw him take quite a few drinks during their frequent meetings, he never saw him remotely close to inebriation.

He knew Langley was keen on contract bridge and was determined to introduce his prospective associate to the more precise form of competitive bridge known as 'duplicate'. In this form of the game there is no luck of the deal. Each pair plays the same set of cards against the other pairs at each 'board' and the results are estimated as 'tops, bottoms, or averages'. Thus, scoring 420 points for bidding and making four spades, not vulnerable, would be a top board if no one in your section did as well, but would be a bottom board if everyone else made an overtrick for 450.

Philip tried hard to get Patty to join him in this venture but she wasn't at all keen, insisting that she preferred the less cut-throat atmosphere of ordinary social bridge. In any event, he decided to join the duplicate club, and began to play the occasional game with mixed results. He was assured by his mentor that he had the makings of a future 'Life Master', but that didn't impress him too much, since Walter was clearly prone to over-complimentary remarks, and any praise from him had to be taken with a large grain of salt. The same measure applied to his hyperbole about Dr. Bosnar's surgical abilities and personal qualities.

What was far more important in his decision to join the clinic was the fact that he found the other two partners likeable, both as physicians and individuals. As for Walter's wife Barbara, she was a pleasant and attractive young lady of Scottish descent, with all the social graces and a natural charm. Phil and Patty soon became quite fond of her and the feeling appeared to be mutual.

After much soul-searching, he made up his mind to accept Walter's persistent invitations to join the group. First, he checked out the facilities with the proverbial fine tooth comb and was favorably impressed. The lab seemed well run and so was the business office, and the entire complex was cheerful and nicely furnished. The other partners joined Langley and Bosnar in a preliminary meeting and discussion, and it was agreed that the new partner's starting share of gross receipts, minus deductions for rent and overhead, would come to $18,000 annually. This amount seemed quite reasonable since his current net income by recent calculation only came to $16,500. It was estimated – based on the increased practice to date and a corresponding increase in surgery – his net income should reach $25,000 or more within two years, and he thought that was more than satisfactory.

Before signing the partnership papers, however, he discussed the move in detail with Patty and told her he couldn't see any objections to the project and she agreed without reservation. He also went over the partnership agreement with his legal and accountancy firm. They found it satisfactory in all respects and thought their client was making the right decision.

He hated to let his nurse go. Flora Kennedy had been a first-rate secretary, receptionist and office nurse for over eighteen months, ever since Mrs. Cranbourne left. She was as helpful and efficient as her predecessor had been the very opposite, and she always displayed an admirable empathy with his patients. It was too bad the Langley group had no room for another staff member at the present time, but he promised to let her know as soon as a vacancy occurred. To his surprise, she wasn't the least bit upset and told him there were lots of part-time opportunities for office nurses in Edwardia, and although she hated to leave his practice, she wouldn't be placed in any hardship, much to his relief.

It was a nice feeling to drive into the clinic parking lot after lunch each day. The premises were impressive, and the atmosphere was relaxed and cordial throughout. Besides, it was good to get away from the combative atmosphere of vying for referred cases, and to know that most of his colleagues who'd been sending him patients would continue to do so. He made it clear that under no circumstances would these patients be directed anywhere but back to the referring doctor, and certainly not to the clinic physicians.

It now seemed that an increasing proportion of his new patients chose St. Peter's hospital for their surgical admission, and he thought that was a pity, but made no attempt to interfere with their choice. He was aware that O'Dwyer had noticed the change and was registering his approval with a broad grin of 'I told you so'.

Bill Evanston and Ron McClure, his new partners, were good physicians and amiable fellows, and their referrals were always well worked up, as were those of Walter Langley. They didn't push their patients for surgery and Philip appreciated that desirable element. It was too easy a pitfall in group practice to advocate surgery in preference to non-operative management, since that was the way the fee schedule was unfairly oriented. Over the years, experience had made him more conservative, and he was often criticized for this trend by some of his more aggressive colleagues. But others admired his objectivity and shared his attitude toward the fee schedule, with its bias against surgical conservatism. Unfortunately, advising a mother that her child didn't need a tonsillectomy carried a much smaller reward than performing the unnecessary operative procedure.

Phil and Patty were convinced the world was once again gearing up for widespread armed conflict. To anyone taking an intelligent interest in world affairs in these days of instant communication and a shrinking planet, it was obvious the next killing grounds would be in Vietnam. The French colonial power in Indochina had been utterly destroyed by the little brown men of the Viet Minh, in the military debacle of Dien Bien Phu. This event also represented the power of Marxism against traditional regimes, whether monarchical, ecclesiastic or colonial. It demonstrated that modern military technology backed by well equipped troops was no match for determined guerilla-style native troops, fighting on familiar terrain and with little regard for casualties. It drove home the lessons of the war against the Japanese: those learned in the reeking jungles of Southeast Asia against the elusive Japanese fighting men. They were warriors who could subsist on the land in which they fought.

The one lesson that still had to be learned was of paramount importance at the present time. In opposing a doctrinaire communist regime such as that of Ho Chi Minh it was pointless to support an unpopular, corrupt and autocratic leader like Ngo Dhin Diem, just as the American support of Syngman Rhee in South Korea had been such a diplomatic blunder. These ill-chosen allies were Fascist-minded dictators who failed to offer the populace an acceptable alternative to the hated communist regime. The West needed men who could exemplify fundamental democratic ideals and – at the very least – provide honest government in the interest of the many rather than the few.

To the long-suffering peasants in the rice-paddies and villages of South Vietnam, hunger and repression were the same, whether under the banner of Marxism or anti-Marxism, and the will to resist the foe soon became weak and unreliable. Such conditions could only lead to mass defection of troops and a lack of cooperation from the native peoples. According to the so-called 'Domino Theory', the Indochinese subcontinent might well fall, nation by nation, to communist subversion and takeover. Even if that were a valid scenario, the anticommunist West, especially the U.S.A, must fight for the hearts and minds of the people rather than relying on the destructive power of massive military force alone.

Thank God the H-bomb couldn't be employed in a place like Vietnam, unless one was prepared to use it against the city of Hanoi on a preemptive basis. To the Pentagon hawks, however, and probably to their Soviet opposite numbers, such an idea was not entirely unthinkable.

Desmond Gates had recently left the Handleigh School for Boys and accepted a post as Assistant Headmaster at the prestigious Sentinel Lake Academy. It was a fine private school located in a matchless setting on the water's edge, and the headmaster was a congenial young chap who was planning to return to his native Ireland within the next two years. Phil and Patty drove out to the school one sunny afternoon and found that, although Des was in his element, Prilly was still lonesome and found the other teachers' wives a bit of a bore. There were some excellent tennis hardcourts and they watched as the headmaster gave Des a good game. It was obvious that Des had found his ideal milieu.

The other activity that provided an outlet for Desmond's towering vanity, was his appointment as director of the Edwardia Players, an amateur theatrical group of no mean talent and range. It was perfect for Desmond's thespian interests and ambitions. Whenever he found the leading actor not to his liking he had no hesitation in taking over the part himself. Needless to say, with his flair for the spectacular and his new positions and conversational abilities, he was becoming a popular social lion. The Bosnars were now meeting him at all the cocktail parties, with his pretty little wife in tow and appearing to bask in her husband's glory. But, Phil and Patty asked each other, for how long? At the same time, they were disheartened that their son – who always idolized Gates when he was his guru in English Literature – seemed of diminishing interest to his paragon, and the point wasn't lost on their perceptive son.

The province-wide surgical pledges and audits had now risen to over 80 percent, and were still coming in from the outlying areas in the interior. The main reason, without a doubt, was that the Surgical Association had put its weight solidly behind the Section of General Surgery in asking its members to comply, and the result was gratifying. It was agreed in closed session discussions that the entire project could be considered a great success, and they were delighted when they received a letter of commendation from the American College of Surgeons. It was Philip's devout hope that the Royal College of Surgeons of Canada wouldn't lag too far behind its American counterpart in adding its own plaudits. Perhaps there were too many officials like Fraywell (his nemesis since the Vanwey years) in the national medical organization, and that might account for their slowness in tackling such a vital threat to ethical surgical practice. (***As it happened, their Royal College sent its congratulations one year later.***)

It had taken a long time, but Philip finally made it to the chess championship of Edwardia. It had been tough to beat those last two opponents, both former city champions, but the format of the finals was a very fair one. The first player with two more wins than his opponent, after playing at least ten games, was declared the winner. Drawn games counted as half a point, wins as one point, and losses as zero. A double stop-clock was always used, and the old gentleman who was their perennial adjudicator was the undisputed referee whose word was law.

The Daily Edwardian published a weekly account of the annual Open Chess Tournament. It was surprising how many people in Edwardia were interested in these matches, considering the fact that most of them weren't even chess players; and Philip's patients were always asking him how the match was going and did he think he would win. Unlike most of his fellow club members who had considerable difficulty in sleeping after a tough game, he had no such problem. Before going to bed, he set up the pieces on a chess board and played out the last game, first from memory and then from his notes. Next, he analyzed the game and made some annotations, and then he was ready for bed and thought no more of chess until the next session.

It was the same with bridge, except that it was easier to analyze bridge hands with Patty and other players. In both games, he always went through the chess and bridge journals in detail, playing out games and hands, often while watching a dull TV program. Both games supplied a strong entertainment factor in addition to sharpening up the mind, and they were good exercises in self-criticism (and more than a modicum of humility).

Just as the chess club had put Philip into contact with men of all ages and from all walks of life, so the duplicate bridge club introduced him to men and women from a wide cross-section of society, but mostly an older age group than the chess players. One of the most interesting, and a talented bridge player, was Harry (born Hari) Bekassy, a Hungarian who'd emigrated to Canada after World War 2 and settled in British Columbia. Bosnar and Bekassy became good friends in fairly short order, mainly through the intermediary of Walter Langley, who'd known Bekassy for years. As the surgeon got to know this engaging European, he learned a surprising amount of detail about his exciting background.

Harry's family in Europe was well-to-do, serving as managers of the vast Esterhazy estates. They were Roman Catholic, and one of their number was an archbishop, while another became a leading actor on stage and screen, both in Europe and Hollywood. Just before the German Anschluss with Austria, Harry Bekassy had been an engineering student at the University of Vienna and – like so many of his fellow students – became a fervent Nazi and devoted admirer of Adolph Hitler. He enlisted enthusiastically in the Wehrmacht and rose in the ranks to become an Oberleutenant in General Erwin Rommel's Afrika Corps. He also became a member of the special 'Inner Elite Group' who were privy to a clandestine assignment: to act as a life-and-death protective squad that would shield the Führer from any attempted assassination.

By the time the debacle of El Alamein had overtaken Rommel's forces, and following Hitler's blind refusal to send further war supplies and reinforcements to North Africa, fanatical support for the Führer had been replaced by a growing fear that he was quite mad and would lead Germany down the road to disaster. Members of the Inner Elite Group were now discussing the drawing of lots to decide who should have the honor of killing their crazy leader if the opportunity arose. Although they had a sneaking feeling that their beloved Field Marshal probably felt the same way, they dared not discuss the matter with him.

Bekassy described the masterly retreat of the German army across North Africa in excruciating detail, with death and destruction on all sides and incessant bombardment from the air, yet with the preservation of a viable fighting force in spite of all. Thus, the great Rommel prove himself a genius of retreat as well as attack, and the loyalty of his troops was redoubled.

Other fascinating details would be forthcoming in due course, but for now Philip knew Harry only as a pleasant companion, a good bridge player and the popular catering manager of the Maklin Bay Golf and Country Club. Philip had never joined that club, as golf was never his game, but the medical society functions were held there and he sometimes had lunch at the club with friends who were members.

Now, whenever he happened to be at the club, Harry made a point of coming over and giving him special attention. In a way the situation was a strange one. He felt sure Bekassy was aware of his Jewish identity, yet he revealed nothing but cordiality and respect, reminding him – in an ironic twist of fate – of a time so long ago when a certain Count Rudi had treated him the same way. Did people like these, he wondered, ever really renounce their warped doctrine, or was it only a reaction to defeat and disillusion?

This year, the meeting of the C.P.S.A. would be held in Vancouver and Philip was due to give a paper on diaphragmatic hernias. There were three superb cases for presentation and each was memorable in its own way, The first was a large, obese female of 86, well-preserved but extremely short of breath. As a young woman in her twenties she had suffered very severe injuries in a train wreck. Her lower left chest was crushed, but there was no injury to the spleen. Since that accident, she'd been chronically short of breath and was receiving treatment for recurrent attacks of congestive heart failure. When Philip investigated her for left upper abdominal pain and a marked increase in shortness of breath, he found a massive traumatic hernia of the diaphragm on the left side, with her stomach and some of her intestine in the left chest cavity. As for the left lung, it appeared to be compressed to about a quarter of its natural size. With the expert help of the her cardiologist and referring physician, he got her into the best possible condition for surgery and went ahead with the operation.

He opened the left chest in the usual fashion with removal of a rib, and got excellent exposure of the situation. The hole in the diaphragm was some seven inches across and the stomach, spleen, and a foot of colon were in the thorax, compressing the lung. Separating the adhesions, particularly to the spleen, was a bit tricky, but the visceral contents went back easily into the abdomen and Philip was able to freshen up the diaphragm edges and repair the gap with a double layer of strong Dacron sutures. He closed up the chest, with the anesthetist doing his best to inflate the left lung, and sewed in a large suction tube which was connected to siphonage bottles and a motorized suction device. The fact that his patient did so well after surgery was far less surprising than the discovery that her left lung re-expanded completely, after some sixty years, and her shortness of breath became a thing of the past. He had little doubt that her congestive heart failure would disappear, too.

The second case was that of a young man in his late thirties and of medium build, who'd been involved in a car collision some five years previously. Since that time he'd complained of upper abdominal flatulent indigestion and a feeling of pressure in the left chest. He'd been X-rayed and diagnosed as *Eventration* of the left diaphragm, based on a severe soft tissue injury to the neck (This medical term is used to describe a paralysis of the diaphragm, in this case secondary to damaging of the nerve to the diaphragm, known as the **Phrenic Nerve**, and situated in the neck. What happens next is the pushing up of the diaphragm into the chest cavity, where there is negative pressure, by positive pressure in the abdomen.)

There were a few things wrong with this diagnosis.
To start with, the patient insisted his injury was to the chest, while the neck simply sustained a mild 'whiplash' injury; besides, none of the other nerves in the neck were affected. When Philip listened to the patient's chest there were loud splashing sounds that changed in volume and location with the patient's changing position. He arranged with the new chief of radiology at the Chelmsford to do a special procedure under his guidance. After giving the patient a small quantity of barium emulsion to drink, he used the tilting table and fluoroscoped the area in question. It was quite easy to demonstrate a large traumatic hernia of the diaphragm, with the stomach and some coils of small intestine flopping back and forth between thorax and abdomen. The diagnosis was crystal clear, the operation straightforward, and the results gratifying to all concerned.

The third case was a woman in her mid-fifties, stocky but not obese. She worked in a warehouse, did a lot of heavy lifting and found the job stressful. Over the past two years she had developed severe and progressive symptoms of ***Reflux Esophagitis***. (This is a condition in which the digestive juices of the stomach are regurgitated into the lower gullet, setting up a severe inflammation that may progress to ulceration and even stricture.) Since such a condition had always been considered in the past, with some special exceptions, to be associated with ***Hiatus Hernia***, (the commonest type of diaphragmatic hernia), and since there was no evidence of such a hernia in this case, the correct diagnosis in this case had been sidetracked. The symptoms were quite characteristic: severe heartburn, bitter-sour regurgitation into the throat and mouth, and difficulty with swallowing. All these symptoms were far worse at night-time.

The usual medical management was totally unsuccessful in this patient. It included administration of antacids; avoidance of alcohol, cigarettes, coffee, and highly spiced foods; no eating or drinking after dinner at six o'clock; and raising the head of the bed on ten inch blocks, with extra pillows if necessary. Analysis of the stomach contents showed a very high level of hydrochloric acid, and ***Esophagoscopy***, (direct inspection of the gullet's interior through an illuminated metal tube) revealed advanced inflammation and early ulceration of the lower gullet, but no sign of malignancy.

The operation was performed through the upper abdomen. Repair of the hiatus in the diaphragm was unnecessary in the absence of hernia, so the valvular mechanism between the stomach and gullet was restored by a technique that placed an acute angle between the two structures like that adjoining the bulge in a glass retort. In addition, the Vagus Nerves were severed to reduce acid secretion, and the outlet of the stomach was widened by a procedure called ***Pyloroplasty***. In view of the ulceration and inflammation of the lower esophagus, the usual gastric tube was not inserted. Instead, Philip chose to perform a ***Tube Gastrostomy***.

Tube gastrostomy is a procedure that was first pioneered in California, in which a multiperforated drainage tube is sewn into the stomach with absorbable sutures and brought out through the belly-wall to come through the skin of the upper abdomen – away from the main incision – and attached to a drainage device. Once the patient is eating well and the bowel function is back to normal the tube is easily removed and the hole closes spontaneously. The reason there is no leakage is that the stomach wall is inverted around the tube in the manner of an oldfashioned leak-proof inkwell.

It was after the successful outcome of this case that Philip began to acquire a special interest in two special features associated with this particular condition. The first was an ongoing search for genuine cases of reflux esophagitis unassociated with hiatus hernia, and the second was a growing commitment to the use of tube gastrostomy as a preferable alternative to long-term nasogastric suction. In geriatric patients, in patients with emphysema or chronic bronchitis (or both), in heavy smokers and patients with laryngeal problems, there was little doubt that tube gastrostomy cut down considerably on postoperative pulmonary complications. Philip tried hard to get his surgical colleagues, both in Edwardia and across the province, to share his enthusiasm for this procedure, but with little success. Perhaps, in the course of time, the light would dawn.

In national affairs, the Diefenbaker government was struggling to undo the negative effects resulting from decades of Mackenzie King's policies, especially the distancing of Canada from her British mother country. The influence of French Canada was never far away and might still result in the overthrow of the Conservative government.

On the international front, the rift between Mao tse-Tung's doctrinaire Marxist state and Khrushchev's post-Stalinist Russia had started to widen, while Russian foreign policy veered toward an accommodation with the capitalist West. With the decline and death of Dulles, it was now possible for Russia to pursue detente with the U.S.A. Khrushchev toured America as an honored guest and these days, in TV thrillers about the foreign menace, it was Communist China rather than the Uss.R. that was the mortal enemy. Khrushchev made an impassioned plea at the U.N. meeting in New York, for worldwide disarmament! God was in his heaven and all seemed right with the world.

It was precisely at this promising time in twentieth century history that the tragicomedy of the U.2 incident took center stage and put the situation back to square one. It was a postmortem tribute to the manic policies of the late John Foster Dulles and his bungling cohorts in the Pentagon. It was hard to understand why the U.S.A. would choose this particular time for sending a spy plane over the U.S.S.R, and even harder to believe that the intelligence experts couldn't conceive of the U.2 being shot down by a Russian missile. What was most incomprehensible was that the American pilot wasn't under the strictest orders never to be taken alive; that he wouldn't have been well supplied with cyanide pills to do the job if he were unable to crash his plane into a flaming ruin. Could such incredible military stupidity be trusted with the nuclear forces at its command?

The Langley Clinic was running smoothly and work was picking up in a satisfactory manner. In addition, Philip was still getting outside work and his patients seemed well satisfied. They were also a source of good public relations for the clinic. There was a steady growth of his patient base, resulting from person-to-person recommendation rather than the more precarious factors of solo referred practice. There was only one small fly in the ointment and that was his increasing awareness of a widespread antipathy among the city doctors toward Walter. As far as Philip was concerned, such hostility was for reasons unknown, and he could only hope they'd be dispelled in time, or at least not spread to their group as a whole.

He discussed the problem with his good friend Cliff Robins, and it was the latter's opinion that it was simply a matter of professional jealousy of Langley's ballooning practice; not unlike that which led to the Stanovitsky tragedy. Oddly enough, it wasn't a G.P. but Reg Asquith, successful internist and rising leader in medical politics, who exhibited the greatest degree of hostility. Philip even got the feeling that some of Asquith's hostility included him, but perhaps that was simply due to their widely divergent political viewpoints.

James Bosnar was growing rather restless and declared his intention of leaving college and going over to England, where he would seek his fortunes. Phil and Patty raised no objection, as long as he had something definite in mind and was prepared to decide where his career and his future lay. From a financial point of view, Philip made his position quite clear. It was up to his son to get a job, and he would match his earnings, dollar for dollar, until he had enough to get him overseas, with a few hundred dollars to spare for the first month or so. Of course, the young man would initially be staying with his grandparents in London, and then he'd have to stay in touch with his parents in Canada, in the sure knowledge that they'd never leave him in the lurch. If things didn't work out, they'd send him a return ticket and he could continue his education in Edwardia.

As for Florian, now that she'd successfully completed her grade 12s, and despite a procession of heartbroken swains, she was showing considerable maturity and independence. Recently, she'd landed a secretarial job in the provincial department of highways, but she still had her mind set on modelling.

It was going to be a difficult year for Patty, as she watched her precious offspring poised to disperse, leaving her to wonder how she would fill the empty hours. Knowing his beloved almost better than she knew herself, Philip was confident that time would never hang heavy on those busiest of hands, and if nothing else, she'd find the time to spoil him even more than ever before. As he was fond of kidding her, if she hadn't been born an Irish Catholic she would, beyond question, have filled the bill as the archetypal Jewish mother and wife.

Dinner at the Bradfords was always a special event. The first time was a bit of a fiasco. They had invited the Bosnars for the forthcoming Friday evening, and they drove out into the countryside and through the densely wooded driveway to the Bradfords' large Tudor-style cottage. When they got there, there were no signs of life and the house seemed in total darkness. Even the outside lights weren't on, but they decided to try the bell anyway. It was a loud bell and its peals should have been audible for half a mile, yet there was no response whatever from the darkened abode, from which no signs of human occupancy emerged.

Phil and Patty were just about ready to give up when there was a sound of ponderous bolts being withdrawn and the door creaked open cautiously. There stood the colonel, in dressing gown and slippers, and behind him his good wife in similar apparel. Both looked as if they'd just been awakened from a deep sleep. It turned out that they'd got their dates mixed up and thought their invitation was for the following Friday. At least that was what the colonel thought, but Mrs. Bradford wasn't so sure. They were still anxious for the visitors to come in, but the Bosnars apologized for disturbing them and agreed to return the following week. The drive had been pleasant and Patty didn't mind, in the slightest, being taken to dinner at the Swiss Alpine Restaurant.

The following Friday evening the Bosnars returned as promised. Among his many accomplishments, the colonel claimed to be a pretty good cook, and they found him out in his first lie. He wasn't a pretty good cook, he was a superb chef and his cuisine, mainly Anglo-Indian, was strictly Cordon Bleu. Although the baked putrefaction of the famous (infamous?) Bombay Duck was eaten sparingly by Philip and never passed Patty's lips, the curried chicken was delicious and the baron of beef superb, as were the accompanying mixed vegetables and rice. True to his medical tradition, Bradford produced a syringe and long needle and used these to inject port wine into several levels of the roast beef, producing a wonderful bouquet as well as augmenting the taste. As for the Cherries Jubilee and Irish coffee that followed, they were a gourmet's dream.

The colonel was about to set up his chess board for their obligatory game when his wife decided it was high time she introduced her friends to some of her African experiences. The story that followed was riveting.

"The African elephant is one of God's most magnificent creations, but the species has been all but eliminated. First by ivory hunters acting with government permission and more recently by poachers, acting in defiance of the law and perfectly prepared to kill the antipoaching police rangers who patrol the area.

As an artist, sitting in an open clearing day after day with my easel, paints and brushes,

I was able to watch the wonderful domestic scenes of mutual affection and concern exhibited by these great animals. At no time did they make the slightest threatening move toward me but behaved as if they regarded me as a friend. I knew that sooner or later the poachers would show up and I wasn't wrong.

There were three of them, and their leader was a big fat ugly Bantu who carried a great cannon of a hunting rifle and massive ammunition. As soon as the elephant family spotted them, the mighty bull elephant charged and the adult animals started to gather protectively around the calves. The number one poacher let off a wild round with a thunderous roar and missed the bull completely.

Unfortunately, his exploding bullet found its fatal mark in one of the calves and right away the herd began letting out piteous cries of grief."

Their narrator paused for breath and Patty asked the obvious question.

"Did the bull elephant kill the guilty poacher?"

"Oh yes, but not as you might think. Nearby, there was a huge ragged tree stump, all black spikes and insect havens. The bull picked up the poacher quite delicately in his trunk and deliberately impaled him on the highest spike. Then the entire herd mounted continuous guard on the condemned man, walking round and round the dead stump and trumpeting as if in cadence with the poacher's screams. That unlucky fellow was going to die a very slow and nasty death and there wasn't a thing anyone could do about it."

The chess was excellent, but for once Philip didn't sleep well that night following the game. It wasn't the game, however, that kept him awake. It was that terrible scene of animal retribution in a sun-drenched clearing halfway across the world.

CHAPTER 39

1927 contd

It was his sister Pauline who first discovered the concealed drawings of their father. It seemed strange that he'd never shown them to his children, as they were superb. It wasn't that the large mahogany writing-desk in the study was off limits, but the fact that it was nearly always kept locked. The study was the larger of two adjoining rooms of the ground floor parlor, and the one that contained the bookcases and impressive H.M.V. gramophone, along with an impressive record collection.

Pauline's curiosity was always irresistible, and after she had searched the inner compartments of the writing desk and cabinet – accidentally left unlocked – to her satisfaction, she found nothing except a set of bills, receipts, insurance policies, and other official documents, all neatly arranged in the various drawers, and all of no particular interest to her. In the bottom lefthand drawer, however, she found the treasured collection of their father's drawings, some unfinished and some merely outlined for future completion.

The drawings were detailed studies of historic court scenes from different periods, going back to the days of the Renaissance; they showed lifelike figures in their rich attire, with the folds and ruffles of their garments brilliantly shaded in light and shadow. The viewer could distinguish between different textures of clothing and could almost hear the rustle of silks and satins. The necklaces and bracelets seemed almost to glint and tinkle in the cunning shafts of light illuminated each scene. Philip knew that with all his artistic skills he could never match the extraordinary perfection of these pencil-works. Next to the art book, of high quality matte paper, was a set of Venus pencils, all carefully sharpened to points of different shapes and degrees of hardness.

By agreement with Pauline it was decided to confess their discovery to their parents, but their Dad refused to say much about these exquisite drawings except to concede that he'd always been interested in the study of historic costumes in different countries. Apparently, there had been other collections, representing Russian, Polish, and French history, but these had been lost along with other precious items on the panicky journey across the English Channel in the winter of 1915, when Philip was thought to be dying of 'double pneumonia'. Only the English historical scenes now remained and these weren't meant to be seen until completed sometime in the future.

From time to time Philip's parents would go off for an afternoon or evening by themselves to the exciting Westend of London (in fact it was on one such occasion that Pauline made her discovery of the unlocked desk). As a rule this was for a meal and some shopping, and his father usually managed to include a walk along Charing Cross Road, where he'd browse briefly at the outdoor book-stalls displaying secondhand books, of every kind and vintage and at giveaway prices. He picked up the occasional worthwhile bargain, and two of these were the handsomely bound and superbly illustrated works on the Crimean War and the Boer War. Philip loved to copy some of the heroic illustrations from these books, such as the Charge of the Light Brigade and the British Relief of the Siege at Mafeking. Not only did these exercises help him to improve his drawings but they served to fill him with an abiding sense of British heroism and military pre-eminence, as well as the righteousness of her wars.

Before the age of thirteen he was never disturbed by any uncomfortable doubts in such matters, and believed without question in the universal desirability of a benign Pax Britannica. His peaceful state of mind, however, now began to encounter growing doubts as he read more and more about these wars in books authored by men of high academic repute and objectivity. It now appeared that Britain's involvement in these famous wars wasn't always based on altruistic considerations.

He learned that with the crumbling of the Ottoman Empire in the middle of the last century there was a growing struggle between France and Imperial Russia over future control of the biblical Holy Shrines. This was based to some extent on traditional schisms between the Church of Rome and the Eastern Orthodox church.

As he delved further into the political complexities of the past century and the machinations of the nations for power, he began to acquire a new insight into history. He learned that the more pragmatic conflicts of the late eighteenth century were those involving future control of the emerging nations in southeast Europe: Serbia, Bulgaria, Rumania and Greece. He read how Turkey felt herself compelled to declare war on Russia, but was opposed by a Russian fleet that dominated the Black Sea and threatened a break-out into the 'forbidden' Mediterranean. He also read how the French and British found it expedient at this juncture to protect their own interests in the region by going to war with Russia.

He was distressed to learn that despite a shameful squandering of brave young lives in futile battles the Crimean War was ultimately lost by Russia, but hardly won by either France, Britain or Turkey. The degree to which this was a war of thinly concealed expansionism was confirmed by Philip's further discovery that the tiny nation of Sardinia had joined the Western Allies as an effort – successful as it proved! – toward the future consolidation of a united Italy.

Without giving way to a bitter sense of cynicism and abandonment of his childish illusions and hero worship, Philip enjoyed – instead – a sense of intellectual emancipation, as he began to review British history in the light of authentic information rather than patriotic propaganda. It made him feel more and more adult as his researches expanded. The Boer War now came to be seen not as a vicious and treacherous attack by backward Dutch chauvinists against the natural order and authority of British Rule in South Africa, but the courageous attacks of lightly armed Boer commandos fighting for independence against the military might of Britain. It seemed that eventually all the colonies of the British Empire would fight for increased independence; if necessary by force of arms, and ultimately with success.

Could Britain really be condemned, he asked himself, for attempting to oppose these changes, and was the disruption of the glorious Empire something to be desired? The world had already seen the replacement of stable conservative regimes by revolutionary anarchy, and Philip had an intuitive dread of the world-wide disorder which might engulf the world's shrinking globe with purely nationalistic wars rather than colonial conflicts.

"An expanding knowledge", a wise man once said, "simply enlarges our horizons of visible ignorance", but it did more than just that. It shook ones complacency, and destabilized ones beliefs. The most traumatized element in Philip's case was his social conscience, and he realized that henceforth it would be his duty to question the status quo and to regard popular viewpoints with caution, if not with suspicion. It had been so easy to view the Great War as the result of German aggression, in which a wildly militaristic Kaiser had seized on the assassination of an Austrian archduke – by a crazy Serbian student in Bosnia – as an excuse to wage war on the western European alliance.

Now, as Philip studied the origins of that tragic war in more extensive detail, it seemed that no involved nation was without blame, with the possible exception of Belgium. Austria-Hungary had aggressive plans against Serbia; Serbia had subversive counter-plans, both in occupied Bosnia and in Austria itself, and the assassination was planned and executed with Serbian approval. Austria-Hungary found good reason to seek revenge for the murder of the royal heir-apparent and his wife, and Russia promptly ordered full mobilization of its army against Austria-Hungary in order to protect the Slavs of Serbia. France seized this opportunity to avenge itself for her defeat in the 1870 Franco-Prussian War by mobilizing against Germany, thus fulfilling its treaty obligations with Imperial Russia. Finally, Great Britain and her Empire joined in the war against an expanding Germany, a nation bent on conquest and even threatening Britain's long acknowledged naval superiority.

To be perfectly fair, it appeared (at least in the beginning) that the British government and people weren't too keen on going to war, and it took the brutal German invasion of Belgium, in defiance of all the treaties guaranteeing Belgian neutrality, to turn the tide and make the British government and people determined to fight against 'the common enemy'. It was NOT a noble war; it was a horrible, stinking war of human attrition and human suffering, with soldiers fighting filthy mud, bitter cold, frostbite and infection, as well as bullets, shells, bombs, and mustard gas; while the strutting generals played with their battle-maps and moved millions of young men to their doom in a macabre game of military chess.

The Army of Tzar Nicholas the 2nd deserted, and Russia turned to revolution and Bolshevism. The German Army ran out of the means and the will to continue the war and suffered a revolution that swayed from extreme socialism to extreme conservatism. France exacted her revenge by occupying the industrial Ruhr and repossessing the Alsace-Lorraine, and Philip thanked God that only Britain, of all the European Allies, showed a sense of mercy and a distaste for vengeance. This, after all was the great nation with the great heart, the country of his childhood dreams and devotion, and its compassion took away some of the bad taste he'd recently felt about the aftermath of that dreadful war.

As for the United States of America, when at last it came into the conflict, it showed itself to be a true friend in time of need, and in the subsequent matter of reparations it proved itself to have a national conscience similar to that of Great Britain. Its efforts on behalf of the new League of Nations were to be applauded, and both Britain and France owed a great debt of gratitude to their friends across the Atlantic.

Henceforth, Philip told myself, he would judge all current events in the light of antecedent history, on the basis of common morality and an aversion to narrow chauvinism and jingoism. As for political parties, it wasn't policies that counted, but deeds and their results in human terms. There was room for national pride, but never at the expense of the common man or the national conscience.

He remembered how excited he used to get whenever he got a new German stamp to add to his growing collection. It made him feel like a millionaire as he watched the zeros multiply on each successive issue: 10,000 Marks, 50,000 Marks, 100,000 Marks. Gloating over these enormous figures, one could all too easily become afflicted with a miserly sense of financial power, and even the most exotic stamps from far off places paled into insignificance beside these magnificent Reichspost beauties. It was only lately that he was able to equate these stamps with the postwar German misery of runaway currency inflation and the newsreel pictures of starving Germans, their children displaying the swollen bellies and withered limbs of famine. The suffering of war didn't necessarily end with the declaration of peace, and the hardship endured by these people, regardless of who really started the Great War, might well prove to be the incendiary fuel for a future conflict of unimaginable ferocity.

On his fourteenth birthday, Philip gave away all his carefully preserved stamps, dividing them among those of his friends who were starting or building up their own collections. For some reason he felt no pangs of regret; nor did he feel particularly noble.

Some of his childhood idols were falling and the world was no longer one of illustrious monarchs and heroic warriors, nor was it one that could only please the Almighty by adherence to the 'one true religion', whichever that might be. In wars between nations, clergymen of the same faith, even the same specific sect, prayed for victory – each against the other.

The transition from childhood to adulthood was not to be without pain, (Philip appreciated that increasingly with each passing day), but objectivity must never be at the expense of dreams, and his own dreams still soared far and wide. Perhaps he'd inherited the indomitable optimism of his father, perhaps the driving intensity of his mother. If so, he was deeply grateful for both, and for their generous love.

CHAPTER 40

1961-62

The commendation from the Royal College of Surgeons of Canada finally arrived, and those who had worked so hard for their rather thankless objective – both in the B.C. Section of General Surgery and the C.P.S.A. – felt justly proud. The current number of positive pledges and audits had reached over ninety percent, and even allowing for errors, this still meant an overwhelming majority of the surgeons. There were still those cynics who argued that the solicitation and dichotomy would simply be channeled into different forms, but this in no way detracted from the deep feeling of satisfaction with a difficult job well done, and Philip knew he'd always remember those who labored so selflessly toward their objective.

      The clinic practice was going well, and there was no shortage of interesting cases. In particular, there were a good many cases of arterial deficiency in the legs that responded well to Endarterectomy (the surgical removal of deposits clogging the bloodvessel) when the blockage was localized, and by *Lumbar Sympathectomy* for cases that were too far gone and were associated with spasm rather than blockage. (In this operation the surgeon removes a chain of nerves near the lower spine that govern the constriction of arteries in the leg). Philip's main source of bloodvessel surgery, however, was in the field of varicose veins. Actually, it wasn't a case of operating for the unattractive appearance of these veins so much as removing those veins that had lost their valvular competence: a competence that helped carry impure blood upward toward the heart against the force of gravity.

      It appeared to him that the treatment of this condition had come full circle over the past century. First, there was the direct surgical removal of the affected veins, leaving the remaining competent veins that were more than enough to take up the slack. Unfortunately, death from hemorrhage or septicemia was all too frequent and the procedure was abandoned. Next came the injection of the affected veins with various sclerosant solutions and at first the results seemed quite spectacular; as a matter of fact Philip had been in charge of some large outpatient Injection Clinics during his residencies and became an enthusiastic supporter of the method. The favorable results, however, were only short-lived and sometimes made the condition worse by virtue of destroying residual healthy valves, and if this included valves in the deep veins the results could be really serious.

      With World War 2, like so many medical advances during wartime, there came a rush of new approaches to this condition, pioneered by men like Clark in Canada, Garber in South Africa and others in Britain and the U.S.A. At first, the operation consisted of tying off the main superficial vein at the groin, above the main valve and flush with the junction to the main deep vein. Later on, as recurrences started to appear, direct sclerosant injections into the ligated vein were added, then multiple ligations at different levels. Then came the operation of vein stripping, at first with stripping devices encircling the vein and then flexible cables entering the vein along its full length. The best of these was the Myers stripper, but Philip found the flexibility factor somewhat deficient and the expanded ends a bit too sharp, so he blueprinted his modifications and contacted the firm of Allen and Hanbury, one of the more liberal instrument companies in Britain. This firm delighted him by constructing a perfect set of 12 vein strippers, of various caliber's and head-size, as designated in his drawings. The bill for this excellent craftmanship was beyond belief: it came to 30 pounds Sterling, and he would always be grateful for this outstanding bargain.

Of course the most important aspect of management was diagnosing which valves in which veins were affected, and then removing the ones involved, along with division of the superficial branches. For the more serious type of venous incompetence, that of the deep veins, the operation consisted of dividing the 'perforator' veins which had defective valves, but never interfering with the deep vein itself. The results were excellent and the scars were usually negligible as long as they were properly placed. As far as sclerosant injections were concerned, these were reserved for residual or recurrent varicosities and did their job well.

Some of the surgeons found these operations tedious and underpaid but Philip found them rewarding insofar as patient satisfaction was concerned. After the first few years, more and more serious vein problems found their way to his office, and his precious strippers were put to good use. Each case presented a different aspect of the problem. Some involved considerable surgery, some the simplest surgery, and some no surgery at all.

James had been earning his travelling money by selling encyclopedias door to door and 'moonlighting' in the evenings by teaching dancing at the Arthur Murray Studios. When he had enough money, his father matched it as promised and added an extra $500 for good measure. The young man left Edwardia with the blessings of the Bosnar family and Patty put on her bravest front; Philip hoped his son would find what he was looking for on the other side of the Atlantic and he knew how his own father must have felt when he first left home.

Florian now completed her course at modelling school and would be off to Vancouver next year to pursue her chosen career as a model. In the meantime she was doing well with her present job in the provincial government, and had recently received an unexpected promotion. She was picking up very valuable secretarial and management skills which could prove valuable in the future, while Phil and Patty were happy to have their independent daughter staying with them for another year. It was hard to understand why she'd never considered a nursing career like that of her mother, and they had to accept the truth that both their children had chosen their own paths in life and weren't satisfied with merely trying to imitate their parents.

A recent arrival in Edwardia was Mike Reston, an experienced thoracic surgeon who'd been practicing in Calgary for the past twenty-five years and now wished to live on the West Coast. His primary interest was lung surgery but he was interested in getting a cardiac surgery team started in Edwardia, a project that was encouraged at the Chelmsford. He asked Philip if he'd be willing to act as a member of such a team and he agreed, but pointed out that the first order of business was to get a pump-oxygenator and a competent pump technician. In the meantime, he helped Reston in the O.R. whenever he could, and made sure he didn't try for too much too soon, as he was rather eccentric and a bit overconfident. Philip's plan was to start with a pump team that wouldn't be restricted to heart cases.

Malignant melanoma is one of the most dangerous and incurable forms of cancer in the human body, except in its very earliest stages. In recent years there had been a definite break-through in the United States by the use of Isolated Perfusion, (a method for circulating highly toxic chemotherapeutic agents through the affected lower limb without permitting the chemicals to enter the general bloodstream). For this purpose, the main artery is exposed in the groin and temporarily clamped off, along with the accompanying main vein. A cannula is inserted into the vein and connected through a system of tubes to the special pump; the entire system is prefilled with matched blood, and a supply of oxygen is fed into the circuit through an ingenious device known as an 'Oxygenator'.

The blood in the circuit is loaded with a given quantity of the chemotherapeutic agent, and an anticoagulant is used to prevent clotting. The blood is then pumped at a given rate through another set of tubes where it is warmed to the body temperature and enters the main artery through a second cannula. This isolated arterial perfusion is then continued for a specific length of time calculated by the cancer specialist. Some of the reported results were very encouraging and Philip thought it would be an excellent opportunity for the medical staff to get acquainted with the use of this sophisticated technology before embarking on a cardiac surgery program.

A special investigatory committee was set up by the Chief of Staff and Dr. Bosnar was chosen as chairman; it included two internists with a special interest in cancer, a cardiologist of distinction, and a second surgeon, Dr. Gregory Barfleet, who wasn't a particular favorite of Philip's, as he was inclined to play politics with most projects. In any event, the committee contacted a highly qualified team at the Swedish Hospital in Seattle where an isolated perfusion program had recently been started. They were running a parallel experimental animal program with dogs, in order to remain alert for unexpected side effects or technical problems. The head of the group was kind enough to invite Philip Bosnar and Chris Dukes, Edwardia's leading cardiologist, down to Seattle for a day-long series of demonstrations at the Swedish.

The weather on that particular day turned particularly bad, and the travellers hoped this wasn't a forewarning of bad luck. The snow fell heavily and their plane almost didn't take off; by the time they arrived in Seattle a full-scale blizzard was under way. It was almost two hours later that they arrived at their destination, and their hosts immediately went into action and demon-strated their procedures in the utmost detail, with a generosity so typical of American medical centers and – sad to say – never quite matched in the Canadian Medical Centers.

The rest of the day was spent in a point-by-point review of every technical detail, no matter how small. By the time the demonstrations were through, Bosnar and Dukes had completely run out of questions. When they expressed their profound thanks they were invited to stay in touch with their hosts and to let them know if they ran into any problems. They even volunteered to send up a member of their team if necessary, and the Canadian visitors were overwhelmed.

When they reported their visit to the committee there was a strong feeling that they should go ahead. But Greg Barfleet decided the time had arrived to pour cold water on the whole idea, and slowly but surely began to sway the others into a negative frame of mind and a timid excess of caution over zeal. Some of Philip's more forthright colleagues suggested to him later that "good old Two-Face," only opposed those projects favoring a competitor, and that he would have been an enthusiastic proponent if only he were in charge of the enterprise.

The upshot of the meeting, on a motion by Barfleet, was that they should ask the Vancouver cardiovascular surgeons whether it would be wise for Edwardia to go ahead, and only a moron could have failed to predict the answer. Philip received a friendly letter from Brigadier-General Jowett, Chairman of the Cancer Society, commending him and the committee for their work on the pump-oxygenator project, but stating that in view of the negative opinion from Vancouver he felt they should drop the idea until a later time. Philip replied immediately.

> **'Dear General Jowett:**
>
> **Please accept my thanks on behalf of our committee for your kind remarks. It would be dishonest of me not to express my personal disappointment at your decision and my feeling that you have been incorrectly advised in this matter.**
>
> **In the first place I believe that asking a neighboring center in B.C. that is in the process of developing a similar program if we should go ahead with our own, was a big mistake. In the second place, if we are ever to establish a local cardiac surgery facility, it is essential that we start with an adequate experience in the operation of a pump-oxygenator. The use of such equipment in the treatment of malignant melanoma by a process known as Isolated Perfusion is a recognized major advance and justifies our best endeavors, rather than a timid withdrawal.**
>
> **Medical progress in a center such as Edwardia can either go forward or backward: it cannot stand still. Let us hope that we will not, at some future date, look back at our present withdrawal from the project under discussion as one of the major setbacks in the advance of our city's patient-care.**
>
> **With respect, Sir,**
> **I remain yours sincerely,**
> **Philip Bosnar'**

The triumph of John Kennedy over Richard Nixon in the American presidential elections was like a blood transfusion to a great nation that was in progressive moral hemorrhage. Admittedly, the outgoing president had been showing signs of a reawakening conscience since the death of Dulles, and his courageous warning against the malign workings of what he called the 'Military-Industrial Complex' was one that – for Philip at least – would serve as a solitary beacon in his unilluminated term of office. Now, this vigorous attractive and young new leader could pull his country out of the swamplands of national and international failure into a brighter future and a genuine leadership of the free world. Not only that, but even the kindest observer would have to admit that the gorgeous Jackie was a somewhat more delectable first lady than poor dowdy Mamie.

In a way, one had to feel sorry for the Eisenhowers; they were never really meant for greatness. It had literally been thrust upon them. Now, their lack of distinction was magnified by the blazing charisma of the youthful Kennedys, and it didn't seem quite fair. Not that the new president's first year in office was going to be a picnic, even with the expert help of his politically astute brother Robert.

Cuba was emerging as a rigidly doctrinaire communist regime in the Caribbean, so very close to Florida, and a Soviet military base there was a growing possibility. Khrushchev's policy of detente with the U.S. had been destroyed in the wreckage of the U.2 and the Berlin Wall was a threat that grew ever more ominous. Vietnam was becoming a quagmire that could and would swallow up soldiers, weapons and resources from America, all in a vain effort to stop a communist tyrant in the north and promote a rightwing dictator in the south.

On his home front, the new president had to cope with a C.I.A. that was almost an autonomous instrument of foreign political and military policy; and scheming away in the omnipotent anti-red bastion of the F.B.I. was the monstrous John Edgar Hoover, whose beady eyes saw only communists but never fascists, trouble-making niggers but never lynch-fomenting Ku Klux Klanners. Now, by the grace of God, there were no longer the Thomases, McCarthys and their committees to augment the paranoia of the number one G-man, and there was no J.F.Dulles to compound the felony. Perhaps the F.B.I. would now be able to devote part of its excessive resources to fighting the rising menace of organized crime, that was increasingly invading the labor unions, especially the Teamsters and the Dockworkers.

Florian produced an unexpected bonus from her civil servants' union: two half-priced charter flight tickets to London. Patty was overjoyed at the opportunity to check up on the fortunes of their wandering boy. Philip had to admit that James kept in touch with them pretty faithfully, and the grandparents in London let them know from time to time how matters were going for him. The young man had only accepted their hospitality for a couple of weeks before going off to seek his own quarters; taking odd jobs to provide an income while he pursued his destiny. When he wrote Phil and Patty that he'd won a scholarship to the Webber-Douglas School of Acting they were delighted, and once again Philip assured him that he'd continue to match his income, dollar for dollar or, more exactly, pound for pound, but on one condition. If he ever found himself in difficulties he was to let them know immediately. Meanwhile, his anxious mother would now be able to see how things really were, instead of just relying on reports.

There was only one of Colonel Bradford's stories that Philip found difficult to believe, although his closest friends who'd known the old gentleman far longer insisted they'd never caught him out in a lie. It was about a transatlantic crossing from New York to Southampton on a Cunard liner; on board was the world chess champion of his day, the redoubtable Pillsbury of the U.S.A, and he was available to play any opponents on the ship, either jointly or separately, for a fee. The youthful Bradford approached the champion and said that although he was strictly an amateur he'd like to take one of three boards, but declined the offered odds of Queen's Rook. He played exceptionally well, while the champion played rather loosely and finally resigned the game to his unknown opponent, thus giving him one of the high points of his colorful life.

Philip simply couldn't swallow this story: it was just too good to be true. (*Yet, many years later, he was reading some historical anecdotes in a book of chess memorabilia when he came across a remarkable item. It concerned a game played by the American world chess champion, Pillsbury, while crossing the Atlantic. The game was against an amateur played without odds, and his opponent had beaten him fair and square – even though it was a three board simultaneous game. The opponent was described as a tall young British engineer.*)

Bosnar's own chess was consolidating to a satisfactory level that he hoped would last him the rest of his life, and he was beginning to concentrate a bit more on duplicate bridge. Walter Langley served as his slave driver, pushing him toward the twin objectives of winning tournaments and becoming Life Master. The game wasn't played for money but for 'master points', and if one was a tournament winner there were trophies. Although Walter and Philip weren't exclusively a bridge partnership, they played as partners quite often. They sometimes discussed the pros and cons of various bidding systems, usually over drinks (for which Walter had a considerable capacity but seemed to handle well).

As far as ever becoming a Life Master, this seemed an ambition that was impossibly remote. Winning or placing in the club games was rewarded with 'fractional' rating points, usually 4 or 5. 100 fractionals were translated into a single Master point, and 50 master points gave a player the rating of Junior Master. 100 master points made the player a full Master, and 200 made one a Senior Master. Eventually the proud possessor of 300 master points became a life master, if at least two-thirds of the points had been won at major regional or national tournaments. What an impossible dream!

Harry Bekassy was still regaling Philip with fascinating stories of his background and yet, strangely, never indicated any curiosity about his listener. He knew only that Philip was born in France of Polish parents, was brought up in England, came out to Canada before the second World War, and served as a surgeon in the Canadian Army. As for Harry, after the retreat from El Alamein he'd found himself caught up in the battle of Kasserine Pass, in which Wehrmacht troops faced American soldiers for the first time.

According to version, the U.S. troops and their commanders were so green it was "like shooting fish in a barrel," as he put it. Right from the start the Germans took the high ground and brought up mortars and light howitzers into the crannies and ledges of the rocky heights, so they could look straight down the throats of the green American troops. These had blithely chosen to hunker down in the exposed valley, and according to one of Harry's witty commanders, seemed to be suffering from an acute shortage of Mom's apple pie. The carnage that followed was awful, and there were G.I. bodies everywhere, while American firepower seemed directed at the clouds.

"If it had been the British Commonwealth forces instead of the Americans," Bekassy observed, "they would have finished us off by nightfall."

Patty and Florian returned from their trip to England with mostly good news. Philip's parents were both in good health, and his father had at long last given up smoking on his physicians advice: perhaps 'ultimatum' was a more accurate word, since the chronic bronchitis and emphysema were becoming a real threat. As a result of giving up his precious cigarettes, he'd put on quite a lot of weight, but was still working as hard as ever, and his factory still lacked an elevator. Whenever Philip had remonstrated with him in the past about this point, he always joked that climbing stairs was the best possible exercise to keep him fit. His dear Mum had become quite a

TV fan, and her favorite sport on the 'telly' was boxing, which she watched with all the concentration of a veteran fight fan.

Clayton was doing well with his first G.P. job on the eastern outskirts of London, as junior partner in a large panel practice, and he celebrated the reunion with his Canadian relatives by taking Florian across to Paris, where they visited with the large family of her grandfather's oldest sister. They had a marvellous time and visited almost every one of the historic Paris landmarks, from the Louvre to the Eiffel Tower, and from the Palace of Versailles to the Church of the Sacre Coeur in the Montmartre.

Patty and Florian had a wonderful reunion with James, who was looking well and was now over six feet tall, with fading memories of his annoying shortness up to the age of sixteen. He was obviously enjoying his work with the drama studio, and his diction was already far more English than Canadian. There was only one fly in the ointment and that was the revelation that their once-pampered son was now living in a dreadful garret in the depths of the Soho district. Not only that, but he didn't seem to mind in the slightest. Of course his mother worried about whether he was eating enough or getting the right food, but he hadn't lost any weight, and in fact was looking extremely fit and strong. While she was in England, Patty was able to get in touch with many of her own family members and there were some joyful reunions.

Although she still remained untempted by duplicate bridge, Patty thoroughly enjoyed the regular social bridge games. There were four couples with whom the Bosnars played on a regular basis. They were the Peters, the Varneys, the Jessops and Langleys, all four of them G.Ps and wives. They played at each others homes once a month, taking turns; first, drinks were served, then two tables of bridge with one couple sitting out on a rotational basis, and a midnight snack before departure.

Each late summer, with the exception of the Langleys, who were otherwise involved, the rest of the group travelled to Yellow Point, on Vancouver Island, for a weekend of relaxation and bridge. They rented a large cottage, with four bedrooms and two bathrooms, and had their meals up at the main lodge. It was a wonderful retreat from the daily wear and tear of medical practice and housework. The mornings were spent in walking along the sea front, swimming in the pool, or just loafing in the sun. The rest of the day was mostly taken up with bridge, and when the sun went down a crackling fire was started with logs of driftwood in the great stone fireplace.

After the ladies had retired to bed, the men got down to serious bridge and serious drinking. There was only one irritating factor and that was the persistent questions put to Philip about the absent Walter Langley, which Philip found objectionable. Was Walter having trouble with his wife, with his drinking, with his patients? Philip made it clear that he didn't appreciate the inquisition, even though he understood that it was mostly tongue in cheek, a method of needling him. On a more serious note, however, he realized they held no great opinion of his partner and were unhappy that Philip had joined his group practice. It was difficult to guess their motives since none of the three referred their surgery to him, anyhow.

It was usually Bill Varney who led the needling and seemed the most hostile to Walter Langley.

"He made a pretty shrewd move when he got you, Philip," he remarked, "I guess he wanted to add some respectability to his group."

"You're entitled to your opinions, Bill, but I don't see it that way at all."
As for the innuendos about alcohol and marriage difficulties, Philip insisted he knew nothing about these. Fortunately, the exchanges never erupted into angry confrontations, and they all staggered to bed about 1 a.m, saturated with bridge, pleasantly drowsy and ready for the morrow.

The Bosnars' old friend from the days of Vanwey, George Freikopf, was dead. They got the news from Ruth Steffanson, and in a way it was a merciful relief. Philip remembered when he came out to consult him professionally in the summer of 1958. This active and athletic man, always a winner in life, (whether it was American politics, business, gambling, or his family), was seriously incapacitated by a severe and persistent attack of sciatica. He had seen several doctors in Edmonton but to no avail, and he'd obtained no appreciable relief from medication, physiotherapy – including pelvic traction – and a spinal support. He was eager for Philip to go ahead with the injection treatments that had been so successful in his Saskatchewan practice. When Philip examined him, he was concerned about the degree of nerve damage that was manifest: there was a significant degree of foot drop.

X-rays were taken and showed nothing unusual, but blood examination revealed a marked degree of anemia, and Philip began to have his suspicions about the possibility of a spinal cord tumor, especially when Freikopf remembered to tell him that he was losing weight. Philip told him about his concerns and advised him to get an appointment with the leading neurosurgeon in his own city; moreover, he thought it unsafe to try a caudal block and George understood.

A letter from Dorothy Freikopf, written a month later, reported that surgical exploration disclosed a *Malignant Myeloma* (a tumor of the bone marrow) and George would be receiving radiotherapy treatments over a considerable period of time. Philip knew that this condition, usually called *Multiple Myeloma*, was characterized by the development of widely scattered tumors throughout the skeletal system and that the prognosis was very grave.

Shortly after receiving the bad news, Phil and Patty took a trip to Edmonton to see how their friend was getting along. In typical fashion, he was taking his disability in stride, with a laugh and a wisecrack, and he had no hesitation in resuming his flirtatious overtures to Patty, whom he still claimed to adore. He played golf whenever he could, but usually came back with one or more broken ribs (pathological fractures), although that hardly slowed him down.

He required frequent blood transfusions and insisted they only made him cranky. He still loved to play bridge, but when they observed his game they saw that not only had he lost his skill but he was no longer the good card-holder of former days. Handsome lucky George hadn't lost his looks; but aside from that his luck had finally run out and his days were numbered.

The Bay of Pigs attempted invasion of Cuba was an unmitigated disaster, an inheritance from the Eisenhower-Dulles regime, an absolute guarantee of Fidel Castro's future implacable enmity on the one hand, and of a consolidating Soviet base in the western Atlantic on the other. This shocking miscalculation was followed by civil war in South Vietnam and a growing unpopularity of the corrupt President Ngo Binh Diem and his brother Nhu.

Meanwhile, the rift between Catholic and Buddhist in the south overshadowed the threat from the Viet Cong and Russian-backed forces of Ho Chi Minh; while the American armed forces were clearly going to be sucked into this morass in increasing numbers with each passing month, first as military advisers and ultimately as fighting troops.

In Europe, the building of the Berlin Wall had effectively closed off the last open gate of the Iron Curtain in the divided city, and the hopes for a unified Germany vanished, not an unmixed blessing.

On the U.S. home front the popular young president was showing strength in the matter of black civil rights where his predecessor had shown only weakness. The heydays of the K.K.K. and their champions in state governments and sheriff's departments were coming to a close; but the sinister J. Edgar Hoover was still trying to destroy the power of his hated enemy, Dr. Martin Luther King, and that of his growing movement across the country.

An unexpected patient who arrived from the prairies was Jim Griffiths, whom Philip had known when he was Reeve of Lampman. At that time they had a fairly active feud going when Griffiths refused to pay more than 33 percent of his fees for patients covered by the township's medical scheme. On this occasion he came to see him in Edwardia because he was suffering from a massive abdominal hernia and knew that Dr. Bosnar had repaired some of these in the past on Lampman patients, some under local anesthesia. Griffiths was quite unsuitable for general anesthesia as he had a very bad chest, with lung fibrosis and a longstanding advanced kyphosis (a hump-back curvature of the thoracic spine).

Philip had him thoroughly checked out by an internist, then admitted him two days before surgery so they could get him into optimum shape for surgery. It was strange operating on the old gentleman while he was sitting up and they chatted about old times and the changing political scene in Saskatchewan. The patient was given an oxygen mask that he could use whenever he felt short of breath, and received a mild tranquilizer in his intravenous infusion.

After preparing the operative field in the usual fashion, and with a nurse seated beside the patient and watching his condition, Philip injected a dilute solution of Procaine into the abdominal wall, using a 'fan' technique that only required two tiny needle pricks through which the long needles were progressively advanced. After entering the abdominal cavity, a highly diluted solution of the local anesthetic was flushed over the intestines and then suctioned off. This cut off the visceral sensations that could produce considerable discomfort, nausea and vomiting.

Because of the size of the abdominal defect no attempt was made to close it, but a Tantalum mesh patch was used instead, and sutured into the freshened margins of tissue with Dacron sutures. In time, new fibrous tissue would grow into the tiny apertures of the metallic mesh and the body would develop a strong abdominal wall where there had been none. The happy patient was entirely comfortable during the operation and he was discharged a few days later, none the worse for wear. It was an operative method Philip had used in several similar cases and the results were rewarding.

Their good friends the Torwalds were doing splendidly and proceeding from strength to strength. They had sold their second motel at a handsome profit and invested in a much larger motel close by the Royal Harbor. It was a superb location with an excellent future, since it was only minutes away from the arrival point of ferries from the U.S.A, and the area was the hub of tourist throngs. In addition to this business Hank and Mattie had also purchased a taxicab company, and astutely secured a franchise for the airport bus service.

Whatever they now touched seemed to turn to gold, and they had purchased a beautiful new beachfront home in the prestigious Elm Bay district close by the Golf and Country Club. Mattie had a skilled eye for antiques and did very well at the estate auctions that were always going on; her new home was becoming filled with these antiques and she exhibited them with justifiable pride. One welcome development in this expansion of the Torwald interests was the hiring of Alf Steffanson as treasurer and business manager of the transportation division, and he was doing an excellent job, both for the owners and for his own advancement.

Then came a great disappointment with its train of tragic consequences. Over the years, young Kitty Torwald had grown up into a beautiful young lady, while Billie Torwald was still boyishly good-looking but a bit on the wild side. His parents decided that some old country discipline would do him no harm, so he was sent off to one of Scotland's most prestigious private schools, for several years. He returned to Edwardia with a cultured diction and a broadened education, but little change in his wild streak, while his boyish charm was even more evident than before.

When it was announced that Billie was now taking over as the new president of the transportation company, the world of Alf Steffanson seemed to collapse around him, and he felt betrayed and humiliated by his friends. He had every reason to believe that when the position of president became vacant he would be the logical choice, and his feelings were made far worse at being preempted by a schoolboy with no business experience whatever.

Since that terrible turn of events, Alf became withdrawn, and his entire personality seemed to shrink within himself. Perhaps his deep belief in the doctrines of free enterprise capitalism had now become tainted by the corruption of nepotism. Was it only just a few years ago, Philip asked himself, that he'd allowed himself to get into such a terrible argument with Ruth Steffanson on the subject of nepotism? She'd always been a strong advocate of the overriding importance of family ties, and could see nothing wrong with family preference in awarding jobs or influencing advancement. Philip's own view, which he'd long held and advanced, perhaps too forcefully, was that this was simply a modern form of tribalism and that the 'Old school tie' system, which he'd always found so repugnant, was simply another form of nepotism.

He wondered now if, whenever Ruth saw him, she would remember the vehemence of his arguments and dislike him for their prophetic quality. In a way he could hardly blame her, since he felt a bit guilty when he thought back to some of his warnings on the subject.

The final tragic chapter of this affair was yet to come. Billie moved to Vancouver to oversee the development of a branch office, and it was said that he fell into bad company. In any event, he was out hunting one day with some of these new friends when he was shot 'by accident' with his own rifle; the inquest raised no question of foul play, but there were many who knew him well and insisted it was no accident but a case of planned murder. Against the urging of some friends in Vancouver, Hank refused to pursue an enquiry, and from the moment of their son's death the joy seemed to go out of the Torwalds' life, and all their wealth and possessions became just so many ornaments. It was a desperately sad ending to all their ambitions and hard work, as well as a shocking lesson in the evils of nepotism.

The sale of the Stanovitsky practice went smoothly, with satisfaction on all sides. Fred

Jurgens was a topflight general practitioner, young, attractive to his patients, and thoroughly conscientious. The office nurse, Sally Beakin, who'd been a loyal fixture in the Stanovitsky practice, had nothing but praise for her new boss, and everything seemed to be working out beautifully; until unexpected problems began to arise. Once every few months, he would suddenly disappear for as long as two weeks at a time.

The usual pattern was that in the middle of an afternoon office he'd tell his nurse he was just slipping out to get some cigarettes. Then, when he didn't reappear for the next hour, she'd phoned Mrs. Jurgens at home to see if the doctor might have driven back to his house for some reason. Next came phone-calls to both hospitals and the police, but all with negative results.

Eventually, Philip got the whole story, and was saddened to learn that this fine young physician had a severe drug problem. It started when he was serving in the Canadian Navy during the closing months of World War 2, when he was prescribed some antidepressant medication for attacks of depression. After a while he found himself becoming more and more drug dependent, and when he periodically felt himself going out of control, he'd drop whatever he was doing, and take off to some hiding place or other until he felt fit to return. He had tried several remedial programs over the years but the condition always seemed to return, no matter how hard he fought against it.

It was a tribute to Jurgens' popularity with his patients that the practice didn't fall off, and his sympathetic nurse handled the difficulties remarkably well, but Philip was afraid he'd lose his hospital privileges and decided to tackle O'Dwyer directly, with no concealment. He proposed that an emergency substitution system should be set up so that, whenever Jurgens disappeared on one of his 'trips', there would be another staff physician available, on a rotational basis, to take over his hospital patients until he returned.

"Great idea, Phil! He's a fine guy and we'd all hate to see him go down the drain. Naturally we'll keep this matter as quiet as possible and perhaps we can get him over his problem, but even if we can't we must try and keep him from losing everything."

"I fully agree, and as long as he continues to practice good medicine and shows no signs of faulty performance we should do whatever we can."

"That's a deal, Phil, and thanks for coming to see me."
Thank God the friendly conspiracy worked, and not only Jurgens' practice was saved but Philip was pretty sure the same was true for his marriage, and he felt enormously gratified.

One of the year's biggest surprises for Philip was a most unlikely win in the two-day Men's Pairs event at a major Regional bridge tournament, and the victory was made sweeter by the presence of some of the greatest names in the game, including the famed Charles Goren and Oswald Jacoby. The graciousness of Goren, which was his trademark, was manifest in the way he posed for the press photograph with one arm around Philip's shoulder and one around that of his superb partner, Tony Bright. That picture was one he would always treasure, and now for the first time he actually began to think about the possibility of becoming a Life Master.

CHAPTER 41

1962-63

Now that he was once again entering the exciting world of investment, Philip had to shake off the disturbing memory of 1955 and the ill-fated Crestwell mines. Walter Langley on the other hand was wildly excited about his latest enterprise. He was always on the lookout for opportunities to make money outside the confines of medical practice. Not that he was alone in this respect: an increasing number of local doctors were heavily invested in real estate, especially apartment houses. Of course pathologists and radiologists enjoyed a special edge in this regard as they were able to set up private laboratories and X-ray facilities outside the confines of hospitals, and these private enclaves were turning out to be veritable gold mines.

Thus, when Walter – through his wide circle of friends and acquaintances – was able to get in on the promising new Athos molybdenum mines north of Kamloops, his enthusiasm knew no bounds. What spurred his optimism most of all was the news that Bing Crosby Enterprises were also heavily invested in this venture, so when he was offered a large block of vendor shares in the mines he had no hesitation in accepting the commitment, with the idea of making the shares available first to his partners and then to close friends. One of these was Duane Elliot, professor of geology at Edwardia University College. He was shown a few samples obtained by the diamond-drilling crew when he visited the location, and he became enthusiastic about the results of the ore assay. These results pointed to levels of molybdenum well above commercially viability.

A meeting was held between the four clinic partners and it was decided that they should invest jointly in a major portion of the vendor shares, since there seemed little doubt that when the shares came onto the market they'd sell for at least double the present rate. If any partner wished to pull out he'd still be assured of a handsome profit, although it seemed that staying in was a better proposition.

Walter soon became one of the directors in the new company and was increasingly involved in meetings, both in the province and ultimately as far away as California. With each passing month his optimism grew, and it became infectious to the point when all three of Philip's partners descended on the Bosnar abode one evening in a state of high excitement. They were there in fact to discuss the possibilities of a world tour on the basis of the fortune that lay within their grasp!

Within weeks, many other doctors invested in the mine, along with lawyers, dentists, and others outside these professions who were known to be shrewd investors. There were a few worrying points that concerned Philip, however. First was the fact that he'd disposed of all his savings in this project; second was Walter's absence from his practice for increasing periods; third was the observation by all three partners that he was drinking rather heavily and putting on too much weight.

The most worrying observation of all was the drop in their total patient load, and this also meant a drop in the amount of surgery being referred to Philip. To remedy this situation it was unanimously decided to take on another partner, and they accepted the application of a personable and capable young G.P. from Prince George who soon turned out to be an excellent choice. He had a great sense of humor, was conscientious, and the patients liked him.

The news from James in London was good insofar as he was now working as assistant stage manager in the Bristol Old Vic (what was irreverently called 'Ass-man' in the profession) and was earning a living. His latest letter signalled a new-found independence, and he stated in no uncertain terms that he wished no further financial support from his father; he also declared that he had decided to remain in Britain, and this was a decision very hard for Patty to accept, but as usual she took it bravely. She wrote to convey their congratulations and good wishes, and made it clear that if he found himself in difficulties his parents would always stand behind him.

As for Florian, she moved to Vancouver, where she was doing modelling on a regular basis for the T.Eaton company. Fortunately, she was able to come home for the occasional week-end so they didn't feel entirely isolated from her.

For the recent past, Philip had alternated as city chess champion with Rudy Trofino, and their annual matches were closely followed in the daily papers. To win the championship, it was necessary to play a minimum of six weekly games and win by not less than two of these. For some reason he found it impossible this year to go ahead by more than one game no matter how hard he tried. The struggle had continued far too long and he felt sure the public must be getting tired of reading the weekly results. Finally he decided, and his opponent agreed, that the next game would be decisive one way or another.

As White, he was able to establish a strong initiative and press the advantage to a winning position, yet somehow, try as he might, he simply couldn't convert his superior position to a clear win. Even with analysis at the end of the evening by their adjudicator, a clear win couldn't be found, and Philip proposed that he and Trofino be declared joint winners for this year. When he got home, he set up the pieces and looked over the position, but still found no win. After a light snack he went to bed and slept a dreamless slumber. At exactly 4 a.m. by the bedside clock he sat bolt upright, declared, "Mate in seven!" and went back to sleep.

The following morning he could hardly wait to set up the chess board once again, and there it was: checkmate in seven against any defense. It was a simple matter of what is known as 'triangulation', a maneuver in which the queen exercises a series of checking moves in diminishing triangles against the opposing king, and one that Philip had completely overlooked. The really exhilarating point was that his subconscious thought processes hadn't overlooked the winning combination, and he realized, as never before, what an enormous advantage this was for the human mind. It was a mechanism by which the brain could go on reasoning, calculating, and analyzing, while the conscious mind blissfully slept and recharged its batteries.

Harry Bekassy came up to the Bosnar home for the occasional meal, and was always a welcome guest. Patty liked him despite his Nazi background and he in turn was very fond of her and thought she was a culinary artist in the finest tradition of great Jewish cooking. When he'd first come to Canada after the second world war he landed in Montreal and became an apprentice chef in the Queen Elizabeth Hotel. The head chef told him that if he ever wanted to become a master cook he had to learn all about Jewish Kosher cooking techniques.

The ironic humor of the situation wasn't lost on Bekassy, but he applied himself to the many books on the subject and then got himself a job as catering chief to a Jewish holiday resort in the Gatineaus of Quebec, where he learned and practiced all the finer points of Jewish cooking and hobnobbed with the residents on a friendly basis so alien to his past. As far as Patty was concerned, Harry swore she was one of the few non-professional cooks who'd mastered the arcane art that was the true basis of cordon bleu – as against mere gourmet – cuisine.

Giving up the violin over the past few years had been made easier by a combination of circumstances. It was too difficult to get a regular piano accompanist, and taking part in the string section of the symphony orchestra would have demanded too much of Philip's time. Moreover, over the years his precious violin had developed first one and then a second major crack on the underside, and it wasn't worth bothering with expensive repairs of doubtful outcome.

After forty years of devotion as an amateur performer he had no wish to witness his own decline as an instrumentalist, and this was bound to occur sooner or later. As a substitute, he diverted his musical energies into a much greater appreciation of recorded music, especially with the replacement of the old 78s (with their poor quality) by the vastly superior 45s and 33s. In addition, the new sound systems were so greatly improved that he was eager to get a really good set.

He'd heard and read a good deal about the Philip Hamlin Black Box stereo system that recently won the International Grand Prix at the Brussels World Fair. The Hamlin music store was located in Seattle, and it seemed a good time to take another trip to that fine city. He and Patty took the ferry to Port Angeles and drove down in their new Plymouth convertible that had replaced their aging Monarch a year ago. After checking in at the Olympic Hotel they made the Hamlin store their first stop and were treated to a demonstration of the Black Box system. It was overwhelming: recorded sound with a realism beyond anything they'd ever heard before, with a stereo effect that was remarkable. The price was reasonable and the Bosnars knew they had just purchased many thousands of hours of unlimited joy.

When they got back, Philip had a special rotating antenna installed on the roof so they could pick up broadcasts from nearby cities, and Philip began to tape-record some of the best programs (with silent thanks to the late Emil Stanovitsky). No longer the instrumentalist, he could now sit back with Patty and enjoy the Longine Symphonettes and Metropolitan Operas from Vancouver and the excellent classical programs from Seattle; they had truly entered a new and unlimited world.

Old Judge Tompkins, now in his nineties, looked just the same as he had twenty years ago, sitting up on his courtroom throne in far-off Vanwey. He'd moved to Edwardia on retirement, and still enjoyed playing golf two or three times a week, rain or shine. Lately he'd found it difficult to continue because of a painful lump on his upper back and asked his G.P. to be referred to Dr. Bosnar. When Philip he examined the old judge, he found a soft rubbery tumor hanging down from the region of the left shoulder blade, slightly tender to pressure, and quite mobile. According to the patient, he'd been aware of this lump for many years but it had never bothered him before; doctors in the past had always reassured him that it was harmless.

"They all said the same thing. It was an innocent fatty tumor and they advised me not to have it removed as long as it didn't bother me. This is the first year it's given me any trouble and I believe it's getting quite a bit larger."

"In my opinion it doesn't feel like a fatty tumor. The best thing to do is to remove it under a local anesthetic, and then we can find out exactly what it is."

Arrangements were made to do the case in the outpatient O.R. at the Chelmsford, since it looked like a straightforward procedure. This proved to be an inaccurate assessment, as the tumor – although well-encapsulated and looking quite benign – was much more extensive than it appeared at first sight, and extended under the shoulder blade to its root between the third and fourth ribs.

The operation was completed under local anesthetic without pain or discomfort to the patient, and on initial examination of the specimen it was obvious that it had been completely removed. Its color was a grayish white and quite unlike the yellow color of a fatty tumor. Philip wasn't entirely surprised, therefore, to learn that it was a *Neurofibroma*, composed of nerve tissue and fibrous elements, and the absence of any sign of malignancy in the laboratory sections was a great relief, if rather unexpected.

The old judge did very well and resumed his golf game with no further discomfort, but one month later he returned with extreme shortness of breath. An X-ray of his chest removed all doubts: both lungs were completely riddled with secondary tumors, and there was no treatment that would be of the slightest use. Once again, and he'd encountered such situations in the past, it was the clinical progress of the case, the 'Natural History', that determined the pathological nature of the condition, rather than the microscopic appearance, especially in this type of tumor. He checked with the judge's own physician and arranged for hospital admission, since he would require special respiratory care to keep him comfortable.

When Philip explained the nature of the tumor and the hopeless prognosis to the patient, he wasn't in the least bit upset, and had only words of thanks.

"After all, Doctor, at least you've allowed me to play golf again before I die, and you've taken away my pain. Now, if you have the time, I'd like you to sit down and let me tell you all about the trial in Vanwey."

"Surely that isn't necessary, Judge. It was so long ago."

"Maybe so, but I've never forgotten and I don't think I've ever really forgiven myself. I showed favoritism to Doctor Tom because he always used to look after my family, and I showed favoritism to Standwick because he used to be my law partner and I admired his shrewd mind so much."

"I really don't think you should tire yourself out."

"You were a stranger, an outsider from England, so I ruled against you and that was terribly wrong. I'm asking your forgiveness."

"Granted, and now you don't have to feel guilty any more." The old gentleman died peacefully in his sleep one month later.

As a bizarre aftermath to this episode, Standwick's wife came to see Dr. Bosnar several weeks later, referred to him by her G.P. at her own request. She was staying on Galiano Island, where her family had a winter cottage and ran a small motel with hired help. The problem for which she sought his opinion was a breast lump that luckily had no features suggestive of malignancy. He admitted her for excisional biopsy, namely removal of the entire lump and microscopic examination, and the benign nature of the condition was confirmed beyond doubt.

Over the years, Mrs. Standwick had consulted him on several occasions for various minor surgical conditions, always by requested referral, and he wondered – with mildly malicious humor – if her husband would ever show up himself as a patient. Perhaps they were no longer together and she was showing her complete independence!. Philip's memories of that corrupt and bigoted lawyer were still unpleasant and he would be happy if he never saw him again.

It was Ian Firth, the publisher of the Daily Edwardian, who first made the suggestion, and Philip thought it was great. Firth had been reading about Sammy Reshevsky, the U.S. chess champion, acknowledged as one of the world's leading players, and was interested to note that the champion gave chess exhibitions across the country from time to time, his fee depending on the number of 'boards' he had to play. The publisher contacted Reshevsky and made the necessary arrangements. There would be a simultaneous set of games against not less than twenty players. Philip pointed out that to any good player this was no impossible feat and that he himself had played several such simultaneous matches and found them not unlike ordinary Rapid Chess.

By the time the exhibition was held, they had managed, by virtue of publicity in the papers, TV and radio, to get a gratifying forty players eager to try their skills against this world-famous player. The hockey arena was hired for a Sunday afternoon and the tables and boards were set up in a giant rectangle, with a barricade separating the players from the spectators. Each player was charged $10 and had to bring his own chess set, while the viewers were charged five dollars each.

On the morning of the match, the diminutive Reshevsky arrived by plane and Philip recognized him immediately from his many photographs in all the chess magazines. After introductions, Firth and Bosnar drove him to the Prince Albert Hotel and checked him into his suite. They asked if he wished to rest but he insisted that he felt quite alert and would be happy if they stayed and chatted. Reshevsky turned out to be charming and unaffected and they enjoyed his company. At noon they went down to the dining room and had lunch together, then they left him and arranged to pick him up at 2 o'clock and drive him to the arena.

The games commenced at 2.30 sharp, and the place was packed with spectators, far beyond their expectations. The rules were simple: at each board the champion would play the white pieces and make the first move, then proceed to the next board. It was expected that each player would have his next move ready by the time Reshevsky, walking around the inside of the rectangle, reached him; if not, then the champion would move on without waiting.

Philip wasn't surprised when his opponent played the Exchange Variation of the Queen's gambit. It was Reshevsky's favorite opening and he'd won many important matches with it. His moves came with inexorable predictablity and – sure enough -the pressure started to build up on the Queen's side of the board and Philip realized something quite unorthodox was called for. After all, this brilliant veteran knew all the standard continuations and had doubtlessly analyzed them to death. What was needed was an audacious bluff, full of threat but lacking in substance.

The champion was a man of pride and he disliked appearing to exert any effort as he walked around the rectangle, making move after move in a regular unhurried cadence. If Philip could upset his equilibrium, even in the slightest degree, by a move that was quite outside the accepted variations, his opponent might be forced to stop and think, and this was something he wouldn't wish to reveal in front of such a large audience. Perhaps if Philip offered his Queen's Bishop's Pawn he could open up the position and threaten an attack on his opponent's King. Reshevsky had castled on the Queen's side and that could possibly make his king vulnerable; alternatively, the gambit might provide a possibility of perpetual check, which would mean a draw.

Philip could hardly wait for the great man to arrive at his board, and found himself breathing hard and almost shaking with excitement. After what seemed like an eternity, his famed opponent arrived in front of him, stopped, frowned, changed his footing from side to side and said, "Hmm. Most interesting." Then, while Philip registered the incredible scene in slow motion, his opponent reached over, shook his hand and declared, "A very nice draw, Doctor, most enjoyable."

For the next twenty-four hours Philip remained on cloud nine, and he knew that this would be the high point of his life as a chess player and one that he could never match. When Firth and Philip bade Reshevsky goodbye at the airport the following morning, the visitor was kind enough to refer to their game: it was one of only two draws (no losses, however!), the other being against the redoubtable Neville Starling, former city champion. The American graciously posed for a news photographer with the two them, and Philip's cup was full to overflowing. This would be another picture he'd always treasure.

In addition to paying his fee, Ian Firth presented the departing visitor with a magnificent Eskimo sculpture on behalf of the Daily Edwardian, and they were sad to learn later on that the piece had crumbled to dust in the plane's vibrations. Firth immediately purchased a second sculpture almost identical with the first, and had the specialty store take responsibility for delivering the gift safely to Reshevsky in New York. When they learned it had arrived intact they both felt very much better.

As for Philip's chess career, he decided that after this high point he'd be giving up the game except for the occasional friendly bout, and never as a serious contender. Perhaps the most important consideration was that, with both youngsters away from home, he wished to spend more time with Patty in the evenings and perhaps they could get involved in joint activities at the bridge table. She had become a most enthusiastic player and her skills had sharpened steadily, but she was still cool to the prospect of duplicate bridge, which she thought was too cut-throat.

In addition to their monthly dinner and bridge evenings with doctors and their wives, which they thoroughly enjoyed, there were other social opportunities for bridge games, especially the annual get-together in Yellow Point. By mutual consent, it had been decided from the very first year, that certain rules would be followed at the annual long weekend at Yellow Point. The late evening stag sessions would have a set objective, namely the selection of the next day's fireplace attendant. The partnerships were on a rotational basis and at the end of the evening the man with the low score drew the job; this included the gathering of suitable driftwood from the beach, chopping it into appropriate size, and keeping the fires going during the day.

So far, Philip had been fortunate enough to avoid this menial task, but he'd reckoned without the plans of his fellow players. On the third night of their recent Yellow Point outing he noticed something peculiar: no matter who was his partner they seemed to end up with a negative score. They either got too high in their bidding, or failed to reach a sure-fire game or slam. The hands were played poorly and the defense was atrocious. Needless to say, it was a setup, and he enjoyed the secret amusement of his conspiratorial opponents even while being victimized.

The next morning, before breakfast, he wandered down to the beach and found a few slender logs of driftwood that were fairly dry and carried them up to the back of the bungalow, where he could chop them down to correct size. Quite by chance, he noticed a tarpaulin covering what looked like a lawn mower. When he lifted the tarp and examined the area more closely, he was amazed to find that what looked like a mower was, instead, a simple power saw complete with cable and plug for connection to an outside socket at the back of the house. As if that weren't enough, there was a huge pile of small logs, all ready for the fireplace and most welcome from his point of view. Nobody in the happy group had ever looked!

Philip decided it was only fair for him to turn the tables on the conspirators. Without a word about his discovery, he staggered into the cottage carrying a great load of firewood, breathing heavily. There was considerable comment over the breakfast table regarding this mighty feat of strength and endurance, but he brushed the praise aside with due humility, and with the fear that he might burst out laughing at any moment.

It was a wonderful weekend and they all had a tremendous time that would be long remembered. Philip told the others that he and Patty would be driving off first, and left a note on the center table while they were busy packing and getting ready to leave. The note was short and sweet!

'Look under the tarp at the back of the house, dear friends, and learn my special secret. Better late than never!'

It hadn't been a good year for the clinic partnership, but Philip's surgery was starting to pick up again. Langley, who'd previously been the busiest of the G.Ps, was hardly ever around and seemed entirely caught up in the excitement of his new professional and social role as a business entrepreneur; he left the clinic to ride along smoothly in his absence. The new associate, Herb Rollins, was doing nicely but could hardly compensate for the increasing absence of the wandering Langley. There was also increasing concern in the group about what was perceived as a change in Langley's behavior, and one incident in particular revealed to Phil and Patty just how deep this change had become.

It was late September and they were gathered at the Langley home for the monthly bridge session, along with the Peters, the Varneys, and the Jessops. As usual, Walter's wife Barbara had excelled herself with preparations for the evening, and they all looked forward to sampling the delicious snacks for which she was famous. She was a truly sweet person, a devoted wife and mother, and the Bosnars were very fond of her.

Walter seemed to be drinking rather heavily and looked a bit restless when they first arrived, and they had the distinct impression that he and Barbara had been interrupted in the middle of an argument. There was a ring at the door and a rough-looking fellow dressed in hunting attire was ushered in with the utmost cordiality by Walter, but without any introductions to the bridge group. The guest followed his host into the bedroom and when they emerged, Walter was dressed for hunting.

The scene that followed must have been sheer hell for Barbara and they all felt terribly sorry for her. Her husband announced, in the nastiest bellicose fashion, that he didn't give a Goddamn about her arrangements, he was going hunting with his pal and wouldn't be back for days. Phil and Patty had always considered the Langleys such a loving happily married couple that they were absolutely stunned, but all the guests acted as though nothing untoward had occurred and the evening went off fairly smoothly, with Barbara rising to magnificent form.

Over the next few weeks, Walter seemed to return to his former self and there was no evidence of abnormal behavior or excessive drinking, and when he mentioned the hunting incident, it was with the deepest of regrets and apologies. He insisted he loved his wife dearly and she deserved his deepest devotion. So, when he asked Philip to accompany him to Seattle in late October for the Regional bridge tournament, he agreed, although Patty expressed her misgivings. As it turned out, however, Walter's behavior was exemplary during the entire trip, although the standard of their game left much to be desired; perhaps they had too much on their minds and were still too preoccupied with their molybdenum bonanza.

The papers and TV broadcasts in Seattle were filled with the expanding menace of the Cuban missile crisis, and matters seemed to be deteriorating moment by moment. This time, the U.2 lived up to its potential as spy in the sky and was not shot down, and this time the evidence produced by Adlai Stevenson at the U.N. General Assembly was terrifying, not only to the U.S.A. but to the whole world. There, for all to see, were the nuclear missiles on Cuban soil, poised at the North American continent, like a gun aimed at its heart.

That the Soviet Union could take such an unspeakable gamble could only mean that Khrushchev was now under the fist of his nation's military hawks and was doing their bidding. President Kennedy was taking an equal and opposite gamble and perhaps that was the safest way, after all. There could be no question that the American blockade of Cuba against the passage of Russian ships was a clear act of war, but the mere demonstration of a willingness to go to war on this issue was the one antidote that could neutralize the Communist venom in the situation; while any less determined action might only invite increasing aggressiveness on the other side.

Philip began to worry about his continued presence in Seattle and away from home in these perilous times. It wasn't the threat of being reduced at any moment to nuclear ash, since the only fate to fear in a thermonuclear attack was survival, with all its horrors. It was the thought that getting back to his loved ones in Edwardia might become impossible if the situation came even closer to war. It was therefore with a great feeling of relief, for so many reasons, that he learned of the resolution of the crisis, with Khrushchev withdrawing his missiles from the Caribbean island under the watchful eye of the U.S. Navy. At the same time Philip wondered if the knives would be sharpening in the Kremlin for the liquidation of their humiliated leader by his political enemies.

Happy as he was to get back to his darling Patty, it seemed that there was a price to pay for this happiness and for the easing of the thermonuclear threat, one that had come so very close. It was the revelation by Langley that the entire molybdenum enterprise had proved to be one giant fraud, and that the three original directors had fled the country without renewing the option on the mine. Investigation produced the unpleasant information that the diamond drilling reports were faked and no genuine diamond drilling had actually taken place. The samples that were produced had undoubtedly been 'salted' into the mine from high-grade ore obtained elsewhere, and the shares were worthless.

It hardly seemed worthwhile pursuing the vanished directors for criminal fraud and possibly throwing a lot of good money after bad. It was better to lump it, and to have the doubtful consolation of knowing that even such a shrewd outfit as Bing Crosby Enterprises had swallowed the bait. All kinds of stories now began to circulate. The directors who absconded after dumping all their shares at considerable profit were said to have pulled similar stunts in other provinces; warrants were out for their arrest, both in Canada and the U.S.A. Professor Elliot suffered a sudden heart attack at his home and died on his way to hospital. Since he'd always been healthy and athletic there was some speculation about the possibility of suicide, but no proof to back this up.

Serious cracks were beginning to appear in the clinic's facade. Bill Evanson divorced his wife and married the clinic's lab technician, a pretty little brunette from Yugoslavia who'd recently parted from her Rumanian husband, a pediatrician. The loyal business manager and receptionist of the Langley Clinic left to get married to Philip's friend, Glen Parsons. And Walter was becoming a serious problem.

Evanson arrived at Philip's house at noon one day, with an extremely bellicose Langley in tow, smelling of liquor.

"I've tried to tell this stubborn bugger he can't keep on squandering his practice but he won't listen to me. Perhaps he'll listen to you."

But Walter was in no mood to take anyone's advice, and exploded,

"Balls. I can bloodywell take care of my problems my own way. I don't need any busybody telling me what to do, so lay off both of you".

Philip knew it was hopeless and said no more; the whole world seemed to be turning topsy turvy in dear old staid and uneventful Edwardia, land of the lotus eaters.

The worst, however, was yet to come. It was an unusually beautiful day in November, and Philip felt like telling all his patients in the waiting room to go home so that he could play hookey. He felt an urge to go walking briskly along the sea front and intoxicate himself with fresh air and bright sunshine. He was overwhelmed by a sense of wanting to escape from an oppressive feeling of confinement when his phone rang. It was Barbara Langley and she sounded deeply upset. She spoke very quietly, almost as if afraid to hear her own shaky voice.

"I just can't go on this way any longer, Philip. I've tried and tried but nothing seems to work. He's becoming impossible to live with and I can't take it any more."

"I'm sure things will get better, once the disappointment over the investment fiasco fades away."

"You're wrong, Philip. It goes much deeper than that."

"Can I come and see you so that we can talk it over?"

"Maybe. I'll let you know tomorrow, but I don't think I can go on living this way."

Philip's phone rang at 7 o'clock the following morning. It was Bill Evanson at the other end, and what he heard chilled his blood.

"I'm over at Walter's. Barbara killed herself with sleeping pills during the night and the police are here now. The whole business is a rotten mess and I think you'd better get over here right away."

When Philip got there, the entire household was in an uproar. There was Walter, collapsed in a chair and weeping. A mixed group of police, friends and neighbors crowded the hallway and bedroom, and Barbara's body was just being removed to an ambulance that would take her to the city morgue. Philip stayed long enough to exchange a few words with an uncomprehending Walter, then left as some of the bereaved husband's closest friends took over.

The next few days were a nightmare. Phil and Patty found it difficult to stay very long at the reception in the Langley home following the funeral. The sight of Walter slumped in a chair, weeping continuously – while friends kept bringing him food and drink – was just too much, and Philip contrasted his present appearance with that of the handsome physically fit athlete of only a few short years ago.

The official version of Mrs. Langley's death was 'Heart Failure'. The partnership was dissolved by mutual consent and Philip returned to private practice, but in dire financial straits. First, he had to find an office he could afford, and furnish and equip it from scratch. When he first moved to the Langley building, Philip had sold his own office furniture and major equipment for a song, and now he had to purchase these once more. Happily, as a stop-gap, Jack Anderson – a likeable pediatrician who was a special favorite of his – allowed Philip to use his office for two afternoons and one morning a week.

Next, he contacted his ever-loyal former nurse, Flora Kennedy, and she said she'd be delighted to come back and work for him. Finally, he held a heart to heart conference with his good friend and accountant, Mr. Wilson junior, and told him his exact financial position.

"No problem at all," he told Philip in his usual upbeat manner. "Just how much do you need?"

Philip said that ten thousand would be enough to see him through the next six months or so, and Wilson assured him his firm could manage that easily at an interest rate of only five percent. It was a great load off Philip's mind and he thanked him.

For some reason, all his medical colleagues in the city seemed to understand what he'd come through in the past year and were remarkably supportive, for which he felt most grateful. Nevertheless he began to review his options. Just what was his future in Edwardia? He'd held all the top professional positions he could have wished for, both in the city and the province, albeit of the non-paying variety. His surgical load was reaching an acceptable level, and despite the disappointing failure of the Langley medical group he'd emerged with his reputation intact, even if his pockets were rather empty. So it now seemed he was destined to settle into a plush-lined rut, with no foreseeable challenges and no beckoning heights to climb.

Even though his first taste of group practice had turned bitter in his mouth, he was convinced it was the best way to practice medicine in this modern era and the day of the independent primadonna attitude was rapidly becoming outdated. If only a large group practice were available, it would be just what he needed at this time to restore his faith and confidence. He found it ironic to learn belatedly about other groups in town that were thinking of approaching him when Walter Langley induced him to join his clinic. All those surgical positions had, of course, long since been filled.

It was at this precise moment in time that Philip heard about the new Community Health Center being started in the city of Saint Pierre Dulac, situated near the eastern end of Lake Superior. It was apparently modelled after the Kaiser-Permanente clinics of the United States and Philip's interest was aroused. When he told Patty about it she became quite excited, but tried not to show it.

"I think you should go ahead and get some particulars," was all she said, calmly.

What she thought, of course, was that he shouldn't overlook what could be a real opportunity. She felt it might be just what her darling was looking for at this time. Philip Bosnar knew his beloved Patricia all too well!

CHAPTER 42

1963

As president of the duplicate bridge club, the least Philip could do was to persuade Patty to come up at least once and play in one of the club games. It wasn't a resounding success: she found the atmosphere too professional and the competition too cut-throat. In fact she thought the players were so unfriendly that she swore she'd never play duplicate bridge again. Had he given up chess at the wrong time, he wondered, or should he try again? There was another answer and he jumped at the opportunity. A city-wide championship in contract bridge, the non-duplicate variety, was to be played on a knockout basis at the homes of the participants, and Patty – God bless her! – agreed to participate. The fortunes smiled on them and they came through the event as winners. One of their opposing pairs was a couple of the strongest and most arrogant players in the duplicate club, and a clear victory against them brought gladness to Patty's heart.

When a woman needs a morale booster she usually seeks a new outfit for her wardrobe. Patty was different; she nearly always looked for something to buy her beloved (and spoiled!) husband, usually a new suit or overcoat. In these uncertain times, however, when their future was being reviewed, she decided that what he really needed was nothing less than a new car, and she had spotted the exact model for the occasion. It was a classic two-seater Jaguar coupé, gleaming white in color, with great rolled fenders and gorgeous lines: lean of body and long of hood, with a precision stickshift and responsive clutch. It was secondhand, well preserved by the previous owner, in perfect shape and a clear bargain. Patty had fallen in love with it on first sight, and Philip soon followed. It looked like a sleek motorized greyhound and his sales resistance simply melted away. He got a good price for his Plymouth convertible and his conscience was eased.

John Kalatannas was a quiet fellow whom Philip had first met in '58, when the young man dropped into the chess club one evening. As he watched one of the best games he made an impressive observation.

"The first seventeen moves are the same as the game between Keres and Evans in 1947 at Budapest." After several such occasions, Philip took the trouble to check the accuracy of these remarks in his own chess library and was surprised to confirm the newcomer's accurate memory. Then he watched him play the occasional game and realized that this blond young man with the gaunt face and pale blue eyes was a gifted player of rare talent. When he asked Philip for a few games, he found that although Kalatannas could always mount a good attack and reach a winning position he seemed to become agitated toward the end of the game and was inclined to let his victory slip away.

Since Philip was interested to know something about his background he offered to drive him home one rainy night. Kalatannas lived quite a long way from the club and usually walked, so their slow drive on this occasion made it possible to learn a good deal about this unusual and intriguing person. He was originally from Finland, where he became a well trained cartographer and – in surprising addition – an accredited hockey coach. He had come to Canada in 1950, first to Montreal, then to Edmonton, and finally to Edwardia. He was an expert linguist and spoke English fluently. As for chess, he'd been interested in the game since the age of eleven and was fortunate in possessing a natural photographic memory.

Just as Philip was looking forward to watching this new addition to the chess club rise rapidly to the top and perhaps later mature into a world class player, the young man decided to go back to Finland. His mother was very ill and he felt that perhaps his future lay in his native land after all. For the next few years, Philip read all the chess journals carefully, looking for some evidence that his predictions had been accurate, but there wasn't a single mention of the name Kalatannas. Then, suddenly, the Finlander was back in town and playing at the club.

Since Philip was no longer competing in club play, he was looking forward once again to the young man's predicted rise in the chess ranks when he got a phone call from him, asking, "Can I see you privately, Dr. Bosnar?" He was invited to visit the Bosnar home the following Saturday afternoon, and perhaps they could have a game as well.

What Kalatannas had to tell Philip made his blood boil. Despite repeated and frustrating efforts to obtain a job through the city employment agencies he'd remained without work and was running out of funds. He was now a married man with a baby on the way, and was eager to become a good Canadian and a productive member of society. Philip promised he'd make a personal representation on his behalf at the employment office and Kalatannas was humbly grateful. Before his visitor left, Philip insisted they have at least one game of chess and enjoy a cool beer together; the game was a tight one but his opponent was too good and scored a clear win. Once again, however, Philip noticed that the closer they got to the end of the game the more nervous and jumpy his opponent became, and it reminded him of a famous short story, one of his favorites.

'*The Chessplayer*', written by Stephan Zweig, was an absorbing yarn in which the leading character taught himself and practiced his game under cruel conditions as a prisoner of the Nazis. Later on, he found it hard to finish off a winning game because of mounting nervous tension. Philip wondered if Kalatannas had been traumatized by some terrible experience as a child during the years of World War 2 and developed the same syndrome.

The following Monday, Philip presented himself at the employment office and asked to see the person in charge. She was an officious type, but polite and respectful, and when he explained the purpose of his mission she pulled the Kalatannas file and showed him the contents. To his amazement, the last entry contained the comment, 'No special qualifications or skills'.

Philip proceeded to tell her all he knew about this intelligent young man and his versatile abilities. In addition, he presented a resumé Kalatannas had given him during the Saturday meeting, and this gave all his credentials – including a degree in machine lubricants and a fine record in track and field coaching. The lady expressed great consternation and Philip told her he expected a prompt rectification of the injustice or he'd go straight to the media. Happily, this action proved unnecessary and his Finnish friend obtained suitable employment the following week as a cartographer with the B.C. civil service.

As for his chess prowess, although Kalatannas became a formidable player, he never reached the heights Philip had anticipated, and as his nervousness seemed to increase his game declined. Nonetheless, Philip consoled himself that as long as Canada now had a loyal new citizen who could contribute to the service of his country, it really wasn't too bad a deal. As Patty commented succinctly when Philip talked about the episode, "After all, darling, there's more to life than chess."

Philip's reply from the Community Health Center in St. Pierre arrived promptly, along with an impressive prospectus and outline of the aims and objects of the clinic. It was due to open officially on September the 1st, 1963, and the initial complement of doctors would be thirteen. There were two well equipped hospitals in St. Pierre which had recently been brought thoroughly up to date, and the city had a population of around 85,000 with an additional service area of about 70,000.

The city's main industrial base was related to one of Canada's leading steel companies, West Cambrian Steel, and the area was enjoying a period of increasing prosperity. Dr. Bosnar was requested to complete the accompanying form if interested. He had no hesitation in going ahead and supplying them with a bare minimum of his credentials, but he hadn't yet made up his mind one hundred per cent.

It was a beautiful, golden morning in early spring when he received a surprise phone call from a Dr. Jim Appleton, Medical Director of the Ontario clinic; he was calling from Vancouver and wanted to know whether he could get together with Dr. Bosnar if he came over on the morning flight. Philip arranged to pick him up at the airport and then take him to the Edwardia Union Club for lunch before going up to the house. During the past two years the club's name had been changed from the original 'British Empire Club', first to the 'Empire Union Club' and then – quite recently – to the 'Edwardia Union Club'.

The man he met at the airport looked about forty years old. He had a pleasant smiling face, and Philip took an instant liking to him. He turned out to be an American, but quiet and relaxed, the antithesis of the typical boisterous American. When Philip mentioned lunch at a union club, Appleton – a confirmed socialist – was sure he'd met a kindred spirit: one with membership in a labor union club. His astonishment when they entered the club's premises, with its paintings and statuettes of past colonial glories, was almost hilarious. Then, after they sat down in the dining room, Philip revealed the origin of the club's name and they both laughed heartily, especially when he informed his guest that he himself was a staunch conservative, albeit of the moderate Center.

After an excellent meal they drove up to the house on Imperial Drive and he introduced Dr. Appleton to Patty, who liked him immediately. Then all three got down to a serious conversation and the visitor told the Bosnars he was looking for someone to head up the department of surgery at the Community Health Center. After reviewing his more detailed credentials, he thought Philip Bosnar should be the one to fill that position. The original candidate for the appointment had been an Associate Professor of Surgery at Dalhousie, but when he learned of the violent opposition to the new clinic from the medical establishment, he backed off.

Appleton and Bosnar talked at length about their philosophies on the ethics, moralities and economics of Medicine in the 60s, and appeared to be on common ground despite the fact that Philip was no socialist. In addition, they concurred in the pragmatic position that major group practice was undoubtedly the wave of the future. It was now time for a scotch and soda and some quiet relaxation to good music. Their guest was soon overwhelmed by the glorious sounds emerging from the Hamlin system, and insisted that if his host decided to accept the offer he must be sure to bring out the stereo system as well.

Later, the two men went outside into the brilliant afternoon and took in the gorgeous scenery below as they slowly strolled along the terrace for the next half hour. When they got back to the house, Appleton remarked with a rueful grin, "You'd never leave all this to come out to St. Pierre," but Patty replied, "That depends on what there is to look forward to at the other end," and he agreed.

He said goodbye to Patty and hoped it was just Au Revoir, then Philip drove him back to the airport in time to get the 5 o'clock plane back to Vancouver. En route, he promised to keep in touch and said that he'd try to get out to St. Pierre sometime soon, at which time he hoped to give his final answer. In the meantime, Appleton promised to keep the offer open until he had the surgeon's final decision. Philip had to admit the Medical Director had made an extremely good impression on both him and Patty. Just before he passed through the boarding gate, the Director said, as if by afterthought, "By the way, Dr. Bosnar, we'd start you off at our top retainer of $24,000 if you decide to join us."

Although Philip's opinion of the Canadian legal profession over the years had steadily deteriorated, he conceded that it was unfair to generalize. He was outraged by the holier-than-thou attitude of most lawyers toward the medical profession, and the situation seemed to be getting worse, year by year. The dangers were two-fold. Not only were lawyers growing bolder in attacking his profession more viciously as time went by, but when they ascended to the judge's bench they were already conditioned to find in favor of the plaintiff against any defendant doctor, with awards that were starting to grow by geometric progression.

One of the brightest legal lights in Edwardia was a short, compact and boyish-looking lawyer named Hubert Greystone, and the first time he and Philip met, at a cocktail party, they'd both had a drink too many and launched into a fearsome argument on the subject of iniquitous lawyers and untrustworthy doctors. No quarter was given and no quarter asked, but by the end of the evening they were well on their way to becoming fast friends, with great mutual respect and admiration.

Greystone liked the forthright quality of Dr. Bosnar's attack and the surgeon was genuinely charmed by the lawyer's sarcastic wit. He was reputed to be a strong contender for future prominence in the provincial Liberal party, (which had fallen on evil times under the onslaught of the rampaging Social Credit machine), and Philip was convinced of his illustrious future. After a while, as their conversations on medicolegal matters became lengthier, more detailed and more temperate, Greystone reached the conclusion that he'd like to use Dr. Bosnar from time to time as a consultant in some of his court cases involving the specialty of surgery.

Not only was Philip soon engaged in the capacity of a second opinion and expert witness, but he served as a guide to Greystone's cross-examination of the doctor or doctors concerned. Instead of being subpoenaed to appear in court, as was the current degrading custom adopted by lawyers in such cases, Philip accompanied the lawyer to his quarters in the courthouse, then sat by his side at the counsel's table in the courtroom throughout the case. His meal-breaks were taken alongside the lawyers for both sides on most occasions, and at the end of the trial he was often asked by opposing counsel if he might be available for one of his subsequent cases. When advising on cross-examination, Philip had one golden rule: do nothing and say nothing to embarrass or humiliate the doctor in the witness box. It was unnecessary at best and objectionable at worst.

At the end of April, three weeks after Philip's fiftieth birthday, Greystone asked the surgeon to accompany him to a case being tried in Vancouver, and booked him into a top-floor suite at the Bayshore Inn hotel. The case went very well for the plaintiff, a patient suing his employers for injuries received in a construction accident as the result of inadequate safety precautions. It wasn't necessary to crucify the doctor concerned, and Philip could only wish that a precedent could be set: one that would combat the current game of setting doctor against doctor in the most adversarial possible manner, making a mockery of the myth that physicians always covered up for each other. Such a cover-up wasn't necessary and wouldn't work anyhow under careful cross-examination.

Philip appreciated the opulent daily basket of fruit and wine that was sent to his room, and the delicious Polynesian meals he enjoyed in company with Greystone and his opposite number. As for his final cheque, it was more than generous, and he decided to fly on to St. Pierre and see things for himself. He booked a morning flight via Vancouver, Winnipeg and Fort Francis, phoned Patty to tell her of his decision, and phoned Jim Appleton, who promised to meet Philip at the airport.

When he left Vancouver, the skies were heavily overcast, the rain was coming down hard and the air was chilly, but when he arrived in St. Pierre's airport the skies were an unblemished blue, the air was warm and the sun was shining brightly. The city was faintly visible on the horizon and he could see no smoky haze above it to indicate the presence of a large steel mill.

Jim Appleton was there to meet him as promised, and before driving him into town he turned north instead and drove through a tranquil wooded area to a lovely stretch of sandy beach on the eastern shore of Lake Superior. Philip could hardly believe his eyes. It had never crossed his mind that there could be such gorgeous country so close to a city whose economy depended on the steel industry, and he knew his driver had just used a powerful psychological ploy to influence his decision.

They turned south once more, and drove past densely wooded hills and extensive farmland areas before entering St. Pierre, and finally the heart of the city. The temporary offices of the Community Health Center were situated in an upstairs suite above a furniture store and next to a small hotel and restaurant. From the windows of the office suite, Philip could look along the busy mainstreet and its stores and get a rough idea of the essential character of the city. It was one of low buildings: two or three storey buildings for the main part and four storeys at most. It was somewhat reminiscent of Edwardia during the early fifties, before the taller buildings of ten to twenty floors began to appear one by one, until now there were entire blocks of tall apartment buildings and office complexes (but no skyscrapers as yet).

After Philip was introduced to Beryl Farnham, a pleasant young lady who was Appleton's secretary, and Dr. Bob Gaylord who appeared to be the assistant director, Appleton suggested that he drive his visitor around town. Since it was such a perfect day, Philip said he'd prefer to walk and they set off along Coburn Street, St. Pierre's main thoroughfare. Even though they were quite close to the steel plant and its tall stacks, there was no evidence of smoke and grime, and the air smelled fresh and clean. The stores, in general, were smaller than those of Edwardia but otherwise quite comparable, and the roadway and sidewalks were uncluttered and unpolluted.

They walked down to the waterfront and past the railroad area to the imposing compound of West Cambrian Steel. Thousands of automobiles were parked in the employees' parking lot, and there were company railway engines and freight cars unloading iron ore from the north shore of Lake Superior. There were also company lake freighters tied up at the extensive docks, unloading coal from company mines in Pennsylvania. It was an impressive sight, and Philip was struck by the fact that the city's industrial base didn't exact its price by belching forth filth into the streets, air and water of St. Pierre.

After a sandwich lunch, his host and guide drove Philip to the two hospitals, one Catholic and one Protestant, separated by less than a block. They were located in the residential part of town and well away from the commercial area. St. Matthew's Hospital looked brand new, and had obviously been completely updated in the recent past. By contrast, the Broughton Hospital looked much older and still needed to be brought up to date in order to match its gleaming sister institution. Philip couldn't help noting, as he looked around, how many trees there were on most of the streets, and how the city fathers had taken precautions to preserve green areas across the entire length and breadth of St. Pierre Dulac – named after Frère Jean St. Pierre, the Jesuit explorer who established one of the first Catholic missions and schools for the Canadian Indians in this area.

That evening, Philip was invited to dinner with the Appletons at their small home in the east end of town, two blocks past a golf course. The director's wife, Beth, proved to be an intelligent and gracious hostess. She poured drinks for the two men, introduced their lively children, two girls and a boy, and it was obvious from her girth that there would soon be another addition to the family. The interior of the house was tastefully furnished in American Colonial style and it was apparent that Beth Appleton was a true daughter of the South, hailing from Georgia and thoroughly steeped in American history. Like her husband, who came from Virginia, she was a socialist and an idealist who shared his attitudes about medical service to the community.

After dinner, which was simple but delicious, Philip's host related the early history of the Community Health Center, with occasional comments and additions from his wife. Over the past ten years there'd been an increasing state of conflict between the steelworkers and the local doctors. The periodic union contract included coverage of medical insurance premiums with the Global Life Company; unfortunately, this did not cover any extra-billing charges over and above the standard fee schedule, charges that got heavier and more widespread each year. In an effort to absorb such additional costs, each new union contract included a corresponding increase in fee coverage, but to no avail, since there was always further additional extra-billing by the doctors, with no reduction in the sums paid out of the patient's own pocket.

As this became more and more of a no-win situation, there was a strong movement for a union-sponsored health plan, with a group of doctors willing to work on a retainer system based on individual qualifications and experience. Such a system, which wasn't tied to the usual fee-for-service base, was similar to the Kaiser-Permanente plan, but had its grass roots in the mine contract groups of the United States.

The leader of the movement toward such a method of health service delivery was an American medical economist and devout socialist, Jonathan Grey of Detroit, where a prototype community Health Center had recently been set up, with a medical staff of ten doctors. The fearless protagonist of the Cambrian District Community Health Center was Bill Trevor, a tough-minded union leader who'd been a stubborn fighter for its successful initiation. His first act was to obtain official blessings from the international office of the United Steelworkers of America. The second was the formation of a Board of Directors of the Community Health Association, which was given a provincial charter by the Ontario government to act as a medical insurance organization, with a contract on a non-profit basis. It was to provide medical coverage for the families of enrolled members in the Health Plan. Those union members not enrolled would continue to obtain coverage under the Global 'Lifemed Plan' as before.

To act as Medical Director, the Board hired Jim Appleton, a man experienced in mine contract medical groups in the Pittsburgh area and a close friend of Jonathan Grey. The Director was authorized to engage the services of a medical group, consisting – initially – of thirteen physicians and surgeons, with a base of six G.Ps, two surgeons, an obstetrician-gynecologist, an internist, a pediatrician, an anesthetist and a radiologist.

Appleton moved up to St. Pierre with his family and immediately tried to engage local medical personnel to fill vacancies in the new group practice, but encountered only hostility and obstructionism. This entrenched attitude of opposition extended to the managerial and supervisory personnel of the steel plant, the lawyers, dentists and merchants of the city, and above all, the 'St. Pierre Gazette', run by the entrenched Grogan family. Any derogatory statements made about the new 'Union Clinic' were reported in the local paper with obvious enthusiasm, then reprinted in the Toronto papers.

"I'm telling you all this, Dr. Bosnar, so you'll have some idea of what you'll be up against. I wouldn't want you coming here under false pretenses."

"I realize there will probably be a lot of antagonism to face before getting the Center to function smoothly. Do you have any plans to combat this antagonism?"

"I've been here for the past year, and I've done everything possible to get friendly relations with the city doctors and the two hospitals. In fact my first attempt at recruitment was with the local doctors, but they all turned me down, sometimes with a fair amount of unnecessary abuse."

"How about the Ontario College and the provincial Medical Association?"

"My husband likes to downplay their hostility but it's no secret that they're solidly against the Center."

The revelations continued until 11 o'clock, and by the time Philip left they were on a Jim, Beth, and Phil basis. Jim drove him to the hotel and they arranged to meet there for breakfast the following morning.

Before leaving St. Pierre for his return trip, Philip visited the Clinic building, located near the western end of town. It was still under construction, and it was hoped that it would be ready for business by September the 1st, the promised date. He went over the blueprints with Appleton and had some suggestions for the layout of the surgical department and minor O.R.; the fact that it would adjoin the X-ray department was a big plus, while the location of the building interested him.

"Tell me, Jim, what made you choose this place for the Clinic?"

"I'm glad you asked, Phil. Our application to locate the building across the street from the two hospitals was turned down by City Council. The reason given was that it would create a traffic hazard because of all the patients driving to and from our building. Actually, this area here may turn out to be the better one in the long run. Quite a few people believe this place will be the center of town within the next ten years."

Philip's plane left on time and he wondered what he would say to Patty when he got back. He'd given Appleton a provisional affirmative, promising to confirm it by letter as soon as possible, and he owed it to the director not to keep him waiting too long.

When he got back to Edwardia, he gave Patty all the details of his trip, and somewhat to his surprise, she didn't appear upset in any way. She just asked him what the city of St. Pierre was like and he lied, quite deliberately.

"Well, Patty, I don't have to tell you what a steel city is like. Just think of a smaller version of Pittsburgh and you've got the picture."

"Is the air clean or did you see smog?"

"There was no smog while I was there."

"How about the streets and buildings. Were they grimy and blackened or were they clean?"

"They were clean enough, I guess."

"And the hospitals?"

"The Catholic hospital looks brand new and the Protestant hospital needs a bit of renovation, but they're both up to standard."

"Then we're going, darling, and don't try to fool me."

"I can't ask you to leave this glorious part of Canada and our daughter and friends while I build up a new career and face new antagonisms. It hardly seems worth it."

"You know you're just dying to meet a new challenge, and Edwardia has little more to offer. You've done all you could to improve surgical standards in this part of the country and in return you've held most of the important positions. Now you can leave with an excellent record behind you and the possibility of some genuine pioneering ahead of you."

"Thanks, darling. You've echoed some of my own thoughts. I'm fifty years old now, and it's time for a change, a new objective. The money is quite acceptable and I have an opportunity to mold the clinic along the lines I believe in. I'll write Appleton tomorrow and finalize my acceptance."

Florian was able to come over and stay with them quite frequently. She had no desire to come to Ontario with her parents and they could hardly blame her. She was doing well with her modelling and was deeply in love with a young man who was in charge of display at Eaton's in Vancouver. They were hoping to get married some time in the near future if all went well, and after the Bosnars met him at their home once or twice they approved of the match.

Now, all that was left was to wind down the practice by August and leave Patty behind to sell the house, auction off some of the furniture, arrange to leave some for Florian, and have the rest of their possessions shipped out. It wouldn't be easy to leave this delightful place, but home, after all, is where the heart is, and many of their thoughts were already with the distant city of St. Pierre and its new Health Center.

The past two years had been a roller coaster of emotional highs and lows and needed to be put into perspective. What had been happening during this time in the world around them?

Adolph Eichmann, kidnapped by the Mossad in '60, was tried and found guilty in a Jerusalem court, then executed last year.

Algeria obtained its independence under the leadership of Ben Bella, combining Islam and Socialism with an abiding hostility to the West. Would other Moslem regimes follow this example?

Willy Brandt, the immensely popular Mayor of Berlin, used his type of Socialism to make West Germany a staunch ally of the West, and his own preference to form a close friendship with John Kennedy.

The Shah of Iran announced his official recognition of the State of Israel, in keeping with his attempts to bring his country out of the dark ages. For his pains, he was viciously attacked by the fundamentalist opposition and threatened by an outraged Nasser.

On the medical front there had been some sensational advances, especially in the field of biochemistry.

The three-dimensional structure of myoglobin (the muscle's oxygen-carrier) had been defined by X-ray analysis, and the structure of DNA as well as the mechanism of protein construction was becoming elucidated in striking detail.

The importance of autoimmunity was revealed in the etiology of an increasing number of diseases; the value of ultrasound as a diagnostic weapon was clearly demonstrated and the implantable cardiac pacemaker had become a practical reality.

Philip Bosnar felt truly blessed to be living in such an exhilarating scientific era, and privileged to be a part of the headlong rush of modern history.

CHAPTER 43

1927-28

This was a year when the whole world seemed to be holding its breath, yet life in Grantham Square had never been more serene. At fourteen going on fifteen, he was still much too small for his age and greatly troubled with a persistent acne that seemed to resist the lotions supposed to be an absolute cure. At least the little metal blackhead remover did in fact remove blackheads, but it failed to slow the onslaught of this facial affliction in new areas. Perhaps this was emblematic of a transition toward manhood. As it started to clear, he was ready to start the daily shaving routine that would represent his rite of passage into the real adult world, where men were men and sought out their women.

He often wondered what it would be like to be with a girl of his own age, to be involved in a love affair and true sexual union. Perhaps, like too many chocolates, he should avoid such thoughts lest they aggravate his acne, quite apart from bringing on unwanted and unfulfilled erections. The day would come within the next year or two when he might be ready for such an encounter, but it had to be the right girl and the right opportunity. He knew all about the primary obligation of the male to avoid getting the female pregnant, by taking the appropriate precautions, and made himself a promise that he would never be guilty of careless dereliction. At least, for the present he hadn't encountered any young female who could arouse his passions, and perhaps in his present inadequate size and facial eruption it was just as well; next year might well be different, but matriculation came first, beyond all romantic or carnal considerations.

He began to take a greater interest in his parents' friends and other people who crossed their day-to-day life. First there were the Kaludins who were business friends of his Dad. Mr. Kaludin was a religious orthodox Jew who spoke English with great difficulty but was a kind and gentle man with a genuine love for the Bosnar family. Aside from her religious orthodoxy, his wife was the very opposite of her husband. She was highly intelligent, spoke perfect English with cultured accent, and was enormously ambitious for their only daughter Miriam, a year older than Pauline. Miriam was as plain as Pauline was beautiful, but she had an alert mind and strong views of her own.

Philip always enjoyed his conversations with Miriam, and he never betrayed her secret failure to share the strict orthodoxy of her parents and the fact that she went through the motions in order to avoid offending them. She was hoping to get a degree in oriental languages and perhaps land a professorship later on. Philip hoped she'd achieve her ambition, and even more, that she would meet the right man some day, one who could see her inner beauty and fall in love with her, God willing!

Arthur Friedman was always a popular visitor to their home. Despite his Jewish heritage, he was the personification of a true Aryan as described by the Nazi genetic doctrinaires; tall and strongly built, with very fair hair, brilliant blue eyes and perfect Nordic features. His elderly parents, still living, had escaped from the recurrent pogroms of Czestokova in the Russian-controlled Poland of the Tzars, bringing their infant son with them to the land of opportunity and tolerance. He in turn fulfilled their ambitions for him by working his way up, through scholarship after scholarship, to become an analytical chemist at Shell Industries.

For years he'd been employed at projects far below his capacities, until he forced the issue by gaining a D.Sc. degree for original work on lubricants, and now he was chief of the department of motor oils in the main branch of Shell Laboratories. Despite his imposing appearance he was a very sick man who suffered from recurrent kidney stones, and he often had to enter London's famous St. Peter's Hospital for treatment. The progressive affliction had already cost him one kidney and countless hours of agonizing pain.

Philip loved to spend time and converse with this fine individual, whose intelligence and eloquence were an inspiration. Friedman was knowledgeable on a wide range of topics, totally broadminded on matters of religion and politics, but – until recently – had never considered marriage. Now, at the age of forty-one, he'd met the woman of his dreams while on a business trip to Geneva. She, too, was an industrial chemist and was Swedish by birth and heritage; her photo showed her to be a very attractive young lady. Friedman hoped to marry her in September and the wedding would take place in Stockholm, at the home of the bride's family. Perhaps that was just as well, since he was marrying a Gentile and wished to spare his Hasidic parents any undue pain. The entire Bosnar family loved this wonderful man, strong yet gentle, robustly built yet in truth a semi-invalid, and they were delighted with the news of his forthcoming wedding.

Mr. and Mrs. Laskovitch, who lived in the Maida Vale district with their two daughters, were great favorites of the Bosnars. The father was an immensely strong man, with giant forearms and fists like hams, and his gruff exterior concealed a very kind heart. It was said that when he was a young man in Cracow it was the drunken ruffians and Cossacks who fled from him during the pogroms rather than the other way around. He was invited to join a small gang of local Jewish thugs who weren't above terrorizing their own people, but chose instead to come to England, raise a religious family and become a successful jeweller with offices in fabled Hatton Gardens. The resplendent gold-plated pocket watch that Philip's father gave him for his Barmitzvah came, like most items of his family's jewelry, from Mr. Laskovitch, always at the most reasonable prices.

Mrs. Laskovitch was the perfect wife for this modern Samson; she was a large, jolly woman with a wonderful sense of humor and a loud, infectious laugh. The two daughters were great favorites with Pauline and Philip. Rosa, aged eighteen, was a natural comedienne, the life of any party and popular with boys, while Lily, aged twenty, was the quiet and thoughtful one. (*Yet oddly enough it was Lily who would be the one to marry first and Rosa to marry much later*). Their mother was a wonderful cook and a gracious hostess and both daughters inherited these characteristics. Their future husbands were to be envied.

Sadie Cohen and Fanny Perlmutter were two dear old maids in their middle fifties, who lived together in a small flat in the Victoria Park area, and who were always made welcome whenever they invited themselves for dinner in the Bosnar home. They were quaint and oldfashioned, hilariously eccentric, and with the oddest views on everything from unprocessed vegetarian diets to what they called, "healthy clothing". Philip found them quite entertaining, and whenever they invited him out for afternoon tea, – usually cucumber or watercress sandwiches with scalding hot tea and lemon – they made sure he showed not the slightest lapse of table manners.

"Good manners," they never tired of telling him, "are the only true mark of a gentleman." Much as he liked them and enjoyed their offbeat behavior he had to acknowledge that they were probably lesbians; yet somehow that realization in no way affected his regard for them. His parents, who'd no doubt reached the same conclusion many years ago, had exactly the same attitude, while Pauline simply found the whole situation hilarious.

'Old Mandy' was their loyal and perennial charwoman who came every week, rain or shine, and turned their orderly and spotless home upside down; so that at the end of her labors, after hours of energetic scrubbing on hands and knees, the house could once more look as orderly and spotless as when she started. She was ugly beyond description and wore a multilayered set of ragged clothes that belonged to the brush of a Hogarth and the pen of a Dickens. Yet his beloved Mum, the acknowledged feudal duchess of the Bosnar family, treated her with respect and consideration, and invariably made her sit down at the kitchen table for lunch or the occasional cup of tea. It was a true lesson in noblesse oblige and one he could never forget.

Mandy was Cockney to the core and tough as nails, and she adored the Bosnar family. She was notorious for her Saturday night bottle fights outside the pubs of Whitechapel. The ritual was time-honored and stylized. Each female combatant grabbed a handful of her opponent's hair with one hand and wielded a broken bottle with the other. The fight was considered over when one or the other cried "Enough!" and if the fight still continued the two would be pulled apart and disarmed by the respectful onlookers. Old Mandy bore her scars on face and arms with the same panache as a Heidelberg student with his saber-cut. There was probably not a single house surgeon in the London Hospital Casualty Department who didn't know this old warrior almost as well as the Bosnars did.

Mr. Tilson, known by the fearful residents of Grantham Square as "The Antisemite", descended upon this enclave of Lord Tredegar's vast London estate on the first Monday of each month, and his heavy knock on the door struck terror into the heart of anyone delinquent with the rent. He was tall and broad, ramrod straight, red-faced and goodlooking in a hard military manner, like a Roman Centurion. He walked with a limp, the result of a war wound for which he'd received a medal, and on his left cheek he had a purple `Port Wine Stain' with which he'd been born and which darkened when he was angered. As he limped along with his strong purposeful stride, the leather satchel at his side, suspended by a shoulder strap, bounced against the hip of his disabled leg with a rhythmic slap. Philip's fearless Mum always greeted him in person when she heard his knock, with a polite smile and a request that he wipe his shoes carefully on the mat before entering her home.

He was always most respectful and asked how she was, how was Mr. Bosnar and how were the children. She in turn would ask him about his own family and showed genuine interest in his answers. She would invite him to sit down and have some tea with her and he always accepted with gratitude. The subject of overdue rent never seemed to came up, and Mr. Tilson was always intrigued by the little French expressions she allowed to slip out whenever she was putting on her aristocratic act. Finally, when she signalled it was time for him to leave, she would say in the most casual manner, "By the way, Mr. Tilson, I believe we owe you some rent, would next month be agreeable?"

"Any time that's convenient Mrs. Bosnar," he'd reply in the most pleasant tone of voice, and Philip knew he would cover the deficit himself until the arrears were made good – and of course they always were. Whatever his mother's magic spell with people like this, it always worked.

Philip's greatest disappointment toward the end of this year was his erstwhile idol, the reverend Doctor (Ph.D.) J.K. Goldbloom. His youngest son, Herzl, named for the father of Zionism, and the apple of his eye, had eloped with a SHIKSA, tragedy of tragedies! The distraught parents announced that their son was dead and invited all their friends to attend the funeral ceremony, with Goldbloom chanting the Kaddish, (the prayer for the dead), over his lost son. Not one member of the Bosnar family attended; Philip's idol had collapsed on the clay feet of outdated bigotry. The Bosnars all hoped that one day, when the young couple brought forth their offspring in the fullness of time, sanity and decency would be reborn and the sundered family reunited.

At about this time, Philip began to re-examine his recent negative feelings about Zionism, as more reports were beginning to filter through the press about a certain Adolph Hitler, leader of the National Socialist party in Germany and a maniacal racist who was driven by a desire to eradicate all 'inferior races' from Aryan Germany. Four years ago this evil man, aided by the fascist General Ludendorf, had attempted a takeover of the legitimate government by a violent 'Putsch'. The attempted armed coup was a miserable failure and Hitler was sentenced to a five year prison term.

According to reports emanating from Germany, the power of the Nazi network resulted in a comparatively short and comfortable period of incarceration for the prisoner, during which he was able to continue his political activities and write the first volume of his book, 'Mein Kampf'. Then, released after nine months, he was ready to resume his unholy mission.

The Nazi philosophy stated that the most important element of the State was a racially homogeneous population, 'Das Volk'; that it should be ruled by a single leader of the highest qualities, 'Der Führer' and that it should declare war on its three main enemies: Democratic government, Marxism, and most dangerous of all – the Jew. Meanwhile, few people seemed to be aware that a small corner of the European carpet was starting to smolder, and Philip felt that perhaps the western nations would all pay dearly one day for their blind complacency. After all, they argued, Europe was at peace, and the spirit of revenge following the Great War had been neutralized by the Treaty of Locarno and the U.S.-sponsored Dawes Plan. Yet, as he scanned the News Chronicle, the Evening Star and the Daily Worker, Philip had an uncomfortable feeling, almost a premonition, of impending disaster, and he wondered if he was destined to become a latterday Jeremiah, a modern prophet of doom.

To combat these feelings there were always the side-splitting comic antics of Mr. Kalman and Mr. Spielmann. His parents called the former "The Chinaman" because of his remarkable resemblance to a Chinese Buddha, and he was one of nature's true clowns, with countless tumbling acts and hilarious brushes with disaster, all contrived, and not unlike those of Buster

Keaton and Charlie Chaplin. Mr. Spielmann was called "The Cousin" because of his distant relationship to Philip's Dad, and his endless store of ad lib jokes kept them in stitches.

The Chinaman was a perennial bachelor, but they never felt very sorry for him, since
he was always in the company of the most attractive women, loved parties and loved children;
Pauline and Philip had always been two of his favorites and he enjoyed performing for them. As for
The Cousin, the funnier his jokes the more his wife refused to laugh and scolded him for what she
called his "foolishness". When she was unable to control herself and burst out laughing, she could
have murdered him for breaking through her defenses. Philip thought The Cousin could have become one of the leading comedy writers of Yiddish literature, and felt that – for the most part – he
was casting his pearls before swine; yet he was one of the happiest men he ever met in his life.

Philip had one severe addiction, and that was the cinema. That was where he spent
most of his allowance each week, and he'd become a true film connoisseur. It was a matter of pride
for him to memorize not only the names of the lesser actors, but the director, the script writer, the
make-up artist and even the entire musical score. It made him feel quite flattered that the foremost
film critic, Eric Dunstan of the Star, praised the same films that he liked and downgraded those he
disliked. As far as Philip was concerned, the greatest directors were the legendary D.W.Griffiths,
Cecil B.de Mille, and the German genius, Fritz Lang. It was a pity that Griffiths's epic 'Birth of a
Nation' seemed to extoll the virtues of the notorious Ku Klux Klan, since that detracted from his
greatness. As for Philip's favorite actors, they were Richard Barthelmess, Emil Jannings, the inimitable Chaplin and the incomparable Garbo.

The musical scores he enjoyed most, even back in the days of the solitary piano im-
proviser, were those based on the classics: the pathos of a Humoresque, the drama of a Grieg Piano
Concerto, the tragedy of a Tchaikovsky Pathetique, the terror of a Night on Bald Mountain. The
wondrous combination of visual story, inspiring sound and gripping plot transported him out of the
everyday world and expanded the horizons of his emotional imagination. He could identify with
the heroes, fight the villains, make love to the heroines, and weep for the victims of grim tragedy.
The silver screen opened up an expanding world of vicarious experience and helped him to augment his reading with conceptual imagery and the inner sound of mood music. It was no use pretending: at heart Philip Bosnar was an incorrigible dreamer.

His next birthday would be his fifteenth. He was still much smaller than he wished
and yet his inner self was growing in strength and in confidence. He no longer experienced those
feelings of rivalry and conflict with his sister but felt, instead, a sense of concern and responsibility
for her safety and well-being, one that involved a willingness to fight on her behalf if necessary.
There were similar feelings of protective responsibility toward his mother, and he was aware that
his changing sense of perspective within the family group represented a subtle change toward true
conceptual manhood and adult commitment.

April the ninth 1938, his fifteenth birthday! Now at last he knew that real honest-to-
goodness manhood was entering his body and replacing his boyhood. He began to feel an urgency
about his obligations and the necessity to help out in the financial problems of the family. Unless he
could pass his matriculation exams in the coming year with honors, and with marks that would
guarantee him obtaining scholarships to continue his studies, he must be prepared to go out and

earn a living: but doing what? He hadn't even made up his mind definitively about his chosen career in the event of being able to continue his education.

The English language, its complexities and nuances, fascinated him, yet he couldn't aspire to become a writer; that required a special talent and a wealth of experience. Besides, it so often entailed many years of abject poverty and dependency. The Law was attractive, with its use of the spoken word in the courtroom to attain ones objective; but was the objective consistent with justice, or was it only a matter of the more astute advocate winning his case at all odds, without regard to the merits and justice of the verdict? It was a troublesome thought. How about a career in the diplomatic service, one in which a sound knowledge of modern languages could be put to good use? That was a distinct possibility, but it would be a long haul and he wouldn't be blessed with the almost mandatory background of a schooling at Eton's or Harrows and a University degree from Oxford or Cambridge.

During the past year it had been science rather than the arts that beckoned him with its irresistible siren song. The incredible advances in atomic physics, in synthetic chemistry – especially organic chemistry – and the awesome advances in medicine; these were attractive fields in which to consider a career, and he was tempted to commit himself along these lines. In the end he felt sure it would narrow down to a decision between Law and Medicine and he felt equally sure that by the time of his matriculation his mind would be made up, once and for all. As for the opposite sex, he knew he was physically more than ready for a serious liaison, yet his involvement must be tempered by the responsibilities that were falling upon him and which he welcomed as his due in this year of his established manhood.

The world was getting smaller, and events that were happening in far off lands seemed much closer at hand. The thrilling solo flight of a young American named Charles Lindbergh, across the Atlantic Ocean to Le Bourget Airport in France and into the hearts of a cheering French multitude, meant that, like Philip's own mature status, Man's flight had come of age and his planet had shrunk quite measurably. What the airplane had accomplished in the air, the wireless of Marconi was also accomplishing in the radio-waves of their atmosphere, and news could travel that much faster from the remotest corners of the earth.

On the world's political scene, Josef Stalin had consolidated his position by getting rid of his last former supporters, Trotsky and Zinoviev, now seen only as rivals and therefore consigned to exile and probably to eventual death. Thus, the socialist dreams of Marx, Engels and Lenin had ended in totalitarian dictatorship, and emancipation of the 'proletarian' masses vanished into a police state, with Siberian exile or worse for those who dared to rebel.

As an ideological conservative, Philip Bosnar abhorred the Stalin regime, yet in some ways he couldn't help feeling even more fiercely opposed to the fascist dictatorships that appeared to be springing up all over the world – and were hardly a happy alternative to the Soviet system. He valued the concept of a democratic society, he believed in free enterprise and honest competition, yet he deplored class privilege and racial, religious, or social intolerance. It was now almost ten years since the end of the Great War: were they now entering into a new era, one of international stability and peace?

When Philip was twelve years old, the Treaty of Locarno between Britain, France, Belgium, Italy and Germany was hailed as the gateway to a millenium, in which mankind could at long last aspire to the intellectual status of Homo Sapiens rather than merely Homo Erectus. What had been the results of this treaty so far? The French Foreign Minister, Monsieur Briand, had been awarded the Nobel Peace prize; the German Foreign Minister, Herr Stresemann, had gained Germany's entrance into the League of Nations and a permanent seat on its prestigious Council, (as well as the withdrawal of foreign troops from the Rhineland!) As for the British Foreign Secretary, Austen Chamberlain had become instantly recognizable across the world as the polished paragon of English diplomacy, with his faultless diction and ubiquitous monocle.

This year, the American Secretary of State was working with his French counterpart to formulate a new treaty, the Kellogg-Briand Pact. It would be a worldwide multilateral pledge to 'renounce war as an instrument of national policy'. Were these more high-sounding but empty phrases in which rhetoric substituted for honest commitment, or were we in truth emerging from the dark ages? The questions multiplied, but only history could provide the answers. Philip devoutly believed in an optimistic philosophy, yet he was not unaware of the incredible dangers of a blind and ignorant euphoria which could fly in the face of reality.

(Ten years later a simpering British Prime Minister would wave a sheet of paper at the cheering crowds and promise them "PEACE IN OUR TIME".)

CHAPTER 44

Retrospective and Prospective

The journey to St. Pierre without his beloved Patty was a lonely but unforgettable one, and since he was in no particular hurry, Philip decided to take an entire week, enjoying the changing scenery and getting his mind clear for the forthcoming challenge. In addition, the leisurely pace of the drive enabled him to reflect on some of the most memorable aspects of his fourteen years of life and practice in Edwardia. With a broad smile on his face he thought of the radiology brothers and their incredible antics.

Charles Faversham and his brother, Dick, were two of the finest comedians he'd ever met. They were both radiologists, and while Dick always looked as if he had something hilarious on his mind, Charlie's appearance was that of a minister preparing a somber sermon for his flock, especially when he was devising some outrageous practical joke. Philip had experienced the ingenuity of their humor at both first and second hand on more than one occasion. Thus, for example, there was the time they hired a professional actor to assume the role of a federal health planner from Ottawa who had just arrived in Edwardia to address the Medical Society membership on Ottawa's plans for State Medicine.

The script of his address was written with fiendish wit by the Faversham brothers in a manner that was sure to arouse the greatest wrath from the outraged listeners. The bogus expert extolled the salary system for doctors, and with feigned relish, said he looked forward to the day when all doctors served the public as civil servants. By the time the audience was ready to assemble a lynch mob, the actor took off his pince-nez, his false beard and mustache, and introduced himself to the meeting as a hired actor. The Favershams came forward and apologized to the membership for the practical joke and everybody laughed and applauded with genuine enthusiasm: everybody except John Kinsley, who stomped out of the room, his face darkened with unremitting anger.

There was the time when old Steve Finnegan decided he should retire. He was an ancient leprechaun of a man whose great loves of his life were his operative surgery, his Catholic faith, whisky, cigarettes, and his native Ireland, though not necessarily in that order. As the centerpiece of the retirement party, the brothers-in-mischief had fashioned a contrived life story, complete with slides, movie clips, and mood music. Accompanying the presentation was a narration by Charlie, delivered with great solemnity and authority, with only the faintest trace of an underlying giggle.

The assembled doctors were shown scenes of the birth of 'Stefan Finikovsky' in the city of Minsk, surrounded by the scores of Russian peasants who were his doting relatives. In the background there was the stirring music of a Cossack choir singing traditional Russian Orthodox music, while an imposing priest in magnificent robes conducted the baptismal ceremonies. There were scenes of the baby growing up to be a boy, each with Finnegan's ancient face, then a teenager, still with Finnegan's ancient face, and finally, a young man with Finnegan's ancient face taking leave of his family and friends in Minsk, with the sound of balalaikas in the background playing Russian folk music.

Next, he was shown on an endless train of the Trans-Siberian railroad, as it traversed the vast frozen steppes on its way westward. The audience then saw him on a large ship, crossing the Atlantic in company with hordes of other steerage passengers. They witnessed his arrival in New York under the welcoming gaze of the statue of Liberty, a lady who wasn't above giving him a friendly wink.

They were treated to a detailed review of his progress in the New World, starting with his adoption by an Irish-American family who later moved to Canada. They were told how he trained to become a hospital orderly, then studied to become a veterinarian but couldn't stand the smell of animals, so he becomes a surgeon instead. His move to the west coast was faithfully chronicled, along with his decision to change his name to Stephen Finnegan.

The Sisters at St. Peter's Hospital were shown delighted to have an Irish son of the faith on their medical staff, and he soon rises to the top. Even so, he continues to take annual postgraduate trips in order to keep abreast of the latest advances in technique. At this point they were shown a picture of their hero wearing little more than a Hawaiian lei, closely surrounded by an amorous group of bare-bosomed beauties in similar attire.

This masterpiece of collage brought the house down, and the presentation concluded in a wild uproar of applause, laughter and congratulations. It was a brilliant piece of work, and must have taken weeks of intense preparation on the part of the Favershams. Above all, it was a true labor of love.

The third occasion recalled by Philip as his purring Jaguar consumed the miles of his long drive, took place only six months ago, and it involved Dick Faversham as the stage manager and Philip Bosnar as the intended victim. Dick asked him to be guest speaker at the annual meeting of the Radiographers' Society and he reluctantly accepted. When he enquired what kind of subject Dick had in mind he promised to let him know in good time.

One week before the meeting he told Philip it was to be a humorous address, and as an example, he gave him a copy of the previous year's address given by his brother, the inimitable Charlie. It was entitled 'The See-through Machine' and was all about a mythical new type of X-ray machine that could see through brick walls and even penetrate lead, but unfortunately blasted everything and everybody in range with lethal radiation. It was hoped that Model 2 would cut down on some of these undesirable side effects, and succeeding models even more so. The whole speech was outrageous but it was black humor at its very finest.

How in God's name, Philip complained, could anyone be expected to follow an act like that!? He began to feel uneasy about the entire prospect but realized he could hardly back down, so he started a desperate search for a suitable subject but kept coming up empty. Two days before the meeting he decided on his title: 'A surgeon's son brings up his father on the facts of life and more'. Not exactly side-splitting but it might just work.

The fatal evening arrived and the dignified chairman of the meeting, after disposing of some routine duties, asked Dr. Richard Faversham to introduce the guest speaker. Dick was in fine form and launched with great relish into a fabricated story of Philip Bosnar's life and background, alternating at times with a minimum of true fact. He commenced with an account of his birth in Paris, France, where he was raised by a maiden aunt who was one of France's leading Can-Can dancers. He continued with Philip's education in England and training as a surgeon before coming to B.C, then went on with a list of his numerous accomplishments in such esoteric fields as cribbage, checkers, and tiddlywinks.

The further he got, the more hysterical the audience became, and some of the laughter was getting out of hand. Faversham's wife, sitting next to him, gave him a look that could kill as she comprehended the deep hole he was gleefully digging for Philip, while poor Patty threw her husband a glance of pure desperation, wondering what the devil he could do to follow this side-splitting stuff. The introduction drew to a merciful close as Dick concluded, "Last but not least, at the recent International Yo-yo Championships in Toledo, Ohio, our versatile guest speaker took top honors. It is with great pleasure that I give you a man whose name is a household word..." Dick leaned over to read the name-card in front of Philip, "I give you Dr. Philip Botulus," and sat down to a pandemonium of applause.

Philip waited until the last sound had faded into silence before rising to address the audience.

"Mr. Chairman, Ladies and Gentlemen, permit me on your behalf to propose a hearty vote of thanks to Dr. FlavourHam for his most amusing address," and sat down. There was a momentary embarrassed silence, then loud clapping as the audience and Chairman realized the guest speaker had just turned the tables on his witty friend, and showed its approval. Only then did Philip go ahead with his prepared speech, and – by the grace of God – his listeners were now conditioned to laugh at each humorous phrase in his address, far more than it deserved, and much to Patricia's relief.

He drove up through Roger's Pass and stayed overnight at the town of Golden, before crossing over into Alberta and taking in the matchless grandeur of the Rockies at Banff. As he drove through the breathtaking scenery he thought of the many episodes which had enriched his professional life in Edwardia and enlarged his understanding of the broader problems in his profession, with their relationship to the public at large. He'd left the plush-lined rut of surgical practice in the land of lotus eaters and was on his way to join a controversial Health Center, with the prospect of facing some deeply entrenched antagonisms from the very outset; yet he felt exhilarated rather than apprehensive.

What sort of conservative was he? he mused. He believed devoutly in the free enterprise system but shared some of the social values and concerns of the political left. He opposed the rigid and inhumane autocracies of communism, but that didn't blind him to the crimes against humanity perpetrated by the fascist regimes of South America, Asia and the rest of the world.

He grimaced as he thought of the insatiable political ambitions of Reg Asquith, a recent arrival from England who was a vitriolic rabble-rouser against anything that smacked of "Commie-style Medicine." He was a clever internist who'd risen through the ranks in Edwardia and the C.M.A. (Canadian Medical Association). He had mounted his crusade against any National Health Insurance Plan controlled by `Big Government', and told the doctors what they wanted to hear, first in their own city, then their province and eventually in the entire nation. He knew the art of effective public speaking and could rally the large majority of doctors against the threat of `State-controlled Socialized Medicine'.

Philip remembered the joint meeting of the British and Canadian Medical Associations held in Edinburgh at the end of July, 1959. It had been a gala affair and a resounding triumph for Dr. Peter Banks, joint President of high repute and a fugitive from Britain's state medicine to the freedom and beauty of Canada's Pacific shores. Even the weather cooperated, and the sun was never brighter nor the temperature warmer than during that week in Scotland's proudest city. Like many of his Canadian colleagues who attended the meeting, Philip was entranced by the splendors of Edinburgh Castle and its parkland grounds, the Waverly Monument, Princes' Street, Holyrood Palace, King Arthur's Seat and the War Memorial. They were all prized targets for their clicking cameras as the weather smiled on the visiting photographers, and his own pictures turned out much better than anticipated.

On the second night Philip stayed in the city of Medicine Hat, and the following morning headed for the long journey across the southern prairies. He couldn't help chuckling as he recalled the unexpected letter that arrived last October from his former pal, Skinny Thompson. Skinny had, for reasons that were not explained, decided to leave Britain and come to Canada. Since he understood that Philip was 'in a position of considerable professional influence in British Columbia,' (although he didn't reveal his sources of information), would he please try and secure a suitable appointment for him as head of a diagnostic radiology department in one of the major medical centers? The circle was now complete, yet Philip felt no particular satisfaction, only an overpowering desire to laugh at the absurdity of the whole affair and the unmitigated gall of Skinny Thompson, a friend of opportunity whose eye had never wandered too far from the main chance.

To salve his own conscience, Philip made a determined investigation of the opportunities in diagnostic radiology across the province before writing that there was nothing available at the present time. He had no intention of holding his breath for Skinny's reply, nor had he given more than a fleeting thought to writing a sardonic 'Thank you' for pre-empting him out of the Grant-Sutton job so many years ago, thus pointing his destiny toward his beloved Patricia Clancy and life in his adopted country, Canada.

The weather remained pleasant for the long and monotonous drive across Saskatchewan. Philip would like to have headed south for a quick tour of Vanwey but it was obvious he could hardly do that without at least some attempt to contact old friends. But that would have meant a stay of at least three or four days, so he stayed on course and headed for Manitoba.

On the third night he stopped at Brandon and had the car checked out the following morning. It was in great shape and was a real joy to drive; not only that but it was the object of great admiration by car buffs wherever he stopped for either gas, meals or accommodation.

As he drew ever nearer to his destination, he began to reflect on the degree of hatred and bigotry that could be aroused by the political aspects of medical practice. The Doctors' Strike of last July in Saskatchewan had been a filthy business, with appalling accusations and insults. There was even the denial of hospital privileges to doctors who opposed the strike or set up group practices under the government plan. Not a single rebuke came from the provincial College of Physicians and Surgeons, nor from the Medical Associations; on the contrary, the official bodies of organized medicine in Saskatchewan appeared to encourage the excesses of the striking doctors.

Even the Canadian Medical Association and Royal College of Canada failed to set any moral or ethical guidelines in the confrontation.

What should have been a civilized dispute between opposing viewpoints became a nasty war of slander, threats, and intimidation. Those who supported the provincial medical plan of the duly elected C.C.F. government were labelled as communists or worse, and the Saskatchewan newspapers fanned the flames of bigotry and political extremism. The pillars of the community who'd always been staunch opponents of labor unions – namely the business leaders, service clubs, and Chambers of Commerce – were now unrestrained in their support of the doctors' strike, and were guilty of exacerbating the intensity of conflict.

In the end, it was the doctors themselves who settled for a Provincial Medical Insurance Act similar in its most important elements to the original Act that precipitated the strike. What a shameful waste of human resources and communal harmony; what a squandering of the noble public image of the medical profession!

On the fourth night, Philip stopped at Kenora and spent an extra day touring the Lake of the Woods district and enjoying its serene beauty, before heading for Fort William on the western shore of Lake Superior. As he thought about his new appointment, Philip found it hard to understand the intensity of the antagonism toward the new community Health Center in Saint Pierre. It wasn't as if organized medicine in Ontario was facing a government takeover of provincial health insurance. It was simply a choice by the steelworkers between the private medical insurance plan, which had covered them so far and the new Community Health Center, which guaranteed total coverage without fear of any out-of-pocket charges outside the plan.

Unlike the Saskatchewan debacle, there could be no charge of strike-breaking applicable to this situation, and in fact, local doctors were the first to be invited into the clinic. Not only that, but the Health Center declared itself in favor of normal cross-consultation with the solo specialists. Nevertheless, when Philip applied to the Ontario College of Physicians and Surgeons for a license to practice in the province, the Deputy Registrar's reply was hostile and suggested that the College was none too happy with the propriety of the Community Health Center. The innuendo was unmistakable, and it was Philip's intention – at the earliest opportunity – to make the College and any other organized group opposing the clinic put up or shut up. If there were valid objections they should be dealt with openly and not by dark hints, whispers and elbow nudges.

The journey along the north shore of Lake Superior, once he left Fort William, with its view of the oblong hill on the offshore peninsula, so aptly named the 'Sleeping Giant', was disappointing. Philip had expected to see more of this magnificent inland sea of fresh water, but the visual access was rather restricted when one considered that this was part of the Canadian transcontinental highway.

When he reached the town of Wawa he took time to drive into the little harbor at Michipicoten in order to gaze across the vast expanse of water from which all the other great lakes derived their flow as far as Lake Ontario and ultimately emptied into the Gulf of St. Lawrence. That evening he feasted on delicious Lake Superior trout at the Wawa Inn and stayed there overnight.

The following morning he got off to an early start and headed south at a leisurely pace along Highway 17, fascinated by the multicolored rocks along the roadside and an occasional glimpse of the lakeshore far below to the right. This was awe-inspiring country, and close scrutiny revealed countless glimpses of the Canadian Shield. The colors were an artist's dream: the vivid reds, yellows and light browns of rocks and trees offsetting the brilliant turquoise, green and silver of shimmering water that stretched far to the west. This had to be the breathtaking backdrop which inspired the Group of Seven and still drew painters from every part of Canada.

By the time he entered the northern outskirts of 'San Pete' (as most of the people around this region seemed to call the city in preference to the French version), the earlier rain clouds had cleared and the city glowed clean and bright in the sun. Yesterday had been heavily overcast and the skies remained dark following the cloudburst over Dryden. Today, the warm sun on Philip's face put him into an upbeat mood. He checked in at a motel a short distance from the Community Health Center and phoned Dr. Appleton at his office number. They arranged to meet at the Center, and after a shower and change, Philip walked over and was impressed with the amount of new construction going on in the area surrounding the new clinic.

The Cambrian District Community Health Center was an impressive three-storey edifice with an attractive facade of light brown brick and white stone, with shrubs and lawn around the front and sides and a large parking area in the rear. Jim Appleton drove up in his Volkswagen Beetle and greeted Philip warmly before unlocking the door to the doctors' entrance and taking him on a grand tour of the interior.

On the ground floor there were offices and consulting rooms, with color-coded waiting rooms and adjoining nurses' and reception areas. In the surgical area there was a minor operating room as well as facilities for examination of the terminal colon by direct inspection, known as 'Sigmoidoscopy', with biopsy if necessary. In the center of the main stairwell there was a decorative central atrium stretching from skylighted roof to basement, with a large collection of polished rocks at the base, each about the size of a small melon and all collected from the surrounding area of the countryside.

There was a central reception area where patients picked up their routing slips and received directions to the different departments. Next to the surgical area was the X-ray department, and Philip was pleased to note that the radiology viewing room adjoined his designated consulting room. In the front western corner was the pediatrics department, and in the rear western corner was the laboratory, with washrooms next door. The basement housed the record rooms and secretarial offices, as well as physiotherapy and maintenance facilities.

On the second floor there were offices for family practice and internal medicine, obstetrics and gynecology. There was also a beautifully equipped optometry department, business offices, the Medical Director's offices and reception room. On the third floor there was a magnificent conference room and library, although there weren't many books so far. There was also a coffee room for non-medical staff, and additional washroom facilities. A roomy and well-designed elevator ran smoothly from basement to third floor and was easy to operate; in addition there was a back staircase supplementing the main stairwell.

It was hardly surprising that the clinic building had won the prestigious Massey Award for outstanding architectural design, and Philip shared Jim Appleton's pride.

"We've had our lumps, you know," the director told Philip ruefully. "A couple of months ago the foundations started to sink on the north side. There was great worry among the directors of the Community Health Association and wild rejoicing in the local Medical Society."

"My God, that must have caused your guys to hit the panic button."

"It sure did. Fortunately, the contractors picked up the problem early enough to take the necessary steps. They were able to prop up the subsiding corner, pour additional concrete and see to the insertion of deeper steel pilings before too much harm was done."

"That was a stroke of luck!"

"I guess we were lucky the whole basement didn't collapse. Even so, it cost the Association an extra one hundred thousand dollars, and we had to ask our subscribers to cough up an extra twenty-five dollars each, over and above their original contribution of one hundred and twenty-five dollars."

"How many subscribers do we have?"

"So far, we have forty-five hundred who've signed up out of a possible six thousand, and I guess we were lucky at that."

"How so?"

"There's been an enormous campaign against our Center and even the patients are feeling the pressure. The new doctors joining the clinic have been called all sorts of derogatory names, both by solo doctors to their patients and by reports in the news media, especially TV."

"What was actually said?"

"Our new medical recruits were called misfits and renegades. The president of the St. Pierre Medical Society appeared on TV to say we'd be ostracized socially if not professionally."

"It's amazing the way doctors can behave toward each other in this type of situation. I'm sure most of them are decent fellows, but on political issues they become unreasonable. Then they end up painting themselves into a corner from which they're unable to negotiate or at least compromise."

"Not only that but they get their wives thoroughly wound up and involve their friends and fellow-members in the various clubs and the cocktail circuit."

"What happens when the new doctors arrive and they run headlong into this unpleasant situation? Do you think they'll be scared off?"

"Let's face it, Phil. Some of our young guys will be scared off, some will leave when they've saved enough money to start on their own and some will leave when they disagree with our policies or direction."

"Well, Jim, I'd sooner have your pragmatic pessimism than an unrealistic pie in the sky attitude."

"Glad to hear it. After all, there aren't too many of us who are really committed to the ideas behind this Health Center, but with just a few strong ones among us, we'll survive."

There were a few workmen putting finishing touches to the interior of the building and they'd still be working when the place was opened for 'business' on Monday morning, September the 2nd, but would be through in time for the official opening ceremonies on the 16th. Beryl Farnham, Jim's indispensable Girl Friday, arrived to tell Philip she'd found a temporary residence for him on the eastern outskirts of the city. It turned out to be a really fine basement suite in a large house on the waterfront. It was owned by a widowed and motherly Italian lady who lived there with her son and grandson. The suite was roomy and well-furnished. It included a bedroom, bathroom, combined kitchen, dining room and large living room. There was even space for Philip's car in the double garage, which was a distinct bonus as he would hate to leave his gorgeous Jag out at night as an irresistible target for some covetous aficionado.

During the next few days Dr. Bosnar met some of the other clinic doctors who'd been arriving in town during the past week or two.

Alf Olmano was a large easy-going young man of Finnish stock, a native son of San Pete, and a man whose slow manner concealed a high intellect.

Mike Fowler was short and compact, serious and dedicated; he, too, was a native son of this city and it must have been difficult for these two to commence their professional lives as family physicians at the Center and face the enmity of their former school chums.

Ted Novak's family had fled Hungary after the Soviet invasion of '56 and it was soon obvious that he was the golden boy of the new group as far as Jim Appleton was concerned. He'd graduated from the medical school of Western University in London, Ontario, with high academic honors, and was a man of great European charm, a fine conversationalist with a forceful manner and keen sense of humor.

Bob Gaylord, an American, was the man Philip Bosnar had met previously when he flew out to see Appleton in May. Although he still behaved as if he were assistant Medical Director, it appeared that he held no such official position. Aside from Appleton, he was the oldest of the new G.Ps in the Center, and had served in the U.S. armed forces as senior lab technician in an army hospital.

Gordy Alsop was a sparrow-like young chap from the maritimes, very bright and cheerful, and the only unmarried member of the medical staff.

Mark Caplan was a handsome Jewish radiologist in his early forties. His dark good looks, brilliant toothy smile and jet black curly hair made him an instant favorite with all the females in the institution. He was a victim of multiple sclerosis and almost wheelchair-bound; nevertheless he was always joking and laughing and appeared to be quite irrepressible.

Tony Donovan, the Ob.Gyn. specialist, was an Englishman who'd only been in Canada for the past five years. He was the no-nonsense type who believed in getting on with the job at hand without frills or fanfare. He was short and stocky, with boyish good looks, and he walked as though marching on parade.

Stuart Atkins, the group's cardiologist and internist, had an impeccable background in his specialty, having trained in the world-famous cardiovascular department at the Cleveland Clinic. To look at, he projected the appearance of a chubby choirboy, with bright red cheeks and a happy outgoing manner.

Jack Grier, the group's anesthetist, was a thin, stooped, hasidic-looking Jewish chap who'd trained at the Mount Sinai Hospital in Toronto; he had an apologetic manner that made him the last sort of individual who could be expected to stand firm under pressure. Perhaps that was an unfair judgement, and only time would tell.

Last, but not least, there was Brigitte Fleischmann, the group's well-qualified pediatrician who came to Canada from Germany with her parents after World War 2, and who seemed an ideal recruit for the Health Center.

As for Gustave Pelletier, the other surgeon, he was taking his Canadian F.R.C.S. exams and wouldn't be joining them for a few months.

After settling comfortably in his new basement quarters on the waterfront, there were several items requiring Philip's prompt attention. Although he'd been granted interim privileges in general surgery at both hospitals it was now necessary for him to fill in the exact procedures he requested from a lengthy list covering all branches of surgery. On the advice of Jim Appleton, he included every single operative and related procedure he'd previously performed in Edwardia and waited for nature to take its course. Would there be calm acceptance by the power structure or would there be a major storm of objections? As it happened, there were quite a few items on the 'Laundry List' (the name he instantly appended to this document and would use forever after) that he wouldn't mind trading off for some new additions at some future time.

On the Thursday afternoon prior to the opening of the Center, Dr. Appleton introduced his medical staff members to the Sister Superior at St. Matthew's Hospital. She seemed very pleasant and gracious, yet Dr. Bosnar detected a certain indefinable chill in her attitude that told him they weren't the most welcome of strangers. They were invading the hitherto isolated tranquillity of the city's medical community which it was supposed to have been prior to the arrival of the new clinic. Dr. Bosnar wondered just how accurate that assessment was, and whether it had been – in actual fact – a sequestered hierarchy of sheltered practices and rigidly patterned referrals, without fear of unwanted intruders and with a captive patient population; under-doctored and under-serviced.

After fifteen minutes of polite but unconvincing cordiality they were turned over to an elderly Sister who showed them through the hospital from sixth floor to basement. The top two floors were the surgical wards, consisting of four-bed public rooms, two-bed semiprivate rooms and large single private rooms. Each floor had a central nurses' chart room, lounge, and conference room, plus a visitors' and patients' lounge.

The fourth floor was the operating suite, with a doctors' lounge and changing quarters, an anesthetic recovery room, a nurses' lounge and changing room, and five large and well-equipped operating rooms.

The third floor was the obstetrical department, and an annex at the rear of the building had been converted to an isolated psychiatric wing.

The second floor was for internal medicine, cardiology and pediatric cases and the first floor was for geriatric and longterm care patients.

Most of the first floor was assigned to the admitting department, the emergency and outpatient departments, the X-ray department and pathology labs.

The basement was huge and was fully utilized for physiotherapy, occupational therapy, nursing school, medical library, cafeteria and conference room, as well as the usual engineering, supplies, and maintenance areas.

There was an impressive Chapel that could be entered from the second floor or from a special staircase off the entrance, and the front of the hospital presented a most attractive facade to passing traffic on Crofton Street.

The doctors' parking lot was between the hospital front and the street's sidewalk, while the extensive visitors' parking lot was at the rear, with a view of the Lake, and unfortunately, of the Gulf Company oil tanks as well.

The next day the same routine was followed at the Broughton Memorial Hospital. They were introduced to the lay administrator, an elderly white-haired gentleman who was very pleasant but apologized that he was too busy to show them around the hospital. They gasped with disbelief and amazement when he handed them over to the JANITOR! for their tour, and Jim whispered to Philip that now they knew where they stood in the pecking order of this institution. Yet, to be fair, the facilities were similar to those of St. Matthew's, although the whole place had a dingy gray look quite unlike the sparkling brightness of its neighboring building. Its only advantage was the presence of a fine separate building, joined by basement tunnel, housing the nurses' residence and a large conference room for medical staff meetings.

It was hard to understand why these two hospitals, with such a history of mutual antagonism and mistrust, had the same doctors on the active medical staff of both institutions, instead of the far commoner custom of active staff on the one and associate staff on the other. It would make far more sense for the two hospitals, located within spitting distance of each other, to join together in one united organization, with a great saving in space and expense. *(In the fullness of time there would be many other incongruities that defied ones sense of reason even more; and were a testimonial to the ability of intellectual people to persist in their ingrained stupidities and sacrifice progress on the altar of prejudice.)*

At 10 a.m. on Monday, September the 2nd, 1963, with the sound of hammering and drilling both inside and outside the building providing the only fanfare, the Cambrian District Community Health Center opened its doors and the patients started filing in. All departments seemed to get into gear in reasonable time and manner, and as far as one could tell, there were no major snafus. There was one novel feature in the building, the Red Phone, a special brainchild of Appleton. The idea was that, when a patient was told to make another appointment with the family physician or a specialist in the group, he or she could pick up one of the many red phones on the first two floors and the appointment could be made and verified through a central office. When the patient returned and checked in at the reception desk, a routing slip would be available for the appropriate office at the appointed time.

Many of the patients were Italians and for Philip it was a nice feeling to get off on the right foot by addressing them in what he hoped was their native tongue: *"Buono giorno Signora. Avete dolore? Dove il daneggia? Per Quanto Tempo"* (Good-day Madam. How are you? Are you in pain? Where does it hurt you? How long have you had it?). This led to an early bond of mutual confidence, but he had to be careful that the patient didn't gallop off into a rapid Italian monologue beyond his slightest comprehension. As a rule, however, the patient would be encouraged by his linguistic courage to break into quite acceptable English and a bond of understanding was duly forged. He was glad he'd taken the trouble to coach himself into using these rudimentary phrases in Italian. His knowledge of pronunciation in this most musical of languages had come from the operas of Rossini, Donizetti, Verdi, Puccini and so many others from sunny Italy, and he practiced his Mediterranean diction with the aid of a small tape-recorder that he kept in his car.

On the afternoon of September the 3rd, Jim Appleton drove Philip Bosnar over to the office of Dr.Glenn Morecombe, Chief of Surgery at St. Matthew's Hospital, after phoning him ahead of time. With a sense of growing disbelief, Philip followed the director up two flights of dilapidated stairs that were covered with worn oilcloth of unrecognizable design; there was no elevator. When they got to the tiny waiting room, with a few ancient and rickety chairs and side tables, the receptionist ushered them into the consulting room.

Morecombe was sitting behind his desk and trying to look as important as possible; it seemed he was too busy writing in a small notebook to be bothered getting up. But he found it difficult not to take Philip's proffered hand when Jim introduced them. The busy surgeon now launched into a protracted account of his own training and qualifications, his army experiences in Britain during World War 2, and his difficulties in getting established as a surgical specialist in San Pete.

He was tall and thin, looked awkwardly folded up in an inadequate armchair, and had a lugubrious expression vaguely reminiscent of Stan Laurel; Philip wondered when he would meet his Oliver Hardy counterpart and had to suppress a desire to burst out laughing. It was obvious Morecombe was trying to prepare his surgical visitor for similar obstacles, presumably at the hospital level, with a pretense that this was standard fare for any new surgeon.

Philip's introduction to Dr. Herb Slater, Chief of Surgery at the Broughton Memorial Hospital, took place in the front lobby of that hospital on the following day. He was a somewhat rotund gentleman in his late fifties, rather short, red-cheeked and prosperous-looking. He seemed friendly enough but one got the impression that here was the traditional 'King of the Hill', one who wasn't afraid or suspicious of any newcomer as long as he himself remained in control of things.

The clinic surgeon had now met a major part of the professional power structure and in due course would encounter the political power base and the red-neck fanatics. The prospect didn't worry him unduly as he felt sure he could handle such people, given time, opportunity and firm determination.

This past year had been exceptionally eventful, and not just from a personal point of view. Early in the year, the last of the Soviet missiles were removed from Cuba, and the threatened millions in North America could breathe more easily. In April, Lester Pearson, the Bosnars' most unbeloved politician, became the new Prime Minister, and Canada was destined to draw still further away from her mother country, while the brilliant promise of the Diefenbaker years died not with a bang but a whimper.

In June, John Kennedy thrilled 150,000 Germans gathered at the West Berlin City Hall by declaring, "Ich bin ein Berliner." (I am a citizen of Berlin). It was two years since the Soviets erected the infamous Berlin Wall, following the disastrous failure of the Vienna summit meeting between Khrushchev and Kennedy.

In Britain, the government of Harold Macmillan was rocked by the Profumo scandal, in which the Secretary of Defense was found to be consorting with a 'high society prostitute' who was sharing her favors with a Russian naval attaché. To make matters worse, it was revealed that Kim Philby, former head of the Foreign Office's counter-intelligence division, had been working for the Soviets since the early '40s, and was the 'Third Man' who warned Burgess and Maclean to defect. It seemed that Britain's vaunted national security system was alarmingly insecure!

By contrast, on this continent matters seemed much more reassuring by the establishment of a telephone 'Hot Line' that could instantly connect the U.S. President with the Soviet leader in any emergency situation; and in October J.F.K. had signed a nuclear test ban treaty at the White House. Meanwhile, at a civil rights demonstration in Washington, the great Martin Luther King had aroused the conscience of racist America with the stirring words of a speech that resounded like a religious anthem.

"I HAVE A DREAM."

Book Three

Assault on the Ramparts

CHAPTER 45

1963

On his first Sunday morning call to the emergency department of the Broughton Memorial Hospital, Philip was the victim of either conscious or subconscious sabotage. Seated in a well-worn armchair of simulated leather at the nurses' desk, he was writing provisional orders for a patient who'd just been brought in for severe vomiting of blood from a known duodenal ulcer. The nurses were projecting mixed attitudes toward the new surgeon: some curiosity, some hostility and some admiration.

While he was pondering his orders, the head nurse balanced a dish of light amber liquid on the back of the left armrest, ostensibly because there was no room on the desk. As soon as Philip got up, the dish tipped over and emptied its contents down his pants. It seemed inappropriate to hurl accusations, so he took the incident in good grace with a smiling, "I sure hope this liquid isn't what I think it is!"

It turned out to be a harmless dilute solution of Phisohex. Everyone laughed and he felt he may have broken the ice and even made one or two valuable friends among the nursing staff. Needless to say, these hospital nurses had their own efficient grapevine.

Pending approval of Philip's application for privileges on the 'laundry list', he was instructed by both hospital administrations that it was mandatory to contact the Chief of Surgery before embarking on any operative procedure. This rule, he was informed, was so that – as a newcomer to the medical staff – he might be supervised by the Chief or his delegate. The first occasion was a young man who'd shot himself accidentally in the left elbow region while handling his loaded hunting rifle carelessly. He was admitted to the surgical ward of St. Matthew's under the care of Dr. Bosnar, who phoned Morecombe. The Chief of Surgery said he was tied up at the moment but would be sending someone else to watch the surgery.

After the customary preliminaries, the patient was taken up to the O.R. and put to sleep by Jack Grier. Once Philip got started on the actual exploration of the gunshot wound, the side door was pulled open a short distance to reveal a friendly-looking, rather handsome chap of about forty, who gave him a cheery wave of the hand.

"Anything interesting, Dr. Bosnar?"
Philip pointed to the X-ray films on the viewing box.

"There's no evidence of any significant injury to the nerves or vessels, so it's simply a matter of removing some bone chips and debriding the wound. There's a bit of muscle damage but that should be easy to repair."

"How about the bullet?"

"That came out through the exit wound. Would you care to scrub in?"

"You seem to have everything pretty well under control. By the way, my name's Don Foley. Welcome to San Pete."

That was Philip's agreeable introduction to one of the community's most influential doctors and an implacable foe of the Community Health Center. Unlike the cruder rednecks among the solo practitioners, he was a sophisticated charmer and a dangerous opponent. Not only was he a man of considerable political influence, but his father had been one of the area's most successful doctors and left his son a legacy of wealth and influence in the Anglosaxon corridors of St. Pierre.

After the operation was successfully concluded, the dressings applied, the O.R. report dictated and the orders written, the two surgeons sat down together in the O.R. lounge and had some coffee. Philip learned that Foley was planning to build a Medical Arts Building between the two hospitals and that it should be ready for occupancy by the spring of 1965. The hazards of traffic congestion had mysteriously disappeared since the clinic's original application to the city council and its rejection. Foley would finance the initial phase, and the other solo doctors would each invest in the building and become shareholders.

Philip's first unpleasant encounter occurred in the Memorial emergency department. He was called to attend a middle-aged steelworker whose lower abdomen had been gashed by the corner of a steel plate at the mill. The plant doctors had referred him to Dr. Slater by force of habit, but the patient insisted on seeing a Community Health surgeon.

Examination revealed that although there had been a good deal of bleeding during the first few minutes following the accident, the actual damage consisted of a two inch laceration involving skin and superficial fat, but no deeper injuries. Philip irrigated the wound with lukewarm saline and injected some local anesthetic under the wound edges before proceeding.

At this point, a man of about his own age demanded to see him, his face almost purple with rage and hostility. He was Dr. McBride, Chief of Emergency, and he wanted to know why Dr. Bosnar had gone ahead without notifying him first.

"Why don't you check my credentials and you'd have your answer if you really need one?" was Philip's cool retort. He cleansed the patient's laceration with hydrogen peroxide and sutured it with a few dacron stitches. By this time the rest of his supervisory team had arrived: two more solo doctors who sat down and watched the epoch-making procedure with equal parts of malice and embarrassment. Just as Philip's nurse was about to cut off the ends of the sutures he stopped her and enquired in a loud imitation of Dr. McBride's voice:

"Nurse, are you sure you have your privileges for cutting the ends off these sutures?" His official observers rose and departed in some confusion, and the patient and nurse joined him in some hearty guffaws.

During the next few weeks, both chiefs of surgery dropped into the O.Rs from time to time whenever Philip was doing a major case, and on each occasion he invited them to scrub in and take over from his assistant. The invitation usually resulted in their rapid departure.

On September the 16th, the official opening of the Cambrian District Community Health Center took place with a brief ceremony at the clinic building, with a minimum of pomp and circumstance. Jim Appleton was one of the main speakers in what was essentially an indoctrination session, mainly for the benefit of the nurses and non-medical personnel of the institution.

As one of the listeners, Philip couldn't help feeling it was the new doctors in the clinic who were in need of such initial indoctrination, rather than the others. In addition, he couldn't agree with the repeated references to 'comprehensive medical care' in the C.H.C. (Community Health Center), and felt he simply had to say something on the subject.

"Mr. Chairman," he declared, "I very much doubt whether there's a single facility in the entire world with the capability of providing full comprehensive medical care. I do believe, though, it should be possible for us to provide high quality medical care for at least seventy per cent of the conditions we're called upon to treat, and I hope within the next ten years the figure will rise to at least eighty-five per cent."

That evening, official celebrations took place at the new Garibaldi Hall, with a banquet to which staff members and their spouses were all invited. There was a head table for the various speakers and a small press contingent was in evidence. The first speaker was the Mayor, and after a few perfunctory and mildly complimentary remarks about the new 'Union Clinic' – a Freudian slip rather than a misconception – he apologized for having to leave early as he had another pressing engagement. The act of waving away the press photographer was silent confession of his embarrassment at participating in these festivities and thereby alienating his medical friends.

The popular use of the term Union Clinic by opponents of the C.H.C. was intended mainly as an irritant to the Center's medical staff. What lay behind the misnomer was an implied insult: 'You poor bastards are salaried employees of a goddamn labor union and can only look after union members and their families.' The factual knowledge that the group doctors were engaged by the Medical Director and were answerable to him – and not to any union – was ignored, as was the news that the clinic would soon be looking after a growing number of patients who weren't steelworkers or their families.

The main speaker was the national director of the U.S.W.A. (United Steelworkers of America), and he was followed by the international director of the U.S.W.A. and Jonathan Grey, the able administrator of the Detroit Group Health Center and one of the founders of the St. Pierre Center. There were many tributes to the tenacity of Bill Trevor, Past President of the local steelworkers' union and proud father of Beryl Farnham, the Medical Director's matchless secretary. It was Trevor who'd been the inspiration for the Health Center, and it was his stubborn persistence that allowed the dream to become reality in the face of the severest opposition and numerous setbacks. There was no recrimination in the speeches and no invidious comparisons with solo doctors, but rather a sense of pride and a rejoicing in the quality of their institution and its medical staff.

Philip's sojourn in the basement suite of the Benedetto house was pleasant and comfortable. Young Gino, the 9-year-old grandson of the widowed landlady, was a delightful young fellow who thought the doctor's Jaguar must be, without question, the most beautiful car ever made. He loved to ride with Philip whenever he went on a shopping trip. For his part, Philip was happy to augment the boy's weekly income by paying him to wash and polish the car to within an inch of its life. It was nice to see the proud gleam in Gino's dark Italian eyes matching that on the Jag's ivory-white surface.

Except for an occasional hot meal at one of the nearby restaurants, Philip managed quite well in his own kitchen and kept the refrigerator well stocked at all times. Every weekend, he put through a long distance phonecall to Patty and they declared how much each loved and missed the other. She wasn't having much luck getting a decent price for their beautiful home; the house market in Edwardia was at an all time low, with the possible exception of the Japanese invasion scare during World War 2.

They agreed that they might have to settle for a lot less than $35,000, the amount they'd hoped to get for their house at the very least. As for the furniture, Florian could take whatever she could use in her apartment and the rest would have to be sold by auction at giveaway prices. It was a buyer's market, so that was that, but they weren't selling their Hamlin sound system. It was one precious item that would be coming out to San Pete, along with their books, clothes and sundry paraphernalia.

Both Morecombe and Slater were showing signs of diminished enthusiasm in their supervisory function toward Philip's operative surgery, and he decided to put the finishing touches to the absurd charade. Whenever he was called out in the middle of the night for emergency surgery, he'd phone one of them to come down and watch him operate. Sure enough, it wasn't very long before they capitulated and told him it wouldn't be necessary for them to be notified for any of his cases, whether emergency or elective, and he knew he'd won his first important battle in this campaign of professional harassment.

Jim Appleton called a general meeting of the medical staff, and it was decided that they should have a small executive committee that could meet with the board of the Community Health Association from time to time, so the doctors could have a significant input into the affairs and policies of the Center. Philip was elected to serve on the executive, along with Bob Gaylord and Stuart Atkins. Jim Appleton, of course, would be their chairman.

Meeting with the board members was an important event for Philip. The President was Bill Trevor, stubborn champion of steelworkers' rights and a man of indomitable will. Philip liked and admired him, even though he knew he'd be a rough customer if they ever got into a debate over the powers of the doctors vis-a-vis the Board. He was a man of sardonic good humor and, in his own way, an idealistic reformer. There were two other union members on the Board: Don Brighton and Al Smithwick, both men of considerable labor experience, with keen minds when it came to negotiations. The two representatives of the ecclesiastic domain were Dean Blalock of the Anglican Church and Monsignor O'Grady of the Roman Catholic Church, both congenial individuals and a combined force for compromise rather than confrontation.

Jonathan Grey, the American Enfant Terrible of Socialized Medicine was the brains behind the Board, just as Trevor was the brawn, Brighton the conscience, and Smithwick the ideology. Blake Robinson was the sole representative from the business community, but from Philip's vantage point he didn't seem genuinely in tune with their beleaguered enterprise. At least he represented a respectable conservative voice on the Board, and Philip was thankful for the balance this provided.

It was Dr. Bosnar's stated aim and object to remove, as soon as possible, each objection levelled by the solo M.Ds against the structure and function of the C.H.C, until it eventually acquired its proper place, not just in the community but in its relationship to organized medicine.

During his first two weeks in San Pete, he made it his business to review the history of the Center and was greatly assisted by Appleton, who answered all his colleague's most searching questions with open honesty. As for Beryl Farnham, she was always ready to dig up any material that might be relevant to his enquiries. The more Philip read and learned during this time, the more proud he became of his decision to join this new and challenging institution.

The original models for the Center were the Health Insurance Plan of Greater New York and the Kaiser Foundation Plan in California. As described in an article published in the *Ontario Medical Review* of January 1961, these were closed panel group practices based on pre-payment and an emphasis on preventive medicine.

There was, from the very outset, a strange inconsistency of attitude toward the concept of 'Closed Panel' medical practice by the city's solo practitioners and by the provincial and national bodies of the medical establishment. Their repeated objection to the notion of a locked-in group of patients at the Health Center – and medical care denied to any other patients – was in sharp conflict with the unspoken fear that eventually the C.H.C. would be open to the entire community.

The official medical publications, both provincial and national, had to admit (albeit reluctantly) that there was nothing innately unethical about closed panel practice. Perhaps they were sensitive to the knowledge that they'd never registered any objections to management-sponsored and industry-based closed panel groups, such as the Inco plan of Sudbury, which paid its doctors on the basis of fee-for-service. Incidentally, it might have been noted that such groups were never referred to as 'Management Clinics'.

From Philip's point of view, the most vulnerable of all closed panel systems to adverse criticism and the one most stubbornly supported and mismanaged was the D.V.A. (Department of Veterans' Affairs) hospital system. Since the Mackenzie King government had refused to bring in conscription at the outset of World War 2, and assured the nation that those remaining on the civilian home front were just as important to the war effort as the armed forces, it was hard to justify the segregation of war veterans in an exclusive and restricted system. Such a segregation seemed to have little to do with improved medical care; and if, in fact, the medical care of veterans proved superior to that available to the rest of society, it would be a refutation of the government's wartime arguments and assurances.

Reviewing the Health Center's history, Philip learned that the first hurdle to be cleared was the choice of location for the C.H.C, and some of the national union leaders were strongly in favor of Hamilton. That was when Bill Trevor proved his mettle and was able to persuade his friends in the national office of the U.S.W.A. that St. Pierre would be the ideal place for such a project.

The second hurdle was that of obtaining a Canadian medical director, even though Dr. Appleton's experience and reputation would otherwise have made him an ideal candidate for the position. He and Jonathan Grey had come up through the ranks of the United Mineworkers' Medical Center at Struperville, Pennsylvania. Appleton became its Medical Director while Grey became Organizational Manager of the enterprise. After the first few years, both had become somewhat disillusioned by the shift in emphasis from excellence in health care to power politics and doctrinaire rigidity. Although both were devout socialists in their attitudes toward medical care of the public, they were aware of the necessities imposed by day-to-day pragmatism and were keen to put their practical philosophies to work in institutions such as the new C.H.Cs in Michigan and Ontario.

Dr. Gordon Williams, the person first selected as Medical Director for the Center, was a Canadian physician with some experience in heading a private group practice in Fort William. But at the very last moment he backed down under the pressure of opposition from San Pete's solo doctors and some of his own friends, as well as the proclaimed hostility of organized medicine. Ultimately, it was his wife's fear of social ostracism, and perhaps his lawyer's advice, that made Williams change his mind, and the Board went ahead and engaged Appleton, a man of much greater experience and true social commitment.

Meanwhile, the journals of organized medicine waxed hot and cold on the subject of closed panel practice. In a way they had been preempted by a most atypical decision of the union leaders of San Pete. As a general rule, when a choice had to be made by a labor union such as the United Steelworkers at the local level, the majority decision was binding on the minority who'd voted the other way.

In the selection of the new Health Center, however, the members were given annual dual choice. Each could elect to remain with the private medical insurance plan and its solo physicians, or sign up with the Center and its own group of physicians. For the weathered stalwarts of the labor movement this was akin to heresy, but to the clinic's doctors the decision was heaven-sent.

The most concrete bonus of the dual choice system was a decision by the O.M.A. (Ontario Medical Association) that the C.H.C's patients had a free choice of doctor, since they had voted to have their medical care given by the Center's physicians. Paradoxically, after facing the wrath of the St. Pierre Medical Society, the O.M.A. switched back in its policy and declared, in May of 1961, that it disapproved of closed panel clinics and supported the distribution of a special pamphlet in San Pete entitled, **'Choose your own doctor'**, attacking closed panel clinics as endangering the welfare of the community, increasing the cost of medical care and '**...alien not only to the best practice of medicine but also to the democratic rights of free people.'**

Philip couldn't help smiling at this new pose by the medical society as fearless guardian of democratic freedoms, fighting against an entrenched and privileged bastion of medical tyranny, with captive patients being looked after by wage-slave doctors. Even the Soviet revisionist writers of history would envy such a performance, at least for its brazen hypocrisy.

What then were the true details? In 1956, St. Pierre had approximately 1 doctor per 1400 population, at a time when the Ontario average was 1 per 850. Sudbury, another so-called 'Northern Ontario' city, had 1 per 831 and by 1956 had increased its doctors to 1 per 697 while San Pete remained at 1 per 1400. It was almost impossible to get a house call in San Pete, there was no doctor available for night calls and weekends were virtually devoid of medical coverage. It wasn't uncommon to see signs in doctors' offices stating, 'Sorry, No New Patients,' after a specified date, because the doctors already had too many patients in their practices.

In 1960, the *Cambrian Leader* reported the death of a 3-year-old boy who'd swallowed an overdose of his mother's pills. No doctor was available to deal with the emergency, and there was a public outcry for more doctors in San Pete. The medical insurance plan for the steelworkers had failed over the years to provide increased and expanded medical benefits, and the city doctors in 1958 had all opted out of P.S.I. (Physicians' Services Incorporated), a doctor-sponsored nonprofit insurance plan that paid 90 percent of the fee schedule and was better than most of the other insurance plans.

All these factors made San Pete an ideal place to introduce a Community Health Center, with a much wider list of medical and paramedical benefits than other insurance schemes, and a guarantee of no extra-billing. It was also clearly stated by the Community Health Association, in October of 1959, that the plan would eventually be made available to the entire community.

Meanwhile, an active war of words was taking place in the Cambrian Leader, and the public was having a field day drawing up sides, with loyalties arraigned for and against innovation in health care. On April 2, 1960, a full- page advertisement by the solo doctors appeared in the Cambrian Leader. In what was named a 'Statement of Policy,' they declared certain principles:

1. Freedom of choice of physicians.
2. Payment of physicians on a fee-for-service basis.
3. Preservation of the solo system of family practice.
4. Maintenance and preservation of the present high standard of medical care and public health.
5. Continued provision of care for those in unfortunate circumstances.

Two weeks later, the steelworkers took out their own full-page advertisement, pointing out that the medical society's position didn't help to diminish the existing problems of medical care. They didn't believe all solo M.Ds were in opposition and reaffirmed their support for the Health Center plan. In conclusion, they stressed their responsible approach and their wish to cooperate with the medical profession at all levels.

The following Saturday the St. Pierre Medical Society had yet another full-page advertisement in the Cambrian Leader, further detailing its objections to the closed panel system and outlining a comparison with the existing system. **'Although it is beyond our power, it stated, 'to decide a policy for the local union members, we feel that our accumulated knowledge of medical care may be of help to the union members in preventing their executive from leading them into a very unhappy and costly experiment.'**

A long period of newspaper silence ensued, but it was eventually broken by an article published March 2 on the front page under the heading:
'Doctors Won't Enter Union Health Center.'
'The position of the local doctors remains exactly the same. Briefly, the Saint Pierre Medical Society feels that medical practice as proposed in the union clinic is not in the best interests either of the union members or the community at large.' The article went on to attack the CHC as representing **'a backward step that could only result in deterioration of the quality of medical care provided to the community, and members of the Medical Staff will not be joining the staff of this clinic. The position taken is in full agreement with the policy of the Ontario and Canadian Medical Associations.'**

The Toronto papers were quick to pick up the story and it appeared across Ontario on March 3. The Community Health planners immediately contacted the O.M.A, who denied knowing about the statement, one that broke an almost two year agreement of silence.

The reply by the steelworkers took the form of another full-page advertisement in the Cambrian Leader; and the OMA had been forewarned in a letter stating, **'I hope you can appreciate that we now have to answer this unwarranted attack.'** The advertisement was entitled **'An Open Letter To The Doctors of Saint Pierre.'** It praised group practice, citing the origin of such world-renowned institutions as the Mayo Clinic. It denied the charge that the union would run the

CHC and insisted that **'...a board of directors similar to a hospital board would establish policy, and the declaration that the union has no intention of telling doctors how to practice medicine has been made clear to everyone.'**

It blamed the local doctors for not increasing their numbers, not attracting more specialists, and for extra- billing their patients. **'Once again we invite qualified local physicians who are truly concerned with the public interest to join us in this program.'** The last statement enraged the medical society but the entire advertisement boosted enrollment in the C.H.C. and the number now exceeded 4,500 families. Along with additional small groups of patients eager to enroll in the Center, the numbers now approached 5,000, and it was becoming obvious that it was going to need more doctors before long.

Slowly and steadily, day by day, the Health Center began to settle into a smooth routine, and a wonderful feeling of comradeship began to develop between all members of the medical and non-medical staff. The regular office hours for family practitioners were 10 a.m. to 12 noon and 1.30 to 5 p.m. on weekdays, and 10 a.m. to 12 noon on Saturdays. In addition, there was an evening emergency clinic from 7 to 9 p.m. on weekdays and 3 to 5 p.m. on weekends. Operating schedules commenced at 8 a.m, but could start for each particular surgeon according to available operating time and priority of booking.

At Saint Matthew's Hospital, the Sister in charge of the O.R. was barely able to conceal her antagonism to the clinic's surgeons. She resisted new and different routines of 'prepping' and draping the operative patient, preferences of their anesthetist in technique and equipment, the surgeon's choice of instruments and sutures, and even his methods of positioning, lighting and assistance.

It was clear that part of this attitude was because she was accustomed to the routine of the solo surgeons and anesthetists with whom she'd worked for years. But there was, nevertheless, a feeling that the clinic surgeons were interlopers and she and her nurses weren't about to turn their backs on the entrenched surgical staff by showing a willingness to cooperate with the clinic doctors. This subtle but tangible feeling was evident in some but not all of the O.R. nurses.

At the Memorial Hospital, the O.R. supervisor was basically down to earth and no nonsense, yet with no particular hostility. At the same time, it was clear that the O.R. nurses were maintaining a watching brief on the clinic surgeons: newcomers who'd invaded this hitherto closed domain. By and large, however, Philip couldn't help feeling that the nursing staffs at both hospitals were becoming more friendly and cooperative, with few exceptions.

One or two senior nurses in the emergency department and surgical floors of the Memorial remained hard line, while at St. Matthew's, aside from the OR supervisor, only the Sister in charge of pediatrics showed a clear hostility. She was fond of quoting the surgical opinions of Dr. Morecombe as if repeating the Sermon from the Mount, and it was obvious that – all textbooks and authorities to the contrary – his were the only decisions she would accept.

Sooner or later she and Philip were bound to be on a collision course, but a sort of armed truce was maintained in the meantime, while the rest of the nuns showed him open friendliness and cooperation, almost without exception. The Mother Superior, although outwardly cordial, still seemed remote, and he remained convinced she was no friend of the Health Center or its doctors. By contrast, The Sister in charge of records went out of her way to show him every warm courtesy, and he felt that she was a true ally in any future hospital difficulty.

The political situation in Ottawa during '61 and '62 was in peculiar contrast to the Ontario government's hands-off attitude toward the Community Health Center. Prime Minister John Diefenbaker appointed Justice Emmet Hall to the Royal Commission on Health Services, and Hall's findings of certain defects in the medical coverage provided by most private insurance plans were widely reported in the press. There now seemed little doubt that in due course there would be a national (and provincial) prepaid health insurance plan. In truth, it could be argued that the Saskatchewan doctors' strike was a direct outcome of John Diefenbaker's policies just as much as those of the C.C.F. premiers, Douglas and Lloyd. It was in the context of these developments that extensive coverage of St. Pierre's medical upheaval appeared in Maclean's magazine and Canadian Doctor.

Meanwhile, there also seemed little doubt that the Kennedy administration was showing an interest in similar programs of health care delivery for the United States. It would take a vigorous young fighter for a better social order, a man like President Kennedy, to face up to an entrenched American Medical Association, with its iron grip on the privatized fee-for-service status quo. Here was a man who could inspire his people to new heights of commitment and responsibility, by exhorting them, **"Ask not what your country can do for you. Ask what you can do for your country!"**

As Philip got to know and understand his fellow doctors in the clinic during the next few weeks, and as he listened to some of their comments vis-a-vis the C.H.C. management, he couldn't help feeling that Appleton might be well advised to exhort them along the same lines. It was an attitude which might prove essential in facing outside opposition during the days and years to come. Such an attitude wouldn't preclude honest discussion of any differences with the Board on issues of management and policy. After all, that was one of the reasons for the selection of an executive committee to represent the medical staff.

Philip's beloved Patricia arrived in early October, looking more beautiful than ever. The plane that brought her also brought their glamorous Gigi, who glanced around imperiously from her cage as if wondering where the press photographers were hiding. She looked resplendent with her glowing chocolate-colored coat and bejewelled collar, and as soon as she was released she bounded over to give Philip a welcoming tongue across the cheek before he and Patty had a chance to kiss and hug each other. Apparently, their prize French poodle had behaved with impeccable manners during the flight, as befitted her aristocratic heritage, and Patty was very proud of her.

They picked up the luggage and drove into town, with the brilliant colors of crimson, orange and gold illuminating the landscape and heralding the arrival of the fall season. Patty was enthralled by the glorious panorama and commented on the view from the air.

"You know, darling, when we were flying over the hills in our approach to Saint Pierre, it looked as if the whole countryside was on fire. I found it hard to believe that trees could produce extraordinary colors like those I was seeing for the first time."

"That's because of the Ontario maple and the Cambrian rocky soil. They combine to provide a painter's dream and a photographer's paradise."

When they got to the Benedetto house, Philip introduced his wife to Mrs. B. and her grandson. Gigi was on her best behavior and became an instant favorite with both the Benedettos. This was just as well since the Bosnars would be staying here with Gigi for a few days before making more permanent arrangements. Patty was pleasantly surprised at the spaciousness and convenience of Philip's basement apartment and complimented the beaming Mrs. B. on the excellence of the furnishings and appliances.

After a lunch of cold chicken, Patty unpacked, freshened up and changed. After a while, jet lag caught up with her; she fell asleep and didn't awaken for the next two hours. That evening, they went out for dinner and young Gino was only too happy to look after their dog, especially as Philip promised to bring him back a large ice-cream cone of his favorite flavor.

During their leisurely meal in the dining-room of the Coronet Hotel nearby, Philip got down to an important question.

"Tell me, Patty, have you decided whether you want to live in a house or an apartment?"

"Definitely an apartment, now the children are no longer living with us and are so far away."

"Well, in that case I think I've got just the right place. I've spoken to the manager of the building and we can move in right away. It's a modern six-storey apartment block near the water, with light brown brick facade and ample balconies. There are also adjoining tennis courts and a boat club."

"That sounds marvellous. Does the tennis club belong to the building?"

"No. It's run jointly by the Rotary club and the YMCA and the membership fee is very reasonable."

"It's been so long since I've played. I wonder if I'll remember how to hit the ball."

"You'd be surprised, darling, how quickly you'll catch on. Don't forget I've always said you're a natural athlete, unlike your husband."

"Now you're putting me on. Anyhow, there's lots of time to think about tennis. First we'll have to see how soon our stuff gets here from Edwardia and we have to shop for some furniture and drapes."

"I should mention that the name of the building is 'Lakeside Manor' and our apartment, to start with, would be on the second floor. According to the manager, there should be an excellent corner suite on the top floor available by next summer. By the way, there's a nice underground garage and that should be a real bonus during the winter months."

Over the next couple of weeks, the remainder of their possessions arrived safely, and Patty selected some basic teak furniture and drapes from a first rate store in a nearby shopping mall. It was all essentially 'Danish Modern' and looked good in their new apartment. This had recently been painted a pleasant ivory color and had beautiful hardwood floors, so there was no hurry to purchase any rugs for the time being. As for Gigi, they assured the manager that she was the best behaved dog in Canada and he appeared to believe them.

By the time they had the stereo sound system set up and their books, records and reel-to-reel tapes in place, they felt they had genuinely become true residents of the new abode. It was nice to walk out onto the balcony and look south across the lake at the huge freighters destined for far-off places; at the sailboats from the boat-club close by, and the tennis players below. This was no primitive life in a grimy steel city, but an exciting slice of Canadian activity and recreation in the heart of the Cambrian Shield with all its natural majesty; and here they were with all this at their very doorstep. Patty was thrilled, and Philip was delighted for her, since he knew how she must have concealed her hidden fears about the kind of environment for which she'd exchanged her life in Edwardia.

Gus Pelletier arrived in November, fresh from his success in the Fellowship exams, and ready to go to work. He was big, bluff, hearty and very French-Canadian, yet he spoke English with only the slightest trace of a Gallic accent. He was in his early forties and had been practicing in a small city near Minneapolis, where he'd done his postgraduate surgical training at the University Hospital. With such good training and practical experience he should be a welcome addition to the Center's surgical department and to Philip, personally. It was going to be good for the two of them to work together on the more complex cases such as thoracic and arterial surgery in which Pelletier expressed a special interest.

He had a great sense of humor, balanced by a quick temper, and he loved company. Since the new doctors and their wives hadn't been overwhelmed by invitations from the St. Pierre establishment to join its various clubs and organizations, it was going to be necessary to socialize among themselves, and as far as Phil and Patty were concerned, that was just fine.

Without being conceited, they could declare openly that it was the loss of the so-called establishment and not theirs. As a matter of fact, the only clubs the Bosnars were interested in were the duplicate bridge club and the tennis club, while the only organizations they were keen about were the theater society and symphony society, and in all of these no special invitations were necessary. To be perfectly fair, however, Philip had to recognize that some of the other clinic doctors and their wives – especially the younger ones – felt the social exclusion far more keenly, and he tried to imbue them with his own attitude of proud independence.

There were two people at the clinic for whom Philip developed an enormous respect during these early months. The first was the administrator, Earl Formby, a tall and laconic individual with the cadaveric leanness of a Dachau survivor. He was a man of infinite good humor, patience and industry, who quietly shepherded the Center through its most difficult birth pangs and was largely responsible for getting the Center open for subscribers by September 1. It must have required long hours of hard work on his part, without fuss or complaint.

The second was Philip's office nurse, Amy Butler, a totally selfless woman in her middle thirties, for whom no effort on behalf of her two surgeons was too much trouble. She was excellent with their patients and a ready learner of new methods. Since she did most of the surgical dressings, it was gratifying for Philip to see how quickly she picked up his particular preferences in materials and techniques, and when it came to helping him in the minor surgery room, she was always ready, willing, and able, beyond all expectations.

One quiet day at the office, early in the last week of November, with the first chill winds of impending winter assaulting the window panes of the minor operating room, Philip was removing a benign tumor from the shoulder of a young woman under local anesthesia when the door opened and Gus Pelletier slipped into the room, his face grim and pale.

"Did you hear the news about President Kennedy? He's just been shot and he's not expected to live."

Philip stared at him in stunned disbelief, and as soon as his associate quietly left, he felt his knees give way and the blood drain from his head.

"You'll have to excuse me," he apologized to his patient, "but I have to sit down for a few minutes before I can continue."
Needless to say, the patient was also deeply disturbed and fully understood his reaction.

When he was finished, and after telling his nurse that he was going home for the next two hours, he drove back to the apartment and found Patty in tears and totally devastated by the tragedy. She was an ardent admirer of the young President, since he represented to her all that was forthright and honorable in a political leader. Beyond mourning his loss, her heart went out to the tragic widow and her little children.

That such a monstrous act of murderous hatred could take place in the course of a peaceful motorcade in Dallas, Texas, drove home a terrible lesson. This was what blind political extremism could lead to, even in a modern democracy, and it gave one shuddering pause.

CHAPTER 46

1964

It seemed to take both Bosnars until the new year before they really got over the killing of President Kennedy and felt able to resume normal living. At first, it appeared that a lone deranged assassin, filled with obsessive communist compulsions, had gunned down his smiling and unwitting victim from ambush in the Dallas book-repository. The building couldn't have been better situated, on the route of the presidential motorcade, for the purpose of assassination.

All this changed when they watched the TV screen in horror, as a small time hoodlum and nightclub owner named Jack Ruby pressed his handgun into the chest of Lee Harvey Oswald and shot him dead. The gunman had entered the underground garage of the gaol without challenge and performed his heinous deed at close quarters, without a single hand raised to stop him. It was almost as though the detectives escorting Oswald stood aside so the target would be unimpeded.

Now a terrible thought crept into the public mind. Was this possibly a deep and sinister conspiracy, with Oswald merely a gullible and expendable patsy? The infamous J.Edgar Hoover could hardly wait to deliver his verdict of the FBI's rush to judgement: there was no conspiracy! It was Philip's instinctive conviction that Ruby would never be legally executed, and Patty believed he'd never be permitted to leave prison alive.

By the year's end, the continuing struggle to normalize relationships between solo and clinic M.Ds was an increasing preoccupation, while the arrival of the snows of winter occupied much of Phil's and Patty's attention as they got out their heavy clothing and snow boots to face the sub-zero temperatures. This was all so different from Edwardia. The hush produced by the great white winter blanket was now accentuated by the departure of the noisy birds. Gone, too, were the blaring ships' horns heralding the passage of the great freighters. The Bosnars had started to get used to the sight and sounds of the mighty man-made sea monsters, but these would now be returning to their lairs, awaiting the spring thaws.

Meanwhile, the surrounding countryside became a gleaming white fairyland, while the city bore its slushy inconveniences with an affectionate stoicism; and getting stuck in the snow or helping a fellow-driver in similar difficulties were events that evoked only the mildest of profanity. This was the season when fractures and dislocations would be on the increase, as people slipped and fell on icy steps or sidewalks. Emergency rooms were kept busy, while the run on splints and plaster kept hospital orderlies on their toes, making sure there were no sudden unexpected shortages.

Philip's closest office neighbor was the radiologist, Mark Caplan, with whom he always took the opportunity to spend some time, discussing X-rays, drinking tea and sharing cigarettes. To be more accurate, Mark usually shared Philip's, since his method of cutting down on smoking was to let himself run out of cigarettes. It was typical of the man. He could be outrageous yet delightful at one and the same time, and everyone loved him. It wasn't just sympathy for his multiple sclerosis affliction and the fact that he needed two canes to get around his office. It was his unfailing and infectious good humor and sparkling personality, both of which reflected an unflagging courage rather than the well-known euphoria of his neurological disorder.

Caplan's father was a well-known thoracic surgeon, and he was the first to break the anti-Jewish barrier against staff appointments at the Toronto General Hospital. Mark had qualified in his fathers specialty but had to switch to radiology when he became incapacitated by the dread multiple sclerosis. In many ways, the Group Health Center was an ideal place for him, and hed be able to function for an extended period of time in this protected environment. Moreover, in view of his qualifications and experience, he was the only C.H.C. doctor other than Appleton and Bosnar who was started at the top annual retainer of $24,000. He'd been subjected to considerable adverse pressure prior to joining the Center, and when he confided the exact circumstances to him Philip was shocked.

Henry Jones was the unlikely name of a Jewish solo general practitioner in San Pete. He was one of the worst redneck fanatics in the local medical society, and when he learned that one or two of the Union Clinic doctors would be Jews, he became wildly agitated; claiming this would be a source of antisemitism in a city where such a problem hadn't existed up to now. (Perhaps that was because most of the Wasp prejudice had been directed against Catholics in general and Italians in particular). In any event, Dr. Jones made it his business to contact Caplan's professional friends in Toronto and ask them to exert pressure on the wayward radiologist not to come to the C.H.C. No doubt hed made the same attempt with Jack Grier but no word of this had so far reached the group doctors.

The first time Philip met Jones, he took an instant dislike to him. He was about the same age as the clinic surgeon, fairhaired and graying, of stocky build and Gentile countenance, complete with upturned nose and short military brush mustache, with an arrogant manner to match. On the first three occasions that Philip passed him in the corridor at Memorial Hospital, Jones looked right past him and failed to answer his "Good Morning," with so much as a grunt. On the fourth occasion he seized Jones by the lapels and spoke very quietly, through clenched teeth.

"Listen, chum. When I say 'Good Morning' to anyone, I expect to be answered unless he's deaf and dumb, or unfamiliar with the English language. Is that clear?"

"Yes, it's clear."

That was the last time Philip's greeting ever went unanswered from Jones or anyone else in San Pete, and he felt that one more step had been taken to break down the ridiculous wall between men of healing, especially when they practiced in the same hospitals of the same city.

A few short months after the opening of the Health Center, the solo doctors placed the following warning in the *Canadian Medical Association Journal*:

'The Medical Society has established an information service to advise doctors contemplating practice in the area on matters of local importance. The establishment of a community-sponsored clinic in our area has given rise to certain misunderstandings within the profession, and newcomers in their own interest should investigate the situation before making commitments.' At least the C.H.C. was now recognized as a consumer-sponsored rather than a union clinic, even though prospective applicants to their medical staff were being warned off. What this warning did not say, was that membership in the medical society required an undertaking not to engage in normal cross-referral patterns with the Health Center, a policy that should have brought sharp condemnation from the O.M.A, the C.M.A. and the Ontario College.

One of Philip's staunchest allies from the earliest time was Dr. Michael Leslie, a fine Englishman – of courtly manners and pleasant disposition – who was the pathologist in charge of the laboratory at St. Matthew's. Not only was he fully aware of the hostility directed against the doctors of the new group by the solo M.Ds, but he refused to go along with their sentiments or actions, and his days in San Pete were probably numbered. In the meantime, he kept Philip informed of what was going on below the surface and warned him of the dangerous enmity of Glenn Morecombe.

"You must remember, Dr. Bosnar," he warned, "that until you arrived he was never challenged on the scope of his operative procedures or dogmatic opinions. Now, with potential rivals of your caliber, that's no longer true and he's not likely to thank you for it."

Leslie's counterpart at the Memorial was Dr. George Filmore, who, at age sixty, displayed the mental senility of a much older man and a clumsy irrational spite against the C.H.C. His pathology reports were as untrustworthy as Leslie's were reliable, and Philip had no hesitation challenging those opinions he doubted and getting a second opinion, especially when it came to questions of malignancy.

Dr. Sidney Frasier was a young solo G.P. with a special interest in psychiatry. He was the son-in-law of Herbert Manderly, chairman of the board at the Memorial Hospital and a power in both the legal profession and the provincial government. For some reason that Philip couldn't fathom, Frasier, no friend of the Center, chose to keep him informed of certain events of which hed so far been unaware. He described a meeting of the Memorial medical staff that took place one month before the clinic opened its doors. Freddy Stewart, president of the medical staff, was reading out the new applications for membership in the active medical staff and discussed the various ways in which privileges could be curtailed. According to Frasier, when he got to Bosnar's name he read out his credentials in detail and declared his own viewpoint: "There's no way we're going to tell this guy just what he can and what he can't do."

Philip was fascinated by the information and asked, "Were both Slater and Morecombe present at that meeting?"

"I'm not sure about Morecombe, but you should know that although Slater's the more powerful of the two, it's Morecombe who tries to enforce any limit of surgical operating privileges."

It wasn't long before this prediction was confirmed. Tony Donovan began to complain of harassment from Morecombe, who repeatedly questioned the scope and indications of his surgical procedures, taking upon himself the prerogatives of chief of gynecology. Next in line was Gus Pelletier, who was told by Morecombe that he couldn't operate on a case of imperforate anus in an infant, since these "always go to Sick Children's in Toronto."

Bill Greston, the radiologist at Memorial who seemed quite friendly whenever he and Philip met and was no great admirer of Morecombe, interpreted the situation more accurately for Philip.

"What the mighty Glenn means is that such cases always go to Toronto unless he does them."

This statement made a lot more sense when Sister Maude, in the records department at

St. Matthews, showed him the laundry list of Morecombes privileges, in strictest confidence. They covered every facet of general surgery, thoracic surgery, urology, orthopedics, neurosurgery, plastic surgery, obstetrics and gynecology, and even anesthesia.

"How could that be?" Philip asked.

"He's supposed to have had an awful lot of training in many fields of work, according to his figures. Besides, he's been very generous to our hospital since doing so well with his mining investments several years ago."

She gave Philip a very strange look and he knew she could tell him much more.

Oddly enough, it was Dr. Slater who precipitated Philip's first strong reaction, and it was in connection with a patient booked for surgery under Gus Pelletier. It was a case of **Sacral Teratoma** (a congenital tumor of the tailbone region) in an infant, and Pelletier had dealt with several of these during his residency on a pediatric surgical service. He was now informed that he'd have to send the patient to Toronto. Philip's enquiries revealed that both Slater and Morecombe had handled such cases in the past.

The booby trap in such situations was no secret: should anything go wrong with the disputed case, the surgeon is placed in an impossible position. As far as Philip was concerned, Pelletier had been given the kiss of death. He wasted no time in getting Slater on the phone and giving him his opinion in no uncertain manner; and concluded on a personal note, delivered in a calm and pleasant tone of voice.

"I think this might be as good a time as any to tell you where I stand regarding any attempt by you or Morecombe to interfere with the legitimate privileges of our clinic doctors. Speaking for myself, I'd like you to understand that I didn't come thousands of miles to this city in order to roll over and play dead. If that's clearly understood I believe we can become friends."

His first real encounter with Morecombe concerned an interesting patient to him by Dr. Atkins, the groups cardiologist. Mrs. G. was a 65-year-old Italian-speaking lady who weighed almost 200 lbs. and had a bad heart. For many years she had been increasingly disabled by a huge abdominal hernia at the site of a previous operation for 'stomach ulcers' at the age of 30. During the past year, the hernia had become quite fixed and impossible to control, so there was no reduction on lying down. Whenever she got out of bed, she tended to overbalance to her left because of the hernia's magnitude. As far as her weight was concerned, the patient had been entirely unsuccessful in her attempts to reduce, and Atkins felt her heart condition was now in sufficient control to permit consideration of surgical repair.

Philip admitted the patient to St. Matthew's Hospital, and when X-rays that were taken from side to side revealed a major portion of the large bowel in the hernia, he placed her on a special bowel routine for possible colon resection. She took the anesthetic very well, and Philip was able to free the margins of the hernia so that he could explore the entire abdomen and exclude any other intra-abdominal condition. After dividing surrounding adhesions as completely as possible, he checked the situation for Loss of Domicile involving the colon, and found that this was indeed the case. (This is a situation in which the organs cannot be returned to and kept confined in the abdominal cavity without causing gross pressure on the diaphragm and impairment of breathing),

The surgeon's impression was confirmed by Jack Grier, who monitored her respiration during the entire procedure. It was therefore necessary to resect that portion of the colon occupying the hernia, along with redundant skin and fat. Fortunately, a total isolating technique could be used, thus avoiding infective contamination. After joining up the bowel securely, Philip was able to repair the large gap in the abdominal wall with a double layer of Teflon mesh, sewn in place as a reinforcing patch. The operative specimen, quite formidable in size, was placed in a large covered basin and sent down to the lab for routine pathological examination.

The patient did very well in the postoperative period and was discharged ten days later without complication, with her colon functioning normally and with a new-found ability to stand or walk without overbalancing. A few days after the patients discharge, Mike Leslie told Philip about Morecombe's reaction to the case. He'd stormed into the lab and asked to see the specimen, then declared that it was **"absolutely unconscionable to put this poor old lady through such a horrendous procedure."**

Philip's reaction to this information was straight-forward and effective. He arranged to present the case at the next surgical ward rounds. After the X-rays were shown, the operation described, the opinions of the anesthetist and assistant presented and the patient introduced, there was much favorable comment, albeit subdued. It was at this point that Philip asked Morecombe, point blank, if he had any critical comment. The chastened Chief of Surgery seemed to have some difficulty getting his words out, but managed to mumble that it was a good thing she'd withstood the surgery. He knew to a certainty that he'd better tread more carefully in future, and the lesson wouldn't be lost on some of the others

During the early months of '64, Philip encountered a strange phenomenon. Parallel to the continued antagonism toward the C.H.C. on a political level, there was an increasing level of dialogue between the doctors of both sides. Only a residual contingent of rednecks maintained the ban on such interchange. Increased dialogue between the two sides also meant more direct accusations in the doctors' lounges at both hospitals. Rather than ignoring them, as was the tendency with his colleagues in the Center, Philip welcomed the opportunity of refuting the allegations in no uncertain manner.

When it was claimed by some that the Health Center would perish within five years, he contended that it might even outlast solo practice as it existed at the present time. He even suggested, not entirely with tongue in cheek, that the C.H.C. might be the final independent bastion of conservative medicine when government took over National Health Insurance. He felt no guilt in relishing the obvious discomfort on the faces of the clinics detractors. Almost simultaneously, he began to receive a series of hints, at first subtle and later quite open, that if he switched to solo practice he'd be warmly welcomed. The price of his clearcut refusal was a noticeable hardening of opposition, but now tempered by a growth of professional respect.

In March, a strange interview took place in the Boardroom of St. Matthew's Hospital between Morecombe and Bosnar. It concerned the laundry list of privileges the clinic surgeon had filled out and submitted to the administrative offices of both hospitals. Evidently, it had been decided that Morecombe would be acting for both surgical departments, and this interview was a kind of bargaining session, so the applicant could trade one privilege at the expense of another.

It was all so dishonest, but Philip had anticipated this type of nonsense by applying for a much wider range of procedures than he intended to use. In this way he was able to retain just about all of the operations he wished to pursue and relinquish those he didn't. Thus, when the field of major urology was removed from his list, with considerable relish on Morecombe's part, Philip made no objection. A new urologist, Leo Kossov, had just arrived in town and was anxious to do all the urology cases referred from the clinic. Even so, Philip retained certain procedures in the broad field of urology in which he had a long and successful background, and no objection was raised.

The whole charade struck him as so artificial and absurd that he decided to take some further action, mainly in order to prevent abuse of the system against his group colleagues at some future date. Accordingly, he sent off a letter to the Section of General Surgery in the O.M.A, asking for a clarification of exactly which privileges should be granted – as a very minimum – to qualified specialists in General Surgery who worked in major community hospitals such as those of Saint Pierre. The reply left him disgusted but not entirely surprised:

'At our recent meeting it was decided that the matter of surgical privileges should be left to the appropriate hospital departments, committees and chiefs.' What a glorious invitation to the corrupters of professional and political power.

Following a meeting of the clinics Medical Executive Committee, it was recommended that each member of the clinics medical staff send an individual application for membership in the Medical Society. The answer to each application was identical, unprincipled, and transparent:

'I regret to inform you that no motion was received from the floor approving your application to the local society and accordingly your membership requirements have not been met at this time.'

A similar but more specific response was obtained at a later date from the Physicians Services Incorporated, usually called the 'P.S.I', the insurance plan sponsored by the Ontario Medical Association. Several smaller groups of patients who now wished to get their services from the Health Center were still getting their coverage from P.S.I, and these included teachers, biologists at the government forestry and insect laboratories, and other middle-class professionals. They were suddenly turned down by P.S.I, since the C.H.C. was still considered to be a closed panel group, incompatible with the charter of their insurance scheme. The Center's attempts to obtain a copy of this charter were unsuccessful.

Most of the family physicians in the group got along well with each other and had a good relationship with the specialists. But Bob Gaylord still tended to act as associate medical director and Ted Novak always gave the impression that he was a considerable cut above the other G.Ps. Both were older men, but their maturity didn't prevent them from vying with each other for prominence in the group, and each came to Philip to present his own particular version of the conflict. Happily, their wives got along famously and seemed well aware of their husbands foibles. Both couples were fond of entertaining, and it wasn't too long before the combatants appeared to patch up their differences.

There was one interesting difference between the two, however, that never changed. Gaylord always projected toughness, yet was deeply hurt by the hostility of the solo doctors and wanted nothing whatever to do with them. Novak, on the other hand, was a smooth middle-European charmer who relied heavily on his social graces to overcome antagonism, and he tried to woo the opposition in the doctors lounges at both hospitals with exaggerated congeniality. To Philip's shame, he felt compelled to reveal his opinion of such behavior by labelling it the "coffee-pouring syndrome" (and over the years the name stuck. Yet these two men were excellent family physicians and were popular with their patients, to the greater glory of the clinic.

One of the bones of contention between the Medical Executive and the Board of the Association, at their regular meetings, was the inordinately high proportion of funds designated as 'overhead and reserve'. Although medical management and decision were the strict preserve of the doctors, fiscal management and decisions were the exclusive preserve of the board, yet the doctors felt they should have some say in the apportioning of income between the M.Ds and the Group Health Association. Those who were most vocal in their criticism of the present arrangement were Tony Donovan and Gus Pelletier. The medical group's irritation was augmented by the fact that all the hiring and firing of nurses and non-medical staff, as well as decisions governing their salaries and assignments, were the province of the board and its administrator.

Philip discussed these matters fully with his colleagues at their Executive meetings, and in addition, had many a private heart-to-heart chat with Jim Appleton, who – in many ways – was the man in the middle. At the joint meetings, Bill Trevor always used pre-emptive tactics to blunt any criticism of the management. He was a veteran of negotiation meetings and when it came to debating techniques he was nobody's dummy.

"Before we get to other matters," he would say, taking the head seat at the long conference table, "we should deal with the latest patient complaints." As if on cue, Jonathan Grey would rise to defend the doctors and Philip had to smile at the ingenuity of the scenario. He would insist on dealing with the patients complaints, one by one, and most of these turned out to be either trivial or baseless. When they had been discussed and often found to be based on misunderstandings of the Centers normal function and procedure, they got down to business, and there was a grudging acceptance by the Board members of the points made on behalf of the doctors.

The 60 percent figure for overhead was adjusted to 55 percent and it was clear that within the year it should be possible to bring it down to 50 percent. The important point was that the average income of the group doctors should be at least equivalent to that of the solo doctors in town. Otherwise the Center would be facing a wave of dissatisfaction from doctors already smarting at being targets of hostility against the steelworkers' union.

After the first ten months the members of the medical executive began to feel, like their medical director, that they were men in the middle, and it was now their added responsibility to keep peace and trust between the doctors and the Board, which wasn't too easy. The medical staff members felt themselves caught between a hostile medical establishment and a suspicious Group Health Association; and Philip realized it would need all his experience and diplomacy to help Appleton keep a lid on the situation. There was also a growing discontent on the part of some specialists at the small income differential between them and the general practitioners. Conversely, the G.Ps argued, since this Center was built on socialist-leaning principles, that the disparity should be reduced still further. As for Philip, he felt that both views were wrong: furthermore, they presented a danger of polarization just when a united front was essential.

The situation reached its climax in the most bizarre and unexpected manner. As the one in charge of the Centers surgical department, Philip began to receive an increasing number of complaints from Jack Grier about booking times in the O.R. It seemed that Gus Pelletier was becoming more demanding about getting his cases booked at 8 a.m, ahead of Donovan and Bosnar. This wasn't always convenient or medically desirable. For example, certain high risk cases were best done ahead of the others, while those with a high possibility of infection should be done last on the list.

Since he had no desire to act in a heavy-handed manner, Philip suggested that as a general rule it was up to the anesthetist to arrange the order of cases, based on accepted criteria. But Grier would have none of it.

"He just bullies me whenever I try to change the order of the cases and I have to give in," he whined. The timid, apologetic Jack Grier was nature's answer to the aspiring bully, an unresisting victim, and Philip knew what the answer would be if he asked him, "Are you a man or a mouse?", so he suggested a meeting instead. It would be between the four of them at the Bosnar apartment and they'd thrash things out and arrive at an amicable settlement.

At 8 p.m. on a Friday evening in late July they were all assembled, and Philip poured drinks for his guests. There was a strange air of excitement, and Grier seemed especially agitated and talkative about nothing in particular. When all seemed comfortable, Philip opened the discussion.

"As you know, chaps, we're here because of some problem in relation to our surgical bookings and I thought it might be a good idea if we each expressed our opinions."

"You're wrong, Phil." Gus Pelletier declared, "That's not why were here."

"It's something much more important," Tony Donovan chimed in, "and we feel it's high time you decided where you stand on the key issues."

"Key issues? I don't know what the bloody hell you're both talking about."

"Well, the three of us met last night at my place," Gus replied. "Jack was there and we'll let him do the talking for us."

Self-effacing Jack Grier a SPOKESMAN for two such aggressive types? Philip felt like laughing out loud. Was the anesthetist on amphetamines, he wondered, as he noted the brightness of his eyes and agitated manner, or was he simply being manipulated by these two forceful characters.

"Well," echoed Grier excitedly, "we've decided the G.Ps are running the show and the specialists are getting the short end of the stick. We carry all the major responsibility and face all the flack in the hospitals while they have the majority voice in running the operation, especially as the medical director is a G.P. and on their side."

"Anything else?"

"Absolutely. We don't like the way the Medical Executive Committee is making decisions for the rest of us and keeping us in the dark about what the Board is up to."

"Is that the end of your speech, Jack, or is there more?" Grier was eager to continue but Pelletier drew him back and took up the argument.

"Look, Phil. We're just as anxious as you are to make this clinic of ours a success. But you have to understand that we can't let the Board walk all over us and we can't let our G.Ps run the whole show.

Now it was Tony Donovan's turn and he was working himself up into a rage.

"Personally," he declared, "I think we might be better off without any G.Ps at all. I happen to know there are quite a few clinics like ours in the States which don't have any G.Ps and they get along just fine. If necessary we can have the internists do most of the adult family practice and the pediatrician do the childrens family practice, and if needed I'd be prepared to do my share."

"You guys amaze me," Philip exploded. "If our family physicians got hold of this stuff they'd probably say they can manage without specialists and refer all their cases to outside consultants. Or else they'd leave. Either way it would be the end of the Group Health Center and I'm not prepared to let that happen.

He poured himself another scotch and soda and invited his guests to help themselves. Inside, his stomach was acting up and he knew he was going through too many cigarettes, but his blood was up and he had to continue.

"If the three of you are hell-bent on getting rid of your Executive Committee you'll only get rid of your bargaining position with the Board, but in any event the decision should be made by the entire medical staff. As far as our medical director is concerned I've heard some of the G.Ps complain that he tends to favor the specialists, so you can pay your money and take your choice. You should remember, though, that Jim Appleton is both a family physician and a specialist with degrees in Public Health. He's also the most experienced man you could possibly get to run our type of group practice. Speaking for myself, I trust the man, and I trust his judgement and fairness."

"You're a dreamer, Phil," was Pelletier's comment, and the other two obviously felt the same way, so Philip decided it was time to end the conversation.

"If you fellows have nothing more to say I suggest we adjourn this meeting, but I don't want to hear any more complaints about the operating schedules. That's what this evening's meeting was supposed to settle."

Half an hour later his guests were ready to leave, and by that time the intensity and tension had faded and they were back to their previous relaxed and friendly relations, with a few wisecracks thrown in for good measure about stubborn Limeys and thick-headed French-Canadians.

It seemed almost impossible, but his beloved wife had finally succumbed to the challenge and excitement of duplicate bridge. It was after Philip left Edwardia that Harry Bekassy had persuaded her to be his partner at a couple of events in the Regional Tournament held at the Prince Albert Hotel. Much to her surprise, after the first couple of games, Patricia found she was really enjoying herself, and by the end of the tournament she'd picked up her first master points by placing well in her 'sections'. It was the perfect antidote to her disappointment at getting a mere $25,000 for their house, and her enthusiasm began to grow with each new game. By the time she got to Saint Pierre she was more than ready to take part in the weekly club games held at the Oddfellows Hall and the Bosnars started to build up a partnership they hoped would eventually result in club championships and perhaps carry them even further in the world of duplicate bridge.

Since the duplicate players represented a good cross section of local society, with a preponderance of teachers and other professionals, it provided them with an early access to the citizens of the community at large, and an opportunity to exchange information and views. The only other doctor in the club was Mark Caplan, and what he lacked in playing ability he more than made up in enthusiastic devotion to the game. Philip was happy to observe that there was no evidence whatever of any antagonism toward him or Mark as participants in the new and controversial Health Center. Perhaps this would be one of the activities through which one could break down some of the misconceptions and prejudices concerning the C.H.C. There would undoubtedly be others.

During the summer months there were two very welcome visits from surgeons who practiced in other centers. The first was Dr. Grant Walters of Sudbury, a well-known and highly respected general and thoracic surgeon. He toured the entire Center in complete detail and spent a long time discussing the set-up of the institution with Philip, over a pot of tea in Caplan's office. He was cordial and sympathetic to the clinic's aims and problems despite the fact that he was probably wedded to the traditional method of solo, fee-for-service practice. They didn't dwell on their differences but rather on their common purposes, and it was refreshing to discuss ones outlook with a man of his caliber and open mind.

The second visitor was Dr. Sam Barnet, whose family lived in this part of Ontario, and who was a good friend of Mark Caplan. Barnet was a general surgeon on staff at the Mount Sinai Hospital in Toronto, and was deeply involved in the development of chemotherapy, with special emphasis on the treatment of breast cancer. This preoccupation with improving the scope and safety of anticancer drugs, meant a sharp decrease in his operating volume and a corresponding decline in income. But he was a man with a mission and one to be admired. He told Philip hed be only too happy to give him any assistance he might need in the chemical management of malignancy and the clinic surgeon was grateful. The opportunity for Barnets help came sooner than expected.

Brigitte Fleischmann, their shy and extremely likeable pediatrician, was a quiet and efficient worker, and one who was averse to making waves. Her husband, Kurt, was the exact opposite, loud and aggressive, but with a deep and abiding loyalty to the Center. Unfortunately, at meetings such as their occasional dinners with doctors and spouses – held in the Bertram Giles suite of the Great Lakes Hotel – Kurt Fleischmann drank too much and got rather noisy about opponents of the Health Center. At such times Philip almost expected to hear him declare, "Achtung everybody. I give you a toast to our fine clinic. Today, San Pete, tomorrow the world!" Of course it never got that far, but it sometimes came quite close, much to the embarrassment of his blushing spouse. Yet he was a well-meaning fellow, utterly devoted to his wife and son, with a massive sense of humor and a large fund of jokes to match.

One day, as Philip was leaving the Center about 5.30 p.m, Brigitte approached and said she'd been waiting for him, as she had a worrying case she wanted to discuss. It was a patient who, over a two month period, had developed a large, hard lump in the lower left neck. There was no pain or tenderness and no fever.

"What about other symptoms?"

"Slight weight-loss and slight loss of appetite, nothing else."

"What about the blood-count, tests for mononucleosis, Tb?

"Nothing abnormal."

"How old is the child?"

"It's not a child. It's a 44-year-old man and he's always been completely healthy. To tell you the truth it's my husband."

"Look, Brigitte, we may be dealing with something serious so I want him to come to my office at 2 o'clock tomorrow for a complete history and physical and then I'll arrange for some X-rays and a formal excision of the lump for microscopic examination and special studies.

The physical was completely negative except for a cluster of hard lymph nodes in the left side of the neck, strongly suggestive of a secondary malignancy. There were no other enlarged nodes or masses and Philip began to feel gloomy about the patients prospects. X-rays of his chest and digestive tract were negative, as were his liver function studies and his stool test for occult blood. The surgical specimen was eventually reported as **'Metastatic carcinoma with a probable primary in the pancreas.'**

Even though Philip re-examined the patients abdomen on several occasions he could feel no evidence of a tumor mass despite maximum relaxation, with both knees raised and the legs supported on pillows. This must be the dreaded infiltrating type of cancer in the body rather than the head of the pancreas, the kind that would spread through the blood-stream and was inoperable by the time any symptoms or masses were apparent.

Philip discussed his findings and opinions openly with both the Fleischmanns and their reaction was splendid.

"I'm not going to recommend an operation to explore your pancreas, Kurt, as it will add nothing to your chances. Any attempt to remove your entire pancreas would be futile at best and only bring you increasing problems, possibly even shortening your life. Instead, I would recommend a course of chemotherapy that might have to be repeated from time to time. An expert at the Mount Sinai Hospital in Toronto has been kind enough to give me his preferred method and a formula that minimizes undesirable side effects such as nausea, and that's the one I intend to use. The name of the chemical agent is 5-fluouracil and it will be given intravenously over a period of time, with hospital supervision."

"What about radiation treatment?"

"That has been found to be of little use in this type of cancer and could also make you extremely ill."

"In that case we'd like you to go ahead with your recommended treatment, and we both feel the same way as you about not exploring my belly by operation."

By the grace of God, Kurt did remarkably well with this regime and within a few months was maintaining his weight, eating and enjoying his food as before and presenting no new evidence of tumor growth or metastases. Perhaps they were in for a new age of miracles.

Philips relations with Pelletier, Donovan, and Grier seemed to have returned completely back to normal, although the first seemed more aggressive than before, the second more arrogant, and the third more humble than before, albeit with a growing sense of humor (even if he did forget the punch lines of his jokes). At the same time there was also a growing level of lobbying going on, with Pelletier and Donovan persuading the others to scuttle the medical executive committee, the one by sweet-talk and entertainment at his home and the other by dogmatic declarations and unremitting propaganda.

Eventually, at a general meeting of the medical staff, the executive was dissolved and policy decisions henceforth would be taken at town-hall-style meetings. This was a time for Appleton to move strongly and swiftly in order to assert his authority, but he believed in the ultimate freedoms of democracy and was content to let nature take its course.

Meanwhile, two new doctors joined the Center. Peter Lawton was a well-trained and well-qualified specialist in Ob.Gyn, and would lighten Tony Donovan's increasing load to a fair degree, while Sam Posner was a general internist with fine credentials, who would be a valuable addition to the medical department. Eventually, it was hoped to have at least two specialists in each department, both for improved patient care and for the reduction of specialist stress and isolation. It was a principle supported by both Appleton and Bosnar, and they hoped it wouldn't be opposed

by the group's original specialists. As for hospital privileges for the newcomers, there were countless inexcusable delays, but in the end there was no way they could be denied their rightful place on
the hospital's medical staffs.

In the absence of a medical executive in the Center, Philip proposed at the next general meeting that they take steps forthwith to establish an independent partnership of the clinic
doctors, to be known as the Lakeside District Medical Group; and they should have an annual
renewable contract with the Board of the Group Health Association. Dr. Appleton was to be their
duly elected medical director and in no way an employee of the Association. Re-election would
take place at five year intervals. These motions were carried unanimously and for the moment, at
least, there was a feeling of strength, unity and harmony among the clinic doctors.

CHAPTER 47

1965

It was a sad day for St. Matthew's Hospital, for the city of Saint Pierre, and for Philip Bosnar in particular, when Michael Leslie was forced to resign. This fine and upright Englishman was one of the best pathologists he'd ever known, accurate and honest. Philip would miss his expertise and his boyish sense of humor, and San Pete's loss was going to be Sudbury's gain. Leslie had at last succumbed to pressure from the medical society for being too friendly and cooperative with the Health Center doctors, and when the Sister Superior cancelled the expected increase in his none too generous annual stipend, he decided that the handwriting on the wall was all too clear and accepted an offer from Sudbury at a much higher income.

Now, until such time as a new pathologist could be found, the city doctors would be at the mercy of Dr. George Filmore's incompetence spread across both hospitals. As a prime example of his premature senility, his initial opinion on the biopsy of Kurt Fleischmann's lymph nodes was *'Ovarian Carcinoma Metastasis in Lymph node'*! When Philip pointed out that the patient was a male, the pathologist changed the written report to 'Pancreatic Carcinoma' without a trace of embarrassment, and the surgeon made sure that slides were sent to the Princess Margaret Hospital pathologist for official confirmation.

The Princess Margaret radiotherapy team, headed by Drs. Ash and Ault, held regular clinics at the Memorial Hospital for both follow-up and new patients, and in late summer Bosnar and Pelletier arranged to meet them in the surgeon's lounge on the O.R. floor. They introduced themselves and had a polite and informative chat over cups of the execrable coffee served in those hallowed quarters. Although both visiting cancer experts were less than effusive, they weren't openly hostile, and Philip found that he liked and respected them. Ash was a great bear of a man, with ruddy face and heavy black Mack Sennett mustache, while Ault was a pale and thoughtful antithesis to his ebullient colleague. (*In years to come Philip would learn to value these two men as sincere and helpful professional friends, and he could always pick up a phone at any time and discuss problem cancer cases with them without going through all the red tape.*)

Gus Pelletier had strong opinions concerning the operative repair of infant hernias, which he considered weren't always handled too well by general surgeons. One morning he was assisting Philip with a recurrent hernia in a 2-year-old boy, and dissection revealed the fact that there was still a large and well-developed congenital hernial sac. Pelletier exploded and exclaimed, "The bloody fool who operated on this kid the first time either didn't know how to find a congenital sac or didn't remove it properly."

The senior scrub nurse, who'd worked in the O.R. for many years and had strong loyalties, turned beet-red and addressed Pelletier angrily.

"That remark was uncalled for. Dr. Brady is one of our best surgeons and he's the one who did the first operation!"

A short while after this incident she left the hospital, and so did the O.R. Sister; whether this was by coincidence, or a decision that they weren't going to work for such brash intruders into the established surgical order, was something Philip would never find out. In any event it wasn't long before the irrepressible Pelletier made a similar observation in a parallel case, a 5-year-old boy.

"Now you can see Dr. Bosnar demonstrating the right way to operate on a pediatric inguinal hernia by dissecting out the congenital sac completely."
The patient was his own son and the apple of his eye, and Gus was quite emotional in his gratitude toward Philip.

There were two cases during the next month that involved both Philip Bosnar and Tony Donovan, one that wasn't without its amusing side and the other with an unexpected dark side. In the first, Philip was called to the emergency department of St. Matthew's Hospital at 9 o'clock on a Sunday evening. The boyish Dr. Mike Fowler was waiting for him when he arrived and introduced him to the patient, a pale and slender young woman who was having considerable pain in her lower right abdomen. After examining her carefully Philip felt convinced that this was a case of tubal pregnancy with intra-abdominal bleeding, and he suggested calling Dr. Donovan.

"But Dr. Donovan's already seen her and thinks she's got acute appendicitis."

"I'm afraid I have to disagree. I know she's missed no periods and had no vaginal bleeding, but she had a bout of faintness at the onset of her attack, even mentions spots before her eyes. Her temperature's normal, her pulse rate's fast and her blood-pressure's below normal."

"Any other suggestive features?"

"Definitely. Her tongue is clean, she has no digestive upset and I thought I could detect a small tender mass in her right tubal region on pelvic examination. In my opinion we should get her up to the O.R. as soon as possible, and without waiting for all the lab tests to come back."

"Why don't you go ahead and get the O.R. set up, Dr. Bosnar, while I phone Donovan, give him your opinion, and get the lab to speed up."
By the time everything was ready in the O.R. and Grier was getting his equipment set up, Tony Donovan arrived and seemed a trifle irritated.

"I still think you'll find a pelvic appendicitis." "Well, Tony, I intend to play it safe by employing a midline incision, and then we'll see."

The abdomen was quickly entered and as soon as blood welled up from the pelvis they all knew that this was indeed a ruptured ectopic (tubal) pregnancy. At this point there was a phone call for Donovan and while he was gone Philip used the suction tube and saline irrigation to clear the pelvis. When Donovan returned he asked Philip to go ahead without him as he had a patient in labor at the other hospital. By this time, everything was under control and Fowler assisted enthusiastically as Philip removed the right Fallopian tube and its contents along with a few clots. When the field was clean and dry he was able to note an appendix that looked quite innocent, and a normal left tube as well as two healthy ovaries. He closed up the abdomen and looked forward to discharging the patient within the week.

The second case was a 12-year-old girl, rather precociously developed for her age. She'd been admitted overnight to St. Matthew's with fever, vomiting and abdominal pain. Her blood count and urinalysis were unremarkable but her abdominal X-rays revealed some dilatation of the small and large bowel and a possible soft tissue mass in the lower abdomen. Physical examination revealed premature enlargement of the breasts, a possible mass deeply located in the lower belly, and marked associated tenderness. There were two other unexpected features. According to her mother she had menstruated briefly once or twice, and then no more for the next two months; not even spotting. An enterprising night supervisor had sent a urine specimen for a pregnancy test and it came back positive.

After discussing the case with Donovan and having him confirm his findings, plus the paradox that she appeared to be a virgin, Philip sat down with the patient's mother and had a lengthy, frank and painful discussion of his findings. The mother was certain her daughter had never shown any undue interest in boys and was confident that pregnancy was out of the question, although she understood that actual penetration wasn't essential for the occurrence of conception.

It was a difficult situation, and Philip was glad he and Tony were in agreement that exploratory Laparotomy (surgical opening of the abdomen) was indicated, since the girl was showing no improvement with anti-emetics and intravenous fluids and was – if anything – getting worse, with a rising pulse-rate and temperature.

The abdominal exploration was performed that afternoon with Donovan assisting, and the nature of the condition was soon apparent. The presence of a soft tissue mass was confirmed right away. It consisted of a conglomerate of grossly enlarged Lymph nodes, each about the size of a plum instead of the normal size of a pea. This was no ordinary *Mesenteric Lymphadenitis* (a condition quite common in children and young adults, in which inflamed lymph nodes can simulate appendicitis) but some type of lymphoid tumor. There was no sign of appendicitis or abscess formation, and the female pelvic organs were small and undeveloped but otherwise normal. Generous biopsies of the lymph node mass were taken and the abdomen closed, but only after excluding any obstructive factor or other abnormality.

Preliminary studies of the slides indicated a diagnosis of *Giant Follicular Lymphoma* (a rather unusual type of lymph node tumor), and Dr. Bosnar asked Dr. Filmore to forward the slides to the Princess Margaret Hospital laboratory. Next, he had a long talk with the patient's mother and explained the findings at surgery. He also advised a transfer to the Princess Margaret Hospital in Toronto as soon as the girl could travel by air.

Over the next twenty-four hours, with continued IVs and gastric suction, the girl showed a steady improvement, and within three days was taking food and walking, with a normal temperature and her bowels moving normally. In addition to dictating an extensive case report addressed to Dr. Ash, Philip phoned him and told him about the red herring factor, namely the positive pregnancy test.

Two days after surgery the laboratory discovered that an error had occurred as two specimens got mixed up that first night when the pregnancy test was ordered. The patient's mother was understandably rattled when she got the news, but at the same time showed considerable relief.

One week later. Dr. Ash phoned to tell Philip that the diagnosis of Giant Follicular Lymphoma had been confirmed and that a course of radiotherapy would be carried out. He sounded quite optimistic and said he'd be sending him a full report, yet some intuitive feeling told Philip that this case was far from over.

The fall of '64 in the Cambrian countryside was incredibly beautiful, and Philip was happy to start doing some more photography. Even the sides of the Trans-Canada Highway were ablaze with color, and on the nearby hillsides it seemed as though nature was determined to put on its most resplendent display. The fallen leaves on the ground revealed an array of colors, ruby, gold, and emerald, and the earth became covered with these jewelled emblems of the changing season.

There was one favorite spot where, once or twice a week, Philip would drive to the top of a hill and gaze down on the valley below, in all its lush glory. This was not only a place to delight the photographer but one in which to refresh ones soul and drive out the trials and tribulations of life's ever-present conflicts. The contemplation of nature's priceless bounty, along with the happiness derived from ones beloved partner in life, made everything else worthwhile, and brought harmony out of chaos.

When Philip learned through the center's grapevine that Jack Grier would be leaving in the new year, he was disappointed and even angry. First, Grier was an excellent anesthetist with a special talent in regional anesthetic techniques. Second, despite all his irritating peculiarities and evidence of weakness under pressure, Philip had grown to like Grier and felt he was beginning to fit in more with his colleagues. Third, he realized that the new position their anesthetist would be filling in Toronto was a definite step upward. Nevertheless, there seemed to Philip something amoral about jumping at the first tempting opportunity to leave the Center. It was so soon after trying to destroy its effective operation, by alienating the G.Ps on the one hand and eliminating the essential medical executive on the other. He must have known how Philip felt since he never once approached him to discuss his forthcoming departure.

Perhaps it should have been no surprise to learn that both Pelletier and Donovan supported Grier's decision and encouraged him to accept the offer. In examining his own opposite attitude, Philip recognized that, to him, joining an organization of this kind was like a marriage, and one didn't abandon such a union at the first overtures from a seductive temptress, even if there were quarrels within the marriage. It was all a matter of loyalty, of fidelity, and of commitment.

Jim Appleton lost no time in placing an advertisement for an anesthetist in both the Canadian and British medical journals, and by mid-November there were eleven applications. These were eventually narrowed down to two, both from England: a Dr. Sidney Raffles in Liverpool and a Dr. Vincent Cassidy in London. Without wasting any time Philip flew over to London in order to interview the candidates in person and to seize the opportunity of seeing his family once again.

The flight, by way of Shannon in Ireland, was a smooth and pleasant one, and the weather was surprisingly mild on arrival in London. His Dad, God bless him, was there to meet him in his spotless limousine; he must have polished it for days to have it reach its present glowing perfection. He had finally accepted his physician's insistent advice to give up smoking, and was starting to put on weight. Not only that, but he was still carrying on his business in the Farringdon Road area and putting in a full day's work without the slightest complaint.

Philip's beloved Mum, as tiny and sprightly as ever, was overjoyed to see him once again, but he was sad to learn that she was being treated for repeated attacks of depression, now that her children had all departed from her home and she was seeing them less often. She had even lost interest in cooking the superb meals for which she was so famous. Nevertheless, Philip's arrival gave her the excuse she needed to revive her enthusiasm for that art.

Clayton was now practicing in Grays, Essex, and Philip spent many happy hours there, renewing old times with the brother who had always been more of a son. He was happy to see Clayton's wife Martha again and their delightful children, a little girl and a new baby boy – named Philip after his Canadian uncle. The house, offices and grounds were all in splendid shape, and it was evident his sister-in-law was a dedicated wife and mother. As for Clayton, he was deeply involved in the academic side of family practice and community medicine, and his papers and lectures on the subject were beginning to gain the notice of the profession at large. One or two leaders in the postgraduate education of Britain's G.Ps had become his close friends, and Philip felt sure his brother was destined for a bright academic future.

The high point of his London visit was seeing his wandering son once more. James had grown into a handsome young man, well over six feet tall, and although very slender, strongly built. His face showed many new lines that bore testimony to the hardships of an aspiring actor in a metropolis overflowing with acting talent. His voice was strong and resonant, his accent a polished English, his bearing aristocratic, and his politics far, far left. In the Maoist lexicon of his son, Philip's moderately conservative views identified him as a cryptofascist, and they were destined for many a political duel in the coming years.

Meanwhile, James was holding body and soul together in reasonable fashion. At the present time he was living with his current lady-love in her cottage, located in a secluded wooded area of Woolwich. She was a most attractive young woman who earned her own living as stage and costume designer, and Philip was afraid she was much more in love with his son than he with her.

During his first week in London, Philip was able to contact both Dr. Raffles and Dr. Cassidy. The first, who was the Center's first choice, conveyed his regrets and reported his wife's objection to leaving Britain and living in North America.

"I'm afraid I can't budge her on that point, old chap, so all bets are off. Sorry." At least he seemed contrite.

Dr. Cassidy sounded pleasantly Irish over the phone, with a cultured 'south-of-the-border' brogue. He said he'd be glad to meet Dr. Bosnar in front of St. Cecilia's Hospital at 12 noon. He arrived fifteen minutes late, very charming and very apologetic.

"I'm afraid our London traffic situation has snarled itself into a hopeless impasse. As for bus schedules, they're meaningless."

They had a leisurely lunch at one of Longrow Street's friendly pubs; the meal was tasty and the Bass Ale – at room temperature – was delicious. They strolled back to St. Cecilia's Hospital, went through the admitting area and through the back into the familiar courtyard that brought back a thousand happy memories.

After a short walk they sat down on a bench in the cool but sunlit air, with only a passing student or pretty nurse as diversion, and talked about the Health Center and its opportunities for a specialist with Cassidy's experience. Without scaring him, Philip gave him some idea of the hostile atmosphere in San Pete, but expressed his optimism that this would disappear in time. The financial terms were agreeable, and Cassidy said he'd be happy to join the clinic at the beginning of the new year. No papers were signed but Cassidy seemed quite definite about his intention to join the Center, so Philip felt confident he would come as promised.

A few days before Philip was due to leave, Pauline arrived with her husband at their parents' house in Hendon. Irving was still at the same job with the same company and Pauline was helping the family coffers by working in a lady's fashion boutique on Oxford Street. They seemed happy enough, but Philip could see no sign whatever of genuine romantic feelings between them, and he felt sad for his sister. She was always the incurable romantic as a girl and still showed signs of her earlier beauty.

"Perhaps I shouldn't tell you this, Phil", she said to him quietly, when she got him alone, "but I thought you ought to know that Dora Henderson has been very ill lately."

He phoned Dora's number and was answered by her niece.

"She's still in the Brenthaven Hospital, in the new cardiac unit, and I'm sure she'd love a visit from you, Dr. Bosnar. She still talks about you whenever Canada is in the news, and takes pride in your career."

He caught the morning train the following day, and after arrival took the familiar walk to the hospital, the one that seemed so unreal and tragic a quarter of a century ago. When he was shown into her room, carrying his awkward load of flowers and fruit-basket, her pale face broke into a flashing smile and she quipped with wicked humor, "Carrying gifts to the dying, Phil, all the way across the Atlantic?"

"Don't put on that Camille act with me, Dora," he bantered, "I've just spoken to your doctor, and he says that you've made an excellent recovery from your recent heart attack. He says that if you keep your blood-pressure down with regular medication and cut down on your gruelling work schedule you'll be as good as new."

They conversed easily for the next half hour and her present frailty and snowy white hair seemed, by a strange paradox, to restore the bygone image of a young and vivacious beauty with 'the smile of angels'.

"Well, Dora, I must be going now."

"Would you give me a kiss before you go. After all, I'm toying with the idea of writing a novel, with you as the central character."

He gave her a gentle kiss and knew he'd never make any attempt to contact her again. Now that he felt reassured she was making a good recovery it was time to cut off the past, once and for all.

"Goodbye, Dora, and all the best." Her eyes were far away.

"I had all the best, Phil, and let it all go."

When Philip got back to San Pete, the snows of winter were already deep on the ground and the relations between Tony Donovan on the one side and his Ob.Gyn. partner and the Medical Director on the other had become equally frigid. It became painfully obvious that the bellicose Tony was a confirmed loner and could never fit into the team atmosphere of a medical group, no matter what changes were made at his behest.

At the beginning of May he handed in his resignation, and the rest of the clinic doctors tried hard not to reveal their sense of relief. Lately he'd been behaving like a bull in a china shop. The group would have been satisfied to let him go without the mandatory ninety day notice, but he created an unacceptable situation when he began to phone all his patients, giving them his new office address and requesting that they make an appointment with him as soon as possible. This was outrageously unethical and he was asked to cease and desist.

When he paid no attention to the warning, Jim Appleton and Peter Lawton decided the College should be notified, and the entire medical staff agreed. Whatever action the College eventually decided to take, it was too little and too late, and Tony Donovan's bitterness toward the C.H.C. was now engraved in stone. He moved out of the Lakeshore Manor into a house near the hospitals, where he set up an office, with his gracious wife – of whom Phil and Patty were very fond – acting as receptionist. To his credit, he made no attempt to cozy up to the local medical society, preferring to be the cat that walks alone.

The departure of two of its medical staff before the end of the Center's second year seemed to set off a sort of chain reaction and Philip wondered where it would stop. To make matters worse, both defectors tried to dislocate the institution's structure before leaving. The next one to leave, however, was no defector. His departure was nothing more than the reaction of a sensitive personality (concealed under a tough exterior) to the innuendoes and antagonisms of his professional colleagues in solo practice.

Bob Gaylord's letter of resignation contained poignant passages. **'A disgraceful situation exists in this city. I am referring to the manner in which certain physicians in Saint Pierre, under the banner of the local medical society, have treated the Community Health Center staff. It is possible that I would have remained here indefinitely had it not been for this situation, but I do not choose to spend my life in an atmosphere of hate, vindictiveness and paranoid delusions.'** Later on in the letter he stated, **'Some of these medical society physicians have said that we should not take the insults, segregation, and efforts to destroy this program in a personal way. Perhaps I am being overly sensitive but I have taken each and every affront personally.'**

He departed with his colleagues' best wishes and informed them that he planned to resume his training in Pathology and then, perhaps, return to upper Michigan as a pathologist and stay in touch with his friends in San Pete. His departure would be a great loss to them and Philip resented seeing him driven from their midst.

Worrying cases and situations are no stranger to any surgeon, and different individuals react in different ways to such stresses. In the old days, before Philip went into the army, he would probably have reacted by drinking more scotch, whereas now it was his duodenal ulcer that demanded a greater and more frequent intake, not of scotch but of antacids.

He was fortunate in never suffering any bleeding episodes; nor were there any obstructive features, a detail confirmed in his recent X-ray examination. At least his general health was fine, and Stuart Atkins assured him that his lungs and cardiovascular system were those of a much younger man. It was, therefore, an unpleasant surprise when he awoke one early morning in early March at about 2 a.m. with a steady cramplike pain all over his belly; one that didn't fluctuate, yet wasn't severe enough to consider an early perforated ulcer.

His natural inclination was to try the bathroom first and see if he could get any relief by passing stool or flatus, but the pain only got worse. He tried to tough it out to a more civilized hour, but by 4 a.m. and after three more drinks of antacid, he decided to stay up and take some further action. His provisional diagnosis was acute appendicitis in the early obstructive phase, before localization of pain and tenderness.

First, he phoned St. Matthew's from the living room in order to avoid waking Patty. They had no available surgical beds but could make room for him in the Intensive Care Unit. He told them that this would be strictly against his policy and he believed in practicing what he preached. Next, he phoned the Memorial and they were able to accommodate him in a private room on the main surgical floor. By this time Patty was awake and he told her he had to go to the hospital because of an emergency, and she went back to sleep.

By the time he'd undressed in the emergency department and had his vital statistics recorded, his vital signs taken and his lab specimens obtained, it was time to call Gus Pelletier and he came over right away. After examining the patient he came to the same conclusion about his diagnosis and stated that he'd place him on an observation routine for a few hours and then probably operate. By this time it was 7 a.m. and Philip phoned Patty and told her the exact truth of what had transpired during the night. She was justifiably angry with him but realized that there had been no point in waking her until now.

Within thirty minutes she'd picked up all the essentials for his hospital stay, packed them neatly and driven over to the hospital in her new Austin car. As his devoted wife, she couldn't conceal her anxiety, but as an experienced surgical nurse she knew there was little to worry about and only hoped the operation wouldn't be too long delayed.

When localization of symptoms and signs in the lower right quadrant of Philip's belly finally occurred, the pain was much sharper and more intense yet much more bearable, since it had changed from so-called 'Protopathic' obstructive cramp to non-obstructive 'Epicritic' pain. The operation went smoothly, the appendix was large and purulent but not ruptured or gangrenous, and Gus left Philip a specimen of his abdominal fat in a bottle to indicate that he'd been putting on a bit too much weight. Within one week the patient was back at work and felt fine; it was his first personal experience of surgery (other than tonsillectomy) and it was much better than he'd expected.

There was only one disturbing element during the postoperative period, and that had nothing to do with the operation itself. Three days after surgery, Gus came to see Philip with some unpleasant news.

"Remember that weird case of Giant Follicular Lymphoma?"

"The one with the wrong pregnancy test?"

"That's the one. Well, yesterday we got a writ from Ronald Carston, the lawyer who's Chairman of the Board at St. Matthew's, claiming that you and the Community Health Center are responsible for permanent damage to the young girl. He's taking you and the clinic to court for damages."

"I can't imagine on what grounds."

"You're accused of mishandling the management of the case and being responsible for radiation treatment that will destroy her ovarian function and permanently impair her future chances to have children."

"Has anything been done about this so far?"

"Jim immediately contacted the C.M.P.A. (Canadian Medical Protective Association). He told them about the case and informed their secretary that a full report would follow. He advised that we say nothing to the lawyer or the family but just sit tight and await developments."

"That's their typical attitude. What about the media? If they get hold of this business through a friendly leak they could have a field day."

"I don't think that's likely, as they'd have to implicate the Princess Margaret guys because of the radiotherapy,"

Two weeks later Philip got a lunchtime phone-call from a very irate Dr. Ash, who was in town with the Ontario Cancer Clinic's regular follow-up session. He'd just learned about the legal action against Philip and the Health Center.

"That you, Bosnar? I've just got off the phone to Morecombe, and I guess I blew my top. I asked him what kind of shyster St. Matthew's had as Chairman of the Board when he could take on a phony case like this, especially as he's suing the wrong people. We were the ones at the Princess Margaret who decided to radiate the patient, and we don't leave our females with depleted ovarian function in such cases."

Dr. Ash sounded as if he was still ready to blow his top.

"Frankly, the whole thing stinks of politics and I'm disgusted. I told Morecombe that Carston should resign as Chairman of the Hospital Board. When you see Morecombe, you might ask him who put the family and their lawyer up to this rotten mischief."

A few days later the legal action was withdrawn. According to Carston's letter of self-justification: **'Additional facts have now come to my attention, but I am still convinced that if the surgeon had spent a little more time with the mother this entire unpleasantness could have been avoided.'**

Philip's reply was as acerbic as he could make it.

'Your letter of May 12 deserves to be treated with the same degree of contempt as your original unsupported allegations. The time I spent with Janice Layton's mother following my first examination of Janice was in excess of four hours during the first two days alone, a fact that completely refutes your most recent accusation.'

On the advice of the Canadian Medical Protective Association, Mrs. Layton was informed that she and her family should seek future medical attention by non-clinic doctors. In spite of this request she wrote and asked Dr. Bosnar if she could come and talk to him and he agreed; perhaps he might discover who were the people involved in this dirty business. The interview was unsatisfactory, however, and left a bad taste in his mouth. The poor woman had obviously been pressured by more than one person but was afraid to divulge who they were.

Philip learned later that the situation had been exacerbated by the fact that following her radiotherapy Janice was re-explored at the Ontario Pediatric Center in Toronto and had her appendix removed. The intern looking after her informed Mrs. Layton, "it was probably her appendix from the very start", an unhelpful statement that was not only slanderous but revealed a total ignorance of the recorded pathology findings. Following this experience, the medical staff of the center seemed to draw closer together, and a medical executive was re-established along its original lines.

Now that Bob Gaylord was gone it seemed that Ted Novak seemed determined to expand his position in the group and fill the void. He wasn't one to hide his light under a bushel and soon got himself elected to the executive in Gaylord's place. There was no doubt that he had a fine academic base and that his manner with patients inspired confidence; it was his constant desire to 'grandstand' that made him so controversial and brought him occasional humiliation but rarely a desire to mend his ways.

There were examples, such as the time he excitedly called Philip up to his office to see one of his patients in urgent consultation. His manner radiated gratification. "This dear lady was seen last week by Dr. Olmano for vague abdominal discomfort and I can't blame him for missing the diagnosis because the patient admits being distended with gas at that time. Today I discovered the presence of an ***Aortic Aneurysm*** and I would like your expert confirmation."

(This condition is a ballooning of the main arterial trunk in the abdomen and represents a major danger to the patient).

Ten minutes later Philip gave him his verdict without frills.

"This is a thin and highly nervous young lady with chronic anxiety related to her abdominal viscera, and with a clearly visible and palpable aortic pulsation that's quite common in such patients. There is no audible bruit and no widening of the aortic column. She should be reassured about these findings and checked for any overlooked stressful situation."

Another occasion was a call from the emergency department at the Memorial at 5 a.m. It was the irrepressible Novak.

"Sorry to get you up at this awful hour, Dr. Bosnar, but I have a woman here with a very large Pneumothorax following a car accident, and she needs your expert help." (Pneumothorax is a condition in which air leaks from the lung into the chest cavity and collapses all or part of the same lung). Ted certainly knew how to lay it on!

The patient was a lady in her mid-forties who was the front seat passenger in a car driven by her boyfriend after a party with friends that included a few drinks. Their car hit a parked truck and the patient sustained a chest injury. Philip examined her carefully and checked out the X-rays.

"This lady has bruised a rib but no pneumothorax, Ted."

"But just look at this line showing the edge of the collapsed lung."

"That line is the edge of the scapula (shoulder blade) because the film was taken with the shoulders thrown forward. I've just injected the painful area with some local anesthetic and she feels much better. Now I'd better get back for some shut-eye as I have an eight o'clock gastric resection."

Ted Novak's first appearance at a meeting with the Board of the Community Health Association was a memorable one. As usual, the meeting started with the customary recitation of patients' complaints, no matter how trivial or even spurious. It had been some considerable time since the last joint meeting and the Board members knew that the doctors had a few important axes to grind. To Ted Novak, however, this was a personal challenge.

"I know there have been quite a few complaints about my fellow doctors, but they're very busy, although not as busy as I am. I'd really like to help when they're in difficulties, but I'm only one man."

At this point Philip shattered the stunned silence by breaking into loud guffaws of laughter that soon spread to the others and broke the tension. (From that time forth Novak was known as 'I'm-only-one-man Novak', but his conceit and vanity continued unabated, while his charm and conviviality remained beyond compare).

Before getting into the nitty-gritty of the agenda, Philip felt it essential to bring the meeting back to sanity and he spoke out frankly.

"Mr. Chairman, before we close the subject of patients' complaints, I feel compelled to relate a small incident that occurred during the first month of our clinic's existence. It was just after 6 p.m. and I was entering my car in the parking lot, planning to go over to the Memorial Hospital and check out a post-op patient before going home for dinner. The doors of the Center were locked until 7 p.m. and I saw a large and menacing individual pounding on the back door and cussing his head off. 'I put money into this fucking building', he complained, 'and now the fucking place is shut and I can't get in.' I tried to explain to him that the place would be open again in one hour but if he couldn't wait I'd be glad to drive him to the hospital. He continued to rant and rave about owning part of the building until I lost my cool. 'Listen, buster,' I said, 'if I had the time I'd take out one of these fucking bricks that you own and ram it in your fucking mouth.' He quietened down immediately and apologized, and when I saw him months later as a surgical patient he behaved like a perfect gentleman."

The rest of the meeting was productive and a good deal was accomplished, to everyone's satisfaction.

1965 was obviously destined to be one of growing pains and early, transitional adjustment. The latest development was the departure of the Health Center's estimable administrator, Earl Formby. He had done his difficult job with quiet efficiency, and without any political or ideological overtones. For the purpose of smoothing the C.H.C's birth-pangs, this technocrat had been the ideal midwife, and he felt it was now time to move on, although Philip wished he'd stay. His departure represented a certain loss of permanency in their institution and Philip was worried. Formby was leaving them to take a teaching post in the University of Saskatoon's department of medical administration and they all wished him well.

There was one more disturbing development in the center that had been slowly growing in dimension during the past six months: the growth of a dissident trio. The key figure in this trio was, without a doubt, Gus Pelletier, that most likeable and persuasive fellow. The second was their new internist, Sam Posner, a child of the European Holocaust, a young man who lost most of his family before coming to Canada at the age of fourteen. He was an individual who always seemed on guard against hidden threats and one whose suspicions were easily aroused. The third was Gil Thayer, a jolly Englishman who joined the family practice department last June and since then had been an inseparable companion and ally of Pelletier. He'd previously practiced in rural Newfoundland and found it too lonely a career. Now he was no longer alone in practice and whenever he was at the hospitals he never left Gus Pelletier's side.

At their medical staff meetings in the Center, the threesome always voted as a bloc, in uniform opposition to the medical director and his majority supporters. Thayer and Posner sent all their surgical cases to Pelletier and Philip thought that was fair enough, since he got most of the referred surgery from the remainder of the staff. What worried him much more was the lack of team spirit manifest in this trio, and he dreaded the possibility of small power cliques being formed in their expanding organization, and threatening its healthy atmosphere and morale. Now, for the first time, Philip knew – with clear certainty – that despite the ferocity of its outside opposition, the greatest threat to the survival of their Health Center would come from within the group itself.

Meanwhile on the home front, Phil and Patty moved into a spacious corner suite on the top floor of the Lakeshore Manor, with a splendid view from every window, and Patty was delighted with her new abode. She would soon be flying out to Edwardia, where Florian was planning to get married in July, and it was time for a mother to be with her daughter and supervise some of the initial arrangements. The Bosnars prayed that Florian had chosen well, and that she'd have as romantic, happy, and durable a marriage as theirs.

On the national scene, the Bosnars saw that their stupid Prime Minister was still doing his best to draw Canada into the U.S. orbit and away from its mother country. His latest act of egregious insult to the country's British affiliations, by changing the time-honored national flag, was an outrage as far as Philip was concerned, and would accomplish nothing in return. Removing the nation's precious Union Jack and substituting what looked like a ketchup-colored, badly drawn Star of David, would offend the anglophiles and do nothing to appease the francophiles. At the very least, the deluded national leader of the Canadian nation could have retained a smaller Union Jack in the top left hand corner of the new flag and added some Fleurs de Lis or even a Cross of Loraine if he wished, thus keeping far more Canadians happy without destroying their history.

In sharp contrast to the ineffectual leadership of Lester B.Pearson, the Presidency of Lyndon Johnson was producing some startling results. This archetypal conservative Democrat from the deep South had brought in the most powerful legislation in support of civil rights and against poverty that anybody could possibly have imagined. He had taken the ideological ball left him by his liberal predecessor and run with it all the way. Philip's dislike and distrust of this coarse vulgarian were now replaced by an abiding admiration, but he couldn't see how even his determined leadership could stop the hopeless entrapment of American soldiers in the military quicksands of Vietnam. It seemed a war the U.S. couldn't possibly win, and Philip began to wonder whether the enemy was just the Viet Cong peasant fighters or they were being supported by North Vietnam forces and even the Chinese and Russians. Who could really tell, and who could reverse the inexorable march toward ultimate tragedy?

As far as duplicate bridge was concerned, Patty was becoming even more devoted to the game than her husband, and along with a few of her friends had started a second club in the city, with weekly games on Wednesday afternoons. The new club used the premises of the elegant new Y.M.C.A. building located across from the Health Center, and Patty was its first president. Because of Philip's schedule, he was unable to join her for these games, but on most Thursday evenings he was able to do so for those held at the technical college, about ten blocks north of the Center. They had been doing quite well in their club games and started to travel around to nearby cities for sectional and regional tournaments, both in Canada and the U.S.A. Since Philip was getting much closer to becoming a 'Life Master' they decided to take in the regional tournament which was being held Minneapolis.

One of the most important elements of these tournaments was the social aspect. Not only were there usually several players from their own city, but they arranged to make their hotel reservations so that their rooms were on the same floor, and they usually took their meals together as a group. Alas, there was also the bad habit of congregating for a party after the evening games, starting close to midnight and continuing until about 2 a.m. In addition, Phil and Patty got to know players from other areas and an increasing number of the game directors, especially those from Toronto.

Patty was anxious to be the one who put Philip over the top as a Life Master, and was deeply disappointed when their first game at the Minneapolis Regional turned out to be a disaster. But somehow, their second event seemed to turn out much better, and they got into a good bidding rhythm that, with sound play and a bit of luck, gave them some very good boards. After the game, Patty asked Philip how he estimated their score, and he said he expected it to be in the 180s (as against an average of 156) but fortunately he was wrong. Their 196 figure was good enough for a second place finish overall and gave Philip his Life Master ranking, the first in the Algoma geographic unit that stretched south to Northern Michigan and east to Elliot Lake.

The Bosnars threw quite a party that night with their friends, and Philip vowed that his next project was to put his darling Patricia 'over the top' within the next few years and make her the first lady Life Master in their unit.

CHAPTER 48

1965-66

It appeared that things were settling down nicely in the Center these days, and the atmosphere between the medical society doctors and those of the Center was slowly but surely improving. Perhaps the situation was almost too calm. One of Philip Bosnar's primary aims was that some kind of clandestine contact should be established between the two sides of the medical profession in the city: the kind of concealed diplomacy that must surely be taking place between the U.S.A. and the U.S.S.R, even at the worst moments of the cold war.

Oddly enough, the first approach was from the other side. Cedric Blore was one of the most respected doctors in the city, a family physician of considerable experience, a historian of some repute who was also very active in the local army reserve, with the rank of Lt. Colonel. He was a good speaker and a polished gentleman, and from the very first he had distanced himself from the medical feud. He approached Philip one day as they were about to enter their cars in the doctors' parking lot at the Memorial. As usual, he was smoking his cigarette fiercely and coughing as though he was destroying some lung tissue with each deep inhalation. He spoke first.

"If you have a moment, Dr. Bosnar, I'd like a word with you."

"By all means, Dr. Blore. Please call me Phil and perhaps you won't mind if I call you Cedric."

"Great idea, but my friends call me Sid. People like you and me don't have to stand on formalities, do we?"

"Certainly not."

"I just wanted to tell you I was in Kingston last week for an army get-together and met some of your buddies from Thorburn."

"It's a small world alright, even in a country the size of Canada."

"Anyhow, they remembered you well and called you their Renaissance Man when you were chief of surgery, because of your knowledge of language, music, chess, and bridge."

"Memories produce their own exaggerations, don't they?"

"Maybe, Phil, but I told them I agreed with their evaluation."

"I think you and I should have lunch together and talk about the local insanity, don't you, Sid?"

That was the start of a series of lunches they had together in a quiet corner of the dining-room at the Lakes Motor Hotel, a few blocks from the Health Center. They discussed ways and means of improving relations between the two sides, and especially the possibility of expanding the present medical society to include the clinic doctors. They talked about opening up some of the more important hospital appointments to clinic doctors, and the avoidance by either side of any public statement offensive to the other doctors. Philip knew Blore had the ear of some of the leading solo doctors such as Darren Markovsky, Don Foley, and Herb Slater as well as the new administrator at the Memorial, and this should prove most helpful.

There was far more interchange these days in the surgeons' lounges of both hospitals, and only the diehard rednecks showed open hostility. The others avoided controversy apart from the occasional needling remark made in fun. It was nice for Philip to know that his surgical work was well regarded, and his discussions at ward rounds brought favorable comments. God knows he didn't need the flattery, as his ego was no shrinking violet, but it established a sort of professional link with the downtown practitioners that cut through political prejudice to some extent. It did NOT translate into referral of surgical cases, but there were renewed attempts to woo him away from the C.H.C. into solo practice. When he made it clear that he wouldn't budge, he became known as a "hardliner", along with Jim Appleton and Wilfred Jarvis, the Center's new administrator.

The abolition of the medical executive at the Health Center hadn't brought any particular benefits to the group, and in fact simply produced a system of decision by meetings in town-hall style, in which the Medical Director had to cope with those persistent loud voices that found it easier to complain than suggest constructive improvement. A newly elected executive committee, despite its faults, would be far better than a pseudo-democratic anarchy.

Jim Appleton was an excellent Medical Director but a hopeless chairman at meetings. Philip wished his friend would be a little more forceful and follow Roberts' Rules of Procedure or some similar protocol, in order to keep the meetings under a semblance of control. One particular point he found most galling was that two of the members most responsible for abolishing the original executive committee had since turned around and left. At least the medical group had gained a valuable educational experience: a lesson that giving in to unreasonable demands was no way to keep the complainers from leaving whenever they felt like it.

Gus Pelletier was getting very restless, and kept telling Philip that with the amount of surgery they were doing they should be making far more money. Philip reminded him that this was Canada and not the United States, but he still grumbled and insisted that the reason he wasn't getting any thoracic surgery from downtown was because he worked at the Health Center. He said that his special training in this field made no difference at all. Finally, when all of Philip's arguments had been exhausted, Gus came out with his plans.

"I'm going down to the States in three weeks, Phil, to meet with some of my old buddies. While I'm down there I hope to see my old chief Dr. Grosfeld, and find out if there's any chance of getting set up in a surgical practice in Minnesota. Let's face it, I'm not cut out for this kind of practice, and I don't believe I have a future here."

"Well, Gus, I'd hate to see you go, because it's been a good relationship in spite of our differences, but I guess you know what's best for you and your family and I wish you luck."

"It's been good working with you, and you know I've learned a good deal from our association."

"We've both learned from each other, one way or another."

"Whatever happens, Phil, I won't make any move without letting you know first."

In a way Philip was relieved. He liked Pelletier a lot and hoped he would do well, no matter what his decision. At least he wasn't thinking of going downtown; that would be awful.

Meanwhile, at St. Matthew's Hospital, one of its most durable figures was about to depart the scene. He was the tiny, elfin radiologist, 'Lofty' Percroft, always cheerful and friendly, rather behind the times in his field, but with broad interests that included prospecting and landscape painting. At the age of seventy-five he felt it was time to enjoy his hobbies, and all the doctors in the city wished him well. His place was taken by a much younger and thoroughly up-to-date Italian, Dr. Guiseppi Alfredi, a man with a sharp mind and a mercurial temper. Philip got along very well with him, but he deplored his tendency to write ill-tempered X-ray reports to some of his C.H.C. colleagues, and he intended to raise the subject in a diplomatic manner when a suitable opportunity arose.

One of Philip's patients developed a severe pneumonia following a stomach resection for cancer. He was responding well to treatment in consultation with Dr. Steve Vandam, the group's recent addition to the department of Internal Medicine. At Vandam's request, Philip had been ordering daily chest X-rays and these were read by a locum radiologist in the absence of Alfredi who was away at a radiology meeting in Montreal. After Alfredi's return, the nurses watched apprehensively as Philip picked up the latest X-ray report during his evening hospital rounds:

'I don't know how I am expected to report on this X-ray when there is no information whatever on the request form. This kind of deficiency is inexcusable!'

Philip defused the situation with a chuckle, and remarked, "I guess the poor chap must be swamped with the back-log and forgot to check the previous request forms on this patient. They carry all the detailed clinical information he could want."

Pulling the X-ray report from the chart, he crumpled it up, put it in his pocket and told the wide-eyed nurses he'd be clearing up the misunderstanding with the fiery radiologist in person.

The next morning, after his first two operations at the Memorial, Philip came over to St. Matthew's and found a note for him at the switchboard: **'See me in my office as soon as possible.'** and signed 'M.F. Prentice. Assistant Administrator.' During the past few months Philip had heard a lot of reports about this worthy gentleman, none of them favorable, but he'd never actually met him. He was said to be obsessed with his own importance and always ready to create difficulties in situations that could otherwise be handled smoothly.

When Philip entered his office, Prentice didn't bother to get up, and after his visitor sat down he busied himself for a few moments with some writing at his desk. Then he looked up with a nasty expression and started to speak in a belligerent tone of voice.

"You have absolutely no right to destroy any part of the hospital charts, Dr. Bosnar. They are hospital property and if you ever..." but at this point Philip interrupted.

"You'd better stop right there before you say too much. I presume you're referring to that unfortunate X-ray report written under stress and based on a misunderstanding. I felt it unwise to leave such a document on the chart, and fully intended to clear up this matter quietly and tactfully with Dr. Alfedi in person. Any indiscreet handling of this affair could easily jeopardize the excellent rapport Dr. Alfredi and I have enjoyed so far."

Unfortunately, Prentice had other ideas, and became hostile, arrogant and rude, until Philip felt he'd had a stomach-full. He rose up, leaned over the table, and spoke very softly.

"Listen, you officious pipsqueak, don't ever use that tone to me. I eat people like you and always spit them out."

His interviewer looked crushed, and Philip knew he'd never have any trouble with him again.

The temperamental Guiseppi and Philip had no further problem from that time forth, and a few months later the self-important assistant administrator at St. Matthew's was replaced by a delightful Irishman with a far more affable disposition. Shawn Dunleavy was his name, and he and Philip soon became good friends.

Don Foley's new Medical Arts Building was now completed and renting. All over town most of the doctors in solo practice were abandoning their dingy offices and renting space in the new building as shareholders. There was a fanfare of publicity in The Cambrian Leader, which declared that the edifice would undoubtedly win an architectural award, and described its features in detail, including a large pharmacy on the ground floor. Its location between the two hospitals wasn't considered by the City Council to be a traffic hazard, and its parking lot was invitingly located adjacent to the Memorial Hospital visitors' parking lot. Although the offices and examining rooms were said to be up to standard, the exterior failed to live up to the architect's expectations. It was in natural unpolished steel, dark grayish brown in color, and with its small windows it presented more the look of a penitentiary than a doctors' building.

The Medical Arts building never came close to being considered for an architectural award much to the disappointment of the medical society, which regarded this place as its new home. Two of the prospective renters who were seen to enter the new office-building on a tour of inspection were Gus Pelletier and his constant companion, the jovial Gil Thayer. Gus had returned from Minnesota in a state of bitter disappointment, and Philip wondered if he might conceivably be considering a switch to downtown practice. There was only one thing to do and that was to ask him directly. Pelletier answered angrily.

"Jesus Christ, everybody seems to know my business better than I do. If I make up my mind to go downtown you'll be the first to know. In the meantime I wish people would stop asking me questions and leave me alone."

Philip left him alone, and in due course he left the Center along with Thayer, and moved into the Medical Arts building.

As for Thayer, who had inherited a large general practice from Bob Gaylord, he took most of these patients with him, thus providing a considerable base for referred surgery to his friend and mentor, along with those families who previously had Pelletier as a surgeon. It was going to be hard for the Center to fill the gap.

Two aftershocks hit the group following this critical event. The first was a letter from Pelletier accusing Appleton of **'malfeasance of funds'**, and giving this as his reason for resigning from the group. When Philip asked Jim how he was going to reply to this libelous accusation, he said he was going to ignore it. The surgeon exploded with frustration:

"For Christ's sake, Jim, if you don't ram this accusation down his throat and make him retract, you might as well send him an admission and apology. It's not only an affront to your honesty but it spills over onto all of us who've trusted and supported you through thick and thin."

Sadly, he never changed his mind. Appleton was a man of peace, and could show a great deal of courage and fortitude in pursuing that goal, but he hated hostile confrontation and Philip felt this might ultimately prove his undoing.

The second shock came later and consisted of a major article prominently published in the Cambrian Leader, entitled: '**Doctors Give Reasons For Leaving Community Health Center**', in which Pelletier and Thayer tried to join their newfound buddies in the medical society by bad-mouthing their former medical institution. It wasn't an edifying performance and – to his credit – Tony Donovan refused to voice his own criticism, nor did he ever show the slightest interest in joining the stampede to the new Medical Arts building. He remained content to practice out of his own home on East Crofton Street, near the Memorial Hospital and with its own small parking lot.

Shortly thereafter, Sam Posner announced his intention of leaving in a few months to take up practice in Ann Arbor, Michigan. For some reason he and Philip had never established any kind of a warm relationship, but perhaps the surgeon was partly to blame, even if the internist was inclined to be a bit of a loner in their group. Philip had never cultivated him on a personal basis, a failure in sharp contrast to the beguiling Gallic manner in which Gus Pelletier was such a past master, one that he envied but couldn't emulate. In his own way Philip, too, was a loner, and found it difficult to take the initiative in forming friendships (especially those that might produce surgical referrals); yet as far as the medical group was concerned he was a true and dependable team player.

There was one redeeming factor during these dark days, and that was the arrival of new doctors in the group. Of these, none was more welcome than Bruce Campbell from London, England. This young and brilliant surgeon – of Scottish ancestry but English accent – had come to them via the University of Cambridge, where he took his medical studies, and St. Bartholomew's Hospital, where he'd been surgical registrar. During the intervening years he'd trained in general surgery, pediatric surgery and urology, and his arrival at this time was providential, whatever his reasons.

The Health Center's urology connection had recently been terminated when Ivan Kossov finally succumbed to downtown pressure and abandoned them. Before that decision, he'd given them good service in his specialty and the arrangement was mutually satisfactory, but the medical society members made life difficult for him and referred their urology elsewhere, out of town. Now that the moment of truth had arrived for him, he was no longer the fiery critic of the solo practitioners and instead became the newest opposition to the Community Health Center.

The arrival at precisely this time of a surgeon with urological training was serendipity beyond Philip's wildest dreams, and with his engaging personality, made him an ideal acquisition for their group. Philip soon found him to be a good general surgeon, slow and careful, and easy to work with. His pediatric surgery was even better than Pelletier's, and he didn't bristle at any suggestions from his senior surgeon, as did his predecessor.

Philip remembered all too well the incident of the abdominoperineal resection which Pelletier had booked. Because of his favorable experience with the combined surgical approach, with one surgeon working from above and one from below (a time-saving method first developed in England and first used by Philip with John Kinsley in Vanwey, long ago), he had offered Gus a suggestion.

"How about doing this case by the combined method of Lloyd-Davies? With the two of us it should work just fine."

"Christ Almighty! You may be the big cheese in our surgical department, but nobody tells me how to do my cases."

By contrast, the very first abdominoperineal resection Philip performed with Campbell was done by the combined method, went very smoothly, and took half the time that was used by Pelletier; but then Gus was an old-style surgical Primadonna and Bruce was not. (***Eventually the combined technique for this major procedure became widely accepted in both hospitals, just as it was elsewhere***).

The partnership contract was now complete and ready for signing. It established once and for all that they were an independent medical body, 'The Cambrian District Medical Group', one that would negotiate an annual contract with the Cambrian District Community Health Association. The central governing body was to be the Medical Executive Committee, and the terms of office – by election – would be staggered in the interests of continuity. The Medical Director would be elected by the Medical Group and would hold office for a term of five years, but would be eligible for re-election at the end of that time. It wasn't a perfect document by any means, but in the main was good enough to serve their purpose. It made it quite clear, for anyone who wanted the plain truth, that the doctors in the C.H.C. weren't the falsely reported 'Slaves of the Unions.'

The clause on compulsory retirement at age 65 worried Philip not only for personal reasons, but because it went against his concept that mental and physical competence were far more important than chronological age. For some perverse reason, even his own profession seemed unable to accept this fundamental point of physiology versus calendar in evaluating functional ability. As if to underscore this medical blind spot, the partnership voted overwhelmingly in favor of the retirement clause.

When Philip discussed this matter with Appleton he was given a reassuring answer.

"Come on now, Phil! You know you'll be going strong for at least another twenty years and there's no way that clause will be enforced in your case. In the next few years we'll introduce a subclause that gives the executive committee the right to make an exception in individual cases."

"That isn't the point, Jim. It's the whole principle that's wrong and should be opposed, not just by the older men like me but by the younger fellows. On a personal level I know only too well where you stand, but who knows if you'll still be Medical Director when I reach the age of 65."

An interesting and possibly disturbing new equation was entering the fluctuating battle lines between the solo and group doctors in the Center. The new members were less acquainted with the 'ancient history' of its origins in 1962-63 than their predecessors, and thus, in the absence of specific indoctrination, were much cozier with the downtown group. This was a development to be expected, even if some of the Board members interpreted it as kow-towing to the clinic's foes in organized medicine and downtown.

Ironically, the reverse was true on the other side. There, the newer arrivals in solo practice, both family physician and specialist, tended to surpass their seniors in overt antagonism toward the Community Health Center, particularly its original members. This had to mean that their indoctrination was far more stringent than the group's, and could only serve to perpetuate a feud that lost its validity as time went by. Philip was reminded of the years when the Führer was able to declare, with each successive hostile act in Europe, that this was his last territorial demand. In the same way, with each successive 'final' requirement by the medical society for cessation of hostilities, as soon as the clinic eliminated the latest point of contention a new one was immediately discovered; and it was easy to understand the Board's attitude of cynicism.

On a strictly personal level, Philip felt he was now being fairly treated in both hospitals, with good cooperation on the surgical floors, the O.Rs and the emergency departments, although there was evidence to suggest that Community Health emergencies were sometimes shunted to solo doctors, and those patients with no designated doctor were always directed downtown. Stuart Atkins enjoyed a certain advantage in this respect, since he was the only fully trained cardiologist in the city, but he neutralized this plus factor by being hard to find during after-office hours.

The group's new pediatrician, Clara Popescu, was a Romanian with a slight accent and a motherly manner that made her very popular with her little patients and their parents; and Tad Pratek was a recent arrival in the family practice department. He was a refugee from Poland. As a boy he'd worked in the railyards at Oswiecem during the hideous days when the place was known as Auschwitz, and perhaps this was in some way connected to his intense interest in human nutrition and the stringent management of intractable overweight.

Several of the Center's doctors were involved in city-wide activities. The Appletons were involved in the local Theater Society, and Jim was active in the flying club and skating club. The Caplans were heavily involved in the various duplicate bridge clubs. The Lawtons were involved in the theater group and local musical activities, as well as church matters. Stuart Atkins was the most heavily involved in church activities, and was a leading member of the church choir and the local Light Opera Society. A number of the medical group were active in golf, tennis and skiing, yet in spite of these activities there was still no evidence of the various service clubs opening their membership to doctors working in the Center; and some of the newer recruits such as Bruce Campbell were incensed at the stupidity of this persistent social blockade. Phil and Patty hoped this resentment wouldn't become an obsession but realized how the younger members of the Cambrian District Medical Group must feel.

The Steel Club, situated on the waterfront and owned by Sir Bertram Giles, was the crown jewel of San Pete's clubs, and Philip was told in confidence by one of its members, a dentist and fellow bridge player, that it would never admit a member from the C.H.C. under any circumstances. Philip replied that any club with a notorious vulgarian like Giles as its founder was hardly the place the Bosnars would wish to join. There were many stories about this ruthless giant of industry, and aside from his talent for making money out of successful enterprises, Sir Bertram was notorious for his coarse manners and boorish behavior. He had developed one of the most productive iron mines in the northern Lake Superior area and his Cambrian Steel mill rivalled those in Hamilton. Nevertheless, he was capable of petty meanness. For example, following an occasion at the Grosvenor Hotel when he thought his waitress was too slow in serving his lunch, he purchased the hotel and sacked the offending employee.

There was a legend concerning one of the most famous Parisian restaurants, which may have stretched the truth but was in keeping with his reputation. The story was that he'd invited a group of British business friends over to dine as his guests in the renowned dining room. When the sommelier brought the wine Giles had ordered, he tasted it and declared it to be inferior. Before the horrified gaze of his guests he repeated the process several times, bottle after bottle, before accepting the wine as satisfactory. What he failed to tell his dining companions was that he'd recently bought the restaurant and wished to impress his competitors with his inflexibility of purpose and refusal to be denied once he made up his mind.

One of Sir Bertram's first acts on taking up residence in the town of Saint Pierre in the '40s was to get himself a personal physician. He didn't consider any of the local doctors good enough, and certainly wouldn't consider his company doctor. Instead, he travelled to Toronto, made some enquiries, and found himself a senior surgical resident, Herbert Slater, a man with a good training in orthopedics as well as general surgery. He brought him out to his steel town, set him up in an office building close to the steel plant, and gave him a permanent contract to take care of any major industrial injuries. From that time forth Dr. Slater became the power and the glory of the local medical profession and his word was law; he had the lion's share of referred surgery and it took a very brave man to oppose him in any way.

The automatic referral of major trauma cases to Slater came grinding to a halt when one of the steelworkers asked specifically to be attended by Dr. Bosnar, since he'd operated on his brother a month before. There were two plant doctors at Cambrian Steel. Andrew Grant was a short jolly Scot and Jason Brackett was a tall Maritimer from Prince Edward Island, with military bearing and a face to match. It was Brackett who was on call when Philip phoned to report his findings.

"Thought I'd better tell you what I found when I examined that steelworker you sent over to St. Matthew's emergency, Dr. Brackett. As you know, he had a girder roll across his right foot and almost sever it at the ankle."

"Looked pretty hopeless to me, Philip. Guess you'll have to amputate, eh?"

"Maybe, but it's worth a try and salvage the foot."

"You must be kidding."

"No, I'm not. Although he's broken all his metatarsals into small pieces, and had his extensor tendons mangled, along with loss of overlying skin, I'm sure there's an adequate arterial blood supply."

"Sure hope you're right, old man. Lot's of luck!"

After extensive multi-stage surgery, the foot was salvaged and was able to function surprisingly well. It was only necessary to enlist the services of an expert shoemaker to make the requisite footwear for the shortened right foot, and the patient was able to return to full duties at his previous job within six months of the accident. As an extra bonus, clinic patients in the steel plant were henceforth referred to group doctors following any industrial accident, and Philip acquired a new friend in the person of Jason Brackett. For Philip Bosnar, it represented another crack in the Steel Curtain.

Edwardia looked stunning in the glorious sunshine of a perfect July, and the gardens were ablaze with masses of rhododendrons in every conceivable color, while the trees seemed overburdened with their lush foliage in every shade of green. Phil and Patty had flown out for their beloved daughter's wedding to Neville Sternway. They checked into the Royal Harbor motel, run by their good friends the Torwalds, and made sure they got there a week ahead of the ceremonies.

The wedding took place at the Anglican Church of the Divine Blood, and Florian looked angelic and rapturous, while Neville looked solid and supportive, with an expression of sublime happiness that softened his rugged features. Aside from Patty having to bring her husband back to his seat almost forcibly after the minister asked, "Who giveth this woman—?" and Philip reluctantly conceded, "I do", the marriage ceremony was a resounding success, and the crowded church got full measure.

Patty, with her glowing good looks, looked more like a sister of the bride than her mother, and the Purcell Fanfare was resoundingly performed by the organist. Florian's close friend Cindy Pringle sang beautifully, with her trained soprano voice echoing to every corner of the old church and bringing murmurs of appreciation.

The reception was held on the spacious lawn of the Pringles' fine home on Gideon Bay, and the champagne flowed freely. The Steffansons were there, the Torwalds and the Jacksons, the Southerbys and even the Gates, but only a select few from the medical profession. The guests included close friends of the bridal couple and their parents, and among the medical couples were Cliff Robins and his wife Melanie, who posed seductively with two of her fellow-models for the delighted photographers. Melanie had certainly fulfilled her promise of becoming a captivating brunette beauty, and displayed a natural flirtatious manner that was as innocent as it was dangerous, while her placid husband took it all in his stride.

After the reception, the bride and groom departed for Galiano Island where they would honeymoon at a secluded lodge belonging to their good friend, Marty Southam. Marty was Italian on her mother's side and aristocratic English on her father's side. She was independently wealthy, wrote a large amount of poetry that was occasionally published, and ran a motel attached to the lodge. She was a unique and independent soul and had known Neville since he was a little boy.

Phil and Patty left a dozen bottles of champagne with the Pringles, a few with the happy newlyweds, and brought the rest back to their motel, where, for the next few days, the father of the bride made every effort to finish off the celebrations with the effervescent brew, while he prayed for Florian's happiness.

One evening after getting back to San Pete, Philip received a phone call from Beth Appleton: would he be willing to read a part in the new play that was being put on by the San Pete's Theater Society? The part was that of Noah in the play of that name by André Obey. The role was due to be played by an experienced actor from Toronto but he wouldn't be available until about two weeks prior to the opening performance. Until that time it was necessary to have someone read the lines at rehearsals, and Beth Appleton thought Philip might fill the bill, especially as he knew a fair amount about the theater and had a son "in the trade." With a certain amount of trepidation, he accepted, and soon found that a good many of his evenings were taken up by endless rehearsals.

The rest of the cast were surprisingly effective in their parts, which included the members of Noah's family and some of the animals on board the Ark, cleverly mimed by the actors – especially Peter Lawton as the tiger and Bill Semple as the bear. Semple, a high school vice-principal, was six foot three inches of beef and brawn and performed his bear-hug act with verve and relish, eventually cracking one of Philip's ribs.

The director of the play, Drew Robson, was a short, compact-looking theatrical genius whose huge reddish graying beard concealed his youthful years. As the rehearsals progressed, Robson made it clear that he'd tolerate no deviation whatever from his strict "blocking instructions", namely the exact on-stage position of every actor in each scene. Occasionally he'd yell out, "Hey! You've just walked off the side of the Ark into the floodwaters." Of course, he could visualize the Ark – still in the imaginary phase, awaiting construction – and his cast could not. By the time the completed Ark was on stage, Philip began to wish they were back in the imaginary phase; climbing up and down the wooden ladder between decks in his light canvas slippers was agony to his untoughened flat feet, and he felt like a victim of the notorious Bastinado endured by prisoners in less civilized countries.

About two weeks before opening night Drew Robson approached Philip with a complaint.

"Look, Doctor, you still haven't learned your lines and time's getting pretty short."

"I don't get it, Drew. I thought I was just reading my lines until your lead actor arrived from Toronto. Why in hell would I need to memorize the part?"

"For Christ's sake, Doctor, I thought you realized by now that you're It! We dropped the idea of the Toronto actor weeks ago, so you'd better get busy and memorize your part." That was one of the qualities he admired about this gnome-like dynamo: no apologies or explanations, just listen to his instructions and follow them without question.

A week later they reached their moment of crisis. Drew Robson no longer worried about Philip's memorization of the lines and cues and in turn the substitute actor discovered that his ability to memorize was undiminished since his student days. What was far more worrying was the crystal-clear recognition that he and the director had entirely different concepts of Noah's nature and personality, and that was serious.

Philip visualized a man of humble origins and totally uncluttered faith, who nevertheless had the innate constructive skills to assemble a mighty ocean-sailing craft: one that could survive the heaving flood waters and bring its cargo of human and animal survivors to a safe landing on the mountain top. Robson saw him as a much simpler son of the soil, a bit of an eccentric dreamer, with an inexhaustible vigor that enabled him to hop around his ship with the agility of a monkey. Philip felt the moment of truth had arrived.

"Drew, I'm sorry. I know exactly how you want Noah portrayed but I can't do it that way as I don't believe the alternative interpretation."

"Of course you can. In fact I'm sure you'll manage."

"Just hear me out. I know just the man who can do this part exactly as you want it and with total conviction. He even knows the lines by heart. It's you, Drew, and you look absolutely perfect for the part."

There was a moment of stunned silence before he replied.

"O.K. doctor. We'll do it your way. Maybe it'll work."

"I promise to give it my best shot."

By the grace of God the play was a great success, and there were some incidents that would stick in Philip's memory forever, although he determined never again to be inveigled into another stage performance, no matter what the excuse.

During the first act he started to become aware of a certain intangible communication taking place between him and the people in the audience as he delivered his lines. They grew silent at exactly the right moments, became amused or excited at just the right moments, and applauded in all the right spots. This, no doubt, was the magic chemistry that kept actors intoxicated even when low earnings failed to justify their efforts, and Philip's emotional bond with his dedicated son was strengthened even more than before.

When it got to the final scene where Noah, on his knees, berated his God for failing to bring the voyage of the Ark to a truly satisfying conclusion, the chemistry flooded across the footlights and Philip knew the play was a genuine success. As for the director, who'd been standing in the shadows in the back of the theater, he bounded to the backstage after the performance, gripped Philip's hand and yelled in his ear,

"Goddammit, Doc, your way was right, after all."

The final performance took place on the Saturday evening to a packed house. There were two surprise visitors in the audience and they came backstage with Patty after the performance. Philip could scarcely believe his eyes when he saw who they were. Doug and Jenny Conway had quietly driven from Sudbury without advance notice, taken their place in the audience and watched the entire play, with Doug taking pictures with his huge press camera, using infra-red film. During the first intermission the visitors sought out Patty, who was delighted but totally astonished at their unexpected presence.

It seemed that Doug had picked up a copy of the Cambrian Leader and read a review of the play in which Philip's name was mentioned. The Conways made up their minds, there and then, to surprise their friends and see the play.

"We didn't know you were into acting, Phil. When did this start?"

"Believe me, I'm not into it. You've just seen my first and last performance."

"But we loved your performance, old sport, and I'm sure James would be proud of his old man."

"Good God! If he ever found out that I poached on his territory he'd have my hide, and rightly so."

Philip went on to explain how the fates had put him into his one and only stage performance as an actor. Since he and Patty were expected at an after-theater party that was being thrown by leaders of the theater group in San Pete, they apologized to the Conways for leaving them so quickly and arranged to meet them the following morning for a late breakfast.

It had been an interesting experience in many ways. Philip became more widely known in the community, and made a number of new friends in the 'theater crowd'. Among these were Flora Mottram, the wife of Art Mottram – a downtown gynecologist. She was and an extremely active social leader in the community, and had watched several performances of the play with her husband. They were both more than kind in their comments.

Another new friend was Klars Kennonen, a massive Viking of a man from Finland who ran the locomotive at the steel plant and was a true devotee of the local theater.

"Doctor Bosnar," he said to Philip with the deepest sincerity, "When you announced during the storm that you lost your rudder, my eyes filled with tears."

(In years to come he, too, would enter their widening circle of friends from all walks of life and help to enrich their experience in this Great Lakes steel city, so far and so different from Edwardia).

CHAPTER 49

1967

One bastion of the hospital power-structure in San Pete had to be levelled if there was any hope of challenging the lines of permanent authority, and that was the unrestricted terms of office allotted to department chiefs. Philip Bosnar's decision on this point was made one evening when he happened to be in the doctors' dictating area adjoining the cloakroom and records room at St. Matthew's Hospital. He noticed Morecombe hard at work inside the file-room, perusing a stack of hospital charts, and decided to see if his suspicions were correct.

"Catching up on some of your charts, Dr. Morecombe?"

"No. I'm reviewing last month's surgical charts as part of our quality control."

"Do you share this chore with your fellow surgeons?"

"Of course not. It's my job, not theirs."

"Who reviews your charts, then?"

"I do. Why do you ask?"

"Well, during my term as chief of surgery at Edwardia's leading hospital it was the accepted rule that monthly review of surgical charts was shared among all members of the surgical staff. In a way I guess it was a modern application of the biblical advice to mere mortals like us: Judge not lest ye be judged."

Following this encounter, Philip began to do his own review of surgical charts, on the basis of a statistical study of postoperative complications and deaths, going back to 1963. He found a distinctly selective system. Slater, Morecombe, Foley, and Duncan were a protected group whose less fortunate results were shielded from the light of critical analysis at surgical ward rounds. Rudi Abel, a late-comer to the ranks of the solo surgical establishment, Campbell, Bosnar, Donovan and even Pelletier, were the unprotected group, hand-picked for criticism and restriction of operative privileges.

One of the worst examples of restriction was the four week-old baby Joyce O'Grady, a patient of Brigitte Fleischmann, suffering from congenital obstructive jaundice. She'd been beautifully worked up by the pediatrician, both diagnostically and metabolically, and was ready for operative exploration, with a provisional diagnosis of obstructed bile-ducts. Dr. Bosnar was asked to perform the necessary surgery.

On the evening prior to the planned surgery, he received a phone call from Morecombe informing him that such cases couldn't be handled in San Pete and had to be referred to the Ontario Pediatric Center in Toronto. The following afternoon the parents came to see him in his office. They were furious with the hospital authorities.

"Dr. Bosnar, we saw the Mother Superior yesterday and told her that we wanted you to operate on our baby, and nobody else. We told her how happy we were at the way you handled our oldest daughter's terrible compound leg fracture and what a wonderful result you got. We told her about the many friends who praised your work and about your great reputation but it made no difference."

Mrs. O'Grady had become quite breathless and was beginning to weep, so her husband took up the complaint with even greater emotion.

"We're an Irish-Canadian family and faithful Roman Catholics and we've always been strong supporters of the Sisters' hospital. We've worked hard to raise money and help it grow. Now we'll never go near that place again. As far as we're concerned they're really prejudiced against this place and its doctors, especially you, its head surgeon. So we want our baby transferred to the Memorial Hospital, and would like you to operate as soon as possible. As a matter of fact that's just what we told the Mother Superior before we left her office."

"I appreciate your confidence and share your anger, but you must face certain considerations. Although you understand that your baby's condition has a very high mortality rate and a low success rate for surgery, you've chosen me as your surgeon and I in turn feel confident I can perform the necessary surgery with the competence of an experienced general surgeon." At this point the O'Gradys appeared to brighten.

"Unfortunately, the actions of St. Matthew's Hospital must be regarded as nothing less than the kiss of death, and it wouldn't be fair to you or your baby for me to go ahead in the face of such a psychological handicap."

Philip saw the disappointment on the faces of his listeners.

"But Dr. Fleischmann speaks so highly of your surgical ability and we have felt so safe up to now. Are you sure you wouldn't be willing to go ahead even though we know our baby may not survive?"

"I'm sorry, but my answer still has to be No."

The following day Brigitte Fleischmann accompanied the O'Gradys and their baby to Toronto on the morning flight. Sadly, despite the best efforts of the fine pediatric surgeons at the Ontario Pediatric Center, the baby died forty-eight hours after surgery. There was one grim irony that deepened the wound felt by the bereaved parents. At the time of the tiny patient's admission, the senior resident recognized Bosnar's name on Dr. Fleischmann's letter of introduction and said he knew him well from Edwardia, where the resident had been in general practice. When he asked why they didn't get Dr. Bosnar to do the operation, the O'Gradys broke down and told him the entire story. For the rest of their lives they'd never be free of the thought that their chosen surgeon might have saved their little girl except for prejudice and immoral interference by the authorities in St. Matthew's.

After this tragic event, Philip brought up the subject of rotating the chiefs of hospital departments at both hospitals.

"Mr. Chairman, I'd like to remind this meeting that we are the medical staff of non-university, community hospitals, and our department chiefs are NOT professors and shouldn't be granted unlimited powers and tenure. I move that we limit their term of office to three years, commencing September the 1st of this year, following the summer vacation break."

The motion was carried at both hospitals by a large majority and it seemed that a feudal era had passed by.

It was hard for Philip to give up his beloved white Jaguar coupe, with its gorgeous flaring side-fenders and matchless handshift. He and Patty were returning from a trip to Chicago, where they'd killed two birds with one stone: a surgical convention that was most informative and an enjoyable regional bridge tournament that brought his darling closer to Life Mastership. The weather was very cold, which was to be expected for February, but it didn't start to snow until they crossed the great suspension bridge at Mackinaw City.

By the time they were ten miles out from St. Ignace, the blizzard struck full force, and they were driving into a steady barrage of snowflakes, challenging but never quite overwhelming the excellent windshield wipers. Half an hour later, at 9 p.m, they were in deep trouble: it was their first experience of a total 'White-out'. Suddenly, there were no boundaries to Interstate Highway 75, only a great white expanse of snow stretching on both sides as far as the eye could see. No lights could be detected anywhere, not those of other cars coming from the opposite direction, of nearby towns and villages; not even the occasional roadside farm-house. Driving was becoming increasingly difficult, and a new element of danger began to intrude itself into the forbidding picture: it was getting cold, very cold, and colder by the minute.

Patricia didn't voice her fears, bless her brave heart, but she knew if they were forced to stop for any reason the result would be disaster for them both. The car's English heater wasn't intended for this type of situation, and any attempt to go looking for a friendly house off the highway would result in one frozen body in the frigid outdoors and another in the car's unheated interior.

It was now imperative to keep up their steady speed of 60 m.p.h. and try to make it to Sault St. Marie, Michigan, before they got into serious trouble. The Good Lord and man's ingenuity provided them with the saving factor, one that made it possible to complete their journey without driving off the highway into a roadside drift and oblivion. At the border of the roadway, otherwise obscured by the great white expanse of borderless snow, was a series of reflectors mounted on poles at regular intervals; each throwing its beam of light off the car's headlights. By keeping his eyes focussed on these reflectors, Philip was able to complete the journey in safety.

On arrival at their destination, they got the car warmed up inside a garage while they defrosted themselves in a cozy restaurant, with a glorious hot meal and fortifying drinks of wine. Patty was feeling much better, and noticed that her husband's eyes were exhibiting the condition known as '*Nystagmus*.' (This is a symptom in which the eyes move involuntarily and rhythmically from side to side, and in this case was a legacy of the life-saving reflectors). By the time they were ready to resume their journey, Philip's nystagmus had disappeared and the blizzard had stopped, so that driving was much less hazardous for the rest of the journey, especially in their newly warmed vehicle.

Three days later and with a heavy heart, Philip traded in his beautiful Jaguar for a far less sporty, burgundy-colored Volvo. No longer would he feel the surging power of his classic automobile; no longer would he have difficulty getting to the twin batteries – by turning the wheels and removing the front boards -and no longer would he feel the brave little heater resigning in defeat before the northern winter's onslaught.

'Interselection' had been introduced last year by the Community Health Association, making it possible for any clinic patient to switch from C.H.C. to solo medical care at any time before the annual dual choice, but even this failed to produce any visible change in the stubborn position of the local medical society. There was to be a district O.M.A. meeting in Sudbury, and Philip Bosnar and Peter Lawton, the Health Center's Ob.Gyn. specialist, decided to attend with their wives.

Jeannie Lawton and Patricia got along extremely well. Both had been nurses prior to marriage and both had a strong sense of loyalty to the clinic, as well as a shared interest in music and theater. They all drove out in Lawton's spacious Pontiac sedan and arrived in time to get registered into their hotel rooms at the Sheridan Hotel. After getting cleaned up and changed, they went down for drinks and dinner, and discussed a plan for action on the following day.

The first meeting, which was being held at the spacious university complex, was to be devoted to business matters, and Philip said he intended to use the opportunity to launch a counter-attack against the San Pete's Medical Society, while their wives could bring them luck by going out shopping.

"How about you, Peter?" Philip asked his friend. "Would you like to say a few words on the same subject?"
But he knew all too well that Lawton was a thinker rather than a speaker, and wasn't surprised when he said he wasn't sure.

"You know, Phil, they may not give you a chance to speak on that matter. I happen to know the society has sent a strong contingent to this event, headed by John Duncan, and they have a lot of pull in Sudbury."

"Good. The more the better! Let them try and refute any of my statements."

The following morning he and Lawton arrived at 8.45 at the auditorium where the meeting was being held, and the only other person present was Dr. Evans, the elderly Chairman, who was busy arranging chairs and microphone on the speaker's platform. Philip introduced himself right away and told him that he had an important item to bring up during the meeting, but the Chairman replied that since he wasn't listed on the printed agenda it was extremely doubtful. Perhaps at the end of the listed agenda – "if there is time" – Dr. Bosnar might say a few brief words, but he knew that this would be futile.

Seated in the front row when the meeting started promptly on time, he sat poised and waiting for the first possible opportunity. Seated on the speaker's platform were the president of the Sudbury Medical Society and the president and secretary of the O.M.A. District 9; and these were the ones who answered the questions from the floor. Philip's chance came at the end of the discussion on 'Public Relations'.

"Are there any questions?" asked the chairman, and when nobody else came forward, Philip leaped to his feet.

"Mr. Chairman, I have a question, and since it's rather a long one I'll use the platform microphone, with your kind permission."

The Chairman looked stunned as Philip bounded up to the platform and spoke his piece.

"In the city of St. Pierre, a situation has been developing over the past few years which threatens to spill over into a public scandal, and that can only do great harm to the public image of our profession. This image is already extremely vulnerable by virtue of the recent media onslaught."

He then went on to summarize the history of the conflict between the two sides, and the exclusion of the clinic doctors from the official medical society.

"Like every one of my clinic colleagues," he concluded, "I'm a member of the O.M.A. yet I'm excluded from a branch society of the O.M.A. and of this District. One can only shudder at the thought of this entire injustice coming to the attention of the public at large, and I urge this meeting to take action before it's too late. My question is: How long must we wait before rectifying this unhappy situation?"

The fifth row of the auditorium was filled with society members from San Pete, and they rose, one after the other, to voice angry rebuttals to Philip's remarks. It was at this point that they were unexpectedly shot down in flames by none other than their erstwhile St. Matthew's pathologist, Michael Leslie, who'd been sitting quietly and unobtrusively in the second row.

"Mr. Chairman," he declared loudly, "I can vouch for the absolute truth of everything Dr. Bosnar has said to this gathering. If anything, he has understated his complaints."

Before Philip left the platform all three official speakers came forward to shake his hand and congratulate him on his forthright remarks, and he in turn stepped down to shake Leslie's hand and thank him for his strong support.

When they got back to the hotel and got together with their wives for lunch, Philip and Peter found that the ladies had defied the bitter cold and walked bravely to the nearest shopping area, where they did a little shopping and had their hair done. Unhappily, they also managed to get their ears and noses painfully frost-bitten, but not beyond recovery. They were eager to learn about the morning's events and were happy their husbands had got the C.H.C. position across to the meeting at large. As Philip pointed out, the best antidote to clandestine acts of antagonism is open exposure, and in this they couldn't have been more successful.

That evening, at the official banquet their two wives looked resplendent in their magnificent evening gowns and their spouses were proud to squire them in their smart black tie and tuxedo dinner attire. On their way into the banquet hall the quartet was warmly greeted by Dr. George Walker, and Philip introduced him to the rest. The Sudbury surgeon was gracious in his welcoming remarks and boyishly effusive in his compliments to the ladies. When the two couples were seated at their table, far removed from John Duncan and his entourage, they were visited by a surprising number of the local doctors. These introduced themselves cordially and uttered favorable comments about the morning's proceedings. Among them, and with an embarrassing degree of friendliness, were the four men who had occupied the speaker's platform during the morning session.

On the final evening of the convention Philip and Peter took their beautiful wives to the dinner-dance hosted by the local medical society at the city's leading night-spot. All four had an evening that was both enjoyable and interesting, and felt in no way inhibited by the tightly grouped contingent from San Pete's Medical Society, headed by the Dr. Duncan.

John Duncan, a tall athletic man in his early forties, was a rising surgeon in San Pete and – with his wide circle of hunting and skiing friends – was popular with the solo G.Ps, all six feet three inches of him. He was good at his work, quite knowledgeable in his specialty of General Surgery, and he had a ready and acerbic wit. His mentor Don Foley had shown him great kindness during his first year in San Pete, and Duncan showed his appreciation with a fierce and abiding loyalty. In the O.R. he was known to roar at the nurses, but they put this down to his macho image and made remarkable allowance for his boorishness.

As for Philip and his fellow clinic doctors, Duncan rarely missed an opportunity to put them down, but almost never to the point of outright rudeness. When he forgot himself and crossed that line, Philip had no hesitation in returning the compliment. Unlike most of his friends and colleagues, he had no fear of the man or his wit. In fact he took the opportunity one day, in the Memorial surgeon's lounge, to declare in front of Duncan's admiring throng,

"People whose wit is always directed at someone else but never at themselves suffer not only from conceit, which is permissible, but vanity, which is a serious character flaw." *(Since that time they had settled for an armed truce and eventually got along much better).*

During the dance, Phil and Patty ran into the Herberts. Wilf Herbert was an internist with a history of heart trouble, and when the Health Center arrived in San Pete he had developed a severe anxiety reaction. He left town in a huff, but later returned and decided to live and let live. The orchestra had just finished a smooth tango when Wilf introduced his wife to the Bosnars, as they were standing next to them during a break in the music. He excused himself to get his wife's cigarettes from the table and while he was gone Mrs. Herbert innocently engaged Patricia in a conversation about "the terrible socialist menace of the Union Clinic." She said she hoped that, as newcomers, the Bosnars were keeping up the "Good Fight." Her husband arrived back in time to catch the end of his wife's foot disappearing into her mouth, so to speak, and after goodnaturedly explaining the faux pas the couple joined Phil and Patty in great hoots of laughter, drawing disapproving glances from Duncan's table.

Before leaving Sudbury, Phil and Patty contacted their longtime Vanwey friends, the Conways, and learned that Doug was about to enter hospital with severe circulatory problems in his legs. He was under the care of a experienced vascular surgeon, and would require extensive arterial surgery. They drove out to visit the patient and found him in great form. He checked out their fruit basket and declared that he found no hidden cigarettes or booze.

"You know, sport, since I quit drinking and the alcohol stopped flowing through my goddam arteries they've been clogging up. So I guess a guy can't win. Anyhow, as long as we can keep you frigging surgeons wealthy, it isn't a total loss." His wit had certainly not lost its bite and they loved him for it. On certain occasions, however, when he grew viciously sarcastic with his wife Jenny (for some private and mysterious reason), they knew he loved her none the less. Philip could only hope that his friend's operation went well and that his rugged vigor and wit would remain unimpaired.

Most cases of head injury in San Pete were treated by the solo surgeons downtown, except for Gus Pelletier. Bruce Campbell and Philip Bosnar weren't at all keen to get involved in handling these cases, since they were used to having them turned over to the nearest neurosurgeon. In Philip's case there was always a neurosurgeon available in Edwardia to handle acute head trauma, and he'd only been called upon to operate on such cases twice in his entire practicing career.

One occasion was in Edwardia, when the only neurosurgeon was out of town and the brain injuries were too severe for the patient to survive. The other was back in Vanwey, when he was able to save the life of a little boy who'd sustained a severe depressed fracture of the skull with intracranial hemorrhage. The trouble with sending such cases out of town was the time element, often the deciding factor in the patient's chances of survival.

The downtown surgeons now decided it was high time the Community health surgeons took care of their own head injury cases, and rather than argue the point Philip arranged to visit his old friend Heiko Noguchi, who was now head neurosurgeon at one of the major hospitals in Wisconsin.

During his drive down highway 75 to Lake Michigan and westward along Highway 2, Philip reflected on the irony that this fine specialist, who'd been so shabbily treated in Canada, was so successful in the U.S.A. In fact he was the author of an authoritative new section on neurosurgery in a recent textbook of emergency surgery.

After checking into a conveniently located motel Philip, phoned his friend, who insisted that he join him for dinner at his home. It was a pleasant informal meal and Philip was delighted to meet Noguchi's wife and daughter. Mrs. Noguchi was an interesting and attractive English schoolteacher who'd recently migrated to America, and it was obvious that she and Heiko were deeply in love. Their little girl looked like her mother but had her father's bright black eyes.

The next few days were instructive and exciting. Philip met Heiko each morning at his hospital and the neurosurgeon showed him as much as possible, with the accent on '*Carotid Angiography*' (injection of a special radio-opaque liquid into the main artery of the head and taking X-ray pictures) for difficult cases of head trauma, and the placement of exploratory burr-holes.

They discussed, in some detail, the possibility of obtaining a neurosurgeon for St. Pierre, but Heiko felt that a base population of 150,000 was unlikely to attract such a specialty. He thought a better avenue would be the establishment of a rapid airlift for acute head-injury cases to an appropriate center, providing it was close enough and the time element wasn't too pressing, as in '*Epidural Hemorrhage*' (where injury to an artery inside the skull produces hemorrhage between the bone and the fibrous envelope surrounding the brain and causes a progressive rise of pressure that may be rapidly fatal if unrelieved).

In the meantime Noguchi suggested that his guest learn as much as possible about the practical aspects of modern head injury management, and gave him a letter of introduction to his friend, the Professor of Neurosurgery at the University Hospital in Minneapolis. The idea was that Philip would be given a two-week crash course in exploration of the brain for critical head injury and additional details of total management, including induced hypothermia and brain-shrinking techniques.

The professor turned out to be an extremely helpful gentleman, and showed a great deal of understanding for Philip's particular situation. He was of the opinion that his Canadian visitor was asking for something that should now be compulsory training for all general surgeons. This would avoid loss of life in those cases where there was a time urgency, and reserve transportation for only those patients in whom no such acute urgency existed. The professor phoned the Hennepin County Hospital and spoke to the neurosurgeon in charge of acute head injuries, explaining Dr. Bosnar's needs. It was decided that he should be on emergency call for such cases over a two week period.

Philip managed to get a motel reasonably close to the Hennepin County Hospital and drove there to introduce himself to his mentor. Unlike his counterpart at the University Hospital, this individual seemed cold and detached and Philip had grave doubts about how much trouble he'd take to show him the things he wanted. That night, at 2 a.m, the emergency nurse called Dr. Bosnar to come over for a case of a gunshot wound to the head. He got there in no time flat, breaking all speed limits with his Volvo on the relatively deserted streets, and arrived in time to observe the smooth but rapid measures taken to keep the unconscious patient alive. She was a large, middle-aged woman who'd been shot in the head by her husband in the course of a drunken family argument.

It was a pretty hopeless case, but everything possible was done both before, during, and after the operation, and Philip stored up a good deal valuable information that would be applicable in more favorable cases. The neurosurgeon noted his presence with a cold eye but Philip felt that he was impressed nonetheless.

The next morning he accompanied the chief on ward rounds and his presence was barely acknowledged. After a while they stopped at the bed of a very old lady who, although sputters, was moaning and holding her free hand to her belly. The chief turned to Philip and said, almost accusingly,

"I understand you're a hotshot general surgeon. Why don't you tell me what's wrong with this old girl? She's forty-eight hours after craniotomy for subdural hematoma, and seems to be having abdominal pains for some reason or other."

The attending nurse turned the patient's bedclothes down to the groins and raised the bed-gown. Examination of the abdomen was negative except for excessive intestinal sounds and Philip drew the bedclothes down another six inches in order to complete his examination. Then he turned and gave his opinion:

"I would suggest to you, doctor, that you get your own general surgeon to operate on this old lady just as soon as possible, preferably under a local anesthetic. She has a strangulated femoral hernia."

It was the oldest pitfall in the book, and proved once again that this diagnosis could be so easily missed if the patient's groins and upper thighs weren't fully exposed. In any event, from that time forth to the end of his stay, Philip 'owned' the department, and nothing was too much trouble for his instructor to provide him with just the kind of crash refresher course he'd hoped for. He even introduced him to his hospital associates as "my friend Dr. Philip Bosnar from Canada", and in return Philip made a point of arriving for each and every head trauma emergency, day or night, within minutes of being called.

Before leaving Minneapolis, Philip contacted Brigitte Fleischmann and arranged to meet her at her office building. It was a sad loss for the Center when this fine individual gave in to her loneliness and feeling of isolation after Kurt's death and left San Pete. Her relatives in Minnesota were the ones who finally persuaded her to make the move. She was looking well and revealed that she was working in a private group practice with eight specialists but no general practitioners.

The building was a good one with offices, examining rooms, and waiting areas above average, but the facilities were in no way comparable to those of the Health Center in San Pete. It was interesting to learn that the internists and pediatricians in this small clinic actually took care of the family practice. Philip asked if she preferred her new position to that in the C.H.C, and she replied that she preferred the Health Center in many ways except for the strife with the downtown solo doctors.

Philip took her out to dinner and found that she'd recovered well from the death of Kurt, that she worshipped his memory and would never marry again, and that her boy was growing up rapidly and looking more like his late father every day. He wished her all the luck in the world, and felt sure she would meet another man some day to whom she could once again give her love, and who would become a substitute father for her growing son.

Just before leaving Minneapolis, Philip found himself unable to resist a fascinating double bill at the leading movie theater in town. It was showing two classical music productions from Britain. First, the Gaieté Parisienne and then the Tales of Hoffman, both with the stirring music of Jacques Offenbach; with everything from raucous Can-Can of the Gaieté to the sinister passages from Hoffmann's encounter with the demonic Doctor Miracle of The Tales. It was an incredible feast for eye and ear, and Philip left the theater in a state of sensory intoxication. The next morning, driving back to San Pete, he couldn't get the music out of his mind and he knew which records he must buy as soon as possible; to be played over and over again in days to come.

It was good to get back to England for a two week holiday, this time the two of them together. Needless to say, Philip's parents insisted that they stay with them in their Hendon home, but this was impractical as his mother was in precarious health and his father far from vigorous, although he still refused to retire from his business. Philip's mother was having trouble with her eyes and would probably require a cataract removal. She was also having problems with her memory and was subject to fits of depression, although she never once revealed these problems during their time together. His father was far too heavy following his abandonment of cigarettes, and was due to have an operation for a large and long-neglected hernia. Clayton had been hoping to persuade them both to move into a suitable nursing home and had written Philip on the subject. It was agreed that the two brothers would share the expenses if and when the fateful day arrived within the next few years.

Phil and Patty finally consented to stay with his parents for the first couple of days and then moved into a hotel. Philip was sad yet relieved to note that his Mum no longer spent as much time practicing her artistry in the kitchen, and that she and his Dad no longer had all their meals at home, but frequently ate out at one of the neighborhood restaurants. Nevertheless, London's leading Chef de Cuisine – as far as family and friends were concerned – showed that she hadn't lost her touch, by putting on one of her inimitable feasts before her loved ones left.

Rafael Bosnar was now a pillar of the local 'Reform' synagogue. It was simply his way of showing the depth of disappointment and revulsion he felt about the betrayal of the Russian Revolution by its despotic rulers. Yet the more Philip spoke to him, the more he realized his father had little in common with religious orthodoxy, but a genuine commitment to the aims and objects of postwar Zionism.

Young James, the actor, was looking great. He'd lost his earlier slouch and was a fine figure of a man, tall, lean, muscular and straight as a die. He was doing quite well in his chosen profession and was currently in a two-year contract with the B.B.C. He was living as man and wife with a gifted young artist, the fair-haired and blue-eyed daughter of an Irish poet, in a pleasant flat located in the Woolwich district, close by the Thames. They seemed very much in love and shared extreme left-wing political views, so that by comparison Philip emerged as an ultra-conservative opponent of the downtrodden masses. Personally, he found his son's paramour a somewhat cold dish, an aloof young lady who made little attempt to join in the affectionate family reunion or conversation, no matter what the subject. As for James, love seemed appropriately blind and he appalled his father by insisting that what attracted him most at first was that she was so much like his mother. The Saints preserve us!, thought Philip.

At the present time, James was involved in the recording of a radio series on the life of Jesus, based on a work by Dorothy Sayers, and had been appropriately cast as Doubting Thomas. His parents were invited to one of the recording sessions at the B.B.C. studios and were quite intrigued. They had a long conversation with the director, who told them he was very impressed with their son and predicted a successful future for him. James certainly had a resonant voice of good deep timbre, and gave each word full meaning, so Phil and Patty were inclined to believe the director wasn't simply flattering the young man in order to make his parents feel good.

Meanwhile, despite his firmest protestations, they made it clear that he could always count on them if he found the going too tough financially between contracts and assignments. They were under no illusions about the difficulties that could confront a struggling actor in such a highly competitive, crowded, and mostly underpaid profession.

Clayton was going from strength to strength. He had a highly successful general practice in a small country town in Essex, and was becoming increasingly involved in the academic aspects of family practice. He was active in a national group concerned with the upgrading of Britain's G.P. standards, and was on the National Board of Examiners. In addition, he was doing a lectureship at King's College Hospital and attending special weekly seminars at the Royal Society of Medicine. These were chaired by the famed expert Dr. Ernst Schumann and were devoted to the psychosocial and family unit aspects of illness and 'non-wellness', with strong Freudian overtones. Clayton was becoming known within an expanding sphere of his profession for his eloquent addresses and erudite publications. Philip admired these for their literary content even as he was prepared to dispute their scientific basis.

Phil and Patty visited Clayton's splendid new home, to which his offices were attached, and were delighted to see how well his devoted wife Martha was looking after her busy husband and bringing up their three attractive children, two boys and a girl. She was a quiet and thoughtful young lady of impeccable manners and charm, an excellent listener rather than a talker, and she was enormously proud of her husband. In addition to running the household, she was a considerable help to the office nurse, helping out with the phone, the books and the typing. She and Patty got along like the proverbial 'house on fire' and both loved to witness the spirited exchanges between the brothers, each waiting for that briefest of pauses to move in with arguments, rebuttals, and refutations. They loved each other dearly, but that would never diminish the intensity of their debates.

Unlike Clayton, Philip believed his duty to his patient was first and foremost a personal one, and more remotely a family matter. Besides, as far as the mighty Sigmund Freud was concerned, he'd never fallen under the spell of his magnificent sophistries, in which words were fitted into a new convoluted glossary that sought to explain – by their very obfuscation – all aberrant adult behavior in terms of juvenile sexual experiences and parental conflicts or obsessions. So far as genuine psychosis was concerned, Philip was confident that this was primarily either the result of organic disease of the brain or due to chemical disorders, including genetic biochemical imbalances. Despite the force of his arguments, Clayton always had a good answer for each of his brother's points and Philip could see why his readers and listeners found him so compelling a communicator.

Phil and Patty visited Pauline and her husband. Both had changed very little since the last time they saw them, but Irving looked more dynamic and seemed to command more respect and admiration from Pauline. She confided to Philip that even their fiercely critical mother-in-law had changed her disparaging attitude toward him. When Philip learned the reason, his admiration knew no bounds.

One day, this most patient of men had permitted his slow anger to burst into flame when he realized at long last that his chances for promotion had evaporated, and he told his employers at Ford's of Dagenham to go to hell. He then went to his bank manager, raised a loan via a second mortgage on his home, bought himself a beautiful new taxicab, large, black and shiny, and proceeded to take the gruelling course required of every cab driver before he could get his license. All this was done with the complete approval of Pauline; in fact her unstinted support and encouragement. His unceasing efforts to become the finest taxi driver in Greater London were his salvation, at the very moment when his self-esteem was at its lowest.

There was one more hurdle to cross, however, and that was the pressure from the large taxicab syndicates to join their staff rather than tough it out as an independent, a 'loner'. He was even visited by a few goon squads, but when they saw his short, stocky figure facing them with a look of dogged determination on his broad face and a large tire-iron in his hand their enthusiasm faded. By the grace of God, he'd survived the early years of difficulty in his new career and was now doing very well, with his account books showing healthy black ink and all his debts paid off. The entire family was very proud of him.

Philip saw Morrie Kahn only once at his parents' home. He was still a welcome guest there whenever he decided to visit with his wife. He still looked like Charlie Chaplin without the mustache, but sadly without the laughter lines that adorned his pleasant features when he was a young and incorrigible jokester and lover of life. Now, with the blessing of his equine-featured wife, he was a dour and doctrinaire communist, with a conversation replete with party slogans and quotations from the Daily Worker, and in his heart Philip wept for him.

People like Morrie made him feel, somehow, in political limbo. He was opposed to the socialist system and believed in compassionate capitalism – free enterprise with a social conscience. It was a position that made him the object of suspicion to those of both the extreme right and extreme left, and even made him walk a fine line in his own profession. It was much the same with religion. He believed in the Judeo-Christian ethic but not in the religious dogmas that would take him beyond the belief in a divine Creator. Above all, he was terrified by absolutes, and perhaps this was the true basis of his revulsion against despotic Fascism on the one hand and despotic Communism on the other.

Knowing his son's inner warm humanitarianism, Philip felt confident of his eventual rejection of Communism, but in the case of Morrie Kahn it was already far too late. He had been hopelessly brainwashed and had lost the power of independent thought, and with it, the virtue of humor.

On one of the last days of their London visit, Philip decided to take his parents out for the day, while Patty stayed behind to spend the day with James and have a few heart to heart talks with him. Philip drove his dad's immaculate four-door sedan, still looking as if it had just emerged from the showroom, with his parents comfortably ensconced in the back and admiring the scenery. First, he took the road out along Windsor Park as far as the Castle, and explored the huge structure and its grounds, taking a few pictures en route. Next, he took the road to Oxford and they went through the various colleges in considerable detail. The light grayish brown walls and gothic shapes were a perfect backdrop to the serenity of the quadrangles and their gardens. They sat on the benches enjoying the warm country air and the song of the birds, then strolled in leisurely pace around this classic center of British learning and history.

After a quiet and pleasant lunch at a nearby tea-house they drove out to Cambridge, where the University buildings were of much darker hue yet somehow less somber than their Oxford counterpart. The entrance gates, with their magnificent college shields and brilliant gold lettering, conveyed an artistic impact that served as an enticement to any self-respecting photographer, and Philip's camera was at its busiest. The college gardens, each with its gracious flower beds, its central gazebo and inviting benches, were a perfect place for his parents to rest, enjoy the tranquil scene and be photographed.

Another place that they found memorable was the little round church with its matchless rose-garden, a veritable gem of English Christian heritage. Before departing from this quaint country city of contrasts, they roamed the stalls of the bustling flea-market in the central square, then strolled down the bank of the Cam river where young swains poled their punts languidly along the serene waters, while their ladyfriends reclined appreciatively in the back and trailed their hands in the gentle current.

On the drive back to Hendon, Philip was on the lookout for a suitable place where he could take his parents to a real oldfashioned English dinner, the kind one could only find in a grand Olde English Inn. Eventually, as they were getting closer to the city, he spotted just the right place, an attractive rambling Elizabethan structure, set in spacious lawns with an imposing driveway – as though expecting the arrival of coach and horses. They were a bit early for dinner, so they had lots of time to freshen up and to enjoy a glass of excellent sherry.

When they sat down in the attractive wood-panelled dining room and looked at their menus, they were surprised to find that the dishes were almost entirely Hungarian. Their hosts came over and introduced themselves: a charming middle- aged couple who were refugees from Budapest. They had survived the Nazi occupation and at first had hailed the arrival of Russian troops. But later on, with Russian tanks entering the city to crush a democratic revival, they knew it was time to leave and perhaps never return. They told the diners that they were happy in England, and their children were growing up to be proper English gentlemen and ladies. In time, they hoped to cater to two types of diner: those who preferred the old traditional British fare and those who looked for continental cuisine.

The Bosnars chose the delicious Chicken Paprika, with a smooth white wine that was fruity but not too sweet and came from Hungary's southern border region. The sumptuous meal was climaxed by a mouthwatering Strudel and thick rich coffee served in tiny cups. It was clear to Phil and Patty that Britain was steadily becoming a cosmopolitan nation of refugees, and was undoubtedly the richer for the transition. The same thing was happening in places like the U.S.A. and their own Canada. But would the trickle of recent years become, one day, an overwhelming flood that destroyed its earlier benefits, breeding bigotry instead of international goodwill and understanding? Only time and the march of history would tell.

There was little doubt in their minds that this joint trip had been therapeutic, had brought the old and the new world so much closer together for both of them. It reduced the feeling of alienation that assailed them from time to time, one that phone calls and letters couldn't entirely dispel. It also restored ones sense of perspective after the critical events of the past few years, not only in Ontario but in the world around them.

In China, the Red Guards were converting the Cultural Revolution into a bloody repression of progressive forces. The young students waving their little red books of Mao's sayings were being used as pawns in a demoniacal game that could only lead to disaster for the long-suffering Chinese masses.

In Vietnam, the war was constantly escalating and so were the lists of the dead and dying.

In the U.S.A, the war protests were escalating and so was the drug scene, the sexual revolution, and the repressive activities of J.Edgar Hoover's F.B.I.

In the Middle East, Nasser's avowed plans to annihilate Israel were given a sharp point by the expulsion of the U.N. peace-keeping forces between Egypt and Israel, and touched off the Six Day War, with a resounding defeat for Egypt and Jordan and a kick in the pants for Syria at the Golan Heights. Now, the West Bank, previously seized by the Jordanians, was occupied by Israel, along with East Jerusalem. The Sinai had become a buffer safety zone against Nasser, while the Gulf of Tiran was once again opened to Israeli shipping.

On the home front, the visiting President De Gaulle, in a frenzy of Anglophobia and a senile lack of judgement, roused a hysterical crowd of Franco-Canadians with his impassioned exhortation, "Vive le Quebec LIBRE!". Canada was in for some very troubled times and the banked fires of independence in the province of Quebec threatened to burst into roaring flame and separate Canada's `two solitudes' once and for all.

CHAPTER 50

1967-68

Arranging the O.R. schedule had become far simpler since the New year. On certain days when Campbell had his short cases – mainly cystoscopies – he started at 8 a.m. and carried straight through. On other days, a similar arrangement was made for Peter Lawton and Armand Coté, his new associate in Ob.Gyn. The rest of the days were assigned to Bosnar for time preference, but whether or not he was due to start at 8 a.m, he made it a habit to get to the hospital at the same time, 7.45. As the work for all four members of the clinic's operating team increased, it became essential to engage a second anesthetist, and they weren't kept waiting long.

Roger Grimes was a well-qualified man from Nova Scotia, who answered the Center's advertisement in fairly short order and proved to be a competent specialist in his field. He wasn't quite as good as Cassidy but showed more interest in the actual operation and its technical details.

For a while everything went along smoothly and there were no jarring episodes to disturb working conditions at the hospital. Then Grimes came down with a severe attack of acute *Cholecystitis* (inflammation of the gall-bladder) and was admitted to the Memorial under Dr. Bosnar's care. The patient revealed the fact that he'd suffered from gall-stones for years and had come through several lesser attacks in the past. He was eager to go ahead with surgery on this occasion, and three days after admission his gall-bladder was removed without incident.

He made a rapid recovery and was able to go home on the fifth postoperative day. The only difficulty was that, despite his excellent return to good health, he showed not the slightest inclination to get back to work even after a month had gone by. But he wasn't too proud to come up to the office every two weeks and collect his cheque. As if this weren't enough, he found the time to develop a growing antipathy toward Dr. Appleton and his medical philosophies. Finally, after another six months, he served notice that he intended to leave at the end of the year "in order to accept a better appointment in Alberta."

To add injury to insult, he occupied this period of grace by sounding off about sundry defects of the Center's organization, and even had the effrontery to oppose Appleton at the regular medical staff meetings, even trying to get him replaced as medical director. At least, Philip thought bitterly, Grimes had managed to get his operation performed without so much as a "thank you," and to enjoy a prolonged convalescence at the clinic's expense.

At one of the clinic meetings, the senior surgeon spoke up. "Mr. Chairman, I, too, would like to voice my criticism of what is happening at this beef session."

He'd endured more than enough of the divisive new anesthetist and his antics, and it was time to toughen up Appleton – who was in the chair but not in control.

"We're setting a dangerous precedent by permitting one of our staff, someone who's given us notice of resignation, to continue attending these meetings. And on top of that he now attempts to destroy the structure of the institution he's leaving. I move that Roger Grimes be asked to vacate this meeting at once." The vote was almost unanimous, with only Vince Cassidy abstaining.

Unlike the present defector, three of their staff whom they hated to lose were Brigitte Fleischmann, who went back to Minneapolis to rejoin her family, Mike Fowler and Gordie Alsop. The two young family doctors returned to Western University in London, Ontario, in order to advance their postgraduate training. All three had been loyal, rock-solid individuals, whose departure the C.H.C. could ill afford and was keenly felt by their patients. It was time to place ones confreres at the Health Center into three categories. There were those who intended to stay, those who intended to go downtown, and those to whom the clinic was a useful stopping-off place before leaving for a more permanent career elsewhere.

Of course this was an unfair and over-simplified assessment, but as senior surgeon he was getting tired of seeing his colleagues come and go. Even if they left as friends and supporters, their patients might not want to stay with the clinic. Worst of all, those doctors who left as denigrators of their organization did as much harm as possible before changing sides. They even managed to plant the seeds of disaffection among new recruits.

In view of such negative influences affecting the retention of doctors within the clinic it was decided to introduce two new factors into the agreement between the medical director and his staff. Any new doctor coming on staff at the Center was designated an 'associate,' but would become eligible for partnership after a period of two years, on approval by three quarters of the medical partners. Then, on becoming a full-blown partner, the former associate would be entitled to a share of the annual surplus. The figure for the surplus was arrived at by taking the entire income of subscriber premiums, fee-for-service and additional amounts such as Workman's Compensation and sundry insurance cases, then subtracting overhead expenses and capital reserve. The latter was an agreed amount between the Board of the Association and the Medical Executive.

The surplus was divided equally between Association and medical partnership, thus equalizing the medical incomes still further, a fact that pleased the family physicians but not the specialists. On the other hand, a new productivity bonus system was introduced that might prove a dangerous innovation in a set-up such as theirs. It could easily become an inducement to overservicing (by some) as a means of augmenting income. This was particularly insidious in the surgical specialties, and Bosnar warned Appleton against letting the new system get out of hand, especially if he wanted the surgical department to retain a conservative attitude toward operations and the use of acute hospital beds.

Matt O'Brien, the anesthetist who now joined the Center as a replacement for Grimes, was a very serious but likeable individual; quite unlike his surly and unappreciative predecessor. As time went by, all the clinic doctors working in the O.R. found that O'Brien did his work competently and without complaint. He always checked his hospital patients at any hour of the day or night to make sure they were comfortable and progressing well. He had come to the clinic from Manitoba, and although he seemed to fit smoothly into the clinic's medical group, he was inclined to be a private person and kept very much to himself.

As was the case with Roger Grimes, Cassidy made no attempt to establish any sort of close professional or personal relationship with O'Brien, and the senior surgeon's vague feeling of apprehension on that score refused to go away. Then, out of the clear blue sky, the Head of Nursing at the Memorial Hospital approached him one day with a complaint about the new clinic anesthetist.

"He upsets the nurses on the floors by coming in to examine his postop patients at any time of the day or night and giving them intravenous Demerol if he thinks they haven't had enough to keep them comfortable."

"Surely that shows compassion for his patients."

"Maybe so, Dr. Bosnar, but it also shows a lack of faith in the nurses' judgement, and if we had every anesthetist running around day and night carrying their own doses of Demerol we'd have total chaos."

When Philip discussed the matter with O'Brien he became defensive, but after the surgeon explained the problem more thoroughly, his colleague promised to cut down on the number of visits between midnight and 7 a.m, and to rely more on the night nurses, in accordance with his detailed instructions. To reinforce O'Brien's position, Bosnar emphasized the real meaning of the order 'p.r.n.' (when necessary) followed by 'q.3.h.' or 'q.4.h.' (every 3 hours or every four hours), as he interpreted it. It was the patient's plea for pain-relief rather than the nurse's opinion that was to receive priority. The dangers of narcotic addiction were not supposed to be their primary concern in dealing with a patient's declared pain.

At the Health Center, Philip had become so sensitive to the continuous coming and going of family physicians that it made him wonder whatever happened to the quality known as loyalty. Patty had already put her foot down when it came to the matter of social entertainment.

"I've had it up to here!" she complained one day, "It seems that no sooner do we have a party for your fellow doctors in the clinic than they take off, either to the doctor's building downtown or greener pastures somewhere else."

"You must realize, Patty, that some of our G.Ps announced early on that they'd only be staying for a year or two. As long as they leave the city they can't do us much harm. It's only when they go downtown that it really hurts us. In any event, I certainly understand how you feel."

The most recent departure was that of Ted Novak: master of the grand manner. He'd been most successful in his efforts to narrow the income gap between family physicians and specialists, and was now feeling a bit frustrated by the knowledge that he'd carried the process just about as far as he could. One afternoon, shortly after 5 o'clock, he asked the senior surgeon to spare a few minutes and join him in his office for a cup of tea. Novak was at his most polite, and treated him with a deference one might normally reserve for a prince of the church. His tea guest, on the other hand, was suspicious and on guard.

"You know the extent of my loyalty to this place," Novak commenced, "and you know I've been prepared to make any sacrifice in order to make our Health Center succeed."
The surgeon made no effort to enter the conversation.

"Recently, I've found my patient-load too heavy and I'm afraid I can't maintain my usual high standards without threatening my health and marriage."
His listener remained resolutely mute.

"To cut a long story short, I've just had an offer from the pharmaceutical division of the prestigious `Jensen Therapies' company to head their clinical trials department."

"Don't hesitate, Ted. Take it!"

It was more a command than advice. He'd seen the advertisement in the medical journals three months ago and felt resentful at this delicate distortion of events.

"I'm sure it will give you just the kind of life you'll enjoy, and I wish you all the luck in the world."

His colleague wiped away a non-existent tear and gripped the older colleague's hand warmly.

"I knew I could depend on you for honest advice, Dr. Bosnar."

Blast it! he thought, I really like this guy with all his faults, but I guess I've given him exactly the right push, though I doubt if he really needs it.

It was late in August of '67 when he received a phone-call from Matt O'Brien, and it chilled him to the bone. The anesthetist was calling from the Memorial Hospital.

"I hate to tell you this, Phil, but I've just given Dr. Appleton my resignation, and I didn't want to leave without saying goodbye to you."

"What the hell's happened, Matt, why do you have to leave?"

"I've got a Demerol addiction. It's been with me for years and I just can't lick it. Anyhow, the nurses caught me in the act last night, giving extra Demerol to the patients and some to myself. Dr. Foley was called in as chief of staff, and he told me to leave town right away and get some help."

"For God's sake, man, you should have told me before, and I would have got you some professional help. You don't have to leave right away, and I'll see if we can't get you straightened out right here in San Pete."

"It's no use. I've tried to keep it under wraps but it was just a matter of time. It's best I get away from here before I hurt you guys at the Health Center. That's the last thing you need after treating me so decently."

"Sorry to see you go, and I wish you luck. You've been a damn good anesthetist as far as I'm concerned. Promise me you'll get some professional help as soon as possible."

"I promise."

My God, he thought, I've been blind! All that business with the extra Demerol for patients; his tendency to keep to himself and his morose personality. Somewhere along the line I should have spotted that something was wrong, yet at no time was there the slightest sign of impairment in the performance of his duties. I'm going to miss him.

At the time of Appleton's original recruitment of medical staff for the Community Health Center, he'd spent considerable time at the Western University Medical School in London, Ontario, and obtained friendly cooperation from the teaching staff. Now that the Center seemed to be facing the constant possibility of further staff changes, it was decided that Atkins and Bosnar should spend a few days with him at the Toronto General Hospital; to establish a liaison with the professors at this most conservative of medical establishments.

They were pleasantly surprised at the degree of cordiality they encountered in the departments of Internal Medicine and General Surgery, but were disappointed by the marked coolness in the department of Orthopedics. It was mainly as a result of this coolness and the scanty reports from that department, usually written by a junior resident, that Philip referred his most difficult orthopedic problems to McClusky of Sudbury. That was prior to the arrival of Hector

Thomas, the new solo orthopod in San Pete, and the situation was destined for a strange resolution at a later time.

Just as the hospitals held periodic Cancer Clinic sessions conducted by the consulting staff of the Princess Margaret medical staff, headed by Drs. Ash and Ault, they also had orthopedic clinics from Toronto consultants. These were related mainly to the Crippled Children's organization, and the specialists from the Toronto General Hospital were headed by Professor Dewar. One afternoon, Dr. Bosnar received a phone-call from Mrs. Keynes, the orthopedic clinic's faithful secretary.

"I'm calling on behalf of Dr. Dewar. He'd like to come up to your apartment this evening and visit with you and Mrs. Bosnar. During his recent lecture tour in Australia he met your wife's sisters and would like to describe that meeting to Mrs. Bosnar in person."

"I'm very sorry but this evening would not be convenient." There was a chill in his voice that registered his displeasure at the arrogance and presumption of the request: not even made in person but through an intermediary. There had been little warmth so far in the great man's attitude to the clinic's medical staff, and its senior surgeon wasn't about to dance with delight at the present approach. At the other end of the line, Mrs. Keynes was spluttering with embarrassment and indignation at Dr. Bosnar's lack of appreciation of the honor bestowed upon his household.

"But Dr. Bosnar, the professor is leaving for Toronto on the morning plane."
He decided to take the poor woman off the hook. After all, she was blameless.

"Please tell Dr. Dewar that I'd like him to join us for breakfast tomorrow morning, and I'll be happy to drive him to the airport in time for his flight."

Here, he thought, was one more example of the strange Providential humor. Two of Patricia's sisters were nuns in a nursing order, and the older one was head of the order for the whole of Australia. In addition, the sisters ran one of the finest hospitals on the southeast coast of that vast country 'down under,' with a reputation for excellence that was recognized far and wide. Both nursing nuns had already met the Bosnars' totally agnostic son in London, England, and loved him dearly; and they had always expressed the greatest affection for their sister's non-Catholic husband in their letters, regardless of his origins or religious affiliation. In truth, from a strictly traditional point of view, both were extremely broadminded and emancipated in their viewpoints and had already encountered some antagonisms from their orthodox 'mother-house' in Ireland. They drew their inspiration from such leaders as Pope John the XX111rd rather than Pious the X11th, and Philip looked forward keenly to their first meeting.

Dr. Dewar phoned him at his home at 8.30 a.m. It was Saturday morning and Philip wasn't on emergency call, so he drove down to Dewar's hotel, picked him up and brought him to the Bosnar apartment. The visitor greeted Patty effusively and accepted some coffee but no breakfast. He then proceeded to eulogize her sisters in the most flattering terms, and it was obvious that they'd made a deep and lasting impression on him. He thought their hospital was superb and their knowledge of hospital organization of the highest order.

"Not only that," he added, "but they're so thoroughly modern and broadminded in their attitudes, quite beyond that of most Catholic nursing orders."

He revealed that they'd asked if he knew their "distinguished brother-in-law in Saint Pierre", which must have caused him some discomfort, and made him promise to convey their warmest regards to the Bosnars when he got back to Canada. As the minutes went by, Dewar seemed to shed his stiffness and become more relaxed, more human. He went out onto the balcony and admired the splendid view, and he even made some complimentary remarks to his host about "the bold experiment in the practice of medicine."

On the way to the airport, Dewar questioned him in searching detail about the Community Health Center, and he replied in equal detail: emphasizing the changes that had been made since its inception.

"I guess the opposition from the solo practitioners has pretty well gone by now," the professor remarked.

"Unfortunately not. We're still excluded from the local medical society."

"But that's absolutely scandalous! I know most of the local lads in surgery, Duncan, Foley, Morecombe and others, and find it difficult to believe they could act this way."

He seemed genuinely upset, and by the time they arrived at the airport Philip felt as though he'd acquired, if not a new friend, at least one less opponent. Dewar's parting words as he took his leave were, "Promise me that you'll do everything in your power to get your group into the medical society. If you don't, you'll be just as guilty as they are."

His anger was as reassuring as it was welcome.

One dark and rainy day in late November, Appleton came into Philip's office and joined him for a cigarette and chat. The surgeon could tell at once that Jim had something on his mind, but when he revealed what it was, he was truly shocked. Perhaps he should have considered the possibility.

"You know, Phil, I've been thinking quite seriously of leaving this place and going down to the University of Virginia for an academic appointment. Beth is becoming very pissed off with the local medical scene and sees no future for our family in this divided city."

"You can't leave, Jim! That would be a betrayal of your most loyal supporters and of the Center itself, and it would be a confession of defeat to our opponents downtown."

"You could get along just fine without me."

"That's a load of horseshit and you know it. You're needed here, and we have a good chance of overcoming most of our hurdles in the next few years and moving ahead to a successful future. Right now there's nobody in our group who could take your place, and you're the only one of us who's really trusted by the Association."

The conversation slowly petered out and Philip felt confident he'd nipped a disastrous decision in the bud. Of course he knew how attached Beth had been to both the Gaylords and Novaks and how lost she must feel without them. He knew how much trouble the Appletons were having with their teen-age children, and how easy it was to blame it on the senseless medical feud in a politically divided community, and in a foreign country to boot. He knew how tempting it was for Jim to accept an academic post in Virginia, where his close friend, Jonathan Grey, was now Dean of a renowned medical school, and he felt considerable sympathy for Jim's moral and emotional quandary. Yet he wouldn't be surprised if his friend never again raised the subject of leaving for greener pastures.

Pat Hogan was a short squat leprechaun of a man. He was in his middle forties, was wildly eccentric and had an infectious giggle. Personally, the senior surgeon had grave doubts about the reliability of this latest recruit in the field of clinic 'gas-passers', despite his numerous Irish and English degrees in chemistry, medicine and anesthesia. Like the last two choices who'd proved so unsuitable, this one had been interviewed and recommended by Vince Cassidy, and Philip hoped he'd investigated the candidate more thoroughly than hitherto. But with his usual air of detachment, it was hard to be sure. In any event, most of Cassidy's own talents were becoming absorbed by a steady increase in the number of dental anesthetics he was giving each morning. These were performed in the dental outpatient department at the Memorial and the O.R. suite at St. Matthew's.

The use of the operating suite for dental cases was a blatant refutation of all the principles of asepsis, and should never have been allowed, but the Sisters' administration turned a blind eye to this infraction despite the objections of a good many surgeons. After all, some of these dentists were St. Matthew's strongest supporters and benefactors.

Campbell and Bosnar weren't too happy with the anesthetic arrangement, and would much sooner have seen the newcomer assigned to the dental cases, but their hands were tied. From Cassidy's point of view, the dentals were an easy way to mount up productivity points, since a series of short anesthetics was more remunerative on the fee schedule than one or two major cases. In addition, he was used from time to time by Pelletier for his thoracic cases, and they could hardly tell him that this interfered with their own schedule.

Meanwhile, Hogan's performance in the O.R. was soon becoming more erratic and unreliable. He found it difficult to set up smooth intravenous infusions, and unlike most of the present gas-passers, put his IV needle into the front of the patient's elbow instead of the back of the hand. Complaints began to mount up steadily about his poor techniques, mainly from the O.R. nurses at both hospitals but also from some members of the hospital committees, though never on an official basis.

On one occasion, Hogan missed a sudden cardiac arrest on a middle-aged steelworker having surgery for removal of an extensive tumor on his left arm. It was only Dr. Bosnar's sudden awareness of a darkening of the patient's blood that enabled him to alert the oblivious anesthetist to imminent disaster. He averted it by clearing a blocked airway and performing closed cardiac massage. His colleagues in Ob.Gyn. were having similar experiences, and the clinic surgeons all held a council of war along with Vince Cassidy and Appleton. It was agreed that Cassidy should talk to Hogan and keep an eye on his activities. But nothing came of this agreement and the senior surgeon began to despair of remedying the situation.

The crisis came in a most peculiar fashion. Campbell was due to go overseas the next day, for a visit to his family and a reunion with some of his friends at St. Bart's Hospital. Dr. Bosnar had a list of four major cases at St. Matthews, the first being a gall-bladder removal on the city's popular police chief, a very bulky man in his late fifties. Pat Hogan appeared to be in a strange mood, and he reacted angrily to the surgeon's request that he place the IV. on the left side as it would be in the assistant's way if placed on the right. Both Campbell and the O.R. supervisory Sister were there and looked apprehensive, especially as she had arranged for a number of visiting nursing students from Michigan to watch Dr. Bosnar's cases for that morning.

While he was scrubbing for the first case the Sister came and asked him to cancel the entire operative 'list'. Hogan had stubbornly placed the IV. in the right arm, refused to switch and declared that if anyone else switched it to the left side he'd walk out. Unlike her predecessor, this

O.R. Sister was older, unbiased and thoroughly reliable, and the disconcerted surgeon took her advice, especially as Campbell urged him to do the same.

It wasn't easy to smooth things over, and Philip spent the next few hours in frantic discussions and arrangements, until his head swam. True to form, Cassidy simply washed his hands of the whole business and was no help at all. Moreover, he announced that he had to spend a few days in Toronto in connection with his Canadian qualifications.

Philip saw the Mother Superior and reported the entire affair in detail, then spoke to the Chief of Anesthesia, who not only supported his action but volunteered to do his list two days later, on a Saturday morning usually reserved for emergency and urgent cases. The clinic surgeon expressed his gratitude in the strongest possible terms and felt that this was a silver lining, indeed, to the darkest of clouds.

It was now possible to go around to his patients, one by one, and explain that Dr. Hogan was unwell and Dr. McGraw had kindly offered to do the cases for him on Saturday morning – and they were duly relieved. He then went straight across to the Memorial, where he explained what had happened to the new administrator, a vast improvement on his predecessor (the one who'd dispatched the hospital janitor to show him and his clinic associates around the hospital in '63). Next, he went over the entire situation with the chief of anesthesia, Dick Roberts, a man he liked very much. Roberts was sympathetic and thought Hogan should be taken off anesthesia, and perhaps referred to the College for further training, despite his many degrees.

Don Foley, as chief of staff at the memorial, expressed the same opinion and felt Bosnar had taken the correct decision. He promised to contact the College, and in the meantime Hogan's anesthetic privileges would be suspended at both hospitals. To Philip's amazement, Fred Stewart, president of the Memorial medical staff and one of the downtown G.P. gas-passers, offered to do one of his cases that was booked for the afternoon, an umbilical hernia in a 10 year-old girl, and he was overcome by the friendly gesture.

Saturday's cases went smoothly, without a single hitch, and the following Monday morning, when Don Foley got back from Toronto, the clinic surgeon was delighted to tell him how well everything had gone, in the face of what could have been a serious crisis. Foley's reply was shattering.

"I'm afraid the cease-fire is over and you won't be getting any more help from our anesthetists."

"I don't understand, Don. What's changed ?"

"It's all because of that stupid Steelworkers TV Hour on Sunday evenings. I've been told they were belittling our solo doctors again and that's really put the fat in the fire this time."

"To be honest with you, I didn't watch that particular program, but I've never yet seen a single one of those TV shows in which they've said anything bad about the solo doctors. Let me look into the matter before the Medical Society takes a definite stand."

"I'm afraid you're already too late."

The Steelworker's Hour, which came on about once a month, was actually a full length Hollywood movie preceded by a commercial that took the form of a tribute by one of the key union figures to special social activities by a steelworker. As it happened, several of the doctors in the clinic had watched the program in question, and although the announcer praised the C.H.C. not one word of criticism had been voiced against the solo doctors.

Suddenly, Philip had a disturbing hunch.

"Did the announcer ever use the term `Comprehensive Medical Care,' when talking about us?"

"As a matter of fact, he did."

"Well I guess that may have been enough to fire up the old paranoia."
Campbell had other ideas. He thought it was all the deliberate plan of Dr. Foley, whom he regarded as the real guiding force behind what he termed the "medical mafia" of San Pete. In fact, he called him "The Godfather."

What happened next was beyond belief. Nothing whatsoever was done at the College level about Hogan, and he went back to his gas-passing, even though he was discharged by the C.H.C. medical group. As for Vince Cassidy, he informed Appleton that because of the stresses associated with the turmoil in anesthesia, he felt compelled to leave the Health Center and practice downtown. He went even further in protecting his fragile sensibilities, by leaving town for a prolonged holiday "until things blow over." This was surely non-involvement at its finest!

In July 1968, the President of the St. Pierre Medical Society informed Appleton that a boycott was now in force by the solo anesthetists against the clinic doctors (or more accurately, their patients!) except for emergency cases. On August the 8th, a writ was prepared by the Health Association lawyers against the Society, and for the rest of the year a series of meetings and correspondence took place, first with the O.M.A. and then with the College. The latter proved even less sympathetic than the O.M.A. and Don Foley's statement on behalf of the Society said it all. **"The Community Health Center agreed to provide their own medical services, but then their own anesthetists left. Accordingly it is up to the Health Center to damn well provide their own anesthetists and their doctors shouldn't expect sympathy when they don't deliver what they said they would."**

The ghost of Comprehensive Medical Care had come home at last to haunt the Community Health Center!

They were now facing their first major medical crisis since the opening of the Center and the way out wasn't going to be easy. On a private level, Philip knew that not everyone in the Medical Society was in favor of the anesthetic boycott. Dick Roberts, for one, spoke to him quite candidly and said that he was sure some of the anesthetists would be willing to defy the boycott, but they were afraid they'd lose a major portion of their work, which – after all – depended on referral by the surgeons.

Only Suzie Chan, a diminutive Chinese-Canadian solo anesthetist, was resolute enough to defy the ban and cover the Center's elective lists whenever she could. Almost immediately, she was made to pay the price by losing a large portion of her work and encountering open hostility from the medical society. There was even talk of throwing her out of that august body, but that would have brought the affair out into the open and caused a public scandal.

On the official level, the medical partnership of the Health Center immediately made representations to all the recognized bodies of the medical establishment and the two local hospitals. Most of the replies were noncommittal and achieved little beyond an assurance that the group doctors were not to be deprived of anesthesia in 'genuine emergency cases'. On an unofficial level, Philip learned from several of his solo physician contacts that attempts to form a hospital-based anesthetic group, available to all patients, was raised repeatedly but always failed at the last moment.

He knew some of the worst diehards in the opposition, and they always seemed to have the final say in such matters. On the other hand there was Art Mottram, an Ob.Gyn. specialist in solo practice, who used to tell him about some of the past feuds in San Pete's medical fraternity. They had occurred long before the C.H.C. was conceived. Mottram had little taste for some of the latest happenings and he had little use for such self-appointed 'gods' as Glenn Morecombe; even less for someone like Tony Donovan, whom he characterized as "an arrogant turncoat." Some of these confidences, and those of people like Dick Roberts and Cedric Blore, were in sharp contrast to the bland pretensions of Don Foley, who insisted that all physicians were honorable people, and that San Pete's doctors had been a peaceful and harmonious group prior to the opening of the Health Center.

A private chat with the new Administrator at the Memorial revealed the fact that the hospital Board, although opposed to the anesthetic boycott, felt they weren't in a position to interfere by direct edict, despite their good intentions. At St. Matthew's Hospital on the other hand, things were quite different, and he was even afforded an insider view in his current capacity as secretary to the Medical Executive Committee of the hospital staff.

The perennial Chief of Staff, Herb Slater, was in the chair at their meetings and he'd mellowed into a reasonable and friendly person. Dr. Bosnar now made it a point, before the end of each meeting, to bring up the subject of the anesthetic boycott and put through a recommendation for corrective action by the hospital administration.

Not only did these recommendations produce no action, but on each occasion the official print-out of Bosnar's minutes carefully omitted all mention of the subject, despite his strenuous objections. After one of these meetings he suggested to the Sister Superior that the best way for her to reverse a previous motion to which she objected, was to erase it from the minutes, and after the meeting he received an unexpected confidence. It was from Darren Markovsky, the family physician who was President of the Medical Society at the time of the media wars between the two sides during '61 and '62.

"You know, Philip, although you're absolutely right in everything you say, you can't win. For one thing, the powers that be in St. Matthew's will make sure you never serve on another committee that has any real influence on hospital policy."

One month later, at a luncheon meeting of the Joint Executive in the board-room of St. Matthew's, the forbidden subject was raised once more, and on this occasion he encountered overt hostility from two new players in the tragicomedy. The first was the Chairman of the Board, Clarence Woodridge. He was the hospital's lawyer, a director of Cambrian Steel and a well-known alcoholic who was periodically hospitalized in a private room at St. Matthew's under the care of Dr. Morecombe. The admitting diagnosis was invariably 'Acute Exacerbation of Gastric Ulcer,' but the treatment was always related to an attack of acute alcoholism.

The second player was the new Sister Superior, Sister Angelica, who was much smarter and younger than her predecessor, but had more virulent prejudices and a venomous tongue. Both she and Woodridge expressed the viewpoint that the lack of anesthesia for clinic patients was really the fault of the C.H.C. and certainly not the responsibility of the hospital. It was cathartic for Philip to blow his stack and say exactly what he thought of this rationalization, in the most unguarded possible language.

After the lunch was over, he buttonholed Woodridge and told him that if the Health Center couldn't rectify matters through the hospitals or College then it would proceed through the courts of law. The lawyer replied with a smirk that such a legal action hadn't the slightest chance of success, and this made the clinic surgeon look forward with great relish to the day his alcoholic opponent would be forced to eat his words.

Wilfred Jarvis, as C.H.C. Administrator, engaged the services of Gregory, Cavendish, Scott and Polson, with offices in the new Professional Tower in downtown Toronto. They immediately dispatched first one and then another young lawyer to San Pete where they interviewed everyone in the Community Health Center remotely connected with the anesthetic boycott. The first lawyer was a large, florid and imposing individual named Peter Scott; he soon apologized that he'd just been called away to another case in Fort William. The second was much quieter and less flamboyant, and he impressed Philip far more. His name was Ronald Polson and he went about his investigation methodically and without fanfare. He spoke to all four surgical specialists and the medical director, as well as the nurses and secretaries who were involved in making the anesthetic bookings. Everything they said was carefully noted and weighed as potential evidence, and it didn't take Philip long to appreciate that this lawyer was involving himself emotionally in their case.

When they had lunch together at a nearby restaurant, the problem was tackled from a broader angle. The legal action was no longer to be confined to the question of the boycott. It was to include the wider issue of exclusion from the local Medical Society. This was a triumph of considerable proportions, as the senior surgeon was getting tired of the remarks so often repeated by some of his immediate colleagues, of whom Armand Coté was the most critical.

A man of impeccable English diction and the most Gallic mannerisms, Coté was the son of an English mother and a French father, born in the Caribbean Island of Martinique and educated in Britain, where he obtained his medical degree and postgraduate training. He was an agnostic and self-professed cynic, and he would often oppose Philip Bosnar's viewpoint by such remarks as: "Don't be such a stupid idealist, my friend. I simply can't see why you're so hellbent on our entry into the local medical society. Personally I don't give a shit."

"As usual, Armand, you've missed the point. I'm not looking for admission to that private club. I want it entirely replaced by a new society open to all M.Ds in this geographic area regardless of whether they are in solo or group practice. I want to tear away the veneer of respectability from dirty tricks such as the anesthetic boycott, once and for all."

But for the moment, Coté remained unconvinced and unconverted, as though by ignoring the problem it would just go away.

A glorious summer had given way to a brilliant fall and Philip was eager to try out his new Nikon 35 mm. camera, an anniversary present from his darling wife. He and Jim planned to take the morning flight to Toronto on Friday, the 22nd of September, and meet with their legal team to formulate the medical group's presentation. The day before the flight, following two short cases performed under local, he took the rest of the day off to prepare the clinic's case against the medical society. In order to keep a sense of proportion, he drove out to the spectacular countryside and selected his photographic scenes carefully. After each shot, he took out his pen and note-pad and wrote out a summary of events in both the overt and underground warfare between the Saint Pierre Medical Society and the medical staff of the Cambrian District Community Health Center, culminating in the recent boycott. Nothing was exaggerated or over-dramatized, but as page followed page, the naked facts spoke for themselves and added up to a massive indictment against the Society's position.

By late afternoon he finished both his photography and case summary, twenty-four shots of the former and eight pages of the latter. He felt confident the pictures would come out well, but how would he fare with his presentation to their tough-minded lawyers?

On arrival at the Toronto International Airport the two clinic representatives phoned Ron Polson and he arranged to meet them for lunch in the main dining room of the Royal York Hotel. It was difficult for Philip to resist kidding their host with a tongue-in-cheek enquiry, just to relax the atmosphere.

"Is this the way you lawyers usually take your lunches?" he asked.

"Only when I eat with wealthy doctors," was the prompt reply, and they got down to a discussion of where matters stood in their proposed case against the medical society: through the College if possible, but if not, then through the courts. The meeting took place at 2.30 p.m. in the offices of Gregory, Cavendish, Smithson, and Heineman, situated in the Professional Tower just off Bay Street. It was sumptuously furnished and decorated, and the visitors knew their legal bill wouldn't be a meager one, but it was worth it just to get the rot stopped, one way or another.

Arthur Fitzpatrick Gregory, senior partner of the firm and Professor Emeritus of the Law faculty of the University of Toronto, was in the chair. He was a small individual, bent with senile arthritis but with an inner vigor that was projected in his bright, birdlike eyes. Seated to his right were Ron Polson and Peter Scott, the former looking sleepy and the latter looking very alert, with ruddy, aggressively handsome features and an imposing shock of light brown hair.

Appleton started things off by introducing Philip to Gregory.

"This is our chief surgeon. Dr. Bosnar, and he is one of the key figures in this matter."

"It's a pleasure to meet you, Sir," said the surgeon, shaking the veteran lawyer's deformed hand carefully. Then, after the amenities were over, he announced, "I would like to read you these hand-written notes that are in summary form. They represent the series of events leading up to the exclusion of our clinic doctors from the Saint Pierre Medical Society, and the present anesthetic boycott."

"Please proceed, Doctor."

"1. Prior to our arrival, the clinic doctors were publicly characterized as 'renegades and misfits' by the Medical Society.

2. It was declared publicly that we would be ostracized personally and socially, if not professionally, by the Society's members."

At this point he was loudly interrupted by Scott.

"But isn't it true that...."

Philip now did his own job of interrupting the interrupter, and made sure he had Gregory's undivided attention.

"Please forgive me, Mr. Gregory, but if my review is to have any impact I must request that you all hear me through without interruption until I'm finished, and then by all means tear my presentation to pieces.

"Go ahead, Doctor. There will be no more interruptions."

"3. Normal cross referral of patients was forbidden from the start.

4. New members of the Society were forced to sign an affidavit promising to maintain the ban on normal cross-referral.

5. Clinic doctors were subjected to considerable harassment and discrimination at both hospitals, including exclusion from key committees. This was at the instigation of Society doctors as detailed in Memorandum A which I hand you now.

6. Legal actions against clinic doctors were encouraged by members of the Society as detailed in Memorandum B which I hand you now.

7. The Society has strenuously opposed the formation of an emergency roster of physicians and surgeons between the solo and Clinic doctors.

8. Acts of hostility against Clinic doctors have compelled some of them to leave the community. I hand you a sample letter.

9. Following the legitimate discharge of Dr Pat Hogan by our group, and in the absence of our senior anesthetist at that time, the initial response of the solo anesthetists was most generous and unselfish, in the finest traditions of our profession.

10.The very next week the Society imposed an official anesthetic boycott on our patients, against which both of our hospitals felt constrained to take no definite action. The exact details are enumerated in Memorandum C which I hand you now.

11.Our aim and object is to replace the existing restrictive medical society with a new one that will be open to all M.Ds. in our area regardless of solo or group practice.

12.This would be the only effective means of removing the cloak of respectability from unethical and immoral acts that are contrary to the highest principles of our profession."

Gregory studied the documents long and hard and in total silence, then turned to his two young partners who were watching his reactions closely. He handed the papers over to them and announced loudly, "**That's our case, gentlemen. Print it!**"

CHAPTER 51

1969-70

For the past two years, the Center had several applicants in orthopedics, E.N.T. (ear, nose, and throat) and ophthalmology, but each was scared off after talking to the downtown doctors, with one notable exception. Dr. Peggy Chapman, who joined the clinic at the end of '68, was a `veddy, veddy British' anesthetist who'd received her additional training at the Montreal General Hospital and was afraid of no man, least of all surgeons. She was tough, resilient and direct, but once the nurses and her fellow doctors got used to these facets of her behavior, they got to like her and found her a tireless and dedicated worker. In addition, she appeared to believe in the basic philosophy and structure of the Health Center and wouldn't be intimidated by the opposition. By this time, the clinic's medical group had no less than four female members on its staff and Philip was impressed with all of them. What was more important, was the fact that the patients were impressed and sometimes preferred them to male doctors.

Now that they had a solid individual on their staff to deliver their anesthetics in conjunction with Suzy Chan, the clinic surgeons could breathe freely once again. They knew that their little Chinese-Canadian savior from the hostile world of solo practice would be leaving within the year, but were now confident they'd soon be able to get a second anesthetist. In the meantime, all their efforts must be directed to breaking the blockade against membership in the St. Pierre Medical Society, preferably by forming a new and broader organization. This would entail actual meetings and repeated communications with the O.M.A. and College, while remaining prepared to absorb their disappointments and keep up the good fight. Unfortunately, 1969 would prove to be a year of confusion and frustration.

On the world scene during these critical times, humankind seemed to be taking one step forward to a glorious destiny and two steps backward into its barbaric past. Dr. Christiaan Barnard, brilliant South African surgeon, electrified the medical world with the first successful human cardiac transplant. This youthful genius, with the charisma of a matinee idol, translated his years of toil and training – with such great surgeons as Wangensteen and Lillehei at Minneapolis and countless hours in the animal labs – into an operation that raised operative surgery to a new and seemingly impossible plateau.

Were there no longer any limits to the range and daring of the modern surgeon's skill? Perhaps, one day in the not too distant future, the entire medical profession could rise to a comparable level of improvisation and courage. It would be a level that would make high-grade medical care to the population at large a feasible moral and economic realization. Just as the heart had always been regarded as the one and only untouchable organ in surgery, and organ transplantation as almost a defiance of the laws of nature, so must Medicine now take a second and unbiased look at such challenging concepts as salaried doctors, group practice and global budgeting.

The break-up of the oil-tanker Torrey Canyon off the coast of Cornwall, and the enormous contamination of the beaches of France, with tragic loss of marine fauna, augured grimly for the future of oceans, beaches, and aquatic wildlife. This was a frightening consequence of human progress in an age when mankind had made itself hopelessly dependent on non-renewable oil as an energy source. The great tankers, with their enormous cargoes of non-degradable bunker oil and their flimsy hulls, ran a dangerous gauntlet of wild seas, fearsome storms and treacherous coastlines, in which the world's precarious ecology was under constant threat. Meanwhile, the multinational cartels looked the other way and the world's governments remained complaisant beyond mere complacence.

The Tet offensive by Communist forces in the endless Vietnam war had finally convinced the most sanguine of American leaders of the ultimate hopelessness of the conflict, and led Lyndon Johnson to bow to the inevitable and relinquish his presidency for good. National morale in the U.S.A. was at its nadir and anarchy was close at hand. The signs were all too obvious, and tragedy was waiting in the wings to shock a great nation out of its moral lethargy. First, the murder of the great Martin Luther King by a southern redneck from the lunatic fringe of the KKK. Could Hoover's FBI have had a hand in this crime, knowing his vitriolic hatred of the civil rights leader?

Then, there was the murder of Bobby Kennedy by a deranged Palestinian, on the eve of his political march to victory. Could this be the long arm of organized Arab terrorism reaching into American politics, with a chosen scapegoat similar to the confused Lee Harvey Oswald in the assassination of J.F.K.?

These were the darkest days for democracy, and not just in the New World. In Czechoslovakia, Alexander Dubcek's attempts to democratize the social and economic system of his oppressed country were crushed by Soviet tanks and troops invading Prague, leading to the downfall of Dubcek and his plans for enlightenment. Meanwhile, the West stood by impotently and a disillusioned electorate brought forth an unsavory pair of reactionaries to assume the Presidency and Vice-Presidency. A once respected nation was facing a crisis of self-confidence that somehow seemed associated with the two men who now controlled its destiny. Their names were Richard Nixon and Spiro Agnew.

During '69, negotiations continued between the C.H.C, the St. Pierre Medical Society, O.M.A. (Ontario Medical Association) and the College, without any solution. Then, in October, OHSIP (the Ontario Health Services Insurance Plan) was introduced by the Robarts government, albeit reluctantly. Since this included unlimited free choice of doctor, it removed the last excuse for the Medical Society's opposition, and it was time for the medical group to strike while the iron was hot. The new scheme also guaranteed, in conjunction with unfettered fee-for-service payment, that the system would ultimately run out of money.

With the advent of the provincial health insurance plan, many of the C.H.C. subscribers now saw no particular advantage in staying committed to the clinic. They experienced a new sense of freedom to see whom they liked and whenever they liked, among a new plethora of doctors, and it felt wonderful. Under the plan of Interselection, they could already choose their own doctor outside the Health Center, with the proviso that they not renew their subscriber membership in the C.H.C. at the next selection time. There also those, of course, who'd expected a medical service millennium when the Center opened its doors, with unrestricted housecalls and other medical benefits, night and day and beyond all reasonable expectation. There were wives with special medical loyalties, women who hadn't been consulted when their steelworker husbands chose the new Health Center against the downtown solo doctor.

All these factors and related ones should have led to a considerable defection of the clinic's subscriber families, but the actual loss was small. It was compensated several times over by the gain of many new groups and individuals other than steelworkers' families. At the same time, it became clear that nothing short of absolute moment-to-moment choice of doctor by clinic patients would satisfy the Medical Society as far as breaking the anesthetic and other cross-coverage boycotts were concerned. It seemed that there'd always be one more stipulation, one more concession, one more capitulation by the Center and only then, PERHAPS, POSSIBLY and MAYBE, professional relationships might be normalized and egregious barriers removed.

Meeting followed meeting with dreary and monotonous lack of progress, and to the Board of the Community Health Association it seemed that their medical group was constantly seeking acceptance and forgiveness by local and provincial medical bodies. As far as Philip was concerned, nothing could be further from the truth, and he made this abundantly clear to his diplomatic counterpart, Cedric Blore. He pointed out that he simply wanted to obliterate all pretexts for restrictive actions by the medical society's hard-liners against clinic patients and their doctors.

The Board of the C.H.C. had stormed at the anesthetic boycott in their own meetings and could hardly wait to take legal action, but most of the doctors in the group wanted action through the College. Both were wrong in their own way. The Board should have publicly flayed those responsible for the boycott, in the media and public meetings, as well as direct confrontation with the hospital authorities. The clinic doctors should never have relied on a sympathetic support from the College but should have INSISTED, via the media if necessary, on fair play and ethical judgment from the province's medical licensing body.

It seemed ironic that, at the very time when their Community Health Association should have been deeply involved in resolving these difficulties, the energies of its union members were absorbed in a prolonged and desperate strike of the steelworkers against the company management. Not only did the Association become a sort of absentee landlord, but there were a few resignations by key members: two representatives from the union's head office in Toronto, and Monsignor O'Grady in San Pete.

A spirit of antagonism seemed to be developing between the medical partnership and the Board, and the Association appeared to be losing enthusiasm for its shining project. A sister health center in St. Catherines, under the auspices of the United Auto Workers, seemed destined for failure, and the financial future of their own Health Center seemed precarious in the extreme.

One move to reverse the threatened decline, was enlargement of their 'in-house' administration by moving Jarvis to the position of Executive Director and appointing Bill Tarkins – a smart young Englishman with a penchant for financial management – to the position of Administrator. Meanwhile, Jarvis, Appleton and Grey were up to their eyebrows in attempts to keep the day-to-day operation of the C.H.C. on an even keel, with no side permitted to rock the boat.

The time seemed right for presenting a joint application by the Community Health

Centers of St. Pierre and St. Catherines to the Ontario Government for a special arrangement of financial coverage, and their stalwart representatives were successful in obtaining a unique provision under OHSIP.

'The Minister may enter into arrangements for the payment of remuneration to physicians or practitioners rendering insured health services to insured persons on a basis other than fee for service.' Thus, the principle of capitation was legally accepted in Ontario as a legitimate alternative to fee-for-service, and an important morale booster had been achieved for the Association.

Without this vital concession, all funds from the government would come directly to the medical partnership and the Board would have no residual fiscal power. The medical partnership, however, had no intention of turning over all its economic clout to the Board. All moneys from fee-for-service patients, Workman's Compensation cases and private insurance patients, would come to the doctors. As far as subscriber patients were concerned, the staff doctors would indirectly bill the Association on a fee-for-service basis.

There was one more factor in the complex equation, and that was the productivity bonus system, with bonus points based on fee-for-service evaluation of such items as hospital visits, emergency duties, house calls, and procedures – medical or surgical, diagnostic or therapeutic. From Philip's point of view, this rewarded the physician who did most active procedures, such as exercise tolerance tests, pulmonary function tests, arteriography, and even electrocardiograms. It also rewarded the surgeon who did the most operations, especially short cases, or practiced rapid surgery. It penalized the physician who spent a long time talking to the patient and practiced slow, methodical, clinical medicine; also the surgeon who performed fewer operations per given number of patients, and who practiced less hurried, careful operative techniques, had long and complex cases, and spent more time with the patient. There were several other areas in which a productivity incentive led to an unnecessary emphasis on 'procedures practice' as a gateway to enhanced earnings.

In any fee-for-service or productivity system, babies with tiny congenital hernias of the navel were more prone to be booked for surgery, and those with questionable inguinal hernias were also finding their way to the OR with minimal findings. Tonsillectomies became epidemic and removal of uteri excessive.

To give credit where credit was due, there was little evidence of widespread abuse of the productivity system by the clinic doctors, but the temptation was always there for the overambitious and the obsessive. It was to the credit of the surgeons, for example, that they turned down most of the children referred to them for tonsillectomy, but as soon as a new specialist in E.N.T. surgery arrived downtown, these same children appeared on the hospital lists for T&As and tubes (removal of tonsils and adenoids plus insertion of fine tubes through the eardrums, presumably for drainage of infected fluid from the middle ear). In all honesty, Bosnar and Campbell found scant justification for this aggressive approach, but (sad to relate) it kept the parents and referring G.Ps equally happy.

Infants with mild club foot deformities, who were making excellent progress with intelligent and attentive use of Dennis-Browne splints, were finding their way to surgical enthusiasts who insisted on performing questionable operative interventions. There were even certain cases of duodenal ulcer, that were perfectly amenable to non-operative measures, referred elsewhere for unnecessary surgery; and the list did not end there. Under such a system of unrestrained free choice plus fee for service, the outcome for government medical insurance was inevitable, namely BANKRUPTCY. Even worse, it encouraged a lowering of discriminating standards and the intrusion of venality.

In January of 1970, the long awaited special meeting with the Council of the Ontario College of Physicians and Surgeons took place at 1.30 p.m. on the second Monday of the month. The Community Health Center was represented by Ron Polson, Jim Appleton and Philip Bosnar and the St. Pierre Medical Society was represented by Bruno Torelli and Dr. Harry Pribble. Torelli was a member of the law firm of Manderly, Lomax and Sprigley, and was a suave, second generation Italian-Canadian. He was also the son-in-law of Dr. Herbert Slater, and his attitude to the Health Center was much more virulent than that of his powerful father-in-law and much closer to that of the implacable Dr. Pribble.

The C.H.C.'s three-man contingent was seated at one end of a large, oblong table, with the Chairman at the other end and Council members on both sides. The opposing contingent would come into this chamber after the first presentation was completed: a sensible arrangement. Polson commenced the proceedings by presenting the case for the 'plaintiff' along the lines of Bosnar's summary and memoranda – previously delivered to the C.H.C.'s Toronto lawyers. It was clear that it made a deep impression as a legal presentation, but the Council members still seemed to remain somewhat cool and unsympathetic. Jim Appleton rose, therefore, to emphasize the harassment aspect of his medical staff's exclusion from the St. Pierre Medical Society.

Then it was Philip's turn, and he attacked the matter from a purely human and moral standpoint.

"Mr. Chairman, honored colleagues, I am here to speak on behalf of a number of young physicians who are the innocent victims of a political war. Looking around this room I would venture a guess about what each of you value most highly, aside from your families, in your personal and professional lives."

He paused for dramatic effect before continuing.

"It is with total confidence that I say it is your personal and professional reputation."

There were vigorous head-noddings and murmurs of assent as he carried on.

"Our medical staff at the clinic, some of them just out of medical school, some just married, are subjected to social and professional ostracism, to innuendo and smears of ethical delinquency and unprofessional behavior. These are nothing short of scandalous. Quite apart from the recent anesthetic boycott against blameless patients and their doctors, only replacement of the present restrictive Medical Society by a broader and more enlightened organization can reverse the campaign of calumny and exclusion. Our honorable profession and our patients deserve better, and I look to you gentlemen to apply the remedy."

There was unconcealed applause from several members of the Council and this was quickly shushed by the Chairman. He thanked the three C.H.C. representatives and requested that they adjourn to the anteroom for coffee.

After about ten minutes of deliberation the Council members joined them and Philip was encouraged by their cordiality and respect. Even the deputy registrar, who'd been so antagonistic during the earliest days of their endeavor, exhibited a remarkable degree of warm friendliness. When the gathering finished its coffee and cigarettes, the threesome were instructed to wait for half an hour while representatives of the St. Pierre Medical Society made their final presentation. In order to avoid an embarrassing encounter, Colson, Appleton and Bosnar went outside into the warm sunshine and discussed their chances, while trying to contain their optimism.

When they were summoned back into the Council room, they found Pribble and Torelli seated to their right and looking very grim. The Chairman cleared his throat and delivered the verdict.

"It has been decided that the present Medical Society in your area is to be discontinued forthwith. It is to be replaced by a new and unrestricted organization that shall be open to all physicians and surgeons in good standing with this College, regardless of solo or group practice. It will be known as the Cambrian District Academy of Medicine."

Philip Bosnar felt like laughing out loud, since the name they'd just chosen was almost identical with that of his Health Center, namely the Cambrian District Community Health Center.

There were ritual handshakes between the two sides and the signing of appropriate documents of agreement. The major battle had been won by the Health Center, but the look in Dr. Pribble's eyes told them that the war might well continue in the form of guerrilla actions for some time to come. At least there could be no cloak of respectability, in future, for actions that discriminated against the Health Center's medical staff and patients, and that was a victory, indeed.

1969 had been yet another year in which the New World revealed its propensity for taking one step forward and two steps backward in Humankind's struggle toward his divinely ordained destiny, that of Homo Sapiens. One didn't need the wisdom and prescience of a Moses, a Jesus, a Mohammed or a Buddha, to recognize the stubborn struggle of mankind's baser instincts against evolutionary progress. As interpreted by Philip and Patricia Bosnar, such progress was toward understanding combined with compassion on the one hand and knowledge combined with judgment on the other. How then, they asked themselves, could a civilization that could send humans to explore the moon and write a glorious chapter in the history of its species, also produce the wholesale slaughter of women, children and old men in a far-off village called Mylai? How could it produce the hideous slaughter of a beautiful actress named Sharon Tate, with her unborn baby and friends, in an act of senseless savagery? Would the future of Humankind's existence on this precious and precarious planet lie in the hands of the Neil Armstrongs among ones fellow-humans or in those of the Calleys and the Mansons?

Everyone rejoiced in the exhilaration of the moon landing, but conversely, all should feel the shame, horror and even the guilt of those horrendous crimes in Mylai and Beverly Hills. It was high time to place price tags on the rights to Life, Liberty, and the Pursuit of Happiness. Those price tags were responsibility, commitment and accountability to fellow humans and the planet as a whole. People everywhere must realize that the massive guilt of the Nazis' European Holocaust, the Khmer Rouge's Cambodian genocide and other similar tragedies (both past and future) was partly theirs, since they shared responsibility for a heinous crime of omission, thus perpetuating the awesome biblical question: **'Am I my brother's keeper?'**

The first meeting of the new Academy of Medicine in San Pete took place at the executive level. Representing the solo doctors were Pribble, Blore and Dartford (a solo internist of strongly entrenched prejudices). The Health Center's representatives were Philip Bosnar, Peter

Lawton and Stuart Atkins, and the first order of business was the picayune issue of the new organization's official name. It appeared that the name selected by the College Council, namely 'The Cambrian District Academy of Medicine,' was too close to that of the Health Center to be palatable to members of the defunct society. The arguments in favor of changing the name to the West Cambrian Academy of Medicine were expressed by Dr. Pribble, first as strident demands and later as plaintive entreaties. In a manner suggestive of Noblesse Oblige by the clinic, Philip and his colleagues graciously acceded to the pleas for a change of title.

When Pribble next suggested that excluding the names of Philip Bosnar and Jim Appleton from present or future presidency of the new academy would be an act of diplomacy to appease the rednecks among the solo practitioners, Philip found it easy to agree, but with a sine qua non: that the names of Foley and Pribble be likewise excluded. The compromise choice was Cedric Blore as the first President and Peter Lawton as the second. Thereafter, the presidency would alternate between solo and clinic doctors.

During the next few meetings they managed to thrash out a new constitution for the Academy. As far as the new executive committee was concerned, each outgoing president would replace one of the present members and terms of office were listed, with Bosnar's name as the last to be replaced. The requirements for membership were clearly unrestricted. The applicant need only be a resident of the broad geographic area served by the Academy and a member in good standing of the Ontario College of Physicians and Surgeons.

It was suggested that one of the first meetings should be in the form of a medico-legal discussion. This, however, was a challenge Philip simply couldn't resist and he minced no words.

"It seems to me that the only medico-legal meetings I've attended so far have consisted of a leading lawyer telling an audience of doctors how to behave in the courtroom, coming dangerously close to telling us how to conduct our practice wherever litigation might be involved. It's high time the situation was reversed and this might be an ideal time to break the pattern."

"Would you care to elaborate, Phil?"

"Gladly. This time let's invite the local lawyers to join us for our meeting. We'll have a senior physician or surgeon, preferably with some medico-legal experience, telling the lawyers how they should behave to doctors in the courtroom and suggesting changes in legal methods and the law itself. For example, doctors questioned in compensation cases should be treated as expert rather than casual witnesses, and certainly not as inferior professionals. If doctors are sued by their patients they must be presumed innocent until proven guilty, and so on, with the lawyers for once being on the receiving end. We could raise the idea of no-fault compensation for the damaged patient, by means of a special ombudsman department, suitably funded."

Despite the enthusiasm of those present in support of his ideas, Philip knew that no such meeting would ever take place. Even the idea of a round table discussion dealing with vexed points between doctors and lawyers would be turned down by the legal profession. It was a pity their own powerful medical profession could expend so much time and energy chasing imaginary bogeymen, but couldn't stand up to the inroads of an arrogant sister profession. There was nothing wrong with the injunction, "Physician, heal thyself," but the legal establishment also needed to be enjoined, "Lawyer, question thine own performance before that of a nobler profession."

It would be a giant step forward, indeed, if the myth of concealment could be exploded once and for all. It was without question a popular one: 'that doctors always shield one of their own when it comes to giving evidence in the courtroom against an accused colleague.' As a matter of fact, the reverse was true in the present decade, and close enquiry among lawyers who were willing to reveal their sources turned up the hidden truth: that many a medico-legal lawsuit originated in pejorative remarks made by one doctor about another.

Phil and Patty remembered only too well the remarks of a prominent local lawyer a year ago. The occasion was a cocktail party given by one of their friends in the dental profession, and the lawyer in question had imbibed a sufficient amount of scotch to make him talkative and a bit unguarded. He introduced himself in a cordial manner, then spoke up.

"I hope you won't mind if I speak to you quite frankly. Personally I think you guys at the Community Health Center have been given a rotten deal. You've had lousy press coverage and you've been on the losing end of a dirty whispering campaign."

"Thanks for your comments but I doubt if there are many people who believe that kind of stuff now they've seen us in action for the past few years."

"You'd be surprised, doctor. I'm sorry to say there are quite a few of my fellow-lawyers who've swallowed that stuff and are only too anxious to see you chaps on the wrong end of some lawsuits."

"That's a bit hard to swallow, unless they're political rednecks."

"Some of them are, and they've got some pals in your own profession who'd be only too glad to provide the material for such lawsuits. What's more, you know there's many a legal action that starts with a remark from a hostile doctor in situations like the one in our community."
(In the years to come there would be many instances of lawsuits against members of the Center's medical staff, but in every case the action was subsequently withdrawn).

An interesting phenomenon was starting to appear in the relationship between solo practitioners and those of the C.H.C. The new Academy was making little difference, but any hostility now had to be clandestine, and no overt actions of discrimination could be carried out. The original big guns of the former St. Pierre Medical Society were visibly mellowing, with a only a few holdouts like Pribble, McBride, and – to a lesser extent – Morecombe. It was from the newer arrivals in solo practice that the clinic encountered its fiercest opposition, and this meant that the initial indoctrination of new solo M.Ds must be as intense as ever.

Although the defectors from the C.H.C. served to fan the flames of enmity, they were still, to a large degree, outside the mainstream of the downtown group, and remained in a state of limbo, with little political credibility. Donovan remained aloof and independent, unaffiliated to the new Academy and retaining his own offices next to the Memorial, on the ground floor of his own home. Pelletier had his offices in the Foley building, and had become a born again Roman Catholic, with ostentatious church attendance and outward renunciation of his former agnosticism. The only residual sign of non-conformity was his absence from all Academy meetings.

With the considerable and frequent turnover of the Clinic's medical staff, most of them in the department of family practice, the Medical Executive Committee at the Center had to check all areas of comparison between their doctors and those in solo practice. One disturbing feature was the introduction of a new siren song beckoning group doctors downtown. It was the replacement of office secretaries, receptionists or nurses by doctors' wives, with what seemed a considerable financial advantage. Jonathan Grey was confident the tax examiners would soon come down like a ton of bricks on these "manipulators," as he called them, especially when they saw the huge salaries paid to their wives. Philip and others remained unconvinced, however, and sought some form of compensation to balance this new differential.

It was finally decided that a Sabbatical system should be put into effect, to be funded out of the Association's overall funds. Each partner of the medical group would receive the equivalent of one month's basic retainer for each year's partnership, up to a limit of seven years. This sum could be used for a period of postgraduate training with pay, or be allowed to accumulate as a retirement package on termination of practice. In addition, there was to be a group life insurance plan, a medico-dental plan and payment of membership fees in the new Academy and the Ontario Medical Association. There would also be an annual book allowance and a 'promotional entertainment' allowance – which simply camouflaged an annual liquor bill. Nevertheless, the temptation of working in their husbands' offices at high salaries remained a potent one for their wives, and the clinic doctors had to be sure they remained closely competitive with solo practice where financial compensation was concerned.

One avenue being explored in depth was the question of group investment into real estate, especially MURBS (Multiple Unit Residential Buildings), which were becoming very popular as a tax-advantaged income. It was Stu Atkins who was first approached by an investment counselor, George Higgins, the son of an Anglican Minister whom the cardiologist knew well through his church activities. The counselor was a partner in Syndvest, Ltd, a new high-powered investment firm with offices in Toronto. It included two financial advisers, a tax expert, a legal expert, an insurance expert and a chartered accountant.

The firm's President, Dwight Crane, was a man with a quick mind and convincing manner, and when Jim Appleton and Philip had lunch with him, he sounded like someone who knew his field thoroughly but wouldn't press his ideas too strongly. He thought it was a good way to bind together a partnership such as theirs, while providing a hedge against exorbitant taxes and gaining a progressive 'Leverage' advantage by obtaining easy credit for further investments on borrowed money. It was their newest member who turned the partnership's hesitation to enthusiastic acceptance. Pat Bradley was their new anesthetist, having joined the group just a month after the arrival of Peggy Chapman. He was a tall, heavy-set Newfoundlander of Irish stock, a man whose rough language concealed a high intellect. He was also a keen student of the stock market and in that respect reminded Philip of his former friend and colleague in Edwardia, John Kinsley.

Bradley spent a good deal of time between cases on the phone to his broker, and often appeared to be giving rather than receiving market advice during these sessions. Since he also had a good record of success with his own investments, Jim and others sought his advice regarding the partnership's possible involvement with Syndvest. His initial reaction was unfavorable, but after spending a considerable time in conversation with Crane, he became convinced that this man was a bright and reliable individual whose financial opinions were sound. The entire medical partnership now entered the new venture with enthusiasm, and looked forward to a successful program of healthy profits and downwardly adjusted taxes. These were heady times, and Philip wondered if his unblemished record as the man with the Anti-Midas Touch was about to be reversed.

In the summer of 1970, the Bosnars had a visit from their son James and his Irish lady-love. Although Phil and Patty were delighted at the reunion, they still found it difficult to feel any warmth toward the quiet and withdrawn young woman. At times, when they were discussing current affairs with their son, she'd throw him a secretive glance or an enigmatic smile, as if sharing some private joke with him. After a few days, she began to let slip the odd remark that revealed her as violently anarchist in her views, the last kind of influence he needed. There was also a suggestion that she was inclined toward antisemitism, and they wondered how this might affect James.

They remembered how deeply affected he'd been when he went to see the film 'Exodus' and then devoured the book by Leon Uris. He could hardly be restrained from going straight to Israel, as a stowaway if necessary, and offering his services to the Israeli army in order to help protect this brave new country from all its enemies. Ah well! they decided, he had the intelligence and would develop the power of making his own decisions, based on knowledge, objective study, judgment and experience. Above all, they were happy to learn how well his drama career was coming along, and to see him looking so well.

The visit lasted two weeks, and although the young couple took their meals with them and spent most of their time in the Bosnar apartment, Phil and Patty made sure their son and his ladylove would have their privacy and their comfort. They did this by booking them into a motel fairly close to Lakeside Towers and taking care of the bill in advance. In the main, it was a happy time, but Patty looked worried and Phil felt uneasy.

Stu Atkins decided it was high time Philip Bosnar got seriously involved in major arterial surgery, and he arranged for him to spend some time with Drs. Humphries and Beven at the Cleveland Clinic, in the department of Peripheral Vascular Surgery. It was at this topflight medical center that Atkins had received most of his cardiology training.

Meeting the two acknowledged leaders in vascular surgery was fascinating for Philip. Humphries, the department head, was mercurial and impulsive, and Beven, the rising star, was quiet and thoughtful. In the first few days, Philip was able to establish excellent personal and professional rapport with both men and had a thoroughly enjoyable time. There seemed no limit to what they were willing to show him, and their hospitality was generous to a fault. He met their families and friends, including star performers like Dr. Favoloro, the brilliant cardiac surgeon from Argentina; and he was shown through their homes and introduced to their many interests. Not only was he given facilities far beyond his expectations in the operating suite – almost as if he were a staff member – but the nurses and technicians were all as helpful as possible. He was able to absorb the finer points of vein and dacron bypass grafts in the lower limb and elsewhere, carotid endarterectomy (clearing out obstructive arterial deposits in the neck), and aortic surgery in the abdomen, by far the most spectacular.

Beven was the master craftsman of carotid surgery and Humphries the supreme leader of aortic surgery. The O.R. nurses showed Philip the best way to set up a vascular surgery operating room, the lights and the instrument tables. The technicians instructed him in the special arts of peripheral and aortic arteriography (the introduction of needles and catheters into the arterial system, injection of radio-opaque liquid and X-ray studies of the arterial system), with emphasis on special tricks of the trade. Altogether, it was a feast of knowledge and specialized training, the kind one rarely obtained in the ordinary courses available at various centers. As if that weren't enough, Humphries and Beven told him where he could get the best possible vascular instruments at the lowest possible price.

On several occasions, their Canadian visitor remarked that he'd never seen surgical instruments of such superb construction and delicacy of operation. They directed him to an instrument maker who had his workshop in Cleveland and made these instruments on direct order, to the exact specifications of the vascular surgeons. Philip found the workshop in a back alley, located in a rather seedy district of the city. It was an unpretentious place, but the interior was spotless and the instruments under construction were handled by an artist. He was a middle-aged German who loved his work and took great pride in his masterpieces. He was delighted to discuss his instruments with Dr. Bosnar, who arranged to contact him in the near future with a substantial order on behalf of the Memorial Hospital in Saint Pierre, and perhaps later, for St. Matthew's Hospital. The instrument maker said it would give him great pleasure to supply their needs at the same prices he charged the Cleveland Clinic.

The Filipino chief resident in vascular surgery at the Cleveland Clinic was a fine surgeon in his own right, and the Greek Junior Resident, who'd fled the Colonels' dictatorship in his own country, had ambitions of becoming a cardiac surgeon and returning to Athens. Both were very helpful to Philip, and he was happy to take them out for drinks and dinner at the finest restaurant of their choice, where they freely discussed their plans and their chiefs.

The weeks fled by and there was hardly any aspect of arterial surgery that Philip didn't see. He even had the pleasure of acquiring some helpful points from Favoloro during one of his special procedures. It was a selective partial occlusion of the major abdominal vein, and was designed to stop the passage of blood clots from the lower limbs into the lungs.

On Philip's final morning at the Cleveland Clinic, Humphries and Beven were both waiting for him in the O.R. suite to say goodbye, and he felt choked up. Humphries spoke up first.

"Well, Phil, you've stolen all our brains and there's absolutely nothing more we can show you. There's no reason at all why you shouldn't be able to go ahead with any of the arterial surgery you've watched since you've been here. If you have any problems that we can help you solve just give us a call."

Beven added his own goodbye.

"We'll be glad to see you here any time. Just let us know before you come down, and we'll set things up for you. If you stay here any longer it would have to be for social reasons only, as we've got nothing more to show you."

As Philip was about to express his appreciation, the O.R. nurses showed up with the huge cake he'd ordered from a bakery a few days earlier. The inscription read:

TO MY O.R. GIRL FRIENDS AT THE CLEVELAND CLINIC.
WITH AFFECTION AND THANKS FROM PHILIP.

They each enjoyed a slice of cake, and the nurses decided that their parting should also be on a light note, by informing their chiefs, with tongue in cheek, "We thought it only fair to tell you we're leaving your service and going up to Canada to work with Dr. Bosnar."
The whole group roared with laughter and parted in the happiest of moods, in which declarations of friendship and gratitude became unnecessary.

Philip returned in time for the death of their beloved Gigi. After giving her owners, indeed her family, so much happiness, she'd finally gone to a well deserved rest. She died of irreversible heart failure, and when the veterinarian put her to sleep it seemed that she was almost grateful. The lives of the Bosnars would never be as full, especially Patty's.

CHAPTER 52

1971—1972

Reviewing the life and times of all the doctors in San Pete since his arrival in this city, Philip was amazed at the huge flux on both sides of the professional boundary. Of the downtown solo M.Ds one of the internists had died suddenly at a very early age from a massive heart attack, one pediatrician with severe psychological problems had committed suicide, one of the G.Ps was seriously ill with obstructive lung disease, two were having problems with alcohol, and four others had left town. At the Health Center they'd lost a total of nine doctors and gained thirteen; one of their G.Ps was having problems with alcohol, one was having serious marital problems, and one was having profound psychological difficulties. The C.H.C. medical staff had been cosmopolitan to a remarkable degree. In addition to Anglo-Canadians and Franco-Canadians, they included American, English, Irish, French, German, Finnish, Polish, Czech, Chinese, Hindu, Iranian, and Caribbean members; white, yellow, brown and black.

Two of the group's women doctors had husbands working on the managerial side of the Lakeside Steel company and that certainly blunted the pro-union label always levelled against their institution. Of far more importance, however, was the recent arrival of Harvey Schafer and his wife, Cynthia Smith-Schafer, both family physicians from the Western University in London, Ontario. She was the daughter of Horatio Smith, Chairman of the South Cambrian Power and Light Company and one of the foremost businessmen and civic leaders in the city. A great mantle of establishment respectability had thus descended at long last upon this health center built by steelworkers, and Philip wondered how such labor stalwarts as Bill Trevor were reacting to the ironic turn of events. San Pete was indeed a place for the unexpected, and a time when anything could happen.

Clayton's visit to North America was a delightful surprise. He'd recently been appointed Professor of Community Medicine at the University of Liverpool, and was becoming recognized as a fine lecturer and writer of medical articles. He'd been invited to visit the University of Chicago for a lecture tour and decided to visit his brother and sister-in-law as well. Phil and Patty were sorry Clayton's wife wasn't able to accompany him as they had a great affection and respect for her.

Philip drove down to Chicago and picked up his brother at his hotel, then drove him back to Canada. They had a pleasant and leisurely trip along the most scenic highways and byways he could find, and Clayton was entranced by the spectacular views of Lake Michigan and Lake Superior en route to the Bosnar abode in San Pete. Phil and Patty were able to put him up comfortably in the apartment, and he found the pull-out bed in the den very much to his liking. The view from the balcony was beyond his wildest imagination and he wondered how his brother and sister-in-law could ever tear themselves away from such a magnificent and ever-changing scene. Philip loved this brother of his very dearly, and he looked forward to many long and fascinating hours of discussion and chit-chat. As for Clayton, they'd never seen him happier, and he adored Patty for her wit, her youthful good looks, her humor and her delicious meals.

Philip took him on a grand tour of the Health Center and introduced him to most of the medical staff and a good many of the nursing and ancillary staff. They had lunch with Appleton and Jarvis, and they discussed everything under the sun in connection with current trends in western society and the delivery of medical care. They drove to both hospitals, where Philip introduced his brother to a good many of the solo doctors and to the nurses on all the floors where he worked. They had coffee together in the O.R. surgeons' lounge at the Memorial, and Clayton got deeply involved in the conversation – most of it in connection with his position as Professor of Community Medicine and his views on the British National Health system.

It was all very pleasant and a few of the solo doctors mentioned that they'd previously heard Clayton as a lecturer at meetings they attended in Britain and Ireland; they were impressed and told Philip so. Those who perused the British medical journals had read some of his articles, and Tony Donovan had known him slightly at St. Clement's Hospital when they were both students, but in different years. The senior staff members of both hospitals arranged a special lunch for Clayton, and it was held in the conference room of St. Matthew's Hospital. By virtue of a profound Freudian slip, Sister Mary Gregory forgot to mention that Dr. Bosnar was invited to the lunch, but Herb Slater picked up the omission and made sure Philip was contacted in time. Unfortunately, he had to cut his presence short since he still had to get back to the O.R. and finish his list. The luncheon, however, was a successful affair and the Bosnar family acquired a number of new admirers.

To round out Clayton's visit, which included several motor trips on both the Canadian side of Lake Superior and the American side as far as Lake Michigan, Phil and Patty decided to host a cocktail party at the Grosvenor Hotel. They invited all their friends, both medical and non-medical, and it was a successful affair in every possible way. There was little doubt that Clayton was the social lion of the affair, and he was at his most charming, his most amusing and his most impressive. Bruce Campbell, in particular, seemed deeply affected by his long conversation with him. Afterwards, he confessed that his meeting with Clayton roused a certain nostalgic yearning to return to Britain, to get back to a university appointment at one of the major teaching hospitals over there. Philip hoped this temptation would fade with the passage of time.

The vascular surgery was starting to pick up in an orderly fashion, but since the radiologists at both hospitals were unwilling to get into arteriography, perhaps because of the time involved, it meant that Philip would have to spend the extra time himself in the performance of these investigations. It also meant that he'd have less time for office appointments, and he hoped this wouldn't cut too deeply into his regular general surgery.

The only vascular cases he got at first from the solo doctors were emergency femoral embolectomies for blood clots blocking the circulation in the leg. The operation consisted of opening the artery at the upper end and passing down a special catheter as far as possible, then blowing up the terminal balloon and pulling out the clots. The next type of case that came his way was the localized blockage of a peripheral artery that required only a removal of the obstructive plaque by specific *endarterectomy*. Then came the arterial bypass grafts from groin level to just above or below the knee, using a portion of the superficial thigh vein or, if this proved unsuitable, a special Dacron graft. Every time he irrigated the artery with anticlotting solution he gave silent thanks to the generous technicians who'd made the splendid irrigation cannulae for Philip to take back with him from the Cleveland Clinic.

With each successive case, the O.R. nurses became more proficient and his assistants more skilled in synchronizing their movements with his procedure. Both hospitals had put in a handsome order for vascular instruments from the little German craftsman in Cleveland, and they were more than satisfied with their quality and performance. Next came the aortic grafts for either aneurysm (ballooning) or blockage, using knitted Dacron grafts which had to be preclotted, and joining the lower end to the main artery of the lower limb either above or below the groin, depending on the patency at each level.

At the surgical ward rounds, Philip gave his fellow surgeons extensive information from his Cleveland notes, based on his personal sessions with Humphries and Beven, and these proved very popular; in fact one or two of the solo surgeons started to try their hands at some of the simpler arterial cases, although none were doing arteriograms. Campbell started to refer some of his patients with kidney problems for aortograms and renal arteriograms and this hastened Philip's proficiency, for which he was grateful despite the time involved.

He was appreciative of the new arteriography equipment purchased by the Memorial Hospital for its X-ray department, even though it was rather clumsy and leaked badly during the injection of dye. Despite the fact that most of the elective downtown arterial surgery was going to Toronto, one or two cases started to come his way from solo practice and Philip was encouraged.

Finally, he got his first case of carotid endarterectomy for transient strokes; Stu Atkins used his cardiac catheter set-up to get excellent carotid arteriograms, and the case went off smoothly, with a happy result and no complications.

Philip's personal relationship with many of the solo doctors was improving day by day, but sad to say, this made little difference to entrenched antagonisms between the downtown and clinic doctors. The main enmity was directed against the C.H.C's Executive Director and Medical Director, but the ripples of hostility encompassed all the members of the medical group. As far as Don Foley was concerned, his attitude to Philip couldn't have been more amicable, and the group's senior surgeon was glad when Foley occasionally drifted into his operating room to watch a particularly interesting operation. It seemed such an eternity since they'd had that fierce encounter over the ethics of the Health Center.

He shuddered when he remembered the occasion. He had just stepped off the elevator on the ground floor of the Memorial and Foley was on his way up; they were exchanging a few moments of customary banter when some pernicious force turned their words into an unpleasant confrontation. For some reason, Foley let slip a small remark to the effect that the Ontario College of Physicians and Surgeons was questioning the C.H.C's method of so-called Closed Panel group practice, and its ethics.

"Goddammit, Don, I've had a gut-full of innuendoes about our patterns of practice. You know bloody well that we're far less restrictive than you guys have been, and you get more of our referred patients by a country mile than the other way around."

Foley muttered a few words and tried to close the elevator but Philip kept his foot in the gate, and noted that the other man was looking very pale. As for Philip, he had one more thing to say.

"As far as I'm concerned, it's time for you to put your money where your mouth is, and the same bloodywell goes for the College."

These days, since the formation of the new Academy, that kind of accusation was a thing of the past, but it had been replaced by a brand new complaint. It had to do with the question of advertising, and it related to articles and lectures by the Community Health Center's Executive Director and its Medical Director. Where Appleton was concerned there was no truth to the accusation that he was guilty of advertising the excellence of the Health Center, or of any implication that its standards of medical care were superior to those of solo practice in the city. In 1963 he had been brought before the College on charges originating with the Medical Society but nothing came out of the encounter, and the issue of a periodic instructional pamphlet to the C.H.C's subscribers continued, with no attempt to draw pejorative comparisons.

Jarvis, on the other hand, had allowed the enthusiasm for his favorite system of subscriber-oriented group practice to make him guilty of superlatives from time to time, and that annoyed the system's detractors and embarrassed the group doctors. As a matter of fact, the latter repeatedly registered their opposition to this type of article or lecture and pleaded for restraint. For their pains, they were considered by some members of the Association Board to be trying for acceptance by the medical orthodoxy, rather than seeking to remove irritants used to justify unreasonable acts of enmity.

The recent news that Philip received from England was disquieting. His father's health was failing to the extent that he was considering retirement from his business, and his mother had consented to having her cataracts removed but was having some prolonged bouts of depression. It seemed that there was a perfect antidote to the situation, and Patty expressed her enthusiastic agreement: they would arrange for his parents to come for a two-week visit to San Pete. Accordingly, they purchased return tickets at the local Air Canada office: Heath Row to Saint Pierre via Toronto, and arranged for a stewardess escort at each point of arrival and departure. In addition, they were fortunate in being able to rent an apartment immediately below theirs, which – by a stroke of luck – was going to be empty for a month, with its occupants going abroad.

The great day came, and it was a wonderful sight to see his Mum and Dad coming off the plane with a pretty stewardess escorting them; they both looked alert and radiant and the reunion was an emotional feast. It was a memorable two weeks, full of love and warmth, with leisurely meals and discussions, drives into the surrounding countryside on both sides of the international border, a short tour of the Community Health Center, and a look at the two hospitals. The visitors were able to retire to their own apartment whenever they felt like it and take a siesta whenever they felt tired.

It was hilarious for Philip to see his dear Mum overwhelmed by the superb Jewish cuisine of her beloved Irish daughter-in-law, and all in all, it seemed that his parents had reached a high point of happiness in their lives. He noticed that his Dad looked much frailer than he'd ever seen him, but his mind was as sharp as ever and the love he held for his beloved Klara was as deep as ever. It was more than affection and devotion. It was the romantic love of youth and gave them both a radiance rarely seen at their age. Phil and Patty wondered if they would ever see them again, and were glad they'd made the right decision in bringing his parents out in the twilight of their lives.

There were many decisions to be made these days, since the Health Center had an unreliable relationship with the provincial government that could change from year to year. This meant that the financial position of the enterprise became very unstable, and there were serious fears about its future. Nevertheless, it seemed that it was still growing, with five new subscribers arriving for every three subscribers who withdrew. The promise to the original steelworkers who subscribed $135 for the construction of the Clinic building, that their premiums would be cancelled on reaching retirement age, was suddenly made inoperative by the new government plan, and there were feelings of betrayal.

So great was the sense of the steelworkers' Community Health Center becoming simply a group practice controlled by the government and the doctors, that Wilfred Jarvis felt constrained to circulate a letter of assurance, which diminished but didn't abolish the disillusionment. **'The Community Health Center is still owned and operated by the people who put it up in the first place. It's still your center and even with all the changes we've had to make as things changed around us we still have the same aims as in the days when you started it. How well we can meet these aims depends on how strong you make us'.**

This was an unconcealed appeal for steadfast loyalty, and perhaps a quixotic dream. The first ethnic Italians who were the bulwark of the original subscriber group had produced a second generation who were increasingly oriented toward the Anglo-Canadian establishment. They were the three-piece-suit button-down-collar young businessmen and professionals who had little in common with the basic values of the older generation. When it came to a loyal support of their Health Center they would be far less dependable than their parents.

Yet paradoxically, it seemed to Philip that the real threat was not that their patient numbers would fall, but rather that they might grow too large and too impersonal. The number of patients using the Center for all or part of their medical services had increased by almost 90 per cent since the days before provincial Medicare, while the total number of visits to the group doctors rose by about 25 per cent. The falsely circulated myth that the Health Center was closed to all but members of the steelworkers union had been exploded, and the city's patients felt free to go wherever (and whenever!) they wished. A city-wide questionnaire done by an independent group revealed that **'Consumers of care at the Community Health Center perceive greater accessibility of certain diagnostic services, perceive the waiting time to see the doctor to be shorter, and find the locational convenience more desirable. However, patients using solo doctors reveal consistently more positive attitudes toward doctors in general and find their own doctor showing more concern for their welfare than do patients at the Community Health Center.'** This study pinpointed the negative impact of their frequent doctor turnover, particularly the family physicians. Philip hoped their latest crop of G.Ps from the Western University Medical School and hospitals would prove more durable.

One of the most prevalent questions facing both the Association Board and Medical Group was the issue of expansion. There was a majority opinion that they should expand progressively and build a large extension onto the present facility. The argument was that if they became large enough they could break the stranglehold on major hospital appointments, held so far by solo doctors. Stu Atkins went so far as to hope the clinic would eventually eliminate solo medical practice in San Pete and take over both hospitals.

Philip was one of the minority who felt that such expansion would make them much more impersonal, and increase the bureaucratic superstructure of what had been, in essence, a sort of family enclave. It was enough for the biblical David to fell the monstrous Goliath without his own people becoming the new Philistines. Even the physical separation of the doctors in a building double the size of the present one might introduce an element of alienation; replacing the present sense of closeness where it was customary for them to walk into each other's office at any time rather than using the phone.

Once it was clear that the majority had made its voice clear, Philip wasn't prepared to fight the issue; especially as he agreed with the viewpoint that the medical partnership should invest in part ownership of the new building extension. This would represent each partner's financial stake in an expanded Community Health Center, and might even increase a sense of commitment and loyalty.

The fortuitous discovery, that the land adjoining their present facilities was now available for the proposed extension, made the time ripe for discussing the situation with the Association, and the doctors set up a special meeting with the Board. Although they were prepared for some degree of opposition, the doctors were shocked by the Board's adamant refusal to consider their suggestion. Bill Trevor and Jonathan Grey told them flatly that the subscribers would never stand for the Health Center extension being partly owned by the doctors as a real estate equity; and even if they did, the property had been legally deeded to the two hospitals in the event that the Health Center was ever discontinued. Another factor was the real prospect of an agreement with the Robarts administration to help it fund the new building to the tune of $900,000.

This turn of events was disappointing news for the medical group and didn't help to allay the feeling that the Board was antagonistic to the medical partnership on matters of finance; and that in this respect Wilfred Jarvis was the Board's hired man and therefore in the Association's corner, while Jim Appleton was caught in the middle. By way of compensation for the doctors' failure to be part owners of the new building, Jarvis suggested some increases in the Sabbatical Plan, but that only raised fresh objections. The newer doctors complained that this Plan clearly favored the most senior partners, as if that were somehow unfair.

Between arteriography, arterial surgery and cardiac pacemakers, Philip was beginning to get less of his wide range of general surgery, but fortunately there was still a healthy range and a sufficient number of worthwhile cases that could be presented for discussion at ward rounds. As for Bruce Campbell, his urology had expanded steadily, but he was still able to handle his own general surgery cases, and his pediatric surgery was as impeccable as ever. Philip was happy to observe his own excellent standing and rapport, especially with the pathology department at St. Matthew's and the radiology department at the Memorial. Such relationships were vital to the reputation of a surgeon and transcended all other aspects of professional evaluation, except – perhaps – that of the anesthetists.

Aside from the occasional solo surgeon who came in to watch one of his cases and the rare occasion when one of the downtown G.Ps gave him an emergency assist, there was never an occasion when any of the downtown physicians came into the O.R. when he was working, and he wondered how they could faithfully decide who was the best surgeon for any particular type of case. He knew that in community hospitals such as theirs this was a question that could always be asked, and for that reason – at the very least – he was thankful to be working in a group practice; although he would have preferred honest and unprejudiced competition, based on knowledge, judgement, experience, operative technique, and above all, results.

This was a time of considerable political activism, in which the status of community health centers was coming under major scrutiny by the United Steelworkers and other unions, the political parties, the various bodies of organized medicine, and both the medical and lay press. The World Health Organization sponsored a comparative review of those steelworkers who'd chosen to remain with their own solo doctors under the Dual Choice plan and those who chose to obtain their medical care as subscribers to the Community Health Center. The results were favorable to the C.H.C. and showed that its subscribers:-

1. Spent 24 percent less time in hospital, mostly due to less admissions.
2. Had fewer surgical operations per capita.
3. Were more likely to have seen a doctor once or more per annum.
4. Were more likely to get check-ups and immunizations.
5. Were more likely to be attended by an 'appropriate' specialist.
6. Were found to undergo more X-ray and laboratory investigations on an out-patient basis.

The study was carried out by Professor Malcolm Prevost of Toronto. He initially obtained full cooperation from the solo medical practitioners, but after the publication of his findings he was viciously attacked in the local press, and his findings discredited. Both the initial cooperation and subsequent attack were led by Don Foley, who was smarting at being faulted by his followers for having agreed to the survey.

The kidnapping of James Cross, a senior British diplomat, in Quebec, and the kidnap-murder of Labor Minister Pierre Laporte by terrorists of the extreme French-Canadian separatist movement, were answered firmly by Prime Minister Trudeau. Despite considerable opposition from his political enemies and the usual misguided bleatings by civil rights and human right groups – who always seemed to forget the rights of the victims of crime – he invoked the War Measures Act and rounded up a wide assortment of suspected supporters of the terrorists. Even though these firm actions failed to prevent Laporte's cowardly murder, they did obtain the release of Cross, and proved that Trudeau was prepared to stand up resolutely against the forces of separatism and terror. The 51-year-old bachelor Prime Minister displayed courage in his private life as well, by wedding a 22-year-old flower child from among his adoring host of female admirers.

In the United States, Lieutenant Calley was sentenced to life imprisonment at hard labor for the murder of at least twenty civilians at Mylai (but more probably more than a hundred men, women and children) and Charles Manson and his grisly entourage were sentenced to death for the appalling slaughter of their Hollywood victims for no apparent reason other than blood-lust. There seemed little doubt that the U.S. legal system would see these sentences considerably reduced.

The intrusion of the sports world into global politics had reached the point of hilarity, with the Soviet Union's team winning the world ice-hockey championship for the ninth time and completely taking over Canada's native game, while the American table tennis team was to be the sacrificial lamb for the Chinese magicians of that game, in order to highlight an easing of tensions between the two nations.

In Southeast Asia, the miserable war that kept enlarging like a colony of deadly bacteria on a Petri dish, and could never be won, was sapping the morale of a declining superpower and draining the blood of its fighting men. President Nixon had launched an undeclared war in Cambodia, and soon its historic heritage and glorious temples would be ravaged and forever degraded.

In Northern Ireland, men were slaughtering each other for different interpretations of history and Christianity, while at the same time their fellow humans were driving vehicles on the surface of the moon for the very first time.

It was high time the Bosnars visited their daughter and her new baby, so they booked flight to Edmonton for the Christmas week. Her husband was working at the huge Carlton department store, with special responsibility for display and interior design. The family had moved to Alberta two years earlier, and although they hated to leave their beautiful province, it was such a great opportunity for advancement and financial security that they couldn't think of turning it down.

On arrival, Phil and Patty found the city incredibly cold, but the apartment was warm and comfortable and the decor revealed Neville Sternway's superb artistic touch. Florian looked very happy and in excellent health, and her husband looked strong and vigorous. He was very helpful around the apartment, in sharp distinction to his father-in-law, who'd never become adequately domesticated. Of all their experiences on this visit it was Phil and Patty's tiny granddaughter who took their breath away. She was a golden-haired fairy princess and her smile was devastating.

Over the next few days they met the many new friends of Florian and Neville, and it became evident that their daughter and her husband were accomplished party-givers. When Phil and Patty complimented them, they insisted it was only because they'd become such experienced party-goers in this hospitable and socially active northern city.

The Christmas dinner was delicious and they all had a wonderful time, none more so than tiny Martina Sternway. The opening of gifts on Christmas morning was a spectacle of delighted surprises and wishes come true, and Martina's squeals of joy were music to the ears of their grandparents.

The grandparents left Edmonton in the secure knowledge that their Florian had a happy marriage, a devoted and successful husband, a lovely little first-born child and a promising future. They could ask for nothing more in these days of common-law marriages and burgeoning divorces.

The Bosnars returned to a snowbound domain in which the snowplows never seemed to be at rest and all the street corners had large snowbanks. Philip was approaching one of these on a dark Thursday evening in February, on his way to St. Pierre College. Patty had gone ahead before him, as she was due to attend a meeting of the bridge club's executive committee prior to the regular bridge club game. She had become involved in the management aspect of the city's duplicate bridge activities and took her job seriously.

Last year she and her fellow executive members were successful in obtaining premises at the College for their two evening sessions, and as Philip was approaching the large compound of low flat buildings . . . . he awoke with blood streaming down from a large open wound on the left side of his head. He felt his wound carefully with his fingers and winced with pain. It seemed to extend from his left temple to the top of his head but the skull felt intact. There was also a smaller wound just below his right kneecap but nothing to suggest any broken bones. Although he was still unsure of his name, his wife's name and whom he knew, he was thinking with some clarity as he looked at his wristwatch, which registered 7.30 p.m., and realized he must have been unconscious for about thirty-five minutes, and that he'd probably been involved in a major collision.

Now a great feeling of peace and contentment swept over him as he thought: This is probably IT – not a bad way to die. Anyhow, I've had a bloody good and interesting life so I can't complain. I'm not quite sure of details but I know I've got a hell of a lot to be thankful for. At that moment, one of the ambulance men – whom he recognized immediately – noticed his movements and exclaimed, "So you're finally awake, Dr. Bosnar!" and the injured man suddenly knew who he was and wanted his adorable Patty with him. He also knew that it wasn't his time to die.

They took him to the X-ray department at St. Matthew's Hospital, where his head and neck were filmed and no fractures were found. He was also able to confirm that the X-ray table felt extremely hard to a patient with a head injury. Bruce Campbell arrived, checked his injuries, and sewed up his wounds under local. At this point Patty arrived, and she was overcome with relief to see her husband conscious and not in desperate shape. He was fitted with a cervical collar for 'acute neck strain' and admitted to a private room on the fifth floor, where he was checked frequently by his night nurse for evidence of any neurological deterioration.

The next morning, despite the protestations of his good friend Campbell, he won his wish to be discharged and phoned his wife. Once home, he demolished a large breakfast of bacon and eggs and felt much better. His right knee felt a bit stiff, but he was able to walk around the apartment without a limp. The cervical collar was a slight nuisance, but he could put up with it for a while, and apart from the Boris Karloff suture line down the right side of his head to the right temple, he didn't look like a recent escapee from the next world. As for this world, Philip Bosnar felt it was his oyster once again.

"Patty darling, why don't we fly to Toronto on Monday and play in the Canadian Nationals? I see from the Bulletin that the two session Mixed Pairs event is on Tuesday and I think we ought to play in that, at the very least."

"You must be joking. You heard Bruce Campbell say that you were to take a two week rest, and I think that's exactly what you ought to do. After all, you've had a severe concussion."

"You wouldn't want me to perish from boredom, would you? If we go ahead and play it will take my mind off my injuries and I'll probably be able to get back to work in a week's time."

The Friday edition of the Cambrian Leader carried an interesting version of Philip's accident. It was in a small column at the foot of the page, entitled: *'Local Man Involved in Car Accident'*. The report read: *'Dr. Philip Bosnar, aged 59, was involved in a car collision at the corner of Bramwell Road and Cornwall Street. The accident occurred at 7 p.m. etc, etc'.*
There wasn't a single word about the exact nature of the accident; that a woman driver from Michigan was entering Bramwell Road from Cornwall Street when her vision was impaired by the falling snow, the darkened sky, and the large snowdrift obscuring the STOP sign.

The article was an amusing contrast with such headlines as 'Prominent Local Surgeon', 'Eminent Local Surgeon', 'Eminent Local Physician', 'Leading Local Doctor', reporting solo M.Ds doing everything from growing a beard to slipping on a banana peel – always displayed with pictures at the head of the page – but never a similar story referring to any doctor from the Health Center. There was never a word about such innovations in the C.H.C. as Dr. Stuart Atkins' cardiac catheterization program or other medical advances in the community clinic.

One inch headlines and front page coverage were available, however, for an article with the heading, **'Woman Sues Community Health Doctors For Damage To Right Arm'**, which went on to imply that the patient might lose the right forearm and hand as a result of cardiac catheterization. (*The fact that the case was subsequently withdrawn and the patient never lost so much as a fingernail failed to neutralize the sheer venom of this libelous article, and it would take another publication of a medico-legal claim against the Health Center, many years later, to produce a successful libel suit against the same newspaper.*)

CHAPTER 53

1972-73

Patricia Bosnar needed fourteen more master points to become a Lifemaster in duplicate bridge and Philip was determined to put his injuries out of mind and concentrate on playing as good a game as possible. After the first four rounds of play he could tell that his partner was operating on all cylinders, and that they were clicking so far as telepathy was concerned. This was a subtle ingredient possessed by few partnerships, even the closest of married couples, and all of a sudden he felt that they had a chance in this important Mixed Pairs event. The rest of the afternoon session was a romp, with board after board going in their favor. When they broke for dinner, they knew they had a good score, maybe in the 190s, with an average of 156.

They were enjoying a leisurely meal with some of their bridge friends when a few late arrivals came over to their table and told them they'd broken the 200 mark and recorded a 203. Now they had a clear run at overall placement at the end of the evening session. The second game wasn't quite as good as the first, but it got stronger with each round and Philip felt sure they should place about third overall, thus bringing his beloved partner much closer to her Lifemaster ranking.

After the game, they retired to the hotel suite of two friends from the San Pete bridge world, and had some drinks with the rest of the accumulating company. Suddenly, a couple burst into the room shouting, "The Bosnars have done it! They've come first overall and Patty is now the first woman Lifemaster in the Cambrian International Unit." Phil and Patty left the party in a confusion of happiness and disbelief, went downstairs to the huge convention hall where they'd been playing, and checked the score. There it was – no error – and they'd won with a total score of 398: not a really great score, but just enough to achieve a narrow win, and giving his darling far more than the points she needed.

The next morning, the Toronto papers were full of the news that an unseeded pair from 'Northern Ontario' had taken the Mixed Pairs event. The news brought a pleasant bonus when Philip's old friend and partner from Vanwey, Al Masters, showed up with his wife at the Royal York Hotel to offer their congratulations. The Bosnars were happy to learn that Al was doing well in a surgical practice on the outskirts of the city, away from the rigors of the University center, and in a comfortable professional environment; and he in turn was fascinated by the amazing progress made by the Cambrian District Community Health center against all odds. Masters was also deeply interested in the changes that had taken place in the C.H.C. organization since its inception. Stella Masters and Patty exchanged news of their respective families while Al and Phil reminisced about the old days, both good and bad, in a far off dusty prairie town long ago, and realized how much they had missed each other.

When the Bosnars got back to San Pete, there was much excitement in the duplicate bridge community, but this later turned to anger when the Cambrian Leader buried the news of their success in a small three-liner at the foot of page 3, despite the fact that the bridge tournament news had been telexed to its editor as soon as the Mixed Pairs results were announced. It was one more petty example of selective reporting in a divided community, and it didn't go unnoticed in the local bridge world – which included a good many teachers and other professionals – nor did it affect the Bosnars' feeling of success.

One week later Philip was back at work, having discarded his cervical collar and had his sutures out in the meantime. His colleagues thought he was being a trifle hasty, his wife agreed, and his lawyer was furious.

"How on earth can I get you a decent settlement for this accident when you won't even take a month or two off, at the very least?"

Philip received a very nice letter from the driver of the other car, full of concern for his injuries and her prayers for his full recovery. The front of her car had rammed into the left side of his Volvo, and only the special steel safety column – just behind the front window – had prevented his head from being caved in by the impact. As for his car, it was a total wreck and not worth any attempt at salvage. So, after two weeks of driving a rented car, he decided to get a new Datsun XK 140 sports model, complete with superb manual stick shift.

There appeared to be no lasting effects from the accident and it wasn't until three months after the event that Philip learned the actual details. Trudy Maclean, a part-time nurse on the long-stay surgical floor at St. Matthew's, had witnessed the entire accident. She'd seen him driving along Crecy Road toward the college compound shortly before seven, at about twenty miles an hour, and observed the collision when the other car plowed into the left side of his Volvo. He appeared to have taken automatic evasive action, driving up the snowbank on the right side of the road, and the next thing the witness recalled was seeing people trying to pull him from the front seat of the car, where he appeared to be jammed. There was also some panic as the engine started to catch fire. None of these important details were available from the police or ambulance men who brought him to the hospital, but experience had taught him that this was par for the course in accident cases, and a longtime source of irritation to those who had to deal with them.

During the past couple of years there had been a subtle change in the composition of the medical group at the Center. There were more women doctors, and these were not only successful and well-liked, but some were married to lawyers, some to husbands on the management staff of Cambrian Steel, and one was the daughter of a leading city businessman and public figure. Some of the new C.H.C. doctors were poorly indoctrinated into the modern concept of a consumer-sponsored health center, with its level of consumer control and input. Some regarded the Board of the Community Health Association as an adversary, more concerned with the success and acclaim of the enterprise than the well-being and satisfaction of its doctors. The increase in fee-for-service practice resulting from the provincial health scheme was as popular with the newer doctors as it was suspect to the Board, and there were those in the medical group who would be quite happy to see capitation payments completely eliminated.

To the public at large the Community Health Center was now the new medical establishment: the new political respectability and the wave of the future. Patricia Bosnar found herself wooed by the wives of the steel plant's top executives, and invited into the top echelons of San Pete's class-divided society; but she remained unimpressed by the smiling blandishments of her husband's erstwhile detractors. Soon (shudder!), the Bosnars might even become fashionable, and that was a fate to be avoided at all costs.

It was clear that the Health Center was winning the battle of numbers. The medical staff had increased from 13 to 23 and the ancillary staff from 38 to 120. After a good deal of dithering and double talk from the provincial government, there was now a solid commitment sufficient to justify plans for a million dollar expansion to the original building, with facilities for a large dental unit and a minor operating room for day surgery and anesthesia.

Rumors of the current plans to expand the Center soon reached the downtown doctors (as did any other proposals and plans within the clinic organization!), and immediately produced a hostile reaction, with renewed hardening of attitudes and a marked cooling of the friendlier relations prevailing between the two sides. As in the past few years, the main antagonism no longer came from the Old Guard but rather from the more recent solo recruits. Reporting to the Board, Jim Appleton declared: "With the commencement of construction of the new building, local political problems have become much worse. The solo practitioners have out-recruited the Group this year and have secured six new general practitioners. Two members of the medical group were on the executive committee of St. Matthew's but following elections there are none."

One ironic development at this time was the C.H.C's decision to supply resident G.Ps and visiting specialists to smaller outlying communities both north and south of San Pete. These communities had first approached the Center for such services, but following strenuous objections by leaders of the solo practitioners, they withdrew their earlier invitations and the solo doctors promptly moved in to fill the void they had created.

A disturbing feature in the relationship between the Medical Group and the Board of the Association was that all discussions between the two sides seemed to focus on allocation of funds between the two sides. In addition, the Board had developed its own Old Guard headed by its crusty President, who seemed incapable of accepting the changing nature of the Center, its evolutionary development, and the dialectical relationship with downtown practice.

At a special meeting of the Board and the Medical Executive to which Dr. Bosnar was invited – he was no longer a member of the Executive – he felt he must challenge Trevor's intransigent position and clarify the situation once and for all.

"Mr. Chairman, it seems to me that all your remarks indicate a misconception on your part, and I'm forced to ask if you still consider Dr. Appleton an employee of the Association, rather than a member of the medical partnership that elected him to the post of Medical Director?"

"As far as I'm concerned, Dr. Bosnar, nothing has changed since this place was started. The Association, acting for the steelworkers, chose Dr. Appleton to be our Medical Director with the power to recruit a staff of doctors. He was our appointee then and he still is."

"I'm sorry you feel that way, Mr. Chairman. It reinforces my fear that yesterday's reformer so often becomes today's hardline dogmatist."

"I think that's an unfair comment, doctor, and I'm sure the members of our Board feel the same way I do about the medical director's position in our institution."

"Why don't we find out by polling the Board members?" In an atmosphere of tense embarrassment, the members of the Board all voted against Bill Trevor's rigid and outdated interpretation, with Wilfred Jarvis abstaining.

One week later, Trevor resigned from the presidency and Al Smithwick was elected to fill the vacancy. Smithwick lacked the gritty determination of his predecessor but was no less committed to the original ideas that produced their center a decade before. Without Trevor there would never have been a Community Health center in San Pete, but with his continued presidency of the Association the entire project might have capsized on a mounting wave of dissension and distrust. Philip liked and admired Bill Trevor, but this fine old warrior had outgrown his usefulness to the institution he'd fathered.

Phil and Patty now learned that their beloved son had broken up with his Irish ladylove and was now looking after his daughter as a single parent. Little Magdalena's mother had exhibited a strange noninvolvement with the beautiful child from the moment of her birth, and now seemed quite happy to leave her to the care of her father while she went off with her new boyfriend, the loutish manager of a rock group. It was all too tempting to conclude that this was the way with the current generation of young parents, and even more so in the bohemian world of painters and actors.

It wasn't going to be easy for James, with his irregular hours and uncertain commitments in various aspects of theater life. His work included radio, television, films and live theater, and he had to be available at all times, which meant he'd now be burdened not only with the extra work of looking after a motherless child, but with getting hold of a baby-sitter at the drop of a hat. Phil and Patty therefore encouraged their son's decision – during a lull in his professional schedule that actors euphemize as 'Resting' – to come and visit them with their grand-daughter.

They had a heartwarming meeting at Toronto's International Airport, and after all the hugs and kisses were exhausted they went across to the restaurant in Terminal 2, where the tired travellers could relax and shake off their jet-lag. James was looking healthy and vigorous and his 3-year-old daughter looked well-fed, well-dressed, healthy and beautiful. But there was a sadness in her eyes, and a nervous reaction to any sudden sounds that worried her grandparents.

It was fortunate that their waiter was attentive and seemed to have an empathy toward the sad little girl with the big brown eyes, and she responded by settling down and enjoying her meal. At first she didn't seem to remember the affectionate strangers who'd greeted her and her father, but they felt sure that once she reached their apartment in San Pete she'd feel at home and remember them as her loving grandparents. It proved to be a delightful visit and they all had a wonderful time together, so that by the time their treasured visitors left at the end of two weeks, the little darling was back to her happy laughing self and gladly returned the adoration of her grandma and grandpa.

Unfortunately, It was far from a favorable time for the Health center as far as the political climate in Toronto's Queen's Park was concerned. Dr. Richard Potter, the current Minister of Health, seemed to have no idea whatsoever of the history or significance of the Community Health center's organization, and regarded it as an experimental venture of little importance and no particular future. Steeped as he was in the traditional pattern of medical practice, he was prone to making stupid and ill-advised statements, and Philip soon got into the habit of calling him Dr. "Potty" (the colloquial English equivalent of 'daft' or 'balmy').

According to the Toronto papers, Dr. Potty **'questioned the success of experimental community health clinics...'** He asked 'why taxpayers throughout the province should have to pay to set up such community clinics when there are already hundreds of health clinics established by doctors themselves?' Such asinine remarks were in response to complaints from the O.M.A. about unfair competition, and augured poorly for adequate funding of community health centers such as the one in San Pete. Fortunately, there were government officials in the health services area who were able to circumvent Dr. Potty's official position, and they found ways to supply operational funds to a number of health centers across the province, especially those of St. Pierre and St. Catherines. Some of these officials now proposed the setting up of a special body, the Program Development and Implementation Group (PDIG), to pursue the formation of community health centers and the funding of these by means alternate to fee-for-service.

By the self-defeating quirks so typical of government organizations, the large and well-established C.H.Cs of St. Pierre and St. Catherines weren't included under PDIG, but came instead under the Special Projects Branch (SPB) of the provincial health ministry. By a stroke of good fortune, however, the Director of Integrated Health Care in the Ministry chose this particular time to visit the San Pete Health center, and Dr. Bosnar met him in the surgeons' lounge at St. Matthew's Hospital, where he was doing his morning O.R. List. The meeting proved to be a pleasant surprise, as the visitor turned out to be Dr. Brian Loftus, whom he'd known and admired as an intern at St. Peter's Hospital in Edwardia when he'd practiced there. He knew him as a man of principle and dedication, and was happy to see him in his present position.

Loftus was presently engaged in touring the province and exploring alternative methods of payment for medical services. It was obvious, while listening to him and watching the reactions of the downtown doctors, that the idea of salaried doctors was no longer anathema to solo practitioners, especially if it kept the average doctor's income at its present level. The more Philip observed the overall reaction during the past year, the more favorable the idea of a salary system seemed for the medical profession, especially when combined with eight-hour shifts of duty, overtime pay, paid sick leave, sabbaticals for postgraduate education, and retirement pensions. Arrangements were made for another meeting between Philip and Loftus the following week, in order to have a detailed discussion on current problems between the CHC and the medical establishment.

They met on the Wednesday afternoon at the office of Brian Loftus in the Health Ministry complex, and after reminiscing about Edwardia and the people they'd known there, they got down to a detailed discussion of the present status of Health Care Delivery, in Canada at large and Ontario in particular. It was abundantly clear that Loftus didn't share the muddle-headed views of his eccentric Minister, and that his own views were idealistic and very much in the socialist mold. He was forced to admit, however, that a salaried scheme, with all its related benefits, would be twice as expensive as the present system of fee-for-service, and that a global budget or capitation method might be the best compromise.

They talked about moment-to-moment free choice of doctor and the temptations presented by remuneration based on productivity, and it was clear that they shared many viewpoints. Then Loftus took his visitor by complete surprise with his next idea.

"What would you say to the construction of a third hospital in your community for the specific use of your Health center medical staff?"

"Why would you think of something like that after we've been here for ten years?"

"Everybody here knows or should know how much grief your people have had at the hospitals, especially with the anesthetic boycott and being kept off important staff positions."

"All that sort of stuff can be blamed on the previous antagonism of the College, the O.M.A, and organized medicine in general, against our pattern of practice. Goddamit, there were even articles that downgraded group practice as compared with solo practice. In view of that kind of opposition at the outset, the right time to consider a separate hospital for our beleaguered center was in the early sixties, rather than the planned extension to the Memorial Hospital, which needs renovating anyhow."

"I still think it's worth considering as a way of avoiding all that kind of bullshit in the future, and I believe it would be possible to persuade the Premier of the feasibility of such a move, especially if the hospital was simply an extension of your present Health center building."

"I hate to disagree with you, Brian; your idea is a good one but ten years too late. It would only open up all the old wounds and create a lot of new ones, not only in San Pete but across the province. In any event, I doubt if the Premier would be prepared to face the combined hostility of the medical establishment and its supporters in the general population."

"There's no chance of rebuilding the Memorial hospital, you know."

"Of course I know, but I think our community would be short-changed if the Memorial doesn't have it's O.R. suite expanded and updated, and the bed-space increased. Our medical group would benefit as much as anyone, and in time our patients would use the Memorial increasingly and St. Matthew's less and less."

"What about all your Italian patients, and the other Catholic families who go to your clinic?"

"There's already been a major swing by these patients our Clinic doctors."

"Glad to hear it, Philip. Well, I wish you all the best, and if there's anything I can do for you and your group please let me know."

Even though nothing concrete was accomplished by this meeting, it was good to know they had a friend in the government who wasn't firmly wedded to entrenched ideas of healthcare delivery.

When Gus Pelletier first left the C.H.C. he was quoted as calling Philip Bosnar, "Appleton's Mouthpiece," and Philip ignored the remark. But since that time, he'd also been characterized by some of the downtown doctors as "the power behind the throne", and although he considered this untrue, he had to admit an inclination to take the initiative in refuting any false accusations against the Center. After all, this was the institution in which he'd chosen to practice for the final segment of his professional life.

The first time he reacted strongly to such an accusation was in '65, when the center was visited by Richard Clauson, a staff writer for 'Canadian Medical Practice'. He spent an entire day with Jarvis, who showed him all over the facilities and went over the financial books with him in considerable detail. Clauson was also given access to the many studies that had been made to verify the cost savings produced by the C.H.C's mode of medical practice. He expressed complete endorsement of their system as a successful and praiseworthy enterprise, and the executive director was glowing with justifiable pride following the day's tour.

The article that came out in the medical journal, however, was anything but complimentary, and portrayed the center as a fiscally inefficient system full of problems and unsatisfactory methods of practice; so that the Community Health system came out as quite inferior to solo fee-for-service practice. Jarvis could hardly believe what he read, Appleton was outraged, and Philip couldn't wait to sit down and write a red-hot rebuttal of the article in unadorned language. He prevailed upon Appleton to cosign the letter and it was duly sent off to the journal, where it was eventually published, but not before the dismayed editor asked if they were really serious about having the letter published in its present form. Philip's reply was a resounding "Yes!" It was the worthy Mr. Clauson, however, who was permitted the last word, in a lengthy and convoluted piece of self-justification that was given prominent display in the journal. But the writer's objectivity had been clearly challenged and – in the eyes of a good many readers – clearly discredited.

An even more discouraging experience had been the Kirk Lyon affair in 1966-67. Dr. Kirk Lyon was a highly respected physician who'd held some of the most prestigious appointments in the medical profession, both nationally and provincially. He was commissioned by the Canadian Medical Association to prepare an impartial study of group practice in Canada, and as chairman of a special committee devoted to this major project, he visited the Health center in San Pete. This after all was the prototype of a community-sponsored group practice, as distinct from private group practice.

Dr. Lyon went through the institution with the proverbial fine-toothed comb, and was shown every possible facility and cooperation by Jarvis, Appleton, and various members of the staff – both medical and ancillary. At the end of his detailed review, he declared that he was impressed by the excellence, efficiency and innovation of the institution, and he felt it might well represent the wave of the future in medical practice.

A book on group practice in Canada, published under the auspices of the Canadian Medical Association, was released soon after Dr Lyon's visit, and although generally favorable to group practice, was anything but favorable to 'Union Sponsored Clinics', which it regarded as distinct from 'Consumer Sponsored Clinics'. The main report was presented by a special committee of which Kirk Lyon was the chairman, and the pejorative comments were, in large degree, his responsibility. For example, it stated: 'While union members may be considered to be consumers, their composition as a national or international special interest group makes them into something somewhat different from a locally inspired group of previously unassociated consumers coming together for the primary purpose of establishing a medical group. The original purpose of the union was not to establish a medical group, since the union had existed long before a project of this nature was envisaged.'

This was hair-splitting sophistry at its worst, and would put the polemics of the most ardent Marxist theoretician to shame. The report went on to state: 'Doctors joining a medical group of this nature should be alert therefore to protect their own interests in the face of a large organization that is potentially much more powerful than the ordinary consumer sponsored group.' Then, as if realizing the absurdity of this remark, the writer continued: 'An important law of economics continues to operate in favor of doctors however, as long as the demand for medical services exceeds the supply – thus giving the profession a very strong bargaining position in most situations.'

After pointing out the theoretical advantages of practicing in such a group with 'outside' sponsorship, the writer continued: 'It is the overall impression of the Special Committee on Group Practice, however, that everything else being equal, there appears to be no advantage to the public or the profession in outside sponsorship of groups. The profession, by accepting positions in such groups, are tending to put their destinies into the hands of others – while it would be undoubtedly in their greatest interest to establish their own group practices where at all possible. In conclusion, therefore, the Committee would strongly recommend against this type of arrangement.'

Philip and others in the group found it incredible that Dr. Kirk Lyon could possibly put his name to such a statement after his visit and euphemistic appraisal of the Health center a short time previously, but the surgeon thought of one of the most important corollaries of his father's favorite dictum: "Man proposes, God disposes." It was that one of the greatest blessings of Time is that it uncovers Truth, and the truth was uncovered in this matter when Bosnar and Appleton attended the First International Congress on Group Practice in Winnipeg.

A bonus of this interesting conference for Philip was meeting his old friend Bill Govern from the dusty prairies of yesteryear. He was now practicing in Edmonton, was involved in computer systems for physicians and hospitals, and prominent in Alberta's medical politics. He'd become a confirmed conservative in sharp contrast to his earlier socialist viewpoint, but still displayed an undiminished capacity for good food and drink. Philip introduced him to Appleton and assured him that their Health Center wasn't a communist enterprise. To do him justice, he showed a deep interest in the details and history of the C.H.C. set-up, and appeared impressed. They exchanged affectionate greetings to each other's wives and parted with a promise to keep in touch, somewhat in the manner of similar promises made by shipboard companions. (Other times, other places!).

At one of the luncheon meetings held during the conference, Bosnar and Appleton observed a distinguished- looking gentleman who approached their table then sat down directly opposite them. They soon recognized him as Dr. Kirk Lyon, and he seemed to recognize them. In any event, they exchanged polite smiles and took no further notice of each other. Finally, when coffee was served, Dr. Lyon unexpectedly spoke up, and his manner was apologetic.

"I suppose you and your group have often wondered why I was so critical of your clinic in my book after praising it so highly during my tour of your place."

"Yes, Dr. Lyon, it was rather puzzling to say the least."

"Well, I owe you an explanation at the very least. Not an excuse, just an explanation."

"I'm sure Dr. Appleton and I would be most interested, and we can pass your explanation on to our colleagues when we get back."

"Following my visit to your center I was guest of honor at a dinner meeting of the St. Pierre Medical Society, and I was asked to convey my impressions of group practice in Canada. I did so to the best of my ability but without being too specific."

"And did you tell them about your tour of our facilities?"

"I told them exactly what I told your people, stressing the points that impressed me the most."

"That must have made you popular."

"I was entirely unprepared for the violence of the reaction. They told me in no uncertain terms that as a former president of the O.M.A. I wasn't expected to praise the enemy but to concentrate on the weak points of your set-up, and present those to my committee. That's just what I did and I'm not proud of it."

"Well, Dr. Lyon, at least you've cleared up the mystery of your about-face, and perhaps you may find it possible one day to tell our divided profession the truth."

The news of the surprise attack on Israel by Egypt and Syria came as a terrible shock to Phil and Patty, and the report that hostilities were launched on Yom Kippur, the holiest day of the year for the Jewish people, added a sinister touch to this latest war against a tiny state that was still the only democracy in the Middle East. Was the Arab world still seeking that 'Final Solution' Hitler's minions couldn't quite complete? It had been little more than a year since Palestinian terrorists slaughtered eleven Israeli athletes at the Munich Olympic games for the crime of being citizens of a Jewish state, while the world expressed shock, but the Games continued with scarcely a pause for breath.

Now the world watched once again as the combined forces of Egypt, Syria, Iraq, and Jordan launched an onslaught that was led by five thousand tanks, more than those used in the Nazi invasion of Russia, and with the latest ground to air missiles from the Soviets that could wipe out all the Israeli planes. This time, unlike the Six Day War, the Israelis – even though they had advance warning of the attack – decided not to strike the first blow, and paid the price. The former military hero and current Minister of Defense, Moshe Dayan, now bore the brunt of the blame for 'the lack of preparedness' and Prime Minister Golda Meir, his most loyal defender, knew her days of leadership were numbered. Yet for all the dire forebodings, opinions, and recriminations, it was the Israeli forces that prevailed, and the new war hero was a beefy, pugnacious and flamboyant soldier in the image of 'Blood and Guts' General Patton. His name was (Major-General) Ariel Sharon, and only the Soviet threat of nuclear intervention forced him to halt his encirclement of the Second Egyptian Army.

At the same time, the Nixon administration, reeling from the Spiro Agnew scandals and the Watergate conspiracy, was hardly in a position to call Brezhnev's bluff, and meekly acceded to an unsatisfactory ceasefire that could produce no real peace. At the time of the ceasefire the Israeli forces were less than fifty miles from Cairo and less than thirty miles from Damascus; a decisive defeat of the combined Arab forces was averted and nowhere was there a word of criticism for one more international hypocrisy, this time based on the need for Arab oil – the newest and heaviest chip in the game of world power politics.

What a year this past twelve months had been! Two past presidents of the U.S.A, Harry Truman and Lyndon Johnson, were dead, and so was a former King of England, the tragic Edward Duke of Windsor. The C.I.A. and major American business interests, having failed in 1970 to prevent the election of President Allende, succeeded in having him murdered in a military coup. Nobody could dispute that Allende was an avowed Marxist, but he was also the legal winner of a democratic election and was now replaced by a fascist dictator.

In wartorn Indochina, a ceasefire had been arranged and the first prisoners of war were starting to come home, but the future looked bleak indeed for the devastated land and people of this unhappy region, and Philip felt in his bones that there would be much bloodshed for years to come.

At least there was one bright happening during the past year that gave him great satisfaction, and that was the dethroning of the latest victor in an endless procession of Russian World Chess Champions by a young challenger from the Western Democracies. To be perfectly honest, Philip much preferred the likeable Boris Spassky to the boorish Bobby Fischer, but he recognized the incomparable genius of the American eccentric who might well prove to be the greatest chess player of all time.

Philip had followed most of Fischer's previous games from the chess journals since his emergence as a chess prodigy in his early teens, and as the present world championship got under way, Philip played out each reported game and analyzed it with a feeling of intense personal involvement.

By Game 11 the American had a comfortable edge of 6 1/2 games to 3 1/2, despite messing up his first game and forfeiting the second game as a penalty for a stupid 'No Show' on the basis of absurd complaints and demands. Just when Fischer appeared to have become invincible, he squandered his position on the fourteenth move and threw the game away, at least as far as Philip's analysis was concerned. The American was playing his favorite 'Poisoned Pawn' variation of the Sicilian Defense with the black pieces, and the game had been adjourned at the thirteenth move. The next day, Spassky's fourteenth move seemed to send his opponent into panic, and instead of moving his queen right back into what appeared to be a fatal trap, he elected to escape, lost the initiative and lost the game.

For the next few days, Philip spent each free moment analyzing every possible variation of the flawed game until Patty exploded, "For God's sake, darling, Fischer's loss of that one game surely isn't the end of the world! I think you've spent more than enough time on it."

"Forgive me, darling, I should have explained. It's not just this one game, though it does let Spassky back into the match. It's the fact that everybody believes Spassky's surprise fourteenth move is a complete refutation of Fischer's favorite variation, one that's brought him many brilliant victories in the past and for which he's famous."

"What do you intend to do about it, beside driving yourself crazy?"

"I'm going to send a cable to Reykjavik and suggest my variation."

"You don't really think Fischer will bother to read it?" "Of course not. He's a hot-head and a boor, and I'm just an unknown chess amateur. Bill Lombardy, his official second, would be more inclined to read it because he respects other people's opinions, even unknown amateurs."

"What's your plan, then?"

"Both contestants have official seconds. Spassky has Geller and Fischer has Lombardy. In addition to managing and advising their virtuosos they often do overnight analyses of the adjourned position between sessions, along with a team of experts, and come up with brilliant moves while the contenders sleep. I firmly believe that's where Spassky's surprise came from."

"I've heard you talk about Lombardy before."

"He and Fischer grew up together as boys, and later on Bill Lombardy became a Catholic priest as well as a gifted chess player, and he remained one of the few close friends of his ornery antisocial friend. He's the one I'm sending my telegram to, with my suggested continuation."

"I hope you find the expense worthwhile. Good luck!"

At no time did he ever receive an acknowledgement to his cable, either direct or indirect. Bobby Fischer never again used the Poisoned Pawn variation in the rest of the games, but he went on to win the match by a decisive score of 12 1/2 to 8 1/2.

(One year later, Philip was finishing dinner and Patty brought him his latest chess journal. He let out a whoop of delight that made Patty wonder what he'd seen in this serious technical publication to produce such a reaction. There it was! In bold print and unmistakable language – a detailed analysis of Game 11 in the last world chess championship by the renowned Soviet Grandmaster, Keres. First, he confirmed Philip's suggested variation for Black's fourteenth move, and then he went on to state that White's surprise fourteenth was the result of overnight analysis by Spassky's support team. Philip's joy was unconfined!)

CHAPTER 54

1973-74

'**W**hy the hell do I still feel like a young man?' Philip asked himself, when he'd passed the dreaded sixty year mark and knew he was now considered a Senior Citizen. As if to reassure him, new developments began to come in rapid succession from all sides. At St. Matthew's Hospital he found himself suddenly placed on several key committees: the Infection Committee, the Tissue and Audit Committee, and the new Angiography Committee. At the Memorial he was approached to take over from Dr. Abel as chief of surgery, which he refused, and to take on the post of Chairman of the Joint Credentials Committee, which he accepted.

Both George Proctor as administrator and Cedric Blore as chief of staff were insistent that Philip Bosnar should reconsider his refusal to become chief of surgery. In reply, he pointed out that he'd already held more than his fair share of top hospital appointments before coming to San Pete and wasn't looking for any more, but he promised to give them his final answer in one month. When he discussed the matter with Bruce Campbell and Jim Appleton they were very persuasive, insisting it was a major breakthrough in the hospital power structure; that after ten years of being frozen out of the surgical decision-making process in both hospitals it was essential for him to seize the opportunity on behalf of the Health Center.

His two anesthetists added their weight to the arguments until he agreed to accept the appointment, but only on condition that there be no interference from either the Memorial medical staff or administration, as he intended to run the department as fairly as possible, without political fear or favor.

No sooner had Philip Bosnar accepted, than Gus Pelletier was appointed chief of surgery at St. Matthews, replacing Frank Brady. Brady was a no-nonsense type of surgeon, but his rough and tough manner concealed a keen mind and a good deal of intellectual sophistication. Over the years, Philip had grown to respect the man and was happy to note that the feeling was mutual, and that Brady's political opposition had become progressively less over the years.

Pelletier, on the other hand, was a smoother surgeon but less sophisticated, and his political opposition to the Health Center remained undiminished. He would certainly get along very well with Mike Callaghan, the E.N.T. (ear, nose, and throat) specialist who was the new chief of medical staff at St. Matthew's.

It was Callaghan who got the lion's share of the Health Center's E.N.T. work and showed his appreciation by maintaining an attitude of cold hostility toward the clinic and its doctors; his main targets were Jarvis, Appleton and Bosnar, and he knew that Bosnar wasn't prepared to let this go unanswered. When Gabor Nagy arrived in the city as a second E.N.T. surgeon, he presented his resumé to the Credentials Committee, and this gave evidence of good training and experience but no Canadian Fellowship degree in his sub- specialty. Since there were a few anesthetists and one or two medical specialists who still had their privileges without their Canadian Fellowship, it was decided to grant Nagy most of the privileges he requested on the laundry list. Any additional requests would be cleared with Callaghan.

After a while, Nagy started to get more and more referrals from the C.H.C. physicians, based on the quality of his work, and Callaghan raged that this was clear evidence of the Health Center's animosity toward him. Maybe that could or should have been a factor, but in truth it simply wasn't. Later on, Callaghan complained to Philip – as Chairman of the Joint Credentials Committee – about his competitor's periodic increases of privileges, and Philip had to remind him that the request for these new privileges was submitted for Callaghan's approval on each occasion and had been passed with his consent. Callaghan's usual reply was that he forgot, or that he'd never given his approval. In any event, aside from the grumbling, complaints and unceasing innuendoes by Callaghan, the work of Gabor Nagy steadily expanded in volume and scope, and there were no repercussions.

When it came to the subject of Canadian F.R.C.S. specialty qualification, it soon became clear that as far as future applications were concerned, the joint Credentials Committee covering both hospitals would have to take a firmer stand. In future, all specialist applications would be required to possess a Canadian Fellowship in the particular specialty or subspecialty. However, interim privileges could be granted if the exams were to be taken within a six month period by the applicant.

There were two interesting situations that arose in connection with this important issue. The first was an application sent to the Health Center in January 1970 by an orthopedic surgeon practicing in a small community about halfway between Thunder Bay and San Pete. He was Siegfried von Taublitz, ex-military surgeon in the Luftwaffe, with impressive German credentials in orthopedics but none in Canada. Appleton wrote to tell him that there were already two highly qualified orthopods in San Pete, and even if he were accepted by the C.H.C. medical group he would be turned down by both hospitals.

Six months later Taublitz was accepted at both hospitals as a solo orthopedist, and by 1974 there was a mounting array of complaints about his work; these were being cautiously whispered but never openly addressed at a committee level. Fortunately, by the time it became Bosnar's responsibility, the problem had already been resolved by Taublitz's decision to curtail his orthopedic work for reasons of ill-health.

The second situation concerned Fred Mansfield. He was a serious and hard-working G.P. who joined the Center in '69 and left one year later to take his postgraduate training in head and neck surgery. He and Percy Blythe, who also stayed with the group from '69 to '70 and left to train in Ophthalmology, were given substantial loans by the medical partnership to enable them to take their specialty training, on the understanding that they would be given specialist appointments at the C.H.C. on their return. It was accepted without saying, that as soon as they received their Canadian Fellowship, the clinic would press for their specialist privileges at both hospitals.

In due course, both men returned in justifiable triumph with their specialty courses completed. Both found themselves, right away, under considerable downtown pressure not to rejoin the Health Center. In the case of Blythe, a studious chap whom Philip liked and respected very much, the pressure translated into a stupid conflict with Jarvis over the set-up of his new department. Each wanted a free hand in the final selection process and the unfortunate result was that

Blythe left town to set up independent practice in Sarnia. As for Mansfield, who returned as devoid of humor as when he left, he informed the medical partnership that he had decided to practice downtown.

As reported to Philip by the newest clinic surgeon Jack Steven's, Mansfield was explicitly warned by his downtown advisers not to rejoin his clinic.

"In a way, Phil, I'm glad you weren't there when he came up to tell us about his decision."

"I was tied up with my delayed last case. We didn't get started 'till after two o'clock."

"Well anyhow, Mansfield told us he'd been to see John Duncan this morning to find out where he stood as far as referrals were concerned."

"He went to see HIM before coming to see US?"

"Hold your horses, Phil, there's more. Duncan warned him that if he rejoined the C.H.C. he'd get no referrals at all from the solo doctors, but if he went downtown the clinic doctors would be bound to use him on an ever-increasing basis."

"Well, that certainly made it plain enough the war's still on. I'm surprised to see it come right out into the open. At least Duncan can be given credit for not concealing the fact."

"Wait! As a result of the morning's interview Mansfield decided to open up his office downtown, and told us so."

"For Christ's sake, Jack, why didn't you throw the self- serving gutless bastard out of the building?"

"We all knew that's what you'd have done, but not everyone has your fierce sense of loyalty."

At the next meeting of the Joint Credentials Committee – covering privileges at both hospitals – Philip recommended Mansfield for interim privileges pending his forthcoming F.R.C.S.C. exams, because of his excellent training program in England. An official confirmatory letter was sent to Mansfield, who then asked for a personal interview with Dr. Bosnar. Philip arranged to see him privately in the boardroom immediately after the next surgical ward rounds at the Memorial.

Mansfield seemed ill at ease, and said he wanted to know which privileges he'd been granted on the laundry list.

"All those in the head and neck surgery column. The limitations are those of your own conscience."

"In what way."

"You know what you can do well, in the interests of your patient, and which cases you'd sooner refer to a special center."

"What about restrictions?"

"Nobody is restricted unless there's clear evidence of diminished performance or ability, and anyone who tries to restrict your privileges on any other grounds will have me to reckon with."

"You mean you won't hold it against me that I left the clinic?"

"Now that you bring it up I have to say that I don't think much of you as a person. A real man would have told Duncan that he and his rednecks could go to hell, rather than submitting to threats of professional boycott."

"Will the Group get its own head and neck surgeon?"

"If we get the right one I'd be in favor of it. If you'd carried on with us you'd have got all the head and neck work that is now done by all three group surgeons, and mine is a fair amount, as you know. Moreover, any other surgeon doing good head and neck work at the present time will retain his privileges in that department."

The interview was over and Mansfield didn't look very healthy. In a way Philip felt sorry for him. He was, after all, the product of his own 'Me First, Me Now' generation, with an entirely different set of values from those of his elders. These were the inglorious days of expediency, infidelity, and materialism.

As far as the administration at St. Matthew's was concerned, Philip had been very happy with Shawn Dunleavy, the pleasant Irishman who replaced Prentice as administrator, and the C.H.C. surgeon looked forward to a more pleasant relationship with the Sisters' hospital. It was true that Callaghan, as chief of staff, still tinged that institution's activities with venom where C.H.C. staff members were concerned, but the new Mother Superior seemed a more decent individual than her predecessors, and all the other Sisters were friendly and cooperative.

Gus Pelletier and Philip Bosnar integrated their weekly surgical ward rounds so that the subject matter of their cases didn't clash, and Philip was pleased to note that their attendance was steadily increasing, especially at the Memorial. At St. Matthew's, Philip gave credit for this increase to the excellent presentations of the pathologist, a gifted East Indian scholar who spent considerable time and effort preparing his material for the rounds. At Memorial it was the change from Rudi Abel, who – although Philip liked him very much as an individual and thought he'd been unfairly treated by the 'Old Guard' – wasn't very good at running ward rounds, and hadn't made much impact as chief of surgery.

Abel was a Jewish refugee from Hitler's Europe, and had left Czechoslovakia with his family at the time of the Sudeten crisis, then settled in England long enough to complete his surgical training and serve with distinction in the British Army before emigrating to Canada. He'd been friendly from the very first, but had never shown any interest in joining the C.H.C. and was evidently committed to throwing in his lot, for better or worse, with the downtown solo practitioners. He got very little referred surgery and derived most of his surgery from what was in fact a general practice. Oddly enough, he got quite a few of his referrals from Tony Donovan, who also handled a fair amount of family practice along with his Ob.Gyn. specialty, and who received in return any of Abel's female patients with the slightest hint of a problem in the field of obstetrics or gynecology. On a personal level, the two were poles apart in background, outlook and manner, but like Cassidy and Pelletier, they got along well.

Jim Appleton was going through a depressing period of disillusionment, undoubtedly compounded by family problems on the home front. In a way he was the agent of his own misfortunes. Among several of those closest to him, Philip had repeatedly urged him to delegate more of his duties and responsibilities to an assistant medical director; both Peter Lawton and Kevin Lam, an excellent family physician with a special interest in psychiatry, would have been willing and able to do the job. Appleton always promised he would comply but never followed through, and as a result he was spending longer hours at the Center and less time at home, where the growth of his children through the difficult teen years of rebellion was fanning the flames of marital discontent and sharpening his own impatience.

Two years previously, the partnership had decided to increase Appleton's productivity income in order to bring it more in line with that of the other family physicians. It was found that his stipend as Medical Director failed to compensate for the time lost in his practice, and consequently his productivity. The long overdue move to increase his compensation failed to diminish his growing discontent, however, as he watched his beloved Health Center appear to lose its idealistic base in a growing wave of materialism.

Eventually, he felt impelled to produced a document entitled: **'Principles, Standards and Goals revisited'**. In this presentation he vented all his frustrations, but at the same time he also planted the seeds of disaffection between himself – as their chosen leader – and the rank and file of group M.Ds, who were far from endorsing Socialism. Philip felt he must write him a personal reply, both as friend and advisor. The Medical Director's memorandum had been written in a vein of disappointment, disillusion and despair, and although it might have some relevance for some of the medical staff, it was grossly unfair for others, and Philip's letter to Appleton registered his feelings in strong rebuttal.

'I'm afraid you've painted a black picture with too broad a brush.' he wrote. **'Your accusations are justified without question as far as some of the G.Ps are concerned, but are unfair to some of your most capable and loyal specialists. Memoranda containing blanket criticism may be a satisfying exercise against frustration, but may also prove self-destructive. As medical director, you have the power and the obligation to voice your disapproval on a one-to-one basis in the privacy of your office. It should be balanced with expressions of approval delivered in the same manner. Only in this way will you separate your supporters from your opponents, encouraging the former and discouraging the latter. The place to debate broad principles and their relation to pragmatic decisions should be the regular meetings of the medical partnership.'**

The past year had been an interesting one. Phil and Patty flew out to Vancouver where their daughter now lived with her family. Neville had gone through several promotions by his firm and had now been transferred from Edmonton to the Vancouver store, where he enjoyed the position of assistant manager. The Sternway family was happily ensconced in a pleasant and spacious town house in North Vancouver, a short distance above the swaying Capilano suspension bridge, the one that had given such a thrill to Florian and Jamie when they were little children so many years ago.

Martina was growing into a lovely child of five, with silky hair the color of ripe corn and large eyes the color of cornflowers. She was the object of her parent's adoration, especially that of her father who treated her like a royal princess, while her mother loved dressing her up and selecting her dolls. As for her 3-year-old brother Paul, he was a sturdy little chap who was the apple of his mother's eye but tended to lose out for affectionate attention from his father, whether he was being treated as a little man or because his sister's radiance was too dazzling. Both children had the coloration and facial characteristics of the Sternways, but that could change in time, and perhaps after puberty the Bosnar-Clancy double helix would start to assert itself.

A delightful addition to their enjoyment of the trip was the visit by Patricia's youngest sister, wearing her smart modern nun's uniform. Sister Josephine was bright, emancipated, and lovable; a worthy sibling to Philip's beloved wife. She thought it hilarious when her brother-in-law suggested that if he'd met her first, he might have married her instead and Patty might have become Sister Patricia; but she still blushed at the thought. Here, Philip felt, was a true daughter of Vatican

2, and he knew in his heart that they had established a deep bond of friendship which no difference of birth or faith could ever loosen.

Florian drove her parents and Sister Josephine around the city, with its sights, stores, and restaurants, and discovered that her saintly aunt loved red bathing suits but hated any sort of seafood. Sister Josephine was taken up to Grouse Mountain on the aerial tram-lift, and thrilled to the breathtaking view of the city below and the skiers taking off nearby on their downhill run. Patty and her sister stayed on for a week, but Philip had to get back to San Pete as he'd arranged a return trip to the Cleveland Clinic, where he looked forward to checking on some of the latest advances in vascular surgery. As he gave her a goodbye hug, he couldn't help feeling that his vivacious and attractive sister-in-law should never have been constricted into a life of celibacy, when she might otherwise have enjoyed the blessings of married life and children, without foregoing a life of good deeds and devotion to God.

The Cleveland Clinic's peripheral vascular department was somehow not the same exciting place he'd known just a few years before. Beven was the new chief, while Humphries had found a fresh challenge in the world of computers, and was deeply involved in his project of computerizing the entire institution in a giant interacting network of integrated management and information. Beven was doing excellent work, especially in liver transplantation, but aside from that there was really little that was new for Philip to see or absorb.

In the evenings after dinner, he stayed glued to the TV screen, as the tragic drama of Richard Nixon's exposure and humiliation was re-enacted in fascinating but horrifying detail during the Watergate Committee Hearings. He wondered if the President's agonized thoughts ever drifted back to the time when he prosecuted (many would say persecuted) the luckless Alger Hiss, and destroyed his name and career on far less convincing evidence. As Philip watched history unfold before his eyes it seemed strange that parameters of decency were now being expounded at the hearings by a southern senator, Sam Ervine, just as a northern judge named Joseph Welch once brought a sense of decency to another committee that was besmirched by a northern senator named Joseph McCarthy.

One day Phil and Patty were discussing their parents. She had lost her father – whom she worshipped – when she was a small girl and he was still a young man. He was a construction supervisor for the county and was walking home one evening when he was hit by a car that apparently went out of control, or at least that was what the driver said. The young man who drove the car belonged to a prominent local family and the police showed little enthusiasm for a follow-up investigation; so that aside from a small insurance policy it was up to the widow to bring up her large family as best she could. Mrs. Bridget Clancy was a woman of strength and character. Fortified by a profound religious faith and the love of her children she managed to give them the start in life she'd once hoped for herself, with resounding success. Some thirty years after the loss of her husband she died suddenly as the result of a heart attack, and Patty grieved beyond words.

Philip's mother had been in failing health for some time, and she finally consented to enter a nursing home as long as her beloved Rafael came with her. They had been comfortably ensconced in a pleasant seniors' establishment for some time, and Philip decided it was high time that he told his father exactly how he felt about him. A similar letter to his mother was pointless, as she was much too confused to absorb anything beyond what she'd always known: that he loved her dearly and admired her fearless attitude toward life. The letter to his father was much easier to write than he imagined.

> **My dear Dad:**
> Now that I have passed my first sixty years of life I feel impelled to tell you how I have felt about you ever since I was a small child. Aside from the deep love I have always had for you, just as I have for my dear Mum, I have always had a boundless admiration for your unfailing goodness, your optimism and your courage in the face of adversity.
> Even though I could never match your shining example when it comes to application of the golden rule, you have been my constant inspiration to go through life doing what I believe to be right, without fear or favor, and never to settle for expediency.
> Whatever my meager accomplishments over the years, they have been important to me mainly in the joy I know they have brought to you. And why not? Without your constant wishes for my success to urge me on I doubt if I would have gone as far as I have, and without your example I may have lacked the courage to face some of my challenges.
> I consider myself a very lucky man to have a father like you and my pride in your qualities as a human being make me exhilarated and inspired. I could never repay you for what you have given me.
> **I love you, Dad.**
> **Philip.'**

Two weeks later, Philip received a phone call from Clayton telling him that their beloved father had just died at the local hospital. He'd passed away with a happy smile on his still handsome face, sitting up in an oxygen tent, and his last words were, "Clayton, be a good boy and read me Phileep's letter again." Philip felt as though the center of his universe and being had collapsed, but was unable to comprehend the depth of his grief. One hour later, the emotional dam suddenly broke, and he covered his face as the sobbing started and continued into the night. His world would never be quite the same again.

Jim Appleton and Philip Bosnar had at least one thing in common and that was their troublesome duodenal ulcers. They were both guilty of cigarette-smoking, although Philip only smoked half as much as Jim, and they both still took a drink of whisky, although the surgeon's was very rare and the director's much more frequent. Despite the fact that Philip's symptoms seemed to be getting steadily worse, his X-rays didn't show the duodenal ulcer to be as deep as he thought. At the same time Jim's X-rays failed to show an ulcer at all and his surgeon began to wonder if, perhaps, he actually had gallbladder disease masquerading as an ulcer. The gallbladder X-ray studies cleared up the mystery. Jim most definitely had gallstones: dozens of tiny 'rice-grain calculi' that were responsible for his miseries.

While waiting for his admission to a private room at St. Matthew's, Philip asked his patient to stay off cigarettes and avoid fatty foods, and he complied. The operation went smoothly and there was no evidence of any ulcer or other complicating feature. The patient made an excellent recovery, and the entire experience seemed to restore his sense of proportion and belief in the Health Center's organization and its future.

The periodic meetings in Toronto between representatives of the Community Health Center and the Special Projects Committee seemed heavily weighted in favor of the Association, and except for the periodic inclusion of the medical director, there was no real representation by the doctors of the group. Jonathan Grey, Wilfred Jarvis and Bill Tarkins were the regulars, and they were sometimes accompanied by Appleton and one or two union representatives of the Board.

On one occasion, Philip announced that he intended to come to the next meeting; after all, he'd only attended one meeting with the Provincial College and that had been highly successful. Appleton was well enough to come along, too, and Philip was glad of his company. In the C.H.C. contingent's preliminary discussion of the course they intended to pursue at the meeting, he noted that Grey was accepted by the others as their spokesman – without question – while the two M.Ds present seemed irrelevant.

At the meeting, there was what seemed like an endless amount of wheeling and dealing between the Committee Chairman and Jonathan Grey, while there were sideline disputes between the government analyst and Tarkins about computer figures. As usual, the clinic's young financial expert was correct and the ministry figures were hopelessly in arrears. Finally, after listening to an obnoxious government member accuse the visitors of asking for too much (when it was obvious they weren't asking enough), Philip felt the time had come for some sign of backbone by the Health Center's representatives. He stood up, put his notes into his briefcase and snapped it shut as loudly as possible.

"Mr. Chairman," he began, "I believe it is unfair to waste the time of your members just as it is for us from St. Pierre. The thousands of patients who come to our Health Center believe the Ontario Government is in favor of our institution and is willing to provide the necessary funds in lieu of fee-for-service to guarantee its survival and growth. Obviously that is not the case and I believe you should say so clearly and unequivocally through the media."
The Chairman rose and put up a placating hand, his face flushed.

"Please sit down, Doctor. I'm sure we can work something out if we just put our heads together. After all, this is still a difficult period of transition, and we are trying to work out a formula that will provide your center with the necessary funds without being more expensive than fee-for-service."

After this little interlude, the atmosphere changed. There was no longer a sense of wheeling and dealing, with each side trying to put one over on the other, and Philip believed some sort of breakthrough had been made. On the trip back to the hotel, for drinks and dinner, he somehow felt that these views were not really shared by the others; almost as though – despite their rejoicing at the final terms of settlement – he had somehow trespassed into their bailiwick.

On the other hand there was little reason for the medical partnership to feel critical about the Association's attitude. In the days when the clinic doctors received not a single cent for huge hospital savings, the figures were a source of pride and were mentioned in glowing published studies. Now that they were being paid a substantial amount for such savings, they were literally squandering hospital bed space.

The best figures came from the surgeons, and the worst from the pediatricians and internists. Since, at the same time, the downtown solo practice figures showed a steady improvement, the clinic had lost a major advantage and lessened its claim to fiscal responsibility. All three surgeons were able to encourage their patients to go home as soon as possible after early postoperative recovery, and arranged for home nursing care and home delivery of prepared meals if necessary. Even a housekeeper could be engaged in certain circumstances.

The group's Ob.Gyn. specialists weren't far behind in the same approach, but in the non-surgical specialties both the admission rate and length of hospital stay appeared inordinately high, even by local standards. Of course, the lure of productivity points favored those doctors who kept their hospital figures high, except for the surgical specialties, where productivity was calculated by procedure and not hospital days.

Over and above this leakage of potential government funds for the C.H.C, there was an increasing degree of unnecessary outside referrals, especially in the surgical fields. The excuse given by the G.Ps was usually that the designated group specialist was unavailable when needed, or that the patient requested a specific outside referral. Investigation of these claims revealed that they were based on little substance, but rather represented a perpetuation of the 'coffee-pourer' syndrome from the days of the affable and ingratiating Novak. Thus, some of these unnecessary referrals were a misguided attempt to patch up relations with the downtown doctors, and perhaps others indicated a flexing of muscles by the large non-specialist segment of the group.

Whatever the reason, they were losing money hand over fist, and Philip felt that either their Medical Director or their Executive Director – perhaps both – should make some attempt to halt the hemorrhage before they faced the same financial problems as those now plaguing the St. Catherine's group.

CHAPTER 55

1975-76

It seemed these days that something was going on all the time to disrupt the smooth and orderly functioning of the Health Center; for example, the recent threat of one new law suit after another against members of the medical staff, never coming to actual trial but always causing considerable anxiety. These cases occasionally found their way into the local press and on one occasion into the local radio and TV. In combating one such combined assault through the media, the clinic doctors were able to enlist the services of an unexpected ally. It was none other than Don Foley, who immediately contacted the appropriate heads of the three media branches and the adverse publicity ceased abruptly, at least for a while. On the other side of the coin there were still occasional complaints to the College about the clinic's method of operation, some with suggestions that it was still engaged in maintaining a closed practice, when it was probably the most open group practice in the country, to its considerable financial disadvantage.

For some peculiar reason most of the writs issued against the Health Center's doctors came from lawyers who enjoyed a close association with St. Matthew's, and never from those associated with the Memorial. The worst of these lawyers was Bruno Corelli, a second generation Italian-Canadian and the latest legal adviser to the Sisters' Hospital, with a particular hostility to the C.H.C. This was part of a strange phenomenon. The parents were devout, hard-working Italian immigrants – mostly from Calabria – who were the backbone of the Health Center's original subscribers. They had always been badmouthed as patients by the downtown doctors, especially the White, Anglosaxon Protestants ('Wasps') and their social friends in the establishment. In the evenings the older generation of Italian men would be seen at the boccia courts around the city as if they were still in their native Calabria, while their wives spent their time raising large families and providing a good home for their bread-winners. Over the years, Philip had come to develop a profound respect and affection for these simple, honest, loyal, and trustworthy people, and the fact that his feelings were reciprocated was a source of great personal and professional satisfaction to him.

To his sorrow, Philip perceived that the second generation, both male and female, were mostly inclined to be overly ambitious and arrogant, with few of their parents' ideals and philosophies. Their overriding goal, it seemed, was to be embraced into the Anglosaxon Establishment. Although the clinic was still looking for some Italian-Canadian doctors to increase its multilingual facilities, Philip harbored distinct misgivings for the future in this context. *(Later on, these fears would be confirmed, with a few exceptions.)*

While such extraneous issues were instrumental in diverting the energies and attention of the medical group from more fundamental problems, there were also an increasing number of unpleasant distractions on the home front. The newer arrivals in general practice from the Western University medical school seemed a more militant lot, and they had no hesitation in making a steadily increasing number of demands. They challenged the authority of their Medical Director in his handling of their schedules and duties, and were seldom without some new complaint. The latest of these concerned the Sabbatical Plan, and every effort was made, particularly by Fred Crowley and Art Spears, both G.Ps, to reduce the seniority differential between recent and longterm members of the group. Unfortunately, they were aided and abetted by one or two of the internists who should have known better, and there was a tendency for the medical partnership to be split into two main divisions: family doctors and specialists.

The family doctors began to hold their own separate meetings, and whenever Appleton was unable (or unwilling) to attend, the division became accentuated, especially with regard to the surgical department. The power of patient-referral now became a potent weapon, and it was used effectively in establishing the growing strength of the non-specialist section. As for the overworked and overstressed Appleton, he found himself in an increasingly difficult position, and tried the impossible and thankless task of being fair to both segments.

As far as Philip's duties at the hospitals were concerned, he could honestly say that he was receiving the utmost cooperation from all sides, but was still disappointed by the poor attendance of clinic G.Ps at surgical ward rounds. This was particularly unfortunate, since the regular scientific meetings at the Center – which included a great deal of interesting surgical material – had gradually waned and then died. The time previously allotted to these meetings was now being utilized for sectional meetings of the family physicians (the term now preferred by the newer G.Ps).

One of the newest arrivals in downtown practice was the Lebanese surgeon Abdel Zaffran, a delightful gentleman with excellent credentials. He was a highly trained general and pediatric surgeon with his F.R.C.S.C. degree and a first-class resumé, and Philip's guess was that he was going to make serious inroads into the surgical practice of Gus Pelletier, who touted his own claims as a pediatric surgeon. After a while there was a noticeable hardening of Pelletier's attitude toward Zaffran, with accusations – made to Philip in confidence – about the new surgeon's propensity for operating on the basis of inadequate indications. Philip couldn't help feeling amused at this spectacle of the proverbial Pot calling the Kettle black.

The climax came when the somewhat naive Zaffran elected to make a presentation at St. Matthew's surgical ward rounds on the subject of Acalculous Cholecystitis (a condition in which the gallbladder becomes the source of severe abdominal symptoms in the absence of any stones). Some surgical authorities expressed doubt as to whether such a condition actually existed, but in all fairness there were clearly established investigations that could establish a firm diagnosis of this biliary disorder. Unfortunately, none of the cases presented by Abdel, (or 'Abbie' as he liked to be called), had any of these investigations carried out prior to his removal of the gallbladder, and that omission was raw meat to the tigerish Pelletier.

After the meeting, he descended on Philip with a request that he join him in open condemnation of Zaffran for his abuse of surgical indications. Philip replied that the first line of approach was to bring the matter forward at the next meeting of the Joint Tissue and Audit Committee for a detailed discussion, to be followed – if indicated – by an appearance of the accused surgeon before the Committee. In the meantime, he promised to take note of any similar incidents at the Memorial involving the new surgeon, and only then would joint action be appropriate.

Time passed, and there no more operations for Acalculous Cholecystitis by Dr. Zaffran, and Pelletier declared he had decided to pursue the matter no further. What he failed to add was that the great Foley himself had given the raging Pelletier a thorough dressing down for attacking this "new boy on the block", especially one whom Foley had persuaded to come to San Pete in the first place. After all, it was pointed out to the chastened accuser, it was by no means uncommon for gallbladders that were surgically removed to reveal no evidence of any stones. Although this point was undeniable, it was hardly to the credit of the surgical profession, and Philip felt that any such case should always be discussed at the Joint Tissue and Audit Committee meetings, without fear or favor. Then, if necessary, a review of the offending surgeon's privileges would follow. In any event, there was little doubt in Philip's mind that, henceforth, the indications for cholecystectomy would be far more stringent.

One of his most difficult problems at surgical wardrounds that he chaired, was the longwinded speaker. Each meeting lasted about fifty minutes, and he tried to introduce about three or four interesting cases; so if one presenter wasted time through poor preparation of records or dwelling on irrelevant detail, it meant that one or more presentation might have to be cancelled.

The worst offender by far was Philip's good friend Rudi Abel, who puttered endlessly through the chart looking for reports that should have been assembled in orderly fashion beforehand, and who repeated himself endlessly while the audience became increasingly restless. No matter how hard Philip tried, he was unable to get him to change his ways or abbreviate his presentation. Then one day, he simply had to cut him short and the yawning listeners loudly applauded, to Philip's great dismay, as he hadn't intended to assail Rudi's fragile pride. Sadly, the damage was done and the injured party salvaged his self-respect by refusing to attend any surgical ward rounds at the Memorial from that day forth. This was regrettable, but the boycott didn't seem to affect the otherwise cordial relations between the two friends, and made the ward rounds go along much more smoothly.

The other offender was Abbie Zaffran, who presented each case as though he were relating a chapter from a Dickens novel, with interminable personal details about the patient having no relevance whatever to the case being presented. Happily, he seemed to improve with the passage of time, but still managed to condense into half an hour of ponderous language what he could have delivered in five minutes with normal presentation.

Frank Miller, new Minister of Health in the province of Ontario, conveyed the impression in both dress and manner that he was more at home on the race-track than in the complex arena of health care, and his advisers were no great help. He and they seemed mired in a bygone era when such anomalies as H.S.Os (Health Service Organizations) and C.H.Cs (Community Health Centers) were not threatening to complicate traditional values. It was hardly surprising, therefore, when he announced that there would be no further development of H.S.Os, perhaps no great tragedy, since some of these were understaffed, fly-by-night, storefront practices. Mr. Miller and his advisory group seemed incapable of differentiating between major Community Health Centers, such as the leading one in San Pete, and the smallest and humblest of the H.S.Os, under which classification the Cambrian District Community Health Center now found itself.

Philip was amazed that none of his colleagues at the clinic seemed to share his rage and resentment at discovering he'd become an H.S.O. staff surgeon without even being consulted. He duly informed both the Medical Director and Administrator that he expected immediate representations to be addressed to Queen's Park, restoring the institution's original status as a consumer-sponsored Health Center. It was his contention that the C.H.C. could hardly lay the entire blame on the Minister of Health for his failure to differentiate between the different types of practice; the C.H.C's management and medical administration were even guiltier for failing to emphasize the difference in the most forceful manner.

It was all very well for Jarvis to write his articles and give his public speeches extolling the virtues of the Health Center. When it came to its recognition by the government as a distinct and widely recognized leader in the field of health care, the clinic's representatives had all become strangely meek and tongue-tied. Where was Jonathan Grey's incisive logic or Trevor's imposing thunder? If the group doctors were to receive all the slings and arrows of their foes for surviving in a controversial form of medical practice, then they might at least be appropriately designated, and not lumped in with these fragile and often nonviable H.S.Os. Perhaps it was a capricious form of snobbery creeping into Philip's soul, a proud commitment toward the day when his Community Health Center would be widely acknowledged as the clear leader in its field.

Pain is a strange inheritance in human evolution and serves us well in drawing our attention to injury, infection, malignancy and other afflictions of our bodies. It is also the focus of a physician's attention, and aside from its diagnostic significance, should be the one symptom that must be relieved as soon as possible and as much as possible. In Philip's case, he was able to keep his nagging ulcer pain in check most of the time, but sometimes at the cost of impatience or irritability. He certainly didn't suffer fools gladly, and hypocrites even less so. His surgical colleagues were most compassionate toward his disability but were reluctant to perform surgery on him, since he'd never bled or obstructed. Nevertheless, he was becoming convinced of the need for surgery by two progressive features that had developed over the past year. The first, that there was early narrowing of the pylorus producing esophageal reflux, especially at night; the second, that the pain had become boring in nature, going through to the back. This, to Philip, was clearcut evidence of pancreatic penetration, and he was determined to have an operation. Unlike many of his surgical colleagues, he didn't try to avoid surgery on himself, but rather welcomed the thought of operative relief of his symptoms and the termination of long drawn out medical therapy – with its danger of metabolic upset and calcium deposits in the kidneys.

One strange feature of pain certainly manifested itself in Philip's case. He could carry out a long operative procedure without the slightest twinge. Yet as soon as he'd finished and taken off his gloves, he became aware of the suffering that had remained dormant while his attention was fixed on the task at hand. The same thing happened if he had a busy office. The symptoms would only return when the last patient had left. When it got to the point of getting up almost every hour during the night to take his antacid and milk, he decided to wait no longer and head for the west coast for the requisite surgery.

It would be a good time to see his daughter and her family, in any event, and he flew out to Vancouver with Patty for a joyous reunion. Florian was looking great and so were the children, and Neville was his usual robust self, full of vigor and good humor. He was very good with the children, but the preference for his lovely 'princess' over his sturdy little son was a bit too obvious, and although he seemed very attentive and warm to Florian, Phil and Patty sensed an undercurrent of disharmony that worried them.

They were comfortably installed in one of the nearby townhouses belonging to friends of Neville and Florian. The owners were away for three weeks, which was opportune, as Philip found it necessary to sit up in an armchair all through the night and take frequent doses of medication. In the circumstances, staying with their daughter's family would have caused a considerable inconvenience.

On the Monday following their weekend arrival, Philip contacted Barney Truscott by phone at his office and gave him a quick rundown of his condition. He'd known Truscott very well during his time of practice in Edwardia. He was a distinguished surgeon of excellent background, having trained under some of the best people at the Mayo Clinic in Rochester, Minnesota. He'd served on the Executive Committee of the Canadian Pacific Surgical Association during Philip's terms of office, and his views on surgery for duodenal ulcer were close to his own. After seeing Philip in his office that very afternoon and giving him a thorough examination, Truscott reviewed the X-rays and lab reports from St. Pierre and arranged for the patient's urgent admission to Vancouver General Hospital, where a private room was reserved for him.

The operation took place on Thursday morning and – according to Truscott's account – was more difficult than expected, with the result that Philip didn't return to his room until 7 o'clock that evening. Patricia and Florian, waiting patiently but with increasing anxiety as the hours went by, were relieved when he was finally put back into bed in his private room and seemed wide awake.

Although Philip and his surgeon were both keen exponents of the technique known as ***Truncal Vagotomy and Jaboulay Pyloroplasty*** (dividing the vagus nerves to reduce stomach acid, and widen the exit from stomach to intestine), they differed on one essential feature. Having encountered many patients who found it difficult to tolerate a gastric tube even though they had good pain tolerance, and others who developed lung complications with the use of such a tube, Philip had become a keen advocate of ***tube gastrostomy***, in which a tube was sewn into the stomach, brought out through a small opening in the abdominal wall, and connected to a drainage device. Most of his patients following gastric surgery tolerated tube gastrostomy better than a nasogastric tube, and he wasn't too happy to wake up with that damned tube in his nose. Unluckily for him, the idea of tube gastrostomy was not yet popular with B.C. surgeons, although he was convinced it would be, in time.

One of the surgical philosophies Dr. Bosnar had always taught, was that the aim and object of postoperative management was the return of normal bodily functions as soon as possible, and one of the reasons for adequate pain relief was to remove the patient's fear of resuming functional activity. Accordingly, as soon as his loved ones left – with his firm reassurance that all was well – he insisted on having the side rails removed from his bed so that he could move freely and get up to the bathroom. His efforts were rewarded with a free and unimpeded torrent of urine and the knowledge that he wouldn't have to put up with a confounded catheter.

After a good night's sleep, he awoke refreshed and was ready to try a little stroll around the room, but found that he wasn't quite as spry as he thought. He was happy to see his friendly surgeon when he dropped by to check on his condition.

"How are you doing today?" he asked.

"Not too bad, all things considered, but the sooner I get this goddamn tube out of my nose the better I'd like it."

"We should be able to take it out in a couple of days."

"Don't you think it's high time you Vancouver guys started using tube gastrostomies? By the way, how did you find my ulcer?"

"The best way to describe your duodenum is that it resembled inflamed concrete. We had to modify our operation to a gastro-jej. It should work almost as well a Jaboulay in your case." (A Gastro-jejunostomy is a hookup between the stomach and the upper small intestine).

Philip was out of hospital on the ninth day, with his sutures out and all systems functioning well. After a few more days of convalescence he was ready to go back home, and in three more weeks was back at work again, albeit on a reduced schedule. The good Lord had brought him across one more hurdle and he was deeply grateful. Patricia had been wonderfully supportive throughout his ordeal, and Truscott had been quietly efficient and compassionate. As for Philip's physical condition, he must have driven the nursing staff crazy by insisting on his daily speed walks around the corridors, wheeling his intravenous stand along with him for the first few days. After developing an unexpected craving for apple juice in the early postoperative period, he was soon back to a normal diet – one he was able to enjoy without the slightest ill effect.

Many new services had been introduced into the C.H.C. since the building expansion: the new oncology program, mental retardation program, speech therapy, nutritionist, family physician psychiatry, and a halfway house detoxification service, among others. But none was more controversial than the nurse-practitioner program introduced by Appleton. He took it upon himself to train some of the nurses in the Center to do physical examinations and participate in a health evaluation unit in the building. In addition, Jarvis arranged with Jonathan Grey for a special nurse-practitioner training course at the University of Virginia, one that would enable them to carry out many of the basic duties of a general practitioner.

This entire enterprise seemed to inflame the worst fears of those doctors in the group who were convinced that their socialist medical director and his echelons of 'Healthniks' were taking over the running of their organization.

Leading the fight, by fair means and foul, by misrepresentation and rumor, were those two stalwarts from Western University, Fred Crowley and Art Spears, who did everything they could to bury the project. Their campaign spilled over to the nursing staff, who registered apprehension about the rules of the College of Nursing concerning limits of responsibility, and about suitable pay raises. The immediate upshot was the start of negotiations to unionize the nursing staff, and their stand – along with that of the medical group – was warmly applauded by their downtown counterparts, but not necessarily from altruistic motives alone. (*Eventually, of course, the nurse-practitioner program would win out over its reactionary opponents and prove highly successful, especially as more patients could be handled by the family physicians without a corresponding increase in medical staff*).

A much needed element was now added to the C.H.C. at this time. The top floor of the new extension to the building (the West Wing) was equipped and staffed to provide a fully up-to-date dental unit, adding one more facet of health care to the institution. As for the surgeons, they were happy with their spacious new office complex, with examining rooms and minor operating room on the second floor. Jarvis was enthusiastic about the possibility of some major day-care surgery being carried out in this new department, but Bosnar felt it wasn't a real possibility, unless there were major improvements in the minor O.R. and a considerable expenditure of funds. It seemed to him that there were always other priorities preempting these surgical requirements, whether in the X-ray department, the cardiology department, or a dozen other requests for equipment and sundry additions. What was needed for true day-care surgery was a proper operating table, a standard hospital operating light that would require structural changes in the ceiling to carry the weight safely, and changing rooms for surgeons, anesthetists, and nurses. Somehow the necessity for these essential items never seemed to rouse the same degree of enthusiasm from the medical director and executive director as the philosophical concept of day surgery.

Frank Brady, former chief of surgery at St. Matthews, former president of the now defunct Medical Society and star of the TV campaign against the C.H.C. in the early 60s, was a keen hunter, whether wildfowl, deer or moose, and had always dreamed of an African Safari. This year he was finally going to get his wish, and arranged to leave for Kenya by way of Britain and Cairo. He planned to stay there for one whole month. When he discussed his forthcoming trip with Philip, scarcely concealing his boyish enthusiasm, the clinic surgeon asked him what he thought of the idea of using a rifle camera that could shoot close-up pictures rather than bullets. Then, he explained, each headshot with the big game's head neatly quartered by the camera's cross hairs, would constitute a genuine hunting trophy that could adorn the walls of his den. Brady thought about it for quite a few moments then shook his head. "No, Phil" he insisted, "it wouldn't be the same."

When he returned to work some six weeks later he sought out Philip and told him what a wonderful experience it had been. The more he saw of these magnificent beasts in their native habitat the more he was filled with a profound repect for their strength and beauty; even a reverence for their position at the head of nature's animal kingdom in the wild.

"You know what? I thought of what you said about hunting with a rifle-camera. I'm going back there some time and that's what I'm going to take with me instead of a real gun."

Sad to say, he never got to realize this new ambition. He succumbed to a fatal heart attack before the end of the year and his passing was mourned by the hundreds of patients who had been part of his huge practice. He'd certainly been one of the most popular doctors the community had ever known, and his initial opposition to the Health Center, especially when extended to live appearances on C.B.C. television, was a formidable obstacle to the clinic's early patient-enrollment.

As for Philip's final judgement of this burly bear of a man, he felt that Brady came out well ahead on points. He was a tough foe but had little true malice. As a surgeon, he was most at home with severe accident cases, a legacy of his years of training in the emergency department of Detroit's Henry Ford Hospital. His surgery was never fancy, but it was fast, confident and bold. Philip wouldn't have chosen him for delicate plastic or pediatric surgery but he was a good man to have in a tough emergency situation.

In many ways he found that Jack Stevens, their newest surgeon, had a very similar operating style. He had come to them primarily for his experience in orthopedics and thoracic surgery. Unfortunately, his orthopedic surgery soon began to diminish, with many cases he could easily handle being referred downtown. In order to compensate for this loss of cases, Stevens began to increase his general surgical practice, making it possible for Bosnar to spend more time with major vascular surgery and its associated arteriography. In the meantime, the productivity bonus had increased from 10 percent of the medical group's income to 25 percent, and Philip found his earning power diminishing. His forthright Gallic colleague, Armand Coté, put the situation to him succinctly.

"For a smart fellow you're really a bit of a chump, Phil. You could make much more money doing a bunch of hernias, hemorrhoids and other short cases instead of these long arterial cases."

"I know, but I really enjoy my arterial work."

"Your enjoyment won't put money in your bank account. I know you're getting very good results, but any bad result and the lawyers will be down your throat, with their surgical experts from Toronto eager to help them. The way I see it you've made a bad bargain."

Philip decided that if the group ever received an application from a surgeon with a background in vascular surgery he might turn this work over to him and content himself with a wider range of general surgery. Campbell of course had the best of all possible worlds with his constant lists of cystoscopic procedures, his major urological operations, and some general surgery; he worked conscientiously, but valued his free time, almost with a religious fervor.

The war in Vietnam had mercifully ended, more with a whimper than a bang. It had been an ignominious defeat for the United States, and TV coverage of the frantic evacuation of Americans and South Vietnamese top brass with their families, fighting for room in the crowded helicopters leaving Saigon, was a sad and desperate sight. As for the poor G.Is, who'd fought and died in the mud and jungles of a far-off land (for a cause they could not comprehend), there were no parades and cheering crowds to greet the survivors when they got home. They were young men whose aged eyes revealed a lifetime of dark experience, and their future was bleak. They had faced many enemies: anti-war demonstrators on the home front, bemedalled senior officers who commanded them to fight a war against women, children and aged, who might – or might not – be Viet Cong. They had to fight alongside South Vietnamese allies who threw down their weapons and deserted when the final phase of the war came upon them, while the politicians in Washington kept expanding a military campaign that was increasingly hopeless year by year.

Richard Nixon had at last resigned in order to escape the ultimate disgrace of impeachment, and the new President was Gerald Ford, a stolid Republican who seemed genuinely relieved that the Vietnamese disaster was over.

Mark Caplan was losing a courageous fight against his nerve-destroying disease, and was in and out of hospital with one complication after another: mainly those associated with his urinary apparatus. Campbell was doing everything possible for the poor chap, but to little avail. At first, Caplan's admissions were to the main surgical floor of the Memorial where he promptly fell in love with the assistant head nurse, the 'divine Lola' Sefton, a blonde and beautiful young lady who was an excellent and thoroughly reliable surgical nurse. That was good for him to fantasize, and Philip was happy to note that the patient's euphoria remained undiminished in the face of his mounting afflictions. Eventually he had to be moved to the chronic care ward at St. Matthew's and Philip was happy to note that the nursing staff gave him the most compassionate attention.

Mark's wife Jessica was a woman of iron character and indomitable will, and she needed both qualities to cope with the enormous problems of looking after the husband she loved so much. Not only was he so helpless physically, but he wasn't the easiest person to deal with because of his unpredictable moods and behavior. She never complained, but only wanted what was best for him. Before her husband's disability became irreversible, she begged Philip to do what he could to make sure Mark would be used at the Center on a part time basis, whenever his condition would allow. Needless to say, Philip was only too happy to go along with the idea, and Jim Appleton informed Mark that his special chair in the X-ray department would always be there for him, whenever he was able to occupy it. In the meantime the group had to employ various locums from time to time, and to rely upon the hospitals for some of its radiology.

One of the best physicians in the Center was undoubtedly the rotund and cheerful cardiologist, Stuart Atkins. Nevertheless, there was no one who gave the Medical Director more grief. Atkins simply wanted to run his own show, with total disregard for the rest of the medical staff. From the very first he had opposed Appleton's proud creation, the red appointment phone; he wanted to be in complete charge of his working hours, whether at the Center or the hospitals.

There was little doubt that hospital duties were his favorite, especially when it came to coronary arteriography and cardiac pacemakers, and the less the number of patients he had to see in the office the better he liked it. He was also obscure in his recollection of when he was supposed to be on emergency call, and was often involved instead with church meetings or rehearsals with the Light Opera Society, of which he was a kingpin. On such occasions, sad to say, he failed to let anyone know where he could be found; the group's complaints multiplied, and the medical director's language became more profane.

"That lazy fat bastard seems determined to fuck up the works, and I don't give a shit if he leaves," he gritted.

"I don't think it would be a smart idea to push him out of our group in spite of all his faults," Philip insisted.

"Balls! I think he's going to hurt us in the long run."

"But he's too valuable to us. He has an excellent reputation in the community and he's the only one of us who's getting a fair amount of referrals from the solo guys. If he went downtown it would be a major triumph for the opposition and a genuine defeat for us. Frankly, I don't think we can afford it."

"Let's hope you're right, Phil."

Philip knew, almost to a certainty, that there would be many anxieties in future with their errant cardiologist. On one recent occasion, when one of the group's internists left to take up an important position in Thailand, and his associate internist had all his arrangements made for a two-week trip to England for a medical meeting, Atkins suddenly decided to leave town. When he was told that this would make things very awkward for the group he was quoted as saying, "I couldn't care less."

There were almost as many complaints about Bruce Campbell's unavailability for emergencies, but aside from occasional long absences away from phone contact, Philip felt many of these complaints were blown out of proportion. By contrast, Jack Stevens was an eager beaver who was always available, whether on call or not, but even that didn't make him immune to criticism by the family doctors. The complaint was that he was too abrupt with his patients; of course this was by sharp contrast with those solo surgeons who were long-winded by comparison, and were at their most charming when seeing a patient referred by one of the clinic G.Ps. As Fred Crowley put it so diplomatically, "The specialist has to please the patient and he damn well has to please me."

Philip sometimes wondered what was being said about himself by these same critical group physicians. That he was too close to Appleton? That he was too involved with vascular surgery to be bothered with run-of-the-mill general surgery? That he was getting close to retirement and should slow down? That his recent gastric surgery meant some degree of residual impairment?

Since the death of their beautiful Gigi, the Bosnars' matchless dog and affectionate friend, Patty felt she wasn't getting enough exercise. When Gigi was alive, Patty used to take her to the spacious park near the waterfront where they could run together, and where the dog could have some extra fun chasing ducks and geese in the pond areas. Now, there were only the long unaccompanied walks and occasional cycling, so Patty joined the swim program at the Y.W.C.A. and the yoga class given by Sarah Duncan, the glamorous wife of San Pete's fire-breathing solo surgeon. She and Patty soon became very friendly and Philip was glad to see this happening, even though (perhaps because!) John Duncan would heartily disapprove. Another activity was tennis singles, and the Bosnars used the courts adjoining their apartment building whenever they could snatch an hour. They played as hard as they could, without a break between games, and that got them feeling extremely fit and alert. In all honesty, nothing could be further from Philip's mind than retirement.

CHAPTER 56

1976

Stanley Featherstone was a tall quiet Englishman who had recently joined the clinic as permanent radiologist. He was a top-grade man in his field, well trained and qualified, and organized in his work to a degree that left Philip Bosnar gasping with admiration and envy. There was little doubt that he was going to be a strong addition to the group, and at some future date might put his managerial skills to good use for the C.H.C.

Herbert Uhlmann, Austrian by birth and a fluent individual with impeccable manners, was the Center's latest addition to its pediatric department, where his expertise in Neonatology (diagnosis and treatment of the newborn infant) and less wasteful use of hospital beds would be a clear bonus.

Gregory Bufold was yet another Englishman, but with a strong family admixture of German ancestry. He was a superb oncologist (medical specialist in cancer), and a better than average internist. He was also a prolific student of the latest advances in his field, and an altogether insatiable workaholic. As far as medical politics were concerned, he liked to work behind the scenes and was a fearsome lobbyist for whatever was his latest cause. Philip foresaw the possibility of future clashes, but they got along extremely well on a professional level, with a healthy mutual respect.

As far as the solo segment of San Pete's medical community was concerned, there was a noticeable change – most of it for the better. There had been a large influx of new solo family physicians, a new crop of pediatricians, a new urologist, a few internists, some new radiologists and pathologists, as well as some new anesthetists. Most of the continuing hostility these days still came, not from the Old Guard but from each new crop of 'Young Turks', although why this still persisted was puzzling. Perhaps it was because they were seduced by the clandestine and rejuvenated Saint Pierre Medical Society. This had never ceased to operate under wraps, while the Ontario College of Physicians and Surgeons appeared to turn a blind eye to the very organization it once ordered abolished. Perhaps the clinic doctors should have taken some official action but it hardly seemed worthwhile; in any event Philip doubted whether the newer M.Ds in the Center would support such a move.

Meanwhile, the onetime 'King of the Hill' Herb Slater was visibly fading, but becoming more likeable in the process. He was doing far less surgery than before and was less active in medical politics, except for a vain effort to get Philip Bosnar elected to the Council of the Ontario College of Physicians and Surgeons, as representative for San Pete. Needless to say, his attempt was bound to fail, considering the reports that Don Foley was the unopposed candidate from the underground society, thus enjoying a comfortable majority.

As for Morecombe, he'd gradually become more cordial to Philip until it was almost embarrassing. By an odd quirk of outlook, when it came to international affairs and twentieth century history they were on the same wavelength. It was only in the matter of surgical opinions that Morecombe seemed to have drifted completely off the mark; he was still convinced of his divine infallibility, yet his convoluted ideas at surgical ward rounds bordered on the irrational, causing his listeners a good deal of awkward discomfort.

Philip's ex-Luftwaffe colleague, the aristocratic Von Taublitz, finally succumbed to his cigarettes after setting fire to his bedroom on more than one occasion, one of them almost ending fatally. At least he lived alone in his house so there was no worry about other lives being endangered. He had become a well-known figure at duplicate bridge games, in which he was an enthusiastic player. it seemed as if he always had three cigarettes going at the same time: the glowing remains of his last cigarette in the ashtray, the one he was smoking and the one he'd just lit, residing side by side in the ashtray and awaiting the next smooth changeover without pause. His death, from cancer of the lungs with widespread secondary malignant deposits, hardly came as a surprise, but his stiff and arrogant sisters who arrived from Hamburg for the funeral were an unpleasant 'Sieg Heil' contrast to this charming, ultrapolite, and always personable gentleman of the old school.

It was a relief to have no further symptoms from his former duodenal ulcer, and Philip was deeply grateful, as it enabled him to devote his attention more fully to the rest of his life and its many pursuits. He still had a huge appetite for music, and Patty shared his appetite to the full. They were happy to know that this love of music was also manifest in their children, as there was so much joy and emotional exhilaration to be obtained from such a wonderful source. As Patty reminded the children, it had been bequeathed to the present generation over the millenia, ever since early man first blew into a blade of grass and beat on a stretched hide.

Philip wasn't playing as much chess as he would like, but still managed to get in the occasional game, although nowhere near as much as in his Edwardia days. Perhaps it was the aftermath of a sad experience he still remembered from '67.

Jerry Frampton was an intelligent and versatile physics teacher at St. Pierre College, and was a strong player at both duplicate bridge and chess, having won several events at both games. Although he was in his mid-forties and looked ruddy and fit, he wasn't a healthy man, with a history of heart disease and the occasional nervous disorders. He was anxious to play chess with Philip, who finally agreed. He invited Frampton up to the apartment, where – after a preliminary drink – they would settle down to a serious game about 8 p.m, while Patty retired to the TV room to watch an interesting program, or more often to read.

The games were enjoyable and close, but there was one disturbing feature. As the position became more complex Philip's opponent became more agitated, and the more disturbed he became the slower his play, so that the games became far too long. After several such evenings they both agreed it would be better to use a stop-clock, and Frampton borrowed one from the YMCA games room and brought it along; they set the clock for twenty moves an hour, which seemed quite reasonable to both of them.

The problem wasn't solved, however. Frampton's nervousness got more pronounced and he declared that the stop- clock just made things worse. So far, Philip was leading in games by a margin of three to one, and his opponent felt sure he could improve his score if he could overcome his agitation. At last he came up with a brainwave: they should play by phone. He would phone his move to Philip, and if the doctor wasn't available he'd leave his move with Patty. In turn, Philip would phone his move to Frampton at certain designated times.

The great contest across the phone-lines got under way, with Frampton opening with the white pieces and playing the Queen's Gambit. It was Philip's own favorite opening, and he felt that the most effective defense by Black was the so-called Nimzo-Indian variation. After about twelve moves they reached a point, in the space of three days, where (despite the chess-books' conclusion that the position gave White a slight edge) Philip felt that Black had the more enterprising opportunities for counterattack. By the twenty-first move it became obvious that White was playing strictly in accordance with the books, so Philip gradually veered away from the official line. By move thirty-four, Black had a dangerous attack shaping up on the kingside and it became apparent that White was underestimating the danger.

At his next move Frampton offered a draw, which Philip politely declined, pointing out that White would lose his queen in the next few moves or be checkmated. Philip's worthy opponent replied that he'd analyze the situation and phone him when he'd reached a conclusion. The days passed and there was no phone-call, but Philip decided that Frampton was taking his own sweet time to make a decision, which was certainly his prerogative. In any event there was no hurry, and there were many more interesting games to come.

The shock came at the next bridge club game as Philip overheard one of the members talking to another.

"Did you hear the awful news about Jerry Frampton? They found him dead in his flat. According to the autopsy he died of a massive heart attack."

Philip felt as if he'd received a physical blow, and he knew the memory of this terrible tragedy would haunt him for years to come. Was it somehow his fault, or was it simply a macabre coincidence?

The Health Center's plans for a dental unit in the new extension of the Center were running into unforeseen roadblocks. The Board of the C.H.C. had hoped to make the dentists employees of the Association, with incomes that compared favorably with those of independent dentists in the community, and with facilities and equipment that were the finest and most modern to be found anywhere. During the past year, unfortunately, the rules and regulations for all segments of provincial health care were being revised. It had been perfectly all right, so far, for a dentist to be employed by various legitimate institutions, including Community Health Centers, or even 'a duly qualified medical practitioner'.

Just as the C.H.C. was presenting its dental proposals, the Health Disciplines Act was changed to exclude employment of dentists by Community Health Centers. A final loophole in the act was seized upon by Jim Appleton in some desperation: namely the clause that permitted a dentist to be employed by a duly qualified M.D. – in this case the group's Medical Director. But once again, with the blessing of the anti-progressive Minister of Health, this clause was removed as well, and dentists were only permitted to make separate contracts for their services to C.H.C. patients in the clinic's facilities. Joint protestations to Toronto from San Pete, St. Catherines, and a few other health centers, were insufficient to get things changed, so the Association had to settle for dentists leasing space in the Center and operating on a fee-for-service basis. As for ancillary staff in the dental unit, these would be employed by the Community Health Association, just as the non-physician staff were also its employees. The will to introduce new facets of broad-ranging health care in the C.H.C. was becoming dulled not only by retrogressive government attitudes, but by the Joint Executive Committee's constant preoccupation with financial matters.

The new Board President was Olaf Bergstrom, personnel manager of the Cambrian Steel Corporation and a powerful voice in the running of his company. He was quiet and courteous in manner but inflexible in negotiations. Unfortunately, this inflexibility was now directed at the medical partnership, which he visualized as an autonomous group practice using the magnificent facilities of the Center "Rent-free!" This unwelcome attitude was manifest most of all during the Sabbatical Plan meetings.

The Sabbatical Committee included Appleton, Bosnar, Bergstrom, Campbell and Jarvis; Bosnar was elected Chairman and their accountant came to some of the meetings by invitation. The funding of the plan was falling woefully behind, and whatever money was set aside by the Board earned a healthy interest for the Association but not for the Plan. With the Board and its President showing an increasing reluctance to set aside sequestered funds for the Sabbatical, and with people like Crowley constantly trying to erode seniority differentials, the plan was in danger of foundering on the rocks of dissension.

Philip found he was losing patience with Bergstrom's intransigence. To compound the situation's problems, the new Board President showed little interest in Philip's contention that group physicians who left to practice downtown should default a portion of their Sabbatical compensation, and the senior surgeon felt that despite Bergstrom's pleasant manner and outward friendliness to individual physicians, he should be replaced. After a while, even the long-suffering medical director arrived at the same conclusion and communicated these views to Jarvis and the Board, although it was obvious that Olaf Bergstrom wasn't the kind of man to give up without a long and stubborn resistance.

There was one aspect of this situation that was rather amusing. The solo practitioners in San Pete, their supporters in organized medicine and the most right-wing members of the medical partnership always blamed the union members of the board for a negative attitude toward the doctors. As a matter of fact, it was people from the managerial and non-union side, men like Olaf Bergstrom and Blake Robinson, who were ultimately the most stubborn and difficult to deal with in negotiations, especially at the level of the Joint Executive Committee.

Ivan Thurston had once been one of the finest family physicians in Southern Saskatchewan. He was a predecessor of Philip Bosnar in Vanwey and one of Peter Forsyth's closest friends. Philip didn't get to meet this exceptional individual until the year he came out of the army, and he was impressed at once with the man's strength of character and broad erudition. Thurston was now an internationally renowned neurologist, with a senior professorship at Harvard Medical School and a special interest in tumors of the brain. He was married to a well-known Boston beauty who was renowned in her own right as a fine poet, and theirs was a happy and thoroughly fulfilled marriage until disaster struck in the summer of 1944. Their only son, a bomber pilot in the United States Air Force, was shot down over Germany and killed. Mrs. Thurston suffered a severe nervous breakdown, and even after her apparent recovery, was unable to comprehend her dreadful loss and refused to believe her son was dead. Any attempt to persuade her of the truth was met with blind rage, and after a while these attacks of anger were followed by more serious symptoms.

By the time of Germany's capitulation in 1945, she awaited – with increasing excitement – the return of her beloved boy from Europe, and when this didn't happen she lapsed into a deepening depression with intervals of agonizing headache and increasing loss of vision. It was at this catastrophic moment in Ivan Thurston's life that he was able, for the first time, to dissociate himself as a physician from his role as loving husband and bereaved father and put his wife's symptoms together to reach a terrible conclusion. Breaking his own inflexible rule never to doctor his own family, he examined his wife carefully, and after completing his ophthalmosopy (visualization of the retina at the back of the eye), he realized that she had a tumor of the brain. Three months later, after surgery and radiation, she mercifully died in her sleep, and her devastated husband was left to grieve the loss of a beloved wife as well their precious son. (Philip wondered what it must be like to be in this poor fellow's position and make such a dread diagnosis on a member of his own family, never dreaming that one day he would find out, although with a far happier outcome).

That summer Patty managed to get in more tennis than usual, and her athleticism on the courts knew no bounds. She even took a few spectacular falls while going for tough shots. By the end of summer she was beginning to complain of pains in her hips and was diagnosed as having bilateral **trochanteric bursitis** (inflammation of the lubricating sacs adjoining the hip joints). Since their son James had recently written to tell his parents he'd just met the lady of his dreams, they thought this would be a great opportunity for Patty to take a few weeks off and visit James in London. Philip would have accompanied her but he had quite a few urgent cases booked for surgery and several important meetings scheduled, so he decided to stay home and let his wife go on her own. She had a marvellous time in London and came home full of enthusiasm and high spirits, insisting that her hip pains had left her despite the many long walks she took around Chelsea and London's Westend.

James had evidently been squiring an attractive young lady considerably younger than himself, then met her even more attractive mother and fell hopelessly in love with her. The object of this new grand passion, Nedda Dumont, was several years older than James, was divorced from her diplomat husband – now living on the Island of Capri – and had three children by her first marriage. These were a 15-year-old daughter who lived with her, a 20-year-old son who lived an independent, gad-about life in London, and a 22-year-old married daughter. Patty found the mother extremely attractive, both physically and intellectually, and she appeared to be very much in love with James. They were planning to get married quietly in an isolated hilltop chapel located in North Wales, where Nedda had lived the simple country life after her divorce, and where an unorthodox Jesuit priest became her close friend and confidant during some very difficult times.

Philip had never seen Patty look so happy and radiant as she related all the details of their son's marriage plans, and when she told him that she was going to join her friends in some cross-country skiing as soon as there was enough snow, he was delighted. One day she was skiing along smoothly when she felt her legs become extremely heavy and fatigued, and she blamed it on picking up too much wet snow on top of her skis. Eventually, however, in spite of clearing her skis, the symptoms grew worse and she had to stop and return home. The next two occasions that she went skiing the same thing happened, and her 'bursitis' pains returned in both hips. She agreed with Philip that she'd better quit this form of activity for the time being, and just get back to her daily walking expeditions instead.

One day she returned home for lunch looking really exhausted; she told her husband that the fatigue and hip pain had become so severe that she found it difficult to cross the street. Philip decided to break his own rules and examine his darling Patricia as simply another patient. She undressed and got into bed without too much fuss and he soon reached his conclusion – with a feeling of gloom and disappointment – that his diagnostic suspicion was fully confirmed. Her peripheral pulses at the ankles and feet were barely perceptible, her groin pulses were grossly diminished and there was a loud 'Bruit' (an abnormal rushing sound) over the abdomen, projected to both groins.

His diagnosis was a blockage of the lower 'Abdominal Aorta' (the large main artery between the diaphragm and the pelvis), at about the level of the third lumbar vertebral body. When he told Patty as gently as he could what his findings indicated, she took the information with calm courage, and he was fiercely proud of her but in agony for her misfortune. Stuart Atkins agreed to see her right away in consultation, and he confirmed his surgical colleague's diagnosis. Philip was still the only surgeon in San Pete doing routine aortic surgery, and that meant getting Patty to a suitable center away from home. He thought about Vancouver but settled for Hugo Tomlinson in Toronto. Tomlinson was a fine vascular surgeon, and in Toronto it would be easier for Philip to take as many trips as might be necessary, before, during and after Patty's surgery.

Atkins wrote Tomlinson a detailed report on his findings, and in addition Philip phoned to tell the Toronto surgeon what led up to the diagnosis, in considerable detail. An appointment was made for Patty to be admitted to the Toronto General Hospital under Dr. Tomlinson, for preliminary assessment and aortography the following week, and Philip was relieved beyond words that time wasn't being wasted. When she met her new surgeon she liked him at once and it was obvious the feeling was mutual. As for Philip, Tomlinson was the kind of individual he respected and admired. After viewing the aortogram he said to Philip, "I believe you first diagnosed your wife's aortic blockage at the level of L.3, Dr. Bosnar. Well, the lumbar aortogram certainly agrees with you."

"I'm most grateful to you for your consideration and I appreciate your prompt attention to my wife's problem. What's your plan now, Dr. Tomlinson?"

"I'm going to try and book her for a bypass in about three weeks and I'm sure you'll agree with me that her femoral arterial system looks just perfect; so we should get an excellent result."

The Bosnars flew back home with a renewed spirit of optimism, but nature and the fates had other ideas. Within a few days her condition got much worse and Patty was barely able to walk across the room. Philip immediately phoned Dr. Tomlinson and gave him the bad news. His response was immediate. "If you can get her to Toronto right away I'll book her for emergency surgery at the earliest opportunity."

Next, Philip phoned John Duncan, who was medical officer for Air Canada and had the authority to arrange for emergency flights to other medical centers. To Philip's great relief Duncan showed great concern when he was given a quick run-down of the situation, and he arranged for the Bosnars to get space on the very next flight out of the city. Philip's appreciation knew no bounds, and the obvious sincerity of Duncan's reaction wiped out most of the antipathy he'd felt for this flamboyant individual over the years.

On arrival in Toronto the Bosnars took a cab to the General Hospital, where Patty was admitted without delay to a private room and was rushed through lab tests, chest X-rays and electrocardiogram. Then she was prepared for surgery and the anesthetist reported that the patient was in perfect physical and emotional shape for the operation, which was booked for the following morning. Philip took a cab to the Park Plaza hotel and checked in without difficulty, but slept very little that night. The next morning he took the subway back to Queen's Park, so that he could get to see Patty and wish her luck before she was moved to the O.R. at 9.45.

By the grace of God and the skill of her surgeon and team, the operation went very well, and his darling wife and sweetheart was brought to the intensive care ward – after her recovery from the anesthetic – with her vital signs highly satisfactory. Everybody seemed pleased with her condition and Philip's relief was enormous.

Over the next few days, after being returned from Intensive Care to her private room, Patty proved what a courageous fighter she was. She used to compliment Philip on being an excellent patient after his gastric adventure in Vancouver, but her postoperative performance left his far behind: not a single complaint about her indwelling nasogastric tube and painful wounds! With an incision that extended from her lower breastbone to the pubis and two more incisions in her upper thighs, Philip knew how she must be feeling, yet there she was looking as pretty as a picture, with a sparkling smile that disregarded the gastric tube and IV adding to her discomforts.

She had overcome the huge initial hurdle of getting up out of bed and was taking a few steps around the room, with every sign of a magnificent recovery to follow. To augment her recovery, she'd become extremely fond of both Dr. Tomlinson and Dr. Smithers, the young and handsome surgical assistant at her operation, who came to see her as often as possible in order to cheer her up. Philip was too grateful, too relieved and too happy to feel more than a twinge of jealousy.

Finally the tube and IV were out, the stitches were removed and Philip's brave darling was walking the corridors with her posture almost fully erect and her spirits high. She even asked her surgeon how long it was since he'd last taken a holiday, and when he told her that it had been almost two years, she said it was high time he took some time off to relax as he was looking very tired. It was a tribute to their doctor-patient relationship that he actually took her advice and arranged to go down to a dude ranch in Arizona and indulge in one of his favorite activities: horseback riding. Patty chose a set of books on Canadian Art that she was sure he would appreciate and Philip arranged to have them delivered to Tomlinson's home.

After they got back, Patty's recovery accelerated at an incredible pace, and the pulses in both her legs were now strong from groin to foot. She was soon walking well, and her posture returned to its former superb quality. Her many friends and family were delighted, and her sisters and young brother – who'd been kept notified throughout – were overjoyed at her remarkable recovery and the excellent prognosis.

As for the convalescing patient, she took a vow that she'd never smoke again, and Philip knew she'd keep her promise. Considering the fact that she'd been smoking three and a half packs of cigarettes daily and always inhaled deeply, this would be no mean task. It was amazing that her heart and lungs were in such excellent shape, and aside from the rapid return of her athletic abilities she found she'd forgotten how to cough.

Meanwhile, the rest of the world hadn't ground to a halt during these days of trial for the Bosnar lovebirds.

In the U.N, under the retrogressive leadership of Kurt Waldheim, the General Assembly had ignominiously declared that Zionism was a form of racism, a resolution that was scathingly equated by the Israeli delegate with a "deep pervading feeling of Antisemitism."

In Spain, the Fascist instigator of the infamous Civil War was dead and the hopes of a return to democracy rested on the strong young shoulders of the new monarch, Juan Carlos.

The history of Continental Africa was being rewritten in blood following the collapse of the British, Belgian and Portuguese colonial dynasties, and the armed forces of Castro's Cuba were openly operating in Angola's 'war of liberation'.

Mighty China had lost two of its giants, first Chou En-Lai then Mao tse-Tung, and now the hunt was on to bring the fearsome Chiang Ching, Mao's widow, and her bloodthirsty Gang of Four to justice and a well deserved retribution.

In the Middle East, Lebanon was in the throes of turmoil and bloodshed between Moslems and Christians, and the intrusion of Syrian troops only added fuel to the flames of conflict; just as in Northern Ireland, where the increasing involvement of British soldiers only served to increase the violence between Protestant and Catholic.

An unknown politician named Jimmy Carter, who most people thought was a country singer and was, instead, a peanut farmer from Georgia, became the new President of the United States and was proving he had the intellectual capacity for the job. At the same time, his nation successfully landed an unmanned spacecraft on the surface of Mars and photographed its lifeless surface, but continued to arm frantically.

In a Philadelphia hotel, on the Fourth of July, a group of celebrating veterans were struck down by a new and hitherto unknown affliction known as Legionnaire's Disease. Was it a toxic chemical that collected in the air conditioning system, a virus, or a bacterium still to be identified?

On the never-ending international terrorist situation, it seemed that at least one nation was prepared to show some genuine courage and concern for the safety of its victimized people. The Entebbe raid was a daring rescue attempt to release the hostages, mostly Israeli and other Jewish civilians, who were being held under threat of death in the Entebbe Airport of Idi Amin's Uganda. Israeli Commandos flew over two thousand miles for their shootout with the hijackers and only two hostages were reported killed out of a total of a hundred and five. While most of the civilized world applauded, the United Nations found it difficult to do likewise, and even came absurdly close to condemning Israel for its 'illegal and violent incursion' into a sovereign foreign nation.

Last but not least, in peaceful and self-absorbed Canada, the darling of the Montreal Olympics was a diminutive 14-year-old girl from Romania, Nadia Comaneci, an athletic virtuoso whose dazzling gymnastic display won the hearts of the millions who watched her, both at the games and at the television sets. Two years earlier it had been Olga Korbut, the tiny elfin sweetheart from the U.S.S.R, who captivated everyone with her gymnastic skills and that magical smile of hers.

Of such stuff, thought Phil and Patty, is the dream of international peace and cooperation kept alive!

CHAPTER 57

1978

The situation regarding referrals was definitely improving. In a way, Don Foley and Philip Bosnar were co-initiators of a new relationship. When they were on emergency call and wished to sign out to another surgeon, they started to use each other from time to time within a stated time period. Thus, for example, if there was some particular activity that would keep one of them out of call from 6 to 11 p.m. during the week, they would sign out to each other for that particular time slot. Philip would first check with his fellow surgeons in the group to see if one of them was available, and he felt sure Foley did the same with his fellow surgeons in solo practice. Eventually, one or two of the other solo surgeons became involved in this system, and finally a full scale emergency call roster for surgeons was established, with all the city's surgeons participating.

In anesthesia, Ob.Gyn, internal medicine and pediatrics, similar comprehensive emergency rosters had already been evolved, but the surgical roster was the final rampart of Fortress Saint Pierre to be breached and it was bound to blunt the edge of mutual hostility. Necessity made it a matter of course that the C.H.C. would be using the downtown orthopedic surgeons to a major degree, and the solo physicians would likewise be using the C.H.C's cardiologist and oncologist. Meanwhile, both sides tried to fill residual gaps in the various specialties and – more importantly – the subspecialties.

It was quite noticeable that some of the downtown surgeons preferred the group anesthetists to their own, and both Pat Bradley and Peggy Kennonen (formerly Chapman) were happy to oblige. Bradley was particularly good at handling critical cases in the Intensive Care Unit and Kennonen was at her best with Cesarean Section cases. Philip was getting the occasional referral from downtown in vascular surgery, and there were always those patients who asked their solo doctors specifically to be referred to Dr. Bosnar.

In the total cross current of referrals, however, the Center was the steady loser, and a careful review of outside referrals by clinic physicians showed a complete disregard for professional justification and fiscal responsibility. The family physicians had grown increasingly powerful in the last few years, and hinted at mass resignation from the Health Center if they lost the power of independent choice in the matter of specialist referrals, whether these appeared necessary or not. Fortunately, none of the surgeons or Ob.Gyn. specialists succumbed to the temptation of buttering up the G.Ps, and Philip was thankful for their moral stand.

The C.H.C's arrangements with government were far from satisfactory. The short range (almost ad hoc) contracts were usually far behind schedule in both financial calculation and signature, and were in effect for a period of only one year. With the news that St. Catherines' Health Center was faltering under increasing financial strain and might have to close its doors, there was an atmosphere of apprehension at the Health Center afflicting both the Board and the group doctors.

Just to add to the insecurity and confusion, the new government committee appointed to deal with the West Cambrian C.H.C. and 'other H.S.Os' eliminated the previous definition of what constituted a capitation patient. It set an arbitrary figure of 36,000 as the Center's fixed capitation patient population, making it impossible for it to increase the enrollment of new patients into its capitation group. Thus, the Ministry of Health came down unabashedly on the side of their angels in this conflict, the angels being those physicians who practiced under the antiquated moment-to-moment free choice of G.P. and fee-for-service system, squandering healthcare funds and encouraging the iniquitous habit of medical shopping. This was a growing custom among the undisciplined patients of an open-ended government-controlled medical service and created a bottomless pit of health care expenditures.

Patty's health was perfect, and aside from some nerve pains in the surgical scars on her upper thighs, she had no symptoms in any way related to her previous circulatory problems and enjoyed her previous wide range of activities. In addition, she continued to look after her husband in a manner that could only be described as pampering, or what their friends called "spoiling him rotten."

Her older sister, Sister Katherine, came over to San Pete for a short visit, with an elderly nun as companion, and Philip found this second sister-in-law to be a wonderful person, with a sharp mind, a gentle and gracious personality and a sterling character. In the space of two weeks they developed a very strong affection for each other. There wasn't much that she missed, and when she visited St. Matthew's Hospital she gave clear evidence of this faculty.

On the walls near the elevator there were two framed collages of photographs. One was of the city's deceased solo physicians and the other was of the solo physicians still living. A few unkind wags in the clinic's medical group referred to these displays as "the dead and the dying of our opposition." In the absence of prior knowledge about these photographic displays, Sister Josephine enquired brightly, "Where is Philip's picture?" and repeated the question to each of the embarrassed hospital nuns whom she encountered. The following week, the photo collection of deceased M.Ds included two C.H.C. doctors who had died, and the collection of the living was taken down; permanently.

The news from England was mixed. Philip's beloved mother had died quietly in her sleep, and it was his fervent hope that she would now be reunited with the one who adored her so much and had been the central focus of her life. Aside from being confused during the past few years between Clayton and Philip, she had enjoyed great happiness from both of their professional careers. At the same time, she'd forged an increasing bond of close affection for her daughter. Pauline had always been number three on her mother's offspring list in the past, but in the end emerged a clear and irrevocable number one in her declining years.

Clayton'S professorship brought him a great deal of satisfaction, as well as the gratification of emerging from the earlier shadow of his "Big Bruvva" in resplendent fashion. The only casualty of his rise to fame was his marriage to the gentle and ever-faithful Martha, a union that burst asunder on the rocks of Clayton's latest extramarital obsession. Unlike the others, this was no transient fancy but the "real thing" and the divorce was inevitable. The first clue Philip had of the crisis in his brother's home life was the paper he sent him: the Stinson Oration of December, 1976, delivered by Professor Clayton Bosnar at the Royal Society of Medicine. It contained a clear philosophical and psychological reorientation in Clayton's attitude toward the practice of Medicine.

Hitherto, as a devout follower of the Ernst Schumann doctrine and a believer in Freudian theories, he had expounded on Schumann's principle of treating the entire family rather than the individual patient. The family, he postulated, was the ultimate unit and what was good for the family must never take second place to what was good for the patient. This was an approach that was the diametric opposite of Philip's own unshakeable belief that when he looked after a patient his primary duty and responsibility was to the patient alone, and the family came second. Now, suddenly, this latest of his brother's many erudite papers sanctified the importance of the individual patient, and relegated the status of the family to a much lower category in the order of things.

The next communication from Clayton was in the form of a personal declaration recorded on a tape cassette. It was an impassioned message and described in detail how he'd fallen hopelessly under the spell of "a new love", one without whom he couldn't live and one who gave him a happiness he'd never known before. He was desperately sorry for the pain this would cause his dear loyal Martha, for whom he still felt great affection, but he must go through with his plans to proceed with a divorce and marry his adored Fleurette Marks. This divine creature was the one with whom he could have a lifelong union of the deepest love and happiness. Philip was sick at heart and so was Patty, but they hoped that Clayton would find true and lasting happiness with his new wife. They also prayed that his academic and professional advance continued unabated, and his children were not too traumatized.

James, in his turn, was extremely happy with his new bride and was enjoying his new life in a large farmhouse outside Cambridge. The house with its small attached orchard was part of Nedda's divorce settlement from her first husband, and between engagements, James was kept busy with renovations on the house and work on the extensive grounds. His little daughter Magdalena and her stepsister Clarissa enjoyed the country life, and all four were ecstatic over the recent arrival of a beautiful baby boy named Bernard. Patty could hardly wait to see her new grandson and Philip wasn't far behind in his joyful anticipation.

The official attitude of the provincial government toward the C.H.C. was leaked by one of its healthcare officials. **"There was a hell of a lot of prejudice against the whole idea of community health centers and a feeling that fee-for-service was what we were used to, and that some of this community health stuff was really way out rubbish."** In other words the San Pete clinic was reluctantly funded by a Ministry that didn't believe in its concept of community health care. The future looked bleak!

As part of the persistent effort to prove that the C.H.C. method of operation was too expensive, the Ministry of Health selected the most cost-efficient fee-for-service group practice in Southern Ontario for a detail by detail cost comparison. Luckily, the C.H.C. came out at the same level of fiscal efficiency, even including hospital savings. It was the accepted rule – one that had always been recognized – that the overhead costs of medical practice were significantly higher in what Toronto liked to call 'Northern Ontario' (even though Saint Pierre was south of Winnipeg, Regina, Calgary and Vancouver!). This economic fact was ignored in the comparison, as was the wellknown differential in hospital savings, which was much higher than in the area around Toronto. There was also no consideration given to the knowledge that the C.H.C. delivered a far wider range of patient services than the chosen private clinic of comparable size.

All these omissions should have invalidated the comparison, but it appeared that whatever the government intended to prove would be proven by hook or by crook. If the politicians who ruled Ontario from the citadel of Queen's Park hoped to buy a favorable reaction and relationship with organized medicine by these tactics, they were due – sooner or later – for an unpleasant surprise.

The weather in London on arrival at Heath Row Airport was perfect: brilliant sunshine, a few small fluffy clouds and unusually high temperatures for September. As Phil and Patty might have expected, their ever-faithful son was there to greet them on their arrival, to help with their luggage and drive them to the hotel they'd booked. A short time later he had to leave for an engagement at a sound studio in the Soho area, where he was doing some dubbing for a German movie.

The visitors checked in at the White House Hotel, across from Regent's Park and a short walk from Great Portland Street underground station. After a quick cleanup and change of clothes they had a leisurely breakfast in the coffee shop. Then they were joined in their suite by Philip's beaming brother and his new paragon, Fleurette; they had driven down from Liverpool the day before and were staying with friends. The brothers greeted each other warmly and Philip had to admit inwardly that their bond of affection could never be broken, even by his brother's present family realignment. Patty had much the same tender feeling toward Clayton, even though she could have kicked him for leaving Martha.

The visit to Cambridge was delightful. James and his wife seemed divinely happy, and their new baby was a delight. Magdalena seemed both happy and thriving, and her older stepsister was a quiet and attractive companion for her. As for the new daughter-in-law, she was charming, intelligent and very good-looking; in truth she had all the social graces that were so lacking in so-called 'Modern Woman'. Phil and Patty believed that Nedda would be a perfect wife for their James, and a warmhearted caring mother for his little girl (by his erstwhile lady-love) and their adorable baby. It was obvious that she was a most competent housekeeper and she spared no effort in entertaining her new in-laws royally, while her husband showed them the wonderful job he was doing with renovations to the house and orchard.

Philip's sister and her husband were doing well, and seemed to be enjoying life. Both were still working and were financially secure, so they could look forward to a reasonably comfortable retirement. Phil and Patty met Pauline and Irving's older daughter and her husband, as well as their two children. These were now university students, had joined the radical left and rejected all the traditional values of their grandparents.

Pauline was still devastated by the loss of her parents: her father, whom she revered as a saint, and her mother – with whom she had developed such a deep bond in her declining years.

Following her parents' deaths, all of Philip's school prizes, as well as his boyhood essays, paintings and sketches, had been turned over to Pauline. He was glad she had them, along with their father's wonderful drawings and the many fine books from the house in Hendon.

Patty had a wonderful visit from her younger brother, who came up to London from his home in Portsmouth. He still had the youthful good looks Philip remembered from the time he first met him, when Francis Clancy was a young schoolboy studying to become a priest. As the two men sat talking and sipping their whiskies and soda, Philip couldn't help thinking that this warm-hearted and fine-looking individual, who'd remained a bachelor all his life, would have made a great priest; instead, he had become a successful executive in the world of finance. He was also the pivot around which the Clancy family revolved, from far off Geelong in Australia to California, Ontario, England, and his native Ireland. He kept in touch with all of these branches of the far-flung clan, and his compassion bound the different parts of the family into a coherent whole.

Philip admired him and understood the enormous regard Patty had for this fine brother of hers. Here was no narrow-minded religious bigot, but a broad-minded and emancipated man of the world, with an abiding affection for his fellow humans and an enviable strength of character to boot. Philip was proud to have him as a brother-in-law and was happy to discover that he and James had become close friends over the years.

As Dr. Bosnar approached the age of sixty-five he began to think of many aspects relating to this important milestone. The first was the clause in the C.H.C. medical partnership contract that terminated partnership at age sixty-five, but Jim assured him that the partnership could be extended by recommendation of the medical executive and approval by the group as a whole. So – for the time being at least – this was no problem. The second was the pressure for retirement from hospital practice, coming mainly from the young turks in solo practice and some of the younger specialists. Mostly, it came from Callaghan, out of enmity, and from Pelletier, whose eye now focused on Bosnar's still considerable surgical practice. He also took careful note of the high proportion of complex operations that Bosnar was still handling with considerable ease and gratifying results.

In the case of Callaghan it was a matter of his hostility to the medical group in general and to Bosnar in particular; in the case of Pelletier it was an expression of the apprehension he felt as each new surgeon arriving in town cost him a proportion of his previous referrals. The problem was intensified by the recent departure of Gil Thayer; he'd left town and gone back east to practice in rural New Brunswick, thus diminishing Pelletier's G.P. referral base. If he could force older surgeons like Philip Bosnar and Rudi Abel to retire, perhaps followed later by Morecombe and Foley, there would be more cases available for him, and the constant pressure of increasing competition would be eased. The third item was the subject of reduced privileges after the age of sixty-five, which had been suggested by these same individuals on several occasions.

At the last meeting of the Joint Credentials Committee prior to the Christmas holidays, Philip brought the matter to a head. He informed the committee members – including Callaghan – that he'd written to both the Royal College of Physicians and Surgeons of Canada and the Ontario College for their recommendations on retirement or reduction of hospital privileges based on chronological age. The replies were almost identical. Neither retirement nor reduction of privileges were to be based on any consideration other than clear evidence of reduced capacity or inferior performance by the individual in question. The Canadian Hospital Association came up with the same reply.

To Bosnar's great satisfaction, several of the members joined him in warning Callaghan not to engage in any sort of vendetta on this issue, and a copy of their deliberations on the subject was sent to Gus Pelletier. The matter was now officially closed and never came up again.

CHAPTER 58

1979

The St. Catherine's Health Center was no longer their companion C.H.C; it had foundered on the reefs of too much political doctrine, too little fiscal realism and a provincial government that couldn't care less. Although this was little understood by most of the partnership, the C.H.C. organization kept its doctrinaire element well in check and refused, at all levels, to be identified with the political aspirations of the N.D.P. or any other party, to its great if unappreciated credit. Even Bill Trevor at his most obdurate would never forget his pragmatic responsibilities in the face of ideological zeal.

To the great relief of the Association, there seemed little likelihood now that the provincial government would permit the San Pete center to perish in the throes of fiscal disaster. Perhaps its very survival was in itself some sort of testimonial to its practicability as an alternative system of medical practice: 'Health Care Delivery', as the new wave of pundits liked to call it.

Philip Bosnar felt there was a vast difference between day to day management of disease in C.H.C. patients and the larger problem of morbidity and mortality in the general population. These latter considerations were tied up with such broader issues as standards of sanitation, adequate food, housing and clothing, the avoidance of deleterious habits and substances, environmental protection, the fight against poverty, improvement of conditions in the workplace, and the diverse fields of public health and – indeed! – of social conscience. Although these were vital issues they were, nevertheless, not the immediate responsibility of the practicing physician except in the matter of patient education. There was also a vast difference between a community health center functioning in a poverty-stricken ghetto and one such as the West Cambrian C.H.C, which conducted its medical services in a mainly affluent segment of society.

Then there was the much-vaunted issue of Preventive Medicine, the darling of the 'Healthniks', those who championed the wider aspects of overall community health rather than the daily nitty-gritty of medical practice. Most real preventive medicine related to the field of public health and social legislation. At the individual level it came down to such items as nutritional instruction, prophylactic inoculations, regular check-ups, screening programs such as mammograms and Pap smears for women in selected age-groups, and colorectal investigations for patients at risk for cancer of the bowel. It was true that an institution such as the C.H.C. was far better geared to such preventive measures, but in the main its doctors treated existing rather than future disorders of the patients who came through its doors.

It wasn't surprising that the Medical Director had a far greater interest in the entire field of preventive medicine; after all, he was fully qualified in the specialty of Public Health. He even carried his concern over such matters into the realm of nuclear proliferation, and was becoming active in the antinuclear movement that opposed not only the proliferation of nuclear arms across the globe but the peaceful development of nuclear energy as well. Philip strongly disagreed with him on nuclear energy, since he felt that this must eventually replace the planet's dwindling supply of biofuels, and was – on the actual rather than the presumed record – less harmful to mankind's endangered environment. As for nuclear arms, he felt that the nuclear stand-off could only be abolished by a lessening of East-West tensions and not by unilateral disarmament. In the meantime, like germ warfare, these weapons were far too dangerous and unpredictable to use, except by maniacs or by accident, and every effort had to be exerted to eliminate such possibilities on both sides of the Iron Curtain.

The two downtown orthopedic surgeons were fully cooperative as far as Philip was concerned and he liked them both. Hector Thomas still worked far too hard but was always available whenever he was needed, and Pandit Mukherjee was an intense individual with a fierce manner but a heart of gold. Philip was glad that Pandit had taken over from Pelletier as Chief of Surgery at St. Matthew's, and he appeared to be doing his job with efficiency and fairness. In view of Philip's own cordial relationship with both of these fine specialists, he was in somewhat of a quandary when, after so many unsuccessful attempts, the group finally got a candidate who was eager to join them as a fully qualified orthopedic surgeon.

Henri Leclerc was a Swiss from Geneva who'd been practicing in Quebec but was now keen to leave that province and practice in an institution such as the Health Center in San Pete. Philip was asked to interview him for evaluation and made sure the candidate's wife was with him on that occasion. Leclerc was a large man in his early forties, without the slightest trace of Gallic accent in his fluent English; his manner was jovial and he had a ready and infectious laugh. His wife was very tall and thin, quiet and serious.

Leclerc said he liked the city and its surroundings and was looking forward to working in the Health Center group. Philip had few worries about him; it was the wife who concerned him. Over the years he'd come to appreciate the degree to which doctors' wives influenced their husbands' decisions as to whether they should stay in the group, go downtown, or leave for another location. It was with these considerations in mind that he tried as hard as he could to gauge Mrs. Leclerc's reactions, and when she assured him that she liked the city, its surrounding area and the idea of her husband working in the Health Center, he gave his full approval to acceptance of the new candidate.

One of the Center's most welcome recent arrivals in the field of general practice was Simon Caplan, younger son of Mark and Jessica Caplan and a charming fellow. He'd inherited his father's good looks but was much more composed in manner and less exuberant. He was also a hard worker, and Philip was happy to use him as his surgical assistant whenever the occasion presented itself. Over and above these attributes, young Simon had developed into a young man of solid character since the time when the Bosnars first knew him as a boy and were invited to his Barmitzvah ceremony and celebrations.

The older Caplan son, Theo, who was more like his mother, was a far more private person and an intense student of the humanities, with a special interest in English literature. This was the subject he now taught at Baysview High, with considerable distinction and a growing reputation. Theo had survived the Hippie phase of the rebellious '60s and become a model of social rectitude, but without abandoning his left wing ideals.

It was a perfect time for young Simon to be working in the Center, for two main reasons. The first was the fact that his father was noticeably failing and wasn't likely to live for more than a year or two at the very most. The second was the fact that he would be a stabilizing influence in the family physician section that, from time to time, tended to be rather divisive within the medical group. They needed more of his kind, and less of the primadonna type.

Don Foley called a meeting of all the general surgeons of San Pete at his home on East Crofton Street – near the Memorial Hospital. It was a warm and lazy Saturday afternoon in late July, and they were all sitting on the back verandah, pleasantly relaxed and facing the peaceful waters of Lake Superior, with the International Bridge visible in the distance. It was a congenial gathering, and as they sat around with their cool drinks they were ready for any cooperative resolution that might be introduced. Foley spoke up when they were all present and settled.

"I thought it would be a good idea at this time to discuss the emergency surgical roster. It seems to me that when one of us reaches the age of sixty-five or has been in practice for twenty-five years, he should be entitled to be taken off the roster. He's earned the right to a bit of peace and quiet in the evenings and weekends, and to spend his energies during the regular hours on elective work. He may still be called for a particular emergency case during regular hours under certain circumstances that we all understand."

John Duncan spoke up next.

"Of course, we're not talking about Herb Slater who's pretty well out of action now, or Glenn Morecombe who's seriously ill. I think we should hear what Phil and Rudi have to say on the subject before we come to any conclusions. After all, they have a pretty big stake in this matter."

"Well, speaking for myself," Philip remarked, "I'm all in favor of the idea and have been for as long as I can remember."

"I'm against it," Rudi Abel protested. "I enjoy my emergency work better than my elective stuff and hate to give it up. Besides, it would have a serious effect on my income."

A lot of discussion followed, tinged by a good deal of embarrassment, since everyone knew Philip was in far better physical shape than Abel, who, although he was the same age, was severely crippled with arthritis. It was finally agreed that Abel had the option of leaving his name on the emergency roster as long as he was well enough. But personally, Philip thought the decision was stupid and shortsighted, even if it was meant to be compassionate. It was also agreed that Philip could be called whenever available for special vascular emergencies occurring 'out of hours'. They all came away from the meeting feeling that at least they'd progressed a long way since the senseless antagonism of the early '60s.

The Bosnars' beloved daughter Florian was now involved in protracted divorce proceedings that gave little assurance of financial support for the two children who'd be living with her, but provided readily available funds for the lawyers in the case. The grounds for divorce were incompatibility and irreconcilable differences, and Florian's custody of the children wasn't disputed. Misfortunes, however, do not come singly nor do they come unmixed. Last December, Florian's small Fiat car had been severely rear-ended by a drunken driver while she was driving along Robson Street. She suffered severe spinal injuries that left her with considerable pain and the possibility of future surgery for a compressed intervertebral disk. Fortunately, she was awarded a generous settlement for her injuries, and this gave her the capital to buy a junior partnership in a newly formed advertising agency.

Ironically, Neville Sternway had always been strongly opposed to having his wife pursue an independent career, but she'd at least won the right to enroll in an evening course in creative writing. She did well in this pursuit, and even wrote several freelance articles for some of the provincial magazines, on a wide range of subjects as diverse as interior residential design and the trucking industry. These first ventures into the field of commercial writing now stood her in good stead for the advertising business, and her copy-writing soon reached a high standard, although she constantly strove to improve its quality and individual style. Her parents were very proud of her, of her sense of independence and her ability to face an uncertain future so confidently and fearlessly.

One day, while Phil and Patty were reflecting on the changing social and moral values in the post-Vietnam era they came to an undeniable conclusion. They were the vanishing dinosaurs of the civilized world as far as marriage was concerned. Here they remained, still married after nearly forty years and still so intensely in love with each other. They had their arguments, their quarrels, their stresses and strains, but they never looked to divorce as an automatic solution. It was natural for them to admire attractive members of the opposite gender and even indulge in harmless flirtations, with their teasing make-believe – but never carried to any serious thought or intent of infidelity. This was one important factor in marital integrity. Another was never allowing devotion and familial affection to replace the original romantic love of their youthful years, with its accompanying passion, to the all too frequent vanishing point. The crux, however, was that both partners in a marriage devote at least as much time and effort to the complex task of making the marriage work as looking after a household and pursuing outside obligations. Phil and Patty both viewed their union as lifelong, and one in which everything – both good and bad – was shared as equally as possible.

Meanwhile, they saw their own children and Philip's own brother caught on the treadmill of divorce, while two of the original doctors in the Health Center were divorced and two others were experiencing increasing marital problems. One of these, to the considerable sorrow of the Bosnars, was Jim Appleton. There were several factors at play and they were cumulative. No longer did his wife Beth see her Jim as a knight in shining armor, bringing much needed health care to an area of poverty and deprivation. To her disillusioned eyes the steelworkers of San Pete were members of an affluent society and not victims in a ghetto of the disadvantaged. The long hours spent by Jim, both during and after regular hours, on the professional and political flux of his endangered institution, left him little time for his domestic responsibilities. There were fierce differences on how to deal with growing children who were busy sowing their teenage oats of rebellion. There had already been trial separations, and divorce loomed on the horizon.

The stresses on Appleton must have been immense, and he sought his release during leisure hours by intense activity in his many hobbies: skiing and skating in the winter months, flying in the summer months, and roughing it in the Cambrian wilderness whenever the spirit moved. This was a man to be admired and yet to be pitied, and Philip felt he needed nothing so much as a stable marriage.

Herb Slater's retirement party was held at the Steel Club and was a gala affair. When Philip Bosnar was asked by the downtown organizer if he'd like to attend, he gladly purchased tickets for Patty and himself. The party was well attended by most of the solo doctors and their wives, but the group doctors were conspicuous by their absence. After cocktails and numerous introductions, the Bosnars were seated at dinner with the Roberts, the Markowskys, the Steve Ramidans and John Duncan (without his wife). It was a better than average meal and the wine flowed freely, loosening tongues and dismissing all lingering restraints.

Philip couldn't resist describing that first time in the Memorial Emergency when he was called to sew up an "itty-bitty" cut and was supervised by a glowering committee of hostile solo doctors, and he emphasized the hilarious aspects of the occasion. Everyone at the table roared with laughter except Mrs. Markowsky. She had been far too well indoctrinated by her husband in the early days of the feared 'Union Clinic' and hadn't yet recovered. Dick Roberts, feeling no pain, insisted on telling Philip how much he enjoyed those occasions when he was called upon to anaesthetize one of his patients.

"You always seem to know exactly what you intend to do and have complete confidence in doing it," he remarked, "It must be great to have that kind of ability."

Philip glanced nervously in Duncan's direction and so did Patty, but there was no adverse reaction, and before Roberts could continue, he said,

"You're the one who always seems in total command of his work. You're always calm and never seem flustered."

"That's just a pose, Phil. I'm never really confident." Happily the conversation was steered into safer channels, and by the end of the dinner they were well into risqué' stories.

It was now time for speeches and presentations to Herb Slater. He was sitting with his plump and affable wife in a state of happy contentment with the entire world, his face flushed with pleasure and his eyes twinkling. In a way he'd been retiring for many years, slowly giving up one surgical privilege after another until limiting himself to minor surgery and surgical assists.

That's something I could never do, thought Philip. When the time comes I'll stop completely, preferably while I'm still at my best. No cutting back to minor surgery or surgical assists: just a clean break and a new activity like writing, both fiction and non-fiction. (In Philip Bosnar's surgical philosophy there really was no such thing as a part-time surgeon. It was like pregnancy, either you were or you weren't).

After the formalities were concluded, the Bosnars went up to the head table and offered the Slaters their congratulations and best wishes, and Herb mumbled some gracious things in return. They stayed another hour for some dancing, which they always enjoyed, then left, feeling satisfied that many former enemies had been converted to friends over the years, without any 'coffee pouring' or compromise on Philip's part.

One of his favorite hobbies was music; he was no longer playing the violin, but he enjoyed listening to his large collection of records, reel-to-reel tapes and the new cassette tapes, some of which were of a very high standard. In addition he was keen on recording some of the excellent broadcasts of classical music that came over the local FM stations. There was one problem with all of these pursuits, and that was the powerful military radar station situated on the Michigan side of the international border. It produced a loud audible BLEEP that came through all of their radio programs and recordings, day and night. Philip tried everything possible to eliminate this pestilential nuisance but to no avail. Even the use of large X-ray cassette-holders arranged as baffles, and wrapping all the wiring in tin foil, only reduced the decibel level of the rhythmic radar obligato by about fifty percent at most, but it still remained penetratingly, maddeningly audible.

When Philip discussed his problem with the owner of the city's leading electronics emporium he sympathized, since he was a classical music buff like Philip, but he had no other solution. He related the story of a similar problem that recently beset music lovers in Chicago. They joined together to send a signed petition to the commanding officer of the offending radar station. In due course, each of the petitioners received a copy of the seven page reply, with detailed instructions, electronic diagrams, and esoteric suggestions for minimizing the problem. **'The best solution of all,'** the document concluded at the bottom of page six, and the reader eagerly turned to the top of page seven, **'is to move right out of this entire area.'** So much for any hopes of eliminating this curse!

The following day, Philip phoned the Michigan radar station and asked for the commanding officer. He came on the line almost immediately, and after introduced himself, Philip told him about the problem and his frustration. The C.O. turned out to be a courteous and cooperative listener, so Philip took the opportunity of assuring him that there were no Canadian plans to invade Michigan, and that not a single tank, amphibious landing craft or bomber was poised for imminent incursion into the U.S.A. The C.O. laughed and replied,

"I believe you, Dr. Bosnar, but there still isn't much I can do to alleviate your problem. Like yourself, my wife and I are both music lovers and if you think you've got problems you should try listening to music where we are."

Philip thanked him for his sympathetic understanding and was encouraged by the C.O's final comment.

"One of these days they're going to shut down the S.A.C. station at Kincheloe and if they do I guess the radar will go, too." At least, Philip thought, this cultured individual had given him a ray of hope for the unknown future.

CHAPTER 59

1980

Glenn Morecombe was dead. He had liver cancer, and Philip Bosnar went to see him in his hospital bed before he was sent home for the last time. Although he was deeply jaundiced his mind was still quite bright and they talked of many things, but not their hostile past or medical 'shop'. He and Philip discussed matters of general philosophy, world affairs and the future, just as if the dying man were going to recover and live for a long time. During the past few years his personal attitude toward Philip had become almost embarrassingly friendly, while professionally he now spoke to him as an equal, which for Morecombe was practically unknown in relation to any of his fellow doctors.

"Phil," he said to his former foe, "it's up to men like you and me to keep the standards of surgery high and make sure we don't have to take second place to the large Centers like Toronto."

His funeral took place in the large United Church on Latham Road and was well attended, although Philip would have expected more from the medical profession; perhaps the younger doctors had better things to do with their time. The service made him furious and he nearly walked out. There were a great many repetitions of "Praise the Lord," and "Glory be to God," with reassurances from the pulpit that the deceased would soon be dwelling with Jesus and the angels, but nary a word about Glenn Morecombe and his accomplishments. He had been a bitter, arrogant and opinionated enemy, but the man had a lot of positive attributes that warranted recognition at this time: his excellent record as a versatile and progressive surgeon, especially in his earlier days, as an enthusiastic teacher of his craft, as a benefactor to St. Matthews Hospital, and last but not least as a fine amateur golfer who'd won many awards in this athletic pursuit. Instead, there was the standard empty patter that seemed to rest on the impertinent assumption that the Divine Creator required constant flattery or he would turn into a petulant tyrant. If this was what religion was all about, then Moses, Jesus, Mohammed and all the other founders of great spiritual faiths had lived and died in vain!

The Ramidan brothers, Jerry and Steve, were members of a totally Anglicized Pakistani family who came to Canada by way of the Barbadoes, where they had built up a highly prosperous import-export business. The entire family had converted from Islam to Roman Catholicism, but the exact background for this conversion was obscure.

Jerry was a solo G.P. and was inclined to be a bit of a playboy, with a talent for sports in general and a fanatical interest in boxing. Since Philip, too, was a bit of a boxing buff who enjoyed watching a well-matched fight (but detested a badly matched one in which a fighter could be seriously hurt), this common interest expanded to others and soon led to a cordial relationship.

Steve, who was older than Jerry, was a urologist, and although he was a sports enthusiast like his brother, he was far more serious and decidedly antagonistic to the Health Center, which he somehow seemed to associate with a Godless Socialism. Day by day, however, as he and Philip got to know each other better at surgical ward rounds and hospital meetings, the atmosphere between them warmed and Philip soon found him to be a valuable ally in many of his projects for hospital improvement. Although Steve Ramidan and Bruce Campbell were fierce rivals in urology, they got along fairly well, but never actually worked together even in such activities as the new Haemodialysis (Artificial Kidney) Committee.

When Steve succeeded Philip Bosnar as Chief of Surgery at the Memorial it was a bit of a blow to Campbell. He'd come to San Pete a few years before his competitor and should therefore have been next in line. Philip had the feeling that Campbell would never quite get over his conviction that he'd been dealt a low blow. George Proctor, the bluff and dependable administrator at the Memorial, assured Philip that the final decision was made on the basis of Ramidan's heavy involvement in all levels of work on behalf of the Memorial, in spite of his entire family's conversion to Catholicism. As a result, although Campbell was well-liked and respected downtown, the overall vote had gone against him. Philip had a high regard for Proctor; he'd shown himself to be a trustworthy friend and when he explained why Campbell hadn't been selected he believed him.

"Campbell's a damn good man," Proctor declared, "but he's still very young so there's no real hurry. Besides he'll be an absolute shoo-in next time around, and you can tell him so, Dr. Bosnar."

"To be perfectly frank, George, I think those comments would work much better if they were spoken by you directly to him."

It seemed quite incredible but the impossible had taken place and – like Mohammed and the mountain – President Anwar Sadat of Egypt, officially still at war with Israel, had come to Tel Aviv and addressed the Knesset. Here was Nasser's successor, once a great admirer of Hitler, and Prime Minister Begin, former firebrand of the Irgun guerilla movement during the British mandate in the forties, meeting in a spirit of peaceful collaboration, and planning a permanent cessation of hostilities. It seemed too good to be true, and Philip kept his optimism in check against the unpredictable vagaries of the future.

Central America was in ferment, with the repressive and corrupt Somoza government of Nicaragua coming under increasing attack from the forces of left wing opposition, and a civil war about to explode.

The new Pope was Polish, thus breaking the tradition of none but Italian Popes that had prevailed since the sixteenth century. It seemed unlikely that he would pursue the moderate policies of John 23rd laid down during Vatican 2.

The mass suicide by the followers of the 'Reverend' James Jones in Guyana revealed with hideous clarity how the perverted manipulation of religion by an obsessed megalomaniac could result in the annihilation of gullible men, women and children, mostly by their own hands.

In Iran, the progressive Shah, long recognized as a staunch friend by the Western democracies, suddenly seemed to become persona non grata. An aging fanatical Islamic fundamentalist who hated the Western Alliance would now rule that strategically important nation, while the U.S and its allies looked the other way.

In Indochina, the tragedy continued, with the wretched Boat People embarking almost daily on hazardous sea voyages, in flimsy overcrowded craft, desperate to escape retribution at the hands of their North Vietnamese masters. Meanwhile, in neighboring Cambodia, the manic regime of Pol Pot proved that distorted Communism could vie with Nazism in heartless cruelty and disregard for human life. Mankind was destined to be witness to a second holocaust in this century and the nations of the world seemed unable to do anything about it. The Western allies had invaded Vietnam for far less cause, and it seemed that human factors were less important than geopolitics in the overall scheme of world affairs.

The Bosnars' earlier anxieties about major oil spills on the high seas were now translating into clear and ever-present dangers, as they witnessed the disastrous oil slick off the coast of France caused by the breakup of an American tanker and – a year before that – the uncontained blowout of a North Sea oil well. Aside from the gigantic losses of nonrenewable fuel resources there was the contamination of the world's seas and shorelines and the tragic loss of sea wildlife, not to mention damage to the unseen flora and fauna of the planet's watery ecology.

Jim Appleton was up for re-election, and for once he had a potent opposition for the directorship. Stuart Atkins was permitting his name to stand as a candidate for the only remaining office he still sought. He'd already held the positions of Chief of Medicine and Chief of Cardiology at the Memorial, and was slated to be Chief of Staff, yet for some reason he seemed to believe he could find the time to serve the Center adequately as Medical Director. Apparently, the pressure to have Atkins to replace Appleton came mainly from the newer G.Ps, under constant brain-washing by Fred Crowley and Art Spears, who could never contain their fierce opposition to Appleton. Philip was sorry to note that they'd been joined by the Schafers, a couple who had so far been happy and content in the group and were such a valuable asset, both as popular G.Ps and through their considerable social contacts in town. Just what caused this shift in attitude was hard to say, but nobody should under-estimate the powerful and unceasing propaganda of Crowley and Spears via the regular meetings of the family physicians; overtly in the Center and covertly in the homes of that worthy pair.

Another unexpected convert to the anti-Appleton cause was Les Capreano. This likeable young man had joined the Health Center only two years ago and had been remarkably successful in his practice, considering the fact that he was severely handicapped by virtue of a bad accident in his youth. He'd been seriously burned in a fire at his home, and sustained permanent contractures of his right upper limb that rendered it essentially useless. In spite of this he'd gone through medical school successfully and graduated with high marks from the Western University medical faculty. When he (somewhat nervously) applied to the C.H.C. he was gladly accepted and Jim Appleton made sure he would be shown every consideration and assistance because of his disability. It soon became evident that this courageous young man was capable of overcoming his handicap to a remarkable degree, both at work and in his sports activities. But when he, too, joined the forces arrayed against Appleton, Philip began to wonder whether there might be some kind of Old Boy's network from the Western Medical faculty, since nearly all of this new alliance consisted of individuals who knew each other well at that medical school before coming to San Pete.

Unfortunately, this enclave was also joined by a few of the specialists in the group, but – thankfully! – by none of the surgeons or the two anesthetists. Pat Bradley was vehemently pro-

Appleton despite being further to the political right of Center than Jim was to the left. Bradley decided to do some lobbying of his own but was only partially successful with those individuals who might be wavering. He became furious and frustrated and expressed his feelings in no uncertain manner.

"Bugger it all, Phil! These are the same guys who were raising a stink only a short time ago because they could never find Stu Atkins when they needed him. Now the stupid bastards don't seem to give a shit about his unavailability or undependability."

"What bothers me even more, Pat, is that a bunch of supposedly smart doctors don't realize that all his hospital jobs and church obligations make it impossible for him to find time for the bloody awful job of medical director."

The fates were kind, however, and the vote went in favor of Appleton by a count of 17 to 14, but the seeds of revolt had been sown and Philip hoped Jim would remain steadfast under the renewed pressure from so many quarters. As for Stuart Atkins, Philip liked this basically decent man and respected his professional abilities as well as his capacity for organization, but he began to suspect that the Atkins ambition was reaching a point beyond control, and he wondered where it would lead him.

During the winter months Phil and Patty got their main exercise by playing indoor tennis at a splendid facility situated a short distance from the Michigan exit off the International Bridge. They took out a membership annually, and this gave them access to the courts, the changing room, lockers and showers. They had many a fine game there and noted that the courts were also popular with several of San Pete's leading businessmen and lawyers. This contact indirectly contributed to the further erosion of antagonism to the Center.

As for cross-country skiing, which Patty would have loved to resume with her friends, Philip strongly discouraged it, as he felt that a combination of exercise and cold temperatures was a bad one for peripheral vascular disorders. It was true that she'd never touched a cigarette since she took the pledge after her aortic bypass, but nicotine left a metabolic memory that rendered the arteries vulnerable to adverse conditions.

Where bridge was concerned, she was playing more regularly than her husband and giving a good account of herself. They both still went to the occasional tournament and managed to win some of the events, but they were no longer 'top of the heap' as far as the local bridge unit was concerned. Several of the newer players were showing a great talent for the game and San Pete now boasted one of the highest club percentages of Lifemasters in the country, both veterans and comparative newcomers. Philip's own game no longer had the insight or hubris of earlier days, but when he really concentrated he could still come up with a good game. In any event it was fun to analyze the daily bridge columns in the newspapers with his wife, and discuss the articles in the bridge journals that came in the mail each month.

Patty had become her husband's unofficial secretary and treasurer, and did most of the letter-writing for both of them as well as the keeping of accounts. At annual income tax time she always had all the cheques, receipts and other pertinent material neatly stacked and ready for their accountant; it left so little for the accountant to do that they often wondered why he charged so much, but he was a good friend and probably managed to find tax exemptions and better ways of income management for them, although Patty had her doubts.

When they first came out to Ontario their finances were at a very low ebb, but it wasn't too late for Philip at the age of fifty to start a savings program, and the R.R.S.P. (registered retirement savings program) with the Canadian Medical Association proved to be a blessing. They had religiously continued to fund this program each year to the limit allowed, and never touched it despite the advice from Dwight Crane, the medical group's investment advisor, to use these funds for real estate purchase. As for their investments through the L.S.M.G. (Lake Superior Medical Group) Company. Ltd, it seemed that their tax exemptions never seemed to cover their losses. Needless to say, Patty – with her unerring sense of judgement about people – never had any faith in the smooth-talking Crane but was too considerate to say "I told you so."

Despite all the plans and endless meetings regarding amalgamation of the two hospitals, it seemed that the medical staffs were no closer to achieving that goal. There were still many irreconcilable differences, rivalries and even hostilities between the two institutions that stood side by side in childish separation. At a lower but more significant level there were many remaining problems between individual doctors that could only be resolved by quiet diplomacy. Don Foley (despite the Godfather nickname bestowed upon him by Bruce Campbell) now made it his business to discuss such matters with Philip on frequent occasions, whether it concerned solo versus solo doctor, group doctor versus group doctor, or solo versus group doctor, and the problems were settled discretely without fuss.

Philip had to admit that in many ways Foley had become a true ally and perhaps even a friend, but the downtown surgeon seemed at pains to conceal this from his large following among the solo doctors. Thus, whenever they were conversing in the hospital corridors and he saw some of his colleagues approaching, Foley would start to walk away in mid-sentence and Philip found this behavior quite unforgivable, regardless of the reason.

In time, The Godfather began to get closer to Philip's fellow surgeons Bruce Campbell and Jack Stevens, even taking them into his confidence from time to time; he also used these avenues to solve problems between the Health Center and the local Medical Society (the one that wasn't supposed to exist but was still a potent political force). In a way it was all rather amusing; despite the earlier expressions of criticism of group versus individual practice, many of the solo doctors were aligning themselves into 'Groups' that worked cooperatively in various small medical buildings around the city, but without any formalized financial agreements between the members beyond rental arrangements. It seemed that they liked to call themselves 'group practices' as if that would lend them some sort of professional glamour, but at least it added force to the dictum that imitation is the sincerest form of flattery.

In spite of Jonathan Grey's dire predictions, there was no action taken by the taxation department or any other disciplinary body against solo physicians putting their wives on their office payroll, mostly as receptionists and nurses – at very liberal salaries. This now became a strong inducement for some of the younger doctors in the C.H.C. to consider solo practice, and acted as a definite counter-attraction to the advantages of the Center's group practice. The advantages to the average patient of a community health center such as the one in San Pete were unquestionable, and were being achieved to a major and constantly increasing extent. The professional advantages to the individual physician in the C.H.C. were also considerable, but could have been much greater with more mutual cooperation and less in-fighting. In the field of doctor education, the rewards could have been significant.

Campbell, Stevens and Bosnar discussed their cases and ideas with each other quite freely, especially during office tea breaks, but this type of interchange, sad to say, was the exception rather than the rule in the other specialties. As for surgical education of the family physicians, most of them resisted the idea, even to the point of claiming that this would simply give the "uppity surgeons" a chance to show their superiority. Yet the net result was a basic lack of surgical understanding by the G.Ps that wasn't helped by their persistent non-attendance at surgical ward rounds in both hospitals. What was equally disappointing was that, had they attended these rounds, they could observe the relative academic standing of their surgeons, the cases they were handling, and their comparative complication and death rates.

Quite aside from considerations of comparative expertise in the various fields of surgery, the needless and mostly unjustified outside referral of surgery was killing the goose for the very people who coveted its golden eggs. The arrangement with government clearly laid out a system of monthly 'Negation', in which each clinic patient receiving medical attention from outside doctors – that could have been provided by the C.H.C. doctors – would result in a corresponding deduction from the capitation payment. Even in the subspecialties, the squandering of professional resources was irresponsible; simple head and neck procedures that had always enjoyed a high rate of success by the group surgeons were now being sent to the downtown subspecialist who had spurned the C.H.C. Perhaps the most irritating referrals of all were the infant hernias and congenital pyloric obstructions that had always produced excellent results in the hands of Bosnar and Campbell but now went to the downtown pediatric surgeon in increasing numbers.

It was, perhaps, some small consolation to learn that the same complaints were being heard from the surgeons in solo practice, and John Duncan was heard to say, "These fucking new G.Ps are getting too big for their goddamn britches." Even Gus Pelletier told Philip in a moment of honest confidence that he was getting worried.

"The bastards know we depend on their referrals for our livelihood," he complained, "so they've got us by the balls." Philip offered his sympathies and suggested joint action by the city's general surgeons, but that called for a level of unanimity among them that was still a long way off.

Phil and Patty were happy to learn that Florian's advertising business was doing well. Her senior partner was a brilliant Welshman who'd started his career with the giant American firm of Walter Thompson but was eager to run his own show and to work in Vancouver, his favorite city. He and Florian got along famously, but although they became good friends they shared no romantic inclinations, somewhat surprising when one considered that both were single and both young and attractive. In addition to the advertising contracts, their firm had also expanded into some small real estate ventures now that Vancouver was in a rapidly expanding market.

Once Florian's divorce went through, Neville moved back to Edmonton, where he was now manager of a new shopping mall recently opened up in that bustling northern city. Florian remained in her North Vancouver townhouse and retained custody of both children, but her family problems weren't over by a long shot. The sibling rivalry between little Paul and Martina became really troublesome following the divorce, to the point that they could hardly be in the same room together without quarrelling violently. Frequent phone calls by both children to their absent father were hardly helpful and poor Florian was bound to emerge as the villain on each occasion. Finally, for better or for worse, Martina decided she wanted to live with her father and Florian agreed to let her go, albeit with a heavy heart.

As far as he was concerned, Philip thought this might well be the best solution for all concerned, and Patty was in vehement agreement. They both also thought that if at any time in the future Martina wanted to return to live with her mother or Paul wished to live with his father then this too might be arranged by mutual consent between their parents; eventually this might lead to a healing of wounds. There was no question that Florian's life as a single mother pursuing a career would become much simpler, and perhaps that would compensate for her loss. At least her worried parents hoped so.

Bruce Campbell's urological practice expanded steadily, so it was decided by the Medical Executive that the Health Center should advertise for another general surgeon. After interviewing one or two unsuitable candidates they came up with one who seemed just right for their purposes. He was Sven Opdahl, a fine-looking blond-haired blue-eyed fellow of Swedish heritage, a man who came highly recommended by his mentors and by the group doctors who knew him at Western University Hospital, where his closest friends nicknamed him 'Seven Up'. Not only was he an excellently trained general surgeon with an impressive resumé but he had done at least a full year's additional training in peripheral vascular surgery.

Even though it had been hoped that Bruno Coppolino would return to the medical group from his lengthy training course in peripheral vascular surgery, they knew he wouldn't be ready for at least another year and it seemed unfair, therefore, to turn down this highly qualified candidate and offend his several friends in the Center. Coppolino had been a student extern with the clinic in 1970 and was a favorite of Bosnar's at that time. He was quiet, pleasant and efficient, and he came from a good Italian family in San Pete. The group surgeons had always hoped he would return to the C.H.C. when he was finished with his postgraduate training at the Ottawa General, but apparently it was not to be.

When Philip first interviewed Opdahl, the young applicant insisted that he had no intention of doing any major arterial surgery for at least two years. In the meantime he would be happy assisting Philip with such cases until he felt quite ready to 'solo' in this tricky field. For the first few months the four surgeons in the expanded department at the Center got along famously, and then the newest recruit began to show a growing hunger for more cases. There were even complaints that he was stealing some of his colleagues' cases: patients who had always faithfully returned to them for any surgery they required. As far as arterial work was concerned he was soon embarking on a widening range of cases, with supreme confidence but painfully slow and hesitant technique. Philip decided that turning over an increasing amount of his arterial work might be the best solution, but the young surgeon remained unsatisfied. Jack Stevens and Bruce Campbell talked the problem over with Philip and decided that the three of them had made a serious error of judgement but would have to live with it, at least for the time being.

Opdahl seemed very anxious to have Dr. Bosnar assist him at his more difficult operations and would always announce to the O.R. nurses that he really wanted him for his knowledge and experience rather than simply as an assistant. Paradoxically, the slightest suggestion on Philip's part during these operations was met with argument and stubborn rejection, usually followed at the end of the procedure by an apology and a confession that he should have listened to him after all. Eventually, Philip told him that he found the task of assisting him too unpleasant, and suggested that he get someone else in future. When the new surgeon responded by becoming abusive, Philip simply walked away and left a handwritten letter for him, containing a detailed analysis of the young man's shortcomings and some suggestions for remedying the problem. In particular, he made it clear that until now he'd always enjoyed assisting every surgeon he'd met, whether or not he was a member of his own group practice.

Meanwhile, both Campbell and Stevens tended to avoid Opdahl like the plague, and he in turn never attended the tea-time discussions at the clinic, nor did he ever discuss his surgical complications or deaths with them.

The relationship of the Community Health Center with the provincial government over the past two years had been a very shaky one, and until some more permanent arrangement could be made the Center needed all the help it could get. This help now came – in its hour of need – in the unexpected persons of both the former and present M.P.P. for the West Cambrian riding. Whenever the Health Center seemed to reach a negotiating impasse with government these two stalwarts made themselves available for advice and assistance, despite the fact that they had consistently refused to join the Board of the Association in former years.

The real surprise was Bishop Blalock, formerly Dean of the Anglican congregation. He was a quiet and gentle man of deep conviction and sterling principle, and suddenly he became the Center's totally unexpected 'Lion in the Streets'. At one of the endless negotiating sessions in Queen's Park, at which both he and the current Minister of Health were present, he exploded and demanded a clearcut commitment to the West Cambrian C.H.C. rather than the usual empty platitudes for public consumption. The result finally came in May of 1978 in the form of a letter from the Minister to the Association Board that read:
'The H.S.O. program and the capitation concept are part of this Ministry's commitment to the development of payment mechanisms which will be available as options to fee for service medicine. We look forward to your continued participation in this project'. This was one small step for the financially teetering Center and one giant step for the hitherto unfriendly Provincial Health Ministry.

The male hormone, the frigid winter temperatures and man's oldest nemesis, Anno Domini, finally combined to assault Philip's urinary system with that most plebeian of all masculine inconveniences, Benign Prostatic Hypertrophy, more commonly called 'Prostate Trouble', and he was ready and willing to have corrective surgery. He had no intention of waiting for complete urinary obstruction and the questionable joys of urethral catheterization. The arrangements were precision-perfect, something like Monty's preparation for the Allied breakthrough at El Alamein. Philip would be admitted to a private room on the fifth floor at the Memorial the night before surgery, Pat Bradley would give him a general anesthetic and Bruce Campbell would perform one of his smooth 'T.U.R'. prostatectomies on him; Philip even knew which nurses would be looking after him following his surgery.

Bradley was puzzled about Philip's choice of a general over his usual low spinal anesthetic for this operation, but the patient firmly reminded him of the general anesthetics he'd been given for one or two extensive dental procedures.

"Don't forget, old chap, you said I took a perfect general and had no nausea, sore throat or any other problems on recovery."

So the stage was set, and even Philip's sweetheart nurses in the O.R. were all set for the big event; but the best laid plans of mice and men gang aft aglay, as his Scottish friends so often warned him.

Philip's urologist was visiting a solo anesthetist the evening before surgery. He was Vincent Cassidy, the former defector from the C.H.C, with whom Bruce Campbell had become inexplicably friendly over the years. Perhaps they were drinking buddies with mutual interests in the Old Country and its medical scene, so they could share nostalgic anecdotes over a glass of good cheer. In any event, the unfortunate Campbell chose the wrong door to open when taking leave of his host and fell down the basement stairs. The following morning he was admitted to Philip's designated private room with a few fractured ribs, and was looked after solicitously by Philip's assigned nurses, while the O.R. was left with a cancelled operation and a disappointed nursing staff.

The symptoms were becoming quite severe at this point and Philip decided that he couldn't wait for his urologist's recovery, so after wishing Campbell a speedy recovery, he left him in Jack Stevens' capable hands and sought his own relief elsewhere. Steve Ramidan was visiting his mother in Calgary where she'd just been hospitalized with a heart attack, and Jim Appleton's frantic phone enquies to Toronto failed to produce any early prospects of relief for Philip's problem in its overcrowded hospitals and overflowing schedules.

At this point the fates must have decided that enough was enough, even for the amusement of the Divine Creator, and Philip's former American colleague Bob Gaylord came to his rescue. Gaylord had successfully completed his pathology course, obtained his specialty papers (the American Board Examinations), become head pathologist at the Saviston Clinic in Northern Michigan, and was now no less than Chairman of the Board at that fine institution. He was able to get Philip a semiprivate room at the Clinic's private hospital and arranged for him to be seen on arrival by the senior urologist, Dr. Eric Swinnerton.

Patty drove her husband down to Clothorpe, where he was soon examined by Swinnerton in the emergency ward of the Saviston Clinic. The urologist was very brusque and uncommunicative but the nurses assured the Bosnars later that this was his usual manner. When Philip mentioned his preference for general anesthesia, Swinnerton informed him curtly that he always used low spinals and that was that. The only available accommodation was a semiprivate room but Philip would be moved to a private room as soon as possible. As for the operation, it might be several days before there was space in the O.R.

All this was anything but reassuring, especially to the patient's worrying wife. She was already unimpressed with the rough-mannered surgeon, and Philip had to persuade her to drive back to San Pete, where he'd phone her as soon as he knew when the operation would take place. After she left, he worked out a schedule of voiding every two hours so that his bladder didn't get too full, as this was the usual precursor to acute retention.

On Sunday, the day after admission, he was keeping himself mentally occupied with a portable computer chess set when he had an unexpected visitor. It was the Clinic's cardiovascular surgeon who happened to be interested in chess. He'd noticed, on passing Philip's room, that the patient was playing computer chess and came in to watch the next few moves of the game. He then asked Philip all about his admission and was given an abbreviated account of the patient's predicament.

"Let me see what I can do," he offered, "I've got a case booked for Tuesday afternoon and I doubt whether my patient will actually be fit for surgery by that time. Maybe I can postpone things for a couple of days and Swinnerton can have my time."

Thus, it came to pass that Philip had his T.U.R. at 2 p.m. on Tuesday afternoon under a low spinal anesthetic, expertly given by the young anesthetist assigned to his case. He supplemented the spinal with intravenous Demerol and Philip was blissfully asleep during the entire procedure. His darling wife was there to greet him when he awakened in his room and she told him she'd booked into a nearby motel. She was enormously relieved that the whole thing was over and was confident that he'd make a good recovery.

Within twenty-four hours he was up and walking in the corridors, with his IV wheeled alongside and his tubes and rubber receptacle concealed inside his pajama trousers. By Friday he was feeling so well that he told Patty to go back home before the snows got too heavy and the roads became treacherous. She agreed reluctantly and he promised to phone her every day. As for Philip's blunt urologist, he came to see him each morning at 7.30 sharp; he was always ahead of the other surgeons on his morning ward rounds. Each day he would check Philip's specimens for blood content, increase the tension on his balloon-catheter and ask him if he had much pain, searching his face for reaction. Philip assured him that the pain was insignificant, and that seemed to open up a camaraderie between them that soon became a friendship.

Swinnerton began to spend more time with him each morning, talking about himself, his family and his various interests, and Philip found that underneath his chilling exterior there was a warm and rather lonely person who needed the very friendships he rejected.

The following Thursday Philip was driven home through a heavy snowstorm by his indomitable wife. She was radiant with joy at his splendid recovery and apparent return to complete normality. Just before their departure for San Pete they were invited to lunch with the Gaylord's at their home in the country a few miles from town. Bob had been a frequent visitor during Philip's stay in hospital and the Bosnars were enormously grateful to him for arranging the hospital admission on such short notice.

The former C.H.C. doctor and his wife Louise were avid for news about the Community Health Center, and their guests in turn were fascinated to learn all about the inner workings of the Saviston Clinic, which was closely affiliated with the Mayo Clinic. They warmly congratulated Gaylord on his rapid rise to the top of the ladder in such a fine institution, and were intrigued to learn that Louise was now heavily involved in working for the Democratic party in Michigan. **(*What they couldn't know and what was so carefully concealed that evening was that their cheerful hosts would be divorced within a few months.*)**

CHAPTER 60

1981

The Bosnars' visit to London was a happy one and a welcome change of pace. James and Nedda were now living in their new house in Southwest London. It was a roomy place done in Tudor style, with a small front garden full of roses and hydrangeas, and a large back garden that included a lawn, flower beds, trees and shrubs. The back garden also led via a locked gate to a park that was the private preserve of the housing conglomerate. This was in the form of a large square of private residences surrounding the park and its well-kept tennis hard court; it was reserved for the exclusive use of the residents. The Cambridge farm had been sold for a decent price and the proceeds were invested in the new home which, however, still carried a substantial mortgage.

James was doing well in his multifaceted career. Aside from major performances on B.B.C. radio – far more important in Britain than in Canada – he was doing a few stage plays, some film work, and the occasional part in a television production. He was superb at dubbing foreign films, and was also in considerable demand for 'Voice Over' work, in which his voice was superimposed on that of a movie or TV actor whose voice was a liability to the role, or as part of a commercial. He'd finally swallowed his objections to commercials, but remained extremely picky about the products or enterprises that were being advertised.

In addition to all these projects he was doing a fair amount of dialogue instruction and translation for various movie directors, including those from the United States, Japan and West Germany, and he had to make frequent trips to Munich, the film Center of Europe. As a result of all these activities, and unlike the vast majority of his fellow actors in London, he was earning a reasonable income for his family.

Nedda was looking quite glamorous, and was busy with their little son Bernard, a gorgeous and affectionate boy who captivated his grandparents beyond all resistance. Nedda was also proving her worth as an excellent and caring mother to Magdalena, the young daughter of Jamie's earlier liaison. She was looking healthier and much less nervous and jumpy than in her earlier days. Nedda's daughter Clarissa by her previous husband was growing into a most attractive teenager and seemed to get along very well with her younger stepsister. As for the Bosnars' son-and-heir, he was a devoted and affectionate husband and father, and his parents were happy for him.

Phil and Patty stayed at their son's home for two weeks, and for part of the time Philip was able to attend an international symposium on peripheral vascular surgery; it was held in the Festival Hall conglomerate on the Thames South Bank. James managed to get in a few games of tennis with his father, who found – to his cost as well as to his parental pride – that his son had become quite a formidable player. Their wives joined them once in a while and all four had a great time on the court.

A proud father also sat in on one of his son's dubbing sessions. It was a Russian film that was being transcribed into English and he marvelled at the way James was able to adjust his spoken words to the mouth movements and facial expressions of the Russian actor. So, it seemed, did the distinguished film director Michael Powell, who was present and who accepted each of the smooth linguistic substitutions on the first take, which apparently was most unusual.

Next, Philip went to see Clayton in his new offices, located in Tavistock Square, close to the offices of the British Medical Association. He'd left his position as Professor of Community Medicine in Liverpool and taken on his new appointment as Chairman of the Farnsworth Foundation, an institution dedicated to the postgraduate education of family physicians. It was a totally academic appointment and removed Clayton almost completely from most of the actual care of patients. It also represented a marked increase in income, but Philip felt sure this would be neutralized by the higher cost of living in London and by Fleurette's easy access to the tempting shops of London's Westend.

The two brothers had lunch together in Clayton's private office and talked for hours about their professional lives, and about almost everything other than his beloved Fleurette, who evidently still enchanted him. During their long conversation, he was interrupted several times by a phone-call from his wife, and he explained to Philip, somewhat lamely, that she was always eager to know just where he was and what he was doing: the thought made his big brother wince.

Philip also arranged to have lunch with his sister and her husband in a small restaurant off Regent Street, and they reminisced at length about their wonderful parents and how much they missed their love and wisdom. Pauline and Irving were both looking well and were obviously happy in their retirement.

Hats off to Health Minister Dennis Timbrell! He had finally bitten the bullet and defied the medical establishment, and his message was carried to the West Cambrian riding by the local M.P.P. The news release by the Health Ministry read: '**The health clinic operated by the Cambrian District Community Health Association is now under a new financial agreement with the Ministry of Health. The new arrangement is the first of its kind under the Ministry's Health Service Organization program and is a precursor to all new HSO arrangements**'. Their project still stood on shaky ground, but at least the fiscal quicksands that threatened them were now a thing of the past, and the stalwarts – like Jarvis, Tarkins, Appleton, Lawton and Bosnar – could breathe deeply once again. Meanwhile, most of the M.Ds in the group were more concerned with their immediate incomes and the Sabbatical Plan, as well as the political jockeying for power within the group. Ah well, Philip reflected, after all is said and done what can you expect from the most individualistic professionals in society, to whom team play is alien except sometimes in the face of a common threat?

Of all the original rednecks in solo practice, none had been more vitriolic than George McBride. It was hard to forget his purple rage when he came with his entourage to watch Dr. Bosnar do his first trivial case in the Memorial Emergency department. Since that time he'd shown the clinic surgeon nothing but naked hostility, but probably no more so than to the rest of the hated institution. His glowering red face, with its deep-set glittering black eyes, also revealed his enmity to anything and anybody remotely connected with Catholicism, and he never set foot in the

Sisters'hospital. A few months ago he'd undergone surgery in Toronto for an extensive abdominal aneurysm, and made a bad recovery. It was rumored that he wouldn't be practicing again on his return, and had asked his office nurse to direct his patients to go to the doctors of their choice. As a result, Philip was asked to see several of McBride's patients requiring elective surgery for various conditions. The clinic surgeon told these patients that before booking them for hospital admission he'd like to check with Dr. McBride.

It wasn't long before he met the recuperating solo G.P. He was coming into the surgeon's lounge at the Memorial for his mid-morning cup of coffee, and Philip seized the opportunity to talk to him while there was no one else in the room. McBride's face had lost its beefy red complexion and his eyes had lost their glitter. When Philip told him he didn't want to operate on his patients without his consent, he grabbed the surgeon by the arm and astonished him with what he said and the way he said it, with a smile instead of a scowl.

"Listen, Phil, of course you should go ahead. I know you're a damn good surgeon and I'm happy to have you operate on my patients. If you give me their names I'll tell them so myself."

After coffee they strolled together up and down the corridor and Philip asked him all about his operation and wished him continued recovery and a happy retirement. McBride seemed quite touched, and Philip felt a great sense of relief at the healing of a deep rift. Two months later McBride suffered a massive stroke and after a while was transferred to the Chronic Care wing of St. Matthews! Thus did the inexorable advance of events break asunder the constraints of prejudice. As Philip's father would say, "Man proposes, God disposes."

What is it about the relationship between doctors and nurses that is so very special? It was a question Philip had asked himself with increasing frequency over the years, as he watched a deepening and widening chasm between the nursing and medical profession. It was so completely different from his earliest days as a practicing surgeon. To some degree it was the fault of doctors, to a greater degree it was the fault of the new training schools for nurses, to an even greater degree it was the fault of the nurses'unions, and to the greatest degree it was the fault of the new hospital administrations.

Remembering the enjoyment he got from lecturing to the nurses in those early days, and the eagerness of the nurses to learn new ideas and new techniques at these lectures, Philip Bosnar deplored the fact that – by and large – the medical profession had defaulted on its responsibility to maintain the education of nurses, and allowed that education to move from hospital to college classroom. The nurses' training schools emphasized the separation of the two professions, and encouraged a certain sense of competition and even alienation. The labor unions promoted the idea that the doctors made far too much money, 'had it pretty soft'and left most of the dirty work to the nurses. The new administrators in both hospitals, now that the amiable George Proctor had been replaced by an ambitious technocrat, made the nurses aware of their duty to protect the hospital from litigation, even if that meant policing staff doctors and reporting real or imagined deficiencies.

There were two instances that illustrated some of these changing attitudes. The first was an elderly lady who was a surgical cancer patient of Philip's in the Memorial. She was due to be discharged the following day, but before her discharge he advised that she have a final sigmoidoscopic check-up. This was a common instrumental examination of the terminal large bowel,

616   BEYOND THE CITADEL

and if done carefully it should cause minimal discomfort to the patient. Since he'd performed several such examinations on this patient prior to her present admission she readily agreed without apprehension. Half an hour later he was informed that she now adamantly refused, and when he came to see her he found her shaking and in tears. The nurse on duty had given her an operative consent form to sign (Hospital Regulations!) and she refused, thinking this was something different and to be feared. Philip took the form, and in full sight of patient and nurse, tore it up. He then proceeded with the sigmoidoscopy, and the patient returned to her bed none the worse and greatly relieved, since the examination revealed no residual abnormality.

He knew the nurse well and had a high regard for her, so he had no hesitation in discussing the matter with her in confidence.

"You must realize, Dr. Bosnar," she explained, "that we have no choice in the matter. We're told by the head of our hospital nursing department that our first duty is to protect the hospital from litigation."

"And how do you feel about this?"

"Like most of the older nurses I feel that my first duty is to the welfare of the patient and to trust the staff doctor's judgement."

"Of course! And we doctors should trust the nurses, and the patients should trust us both, otherwise the whole system breaks down."

The second incident occurred in St. Matthew's Hospital. Late one morning Gus Pelletier burst into the surgeons' lounge in a towering rage. He'd been conducting his regular morning rounds on the sixth floor surgical ward, and when he asked for a nurse to accompany him, he was told they were too busy, and they were backed up by a belligerent head nurse.

"What did you say or do?" asked Philip.

"To tell you the truth I was too fucking mad to say anything, but I certainly don't plan to put up with that kind of shit."

Philip decided to investigate the situation for himself, went up to the sixth floor and waited for a nurse to accompany him on his ward rounds. They were all unusually busy, sitting and writing at the nurses' desk. The head nurse was also there, her face a study of stubborn bellicosity.

"I'm sorry, Dr. Bosnar, but these are new times and you doctors can't expect to have the nurses running around after you and neglecting their other duties."

"I've no intention of debating the issue with you at this time. Any nurse who accompanies me will learn a good deal about my plans for managing patients' problems and speeding recovery. She in turn can help me by disrobing and positioning them for my examination. I can also learn a lot from the nurse's comments in front of the patient. Later on, if the patient has any questions about what I said, the nurse can provide an explanation."

The head nurse started to splutter and bluster, especially since the seated nurses seemed to agree with his remarks, but Philip cut her short.

"The nurse who accompanies me benefits the patient. Your divisive and uncooperative philosophy does not."

He took one of the smiling nurses by the arm, helped her up from her chair and had her accompany him on his rounds. When he returned he thanked her in front of her redfaced boss to whom he now turned.

"Don't let me hear that you've taken out this episode on any of your junior nurses or there'll be trouble, I promise you!"

His next move was to get in touch with Mukherjee, who was doing such an excellent job as Chief of Surgery. They liked and respected each other and always got along extremely well. When Philip gave him all the details he promised to take appropriate action, and within a month there was no longer any problem getting a nurse to accompany him. He always made allowances when the nurses were shorthanded, but many of his colleagues now did their ward rounds on their own, a move that could only compound the problem and – in time – destroy the precious relationship between doctor and nurse.

The real truth was that Philip Bosnar loved most of the nurses with whom he worked and would have been unable to do his best work for the patient without that love. In some cases the love reached the point of true physical attraction, but marital infidelity never tempted him to the point of having an affair, not even a one night stand, unlike some of his more easily diverted fellow doctors. Not all such liaisons were necessarily initiated by the doctors. In this modern era of feminine emancipation there were more than a few aggressively flirtatious advances by nurses to doctors, and unless backbone ruled over pelvis, the results could be serious. In three or four cases such affairs had actually led to the breakup of marriages, and where there were children this was particularly sad.

As it happened, there were three or four hospital nurses whom Philip found enormously attractive and with whom he established a particularly deep bond of friendship over the years. One was Lola Sefton, that tall and beautiful blonde popularly known as The Divine Lola; she was assistant head nurse on the main surgical floor at the Memorial. Betsy McShane, the outwardly tough but inwardly warmhearted head nurse, was fond of teasing them both about their attraction and affection for each other, and it was a standing joke that in no way impaired a wonderful professional relationship. Nurse Sefton was a superb surgical nurse, and on their ward rounds they made an effective team second to none.

Another favorite was Cathy Nichols, who'd been chief scrub nurse at the Memorial O.R. when he first arrived in San Pete. Not only was she a strikingly good-looking brunette, tiny in stature yet strong in professional competence, but she proved to be a true and dependable friend over the years, and their deep mutual fondness never waned. They loved working together in the O.R. and when she later moved to a medical floor, because of ill health, he felt that he was the loser.

As for the series of office nurses with whom Philip had worked since Amy Butler in 1963, he loved nearly all of them, and most of them reciprocated his affection, but within clearcut and unbreachable bounds of propriety. As with the hospital nurses, affection was one thing but excessive familiarity could be highly destructive and no nurse ever called him by his first name. On the other hand, if they met out of working hours professional restraints were off and they talked to each other as familiar friends. It was his devout hope that the entire medical and nursing professions would preserve this type of mutually affectionate yet respectful attitude, without which the care of patients lost many of the advantages of a truly cohesive and understanding medical team.

It seemed hard to believe that Mark Caplan was no longer with them. Philip's regular visits to this remarkable man, during the years of his purgatory in the chronic care wing at St. Matthew's, were a mixture of pleasure and sadness. It was wonderful to see Mark's spirits remain high and his puckish sense of humor still there, while his body gave way – inch by miserable inch – to inexorable disease. His courage was enormous and he would never complain about his endless days of misery and boredom, with the constant threat of bedsores, problems with bowel and bladder, loneliness, nauseating smells, and unappealing hospital food. Whenever he saw a visitor he would brighten up, ask for a cigarette, and once in a while allow himself to be taken to the cafeteria in a wheelchair when Patty and her bridge friends came to see him as a group and treated him to coffee and cakes.

His wife, Jessica, needed all her remarkable strength of character to sustain her through these incredibly difficult years, and when at last her beloved husband faded quietly away to a peaceful end, it was a merciful relief for her, especially knowing that his suffering was over. He had lived to see the growth, development and success of his two sons in their chosen fields; and throughout his ordeal had been sustained by the deep love and devotion of his loyal wife. He'd made friends with everyone he ever met and it was doubtful whether he'd ever made an enemy.

When Simon Caplan left the Center to embark on a postgraduate training period in Diagnostic Radiology, it was a great loss to the clinic group, but it was nice to know that he would be pursuing his father's specialty. No doubt his clinic colleagues would be seeing him from time to time as a radiology locum at the Center, and whenever Philip saw his good looks and invariable good humor, he would remember Mark – a friend for whom he had the deepest regard and greatest admiration.

CHAPTER 61

1982

The situation with Opdahl had taken on new dimensions. From time to time he would phone Bosnar at his home, usually at dinnertime, with some new and outlandish complaint, and he tended to become somewhat strident when Philip suggested he discuss these matters with him at the office or hospital. Occasionally, he would even book one of Bosnar's surgical cases under his own name, on the pretext that he'd seen the patient on one occasion when his fellow-surgeon was engaged elsewhere. He didn't seem deterred by the fact that the patient was already booked electively under Bosnar's name and that no emergency had arisen in the interim. When Philip changed the booking back to its original status, Opdahl was absolutely livid and no explanation on Philip's part made the slightest difference.

Then, as if a another facet of his character had broken through to the surface, he would stop Bosnar in a hospital parking lot and tell him how sorry he was for behaving so abominably. He confessed that his unbridled ambition tended to get out of hand and caused him to behave in an arrogant and ruthless manner. He told Philip how much he admired his knowledge, experience and operative technique, and on each such confessional he promised to mend his ways. But Philip always told him, "Don't tell me with words. Show me with deeds."

Matters didn't get better; they got worse as office politics entered the picture. The astute Sven had aligned himself heavily with the anti-Appleton faction, with whom he now socialized quite ostentatiously. The surgical referrals took a sharp turn in his direction and away from his fellow-surgeons. Dependable sources of referred work from such F.Ps (Family Physicians) as the Schafers suddenly dried up and went to the new 'Golden Boy'.

It seemed to the Bosnars that the end of the 70s and beginning of the 80s was shaking the world out of its preoccupation with the Cold War as the be-all and end-all of international affairs, and was opening up new possibilities for an era of peace and understanding. At the same time, however, it appeared to confront the world with terrible new dangers.

In the Middle East, the impossible had become the incredible and then the factual. The ultra-hardline Menahem Begin finally signed a peace treaty with Anwar Sadat, returning Egyptian territory won in the Six Day War in exchange for an end to armed hostilities, either declared or guerilla. No matter the arm twisting by Jimmy Carter, the differences over East Jerusalem and the fact that eighteen Moslem nations now cut off diplomatic relations with Egypt, it was the first break in a seemingly hopeless impasse and a ray of sunshine through the black clouds.

The disgusting and clownish tyrant of Uganda, President Idi Amin Dada, who terrorized his own people with torture and death, now was in full flight with the bedraggled remains of his armed thugs. The thought that this grotesque monster had actually been elected President of the

Organization of African States sickened Phil and Patty. It reminded them of Phil's fear, at the end of the Second World War, that the change from British Colonialism to independent Nationalism – in some places – might simply produce despotism.

In the Far East, the rift between China and the U.S.S.R. had grown so deep that Brezhnev finally described the Chinese regime as the most dangerous single threat to world peace. Perhaps there was something to learn about huge differences in outlook and philosophy between nations who prided themselves as followers of the doctrines of Marx and Lenin.

In Britain, the voters had elected the first woman in its parliamentary history to become Prime Minister, and she seemed a true conservative of the old school, but far more hawkish than her predecessors.

Meanwhile, President Carter and Secretary Brezhnev had successfully negotiated another arms treaty, to the obvious dismay of military-industrial establishments on both sides.

In devastated Cambodia, the new government had convicted the genocidal fanatic, Pol Pot, and his accomplice, Leng San, for their hideous crimes in the name of Communism. Unfortunately, the criminals escaped and were nowhere to be found.

In Iran, a country gone mad with religious fundamentalism and vitriolic hatred of America, the reluctant admission of the ousted Shah to the U.S.A. for life-saving surgery was seized as a pretext by Iranian fanatics for an invasion of the American Embassy in Teheran and imprisonment of American hostages who were there. The impotence of the United Nations and of the vaunted might of the United States to do anything against this heinous crime, a flagrant disregard of international law, made the Bosnars feel physically sick.

With the arrival of the 80s the world was witness to the spectacle of the U.S.S.R. duplicating the horrible mistake their western foes had made in Indochina. They invaded Afghanistan, but in this case to save Communism. The doctrines of Marx and Lenin had surely acquired chameleon qualities.

That undistinguished B-movie actor, Ronald Reagan, had become the new President of the United States, but Phil and Patty doubted whether all his huffing and puffing would really change things very much, and the release of the embassy hostages at the change of presidencies in Washington was obviously intended as an affront to Jimmie Carter for daring to try a rescue attempt in Iran, no matter that the total foul-up which occurred was the result of Pentagon incompetence.

February of 1981 couldn't have been a worse time for the accident, but 'Que Sera, Sera,' (What will be, will be) as Doris Day repeatedly informed her rapt audience in Hitchcock's The Man Who Knew Too Much, back in the 50s. The doctors' parking lot at St Matthew's was at its worst, and Philip had always considered it a death-trap in the winter months, especially after witnessing several falls on the snow and ice that covered its uneven tilted surface. A few years ago, at a medical staff meeting, he'd brought up the subject and proposed that the administration take the necessary steps to make the area safe. The motion was carried unanimously but had produced no major results up to the present.

To the left of the parking lot, facing the hospital Chapel, there was a raised sidewalk which was supposed to be kept clear by the maintenance staff. So far, even on the worst days of snowfall, only one or two small areas were cleared, to enable the doctors to go from the sidewalk onto the treacherous surface of the parking lot and vice versa, when driving into or out of the hospital. On this particular morning Bosnar arrived at about 7.50 a.m. for an 8 o'clock case and found the parking lot as slippery as a skating rink, while the sidewalk was heavy with totally uncleared snow. He slithered up the sloping surface in company with two other doctors. They were Jack Collins, a solo family physician and Frank Guzzo, one of his favorite G.Ps. in the clinic. Both agreed that the conditions were dangerous and something must be done to remedy the situation right away. All three left a message for the maintenance department with the central phone operator, and Philip felt sure that it should add considerable weight to the complaint – since Collins had always been a staunch supporter of St. Matthews.

At a 9.45 Philip had finished his surgery and ward rounds and was ready to drive the short distance to the Memorial. Even with the deep treads of his snowboots, he wasn't keen on walking across and returning later on uncertain terrain. As he entered the parking lot, he noticed that not a single shovelful of snow had been removed from the sidewalk, and since Bruce Campbell was just turning on his car's ignition for his way out, Philip stood perfectly still. Without the slightest warning, his feet flew out on the thin icy crust covered by the snow, and he went down hard. When he got to his feet, he looked at his aching left wrist and saw the telltale 'dinner fork' deformity which was so severe that it guarantied a pretty bad fracture. Bruce offered to get Philip a wheelchair but the injured surgeon was too furious to accept.

"To hell with it," he growled, "I'll bloodywell walk."

His good samaritan helped his friend to the emergency department, where they fixed him up with a sling and took him across to the X-ray department. The films showed a nasty multiple fracture, with a number of fragments that looked like large teeth, and severe displacement. When he returned to the emergency department he was met by a concerned-looking Sister Mary Joseph, the new Mother Superior, who naively asked, "Are you in pain?"

"No, Sister," Dr. Philip Bosnar replied, "I'm in anger."

He proceeded to remind her, in blunt language, of repeated complaints about unsafe winter conditions in the doctors' parking lot and the administration's failure to do much about it. Bruce Campbell returned in the nick of time and rescued Philip from becoming too abusive. He accompanied him in the elevator to the O.R. on the fourth floor, where Jacques Leclerc was ready to go ahead with reduction and plaster as soon as possible. But he changed his mind when he realized the patient had eaten a substantial breakfast. Grant Fraser, the group's newest anesthetist from Glasgow was standing by and Philip asked, "How about an IV regional instead of a general?" All agreed, and half an hour later he was wheeled into the O.R, where the portable X-ray arm was in readiness.

The procedure was reasonably painless except for the insertion of the upper traction pin at the elbow level. Once the displacement was completely corrected and everyone was happy with the X-rays, Leclerc applied a plaster cast from knuckles to axilla, incorporating both upper and lower traction pins, with the elbow at right angles. As soon as Bosnar was allowed to get up in the recovery room he phoned his darling Patty and brought her up to date.

"Why didn't you call me sooner?" she asked him.

"I didn't like to worry you," he replied lamely. "By the way, Pat Bradley's here now and he's offered to drive me home, so don't you bother to come up."

When he got back to the doctors' changing room, Abbie Zaffran showed genuine concern and a compassion that was truly touching. He helped Philip get dressed and made sure his overcoat was properly buttoned and his hat correctly placed on his head, with an almost motherly touch. It was a kindness he'd never forget.

It was going to be a slow recovery, and Leclerc doubted whether Philip would be able to operate for another six months at the earliest, but the stubborn patient was determined to prove his orthopod wrong. He started to exercise his left shoulder and fingers until he found himself doing it automatically during every spare moment, and sometimes awakened during the night to find he was still doing his exercises (in a sort of manual sleepwalking).

Next, he made arrangements to resume office practice two weeks after his accident, and in the interim, he flew to Toronto with Patty for a surgical meeting. Jack Stevens came out to the same meeting and sat next to Philip in the auditorium, giving him an opportunity to act as guardian angel. In the evenings, all three arranged to have drinks and dinner together at various restaurants, and Stevens would sing her husband's praises to Patricia.

"I could tell by his expression that he was having a lot of pain even though he never complained."

Philip hated to spoil his act but insisted, "Actually I've had very little pain, and if I scowled, it was because I disagreed vehemently with some of the speakers."

After a month of office appointments, Patty decided Phil was due for a break and she was aided and abetted by Campbell and Stevens, who showed him every consideration and were obviously concerned for his health and welfare. Neither reaction was evident in the behavior of the clinic's youngest surgeon, but perhaps he wasn't one to reveal his warmer sentiments. Patty, that infallible judge of human nature, had met Opdahl on several occasions and found him objectionable from the very first, mainly for a certain arrogance in his manner; moreover she was unwilling to make any excuses for his churlishness.

The Bosnars flew out to Vancouver and had a great time with Florian and their rapidly growing grandson Paul. They met her many friends and visited her business premises in the heart of the downtown area. After that, they took the ferry to Edwardia, where they spent a few days renewing old friendships. It was a wonderful release for both of them, after the anxieties of Philip's accident and the recent disharmonies of the surgical department at the Center.

Returning refreshed and hardly aware of his temporary disability, Philip was ready for work. Not only did he continue with his office routine, but he went up to both hospitals on a regular basis, attending ward rounds and staff meetings, and above all, maintaining his visibility lest some of his younger colleagues write him off prematurely. He also spent far more time with both Appleton and Jarvis.

It seemed that Appleton was retreating into some kind of psychological shell. Since his divorce, he'd been having a highly visible affair with a pleasant, goodlooking new ladyfriend, Susan Dafoe, and the couple seemed destined for eventual marriage, or at least some sort of permanent arrangement. Unfortunately, most of the doctors' wives in the Center took a very dim and biased view of this development. They conducted a thinly veiled campaign of ostracism against the woman they saw (quite erroneously) as the reason behind the Appleton divorce, and it made Jim angry and resentful.

His relationship with Jarvis had also been deteriorating steadily. This was partly due to the fact that the administrator kept expanding his domain, with increasing staff and impressive quarters in the new building, while the medical director kept reducing his already low profile. Philip couldn't contain his impatience and spoke up without mincing words.

"For God's sake, Jim, when you give yourself such a low profile as Medical Director you give the medical group a low profile. You should be expanding your office space, not contracting it, and you should have several assistants, if only to avoid overloading poor Beryl Farnham."

"Perhaps you're right, Phil, but it's not in my nature."

"Wilf Jarvis often complains that you don't keep him informed enough about what's going on at the doctors' level, yet I often see you trotting over to his palatial department but never see him coming over to see you. That not only creates a bad image but encourages the idea that it's the Association and not the medical group that makes this place run. I'd hate to see this become a self-fulfilling prophesy."

"I guess I've been at fault. I've known in my gut for some time that Wilf was winning some sort of power struggle he started, and perhaps now's the best time to fight back."

"Frankly, I feel that Jarvis is a damn good man but he's got too ambitious and if he tries to do that at the expense of our Medical Director then perhaps he should go."

"You're fucking right! It's time I fought back."

"If you don't, Jim, I'm afraid some of your supporters may abandon you and you'll be replaced by someone who views this place in an entirely different light."

Bosnar's interviews with Jarvis were pleasant enough, and seemed fully informative about what was going on behind the scenes with the Board. The Administrator's declining opinion of Appleton was matched by a rising opinion of and indeed a dependence on Jonathan Grey, the distant but pervasive genius of the Association. Philip tried to tell him how wrong he was but clearly failed.

By mid-June, he was ready to start operating, his cast and pins having been removed and his physiotherapy continuing with excellent results. Everything was going along well, although it was obvious that Opdahl had made serious inroads into the senior surgeon's practice during his period of incapacity. He wasn't one to let grass grow under his feet! Nevertheless, Philip was well pleased with his progress and continued to find he was operating without the slightest difficulty or fatigue. In fact, Pandit Mukhejee congratulated him on the degree to which he'd recovered full motion of his fingers, wrist, elbow and shoulder. He felt it was a tribute to Leclerc's treatment and the patient's persistence in exercising the stiffened areas of his left upper limb.

Then, in late July, the patient began to get symptoms of 'Carpal Tunnel Syndrome' in the left hand, most severe after he went to bed, and he found it difficult not to feel somewhat discouraged. (This syndrome is a well-known condition of nerve compression in the wrist compartment). Philip had operated on many such cases with complete success and this knowledge tempered his pessimism. Jacques Leclerc arranged to operate on Philip in one month if the condition failed to improve. He embarked on an intensive course of physiotherapy, anti-inflammatory drugs and a night-splint, and was happy to note a marked improvement in three weeks. Then, when nerve-conduction studies showed a similar improvement, the operation was cancelled and there was a great sigh of relief from all concerned.

The news of the latest departure from the clinic's ranks hit Philip Bosnar very hard, and he knew it was a blow from which it would be difficult to recover. Last year, Bruce Campbell had finally taken over as Chief of Surgery at the Memorial. He was well-liked and respected downtown, but he was becoming frustrated and disillusioned with some of the rebellious elements within the Health Center, and Philip was sure this was one of the factors in Bruce's decision, although there were others.

Last October, Philip had supported Bruce's bid for an increase in his basic retainer, on the grounds that he performed a service in two specialties, general surgery and urology. But this increase was fought bitterly by some of the recalcitrant F.Ps (Family Physicians, formerly known as G.Ps), who claimed that such an advantage to the clinic was offset by the difficulties they sometimes had in finding him during his emergency on-call hours.

Another major factor was the serious problem which had arisen between Bruce and his very pretty and very English young wife. Rumor had it that she'd accused him of fooling around with the wife of one of the clinic physicians, but Philip found that hard to believe. A contributory factor was Cynthia Campbell's love of horses, which had been quite intense since the days of a childhood she hadn't completely outgrown. A move to Southern Ontario, with its farmlands and livestock, grew uppermost in her mind until it became almost an ultimatum to her husband.

Last but not least, there was Bruce Campbell's inability to tolerate the totally self-centered and undiminished arrogance of Sven Opdahl. It was Bruce who first pointed out that their youngest surgeon's closest cronies called him "Seven Up", while those who tolerated him called him Sven, and those who couldn't abide him called him Opdahl or worse. That made it easy to anticipate where one would most likely get the major surgical referrals.

When Bruce Campbell came to see Phil Bosnar and tell him about his decision, he looked uncomfortable and downcast and Bosnar felt sorry for his friend's discomfort.

"I've accepted an offer to take over a urological practice in Broadleigh, a city of some ninety thousand near Toronto. One of their four urologists recently died and another is retiring and turning over his practice."

"Won't you hate leaving all that general surgery you enjoyed so much, Bruce?"

"Of course I will, and I'll miss working in the Health Center, but most of all I'll miss working with you. I like to think you and I made a damn fine combination, and it's too bad there aren't more like you to make this place successful."

"I'm going to miss you a hell of a lot, Bruce, and so will a lot of others, but you have to do what you feel is best for you and your family."

"You know, Phil, you had to make a pretty tough decision yourself when you reached the crossroads of your life at the age of fifty and left Edwardia. Well, for me the crossroads have come at the age of forty-five. I guess you age more slowly than most of us."

When the time came for him to leave, there was considerable consternation in the clinic, but most of all in the surgical department. Where on earth would they find another fine general surgeon who was also a trained urologist? The chances were pretty slim and probably hopeless.

Both Jack Stevens and Bruce Campbell now thought it would be a great idea if Philip took a couple of weeks off before Campbell's departure, and Patricia agreed with unconcealed enthusiasm. They flew to London and booked into a fine hotel-cum-pub just a short distance from their son's home, as they knew Florian planned to come over with young Paul at about the same time. They had a great time together, all three generations, although Clarissa had gone off to live with her father on the Isle of Capri. Bernard was still a striking-looking little lad, as affectionate as ever but full of mischief, and Magdalena was developing into a brunette beauty of no mean standard. She was clearly determined to follow her own independent path in life.

When Bosnar got back, life in the surgical department of the Health Center seemed strange in the absence of Bruce Campbell, and their over-ambitious young surgeon was hardly the man to fill the void. Since Leclerc was now doing the clinic's orthopedics, Bosnar was glad Jack Stevens was getting himself involved in colonoscopies. They occupied several hours a week of his office time and got him really keen on the subject of colonic tumors, a field in which he was becoming increasingly expert. He and the senior surgeon formed an excellent team in combined simultaneous abdominoperineal operations, regardless of who did the upper or lower part of the procedure. Jack was a bold and competent surgeon, although a bit too fast for Philip's taste, where Bruce had been rather slow and cautious.

As for their surgical primadonna, he was using Bruno Coppolino more and more as his assistant. The former extern was now back in town and doing general and vascular surgery. If only they'd been able to wait they would now have him as their third surgeon, along with his easy manner, pleasant attitude and quiet competence. It was a double loss, since Opdahl would have gone elsewhere, perhaps downtown. At least it was nice to know that the amiable Coppolino was using Opdahl as his occasional assistant for arterial surgery, thus returning the compliment as far as the clinic was concerned, although these two individuals were as different as it was possible to imagine.

Bosnar had occasion, from time to time, to call Coppolino into consultation, especially in those cases where the circulatory deficiency was beyond arterial surgery and the clinic surgeon thought sympathectomy (ablation of the nerves causing arterial constriction) might avoid or limit amputation for the unfortunate patient. Coppolino not only endorsed Philip's opinions but did so in a manner that expressed a high regard for the expertise of his older and more experienced colleague, and the clinic surgeon appreciated his courtesy and cooperative attitude. In other circumstances they might now have been working together in the same group practice, but capricious fate preferred the ironic reversal.

Jim Appleton's downfall started with the resignation of Art Spears. Almost since their arrival, he and Fred Crowley had embarked on a course of opposition to their Medical Director, although in the case of Spears the opposition was less doctrinaire and certainly less vitriolic. When he set up his own office across from his residence on Park Road and inserted an ostentatious advertisement in the local press, the Medical Director exploded. He wrote the defector a scathing letter and accused him of stabbing the Health Center in the back. It was a perfect setup for Spears, who now played the injured party to the limit and showed the letter to all his friends at the clinic.

What followed was a major attempt to unseat Appleton, which was only narrowly defeated, thanks once again to a small loyal group which included Pat Bradley, Jack Stevens and Philip Bosnar; but their chastened Director was forced to send an apology to Spears. Philip felt sure Jim's lack of diplomacy in handling the matter had a lot to do with his anger at the rejection of his ladylove by many of the clinic doctors and most of their wives.

The second factor in this sad series of events was the Ontario doctors' rebellion against the Provincial Government over its stand on the schedule of medical fees. It was no new disagreement by any means, but simply the heating up of an old issue to the boiling point. The O.M.A. sponsored a controlled action by its members: a shut-down of doctors' offices and suspension of medical coverage except for emergency work.

Although the Health Center kept its doors open, most of the clinic doctors honored the slowdown and attended an 'Educational Day' at the Lakeshore Inn. In actual fact this was a series of meetings and speeches in which the doctors gave vent to their feelings of betrayal by the government. Emergency services at both hospitals continued unabated, and even moderately urgent cases were attended on the wards and in the O.Rs.

There was no genuine doctors' strike, and the situation wasn't nearly as bad as the media were reporting. Although it was true that the fee-for-service system was being milked to the limit, and a good deal of extra-billing was hard to justify, the government wasn't being fair in carrying out its part of the bargain. Since it was the government's decision to maintain the fee-for-service system, it really couldn't justify the widening gap between the O.M.A.'s fee schedule and that of the Health Ministry, especially with major increases in office costs.

It seemed to Philip that the Ontario government was using the recent Wage and Price Control legislation as an excuse for reneging on its agreement with the O.M.A. That agreement amounted to a commitment to narrow the gap between the two fee schedules to an acceptable level over the next few years. It had been shelved for the duration of the controls, but once the controls were off the government seemed determined to return to square one – as though the agreement prior to controls had never been reached. Listening to recorded speeches from their O.M.A. representatives in the Toronto heartland, Philip thought how sterile they sounded and asked if he could address the gathering from the platform and the chairman graciously assented.

Philip expressed his thoughts as succinctly as possible, pointing out where the medical profession was just as much at fault as the government in the present impasse. He reminded the audience that fee-for-service wasn't engraved in stone and was beset by many disadvantages, and that doctors were too preoccupied with internecine warfare to present a truly united front. The loud applause that followed his remarks surprised him, as did the many favorable comments from downtown solo practitioners over the next few days.

It was at this sensitive and critical point that his good friend, Jim Appleton, threw caution to the winds and wrote a letter to the O.M.A. denouncing the Ontario doctors' action against the government. He wrote it on Health Center stationery and signed it as Medical Director of the Cambrian District Medical Group. There was an immediate howl of protest, not only from downtown but within the medical group itself; and from the rednecks within the O.M.A. Worse still, it caused Frank Guzzo, one of their finest F.Ps, to resign in protest and transfer his practice to the Foley Medical Building. Jim Appleton's follow-up letter, explaining that he'd written as an individual and not on behalf of the clinic's medical group, was too little and too late.

CHAPTER 62

1982 cont'd

Freddy Stewart was dead. Even in the earliest days he'd never shown the extreme antagonism to the Community Health Center that was prevalent at the time. At the very worst he would direct some witty wisecracks at the group but never with malice. It was Stewart who, it was reported, had read out Bosnar's resume' in his capacity as Staff President at the Memorial and observed (incorrectly as it turned out) that nobody could limit this new surgeon's operating privileges. Later, when the Center first ran into its anesthetic crisis with Pat Hogan, he was one of those who volunteered his services for Philip's afternoon case.

Slowly but surely, a strong bond of mutual respect and liking developed between them, and on one occasion he invited Philip to his home for a game of chess, with Steve Ramidan and John Webber as onlookers. (Webber had been one of the most rigid supporters of the anesthetic boycott and swore he would never raise a finger to help "any doctor working for the Union"). They actually played three quick games in which Stewart proved himself a good tactician but lacking in strategy. Philip complimented him on his ability and he glowed with pride, although the games were noteworthy more for the wonderful cordiality of the occasion than their high standard.

Several months later Philip returned the invitation and Freddie Stewart accepted. It was later on, when the games were finished and they sat drinking their scotch whiskies to an accompaniment of quiet recorded music, that Stewart began to reveal more of his background, of which Philip already knew a good deal. Freddy was a genuine war hero, having served with the Canadian Army in the Italian Campaign and given up his right leg and the function of his left shoulder in the Allied campaign against the Nazi enemy.

After the tragic death of his wife from advanced cancer he became severely addicted to alcohol, and it was still a serious problem. He was also a very heavy smoker and that didn't help his bronchitis and emphysema. Above all, he was a man of considerable imagination and intellect, who hid these virtues behind the mask of a buffoon. During all the years Philip knew him he never detected the slightest evidence of malice in Freddy, only goodwill and a warm personality. The impersonal funeral for this man of genuine worth only reminded Philip that he would miss him very much.

Shortly after Philip's letter to the Board, a special joint meeting of the Board and the Medical Executive took place, and he was invited to attend. The Chairman opened the meeting by apologizing to him on behalf of the Association for any embarrassment or injury they had caused him by virtue of the decision to engage Professor Jenkins to write the official History of the Health Center. He claimed (and Philip believed him) that as new President of the Board he had no idea that there was any question of Philip being the designated author.

At this point Philip informed the meeting in no uncertain terms about the sequence of events and his disappointment at the way he'd been sidetracked while a decision was being finalized behind his back. Jarvis now rose to present himself as the injured party falsely accused of double-dealing, and read out a letter from the absent Jonathan Grey offering congratulations for his wise selection of Zachary Jenkins to author of the forthcoming Community Health Center history. It all seemed like a piece of Byzantine deception that had backfired and it was entirely possible that the fault lay with Grey rather than Jarvis, a man for whom Philip still retained a healthy degree of respect and admiration.

Stanley Featherstone now rose, and with the expression of a cat poised to swallow a canary, suggested that the meeting might like to hear his abbreviated history of the C.H.C, entitled 'The Ants and the Bees'. It was about a colony of blue ants who were good workers and lived on an ant-hill. A number of bees also lived in the same area. They had been away for many years learning how to make honey and felt they had the sole rights to make that honey. Since the ant families often needed honey when they were sick, they were compelled to go to the beehive whether they liked it or not. Some of the ants found the resident bees overbearing and slow in delivering honey when required or when convenient to the ant population.

The story continued, in Featherstone's drily humorous manner, with the ants building their own beehive and filling it with a sufficient number and variety of tame bees to provide all the honey needed by those ants who wished to use the new beehive. The tame bees and their honey-making were under the direction of Super-bee, while the administrator of the new beehive was known as Super-ant and the group that assisted him in running the hive was known as a 'Plank'. In addition to the cold war between the resident bees and the newcomer tame bees, there were disputes between the tame bees and the members of the Plank that became worse as the tame bees suspected the Plank was gaining too much control of the hive. The situation became critical when Super-ant and his associates decided that the glorious history of the blue ants' hive should be written by an imported writer who would concentrate on the ants' contribution.

Super-bee and his fellow tame bees (no longer willing to be considered tame) felt it was more appropriate for the history to be written by one of their own. They were the ones making the honey and they had the very able bee willing to write the history from the bees' viewpoint. Besides, they had been the ones who had to face the hostility of the resident bees and their supporters ever since the building of the new beehive. When Super-ant and his supporters went ahead with their own history writer it was the beginning of the end and the ants' beehive was finally sold.

It was a brilliant allegory and its conclusion was a clear warning to the Association and its manager. It was received with a variety of reactions, from appreciative laughter to awkward silence, and in the case of Al Smithwick by deep anger, leading to his eventual resignation from the Board.

A few days later, Jim Appleton dropped his bombshell in a memorandum to the Joint Executive Committee and Wilfred Jarvis. It stated that it would be counterproductive if the History were used to manipulate the structure and function of the C.H.C. He concluded with the extraordinary opinion that the History, as far as he was concerned, was a 'NON-ISSUE'! At this point Philip felt as though his friend Jim had dealt him a massive blow to the body and he felt physically sick. The memorandum continued with a justification of the decision by Zachary Jenkins to write the History and his right to do so. Surely, Philip insisted, and his colleagues with him, it was the

Board's unilateral decision to commission Jenkins and fund his book from C.H.C. coffers that was the real issue.

When Philip had swallowed his bile and recovered his equilibrium after reading Jim's convoluted and bloodless dissertation, he mourned the loss of that outraged supporter who, less than a year ago, was prepared to do ultimate battle to ensure that the writing of their history would remain securely in Philip's hands. The letter Philip now wrote to Jim Appleton expressed his disappointment at his untimely capitulation. He predicted his imminent rejection as Medical Director by the medical partnership.

'It is with deep regret' he wrote, 'that I can no longer support you in that office. I am sorry to report that you have also lost the support of others who have always been steadfastly in your corner up to this time.'

By a strange quirk of fate, Doug Mottram became one of Philip Bosnar's prime sources of local folklore concerning the past history of St. Pierre's medical profession in the period preceding the arrival of the C.H.C. When Philip first met him in the surgeon's lounge at St. Matthews he'd been cold and aloof, with the appearance and manner of an army general faced with a new and insubordinate officer. He was Chief of Ob.Gyn. and reserved his main hostility for Tony Donovan. When Donovan led the first exodus from the Center, Mottram became friendly with Philip and expressed his attitude quite freely about "turncoats" like Donovan and "self-appointed gods" like Glenn Morecombe. He revealed to the clinic surgeon that in earlier days it was Herb Slater, before his mellowing years of seniority, who ruled the local doctors with a combination of naked force and generous inducements. Slater made it quite clear that he was the final arbiter of which new doctor could come to San Pete and who could stay. The price of admission and of survival was to keep in the good graces of the Emperor Slater, and the rewards were more than generous.

There were many other similar confidences and these dovetailed nicely with those that were periodically relayed to Philip by Dick Roberts (leading anesthetist at the Memorial) and others. When the time came for the solo and group doctors to bury the hatchet with the formation of the new Academy, it was Mottram's chuckling voice that was heard loudly at a Memorial staff meeting, exclaiming, "Oh good! Now we can all go back to fighting among ourselves."

Flora Mottram, Doug's socially prominent wife, was extremely active in the local art and social circles, and when Philip had his thespian stint with the local theater group in the play 'Noah', she and Patricia found themselves in overlapping social circles. As a result, not only were they thrown together increasingly at various ladies' gatherings, but Doug Mottram and Philip became frequent companions at cocktail parties and other social functions, and developed a pleasant and comfortable relationship. It was nice to see this otherwise rather stiff and austere individual when he and Philip were in each others company, and Flora Mottram cherished a picture taken by a mutual friend that showed her relaxed husband making a winning shot against Philip in a game of tabletop 'deck football'.

Philip was sorry when Doug Mottram died of a stroke, and felt that in some ways the fates had revealed more of the true person to him than to most – despite their vast differences in medical politics – and his widow assured him that this was truly so. After Doug's untimely death, she remained a good friend of Phil and Patty, and they were pleased to see her throw herself enthusiastically into sponsoring the artistic life and growth of their city in all its aspects.

Jim Appleton's days as Medical Director were numbered and there was no hope of rescuing him from his own actions, yet once again he came up with one of those extraordinary changes of direction that Philip found so upsetting. Barely two weeks after that awful memorandum in which he defined the History as a non-issue he wrote two letters to Jenkins on successive days and the contents made astounding reading. Both castigated the author on his political bias in favor of the role played by the steelworkers' union and its representatives, rather than the medical group, in allotting credit for the success of the C.H.C..

A long paragraph in the second letter said it all.

'The overall theme is that of long suffering and underprivileged steelworkers and their representatives and administrators engaged in a struggle against powerful and avaricious physicians both without and within the program, save for one lonely slightly progressive medical director, who capitulated unendingly to the forces of evil in the medical profession. Why didn't you congratulate our medical staff for turning every attack on them by the local profession into an advantage and increasing security and growth of the program? Your book is a scathing indictment of the medical profession. In other context it might perhaps be deserved, but it is an especially scathing indictment of members of the Cambrian District Medical Group whose presence, cooperation and program development have made the whole production possible. There is no recognition in your manuscript of the fact that we have attracted from among the general medical graduates good quality physicians who have been willing to have themselves tarred with the Union Clinic brush and as a result have been castigated, ostracized and belittled by their colleagues in solo practice and organized medicine. At the same time administrators, union board members and authors become public defenders and heroes among their own colleagues. When the flames of controversy are fanned the doctors take the battering and the administration and the board take the glory. Is the sensitivity of our physicians not then quite understandable?'

This time, Philip was sorry to observe, it was a case of far too much far too late, and he felt that much of the belated criticism was unfair. The author had faithfully discharged his commission from the Association to write a detailed history of the C.H.C. according to his research, his interviews, and his political background as an intellectual activist for the British Labor Party. The last paragraph of Jim's second letter to Jenkins summed up the crux of the omission from the History that was bound to be the result of authorship by him rather than by Philip or another senior group doctor. For that reason it was to the Board that all of these objections should have been made.

As the Appleton letters to Zachary Jenkins stated, the author could write anything he damn-well pleased and in fact had done a very good job on the History according to his own lights. That wasn't the issue; it was the pre-empting of an author chosen by the medical partnership, who would have given the group doctors their rightful recognition and appreciation, by one who would nonetheless emphasize the role of the Association, the Board and the Executive director.

The international scene for the past twelve months had been a sad one and its train of tragic events made the problems of the medical scene in San Pete seem trivial in the extreme by comparison.

A new war had broken out, this time between Britain and Argentina over a tiny group of windswept islands in the Southern Atlantic. The only good to come out of the sorry affair was the opportunity for Argentineans to throw out their corrupt and repressive generals who had misgoverned the nation and thrown it into a war designed to recapture some degree of support, on a wave of patriotic wartime fervor. Other byproducts of this miniwar were the proof that aluminum superstructures on British vessels burned furiously when hit by French Exocet missiles, and the fact that Prime Minister Thatcher gained rather than lost national popularity in a country not yet fully recovered from the last war.

There were unsuccessful assassination attempts against President Reagan and Pope John Paul 11, both by mentally deranged individuals. In Egypt a group of religious fundamentalists in the army were more successful, in their assassination of President Anwar Sadat. He had finally and inevitably paid the price for the Camp David accords with Israel, and one could be sure that Prime Minister Begin would become steadily more intransigent and lead his Likud Party into a rigidly uncompromising nationalism.

Disturbing questions now arose. Would his Zionism, tainted by ultranationalism, force Begin into a vengeful campaign against the P.L.O, the terrorist organizations and Arab States that fostered them? Would he be able to control his avenging armies, headed by such strong-willed militarists as General Sharon, hero of the Yom Kippur War? As far as the Likud Party was concerned, the murder of Sadat had been ordered by the renegade Palestinians and terror could not go indefinitely unanswered.

Chapter 63

1983

When Jim Appleton resigned his position as Medical Director in the face of major opposition from the partnership, Philip knew an era had passed for the Health Center and it would never be quite the same again. The entire staff, both medical and non-medical, threw Jim a great party at which they wished him bon voyage on his journey to the Bahamas. That was where he planned to take a three month Sabbatical leave of absence in the field of Public Health, accompanied by his new and radiant bride.

The tug-of-war for a new medical director began almost at once and Philip was approached early by several of the partners, but he made it clear at once that under no circumstances would he consider taking such a position. There were, in fact, only three partners whom he would consider for the job. The first of these was Peter Lawton, who shared Appleton's viewpoints but wasn't under the influence of Grey and Jarvis. Unfortunately, he often became tongue-tied at meetings and this could prove disastrous at times of dissension. The second was Kevin Lam, who was dynamic and decisive, but had already been characterized by his critics as an 'Appleton clone',which was both untrue and unfair, but made his election most unlikely. The third, oddly enough, and one who would really shake up the old guard in the Board, was the quiet but highly efficient Stan Featherstone, author of that magnificent skit, 'The Ants and the Bees.'

As Featherstone's name came to the forefront, another contender for the position suddenly emerged, complete with a solid block of supporters headed by the Schafers, and with a tireless lobbyist in the person of the firebreathing oncologist, Tom Bufold. The candidacy of Fred Crowley had been carefully prepared and cunningly concealed, and Philip shuddered at the thought of having such a volatile and disruptive individual as new Medical Director. It would certainly hasten his own retirement and might lead to a major walkout by some of the older partners.

After a series of elections in which there was a tied vote between Crowley and Featherstone, despite passionate lobbying of a few waverers by Pat Bradley, it came down to a one vote majority in favor of the unflappable and uncharismatic radiologist, with one abstention. At this point, there was a determined effort by the hard core of Crowley's support to challenge the validity of Philip Bosnar's vote. However, at a meeting of the medical executive a year ago and with Crowley as one of the members, it had been determined that after the age of sixty-five a clinic doctor could retain his partnership on a year-to-year basis. It would be done by executive decision, up to the age of seventy-one, and Philip was not yet seventy. Thus, the vote held by a tenuous thread, but battle lines had been drawn; and in the long run Jim Appleton was proven almost right when Philip once jokingly asked him whether he thought the historical prediction, "Aprés moi, la déluge" applied to him and he answered, "Of course it does."

The incursion by Palestinians across the Lebanese border and the rocket attacks on Northern Israeli settlements could only be tolerated for just so long by Menahem Begin, his Likud party and a large segment of the Israeli population. All he could see, so far, in exchange for giving up the Sinai Peninsula to Egypt – including the oilfields developed by his engineers – was the murder of the Egyptian leader with whom he had signed a peace treaty, and continued hostility from his Arab neighbors.

There was only one solution left to the hardliners: the invasion of Lebanon and expulsion or destruction of the P.L.O. organization hiding in Beirut and the Palestinian refugee camps. In both places the P.L.O. guerillas had surrounded themselves with their families: women, children and the elderly, so the Israeli Army had to attack through their homes and human buffers before getting to the P.L.O. core. What an ingenious method of branding the invaders as heartless monsters and swinging world sentiment to the Palestinian cause. What a stupid lack of foresight by Israeli hardliners and militarists, when unfavorable world opinion could eventually destroy Israel much more effectively than the P.L.O. at its worst.

One evening following their return from the Bahamas, the Appletons visited Phil and Patty, bearing gifts. There were two dark crayon portraits of young native children, one a shy little girl and the other a rambunctious little boy. In addition, they brought along two busts of adult Bahamians, a male and a female, carved in mahogany. The travellers recounted their experiences on the Islands, where they'd been treated like visiting royalty and had a wonderful time. They were determined to go back whenever they could and it seemed to Phil and Patty that the Caribbean Sabbatical had been just the antidote the Appletons needed to overcome their feeling of rejection during the events of the past year.

As if the fates were determined to compound the changes that came over the Health Center during these days of upheaval, the indomitable figure of Bill Trevor would no longer tower over the institution he founded. He died of rapidly advancing lung cancer at the age of seventy-one. It was hardly surprising, since he was a lifelong cigarette smoker despite his obsessive concern for the better health of his community. His memory would not die, however, and he would always be remembered as the driving force behind the origin of the Health Center. Despite their differences, Philip recognized Trevor's greatness and his invincible spirit. He would not easily be replaced in the trade union movement of their city, indeed the nation.

Sven Opdahl was now practicing as if he were an entirely independent surgeon in the clinic, with his own referral base and his own political group. Pursuing this independent line, he made a startling and one-sided decision to refer all of the clinic's arterial surgery to Coppolino. This was done without consulting either his fellow surgeons or the new Medical Director. Had he wished to give up vascular work after his initial avidity for this demanding field of expertise, he could have returned it to Philip, who would then have worked out a happy arrangement with Coppolino. It would have been one in which they would assist each other in such cases and mutually develop a program advancing the scope of vascular surgery in the community.

It was all part of a pattern in Opdahl's arrogant behavior. Their last clash had been over the purchase of an ultrasonic monitoring device for impaired arterial circulation in the limbs, particularly the legs. George Proctor had called Dr. Bosnar into his office one day, and asked if he had any ideas for improved equipment in the vascular diagnostic department: specifically for arterial cases which might require surgery. Bosnar suggested an inexpensive Doppler apparatus that was portable and would give the patients good service, until such time as they could set up a full modern vascular laboratory equivalent to those in major centers. The apparatus finally chosen seemed to fit the bill perfectly. Shortly after its purchase, an irate Sven Opdahl phoned Philip at his home. He still seemed to favor his senior partner's dinner hour for complaints.

"You had no right to advise such a purchase, Dr. Bosnar. Bruno and I were in the process of forming a vascular surgery committee and then we were going to select suitable equipment far superior to the one you selected."

"I don't believe I owe you any explanation, Sven, especially as you chose to keep the subject of such a committee so completely secret. It would, I presume, have included anyone with a special interest in this field of surgery."

"Oh, of course. We certainly meant to include you."

"Did you really? Well, for your information, the first time the present administrator asked me was when I was still chief of surgery at the Memorial and this recent purchase was simply the end result of that enquiry. We certainly weren't aware that the major purchase of a full vascular lab was on the books at this time. Perhaps it would be better if you could learn to communicate with your fellow surgeons."

As time went by, Philip had the feeling that Opdahl was gathering a block of supporters in the Center who might eventually defect downtown, and that viewpoint was shared by quite a few of his closest colleagues.

At the urging of his friends, both in the Clinic and downtown, Philip sued the administration of St. Matthew's Hospital for his injuries. The amount wasn't great by American standards, but the action was necessary to send an unmistakable signal that the safety and welfare of all the doctors on hospital staff were still a responsibility of hospital management. The hospital lawyer, Anthony Brutelli, no friend of either Philip or the C.H.C, fought the case fiercely, almost vindictively. His defense was that the accident was due either to the surgeon's personal carelessness or defective footwear, and in any event, Dr. Bosnar should be ready for retirement at his age.

This comment afforded Philip's professional peers in surgery and anesthesia an opportunity to write out glowing refutations, stating that they would unhesitatingly choose him as their personal surgeon as soon as his recovery was complete. In the end, the chagrined Brutelli capitulated and a settlement was made. More importantly, the doctors' parking lot was resurfaced and levelled, while snow removal was stringently enforced. Philip's orthopod, Jacques Leclerc, felt the hospital had got off much too lightly, because there was always a chance of subsequent arthritis in the injured wrist as a sequel to the accident, but Philip was satisfied with the result and let the matter rest.

With the media constantly reminding the public of worldwide terrorism, the horrid civil war in Northern Ireland and the miserable happenings in Israel, Philip and his wife both agreed that the so-called civilized world was largely to blame. First, what was a terrorist act? It wasn't the bombing of British troops in Belfast but it certainly WAS the bombing of innocent civilians in a pub or a shopping area in Derry. It wasn't the bombing of a U.S. marine base in Beirut but it certainly WAS the bombing of a civilian airport in Tel Aviv. It wasn't the killing of Israeli soldiers by Palestinians in Gaza but it certainly WAS the murder of Israeli athletes in Munich. The underlying or purported political grievance was not the essence of terrorism. It was the selection of innocent and defenseless civilians as targets for hijacking, hostage-taking and murder. Sooner or later, it would turn those fighting terrorism into similar tactics and rationalizations. That was what the Bosnars feared might happen in Israel, under the increasingly hardline government of that troubled nation.

Philip's seventieth birthday was celebrated with a great party held in the officers' mess at the local Armories. Most of the arrangements were made by Pat Bradley, who was medical officer in the army reserve with the acting rank of Major. The invited guests included friends from bridge, tennis and art circles. There were doctors from the clinic and downtown, but only those whom the senior surgeon regarded as his closest friends in the profession, regardless of their political affiliations, along with their spouses. The bar was hyperactive and the bartenders proved they were practiced experts at their craft. The dinner was delicious and was catered by Joe Farentino, who ran the Gioconda restaurant downtown and regularly managed all the regimental dinners at the armories.

The festivities included a number of laudatory speeches, full of sentimental hyperbole that owed much to the pre-dinner refreshments and the table wine. The main tribute came from Armand Coté, who waxed quite witty and eloquent as he made the presentation of Philip's birthday gift from the medical group, an attractive set of Eskimo carvings. The Bosnars had a fine time and both agreed that the affair had gone off without a hitch. Nobody got mad and nobody got falling-down drunk.

The celebration of the Health Center's twentieth anniversary was another gala affair. It was held at the new Hilton Hotel on the waterfront, and was attended by the non-medical staff who constituted a large majority; by the medical staff; by Board representatives of the Association; by local civic leaders; by members of the provincial government and the International Steelworkers' Union. Accompanying these personnel were their spouses, and the assembly could just as easily have been mistaken for the top echelons of traditional organized medicine rather than the minions of an erstwhile 'Union Clinic Looking around the vast banquet hall, one was filled with a dizzying sensation of success and even of a new social and professional establishment.

Among the dignitaries at the head table were Jonathan Grey as the Center's éminence grise, Wilfred Jarvis as Executive Director, Dale Christoff as Chairman of the Board, Stan Featherstone as new Medical Director and Jim Appleton as original and Emeritus Medical Director. Paul Haskins was there from the head office of the United Steelworkers of America, and Dr. Bertram Macintosh from the Ontario Health Ministry.

After a long interval for cocktails, and the slow filling of tables by late arrivals looking for their designated places, dinner was served, the wine flowed freely and the great gathering settled comfortably to the banquet sounds of good food being handled with gusto, clinking wine glasses, conversation and laughter. Women stole surreptitious glances at the evening wear of those at nearby tables and men tried to look comfortable in their suits and ties, since these were the days of casual male attire in the workplace and not infrequently at evening social events.

Patty was happy that she and Phil hadn't been assigned to the head table but disappointed that none of their many friends were at their own table. Instead, their assigned dinner companions were three of the clinic's youngest F.Ps and their wives. They in turn must have felt less than comfortable in the company of a senior surgeon and his wife, with a full generation gap. Fortunately, he was able to break the ice by getting off a few harmless jokes and guiding the conversation along humorous lines. Despite the relaxed and jovial feeling at the table, however, it was obvious that there was little in common between veterans of the Health Center and this new breed who had little emotional involvement in its history.

Eventually, it was time for introductions at the head table and then the speeches. Phil and Patty glanced at each other from time to time as they reacted in unison to the paeans of mutual praise and thinly veiled self-congratulation coming from the speakers. There was a noticeable absence of any reference to the courage and dedication of those doctors who stuck with the clinic through its darkest days. Only Featherstone had a few passing words of appreciation for "those stalwarts, Drs. Appleton and Bosnar," and this subdued tribute was followed by scattered applause. Appleton's remarks in response sounded petulant, revealing a persistence of the anger he'd expressed in his letters to Zachary Jenkins. As far as he was concerned, this present celebration was simply more of the same and Philip had to agree with his sentiments.

The speeches finally came to an end, various awards were presented and a dance band took charge of the festivities. Patty was only too glad to get away from the table and trip the light fantastic on the dance floor with her beloved. There was no doubt the Association had every reason to celebrate the twenty-year survival and triumph of the Cambrian District Community Health Center, but it was BECAUSE OF and not IN SPITE OF its doctors. As for the local civic leaders and government spokesmen, Patty wanted to ask them, "Where were you when we really needed you?"

CHAPTER 64

1984

It didn't seem possible but it finally happened. They were taking down the radar installation across the water and from now on the rhythmic, brassy bleep would no longer haunt the Bosnars' musical reception. Philip could get rid of the lead-lined X-ray film-holders and unwrap the metal foil from all the stereo wiring. The SAC bomber station was being dismantled and would soon be replaced by a new penitentiary, and Northern Michigan's despair at the drastic change would match Philip's elation at once again listening to unpolluted music. He should somehow feel guilty but was too occupied in a frenzy of recording from radio and phonograph on to cassette tapes. It all seemed like a dream, and he wondered what it would be like when mankind's progressive pollution of land, water and air also came to a merciful end.

Whenever they used to drive through Coppercliff and Sudbury, Phil and Patty were appalled by the despoliation of all three environments by the deadly fumes emerging from the chimney stacks carrying noxious gases from the nickel ore smelters that were the source of the area's livelihood. Yet in recent times it was truly miraculous to see what had been accomplished by public pressure, civic pride and a determination to change things. The dirt and devastation had been replaced by renewed growth of grass and trees, clean streets and gleaming buildings, and fish were returning to the lakes while the air that one breathed no longer smelled like a cesspool.

When Phil and Patty thought of some of the beautiful places in Canada where the inhabitants had to inhale the stench of unregulated pulp-mills from which they derived their daily bread, their hearts bled for the almost casual and careless environmental pollution. It had taken some sensible decisions by the authorities to close down that SAC station and its associated radar installation in neighboring Michigan, and it would take similarly wise decisions in their own country to stop the fouling of their own environment.

The investment campaign was in deep trouble and Dwight Crane was being charged with fraud. It was a group of physicians in the Toronto area who initiated the proceeding and despite Philip's steady losses due to Crane's phony promises he somehow felt sorry for him. He was like a faulty automobile with an excellent motor, a smooth steering mechanism, but no reverse gear, no brakes and no rear view mirrors. Most of the ventures in his recommended portfolio were losers and had it not been for their R.R.S.P. program the prospects for a comfortable retirement would have been bleak indeed for the Bosnars.

To add to Philip's still unblemished record as possessor of the anti-Midas touch, the income tax ferrets now descended upon the medical partnership with a new decision. Their accumulated Sabbatical Plan savings would now be taxed as total earned income for 1984-1985, thus wiping out a large portion of this financial benefit. Philip had pressed very hard for an amortized system of payment at retirement, preferably over a ten year period and at an agreed rate of interest, but all such suggestions were now irrelevant and all protests from their accountants and lawyers were fruitless.

In a way this tax decision precipitated the departure of three members of the medical partnership. Angus McTavish, one of the group's finest and least troublesome G.Ps went into the Foley medical building, and although he assured Philip that this was because of the dissensions within the group, the real reason appeared to be that his wife now became his office nurse and receptionist. As for the Schafers, they moved into the new doctors' building across the road from Memorial Hospital, and their excuse was that they couldn't continue to work under Featherstone as their medical director.

It was obviously only a matter of time before the Crowley-Opdahl conglomerate moved out in a separate partnership downtown, and like many of his colleagues Philip almost welcomed the inevitable defection, although he worried about such valuable physicians as Atkins and Dubois being inveigled into this plan. Atkins seemed to have transferred his dislike of Appleton to a growing distrust of Featherstone, while Hector Dubois – one of their finest family physicians – was fearful that the clinic was in danger of falling apart.

One of the major casualties of the present schism within the partnership was Jack Stevens, and the irrepressible Armand Coté was quite direct in keeping Philip informed of what was being whispered.

"You know what good friends the Stevens are with Freda and me but I have to tell you that there is a real campaign being waged against Jack. Most of it comes from Fred Crowley who's supposed to be a good friend of his and it's being organized by Sven."

"What sort of gossip are they spreading?"

"Well, Fred thinks that Jack is in Featherstone's pocket and he echoes Opdahl's criticisms of his surgical work."

"Exactly what are those criticisms?"

"Too fast and too careless. Too many mistakes. Bad public relations with patients and families as well as with the G.Ps."

"I think those criticisms are politically motivated and are just a way of discrediting him."

"Frankly I've never understood his continuing friendship with Fred Crowley."

"The self-appointed critics probably have a few juicy items circulating about me."

"Well, Crowley simply hates your guts for your earlier support of Appleton and your present support of Featherstone. His main concern is getting you retired and out of the way."

"How about our overly ambitious young surgeon."

"He probably hates your guts, too, but mostly as a rival who stands in his way. He admires your knowledge and your operative technique but would be happy to see you retire. Sometimes I think he's actually afraid of you."

"I certainly hope so. He needs somebody who can handle his bloody arrogance and hype."

"You're right about the hype. He's very convincing though, especially with the patients' families and with his G.Ps, and hands them a pretty good line."

"Just as long as he doesn't talk some of our better guys into joining the exodus, whenever it comes."

In sharp contrast with the substance of this conversation was the behavior of Opdahl at surgical ward rounds. Although he always made a point of sitting as far away from Jack Stevens and Philip as possible, and usually close to Pelletier, he was enthusiastic in endorsing Philip's opinions, almost without exception. This was in sharp contrast to his first year or two, when he was only too eager to contradict his senior colleague's views, no matter what. Perhaps he was now trying to convince the downtown surgeons that he held no personal or professional animosity toward Philip, but few if any were convinced.

Philip's relations with Jim Appleton had improved steadily over the past year. At first he had to seek out the deposed director in his new quarters on the ground floor of the clinic extension, and chat with him about a variety of matters. As far as their new Medical Director was concerned, although Jim had supported him strongly against the attacks of the Schafers, Fred Crowley and the others, he was far from an unqualified admirer of Stanley Featherstone; even less of his Korean wife, Cathy, whom he called "Catherine the Great" or more colloquially, "The Empress." These views were clearly shared by the new Mrs. Appleton and – sad to say – by an increasing number of the doctors who'd voted for Featherstone.

After a while, it was Jim who came up to the surgical offices on the second floor and joined Philip and Jack Stevens for tea, and it was nice to know that there were few residual hard feelings. Their junior surgeon hardly ever joined them at these times.

Meanwhile, although he had frequent contact with the new Medical Director, Philip didn't feel that he had any real influence on his decisions, but was careful not to press the point. At first, Stan Featherstone had fallen quite heavily under the hype-laden influence of the persuasive Sven Opdahl, but as the months went by he became progressively more disillusioned and finally was no longer entranced. Philip felt sure that once Stan learned how to evaluate the members of his medical group a bit more accurately, his managerial skills would make him a fine Director, albeit a far more expensive one than his predecessor.

Under the productivity bonus system, which was based on the fee schedule, a well-organized and highly capable radiologist like Featherstone could make a fortune and did. Added to that was the retainer for his duties as Medical Director and the extra fees he earned on weekends by going up to the Northshore towns and reading their X-rays; all this came to a sum that was far out in front of the other specialties and seemed quite obscene to the G.Ps. How people like Wilfred Jarvis reacted to these income figures could only be imagined, but one felt sure the descriptive language would be colorful.

Jim Appleton, to his credit, was now running a highly efficient and busy family practice, with an expanding income, but he regarded Stanley's income as quite beyond the bounds of propriety and certain to cause dissension. In a way, Philip could understand his feelings. While he was still medical director Jim had to let Jacques Leclerc go because of his demands for a greatly increased retainer. He pointed out to Leclerc that any major discrepancy between the earnings of different members of the surgical department would cause too great an upheaval. As a result, the Center lost its orthopod to downtown solo practice, even though he did continue to give the group doctors his unrestricted service and to use the clinic anesthetists and medical consultants as if he were still with the Center.

In a strange and disturbing fashion, once he was in solo practice he was far more accessible for emergency call, and his wife was even less rude – almost to the point of charm –

when they tried to contact her husband by phoning his home. In any event, having previously established the point in question, Jim could hardly view the present huge differential in incomes in the partnership with any degree of equanimity.

At this worst period of internal dissension among the group doctors it seemed almost ironical that the current Minister of Health, Larry Grossman, should come out wholeheartedly in favor of the C.H.C. type of set-up.

'Community Health Centers will no longer be considered an experiment. We will no longer view them as HSOs that have not fully matured. The CHC is a distinct, different and important element in the health services systems and will receive stable and ongoing funding.' He went even further and undertook that his ministry would **'foster their further development and where possible remove obstacles to the development of these organizations.'** Philip's former lonely and stiffnecked opposition to becoming a member of an H.S.O. without his consent had been vindicated at last!

On the recruitment front, there had been a completely new crop of doctors, including several excellent Family Physicians (F.Ps), a new Pediatrician and a new Internist with a special interest in Respiratory Medicine. The newer M.Ds were more than ready for a change in direction for the Center and for reduced powers in the hands of the Board, the Medical Director and the Executive Director. They had little time for older ideas and older values within the C.H.C. and Philip felt that they probably considered someone like him as a venerable figure from a remote historic past. There were many changes that they had in mind, and as the Health Center passed its twenty-first year this was clearly going to be a period of great upheaval.

A number of meetings took place during the year regarding revisions to their partnership agreement, especially those concerning retirement from the Cambrian District Medical Group. This didn't mean retirement from practice but simply severance from the partnership, with its special benefits, including voting rights. Of course, Crowley pressed his ulterior motives hard but had to settle for a compromise, namely that after the age of 65 the individual could retain full partnership by executive decision, on an annual basis to the age of 71. Only Stuart Atkins and Greg Bufold expressed vehement opposition to the 71 limitation and that was rather surprising.

Since this was the year of Philip's seventy-first birthday, he was offered a part-time appointment with greatly reduced office hours and a corresponding reduction of operative work, but still enough to keep his skills properly honed. His annual income was reduced by about forty percent, yet in some ways he had a freedom that made the new arrangement worthwhile. He resigned from most of his committee memberships at the Memorial but still remained active in an advisory capacity – especially at the planning level and the drafting of new medical staff regulations in the hospital. At the same time, there were many surreptitious approaches from solo practitioners urging him to come in from the cold, as it were, and practice as an independent surgeon, available to both downtown doctors and the C.H.C, but Philip had no difficulty resisting the temptation.

One of the new developments within the C.H.C. was the idea of contractual arrangements with outside subspecialists where it was unsuccessful in recruitment or where it wasn't worthwhile engaging a fulltime doctor. Thus, the group had a perfectly satisfactory contract with one of the downtown urologists and in due course there would undoubtedly be others.

This was another way to bridge what was once a gulf and was now no more than a shallow ditch separating the aims and objects of the solo and the group doctors. Their common foe was the increasing and restrictive powers of hospital administrations, translating government pressures on hospital budgets into curtailment of the rights and powers of the medical staff.

At about the same time, the clinic doctors were taking steps to make sure that there would be no similar encroachment within their Center. In 1981 the Cambrian District Medical Group had signed a memorandum of agreement with the Board of the Association, designated as a **'Declaration of Intent'**, which set forth clear separation of function and authority.

'Inasmuch as the Board and the Medical Group are desirous of drafting and signing an agreement that will assure an effective relationship between them, and that will enhance the development of policy and program decisions and that will improve and accelerate the decision making process, both parties agree:

> **1. that the existing Medical Services Agreement is no longer acceptable to either the Medical Group or the Board;**
>
> **11. that past policy and program decisions shall be reviewed by the Joint Executive Committee who will make recommendations to the Partnership and the Board;**
>
> **111. that future policy and program decisions be approved by the Joint Executive Committee at least until the existing agreement has been replaced;**
>
> **1V. that there shall be joint responsibility and authority by the Partnership and the Board on all fiscal and program matters;**
>
> **V. It is mutually agreed that the sponsors must be secure against depreciation and the cost of replacement of the physical plant, and the Sabbatical Leave Plan for the Medical Group shall remain a liability against the assets of the Association. The specific terminology and form of the final Medical Services Agreement to be signed by both parties shall take into consideration the legal and fiscal responsibilities of each party as determined after expert testimony from mutually acceptable specialists in law and finance.'**

The item about the Sabbatical Plan, of course, was now null and void, but the rest of the agreement was finally in force, thanks in large measure to the cooperative and progressive Chairman of the Board, Dale Christoff, a man one could work with and respect. There would be no more endless debates with the quiet but inflexible Bergstrom, no more inflammatory references to "Rent-free" use of the premises by the doctors, no more mutual paranoia, thank God.

'It was', to quote the immortal Dickens, **'the best of times, it was the worst of times,'** Now was the best of times for the newest members of the group's medical staff, and perhaps the worst of times for an old warhorse like Philip Bosnar.

CHAPTER 65

1984-85

Darren Markowsky was one of two early foes of the clinic who came around completely in the early '80s. As President of the St. Pierre Medical Society in '62 he'd appeared on national TV along with the late Frank Brady to pronounce the social and professional ostracism of the C.H.C. doctors to the world at large, but primarily to the city's establishment and the membership of the O.M.A. across the province.

In his personal attitude Philip had never found him particularly bitter until the days of the anesthetic boycott, when he swore that he would never give his services to any Union Clinic surgeon. Later on, however, he seemed to mellow to a large extent and was no doubt embarrassed by his wife's behavior at their table during the Slater retirement party.

During the past few years he had given up first his general practice and then his anesthesia but made himself available for 'surgical assists'. He soon became one of Philip's most willing assistants on those occasions when it was inconvenient to get one of the regular clinic assistants during busy office hours. Markovsky was always eager to do his best and seemed to enjoy Philip's operations, while the surgeon was happy to use him because of his evident enthusiasm.

John Webber had been one of the most implacable foes of the 'Union Clinic' since its inception and exuded an aura of hatred toward its doctors. This reached its peak at the time of the anesthetic boycott and on one occasion he lost his temper with Philip in the surgeon's lounge at the Memorial. At least he didn't aim his fist at the clinic surgeon's jaw as he'd once done to both Appleton and Lawton at a medical meeting in Northern Michigan. When he tried to rationalize the boycott, Philip told him to "stop spouting such absolute bullshit!", and he responded by accusing Philip of reporting him to the Ontario College for refusing to give an anesthetic for one of his clinic patients. Since Webber wouldn't back down in front of the other doctors who were present, Philip told him that he'd write the College forthwith and insist that they confirm or deny the accusation. When the anemic College denial finally arrived, Philip posted it prominently on the bulletin board and since that occasion the personal and professional relationship between them became progressively more cordial.

Webber had given up both his general practice and his anesthesia and made himself available for emergency surgical assistance. By the year 1981 he outdid even Markovsky by his eagerness to assist Philip, regardless of the time of day or night, and the surgeon was embarrassed to find the extent to which his former foe became one of his most devoted fans. He recalled his discomfort when Webber burst into the surgeon's lounge one morning after one of Philip's operations for reflux esophagitis, and declared, "It sure is a pleasure to assist a real surgeon who's also a real gentleman for a change!"

Philip had the good sense to laugh out loud as if to emphasize that his assistant had simply delivered a wisecrack, and that seemed to defuse the situation.

For the past few years, especially since 1980, Philip had wondered about 1984 and how close it would be to the predictions of George Orwell in his book of that name. In some ways the writer was close to the truth.

The military dictatorships of Central and South America were terrorizing their subjects with repression, torture and murder.

The Stalinist regimes of East Germany, Czechoslovakia, Hungary, Bulgaria, Albania and Poland weren't much better, and North Korea was no haven of freedom in the orient, while China, Vietnam, Cambodia, Indonesia, and even South Korea were large question marks.

In Africa, many of the black rulers oppressed their own people as much as the white rulers of South Africa did with their black subjects and those who opposed Apartheid.

In the Arab world, many of the nations were guilty of oppression, and even in the democratic government of Israel there was increasing repression in the occupied territories, and Philip's Zionist zeal cooled as he saw the first signs of possible fascism.

In Iran the fanatical Ayatollah was conducting a campaign of repression that made the late Shah seem like a veritable saint by comparison, while both Iran and Iraq were finding new ways to kill off their youth on expanding bloodstained battlegrounds.

Here in enlightened, democratic Canada, every doctor was under constant surveillance by a plethora of Big Brothers. There was the provincial government with its Ministry of Health, the C.M.A, the O.M.A. and the Ontario College of Physicians and Surgeons. In the legal profession there were countless lawyers ready to pounce on any medical slip or infraction, real or imagined, and in the hospitals there were administrators in growing numbers, as well as supervising and disciplinary medical committees at every possible level.

In the C.H.C. there was the Board and its Executive Director, viewed by many of the group doctors as Big Brother, although some felt it was really their own Medical Director.

Now there was also the all-knowing, all-seeing computer, and the Center had at last become fully computerized! There was ample reason for the emergence of a galloping paranoia, yet – in truth – even with all these various levels of real and imagined Big Brotherhood, doctors could still practice their healing profession according to their personal conscience and the best of their ability, and shouldn't be wasting their time looking over their shoulder.

A review of world events leading up to the fateful year of 1984 seemed to echo the French maxim: 'Plus ça change, plus c'est la même chose.' In the five years since the overthrow of the Somoza government in Nicaragua by the political left, there seemed little improvement in human liberty, and the Soviet invasion of Afghanistan proved that Russia was capable of repeating the U.S.A. mistakes of the Vietnam War.

In a year when their Voyager 1 revealed the marvels of the planet Saturn, the Americans voted a B-movie actor to be their President, and a year later found a new enemy that was impervious to nuclear missiles. It was known euphemistically as AIDS and all it did was destroy the body's own defense mechanisms. This deadly plague appeared to have found its origin in homosexual promiscuity but was spreading to heterosexual partners, users of contaminated needles among drug addicts, and even innocent recipients of virally infected blood transfusions.

One year later Leonid Brezhnev died and his leadership was taken over by another sick man, Yuri Andropov, ex-chief of the K.G.B, while a lukewarm Detente continued alongside the still torrid Cold War.

In the twelve months preceding George Orwell's year of the Big Brother, Israel's invasion of the Lebanese Anarchy produced the dispersal of Yasser Arafat's PLO to new centers of continued terrorism. It also produced the massacres of Sabra and Shattila by the Christian Militia, with Sharon's commanders looking the other way. The Israeli senior officers insisted they could never have stopped this act of vengeance for the murder of a revered Christian leader, Amin Gemayel, but their word was doubted.

As a sequel to Iran's seizure of the U.S. embassy in Teheran in '79, the U.S. Embassy in Beirut was bombed, with the double loss of forty dead and the sanctity of diplomatic territory for all time. Then, as if this were now the real main event, the U.S. marine base in Beirut was bombed with the loss of 216 lives and countless wounded. It was only natural that America should seek early revenge. Unfortunately it sought that vengeance in tiny, defenseless Grenada, and national pride was assuaged as long as one didn't gag at the uneven contest of arms between superpower and minipower.

In February of '84 Andropov died, quite predictably, and his place was taken by the aging, ailing Chernenko. He would have just enough time before his own death to call for peaceful co-existence with the United States of America, while the world held its breath and wondered whether the vitriolic hatred of those who saw Russia as the Evil Empire could abide such a concept. At least, the nightmare of totalitarian repression and expansionism seemed somewhat further away after all, in this most fateful of years (at least by fictional prediction).

The actual events of 1984 proved to be merely the culmination of five previous years in which the cataclysmic had become the ordinary. It seemed as though the fateful year was not so much a conclusion of all that had preceded it during recent years as it was a signpost of more stupendous changes yet to come, and for the first time Philip wanted to live many more years in order to witness those changes.

Stanley Featherstone was anxious to get a special amendment to the medical partnership agreement, extending the term of office of the medical director from five to ten years and requiring a majority of eighty percent to replace him by special resolution. Opposing him violently on these issues were Crowley, Opdahl, Atkins and at least ten others but, of these, five had already made up their minds to leave the group unless Crowley was able to take over the directorship by a coup d'état at the appropriate moment. The clinic's most painful loss would be Les Capreano, whom they liked so much and for whom they had tried to do their best. Their least regrettable loss would be that born troublemaker Angus Sharnton, who'd only been with them for two complaint-filled years as associate cardiologist to Stuart Atkins.

As far as Wilf Jarvis was concerned the decision of Atkins to defect was a devastating blow to the Health Center organization, and he blamed it largely on the antipathy of Jim Appleton and – later on – that of Stan Featherstone. It was an opinion shared by most of the Board and by many of the group doctors, but it was absolutely wrong. Stuart had, for many years, harbored a secret desire to leave the Center, and he and his wife showed an increasing affinity for social involvement with the downtown doctors and their wives.

Strange paradoxes come in all shapes and sizes. Although Stuart Atkins was the one member of the group's partnership who expressed a clear desire to eliminate all solo practice in San Pete and have the Health Center as the only viable medical practice in the city, he managed to maintain the friendliest of relations with those he planned to smother. Another factor was his oddball and unexplainable attachment to Fred Crowley, which was much stronger than his antipathy toward Opdahl and his unconcealed liking for Philip, at least on a professional level. Last but not least there was the perverse influence of Stuart's associate in the department of cardiology, and the vulnerable senior cardiologist became a latter-day Othello beset by more than one Iago.

Eventually, two compromise resolutions were reluctantly adopted by a badly split partnership. The first was that the elected Medical Director should serve for a period of eight years and the second was that his earlier retirement from this office could be obtained by a special resolution supported by a seventy percent majority of the partnership. Needless to say, with a new crop of doctors that would be replacing the eight presumed defectors, it was unlikely that there would be any kind of a majority to vote against their present Medical Director in the foreseeable future.

In the meantime, before committing themselves to a leasing arrangement in the new suite of professional offices within three blocks of the hospitals, there were numerous meetings between representatives of the defecting group and members of the Board. Most of these meetings were with Wilf Jarvis and Jonathan Grey, who was spending a great deal of time at the Health Center during these revolutionary times. It took a considerable amount of persuasion on Philip's part to convince these worried gentlemen of the Board that Armageddon wasn't about to engulf their institution, and that this was simply another crisis to be faced, endured and soon overcome, although the echoes might resound for some time to come.

When Philip heard that his old friend, Doug Conway, was desperately ill, he drove out to Sudbury and went to see him in his hospital room. The arterial disease had now spread throughout Doug's system and yet, miraculously, his brain was spared and he was as sharp as ever. Since Philip knew that his friend was writing a history of the nickel-mining industry in Ontario, he brought him a book on the early history of the region between Saint Pierre and North Bay; it was an arcane piece of work that he felt sure would be of value to Doug and the ailing writer was most appreciative. They talked about old times and laughed so uproariously that a disapproving nurse came in to see what was going on and Philip assured her that they were just two old reminiscing buddies. When he talked about his wife Jenny, however, Doug's wit grew acerbic and he seemed to blame her for his deterioration, which was unfair since she had faithfully stuck with him during his worst years of alcoholism.

Jenny wrote the Bosnars three months later that Doug died shortly after Philip's visit, and they drove out to see her. Her son Kenneth was with her and they were glad to see what a fine young man he'd become. He was intelligent and courteous, and the Bosnars were happy to observe the kindness and consideration he showed to his mother. He'd always been regarded as the black sheep of the family, knocking around Southern California as a tennis bum, while the Conway daughter Doreen was always the apple of her parents' eyes, especially her doting father. Nevertheless, this goodlooking young man appeared to have turned out well and Philip felt justifiably proud since, after all, he was the one who had delivered Kenneth by Cesarean Section, back in his early days in Saskatchewan. As for the petite Jenny, as plump and pretty as ever, she was showing early but unmistakeable signs of Altzheimer's Disease and the Bosnars were deeply saddened.

By September, all those who had committed themselves to moving out of the Center were gone; they'd moved into their impressive new building on Fortas Avenue and left a large hole in their former institution. Some of them took their nurses with them and they had also taken the medical partnership's lawyer with them; he would now act on their behalf. Since all the arrangements, both business and legal, were being fashioned long before the defectors handed in their three month notices of resignation, and two of them were actually serving on the Executive Committee at the time, there were muttered complaints about a serious conflict of interest. There was also the matter of their lawyer who, while still on financial retainer to the partnership, had drawn up the new C.H.C's medical partnership contract – including a change of mandatory notice of resignation from six months to three months – which hardly seemed kosher in the circumstances.

Last but not least there was a little item concerning the young and attractive surgical secretary. Lisa Krumchak had been in charge of booking office appointments in the clinic's surgical department and this was a pivotal job as far as the group surgeons were concerned. Those patients who were specifically referred to a named surgeon were simply fitted into the first available slot and that was no particular problem.

Both medical directors had – rather naively – tried to counteract the solid echelon of 'political referrals' by encouraging nonspecific referrals to the department of surgery, leaving it up to the surgical secretary to sort things out; but Nature Abhors a Vacuum and guile soon filled this void in the surgical booking system. It was Bruce Campbell who first drew Philip's attention and that of Jack Stevens to what was going on.

"Have you chaps noticed how the best cases among the unspecified referrals are mostly going one way and the minor stuff is coming to the two of us?"

"I wondered why the sly devil was wooing our Lisa so hard and always showering her with praise." Jack Stevens grumbled.

"Yes, but haven't you wondered how she knows which cases to send to each of us?" Bruce asked.

"I think I've got it figured out," Jack replied, "all our sweet-faced secretary has to do is to ask the patients the condition for which they're being referred, and as they say in the ads for men's perfume, 'the rest is easy.'"

They decided not to make any particular fuss about it but just watch, wait and see. Sooner or later, they decided, the evidence would be strong enough to warrant serious measures, but in the meantime three events decided the issue for them. The first was Bruce Campbell's decision to leave; the second was Sven Opdahl's decision to leave; and the third was Opdahl's decision to take Lisa Krumchak with him as his secretary-receptionist. He tried to take his office nurse with him as well but she declined with thanks. She was a far better judge of character than the unworldly Lisa.

By the end of 1985 all sense of loss, conflict, and commotion in the Center seemed to disappear in a new wave of optimism, as the medical staff was successful in engaging the services of first-class replacements to fill the vacancies. Among the Board members, however, only Dale

Christoff had kept his head and refused to join the doomsayers. More and more, this doughty individual had become Philip's favorite on the Board, one who could swallow the impudent jibes of Featherstone's 'Ants and Bees' and still look confidently to the future. Giving substance to this impression, Christoff sent a strongly worded letter to the medical partnership in support of the new Medical Director and opposition to the idea of mandatory retirement by any member of the medical staff on the basis of age. He showed them that he could speak powerfully for the steelworkers and the community at large without denigrating his medical comrades in arms.

CHAPTER 66

1986

Philip Bosnar's mind was fully made up: he would retire from practice at the end of this year. A combination of factors had finally solidified his decision. In the first place, this was his fiftieth year since graduating in medicine and that was a good time to call it quits. In the second place, his beloved wife and children were of one mind, that he now enjoy a well-earned rest from the demands of surgery and indulge his other interests to a much greater degree. In the third place there was his strong desire to embark on a writing career, with articles on a wide range of subjects and perhaps some fiction as well.

The idea of continuing to earn a good living by making himself available for surgical assists held not the slightest attraction for him; neither did the suggestion that he confine himself to less demanding areas of operative surgery.

It was always his conviction that there was no such entity as a partial surgeon or a part-time surgeon. Of one thing he was quite sure and that was that instead of their customary two to four weeks in southern Florida or the Caribbean, he and Patty could – following his retirement – spend three winter months in their favorite haunts on Gasparilla Island, Sanibel Island or Naples on the Gulf Coast of Florida. There, they could play tennis to their heart's content, enjoy the beach and ocean and have the occasional bridge game.

Florian and James were both determined – on the other hand – to see their parents move back to Edwardia, which would save them the long and arduous annual drive to Florida. They would be close to Florian, and James would find it much easier to fly out directly from London to Vancouver. As for Patty, despite the painful idea of leaving her many close friends in San Pete, she seemed to be getting more and more enthusiastic about the idea of moving back to the tranquil beauties of Edwardia and leaving the snows of Ontario behind, forever.

The introduction of Bill 94 by the provincial government seemed an act of bad faith toward the medical profession, yet Philip would be the last person to condone freewheeling 'extra-billing'. What worried him most was that, with each new dispute between government and doctors, public opinion of their healing profession went progressively downward, and to him that meant an erosion of faith, such a vital ingredient of patient care. Now that he had his new word processor and had started his articles, he decided to write to the local paper and explain the background to the current impasse so that the public could get a clearer picture of the issues involved.

'Aside from the inevitable polarization precipitated by Bill 94' he wrote, **'in which some elements of the media have played an accessory role, the objective and rational discussion of key points in the ongoing dispute have never been clearly presented, either by the Ontario Government or the Ontario Medical Association.'**

He went on to recount the introduction of a physician-sponsored prepaid health insurance plan in Ontario and the two essential changes in the fee schedule by which doctors would be paid for their services. The first was the acceptance of a ten percent discount on the O.M.A. fee schedule to pay for the secretarial and administrative costs of running the plan efficiently; in effect, a collection fee.

'Now, in 1986, the discount figure between the O.M.A. fee schedule and the O.H.I.P. Schedule of Benefits (the government fee schedule) has reached approximately 30 percent and could in time become 50 percent or more.'

The second initial change was a conversion of the minimum fee schedule to a maximum fee schedule. He discussed the economic factors producing this divergence.

'The obvious question that must be addressed is a fairly simple one: Has the overall rise in the O.M.A. fee schedule been excessive over the past 30 years or is the government trying to impose a bureaucratic and financial grip on doctors, unique among professions? An examination of the 30-year rise in the price of food, housing, rent, clothing, automobile and other related costs as well as the general rise in wages and incomes would indicate that the increase in O.M.A. fees has not been excessive. In fact, it has tended to lag behind the overall rise of the related figures referred to above. Parenthetically, the government has never accused the O.M.A. of being out of line with its increases.'

Lest he appear to have converted to a philosophy of totally unfettered extra-billing or the apostle of charging fee-for-service, there were one or two more items that required addressing.

'Personally, like many other doctors in this province, I am against the idea of indiscriminate and rampant extra-billing. I do not believe that any individual doctor should have the right to say, "I'm worth it!" This should be a decision made by his or her peers in the profession, based on professional record and reputation, experience, judgement, unique contribution and skills, etc. and not on what the traffic will bear.'

He had to admit to himself that he had Art Spears in mind when he wrote this particular paragraph. That young man, so full of lofty pontifications about professional ethics and the most idealistic and non-venal approach to Medicine, was no sooner out of their Center than he was busy extra-billing all his patients, proving himself a fanatical convert to fee-for-service at its very worst. Philip still felt very strongly that the fee- for-service method encouraged active procedures, overservicing and overutilization, while discouraging medical and – more importantly – surgical conservatism, as well as the concept of prevention versus cure. Nevertheless, since there was such an entity as a fee schedule, it was still the barometer of relations between their profession and the government.

The article suggested a solution.

'Perhaps the simplest negotiation would be to have a single unified fee schedule with annual compilation of administrative, secretarial and other bureaucratic costs, slight annual variations, but certainly not in the order of a growth from 10 percent to 30 percent without mutual consent.'

Finally, he offered a critical comment about some of the tactics being used in the present impasse.

'Confrontation and doctor strikes are not the answer. Vote-seeking tactics are not the answer. Vituperative doctor-bashing columnists in some of our leading newspapers should be counterbalanced by a fair-minded press with columnists of the opposing viewpoint. In a demo-

cratic society, binding arbitration is a far more desirable alternative to unilateral, high-handed, legislative fiat.'

At the very next surgical ward rounds in St. Matthew's Hospital, with Pandit Mukherjee in the chair and before the first case was presented, Sven Opdahl rose to his feet and addressed the meeting, which included most of the general surgeons, orthopedic surgeons, urologists, the head pathologist, and the two plastic surgeons.

"Before we start the case presentations, Mr. Chairman, I believe we all owe a great debt of gratitude to Philip Bosnar for his fine article that sets the record straight for the public. It should clear up a lot of wrong ideas and put our profession in a much better light."

There was loud and prolonged applause and beyond a brief "Thank you," there was really nothing for Philip to say; but he could sense an unspoken feeling of guilt on the part of Opdahl.

Jack Stevens had a truly fine hobby, namely cooking, at which he was most competent and unreserved. Philip had been invited to several spur-of-the-moment meals at his house when his wife Janice was away. He could certainly vouch for the excellence of his surgical partner's food and the ease and panache with which he served it. One day Jack approached him with a novel idea: he'd invite all the general surgeons in town to a dinner at his house, which he would prepare and serve on his own.

The guests all arrived between 7 and 7.30 on a Friday evening, soon after Philip's 73rd birthday, and had their preliminary cocktails prior to the meal, thus breaking the ice as early as possible. When they came to the magnificently appointed dining table they found their place cards and checked their seating. Jack was seated at the head of the table and Don Foley at the other end. Philip was seated at Foley's left and Opdahl was at Philip's left. Opposite Philip were Abbie Zaffran, Gus Pelletier and John Duncan; all were in fine spirits and jokes were soon flying fast and furious. Stan Abel was away in Toronto having some reconstructive surgery for his arthritic joints. Ironically, he'd been forced to retire a year ago after so adamantly resisting being taken off the emergency call roster. True to form, Opdahl apologized to his host that he might have to leave early since he had a long-standing commitment to another meeting later on that evening.

The meal was a resounding success and Cordon Bleu in every respect: commencing with a crabmeat cocktail with a medium Chablis, a tasty sherry consommé, a crisp endive, cucumber and watercress salad with Roquefort dressing, a palate-clearing glass of Chardonnay, and superb leg of lamb with tangy mint sauce, washed down with a pleasant Mommesin. Fresh fruit desert was followed by assorted cheeses and English crackers, and then some strong coffee and Hennessy five star brandy. They all complimented their host on the superb banquet he'd prepared, loosened a few buttons and were settling into a comfortable slouch when Don Foley unexpectedly rose to his feet.

"We are all assembled here this evening," he declared, "in order to celebrate Philip's fiftieth year in practice since graduating in early 1936, and to pay our respects."

He then proceeded in his usual humming and hawing manner to shower Philip with eulogies that the recipient felt had a certain posthumous quality to them. Controlling himself carefully against any breach of etiquette, he responded with a degree of mock gravity but emphasized his honest appreciation of the gesture. After thanking his host for the superb meal and Foley for his remarks he added, "I hope all of you enjoy your surgical careers as much as I have so far enjoyed mine. By the time I retire in about ten years from now I look forward to attending similar celebrations to honor each of you and perhaps coming to some of your retirement parties." The joke wasn't lost on them and there were appreciative guffaws, some ribald responses and lots of goodnatured kidding.

Next came a presentation by Foley on behalf of the assembled surgeons. It was a handsome pewter beer mug with an engraved message that was read out by a sentimental Godfather, **'To our esteemed colleague, Philip Bosnar, with abiding affection and respect for his fifty years of devoted service in the practice of Medicine. From his surgical colleagues in Saint Pierre.'** They all toasted him and he toasted them in return and told them how much he would value their thoughtful gift (and that was the absolute truth). They retired to the living room with their brandy refills and Opdahl, now feeling no pain whatever, made a few phone calls and came back to inform them that he would be staying. In point of fact he was one of the very last to leave, at 1.30 a.m.

This had been a strange year in so many ways. Philip had never enjoyed his surgery more and his work seemed easier than it had ever been, no matter how difficult or involved the case might be. His relationship with doctors on both sides of their former lines of battle could hardly be better and the nurses were never more cooperative. Could this be in anticipation of a forthcoming departure?

Patty's health was excellent and she was as loving, athletic and vigorous as ever. Florian's business was doing well and her daughter Martina was spending more and more time with her in Vancouver, while Paul was going out to Edmonton periodically to stay with his father. In addition, Neville and Florian had established a new long-distance friendship without romantic renewal but with a new understanding replacing the old bitterness. In the old country, their son Peter's career was obviously successful, and he and Nedda remained happily married.

Phil and Patty felt unduly blessed by the intense love and respect their children had for them, undiminished by the distance that separated them. Their letters, Patty's replies (she was still correspondent for both of them) and their long-distance phone calls combined to shorten the physical distance, and there were always the periodic visits. Their grandchildren were maturing well and were very precious to them, and they were in close and affectionate touch with Patty's young brother and her two sisters in Australia. Only Philip's brother, Clayton, whom he loved so dearly, seemed lost to him, and if that was the cost of his newfound happiness in a second marriage, then so be it!

Over the years the Bosnars had watched their city grow in size and character. The waterfront was a most successful project and one could now take long walks along the lakeside and enjoy the view at all times of the day. Culturally, the West Cambrian Players were a thriving theatrical enterprise as were the Opera Society and Symphony Orchestra. The Cambrian Steel Company was emerging from a period of doldrums and promised to become an economically viable enterprise once more, with an expanding workforce despite increasing automation. The Forest Pathology laboratories were among the finest in the world and boasted one of the highest concentration of Ph.Ds to be found anywhere outside university centers. Last but not least, their Community Health

Center had become the most successful of its kind in the whole of Canada, with a medical staff of forty-one specialists and family physicians, and well over two hundred ancillary staff.

Among many others, including their most vehement opposition, the Kennonens always insisted that without the stubborn efforts and unaltered vision of a hard-nosed surgeon named Philip Bosnar there would be no such entity today as their Health Center. Klars Kennonen, whom Philip first met as an enthusiastic member of the West Cambrian Players – working hard behind the scenes – had given up his job as locomotive engineer at the steel company and gone into private real estate. He had shrewdly bought up old houses, renovated them with the help of staunch hardworking Finnish workmen, then rented them at a tidy profit. In the process, both he and Peggy had changed from ardent socialists to exponents of conservative capitalism, and Philip often kidded them unmercifully on their conversion. They had done well enough to accept such kidding laughingly and to look forward to Peggy's early retirement from anesthesia.

Both Kennonens were still extremely loyal to the Clinic despite their many political and organizational differences with both the Board and the medical directorship, and they'd always remained the best of friends with Patty and Phil. Klars, who was built like a viking and had a Falstaffian sense of humor, never failed to become moist-eyed when he recalled Philip's desperate cry as Noah: "I have lost my rudder!" and his wife was quick to point out that her favorite surgeon had never lost his rudder in steering their endangered Health Center through its storm-tossed voyage to present times.

Toward the end of October, Philip was approached by Les Capreano regarding the forthcoming annual meeting of the O.M.A's West Cambrian District to be held in San Pete. Les was now President of the West Cambrian Academy of Medicine and he wanted to know if Philip would consent to be keynote speaker at the banquet on the last evening of the meeting; to be held in the Sheraton-Lakes Hotel on the Northern Highway. Philip asked if he could be given a few days to think about it before giving his answer, and Capreano replied that he hoped he would consent, as the program committee had unanimously agreed on Dr. Bosnar as their choice for the speech. After discussing the matter with his good friend 'Sonny' Sangarillingham, St. Matthews' brilliant pathologist – who thought Philip should discuss his fifty year experience in surgery – he agreed.

The banquet was well attended, with many from out of town, and the atmosphere was pleasant and relaxed, including continual introductions of the wives and husbands of doctors, both clinic and solo. Seated at the Bosnars' table were the Appletons, Stevens and Lawtons, and drinks and food passed by smoothly in an atmosphere of warm congeniality. Following a dance exhibition by several talented local children, Don Foley mounted the platform and introduced Philip Bosnar as the after-dinner speaker, with a customary flow of hyperbole.

After a few preliminary remarks, Philip launched into his main address, entitled **'Changing Times and Horizons.'** He started by confessing that when he was asked to talk about his fifty years in general surgery it was an offer he couldn't refuse since it enabled him to present his ideas and prejudices as well as his early dreams and later experiences to an audience of colleagues and spouses, mostly younger than himself. In 1936 he had envisioned a world of Medicine in which no patient would be denied good medical care because of an inability to pay. It was the dawn of modern chemotherapy, starting with Prontosil and the sulfonamides, then progressing to the penicillins and now the expanding array of antibacterial, anti-parasitic, antifungal and antiviral agents.

It was an era in which surgical operations were destined to be replaced by molecular therapy, and one in which the secrets of immunology would be unlocked and provide a pathway to future cures. He stressed the vital importance of biochemistry in all aspects of medical and surgical practice.

He spoke of the decline of old surgical operations and the introduction of new ones, especially organ transplants. He pointed to the decline of past diseases such as Tuberculosis and Polio, and the arrival of new diseases such as Aids and Legionaire's Disease. He discussed the social and medical challenge of Aids and emphasized the importance of the condom in prophylaxis.

In his discussion of the marvels of modern technology he warned about overuse and excessive expectations, as well as the rising financial burden in a restricted governmental budget. He voiced his concern over narrowing fields of specialization and subspecialization, and emphasized the importance of preserving general surgery from ultimate extinction. As far as hospitals were concerned he deplored the proliferation of non-medical administration and the decline of doctors' authority. He condemned the alienation between the nursing and medical professions and called for a return of doctors to the realm of nurses' education, preferably in a hospital environment.

He criticized the growth of medicolegal litigation and called for a lessening of lawyers' interference in the practice of Medicine and a strengthening of the medical profession's reaction to a growing dominance of the legal profession. He expressed his disapproval of the tendency toward overcentralization of specialist services in major centers and demonstrated how wasteful and inconvenient this was in a country of vast distances such as Canada.

In discussing the World Health Organization he found fault with its unrealistic utopian definition of good health in a world where enormous segments of the third world still lacked adequate food, shelter, clean water and basic hygiene. He compared what constituted the everyday medical concerns of Canadian patients with those of the third world and suggested a revised perspective. A possible plan was suggested for new medical graduates, following their rotating internship, to spend some time in the disadvantaged areas of the world before returning to continue their careers in the land of plenty. He warned against the facile acceptance of statistical reviews and suggested that individual experience should not be undervalued. In conclusion, he pointed to the future of Medicine in a golden era of new and startling discoveries and told his young audience how much he envied them their unlimited horizons.

The speech was followed by total silence and Philip was afraid he'd gone too far, especially in the presence of doctors' spouses, but he was quite wrong. As he was about to leave the platform there was a thunderous sound as the entire audience rose in a standing ovation that lasted for what seemed an eternity. John Duncan came rushing down the aisle – all six foot four inches of him – to shake his hand and yell, "That was great, Philip, just great!" Other congratulations engulfed him and he felt that his efforts hadn't been wasted after all. As for his adorable Patricia, she seemed lost in a sort of happy delirium, but she must have shared his pride since she had also shared the many controversial views conveyed in his address and held by both for so long.

The remainder of 1986 was a whirl of retirement parties and presentations, from the

Academy, the Board, the group medical partnership and the ancillary staff of the Group Health Center: nurses, secretaries, lab workers, X-ray technicians, physiotherapists and all the others. There were speeches, humorous as well as serious, in which Philip Bosnar was compared with everyone from Louis Pasteur to Sir William Osler and he tried very hard not to laugh at the wrong moments. The gifts were all beautiful and everyone seemed to be having such a wonderful time that Philip thought it was a pity one couldn't have a retirement annually.

EPILOGUE

Phil and Patty sat by the pool of their rented villa in Naples, Florida, and reviewed the history of 23 years with the Community Health Center and especially the past few years.

"Well, Patty darling, we started with thirteen doctors and finished with over forty. Stu Atkins has been replaced by an even better cardiologist who's extremely well liked by his colleagues and patients and is always available."

"How about the new surgeon, the one who looks like a schoolboy?"

"He's a much better surgeon than Opdahl, and as modest as his predecessor was egotistic. He has a great sense of humor and is easy to work with."

"Is he married?"

"Sure is. His wife is a first class family physician and is well liked in the Center."

"Any other acquisitions?"

"We've an excellent rheumatologist and four new G.Ps, three of whom are women. We also have a damn good ophthalmologist and the prospect of an E.N.T. surgeon."

"Is everything peaceful now with the Medical Director?"

"I doubt if it will ever be. Palace revolts are almost built into the system, with a new set of rebels from one time to the next. The next rebellion will come from some of the newer specialists with the help of a few longtime members of the partnership, and I believe Jim Appleton may even try a comeback."

"Will the Center survive, do you think?"

"Not only will it survive but it will progressively become more respectable and may ultimately replace traditional systems as the method favored by the medical establishment."

"Does that mean that you've successfully challenged the Citadel?"

"My longtime objective has been to reach beyond the Citadel, if possible, to a system that stresses the team approach to patient care. One that doesn't squander our country's resources in its search for good medical care for all patients. Our Health Center in San Pete is just the first faltering step."

"What about the fee-for-service system?"

"I believe it must go, but its demise will be resisted to the very last questionable investigation, procedure, medication, emergency room care and hospitalization. Doctors are human, even the least venal among them, and they cannot escape the temptation to use and abuse the present system that favors expensive so-called 'productivity', which means doing things."

"What things?"

"Those activities that are rewarded by a fee schedule which punishes cost-saving conservatism in the rational management of sickness."

· · · · · · · · · · . The funny little man came down the railway carriage, yelling, "Peanuts and CocaCola!" then stopped to ask Philip, "Well, Doc, how do you like Canada?" and he replied: "Great country!"

"Land of opportunity," chimed in their dour-faced porter.

"Too bad you didn't make it to professor of surgery at one of our major universities, old sport," said Doug Conway, sitting in his editor's office of the Vanwey Tribune, "I was ready to bet anyone you would."

But Philip's beloved mother and father would have none of that, and proudly declared in perfect unison, "What our Phileep did to make his profession better was much more important." They were seated in the spotless kitchen of number twelve Grantham Square and Philip could hear the sounds of a tennis game in the park.

At that moment a little golden-haired girl interrupted her game of hopscotch outside her uncle's fish and chip shop on the Mile End Road to say, "I'm so happy you married the girl you really love, Phil. You'll always be in love with her, but I still want you to write about me in your book. You WILL write one, you know." .   ·   ·   ·   ·   ·   · · · "That must have been quite a wild daydream, my darling," said Patty as she gently lifted her husband's arm from across her face. "You were certainly thrashing around in your sleep."

"To be truthful, Patty, it was a very non-violent dream. I'd tell you about it but it would only sound too crazy. You know how mixed up dreams can be."

Yes, but she also knew who could translate so many dreams into reality.

The End